D0390481

THE BEST OF THE BEST

20 Years of

THE YEAR'S BEST
SCIENCE FICTION

ALSO BY GARDNER DOZOIS

ANTHOLOGIES

A DAY IN THE LIFE
ANOTHER WORLD
BEST SCIENCE FICTION STORIES OF THE
 YEAR #6–10
THE BEST OF ISAAC ASIMOV'S SCIENCE
 FICTION MAGAZINE
TIME-TRAVELERS FROM ISAAC ASIMOV'S
 SCIENCE FICTION MAGAZINE
TRANSCENDENTAL TALES FROM ISAAC
 ASIMOV'S SCIENCE FICTION MAGAZINE
ISAAC ASIMOV'S ALIENS
ISAAC ASIMOV'S MARS
ISAAC ASIMOV'S SF LITE
ISAAC ASIMOV'S WAR
ROADS NOT TAKEN
 (with Stanley Schmidt)
THE YEAR'S BEST SCIENCE FICTION
 #1–20

FUTURE EARTHS: UNDER AFRICAN SKIES
 (with Mike Resnick)
FUTURE EARTHS: UNDER SOUTH
 AMERICAN SKIES
 (with Mike Resnick)
RIPPER! (with Susan Casper)
MODERN CLASSIC SHORT NOVELS OF
 SCIENCE FICTION
MODERN CLASSIC OF FANTASY
KILLING ME SOFTLY
DYING FOR IT
THE GOOD OLD STUFF
THE GOOD NEW STUFF
EXPLORERS
THE FURTHEST HORIZON
WORLDMAKERS
SUPERMEN

COEDITED WITH SHEILA WILLIAMS

ISAAC ASIMOV'S PLANET EARTH
ISAAC ASIMOV'S ROBOTS
ISAAC ASIMOV'S VALENTINES
ISAAC ASIMOV'S SKIN DEEP
ISAAC ASIMOV'S GHOSTS
ISAAC ASIMOV'S VAMPIRES
ISAAC ASIMOV'S MOONS

ISAAC ASIMOV'S CHRISTMAS
ISAAC ASIMOV'S CAMELOT
ISAAC ASIMOV'S WEREWOLVES
ISAAC ASIMOV'S SOLAR SYSTEM
ISAAC ASIMOV'S DETECTIVES
ISAAC ASIMOV'S CYBERDREAMS

COEDITED WITH JACK DANN

ALIENS!	MERMAIDS!	DINOSAURS!	INVADERS!	CLONES
UNICORNS!	SORCERERS!	LITTLE PEOPLE!	ANGELS!	NANOTECH
MAGICATS!	DEMONS!	DRAGONS!	DINOSAURS II	IMMORTALS
MAGICATS 2!	DOGTALES!	HORSES!	HACKERS	
BESTIARY!	SEASERPENTS!	UNICORNS 2	TIMEGATES	

FICTION

STRANGERS
THE VISIBLE MAN (Collection)
NIGHTMARE BLUE
 (with George Alec Effinger)

SLOW DANCING THROUGH TIME
 (with Jack Dann, Michael Swanwick,
 Susan Casper, and Jack C. Haldeman II)
THE PEACEMAKER
GEODESIC DREAMS (collection)

NONFICTION

THE FICTION OF JAMES TIPTREE, JR.

THE BEST OF THE BEST

20 Years of

THE YEAR'S BEST
SCIENCE FICTION

Gardner Dozois

st. martin's griffin ✹ new york

THE BEST OF THE BEST. Copyright © 2005 by Gardner Dozois.
Foreword copyright © by Robert Silverberg. All rights reserved.
Printed in the United States of America.
No part of this book may be used or reproduced in any manner
whatsoever without written permission except in the case of brief
quotations embodied in critical articles or reviews. For information,
address St. Martin's Press, 175 Fifth Avenue, New York,
N.Y. 10010.

www.stmartins.com

Library of Congress Cataloging-in-Publication Data

Best of the best : 20 years of the Year's best science fiction /
    [edited by] Gardner Dozois.—1st ed.
        p.   cm.
    ISBN 0-312-33656-X (pbk)
    EAN 978-0312-33656-1
    ISBN 0-312-33655-1 (hc)
    EAN 978-0312-33655-4
      1. Science fiction, American.   2. Science fiction, English.
I. Dozois, Gardner R.   II. Year's best science fiction (New
York, N.Y.)

PS648.S3B499   2005
813'.0876608—dc22

                                        2004051411

FIRST EDITION: FEBRUARY 2005

10 9 8 7 6 5 4 3 2 1

contents

ACKNOWLEDGMENTS   *vii*

FOREWORD • *Robert Silverberg*   *xi*

PREFACE • *Gardner Dozois*   *xvii*

BLOOD MUSIC • *Greg Bear*   1

A CABIN ON THE COAST • *Gene Wolfe*   19

SALVADOR • *Lucius Shepard*   28

TRINITY • *Nancy Kress*   42

FLYING SAUCER ROCK AND ROLL • *Howard Waldrop*   78

DINNER IN AUDOGHAST • *Bruce Sterling*   93

ROADSIDE RESCUE • *Pat Cadigan*   103

SNOW • *John Crowley*   109

THE WINTER MARKET • *William Gibson*   121

THE PURE PRODUCT • *John Kessel*   137

STABLE STRATEGIES FOR MIDDLE MANAGEMENT • *Eileen Gunn*   152

KIRINYAGA • *Mike Resnick*   162

TALES FROM THE VENIA WOODS • *Robert Silverberg*   177

BEARS DISCOVER FIRE • *Terry Bisson*   191

EVEN THE QUEEN • *Connie Willis*   199

GUEST OF HONOR • *Robert Reed*   213

NONE SO BLIND • *Joe Haldeman*   238

MORTIMER GRAY'S *HISTORY OF DEATH* • *Brian Stableford*   246

THE LINCOLN TRAIN • *Maureen F. McHugh*   293

WANG'S CARPETS • *Greg Egan*   303

COMING OF AGE IN KARHIDE • *Ursula K. Le Guin*   328

THE DEAD • *Michael Swanwick*   342

RECORDING ANGEL • *Ian McDonald*   352

A DRY, QUIET WAR • *Tony Daniel*   363

THE UNDISCOVERED • *William Sanders*   380

SECOND SKIN • *Paul J. McAuley*   400

STORY OF YOUR LIFE • *Ted Chiang*   418

PEOPLE CAME FROM EARTH • *Stephen Baxter*   454

THE WEDDING ALBUM • *David Marusek*   464

10^{16} TO 1 • *James Patrick Kelly*   502

DADDY'S WORLD • *Walter Jon Williams*   520

THE REAL WORLD • *Steven Utley*   541

HAVE NOT HAVE • *Geoff Ryman*   561

LOBSTERS • *Charles Stross*   577

BREATHMOSS • *Ian R. MacLeod*   597

LAMBING SEASON • *Molly Gloss*   647

acknowledgment is made for permission to reprint the following materials:

"Blood Music," by Greg Bear. Copyright © 1983 by Davis Publications, Inc. First published in *Analog Science Fact/Science Fiction*, June 1983. Reprinted by permission of the author.

"A Cabin on the Coast," by Gene Wolfe. Copyright © 1981 by Gene Wolfe. First Published in *Zu den Stemen* (Goldmann, Verlag, Munich), edited by Peter Wilfert. First published in English in *The Magazine of Fantasy & Science Fiction*, February 1984. Reprinted by permission of the author and the author's agent, the Virginia Kidd Literary Agency.

"Salvador," by Lucius Shepard. Copyright © 1984 by Mercury Press, Inc. First published in *The Magazine of Fantasy & Science Fiction*, April 1984. Reprinted by permission of the author.

"Trinity," by Nancy Kress. Copyright © 1984 by Davis Publications, Inc. First published in *Isaac Asimov's Science Fiction Magazine*, October 1984. Reprinted by permission of the author.

"Flying Saucer Rock and Roll," by Howard Waldrop. Copyright © 1984 by Omni Publications International, Ltd. First published in *Omni*, January 1985. Reprinted by permission of the author.

"Dinner in Audoghast," by Bruce Sterling. Copyright © 1985 by Davis Publications, Inc. First published in *Isaac Asimov's Science Fiction Magazine*, May 1985. Reprinted by permission of the author.

"Roadside Rescue," by Pat Cadigan. Copyright © 1985 by Omni Publication International, Ltd. First published in *Omni*, July 1985. Reprinted by permission of the author.

"Snow," by John Crowley. Copyright © 1985 by Omni Publications International, Ltd. First published in *Omni*, November 1985. Published by permission of the author and his agent.

"The Winter Market," by William Gibson. Copyright © 1986 by William Gibson. First published in *Stardate*, February 1986. Reprinted by permission of the author and his agent, Martha Millard.

"The Pure Product," by John Kessel. Copyright © 1986 by Davis Publications, Inc. First published in *Isaac Asimov's Science Fiction Magazine*, March 1986. Reprinted by permission of the author.

"Stable Strategies for Middle Management," by Elleen Gunn. Copyright © 1988 by Davis Publications, Inc. First published in *Isaac Asimov's Science Fiction Magazine*, June 1988. Reprinted by permission of the author.

"Kirinyaga," by Mike Resnick. Copyright © 1988 by Mercury Press, Inc. First published in *The Magazine of Fantasy & Science Fiction*, November 1988. Reprinted by permission of the author.

"Tales from the Venia Woods," by Robert Silverberg. Copyright © 1989 by Agberg Ltd. First published in *The Magazine of Fantasy & Science Fiction*, October 1989. Reprinted by permission of the author.

"Bears Discover Fire," by Terry Bisson. Copyright © 1990 by Davis Publications, Inc. First published in *Isaac Asimov's Science Fiction Magazine*, August 1990. Reprinted by permission of the author.

"Even the Queen," by Connie Willis. Copyright © 1992 by Davis Publications, Inc. First published in *Isaac Asimov's Fiction Magazine*, April 1992. Reprinted by permission of the author.

"Guest of Honor," by Robert Reed. Copyright © 1993 by Mercury Press, Inc. First published in *The Magazine of Fantasy & Science Fiction*, June 1993. Reprinted by permission of the author.

"None So Blind," by Joe Haldeman. Copyright © 1994 by Bantam Doubleday Dell Magazines. First published in *Asimov's Science Fiction*, November 1994. Reprinted by permission of the author.

"Mortimer Gray's *History of Death*," by Brian Stableford. Copyright © 1995 by Bantam Doubleday Dell Magazines. First published in *Asimov's Science Fiction*, April 1995. Reprinted by permission of the author.

"The Lincoln Train," by Maureen F. McHugh. Copyright © 1995 by Mercury Press, Inc. First published in *The Magazine of Fantasy & Science Fiction*, April 1995. Reprinted by permission of the author.

"Wang's Carpets," by Greg Egan. Copyright © 1995 by Greg Egan. First appeared in *New Legends* (Tor). Reprinted by permission of the author.

"Coming of Age in Karhide," by Ursula K. Le Guin. Copyright © 1995 by Ursula K. Le Guin. First published in *New Legends* (Tor). Reprinted by permission of the author and the author's agent, the Virginia Kidd Literary Agency.

"The Dead," by Michael Swanwick. Copyright © 1996 by Michael Swanwick. First published in *Starlight 1* (Tor). Reprinted by permission of the author.

"Recording Angel," by Ian McDonald. Copyright © 1996 by Interzone. First published in *Interzone*, February 1996. Reprinted by permission of the author.

"A Dry, Quiet War," by Tony Daniel. Copyright © 1996 by Dell Magazines. First published in *Asimov's Science Fiction*, June 1996. Reprinted by permission of the author.

"The Undiscovered," by William Sanders. Copyright © 1997 by Dell Magazines. First published in *Asimov's Science Fiction*, March 1997. Published by permission of the author.

"Second Skin," by Paul J. McAuley. Copyright © 1997 by Paul J. McAuley. First published in *Asimov's Science Fiction*, April 1997. Reprinted by permission of the author.

"Story of Your Life," by Ted Chiang. Copyright © 1998 by Ted Chiang. First published in *Starlight 2* (Tor). Reprinted by permission of the author and the author's agent, the Virginia Kidd Literary Agency.

"People Came from Earth," by Stephen Baxter. Copyright © 1999 by Stephen Baxter. First published in *Moon Shots* (DAW). Reprinted by permission of the author.

"The Wedding Album," by David Marusek. Copyright © 1999 by Dell Magazines. First published in *Asimov's Science Fiction*, June 1999. Reprinted by permission of the author.

"10^{16} to 1," by James Patrick Kelly. Copyright © 1999 by Dell Magazines. First published in *Asimov's Science Fiction*, June 1999. Reprinted by permission of the author.

"Daddy's World," by Walter Jon Williams. Copyright © 1999 by Walter Jon Williams. First published in *Not of Woman Born* (Roc Books). Reprinted by permission of the author.

"The Real World," by Steven Utley. Copyright © 2000 by SCIFI.COM. First published electronically on *SCI FICTION*, September 6. Reprinted by permission of the author.

"Have Not Have," by Geoff Ryman. Copyright © 2001 by Spilogale, Inc. First published in *The Magazine of Fantasy & Science Fiction*, April 2001. Reprinted by permission of the author.

"Lobsters," by Charles Stross. Copyright © 2001 by Dell Magazines. First published in *Asimov's Science Fiction*, June 2001. Reprinted by permission of the author.

"Breathmoss," by Ian R. MacLeod. Copyright © 2002 by Dell Magazines. First published in *Asimov's Science Fiction*, May 2002. Reprinted by permission of the author and his agent, Susan Ann Protter.

"Lambing Season," by Molly Gloss. Copyright © 2002 by Dell Magazines. First published in *Asimov's Science Fiction*, July 2002. Reprinted by permission of the author.

foreword

Robert Silverberg

Gardner Dozois's annual anthology, *The Year's Best Science Fiction*, began publication in 1984 and by now is a series that comprises twenty hefty volumes, which require close to three and a half feet of shelf space. You will find that three-and-a-half-foot expanse of Dozois anthologies in any science-fiction library worthy of the name. Their presence is essential, for the Dozois book is the definitive historical record of the most fertile twenty years in the history of the science-fiction short story. Volume by volume, each anthology is an exciting and memorable collection. Taken all in all, though, they form a whole rather greater than the sum of their parts: an extraordinary editorial achievement, a unique encyclopedic text. And now we are given a book that offers us The Best of the Best—editor Dozois's selection of the finest of the hundreds of stories that make up those twenty anthologies.

In no way does this book, good as it is, *replace* those twenty anthologies. No one volume possibly could. It serves, rather, as a marker, a signifier, which by the luminous excellence of its material reminds us of the magnitude of Gardner Dozois's total accomplishment in assembling this wondrous series.

The science-fiction short story's illustrious history goes back a long way. Beyond doubt the Greeks and the Romans wrote them—tales of robot warriors and imaginary voyages, some of them voyages to the moon. Closer to our own day, Hawthorne, Poe, and Verne produced what was unquestionably science fiction. More than a century ago H. G. Wells, the first great modern master of the form, filled the popular magazines of his day with dozens of s-f stories—"The Country of the Blind," "The Crystal Egg," "The Star," and many more—of such surpassing inventiveness that they have held their own in print ever since. From 1911 on, the Luxembourg-born gadgeteer Hugo Gernsback began publishing science fiction as a regular feature of his magazines *Modern Electrics* and *Science and Invention*, and it proved so popular that in 1926 Gernsback launched *Amazing Stories*, the first magazine devoted entirely to it. (Because new stories were so hard to find at first, Gernsback filled many of the early issues with the work of Poe, Verne, and Wells.) *Amazing* built an avid readership and before long had a vigorous pair of competitors: *Wonder Stories* and *Astounding Stories*. Those were followed by a host of others, gaudy pulp magazines with names like *Startling Stories*, *Planet Stories*, *Cosmic Stories*, and *Super Science Stories*, and then, after World War II, came a group of less flamboyant-looking magazines aimed at more sophisticated readers, most notably *Galaxy Science Fiction* and *Fantasy and Science Fiction*.

Though much of the material in the science-fiction magazines of the 1930s and 1940s was crude and ephemeral, some was not, and, inevitably, book publishers began to collect the best of it in anthologies. The first such volume was Phil Stong's *The Other Worlds* (1941), which drew on the pulps for stories by Lester del Rey, Theodore Sturgeon, Murray Leinster, Harry Bates, and other well-known s-f masters of the day. Two years later, the knowledgeable Donald A. Wollheim edited *The Pocket Book of Science Fiction*, with stories by Sturgeon, Wells, Robert A. Heinlein, and more. Then, just after the war, came two major collections, both of them still of major significance: *Adventures in Time and Space*, edited by Raymond J. Healy and J. Francis McComas, and *The Best of Science Fiction*, edited by Groff Conklin. The Healy–McComas book, studded with classics like Asimov's "Nightfall" and Don A. Stuart's "Who Goes There?", was drawn largely from the pages of John W. Campbell's *Astounding Science Fiction*, the dominant magazine in the field during the 1940s. The Conklin anthology also leaned heavily on Campbell's magazine, but cast a wider net, with extensive representation of stories from the previous decade, including many from the Gernsback magazines, as well as work by Poe, Wells, and Arthur Conan Doyle.

As the science-fiction magazines grew in number and quality in the post-war years, an inevitable next development was the coming of anthologies devoted to the best stories of a single year. The first of these was edited by Everett F. Bleiler and T. E. Dikty, a pair of scholarly science-fiction readers with long experience in the field, and it was called, not entirely appropriately (since it drew entirely on material published in 1948), *The Best Science Fiction Stories: 1949*.

Science fiction then was a very small entity indeed—eight or nine magazines, a dozen or so books a year produced by semi-professional publishing houses run by old-time s-f fans, and the very occasional short story by the likes of Robert A. Heinlein in the *Saturday Evening Post* or some other well-known slick magazine. So esoteric a species of reading-matter was it that Bleiler and Dikty found it necessary to provide their book, which was issued by the relatively minor mainstream publishing house of Frederick Fell, Inc., with two separate introductory essays explaining the nature and history of science fiction to uninitiated readers.

In those days science fiction was at its best in the short lengths, and the editors of *The Best Science Fiction: 1949* had plenty of splendid material to offer. There were two stories by Ray Bradbury, both later incorporated in *The Martian Chronicles*; Wilmar Shiras's fine superchild story "In Hiding;" an excellent early Poul Anderson story, one by Isaac Asimov, and half a dozen others, all of which would be received enthusiastically by modern readers. The book did fairly well, by the modest sales standards of its era, and the Bleiler–Dikty series of annual anthologies continued for another decade or so.

Toward the end of its era the Bleiler–Dikty collection was joined by a very different sort of Best of the Year anthology edited by Judith Merril, whose sophisticated literary tastes led her to go far beyond the s-f magazines, offering stories by such outsiders to the field as Jorge Luis Borges, Jack Finney, Donald Barthelme, and John Steinbeck cheek-by-jowl with the more familiar offerings of Asimov, Sturgeon, Robert Sheckley, and Clifford D. Simak. The Merril anthology, inaugurated in 1956, also lasted about a decade; and by then science fiction had become big business, with new magazines founded, shows like *Star Trek* appearing on network television, dozens and then hundreds of novels published every year. Since the 1960s no year has gone by without its Best of the Year collection, and sometimes two or three simultaneously. Such distinguished science-fiction writers as Frederik Pohl, Harry Harrison, Brian Aldiss, and Lester del Rey took their turns at compiling annual anthologies, along with veteran book editors like Donald A. Wollheim and Terry Carr.

When word went forth in 1983 that one more Year's Best anthology was being assembled, this one under the editorship of Gardner Dozois, it was reasonable to expect a creditable job. Dozois was, after all, a capable and well-known writer himself, who had begun his career precociously with a short story in 1966 and from 1971 on had brought forth a great deal of impressively powerful work; he had edited a string of theme anthologies (A Day in the Life, 1972, Future Power, 1976, Another World, 1977, and many others); and for five years beginning in 1977 had taken over the editorship of Lester del Rey's Best Science Fiction Stories of the Year anthology. But no one, I think, was quite prepared for the magnitude and comprehensiveness of The Year's Best Science Fiction: First Annual Collection, the 1984 inaugural volume of the new Dozois anthology, nor could anyone have anticipated that the series would, in time, come to be the defining summation of a glorious era in science fiction.

I have the first volume of the Dozois series before me now. It looks surprisingly like the most recent one: a thick book (575 pages; the twentieth volume has 648) that announces its name in bold letters emphasizing the words SCIENCE FICTION, proudly asserts that it offers "Over 250,000 words of Fantastic Fiction" (the subhead on the most recent volume reads, "More than 300,000 words of Fantastic Fiction"), and lists on its cover the names of thirteen of its twenty-five contributors.

Those contributors were a stellar group, of course: Poul Anderson, Kim Stanley Robinson, George R. R. Martin, Joe Haldeman, Greg Bear, Connie Willis, Dan Simmons, Avram Davidson, R. A. Lafferty, etc., etc., etc. Some, like Bear and Willis and Simmons and Robinson, were just entering their years of greatness. Some, like Davidson and Lafferty, were nearing the end of important careers. Taken all together, the stories represent a shrewd cross-section of what was already a potent period in the history of the s-f short story, a period that would see even greater accomplishments a couple of years later when Dozois became editor of the ranking s-f monthly, Isaac Asimov's Science Fiction Magazine.

But that first volume was not distinguished merely by the excellence of its fiction. What gave it special importance and, eventually, immense historical value, was the sixteen-page essay "Summation: 1983," in which Dozois provided a penetrating, closely analytical account of the year's activities in the world of science-fiction publishing: comings and goings among editors and publishers, sales figures for best-selling books, circulation figures for magazines, thematic trends in current science fiction, news of awards and conventions, comments on recent s-f movies, obituaries. No previous best-of-the-year anthology had provided anything comparable. Each of the nineteen subsequent volumes has had a similar summation section, each at least as lengthy as the first and some much longer indeed; in and of themselves they form a continuing chronicle of the evolution of science fiction in the late twentieth century that will be of value to critics, historians, and readers for decades to come.

The stories chosen by Dozois in these first twenty volumes also constitute a statement about the nature of the s-f short story in that two-decade period—a statement filtered through the sensibility of just one reader, of course, but a highly informed one, steeped in the history of the field, imbued with a sense of science fiction's value both as entertainment and intellectual stimulation, and further augmented by the editor's own innate knowledge, as a skilled practitioner himself, of the art of the short story. Over the years Dozois's story-picking expertise has been confirmed by reader approval, demonstrated through the great number of Hugo awards conferred on Dozois–chosen stories and by the many awards given to the anthology itself.

Dozois's task as anthologist was complicated, in an odd way, when he became editor of *Isaac Asimov's Science Fiction Magazine* in 1985. *Asimov's* had already established itself as the outstanding magazine of the field by then, but under Dozois's guidance it attained an even more powerful position of dominance, as is shown by the unparalleled fourteen Hugo awards for Best Editor that he received during the nineteen years of his stewardship of the magazine. John Campbell's *Astounding* was similarly dominant in its day, more than half a century ago—but Campbell was not also the editor of a Best of the Year anthology. When Healy and McComas, in 1946, chose twenty-five of their thirty-three stories from the Campbell *Astounding*, no one was particularly surprised or upset: everyone knew that most of the superior stories of the era had been published there. And, since science-fiction writers tend naturally to gravitate toward their era's top magazine, a similar concentration of the best work began appearing in the Dozois–edited *Asimov's*. But Dozois as anthology editor could not allow himself to draw as extensively on his own magazine as Healy and McComas had drawn on Campbell's, lest his book seem merely self-promoting; and so he was faced with the perplexing necessity of finding worthy stories for his anthology that had originally appeared in magazines competitive with his own.

Examining a few randomly chosen volumes of the Dozois series, we can see how well he managed this tricky task. The seventh volume, published in 1990, contains twenty-five stories, of which just nine originated in *Asimov's*: an admirable show of objectivity. The eleventh volume, from 1994, includes only seven *Asimov's* items out of twenty-three. The twentieth volume, released in 2003, shows an eight-for-twenty-six ratio. Surely the practice of this sort of discipline required Dozois to eliminate from his anthology a great many stories from his magazine that must have seemed as worthy of reprinting as the ones he did choose for the book; but the fact remains that he compelled himself to look far and wide for stories and the contents pages of his anthologies display a broad range of fiction from every appropriate source in the field.

One does see a certain group of authors appearing regularly in volume after volume: Connie Willis, Bruce Sterling, James Patrick Kelly, Michael Swanwick, Ian McDonald, John Kessel, Nancy Kress, Lucius Shepard, Mike Resnick, Greg Egan, Walter Jon Williams, and four or five others. The presence of such a cast of constant favorites would hardly be a surprise in any ongoing series of anthologies, which, after all, represent by definition the personal tastes of the series' editor; but in fact Dozois's little group of regulars were chosen for one anthology after another primarily because they were consistently doing the best work in the field. New writers joined the group every year: Robert Reed, for example, an unknown writer when the series began, came in with the ninth volume and has scarcely missed one since. The contents page of the twentieth volume gives us Maureen F. McHugh, Charles Stross, Alexander Irvine, Alastair Reynolds, Charles Coleman Finlay, and three or four more whose names would have meant nothing to readers a decade or so ago, but who can be expected to turn up on future contents pages of the Dozois anthology with great regularity in the years to come. More than thirty years after he first edited a science-fiction anthology, Gardner Dozois still maintains the ability to spot fresh new talent.

And now, to mark the completion of the first twenty years' run of *The Year's Best Science Fiction*, Dozois has selected *The Best of the Best*. Every writer whose work is included here knows what an immense honor it is to be chosen. For Gardner Dozois himself the book is the capstone of two decades of remarkable work. Let him revel in the pleasure of knowing that he has given us, here, a volume that takes its place instantly among the classic science-fiction anthologies of all time.

preface

When I started work on *The Year's Best Science Fiction, First Annual Collection*, back in 1983 (the book appeared in 1984), I was thirty-six, just past having been a hot young Turk in the '70s, beginning to brown and curl a bit, my son was fourteen, most of the famous SF writers of the Campbellian Golden Age of the '40s and the Gold/Boucher Age of the '50s were not only still alive but available to be talked to at most science-fiction conventions, and most of my peers and contemporaries were, if not new writers anymore, still on the young ends of their careers and not really well-known yet . . . and I knew several young hopefuls, like a local fan called Michael Swanwick, who had only four or five sales under their belts. It would be two years yet before I took over the editorship of *Isaac Asimov's Science Fiction Magazine*.

Now, as I sit typing in 2004, I'm an old man, my son has two children of his own (six and eight, respectively), most of the Big-Name writers who dominated the genre then are dead, and my peers and contemporaries, those of them who are still alive, are no longer Hot Young Turks, but rather the Big-Name writers of the field, and they are as gray and wrinkled and sagging as I am. Michael Swanwick is a multiple Hugo-winner. And my almost-twenty-year career as editor of *Asimov's* is behind me and being coolly evaluated by critics and historians. Time washes you away in a flood, and by the time you can turn your head and look back, the beach has dwindled to a thin tan line behind you. There is no further shore.

So, after having completed twenty-seven Best-of-the-Year anthologies over a period of twenty-eight years (the time and number discrepancy is because I turned out six volumes of an earlier Best-of-the-Year series in the '70s, for Dutton, before starting on *this* series—which started out with the now-defunct publisher Bluejay Books, and switched to St. Martin's Press in 1987, with the *Fourth Annual Edition*, when Bluejay folded), it seemed time for a retrospective, a look back.

By the time you read these words, there will have been twenty-one volumes of *The Year's Best Science Fiction* published. Those twenty-one volumes together contain 6,306,634 words of fiction, written by one hundred and eighty different authors. When the idea of putting a *Best of the Best* retrospective anthology together first occurred to me, it seemed like a straightforward task, perhaps even an easy one. It was not. In fact, this may have been one of the hardest jobs I've ever had to do (as far as putting anthologies together is concerned anyway; shoveling coal in the hot sun is considerably harder by any absolute standard, believe me). For one thing, in order to figure out what stories in those volumes were really the best, I had to *reread* a significant proportion of those 6,306,634 words, especially as I found that I barely remembered some of the stories from earlier volumes.

Doing all that reading was not the hardest part, though. Looking back through the twenty-one volumes only served to remind me how *many* good stories had appeared in them over the years. Even with a retrospective volume as large as this one, I couldn't possibly get all of them, or even a significant proportion of them, into the book. Even a book twice the size of this one wouldn't be big enough to include all the stories that probably *should* be included. Since all of those stories were to my taste in the first place—which should hardly come as a surprise—and since taste was the usual winnowing-screen I would employ in selecting which stories to use from someone *else's* anthology or magazine, how was I going to cut the huge crop of contenders down to a manageable number?

For starters, for symmetry's sake, I decided to limit the choice to the first twenty volumes. In the unlikely event that I live long enough to produce an additional nineteen volumes, perhaps we can have a *Best of the Best II*. Then, although novellas have always been among my favorite stories in the *Bests*, and there are easily a dozen or more that *ought* to be in the multidimensional, infinitely-expansible version of this book (Michael Swanwick's "Griffin's Egg," Frederic Pohl's "Outnumbering the Dead," Ursula K. Le Guin's "A Woman's Liberation," Kim Stanley Robinson's "Green Mars," William Barton's "Off on a Starship," Lucius Shepard's "R&R," Nancy Kress's "Beggars in Spain," Robert Silverberg's "Sailing to Byzantium," Judith Moffett's "Tiny Tango," Greg Benford's "Immersion," Greg Egan's "Oceanic," Ian McDonald's "The Days of Solomon Gursky," John Kessel's "Stories For Men," and so many more), here in the real world where practical considerations of length exist, I clearly had room for no more than a few of them, if I wanted to get a large selection of authors representative of twenty years' worth of *Best* volumes into the book.

I was still left with the most difficult problem, though—how do you decide what the word "Best" means in this context? Do I go for the best-known stories, stories such as Nancy Kress's "Beggars in Spain" and James Patrick Kelly's "Think Like a Dinosaur," which have been reprinted very widely and which most people have already seen, or do I go with other good stories by the same authors that haven't been as ballyhooed? If I didn't use the most famous stories, many people were going to be disappointed that they weren't there. On the other hand, if I used them exclusively, I'd produce a book full of stuff that everyone's already read and that's largely duplicable elsewhere. The only solution I could see was to walk a tightrope between the two, putting in some of the most famous stories and in other cases picking more obscure and unfairly overlooked alternatives instead—although I'm aware that I'm taking a chance of pleasing nobody with this approach.

The biggest decision I came to, though, was that I had to pick the stories that had made the strongest impression on me as a *reader*, stories that really moved or excited or impressed me, both on first reading years ago and on rereading now, stories that made me put down the book when I finished them, and stare off through the air, and shiver, remembering the wonders I'd just experienced—and that I had to pick them with no (or as little as possible, anyway) consideration for demographics, for whether I had enough big-name writers, or enough women writers, or enough Brits, or whatever, or whether or not I'd selected stories from all the important markets that ought to be represented. So don't even bother to tell me that there's too many stories from *Asimov's* here (although several of them are from before I took over as editor, and *Asimov's has* been the dominant American SF magazine of the '80s and '90s, under three different editors), I already know. Or that there's not enough stories from *Interzone*, or that there ought to be something from *Science Fiction Age*. I picked the stories I had the strongest emotional reactions to, and let the chips fall where they may, as far as demographics were concerned, although no doubt I'm buying myself a lot of trouble with the critics by dong so. I have no doubt that a different editor could have gone through this same pool of stories and come up with a totally different selection of stories that would have been equally valid and equally defensible as deserving the title *Best of the Best*, that in fact no two readers would come up with the same list if asked to select one. Hell, a day earlier or a day later, I might well have come up with a different list myself.

But it's reassuring to remember that there really *have* been a lot of good stories published in this series over the course of two decades. If ever the term "embarrassment of riches" applies, it applies here. So I like to tell myself that even if I'd closed my eyes, stabbed out a finger, and picked stories at random, you'd probably still be getting a pretty good anthology out of it.

In closing, I'd like to thank Jim Frenkel, my editor at Bluejay, who not only proposed the idea of me doing a new Best-of-the-Year series in the first place, after my Dutton series had died, but who insisted that it be a really big *fat* volume, as big as possible; I was against this idea, thinking that people wouldn't want to spend the extra money for a big hardcover volume, but over the years almost every positive review has mentioned the size of the *Best* as a selling point and most reader feedback indicates that people like it big, so he was right and I was wrong. If he'd listened to me, the series might have died long ago. I'd also like to thank my own editors at St. Martin's over the years, Stuart Moore, Gordon Van Gelder, Bryan Cholfin, and, today, Marc Resnick.

I'd also like to thank the often-unsung acquisitions editors who had the good taste to buy these stories in the first place: Ellen Datlow, Shawna McCarthy, Ed Ferman, Kristine Kathryn Rusch, Gordon Van Gelder, David Pringle, Peter Crowther, Constance Ash, Stanley Schmidt, Greg Bear, David Bischoff, and Patrick Nielson Hayden, as well as all the editors over the last twenty years who bought all the stories in those twenty volumes that didn't happen to make the cut for this particular retrospective. I'd like to thank the *writers*, who labored long into the night over keyboards in lonely rooms to write all the stories in this anthology, and all the other stories in the twenty volumes of the *Best*, and all the good stories that didn't make it into any of them in the first place—because there've always been more good stories than we have room to use, every year from the beginning to now.

And lastly, I'd like to thank you, the readers, for buying and appreciating the volumes of this series, and thus making it a success. May you continue to enjoy future volumes, and may you enjoy the one you hold in your hands at the moment.

—Gardner Dozois

THE BEST of THE BEST

20 Years of

THE YEAR'S BEST
SCIENCE FICTION

blood music

GREG BEAR

Born in San Diego, California, Greg Bear made his first sale at the age of fifteen to Robert Lowndes's *Famous Science Fiction*, and has subsequently established himself as one of the top professionals in the genre. He won a Nebula Award for his pyrotechnic novella "Hardfought," a Nebula and Hugo Award for the famous story which follows, "Blood Music," which was later expanded into a novel of the same title, and a subsequent Nebula and Hugo for his story "Tangents." He added another Nebula Award to his collection for his novel *Darwin's Radio*. His other books include the novels *Hegira, Psychlone, Beyond Heaven's River, Strength of Stones The Infinity Concerto, The Serpent Mage, Eon, Eternity, The Forge of God, Anvil of Stars, Moving Mars, Heads, Legacy, Queen of Angels, Slant,* and *Dinosaur Summer*, as well as the collections *Wind from a Burning Woman* and *Tangents*, and, as editor, the original anthology *New Legends,* one of the best anthologies of the '90s. His most recent books are the novels *Vitals* and *Darwin's Children*, and the monumental collection *The Collected Stories of Greg Bear.* He has had stories in our First and Fourth annual collections. He lives with his family just outside of Seattle, Washington.

Bear has a sweeping, Stapeldonean vision of how different the future must inevitably be from the present. This vision of the strange, inhuman future to come is featured powerfully in the story that follows, which may be the first true nanotech story, even though it was written several years before the term "nanotechnology" was even coined—a chilling story that warns us that that inhuman future may not be hundreds of years away, or even decades away, but may instead lay waiting for us only next week, or tomorrow, or today . . . and that the true frontiers of exploration may not lay Out There, but rather deep inside.

There is a principle in nature I don't think anyone has pointed out before. Each hour, a myriad of trillions of little live things—bacteria, microbes "animalcules"—are born and die, not counting for much except in the bulk of their existence and the accumulation of their tiny effects. They do not perceive deeply. They do not suffer much. A hundred billion, dying, would not begin to have the same importance as a single human death.

Within the ranks of magnitude of all creatures, small as microbes or great as humans, there is an equality of "elan," just as the branches of a tall tree, gathered together, equal the bulk of the limbs below, and all the limbs equal the bulk of the trunk.

That, at least, is the principle. I believe Vergil Ulam was the first to violate it.

It had been two years since I'd last seen Vergil. My memory of him hardly matched the tan, smiling, well-dressed gentleman standing before me. We had made a lunch appointment over the phone the day before, and now faced each other in the wide double doors of the employees' cafeteria at the Mount Freedom Medical Center.

"Vergil?" I asked. "My God, Vergil!"

"Good to see you, Edward." He shook my hand firmly. He had lost ten or twelve kilos and what remained seemed tighter, better proportioned. At university, Vergil had been the pudgy, shock-haired, snaggle-toothed whiz kid who hot-wired doorknobs, gave us punch that turned our piss blue, and never got a date except with Eileen Termagent, who shared many of his physical characteristics.

"You look fantastic," I said. "Spend a summer in Cabo San Lucas?"

We stood in line at the counter and chose our food. "The tan," he said, picking out a carton of chocolate milk, "is from spending three months under a sunlamp. My teeth were straightened just after I last saw you. I'll explain the rest, but we need a place to talk where no one will listen close."

I steered him to the smokers' corner, where three die-hard puffers were scattered among six tables.

"Listen, I mean it," I said as we unloaded our trays. "You've changed. You're looking good."

"I've changed more than you know." His tone was motion-picture ominous, and he delivered the line with a theatrical lift of his brows. "How's Gail?"

Gail was doing well, I told him, teaching nursery school. We'd married the year before. His gaze shifted down to his food—pineapple slice and cottage cheese, piece of banana cream pie—and he said, his voice almost cracking, "Notice something else?"

I squinted in concentration. "Uh."

"Look closer."

"I'm not sure. Well, yes, you're not wearing glasses. Contacts?"

"No. I don't need them anymore."

"And you're a snappy dresser. Who's dressing you now? I hope she's as sexy as she is tasteful."

"Candice isn't—wasn't responsible for the improvement in my clothes," he said. "I just got a better job, more money to throw around. My taste in clothes is better than my taste in food, as it happens." He grinned the old Vergil self-deprecating grin, but ended it with a peculiar leer. "At any rate, she's left me, I've been fired from my job, I'm living on savings."

"Hold it," I said. "That's a bit crowded. Why not do a linear breakdown? You got a job. Where?"

"Genetron Corp.," he said. "Sixteen months ago."

"I haven't heard of them."

"You will. They're putting out common stock in the next month. It'll shoot off the board. They've broken through with MABs. Medical—"

"I know what MABs are," I interrupted. "At least in theory. Medically Applicable Biochips."

"They have some that work."

"What?" It was my turn to lift my brows.

"Microscopic logic circuits. You inject them into the human body, they set up shop where they're told and troubleshoot. With Dr. Michael Bernard's approval."

That was quite impressive. Bernard's reputation was spotless. Not only was he associated with the genetic engineering biggies, but he had made news at least once a year in his practice as a neurosurgeon before retiring. Covers on *Time*, *Mega*, *Rolling Stone*.

"That's supposed to be secret—stock, breakthrough, Bernard, everything." He looked around and lowered his voice. "But you do whatever the hell you want. I'm through with the bastards."

I whistled. "Make me rich, huh?"

"If that's what you want. Or you can spend some time with me before rushing off to your broker."

"Of course." He hadn't touched the cottage cheese or pie. He had, however, eaten the pineapple slice and drunk the chocolate milk. "So tell me more."

"Well, in med school I was training for lab work. Biochemical research. I've always had a bent for computers, too. So I put myself through my last two years—"

"By selling software packages to Westinghouse," I said.

"It's good my friends remember. That's how I got involved with Genetron, just when they were starting out. They had big money backers, all the lab facilities I thought anyone would ever need. They hired me, and I advanced rapidly.

"Four months and I was doing my own work. I made some breakthroughs"—he tossed his hand nonchalantly—"then I went off on tangents they thought were premature. I persisted and they took away my lab, handed it over to a certifiable flatworm. I managed to save part of the experiment before they fired me. But I haven't exactly been cautious . . . or judicious. So now it's going on outside the lab."

I'd always regarded Vergil as ambitious, a trifle cracked, and not terribly sensitive. His relations with authority figures had never been smooth. Science, for him, was like the woman you couldn't possibly have, who suddenly opens her arms to you, long before you're ready for mature love—leaving you afraid you'll forever blow the chance, lose the prize. Apparently, he did. "Outside the lab? I don't get you."

"Edward, I want you to examine me. Give me a thorough physical. Maybe a cancer diagnostic. Then I'll explain more."

"You want a five-thousand-dollar exam?"

"Whatever you can do. Ultrasound, NMR, thermogram, everything."

"I don't know if I can get access to all that equipment. NMR full-scan has only been here a month or two. Hell, you couldn't pick a more expensive way—"

"Then ultrasound. That's all you'll need."

"Vergil, I'm an obstetrician, not a glamour-boy lab-tech. OB-GYN, butt of all jokes. If you're turning into a woman, maybe I can help you."

He leaned forward, almost putting his elbow into the pie, but swinging wide at the last instant by scant millimeters. The old Vergil would have hit it square. "Examine me closely and you'll . . ." He narrowed his eyes. "Just examine me."

"So I make an appointment for ultrasound. Who's going to pay?"

"I'm on Blue Shield." He smiled and held up a medical credit card. "I messed with the personnel files at Genetron. Anything up to a hundred thousand dollars medical, they'll never check, never suspect."

He wanted secrecy, so I made arrangements. I filled out his forms myself. As long as everything was billed properly, most of the examination could take place without official notice. I didn't charge for my services. After all, Vergil had turned my piss blue. We were friends.

He came in late at night. I wasn't normally on duty then, but I stayed late, waiting for him on the third floor of what the nurses called the Frankenstein wing. I sat on an orange plastic chair. He arrived, looking olive-colored under the fluorescent lights.

He stripped, and I arranged him on the table. I noticed, first off, that his ankles looked swollen. But they weren't puffy. I felt them several times. They seemed healthy but looked odd. "Hm," I said.

I ran the paddles over him, picking up areas difficult for the big unit to hit, and programmed the data into the imaging system. Then I swung the table around and inserted it into the enameled orifice of the ultrasound diagnostic unit, the hum-hole, so-called by the nurses.

I integrated the data from the hum-hole with that from the paddle sweeps and rolled Vergil out, then set up a video frame. The image took a second to integrate, then flowed into a pattern showing Vergil's skeleton. My jaw fell.

Three seconds of that and it switched to his thoracic organs, then his musculature, and, finally, vascular system and skin.

"How long since the accident?" I asked, trying to take the quiver out of my voice.

"I haven't been in an accident," he said. "It was deliberate."

"Jesus, they beat you to keep secrets?"

"You don't understand me, Edward. Look at the images again. I'm not damaged."

"Look, there's thickening here"—I indicated the ankles—"and your ribs—that crazy zigzag pattern of interlocks. Broken sometime, obviously. And—"

"Look at my spine," he said. I rotated the image in the video frame.

Buckminster Fuller, I thought. It was fantastic. A cage of triangular projections, all interlocking in ways I couldn't begin to follow, much less understand. I reached around and tried to feel his spine with my fingers. He lifted his arms and looked off at the ceiling.

"I can't find it," I said. "It's all smooth back there." I let go of him and looked at his chest, then prodded his ribs. They were sheathed in something tough and flexible. The harder I pressed, the tougher it became. Then I noticed another change.

"Hey," I said. "You don't have any nipples." There were tiny pigment patches, but no nipple formations at all.

"See?" Vergil asked, shrugging on the white robe, "I'm being rebuilt from the inside out."

In my reconstruction of those hours, I fancy myself saying, "So tell me about it." Perhaps mercifully, I don't remember what I actually said.

He explained with his characteristic circumlocutions. Listening was like trying to get to the meat of a newspaper article through a forest of sidebars and graphic embellishments.

I simplify and condense.

Genetron had assigned him to manufacturing prototype biochips, tiny circuits made out of protein molecules. Some were hooked up to silicon chips little more than a micrometer in size, then went through rat arteries to chemically keyed locations, to make connections with the rat tissue and attempt to monitor and even control lab-induced pathologies.

"*That* was something," he said.

"We recovered the most complex microchip by sacrificing the rat, then debriefed it—hooked the silicon portion up to an imaging system. The computer gave us bar graphs, then a diagram of the chemical characteristics of about eleven centimeters of blood vessel . . . then put it all together to make a picture. We zoomed down eleven centimeters of rat artery. You never saw so many scientists jumping up and down, hugging each other, drinking buckets of bug juice." Bug juice was lab ethanol mixed with Dr. Pepper.

Eventually, the silicon elements were eliminated completely in favor of nucleo-proteins. He seemed reluctant to explain in detail, but I gathered they found ways to make huge molecules—as large as DNA, and even more complex—into electro-chemical computers, using ribosome-like structures as "encoders" and "readers" and RNA as "tape." Vergil was able to mimic reproductive separation and reassembly in his nucleoproteins, incorporating program changes at key points by switching nucleotide pairs. "Genetron wanted me to switch over to supergene engineering, since that was the coming thing everywhere else. Make all kinds of critters, some out of our imagination. But I had different ideas." He twiddled his finger around his ear and made theremin sounds. "Mad scientist time, right?" He laughed, then sobered. "I injected my best nucleoproteins into bacteria to make duplication and compounding easier. Then I started to leave them inside, so the circuits could interact with the cells. They were heuristically programmed; they taught themselves. The cells fed chemically coded information to the computers, the computers processed it and made decisions, the cells became smart. I mean, smart as planaria, for starters. Imagine an *E. coli* as smart as a planarian worm!"

I nodded. "I'm imagining."

"Then I really went off on my own. We had the equipment, the techniques; and I knew the molecular language. I could make really dense, really complicated biochips by compounding the nucleoproteins, making them into little brains. I did some research into how far I could go, theoretically. Sticking with bacteria, I could make a biochip with the computing capacity of a sparrow's brain. Imagine how jazzed I was! Then I saw a way to increase the complexity a thousandfold, by using something we regarded as a nuisance—quantum chit-chat between the fixed elements of the circuits. Down that small, even the slightest change could bomb a biochip. But I developed a program that actually predicted and took advantage of electron tunneling. Emphasized the heuristic aspects of the computer, used the chit-chat as a method of increasing complexity."

"You're losing me," I said.

"I took advantage of randomness. The circuits could repair themselves, compare memories, and correct faulty elements. I gave them basic instructions: Go forth and multiply. Improve. By God, you should have seen some of the cultures a week later! It was amazing. They were evolving all on their own, like little cities. I destroyed them all. I think one of the petri dishes would have grown legs and walked out of the incubator if I'd kept feeding it."

"You're kidding." I looked at him. "You're not kidding."

"Man, they *knew* what it was like to improve! They knew where they had to go, but they were just so limited, being in bacteria bodies, with so few resources."

"How smart were they?"

"I couldn't be sure. They were associating in clusters of a hundred to two hundred cells, each cluster behaving like an autonomous unit. Each cluster might have been as smart as a rhesus monkey. They exchanged information through their pili, passed on bits of memory, and compared notes. Their organization was obviously different from a group of monkeys. Their world was so much simpler, for one thing. With their abilities, they were masters of the petri dishes. I put phages in with them; the phages didn't have a chance. They used every option available to change and grow."

"How is that possible?"

"What?" He seemed surprised I wasn't accepting everything at face value.

"Cramming so much into so little. A rhesus monkey is not your simple little calculator, Vergil."

"I haven't made myself clear," he said, obviously irritated. "I was using nucleoprotein computers. They're like DNA, but all the information can interact. Do you know how many nucleotide pairs there are in the DNA of a single bacteria?"

It had been a long time since my last biochemistry lesson. I shook my head.

"About two million. Add in the modified ribosome structures—fifteen thousand of them, each with a molecular weight of about three million—and consider the combinations and permutations. The RNA is arranged like a continuous loop paper tape, surrounded by ribosomes ticking off instructions and manufacturing protein chains . . ." His eyes were bright and slightly moist. "Besides, I'm not saying every cell was a distinct entity. They cooperated."

"How many bacteria in the dishes you destroyed?"

"Billions. I don't know." He smirked. "You got it, Edward. Whole planetsful of *E. coli.*"

"But Genetron didn't fire you then?"

"No. They didn't know what was going on, for one thing. I kept compounding the molecules, increasing their size and complexity. When bacteria were too limited, I took blood from myself, separated out white cells, and injected them with the new biochips. I watched them, put them through mazes and little chemical problems. They were whizzes. Time is a lot faster at that level—so little distance for the messages to cross, and the environment is much simpler. Then I forgot to store a file under my secret code in the lab computers. Some managers found it and guessed what I was up to. Everybody panicked. They thought we'd have every social watchdog in the country on our backs because of what I'd done. They started to destroy my work and wipe my programs. Ordered me to sterilize my white cells. Christ." He pulled the white robe off and started to get dressed. "I only had a day or two. I separated out the most complex cells—"

"How complex?"

"They were clustering in hundred-cell groups, like the bacteria. Each group as smart as a four-year-old kid, maybe." He studied my face for a moment. "Still doubting? Want me to run through how many nucleotide pairs there are in a mammalian cell? I tailored my computers to take advantage of the white cells' capacity. Four billion nucleotide pairs, Edward. And they don't have a huge body to worry about, taking up most of their thinking time."

"Okay," I said. "I'm convinced. What did you do?"

"I mixed the cells back into a cylinder of whole blood and injected myself with it." He buttoned the top of his shirt and smiled thinly at me. "I'd programmed them with every drive I could, talked as high a level as I could using just enzymes and such. After that, they were on their own."

"You programmed them to go forth and multiply, improve?" I repeated.

"I think they developed some characteristics picked up by the biochips in their *E. coli* phases. The white cells could talk to each other with extruded memories. They found ways to ingest other types of cells and alter them without killing them."

"You're crazy."

"You can see the screen! Edward, I haven't been sick since. I used to get colds all the time. I've never felt better."

"They're inside you, finding things, changing them."

"And by now, each cluster is as smart as you or I."

"You're absolutely nuts."

He shrugged. "Genetron fired me. They thought I was going to take revenge for what they did to my work. They ordered me out of the labs, and I haven't had a real chance to see what's been going on inside me until now. Three months."

"So . . ." My mind was racing. "You lost weight because they improved your fat metabolism. Your bones are stronger, your spine has been completely rebuilt—"

"No more backaches even if I sleep on my old mattress."

"Your heart looks different."

"I didn't know about the heart," he said, examining the frame image more closely. "As for the fat—I was thinking about that. They could increase my brown cells, fix up the metabolism. I haven't been as hungry lately. I haven't changed my eating habits that much—I still want the same old junk—but somehow I get around to eating only what I need. I don't think they know what my brain is yet. Sure, they've got all the glandular stuff—but they don't have the *big* picture, if you see what I mean. They don't know *I'm* in here. But boy, they sure did figure out what my reproductive organs are."

I glanced at the image and shifted my eyes away.

"Oh, they look pretty normal," he said, hefting his scrotum obscenely. He snickered. "But how else do you think I'd land a real looker like Candice? She was just after a one-night stand with a techie. I looked okay then, no tan but trim, with good clothes. She'd never screwed a techie before. Joke time, right? But my little geniuses kept us up half the night. I think they made improvements each time. I felt like I had a goddamned fever."

His smile vanished. "But then one night my skin started to crawl. It really scared me. I thought things were getting out of hand. I wondered what they'd do when they crossed the blood-brain barrier and found out about *me*—about the brain's real function. So I began a campaign to keep them under control. I figured, the reason they wanted to get into the skin was the simplicity of running circuits across a surface. Much easier than trying to maintain chains of communication in and around muscles, organs, vessels. The skin was much more direct. So I bought a quartz lamp." He caught my puzzled expression. "In the lab, we'd break down the protein in biochip cells by exposing them to ultraviolet light. I alternated sunlamp with quartz treatments. Keeps them out of my skin and gives me a nice tan."

"Give you skin cancer, too," I commented.

"They'll probably take care of that. Like police."

"Okay. I've examined you, you've told me a story I still find hard to believe . . . what do you want me to do?"

"I'm not as nonchalant as I act, Edward. I'm worried. I'd like to find some way to control them before they find out about my brain. I mean, think of it, they're in the trillions by now, each one smart. They're cooperating to some extent. I'm probably the smartest thing on the planet, and they haven't even begun to get their act together. I don't really want them to take over." He laughed unpleasantly. "Steal my soul, you know? So think of some treatment to block them. Maybe we can starve the little buggers. Just think on it." He buttoned his shirt. "Give me a call." He handed me a slip of paper with his address and phone number. Then he went to the keyboard and erased the image on the frame, dumping the memory of the examination. "Just you," he said. "Nobody else for now. And please . . . hurry."

It was three o'clock in the morning when Vergil walked out of the examination room. He'd allowed me to take blood samples, then shaken my hand—his palm was damp, nervous—and cautioned me against ingesting anything from the specimens.

Before I went home, I put the blood through a series of tests. The results were ready the next day.

I picked them up during my lunch break in the afternoon, then destroyed all of the samples. I did it like a robot. It took me five days and nearly sleepless nights to accept what I'd seen. His blood was normal enough, though the machines diagnosed the patient as having an infection. High levels of leukocytes—white blood cells— and histamines. On the fifth day, I believed.

Gail came home before I did, but it was my turn to fix dinner. She slipped one of the school's disks into the home system and showed me video art her nursery kids had been creating. I watched quietly, ate with her in silence.

I had two dreams, part of my final acceptance. In the first, that evening, I witnessed the destruction of the planet Krypton, Superman's home world. Billions of superhuman geniuses went screaming off in walls of fire. I related the destruction to my sterilizing the samples of Vergil's blood.

The second dream was worse. I dreamed that New York City was raping a woman.

By the end of the dream, she gave birth to little embryo cities, all wrapped up in translucent sacs, soaked with blood from the difficult labor.

I called him on the morning of the sixth day. He answered on the fourth ring. "I have some results," I said. "Nothing conclusive. But I want to talk with you. In person."

"Sure," he said. "I'm staying inside for the time being." His voice was strained; he sounded tired.

Vergil's apartment was in a fancy high-rise near the lake shore. I took the elevator up, listening to little advertising jingles and watching dancing holograms display products, empty apartments for rent, the building's hostess discussing social activities for the week.

Vergil opened the door and motioned me in. He wore a checked robe with long sleeves and carpet slippers. He clutched an unlit pipe in one hand, his fingers twisting it back and forth as he walked away from me and sat down, saying nothing.

"You have an infection," I said.

"Oh?"

"That's all the blood analyses tell me. I don't have access to the electron microscopes."

"I don't think it's really an infection," he said. "After all, they're my own cells. Probably something else . . . some sign of their presence, of the change. We can't expect to understand everything that's happening."

I removed my coat. "Listen," I said, "you really have me worried now." The expression on his face stopped me: a kind of frantic beatitude. He squinted at the ceiling and pursed his lips.

"Are you stoned?" I asked.

He shook his head, then nodded once, very slowly. "Listening," he said.

"To what?"

"I don't know. Not sounds . . . exactly. Like music. The heart, all the blood vessels, friction of blood along the arteries, veins. Activity. Music in the blood." He looked at me plaintively. "Why aren't you at work?"

"My day off. Gail's working."

"Can you stay?"

I shrugged. "I suppose." I sounded suspicious. I glanced around the apartment, looking for ashtrays, packs of papers.

"I'm not stoned, Edward," he said. "I may be wrong, but I think something big is happening. I think they're finding out who I am."

I sat down across from Vergil, staring at him intently. He didn't seem to notice. Some inner process involved him. When I asked for a cup of coffee, he motioned to the kitchen. I boiled a pot of water and took a jar of instant from the cabinet. With cup in hand, I returned to my seat. He twisted his head back and forth, eyes open. "You always knew what you wanted to be, didn't you?" he asked.

"More or less."

"A gynecologist. Smart moves. Never false moves. I was different. I had goals, but no direction. Like a map without roads, just places to be. I didn't give a shit for anything, anyone but myself. Even science. Just a means. I'm surprised I got so far. I even hated my folks."

He gripped his chair arms.

"Something wrong?" I asked.

"They're talking to me," he said. He shut his eyes.

For an hour he seemed to be asleep. I checked his pulse, which was strong and steady, felt his forehead—slightly cool—and made myself more coffee. I was looking through a magazine, at a loss what to do, when he opened his eyes again. "Hard to figure exactly what time is like for them," he said. "It's taken them maybe three, four days to figure out language, key human concepts. Now they're on to it. On to me. Right now."

"How's that?"

He claimed there were thousands of researchers hooked up to his neurons. He couldn't give details. "They're damned efficient, you know," he said. "They haven't screwed me up yet."

"We should get you into the hospital now."

"What in hell could other doctors do? Did *you* figure out any way to control them? I mean, they're my own cells."

"I've been thinking. We could starve them. Find out what metabolic differences—"

"I'm not sure I want to be rid of them," Vergil said. "They're not doing any harm."

"How do you know?"

He shook his head and held up one finger. "Wait. They're trying to figure out what space is. That's tough for them: They break distances down into concentrations of chemicals. For them, space is like intensity of taste."

"Vergil—"

"Listen! Think, Edward!" His tone was excited but even. "Something big is happening inside me. They talk to each other across the fluid, through membranes. They tailor something—viruses?—to carry data stored in nucleic acid chains. I think they're saying 'RNA.' That makes sense. That's one way I programmed them. But plasmidlike structures, too. Maybe that's what your machines think is a sign of infection—all their chattering in my blood, packets of data. Tastes of other individuals. Peers. Superiors. Subordinates."

"Vergil, I still think you should be in a hospital."

"This is my show, Edward," he said. "I'm their universe. They're amazed by the new scale." He was quiet again for a time. I squatted by his chair and pulled up the sleeve to his robe. His arm was crisscrossed with white lines. I was about to go to the phone when he stood and stretched. "Do you realize," he said, "how many body cells we kill each time we move?"

"I'm going to call for an ambulance," I said.

"No, you aren't." His tone stopped me. "I told you, I'm not sick, this is my show. Do you know what they'd do to me in a hospital? They'd be like cavemen trying to fix a computer. It would be a farce."

"Then what the hell am I doing here?" I asked, getting angry. "I can't do anything. I'm one of those cavemen."

"You're a friend," Vergil said, fixing his eyes on me. I had the impression I was being watched by more than just Vergil. "I want you here to keep me company." He laughed. "But I'm not exactly alone."

He walked around the apartment for two hours, fingering things, looking out windows, slowly and methodically fixing himself lunch. "You know, they can actually feel their own thoughts," he said about noon. "I mean, the cytoplasm seems to have a will of its own, a kind of subconscious life counter to the rationality they've only recently acquired. They hear the chemical 'noise' of the molecules fitting and unfitting inside."

At two o'clock, I called Gail to tell her I would be late. I was almost sick with tension, but I tried to keep my voice level. "Remember Vergil Ulam? I'm talking with him right now."

"Everything okay?" she asked.

Was it? Decidedly not. "Fine," I said.

"Culture!" Vergil said, peering around the kitchen wall at me. I said good-bye and hung up the phone. "They're always swimming in that bath of information. Contributing to it. It's a kind of gestalt thing. The hierarchy is absolute. They send tailored phages after cells that don't interact properly. Viruses specified to individuals or groups. No escape. A rouge cell gets pierced by the virus, the cell blebs outward, it explodes and dissolves. But it's not just a dictatorship. I think they effectively have more freedom than in a democracy. I mean, they vary so differently from individual to individual. Does that make sense? They vary in different ways than we do."

"Hold it," I said, gripping his shoulders. "Vergil, you're pushing me to the edge. I can't take this much longer. I don't understand, I'm not sure I believe—"

"Not even now?"

"Okay, let's say you're giving me the right interpretation. Giving it to me straight. Have you bothered to figure out the consequences yet? What all this means, where it might lead?"

He walked into the kitchen and drew a glass of water from the tap then returned and stood next to me. His expression had changed from childish absorption to sober concern. "I've never been very good at that."

"Are you afraid?"

"I was. Now, I'm not sure." He fingered the tie of his robe. "Look, I don't want you to think I went around you, over your head or something. But I met with Michael Bernard yesterday. He put me through his private clinic, took specimens. Told me to quit the lamp treatments. He called this morning, just before you did. He says it all checks out. And he asked me not to tell anybody." He paused and his expression became dreamy again. "Cities of cells," he continued. "Edward, they push tubes through the tissues, spread information—"

"Stop it!" I shouted. "Checks out? What checks out?"

"As Bernard puts it, I have 'severely enlarged macrophages' throughout my system. And he concurs on the anatomical changes."

"What does he plan to do?"

"I don't know. I think he'll probably convince Genetron to reopen the lab."

"Is that what you want?"

"It's not just having the lab again. I want to show you. Since I stopped the lamp treatments, I'm still changing." He undid his robe and let it slide to the floor. All over his body, his skin was crisscrossed with white lines. Along his back, the lines were starting to form ridges.

"My God," I said.

"I'm not going to be much good anywhere else but the lab soon. I won't be able to go out in public. Hospitals wouldn't know what to do, as I said."

"You're . . . you can talk to them, tell them to slow down," I said, aware how ridiculous that sounded.

"Yes, indeed I can, but they don't necessarily listen."

"I thought you were their god or something."

"The ones hooked up to my neurons aren't the big wheels. They're researchers, or at least serve the same function. They know I'm here, what I am, but that doesn't mean they've convinced the upper levels of the hierarchy."

"They're disputing?"

"Something like that. It's not all that bad, anyway. If the lab is reopened, I have a home, a place to work." He glanced out the window, as if looking for someone. "I don't have anything left but them. They aren't afraid, Edward. I've never felt so close to anything before." The beatific smile again. "I'm responsible for them. Mother to them all."

"You have no way of knowing what they're going to do."

He shook his head.

"No, I mean it. You say they're like a civilization—"

"Like a thousand civilizations."

"Yes, and civilizations have been known to screw up. Warfare, the environment—"

I was grasping at straws, trying to restrain a growing panic. I wasn't competent to handle the enormity of what was happening. Neither was Vergil. He was the last person I would have called insightful and wise about large issues.

"But I'm the only one at risk."

"You don't know that. Jesus, Vergil, look what they're *doing* to you!"

"To me, all to me!" he said. "Nobody else."

I shook my head and held up my hands in a gesture of defeat. "Okay, so Bernard gets them to reopen the lab, you move in, become a guinea pig. What then?"

"They treat me right. I'm more than just good old Vergil Ulam now. I'm a god-damned galaxy, a super-mother."

"Super-host, you mean." He conceded the point with a shrug.

I couldn't take any more. I made my exit with a few flimsy excuses, then sat in the lobby of the apartment building, trying to calm down. Somebody had to talk some sense into him. Who would he listen to? He had gone to Bernard . . .

And it sounded as if Bernard was not only convinced, but very interested. People of Bernard's stature didn't coax the Vergil Ulams of the world along unless they felt it was to their advantage.

I had a hunch, and I decided to play it. I went to a pay phone, slipped in my credit card, and called Genetron.

"I'd like you to page Dr. Michael Bernard," I told the receptionist.

"Who's calling, please?"

"This is his answering service. We have an emergency call and his beeper doesn't seem to be working."

A few anxious minutes later, Bernard came on the line. "Who the hell is this?" he asked. "I don't have an answering service."

"My name is Edward Milligan. I'm a friend of Vergil Ulam's. I think we have some problems to discuss."

We made an appointment to talk the next morning.

I went home and tried to think of excuses to keep me off the next day's hospital shift. I couldn't concentrate on medicine, couldn't give my patients anywhere near the attention they deserved.

Guilty, angry, afraid.

That was how Gail found me. I slipped on a mask of calm and we fixed dinner together. After eating, holding onto each other, we watched the city lights come on in late twilight through the bayside window. Winter starlings pecked at the yellow lawn in the last few minutes of light, then flew away with a rising wind which made the windows rattle.

"Something's wrong," Gail said softly. "Are you going to tell me, or just act like everything's normal?"

"It's just me," I said. "Nervous. Work at the hospital."

"Oh, lord," she said, sitting up. "You're going to divorce me for that Baker woman." Mrs. Baker weighed three hundred and sixty pounds and hadn't known she was pregnant until her fifth month.

"No," I said, listless.

"Rapturous relief," Gail said, touching my forehead lightly. "You know this kind of introspection drives me crazy."

"Well, it's nothing I can talk about yet, so . . ." I patted her hand.

"That's disgustingly patronizing," she said, getting up. "I'm going to make some tea. Want some?" Now she was miffed, and I was tense with not telling.

Why not just reveal all? I asked myself. An old friend was turning himself into a galaxy.

I cleared away the table instead. That night, unable to sleep, I looked down on Gail in bed from my sitting position, pillow against the wall, and tried to determine what I knew was real, and what wasn't.

I'm a doctor, I told myself. A technical, scientific profession. I'm supposed to be immune to things like future shock.

Vergil Ulam was turning into a galaxy.

How would it feel to be topped off with a trillion Chinese? I grinned in the dark and almost cried at the same time. What Vergil had inside him was unimaginably stranger than Chinese. Stranger than anything I—or Vergil—could easily understand. Perhaps ever understand.

But I knew what was real. The bedroom, the city lights faint through gauze curtains. Gail sleeping. Very important. Gail in bed, sleeping.

The dream returned. This time the city came in through the window and attacked Gail. It was a great, spiky lighted-up prowler, and it growled in a language I couldn't understand, made up of auto horns, crowd noises, construction bedlam. I tried to fight it off, but it got to her—and turned into a drift of stars, sprinkling all over the bed, all over everything. I jerked awake and stayed up until dawn, dressed with Gail, kissed her, savored the reality of her human, unviolated lips.

I went to meet with Bernard. He had been loaned a suite in a big downtown hospital; I rode the elevator to the sixth floor, and saw what fame and fortune could mean.

The suite was tastefully furnished, fine serigraphs on wood-paneled walls, chrome and glass furniture, cream-colored carpet, Chinese brass, and wormwood-grain cabinets and tables.

He offered me a cup of coffee, and I accepted. He took a seat in the breakfast nook, and I sat across from him, cradling my cup in moist palms. He wore a dapper gray suit and had graying hair and a sharp profile. He was in his mid sixties and he looked quite a bit like Leonard Bernstein.

"About our mutual acquaintance," he said. "Mr. Ulam. Brilliant. And, I won't hesitate to say, courageous."

"He's my friend. I'm worried about him."

Bernard held up one finger. "Courageous—and a bloody damned fool. What's happening to him should never have been allowed. He may have done it under duress, but that's no excuse. Still, what's done is done. He's talked to you, I take it."

I nodded. "He wants to return to Genetron."

"Of course. That's where all his equipment is. Where his home probably will be while we sort this out."

"Sort it out—how? Why?" I wasn't thinking too clearly. I had a slight headache.

"I can think of a large number of uses for small, superdense computer elements with a biological base. Can't you? Genetron has already made breakthroughs, but this is something else again."

"What do you envision?"

Bernard smiled. "I'm not really at liberty to say. It'll be revolutionary. We'll have to get him in lab conditions. Animal experiments have to be conducted. We'll start from scratch, of course. Vergil's . . . um . . . colonies can't be transferred. They're based on his own white blood cells. So we have to develop colonies that won't trigger immune reactions in other animals."

"Like an infection?" I asked.

"I suppose there are comparisons. But Vergil is not infected."

"My tests indicate he is."

"That's probably the bits of data floating around in his blood, don't you think?"

"I don't know."

"Listen, I'd like you to come down to the lab after Vergil is settled in. Your expertise might be useful to us."

Us. He was working with Genetron hand in glove. Could he be objective? "How will you benefit from all this?"

"Edward, I have always been at the forefront of my profession. I see no reason why I shouldn't be helping here. With my knowledge of brain and nerve functions, and the research I've been conducting in neurophysiology—"

"You could help Genetron hold off an investigation by the government," I said.

"That's being very blunt. Too blunt, and unfair."

"Perhaps. Anyway, yes: I'd like to visit the lab when Vergil's settled in. If I'm still welcome, bluntness and all." He looked at me sharply. I wouldn't be playing on *his* team; for a moment, his thoughts were almost nakedly apparent.

"Of course," Bernard said, rising with me. He reached out to shake my hand. His palm was damp. He was as nervous as I was, even if he didn't look it.

I returned to my apartment and stayed there until noon, reading, trying to sort things out. Reach a decision. What was real, what I needed to protect.

There is only so much change anyone can stand: innovation, yes, but slow application. Don't force. Everyone has the right to stay the same until they decide otherwise.

The greatest thing in science since . . .

And Bernard would force it. Genetron would force it. I couldn't handle the thought. "Neo-Luddite," I said to myself. A filthy accusation.

When I pressed Vergil's number on the building security panel, Vergil answered almost immediately. "Yeah," he said. He sounded exhilarated. "Come on up. I'll be in the bathroom. Door's unlocked."

I entered his apartment and walked through the hallway to the bathroom. Vergil lay in the tub, up to his neck in pinkish water. He smiled vaguely and splashed his hands. "Looks like I slit my wrists, doesn't it?" he said softly. "Don't worry. Everything's fine now. Genetron's going to take me back. Bernard just called." He pointed to the bathroom phone and intercom.

I sat on the toilet and noticed the sunlamp fixture standing unplugged next to the linen cabinets. The bulbs sat in a row on the edge of the sink counter. "You're sure that's what you want," I said, my shoulders slumping.

"Yeah, I think so," he said. "They can take better care of me. I'm getting cleaned up, going over there this evening. Bernard's picking me up in his limo. Style. From here on in, everything's style."

The pinkish color in the water didn't look like soap. "Is that bubble bath?" I asked. Some of it came to me in a rush then and I felt a little weaker; what had occurred to me was just one more obvious and necessary insanity.

"No," Vergil said. I knew that already.

"No," he repeated, "it's coming from my skin. They're not telling me everything, but I think they're sending out scouts. Astronauts." He looked at me with an expression that didn't quite equal concern; more like curiosity as to how I'd take it.

The confirmation made my stomach muscles tighten as if waiting for a punch. I had never even considered the possibility until now, perhaps because I had been concentrating on other aspects. "Is this the first time?" I asked.

"Yeah," he said. He laughed. "I've half a mind to let the little buggers down the drain. Let them find out what the world's really about."

"They'd go everywhere," I said.

"Sure enough."

"How . . . how are you feeling?"

"I'm feeling pretty good now. Must be billions of them." More splashing with his hands. "What do you think? Should I let the buggers out?"

Quickly, hardly thinking, I knelt down beside the tub. My fingers went for the cord on the sunlamp and I plugged it in. He had hot-wired doorknobs, turned my piss blue, played a thousand dumb practical jokes and never grown up, never grown mature enough to understand that he was sufficiently brilliant to transform the world; he would never learn caution.

He reached for the drain knob. "You know, Edward, I—"

He never finished. I picked up the fixture and dropped it into the tub, jumping back at the flash of steam and sparks. Vergil screamed and thrashed and jerked and then everything was still, except for the low, steady sizzle and the smoke wafting from his hair.

I lifted the toilet lid and vomited. Then I clenched my nose and went into the living room. My legs went out from under me and I sat abruptly on the couch.

After an hour, I searched through Vergil's kitchen and found bleach, ammonia, and a bottle of Jack Daniel's. I returned to the bathroom, keeping the center of my gaze away from Vergil. I poured first the booze, then the bleach, then the ammonia into the water. Chlorine started bubbling up and I left, closing the door behind me.

The phone was ringing when I got home. I didn't answer. It could have been the hospital. It could have been Bernard. Or the police. I could envision having to explain everything to the police. Genetron would stonewall; Bernard would be unavailable.

I was exhausted, all my muscles knotted with tension and whatever name one can give to the feelings one has after—

Committing genocide?

That certainly didn't seem real. I could not believe I had just murdered a hundred trillion intelligent beings. Snuffed a galaxy. It was laughable. But I didn't laugh.

It was easy to believe that I had just killed one human being, a friend. The smoke, the melted lamp rods, the drooping electrical outlet and smoking cord.

Vergil.

I had dunked the lamp into the tub with Vergil.

I felt sick. Dreams, cities raping Gail (and what about his girlfriend, Candice?). Letting the water filled with them out. Galaxies sprinkling over us all. What horror. Then again, what potential beauty—a new kind of life, symbiosis and transformation.

Had I been thorough enough to kill them all? I had a moment of panic. Tomorrow, I thought, I will sterilize his apartment. Somehow, I didn't even think of Bernard.

When Gail came in the door, I was asleep on the couch. I came to, groggy, and she looked down at me.

"You feeling okay?" she asked, perching on the edge of the couch. I nodded.

"What are you planning for dinner?" My mouth didn't work properly. The words were mushy. She felt my forehead.

"Edward, you have a fever," she said. "A very high fever."

I stumbled into the bathroom and looked in the mirror. Gail was close behind me. "What is it?" she asked.

There were lines under my collar, around my neck. White lines, like freeways. They had already been in me a long time, days.

"Damp palms," I said. So obvious.

I think we nearly died. I struggled at first, but in minutes I was too weak to move. Gail was just as sick within an hour.

I lay on the carpet in the living room, drenched in sweat. Gail lay on the couch, her face the color of talcum, eyes closed, like a corpse in an embalming parlor. For a time I thought she was dead. Sick as I was, I raged—hated, felt tremendous guilt at my weakness, my slowness to understand all the possibilities. Then I no longer cared. I was too weak to blink, so I closed my eyes and waited.

There was a rhythm in my arms, my legs. With each pulse of blood, a kind of sound welled up within me, like an orchestra thousands strong, but not playing in unison; playing whole seasons of symphonies at once. Music in the blood. The sound became harsher, but more coordinated, wave-trains finally canceling into silence, then separating into harmonic beats.

The beats seemed to melt into me, into the sound of my own heart.

First, they subdued our immune responses. The war—and it was a war, on a scale never before known on Earth, with trillions of combatants—lasted perhaps two days.

By the time I regained enough strength to get to the kitchen faucet, I could feel them working on my brain, trying to crack the code and find the god within the protoplasm. I drank until I was sick, then drank more moderately and took a glass to Gail. She sipped at it. Her lips were cracked, her eyes bloodshot and ringed with yellowish crumbs. There was some color in her skin. Minutes later, we were eating feebly in the kitchen.

"What in hell is happening?" was the first thing she asked. I didn't have the strength to explain. I peeled an orange and shared it with her. "We should call a doctor," she said. But I knew we wouldn't. I was already receiving messages; it was becoming apparent that any sensation of freedom we experienced was illusory.

The messages were simple at first. Memories of commands, rather than the commands themselves, manifested themselves in my thoughts. We were not to leave the apartment—a concept which seemed quite abstract to those in control, even if undesirable—and we were not to have contact with others. We would be allowed to eat certain foods and drink tap water for the time being.

With the subsidence of the fevers, the transformations were quick and drastic. Almost simultaneously, Gail and I were immobilized. She was sitting at the table, I was kneeling on the floor. I was able barely to see her in the corner of my eye.

Her arm developed pronounced ridges.

They had learned inside Vergil; their tactics within the two of us were very different. I itched all over for about two hours—two hours in hell—before they made the breakthrough and found me. The effort of ages on their timescale paid off and they communicated smoothly and directly with this great, clumsy intelligence who had once controlled their universe.

They were not cruel. When the concept of discomfort and its undesirability was made clear, they worked to alleviate it. They worked too effectively. For another hour, I was in a sea of bliss, out of all contact with them.

With dawn the next day, they gave us freedom to move again; specifically, to go to the bathroom. There were certain waste products they could not deal with. I voided those—my urine was purple—and Gail followed suit. We looked at each other vacantly in the bathroom. Then she managed a slight smile. "Are they talking to you?" she asked. I nodded. "Then I'm not crazy."

For the next twelve hours, control seemed to loosen on some levels. I suspect there was another kind of war going on in me. Gail was capable of limited motion, but no more.

When full control resumed, we were instructed to hold each other. We did not hesitate.

"Eddie . . ." she whispered. My name was the last sound I ever heard from outside.

Standing, we grew together. In hours, our legs expanded and spread out. Then extensions grew to the windows to take in sunlight, and to the kitchen to take water from the sink. Filaments soon reached to all corners of the room, stripping paint and plaster from the walls, fabric and stuffing from the furniture.

By the next dawn, the transformation was complete.

I no longer have any clear view of what we look like. I suspect we resemble cells—large, flat, and filamented cells, draped purposefully across most of the apartment. The great shall mimic the small.

Our intelligence fluctuates daily as we are absorbed into the minds within. Each day, our individuality declines. We are, indeed, great clumsy dinosaurs. Our memories have been taken over by billions of them, and our personalities have been spread through the transformed blood.

Soon there will be no need for centralization.

Already the plumbing has been invaded. People throughout the building are undergoing transformation.

Within the old time frame of weeks, we will reach the lakes, rivers, and seas in force.

I can barely begin to guess the results. Every square inch of the planet will teem with thought. Years from now, perhaps much sooner, they will subdue their own individuality—what there is of it.

New creatures will come, then. The immensity of their capacity for thought will be inconceivable.

All my hatred and fear is gone now.

I leave them—us—with only one question.

How many times has this happened, elsewhere? Travelers never came through space to visit the Earth. They had no need.

They had found universes in grains of sand.

A cabin on the coast

GENE WOLFE

Gene Wolfe is perceived by many critics to be one of the best—perhaps *the* best—SF and fantasy writers working today. His most acclaimed work is the tetralogy *The Book of the New Sun*, individual volumes of which have won the Nebula Award, the World Fantasy Award, and the John W. Campbell Memorial Award. He followed this up with a popular new series, *The Book of the Long Sun*, that included *Nightside the Long Sun*, *The Lake of the Long Sun*, *Caldé of the Long Sun*, and *Exodus from the Long Sun*, and has recently completed another series, *The Book of the Short Sun*, with the novels *On Blue's Waters*, *In Green's Jungles*, and *Return to the Whorl*. His other books include the classic novels *Peace* and *The Devil in a Forest*, both recently rereleased, as well as *Free Live Free*, *Soldier in the Mist*, *Soldier of Arete*, *There Are Doors*, *Castleview*, *Pandora by Holly Hollander*, and *The Urth of the New Sun*. His short fiction has been collected in *The Island of Doctor Death and Other Stories and Other Stories*, *Gene Wolfe's Book of Days*, *The Wolfe Archipelago*, the World Fantasy Award–winning collection *Storeys from the Old Hotel*, *Endangered Species*, and *Strange Travelers*. He has had stories in our First, Second, Fifth, and Fourteenth collections. His most recent book is a new novel, *The Knight*. Coming up is another novel, *The Wizard*, the sequel to *The Knight*, and a new collection, *Innocents Aboard*.

Here he confronts us with a power old and cold and strange, one as chameleonic as it is implacable.

It might have been a child's drawing of a ship. He blinked, and blinked again. There were masts and sails, surely. One stack, perhaps another. If the ship were really there at all. He went back to his father's beach cottage, climbed the five wooden steps, wiped his feet on the coco mat.

Lissy was still in bed, but awake, sitting up now. It must have been the squeaking of the steps, he thought. Aloud he said, "Sleep good?"

He crossed the room and kissed her. She caressed him and said, "You shouldn't go swimming without a suit, dear wonderful swimmer. How was the Pacific?"

"Peaceful. Cold. It's too early for people to be up, and there's nobody within a mile of here anyway."

"Get into bed then. How about the fish?"

"Salt water makes the sheets sticky. The fish have seen them before." He went to the corner, where a showerhead poked from the wall. The beach cottage—Lissy called it a cabin—had running water of the sometimes and rusty variety.

"They might bite 'em off. Sharks, you know. Little ones."

"Castrating woman." The shower coughed, doused him with icy spray, coughed again.

"You look worried."

"No."

"Is it your dad?"

He shook his head, then thrust it under the spray, fingers combing his dark, curly hair.

"You think he'll come out here? Today?"

He withdrew, considering. "If he's back from Washington, and he knows we're here."

"But he couldn't know, could he?"

He turned off the shower and grabbed a towel, already damp and a trifle sandy. "I don't see how."

"Only he might guess." Lissy was no longer smiling. "Where else could we go? Hey, what did we do with my underwear?"

"Your place. Your folks'. Any motel."

She swung long, golden legs out of bed, still holding the sheet across her lap. Her breasts were nearly perfect hemispheres, except for the tender protrusions of their pink nipples. He decided he had never seen breasts like that. He sat down on the bed beside her. "I love you very much," he said. "You know that?"

It made her smile again. "Does that mean you're coming back to bed?"

"If you want me to."

"I want a swimming lesson. What will people say if I tell them I came here and didn't go swimming."

He grinned at her. "That it's that time of the month."

"You know what you are? You're filthy!" She pushed him. "Absolutely filthy! I'm going to bite your ears off." Tangled in the sheet, they fell off the bed together. "There they are!"

"There what are?"

"My bra and stuff. We must have kicked them under the bed. Where are our bags?"

"Still in the trunk. I never carried them in."

"Would you get mine? My swimsuit's in it."

"Sure," he said.

"And put on some pants!"

"My suit's in my bag too." He found his trousers and got the keys to the Triumph. Outside the sun was higher, the chill of the fall morning nearly gone. He looked for the ship and saw it. Then it winked out like a star.

———

That evening they made a fire of driftwood and roasted the big, greasy Italian sausages he had brought from town, making giant hot dogs by clamping them in French bread. He had brought red supermarket wine too; they chilled it in the Pacific. "I never ate this much in my life," Lissy said.

"You haven't eaten anything yet."

"I know, but just looking at this sandwich would make me full if I wasn't so hungry." She bit off the end. "Cuff tough woof."

"What?"

"Castrating woman. That's what you called me this morning, Tim. Now *this* is a castrating woman."

"Don't talk with your mouth full."

"You sound like my mother. Give me some wine. You're hogging it."

He handed the bottle over. "It isn't bad, if you don't object to a complete lack of character."

"I sleep with you, don't I?"

"I have character, it's just all rotten."

"You said you wanted to get married."

"Let's go. You can finish that thing in the car."

"You drank half the bottle. You're too high to drive."

"Bullshoot."

Lissy giggled. "You just said bullshoot. Now *that's* character!"

He stood up. "Come on, let's go. It's only five hundred miles to Reno. We can get married there in the morning."

"You're serious, aren't you?"

"If you are."

"Sit down."

"You were testing me," he said. "That's not fair, now is it?"

"You've been so worried all day. I wanted to see if it was about me—if you thought you'd made a terrible mistake."

"We've made a mistake," he said. "I was trying to fix it just now."

"You think your dad is going to make it rough for you—"

"Us."

"—for us because it might hurt him in the next election."

He shook his head. "Not that. All right, maybe partly that. But he means it too. You don't understand him."

"I've got a father myself."

"Not like mine. Ryan was almost grown up before he left Ireland. Taught by nuns and all that. Besides, I've got six older brothers and two sisters. You're the oldest kid. Ryan's probably at least fifteen years older than your folks."

"Is that really his name? Ryan Neal?"

"His full name is Timothy Ryan Neal, the same as mine. I'm Timothy, Junior. He used Ryan when he went into politics because there was another Tim Neal around then, and we've always called me Tim to get away from the Junior."

"I'm going to call him Tim again, like the nuns must have when he was young. Big Tim. You're Little Tim."

"Okay with me. I don't know if Big Tim is going to like it."

Something was moving, it seemed, out where the sun had set. Something darker against the dark horizon.

"What made you Junior anyway? Usually it's the oldest boy."

"He didn't want it, and would never let Mother do it. But she wanted to, and I was born during the Democratic convention that year."

"He had to go, of course."

"Yeah, he had to go, Lissy. If you don't understand that, you don't understand politics at all. They hoped I'd hold off for a few days, and what the hell, Mother'd had eight with no problems. Anyway he was used to it—he was the youngest of seven boys himself. So she got to call me what she wanted."

"But then she died." The words sounded thin and lonely against the pounding of the surf.

"Not because of that."

Lissy upended the wine bottle; he saw her throat pulse three times. "Will I die because of that, Little Tim?"

"I don't think so." He tried to think of something gracious and comforting. "If we decide we want children, that's the risk I have to take."

"*You* have to take? Bullshoot."

"That both of us have to take. Do you think it was easy for Ryan, raising nine kids by himself?"

"You love him, don't you?"

"Sure I love him. He's my father."

"And now you think you might be ruining things for him. For my sake."

"That's not why I want us to be married, Lissy."

She was staring into the flames; he was not certain she had even heard him. "Well, now I know why his pictures look so grim. So gaunt."

He stood up again. "If you're through eating . . ."

"You want to go back to the cabin? You can screw me right here on the beach—there's nobody here but us."

"I didn't mean that."

"Then why go in there and look at the walls? Out here we've got the fire and the ocean. The moon ought to be up pretty soon."

"It would be warmer."

"With just that dinky little kerosene stove? I'd rather sit here by the fire. In a minute I'm going to send you off to get me some more wood. You can run up to the cabin and get a shirt too if you want to."

"I'm okay."

"Traditional roles. Big Tim must have told you all about them. The woman has the babies and keeps the home fires burning. You're not going to end up looking like him though, are you, Little Tim?"

"I suppose so. He used to look just like me."

"Really?"

He nodded. "He had his picture taken just after he got into politics. He was running for ward committeeman, and he had a poster made. We've still got the picture, and it looks like me with a high collar and a funny hat."

"She knew, didn't she?" Lissy said. For a moment he did not understand what she meant. "Now go and get some more wood. Only don't wear yourself out, because when you come back we're going to take care of that little thing that's bothering you, and we're going to spend the night on the beach."

When he came back she was asleep, but he woke her carrying her up to the beach cottage.

Next morning he woke up alone. He got up and showered and shaved, supposing that she had taken the car into town to get something for breakfast. He had filled the coffee pot and put it on before he looked out the shore-side window and saw the Triumph still waiting near the road.

There was nothing to be alarmed about, of course. She had awakened before he had and gone out for an early dip. He had done the same thing himself the morning before. The little patches of green cloth that were her bathing suit were hanging over the back of a rickety chair, but then they were still damp from last night. Who would want to put on a damp, clammy suit? She had gone in naked, just as he had.

He looked out the other window, wanting to see her splashing in the surf, waiting for him. The ship was there, closer now, rolling like a derelict. No smoke came from its clumsy funnel and no sails were set, but dark banners hung from its rigging. Then there was no ship, only wheeling gulls and the empty ocean. He called her name, but no one answered.

He put on his trunks and a jacket and went outside. A wind had smoothed the sand. The tide had come, obliterating their fire, reclaiming the driftwood he had gathered.

For two hours he walked up and down the beach, calling, telling himself there was nothing wrong. When he forced himself not to think of Lissy dead, he could only think of the headlines, the ninety seconds of ten o'clock news, how Ryan would look, how Pat—all his brothers—would look at him. And when he turned his mind from that, Lissy was dead again, her pale hair snarled with kelp as she rolled in the surf, green crabs feeding from her arms.

He got into the Triumph and drove to town. In the little brick station he sat beside the desk of a fat cop and told his story.

The fat cop said, "Kid, I can see why you want us to keep it quiet."

Tim said nothing. There was a paperweight on the desk—a baseball of white glass.

"You probably think we're out to get you, but we're not. Tomorrow we'll put out a missing persons report, but we don't have to say anything about you or the senator in it, and we won't."

"Tomorrow?"

"We got to wait twenty-four hours, in case she should show up. That's the law. But kid—" The fat cop glanced at his notes.

"Tim."

"Right. Tim. She ain't going to show up. You got to get yourself used to that."

"She could be . . ." Without wanting to, he let it trail away.

"Where? You think she snuck off and went home? She could walk out to the road and hitch, but you say her stuff's still there. Kidnapped? Nobody could have pulled her out of bed without waking you up. Did you kill her?"

"No!" Tears he could not hold back were streaming down his cheeks.

"Right. I've talked to you and I don't think you did. But you're the only one that could have. If her body washes up, we'll have to look into that."

Tim's hands tightened on the wooden arms of the chair. The fat cop pushed a box of tissues across the desk.

"Unless it washes up, though, it's just a missing person, okay? But she's dead, kid, and you're going to have to get used to it. Let me tell you what happened." He cleared his throat.

"She got up while you were still asleep, probably about when it started to get light. She did just what you thought she did—went out for a nice refreshing swim before you woke up. She went out too far, and probably she got a cramp. The ocean's cold as hell now. Maybe she yelled, but if she did she was too far out, and the waves covered it up. People think drowners holler like fire sirens, but they don't—they don't have that much air. Sometimes they don't make any noise at all."

Tim stared at the gleaming paperweight.

"The current here runs along the coast—you probably know that. Nobody ought to go swimming without somebody else around, but sometimes it seems like everybody does it. We lose a dozen or so a year. In maybe four or five cases we find them. That's all."

The beach cottage looked abandoned when he returned. He parked the Triumph and went inside and found the stove still burning, his coffee perked to tar. He took the pot outside, dumped the coffee, scrubbed the pot with beach sand and rinsed it with salt water. The ship, which had been invisible through the window of the cottage, was almost plain when he stood waist deep. He heaved the coffee pot back to shore and swam out some distance, but when he straightened up in the water, the ship was gone.

Back inside he made fresh coffee and packed Lissy's things in her suitcase. When that was done, he drove into town again. Ryan was still in Washington, but Tim told his secretary where he was. "Just in case anybody reports me missing," he said.

She laughed. "It must be pretty cold for swimming."

"I like it," he told her. "I want to have at least one more long swim."

"All right, Tim. When he calls, I'll let him know. Have a good time."

"Wish me luck," he said, and hung up. He got a hamburger and more coffee at a Jack-in-the-Box and went back to the cottage and walked a long way along the beach.

He had intended to sleep that night, but he did not. From time to time he got up and looked out the window at the ship, sometimes visible by moonlight, sometimes only a dark presence in the lower night sky. When the first light of dawn came, he put on his trunks and went into the water.

For a mile or more, as well as he could estimate the distance, he could not see it. Then it was abruptly close, the long oars like the legs of a water spider, the funnel belching sparks against the still-dim sky, sparks that seemed to become new stars.

He swam faster then, knowing that if the ship vanished he would turn back and save himself, knowing too that if it only retreated before him, retreated forever, he would drown. It disappeared behind a cobalt wave, reappeared. He sprinted and grasped at the sea-slick shaft of an oar, and it was like touching a living being. Quite suddenly he stood on the deck, with no memory of how he came there.

Bare feet pattered on the planks, but he saw no crew. A dark flag lettered with strange script flapped aft, and some vague recollection of a tour of a naval ship with his father years before made him touch his forehead. There was a sound that might have been laughter or many other things. The captain's cabin would be aft too, he thought. He went there, bracing himself against the wild roll, and found a door.

Inside, something black crouched upon a dais. "I've come for Lissy," Tim said.

There was no reply, but a question hung in the air. He answered it almost without intending to. "I'm Timothy Ryan Neal, and I've come for Lissy. Give her back to me."

A light, it seemed, dissolved the blackness. Cross-legged on the dais, a slender man in tweeds sucked at a long clay pipe. "It's Irish, are ye?" he asked.

"American," Tim said.

"With such a name? I don't believe ye. Where's yer feathers?"

"I want her back," Tim said again.

"An' if ye don't get her?"

"Then I'll tear this ship apart. You'll have to kill me or take me too."

"Spoken like a true son of the ould sod," said the man in tweeds. He scratched a kitchen match on the sole of his boot and lit his pipe. "Sit down, will ye? I don't fancy lookin' up like that. It hurts me neck. Sit down, and 'tis possible we can strike an agreement."

"This is crazy," Tim said. "The whole thing is crazy."

"It is that," the man in tweeds replied. "An' there's much, much more comin'. Ye'd best brace for it, Tim me lad. Now sit down."

There was a stout wooden chair behind Tim where the door had been. He sat. "Are you about to tell me you're a leprechaun? I warn you, I won't believe it."

"Me? One o' them scamperin', thievin', cobblin', little misers? I'd shoot meself. Me name's Daniel O'Donoghue, King o' Connaught. Do ye believe that, now?"

"No," Tim said.

"What would ye believe then?"

"That this is—some way, somehow—what people call a saucer. That you and your crew are from a planet of another sun."

Daniel laughed. "'Tis a close encounter you're havin', is it? Would ye like to see me as a tiny green man wi' horns like a snail's? I can do that too."

"Don't bother."

"All right, I won't, though 'tis a good shape. A man can take it and be whatever he wants, one o' the People o' Peace or a bit o' a man from Mars. I've used it for both, and there's nothin' better."

"You took Lissy," Tim said.

"And how would ye be knowin' that?"

"I thought she'd drowned."

"Did ye now?"

"And that this ship—or whatever it is—was just a sign, an omen. I talked to a policeman and he as good as told me, but I didn't really think about what he said until last night, when I was trying to sleep."

"Is it a dream yer havin'? Did ye ever think on that?"

"If it's a dream, it's still real," Tim said doggedly. "And anyway, I saw your ship when I was awake, yesterday and the day before."

"Or yer dreamin' now ye did. But go on wi' it."

"He said Lissy couldn't have been abducted because I was in the same bed, and that she'd gone out for a swim in the morning and drowned. But she could have been abducted, if she had gone out for the swim first. If someone had come for her with a boat. And she wouldn't have drowned, because she didn't swim good enough to drown. She was afraid of the water. We went in yesterday, and even with me there, she would hardly go in over her knees. So it was you."

"Yer right, ye know," Daniel said. He formed a little steeple of his fingers. "'Twas us."

Tim was recalling stories that had been read to him when he was a child. "Fairies steal babies, don't they? And brides. Is that why you do it? So we'll think that's who you are?"

"Bless ye, 'tis true," Daniel told him. "'Tis the Fair Folk we are. The jinn o' the desert too, and the saucer riders ye say ye credit, and forty score more. Would ye be likin' to see me wi' me goatskin breeches and me panpipe?" He chuckled. "Have ye never wondered why we're so much alike the world over? Or thought that we don't always know just which shape's the best for a place, so the naiads and the dryads might as well be the ladies o' the Deeny Shee? Do ye know what the folk o' the Barb'ry Coast call the hell that's under their sea?"

Tim shook his head.

"Why, 'tis Domdaniel. I wonder why that is, now. Tim, ye say ye want this girl."

"That's right."

"An' ye say there'll be trouble and plenty for us if ye don't have her. But let me tell ye now that if ye don't get her, wi' our blessin' to boot, ye'll drown.—Hold your tongue, can't ye, for 'tis worse than that.—If ye don't get her wi' our blessin', 'twill be seen that ye were drownin' now. Do ye take me meaning?"

"I think so. Close enough."

"Ah, that's good, that is. Now here's me offer. Do ye remember how things stood before we took her?"

"Of course."

"They'll stand so again, if ye but do what I tell ye. 'Tis yerself that will remember, Tim Neal, but she'll remember nothin'. An' the truth of it is, there'll be nothin' to remember, for it'll all be gone, every stick of it. This policeman ye spoke wi', for instance. Ye've me word that ye will not have done it."

"What do I have to do?" Tim asked.

"Service. Serve us. Do whatever we ask of ye. We'd sooner have a broth of a girl like yer Lissy than a great hulk of a lad like yerself, but then too, we'd sooner be havin' one that's willin', for the unwillin' girls are everywhere—I don't doubt but ye've seen it yerself. A hundred years, that's all we ask of ye. 'Tis short enough, like Doyle's wife. Will ye do it?"

"And everything will be the same, at the end, as it was before you took Lissy?"

"Not everythin', I didn't say that. Ye'll remember, don't ye remember me sayin' so? But for her and all the country round, why 'twill be the same."

"All right," Tim said. "I'll do it."

"'Tis a brave lad ye are. Now I'll tell ye what I'll do. I said a hundred years, to which ye agreed—"

Tim nodded.

"—but I'll have no unwillin' hands about me boat, nor no ungrateful ones neither. I'll make it twenty. How's that? Sure and I couldn't say fairer, could I?"

Daniel's figure was beginning to waver and fade; the image of the dark mass Tim had seen first hung about it like a cloud.

"Lay yerself on yer belly, for I must put me foot upon yer head. Then the deal's done."

The salt ocean was in his mouth and his eyes. His lungs burst for breath. He revolved in the blue chasm of water, tried to swim, at last exploded gasping into the air.

The King had said he would remember, but the years were fading already. Drudging, dancing, buying, spying, prying, waylaying, and betraying when he walked in the world of men. Serving something that he had never wholly understood. Sailing foggy seas that were sometimes of this earth. Floating among the constellations. The years and the slaps and the kicks were all fading, and with them (and he rejoiced in it) the days when he had begged.

He lifted an arm, trying to regain his old stroke, and found that he was very tired. Perhaps he had never really rested in all those years. Certainly, he could not recall resting. Where was he? He paddled listlessly, not knowing if he were swimming away from land, if he were in the center of an ocean. A wave elevated him, a long, slow swell of blue under the gray sky. A glory—the rising or perhaps the setting sun—shone to his right. He swam toward it, caught sight of a low coast.

He crawled onto the sand and lay there for a time, his back struck by drops of spray like rain. Near his eyes, the beach seemed nearly black. There were bits of charcoal, fragments of half-burned wood. He raised his head, pushing away the earth, and saw an empty bottle of greenish glass nearly buried in the wet sand.

When he was able at last to rise, his limbs were stiff and cold. The dawnlight had become daylight, but there was no warmth in it. The beach cottage stood only about a hundred yards away, one window golden with sunshine that had entered from the other side, the walls in shadow. The red Triumph gleamed beside the road.

At the top of a small dune he turned and looked back out to sea. A black freighter with a red and white stack was visible a mile or two out, but it was only a freighter. For a moment he felt a kind of regret, a longing for a part of his life that he had hated but that was now gone forever. I will never be able to tell her what happened, he thought. And then, Yes I will, if only I let her think I'm just making it up. And then, No wonder so many people tell so many stories. Goodbye to all that.

The steps creaked under his weight, and he wiped the sand from his feet on the coco mat. Lissy was in bed. When she heard the door open she sat up, then drew up the sheet to cover her breasts.

"Big Tim," she said. "You did come. Tim and I were hoping you would."

When he did not answer, she added, "He's out having a swim, I think. He should be around in a minute."

And when he still said nothing. "We're—Tim and I—we're going to be married."

salvador

Lucius Shepard

Lucius Shepard was one of the most popular, influential, and prolific of the
new writers of the '80s, and that decade and much of the decade that followed would see a steady stream of bizarre and powerfully compelling stories by Shepard, stories such as the landmark novella "R&R," which won
him a Nebula Award in 1987, "The Jaguar Hunter," "Black Coral," "A Spanish Lesson," "The Man Who Painted the Dragon Griaule," "Shades," "A
Traveller's Tale," "Human History," "How the Wind Spoke at Madaket,"
"Beast of the Heartland," "The Scalehunter's Beautiful Daughter," and
"Barnacle Bill the Spacer," which won him a Hugo Award in 1993. In
1988, he picked up a World Fantasy Award for his monumental short-story
collection *The Jaguar Hunter*, following it in 1992 with a second World
Fantasy Award for his second collection, *The Ends of the Earth*.

In the mid to late '90s, Shepard's production slowed dramatically, but in
the new century he has returned to something like his startling prolificacy
of old; by my count, Shepard published at least ten or eleven stories in 2003
alone, many of them novellas, including three almost-novel-length chap-
books, *Louisiana Breakdown*, *Floater*, and *Colonel Rutherford's Colt*. Nor
has the quality of his work slipped—stories like "Radiant Green Star,"
"Only Partially There," and "Liar's House" deserve to be ranked among his
best work ever, and his "Over Yonder" won him the Theodore Sturgeon
Memorial Award. And it may be that he's only beginning to hit his stride.
Shepard's other books include the novels *Green Eyes*, *Kalimantan*, *The
Golden*, and the collection *Barnacle Bill the Spacer*. His stories have appeared in our Second, Third, Fourth, Fifth, Sixth, Seventh, Eighth, and
Eighteenth annual collections. His most recent books are two new collections, *Trujillo* and *Two Trains Running*. Born in Lynchburg, Virginia, he
now lives in Vancouver, Washington.

In the harrowing story that follows, the first to make me really sit up and
take serious notice of Shepard as a writer, he shows us that we *do* learn
from the experience of war—the only question is, learn *what*?

Three weeks before they wasted Tecolutla, Dantzler had his baptism of fire. The platoon was crossing a meadow at the foot of an emerald-green volcano, and being a dreamy sort, he was idling along, swatting tall grasses with his rifle barrel and thinking how it might have been a first-grader with crayons who had devised this elementary landscape of a perfect cone rising into a cloudless sky, when cap-pistol noises sounded on the slope. Someone screamed for the medic, and Dantzler dove into the grass, fumbling for his ampules. He slipped one from the dispenser and popped it under his nose, inhaling frantically; then, to be on the safe side, he popped another— "A double helpin' of martial arts," as DT would say—and lay with his head down until the drugs had worked their magic. There was dirt in his mouth, and he was very afraid.

Gradually his arms and legs lost their heaviness, and his heart rate slowed. His vision sharpened to the point that he could see not only the pinpricks of fire blooming on the slope, but also the figures behind them, half-obscured by brush. A bubble of grim anger welled up in his brain, hardened to a fierce resolve, and he started moving toward the volcano. By the time he reached the base of the cone, he was all rage and reflexes. He spent the next forty minutes spinning acrobatically through the thickets, spraying shadows with bursts of his M-18; yet part of his mind remained distant from the action, marveling at his efficiency, at the comic-strip enthusiasm he felt for the task of killing. He shouted at the men he shot, and he shot them many more times than was necessary, like a child playing soldier.

"Playin' my ass!" DT would say. "You just actin' natural."

DT was a firm believer in the ampules; though the official line was that they contained tailored RNA compounds and pseudoendorphins modified to an inhalant form, he held the opinion that they opened a man up to his inner nature. He was big, black, with heavily muscled arms and crudely stamped features, and he had come to the Special Forces direct from prison, where he had done a stretch for attempted murder; the palms of his hands were covered by jail tattoos—a pentagram and a horned monster. The words DIE HIGH were painted on his helmet. This was his second tour in Salvador, and Moody—who was Dantzler's buddy—said the drugs had addled DT's brains, that he was crazy and gone to hell.

"He collects trophies," Moody had said. "And not just ears like they done in 'Nam."

When Dantzler had finally gotten a glimpse of the trophies, he had been appalled. They were kept in a tin box in DT's pack and were nearly unrecognizable; they looked like withered brown orchids. But despite his revulsion, despite the fact that he was afraid of DT, he admired the man's capacity for survival and had taken to heart his advice to rely on the drugs.

On the way back down the slope they discovered a live casualty, an Indian kid about Dantzler's age, nineteen or twenty. Black hair, adobe skin, and heavy-lidded brown eyes. Dantzler, whose father was an anthropologist and had done fieldwork in Salvador, figured him for a Santa Ana tribesman; before leaving the States,

Dantzler had pored over his father's notes, hoping this would give him an edge, and had learned to identify the various regional types. The kid had a minor leg wound and was wearing fatigue pants and a faded COKE ADDS LIFE T-shirt. This T-shirt irritated DT no end.

"What the hell you know 'bout Coke?" he asked the kid as they headed for the chopper that was to carry them deeper into Morazán Province. "You think it's funny or somethin'?" He whacked the kid in the back with his rifle butt, and when they reached the chopper, he slung him inside and had him sit by the door. He sat beside him, tapped out a joint from a pack of Kools, and asked, "Where's Infante?"

"Dead," said the medic.

"Shit!" DT licked the joint so it would burn evenly. "Goddamn beaner ain't no use 'cept somebody else know Spanish."

"I know a little," Dantzler volunteered.

Staring at Dantzler, DT's eyes went empty and unfocused. "Naw," he said. "You don't know no Spanish."

Dantzler ducked his head to avoid DT's stare and said nothing; he thought he understood what DT meant, but he ducked away from the understanding as well. The chopper bore them aloft, and DT lit the joint. He let the smoke out his nostrils and passed the joint to the kid, who accepted gratefully.

"*Qué sabor!*" he said, exhaling a billow; he smiled and nodded, wanting to be friends.

Dantzler turned his gaze to the open door. They were flying low between the hills, and looking at the deep bays of shadow in their folds acted to drain away the residue of the drugs, leaving him weary and frazzled. Sunlight poured in, dazzling the oil-smeared floor.

"Hey, Dantzler!" DT had to shout over the noise of the rotors. "Ask him whass his name!"

The kid's eyelids were drooping from the joint, but on hearing Spanish he perked up; he shook his head, though, refusing to answer. Dantzler smiled and told him not to be afraid.

"Ricardo Quu," said the kid.

"Kool!" said DT with false heartiness. "Thass my brand!" He offered his pack to the kid.

"*Gracias, no.*" The kid waved the joint and grinned.

"Dude's named for a goddamn cigarette," said DT disparagingly, as if this were the height of insanity.

Dantzler asked the kid if there were more soldiers nearby, and once again received no reply; but, apparently sensing in Dantzler a kindred soul, the kid leaned forward and spoke rapidly, saying that his village was Santander Jiménez, that his father was—he hesitated—a man of power. He asked where they were taking him. Dantzler returned a stony glare. He found it easy to reject the kid, and he realized later this was because he had already given up on him.

Latching his hands behind his head, DT began to sing—a wordless melody. His voice was discordant, barely audible above the rotors; but the tune had a familiar ring and Dantzler soon placed it. The theme from "Star Trek." It brought back memories of watching TV with his sister, laughing at the low-budget aliens and

Scotty's Actors' Equity accent. He gazed out the door again. The sun was behind the hills, and the hillsides were unfeatured blurs of dark green smoke. Oh, God, he wanted to be home, to be anywhere but Salvador! A couple of the guys joined in the singing at DT's urging, and as the volume swelled, Dantzler's emotion peaked. He was on the verge of tears, remembering tastes and sights, the way his girl Jeanine had smelled, so clean and fresh, not reeking of sweat and perfume like the whores around Ilopango—finding all this substance in the banal touchstone of his culture and the illusions of the hillsides rushing past. Then Moody tensed beside him, and he glanced up to learn the reason why.

In the gloom of the chopper's belly, DT was as unfeatured as the hills—a black presence ruling them, more the leader of a coven than a platoon. The other two guys were singing their lungs out, and even the kid was getting into the spirit of things. "*Música!*" he said at one point, smiling at everybody, trying to fan the flame of good feeling. He swayed to the rhythm and essayed a "la-la" now and again. But no one else was responding.

The singing stopped, and Dantzler saw that the whole platoon was staring at the kid, their expressions slack and dispirited.

"Space!" shouted DT, giving the kid a little shove. "The final frontier!"

The smile had not yet left the kid's face when he toppled out the door. DT peered after him; a few seconds later he smacked his hand against the floor and sat back, grinning. Dantzler felt like screaming, the stupid horror of the joke was so at odds with the languor of his homesickness. He looked to the others for reaction. They were sitting with their heads down, fiddling with trigger guards and pack straps, studying their bootlaces, and seeing this, he quickly imitated them.

Morazán Province was spook country. Santa Ana spooks. Flights of birds had been reported to attack patrols; animals appeared at the perimeters of campsites and vanished when you shot at them; dreams afflicted everyone who ventured there. Dantzler could not testify to the birds and animals, but he did have a recurring dream. In it the kid DT had killed was pinwheeling down through a golden fog, his T-shirt visible against the roiling backdrop, and sometimes a voice would boom out of the fog, saying, "You are killing my son." No, no, Dantzler would reply, it wasn't me, and besides, he's already dead. Then he would wake covered with sweat, groping for his rifle, his heart racing.

But the dream was not an important terror, and he assigned it no significance. The land was far more terrifying. Pine-forested ridges that stood out against the sky like fringes of electrified hair; little trails winding off into thickets and petering out, as if what they led to had been magicked away; gray rock faces along which they were forced to walk, hopelessly exposed to ambush. There were innumerable booby traps set by the guerrillas, and they lost several men to rockfalls. It was the emptiest place of Dantzler's experience. No people, no animals, just a few hawks circling the solitudes between the ridges. Once in a while they found tunnels, and these they blew with the new gas grenades; the gas ignited the rich concentrations of hydrocarbons and sent flame sweeping through the entire system. DT would praise whoever had discovered the tunnel and would estimate in a loud voice how many beaners they had "refried." But Dantzler knew they were traversing pure emptiness and burning empty holes. Days, under debilitating heat, they humped the mountains, traveling seven, eight, even ten klicks up trails so steep that frequently the feet of the guy ahead of you would be on a level with your face; nights, it was cold, the darkness absolute, the silence so profound that Dantzler imagined he could hear the great humming vibration of the earth. They might have been anywhere or nowhere. Their fear was nourished by the isolation, and the only remedy was "martial arts."

Dantzler took to popping the pills without the excuse of combat. Moody cautioned him against abusing the drugs, citing rumors of bad side effects and DT's madness; but even he was using them more and more often. During basic training, Dantzler's D.I. had told the boots that the drugs were available only to the Special Forces, that their use was optional; but there had been too many instances of lackluster battlefield performance in the last war, and this was to prevent a reoccurrence.

"The chickenshit infantry should take 'em," the D.I. had said. "You bastards are brave already. You're born killers, right?"

"Right, sir!" they had shouted.

"What are you?"

"Born killers, sir!"

But Dantzler was not a born killer; he was not even clear as to how he had been drafted, less clear as to how he had been manipulated into the Special Forces, and he had learned that nothing was optional in Salvador, with the possible exception of life itself.

The platoon's mission was reconnaissance and mop-up. Along with other Special Forces platoons, they were to secure Morazán prior to the invasion of Nicaragua; specifically, they were to proceed to the village of Tecolutla, where a Sandinista patrol had recently been spotted, and following that they were to join up with the First Infantry and take part in the offensive against León, a provincial capital just across the Nicaraguan border. As Dantzler and Moody walked together, they frequently talked about the offensive, how it would be good to get down into flat country; occasionally they talked about the possibility of reporting DT, and once, after he had led them on a forced night march, they toyed with the idea of killing him. But most often they discussed the ways of the Indians and the land, since this was what had caused them to become buddies.

Moody was slightly built, freckled, and red-haired; his eyes had the "thousand-yard stare" that came from too much war. Dantzler had seen winos with such vacant, lusterless stares. Moody's father had been in 'Nam, and Moody said it had been worse than Salvador because there had been no real commitment to win; but he thought Nicaragua and Guatemala might be the worst of all, especially if the Cubans sent in troops as they had threatened. He was adept at locating tunnels and detecting booby traps, and it was for this reason Dantzler had cultivated his friendship. Essentially a loner, Moody had resisted all advances until learning of Dantzler's father; thereafter he had buddied up, eager to hear about the field notes, believing they might give him an edge.

"They think the land has animal traits," said Dantzler one day as they climbed along a ridgetop. "Just like some kinds of fish look like plants or sea bottom, parts of the land look like plain ground, jungle . . . whatever. But when you enter them, you find you've entered the spirit world, the world of Sukias."

"What's *Sukias?*" asked Moody.

"Magicians." A twig snapped behind Dantzler, and he spun around, twitching off the safety of his rifle. It was only Hodge—a lanky kid with the beginnings of a beer gut. He stared hollow-eyed at Dantzler and popped an ampule.

Moody made a noise of disbelief. "If they got magicians, why ain't they winnin'? Why ain't they zappin' us off the cliffs?"

"It's not their business," said Dantzler. "They don't believe in messing with worldly affairs unless it concerns them directly. Anyway, these places—the ones that look like normal land but aren't—they're called. . . ." He drew a blank on the name. "*Aya*-something. I can't remember. But they have different laws. They're where your spirit goes to die after your body dies."

"Don't they got no Heaven?"

"Nope. It just takes longer for your spirit to die, and so it goes to one of these places that's between everything and nothing."

"Nothin'," said Moody disconsolately, as if all his hopes for an afterlife had been dashed. "Don't make no sense to have spirits and not have no Heaven."

"Hey," said Dantzler, tensing as wind rustled the pine boughs. "They're just a bunch of damn primitives. You know what their sacred drink is? Hot chocolate! My old man was a guest at one of their funerals, and he said they carried cups of hot chocolate balanced on these little red towers and acted like drinking it was going to wake them to the secrets of the universe." He laughed, and the laughter sounded tinny and psychotic to his own ears. "So you're going to worry about fools who think hot chocolate's holy water?"

"Maybe they just like it," said Moody. "Maybe somebody dyin' just give 'em an excuse to drink it."

But Dantzler was no longer listening. A moment before, as they emerged from pine cover onto the highest point of the ridge, a stony scarp open to the winds and providing a view of rumpled mountains and valleys extending to the horizon, he had popped an ampule. He felt so strong, so full of righteous purpose and controlled fury, it seemed only the sky was around him, that he was still ascending, preparing to do battle with the gods themselves.

Tecolutla was a village of whitewashed stone tucked into a notch between two hills. From above, the houses—with their shadow-blackened windows and doorways—looked like an unlucky throw of dice. The streets ran uphill and down, diverging around boulders. Bougainvilleas and hibiscuses speckled the hillsides, and there were tilled fields on the gentler slopes. It was a sweet, peaceful place when they arrived, and after they had gone it was once again peaceful; but its sweetness had been permanently banished. The reports of Sandinistas had proved accurate, and though they were casualties left behind to recuperate, DT had decided their presence called for extreme measures. Fu gas, frag grenades, and such. He had fired an M-60 until the barrel melted down, and then had manned the flamethrower. Afterward, as they rested atop the next ridge, exhausted and begrimed, having radioed in a chopper for resupply, he could not get over how one of the houses he had torched had come to resemble a toasted marshmallow.

"Ain't that how it was, man?" he asked, striding up and down the line. He did not care if they agreed about the house; it was a deeper question he was asking, one concerning the ethics of their actions.

"Yeah," said Dantzler, forcing a smile. "Sure did."

DT grunted with laughter. "You *know* I'm right, don'tcha man?"

The sun hung directly behind his head, a golden corona rimming a black oval, and Dantzler could not turn his eyes away. He felt weak and weakening, as if threads of himself were being spun loose and sucked into the blackness. He had popped three ampules prior to the firefight, and his experience of Tecolutla had been a kind of mad whirling dance through the streets, spraying erratic bursts that appeared to be writing weird names on the walls. The leader of the Sandinistas had worn a mask—a gray face with a surprised hole of a mouth and pink circles around the eyes. A ghost face. Dantzler had been afraid of the mask and had poured round after round into it. Then, leaving the village, he had seen a small girl standing beside the shell of the last house, watching them, her colorless rag of a dress tattering in the breeze. She had been a victim of that malnutrition disease, the one that paled your skin and whitened your hair and left you retarded. He could not recall the name of the disease—things like names were slipping away from him—nor could he believe anyone had survived, and for a moment he had thought the spirit of the village had come out to mark their trail.

That was all he could remember of Tecolutla, all he wanted to remember. But he knew he had been brave.

Four days later, they headed up into a cloud forest. It was the dry season, but dry season or not, blackish gray clouds always shrouded these peaks. They were shot through by ugly glimmers of lightning, making it seem that malfunctioning neon signs were hidden beneath them, advertisements for evil. Everyone was jittery, and Jerry LeDoux—a slim dark-haired Cajun kid—flat-out refused to go.

"It ain't reasonable," he said. "Be easier to go through the passes."

"We're on recon, man! You think the beaners be waitin' in the passes, wavin' their white flags?" DT whipped his rifle into firing position and pointed it at LeDoux. "C'mon, Louisiana man. Pop a few, and you feel different."

As LeDoux popped the ampules, DT talked to him.

"Look at it this way, man. This is your big adventure. Up there it be like all them animal shows on the tube. The savage kingdom, the unknown. Could be like Mars or somethin'. Monsters and shit, with big red eyes and tentacles. You wanna miss that, man? You wanna miss bein' the first grunt on Mars?"

Soon LeDoux was raring to go, giggling at DT's rap.

Moody kept his mouth shut, but he fingered the safety of his rifle and glared at DT's back. When DT turned to him, however, he relaxed. Since Tecolutla he had grown taciturn, and there seemed to be a shifting of lights and darks in his eyes, as if something were scurrying back and forth behind them. He had taken to wearing banana leaves on his head, arranging them under his helmet so the frayed ends stuck out the sides like strange green hair. He said this was camouflage, but Dantzler was certain it bespoke some secretive irrational purpose. Of course DT had noticed Moody's spiritual erosion, and as they prepared to move out, he called Dantzler aside.

"He done found someplace inside his head that feel good to him," said DT. "He's tryin' to curl up into it, and once he do that he ain't gon' be responsible. Keep an eye on him."

Dantzler mumbled his assent, but was not enthused.

"I know he your fren', man, but that don't mean shit. Not the way things are. Now me, I don't give a damn 'bout you personally. But I'm your brother-in-arms, and thass somethin' you can count on . . . y'understand."

To Dantzler's shame, he did understand.

They had planned on negotiating the cloud forest by nightfall, but they had underestimated the difficulty. The vegetation beneath the clouds was lush—thick, juicy leaves that mashed underfoot, tangles of vines, trees with slick, pale bark and waxy leaves—and the visibility was only about fifteen feet. They were gray wraiths passing through grayness. The vague shapes of the foliage reminded Dantzler of fancifully engraved letters, and for a while he entertained himself with the notion that they were walking among the half-formed phrases of a constitution not yet manifest in the land. They barged off the trail, losing it completely, becoming veiled in spiderwebs and drenched by spills of water; their voices were oddly muffled, the tag ends of words swallowed up. After seven hours of this, DT reluctantly gave the order to pitch camp. They set electric lamps around the perimeter so they could see to string the jungle hammocks; the beam of light illuminated the moisture in the air, piercing the murk with jeweled blades. They talked in hushed tones, alarmed by the eerie atmosphere. When they had done with the hammocks, DT posted four sentries—Moody, LeDoux, Dantzler, and himself. Then they switched off the lamps.

It grew pitch-dark, and the darkness was picked out by plips and plops, the entire spectrum of dripping sounds. To Dantzler's ears they blended into a gabbling speech. He imagined tiny Santa Ana demons talking about him, and to stave off paranoia he popped two ampules. He continued to pop them, trying to limit himself to one every half hour; but he was uneasy, unsure where to train his rifle in the dark, and he exceeded his limit. Soon it began to grow light again, and he assumed that more time had passed than he had thought. That often happened with the ampules— it was easy to lose yourself in being alert, in the wealth of perceptual detail available to your sharpened senses. Yet on checking his watch, he saw it was only a few minutes after two o'clock. His system was too inundated with the drugs to allow panic, but he twitched his head from side to side in tight little arcs to determine the source of the brightness. There did not appear to be a single source; it was simply that filaments of the cloud were gleaming, casting a diffuse golden glow, as if they were elements of a nervous system coming to life. He started to call out, then held back. The others must have seen the light, and they had given no cry; they probably had a good reason for their silence. He scrunched down flat, pointing his rifle out from the campsite.

Bathed in the golden mist, the forest had acquired an alchemic beauty. Beads of water glittered with gemmy brilliance; the leaves and vines and bark were gilded. Every surface shimmered with light . . . everything except a fleck of blackness hovering between two of the trunks, its size gradually increasing. As it swelled in his vision, he saw it had the shape of a bird, its wings beating, flying toward him from an inconceivable distance—inconceivable, because the dense vegetation did not permit you to see very far in a straight line, and yet the bird was growing larger with such slowness that it must have been coming from a long way off. It was not really flying, he realized; rather, it was as if the forest were painted on a piece of paper, as if someone were holding a lit match behind it and burning a hole, a hole that maintained the shape of a bird as it spread. He was transfixed, unable to react. Even when it had blotted out half the light, when he lay before it no bigger than a mote in relation to its huge span, he could not move or squeeze the trigger. And then the blackness swept over him. He had the sensation of being borne along at incredible speed, and he could no longer hear the dripping of the forest.

"Moody!" he shouted. "DT!"

But the voice that answered belonged to neither of them. It was hoarse, issuing from every part of the surrounding blackness, and he recognized it as the voice of his recurring dream.

"You are killing my son," it said. "I have led you here, to this *ayahuamaco*, so he may judge you."

Dantzler knew to his bones the voice was that of the *Sukia* of the village of Santander Jiménez. He wanted to offer a denial, to explain his innocence, but all he could manage was, "No." He said it tearfully, hopelessly, his forehead resting on his rifle barrel. Then his mind gave a savage twist, and his soldiery self regained control. He ejected an ampule from his dispenser and popped it.

The voice laughed—malefic, damning laughter whose vibrations shuddered Dantzler. He opened up with the rifle, spraying fire in all directions. Filigrees of golden holes appeared in the blackness, tendrils of mist coiled through them. He kept on firing until the blackness shattered and fell in jagged sections toward him. Slowly. Like shards of black glass dropping through water. He emptied the rifle and flung himself flat, shielding his head with his arms, expecting to be sliced into bits; but nothing touched him. At last he peeked between his arms; then—amazed, because the forest was now a uniform lustrous yellow—he rose to his knees. He scraped his hand on one of the crushed leaves beneath him, and blood welled from the cut. The broken fibers of the leaf were as stiff as wires. He stood, a giddy trickle of hysteria leaking up from the bottom of his soul. It was no forest, but a building of solid gold worked to resemble a forest—the sort of conceit that might have been fabricated for the child of an emperor. Canopied by golden leaves, columned by slender golden trunks, carpeted by golden grasses. The water beads were diamonds. All the gleam and glitter soothed his apprehension; here was something out of a myth, a habitat for princesses and wizards and dragons. Almost gleeful, he turned to the campsite to see how the others were reacting.

Once, when he was nine years old, he had sneaked into the attic to rummage through the boxes and trunks, and he had run across an old morocco-bound copy of *Gulliver's Travels*. He had been taught to treasure old books, and so he had opened it eagerly to look at the illustrations, only to find that the centers of the pages had been eaten away, and there, right in the heart of the fiction, was a nest of larvae. Pulpy, horrid things. It had been an awful sight, but one unique in his experience, and he might have studied those crawling scraps of life for a very long time if his father had not interrupted. Such a sight was now before him, and he was numb with it.

They were all dead. He should have guessed they would be; he had given no thought to them while firing his rifle. They had been struggling out of their hammocks when the bullets hit, and as a result they were hanging half-in, half-out, their limbs dangling, blood pooled beneath them. The veils of golden mist made them look dark and mysterious and malformed, like monsters killed as they emerged from their cocoons. Dantzler could not stop staring, but he was shrinking inside himself. It was not his fault. That thought kept swooping in and out of a flock of less acceptable thoughts; he wanted it to stay put, to be true, to alleviate the sick horror he was beginning to feel.

"What's your name?" asked a girl's voice behind him.

She was sitting on a stone about twenty feet away. Her hair was a tawny shade of gold, her skin a half-tone lighter, and her dress was cunningly formed out of the mist. Only her eyes were real. Brown heavy-lidded eyes—they were at variance with the rest of her face, which had the fresh, unaffected beauty of an American teenager.

"Don't be afraid," she said, and patted the ground, inviting him to sit beside her.

He recognized the eyes, but it was no matter. He badly needed the consolation she could offer; he walked over and sat down. She let him lean his head against her thigh.

"What's your name?" she repeated.

"Dantzler," he said. "John Dantzler." And then he added, "I'm from Boston. My father's . . ." It would be too difficult to explain about anthropology. "He's a teacher."

"Are there many soldiers in Boston?" She stroked his cheek with a golden finger.

The caress made Dantzler happy. "Oh, no," he said. "They hardly know there's a war going on."

"This is true?" she said, incredulous.

"Well, they *do* know about it, but it's just news on the TV to them. They've got more pressing problems. Their jobs, families."

"Will you let them know about the war when you return home?" she asked. "Will you do that for me?"

Dantzler had given up hope of returning home, of surviving, and her assumption that he would do both acted to awaken his gratitude. "Yes," he said fervently. "I will."

"You must hurry," she said. "If you stay in the *ayahuamaco* too long, you will never leave. You must find the way out. It is a way not of directions or trails, but of events."

"Where is this place?" he asked, suddenly aware of how much he had taken it for granted.

She shifted her leg away, and if he had not caught himself on the stone, he would have fallen. When he looked up, she had vanished. He was surprised that her disappearance did not alarm him; in reflex he slipped out a couple of ampules, but after a moment's reflection he decided not to use them. It was impossible to slip them back into the dispenser, so he tucked them into the interior webbing of his helmet for later. He doubted he would need them, though. He felt strong, competent, and unafraid.

Dantzler stepped carefully between the hammocks, not wanting to brush against them; it might have been his imagination, but they seemed to be bulged down lower than before, as if death had weighed out heavier than life. That heaviness was in the air, pressuring him. Mist rose like golden steam from the corpses, but the sight no longer affected him—perhaps because the mist gave the illusion of being their souls. He picked up a rifle with a full magazine and headed off into the forest.

The tips of the golden leaves were sharp, and he had to ease past them to avoid being cut; but he was at the top of his form, moving gracefully, and the obstacles barely slowed his pace. He was not even anxious about the girl's warning to hurry; he was certain the way out would soon present itself. After a minute or so he heard voices, and after another few seconds he came to a clearing divided by a stream, one so perfectly reflecting that its banks appeared to enclose a wedge of golden mist. Moody was squatting to the left of the stream, staring at the blade of his survival knife and singing under his breath—a wordless melody that had the erratic rhythm of a trapped fly. Beside him lay Jerry LeDoux, his throat slashed from ear to ear. DT was sitting on the other side of the stream; he had been shot just above the knee, and though he had ripped up his shirt for bandages and tied off the leg with a tourni-quet, he was not in good shape. He was sweating, and a gray chalky pallor infused his skin. The entire scene had the weird vitality of something that had materialized in a magic mirror, a bubble of reality enclosed within a gilt frame.

DT heard Dantzler's footfalls and glanced up. "Waste him!" he shouted, pointing to Moody.

Moody did not turn from contemplation of the knife. "No," he said, as if speaking to someone whose image was held in the blade.

"Waste him, man!" screamed DT. "He killed LeDoux!"

"Please," said Moody to the knife. "I don't want to."

There was blood clotted on his face, more blood on the banana leaves sticking out of his helmet.

"Did you kill Jerry?" asked Dantzler; while he addressed the question to Moody, he did not relate to him as an individual, only as part of a design whose message he had to unravel.

"Jesus Christ! Waste him!" DT smashed his fist against the ground in frustration.

"Okay," said Moody. With an apologetic look, he sprang to his feet and charged Dantzler, swinging the knife.

Emotionless, Dantzler stitched a line of fire across Moody's chest; he went side-ways into the bushes and down.

"What the hell was you waitin' for!" DT tried to rise, but winced and fell back. "Damn! Don't know if I can walk."

"Pop a few," Dantzler suggested mildly.

"Yeah. Good thinkin', man." DT fumbled for his dispenser.

Dantzler peered into the bushes to see where Moody had fallen. He felt nothing, and this pleased him. He was weary of feeling.

DT popped an ampule with a flourish, as if making a toast, and inhaled. "Ain't you gon' to do some, man?"

"I don't need them," said Dantzler. "I'm fine."

The stream interested him; it did not reflect the mist, as he had supposed, but was itself a seam of the mist.

"How many you think they was?" asked DT.

"How many what?"

"Beaners, man! I wasted three or four after they hit us, but I couldn't tell how many they was."

Dantzler considered this in light of his own interpretation of events and Moody's conversation with the knife. It made sense. A Santa Ana kind of sense.

"Beats me," he said. "But I guess there's less than there used to be."

DT snorted. "You got *that* right!" He heaved to his feet and limped to the edge of the stream. "Gimme a hand across."

Dantzler reached out to him, but instead of taking his hand, he grabbed his wrist and pulled him off-balance. DT teetered on his good leg, then toppled and vanished beneath the mist. Dantzler had expected him to fall, but he surfaced instantly, mist clinging to his skin. Of course, thought Dantzler; his body would have to die before his spirit would fall.

"What you doin', man?" DT was more disbelieving than enraged.

Dantzler planted a foot in the middle of his back and pushed him down until his head was submerged. DT bucked and clawed at the foot and managed to come to his hands and knees. Mist slithered from his eyes, his nose, and he choked out the words ". . . kill you . . ." Dantzler pushed him down again; he got into pushing him down and letting him up, over and over. Not so as to torture him. Not really. It was because he had suddenly understood the nature of the *ayahuamaco*'s laws, that they were approximations of normal laws, and he further understood that his actions had to approximate those of someone jiggling a key in a lock. DT was the key to the way out, and Dantzler was jiggling him, making sure all the tumblers were engaged.

Some of the vessels in DT's eyes had burst, and the whites were occluded by films of blood. When he tried to speak, mist curled from his mouth. Gradually his struggles subsided; he clawed runnels in the gleaming yellow dirt of the bank and shuddered. His shoulders were knobs of black land foundering in a mystic sea.

For a long time after DT sank from view, Dantzler stood beside the stream, uncertain of what was left to do and unable to remember a lesson he had been taught. Finally he shouldered his rifle and walked away from the clearing. Morning had broken, the mist had thinned, and the forest had regained its usual coloration. But he scarcely noticed these changes, still troubled by his faulty memory. Eventually, he let it slide—it would all come clear sooner or later. He was just happy to be alive. After a while he began to kick the stones as he went, and to swing his rifle in a care-free fashion against the weeds.

When the First Infantry poured across the Nicaraguan border and wasted León, Dantzler was having a quiet time at the VA hospital in Ann Arbor, Michigan; and at the precise moment the bulletin was flashed nationwide, he was sitting in the lounge, watching the American League playoffs between Detroit and Texas. Some of the patients ranted at the interruption, while others shouted them down, wanting to hear the details. Dantzler expressed no reaction whatsoever. He was solely concerned with being a model patient; however, noticing that one of the staff was giving him a clinical stare, he added his weight on the side of the baseball fans. He did not want to appear too controlled. The doctors were as suspicious of that sort of behavior as they were of its contrary. But the funny thing was—at least it was funny to Dantzler—that his feigned annoyance at the bulletin was an exemplary proof of his control, his expertise at moving through life the way he had moved through the golden leaves of the cloud forest. Cautiously, gracefully, efficiently. Touching nothing, and being touched by nothing. That was the lesson he had learned—to be as perfect a counterfeit of a man as the *ayahuamaco* had been of the land; to adopt the various stances of a man, and yet, by virtue of his distance from things human, to be all the more prepared for the onset of crisis or a call to action. He saw nothing aberrant in this; even the doctors would admit that men were little more than organized pretense. If he was different from other men, it was only that he had a deeper awareness of the principles on which his personality was founded.

When the battle of Managua was joined, Dantzler was living at home. His parents had urged him to go easy in readjusting to civilian life, but he had immediately gotten a job as a management trainee in a bank. Each morning he would drive to work and spend a controlled, quiet eight hours; each night he would watch TV with his mother, and before going to bed, he would climb to the attic and inspect the trunk containing his souvenirs of war—helmet, fatigues, knife, boots. The doctors had insisted he face his experiences, and this ritual was his way of following their instructions. All in all, he was quite pleased with his progress, but he still had problems. He had not been able to force himself to venture out at night, remembering too well the darkness in the cloud forest, and he had rejected his friends, refusing to see them or answer their calls—he was not secure with the idea of friendship. Further, despite his methodical approach to life, he was prone to a nagging restlessness, the feeling of a chore left undone.

One night his mother came into his room and told him that an old friend, Phil Curry, was on the phone. "Please talk to him, Johnny," she said. "He's been drafted, and I think he's a little scared."

The word *drafted* struck a responsive chord in Dantzler's soul, and after brief deliberation he went downstairs and picked up the receiver.

"Hey," said Phil. "What's the story, man? Three months, and you don't even give me a call."

"I'm sorry," said Dantzler. "I haven't been feeling so hot."

"Yeah, I understand." Phil was silent a moment. "Listen, man. I'm leavin', y'know, and we're havin' a big send-off at Sparky's. It's goin' on right now. Why don't you come down?"

"I don't know."

"Jeanine's here, man. Y'know, she's still crazy 'bout you, talks 'bout you alla time. She don't go out with nobody."

Dantzler was unable to think of anything to say.

"Look," said Phil, "I'm pretty weirded out by this soldier shit. I hear it's pretty bad down there. If you got anything you can tell me 'bout what it's like, man, I'd 'preciate it."

Dantzler could relate to Phil's concern, his desire for an edge, and besides, it felt right to go. Very right. He would take some precautions against the darkness.

"I'll be there," he said.

It was a foul night, spitting snow, but Sparky's parking lot was jammed. Dantzler's mind was flurried like the snow, crowded like the lot—thoughts whirling in, jockeying for position, melting away. He hoped his mother would not wait up, he wondered if Jeanine still wore her hair long, he was worried because the palms of his hands were unnaturally warm. Even with the car windows rolled up, he could hear loud music coming from inside the club. Above the door the words SPARKY'S ROCK CITY were being spelled out a letter at a time in red neon, and when the spelling was complete, the letters flashed off and on and a golden neon explosion bloomed around them. After the explosion, the entire sign went dark for a split second, and the big ramshackle building seemed to grow large and merge with the black sky. He had an idea it was watching him, and he shuddered—one of those sudden lurches downward of the kind that take you just before you fall asleep. He knew the people inside did not intend him any harm, but he also knew that places have a way of changing people's intent, and he did not want to be caught off guard. Sparky's might be such a place, might be a huge black presence camouflaged by neon, its true substance one with the abyss of the sky, the phosphorescent snowflakes jittering in his headlights, the wind keening through the side vent. He would have liked very much to drive home and forget about his promise to Phil; however, he felt a responsibility to explain about the war. More than a responsibility, an evangelistic urge. He would tell them about the kid falling out of the chopper, the white-haired girl in Tecolutla, the emptiness, God, yes! How you went down chock-full of ordinary American thoughts and dreams, memories of smoking weed and chasing tail and hanging out and freeway flying with a case of something cold, and how you smuggled back a human-shaped container of pure Salvadorian emptiness. Primo grade. Smuggled it back to the land of silk and money, of mindfuck video games and topless tennis matches and fast-food solutions to the nutritional problem. Just a taste of Salvador would banish all those trivial obsessions. Just a taste. It would be easy to explain.

Of course, some things beggared explanation.

He bent down and adjusted the survival knife in his boot so the hilt would not rub against his calf. From his coat pocket he withdrew the two ampules he had secreted in his helmet that long-ago night in the cloud forest. As the neon explosion flashed once more, glimmers of gold coursed along their shiny surfaces. He did not think he would need them; his hand was steady, and his purpose was clear. But to be on the safe side, he popped them both.

Trinity

NANCY KRESS

Nancy Kress began selling her elegant and incisive stories in the mid-seventies, and has since become a frequent contributor to *Asimov's Science Fiction, The Magazine of Fantasy and Science Fiction, Omni,* and elsewhere. Her books include the novels *The Prince Of Morning Bells, The Golden Grove, The White Pipes, An Alien Light, Brain Rose, Oaths & Miracles, Stinger, Maximum Light,* the novel version of her Hugo and Nebula-winning story, *Beggars in Spain,* a sequel, *Beggars and Choosers,* and a popular recent sequence of novels, *Probability Moon, Probability Sun,* and *Probability Space.* Her short work has been collected in *Trinity and Other Stories, The Aliens of Earth,* and *Beaker's Dozen.* Her most recent books are two new novels, *Crossfire* and *Nothing Human.* Upcoming is a new novel, *Crucible.* She has also won Nebula Awards for her stories "Out of All Them Bright Stars" and "The Flowers of Aulit Prison." She has had stories in our Second, Third, Sixth through Fifteenth, and Eighteenth through Twenty-first annual collections.

People have been searching for God for thousands of years, perhaps from the very beginnings of the human species, but until now it hasn't occurred to anyone that it might be possible to use the sophisticated tools of modern high technology as an aid to that search.

That thought *does* occur to the characters in the unsettling story that follows (one from early in her distinguished career, before most readers had realized that a giant of the form had appeared); what *doesn't* occur to them is that if you look hard enough for something, you just might be unlucky enough to *find* it. . . .

Lord, I believe; help Thou mine unbelief!
—*Mark 9:24*

At first I didn't recognize Devrie.

Devrie—I didn't recognize *Devrie*. Astonished at myself, I studied the wasted figure standing in the middle of the bare reception room: arms like wires, clavicle sharply outlined, head shaved, dressed in that ugly long tent of lightweight gray. God knew what her legs looked like under it. Then she smiled, and it was Devrie.

"You look like shit."

"Hello. Seena. Come on in."

"I am in."

"Barely. It's not catching, you know."

"Stupidity fortunately isn't," I said and closed the door behind me. The small room was too hot; Devrie would need the heat, of course, with almost no fat left to insulate her bones and organs. Next to her I felt huge, although I am not. Huge, hairy, sloppy-breasted.

"Thank you for not wearing bright colors. They do affect me."

"Anything for a sister," I said, mocking the childhood formula, the old sentiment. But Devrie was too quick to think it was only mockery; in that, at least, she had not changed. She clutched my arm and her fingers felt like chains, or talons.

"You found him. Seena, you found him."

"I found him."

"Tell me," she whispered.

"Sit down first, before you fall over. God, Devrie, don't you eat at all?"

"*Tell me*," she said. So I did.

Devrie Caroline Konig had admitted herself to the Institute of the Biological Hope on the Caribbean island of Dominica eleven months ago, in late November of 2017, when her age was 23 years and 4 months. I am precise about this because it is all I can be sure of. I need the precision. The Institute of the Biological Hope is not precise; it is a mongrel, part research laboratory in brain sciences, part monastery, part school for training in the discipline of the mind. That made my baby sister guinea pig, postulant, freshman. She had always been those things, but, until now, sequentially. Apparently so had many other people, for when eccentric Nobel Prize winner James Arthur Bohentin had founded his Institute, he had been able to fund it, although precariously. But in that it did not differ from most private scientific research centers.

Or most monasteries.

I wanted Devrie out of the Institute of Biological Hope.

"It's located on Dominica," I had said sensibly—what an ass I had been—to an unwasted Devrie a year ago, "because the research procedures there fall outside United States laws concerning the safety of research subjects. Doesn't that *tell* you something, Devrie? Doesn't that at least give you pause? In New York, it would be illegal to do to anyone what Bohentin does to his people."

"Do you know him?" she had asked.

"I have met him. Once."

"What is he like?"

"Like stone."

Devrie shrugged, and smiled. "All the particpants in the Institute are willing. Eager."

"That doesn't make it ethical for Bohentin to destroy them. Ethical or legal."

"It's legal on Dominica. And in thinking you know better than the participants what they should risk their own lives for, aren't you playing God?"

"Better me than some untrained fanatic who offers himself up like an exalted Viking hero, expecting Valhalla."

"You're an intellectual snob, Seena."

"I never denied it."

"Are you sure you aren't really objecting not to the Institute's dangers but to its purpose? Isn't the 'Hope' part what really bothers you?"

"I don't think scientific method and pseudo-religious mush mix, no. I never did. I don't think it leads to a perception of God."

"The holotank tapes indicate it leads to a perception of *something* the brain hasn't encountered before," Devrie said, and for a moment I was silent.

I was once, almost, a biologist. I was aware of the legitimate studies that formed the basis for Bohentin's megalomania: the brain wave changes that accompany anorexia nervosa, sensory deprivation, biological feedback, and neurotransmitter stimulants. I have read the historical accounts, some merely pathetic but some disturbingly not, of the Christian mystics who achieved rapture through the mortification of the flesh and the Eastern mystics who achieved anesthesia through the control of the mind, of the faith healers who succeeded, of the carcinomas shrunk through trained will. I knew of the research of focused clairvoyance during orgasm, and of what happens when neurotransmitter number and speed are increased chemically.

And I knew all that was known about the twin trance.

Fifteen years earlier, as a doctoral student in biology, I had spent one summer replicating Sunderwirth's pioneering study of drug-enhanced telepathy in identical twins. My results were positive, except that within six months all eight of my research subjects had died. So had Sunderwirth's. Twin-trance research became the cloning controversy of the new decade, with the same panicky cycle of public outcry, legal restrictions, religious misunderstandings, fear, and demagoguery. When I received the phone call that the last of my subjects was dead—cardiac arrest, no history of heart disease, forty-three Goddamn years old—I locked myself in my apartment, with the lights off and my father's papers clutched in my hand, for three days. Then I resigned from the neurology department and became an entomologist. There is no pain in classifying dead insects.

"There is something *there*," Devrie had repeated. She was holding the letter sent to our father, whom someone at the Institute had not heard was dead. "It says the holotank tapes—"

"So there's something there," I said. "So the tanks are picking up some strange radiation. Why call it 'God'?"

"Why not call it God?"

"Why not call it Rover? Even if I grant you that the tape pattern looks like a presence—which I don't—you have no way of knowing that Bohentin's phantom isn't, say, some totally ungodlike alien being."

"But neither do I know that it *is*."

"Devrie—"

She had smiled and put her hands on my shoulders. She had—has, has always had—a very sweet smile. "Seena. *Think*. If the Institute can prove rationally that God exists—can prove it to the intellectual mind, the doubting Thomases who need something concrete to study . . . faith that doesn't need to be taken on faith . . ."

She wore her mystical face, a glowing softness that made me want to shake the silliness out of her. Instead I made some clever riposte, some sarcasm I no longer remember, and reached out to ruffle her hair. Big-sisterly, patronizing, thinking I could deflate her rapturous interest with the pinprick of ridicule. God, I was an ass. It hurts to remember how big an ass I was.

A month and a half later Devrie committed herself and half her considerable inheritance to the Institute of the Biological Hope.

"Tell me," Devrie whispered. The Institute had no windows; outside I had seen grass, palm trees, butterflies in the sunshine, but inside here in the bare gray room there was nowhere to look but at her face.

"He's a student in a Master's program at a third-rate college in New Hampshire. He was adopted when he was two, nearly three, in March of 1997. Before that he was in a government-run children's home. In Boston, of course. The adopting family, as far as I can discover, never was told he was anything but one more toddler given up by somebody for adoption."

"Wait a minute," Devrie said. "I need . . . a minute."

She had turned paler, and her hands trembled. I had recited the information as if it were no more than an exhibit listing at my museum. Of course she was rattled. I wanted her rattled. I wanted her out.

Lowering herself to the floor, Devrie sat cross-legged and closed her eyes. Concentration spread over her face, but a concentration so serene it barely deserved that name. Her breathing slowed, her color freshened, and when she opened her eyes, they had the rested energy of a person who has just slept eight hours in mountain air. Her face even looked plumper, and an EEG, I guessed, would show damn near alpha waves. In her year at the Institute she must have mastered quite an array of biofeedback techniques to do that, so fast and with such a malnourished body.

"Very impressive," I said sourly.

"Seena—have you seen him?"

"No. All this is from sealed records."

"How did you get into the records?"

"Medical and governmental friends."

"Who?"

"What do you care, as long as I found out what you wanted to know?"

She was silent. I knew she would never ask me if I had obtained her information legally or illegally; it would not occur to her to ask. Devrie, being Devrie, would assume it had all been generously offered by my modest museum connections and our dead father's immodest research connections. She would be wrong.

"How old is he now?"

"Twenty-four years last month. They must have used your two-month tissue sample."

"Do you think Daddy knew where the . . . baby went?"

"Yes. Look at the timing—the child was normal and healthy, yet he wasn't adopted until he was nearly three. The researchers kept track of him, all right, they kept all six clones in a government-controlled home where they could monitor their development as long as humanely possible. The same-sex clones were released for adoption after a year, but they hung onto the cross-sex ones until they reached an age where they would become harder to adopt. They undoubtedly wanted to study *them* as long as they could. And even after the kids were released for adoption, the researchers held off publishing until April, 1998, remember. By the time the storm broke, the babies were out of its path, and anonymous."

"And the last," Devrie said.

"And the last," I agreed, although of course the researchers hadn't foreseen *that*. So few in the scientific community had foreseen that. Offense against God and man, Satan's work, natter natter. Watching my father's suddenly stooped shoulders and stricken eyes, I had thought how ugly public revulsion could be and had nobly resolved—how had I thought of it then? So long ago—resolved to snatch the banner of pure science from my fallen father's hand. Another time that I had been an ass. Five years later, when it had been my turn to feel the ugly scorching of public revulsion, I had broken, left neurological research, and fled down the road that led to the Museum of Natural History, where I was the curator of ants fossilized in amber and moths pinned securely under permaplex.

"The other four clones," Devrie said, "the ones from that university in California that published almost simultaneously with Daddy—"

"I don't know. I didn't even try to ask. It was hard enough in Cambridge."

"Me," Devrie said wonderingly. "He's *me*."

"Oh, for—Devrie, he's your twin. No more than that. No—actually less than that. He shares your genetic material exactly as an identical twin would, except for the Y chromosome, but he shares none of the congenital or environmental influences that shaped your personality. There's no mystical replication of spirit in cloning. He's merely a twin who got born eleven months late!"

She looked at me with luminous amusement. I didn't like the look. On that fleshless face, the skin stretched so taut that the delicate bones beneath were as visible as the veins of a moth wing, her amusement looked ironic. Yet Devrie was never ironic. Gentle, passionate, trusting, a little stupid, she was not capable of irony. It was beyond her, just as it was beyond her to wonder why I, who had fought her entering the Institute of the Biological Hope, had brought her this information now. Her amusement was one-layered, and trusting.

God's fools, the Middle Ages had called them.

"Devrie," I said, and heard my own voice unexpectedly break, "leave here. It's physically not safe. What are you down to, ten percent body fat? Eight? Look at yourself, you can't hold body heat, your palms are dry, you can't move quickly without getting dizzy. Hypotension. What's your heartbeat? Do you still menstruate? It's insane."

She went on smiling at me. God's fools don't need menstruation. "Come with me, Seena. I want to show you the Institute."

"I don't want to see it."

"Yes. This visit you should see it."

"Why this visit?"

"Because you *are* going to help me get my clone to come here, aren't you? Or else why did you go to all the trouble of locating him?"

I didn't answer. She still didn't see it.

Devrie said, "'Anything for a sister.' But you were always more like a mother to me than a sister." She took my hand and pulled herself off the floor. So had I pulled her up to take her first steps, the day after our mother died in a plane crash at Orly. Now Devrie's hand felt cold. I imprisoned it and counted the pulse.

"Bradycardia."

But she wasn't listening.

The Institute was a shock. I had anticipated the laboratories: monotonous gray walls, dim light, heavy soundproofing, minimal fixtures in the ones used for sensory dampening; high-contrast textures and colors, strobe lights, quite good sound equipment in those for sensory arousal. There was much that Devrie, as subject rather than researcher, didn't have authority to show me, but I deduced much from what I did see. The dormitories, divided by sex, were on the sensory-dampening side. The subjects slept in small cells, ascetic and chaste, that reminded me of an abandoned Carmelite convent I had once toured in Belgium. That was the shock: the physical plant felt scientific, but the atmosphere did not.

There hung in the gray corridors a wordless peace, a feeling so palpable I could feel it clogging my lungs. No. "Peace" was the wrong word. Say "peace" and the picture is pastoral, lazy sunshine and dreaming woods. This was not like that at all. The research subjects—students? postulants?—lounged in the corridors outside closed labs, waiting for the next step in their routine. Both men and women were anorectic, both wore gray bodysuits or caftans, both were fined down to an otherworldly ethereality when seen from a distance and a malnourished asexuality when seen up close. They talked among themselves in low voices, sitting with backs against the wall or stretched full-length on the carpeted floor, and on all their faces I saw the same luminous patience, the same certainty of being very near to something exciting that they nonetheless could wait for calmly, as long as necessary.

"They look," I said to Devrie, "as if they're waiting to take an exam they already know they'll ace."

She smiled. "Do you think so? I always think of us as travelers waiting for a plane, boarding passes stamped for Eternity."

She was actually serious. But she didn't in fact wear the same expression as the others; hers was far more intense. If they were travelers, she wanted to pilot.

The lab door opened and the students brought themselves to their feet. Despite their languid movements, they looked sharp: sharp protruding clavicles, bony chins, angular unpadded elbows that could chisel stone.

"This is my hour for biofeedback manipulation of drug effects," Devrie said. "Please come watch."

"I'd sooner watch you whip yourself in a twelfth-century monastery."

Devrie's eyes widened, then again lightened with that luminous amusement. "It's for the same end, isn't it? But they had such unsystematic means. Poor struggling God-searchers. I wonder how many of them made it."

I wanted to strike her. "*Devrie*—"

"If not biofeedback, what would you like to see?"

"You out of here."

"What else?"

There was only one thing: the holotanks. I struggled with the temptation, and lost. The two tanks stood in the middle of a roomy lab carpeted with thick gray matting and completely enclosed in a Faraday cage. That Devrie had a key to the lab was my first clue that my errand for her had been known, and discussed, by someone higher in the Institute. Research subjects do not carry keys to the most delicate brain-perception equipment in the world. For this equipment Bohentin had received his Nobel.

The two tanks, independent systems, stood as high as my shoulder. The ones I had used fifteen years ago had been smaller. Each of these was a cube, opaque on its bottom half, which held the sensing apparatus, computerized simulators, and recording equipment; clear on its top half, which was filled with the transparent fluid out of whose molecules the simulations would form. A separate sim would form for each subject, as the machine sorted and mapped all the electromagnetic radiation received and processed by each brain. *All* that each brain perceived, not only the visuals; the holograph equipment was capable of picking up all wavelengths that the brain did, and of displaying their brain-processed analogues as three-dimensional images floating in a clear womb. When all other possible sources of radiation were filtered out except for the emanations from the two subjects themselves, what the sims showed was what kinds of activity were coming from—and hence going on in—the other's brain. That was why it worked best with identical twins in twin trance: no structural brain differences to adjust for. In a rawer version of this holotank, a rawer version of myself had pioneered the recording of twin trances. The UCIC, we had called it then: What you see, I see.

What I had seen was eight autopsy reports.

"We're so *close*," Devrie said. "Mona and Marlene—" she waved a hand toward the corridor, but Mona and Marlene, whichever two they had been, had gone— "had taken KX3, that's the drug that—"

"I know what it is," I said, too harshly. KX3 reacts with one of the hormones overproduced in an anorectic body. The combination is readily absorbed by body fat, but in a body without fat, much of it is absorbed by the brain.

Devrie continued, her hand tight on my arm. "Mona and Marlene were controlling the neural reactions with biofeedback, pushing the twin trance higher and higher, working it. Dr. Bohentin was monitoring the holotanks. The sims were incredibly detailed—everything each twin perceived in the perceptions of the other, in all wavelengths. Mona and Marlene forced their neurotransmission level even higher and then, in the tanks—" Devrie's face glowed, the mystic-rapture look—"a completely third sim formed. Completely separate. A third *presence*."

I stared at her.

"It was recorded in *both* tanks. It was shadowy, yes, but it was *there*. A third presence that can't be perceived except through another human's electromagnetic presence, and then only with every drug and trained reaction and arousal mode and the twin trance all pushing the brain into a supraheightened state. A third presence!"

"Isotropic radiation. Bohentin fluffed the pre-screening program and the computer hadn't cleared the background microradiation—" I said, but even as I spoke I knew how stupid that was. Bohentin didn't make mistakes like that, and isotropic radiation simulates nowhere close to the way a presence does. Devrie didn't even bother to answer me.

This, then, was what the rumors had been about, the rumors leaking for the last year out of the Institute and through the scientific community, mostly still scoffed at, not yet picked up by the popular press. This. A verifiable, replicable third presence being picked up by holography. Against all reason, a long shiver went over me from neck to that cold place at the base of the spine.

"There's more," Devrie said feverishly. "They *felt* it. Mona and Marlene. Both said afterwards that they could feel it, a huge presence filled with light, but they couldn't quite reach it. Damn—they couldn't reach it, Seena! They weren't playing off each other enough, weren't close enough. Weren't, despite the twin trance, *melded* enough."

"Sex," I said.

"They tried it. The subjects are all basically heterosexual. They inhibit."

"So go find some homosexual God-yearning anorectic incestuous twins!"

Devrie looked at me straight. "I need him. Here. He *is* me."

I exploded, right there in the holotank lab. No one came running in to find out if the shouting was dangerous to the tanks, which was my second clue that the Institute knew very well why Devrie had brought me there. "Damn it to hell, he's a human being, not some chemical you can just order up because you need it for an experiment! You don't have the right to expect him to come here, you didn't even have the right to tell anyone that he exists, but that didn't stop you, did it? There are still anti-bioengineering groups out there in the real world, religious split-brains who—how *dare* you put him in any danger? How dare you even presume he'd be interested in this insane mush?"

"He'll come," Devrie said. She had not changed expression.

"How the hell do you know?"

"He's me. And I want God. He will, too."

I scowled at her. A fragment of one of her poems, a thing she had written when she was fifteen, came to me: "Two human species/Never one—/One aching for God/One never." But she had been fifteen then. I had assumed that the sentiment, as adolescent as the poetry, would pass.

I said, "What does Bohentin think of this idea of importing your clone?"

For the first time she hesitated. Bohentin, then, was dubious. "He thinks it's rather a long shot."

"You could phrase it that way."

"But *I* know he'll want to come. Some things you just know, Seena, beyond rationality. And besides—" she hesitated again, and then went on, "I have left half my inheritance from Daddy, and the income on the trust from Mummy."

"Devrie. God, Devrie—you'd *buy* him?"

For the first time she looked angry. "The money would be just to get him here, to see what is involved. Once he sees, he'll want this as much as I do, at any price! What price can you put on God? I'm not 'buying' his life—I'm offering him the way to *find* life. What good is breathing, existing, if there's no purpose to it? Don't you realize how many centuries, in how many ways, people have looked for that light-filled presence and never been able to be *sure*? And now we're almost there, Seena, I've seen it for myself—*almost there*. With verifiable, scientifically-controlled means. Not subjective faith this time—scientific data, the same as for any other actual phenomenon. This research stands now where research into the atom stood fifty years ago. Can you touch a quark? But it's there! And my clone can be a part of it, can *be* it, how can you talk about the money buying him under circumstances like that!"

I said slowly, "How do you know that whatever you're so close to is God?" But that was sophomoric, of course, and she was ready for it. She smiled warmly.

"What does it matter what we call it? Pick another label if it will make you more comfortable."

I took a piece of paper from my pocket. "His name is Keith Torellen. He lives in Indian Falls, New Hampshire. Address and mailnet number here. Good luck, Devrie." I turned to go.

"Seena! *I* can't go!"

She couldn't, of course. That was the point. She barely had the strength in that starved, drug-battered body to get through the day, let alone to New Hampshire. She needed the sensory-controlled environment, the artificial heat, the chemical monitoring. "Then send someone from the Institute. Perhaps Bohentin will go."

"*Bohentin!*" she said, and I knew that was impossible; Bohentin had to remain officially ignorant of this sort of recruiting. Too many U.S. laws were involved. In addition, Bohentin had no persuasive skills; people as persons and not neurologies did not interest him. They were too far above chemicals and too far below God.

Devrie looked at me wih a kind of level fury. "This is really why you found him, isn't it? So I would have to stop the drug program long enough to leave here and go get him. You think that once I've gone back out into the world either the build-up effects in the brain will be interrupted or else the spell will be broken and I'll have doubts about coming back here!"

"Will you listen to yourself? 'Out in the world.' You sound like some archaic nun in a cloistered order!"

"You always did ridicule anything you couldn't understand," Devrie said icily, turned her back on me, and stared at the empty holotanks. She didn't turn when I left the lab, closing the door behind me. She was still facing the tanks, her spiny back rigid, the piece of paper with Keith Torellen's address clutched in fingers delicate as glass.

In New York the museum simmered with excitement. An unexpected endowment had enabled us to buy the contents of a small, very old museum located in a part of Madagascar not completely destroyed by the African Horror. Crate after crate of moths began arriving in New York, some of them collected in the days when naturalists-gentlemen shot jungle moths from the trees using dust shot. Some species had been extinct since the Horror and thus were rare; some were the brief mutations from the bad years afterward and thus were even rarer. The museum staff uncrated and exclaimed.

"Look at this one," said a young man, holding it out to me. Not on my own staff, he was one of the specialists on loan to us—DeFabio or DeFazio, something like that. He was very handsome. I looked at the moth he showed me, all pale wings outstretched and pinned to black silk. "A perfect Thysania Africana. *Perfect*."

"Yes."

"You'll have to loan us the whole exhibit, in a few years."

"Yes," I said again. He heard the tone in my voice and glanced up quickly. But not quickly enough—my face was all professional interest when his gaze reached it. Still, the professional interest had not fooled him; he had heard the perfunctory note. Frowning, he turned back to the moths.

By day I directed the museum efficiently enough. But in the evenings, home alone in my apartment, I found myself wandering from room to room, touching objects, unable to settle to work at the oversize teak desk that had been my father's, to the reports and journals that had not. His had dealt with the living, mine with the ancient dead—but I had known that for years. The fogginess of my evenings bothered me.

"Faith should not mean fogginess."

Who had said that? Father, of course, to Devrie, when she had joined the dying Catholic Church. She had been thirteen years old. Skinny, defiant, she had stood clutching a black rosary from God knows where, daring him from scared dark eyes to forbid her. Of course he had not, thinking, I suppose, that Heaven, like any other childhood fever, was best left alone to burn out its course.

Devrie had been received into the Church in an overdecorated chapel, wearing an overdecorated dress of white lace and carrying a candle. Three years later she had left, dressed in a magenta body suit and holding the keys to Father's safe, which his executor had left unlocked after the funeral. The will had, of course, made me Devrie's guardian. In the three years Devrie had been going to Mass, I had discovered that I was sterile, divorced my second husband, finished my work in entomology, accepted my first position with a museum, and entered a drastically premature menopause.

That is not a flip nor random list.

After the funeral, I sat in the dark in my father's study, in his maroon leather chair and at his teak desk. Both felt oversize. All the lights were off. Outside it rained; I heard the steady beat of water on the window, and the wind. The dark room was cold. In my palm I held one of my father's research awards, a small abstract sculpture of a double helix, done by Harold Landau himself. It was very heavy. I couldn't think what Landau had used, to make it so heavy. I couldn't think, with all the noise from the rain. My father was dead, and I would never bear a child.

Devrie came into the room, leaving the lights off but bringing with her an incandescent rectangle from the doorway. At sixteen she was lovely, with long brown hair in the masses of curls again newly fashionable. She sat on a low stool beside me, all that hair falling around her, her face white in the gloom. She had been crying.

"He's gone. He's really gone. I don't believe it yet."

"No."

She peered at me. Something in my face, or my voice, must have alerted her; when she spoke again it was in that voice people use when they think your grief is understandably greater than theirs. A smooth dark voice, like a wave.

"You still have me, Seena. We still have each other."

I said nothing.

"I've always thought of you more as my mother than my sister, anyway. You took the place of Mother. You've been a mother to at least *me*."

She smiled and squeezed my hand. I looked at her face—so young, so pretty— and I wanted to hit her. I didn't want to be her mother; I wanted to be her. All her choices lay ahead of her, and it seemed to me that self-indulgent night as if mine were finished. I could have struck her.

"Seena—"

"Leave me alone! Can't you ever leave me alone? All my life you've been dragging behind me; why don't *you* die and finally leave me alone!"

We make ourselves pay for small sins more than large ones. The more trivial the thrust, the longer we're haunted by memory of the wound.

I believe that.

Indian Falls was out of another time: slow, quiet, safe. The Avis counter at the airport rented not personal guards but cars, and the only shiny store on Main Street sold wilderness equipment. I suspected that the small state college, like the town, traded mostly on trees and trails. That Keith Torellen was trying to take an academic degree *here* told me more about his adopting family than if I had hired a professional information service.

The house where he lived was shabby, paint peeling and steps none too sturdy. I climbed them slowly, thinking once again what I wanted to find out.

Devrie would answer none of my messages on the mailnet. Nor would she accept my phone calls. She was shutting me out, in retaliation for my refusing to fetch Torellen for her. But Devrie would discover that she could not shut me out as easily as that; we were sisters. I wanted to know if she had contacted Torellen herself, or had sent someone from the Institute to do so.

If neither, then my visit here would be brief and anonymous; I would leave Keith Torellen to his protected ignorance and shabby town. But if he *had* seen Devrie, I wanted to discover if and what he had agreed to do for her. It might even be possible that he could be of use in convincing Devrie of the stupidity of what she was doing. If he could be used for that, I would use him.

Something else: I was curious. This boy was my brother—nephew? no, brother— as well as the result of my father's rational mind. Curiosity prickled over me. I rang the bell.

It was answered by the landlady, who said that Keith was not home, would not be home until late, was "in rehearsal."

"Rehearsal?"

"Over to the college. He's a student and they're putting on a play."

I said nothing, thinking.

"I don't remember the name of the play," the landlady said. She was a large woman in a faded garment, dress or robe. "But Keith says it's going to be real good. It starts this weekend." She laughed. "But you probably already know all that! George, my husband George, he says I'm forever telling people things they already know!"

"How would I know?"

She winked at me. "Don't you think I got eyes? Sister, or cousin? No, let me guess—older sister. Too much alike for cousins."

"Thank you," I said. "You've been very helpful."

"Not sister!" She clapped her hand over her mouth, her eyes shiny with amusement. "You're checking up on him, ain't you? You're his mother! I should of seen it right off!"

I turned to negotiate the porch steps.

"They rehearse in the new building, Mrs. Torellen," she called after me. "Just ask anybody you see to point you in the right direction."

"Thank you," I said carefully.

Rehearsal was nearly over. Evidently it was a dress rehearsal; the actors were in period costume and the director did not interrupt. I did not recognize the period or the play. Devrie had been interested in theater; I was not. Quietly I took a seat in the darkened back row and waited for the pretending to end.

Despite wig and greasepaint, I had no trouble picking out Keith Torellen. He moved like Devrie: quick, light movements, slightly pigeon-toed. He had her height and, given the differences of a male body, her slenderness. Sitting a theater's length away, I might have been seeing a male Devrie.

But seen up close, his face was mine.

Despite the landlady, it was a shock. He came towards me across the theater lobby, from where I had sent for him, and I saw the moment he too struck the resemblance. He stopped dead, and we stared at each other. Take Devrie's genes, spread them over a face with the greater bone surface, larger features, and coarser skin texture of a man—and the result was my face. Keith had scrubbed off his makeup and removed his wig, exposing brown curly hair the same shade Devrie's had been. But his face was mine.

A strange emotion, unnamed and hot, seared through me.

"Who are *you*? Who the hell *are* you?"

So no one had come from the Institute after all. Not Devrie, not any one.

"You're one of them, aren't you?" he said; it was almost a whisper. "One of my real family?"

Still gripped by the unexpected force of emotion, still dumb, I said nothing. Keith took one step toward me. Suspicion played over his face—Devrie would not have been suspicious—and vanished, replaced by a slow painful flush of color.

"You are. You *are* one. Are you . . . are you my mother?"

I put out a hand against a stone post. The lobby was all stone and glass. Why were all theater lobbies stone and glass? Architects had so little damn imagination, so little sense of the bizarre.

"No! I am not your mother!"

He touched my arm. "Hey, are you okay? You don't look good. Do you need to sit down?"

His concern was unexpected, and touching. I thought that he shared Devrie's genetic personality and that Devrie had always been hypersensitive to the body. But this was not Devrie. His hand on my arm was stronger, firmer, warmer than Devrie's. I felt giddy, disoriented. This was not Devrie.

"A mistake," I said unsteadily. "This was a mistake. I should not have come. I'm sorry. My name is Dr. Seena Konig and I am a . . . relative of yours, but I think this is a mistake. I have your address and I promise that I'll write about your family, but now I think I should go." Write some benign lie, leave him in ignorance. This was a mistake.

But he looked stricken, and his hand tightened on my arm. "You can't! I've been searching for my biological family for two years! You can't just go!"

We were beginning to attract attention in the theater lobby. Hurrying students eyed us sideways. I thought irrelevantly how different they looked from the "students" at the Institute, and with that thought regained my composure. This was a student, a boy—"you can't!" a boyish protest, and boyish panic in his voice—and not the man-Devrie-me he had seemed a foolish moment ago. He was nearly twenty years my junior. I smiled at him and removed his hand from my arm.

"Is there somewhere we can have coffee?"

"Yes. Dr. . . ."

"Seena," I said. "Call me Seena."

Over coffee, I made him talk first. He watched me anxiously over the rim of his cup, as if I might vanish, and I listened to the words behind the words. His adopting family was the kind that hoped to visit the Grand Canyon but not Europe, go to movies but not opera, aspire to college but not to graduate work, buy wilderness equipment but not wilderness. Ordinary people. Not religious, not rich, not unusual. Keith was the only child. He loved them.

"But at the same time I never really felt I belonged," he said, and looked away from me. It was the most personal thing he had knowingly revealed, and I saw that he regretted it. Devrie would not have. More private, then, and less trusting. And I sensed in him a grittiness, a tougher awareness of the world's hardness, than Devrie had ever had—or needed to have. I made my decision. Having disturbed him thus far, I owed him the truth—but not the whole truth.

"Now you tell me," Keith said, pushing away his cup. "Who were my parents? Our parents? Are you my sister?"

"Yes."

"Our parents?"

"Both are dead. Our father was Dr. Richard Konig. He was a scientist. He—" But Keith had recognized the name. His readings in biology or history must have been more extensive than I would have expected. His eyes widened, and I suddenly wished I had been more oblique.

"Richard Konig. He's one of those scientists that were involved in that bioengineering scandal—"

"How did you learn about that? It's all over and done with. Years ago."

"Journalism class. We studied how the press handled it, especially the sensationalism surrounding the cloning thing twenty years—"

I saw the moment it hit him. He groped for his coffee cup, clutched the handle, didn't raise it. It was empty anyway. And then what I said next shocked me as much as anything I have ever done.

"It was Devrie," I said, and heard my own vicious pleasure, "*Devrie* was the one who wanted me to tell you!"

But of course he didn't know who Devrie was. He went on staring at me, panic in his young eyes, and I sat frozen. That tone I heard in my own voice when I said "Devrie," that vicious pleasure that it was she and not I who was hurting him . . .

"Cloning," Keith said. "Konig was in trouble for claiming to have done illegal cloning. Of humans." His voice held so much dread that I fought off my own dread and tried to hold my voice steady to his need.

"It's illegal now, but not then. And the public badly misunderstood. All that sensationalism—you were right to use that word, Keith—covered up the fact that there is nothing abnormal about producing a fetus from another diploid cell. In the womb, identical twins—"

"Am I a clone?"

"Keith—"

"*Am I a clone?*"

Carefully I studied him. This was not what I had intended, but although the fear was still in his eyes, the panic had gone. And curiosity—Devrie's curiosity, and her eagerness—they were there as well. This boy would not strike me, nor stalk out of the restaurant, nor go into psychic shock.

"Yes. You are."

He sat quietly, his gaze turned inward. A long moment passed in silence.

"Your cell?"

"No. My—our sister's. Our sister Devrie."

Another long silence. He did not panic. Then he said softly, "Tell me."

Devrie's phrase.

"There isn't much to tell, Keith. If you've seen the media accounts, you know the story, and also what was made of it. The issue then becomes how you feel about what you saw. Do you believe that cloning is meddling with things man should best leave alone?"

"No. I don't."

I let out my breath, although I hadn't known I'd been holding it. "It's actually no more than delayed twinning, followed by surrogate implantation. A zygote—"

"I know all that," he said with some harshness, and held up his hand to silence me. I didn't think he knew that he did it. The harshness did not sound like Devrie. To my ears, it sounded like myself. He sat thinking, remote and troubled, and I did not try to touch him.

Finally he said, "Do my parents know?"

He meant his adoptive parents. "No."

"Why are you telling me now? Why did you come?"

"Devrie asked me to."

"She needs something, right? A kidney? Something like that?"

I had not foreseen that question. He did not move in a class where spare organs are easily purchasable. "No. Not a kidney, not any kind of biological donation." A voice in my mind jeered at that, but I was not going to give him any clues that would lead to Devrie. "She just wanted me to find you."

"Why didn't she find me herself? She's my age, right?"

"Yes. She's ill just now and couldn't come."

"Is she dying?"

"No!"

Again he sat quietly, finally saying, "No one could tell me anything. For two years I've been searching for my mother, and not one of the adoptee-search agencies could find a single trace. Not one. Now I see why. Who covered the trail so well?"

"My father."

"I want to meet Devrie."

I said evenly, "That might not be possible."

"Why not?"

"She's in a foreign hospital. Out of the country. I'm sorry."

"When does she come home?"

"No one is sure."

"What disease does she have?"

She's sick for God, I thought, but aloud I said, not thinking it through, "A brain disease."

Instantly, I saw my own cruelty. Keith paled, and I cried, "No, no, nothing you could have as well! Truly, Keith, it's not—she took a bad fall. From her hunter."

"Her hunter," he said. For the first time, his gaze flickered over my clothing and jewelry. But would he even recognize how expensive they were? I doubted it. He wore a synthetic, deep-pile jacket with a tear at one shoulder and a cheap wool hat, dark blue, shapeless with age. From long experience I recognized his gaze: uneasy, furtive, the expression of a man glimpsing the financial gulf between what he had assumed were equals. But it wouldn't matter. Adopted children have no legal claim on the estates of their biological parents. I had checked.

Keith said uneasily, "Do you have a picture of Devrie?"

"No," I lied.

"Why did she want you to find me? You still haven't said."

I shrugged. "The same reason, I suppose, that you looked for your biological family. The pull of blood."

"Then she wants me to write to her."

"Write to me instead."

He frowned. "Why? Why not to Devrie?"

What to say to that? I hadn't bargained on so much intensity from him. "Write in care of me, and I'll forward it to Devrie."

"Why not to her directly?"

"Her doctors might not think it advisable," I said coldly, and he backed off—either from the mention of doctors or from the coldness.

"Then give me your address, Seena. Please."

I did. I could see no harm in his writing me. It might even be pleasant. Coming home from the museum, another wintry day among the exhibits, to find on the mail-net a letter I could answer when and how I chose, without being taken by surprise. I liked the idea.

But no more difficult questions now. I stood. "I have to leave, Keith."

He looked alarmed. "So soon?"

"Yes."

"But why?"

"I have to return to work."

He stood, too. He was taller than Devrie. "Seena," he said, all earnestness, "just a few more questions. How did you find me?"

"Medical connections."

"Yours?"

"Our father's. I'm not a scientist." Evidently his journalism class had not studied twin-trance sensationalism.

"What do you do?"

"Museum curator. Arthropods."

"What does Devrie do?"

"She's too ill to work. I must go, Keith."

"One more. Do I look like Devrie as well as you?"

"It would be wise, Keith, if you were careful whom you spoke with about all of this. I hadn't intended to say so much."

"I'm not going to tell my parents. Not about being—not about all of it."

"I think that's best, yes."

"Do I look like Devrie as well as you?"

A little of my first, strange emotion returned with his intensity. "A little, yes. But more like me. Sex variance is a tricky thing."

Unexpectedly, he held my coat for me. As I slipped into it, he said from behind, "Thank you, Seena," and let his hands rest on my shoulders.

I did not turn around. I felt my face flame, and self-disgust flooded through me, followed by a desire to laugh. It was all so transparent. This man was an attractive stranger, was Devrie, was youth, was myself, was the work not of my father's loins but of his mind. Of course I was aroused by him. Freud outlasts cloning: a note for a research study, I told myself grimly, and inwardly I did laugh.

But that didn't help either.

In New York, winter came early. Cold winds whipped whitecaps on harbor and river, and the trees in the Park stood bare even before October had ended. The crumbling outer boroughs of the shrinking city crumbled a little more and talked of the days when New York had been important. Manhattan battened down for snow, hired the seasonal increases in personal guards, and talked of Albuquerque. Each night museum security hunted up and evicted the drifters trying to sleep behind exhibits, drifters as chilled and pale as the moths under permaplex, and, it seemed to me, as detached from the blood of their own age. All of New York seemed detached to me that October, and cold. Often I stood in front of the cases of Noctuidae, staring at them for so long that my staff began to glance at each other covertly. I would catch their glances when I jerked free of my trance. No one asked me about it.

Still no message came from Devrie. When I contacted the Institute on the mailnet, she did not call back.

No letter from Keith Torellen.

Then one night, after I had worked late and was hurrying through the chilly gloom towards my building, he was there, bulking from the shadows so quickly that the guard I had taken for the walk from the museum sprang forward in attack position.

"No! It's all right! I know him!"

The guard retreated, without expression. Keith stared after him, and then at me, his face unreadable.

"Keith, what are you doing here? Come inside!"

He followed me into the lobby without a word. Nor did he say anything during the metal scanning and ID procedure. I took him up to my apartment, studying him in the elevator. He wore the same jacket and cheap wool hat as in Indian Falls, his hair wanted cutting, and the tip of his nose was red from waiting in the cold. How long had he waited there? He badly needed a shave.

In the apartment he scanned the rugs, the paintings, my grandmother's ridiculously ornate, ugly silver, and turned his back on them to face me.

"Seena. I want to know where Devrie is."

"Why? Keith, what has happened?"

"Nothing has happened," he said, removing his jacket but not laying it anywhere. "Only that I've left school and spent two days hitching here. It's no good, Seena. To say that cloning is just like twinning: it's no good. I want to see Devrie."

His voice was hard. Bulking in my living room, unshaven, that hat pulled down over his ears, he looked older and less malleable than the last time I had seen him. Alarm—not physical fear, I was not afraid of him, but a subtler and deeper fear—sounded through me.

"Why do you want to see Devrie?"

"Because she cheated me."

"Of *what*, for God's sake?"

"Can I have a drink? Or a smoke?"

I poured him a Scotch. If he drank, he might talk. I had to know what he wanted, why such a desperate air clung to him, how to keep him from Devrie. I had never seen *her* like this. She was strong-willed, but always with a blitheness, a trust that eventually her will would prevail. Desperate forcefulness of the sort in Keith's manner was not her style. But of course Devrie had always had silent money to back her will; perhaps money could buy trust as well as style.

Keith drank off his Scotch and held out his glass for another. "It was freezing out there. They wouldn't let me in the lobby to wait for you."

"Of course not."

"You didn't tell me your family was rich."

I was a little taken aback at his bluntness, but at the same time it pleased me; I don't know why.

"You didn't ask."

"That's shit, Seena."

"Keith. Why are you here?"

"I told you. I want to see Devrie."

"What is it you've decided she cheated you of? Money?"

He looked so honestly surprised that again I was startled, this time by his resemblance to Devrie. She too would not have thought of financial considerations first, if there were emotional ones possible. One moment Keith was Devrie, one moment he was not. Now he scowled with sudden anger.

"Is that what you think—that fortune hunting brought me hitching from New Hampshire? God, Seena, I didn't even know how much you had until this very—I still don't know!"

I said levelly, "Then what is it you're feeling so cheated of?"

Now he was rattled. Again that quick, half-furtive scan of my apartment, pausing a millisecond too long at the Caravaggio, subtly lit by its frame. When his gaze returned to mine it was troubled, a little defensive. Ready to justify. Of course I had put him on the defensive deliberately, but the calculation of my trick did not prepare me for the staggering naivete of his explanation. Once more it was Devrie complete, reducing the impersonal greatness of science to a personal and emotional loss.

"Ever since I knew that I was adopted, at five or six years old, I wondered about my biological family. Nothing strange in that—I think all adoptees do. I used to make up stories, kid stuff, about how they were really royalty, or lunar colonists, or survivors of the African Horror. Exotic things. I thought especially about my mother, imagining this whole scene of her holding me once before she released me for adoption, crying over me, loving me so much she could barely let me go but had to for some reason. Sentimental shit." He laughed, trying to make light of what was not, and drank off his Scotch to avoid my gaze.

"But Devrie—the fact of her—destroyed all that. I never had a mother who hated to give me up. I never had a mother at all. What I had was a cell cut from Devrie's fingertip or someplace, something discardable, and she doesn't even know what I look like. But she's damn well going to."

"Why?" I said evenly. "What could you expect to gain from her knowing what you look like?"

But he didn't answer me directly. "The first moment I saw you, Seena, in the theater at school, I thought you were my mother."

"I know you did."

"And you hated the idea. Why?"

I thought of the child I would never bear, the marriage, like so many other things of sweet promise, gone sour. But self-pity is a fool's game. "None of your business."

"Isn't it? Didn't you hate the idea because of the way I was made? Coldly. An experiment. Weren't you a little bit insulted at being called the mother of a discardable cell from Devrie's fingertip?"

"What the hell have you been reading? An experiment—what is any child but an experiment? A random egg, a random sperm. Don't talk like one of those anti-science religious split-brains!"

He studied me levelly. Then he said, "Is Devrie religious? Is that why you're so afraid of her?"

I got to my feet, and pointed at the sideboard. "Help yourself to another drink if you wish. I want to wash my hands. I've been handling specimens all afternoon." Stupid, clumsy lie—nobody would believe such a lie.

In the bathroom I leaned against the closed door, shut my eyes, and willed myself to calm. Why should I be so disturbed by the angry lashing-out of a confused boy? I was handy to lash out against; my father, whom Keith was really angry at, was not. It was all so predictable, so earnestly adolescent, that even over the hurting in my chest I smiled. But the smile, which should have reduced Keith's ranting to the tantrum of a child—there, there, when you grow up you'll find out that no one really knows who he is—did not diminish Keith. His losses were real—mother, father, natural place in the natural sequence of life and birth. And suddenly, with a clutch at the pit of my stomach, I knew why I had told him all that I had about his origins. It was not from any ethic of fidelity to "the truth." I had told him he was clone because I, too, had had real losses—research, marriage, motherhood—and Devrie could never have shared them with me. Luminous, mystical Devrie, too occupied with God to be much hurt by man. *Leave me alone! Can't you ever leave me alone! All my life you've been dragging behind me—why don't you die and finally leave me alone!* And Devrie had smiled tolerantly, patted my head, and left me alone, closing the door softly so as not to disturb my grief. My words had not hurt her. I could not hurt her.

But I could hurt Keith—the other Devrie—and I had. That was why he disturbed me all out of proportion. That was the bond. My face, my pain, my fault.

Through my fault, through my fault, through my most grievous fault. But what nonsense. I was not a believer, and the comforts of superstitious absolution could not touch me. What shit. Like all nonbelievers, I stood alone.

It came to me then that there was something absurd in thinking all this while leaning against a bathroom door. Grimly absurd, but absurd. The toilet as confessional. I ran the cold water, splashed some on my face and left. How long had I left Keith alone in the living room?

When I returned, he was standing by the mailnet. He had punched in the command to replay my outgoing postal messages, and displayed on the monitor was Devrie's address at the Institute of the Biological Hope.

"What is it?" Keith said. "A hospital?"

I didn't answer him.

"I can find out, Seena. Knowing this much, I can find out. Tell me."

Tell me. "Not a hospital. It's a research laboratory. Devrie is a voluntary subject."

"Research on what? I will find out, Seena."

"Brain perception."

"Perception of what?"

"Perception of *God*," I said, torn among weariness, anger and a sudden gritty exasperation, irritating as sand. Why not just leave him to Devrie's persuasions, and her to mystic starvation? But I knew I would not. I still, despite all of it, wanted her out of there.

Keith frowned, "What do you mean, 'perception of God'?"

I told him. I made it sound as ridiculous as possible, and as dangerous. I described the anorexia, the massive use of largely untested drugs that would have made the Institute illegal in the United States, the skepticism of most of the scientific community, the psychoses and death that had followed twin-trance research fifteen years earlier. Keith did not remember that—he had been eight years old—and I did not tell him that I had been one of the researchers. I did not tell him about he tapes of the shadowy third presence in Bohentin's holotanks. In every way I could, with every verbal subtlety at my use, I made the Institute sound crackpot, and dangerous, and ugly. As I spoke, I watched Keith's face, and sometimes it was mine, and sometimes the expression altered it into Devrie's. I saw bewilderment at her having chosen to enter the Institute, but not what I had hoped to see. Not scorn, not disgust.

When I had finished, he said, "But why did she think that *I* might want to enter such a place as a twin subject?"

I had saved this for last. "Money. She'd buy you."

His hand, holding his third Scotch, went rigid. "Buy me."

"It's the most accurate way to put it."

"What the hell made her think—" he mastered himself, not without effort. Not all the discussion of bodily risk had affected him as much as this mention of Devrie's money. He had a poor man's touchy pride. "She thinks of me as something to be *bought.*"

I was carefully quiet.

"Damn her," he said. "*Damn* her." Then roughly, "And I was actually considering—"

I caught my breath. "Considering the Institute? After what I've just told you? How in hell could you? And you said, I remember, that your background was not religious!"

"It's not. But I . . . I've wondered." And in the sudden turn of his head away from me so that I wouldn't see the sudden rapt hopelessness in his eyes, in the defiant set of shoulders, I read more than in his banal words, and more than he could know. Devrie's look, Devrie's wishfulness, feeding on air. The weariness and anger, checked before, flooded me again and I lashed out at him.

"Then go ahead and fly to Dominica to enter the Institute yourself!"

He said nothing. But from something—his expression as he stared into his glass, the shifting of his body—I suddenly knew that he could not afford the trip.

I said, "So you fancy yourself as a believer?"

"No. A believer manqué." From the way he said it, I knew that he had said it before, perhaps often, and that the phrase stirred some hidden place in his imagination.

"What is wrong with you," I said, "with people like you, that the human world is not enough?"

"What is wrong with people like you, that it is?" he said, and this time he laughed and raised his eyebrows in a little mockery that shut me out from this place beyond reason, this glittering escape. I knew then that somehow or other, sometime or other, despite all I had said, Keith would go to Dominica.

I poured him another Scotch. As deftly as I could, I led the conversation into other, lighter directions. I asked about his childhood. At first stiffly, then more easily as time and Scotch loosened him, he talked about growing up in the Berkshire Hills. He became more lighthearted, and under my interest turned both shrewd and funny, with a keen sense of humor. His thick brown hair fell over his forehead. I laughed with him, and broke out a bottle of good port. He talked about amateur plays he had acted in; his enthusiasm increased as his coherence decreased. Enthusiasm, humor, thick brown hair. I smoothed the hair back from his forehead. Far into the night I pulled the drapes back from the window and we stood together and looked at the lights of the dying city ten stories below. Fog rolled in from the sea. Keith insisted we open the doors and stand on the balcony; he had never smelled fog tinged with the ocean. We smelled the night, and drank some more, and talked, and laughed.

And then I led him again to the sofa.

"Seena?" Keith said. He covered my hand, laid upon his thigh, with his own, and turned his head to look at me questioningly. I leaned forward and touched my lips to his, barely in contact, for a long moment. He drew back, and his hand tried to lift mine. I tightened my fingers.

"Seena, no . . ."

"Why not?" I put my mouth back on his, very lightly. He had to draw back to answer, and I could feel that he did not want to draw back. Under my lips he frowned slightly; still, despite his drunkenness—so much more than mine—he groped for the word.

"Incest . . ."

"No. We two have never shared a womb."

He frowned again, under my mouth. I drew back to smile at him, and shifted my hand. "It doesn't matter any more, Keith. Not in New York. But even if it did—I am not your sister, not really. You said so yourself—remember? Not a family. Just . . . here."

"Not family," he repeated, and I saw in his eyes the second before he closed them the flash of pain, the greed of a young man's desire, and even the crafty evasions of the good port. Then his arms closed around me.

He was very strong, and more than a little violent. I guessed from what confusions the violence flowed but still I enjoyed it, that overwhelming rush from that beautiful male-Devrie body. I wanted him to be violent with me, as long as I knew there was not real danger. No real danger, no real brother, no real child. Keith was not my child but Devrie was my child-sister, and I had to stop her from destroying herself, no matter how . . . didn't I? "The pull of blood." But this was necessary, was justified . . . was the necessary gamble. For Devrie.

So I told myself. Then I stopped telling myself anything at all, and surrendered to the warm tides of pleasure.

But at dawn I woke and thought—with Keith sleeping heavily across me and the sky cold at the window—*what the hell am I doing?*

When I came out of the shower, Keith was sitting rigidly against the pillows. Sitting next to him on the very edge of the bed, I pulled a sheet around my nakedness and reached for his hand. He snatched it away.

"Keith. It's all right. Truly it is."

"You're my sister."

"But nothing will come of it. No child, no repetitions. It's not all that uncommon, dear heart."

"It is where I come from."

"Yes. I know. But not here."

He didn't answer, his face troubled.

"Do you want breakfast?"

"No. No, thank you."

I could feel his need to get away from me; it was almost palpable. Snatching my bodysuit off the floor, I went into the kitchen, which was chilly. The servant would not arrive for another hour. I turned up the heat, pulled on my bodysuit—standing on the cold floor first on one foot and then on the other, like some extinct species of water fowl—and made coffee. Through the handle of one cup I stuck two folded large bills. He came into the kitchen, dressed even to the torn jacket.

"Coffee."

"Thanks."

His fingers closed on the handle of the cup, and his eyes widened. Pure, naked shock, uncushioned by any defenses whatsoever: the whole soul, betrayed, pinned in the eyes.

"Oh God, no, Keith—how can you even think so? It's for the trip back to Indian Falls! A gift!"

An endless pause, while we stared at each other. Then he said, very low, "I'm sorry. I should have . . . seen what it's for." But his cup trembled in his hand, and a few drops sloshed onto the floor. It was those few drops that undid me, flooding me with shame. Keith had a right to his shock, and to the anguish in his/my/Devrie's face. She wanted him for her mystic purposes, I for their prevention. Fanatic and saboteur, we were both better defended against each other than Keith, without money nor religion nor years, was against either of us. If I could have seen any other way than the gamble I had taken . . . but I could not. Nonetheless, I was ashamed.

"Keith. I'm sorry."

"Why did we? Why did we?"

I could have said: we didn't; I did. But that might have made it worse for him. He was male, and so young.

Impulsively I blurted, "Don't go to Dominica!" But of course he was beyond listening to me now. His face closed. He set down the coffee cup and looked at me from eyes much harder than they had been a minute ago. Was he thinking that because of our night together I expected to influence him directly? I was not that young. He could not foresee that I was trying to guess much farther ahead than that, for which I could not blame him. I could not blame him for anything. But I did regret how clumsily I had handled the money. That had been stupid.

Nonetheless; when he left a few moments later, the handle of the coffee cup was bare. He had taken the money.

The Madagascar exhibits were complete. They opened to much press interest, and there were both favorable reviews and celebrations. I could not bring myself to feel that it mattered. Ten times a day I went through the deadening exercise of willing an interest that had deserted me, and when I looked at the moths, ashy white wings out-stretched forever, I could feel my body recoil in a way I could not name.

The image of the moths went home with me. One night in November I actually thought I heard wings beating against the window where I had stood with Keith. I yanked open the drapes and then the doors, but of course there was nothing there. For a long time I stared at the nothingness, smelling the fog, before typing yet an-other message, urgent-priority personal, to Devrie. The mailnet did not bring any answer.

I contacted the mailnet computer at the college at Indian Falls. My fingers trem-bled as they typed a request to leave an urgent-priority personal message for a stu-dent, Keith Torellen. The mailnet typed back:

TORELLEN, KEITH ROBERT. 64830016. ON MEDICAL LEAVE OF ABSENCE. TIME OF LEAVE: INDEFINITE. NO FORWARDING MAILNET NUMBER. END.

The sound came again at the window. Whirling, I scanned the dark glass, but there was nothing there, no moths, no wings, just the lights of the decaying city flung randomly across the blackness and the sound, faint and very far away, of a siren wailing out somebody else's disaster.

I shivered. Putting on a sweater and turning up the heat made me no warmer. Then the mail slot chimed softly and I turned in time to see the letter fall from the pneumatic tube from the lobby, the apartment house sticker clearly visible, assuring me that it had been processed and found free of both poison and explosives. Also vis-ible was the envelope's logo: INSTITUTE OF THE BIOLOGICAL HOPE, all the O's radiant golden suns. But Devrie never wrote paper mail. She preferred the mailnet.

The note was from Keith, not Devrie. A short note, scrawled on a torn scrap of pa-per in nearly indecipherable handwriting. I had seen Keith's handwriting in Indian Falls, across his student notebooks; this was a wildly out-of-control version of it, al-most psychotic in the variations of spacing and letter formation that signal identity. I guessed that he had written the note under the influence of a drug, or several drugs, his mind racing much faster than he could write. There was neither punctua-tion nor paragraphing.

Dear Seena Im going to do it I have to know my parents are angry but I have
to know I have to all the confusion is gone Seena Keith

There was a word crossed out between "gone" and "Seena," scratched out with erratic lines of ink. I held the paper up to the light, tilting it this way and that. The crossed-out word was "mother."

all the confusion is gone mother

Mother.

Slowly I let out the breath I had not known I was holding. The first emotion was pity, for Keith, even though I had intended this. We had done a job on him, Devrie and I. Mother, sister, self. And when he and Devrie artificially drove upward the number and speed of the neurotransmitters in the brain, generated the twin trance, and then Keith's pre-cloning Freudian-still mind reached for Devrie to add sexual energy to all the other brain energies fueling Bohentin's holotanks—

Mother. Sister. Self.

All was fair in love and war. A voice inside my head jeered: and which is this? But I was ready for the voice. This was both. I didn't think it would be long before Devrie left the Institute to storm to New York.

It was nearly another month, in which the snow began to fall and the city to deck itself in the tired gilt fallacies of Christmas. I felt fine. Humming, I catalogued the Madagascar moths, remounting the best specimens in exhibit cases and sealing them under permaplex, where their fragile wings and delicate antennae could lie safe. The mutant strains had the thinnest wings, unnaturally tenuous and up to twenty-five centimeters each, all of pale ivory, as if a ghostly delicacy were the natural evolutionary response to the glowing landscape of nuclear genocide. I catalogued each carefully.

"Why?" Devrie said. "*Why?*"

"You look like hell."

"Why?"

"I think you already know," I said. She sagged on my white velvet sofa, alone, the PGs that I suspected acted as much as nurses as guards, dismissed from the apartment. Tears of anger and exhaustion collected in her sunken eye sockets but did not fall. Only with effort was she keeping herself in a sitting position, and the effort was costing her energy she did not have. Her skin, except for two red spots of fury high on each cheekbone, was the color of old eggs. Looking at her, I had to keep my hands twisted in my lap to keep myself from weeping.

"Are you telling me you *planned* it, Seena? Are you telling me you located Keith and slept with him because you knew that would make him impotent with me?"

"Of course not. I know sexuality isn't that simple. So do you."

"But you gambled on it. You gambled that it would be one way to ruin the experiment."

"I gambled that it would . . . complicate Keith's responses."

"Complicate them past the point where he knew who the hell he was with!"

"He'd be able to know if you weren't making him glow out of his mind with neurotransmitter kickers! He's not stupid. But he's not ready for whatever mystic hoops you've tried to make him jump through—if anybody ever *can* be said to be ready for that!—and no, I'm not surprised that he can't handle libidinal energies on top of all the other artificial energies you're racing through his brain. Something was bound to snap."

"You caused it, Seena. As cold-bloodedly as that."

A sudden shiver of memory brought the feel of Keith's hands on my breasts. No, not as cold-bloodedly as that. No. But I could not say so to Devrie.

"I trusted you," she said. " 'Anything for a sister'—God!"

"You were right to trust me. To trust me to get you out of that place before you're dead."

"Listen to yourself! Smug, all-knowing, self-righteous . . . do you know how *close* we were at the Institute? Do you have any idea what you've destroyed?"

I laughed coldly. I couldn't help it. "If contact with God can be destroyed because one confused kid can't get it up, what does that say about God?"

Devrie stared at me. A long moment passed, and in the moment the two red spots on her cheeks faded and her eyes narrowed. "Why, Seena?"

"I told you. I wanted you safe, out of there. And you are."

"No. No. There's something else, something more going on here. Going on with you."

"Don't make it more complicated than it is, Devrie. You're my sister, and my only family. Is it so odd that I would try to protect you?"

"Keith is your brother."

"Well, then, protect both of you. Whatever derails that experiment protects Keith, too."

She said softly, "Did you want him so much?"

We stared at each other across the living room, sisters, I standing by the mailnet and she supported by the sofa, needing its support, weak and implacable as any legendary martyr to the faith. Her weakness hurt me in some nameless place; as a child Devrie's body had been so strong. The hurt twisted in me, so that I answered her with truth. "Not so much. Not at first, not until we . . . no, that's not true. I wanted him. But that was not the reason, Devrie—it was not a rationalization for lust, nor any lapse in self-control."

She went on staring at me, until I turned to the sideboard and poured myself a Scotch. My hand trembled.

Behind me Devrie said, "Not lust. And not protection either. Something else, Seena. You're afraid."

I turned, smiling tightly. "Of you?"

"No. No, I don't think so."

"What then?"

"I don't know. Do you?"

"This is your theory, not mine."

She closed her eyes. The tears, shining all this time over her anger, finally fell. Head flung back against the pale sofa, arms limp at her side, she looked the picture of desolation, and so weak that I was frightened. I brought her a glass of milk from the kitchen and held it to her mouth, and I was a little surprised when she drank it off without protest.

"Devrie. You can't go on like this. In this physical state."

"No," she agreed, in a voice so firm and prompt that I was startled further. It was the voice of decision, not surrender. She straightened herself on the sofa. "Even Bohentin says I can't go on like this. I weigh less than he wants, and I'm right at the edge of not having the physical resources to control the twin trance. I'm having racking withdrawal symptoms even being on this trip, and at this very minute there is a doctor sitting at Father's desk in your study, in case I need him. Also, I've had my lawyers make over most of my remaining inheritance to Keith. I don't think you knew that. What's left has all been transferred to a bank on Dominica, and if I die it goes to the Institute. You won't be able to touch it, nor touch Keith's portion either, not even if I die. And I will die, Seena, soon, if I don't start eating and stop taking the program's drugs. I'll just burn out body and brain both. You've guessed that I'm close to that, but you haven't guessed how close. Now I'm telling you. I can't handle the stresses of the twin trance much longer."

I just went on holding her glass, arm extended, unable to move.

"You gambled that you could destroy one component in the chain of my experiment at the Institute by confusing my twin sexually. Well, you won. Now *I'm* making a gamble. I'm gambling my life that you can undo what you did with Keith, and without his knowing that I made you. You said he's not stupid and his impotency comes from being unable to handle the drug program; perhaps you're partly right. But he is me—*me*, Seena—and I know you've thought I was stupid all my life, because I wanted things you don't understand. Now Keith wants them, too—it was inevitable that he would—and you're going to undo whatever is standing in his way. I had to fight myself free all my life of your bullying, but Keith doesn't have that kind of time. Because if you don't undo what you caused, I'm going to go ahead with the twin trance anyway—the *twin trance*, Seena—without the sexual component and without letting Bohentin know just how much greater the strain is in trance than he thinks it is. He doesn't know, he doesn't have a twin, and neither do the doctors. But I know, and if I push much farther I'm going to eventually die at it. *Soon* eventually. When I do, all your scheming to get me out of there really will have failed and you'll be alone with whatever it is you're so afraid of. But I don't think you'll let that happen.

"I think that instead you'll undo what you did to Keith, so that the experiment can have one last real chance. And in return, after that one chance, I'll agree to come home, to Boston or here to New York, for one year.

"That's my gamble."

She was looking at me from eyes empty of all tears, a Devrie I had not ever seen before. She meant it, every demented word, and she would do it. I wanted to scream at her, to scream a jumble of suicide and moral blackmail and warped perceptions and outrage, but the words that came out of my mouth came out in a whisper.

"What in God's name is worth *that*?"

Shockingly, she laughed, a laugh of more power than her wasted frame could have contained. Her face glowed, and the glow looked both exalted and insane. "You said it, Seena—in God's name. To finally know. To *know*, beyond the fogginess of faith, that we're not alone in the universe. . . . Faith should not mean fogginess." She laughed again, this time defensively, as if she knew how she sounded to me. "You'll do it, Seena." It was not a question. She took my hand.

"You would *kill* yourself?"

"No. I would die trying to reach God. It's not the same thing."

"I never bullied you, Devrie."

She dropped my hand. "All my life, Seena. And on into now. But all of your bullying and your scorn would look rather stupid, wouldn't it, if there really can be proved to exist a rational basis for what you laughed at all those years!"

We looked at each other, sisters, across the abyss of the pale sofa, and then suddenly away. Neither of us dared speak.

My plane landed on Dominica by night. Devrie had gone two days before me, returning with her doctor and guards on the same day she had left, as I had on my previous visit. I had never seen the island at night. The tropical greenery, lush with that faintly menacing suggestion of plant life gone wild, seemed to close in on me. The velvety darkness seemed to smell of ginger, and flowers, and the sea—all too strong, too blandly sensual, like an overdone perfume ad. At the hotel it was better; my room was on the second floor, above the dark foliage, and did not face the sea. Nonetheless, I stayed inside all that evening, all that darkness, until I could go the next day to the Institute of the Biological Hope.

"Hello, Seena."

"Keith. You look—"

"Rotten," he finished, and waited. He did not smile. Although he had lost some weight, he was nowhere near as skeletal as Devrie, and it gave me a pang I did not analyze to see his still-healthy body in the small gray room where last I had seen hers. His head was shaved, and without the curling brown hair he looked sterner, prematurely middle-aged. That, too, gave me a strange emotion, although it was not why he looked rotten. The worst was his eyes. Red-veined, watery, the sockets already a little sunken, they held the sheen of a man who was not forgiving somebody for something. Me? Himself? Devrie? I had lain awake all night, schooling myself for this insane interview, and still I did not know what to say. What does one say to persuade a man to sexual potency with one's sister so that her life might be saved? I felt ridiculous, and frightened, and—I suddenly realized the name of my strange emotion—humiliated. How could I even start to slog towards what I was supposed to reach?

"How goes the Great Experiment?"

"Not as you described it," he said, and we were there already. I looked at him evenly.

"You can't understand why I presented the Institute in the worst possible light."

"I can understand that."

"Then you can't understand why I bedded you, knowing about Bohentin's experiment."

"I can also understand that."

Something was wrong. Keith answered me easily, without restraint, but with conflict gritty beneath his voice, like sand beneath blowing grass. I stepped closer, and he flinched. But his expression did not change.

"Keith. What is this about? What am I doing here? Devrie said you couldn't . . . that you were impotent with her, confused enough about who and what . . ." I trailed off. He still had not changed expression.

I said quietly, "It was a simplistic idea in the first place. Only someone as simplistic as Devrie . . ." Only someone as simplistic as Devrie would think you could straighten out impotency by talking about it for a few hours. I turned to go, and I had gotten as far as laying my hand on the doorknob before Keith grasped my arm.

Back to him, I squeezed my eyes shut. What in God would I have *done* if he had not stopped me?

"It's not what Devrie thinks!" With my back to him, not able to see his middle-aged baldness but only to hear the anguish in his voice, he again seemed young, uncertain, the boy I had bought coffee for in Indian Falls. I kept my back to him, and my voice carefully toneless.

"What is it, then, Keith? If not what Devrie thinks?"

"I don't know!"

"But you do know what it's not? It's not being confused about who is your sister and who your mother and who you're willing to have sex with in front of a room full of researchers?"

"No." His voice had gone hard again, but his hand stayed on my arm. "At first, yes. The first time. But, Seena—I *felt* it. *Almost.* I almost felt the presence, and then all the rest of the confusion—it didn't seem as important anymore. Not the confusion between you and Devrie."

I whirled to face him. "You mean God doesn't care whom you fuck if it gets you closer to fucking with Him."

He looked at me hard then—at me, not at his own self-absorption. His reddened eyes widened a little. "Why, Seeny—*you* care. You told me the brother-sister thing didn't matter anymore—but *you* care."

Did I? I didn't even know anymore. I said, "But then, I'm not deluding myself that it's all for the old Kingdom and the Glory."

"Glory," he repeated musingly, and finally let go of my arm. I couldn't tell what he was thinking.

"Keith. This isn't getting us anywhere."

"Where do you want to get?" he said in the same musing tone. "Where did any of you, starting with your father, want to get with me? Glory . . . glory."

Standing this close to him, seeing close up the pupils of his eyes and smelling close up the odor of his sweat, I finally realized what I should have seen all along: he was glowing. He was of course constantly on Bohentin's program of neurotransmitter manipulation, but the same chemicals that made the experiments possible also raised the threshold of both frankness and suggestibility. I guessed it must be a little like the looseness of being drunk, and I wondered if perhaps Bohentin might have deliberately raised the dosage before letting this interview take place. But no, Bohentin wouldn't be aware of the bargain Devrie and I had struck; she would not have told him. The whole bizarre situation was hers alone, and Keith's drugged musings a fortunate side-effect I would have to capitalize on.

"Where do you think my father wanted to get with you?" I asked him gently.

"Immortality. Godhead. The man who created Adam and Eve."

He was becoming maudlin. "Hardly 'the man,'" I pointed out. "My father was only one of a team of researchers. And the same results were being obtained independently in California."

"Results. I am a 'result.' What *do you* think he wanted, Seena?"

"Scientific knowledge of cell development. An objective truth."

"That's all Devrie wants."

"To compare bioengineering to some mystic quest—"

"Ah, but if the mystic quest is given a laboratory answer? Then it, too, becomes a scientific truth. You really hate that idea, don't you, Seena? You hate science validating anything you define as non-science."

I said stiffly, "That's rather an oversimplification."

"Then what do you hate?"

"I hate the risk to human bodies and human minds. To Devrie. To you."

"How nice of you to include me," he said, smiling. "And what do you think Devrie wants?"

"Sensation. Romantic religious emotion. To be all roiled up inside with delicious esoterica."

He considered this. "Maybe."

"And is that what you want as well, Keith? You've asked what everyone else wants. What do you want?"

"I want to feel at home in the universe. As if I belonged in it. And I never have."

He said this simply, without self-consciousness, and the words themselves were predictable enough for his age—even banal. There was nothing in the words that could account for my eyes suddenly filling with tears. "And 'scientifically' reaching God would do that for you?"

"How do I know until I try it? Don't cry, Seena."

"I'm not!"

"All right," he agreed softly. "You're not crying." Then he added, without changing tone, "I am more like you than like Devrie."

"How so?"

"I think that Devrie has always felt that she belongs in the universe. She only wants to find the . . . the coziest corner of it to curl up in. Like a cat. The coziest corner to curl up in is God's lap. Aren't you surprised that I should be more like you than like the person I was cloned from?"

"No," I said. "Harder upbringing than Devrie's. I told you that first day: cloning is only delayed twinning."

He threw back his head and laughed, a sound that chilled my spine. Whatever his conflict was, we were moving closer.

"Oh no, Seena. You're so wrong. It's more than delayed twinning, all right. You can't buy a real twin. You either have one or you don't. But you can buy yourself a clone. Bought, paid for, kept on the books along with all the rest of the glassware and holotanks and electron microscopes. You said so yourself, in your apartment, when you first told me about Devrie and the Institute. 'Money. She'd buy you.' And you were right, of course. Your father bought me, and she did, and you did. But of course you two women couldn't have bought if I hadn't been selling."

He was smiling still. Stupid—we had both been stupid, Devrie and I, we had both been looking in the wrong place, misled by our separate blinders-on training in the laboratory brain. My training had been scientific, hers humanistic, and so I looked at Freud and she looked at Oedipus, and we were equally stupid. How did the world look to a man who did not deal in laboratory brains, a man raised in a grittier world in which limits were not what the mind was capable of but what the bank book would stand? "Your genes are too expensive for you to claim except as a beggar; your sisters are too expensive for you to claim except as a beggar; God is too expensive for you to claim except as a beggar." To a less romantic man it would not have mattered, but a less romantic man would not have come to the Institute. What dark humiliations and resentments did Keith feel when he looked at Devrie, the self who was buyer and not bought?

Change the light you shine onto a mind, and you see different neural patterns, different corridors, different forests of trees grown in soil you could not have imagined. Run that soil through your fingers and you discover different pebbles, different sand, different leaf mold from the decay of old growths. Devrie and I had been hacking through the wrong forest.

Not Oedipus, but Marx.

Quick lines of attack came to me. Say: Keith it's a job like any other with high-hazard pay why can't you look at it like that a very dangerous and well-paid job for which you've been hired by just one more eccentric member of the monied class. Say: You're entitled to the wealth you're our biological brother damn it consider it rationally as a kinship entitlement. Say: Don't be so nicey-nice it's a tough world out there and if Devrie's giving it away take it don't be an impractical chump.

I said none of that. Instead I heard myself saying, coolly and with a calm cruelty, "You're quite right. You were bought by Devrie, and she is now using her own purchase for her own ends. You're a piece of equipment bought and paid for. Unfortunately, there's no money in the account. It has all been a grand sham."

Keith jerked me to face him with such violence that my neck cracked. "What are you saying?"

The words came as smoothly, as plausibly, as if I had rehearsed them. I didn't even consciously plan them: how can you plan a lie you do not know you will need? I slashed through this forest blind, but the ground held under my feet.

"Devrie told me that she has signed over most of her inheritance to you. What she didn't know, because I haven't yet told her, is that she doesn't have control of her inheritance any longer. It's not hers. I control it. I had her declared mentally incompetent on the grounds of violent suicidal tendencies and had myself made her legal guardian. She no longer has the legal right to control her fortune. A doctor observed her when she came to visit me in New York. So the transfer of her fortune to you is invalid."

"The lawyers who gave me the papers to sign—"

"Will learn about the New York action this week," I said smoothly. How much inheritance law did Keith know? Probably very little. Neither did I, and I invented furiously; it only needed to *sound* plausible. "The New York courts only handed down their decision recently, and Dominican judicial machinery, like everything else in the tropics, moves slowly. But the ruling will hold, Keith. Devrie does not control her own money, and you're a pauper again. But *I* have something for you. Here. An airline ticket back to Indian Falls. You're a free man. Poor, but free. The ticket is in your name, and there's a check inside it—that's from me. You've earned it, for at least trying to aid poor Devrie. But now you're going to have to leave her to me. I'm now her legal guardian."

I held the ticket out to him. It was wrapped in its airline folder; my own name as passenger was hidden. Keith stared at it, and then at me.

I said softly, "I'm sorry you were cheated. Devrie didn't mean to. But she has no money, now, to offer you. You can go. Devrie's my burden now."

His voice sounded strangled. "To remove from the Institute?"

"I never made any secret of wanting her out. Although the legal papers for that will take a little time to filter through the Dominican courts. She wouldn't go except by force, so force is what I'll get. Here."

I thrust the ticket folder at him. He made no move to take it, and I saw from the hardening of his face—my face, Devrie's face—the moment when Devrie shifted forests in his mind. Now she was without money, without legal control of her life, about to be torn from the passion she loved most. The helpless underdog. The orphaned woman, poor and cast out, in need of protection from the powerful who had seized her fortune.

Not Marx, but Cervantes.

"You would do that? To your own sister?"

Anything for a sister. I said bitterly, "Of course I would."

"She's not mentally imcompetent!"

"Isn't she?"

"No!"

I shrugged. "The courts say she is."

Keith studied me, resolve hardening around him. I thought of certain shining crystals, that will harden around any stray piece of grit. Now that I was succeeding in convincing him, my lies hurt—or perhaps what hurt was how easily he believed them.

"Are you sure, Seena," he said, "that *you* aren't just trying a grab for Devrie's fortune?"

I shrugged again, and tried to make my voice toneless. "I want her out of here. I don't want her to die."

"Die? What makes you think she would die?"

"She looks—"

"She's nowhere near dying," Keith said angrily—his anger a release, so much that it hardly mattered at what. "Don't you think I can tell in twin trance what her exact physical state is? And don't you know how much control the trance gives each twin over the bodily processes of the other? Don't you even know that? Devrie isn't anywhere near dying. And I'd pull her out of trance if she were." He paused, looking hard at me. "Keep your ticket, Seena."

I repeated mechanically, "You can leave now. There's no money." *Devrie had lied to me.*

"That wouldn't leave her with any protection at all, would it?" he said levelly. When he grasped the doorknob to leave, the tendons in his wrist stood out clearly, strong and taut. I did not try to stop his going.

Devrie had lied to me. With her lie, she had blackmailed me into yet another lie to Keith. The twin trance granted control, in some unspecified way, to each twin's body; the trance I had pioneered might have resulted in eight deaths unknowingly inflicted on each other out of who knows what dark forests in eight fumbling minds. Lies, blackmail, death, more lies.

Out of these lies they were going to make scientific truth. Through these forests they were going to search for God.

"Final clearance check of holotanks," an assistant said formally. "Faraday cage?"

"Optimum."

"External radiation?"

"Cleared," said the man seated at the console of the first tank.

"Cleared," said the woman seated at the console of the second.

"Microradiation?"

"Cleared."

"Cleared."

"Personnel radiation, Class A?"

"Cleared."

"Cleared."

On it went, the whole tedious and crucial procedure, until both tanks had been cleared and focused, the fluid adjusted, tested, adjusted again, tested again. Bohentin listened patiently, without expression, but I, standing to the side of him and behind the tanks, saw the nerve at the base of his neck and just below the hairline pulse in some irregular rhythm of its own. Each time the nerve pulsed, the skin rose slightly from under his collar. I kept my eyes on that syncopated crawling of flesh, and felt tension prickle over my own skin like heat.

Three-quarters of the lab, the portion where the holotanks and other machinery stood, was softly dark, lit mostly from the glow of console dials and the indirect track lighting focused on the tanks. Standing in the gloom were Bohentin, five other scientists, two medical doctors—and me. Bohentin had fought my being allowed there, but in the end he had had to give in. I had known too many threatening words not in generalities but in specifics: reporter's names, drug names, cloning details, twin trance tragedy, anorexia symptoms, bioengineering amendment. He was not a man who much noticed either public opinion or relatives' threats, but no one else outside his Institute knew so many so specific words—some knew some of the words, but only I had them all. In the end he had focused on me his cold, brilliant eyes, and given permission for me to witness the experiment that involved my sister.

I was going to hold Devrie to her bargain. I was not going to believe anything she told me without witnessing it for myself.

Half the morning passed in technical preparation. Somewhere Devrie and Keith, the human components of this costly detection circuit, were separately being brought to the apex of brain activity. Drugs, biofeedback, tactile and auditory and kinaesthetic stimulation—all carefully calculated for the maximum increase of both the number of neurotransmitters firing signals through the synapses of the brain and of the speed at which the signals raced. The more rapid the transmission through certain pathways, the more intense both perception and feeling. Some neurotransmitters, under this pressure, would alter molecular structure into natural hallucinogens; that reaction had to be controlled. Meanwhile other drugs, other biofeedback techniques, would depress the body's natural enzymes designed to either reabsorb excess transmitters or to reduce the rate at which they fired. The number and speed of neurotransmitters in Keith's and Devrie's brains would mount, and mount, and mount, all natural chemical barriers removed. The two of them would enter the lab with their whole brains—rational cortex, emotional limbic, right and left brain functions—simultaneously aroused to an unimaginable degree. *Simultaneously*. They would be feeling as great a "rush" as a falling skydiver, as great a glow as a cocaine user, as great a mental clarity and receptivity as a da Vinci whose brush is guided by all the integrated visions of his unconscious mind. They would be white-hot.

Then they would hit each other with the twin trance.

The quarter of the lab which Keith and Devrie would use was softly and indirectly lit, though brighter than the rest. It consisted of a raised, luxuriantly padded platform, walls and textured pillows in a pink whose component wavelengths had been carefully calculated, temperature in a complex gradient producing precise convection flows over the skin. The man and woman in that womb-colored, flesh-stimulating environment would be able to see us observers standing in the gloom behind the holotanks only as vague shapes. When the two doors opened and Devrie and Keith moved onto the platform, I knew that they would not even try to distinguish who stood in the lab. Looking at their faces, that looked only at each other, I felt my heart clutch.

They were naked except for the soft helmets that both attached hundreds of needles to nerve clumps just below the skin and also held the earphones through which Bohentin controlled the music that swelled the cathedrals of their skulls. "Cathedrals"—from their faces, transfigured to the ravished ecstasy found in paintings of medieval saints, that was the right word. But here the ecstasy was controlled, understood, and I saw with a sudden rush of pain at old memories that I could recognize the exact moment when Keith and Devrie locked onto each other with the twin trance. I recognized it, with my own more bitter hyperclarity, in their eyes, as I recognized the cast of concentration that came over their features, and the intensity of their absorption. The twin trance. They clutched each other's hands, faces inches apart, and suddenly I had to look away.

Each holotank held two whorls of shifting colors, the outlines clearer and the textures more sharply delineated than any previous holographs in the history of science. Keith's and Devrie's perceptions of each other's presence. The whorls went on clarifying themselves, separating into distinct and mappable layers, as on the platform Keith and Devrie remained frozen, all their energies focused on the telepathic trance. Seconds passed, and then minutes. And still, despite the clarity of the holographs in the tank, a clarity that fifteen years earlier I would have given my right hand for, I sensed that Keith and Devrie were holding back, were deliberately confining their unimaginable perceptiveness to each other's radiant energy, in the same way that water is confined behind a dam to build power.

But how could *I* be sensing that? From a subliminal "reading" of the mapped perceptions in the holotanks? Or from something else?

More minutes passed. Keith and Devrie stayed frozen, facing each other, and over her skeletal body and his stronger one a flush began to spread, rosy and slow, like heat tide rising.

"Jesus H. Christ," said one of the medical doctors, so low that only I, standing directly behind her, could have heard. It was not a curse, nor a prayer, but some third possibility, unnameable.

Keith put one hand on Devrie's thigh. She shuddered. He drew her down to the cushions on the platform and they began to caress each other, not frenzied, not in the exploring way of lovers but with a deliberation I have never experienced outside a research lab, a slow care that implied that worlds of interpretation hung on each movement. Yet the effect was not of coldness nor detachment but of intense involvement, of tremendous energy joyously used, of creating each other's bodies right then, there under each other's hands. They were *working*, and oblivious to all but their work. But if it was a kind of creative work, it was also a kind of primal innocent eroticism, and, watching, I felt my own heat begin to rise. "Innocent"—but if innocence is unknowingness, there was nothing innocent about it at all. Keith and Devrie knew and controlled each heartbeat, and I felt the exact moment when they let their sexual energies, added to all the other neural energies, burst the dam and flood outward in wave after wave, expanding the scope of each brain's perceptions, inundating the artificially-walled world.

A third whorl formed in holotank.

It formed suddenly: one second nothing, the next brightness. But then it wavered, faded a bit. After a few moments it brightened slightly, a diffused gloden haze, before again fading. On the platform Keith gasped, and I guessed he was having to shift his attention between perceiving the third source of radiation and keeping up the erotic version of the twin trance. His biofeedback techniques were less experienced than Devrie's, and the male erection more fragile. But then he caught the rhythm, and the holograph brightened.

It seemed to me that the room brightened as well, although no additional lights came on and the consoles glowed no brighter. Sweat poured off the researchers. Bohentin leaned forward, his neck muscle tautening toward the platform as if it were his will and not Keith/Devrie's that strained to perceive that third presence recorded in the tank. I thought, stupidly, of mythical intermediaries: Merlyn never made king, Moses never reaching the Promised Land. Intermediaries—and then it became impossible to think of anything at all.

Devrie shuddered and cried out. Keith's orgasm came a moment later, and with it a final roil of neural activity so strong the two primary whorls in each holotank swelled to fill the tank and inundate the third. At the moment of breakthrough Keith screamed, and in memory it seems as if the scream was what tore through the last curtain—that is nonsense. How loud would microbes have to scream to attract the attention of giants? How loud does a knock on the door have to be to pull a sleeper from the alien world of dreams?

The doctor beside me fell to her knees. The third presence—or some part of it—swirled all around us, racing along our own unprepared synapses and neurons, and what swirled and raced was astonishment. A golden, majestic astonishment. We had finally attracted Its attention, finally knocked with enough neural force to be just barely heard—and It was astonished that we could, or did exist. The slow rise of that powerful astonishment within the shielded lab was like the slow swinging around of the head of a great beast to regard some butterfly it has barely glimpsed from the corner of one eye. But this was no beast. As Its attention swung toward us, pain exploded in my skull—the pain of sound too loud, lights too bright, charge too high. My brain was burning on overload. There came one more flash of insight—wordless, pattern without end—and the sound of screaming. Then, abruptly, the energy vanished.

Bohentin, on all fours, crawled toward the holotanks. The doctor lay slumped on the floor; the other doctor had already reached the platform and its two crumpled figures. Someone was crying, someone else shouting. I rose, fell, dragged myself to the side of the platform and then could not climb it. I could not climb the platform. Hanging with two hands on the edge, hearing the voice crying as my own, I watched the doctor bend shakily to Keith, roll him off Devrie to bend over her, turn back to Keith.

Bohentin cried, "The tapes are intact!"

"Oh God oh God oh God oh God oh God," somone moaned, until abruptly she stopped. I grasped the flesh-colored padding on top of the platform and pulled myself up onto it.

Devrie lay unconscious, pulse erratic, face cast in perfect bliss. The doctor breathed into Keith's mouth—what strength could the doctor himself have left?—and pushed on the naked chest. Breathe, push, breathe, push. The whole length of Keith's body shuddered; the doctor rocked back on his heels; Keith breathed.

"It's all on tape!" Bohentin cried. "It's all *on tape!*"

"God damn you to hell," I whispered to Devrie's blissful face. "It didn't even know we were there!"

Her eyes opened. I had to lean close to hear her answer.

"But now . . . we know He . . . is there."

She was too weak to smile. I looked away from her, away from that face, out into the tumultuous emptiness of the lab, anywhere.

They will try again.

Devrie has been asleep, fed by glucose solution through an IV, for fourteen hours. I sit near her bed, frowned at by the nurse, who can see my expression as I stare at my sister. Somewhere in another bed Keith is sleeping yet again. His rest is more fitful than Devrie's; she sinks into sleep as into warm water, but he cannot. Like me, he is afraid of drowning.

An hour ago he came into Devrie's room and grasped my hand. "How could It—He—It not have been aware that we existed? Not even have *known?*"

I didn't answer him.

"You felt it too, Seena, didn't you? The others say they could, so you must have too. It . . . created us in some way. No, that's wrong. How could It create us and not *know?*"

I said wearily, "Do *we* always know what we've created?" and Keith glanced at me sharply. But I had not been referring to my father's work in cloning.

"Keith. What's a Thysania Africana?"

"A what?"

"Think of us," I said, "as just one more biological side-effect. One type of being acts, and another type of being comes into existence. Man stages something like the African Horror, and in doing so he creates whole new species of moths and doesn't even discover they exist until long afterward. If man can do it, why not God? And why should He be any more aware of it than we are?"

Keith didn't like that. He scowled at me, and then looked at Devrie's sleeping face: Devrie's sleeping bliss.

"Because she is a fool," I said savagely, "and so are you. You won't leave it alone, will you? Having been noticed by It once, you'll try to be noticed by It again. Even though she promised me otherwise, and even if it kills you both."

Keith looked at me a long time, seeing clearly—finally—the nature of the abyss between us, and its dimensions. But I already knew neither of us could cross. When at last he spoke, his voice held so much compassion that I hated him. "Seena. Seena, love. There's no more doubt now, don't you see? Now rational belief is no harder than rational doubt. Why are you so afraid to even believe?"

I left the room. In the corridor I leaned against the wall, palms spread flat against the tile, and closed my eyes. It seemed to me that I could hear wings, pale and fragile, beating against glass.

They will try again. For the sake of sure knowledge that the universe is not empty, Keith and Devrie and all the others like their type of being will go on pushing their human brains beyond what the human brain has evolved to do, go on fluttering their wings against that biological window. For the sake of sure knowledge: belief founded on experiment and not on faith. And the Other: being/alien/God? It, too, may choose to initiate contact, if It can and now that It knows we are here. Perhaps It will seek to know *us*, and even beyond the laboratory Devrie and Keith may find any moment of heightened arousal subtly invaded by a shadowy Third. Will they sense It, hovering just beyond consciousness, if they argue fiercely or race a sailboat in rough water or make love? How much arousal will it take, now, for them to sense those huge wings beating on the *other* side of the window?

And windows can be broken.

Tomorrow I will fly back to New York. To my museum, to my exhibits, to my moths under permaplex, to my empty apartment, where I will keep the heavy drapes drawn tightly across the glass.

For—oh God—all the rest of my life.

flying saucer rock and roll

HOWARD WALDROP

Howard Waldrop is widely considered to be one of the best short-story writers in the business, and his famous story "The Ugly Chickens" won both the Nebula and the World Fantasy Awards in 1981. His work has been gathered in the collections: *Howard Who?, All About Strange Monsters of the Recent Past: Neat Stories by Howard Waldrop, Night of the Cooters: More Neat Stories by Howard Waldrop,* and *Going Home Again.* Waldrop is also the author of the novel *The Texas-Israeli War: 1999,* in collaboration with Jake Saunders, and of two solo novels, *Them Bones* and *A Dozen Tough Jobs.* He is at work on a new novel, tentatively entitled *The Moon World.* His most recent books are the print version of his collection *Dream Factories and Radio Pictures* (formerly available only in downloadable form online), the chapbook *A Better World's in Birth!,* and a collection of his stories written in collaboration with various other authors, *Custer's Last Jump and Other Collaborations.* His stories have appeared in our First, Third, Fourth, Fifth, Sixth, Twelfth, Fifteenth, Sixteenth, and Twenty-first annual collections. Having lived in Washington state for a number of years, Waldrop recently moved back to his former hometown of Austin, Texas, something which caused celebrations and loud hurrahs to rise up from the rest of the population.

In the classic story that follows, one which has assumed cult favorite status over the years, he brings together flying saucers and a rock and roll band — with some rather startling results.

They could have been contenders.

Talk about Danny and the Juniors, talk about the Spaniels, the Contours, Sonny Till and the Orioles. They made it to the big time: records, tours, sock hops at $500 a night. Fame and glory.

But you never heard of the Kool-Tones, because they achieved their apotheosis and their apocalypse on the same night, and then they broke up. Some still talk about that night, but so much happened, the Kool-Tones get lost in the shuffle. And who's going to believe a bunch of kids, anyway? The cops didn't and their parents didn't. It was only two years after the president had been shot in Dallas, and people were still scared. This, then, is the Kool-Tones' story:

Leroy was smoking a cigar through a hole he'd cut in a pair of thick, red wax lips. Slim and Zoot were tooting away on Wowee whistles. It was a week after Halloween, and their pockets were still full of trick-or-treat candy they'd muscled off little kids in the projects. Ray, slim and nervous, was hanging back, "We shouldn't be here, you know? I mean, this ain't the Hellbenders' territory, you know? I don't know whose it is, but, like, Vinnie and the guys don't come this far." He looked around.

Zoot, who was white and had the beginnings of a mustache, took the yellow wax-candy kazoo from his mouth. He bit off and chewed up the big C pipe. "I mean, if you're scared, Ray, you can go back home, you know?"

"Nah!" said Leroy. "We need Ray for the middle parts." Leroy was twelve years old and about four feet tall. He was finishing his fourth cigar of the day. He looked like a small Stymie Beard from the old Our Gang comedies.

He still wore the cut-down coat he'd taken with him when he'd escaped from his foster home.

He was staying with his sister and her boyfriend. In each of his coat pockets he had a bottle: one Coke and one bourbon.

"We'll be all right," said Cornelius, who was big as a house and almost eighteen. He was shaped like a big ebony golf tee, narrow legs and waist blooming out to an A-bomb mushroom of arms and chest. He was a yard wide at the shoulders. He looked like he was always wearing football pads.

"That's right," said Leroy, taking out the wax lips and wedging the cigar back into the hole in them. "I mean, the kid who found this place didn't say anything about it being somebody's *spot*, man."

"What's that?" asked Ray.

They looked up. A small spot of light moved slowly across the sky. It was barely visible, along with a few stars, in the lights from the city.

"Maybe it's one of them UFOs you're always talking about, Leroy," said Zoot.

"Flying saucer, my left ball," said Cornelius. "That's Telstar. You ought to read the papers."

"Like your mama makes you?" asked Slim.

"Aww . . . ," said Cornelius.

They walked on through the alleys and the dark streets. They all walked like a man.

"This place is Oz," said Leroy.

"Hey!" yelled Ray, and his voice filled the area, echoed back and forth in the darkness, rose in volume, died away.

"Wow."

They were on what had been the loading dock of an old freight and storage company. It must have been closed sometime during the Korean War or maybe in the unimaginable eons before World War II. The building took up most of the block, but the loading area on the back was sunken and surrounded by the stone wall they had climbed. If you stood with your back against the one good loading door, the place was a natural amphitheater.

Leroy chugged some Coke, then poured bourbon into the half-empty bottle. They all took a drink, except Cornelius, whose mother was a Foursquare Baptist and could smell liquor on his breath three blocks away.

Cornelius drank only when he was away from home two or three days.

"Okay, Kool-Tones," said Leroy. "Let's hit some notes."

They stood in front of the door, Leroy to the fore, the others behind him in a semicircle: Cornelius, Ray, Slim, and Zoot.

"One, two, three," said Leroy quietly, his face toward the bright city beyond the surrounding buildings.

He had seen all the movies with Frankie Lymon and the Teenagers in them and knew the moves backwards. He jumped in the air and came down, and Cornelius hit it: "*Bah-doo, bah-doo, bah-doo—uhh.*"

It was a bass from the bottom of the ocean, from the Marianas Trench, a voice from Death Valley on a wet night, so far below sea level you could feel the absence of light in your mind. And then Zoot and Ray came in: "*Oooh-oooh, ooh-oooh,*" with Leroy humming under, and then Slim stepped out and began to lead the tenor part of "Sincerely," by the Crows. And they went through that one perfectly, flawlessly, the dark night and the dock walls throwing their voices out to the whole breathing city.

"Wow," said Ray, when they finished, but Leroy held up his hand, and Zoot leaned forward and took a deep breath and sang: "*Dee-dee-woo-oo, dee-eee-wooo-oo, dee-uhmm-doo-way.*"

And Ray and Slim chanted: "*A-weem-wayyy, a-wee,-wayyy.*"

And then Leroy, who had a falsetto that could take hair off an opossum, hit the high notes from "The Lion Sleeps Tonight," and it was even better than the first song, and not even the Tokens on their number two hit had ever sounded greater.

Then they started clapping their hands, and at every clap the city seemed to jump with expectation, joining in their dance, and they went through a shaky-legged Skyliners-type routine and into: *Hey-ahh-stuh-huh, hey-ahh-stuh-uhh,*" of Maurice Williams and the Zodiacs' "Stay," and when Leroy soared his "*Hoh-wahh-yuh?*" over Zoot's singing, they all thought they would die.

And without pause, Ray and Slim started: "*Shoo-be-doop, shoo-doop-de-be-doop, shoo-doopbe-do-be-doop,*" and Cornelius was going, "*Ah-rem-em, ah-rem-em, ah-rem-emm bah.*"

And they went through the Five Satins' "(I Remember) In the Still of the Night."

"Hey, wait," said Ray, as Slim "*woo-uh-wooo-uh-woo-ooo-ah-woo-ah*"-ed to a finish, "I thought I saw a guy out there."

"You're imagining things," said Zoot. But they all stared out into the dark anyway. There didn't seem to be anything there.

"Hey, look," said Cornelius. "Why don't we try putting the bass part of 'Stormy Weather' with the high part of 'Crying in the Chapel'? I tried it the other night, but I can't—"

"Shit, man!" said Slim. "That ain't the way it is on the records. You gotta do it like on the records."

"Records are going to hell, anyway. I mean, you got Motown and some of that, but the rest of it's like the Beatles and Animals and Rolling Stones and Wayne shitty Fontana and the Mindbenders and . . ."

Leroy took the cigar from his mouth. "Fuck the Beatles," he said. He put the cigar back in his mouth.

"Yeah, you're right, I agree. But even the other music's not the—"

"Aren't you kids up past your bedtime?" asked a loud voice from the darkness.

They jerked erect. For a minute, they hoped it was only the cops.

Matches flared in the darkness, held up close to faces. The faces all had their eyes closed so they wouldn't be blinded and unable to see in case the Kool-Tones made a break for it. Blobs of faces and light floated in the night, five, ten, fifteen, more.

Part of a jacket was illuminated. It was the color reserved for the kings of Tyre.

"Oh shit!" said Slim. "Trouble. Looks like the Purple Monsters."

The Kool-Tones drew into a knot.

The matches went out and they were in a breathing darkness.

"You guys know this turf is reserved for friends of the local protective, athletic, and social club, viz., us?" asked the same voice. Chains clanked in the black night.

"We were just leaving," said Cornelius.

The noisy chains rattled closer.

You could hear knuckles being slapped into fists out there.

Slim hoped someone would hurry up and hit him so he could scream.

"Who are you guys with?" asked the voice, and a flashlight shone in their eyes, blinding them.

"Aww, they're just little kids," said another voice.

"Who you callin' little, turd?" asked Leroy, shouldering his way between Zoot and Cornelius's legs.

A *wooooooo!* went up from the dark, and the chains rattled again.

"For God's sake, shut up, Leroy!" said Ray.

"Who you people think you are, anyway?" asked another, meaner voice out there.

"We're the Kool-Tones," said Leroy. "We can sing it slow, and we can sing it low, and we can sing it loud, and we can make it go!"

"I hope you like that cigar, kid," said the mean voice, "because after we piss on it, you're going to have to eat it."

"Okay, okay, look," said Cornelius. "We didn't know it was your turf. We come from over in the projects and . . ."

"Hey, Man, Hellbenders, Hellbenders!" The chains sounded like tambourines now.

"Naw, naw. We ain't Hellbenders. We ain't nobody but the Kool-Tones. We just heard about this place. We didn't know it was yours," said Cornelius.

"We only let Bobby and the Bombers sing here," said a voice.

"Bobby and the Bombers can't sing their way out of the men's room," said Leroy. Slim clamped Leroy's mouth, burning his hand on the cigar.

"You're gonna regret that," said the mean voice, which stepped into the flashlight beam, "because I'm Bobby, and four more of these guys out here are the Bombers."

"We didn't know you guys were part of the Purple Monsters!" said Zoot.

"There's lots of stuff you don't know," said Bobby. "And when we're through, there's not much you're gonna *remember*."

"I only know the Del Vikings are breaking up," said Zoot. He didn't know why he said it. Anything was better than waiting for the knuckle sandwiches.

Bobby's face changed. "No shit?" Then his face set in hard lines again. "Where'd a punk like you hear something like that?"

"My cousin," said Zoot. "He was in the Air Force with two of them. He writes to 'em. They're tight. One of them said the act was breaking up because nobody was listening to their stuff anymore."

"Well, that's rough," said Bobby. "It's tough out there on the road."

"Yeah," said Zoot. "It really is."

Some of the tension was gone, but certain delicate ethical questions remained to be settled.

"I'm Lucius," said a voice. "Warlord of the Purple Monsters." The flashlight came on him. He was huge. He was like Cornelius, only he was big all the way to the ground. His feet looked like blunt I beams sticking out of the bottom of his jeans. His purple satin jacket was a bright fluorescent blot on the night. "I hate to break up this chitchat—" he glared at Bobby— "but the fact is you people are on Purple Monster territory, and some tribute needs to be exacted."

Ray was digging in his pocket for nickels and dimes.

"Not money. Something that will remind you not to do this again."

"Tell you what," said Leroy. He had worked himself away from Slim. "You think Bobby and the Bombers can sing?"

"Easy!" said Lucius to Bobby, who had started forward with the Bombers. "Yeah, kid. They're the best damn group in the city."

"Well, I think we can outsing 'em," said Leroy, and smiled around his dead cigar.

"Oh, jeez," said Zoot. "They got a record, and they've—"

"I said, we can outsing Bobby and the Bombers, anytime, any place," said Leroy.

"And what if you can't?" asked Lucius.

"You guys like piss a lot, don't you?" There was a general movement toward the Kool-Tones. Lucius held up his hand. "Well," said Leroy, "how about all the members of the losing group drink a quart apiece?"

Hands of the Kool-Tones reached out to stifle Leroy. He danced away.

"I like that," said Lucius. "I really like that. That all right, Bobby?"

"I'm going to start saving it up now."

"Who's gonna judge?" asked one of the Bombers.

"The same as always," said Leroy. "The public. Invite 'em in."

"Who do we meet with to work this out?" asked Lucius.

"Vinnie of the Hellbenders. He'll work out the terms."

Slim was beginning to see he might not be killed that night. He looked on Leroy with something like worship.

"How we know you guys are gonna show up?" asked Bobby.

"I swear on Sam Cooke's grave," said Leroy.

"Let 'em pass," said Bobby.

They crossed out of the freight yard and headed back for the projects.

"Shit, man!"

"Now you've done it!"

"I'm heading for Florida."

"What the hell, Leroy, are you crazy?"

Leroy was smiling. "We can take them, easy," he said, holding up his hand flat.

He began to sing "Chain Gang." The other Kool-Tones joined in, but their hearts weren't in it. Already there was a bad taste in the back of their throats.

Vinnie was mad.

The black outline of a mudpuppy on his white silk jacket seemed to swell as he hunched his shoulders toward Leroy.

"What the shit you mean, dragging the Hellbenders into this without asking us first? That just ain't done, Leroy."

"Who else could take the Purple Monsters in case they wasn't gentlemen?" asked Leroy.

Vinnie grinned. "You're gonna die before you're fifteen, kid."

"That's my hope."

"Creep. Okay, we'll take care of it."

"One thing," said Leroy. "No instruments. They gotta get us a mike and some amps, and no more than a quarter of the people can be from Monster territory. And it's gotta be at the freight dock."

"That's one thing?" asked Vinnie.

"A few. But that place is great, man. We can't lose there."

Vinnie smiled, and it was a prison-guard smile, a Nazi smile. "If you lose, kid, after the Monsters get through with you, the Hellbenders are gonna have a little party."

He pointed over his shoulder to where something resembling testicles floated in alcohol in a mason jar on a shelf. "We're putting five empty jars up there tomorrow. That's what happens to people who get the Hellbenders involved without asking and then don't come through when the pressure's on. You know what I mean?"

Leroy smiled. He left smiling. The smile was still frozen to his face as he walked down the street.

This whole thing was getting too grim.

Leroy lay on his cot listening to his sister and her boyfriend porking in the next room.

It was late at night. His mind was still working. Sounds beyond those in the bedroom came to him. Somebody staggered down the project hallway, bumping from one wall to another. Probably old man Jones. Chances are he wouldn't make it to his room all the way at the end of the corridor. His daughter or one of her kids would probably find him asleep in the hall in a pool of barf.

Leroy turned over on the rattly cot, flipped on his seven-transistor radio, and jammed it up to his ear. Faintly came the sounds of another Beatles song.

He thumbed the tuner, and the four creeps blurred into four or five other Englishmen singing some other stupid song about coming to places he would never see.

He went through the stations until he stopped on the third note of the Monotones' "Book of Love." He sang along in his mind.

Then the deejay came on, and everything turned sour again. "Another golden oldie, 'Book of Love,' by the Monotones. Now here's the WBKD pick of the week, the fabulous Beatles with 'I've Just Seen a Face.'" Leroy pushed the stations around the dial, then started back.

Weekdays were shit. On weekends you could hear good old stuff, but mostly the stations all played Top 40, and that was English invasion stuff, or if you were lucky, some Motown. It was Monday night. He gave up and turned to an all-night blues station, where the music usually meant something. But this was like, you know, the sharecropper hour or something, and all they were playing was whiny cotton-choppin' work blues from some damn Alabama singer who had died in 1932, for God's sake.

Disgusted, Leroy turned off the radio.

His sister and her boyfriend had quit for a while, so it was quieter in the place. Leroy lit a cigarette and thought of getting out of here as soon as he could.

I mean, Bobby and the Bombers had a record, a real big-hole forty-five on WhamJam. It wasn't selling worth shit from all Leroy heard, but that didn't matter. It was a record, and it was real, it wasn't just singing under some street lamp. Slim said they'd played it once on WABC, on the *Hit-or-Flop* show, and it was a flop, but people heard it. Rumor was the Bombers had gotten sixty-five dollars and a contract for the session. They'd had a couple of gigs at dances and such, when the regular band took a break. They sure as hell couldn't be making any money, or they wouldn't be singing against the Kool-Tones for free kicks.

But they had a record out, and they were working.

If only the Kool-Tones got work, got a record, went on tour. Leroy was just twelve, but he knew how hard they were working on their music. They'd practice on street corners, on the stoop, just walking, getting the notes down right—the moves, the facial expressions of all the groups they'd seen in movies and on Slim's mother's TV.

There were so many places to be out there. There was a real world with people in it who weren't punching somebody for berries, or stealing the welfare and stuff. Just someplace open, someplace away from everything else.

He flipped on the flashlight beside his cot, pulled it under the covers with him, and opened his favorite book. It was Edward J. Ruppelt's *Report on Unidentified Flying Objects*. His big brother John William, whom he had never seen, sent it to him from his Army post in California as soon as he found Leroy had run away and was living with his sister. John William also sent his sister part of his allotment every month.

Leroy had read the book again and again. He knew it by heart already. He couldn't get a library card under his own name because the state might trace him that way. (They'd already been around asking his sister about him. She lied. But she too had run away from a foster home as soon as she was old enough, so they hadn't believed her and would be back.) So he'd had to boost all his books. Sometimes it took days, and newsstand people got mighty suspicious when you were black and hung around for a long time, waiting for the chance to kipe stuff. Usually they gave you the hairy eyeball until you went away.

He owned twelve books on UFOs now, but the Ruppelt was still his favorite. Once he'd gotten a book by some guy named Truman or something who wrote poetry inspired by the people from Venus. It was a little sad, too, the things people believed sometimes. So Leroy hadn't read any more books by people who claimed they'd been inside the flying saucers or met the Neptunians or such. He read only the ones that gave histories of the sightings and asked questions, like why was the Air Force covering up? Those books never told you what was in the UFOs, and that was good because you could imagine it for yourself.

He wondered if any of the Del Vikings had seen flying saucers when they were in the Air Force with Zoot's cousin. Probably not, or Zoot would have told him about it. Leroy always tried to get the rest of the Kool-Tones interested in UFOs, but they all said they had their own problems, like girls and cigarette money. They'd go with him to see *Invasion of the Saucermen* or *Earth vs. the Flying Saucers* at the movies, or watch *The Thing* on Slim's mother's TV on the *Creature Feature*, but that was about it.

Leroy's favorite flying-saucer sighting was the Mantell case, in which a P-51 fighter plane, which was called a Mustang, chased a UFO over Kentucky and then crashed after it went off the Air Force radar. Some say Captain Mantell died of asphyxiation because he went to 20,000 feet and didn't have on an oxygen mask, but other books said he saw "something metallic and of tremendous size" and was going after it. Ruppelt thought it was a Skyhook balloon, but he couldn't be sure. Others said it was a real UFO and that Mantell had been shot down with Z-rays.

It had made Leroy's skin crawl when he had first read it.

But his mind went back to the Del Vikings. What had caused them to break up? What was it really like out there on the road? Was music getting so bad that good groups couldn't make a living at it anymore?

Leroy turned off the flashlight and put the book away. He put out the cigarette, lit a cigar, went to the window, and looked up the airshaft. He leaned way back against the cool window and could barely see one star overhead. Just one star.

He scratched himself and lay back down on the bed.

For the first time, he was afraid about the contest tomorrow night.

We got to be good, he said to himself. *We got to be good*.

In the other room, the bed started squeaking again.

The Hellbenders arrived early to check out the turf. They'd been there ten minutes when the Purple Monsters showed up. There was handshaking all around, talk a little while, then they moved off into two separate groups. A few civilians came by to make sure this was the place they'd heard about.

"Park your cars out of sight, if you got 'em," said Lucius. "We don't want the cops to think anything's going on here."

Vinnie strut-walked over to Lucius.

"This crowd's gonna be bigger than I thought. I can tell."

"People come to see somebody drink some piss. You know, give the public what it wants. . . ." Lucius smiled.

"I guess so. I got this weird feelin', though. Like, you know, if your mother tells you she dreamed about her aunt, like right before she died and all?"

"I know what feelin' you mean, but I ain't got it," said Lucius.

"Who you got doing the electrics?"

"Guy named Sparks. He was the one lit up Choton Field."

At Choton Field the year before, two gangs wanted to fight under the lights. So they went to a high-school football stadium. Somebody got all the lights and the P.A. on without going into the control booth.

Cops drove by less than fifty feet away, thinking there was a practice scrimmage going on, while down on the field guys were turning one another into bloody strings. Somebody was on the P.A. giving a play-by-play. From the outside, it sounded cool. From the inside, it looked like a pizza with all the topping ripped off it.

"Oh," said Vinnie. "Good man."

He used to work for Con Ed, and he still had his I.D. card. Who was going to mess with Consolidated Edison? He drove an old, gray pickup with a smudge on the side that had once been a power-company emblem. The truck was filled to the brim with cables, wires, boots, wrenches, tape, torches, work lights, and rope.

"Light man's here!" said somebody.

Lucius shook hands with him and told him what they wanted. He nodded.

The crowd was getting larger, groups and clots of people drifting in, though the music wasn't supposed to start for another hour. Word traveled fast.

Sparks attached a transformer and breakers to a huge, thick cable.

Then he got out his climbing spikes and went up a pole like a monkey, the heavy *chunk-chunk* drifting down to the crowd every time he flexed his knees. His tool belt slapped against his sides.

He had one of the guys in the Purple Monsters throw him up the end of the inch-thick electrical cable.

The sun had just gone down, and Sparks was a silhouette against the purpling sky that poked between the buildings.

A few stars were showing in the eastern sky. Lights were on all through the autumn buildings. Thanksgiving was in a few weeks, then Christmas.

The shopping season was already in full swing, and the streets would be bathed in neon, in holiday colors. The city stood up like big, black fingers all around them.

Sparks did something to the breakdown box on the pole.

There was an immense blue scream of light that stopped everybody's heart.

New York City went dark.

"Fucking *wow!*"

A raggedy-assed cheer of wonder ran through the crowd.

There were crashes, and car horns began to honk all over town.

"Uh, Lucius," Sparks yelled down the pole after a few minutes. "Have the guys go steal me about thirty automobile batteries."

The Purple Monsters ran off in twenty different directions.

"Ahhhyyyhhyyh," said Vinnie, spitting a toothpick out of his mouth. "The Monsters get to have all the fun."

It was 5:27 P.M. on November 9, 1965. At the Ossining changing station, a guy named Jim was talking to a guy named Jack.

Then the trouble phone rang. Jim checked all his dials before he picked it up.

He listened, then hung up.

"There's an outage all down the line. They're going to switch the two hundred K's over to the Buffalo net and reroute them back through here. Check all the load levels. Everything's out from Schenectady to Jersey City."

When everything looked ready, Jack signaled to Jim. Jim called headquarters, and they watched the needles jump on the dials.

Everything went black.

Almost everything.

Jack hit all the switches for backup relays, and nothing happened.

Almost nothing.

Jim hit the emergency battery work lights. They flickered and went out.

"What the hell?" asked Jack.

He looked out the window.

Something large and bright moved across a nearby reservoir and toward the changing station.

"Holy Mother of Christ!" he said.

Jim and Jack went outside.

The large bright thing moved along the lines toward the station. The power cables bulged toward the bottom of the thing, whipping up and down, making the stanchions sway. The station and the reservoir were bathed in a blue glow as the thing went over. Then it took off quickly toward Manhattan, down the straining lines, leaving them in complete darkness.

Jim and Jack went back into the plant and ate their lunches.

Not even the phone worked anymore.

It was really black by the time Sparks got his gear set up. Everybody in the crowd was talking about the darkness of the city and the sky. You could see stars all over the place, everywhere you looked.

There was very little noise from the city around the loading area.

Somebody had a radio on. There were a few Jersey and Pennsy stations on. One of them went off while they listened.

In the darkness, Sparks worked by the lights of his old truck. What he had in front of him resembled something from an alchemy or magnetism treatise written early in the eighteenth century. Twenty or so car batteries were hooked up in series with jumper cables. He'd tied those in with amps, mikes, transformers, a light board, and lights on the dock area.

"Stand clear!" he yelled. He bent down with the last set of cables and stuck an alligator clamp on a battery post.

There was a screeching blue jag of light and a frying noise. The lights flickered and came on, and the amps whined louder and louder.

The crowd, numbering around five hundred, gave out with prolonged huzzahs and applause.

"Test test test," said Lucius. Everybody held their hands over their ears.

"Turn that fucker down," said Vinnie. Sparks did. Then he waved to the crowd, got into his old truck, turned the lights off, and drove into the night.

"Ladies and gentlemen, the Purple Monsters . . .," said Lucius, to wild applause, and Vinnie leaned into the mike, "and the Hellbenders," more applause, then back to Lucius, "would like to welcome you to the first annual piss-off—I mean, sing-off—between our own Bobby and the Bombers," cheers, "and the challengers," said Vinnie, "the Kool-Tones!" More applause.

"They'll do two sets, folks," said Lucius, "taking turns. And at the end, the unlucky group, gauged by *your* lack of applause, will win a prize!"

The crowd went wild.

The lights dimmed out. "And now," came Vinnie's voice from the still blackness of the loading dock, "for your listening pleasure, Bobby and the Bombers!"

"*Yayyyyyyyyyy!*"

The lights, virtually the only lights in the city except for those that were being run by emergency generators, came up, and there they were.

Imagine frosted, polished elegance being thrust on the unwilling shoulders of a sixteen-year-old.

They had on blue jackets, matching pants, ruffled shirts, black ties, cuff links, tie tacks, shoes like obsidian mortar trowels. They were all black boys, and from the first note, you knew they were born to sing:

"*Bah bah*," sang Letus the bassman, "*doo-doo duh-du doo-ahh, duh-doo-dee-doot*," sang the two tenors, Lennie and Conk, and then Bobby and Fred began trading verses of the Drifters' "There Goes My Baby," while the tenors wailed and Letus carried the whole with his bass.

Then the lights went down and came up again as Lucius said, "Ladies and gentlemen, the Kool-Tones!"

It was magic of a grubby kind.

The Kool-Tones shuffled on, arms pumping in best Frankie Lymon and the Teenagers fashion, and they ran in place as the hand-clapping got louder and louder, and they leaned into the mikes.

They were dressed in waiters' red-cloth jackets the Hellbenders had stolen from a laundry service for them that morning. They wore narrow black ties, except Leroy, who had on a big, thick, red bow tie he'd copped from his sister's boyfriend.

Then Cornelius leaned over his mike and: "*Doook doook doook doookov*," and Ray and Zoot joined with "*dook dook dook dookov*," into Gene Chandler's "Duke of Earl," with Leroy smiling and doing all of Chandler's hand moves. Slim chugged away the "*iiiiiiiyiyiyiyiiiii's*" in the background in runs that made the crowd's blood run cold, and the lights went down. Then the Bombers were back, and in contrast to the up-tempo ending of "The Duke of Earl" they started with a sweet tenor a cappella line and then: "*woo-radad-da-dat, woo-radad-da-dat*," of Shep and the Limelites' "Daddy's Home."

The Kool-Tones jumped back into the light. This time Cornelius started off with "*Bom-a-pa-bomp, bomp-pa-pa-bomp, dang-a-dang-dang, ding-a-dong-ding*," and into the Marcels' "Blue Moon," not just a hit but a mere monster back in 1961. And they ran through the song, Slim taking the lead, and the crowd began to yell like mad halfway through. And Leroy—smiling, singing, rocking back and forth, doing James Brown tantrum-steps in front of the mike—knew, could feel, that they had them; that no matter what, they were going to win. And he ended with his whining part and Cornelius went "*Bomp-ba-ba-bomp-ba-bom,*" and paused and then, deeper, "*booo mooo.*"

The lights came up and Bobby and the Bombers hit the stage. At first Leroy, sweating, didn't realize what they were doing, because the Bombers, for the first few seconds, made this churning rinky-tink sound with the high voices. The bass, Letus, did this grindy sound with his throat. Then the Bombers did the only thing that could save them, a white boy's song, Bobby launching into Del Shannon's "Runaway," with both feet hitting the stage at once. Leroy thought he could taste that urine already.

The other Kool-Tones were transfixed by what was about to happen.

"They can't do that, man," said Leroy.

"They're gonna cop out."

"That's impossible. Nobody can do it."

But when the Bombers got to the break, this guy Fred stepped out to the mike and went: "*Eee-de-ee-dee-eedle-eee-eee, eee-deee-eedle-deeee, eedle-dee-eedle-dee-dee-dee, eewheetle-eedle-dee-deedle-dee-eeeeee,*" in a splitting falsetto, half mechanical, half Martian cattle call—the organ break of "Runaway," done with the human voice.

The crowd was on its feet screaming, and the rest of the song was lost in stamping and cheers. When the Kool-Tones jumped out for the last song of the first set, there were some boos and yells for the Bombers to come back, but then Zoot started talking about his girl putting him down because he couldn't shake 'em down, but how now *he* was back, to let her know. . . . They all jumped in the air and came down on the first line of "Do You Love Me?" by the Contours, and they gained some of the crowd back. But they finished a little wimpy, and then the lights went down and an absolutely black night descended. The stars were shining over New York City for the first time since World War II, and Vinnie said, "Ten minutes, folks!" and guys went over to piss against the walls or add to the consolation-prize bottles.

It was like halftime in the locker room with the score Green Bay 146, You 0.

"A cheap trick," said Zoot. "We don't *do* shit like that."

Leroy sighed. "We're gonna have to," he said. He drank from a Coke bottle one of the Purple Monsters had given him. "We're gonna have to do something."

"We're gonna have to drink pee-pee, and then Vinnie's gonna denut us, is what's gonna happen."

"No, he's not," said Cornelius.

"Oh, yeah?" asked Zoot. "Then what's that in the bottle in the clubhouse?"

"Pig's balls," said Cornelius. "They got 'em from a slaughterhouse."

"How do you know?"

"I just know," said Cornelius, tiredly. "Now let's just get this over with so we can go vomit all night."

"I don't want to hear any talk like that," said Leroy. "We're gonna go through with this and give it our best, just like we planned, and if that ain't good enough, well, it just ain't good enough."

"No matter what we do, it just ain't good enough."

"Come on, Ray, *man!*"

"I'll do my best, but my heart ain't in it."

They lay against the loading dock. They heard laughter from the place where Bobby and the Bombers rested.

"Shit, it's dark!" said Slim.

"It ain't just us, just the city," said Zoot. "It's the whole goddamn U.S."

"It's just the whole East Coast," said Ray. "I heard on the radio. Part of Canada, too."

"What is it?"

"Nobody knows."

"Hey, Leroy," said Cornelius. "Maybe it's those Martians you're always talking about."

Leroy felt a chill up his spine.

"Nah," said Slim. "It was that guy Sparks. He shorted out the whole East Coast up that pole there."

"Do you really believe that?" asked Zoot.

"I don't know what I believe anymore."

"I believe," said Lucius, coming out of nowhere with an evil grin on his face, "that it's *show time.*"

They came to the stage running, and the lights came up, and Cornelius leaned on his voice and: "*Rabbalabbalabba ging gong, rabbalabbalabba ging gong,*" and the others went "*wooooooooooo*" in the Edsels' "Rama Lama Ding Dong." They finished and the Bombers jumped into the lights and went into: "*Domm dom domm dom doobedoo dom domm dom dobedoobeedomm, wahwahwahwahhh,*" of the Del Vikings' "Come Go With Me."

The Kool-Tones came back with: "*Ahhhhhhhhaahhwoooowoooo, ow-ow-ow-owh-woo,*" of "Since I Don't Have You," by the Skyliners, with Slim singing in a clear, straight voice, better than he had ever sung that song before, and everybody else joined in, Leroy's voice fading into Slim's for the falsetto *weeeeoooooow*'s so you couldn't tell where one ended and the other began.

Then Bobby and the Bombers were back, with Bobby telling you the first two lines and: "*Detooodwop, detooodwop, detooodwop,*" of the Flamingos' "I Only Have Eyes for You," calm, cool, collected, assured of victory, still running on the impetus of their first set's showstopper.

Then the Kool-Tones came back and Cornelius rared back and asked: "*Ahwunno wunno hooo? Be-do-be hoooo?*" Pause.

They slammed down into "Book of Love," by the Monotones, but even Cornelius was flagging, sweating now in the cool air, his lungs were husks. He saw one of the Bombers nod to another, smugly, and that made him mad. He came down on the last verse like there was no one else on the stage with him, and his bass roared so loud it seemed there wasn't a single person in the dark United States who didn't wonder who wrote that book.

And they were off, and Bobby and the Bombers were on now, and a low hum began to fill the air. Somebody checked the amp; it was okay. So the Bombers jumped into the air, and when they came down they were into the Cleftones' "Heart and

Soul," and they *sang* that song, and while they were singing, the background humming got louder and louder.

Leroy leaned to the other Kool-Tones and whispered something. They shook their heads. He pointed to the Hellbenders and the Purple Monsters all around them. He asked a question they didn't want to hear. They nodded grudging approval, and then they were on again, for the last time.

"Dep dooomop dooomop doomop, doo ooo, ooowah oowah oooway ooowah," sang Leroy, and they all asked "Why Do Fools Fall in Love?" Leroy sang like he was Frankie Lymon—not just some kid from the projects who wanted to be him—and the Kool-Tones *were* the Teenagers, and they began to pull and heave that song like it was a dead whale. And soon they had it in the water, and then it was swimming a little, then it was moving, and then the sonofabitch started spouting water, and that was the place where Leroy went into the falsetto *"wyyyyyyyyyyyyyyyyyyyyyy,"* and instead of chopping it where it should have been, he kept on. The Kool-Tones went *ooom wahooomwah* softly behind him, and still he held that note, and the crowd began to applaud, and they began to yell, and Leroy held it longer, and they started stamping and screaming, and he held it until he knew he was going to cough up both his lungs, and he held it after that, and the Kool-Tones were coming up to meet him, and Leroy gave a tantrum-step, and his eyes were bugging, and he felt his lungs tear out by the roots and come unglued, and he held the last syllable, and the crowd wet itself and—

The lights went out and the amp went dead. Part of the crowd had a subliminal glimpse of something large, blue, and cool looming over the freight yard, bathing the top of the building in a soft glow.

In the dead air the voices of the Kool-Tones dropped in pitch as if they were pulled upward at a thousand miles an hour, and then they rose in pitch as if they had somehow come back at that same thousand miles an hour.

The blue thing was a looming blur and then was gone.

The lights came back on. The Kool-Tones stood there blinking: Cornelius, Ray, Slim, and Zoot. The space in front of the center mike was empty.

The crowd had an orgasm.

The Bombers were being violently ill over next to the building.

"God, that was *great!*" said Vinnie. "Just great!"

All four of the Kool-Tones were shaking their heads.

They should be tired, but this looked worse than that, thought Vinnie. They should be ecstatic. They looked like they didn't know they had won.

"Where's Leroy?" asked Cornelius.

"How the hell should I know?" Vinnie said, sounding annoyed.

"I remember him smiling, like," said Zoot.

"And the blue thing. What about it?"

"What blue thing?" asked Lucius.

"I dunno. Something was blue."

"All I saw was the lights go off and that kid ran away," said Lucius.

"Which way?"

"Well, I didn't exactly see him, but he must have run some way. Don't know how he got by us. Probably thought you were going to lose and took it on the lam. I don't see how you'd worry when you can make your voices do that stuff."

"Up," said Zoot, suddenly.

"What?"

"We went up, and we came down. Leroy didn't come down with us."

"Of course not. He was still holding the same note. I thought the little twerp's balls were gonna fly out his mouth."

"No. We . . ." Slim moved his hands up, around, gave up. "I don't know what happened, do you?"

Ray, Zoot, and Cornelius all looked like they had thirty-two-lane bowling alleys inside their heads and all the pin machines were down.

"Aw, shit," said Vinnie. "You won. Go get some sleep. You guys were really bitchin'."

The Kool-Tones stood there uncertainly for a minute.

"He was, like, smiling, you know?" said Zoot.

"He was always smiling," said Vinnie. "Crazy little kid."

The Kool-Tones left.

The sky overhead was black and spattered with stars. It looked to Vinnie as if it were deep and wide enough to hold anything. He shuddered.

"Hey!" he yelled. "Somebody bring me a beer!"

He caught himself humming. One of the Hellbenders brought him a beer.

Dinner in Audoghast

BRUCE STERLING

One of the most powerful and innovative new talents to enter SF in the past few decades, Bruce Sterling sold his first story in 1976. By the end of the '80s, he had established himself, with a series of stories set in his exotic "Shaper/Mechanist" future, with novels such as the complex and Stapeldonian *Schismatrix* and the well-received *Islands in the Net* (as well as with his editing of the influential anthology *Mirrorshades: The Cyberpunk Anthology* and the infamous critical magazine *Cheap Truth*), as perhaps the prime driving force behind the revolutionary "Cyberpunk" movement in science fiction, and also as one of the best new hard-science writers to enter the field in some time. His other books include a critically acclaimed nonfiction study of First Amendment issues in the world of computer networking, *The Hacker Crackdown: Law and Disorder on the Electronic Frontier*, the novels *The Artificial Kid, Involution Ocean, Heavy Weather, Holy Fire, Distraction*, and *Zeitgeist*, a novel in collaboration with William Gibson, *The Difference Engine*, an omnibus collection (it contains the novel *Schismatrix* as well as most of his Shaper/Mechanist stories) *Schismatrix Plus*, and the landmark collections *Crystal Express, Globalhead*, and *A Good Old-fashioned Future*. His most recent books include a nonfiction study of the future, *Tomorrow Now: Envisioning the Next Fifty Years*, and a new novel, *The Zenith Angle*. His story "Bicycle Repairman" earned him a long-overdue Hugo in 1997, and he won another Hugo in 1997 for his story "Taklamakan." His stories have appeared in our First through Eighth, Eleventh, Fourteenth, Sixteenth, and Twentieth annual collections. He lives with his family in Austin, Texas.

Sterling was just another of a jostling pack of new writers when he published this story back in 1985, as yet only recognized by a very few of the *cognoscenti* as a writer to watch . . . and in the years that followed, we have watched him become one of the most significant talents of his generation. Here, in a story which sounds a cautionary note for our own smug belief in the immortality of our *own* society, he reminds us that while prophets may indeed be without honor in their own countries, they remain, after all, *prophets. . . .*

> Then one arrives at Audoghast, a large and very populous city built
> in a sandy plain. . . . The inhabitants live in ease and possess great
> riches. The market is always crowded; the mob is so huge and the
> chattering so loud that you can scarcely hear your own words. . . .
> The city contains beautiful buildings and very elegant homes.
>
> —Description of Northern Africa,
> Abu Ubayd Al-Bakri (A.D. 1040–94)

Delightful Audoghast! Renowned through the civilized world, from Cordova to Baghdad, the city spread in splendor beneath a twilit Saharan sky. The setting sun threw pink and amber across adobe domes, masonry mansions, tall, mud-brick mosques, and open plazas thick with bristling date palms. The melodious calls of market vendors mixed with the remote and amiable chuckling of Saharan hyenas.

Four gentlemen sat on carpets in a tiled and whitewashed portico, sipping coffee in the evening breeze. The host was the genial and accomplished slave-dealer, Manimenesh. His three guests were Ibn Watunan, the caravan-master; Khayali, the poet and musician; and Bagayoko, a physician and court assassin.

The home of Manimenesh stood upon the hillside in the aristocratic quarter, where it gazed down on an open marketplace and the mud-brick homes of the lowly. The prevailing breeze swept away the city reek, and brought from within the mansion the palate-sharpening aromas of lamb in tarragon and roast partridge in lemons and eggplant. The four men lounged comfortably around a low inlaid table, sipping spiced coffee from Chinese cups and watching the ebb and flow of market life.

The scene below them encouraged a lofty philosophical detachment. Manimenesh, who owned no less than fifteen books, was a well-known patron of learning. Jewels gleamed on his dark, plump hands, which lay cozily folded over his paunch. He wore a long tunic of crushed red velvet, and a gold-threaded skullcap.

Khayali, the young poet, had studied architecture and verse in the schools of Timbuktu. He lived in the household of Manimenesh as his poet and praisemaker, and his sonnets, ghazals, and odes were recited throughout the city. He propped one elbow against the full belly of his two-string *guimbri* guitar, of inlaid ebony, strung with leopard gut.

Ibn Watunan had an eagle's hooded gaze and hands callused by camel-reins. He wore an indigo turban and a long striped djellaba. In thirty years as a sailor and caravaneer, he had bought and sold Zanzibar ivory, Sumatran pepper, Ferghana silk, and Cordovan leather. Now a taste for refined gold had brought him to Audoghast, for Audoghast's African bullion was known throughout Islam as the standard of quality.

Doctor Bagayoko's ebony skin was ridged with an initiate's scars, and his long clay-smeared hair was festooned with knobs of chiseled bone. He wore a tunic of white Egyptian cotton, hung with gris-gris necklaces, and his baggy sleeves bulged with herbs and charms. He was a native Audoghastian of the animist persuasion, the personal physician of the city's prince.

Bagayoko's skill with powders, potions, and unguents made him an intimate of Death. He often undertook diplomatic missions to the neighboring Empire of Ghana. During his last visit there, the anti-Audoghast faction had mysteriously suffered a lethal outbreak of pox.

Between the four men was the air of camaraderie common to gentlemen and scholars.

They finished the coffee, and a slave took the empty pot away. A second slave, a girl from the kitchen staff, arrived with a wicker tray loaded with olives, goat cheese, and hard-boiled eggs sprinkled with vermilion. At that moment, a muezzin yodeled the evening call to prayer.

"Ah," said Ibn Watunan, hesitating. "Just as we were getting started."

"Never mind," said Manimenesh, helping himself to a handful of olives. "We'll pray twice next time."

"Why was there no noon prayer today?" said Watunan.

"Our muezzin forgot," the poet said.

Watunan lifted his shaggy brows. "That seems rather lax."

Doctor Bagayoko said, "This is a new muezzin. The last was more punctual, but, well, he fell ill." Bagayoko smiled urbanely and nibbled his cheese.

"We Audoghastians like our new muezzin better," said the poet, Khayali. "He's one of our own, not like that other fellow, who was from Fez. *Our* muezzin is sleeping with a Christian's wife. It's very entertaining."

"You have Christians here?" Watunan said.

"A clan of Ethiopian Copts," said Manimenesh. "And a couple of Nestorians."

"Oh," said Watunan, relaxing. "For a moment I thought you meant real *feringhee* Christians, from Europe."

"From where?" Manimenesh was puzzled.

"Very far away," said Ibn Watunan, smiling. "Ugly little countries, with no profit."

"There were empires in Europe once," said Khayali knowledgeably. "The Empire of Rome was almost as big as the modern civilized world."

Watunan nodded. "I have seen the New Rome, called Byzantium. They have armored horsemen, like your neighbors in Ghana. Savage fighters."

Bagayoko nodded, salting an egg. "Christians eat children."

Watunan smiled. "I can assure you that the Byzantines do no such thing."

"Really?" said Bagayoko. "Well, our Christians do."

"That's just the doctor's little joke," said Manimenesh. "Sometimes strange rumors spread about us, because we raid our slaves from the Nyam-Nyam cannibal tribes on the coast. But we watch their diet closely, I assure you."

Watunan smiled uncomfortably. "There is always something new out of Africa. One hears the oddest stories. Hairy men, for instance."

"Ah," said Manimenesh. "You mean gorillas, from the jungles to the south. I'm sorry to spoil the story for you, but they are nothing better than beasts."

"I see," said Watunan. "That's a pity."

"My grandfather owned a gorilla once," Manimenesh said. "Even after ten years, it could barely speak Arabic."

They finished the appetizers. Slaves cleared the table and brought in a platter of fattened partridges, stuffed with lemons and eggplants, on a bed of mint and lettuce. The four diners leaned in closer and dexterously ripped off legs and wings.

Watunan sucked meat from a drumstick and belched politely. "Audoghast is famous for its cooks," he said. "I'm pleased to see that this legend, at least, is confirmed."

"We Audoghastians pride ourselves on the pleasures of table and bed," said Manimenesh, pleased. "I have asked Elfelilet, one of our premiere courtesans, to honor us with a visit tonight. She will bring her troupe of dancers."

Watunan smiled. "That would be splendid. One tires of boys on the trail. Your women are remarkable. I've noticed that they go without the veil."

Khayali lifted his voice in song. "When a woman of Audoghast appears / The girls of Fez bite their lips, / The dames of Tripoli hide in closets, / And Ghana's women hang themselves."

"We take pride in the exalted status of our women," said Manimenesh. "It's not for nothing that they command a premium market price!"

In the marketplace, downhill, vendors lit tiny oil lamps, which cast a flickering glow across the walls of tents and the watering troughs. A troop of the prince's men, with iron spears, shields, and chain mail, marched across the plaza to take the night watch at the Eastern Gate. Slaves with heavy water-jars gossiped beside the well.

"There's quite a crowd around one of the stalls," said Bagayoko.

"So I see," said Watunan. "What is it? Some news that might affect the market?"

Bagayoko sopped up gravy with a wad of mint and lettuce. "Rumor says there's a new fortune-teller in town. New prophets always go through a vogue."

"Ah yes," said Khayali, sitting up. "They call him 'the Sufferer.' He is said to tell the most outlandish and entertaining fortunes."

"I wouldn't trust any fortune-teller's market tips," said Manimenesh. "If you want to know the market, you have to know the hearts of the people, and for that you need a good poet."

Khayali bowed his head. "Sir," he said, "live forever."

It was growing dark. Household slaves arrived with pottery lamps of sesame oil, which they hung from the rafters of the portico. Others took the bones of the partridges and brought in a haunch and head of lamb with a side dish of cinnamon tripes.

As a gesture of esteem, the host offered Watunan the eyeballs, and after three ritual refusals the caravan-master dug in with relish. "I put great stock in fortune-tellers, myself," he said, munching. "They are often privy to strange secrets. Not the occult kind, but the blabbing of the superstitious. Slave-girls anxious about some household scandal, or minor officials worried over promotions—inside news from those who consult them. It can be useful."

"If that's the case," said Manimenesh, "perhaps we should call him up here."

"They say he is grotesquely ugly," said Khayali. "He is called 'the Sufferer' because he is outlandishly afflicted by the disease."

Bagayoko wiped his chin elegantly on his sleeve. "Now you begin to interest me!"

"It's settled, then." Manimenesh clapped his hands. "Bring young Sidi, my errand-runner!"

Sidi arrived at once, dusting flour from his hands. He was the cook's teenage son, a tall young black in a dyed woolen djellaba. His cheeks were stylishly scarred, and he had bits of brass wire interwoven with his dense black locks. Manimenesh gave him his orders; Sidi leapt from the portico, ran downhill through the garden, and vanished through the gates.

The slave-dealer sighed. "This is one of the problems of my business. When I bought my cook she was a slim and lithesome wench, and I enjoyed her freely. Now years of dedication to her craft have increased her market value by twenty times, and also made her as fat as a hippopotamus, though that is beside the point. She has always claimed that Sidi is my child, and since I don't wish to sell her, I must make allowance. I have made him a freeman; I have spoiled him, I'm afraid. On my death, my legitimate sons will deal with him cruelly."

The caravan-master, having caught the implications of this speech, smiled politely. "Can he ride? Can he bargain? Can he do sums?"

"Oh," said Manimenesh with false nonchalance, "he can manage that newfangled stuff with the zeroes well enough."

"You know I am bound for China," said Watunan. "It is a hard road that brings either riches or death."

"He runs the risk in any case," the slave-dealer said philosophically. "The riches are Allah's decision."

"This is truth," said the caravan-master. He made a secret gesture, beneath the table, where the others could not see. His host returned it, and Sidi was proposed, and accepted, for the Brotherhood.

With the night's business over, Manimenesh relaxed, and broke open the lamb's steamed skull with a silver mallet. They spooned out the brains, then attacked the tripes, which were stuffed with onion, cabbage, cinnamon, rue, coriander, cloves, ginger, pepper, and lightly dusted with ambergris. They ran out of mustard dip and called for more, eating a bit more slowly now, for they were approaching the limit of human capacity.

They then sat back, pushing away platters of congealing grease, and enjoying a profound satisfaction with the state of the world. Down in the marketplace, bats from an abandoned mosque chased moths around the vendors' lanterns.

The poet belched suavely and picked up his two-stringed guitar. "Dear God," he said, "this is a splendid place. See, caravan-master, how the stars smile down on our beloved Southwest." He drew a singing note from the leopard-gut strings. "I feel at one with Eternity."

Watunan smiled. "When I find a man like that, I have to bury him."

"There speaks the man of business," the doctor said. He unobtrusively dusted a tiny pinch of venom on the last chunk of tripe, and ate it. He accustomed himself to poison. It was a professional precaution.

From the street beyond the wall, they heard the approaching jungle of brass rings. The guard at the gate called out. "The Lady Elfelilet and her escorts, lord!"

"Make them welcome," said Manimenesh. Slaves took the platters away, and brought a velvet couch onto the spacious portico. The diners extended their hands; slaves scrubbed and toweled them clean.

Elfelilet's party came forward through the fig-clustered garden: two escorts with gold-topped staffs heavy with jingling brass rings; three dancing-girls, apprentice courtesans in blue woolen cloaks over gauzy cotton trousers and embroidered blouses; and four palanquin bearers, beefy male slaves with oiled torsos and callused shoulders. The bearers set the palanquin down with stifled grunts of relief and opened the cloth-of-gold hangings.

Elfelilet emerged, a tawny-skinned woman, her eyes dusted in kohl and collyrium, her hennaed hair threaded with gold wire. Her palms and nails were stained pink; she wore an embroidered blue cloak over an intricate sleeveless vest and ankle-tied silk trousers starched and polished with myrobalan lacquer. A light freckling of smallpox scars along one cheek delightfully accented her broad, moonlike face.

"Elfelilet, my dear," said Manimenesh, "you are just in time for dessert."

Elfelilet stepped gracefully across the tiled floor and reclined face-first along the velvet couch, where the well-known loveliness of her posterior could be displayed to its best advantage. "I thank my friend and patron, the noble Manimenesh. Live forever! Learned Doctor Bagayoko, I am your servant. Hello, poet."

"Hello, darling," said Khayali, smiling with the natural camaraderie of poets and courtesans. "You are the moon, and your troupe of lovelies are comets across our vision."

The host said, "This is our esteemed guest, the caravan-master, Abu Bekr Ahmed Ibn Watunan."

Watunan, who had been gaping in enraptured amazement, came to himself with a start. "I am a simple desert man," he said. "I haven't a poet's gift of words. But I am your ladyship's servant."

Elfelilet smiled and tossed her head; her distended earlobes clattered with heavy chunks of gold filigree. "Welcome to Audoghast."

Dessert arrived. "Well," said Manimenesh. "Our earlier dishes were rough and simple fare, but this is where we shine. Let me tempt you with these *djouzinkat* nutcakes. And do sample our honey macaroons—I believe there's enough for everyone."

Everyone, except of course for the slaves, enjoyed the light and flaky *cataif* macaroons, liberally dusted with Kairwan sugar. The nutcakes were simply beyond compare: painstakingly milled from hand-watered wheat, lovingly buttered and sugared, and artistically studded with raisins, dates, and almonds.

"We eat *djouzinkat* nutcakes during droughts," the poet said, "because the angels weep with envy when we taste them."

Manimenesh belched heroically and readjusted his skullcap. "Now," he said, "we will enjoy a little bit of grape wine. Just a small tot, mind you, so that the sin of drinking is a minor one, and we can do penance with the minimum of alms. After that, our friend the poet will recite an ode he has composed for the occasion."

Khayali began to tune his two-string guitar. "I will also, on demand, extemporize twelve-line *ghazals* in the lyric mode, upon suggested topics."

"And after our digestion has been soothed with epigrams," said their host, "we will enjoy the justly famed dancing of her ladyship's troupe. After that we will retire within the mansion and enjoy their other, equally lauded, skills."

The gate-guard shouted, "Your errand-runner, Lord! He awaits your pleasure, with the fortune-teller!"

"Ah," said Manimenesh. "I had forgotten."

"No matter, sir," said Watunan, whose imagination had been fired by the night's agenda.

Bagayoko spoke up. "Let's have a look at him. His ugliness, by contrast, will heighten the beauty of these women."

"Which would otherwise be impossible," said the poet.

"Very well," said Manimenesh. "Bring him forward."

Sidi, the errand boy, came through the garden, followed with ghastly slowness by the crutch-wielding fortune-teller.

The man inched into the lamplight like a crippled insect. His voluminous dust-gray cloak was stained with sweat, and nameless exudations. He was an albino. His pink eyes were shrouded with cataracts, and he had lost a foot, and several fingers, to leprosy. One shoulder was much lower than the other, suggesting a hunchback, and the stub of his shin was scarred by the gnawing of canal-worms.

"Prophet's beard!" said the poet. "He is truly of surpassing ghastliness."

Elfelilet wrinkled her nose. "He reeks of pestilence!"

Sidi spoke up. "We came as fast as we could, Lord!"

"Go inside, boy," said Manimenesh; "soak ten sticks of cinnamon in a bucket of water, then come back and throw it over him."

Sidi left at once.

Watunan stared at the hideous man, who stood, quivering on one leg, at the edge of the light. "How is it, man, that you still live?"

"I have turned my sight from this world," said the Sufferer. "I turned my sight to God, and He poured knowledge copiously upon me. I have inherited a knowledge which no mortal body can support."

"But God is merciful," said Watunan. "How can you claim this to be His doing?"

"If you do not fear God," said the fortune-teller, "fear Him after seeing me." The hideous albino lowered himself, with arthritic, aching slowness, to the dirt outside the portico. He spoke again. "You are right, caravan-master, to think that death would be a mercy to me. But death comes in its own time, as it will to all of you."

Manimenesh cleared his throat. "Can you see our destinies, then?"

"I see the world," said the Sufferer. "To see the fate of one man is to follow a single ant in a hill."

Sidi reemerged and poured the scented water over the cripple. The fortune-teller cupped his maimed hands and drank. "Thank you, boy," he said. He turned his clouded eyes on the youth. "Your children will be yellow."

Sidi laughed, startled. "Yellow? Why?"

"Your wives will be yellow."

The dancing-girls, who had moved to the far side of the table, giggled in unison. Bagayoko pulled a gold coin from within his sleeve. "I will give you this gold dirham if you will show me your body."

Elfelilet frowned prettily and blinked her kohl-smeared lashes. "Oh, learned Doctor, please spare us."

"You will see my body, sir, if you have patience," said the Sufferer. "As yet, the people of Audoghast laugh at my prophecies. I am doomed to tell the truth, which is harsh and cruel, and therefore absurd. As my fame grows, however, it will reach the ears of your prince, who will then order you to remove me as a threat to public order. You will then sprinkle your favorite poison, powdered asp venom, into a bowl of chickpea soup I will receive from a customer. I bear you no grudge for this, as it will be your civic duty, and will relieve me of pain."

"What an odd notion," said Bagayoko, frowning. "I see no need for the prince to call on my services. One of his spearmen could puncture you like a waterskin."

"By then," the prophet said, "my occult powers will have roused so much uneasiness that it will seem best to take extreme measures."

"Well," said Bagayoko, "that's convenient, if exceedingly grotesque."

"Unlike other prophets," said the Sufferer, "I see the future not as one might wish it to be, but in all its cataclysmic and blind futility. That is why I have come here, to your delightful city. My numerous and totally accurate prophecies will vanish when this city does. This will spare the world any troublesome conflicts of predestination and free will."

"He is a theologian!" the poet said. "A leper theologian—it's a shame my professors in Timbuktu aren't here to debate him!"

"You prophesy doom for our city?" said Manimenesh.

"Yes. I will be specific. This is the year 406 of the Prophet's Hejira, and one thousand and fourteen years since the birth of Christ. In forty years, a puritan and fanatical cult of Moslems will arise, known as the Almoravids. At that time, Audoghast will be an ally of the Ghana Empire, who are idol-worshipers. Ibn Yasin, the warrior saint of the Almoravids, will condemn Audoghast as a nest of pagans. He will set his horde of desert marauders against the city; they will be enflamed by righteousness and greed. They will slaughter the men, and rape and enslave the women. Audoghast will be sacked, the wells will be poisoned, and the cropland will wither and blow away. In a hundred years, sand dunes will bury the ruins. In five hundred years, Audoghast will survive only as a few dozen lines of narrative in the travel books of Arab scholars."

Khayali shifted his guitar. "But the libraries of Timbuktu are full of books on Audoghast, including, if I may say so, our immortal tradition of poetry."

"I have not yet mentioned Timbuktu," said the prophet, "which will be sacked by Moorish invaders led by a blond Spanish eunuch. They will feed the books to goats."

The company burst into incredulous laughter. Unperturbed, the prophet said, "The ruin will be so general, so thorough, and so all-encompassing, that in future centuries it will be stated, and believed, that West Africa was always a land of savages."

"Who in the world could make such a slander?" said the poet.

"They will be Europeans, who will emerge from their current squalid decline, and arm themselves with mighty sciences."

"What happens then?" said Bagayoko, smiling.

"I can look at those future ages," said the prophet, "but I prefer not to do so, as it makes my head hurt."

"You prophesy, then," said Manimenesh, "that our far-famed metropolis, with its towering mosques and armed militia, will be reduced to utter desolation."

"Such is the truth, regrettable as it may be. You, and all you love, will leave no trace in this world, except a few lines in the writing of strangers."

"And our city will fall to savage tribesmen?"

The Sufferer said, "No one here will witness the disaster to come. You will live out your lives, year after year, enjoying ease and luxury, not because you deserve it, but simply because of blind fate. In time you will forget this night; you will forget all I have said, just as the world will forget you and your city. When Audoghast falls, this boy Sidi, this son of a slave, will be the only survivor of this night's gathering. By then he too will have forgotten Audoghast, which he has no cause to love. He will be a rich old merchant in Ch'ang-an, which is a Chinese city of such fantastic wealth that it could buy ten Audoghasts, and which will not be sacked and annihilated until a considerably later date."

"This is madness," said Watunan.

Bagayoko twirled a crusted lock of mud-smeared hair in his supple fingers. "Your gate-guard is a husky lad, friend Manimenesh. What say we have him bash this storm-crow's head in, and haul him out to be hyena food?"

"For that, Doctor," said the Sufferer, "I will tell you the manner of your death. You will be killed by the Ghanaian royal guard, while attempting to kill the crown prince by blowing a subtle poison into his anus with a hollow reed."

Bagayoko started. "You idiot, there is no crown prince."

"He was conceived yesterday."

Bagayoko turned impatiently to the host. "Let us rid ourselves of this prodigy!"

Manimenesh nodded sternly. "Sufferer, you have insulted my guests and my city. You are lucky to leave my home alive."

The Sufferer hauled himself with agonizing slowness to his single foot. "Your boy spoke to me of your generosity."

"What! Not one copper for your driveling."

"Give me one of the gold dirhams from your purse. Otherwise I shall be forced to continue prophesying, and in a more intimate vein."

Manimenesh considered this. "Perhaps it's best." He threw Sidi a coin. "Give this to the madman and escort him back to his raving-booth."

They waited in tormented patience as the fortune-teller creaked and crutched, with painful slowness, into the darkness.

Manimenesh, brusquely, threw out his red velvet sleeves and clapped for wine. "Give us a song, Khayali."

The poet pulled the cowl of his cloak over his head. "My head rings with an awful silence," he said. "I see all way-marks effaced, the joyous pleasances converted into barren wilderness. Jackals resort here, ghosts frolic, and demons sport; the gracious halls, and rich boudoirs, that once shone like the sun, now, overwhelmed by desolation, seem like the gaping mouths of savage beasts!" He looked at the dancing-girls, his eyes brimming with tears. "I picture these maidens, lying beneath the dust, or dispersed to distant parts and far regions, scattered by the hand of exile, torn to pieces by the fingers of expatriation."

Manimenesh smiled on him kindly. "My boy," he said, "if others cannot hear your songs, or embrace these women, or drink this wine, the loss is not ours, but theirs. Let us, then, enjoy all three, and let those unborn do the regretting."

"Your patron is wise," said Ibn Watunan, patting the poet on the shoulder. "You see him here, favored by Allah with every luxury; and you saw that filthy madman, bedeviled by plague. That lunatic, who pretends to great wisdom, only croaks of ruin; while our industrious friend makes the world a better place, by fostering nobility and learning. Could God forsake a city like this, with all its charms, to bring about that fool's disgusting prophesies?" He lifted his cup to Elfelilet, and drank deeply.

"But delightful Audoghast," said the poet, weeping. "All our loveliness, lost to the sands."

"The world is wide," said Bagayoko, "and the years are long. It is not for us to claim immortality, not even if we are poets. But take comfort, my friend. Even if these walls and buildings crumble, there will always be a place like Audoghast, as long as men love profit! The mines are inexhaustible, and elephants are thick as fleas. Mother Africa will always give us gold and ivory."

"Always?" said the poet hopefully, dabbing at his eyes.

"Well, surely there are always slaves," said Manimenesh, and smiled, and winked. The others laughed with him, and there was joy again.

Roadside Rescue

PAT CADIGAN

Pat Cadigan was born in Schenectady, New York, and now lives in London with her family. She made her first professional sale in 1980, and has subsequently come to be regarded as one of the best new writers of her generation. Her story "Pretty Boy Crossover" has appeared on several critic's lists as among the best science-fiction stories of the 1980's, and her story "Angel" was a finalist for the Hugo Award, the Nebula Award, *and* the World Fantasy Award (one of the few stories ever to earn that rather unusual distinction). Her short fiction—which has appeared in most of the major markets, including *Omni, Asimov's Science Fiction,* and *The Magazine of Fantasy & Science Fiction*—has been gathered in the collections *Patterns* and *Dirty Work*. Her first novel, *Mindplayers,* was released in 1987 to excellent critical response, and her second novel, *Synners,* released in 1991, won the Arthur C. Clarke Award as the year's best science-fiction novel, as did her third novel, *Fools,* making her the only writer ever to win the Clarke Award twice. Her other books include the novels *Tea from an Empty Cup* and *Dervish is Digital,* and, as editor, the anthology *The Ultimate Cyberpunk*. Her most recent book is a new novel, *Reality Used to Be a Friend of Mine*. Her stories have appeared in our First through Sixth, and Ninth through Thirteenth annual collections.

Here she gives us an economically brutal tale about a stranded traveler who gets a little *more* help than he bargained for. . . .

Barely fifteen minutes after he'd called Area Traffic Surveillance, Etan Carrera saw the big limousine transport coming toward him. He watched it with mild interest from his smaller and temporarily disabled vehicle. Some media celebrity or an alien—more likely an alien. All aliens seemed enamored with things like limos and private SSTs, even after all these years. In any case, Etan fully expected to see the transport pass without even slowing, the navigator (not driver—limos drove themselves) hardly glancing his way, leaving him alone again in the rolling, green, empty countryside.

But the transport did slow and then stopped, cramming itself into the breakdown lane across the road. The door slid up, and the navigator jumped out, smiling as he came over to Etan. Etan blinked at the dark, full-dress uniform. *People who worked for aliens had to do some odd things,* he thought, and for some reason put his hand on the window control as though he were going to roll it up.

"Afternoon, sir," said the navigator, bending a little from the waist.

"Hi," Etan said.

"Trouble with your vehicle?"

"Nothing too serious, I hope. I've called Surveillance, and they say they'll be out to pick me up in two hours at most."

"That's a long time to wait." The navigator's smile widened. He was very attractive, holo-star kind of handsome. *People who work for aliens,* Etan thought. "Perhaps you'd care to wait in my employer's transport. For that matter, I can probably repair your vehicle, which will save you time and money. Roadside rescue fees are exorbitant."

"That's very kind," Etan said, "But I *have* called, and I don't want to impose—"

"It was my employer's idea to stop, sir. I agreed, of course. My employer is quite fond of people. In fact, my employer loves people. And I'm sure you would be rewarded in some way."

"Hey, now, I'm not asking for anything—"

"My employer is a most generous entity," said the navigator, looking down briefly. "I'll get my tool kit." He was on his way back across the road before Etan could object.

Ten minutes later the navigator closed the power plant housing of Etan's vehicle and came around to the window again, still looking formal and unruffled. "Try it now, sir."

Etan inserted his key card into the dash console and shifted the control near the steering module. The vehicle hummed to life. "Well, now," he said. "You fixed it."

That smile again. "Occasionally the connections to the motherboard are improperly fitted. Contaminants get in, throw off the fuel mixing, and the whole plant shuts down."

"Oh," Etan said, feeling stupid, incompetent, and worst of all, obligated.

"You won't be needing rescue now, sir."

"Well. I should call and tell them." Etan reached reluctantly for the console phone.

"You could call from the limo, sir. And if you'd care for a little refreshment—" The navigator opened his door for him.

Etan gave up. "Oh, sure, sure. This is all very nice of you and your, uh, employer." *What the hell,* he thought, getting out and following the navigator across the road. *If it meant that much to the alien, he'd give the alien a thrill.*

"We both appreciate this. My employer and I."

Etan smiled, bracing himself as the door to the passenger compartment of the limo slid back. Whatever awkward greeting he might have made died in his throat. There was no one inside, no one and nothing.

"Just go ahead and get in, sir."

"But, uh—"

"My employer is in there. Somewhere." Smile. "You'll find the phone by the refrigerator. Or shall I call Surveillance for you?"

"No, I'll do it. Uh, thanks." Etan climbed in and sat down on the silvery gray cushion. The door slid partially shut, and a moment later Etan heard the navigator moving around up front. Somewhere a blower went on, puffing cool, humid air at his face. He sat back tentatively. Luxury surroundings—refrigerator, bar, video, sound system. God knew what use the alien found for any of it. Hospitality. It probably wouldn't help. He and the alien would no doubt end up staring at each other with nothing to say, feeling freakish.

He was on the verge of getting up and leaving when the navigator slipped through the door. It shut silently as he sat down across from Etan and unbuttoned his uniform tunic.

"Cold drink, sir?"

Etan shook his head.

"Hope you don't mind if I do." There was a different quality to the smile now. He took an amber bottle from the refrigerator and flipped the cap off, aiming it at a disposal in the door. Etan could smell alcohol and heavy spicing. "Possibly the best spiced ale in the world, if not the known universe," the navigator said. "Sure you won't have any?"

"Yes, I—" Etan sat forward a little. "I really think I ought to say thank you and get on. I don't want to hold you up—"

"My employer chooses where he wants to be when he wants to be there." The navigator took another drink from the bottle. "At least, I'm calling it a he. Hard to tell with a lot of these species." He ran his fingers through his dark hair; one long strand fell and brushed his temple. Etan caught a glimpse of a shaved spot near his temple. Implant; so the navigator would be mentally attuned to his employer, making speech or translation unnecessary. "With some, gender's irrelevant. Some have more than one gender. Some have more than *two*. Imagine taking *that* trip, if you can." He tilted the bottle up again. "But my present employer, here, asking him what gender he is, it's like asking you what flavor you are."

Etan took a breath. One more minute; then he'd ask this goof to let him out. "Not much you can do, I guess, except to arbitrarily assign them sex and—"

"Didn't say *that*."

"Pardon?"

The navigator killed the bottle. "Didn't say anything about sex."

"Oh." Etan paused, wondering exactly how crazy the navigator might be and how he'd managed to hide it well enough to be hired for an alien. "Sorry. I thought you said that some of them lacked sex—"

"Never said anything about sex. Gender, I said. Nothing about sex."

"But the terms can be interchangeable."

"Certainly *not*." The navigator tossed the bottle into the disposal and took another from the refrigerator. "Maybe on this planet but not out there."

Etan shrugged. "I assumed you'd need gender for sex, so if a species lacked gender, they'd uh . . ." he trailed off, making a firm resolution to shut up until he could escape. Suddenly he was very glad he hadn't canceled his rescue after all.

"Our nature isn't universal law," said the navigator. "Out there—" he broke off, staring at something to Etan's left. "Ah. My employer has decided to come out at last."

The small creature at the end of the seat seemed to have coalesced out of the humid semidark, an off-white mound of what seemed to be fur as close and dense as a seal's. It might have repelled or disconcerted him except that it smelled so *good*, like a cross between fresh-baked bread and wildflowers. The aroma filled Etan with a sudden, intense feeling of well-being. Without thinking, he reached out to touch it, realized, and pulled his hand back.

"Going to pet it, were you? Stroke it?"

"Sorry," Etan said, half to the navigator and half to the creature.

"I forgive you," said the navigator, amused. "He'd forgive you, too, except he doesn't feel you've done anything wrong. It's the smell. Very compelling." He sniffed. "Go ahead. You won't hurt him."

Etan leaned over and gingerly touched the top of the creature. The contact made him jump. It didn't feel solid. It was like touching gelatin with a fur covering.

"Likes to stuff itself into the cushions and feel the vibrations from the ride," said the navigator. "But what it *really* loves is talk. Conversation. Sound waves created by the human voice are especially pleasing to it. And in *person*, not by holo or phone." The navigator gave a short, mirthless laugh and killed the second bottle. "So. Come on. Talk it up. That's what you're here for."

"Sorry," Etan said defensively. "I don't know exactly what to say."

"Express your goddamn *gratitude* for it having me fix your vehicle."

Etan opened his mouth to make an angry response and decided not to. For all he knew, both alien and human were insane and dangerous besides. "Yes. Of course I do appreciate your help. It was so kind of you, and I'm saving a lot of money since I don't need a roadside rescue now—"

"Never called it off, did you?"

"What?"

"The rescue. You never called to tell Surveillance you didn't need help."

Etan swallowed. "Yes. I did."

"Liar."

All right, Etan thought. *Enough was too much.* "I don't know what transport services you work for, but I'll find out. They ought to know about you."

"Yeah? What should they know—that I make free repairs at the bidding of an alien hairball?" The navigator grinned bitterly.

"No." Etan's voice was quiet. "They should know that maybe you've been working too long and too hard for aliens." His eyes swiveled apologetically to the creature. "Not that I mean to offend—"

"Forget it. It doesn't understand a goddam word."

"Then why did you want me to talk to it?"

"Because *I* understand. We're attuned. On several frequencies, mind you, one for every glorious mood it might have. Not that it's any of your business."

Etan shook his head. "You need help."

"Fuck if I do. Now finish your thanks and start thinking up some more things to say."

The bread-and-flowers aroma intensified until Etan's nerves were standing on end. His heart pounded ferociously, and he wondered if a smell could induce cardiac arrest.

"I think I've finished thanking your employer." He looked directly at the creature. "And that's all I have to say. Under more pleasant circumstances, I might have talked my head off. Sorry." He started to get up.

The navigator moved quickly for someone who was supposed to be drunk. Etan found himself pinned against the back of the seat before he realized that the man wasn't jumping up to open the door. For a moment, he stared into the navigator's flushed face, not quite believing.

"Talk," the navigator said softly, almost gently. "Just talk. That's all you've got to do."

Etan tried heaving himself upward to throw them both off the seat and onto the floor, but the navigator had him too securely. "Help!" he bellowed. "Somebody help me!"

"Okay, yell for help. That's good, too," said the navigator, smiling. They began to slide down on the seat together with Etan on the bottom. "Go ahead. Yell all you want."

"Let me up and I won't report you."

"I'm sure I can believe *that*." The navigator laughed. "Tell us a whole fairy story now."

"Let me go or I swear to Christ I'll kill you and that furry shit you work for."

"What?" the navigator asked, leaning on him a little harder. "What was that, *sir*?"

"Let me go or I'll *fucking kill you!*"

Something in the air seemed to break, as though a circuit had been completed or some sort of energy discharged. Etan sniffed. The bread-and-flowers aroma had changed, more flowers, less bread, and much weaker, dissipating in the ventilation before he could get more than a whiff.

The navigator pushed himself off Etan and plumped down heavily on the seat across from him again. Etan held still, looking first at the man rubbing his face with both hands and then turning his head so he could see the creature sliding down behind the cushion. *We scared it*, he thought, horrified. *Bad enough to make it hide under the seat.*

"Sir."

Etan jumped. The navigator was holding a fistful of currency out to him. The denominations made him blink.

"It's yours, sir. Take it. You can go now."

Etan pulled himself up. "What the hell do you mean, it's mine?"

"Please, sir." The navigator pressed one hand over his left eye. "If you're going to talk anymore, please step outside."

"Step outs—" Etan slapped the man's hand away and lunged for the door.

"Wait!" called the navigator, and in spite of everything, Etan obeyed. The navigator climbed out of the transport clumsily, still covering his eye, the other hand offering the currency. "Please, sir. You haven't been hurt. You have a repaired vehicle, more than a little pocket money here—you've come out ahead if you think about it."

Etan laughed weakly. "I can't believe this."

"Just take the money, sir. My employer wants you to have it." The navigator winced and massaged his eye some more. "Purely psychosomatic," he said, as though Etan had asked. "The implant is painless and causes no damage, no matter how intense the exchange between species. But please lower your voice, sir. My employer can still feel your sound, and he's quite done with you."

"What is that supposed to mean?"

"The money is yours from my employer," the navigator said patiently. "My employer loves people. We discussed that earlier. *Loves* them. Especially their voices."

"So?" Etan crossed his arms. The navigator leaned over and stuffed the money between Etan's forearms.

"Perhaps you remember what else we were discussing. I really have no wish to remind you, sir."

"So? What's all that stuff about gender—what's that got to do with . . ." Etan's voice died away.

"Human voices," the navigator said. "No speech where they come from. And we're so new and different to them. This one's been here only a few weeks. Its preference happens to be that of a man speaking from fear and anger, something you can't fake."

Etan took a step back from the man, unfolding his arms and letting the money fall to the ground, thinking of the implant, the man feeling whatever the creature felt.

"I don't know if you could call it perversion or not," said the navigator. "Maybe there's no such thing." He looked down at the bills. "Might as well keep it. You earned it. You even did well." He pulled himself erect and made a small, formal bow. "Good day, sir," he said, with no mockery at all and climbed into the transport's front seat. Etan watched the limo roll out of the breakdown lane and lumber away from him.

After a while he looked down. The money was still there at his feet, so he picked it up.

Just as he was getting back into his own vehicle, the console phone chimed. "We've got an early opening in our patrol pattern," Surveillance told him. "So we can swing by and get you in ten minutes."

"Don't bother," Etan said.

"Repeat?"

"I said, you're too late."

"Repeat again, please."

Etan sighed. "There isn't anything to rescue me from anymore."

There was a brief silence on the other end. "Did you get your vehicle overhauled?"

"Yeah," Etan said. "That, too."

snow

jOHN CROWLEY

One of the most respected authors of our day, John Crowley is perhaps best known for his fat and fanciful novel *Little, Big*, which won the prestigious World Fantasy Award. His other novels include *Beasts, The Deep, Engine Summer, AEgypt, Love and Sleep*, and *Daemonomania*. His short fiction has been gathered in two collections, *Novelty* and *Antiquities*. His most recent books are a novel, *The Translator*, and a new collection, *Novelties and Souvenirs: Collected Short Fiction*. His stories have appeared in our Third and Seventh annual collections. He lives in the Berkshire Hills of western Massachusetts.

Throughout the centuries, people have spent a great deal of money on the quest for forgetfulness. But, as the bittersweet story that follows suggests, someday it might prove even more expensive to *remember*. . . .

I don't think Georgie would ever have got one for herself: She was at once unsentimental and a little in awe of death. No, it was her first husband—an immensely rich and (from Georgie's description) a strangely weepy guy—who had got it for her. Or for himself, actually, of course. He was to be the beneficiary. Only he died himself shortly after it was installed. If *installed* is the right word. After he died, Georgie got rid of most of what she'd inherited from him, liquidated it, it was cash that she had liked best about that marriage anyway; but the Wasp couldn't really be got rid of. Georgie ignored it.

In fact the thing really was about the size of a wasp of the largest kind, and it had the same lazy and mindless flight. And of course it really was a bug, not of the insect kind but of the surveillance kind. And so its name fit all around: one of those bits of accidental poetry the world generates without thinking. O Death, where is thy sting?

Georgie ignored it, but it was hard to avoid; you had to be a little careful around it; it followed Georgie at a variable distance, depending on her motions and the number of other people around her, the level of light, and the tone of her voice. And there was always the danger you might shut it in a door or knock it down with a tennis racket. It cost a fortune (if you count the access and the perpetual-care contract, all prepaid), and though it wasn't really fragile, it made you nervous.

It wasn't recording all the time. There had to be a certain amount of light, though not much. Darkness shut it off. And then sometimes it would get lost. Once when we hadn't seen it hovering around for a time, I opened a closet door, and it flew out, unchanged. It went off looking for her, humming softly. It must have been shut in there for days.

Eventually it ran out, or down. A lot could go wrong, I suppose, with circuits that small, controlling that many functions. It ended up spending a lot of time bumping gently against the bedroom ceiling, over and over, like a winter fly. Then one day the maid swept it out from under the bureau, a husk. By that time it had transmitted at least eight thousand hours (eight thousand was the minimum guarantee) of Georgie: of her days and hours, her comings in and her goings out, her speech and motion, her living self—all on file, taking up next to no room, at The Park. And then, when the time came, you could go there, to The Park, say on a Sunday afternoon; and in quiet landscaped surroundings (as The Park described it) you would find her personal resting chamber; and there, in privacy, through the miracle of modern information storage and retrieval systems, you could access her: her alive, her as she was in every way, never changing or growing any older, fresher (as The Park's brochure said) than in memory ever green.

I married Georgie for her money, the same reason she married her first, the one who took out The Park's contract for her. She married me, I think, for my looks; she always had a taste for looks in men. I wanted to write. I made a calculation that more women than men make, and decided that to be supported and paid for by a rich wife would give me freedom to do so, to "develop." The calculation worked out no better for me than it does for most women who make it. I carried a typewriter and a case of miscellaneous paper from Ibiza to Gstaad to Bali to London, and typed on beaches, and learned to ski. Georgie liked me in ski clothes.

Now that those looks are all but gone, I can look back on myself as a young hunk and see that I was in a way a rarity, a type that you also run into often among women and less among men, the beauty unaware of his beauty, aware that he affects women profoundly and more or less instantly but doesn't know why; thinks he is being listened to and understood, that his soul is being seen, when all that's being seen is long-lashed eyes and a strong, square, tanned wrist turning in a lovely gesture, stubbing out a cigarette. Confusing. By the time I figured out why I had for so long been indulged and cared for and listened to, why I was interesting, I wasn't as interesting as I had been. At about the same time I realized I wasn't a writer at all. Georgie's investment stopped looking as good to her, and my calculation had ceased to add up; only by that time I had come, pretty unexpectedly, to love Georgie a lot, and she just as unexpectedly had come to love and need me too, as much as she needed anybody. We never really parted, even though when she died I hadn't seen her for years. Phone calls, at dawn or four A.M. because she never, for all her travel, really grasped that the world turns and cocktail hour travels around with it.

She was a crazy, wasteful, happy woman, without a trace of malice or permanence or ambition in her—easily pleased and easily bored and strangely serene despite the hectic pace she kept up. She cherished things and lost them and forgot them: things, days, people. She had fun, though, and I had fun with her; that was her talent and her destiny, not always an easy one. Once, hung over in a New York hotel, watching a sudden snowfall out the immense window, she said to me, "Charlie, I'm going to die of fun."

And she did. Snow-foiling in Austria, she was among the first to get one of those snow leopards, silent beasts as fast as speedboats. Alfredo called me in California to tell me, but with the distance and his accent and his eagerness to tell me *he* wasn't to blame, I never grasped the details. I was still her husband, her closest relative, heir to the little she still had, and beneficiary, too, of The Park's access concept. Fortunately, The Park's services included collecting her from the morgue in Gstaad and installing her in her chamber at The Park's California unit. Beyond signing papers and taking delivery when Georgie arrived by freight airship at Van Nuys, there was nothing for me to do. The Park's representative was solicitous and made sure I understood how to go about accessing Georgie, but I wasn't listening. I am only a child of my time, I suppose. Everything about death, the fact of it, the fate of the remains, and the situation of the living faced with it, seems grotesque to me, embarrassing, useless. And everything done about it only makes it more grotesque, more useless: Someone I loved is dead; let me therefore dress in clown's clothes, talk backwards, and buy expensive machinery to make up for it. I went back to L.A.

A year or more later, the contents of some safe-deposit boxes of Georgie's arrived from the lawyer's: some bonds and such stuff, and a small steel case, velvet lined, that contained a key, a key deeply notched on both sides and headed with smooth plastic, like the key to an expensive car.

Why did I go to The Park that first time? Mostly because I had forgotten about it: getting that key in the mail was like coming across a pile of old snapshots you hadn't cared to look at when they were new but which after they have aged come to contain the past, as they did not contain the present. I was curious.

I understood very well that The Park and its access concept were very probably only another cruel joke on the rich, preserving the illusion that they can buy what can't be bought, like the cryonics fad of thirty years before. Once in Ibiza, Georgie and I met a German couple who also had a contract with The Park; their Wasp hovered over them like a Paraclete and made them self-conscious in the extreme—they seemed to be constantly rehearsing the eternal show being stored up for their descendants. Their deaths had taken over their lives, as though they were pharaohs. Did they, Georgie wondered, exclude the Wasp from their bedroom? Or did its presence there stir them to greater efforts, proofs of undying love and admirable vigor for the unborn to see?

No, death wasn't to be cheated that way, any more than by pyramids, by masses said in perpetuity. It wasn't Georgie saved from death that I would find. But there were eight thousand hours of her life with me, genuine hours, stored there more carefully than they could be in my porous memory; Georgie hadn't excluded the Wasp from her bedroom, our bedroom, and she who had never performed for anybody could not have conceived of performing for it. And there would be me, too, undoubtedly, caught unintentionally by the Wasp's attention: out of those thousands of hours there would be hundreds of myself, and myself had just then begun to be problematic to me, something that had to be figured out, something about which evidence had to be gathered and weighed. I was thirty-eight years old.

That summer, then, I borrowed a Highway Access Permit (the old HAPpy card of those days) from a county lawyer I knew and drove the coast highway up to where The Park was, at the end of a pretty beach road, all alone above the sea. It looked from the outside like the best, most peaceful kind of Italian country cemetery, a low stucco wall topped with urns, amid cypresses, an arched gate in the center. A small brass plaque on the gate: PLEASE USE YOUR KEY. The gate opened, not to a square of shaded tombstones but onto a ramped corridor going down: The cemetery wall was an illusion, the works were underground. Silence, or nameless Muzak like silence; solitude—either the necessary technicians were discreetly hidden or none were needed. Certainly the access concept turned out to be simplicity itself, in operation anyway. Even I, who am an idiot about information technology, could tell that. The Wasp was genuine state-of-the-art stuff, but what we mourners got was as ordinary as home movies, as old letters tied up in ribbon.

A display screen near the entrance told me down which corridor to find Georgie, and my key let me into a small screening room where there was a moderate-size TV monitor, two comfortable chairs, and dark walls of chocolate-brown carpeting. The sweet-sad Muzak. Georgie herself was evidently somewhere in the vicinity, in the wall or under the floor, they weren't specific about the charnel-house aspect of the place. In the control panel before the TV were a keyhole for my key and two bars: ACCESS and RESET.

I sat, feeling foolish and a little afraid, too, made more uncomfortable by being so deliberately soothed by neutral furnishings and sober tools. I imagined, around me, down other corridors, in other chambers, that others communed with their dead as I was about to do; that the dead were murmuring to them beneath the stream of Muzak; that they wept to see and hear, as I might. But I could hear nothing. I turned my key in its slot, and the screen lit up. The dim lights dimmed further, and the Muzak ceased. I pushed ACCESS, obviously the next step. No doubt all these procedures had been explained to me long ago at the dock when Georgie in her aluminum box was being off-loaded, and I hadn't listened. And on the screen she turned to look at me—only not at me, though I started and drew breath—at the Wasp that watched her.

She was in mid-sentence, mid-gesture. Where? When? *Or put it on the same card with the others,* she said, turning away. Someone said something, Georgie answered, and stood up, the Wasp panning and moving erratically with her, like an amateur with a home-video camera. A white room, sunlight, wicker. Ibiza. Georgie wore a cotton blouse, open; from a table she picked up lotion, poured some on her hand, and rubbed it across her freckled breastbone. The meaningless conversation about putting something on a card went on, ceased. I watched the room, wondering what year, what season I had stumbled into. Georgie pulled off her shirt—her small round breasts tipped with large, childlike nipples, child's breasts she still had at forty, shook delicately. And she went out onto the balcony, the Wasp following, blinded by sun, adjusting. *If you want to do it that way,* someone said. The someone crossed the screen, a brown blur, naked. It was me. Georgie said: *Oh, look, hummingbirds.*

She watched them, rapt, and the Wasp crept close to her cropped blond head, rapt too, and I watched her watch. She turned away, rested her elbows on the balustrade. I couldn't remember this day. How should I? One of hundreds, of thousands. . . . She looked out to the bright sea, wearing her sleepwalking face, mouth partly open, and absently stroked her breast with her oiled hand. An iridescent glitter among the flowers was the hummingbird.

Without really knowing what I did—I felt hungry, suddenly, hungry for pastness, for more—I touched the RESET bar. The balcony in Ibiza vanished, the screen glowed emptily. I touched ACCESS.

At first there was darkness, a murmur; then a dark back moved away from before the Wasp's eye, and a dim scene of people resolved itself. Jump. Other people, or the same people, a party? Jump. Apparently the Wasp was turning itself on and off according to the changes in light levels here, wherever *here* was. Georgie in a dark dress having her cigarette lit: brief flare of the lighter. She said *Thanks*. Jump. A foyer or hotel lounge. Paris? The Wasp jerkily sought for her among people coming and going; it couldn't make a movie, establishing shots, cutaways—it could only doggedly follow Georgie, like a jealous husband, seeing nothing else. This was frustrating. I pushed RESET. ACCESS. Georgie brushed her teeth, somewhere, somewhen.

I understood, after one or two more of these terrible leaps. Access was random. There was no way to dial up a year, a day, a scene. The Park had supplied no program, none; the eight thousand hours weren't filed at all; they were a jumble, like a lunatic's memory, like a deck of shuffled cards. I had supposed, without thinking about it, that they would begin at the beginning and go on till they reached the end. Why didn't they?

I also understood something else. If access was truly random, if I truly had no control, then I had lost as good as forever those scenes I had seen. Odds were on the order of eight thousand to one (more? far more? probabilities are opaque to me) that I would never light on them again by pressing this bar. I felt a pang of loss for that afternoon in Ibiza. It was doubly gone now. I sat before the empty screen, afraid to touch ACCESS again, afraid of what I would lose.

I shut down the machine (the light level in the room rose, the Muzak poured softly back in) and went out into the halls, back to the display screen in the entranceway. The list of names slowly, greenly, rolled over like the list of departing flights at an airport. Code numbers were missing from beside many, indicating perhaps that they weren't yet in residence, only awaited. In the *D*s, only three names, and DIRECTOR—hidden among them as though he were only another of the dead. A chamber number. I went to find it, and went in.

The director looked more like a janitor or a night watchman, the semi-retired type you often see caretaking little-visited places. He wore a brown smock like a monk's robe, and was making coffee in a corner of his small office, out of which little business seemed to be done. He looked up startled, caught out, when I entered.

"Sorry," I said, "but I don't think I understand this system right."

"A problem?" he said. "Shouldn't be a problem." He looked at me a little wide-eyed and shy, hoping not to be called on for anything difficult. "Equipment's all working?"

"I don't know," I said. "It doesn't seem that it could be." I described what I thought I had learned about The Park's access concept. "That can't be right, can it?" I said. "That access is totally random . . ."

He was nodding, still wide-eyed, paying close attention.

"Is it?" I asked.

"Is it what?"

"Random."

"Oh, yes. Yes, sure. If everything's in working order."

I could think of nothing to say for a moment, watching him nod reassuringly. Then: "Why?" I asked. "I mean why is there no way at all to, to organize, to have some kind of organized access to the material?" I had begun to feel that sense of grotesque foolishness in the presence of death, as though I were haggling over Georgie's effects. "That seems stupid, if you'll pardon me."

"Oh no, oh no," he said. "You've read your literature? You've read all your literature?"

"Well, to tell the truth . . ."

"It's all just as described," the director said. "I can promise you that. If there's any problem at all . . ."

"Do you mind," I said, "if I sit down?" I smiled. He seemed so afraid of me and my complaint, of me as mourner, possibly grief-crazed and unable to grasp the simple limits of his responsibilities to me, that he needed soothing himself. "I'm sure everything's fine," I said. "I just don't think I understand. I'm kind of dumb about these things."

"Sure. Sure. Sure." He regretfully put away his coffee makings and sat behind his desk, lacing his fingers together like a consultant. "People get a lot of satisfaction out of the access here," he said, "a lot of comfort, if they take it in the right spirit." He tried a smile. I wondered what qualifications he had had to show to get this job. "The random part. Now, it's all in the literature. There's the legal aspect—you're not a lawyer are you, no, no, sure, no offense. You see, the material here isn't *for* anything, except, well, except for communing. But suppose the stuff were programmed, searchable. Suppose there was a problem about taxes or inheritance or so on. There could be subpoenas, lawyers all over the place, destroying the memorial concept completely."

I really hadn't thought of that. Built-in randomness saved past lives from being searched in any systematic way. And no doubt saved The Park from being in the records business and at the wrong end of a lot of suits. "You'd have to watch the whole eight thousand hours," I said, "and even if you found what you were looking for there'd be no way to replay it. It would have gone by." It would slide into the random past even as you watched it, like that afternoon in Ibiza, that party in Paris. Lost.

He smiled and nodded. I smiled and nodded.

"I'll tell you something," he said. "They didn't predict that. The randomness. It was a side effect, an effect of the storage process. Just luck." His grin turned down, his brows knitted seriously. "See, we're storing here at the molecular level. We have to go that small, for space problems. I mean your eight-thousand-hour guarantee. If we had gone tape or conventional, how much room would it take up? If the access concept caught on. A lot of room. So we went vapor-trap and endless-tracking. Size of my thumbnail. It's all in the literature." He looked at me strangely. I had a sudden intense sensation that I was being fooled, tricked, that the man before me in his smock was no expert, no technician; he was a charlatan, or maybe a madman impersonating a director and not belonging here at all. It raised the hair on my neck, and passed. "So the randomness," he was saying. "It was an effect of going molecular. Brownian movement. All you do is lift the endless tracking for a microsecond and you get a rearrangement at the molecular level. We don't randomize. The molecules do it for us."

I remembered Brownian movement, just barely, from physics class. The random movement of molecules, the teacher said; it has a mathematical description. It's like the movement of dust motes you see swimming in a shaft of sunlight, like the swirl of snowflakes in a glass paperweight that shows a cottage being snowed on. "I see," I said. "I guess I see."

"Is there," he said, "any other problem?" He said it as though there might be some other problem and that he knew what it might be and that he hoped I didn't have it. "You understand the system, key lock, two bars, ACCESS, RESET. . . ."

"I understand," I said. "I understand now."

"Communing," he said, standing, relieved, sure I would be gone soon. "I understand. It takes a while to relax into the communing concept."

"Yes," I said. "It does."

I wouldn't learn what I had come to learn, whatever that was. The Wasp had not been good at storage after all, no, no better than my young soul had been. Days and weeks had been missed by its tiny eye. It hadn't seen well, and in what it had seen it had been no more able to distinguish the just-as-well-forgotten from the unforgettable than my own eye had been. No better and no worse—the same.

And yet, and yet—she stood up in Ibiza and dressed her breasts with lotion, and spoke to me: *Oh, look, hummingbirds.* I had forgotten, and the Wasp had not; and I owned once again what I hadn't known I had lost, hadn't known was precious to me.

The sun was setting when I left The Park, the satin sea foaming softly, randomly around the rocks.

I had spent my life waiting for something, not knowing what, not even knowing I waited. Killing time. I was still waiting. But what I had been waiting for had already occurred and was past.

It was two years, nearly, since Georgie had died: two years until, for the first and last time, I wept for her; for her, and for myself.

Of course I went back. After a lot of work and correctly placed dollars, I netted a HAPpy card of my own. I had time to spare, like a lot of people then, and often on empty afternoons (never on Sunday) I would get out onto the unpatched and weed-grown freeway and glide up the coast. The Park was always open. I relaxed into the communing concept.

Now, after some hundreds of hours spent there underground, now when I have long ceased to go through those doors (I have lost my key, I think; anyway I don't know where to look for it), I know that the solitude I felt myself to be in was real. The watchers around me, the listeners I sensed in other chambers, were mostly my imagination. There was rarely anyone there. These tombs were as neglected as any tombs anywhere usually are. Either the living did not care to attend much on the dead—when have they ever?—or the hopeful buyers of the contracts had come to discover the flaw in the access concept: as I discovered it, in the end.

ACCESS, and she takes dresses one by one from her closet, and holds them against her body, and studies the effect in a tall mirror, and puts them back again. She had a funny face, which she never made except when looking at herself in the mirror, a face made for no one but herself, that was actually quite unlike her. The mirror Georgie.

RESET.

ACCESS. By a bizarre coincidence here she is looking in another mirror. I think the Wasp could be confused by mirrors. She turns away, the Wasp adjusts; there is someone asleep, tangled in bedclothes on a big hotel bed, morning, a room-service cart. Oh: the Algonquin: myself. Winter. Snow is falling outside the tall window. She searches her handbag, takes out a small vial, swallows a pill with coffee, holding the cup by its body and not its handle. I stir, show a tousled head of hair. Conversation— unintelligible. Gray room, whitish snow light, color degraded. Would I now (I thought, watching us) reach out for her? Would I in the next hour take her, or she me, push aside the bedclothes, open her pale pajamas? She goes into the john, shuts the door. The Wasp watches stupidly, excluded, transmitting the door.

RESET, finally.

But what (I would wonder) if I had been patient, what if I had watched and waited?

Time, it turns out, takes an unconscionable time. The waste, the footless waste— it's no spectator sport. Whatever fun there is in sitting idly looking at nothing and tasting your own being for a whole afternoon, there is no fun in replaying it. The waiting is excruciating. How often, in five years, in eight thousand hours of daylight or lamplight, might we have coupled, how much time expended in lovemaking? A hundred hours, two hundred? Odds were not high of my coming on such a scene; darkness swallowed most of them, and the others were lost in the interstices of endless hours spent shopping, reading, on planes and in cars, asleep, apart. Hopeless.

ACCESS. She has turned on a bedside lamp. Alone. She hunts amid the Kleenex and magazines on the bedside table, finds a watch, looks at it dully, turns it right side up, looks again, and puts it down. Cold. She burrows in the blankets, yawning, staring, then puts out a hand for the phone but only rests her hand on it, thinking. Thinking at four A.M. She withdraws her hand, shivers a child's deep, sleepy shiver, and shuts off the light. A bad dream. In an instant it's morning, dawn; the Wasp slept, too. She sleeps soundly, unmoving, only the top of her blond head showing out of the quilt—and will no doubt sleep so for hours, watched over more attentively, more fixedly, than any peeping Tom could ever have watched over her.

RESET.

ACCESS.

"I can't hear as well as I did at first," I told the director. "And the definition is getting softer."

"Oh sure," the director said. "That's really in the literature. We have to explain that carefully. That this might be a problem."

"It isn't just my monitor?" I asked. "I thought it was probably only the monitor."

"No, no, not really, no," he said. He gave me coffee. We'd gotten to be friendly over the months. I think, as well as being afraid of me, he was glad I came around now and then; at least one of the living came here, one at least was using the services. "There's a *slight* degeneration that does occur."

"Everything seems to be getting gray."

His face had shifted into intense concern, no belittling this problem. "Mm-hm, mm-hm, see, at the molecular level where we're at, there is degeneration. It's just in the physics. It randomizes a little over time. So you lose—you don't lose a minute of what you've got, but you lose a little definition. A little color. But it levels off."

"It does?"

"We think it does. Sure it does, we promise it does. We *predict* that it will."

"But you don't know."

"Well, well you see we've only been in this business a short while. This concept is new. There were things we couldn't know." He still looked at me, but seemed at the same time to have forgotten me. Tired. He seemed to have grown colorless himself lately, old, losing definition. "You might start getting some snow," he said softly.

ACCESS RESET ACCESS.

A gray plaza of herringbone-laid stones, gray, clicking palms. She turns up the collar of her sweater, narrowing her eyes in a stern wind. Buys magazines at a kiosk: *Vogue, Harper's, La Moda. Cold*, she says to the kiosk girl. *Frio.* The young man I was takes her arm; they walk back along the beach, which is deserted and strung with cast seaweed, washed by a dirty sea. Winter in Ibiza. We talk, but the Wasp can't hear, the sea's sound confuses it; it seems bored by its duties and lags behind us.

RESET.

ACCESS. The Algonquin, terribly familiar: morning, winter. She turns away from the snowy window. Myself in bed . . . and for a moment watching this I felt suspended between two mirrors, reflected endlessly. I had seen this before; I had lived it once and remembered it once, and remembered the memory, and here it was again, or could it be nothing but another morning, a similar morning? There were far more than one like this, in this place. But no; she turns from the window, she gets out her vial of pills, picks up the coffee cup by its body: I had seen this moment before, not months before, weeks before, here in this chamber. I had come upon the same scene twice.

What are the odds of it, I wondered, what are the odds of coming upon the same minutes again, these minutes.

I stir within the bedclothes.

I leaned forward to hear, this time, what I would say; it was something like *but fun anyway*, or something.

Fun, she says, laughing, harrowed, the degraded sound a ghost's twittering. *Charlie, someday I'm going to die of fun.*

She takes her pill. The Wasp follows her to the john, and is shut out.

Why am I here? I thought, and my heart was beating hard and slow. What am I here for? What?

RESET.

ACCESS.

Silvered icy streets, New York, Fifth Avenue. She is climbing shouting from a cab's dark interior. *Just don't shout at me*, she shouts at someone, her mother I never met, a dragon. She is out and hurrying away down the sleety street with her bundles, the Wasp at her shoulder. I could reach out and touch her shoulder and make her turn and follow me out.

Walking away, lost in the colorless press of traffic and people, impossible to discern within the softened snowy image.

Something was very wrong.

Georgie hated winter, she escaped it most of the time we were together, about the first of the year beginning to long for the sun that had gone elsewhere; Austria was all right for a few weeks, the toy villages and sugar snow and bright, sleek skiers were not really the winter she feared, though even in fire-warmed chalets it was hard to get her naked without gooseflesh and shudders from some draft only she could feel. We were chaste in winter. So Georgie escaped it: Antigua and Bali and two months in Ibiza when the almonds blossomed. It was continual false, flavorless spring all winter long.

How often could snow have fallen when the Wasp was watching her?

Not often; countable times, times I could count up myself if I could remember as the Wasp could. Not often. Not always.

"There's a problem," I said to the director.

"It's peaked out, has it?" he said. "That definition problem?"

"Well, no," I said. "Actually, it's gotten worse."

He was sitting behind his desk, arms spread wide across his chair's back, and a false, pinkish flush to his cheeks like undertaker's makeup. Drinking.

"Hasn't peaked out, huh?" he said.

"That's not the problem," I said. "The problem is the access. It's not random like you said."

"Molecular level," he said. "It's in the physics."

"You don't understand. It's not getting more random. It's getting less random. It's getting selective. It's freezing up."

"No no no," he said dreamily. "Access is random. Life isn't all summer and fun, you know. Into each life some rain must fall."

I sputtered, trying to explain. "But but but . . ."

"You know," he said. "I've been thinking of getting out of access." He pulled open a drawer in the desk before him; it made an empty sound. He stared within it dully for a moment, and shut it. "The Park's been good for me, but I'm just not used to this. Used to be you thought you could render a service, you know? Well, hell, you know, you've had fun, what do you care."

He *was* mad. For an instant I heard the dead around me; I tasted on my tongue the stale air of underground.

"I remember," he said, tilting back in his chair and looking elsewhere, "many years ago, I got into access. Only we didn't call it that then. What I did was, I worked for a stock-footage house. It was going out of business like they all did, like this place here is going to do, shouldn't say that, but you didn't hear it. Anyway, it was a big warehouse with steel shelves for miles, filled with film cans, film cans filled with old plastic film, you know? Film of every kind. And movie people, if they wanted old scenes of past time in their movies, would call up and ask for what they wanted, find me this, find me that. And we had everything, every kind of scene, but you know what the hardest thing to find was? Just ordinary scenes of daily life. I mean people just doing things and living their lives. You know what we *did* have? Speeches. People giving speeches. Like presidents. You could have hours of speeches, but not just people, whatchacallit, oh, washing clothes, sitting in a park . . ."

"It might just be the reception," I said. "Somehow."

He looked at me for a long moment as though I had just arrived. "Anyway," he said at last, turning away again, "I was there awhile learning the ropes. And producers called and said, 'Get me this, get me that.' And one producer was making a film, some film of the past, and he wanted old scenes, *old*, of people long ago, in the summer; having fun; eating ice cream; swimming in bathing suits; riding in convertibles. Fifty years ago. Eighty years ago."

He opened his empty drawer again, found a toothpick, and began to use it.

"So I accessed the earliest stuff. Speeches. More speeches. But I found a scene here and there—people in the street, fur coats, window-shopping, traffic. Old people, I mean they were young then, but people of the past; they have these pinched kind of faces, you get to know them. Sad, a little. On city streets, hurrying, holding their hats. Cities were sort of black then, in film; black cars in the streets, black derby hats. Stone.

"Well, it wasn't what they wanted. I found summer for them, color summer, but new. They wanted old. I kept looking back. I kept looking. I did. The further back I went, the more I saw these pinched faces, black cars, black streets of stone. Snow. There isn't any summer there."

With slow gravity he rose and found a brown bottle and two coffee cups. He poured sloppily. "So it's not your reception," he said. "Film takes longer, I guess, but it's the physics. All in the physics. A word to the wise is sufficient."

The liquor was harsh, a cold distillate of past sunlight. I wanted to go, get out, not look back. I would not stay watching until there was only snow.

"So I'm getting out of access," the director said. "Let the dead bury the dead, right? Let the dead bury the dead."

I didn't go back. I never went back, though the highways opened again and The Park isn't far from the town I've settled in. Settled; the right word. It restores your balance, in the end, even in a funny way your cheerfulness, when you come to know, without regrets, that the best thing that's going to happen in your life has already happened. And I still have some summer left to me.

I think there are two different kinds of memory, and only one kind gets worse as I get older: the kind where, by an effort of will, you can reconstruct your first car or your Service serial number or the name and figure of your high school physics teacher—a Mr. Holm, in a gray suit, a bearded guy, skinny, about thirty. The other kind doesn't worsen; if anything it grows more intense. The sleepwalking kind, the kind you stumble into as into rooms with secret doors and suddenly find yourself sitting not on your front porch but in a classroom, you can't at first think where or when, and a bearded, smiling man is turning in his hand a glass paperweight, inside which a little cottage stands in a swirl of snow.

There is no access to Georgie, except that now and then, unpredictably, when I'm sitting on the porch or pushing a grocery cart or standing at the sink, a memory of that kind will visit me, vivid and startling, like a hypnotist's snap of fingers. Or like that funny experience you sometimes have, on the point of sleep, of hearing your name called softly and distinctly by someone who is not there.

the winter market

WILLIAM GIBSON

William Gibson won the Nebula Award, the Hugo Award, and the Philip K. Dick Award in 1985 for his remarkable first novel *Neuromancer*—a rise to prominence as fiery and meteoric as any in SF history. Gibson sold his first story in 1977 to the now-defunct semiprozine *Unearth*, but it was seen by practically no one, and Gibson's name remained generally unknown until 1981, when he sold to *Omni* a taut and suspenseful thriller called "Johnny Mnemonic," a Nebula finalist that year. He followed it up in 1982 with another and even more compelling *Omni* story called "Burning Chrome," which was also a Nebula finalist . . . and all at once Gibson was very much a writer to watch.

Those watching him did not have long to wait. By the late '80s, the appearance of *Neuromancer* and its sequels, *Count Zero* and *Mona Lisa Overdrive*, had made him the most talked-about and controversial (at the heart of the Cyberpunk Wars of the '80s, although he mostly stayed aloof from the actual fighting in the trenches) new SF writer of the decade—one might almost say "writer," leaving out the "SF" part, for Gibson's reputation spread far outside the usual boundaries of the genre, with wildly enthusiastic notices about him and interviews with him appearing in places like *Rolling Stone*, *Spin*, and *The Village Voice*, and with pop-culture figures like Timothy Leary (not someone ordinarily much given to close observation of the SF world) embracing him with open arms.

By now, Gibson is a full-fledged cultural icon, a best-selling author whose novels get respectful feature reviews in places like *The New York Times* and *The Washington Post* and whose stories get made into big-budget major motion pictures, someone who has had a full-length documentary film made about him and who is practically worshiped as a god in SF circles in Japan, and someone whose early work has been imitated hundreds of times, not only in print science fiction but in comics, movies, and even weekly television shows.

Some are no doubt jealous of his success, but even most of them would probably admit, when forced to it, that Gibson is the kind of major talent that comes along maybe once or twice in a literary generation . . . and has earned his accolades.

Gibson's other books include *Virtual Light*, *Idoru*, and *All Tomorrow's Parties*, and a novel written in collaboration with Bruce Sterling, *The Difference Engine*. His short fiction has been collected in *Burning Chrome*. His latest book is another best-selling novel, *Pattern Recognition*. Born in South Carolina, he now lives in Vancouver, Canada, with his wife and family.

In the gripping story that follows, he suggests that people who know *exactly* what they want can be a little frightening—particularly if they need *you* to get it for them. . . .

It rains a lot, up here; there are winter days when it doesn't really get light at all, only a bright, indeterminate gray. But then there are days when it's like they whip aside a curtain to flash you three minutes of sunlit, suspended mountain, the trademark at the start of God's own movie. It was like that the day her agents phoned, from deep in the heart of their mirrored pyramid on Beverly Boulevard, to tell me she'd merged with the net, crossed over for good, that *Kings of Sleep* was going triple-platinum. I'd edited most of *Kings*, done the brain-map work and gone over it all with the fast-wipe module, so I was in line for a share of royalties.

No, I said, no. Then yes, yes, and hung up on them. Got my jacket and took the stairs three at a time, straight out to the nearest bar and an eight-hour blackout that ended on a concrete ledge two meters above midnight. False Creek water. City lights, that same gray bowl of sky smaller now, illuminated by neon and mercury-vapor arcs. And it was snowing, big flakes but not many, and when they touched black water, they were gone, no trace at all. I looked down at my feet and saw my toes clear of the edge of concrete, the water between them. I was wearing Japanese shoes, new and expensive, glove-leather Ginza monkey boots with rubber-capped toes. I stood there for a long time before I took that first step back.

Because she was dead, and I'd let her go. Because, now, she was immortal, and I'd helped her get that way. And because I knew she'd phone me, in the morning.

My father was an audio engineer, a mastering engineer. He went way back, in the business, even before digital. The processes he was concerned with were partly mechanical, with that clunky quasi-Victorian quality you see in twentieth-century technology. He was a lathe operator, basically. People brought him audio recordings and he burned their sounds into grooves on a disk of lacquer. Then the disk was electroplated and used in the construction of a press that would stamp out records, the black things you see in antique stores. And I remember him telling me, once, a few months before he died, that certain frequencies—transients, I think he called them—could easily burn out the head, the cutting head, on a master lathe. These heads were incredibly expensive, so you prevented burnouts with something called an accelerometer. And that was what I was thinking of, as I stood there, my toes out over the water: that head, burning out.

Because that was what they did to her.

And that was what she wanted.

No accelerometer for Lise.

I disconnected my phone on my way to bed. I did it with the business end of a West German studio tripod that was going to cost a week's wages to repair.

Woke some strange time later and took a cab back to Granville Island and Rubin's place.

Rubin, in some way that no one quite understands, is a master, a teacher, what the Japanese call a *sensei*. What he's the master of, really, is garbage, kipple, refuse, the sea of cast-off goods our century floats on. *Gomi no sensei*. Master of junk.

I found him, this time, squatting between two vicious-looking drum machines I hadn't seen before, rusty spider arms folded at the hearts of dented constellations of steel cans fished out of Richmond dumpsters. He never calls the place a studio, never refers to himself as an artist. "Messing around," he calls what he does there, and seems to view it as some extension of boyhood's perfectly bored backyard afternoons. He wanders through his jammed, littered space, a kind of minihangar cobbled to the water side of the Market, followed by the smarter and more agile of his creations, like some vaguely benign Satan bent on the elaboration of still stranger processes in his ongoing Inferno of *gomi*. I've seen Rubin program his constructions to identify and verbally abuse pedestrians wearing garments by a given season's hot designer; others attend to more obscure missions, and a few seem constructed solely to deconstruct themselves with as much attendant noise as possible. He's like a child, Rubin; he's also worth a lot of money in galleries in Tokyo and Paris.

So I told him about Lise. He let me do it, get it out, then nodded. "I know," he said. "Some CBC creep phoned eight times." He sipped something out of a dented cup. "You wanna Wild Turkey sour?"

"Why'd they call you?"

" 'Cause my name's on the back of *Kings of Sleep*. Dedication."

"I didn't see it yet."

"She try to call you yet?"

"No."

"She will."

"Rubin, she's dead. They cremated her already."

"I know," he said. "And she's going to call you."

Gomi.

Where does the *gomi* stop and the world begin? The Japanese, a century ago, had already run out of *gomi* space around Tokyo, so they came up with a plan for creating space out of *gomi*. By the year 1969 they had built themselves a little island in Tokyo Bay, out of *gomi*, and christened it Dream Island. But the city was still pouring out its nine thousand tons per day, so they went on to build New Dream Island, and today they coordinate the whole process, and new Nippons rise out of the Pacific. Rubin watches this on the news and says nothing at all.

He has nothing to say about *gomi*. It's his medium, the air he breathes, something he's swum in all his life. He cruises Greater Van in a spavined truck-thing chopped down from an ancient Mercedes airporter, its roof lost under a wallowing rubber bag half-filled with natural gas. He looks for things that fit some strange design scrawled on the inside of his forehead by whatever serves him as Muse. He brings home more *gomi*. Some of it still operative. Some of it, like Lise, human.

I met Lise at one of Rubin's parties. Rubin had a lot of parties. He never seemed particularly to enjoy them, himself, but they were excellent parties. I lost track, that fall, of the number of times I woke on a slab of foam to the roar of Rubin's antique espresso machine, a tarnished behemoth topped with a big chrome eagle, the sound outrageous off the corrugated steel walls of the place, but massively comforting, too: There was coffee. Life would go on.

First time I saw her: in the Kitchen Zone. You wouldn't call it a kitchen, exactly, just three fridges and a hot plate and a broken convection oven that had come in with the *gomi*. First time I saw her: She had the all-beer fridge open, light spilling out, and I caught the cheekbones and the determined set of that mouth, but I also caught the black glint of polycarbon at her wrist, and the bright slick sore the ex-oskeleton had rubbed there. Too drunk to process, to know what it was, but I did know it wasn't party time. So I did what people usually did, to Lise, and clicked myself into a different movie. Went for the wine instead, on the counter beside the convection oven. Never looked back.

But she found me again. Came after me two hours later, weaving through the bodies and junk with that terrible grace programmed into the exoskeleton. I knew what it was, then, as I watched her homing in, too embarrassed now to duck it, to run, to mumble some excuse and get out. Pinned there, my arm around the waist of a girl I didn't know, while Lise advanced—*was advanced*, with that mocking grace—straight at me now, her eyes burning with wizz, and the girl had wriggled out and away in a quiet social panic, was gone, and Lise stood there in front of me, propped up in her pencil-thin polycarbon prosthetic. Looked into those eyes and it was like you could hear her synapses whining, some impossibly high-pitched scream as the wizz opened every circuit in her brain.

"Take me home," she said, and the words hit me like a whip. I think I shook my head. "Take me home." There were levels of pain there, and subtlety, and an amazing cruelty. And I knew then that I'd never been hated, ever, as deeply or thoroughly as this wasted little girl hated me now, hated me for the way I'd looked, then looked away, beside Rubin's all-beer refrigerator.

So—if that's the word—I did one of those things you do and never find out why, even though something in you knows you could never have done anything else.

I took her home.

I have two rooms in an old condo rack at the corner of Fourth and MacDonald, tenth floor. The elevators usually work, and if you sit on the balcony railing and lean out backward, holding on to the corner of the building next door, you can see a little upright slit of sea and mountain.

She hadn't said a word, all the way back from Rubin's, and I was getting sober enough to feel very, uneasy as I unlocked the door and let her in.

The first thing she saw was the portable fast-wipe I'd brought home from the Pilot the night before. The exoskeleton carried her across the dusty broadloom with that same walk, like a model down a runway. Away from the crash of the party, I could hear it click softly as it moved her. She stood there, looking down at the fast-wipe. I could see the thing's ribs when she stood like that, make them out across her back through the scuffed black leather of her jacket. One of those diseases. Either one of the old ones they've never quite figured out or one of the new ones—the all too obviously environmental kind—that they've barely even named yet. She couldn't move, not without that extra skeleton, and it was jacked straight into her brain, myoelectric interface. The fragile-looking polycarbon braces moved her arms and legs, but a more subtle system handled her thin hands, galvanic inlays. I thought of frog legs twitching in a high-school lab tape, then hated myself for it.

"This is a fast-wipe module," she said, in a voice I hadn't heard before, distant, and I thought then that the wizz might be wearing off. "What's it doing here?"

"I edit," I said, closing the door behind me.

"Well, now," and she laughed. "You do. Where?"

"On the Island. Place called the Autonomic Pilot."

She turned; then, hand on thrust hip, she swung—it swung her—and the wizz and the hate and some terrible parody of lust stabbed out at me from those washed-out gray eyes. "You wanna make it, editor?"

And I felt the whip come down again, but I wasn't going to take it, not again. So I cold-eyed her from somewhere down in the beer-numb core of my walking, talking, live-limbed, and entirely ordinary body and the words came out of me like spit: "Could you feel it, if I did?"

Beat. Maybe she blinked, but her face never registered. "No," she said, "but sometimes I like to watch."

Rubin stands at the window, two days after her death in Los Angeles, watching snow fall into False Creek. "So you never went to bed with her?"

One of his push-me-pull-you's, little roller-bearing Escher lizards, scoots across the table in front of me, in curl-up mode.

"No," I say, and it's true. Then I laugh. "But we jacked straight across. That first night."

"You were crazy," he says, a certain approval in his voice. "It might have killed you. Your heart might have stopped, you might have stopped breathing. . . ." He turns back to the window. "Has she called you yet?"

We jacked, straight across.

I'd never done it before. If you'd asked me why, I would have told you that I was an editor and that it wasn't professional.

The truth would be something more like this.

In the trade, the legitimate trade—I've never done porno—we call the raw product dry dreams. Dry dreams are neural output from levels of consciousness that most people can only access in sleep. But artists, the kind I work with at the Autonomic Pilot, are able to break the surface tension, dive down deep, down and out, out into Jung's sea, and bring back—well, dreams. Keep it simple. I guess some artists have always done that, in whatever medium, but neuroelectronics lets us access the experience, and the net gets it all out on the wire, so we can package it, sell it, watch how it moves in the market. Well, the more things change . . . That's something my father liked to say.

Ordinarily I get the raw material in a studio situation, filtered through several million dollars' worth of baffles, and I don't even have to see the artist. The stuff we get out to the consumer, you see, has been structured, balanced, turned into art. There are still people naive enough to assume that they'll actually enjoy jacking straight across with someone they love. I think most teenagers try it, once. Certainly it's easy enough to do; Radio Shack will sell you the box and the trodes and the cables. But me, I'd never done it. And now that I think about it, I'm not so sure I can explain why. Or that I even want to try.

I do know why I did it with Lise, sat down beside her on my Mexican futon and snapped the optic lead into the socket on the spine, the smooth dorsal ridge, of the exoskeleton. It was high up, at the base of her neck, hidden by her dark hair.

Because she claimed she was an artist, and because I knew that we were engaged, somehow, in total combat, and I was *not* going to lose. That may not make sense to you, but then you never knew her, or know her through *Kings of Sleep*, which isn't the same at all. You never felt that hunger she had, which was pared down to a dry need, hideous in its singleness of purpose. People who know *exactly* what they want have always frightened me, and Lise had known what she wanted for a long time, and wanted nothing else at all. And I was scared, then, of admitting to myself that I was scared, and I'd seen enough strangers' dreams, in the mixing room at the Autonomic Pilot, to know that most people's inner monsters are foolish things, ludicrous in the calm light of one's own consciousness. And I was still drunk.

I put the trodes on and reached for the stud on the fast-wipe. I'd shut down its studio functions, temporarily converting eighty thousand dollars' worth of Japanese electronics to the equivalent of one of those little Radio Shack boxes. "Hit it," I said, and touched the switch.

Words. Words cannot. Or, maybe, just barely, if I even knew how to begin to describe it, what came up out of her, what she did . . .

There's a segment on *Kings of Sleep*; it's like you're on a motorcycle at midnight, no lights but somehow you don't need them, blasting out along a cliff-high stretch of coast highway, so fast that you hang there in a cone of silence, the bike's thunder lost behind you. Everything, lost behind you. . . . It's just a blink, on *Kings*, but it's one of the thousand things you remember, go back to, incorporate into your own vocabulary of feelings. Amazing. Freedom and death, right there, right there, razor's edge, forever.

What I got was the big-daddy version of that, raw rush, the king hell killer uncut real thing, exploding eight ways from Sunday into a void that stank of poverty and lovelessness and obscurity.

And that was Lise's ambition, that rush, *seen from the inside*.

It probably took all of four seconds.

And, course, she'd won.

I took the trodes off and stared at the wall, eyes wet, the framed posters swimming. I couldn't look at her. I heard her disconnect the optic lead. I heard the exoskeleton creak as it hoisted her up from the futon. Heard it tick demurely as it hauled her into the kitchen for a glass of water.

Then I started to cry.

Rubin inserts a skinny probe in the roller-bearing belly of a sluggish push-me-pull-you and peers at the circuitry through magnifying glasses with miniature headlights mounted at the temples.

"So? You got hooked." He shrugs, looks up. It's dark now and the twin tensor beams stab at my face, chill damp in his steel barn and the lonesome hoot of a foghorn from somewhere across the water. "So?"

My turn to shrug. "I just did. . . . There didn't seem to be anything else to do."

The beams duck back to the silicon heart of his defective toy. "Then you're okay. It was a true choice. What I mean is, she was set to be what she is. You had about as much to do with where she's at today as that fast-wipe module did. She'd have found somebody else if she hadn't found you. . . ."

I made a deal with Barry, the senior editor, got twenty minutes at five on a cold September morning. Lise came in and hit me with that same shot, but this time I was ready, with my baffles and brain maps, and I didn't have to feel it. It took me two weeks, piecing out the minutes in the editing room, to cut what she'd done down into something I could play for Max Bell, who owns the Pilot.

Bell hadn't been happy, not happy at all, as I explained what I'd done. Maverick editors can be a problem, and eventually most editors decide that they've found someone who'll be it, the next monster, and then they start wasting time and money. He'd nodded when I'd finished my pitch, then scratched his nose with the cap of his red feltpen. "Uh-huh. Got it. Hottest thing since fish grew legs, right?"

But he'd jacked it, the demo soft I'd put together, and when it clicked out of its slot in his Braun desk unit, he was staring at the wall, his face blank.

"Max?"

"Huh?"

"What do you think?"

"Think? I . . . What did you say her name was?" He blinked. "Lisa? Who you say she's signed with?"

"Lise. Nobody, Max. She hasn't signed with anybody yet."

"Jesus Christ." He still looked blank.

"You know how I found her?" Rubin asks, wading through ragged cardboard boxes to find the light switch. The boxes are filled with carefully sorted *gomi*: lithium batteries, tantalum capacitors, RF connectors, breadboards, barrier strips, ferroresonant transformers, spools of bus bar wire. . . . One box is filled with the severed heads of hundreds of Barbie dolls, another with armored industrial safety gauntlets that look like space-suit gloves. Light floods the room and a sort of Kandinski mantis in snipped and painted tin swings its golfball-size head toward the bright bulb. "I was down Granville on a *gomi* run, back in an alley, and I found her just sitting there. Caught the skeleton and she didn't look so good, so I asked her if she was okay. Nothin'. Just closed her eyes. Not my lookout, I think. But I happen back by there about four hours later and she hasn't moved. 'Look, honey,' I tell her, 'maybe your hardware's buggered up. I can help you, okay?' Nothin'. 'How long you been back here?' Nothin'. So I take off." He crosses to his workbench and strokes the thin metal limbs of the mantis thing with a pale forefinger. Behind the bench, hung on damp-swollen sheets of ancient pegboard, are pliers, screwdrivers, tie-wrap guns, a rusted Daisy BB rifle, coax strippers, crimpers, logic probes, heat guns, a pocket oscilloscope, seemingly every tool in human history, with no attempt ever made to order them at all, though I've yet to see Rubin's hand hesitate.

"So I went back," he says. "Gave it an hour. She was out by then, unconscious, so I brought her back here and ran a check on the exoskeleton. Batteries were dead. She'd crawled back there when the juice ran out and settled down to starve to death, I guess."

"When was that?"

"About a week before you took her home."

"But what if she'd died? If you hadn't found her?"

"Somebody was going to find her. She couldn't *ask* for anything, you know? Just *take*. Couldn't stand a favor."

Max found the agents for her, and a trio of awesomely slick junior partners Leared into YVR a day later. Lise wouldn't come down to the Pilot to meet them, insisted we bring them up to Rubin's, where she still slept.

"Welcome to Couverville," Rubin said as they edged in the door. His long face was smeared with grease, the fly of his ragged fatigue pants held more or less shut with a twisted paper clip. The boys grinned automatically, but there was something marginally more authentic about the girl's smile. "Mr. Stark," she said, "I was in London last week. I saw your installation at the Tate."

"*Marcello's Battery Factory*," Rubin said. "They say it's scatological, the Brits. . . ." He shrugged. "Brits. I mean, who knows?"

"They're right. It's also very funny."

The boys were beaming like table-tanned lighthouses, standing there in their suits. The demo had reached Los Angeles. They knew.

"And you're Lise," she said, negotiating the path between Rubin's heaped *gomi*. "You're going to be a very famous person soon, Lise. We have a lot to discuss. . . ."

And Lise just stood there, propped in polycarbon, and the look on her face was the one I'd seen that first night, in my condo, when she'd asked me if I wanted to go to bed. But if the junior agent lady saw it, she didn't show it. She was a pro.

I told myself that I was a pro, too.

I told myself to relax.

Trash fires gutter in steel canisters around the Market. The snow still falls and kids huddle over the flames like arthritic crows, hopping from foot to foot, wind whipping their dark coats. Up in Fairview's arty slum-tumble, someone's laundry has frozen solid on the line, pink squares of bedsheet standing out against the background dinge and the confusion of satellite dishes and solar panels. Some ecologist's egg-beater windmill goes round and round, round and round, giving a whirling finger to the Hydro rates.

Rubin clumps along in paint-spattered L. L. Bean gumshoes, his big head pulled down into an oversize fatigue jacket. Sometimes one of the hunched teens will point him out as we pass, the guy who builds all the crazy stuff, the robots and shit.

"You know what your trouble is?" he says when we're under the bridge, headed up to Fourth. "You're the kind who *always reads the handbook.* Anything people build, any kind of technology, it's going to have some specific purpose. It's for doing something that somebody already understands. But if it's new technology, it'll open areas nobody's ever thought of before. You read the manual, man, and you won't play around with it, not the same way. And you get all funny when somebody else uses it to do something you never thought of. Like Lise."

"She wasn't the first." Traffic drums past overhead.

"No, but she's sure as hell the first person *you* ever met who went and translated themself into a hardwired program. You lose any sleep when whatsisname did it, three-four years ago, the French kid, the writer?"

"I didn't really think about it, much. A gimmick. PR . . ."

"He's still writing. The weird thing is, he's going to *be* writing, unless somebody blows up his mainframe. . . ."

I wince, shake my head. "But it's not *him*, is it? It's just a program."

"Interesting point. Hard to say. With Lise, though, we find out. She's not a writer."

She had it all in there, *Kings*, locked up in her head the way her body was locked in that exoskeleton.

The agents signed her with a label and brought in a production team from Tokyo. She told them she wanted me to edit. I said no; Max dragged me into his office and threatened to fire me on the spot. If I wasn't involved, there was no reason to do the studio work at the Pilot. Vancouver was hardly the center of the world, and the agents wanted her in Los Angeles. It meant a lot of money to him, and it might put the Autonomic Pilot on the map. I couldn't explain to him why I'd refused. It was too crazy, too personal; she was getting a final dig in. Or that's what I thought then. But Max was serious. He really didn't give me any choice. We both knew another job wasn't going to crawl into my hand. I went back out with him and we told the agents that we'd worked it out: I was on.

The agents showed us lots of teeth.

Lise pulled out an inhaler full of wizz and took a huge hit. I thought I saw the agent lady raise one perfect eyebrow, but that was the extent of censure. After the papers were signed, Lise more or less did what she wanted.

And Lise always knew what she wanted.

We did *Kings* in three weeks, the basic recording. I found any number of reasons to avoid Rubin's place, even believed some of them myself. She was still staying there, although the agents weren't too happy with what they saw as a total lack of security. Rubin told me later that he'd had to have *his* agent call them up and raise hell, but after that they seemed to quit worrying. I hadn't known that Rubin had an agent. It was always easy to forget that Rubin Stark was more famous, then, than anyone else I knew, certainly more famous than I thought Lise was ever likely to become. I knew we were working on something strong, but you never know how big anything's liable to be.

But the time I spent in the Pilot, I was *on*. Lise was amazing.

It was like she was born to the form, even though the technology that made that form possible hadn't even existed when she was born. You see something like that and you wonder how many thousands, maybe millions, of phenomenal artists have died mute, down the centuries, people who could never have been poets or painters or saxophone players, but who had this stuff inside, these psychic waveforms waiting for the circuitry required to tap in. . . .

I learned a few things about her, incidentals, from our time in the studio. That she was born in Windsor. That her father was American and served in Peru and came home crazy and half-blind. That whatever was wrong with her body was congenital. That she had those sores because she refused to remove the exoskeleton, ever, because she'd start to choke and die at the thought of that utter helplessness. That she was addicted to wizz and doing enough of it daily to wire a football team.

Her agents brought in medics, who padded the polycarbon with foam and sealed the sores over with micropore dressings. They pumped her up with vitamins and tried to work on her diet, but nobody ever tried to take that inhaler away.

They brought in hairdressers and makeup artists, too, and wardrobe people and image builders and articulate little PR hamsters, and she endured it with something that might almost have been a smile.

And, right through those three weeks, we didn't talk. Just studio talk, artist-editor stuff, very much a restricted code. Her imagery was so strong, so extreme, that she never really needed to explain a given effect to me. I took what she put out and worked with it, and jacked it back to her. She'd either say yes or no, and usually it was yes. The agents noted this and approved, and clapped Max Bell on the back and took him out to dinner, and my salary went up.

And I was pro, all the way. Helpful and thorough and polite. I was determined not to crack again, and never thought about the night I cried, and I was also doing the best work I'd ever done, and knew it, and that's a high in itself.

And then, one morning, about six, after a long, long session—when she'd first gotten that eerie cotillion sequence out, the one the kids call the Ghost Dance—she spoke to me. One of the two agent boys had been there, showing teeth, but he was gone now and the Pilot was dead quiet, just the hum of a blower somewhere down by Max's office.

"Casey," she said, her voice hoarse with the wizz, "sorry I hit on you so hard."

I thought for a minute she was telling me something about the recording we'd just made. I looked up and saw her there, and it struck me that we were alone, and hadn't been alone since we'd made the demo.

I had no idea at all what to say. Didn't even know what I felt.

Propped up in the exoskeleton, she was looking worse than she had that first night, at Rubin's. The wizz was eating her, under the stuff the makeup team kept smoothing on, and sometimes it was like seeing a death's-head surface beneath the face of a not very handsome teenager. I had no idea of her real age. Not old, not young.

"The ramp effect," I said, coiling a length of cable.

"What's that?"

"Nature's way of telling you to clean up your act. Sort of mathematical law, says you can only get off real good on a stimulant x number of times, even if you increase the doses. But you can't *ever* get off as nice as you did the first few times. Or you shouldn't be able to, anyway. That's the trouble with designer drugs; they're too clever. That stuff you're doing has some tricky tail on one of its molecules, keeps you from turning the decomposed adrenaline into adrenochrome. If it didn't, you'd be schizophrenic by now. You got any little problems, Lise? Like apneia? Sometimes maybe you stop breathing if you go to sleep?"

But I wasn't even sure I felt the anger that I heard in my own voice.

She stared at me with those pale gray eyes. The wardrobe people had replaced her thrift-shop jacket with a butter-tanned matte black blouson that did a better job of hiding the polycarbon ribs. She kept it zipped to the neck, always, even though it was too warm in the studio. The hairdressers had tried something new the day before, and it hadn't worked out, her rough dark hair a lopsided explosion above that drawn, triangular face. She stared at me and I felt it again, her singleness of purpose.

"I don't sleep, Casey."

It wasn't until later, much later, that I remembered she'd told me she was sorry. She never did again, and it was the only time I ever heard her say anything that seemed to be out of character.

Rubin's diet consists of vending-machine sandwiches, Pakistani takeout food, and espresso. I've never seen him eat anything else. We eat samosas in a narrow shop on Fourth that has a single plastic table wedged between the counter and the door to the can. Rubin eats his dozen samosas, six meat and six veggie, with total concentration, one after another, and doesn't bother to wipe his chin. He's devoted to the place. He loathes the Greek counterman; it's mutual, a real relationship. If the counterman left, Rubin might not come back. The Greek glares at the crumbs on Rubin's chin and jacket. Between samosas, he shoots daggers right back, his eyes narrowed behind the smudged lenses of his steel-rimmed glasses.

The samosas are dinner. Breakfast will be egg salad on dead white bread, packed in one of those triangles of milky plastic, on top of six little cups of poisonously strong espresso.

"You didn't see it coming, Casey." He peers at me out of the thumbprinted depths of his glasses. "'Cause you're no good at lateral thinking. You read the handbook. What else did you think she was after? Sex? More wizz? A world tour? She was past all that. That's what made her so strong. She was past it. That's why *Kings of Sleep*'s as big as it is, and why the kids buy it, why they *believe* it. They know. Those kids back down the Market, warming their butts around the fires and wondering if they'll find someplace to sleep tonight, they believe it. It's the hottest soft in eight years. Guy at a shop on Granville told me he gets more of the damned things lifted than he sells of anything else. Says it's a hassle to even stock it. . . . She's big because she was what they are, only more so. She knew, man. No dreams, no hope. You can't see the cages on those kids, Casey, but more and more they're twigging to it, that they aren't going *anywhere*." He brushes a greasy crumb of meat from his chin, missing three more. "So she sang it for them, said it the way they can't, painted them a picture. And she used the money to buy herself a way out, that's all."

I watch the steam bead and roll down the window in big drops, streaks in the condensation. Beyond the window I can make out a partially stripped Lada, wheels scavenged, axles down on the pavement.

"How many people have done it, Rubin? Have any idea?"

"Not too many. Hard to say, anyway, because a lot of them are probably politicians we think of as being comfortably and reliably dead." He gives me a funny look. "Not a nice thought. Anyway, they had first shot at the technology. It still costs too much for any ordinary dozen millionaires, but I've heard of at least seven. They say Mitsubishi did it to Weinberg before his immune system finally went tits up. He was head of their hybridoma lab in Okayama. Well, their stock's still pretty high, in monoclonals, so maybe it's true. And Langlais, the French kid, the novelist . . ." He shrugs. "Lise didn't have the money for it. Wouldn't now, even. But she put herself in the right place at the right time. She was about to croak, she was in Hollywood, and they could already see what *Kings* was going to do."

The day we finished up, the band stepped, off a JAL shuttle out of London, four skinny kids who operated like a well-oiled machine and displayed a hypertrophied fashion sense and a total lack of affect. I set them up in a row at the Pilot, in identical white Ikea office chairs, smeared saline paste on their temples, taped the trodes on, and ran the rough version of what was going to become *Kings of Sleep*. When they came out of it, they all started talking at once, ignoring me totally, in the British version of that secret language all studio musicians speak, four sets of pale hands zooming and chopping the air.

I could catch enough of it to decide that they were excited. That they thought it was good. So I got my jacket and left. They could wipe their own saline paste off, thanks.

And that night I saw Lise for the last time, though I didn't plan to.

Walking back down to the Market, Rubin noisily digesting his meal, red taillights reflected on wet cobbles, the city beyond the Market a clean sculpture of light, a lie, where the broken and the lost burrow into the *gomi* that grows like humus at the bases of the towers of glass . . .

"I gotta go to Frankfurt tomorrow, do an installation. You wanna come? I could write you off as a technician." He shrugs his way deeper into the fatigue jacket. "Can't pay you, but you can have airfare, you want . . ."

Funny offer, from Rubin, and I know it's because he's worried about me, thinks I'm too strange about Lise, and it's the only thing he can think of, getting me out of town.

"It's colder in Frankfurt now than it is here."

"You maybe need a change, Casey. I dunno . . ."

"Thanks, but Max has a lot of work lined up. Pilot's a big deal now, people flying in from all over . . ."

"Sure."

When I left the band at the Pilot, I went home. Walked up to Fourth and took the trolley home, past the windows of the shops I see every day, each one lit up jazzy and slick, clothes and shoes and software, Japanese motorcycles crouched like clean enamel scorpions, Italian furniture. The windows change with the seasons, the shops come and go. We were into the preholiday mode now, and there were more people on the street, a lot of couples, walking quickly and purposefully past the bright windows, on their way to score that perfect little whatever for whomever, half the girls in those padded thigh-high nylon boot things that came out of New York the winter before, the ones that Rubin said made them look like they had elephantiasis. I grinned, thinking about that, and suddenly it hit me that it really was over, that I was done with Lise, and that now she'd be sucked off to Hollywood as inexorably as if she'd poked her toe into a black hole, drawn down by the unthinkable gravitic tug of Big Money. Believing that, that she was gone—probably *was* gone, by then—I let down some kind of guard in myself and felt the edges of my pity. But just the edges, because I didn't want my evening screwed up by anything. I wanted partytime. It had been a while.

Got off at my corner and the elevator worked on the first try. Good sign, I told myself. Upstairs, I undressed and showered, found a clean shirt, microwaved burritos. Feel normal, I advised my reflection while I shaved. You have been working too hard. Your credit cards have gotten fat. Time to remedy that.

The burritos tasted like cardboard, but I decided I liked them because they were so aggressively normal. My car was in Burnaby, having its leaky hydrogen cell repacked, so I wasn't going to have to worry about driving. I could go out, find partytime, and phone in sick in the morning. Max wasn't going to kick; I was his star boy. He owed me.

You owe me, Max, I said to the subzero bottle of Moskovskaya I fished out of the freezer. Do you ever owe me. I have just spent three weeks editing the dreams and nightmares of one very screwed up person, Max. On your behalf. So that you can grow and prosper, Max. I poured three fingers of vodka into a plastic glass left over from a party I'd thrown the year before and went back into the living room.

Sometimes it looks to me like nobody in particular lives there. Not that it's that messy; I'm a good if somewhat robotic housekeeper, and even remember to dust the tops of framed posters and things, but I have these times when the place abruptly gives me a kind of low-grade chill, with its basic accumulation of basic consumer goods. I mean, it's not like I want to fill it up with cats or houseplants or anything, but there are moments when I see that anyone could be living there, could own those things, and it all seems sort of interchangeable, my life and yours, my life and anybody's. . . .

I think Rubin sees things that way, too, all the time, but for him it's a source of strength. He lives in other people's garbage, and everything he drags home must have been new and shiny once, must have meant something, however briefly, to someone. So he sweeps it all up into his crazy-looking truck and hauls it back to his place and lets it compost there until he thinks of something new to do with it. Once he was showing me a book of twentieth-century art he liked, and there was a picture of an automated sculpture called *Dead Birds Fly Again*, a thing that whirled real dead birds around and around on a string, and he smiled and nodded, and I could see he felt the artist was a spiritual ancestor of some kind. But what could Rubin do with my framed posters and my Mexican futon from the Bay and my temperfoam bed from Ikea? Well, I thought, taking a first chilly sip, he'd be able to think of something, which was why he was a famous artist and I wasn't.

I went and pressed my forehead against the plate-glass window, as cold as the glass in my hand. Time to go, I said to myself. You are exhibiting symptoms of urban singles angst. There are cures for this. Drink up. Go.

I didn't attain a state of partytime that night. Neither did I exhibit adult common sense and give up, go home, watch some ancient movie, and fall asleep on my futon. The tension those three weeks had built up in me drove me like the mainspring of a mechanical watch, and I went ticking off through nighttown, lubricating my more or less random progress with more drinks. It was one of those nights, I quickly decided, when you slip into an alternate continuum, a city that looks exactly like the one where you live, except for the peculiar difference that it contains not one person you love or know or have even spoken to before. Nights like that, you can go into a familiar bar and find that the staff has just been replaced; then you understand that your real motive in going there was simply to see a familiar face, on a waitress or a bartender, whoever. . . . This sort of thing has been known to mediate against partytime.

I kept it rolling, though, through six or eight places, and eventually it rolled me into a West End club that looked as if it hadn't been redecorated since the Nineties. A lot of peeling chrome over plastic, blurry holograms that gave you a headache if you tried to make them out. I think Barry had told me about the place, but I can't imagine why. I looked around and grinned. If I was looking to be depressed, I'd come to the right place. Yes, I told myself as I took a corner stool at the bar, this was genuinely sad, really the pits. Dreadful enough to halt the momentum of my shitty evening, which was undoubtedly a good thing. I'd have one more for the road, admire the grot, and then cab it on home.

And then I saw Lise.

She hadn't seen me, not yet, and I still had my coat on, tweed collar up against the weather. She was down the bar and around the corner with a couple of empty drinks in front of her, big ones, the kind that come with little Hong Kong parasols or plastic mermaids in them, and as she looked up at the boy beside her, I saw the wizz flash in her eyes and knew that those drinks had never contained alcohol, because the levels of drug she was running couldn't tolerate the mix. The kid, though, was gone, numb grinning drunk and about ready to slide off his stool, and running on about something as he made repeated attempts to focus his eyes and get a better look at Lise, who sat there with her wardrobe team's black leather blouson zipped to her chin and her skull about to burn through her white face like a thousand-watt bulb. And seeing that, seeing her there, I knew a whole lot of things at once.

That she really was dying, either from the wizz or her disease or the combination of the two. That she damned well knew it. That the boy beside her was too drunk to have picked up on the exoskeleton, but not too drunk to register the expensive jacket and the money she had for drinks. And that what I was seeing was exactly what it looked like.

But I couldn't add it up, right away, couldn't compute. Something in me cringed.

And she was smiling, or anyway doing a thing she must have thought was like a smile, the expression she knew was appropriate to the situation, and nodding in time to the kid's slurred inanities, and that awful line of hers came back to me, the one about liking to watch.

And I know something now. I know that if I hadn't happened in there, hadn't seen them, I'd have been able to accept all that came later. Might even have found a way to rejoice on her behalf, or found a way to trust in whatever it is that she's since become, or had built in her image, a program that pretends to be Lise to the extent that it believes it's her. I could have believed what Rubin believes, that she was so truly past it, our hi-tech Saint Joan burning for union with that hardwired godhead in Hollywood, that nothing mattered to her except the hour of her departure. That she threw away that poor sad body with a cry of release, free of the bonds of polycarbon and hated flesh. Well, maybe, after all, she did. Maybe it was that way. I'm sure that's the way she expected it to be.

But seeing her there, that drunken kid's hand in hers, that hand she couldn't even feel, I knew, once and for all, that no human motive is ever entirely pure. Even Lise, with that corrosive, crazy drive to stardom and cybernetic immortality, had weaknesses. Was human in a way I hated myself for admitting.

She'd gone out that night, I knew, to kiss herself goodbye. To find someone drunk enough to do it for her. Because, I knew then, it was true: She did like to watch.

I think she saw me, as I left. I was practically running. If she did, I suppose she hated me worse than ever, for the horror and the pity in my face.

I never saw her again.

Someday I'll ask Rubin why Wild Turkey sours are the only drink he knows how to make. Industrial-strength, Rubin's sours. He passes me the dented aluminum cup, while his place ticks and stirs around us with the furtive activity of his smaller creations.

"You ought to come to Frankfurt," he says again.

"Why, Rubin?"

"Because pretty soon she's going to call you up. And I think maybe you aren't ready for it. You're still screwed up about this, and it'll sound like her and think like her, and you'll get too weird behind it. Come over to Frankfurt with me and you can get a little breathing space. She won't know you're there. . . ."

"I told you," I say, remembering her at the bar in that club, "lots of work. Max—"

"Stuff Max. Max you just made rich. Max can sit on his hands. You're rich yourself, from your royalty cut on *Kings*, if you weren't too stubborn to dial up your bank account. You can afford a vacation."

I look at him and wonder when I'll tell him the story of that final glimpse. "Rubin, I appreciate it, man, but I just . . ."

He sighs, drinks. "But what?"

"Rubin, if she calls me, is it *her*?"

He looks at me a long time. "God only knows." His cup clicks on the table. "I mean, Casey, the technology is there, so who, man, really who, is to say?"

"And you think I should come with you to Frankfurt?"

He takes off his steel-rimmed glasses and polishes them inefficiently on the front of his plaid flannel shirt. "Yeah, I do. You need the rest. Maybe you don't need it now, but you're going to, later."

"How's that?"

"When you have to edit her next release. Which will almost certainly be soon, because she needs money bad. She's taking up a lot of ROM on some corporate mainframe, and her share of *Kings* won't come close to paying for what they had to do to put her there. And you're her editor, Casey. I mean, who else?"

And I just stare at him as he puts the glasses back on, like I can't move at all.

"Who else, man?"

And one of his constructs clicks right then, just a clear and tiny sound, and it comes to me, he's right.

the pure product

JOHN KESSEL

Born in Buffalo, New York, John Kessel now lives with his family in Raleigh, North Carolina, where he is a professor of American Literature and the director of the creative writing program at North Carolina State University. Kessel made his first sale in 1975. His first solo novel, *Good News from Outer Space*, was released in 1988 to wide critical acclaim, but before that he had made his mark on the genre primarily as a writer of highly imaginative, finely crafted short stories, many of which have been assembled in his collection *Meeting in Infinity*. He won a Nebula Award in 1983 for his novella "Another Orphan," which was also a Hugo finalist that year, and has been released as an individual book. His story "Buffalo" won the Theodore Sturgeon Award in 1991, and his novella "Stories for Men" won the prestigious James Tiptree Jr. Memorial Award in 2003. His other books include the novel *Freedom Beach*, written in collaboration with James Patrick Kelly, and an anthology of stories from the famous Sycamore Hill Writers Workshop (which he also helps to run), called *Intersections*, co-edited by Mark L. Van Name and Richard Butner. His most recent books are a major novel, *Corrupting Dr. Nice*, and a new collection, *The Pure Product*. His stories have appeared in our First, Second (in collaboration with James Patrick Kelly), Fourth, Sixth, Eighth, Thirteenth, Fourteenth, Fifteenth, and Nineteenth through Twenty-first annual collections.

Here, in the story that announced (for me, anyway) Kessel's arrival as a really major talent, he takes us for a taut and hard-edged tour of modern-day America, in company with an unusual and spooky pair of tourists. . . .

I arrived in Kansas City at one o'clock on the afternoon of the thirteenth of August. A Tuesday. I was driving the beige 1983 Chevrolet Citation that I had stolen two days earlier in Pocatello, Idaho. The Kansas plates on the car I'd taken from a different car in a parking lot in Salt Lake City. Salt Lake City was founded by the Mormons, whose god tells them that in the future Jesus Christ will come again.

I drove through Kansas City with the windows open and the sun beating down through the windshield. The car had no air conditioning, and my shirt was stuck to my back from seven hours behind the wheel. Finally I found a hardware store,

"Hector's" on Wornall. I pulled into the lot. The Citation's engine dieseled after I turned off the ignition; I pumped the accelerator once and it coughed and died. The heat was like syrup. The sun drove shadows deep into corners, left them flattened at the feet of the people on the sidewalk. It made the plate glass of the store window into a dark negative of the positive print that was Wornall Road. August.

The man behind the counter in the hardware store I took to be Hector himself. He looked like Hector, slain in vengeance beneath the walls of paintbrushes — the kind of semifriendly, publicly optimistic man who would tell you about his crazy wife and his ten-penny nails. I bought a gallon of kerosene and a plastic paint funnel, put them into the trunk of the Citation, then walked down the block to the Mark Twain Bank. Mark Twain died at the age of seventy-five with a heart full of bitter accusations against the Calvinist god and no hope for the future of humanity. Inside the bank I went to one of the desks, at which sat a Nice Young Lady. I asked about starting a business checking account. She gave me a form to fill out, then sent me to the office of Mr. Graves.

Mr. Graves wielded a formidable handshake. "What can I do for you, Mr. . . . ?"

"Tillotsen, Gerald Tillotsen," I said. Gerald Tillotsen, of Tacoma, Washington, died of diphtheria at the age of four weeks — on September 24, 1938. I have a copy of his birth certificate.

"I'm new to Kansas City. I'd like to open a business account here, and perhaps take out a loan. I trust this is a reputable bank? What's your exposure in Brazil?" I looked around the office as if Graves were hiding a woman behind the hat stand, then flashed him my most ingratiating smile.

Mr. Graves did his best. He tried smiling back, then looked as if he had decided to ignore my little joke. "We're very sound, Mr. Tillotsen."

I continued smiling.

"What kind of business do you own?"

"I'm in insurance. Mutual Assurance of Hartford. Our regional office is in Oklahoma City, and I'm setting up an agency here, at 103rd and State Line." Just off the interstate.

He examined the form. His absorption was too tempting.

"Maybe I can fix you up with a policy? You look like dead meat."

Graves's head snapped up, his mouth half-open. He closed it and watched me guardedly. The dullness of it all! How I tire. He was like some cow, like most of the rest of you in this silly age, unwilling to break the rules in order to take offense. "Did he really say that?" he was thinking. "Was that his idea of a joke? He looks normal enough." I did look normal, exactly like an insurance agent. I was the right kind of person, and I could do anything. If at times I grate, if at times I fall a little short of or go a little beyond convention, there is not one of you who can call me to account.

Graves was coming around. All business.

"Ah — yes, Mr. Tillotsen. If you'll wait a moment, I'm sure we can take care of this checking account. As for the loan —"

"Forget it."

That should have stopped him. He should have asked after my credentials, he should have done a dozen things. He looked at me, and I stared calmly back at him. And I knew that, looking into my honest blue eyes, he could not think of a thing.

"I'll just start the checking account with this money order," I said, reaching into my pocket. "That will be acceptable, won't it?"

"It will be fine," he said. He took the form and the order over to one of the secretaries while I sat at the desk. I lit a cigar and blew some smoke rings. I'd purchased the money order the day before in a post office in Denver. Thirty dollars. I didn't intend to use the account very long. Graves returned with my sample checks, shook hands earnestly, and wished me a good day. Have a *good* day, he said, I *will*, I said.

Outside, the heat was still stifling. I took off my sports coat. I was sweating so much I had to check my hair in the sideview mirror of my car. I walked down the street to a liquor store and bought a bottle of chardonnay and a bottle of Chivas Regal. I got some paper cups from a nearby grocery. One final errand, then I could relax for a few hours.

In the shopping center that I had told Graves would be the location for my nonexistent insurance office, I had noticed a sporting goods store. It was about three o'clock when I parked in the lot and ambled into the shop. I looked at various golf clubs: irons, woods, even one set with fiberglass shafts. Finally I selected a set of eight Spalding irons with matching woods, a large bag, and several boxes of Top-Flites. The salesman, who had been occupied with another customer at the rear of the store, hustled up, his eyes full of commission money. I gave him little time to think. The total cost was $612.32. I paid with a check drawn on my new account, cordially thanked the man, and had him carry all the equipment out to the trunk of the car.

I drove to a park near the bank; Loose Park, they called it. I felt loose. Cut loose, drifting free, like one of the kites people were flying that had broken its string and was ascending into the sun. Beneath the trees it was still hot, though the sunlight was reduced to a shuffling of light and shadow on the brown grass. Kids ran, jumped, swung on playground equipment. I uncorked my bottle of wine, filled one of the paper cups, and lay down beneath a tree, enjoying the children, watching young men and women walking along the footpaths.

A girl approached. She didn't look any older than seventeen. Short, slender, with clean blond hair cut to her shoulders. Her shorts were very tight. I watched her unabashedly; she saw me watching and left the path to come over to me. She stopped a few feet away, hands on her hips. "What are you looking at?" she asked.

"Your legs," I said. "Would you like some wine?"

"No thanks. My mother told me never to accept wine from strangers." She looked right through me.

"I take what I can get from strangers," I said. "Because I'm a stranger, too."

I guess she liked that. She was different. She sat down and we chatted for a while. There was something wrong about her imitation of a seventeen-year-old; I began to wonder whether hookers worked the park. She crossed her legs and her shorts got tighter. "Where are you from?" she asked.

"San Francisco. But I've just moved here to stay. I have a part interest in the sporting goods store at the Eastridge Plaza."

"You live near here?"

"On West Eighty-ninth." I had driven down Eighty-ninth on my way to the bank.

"I live on Eighty-ninth! We're neighbors."

It was exactly what one of my own might have said to test me. I took a drink of wine and changed the subject. "Would you like to visit San Francisco someday?"

She brushed her hair back behind one ear. She pursed her lips, showing off her fine cheekbones. "Have you got something going?" she asked, in queerly accented English.

"Excuse me?"

"I said, have you got something going," she repeated, still with the accent—the accent of my own time.

I took another sip. "A bottle of wine," I replied in good Midwestern 1980s.

She wasn't having any of it. "No artwork, please. I don't like artwork."

I had to laugh: my life was devoted to artwork. I had not met anyone real in a long time. At the beginning I hadn't wanted to, and in the ensuing years I had given up expecting it. If there's anything more boring than you people it's us people. But that was an old attitude. When she came to me in K.C. I was lonely and she was something new.

"Okay," I said. "It's not much, but you can come for the ride. Do you want to?"

She smiled and said yes.

As we walked to my car, she brushed her hip against my leg. I switched the bottle to my left hand and put my arm around her shoulders in a fatherly way. We got into the front seat, beneath the trees on a street at the edge of the park. It was quiet. I reached over, grabbed her hair at the nape of her neck, and jerked her face toward me, covering her little mouth with mine. Surprise: she threw her arms around my neck and slid across the seat into my lap. We did not talk. I yanked at the shorts; she thrust her hand into my pants. St. Augustine asked the Lord for chastity, but not right away.

At the end she slipped off me, calmly buttoned her blouse, brushed her hair back from her forehead. "How about a push?" she asked. She had a nail file out and was filing her index fingernail to a point.

I shook my head and looked at her. She resembled my grandmother. I had never run into my grandmother, but she had a hellish reputation. "No thanks. What's your name?"

"Call me Ruth." She scratched the inside of her left elbow with her nail. She leaned back in her seat, sighed deeply. Her eyes became a very bright, very hard blue.

While she was aloft I got out, opened the trunk, emptied the rest of the chardonnay into the gutter, and used the funnel to fill the bottle with kerosene. I plugged it with a kerosene-soaked rag. Afternoon was sliding into evening as I started the car and cruised down one of the residential streets. The houses were like those of any city or town of that era of the Midwest USA: white frame, forty or fifty years old, with large porches and small front yards. Dying elms hung over the street. Shadows stretched across the sidewalks. Ruth's nose wrinkled; she turned her face lazily toward me, saw the kerosene bottle, and smiled.

Ahead on the left-hand sidewalk I saw a man walking leisurely. He was an average sort of man, middle-aged, probably just returning from work, enjoying the quiet pause dusk was bringing to the hot day. It might have been Hector; it might have been Graves. It might have been any one of you. I punched the cigarette lighter, readied the bottle in my right hand, steering with my leg as the car moved slowly forward.

"Let me help," Ruth said. She reached out and steadied the wheel with her slender fingertips. The lighter popped out. I touched it to the rag; it smoldered and caught. Greasy smoke stung my eyes. By now the man had noticed us. I hung my arm, holding the bottle, out the window. As we passed him, I tossed the bottle at the sidewalk like a newsboy tossing a rolled-up newspaper. The rag flamed brighter as it whipped through the air; the bottle landed at his feet and exploded, dousing him with burning kerosene. I floored the accelerator; the motor coughed, then roared, the tires and Ruth both squealing in delight. I could see the flaming man in the rearview mirror as we sped away.

On the Great American Plains, the summer nights are not silent. The fields sing the summer songs of insects—not individual sounds, but a high-pitched drone of locusts, crickets, cicadas, small chirping things for which I have no names. You drive along the superhighway and that sound blends with the sound of wind rushing through your opened windows, hiding the thrum of the automobile, conveying the impression of incredible velocity. Wheels vibrate, tires beat against the pavement, the steering wheel shudders, alive in your hands, droning insects alive in your ears. Reflecting posts at the roadside leap from the darkness with metronomic regularity, glowing amber in the headlights, only to vanish abruptly into the ready night when you pass. You lose track of time, how long you have been on the road, where you are going. The fields scream in your ears like a thousand lost, mechanical souls, and you press your foot to the accelerator, hurrying away.

When we left Kansas City that evening we were indeed hurrying. Our direction was in one sense precise: Interstate 70, more or less due east, through Missouri in a dream. They might remember me in Kansas City, at the same time wondering who and why. Mr. Graves scans the morning paper over his grapefruit: MAN BURNED BY GASOLINE BOMB. The clerk wonders why he ever accepted an unverified counter check, without a name or address printed on it, for six hundred dollars. The check bounces. They discover it was a bottle of chardonnay. The story is pieced together. They would eventually figure out how—I wouldn't lie to myself about that (I never lie to myself)—but the why would always escape them. Organized crime, they would say. A plot that misfired.

Of course, they still might have caught me. The car became more of a liability the longer I held on to it. But Ruth, humming to herself, did not seem to care, and neither did I. You have to improvise those things; that's what gives them whatever interest they have.

Just shy of Columbia, Missouri, Ruth stopped humming and asked me, "Do you know why Helen Keller can't have any children?"

"No."

"Because she's dead."

I rolled up the window so I could hear her better. "That's pretty funny," I said.

"Yes. I overheard it in a restaurant." After a minute she asked, "Who's Helen Keller?"

"A dead woman." An insect splattered itself against the windshield. The lights of the oncoming cars glinted against the smear it left.

"She must be famous," said Ruth. "I like famous people. Have you met any? Was that man you burned famous?"

"Probably not. I don't care about famous people anymore." The last time I had anything to do, even peripherally, with anyone famous was when I changed the direction of the tape over the lock in the Watergate so Frank Wills would see it. Ruth did not look like the kind who would know about that. "I was there for the Kennedy assassination," I said, "but I had nothing to do with it."

"Who was Kennedy?"

That made me smile. "How long have you been here?" I pointed at her tiny purse. "That's all you've got with you?"

She slid across the seat and leaned her head against my shoulder. "I don't need anything else."

"No clothes?"

"I left them in Kansas City. We can get more."

"Sure," I said.

She opened the purse and took out a plastic Bayer aspirin case. From it she selected two blue-and-yellow caps. She shoved her palm up under my nose. "Serometh?"

"No thanks."

She put one of the caps back into the box and popped the other under her nose. She sighed and snuggled tighter against me. We had reached Columbia and I was hungry. When I pulled in at a McDonald's she ran across the lot into the shopping mall before I could stop her. I was a little nervous about the car and sat watching it as I ate (Big Mac, small Dr. Pepper). She did not come back. I crossed the lot to the mall, found a drugstore, and bought some cigars. When I strolled back to the car she was waiting for me, hopping from one foot to another and tugging at the door handle. Serometh makes you impatient. She was wearing a pair of shiny black pants, pink- and white-checked sneakers, and a hot pink blouse. "'s go!" she hissed.

I moved even slower. She looked like she was about to wet herself, biting her soft lower lip with a line of perfect white teeth. I dawdled over my keys. A security guard and a young man in a shirt and tie hurried out of the mall entrance and scanned the lot. "Nice outfit," I said. "Must have cost you something."

She looked over her shoulder, saw the security guard, who saw her. "Hey!" he called, running toward us. I slid into the car, opened the passenger door. Ruth had snapped open her purse and pulled out a small gun. I grabbed her arm and yanked her into the car; she squawked and her shot went wide. The guard fell down anyway, scared shitless. For the second time that day I tested the Citation's acceleration; Ruth's door slammed shut and we were gone.

"You scut," she said as we hit the entrance ramp of the interstate. "You're a scut-pumping Conservative. You made me miss." But she was smiling, running her hand up the inside of my thigh. I could tell she hadn't ever had so much fun in the twentieth century.

For some reason I was shaking. "Give me one of those serometh," I said.

Around midnight we stopped in St. Louis at a Holiday Inn. We registered as Mr. and Mrs. Gerald Bruno (an old acquaintance) and paid in advance. No one remarked on the apparent difference in our ages. So discreet. I bought a copy of the *Post-Dispatch*, and we went to the room. Ruth flopped down on the bed, looking bored, but thanks to her gunplay I had a few more things to take care of. I poured myself a glass of Chivas, went into the bathroom, removed the toupee and flushed it down the toilet, showered, put a new blade in my old razor, and shaved the rest of the hair from my head. The Lex Luthor look. I cut my scalp. That got me laughing, and I could not stop. Ruth peeked through the doorway to find me dabbing the crown of my head with a bloody Kleenex.

"You're a wreck," she said.

I almost fell off the toilet laughing. She was absolutely right. Between giggles I managed to say, "You must not stay anywhere too long, if you're as careless as you were tonight."

She shrugged. "I bet I've been at it longer than you." She stripped and got into the shower. I got into bed.

The room enfolded me in its gold-carpet green-bedspread mediocrity. Sometimes it's hard to remember that things were ever different. In 1596 I rode to court with Essex; I slept in a chamber of supreme garishness (gilt escutcheons in the corners of the ceiling, pink cupids romping on the walls), in a bed warmed by any of the trollops of the city I might want. And there in the Holiday Inn I sat with my drink, in my pastel blue pajama bottoms, reading a late-twentieth-century newspaper, smoking a cigar. An earthquake in Peru estimated to have killed eight thousand in Lima alone. Nope. A steel worker in Gary, Indiana, discovered to be the murderer of six prepubescent children, bodies found buried in his basement. Perhaps. The president refuses to enforce the ruling of his Supreme Court because it "subverts the will of the American people." Probably not.

We are everywhere. But not everywhere.

Ruth came out of the bathroom, saw me, did a double take. "You look—perfect!" she said. She slid in the bed beside me, naked, and sniffed at my glass of Chivas. Her lip curled. She looked over my shoulder at the paper. "You can understand that stuff?"

"Don't kid me. Reading is a survival skill. You couldn't last here without it."

"Wrong."

I drained the Scotch. Took a puff on the cigar. Dropped the paper to the floor beside the bed. I looked her over. Even relaxed, the muscles in her arms and along the tops of her thighs were well defined.

"You even smell like one of them," she said.

"How did you get the clothes past their store security? They have those beeper tags clipped to them."

"Easy. I tried on the shoes and walked out when they weren't looking. In the second store I took the pants into a dressing room, cut the alarm tag out of the waistband, and put them on. I held the alarm tag that was clipped to the blouse in my armpit and walked out of that store, too. I put the blouse on in the mall women's room."

"If you can't read, how did you know which was the women's room?"

"There's a picture on the door."

I felt tired and old. Ruth moved close. She rubbed her foot up my leg, drawing the pajama leg up with it. Her thigh slid across my groin. I started to get hard. "Cut it out," I said. She licked my nipple.

I could not stand it. I got off the bed. "I don't like you."

She looked at me with true innocence. "I don't like you, either."

Although he was repulsed by the human body, Jonathan Swift was passionately in love with a woman named Esther Johnson. "What you did at the mall was stupid," I said. "You would have killed that guard."

"Which would have made us even for the day."

"Kansas City was different."

"We should ask the cops there what they think."

"You don't understand. That had some grace to it. But what you did was inelegant. Worst of all it was not gratuitous. You stole those clothes for yourself, and I hate that." I was shaking.

"Who made all these laws?"

"I did."

She looked at me with amazement. "You're not just a Conservative. You're gone native!"

I wanted her so much I ached. "No I haven't," I said, but even to me my voice sounded frightened.

Ruth got out of the bed. She glided over, reached one hand around to the small of my back, pulled herself close. She looked up at me with a face that held nothing but avidity. "You can do whatever you want," she whispered. With a feeling that I was losing everything, I kissed her. You don't need to know what happened then.

I woke when she displaced herself: there was a sound like the sweep of an arm across fabric, a stirring of air to fill the place where she had been. I looked around the still brightly lit room. It was not yet morning. The chain was across the door; her clothes lay on the dresser. She had left the aspirin box beside my bottle of Scotch.

She was gone. Good, I thought, now I can go on. But I found that I couldn't sleep, could not keep from thinking. Ruth must be very good at that, or perhaps her thought is a different kind of thought from mine. I got out of the bed, resolved to try again but still fearing the inevitable. I filled the tub with hot water. I got in, breathing heavily. I took the blade from my razor. Holding my arm just beneath the surface of the water, hesitating only a moment, I cut deeply one, two, three times along the veins in my left wrist. The shock was still there, as great as ever. With blood streaming from me I cut the right wrist. Quickly, smoothly. My heart beat fast and light, the blood flowed frighteningly; already the water was stained. I felt faint—yes—it was going to work this time, yes. My vision began to fade—but in the last moments before consciousness fell away I saw, with sick despair, the futile wounds closing themselves once again, as they had so many times before. For in the future the practice of medicine may progress to the point where men need have little fear of death.

The dawn's rosy fingers found me still unconscious. I came to myself about eleven, my head throbbing, so weak I could hardly rise from the cold bloody water. There were no scars. I stumbled into the other room and washed down one of Ruth's megamphetamines with two fingers of Scotch. I felt better immediately. It's funny how that works sometimes, isn't it? The maid knocked as I was cleaning the bathroom. I shouted for her to come back later, finished as quickly as possible, and left the hotel immediately. I ate Shredded Wheat with milk and strawberries for breakfast. I was full of ideas. A phone book gave me the location of a likely country club.

The Oak Hill Country Club of Florissant, Missouri, is not a spectacularly wealthy institution, or at least it does not give that impression. I'll bet you that the membership is not as purely white as the stucco clubhouse. That was all right with me. I parked the Citation in the mostly empty parking lot, hauled my new equipment from the trunk, and set off for the locker room, trying hard to look like a dentist. I successfully ran the gauntlet of the pro shop, where the proprietor was telling a bored caddy why the Cardinals would fade in the stretch. I could hear running water from the showers as I shuffled into the locker room and slung the bag into a corner. Someone was singing the "Ode to Joy," abominably.

I began to rifle through the lockers, hoping to find an open one with someone's clothes in it. I would take the keys from my benefactor's pocket and proceed along my merry way. Ruth would have accused me of self-interest; there was a moment in which I accused myself. Such hesitation is the seed of failure: as I paused before a locker containing a likely set of clothes, another golfer entered the room along with the locker-room attendant. I immediately began undressing, lowering my head so that the locker door hid my face. The golfer was soon gone, but the attendant sat down and began to leaf through a worn copy of *Penthouse*. I could come up with no better plan than to strip and enter the showers. Amphetamine daze. Perhaps the kid would develop a hard-on and go to the john to take care of it.

There was only one other man in the shower, the symphonic soloist, a somewhat portly gentleman who mercifully shut up as soon as I entered. He worked hard at ignoring me. I ignored him in return: *alle Menschen werden Brüder*. I waited a long five minutes after he left; two more men came into the showers, and I walked out with what composure I could muster. The locker-room boy was stacking towels on a table. I fished a five from my jacket in the locker and walked up behind him. Casually I took a towel.

"Son, get me a pack of Marlboros, will you?"

He took the money and left.

In the second locker I found a pair of pants that contained the keys to some sort of Audi. I was not choosy. Dressed in record time, I left the new clubs beside the rifled locker. My note read, "The pure products of America go crazy." There were three eligible cars in the lot, two 4000s and a Fox. The key would not open the door of the Fox. I was jumpy, but almost home free, coming around the front of a big Chrysler. . . .

"Hey!"

My knee gave way and I ran into the fender of the car. The keys slipped out of my hand and skittered across the hood to the ground, jingling. Grimacing, I hopped toward them, plucked them up, glancing over my shoulder at my pursuer as I stooped. It was the locker-room attendant.

"Your cigarettes." He looked at me the way a sixteen-year-old looks at his father; that is, with bored skepticism. All our gods in the end become pitiful. It was time for me to be abruptly courteous. As it was, he would remember me too well.

"Thanks," I said. I limped over, put the pack into my shirt pocket. He started to go, but I couldn't help myself. "What about my change?"

Oh, such an insolent silence! I wonder what you told them when they asked you about me, boy. He handed over the money. I tipped him a quarter, gave him a piece of Mr. Graves's professional smile. He studied me. I turned and inserted the key into the lock of the Audi. A fifty percent chance. Had I been the praying kind I might have prayed to one of those pitiful gods. The key turned without resistance; the door opened. The kid slouched back toward the clubhouse, pissed at me and his lackey's job. Or perhaps he found it in his heart to smile. Laughter—the Best Medicine.

A bit of a racing shift, then back to Interstate 70. My hip twinged all the way across Illinois.

I had originally intended to work my way east to Buffalo, New York, but after the Oak Hill business I wanted to cut it short. If I stayed on the interstate I was sure to get caught; I had been lucky to get as far as I had. Just outside of Indianapolis I turned onto Route 37 north to Fort Wayne and Detroit.

I was not, however, entirely crowed. Twenty-five years in one time had given me the right instincts, and with the coming of the evening and the friendly insects to sing me along, the boredom of the road became a new recklessness. Hadn't I already been seen by too many people in those twenty-five years? Thousands had looked into my honest face—and where were they? Ruth had reminded me that I was not stuck here. I would soon make an end to this latest adventure one way or another, and once I had done so, there would be no reason in God's green world to suspect me.

And so: north of Fort Wayne, on Highway 6 east, a deserted country road (what was he doing there?), I pulled over to pick up a young hitchhiker. He wore a battered black leather jacket. His hair was short on the sides, stuck up in spikes on top, hung over his collar in back; one side was carrot-orange, the other brown with a white streak. His sign, pinned to a knapsack, said "?" He threw the pack into the backseat and climbed into the front.

"Thanks for picking me up." He did not sound like he meant it. "Where you going?"

"Flint. How about you?"

"Flint's as good as anywhere."

"Suit yourself." We got up to speed. I was completely calm. "You should fasten your seat belt," I said.

"Why?"

The surly type. "It's not just a good idea. It's the law."

He ignored me. He pulled a crossword puzzle book and a pencil from his jacket pocket. "How about turning on the light."

I flicked on the dome light for him. "I like to see a young man improve himself," I said.

His look was an almost audible sigh. "What's a five-letter word for 'the lowest point'?"

"Nadir," I replied.

"That's right. How about 'widespread'; four letters."

"Rife."

"You're pretty good." He stared at the crossword for a minute, then rolled down his window and threw the book, and the pencil, out of the car. He rolled up the window and stared at his reflection in it. I couldn't let him get off that easily. I turned off the interior light, and the darkness leapt inside.

"What's your name, son? What are you so mad about?"

"Milo. Look, are you queer? If you are, it doesn't matter to me but it will cost you . . . if you want to do anything about it."

I smiled and adjusted the rearview mirror so I could watch him—and he could watch me. "No, I'm not queer. The name's Loki." I extended my right hand, keeping my eyes on the road.

He looked at the hand. "Loki?"

As good a name as any. "Yes. Same as the Norse god."

He laughed. "Sure, Loki. Anything you like. Fuck you."

Such a musical voice. "Now there you go. Seems to me, Milo—if you don't mind my giving you my unsolicited opinion—that you have something of an attitude problem." I punched the cigarette lighter, reached back and pulled a cigar from my jacket on the backseat, in the process weaving the car all over Highway 6. I bit the end off the cigar and spat it out the window, stoked it up. My insects wailed. I cannot explain to you how good I felt.

"Take for instance this crossword puzzle book. Why did you throw it out the window?"

I could see Milo watching me in the mirror, wondering whether he should take me seriously. The headlights fanned out ahead of us, the white lines at the center of the road pulsing by like a rapid heartbeat. Take a chance, Milo. What have you got to lose?

"I was pissed," he said. "It's a waste of time. I don't care about stupid games."

"Exactly. It's just a game, a way to pass the time. Nobody ever really learns anything from a crossword puzzle. Corporation lawyers don't get their Porsches by building their word power with crosswords, right?"

"I don't care about Porsches."

"Neither do I, Milo. I drive an Audi."

Milo sighed.

"I know, Milo. That's not the point. The point is that it's all a game, crosswords or corporate law. Some people devote their lives to Jesus; some devote their lives to artwork. It all comes to pretty much the same thing. You get old. You die."

"Tell me something I don't already know."

"Why do you think I picked you up, Milo? I saw your question mark and it spoke to me. You probably think I'm some pervert out to take advantage of you. I have a funny name. I don't talk like your average middle-aged businessman. Forget about that." The old excitement was upon me; I was talking louder and louder, leaning on the accelerator. The car sped along. "I think you're as troubled by the materialism and cant of life in America as I am. Young people like you, with orange hair, are trying to find some values in a world that offers them nothing but crap for ideas. But too many of you are turning to extremes in response. Drugs, violence, religious fanaticism, hedonism. Some, like you I suspect, to suicide. Don't do it, Milo. Your life is too valuable." The speedometer touched eighty, eighty-five. Milo fumbled for his seat belt but couldn't find it.

I waved my hand, holding the cigar, at him. "What's the matter, Milo? Can't find the belt?" Ninety now. A pickup went by us going the other way, the wind of its passing beating at my head and shoulder. Ninety-five.

"Think, Milo! If you're upset with the present, with your parents and the schools, think about the future. What will the future be like if this trend toward valuelessness continues in the next hundred years? Think of the impact of the new technologies! Gene splicing, gerontology, artificial intelligence, space exploration, biological weapons, nuclear proliferation! All accelerating this process! Think of the violent reactionary movements that could arise—are arising already, Milo, as we speak—from people's desire to find something to hold on to. Paint yourself a picture, *Milo*, of the kind of man or woman another hundred years of this process might produce!"

"What are you talking about?" He was terrified.

"I'm talking about the survival of values in America! Simply that." Cigar smoke swirled in front of the dashboard lights, and my voice had reached a shout. Milo was gripping the sides of his seat. The speedometer read 105. "And you, *Milo*, are at the heart of this process! If people continue to think the way you do, *Milo*, throwing their crossword puzzle books out the windows of their Audis all across America, the future will be full of absolutely valueless people! Right, MILO?" I leaned over, taking my eyes off the road, and blew smoke into his face, screaming, "ARE YOU LISTENING, MILO? MARK MY WORDS!"

"Y-yes."

"GOO, GOO, GA-GA-GAA!"

I put my foot all the way to the floor. The wind howled through the window, the gray highway flew beneath us.

"Mark my words, Milo," I whispered. He never heard me. "Twenty-five across. Eight letters. N-i-h-i-l—"

My pulse roared in my ears, there joining the drowned choir of the fields and the roar of the engine. Body slimy with sweat, fingers clenched through the cigar, fists clamped on the wheel, smoke stinging my eyes. I slammed on the brakes, downshifting immediately, sending the transmission into a painful whine as the car slewed and skidded off the pavement, clipping a reflecting marker and throwing Milo against the windshield. The car stopped with a jerk in the gravel at the side of the road, just shy of a sign announcing, WELCOME TO OHIO.

There were no other lights on the road, I shut off my own and sat behind the wheel, trembling, the night air cool on my skin. The insects wailed. The boy was slumped against the dashboard. There was a star fracture in the glass above his head, and warm blood came away on my fingers when I touched his hair. I got out of the car, circled around to the passenger's side, and dragged him from the seat into the field adjoining the road. He was surprisingly light. I left him there, in a field of Ohio soybeans on the evening of a summer's day.

The city of Detroit was founded by the French adventurer Antoine de la Mothe, sieur de Cadillac, a supporter of Comte de Pontchartrain, minister of state to the Sun King, Louis XIV. All of these men worshiped the Roman Catholic god, protected their political positions, and let the future go hang. Cadillac, after whom an American automobile was named, was seeking a favorable location to advance his own economic interests. He came ashore on July 24, 1701, with fifty soldiers, an equal number of settlers, and about one hundred friendly Indians near the present site of the Veterans Memorial Building, within easy walking distance of the Greyhound Bus Terminal.

The car did not run well after the accident, developing a reluctance to go into fourth, but I didn't care. The encounter with Milo had gone exactly as such things should go, and was especially pleasing because it had been totally unplanned. An accident—no order, one would guess—but exactly as if I had laid it all out beforehand. I came into Detroit late at night via Route 12, which eventually turned into Michigan Avenue. The air was hot and sticky. I remember driving past the Cadillac plant; multitudes of red, yellow, and green lights glinting off dull masonry and the smell of auto exhaust along the city streets. I found the sort of neighborhood I wanted not far from Tiger Stadium: pawnshops, an all-night deli, laundromats, dimly lit bars with red Stroh's signs in the windows. Men on street corners walked casually from noplace to noplace.

I parked on a side street just around the corner from a 7-Eleven. I left the motor running. In the store I dawdled over a magazine rack until at last I heard the racing of an engine and saw the Audi flash by the window. I bought a copy of *Time* and caught a downtown bus at the corner. At the Greyhound station I purchased a ticket for the next bus to Toronto and sat reading my magazine until departure time.

We got onto the bus. Across the river we stopped at customs and got off again. "Name?" they asked me.

"Gerald Spotsworth."

"Place of birth?"

"Calgary." I gave them my credentials. The passport photo showed me with hair. They looked me over. They let me go.

I work in the library of the University of Toronto. I am well read, a student of history, a solid Canadian citizen. There I lead a sedentary life. The subways are clean, the people are friendly, the restaurants are excellent. The sky is blue. The cat is on the mat.

We got back on the bus. There were few other passengers, and most of them were soon asleep; the only light in the darkened interior was that which shone above my head. I was very tired, but I did not want to sleep. Then I remembered that I had Ruth's pills in my jacket pocket. I smiled, thinking of the customs people. All that was left in the box were a couple of tiny pink tabs. I did not know what they were, but I broke one down the middle with my fingernail and took it anyway. It perked me up immediately. Everything I could see seemed sharply defined. The dark green plastic of the seats. The rubber mat in the aisle. My fingernails. All details were separate and distinct, all interdependent. I must have been focused on the threads in the weave of my pants leg for ten minutes when I was surprised by someone sitting down next to me. It was Ruth. "You're back!" I exclaimed.

"We're all back," she said. I looked around and it was true: on the opposite side of the aisle, two seats ahead, Milo sat watching me over his shoulder, a trickle of blood running down his forehead. One corner of his mouth pulled tighter in a rueful smile. Mr. Graves came back from the front seat and shook my hand. I saw the fat singer from the country club, still naked. The locker-room boy. A flickering light from the back of the bus: when I turned around there stood the burning man, his eye sockets two dark hollows behind the wavering flames. The shopping-mall guard. Hector from the hardware store. They all looked at me.

"What are you doing here?" I asked Ruth.

"We couldn't let you go on thinking like you do. You act like I'm some monster. I'm just a person."

"A rather nice-looking young lady," Graves added.

"People are monsters," I said.

"Like you, huh?" Ruth said. "But they can be saints, too."

That made me laugh. "Don't feed me platitudes. You can't even read."

"You make such a big deal out of reading. Yeah, well, times change. I get along fine, don't I?"

The mall guard broke in. "Actually, miss, the reason we caught on to you is that someone saw you walk into the men's room." He looked embarrassed.

"But you didn't catch me, did you?" Ruth snapped back. She turned to me. "You're afraid of change. No wonder you live back here."

"This is all in my imagination," I said. "It's because of your drugs."

"It is all in your imagination," the burning man repeated. His voice was a whisper. "What you see in the future is what you are able to see. You have no faith in God or your fellow man."

"He's right," said Ruth.

"Bull. Psychobabble."

"Speaking of babble," Milo said, "I figured out where you got that goo-goo-goo stuff. Talk—"

"Never mind that," Ruth broke in. "Here's the truth. The future is just a place. The people there are just people. They live differently. So what? People make what they want of the world. You can't escape human failings by running into the past." She rested her hand on my leg. "I'll tell you what you'll find when you get to Toronto," she said. "Another city full of human beings."

This was crazy. I knew it was crazy. I knew it was all unreal, but somehow I was getting more and more afraid. "So the future is just the present writ large," I said bitterly. "More bull."

"You tell her, pal," the locker-room boy said.

Hector, who had been listening quietly, broke in. "For a man from the future, you talk a lot like a native."

"You're the king of bullshit, man," Milo said. "'Some people devote themselves to artwork'! Jesus!"

I felt dizzy. "Scut down, Milo. That means 'Fuck you too.'" I shook my head to try to make them go away. That was a mistake: the bus began to pitch like a sailboat. I grabbed for Ruth's arm but missed. "Who's driving this thing?" I asked, trying to get out of the seat.

"Don't worry," said Graves. "He knows what he's doing."

"He's brain-dead," Milo said.

"You couldn't do any better," said Ruth, pulling me back down.

"No one is driving," said the burning man.

"We'll crash!" I was so dizzy now that I could hardly keep from being sick. I closed my eyes and swallowed. That seemed to help. A longtime passed; eventually I must have fallen asleep.

When I woke it was late morning and we were entering the city, cruising down Eglinton Avenue. The bus had a driver after all—a slender black man with neatly trimmed sideburns who wore his uniform hat at a rakish angle. A sign above the windshield said, YOUR DRIVER—SAFE, COURTEOUS, and below that, on the slide-in nameplate, WILBERT CAUL. I felt like I was coming out of a nightmare. I felt happy. I stretched some of the knots out of my back. A young soldier seated across the aisle from me looked my way; I smiled, and he returned it briefly.

"You were mumbling to yourself in your sleep last night," he said.

"Sorry. Sometimes I have bad dreams."

"It's okay. I do too, sometimes." He had a round open face, an apologetic grin. He was twenty, maybe. Who knew where his dreams came from? We chatted until the bus reached the station; he shook my hand and said he was pleased to meet me. He called me "sir."

I was not due back at the library until Monday, so I walked over to Yonge Street. The stores were busy, the tourists were out in droves, the adult theaters were doing a brisk business. Policemen in sharply creased trousers, white gloves, sauntered along among the pedestrians. It was a bright, cloudless day, but the breeze coming up the street from the lake was cool. I stood on the sidewalk outside one of the strip joints and watched the videotaped come-on over the closed circuit. The Princess Laya. Sondra Nieve, the Human Operator. Technology replaces the traditional barker, but the bodies are more or less the same. The persistence of your faith in sex and machines is evidence of your capacity to hope.

Francis Bacon, in his masterwork *The New Atlantis*, foresaw the utopian world that would arise through the application of experimental science to social problems. Bacon, however, could not solve the problems of his own time and was eventually accused of accepting bribes, fined £40,000, and imprisoned in the Tower of London. He made no appeal to God, but instead applied himself to the development of the virtues of patience and acceptance. Eventually he was freed. Soon after, on a freezing day in late March, we were driving near Highgate when I suggested to him that cold might delay the process of decay. He was excited by the idea. On impulse he stopped the carriage, purchased a hen, wrung its neck, and stuffed it with snow. He eagerly looked forward to the results of his experiment. Unfortunately, in haggling with the street vendor he had exposed himself thoroughly to the cold and was seized by a chill that rapidly led to pneumonia, of which he died on April 9, 1626.

There's no way to predict these things.

When the videotape started repeating itself I got bored, crossed the street, and lost myself in the crowd.

stable strategies for middle management

EILEEN GUNN

Eileen Gunn is not a prolific writer, but her stories are well worth waiting for, and are relished (and eagerly anticipated) by a small but select group of knowledgeable fans who know that she has a twisted perspective on life unlike anyone else's, and a strange and pungent sense of humor all her own. She has made several sales to *Asimov's Science Fiction*, as well as to markets such as *Amazing, Proteus, Tales by Moonlight,* and *Alternate Presidents,* and has been a Nebula and Hugo finalist several times. She is the editor and publisher of the jazzy and eclectic electronic magazine *The Infinite Matrix* (www.infinitematrix.net), and the chairman of the board of the Clarion West Writers Workshop. Coming up is her first short story collection, *Stable Strategies and Others,* and she is at work on a biography of the late Avram Davidson. After brief periods of exile in Brooklyn and San Francisco, she is now back in Seattle, Washington, where she had formerly resided for many years, much to the relief of the other inhabitants.

In the strange and funny story that follows, a Hugo finalist, she shows us how bioscience may someday make possible career-advancement ploys far more bizarre than any that are possible today. . . .

Our cousin the insect has an external skeleton made of shiny brown chitin, a material that is particularly responsive to the demands of evolution. Just as bioengineering has sculpted our bodies into new forms, so evolution has shaped the early insect's chewing mouthparts into her descendants' chisels, siphons, and stilettos, and has molded from the chitin special tools—pockets to carry pollen, combs to clean her compound eyes, notches on which she can fiddle a song.

From the popular science program Insect People!

I awoke this morning to discover that bioengineering had made demands upon me during the night. My tongue had turned into a stiletto, and my left hand now contained a small chitinous comb, as if for cleaning a compound eye. Since I didn't have compound eyes, I thought that perhaps this presaged some change to come.

I dragged myself out of bed, wondering how I was going to drink my coffee through a stiletto. Was I now expected to kill my breakfast, and dispense with coffee entirely? I hoped I was not evolving into a creature whose survival depended on early-morning alertness. My circadian rhythms would no doubt keep pace with any physical changes, but my unevolved soul was repulsed at the thought of my waking cheerfully at dawn, ravenous for some wriggly little creature that had arisen even earlier.

I looked down at Greg, still asleep, the edge of our red and white quilt pulled up under his chin. His mouth had changed during the night too, and seemed to contain some sort of a long probe. Were we growing apart?

I reached down with my unchanged hand and touched his hair. It was still shiny brown, soft and thick, luxurious. But along his cheek, under his beard, I could feel patches of sclerotin, as the flexible chitin in his skin was slowly hardening to an impermeable armor.

He opened his eyes, staring blearily forward without moving his head. I could see him move his mouth cautiously, examining its internal changes. He turned his head and looked up at me, rubbing his hair slightly into my hand.

"Time to get up?" he asked. I nodded. "Oh, God," he said. He said this every morning. It was like a prayer.

"I'll make coffee," I said. "Do you want some?"

He shook his head slowly. "Just a glass of apricot nectar," he said. He unrolled his long, rough tongue and looked at it, slightly cross-eyed. "This is real interesting, but it wasn't in the catalog. I'll be sipping lunch from flowers pretty soon. That ought to draw a second glance at Duke's."

"I thought account execs were expected to sip their lunches," I said.

"Not from the flower arrangements . . ." he said, still exploring the odd shape of his mouth. Then he looked up at me and reached up from under the covers. "Come here."

It had been a while, I thought, and I had to get to work. But he did smell terribly attractive. Perhaps he was developing aphrodisiac scent glands. I climbed back under the covers and stretched my body against his. We were both developing chitinous knobs and odd lumps that made this less than comfortable. "How am I supposed to kiss you with a stiletto in my mouth?" I asked.

"There are other things to do. New equipment presents new possibilities." He pushed the covers back and ran his unchanged hands down my body from shoulder to thigh. "Let me know if my tongue is too rough."

It was not.

Fuzzy-minded, I got out of bed for the second time and drifted into the kitchen.

Measuring the coffee into the grinder, I realized that I was no longer interested in drinking it, although it was diverting for a moment to spear the beans with my stiletto. What was the damn thing for, anyhow? I wasn't sure I wanted to find out.

Putting the grinder aside, I poured a can of apricot nectar into a tulip glass. Shallow glasses were going to be a problem for Greg in the future, I thought. Not to mention solid food.

My particular problem, however, if I could figure out what I was supposed to eat for breakfast, was getting to the office in time for my ten A.M. meeting. Maybe I'd just skip breakfast. I dressed quickly and dashed out the door before Greg was even out of bed.

Thirty minutes later, I was more or less awake and sitting in the small conference room with the new marketing manager, listening to him lay out his plan for the Model 2000 launch.

In signing up for his bioengineering program, Harry had chosen specialized primate adaptation, B-E Option No. 4. He had evolved into a textbook example: small and long-limbed, with forward-facing eyes for judging distances and long, grasping fingers to keep him from falling out of his tree.

He was dressed for success in a pin-striped three-piece suit that fit his simian proportions perfectly. I wondered what premium he paid for custom-made. Or did he patronize a ready-to-wear shop that catered especially to primates?

I listened as he leaped agilely from one ridiculous marketing premise to the next. Trying to borrow credibility from mathematics and engineering, he used wildly metaphoric bizspeak, "factoring in the need for pipeline throughout," "fine-tuning the media mix," without even cracking a smile.

Harry had been with the company only a few months, straight from business school. He saw himself as a much-needed infusion of talent. I didn't like him, but I envied his ability to root through his subconscious and toss out one half-formed idea after another. I know he felt it reflected badly on me that I didn't join in and spew forth a random selection of promotional suggestions.

I didn't think much of his marketing plan. The advertising section was a textbook application of theory with no practical basis. I had two options: I could force him to accept a solution that would work, or I could yes him to death, making sure everybody understood it was his idea. I knew which path I'd take.

"Yeah, we can do that for you," I told him. "No problem." We'd see which of us would survive and which was hurtling to an evolutionary dead end.

Although Harry had won his point, he continued to belabor it. My attention wandered—I'd heard it all before. His voice was the hum of an air conditioner, a familiar, easily ignored background noise. I drowsed and new emotions stirred in me, yearnings to float through moist air currents, to land on bright surfaces, to engorge myself with warm, wet food.

Adrift in insect dreams, I became sharply aware of the bare skin of Harry's arm, between his gold-plated watchband and his rolled-up sleeve, as he manipulated papers on the conference room table. He smelled greasily delicious, like a pepperoni pizza or a charcoal-broiled hamburger. I realized he probably wouldn't taste as good as he smelled, but I was hungry. My stiletto-like tongue was there for a purpose, and it wasn't to skewer cubes of tofu. I leaned over his arm and braced myself against the back of his hand, probing with my stylets to find a capillary.

Harry noticed what I was doing and swatted me sharply on the side of the head. I pulled away before he could hit me again.

"We were discussing the Model 2000 launch. Or have you forgotten?" he said, rubbing his arm.

"Sorry. I skipped breakfast this morning." I was embarrassed.

"Well, get your hormones adjusted, for chrissake." He was annoyed, and I couldn't really blame him. "Let's get back to the media allocation issue, if you can keep your mind on it. I've got another meeting at eleven in Building Two."

Inappropriate feeding behavior was not unusual in the company, and corporate etiquette sometimes allowed minor lapses to pass without pursuit. Of course, I could no longer hope that he would support me on moving some money out of the direct-mail budget. . . .

During the remainder of the meeting, my glance kept drifting through the open door of the conference room, toward a large decorative plant in the hall, one of those oases of generic greenery that dot the corporate landscape. It didn't look succulent exactly—it obviously wasn't what I would have preferred to eat if I hadn't been so hungry—but I wondered if I swung both ways?

I grabbed a handful of the broad leaves as I left the room and carried them back to my office. With my tongue, I probed a vein in the thickest part of a leaf. It wasn't so bad. Tasted green. I sucked them dry and tossed the husks in the wastebasket.

I was still omnivorous, at least—female mosquitoes don't eat plants. So the process wasn't complete. . . .

I got a cup of coffee, for company, from the kitchenette and sat in my office with the door closed and wondered what was happening. The incident with Harry disturbed me. Was I turning into a mosquito? If so, what the hell kind of good was that supposed to do me? The company didn't have any use for a whining loner.

There was a knock at the door, and my boss stuck his head in. I nodded and gestured him into my office. He sat down in the visitor's chair on the other side of my desk. From the look on his face, I could tell Harry had talked to him already.

Tom Samson was an older guy, pre-bioengineering. He was well versed in stimulus-response techniques, but had somehow never made it to the top job. I liked him, but then that was what he intended. Without sacrificing authority, he had pitched his appearance, his gestures, the tone of his voice, to the warm end of the spectrum. Even though I knew what he was doing, it worked.

He looked at me with what appeared to be sympathy, but was actually a practiced sign stimulus, intended to defuse any fight-or-flight response. "Is there something bothering you, Margaret?"

"Bothering me? I'm hungry, that's all. I get short-tempered when I'm hungry."

Watch it, I thought. He hasn't referred to the incident; leave it for him to bring up. I made my mind go blank and forced myself to meet his eyes. A shifty gaze is a guilty gaze.

Tom just looked at me, biding his time, waiting for me to put myself on the spot. My coffee smelt burnt, but I stuck my tongue in it and pretended to drink. "I'm just not human until I've had my coffee in the morning." Sounded phony. Shut up, I thought.

This was the opening that Tom was waiting for. "That's what I wanted to speak to you about, Margaret." He sat there, hunched over in a relaxed way, like a mountain gorilla, unthreatened by natural enemies. "I just talked to Harry Winthrop, and he said you were trying to suck his blood during a meeting on marketing strategy." He paused for a moment to check my reaction, but the neutral expression was fixed on my face and I said nothing. His face changed to project disappointment. "You know, when we noticed you were developing three distinct body segments, we had great hopes for you. But your actions just don't reflect the social and organizational development we expected."

He paused, and it was my turn to say something in my defense. "Most insects are solitary, you know. Perhaps the company erred in hoping for a termite or an ant. I'm not responsible for that."

"Now, Margaret," he said, his voice simulating genial reprimand. "This isn't the jungle, you know. When you signed those consent forms, you agreed to let the B-E staff mold you into a more useful corporate organism. But this isn't nature, this is man reshaping nature. It doesn't follow the old rules. You can truly be anything you want to be. But you have to cooperate."

"I'm doing the best I can," I said, cooperatively. "I'm putting in eighty hours a week."

"Margaret, the quality of your work is not an issue. It's your interactions with others that you have to work on. You have to learn to work as part of the group. I just cannot permit such backbiting to continue. I'll have Arthur get you an appointment this afternoon with the B-E counselor." Arthur was his secretary. He knew everything that happened in the department and mostly kept his mouth shut.

"I'd be a social insect if I could manage it," I muttered as Tom left my office. "But I've never known what to say to people in bars."

For lunch I met Greg and our friend David Detlor at a health-food restaurant that advertises fifty different kinds of fruit nectar. We'd never eaten there before, but Greg knew he'd love the place. It was already a favorite of David's, and he still has all his teeth, so I figured it would be okay with me.

David was there when I arrived, but not Greg. David works for the company too, in a different department. He, however, has proved remarkably resistant to corporate blandishment. Not only has he never undertaken B-E, he hasn't even bought a three-piece suit. Today he was wearing chewed-up blue jeans and a flashy Hawaiian shirt, of a type that was cool about ten years ago.

"Your boss lets you dress like that?" I asked.

"We have this agreement. I don't tell her she has to give me a job, and she doesn't tell me what to wear."

David's perspective on life is very different from mine. And I don't think it's just that he's in R&D and I'm in Advertising—it's more basic than that. Where he sees the world as a bunch of really neat but optional puzzles put there for his enjoyment, I see it as . . . well, as a series of SATs.

"So what's new with you guys?" he asked, while we stood around waiting for a table.

"Greg's turning into a goddamn butterfly. He went out last week and bought a dozen Italian silk sweaters. It's not a corporate look."

"He's not a corporate *guy*, Margaret."

"Then why is he having all this B-E done if he's not even going to use it?"

"He's dressing up a little. He just wants to look nice. Like Michael Jackson, you know?"

I couldn't tell whether David was kidding me or not. Then he started telling me about his music, this barbershop quartet that he sings in. They were going to dress in black leather for the next competition and sing Shel Silverstein's "Come to Me, My Masochistic Baby."

"It'll knock them on their tails," he said gleefully. "We've already got a great arrangement."

"Do you think it will win, David?" It seemed too weird to please the judges in that sort of a show.

"Who cares?" said David. He didn't look worried.

Just then Greg showed up. He was wearing a cobalt blue silk sweater with a copper green design on it. Italian. He was also wearing a pair of dangly earrings shaped like bright blue airplanes. We were shown to a table near a display of carved vegetables.

"This is great," said David. "Everybody wants to sit near the vegetables. It's where you sit to be *seen* in this place." He nodded to Greg. "I think it's your sweater."

"It's the butterfly in my personality," said Greg. "Headwaiters never used to do stuff like this for me. I always got the table next to the espresso machine."

If Greg was going to go on about the perks that come with being a butterfly, I was going to change the subject.

"David, how come you still haven't signed up for B-E?" I asked. "The company pays half the cost, and they don't ask questions."

David screwed up his mouth, raised his hands to his face, and made small, twitching, insect gestures, as if grooming his nose and eyes. "I'm doing okay the way I am."

Greg chuckled at this, but I was serious. "You'll get ahead faster with a little adjustment. Plus you're showing a good attitude, you know, if you do it."

"I'm getting ahead faster than I want to right now—it looks like I won't be able to take the three months off that I wanted this summer."

"Three months?" I was astonished. "Aren't you afraid you won't have a job to come back to?"

"I could live with that," said David calmly, opening his menu.

The waiter took our orders. We sat for a moment in a companionable silence, the self-congratulation that follows ordering high-fiber foodstuffs. Then I told them the story of my encounter with Harry Winthrop.

"There's something wrong with me," I said. "Why suck his blood? What good is that supposed to do me?"

"Well," said David, "*you* chose this schedule of treatments. Where did you want it to go?"

"According to the catalog," I said, "the No. 2 Insect Option is supposed to make me into a successful competitor for a middle-management niche, with triggerable responses that can be useful in gaining entry to upper hierarchical levels. Unquote." Of course, that was just ad talk—I didn't really expect it to do all that. "That's what I want. I want to be in charge. I want to be the boss."

"Maybe you should go back to BioEngineering and try again," said Greg. "Sometimes the hormones don't do what you expect. Look at my tongue, for instance." He unfurled it gently and rolled it back into his mouth. "Though I'm sort of getting to like it." He sucked at his drink, making disgusting slurping sounds. He didn't need a straw.

"Don't bother with it, Margaret," said David firmly, taking a cup of rosehip tea from the waiter. "Bioengineering is a waste of time and money and millions of years of evolution. If human beings were intended to be managers, we'd have evolved pin-striped body covering."

"That's cleverly put," I said, "but it's dead wrong."

The waiter brought our lunches, and we stopped talking as he put them in front of us. It seemed like the anticipatory silence of three very hungry people, but was in fact the polite silence of three people who have been brought up not to argue in front of disinterested bystanders. As soon as he left, we resumed the discussion.

"I mean it," David said. "The dubious survival benefits of management aside, bio-engineering is a waste of effort. Harry Winthrop, for instance, doesn't need B-E at all. Here he is, fresh out of business school, audibly buzzing with lust for a high-level management position. Basically he's just marking time until a presidency opens up somewhere. And what gives him the edge over you is his youth and inexperience, not some specialized primate adaptation."

"Well," I said with some asperity, "he's not constrained by a knowledge of what's failed in the past, that's for sure. But saying that doesn't solve my problem, David. Harry's signed up. I've signed up. The changes are under way and I don't have any choice."

I squeezed a huge glob of honey into my tea from a plastic bottle shaped like a teddy bear. I took a sip of the tea; it was minty and very sweet. "And now I'm turning into the wrong kind of insect. It's ruined my ability to deal with Product Marketing."

"Oh, give it a rest!" said Greg suddenly. "This is *so* boring. I don't want to hear any more about corporate hugger-mugger. Let's talk about something that's fun."

I had had enough of Greg's lepidopterate lack of concentration. "Something that's *fun?* I've invested all my time and most of my genetic material in this job. This is all the goddamn fun there is."

The honeyed tea made me feel hot. My stomach itched—I wondered if I was having an allergic reaction. I scratched, and not discreetly. My hand came out from under my shirt full of little waxy scales. What the hell was going on under there? I tasted one of the scales; it was wax all right. Worker bee changes? I couldn't help myself—I stuffed the wax into my mouth.

David was busying himself with his alfalfa sprouts, but Greg looked disgusted. "That's gross, Margaret," he said. He made a face, sticking his tongue part way out. Talk about gross. "Can't you wait until after lunch?"

I was doing what came naturally, and did not dignify his statement with a response.

There was a side dish of bee pollen on the table. I took a spoonful and mixed it with the wax, chewing noisily. I'd had a rough morning, and bickering with Greg wasn't making the day more pleasant.

Besides, neither he nor David has any real respect for my position in the company. Greg doesn't take my job seriously at all. And David simply does what he wants to do, regardless of whether it makes any money, for himself or anyone else. He was giving me a back-to-nature lecture, and it was far too late for that.

This whole lunch was a waste of time. I was tired of listening to them, and felt an intense urge to get back to work. A couple of quick stings distracted them both: I had the advantage of surprise. I ate some more honey and quickly waxed them over. They were soon hibernating side by side in two large octagonal cells.

I looked around the restaurant. People were rather nervously pretending not to have noticed. I called the waiter over and handed him my credit card. He signaled to several busboys, who brought a covered cart and took Greg and David away. "They'll eat themselves out of that by Thursday afternoon," I told him. "Store them on their sides in a warm, dry place, away from direct heat." I left a large tip.

I walked back to the office, feeling a bit ashamed of myself. A couple days of hibernation weren't going to make Greg or David more sympathetic to my problems. And they'd be real mad when they got out.

I didn't use to do things like that. I used to be more patient, didn't I? More appreciative of the diverse spectrum of human possibility. More interested in sex and television.

This job was not doing much for me as a warm, personable human being. At the very least, it was turning me into an unpleasant lunch companion. Whatever had made me think I wanted to get into management anyway?

The money, maybe.

But that wasn't all. It was the challenge, the chance to do something new, to control the total effort instead of just doing part of a project. . . .

The money too, though. There were other ways to get money. Maybe I should just kick the supports out from under the damn job and start over again.

I saw myself sauntering into Tom's office, twirling his visitor's chair around and falling into it. The words "I quit" would force their way out, almost against my will. His face would show surprise—feigned, of course. By then I'd have to go through with it. Maybe I'd put my feet up on his desk. And then—

But was it possible to just quit, to go back to being the person I used to be? No, I wouldn't be able to do it. I'd never be a management virgin again.

I walked up to the employee entrance at the rear of the building. A suction device next to the door sniffed at me, recognized my scent, and clicked the door open. Inside, a group of new employees, trainees, were clustered near the door, while a personnel officer introduced them to the lock and let it familiarize itself with their pheromones.

On the way down the hall, I passed Tom's office. The door was open. He was at his desk, bowed over some papers, and looked up as I went by.

"Ah, Margaret," he said. "Just the person I want to talk to. Come in for a minute, would you." He moved a large file folder onto the papers in front of him on his desk, and folded his hands on top of them. "So glad you were passing by." He nodded toward a large, comfortable chair. "Sit down."

"We're going to be doing a bit of restructuring in the department," he began, "and I'll need your input, so I want to fill you in now on what will be happening."

I was immediately suspicious. Whenever Tom said "I'll need your input," he meant everything was decided already.

"We'll be reorganizing the whole division, of course," he continued, drawing little boxes on a blank piece of paper. He'd mentioned this at the department meeting last week.

"Now, your group subdivides functionally into two separate areas, wouldn't you say?"

"Well—"

"Yes," he said thoughtfully, nodding his head as though in agreement. "That would be the way to do it." He added a few lines and a few more boxes. From what I could see, it meant that Harry would do all the interesting stuff and I'd sweep up afterwards.

"Looks to me as if you've cut the balls out of my area and put them over into Harry Winthrop's," I said.

"Ah, but your area is still very important, my dear. That's why I don't have you actually reporting to Harry." He gave me a smile like a lie.

He had put me in a tidy little bind. After all, he was my boss. If he was going to take most of my area away from me, as it seemed he was, there wasn't much I could do to stop him. And I would be better off if we both pretended that I hadn't experienced any loss of status. That way I kept my title and my salary.

"Oh, I see." I said. "Right."

It dawned on me that this whole thing had been decided already, and that Harry Winthrop probably knew all about it. He'd probably even wangled a raise out of it. Tom had called me in here to make it look casual, to make it look as though I had something to say about it. I'd been set up.

This made me mad. There was no question of quitting now. I'd stick around and fight. My eyes blurred, unfocused, refocused again. Compound eyes! The promise of the small comb in my hand was fulfilled! I felt a deep chemical understanding of the ecological system I was now a part of. I knew where I fit in. And I knew what I was going to do. It was inevitable now, hardwired in at the DNA level.

The strength of this conviction triggered another change in the chitin, and for the first time I could actually feel the rearrangement of my mouth and nose, a numb tickling like inhaling seltzer water. The stiletto receded and mandibles jutted forth, rather like Katharine Hepburn. Form and function achieved an orgasmic synchronicity. As my jaw pushed forward, mantis-like, it also opened, and I pounced on Tom and bit his head off.

He leaped from his desk and danced headless about the office.

I felt in complete control of myself as I watched him and continued the conversation. "About the Model 2000 launch," I said. "If we factor in the demand for pipeline throughout and adjust the media mix just a bit, I think we can present a very tasty little package to Product Marketing by the end of the week."

Tom continued to strut spasmodically, making vulgar copulative motions. Was I responsible for evoking these mantid reactions? I was unaware of a sexual component in our relationship.

I got up from the visitor's chair and sat behind his desk, thinking about what had just happened. It goes without saying that I was surprised at my own actions. I mean, irritable is one thing, but biting people's heads off is quite another. But I have to admit that my second thought was, well, this certainly is a useful strategy, and should make a considerable difference in my ability to advance myself. Hell of a lot more productive than sucking people's blood.

Maybe there was something after all to Tom's talk about having the proper attitude.

And, of course, thinking of Tom, my third reaction was regret. He really had been a likeable guy, for the most part. But what's done is done, you know, and there's no use chewing on it after the fact.

I buzzed his assistant on the intercom. "Arthur," I said, "Mr. Samson and I have come to an evolutionary parting of the ways. Please have him re-engineered. And charge it to Personnel."

Now I feel an odd itching on my forearms and thighs. Notches on which I might fiddle a song?

Kirinyaga
MIKE RESNICK

Mike Resnick is one of the best-selling authors in science fiction, and one of the most prolific. His many novels include *Santiago, The Dark Lady, Stalking the Unicorn, Birthright: The Book of Man, Paradise, Ivory, Soothsayer, Oracle, Lucifer Jones, Purgatory, Inferno, A Miracle of Rare Design, The Widowmaker, The Soul Eater,* and *A Hunger in the Soul.* His award-winning short fiction has been gathered in the collections *Will the Last Person to Leave the Planet Please Turn Off the Sun?, An Alien Land, Kirinyaga, A Safari of the Mind,* and *Hunting the Snark and Other Short Novels.* In the last decade or so, he has become almost as prolific as an anthologist, producing, as editor, *Inside the Funhouse: 17 SF Stories about SF, Whatdunits, More Whatdunits,* and *Shaggy B.E.M Stories,* and a long string of anthologies co-edited with Martin H. Greenberg—*Alternate Presidents, Alternate Kennedys, Alternate Warriors, Aladdin: Master of the Lamp, Dinosaur Fantastic, By Any Other Fame, Alternate Outlaws,* and *Sherlock Holmes in Orbit,* among others—as well as two anthologies co-edited with Gardner Dozois. He won the Hugo Award in 1989 for "Kirinyaga," the story that follows. He won another Hugo Award in 1991 for another story in the Kirinyaga series, "The Manumouki," and another Hugo and Nebula in 1995 for his novella "Seven Views of Olduvai Gorge." His most recent books include the novel *The Return of Santiago,* and the anthologies *Stars: Songs Inspired by the Songs of Janis Ian* (edited with Janis Ian), and *New Voices in Science Fiction.* His stories have appeared in our Sixth, Seventh, Ninth, Eleventh, Twelfth, Fourteenth, and Seventeenth annual collections. He lives with his wife, Carol, in Cincinnati, Ohio.

The "Kirinyaga" series, taking place on an orbital space-colony that has been remade in the image of ancient Kenya as a utopian experiment (the stories have been gathered in the collection *Kirinyaga*), has been one of the most talked-about and controversial series in the recent history of science fiction. This, the very first story of the sequence and still one of the best, reminds us that although we like to compliment ourselves, rather smugly, on the brightness and rationality of our tidy, shiny modern world, the Old Ways still exist—and maybe always will.

In the beginning, Ngai lived alone atop the mountain called Kirinyaga. In the fullness of time He created three sons, who became the fathers of the Masai, the Kamba, and the Kikuyu races, and to each son He offered a spear, a bow, and a digging-stick. The Masai chose the spear, and was told to tend herds on the vast savannah. The Kamba chose the bow, and was sent to the dense forests to hunt for game. But Gikuyu, the first Kikuyu, knew that Ngai loved the earth and the seasons, and chose the digging-stick. To reward him for this Ngai not only taught him the secrets of the seed and the harvest, but gave him Kirinyaga, with its holy fig tree and rich lands.

The sons and daughters of Gikuyu remained on Kirinyaga until the white man came and took their lands away, and even when the white man had been banished they did not return, but chose to remain in the cities, wearing Western clothes and using Western machines and living Western lives. Even I, who am a *mundumugu*— a witch doctor—was born in the city. I have never seen the lion or the elephant or the rhinoceros, for all of them were extinct before my birth; nor have I seen Kirinyaga as Ngai meant it to be seen, for a bustling, overcrowded city of three million inhabitants covers its slopes, every year approaching closer and closer to Ngai's throne at the summit. Even the Kikuyu have forgotten its true name, and now know it only as Mount Kenya.

To be thrown out of Paradise, as were the Christian Adam and Eve, is a terrible fate, but to live beside a debased Paradise is infinitely worse. I think about them frequently, the descendants of Gikuyu who have forgotten their origin and their traditions and are now merely Kenyans, and I wonder why more of them did not join with us when we created the utopian world of Kirinyaga.

True, it is a harsh life, for Ngai never meant life to be easy; but it is also a satisfying life. We live in harmony with our environment, we offer sacrifices when Ngai's tears of compassion fall upon our fields and give sustenance to our crops, we slaughter a goat to thank him for the harvest.

Our pleasures are simple: a gourd of *pombe* to drink, the warmth of a *boma* when the sun has gone down, the wail of a newborn son or daughter, the footraces and spear-throwing and other contests, the nightly singing and dancing.

Maintenance watches Kirinyaga discreetly, making minor orbital adjustments when necessary, assuring that our tropical climate remains constant. From time to time they have subtly suggested that we might wish to draw upon their medical expertise, or perhaps allow our children to make use of their educational facilities, but they have taken our refusal with good grace, and have never shown any desire to interfere in our affairs.

Until I strangled the baby.

It was less than an hour later that Koinnage, our paramount chief, sought me out.

"That was an unwise thing to do, Koriba," he said grimly.

"It was not a matter of choice," I replied. "You know that."

"Of course you had a choice," he responded. "You could have let the infant live."

He paused, trying to control his anger and his fear. "Maintenance has never set foot on Kirinyaga before, but now they will come."

"Let them," I said with a shrug. "No law has been broken."

"We have killed a baby," he replied. "They will come, and they will revoke our charter!"

I shook my head. "No one will revoke our charter."

"Do not be too certain of that, Koriba," he warned me. "You can bury a goat alive, and they will monitor us and shake their heads and speak contemptuously among themselves about our religion. You can leave the aged and the infirm out for the hyenas to eat, and they will look upon us with disgust and call us godless heathens. But I tell you that killing a newborn infant is another matter. They will not sit idly by; they will come."

"If they do, I shall explain why I killed it," I replied calmly.

"They will not accept your answers," said Koinnage. "They will not understand."

"They will have no choice but to accept my answers," I said. "This is Kirinyaga, and they are not permitted to interfere."

"They will find a way," he said with an air of certainty. "We must apologize and tell them that it will not happen again."

"We will not apologize," I said sternly. "Nor can we promise that it will not happen again."

"Then, as paramount chief, I will apologize."

I stared at him for a long moment, then shrugged. "Do what you must do," I said. Suddenly I could see the terror in his eyes.

"What will you do to me?" he asked fearfully.

"I? Nothing at all," I said. "Are you not my chief?" As he relaxed, I added: "But if I were you, I would beware of insects."

"Insects?" he repeated. "Why?"

"Because the next insect that bites you, be it spider or mosquito or fly, will surely kill you," I said. "Your blood will boil within your body, and your bones will melt. You will want to scream out your agony, yet you will be unable to utter a sound." I paused. "It is not a death I would wish on a friend," I added seriously.

"Are we not friends, Koriba?" he said, his ebony face turning an ash gray.

"I thought we were," I said. "But my friends honor our traditions. They do not apologize for them to the white man."

"I will not apologize!" he promised fervently. He spat on both his hands as a gesture of his sincerity.

I opened one of the pouches I kept around my waist and withdrew a small polished stone from the shore of our nearby river. "Wear this around your neck," I said, handing it to him, "and it shall protect you from the bites of insects."

"Thank you, Koriba!" he said with sincere gratitude, and another crisis had been averted.

We spoke about the affairs of the village for a few more minutes, and finally he left me. I sent for Wambu, the infant's mother, and led her through the ritual of purification, so that she might conceive again. I also gave her an ointment to relieve the pain in her breasts, since they were heavy with milk. Then I sat down by the fire before my *boma* and made myself available to my people, settling disputes over the ownership of chickens and goats, and supplying charms against demons, and instructing my people in the ancient ways.

By the time of the evening meal, no one had a thought for the dead baby. I ate alone in my *boma*, as befitted my status, for the *mundumugu* always lives and eats apart from his people. When I had finished I wrapped a blanket around my body to protect me from the cold and walked down the dirt path to where all the other *bomas* were clustered. The cattle and goats and chickens were penned up for the night, and my people, who had slaughtered and eaten a cow, were now singing and dancing and drinking great quantities of *pombe*. As they made way for me, I walked over to the caldron and took a drink of *pombe*, and then, at Kanjara's request, I slit open a goat and read its entrails and saw that his youngest wife would soon conceive, which was cause for more celebration. Finally the children urged me to tell them a story.

"But not a story of Earth," complained one of the taller boys. "We hear those all the time. This must be a story about Kirinyaga."

"All right," I said. "If you will all gather around, I will tell you a story of Kirinyaga." The youngsters all moved closer. "This," I said, "is the story of the Lion and the Hare." I paused until I was sure that I had everyone's attention, especially that of the adults. "A hare was chosen by his people to be sacrificed to a lion, so that the lion would not bring disaster to their village. The hare might have run away, but he knew that sooner or later the lion would catch him, so instead he sought out the lion and walked right up to him, and as the lion opened his mouth to swallow him, the hare said, 'I apologize, Great Lion.'

" 'For what?' asked the lion curiously.

" 'Because I am such a small meal,' answered the hare. 'For that reason, I brought honey for you as well.'

" 'I see no honey,' said the lion.

" 'That is why I apologized,' answered the hare. 'Another lion stole it from me. He is a ferocious creature, and says that he is not afraid of you.'

"The lion rose to his feet. 'Where is this other lion?' he roared.

"The hare pointed to a hole in the earth. 'Down there,' he said, 'but he will not give you back your honey.'

" 'We shall see about that!' growled the lion.

"He jumped into the hole, roaring furiously, and was never seen again, for the hare had chosen a very deep hole indeed. Then the hare went home to his people and told them that the lion would never bother them again."

Most of the children laughed and clapped their hands in delight, but the same young boy voiced his objection.

"That is not a story of Kirinyaga," he said scornfully. "We have no lions here."

"It *is* a story of Kirinyaga," I replied. "What is important about the story is not that it concerned a lion and a hare, but that it shows that the weaker can defeat the stronger if he uses his intelligence."

"What has that to do with Kirinyaga?" asked the boy.

"What if we pretend that the men of Maintenance, who have ships and weapons, are the lion, and the Kikuyu are the hares?" I suggested. "What shall the hares do if the lion demands a sacrifice?"

The boy suddenly grinned. "Now I understand! We shall throw the lion down a hole!"

"But we have no holes here," I pointed out.

"Then what shall we do?"

"The hare did not know that he would find the lion near a hole," I replied. "Had he found him by a deep lake, he would have said that a large fish took the honey."

"We have no deep lakes."

"But we do have intelligence," I said. "And if Maintenance ever interferes with us, we will use our intelligence to destroy the lion of Maintenance, just as the hare used his intelligence to destroy the lion of the fable."

"Let us think how to destroy Maintenance right now!" cried the boy. He picked up a stick and brandished it at an imaginary lion as if it were a spear and he a great hunter.

I shook my head. "The hare does not hunt the lion, and the Kikuyu do not make war. The hare merely protects himself, and the Kikuyu do the same."

"Why would Maintenance interfere with us?" asked another boy, pushing his way to the front of the group. "They are our friends."

"Perhaps they will not," I answered reassuringly. "But you must always remember that the Kikuyu have no true friends except themselves."

"Tell us another story, Koriba!" cried a young girl.

"I am an old man," I said. "The night has turned cold, and I must have my sleep."

"Tomorrow?" she asked. "Will you tell us another tomorrow?"

I smiled. "Ask me tomorrow, after all the fields are planted and the cattle and goats are in their enclosures and the food has been made and the fabrics have been woven."

"But girls do not herd the cattle and goats," she protested. "What if my brothers do not bring all their animals to the enclosure?"

"Then I will tell a story just to the girls," I said.

"It must be a long story," she insisted seriously, "for we work much harder than the boys."

"I will watch you in particular, little one," I replied, "and the story will be as long or as short as your work merits."

The adults all laughed and suddenly she looked very uncomfortable, but then I chuckled and hugged her and patted her head, for it was necessary that the children learned to love their *mundumugu* as well as hold him in awe, and finally she ran off to play and dance with the other girls, while I retired to my *boma*.

Once inside, I activated my computer and discovered that a message was waiting for me from Maintenance, informing me that one of their number would be visiting me the following morning. I made a very brief reply—"Article II, Paragraph 5," which is the ordinance forbidding intervention—and lay down on my sleeping blanket, letting the rhythmic chanting of the singers carry me off to sleep.

I awoke with the sun the next morning and instructed my computer to let me know when the Maintenance ship had landed. Then I inspected my cattle and my goats—I, alone of my people, planted no crops, for the Kikuyu feed their *mundumugu*, just as they tend his herds and weave his blankets and keep his *boma* clean— and stopped by Simani's *boma* to deliver a balm to fight the disease that was afflicting his joints. Then, as the sun began warming the earth, I returned to my own *boma*, skirting the pastures where the young men were tending their animals. When I arrived, I knew the ship had landed, for I found the droppings of a hyena on the ground near my hut, and that is the surest sign of a curse.

I learned what I could from the computer, then walked outside and scanned the horizon while two naked children took turns chasing a small dog and running away from it. When they began frightening my chickens, I gently sent them back to their own *boma*, and then seated myself beside my fire. At last I saw my visitor from Maintenance, coming up the path from Haven. She was obviously uncomfortable in the heat, and she slapped futilely at the flies that circled her head. Her blonde hair was starting to turn gray, and I could tell by the ungainly way she negotiated the steep, rocky path that she was unused to such terrain. She almost lost her balance a number of times, and it was obvious that her proximity to so many animals frightened her, but she never slowed her pace, and within another ten minutes she stood before me.

"Good morning," she said.

"*Jambo*, Memsahib," I replied.

"You are Koriba, are you not?"

I briefly studied the face of my enemy; middle-aged and weary, it did not appear formidable. "I am Koriba," I replied.

"Good," she said. "My name is—"

"I know who you are," I said, for it is best, if conflict cannot be avoided, to take the offensive.

"You do?"

I pulled the bones out of my pouch and cast them on the dirt. "You are Barbara Eaton, born of Earth," I intoned, studying her reactions as I picked up the bones and cast them again. "You are married to Robert Eaton, and you have worked for Maintenance for nine years." A final cast of the bones. "You are forty-one years old, and you are barren."

"How did you know all that?" she asked with an expression of surprise.

"Am I not the *mundumugu*?"

She stared at me for a long minute. "You read my biography on your computer," she concluded at last.

"As long as the facts are correct, what difference does it make whether I read them from the bones or the computer?" I responded, refusing to confirm her statement. "Please sit down, Memsahib Eaton."

She lowered herself awkwardly to the ground, wrinkling her face as she raised a cloud of dust.

"It's very hot," she noted uncomfortably.

"It is very hot in Kenya," I replied.

"You could have created any climate you desired," she pointed out.

"We *did* create the climate we desired," I answered.

"Are there predators out there?" she asked, looking out over the savannah.

"A few," I replied.

"What kind?"

"Hyenas."

"Nothing larger?" she asked.

"There *is* nothing larger anymore," I said.

"I wonder why they didn't attack me?"

"Perhaps because you are an intruder," I suggested.

"Will they leave me alone on my way back to Haven?" she asked nervously, ignoring my comment.

"I will give you a charm to keep them away."

"I'd prefer an escort."

"Very well," I said.

"They're such ugly animals," she said with a shudder. "I saw them once when we were monitoring your world."

"They are very useful animals," I answered, "for they bring many omens, both good and bad."

"Really?"

I nodded. "A hyena left me an evil omen this morning."

"And?" she asked curiously.

"And here you are," I said.

She laughed. "They told me you were a sharp old man."

"They were mistaken," I replied. "I am a feeble old man who sits in front of his *boma* and watches younger men tend his cattle and goats."

"You are a feeble old man who graduated with honors from Cambridge and then acquired two postgraduate degrees from Yale," she replied.

"Who told you that?"

She smiled. "You're not the only one who reads biographies."

I shrugged. "My degrees did not help me become a better *mundumugu*," I said. "The time was wasted."

"You keep using that word. What, exactly, *is* a *mundumugu*?"

"You would call him a witch doctor," I answered. "But in truth the *mundumugu*, while he occasionally casts spells and interprets omens, is more a repository of the collected wisdom and traditions of his race."

"It sounds like an interesting occupation," she said.

"It is not without its compensations."

"And *such* compensations!" she said with false enthusiasm as a goat bleated in the distance and a young man yelled at it in Swahili. "Imagine having the power of life and death over an entire utopian world!"

So now it comes, I thought. Aloud I said: "It is not a matter of exercising power, Memsahib Eaton, but of maintaining traditions."

"I rather doubt that," she said bluntly.

"Why should you doubt what I say?" I asked.

"Because if it were traditional to kill newborn infants, the Kikuyus would have died out after a single generation."

"If the slaying of the infant arouses your disapproval," I said calmly, "I am surprised Maintenance has not previously asked about our custom of leaving the old and the feeble out for the hyenas."

"We know that the elderly and the infirm have consented to your treatment of them, much as we may disapprove of it," she replied. "We also know that a newborn infant could not possibly consent to its own death." She paused, staring at me. "May I ask why this particular baby was killed?"

"That *is* why you have come here, is it not?"

"I have been sent here to evaluate the situation," she replied, brushing an insect from her cheek and shifting her position on the ground. "A newborn child was killed. We would like to know why."

I shrugged. "It was killed because it was born with a terrible *thahu* upon it."

She frowned. "A *thahu*? What is that?"

"A curse."

"Do you mean that it was deformed?" she asked.

"It was not deformed."

"Then what was this curse that you refer to?"

"It was born feet-first," I said.

"That's it?" she asked, surprised. "That's the curse?"

"Yes."

"It was murdered simply because it came out feet-first?"

"It is not murder to put a demon to death," I explained patiently. "Our tradition tells us that a child born in this manner is actually a demon."

"You are an educated man, Koriba," she said. "How can you kill a perfectly healthy infant and blame it on some primitive tradition?"

"You must never underestimate the power of tradition, Memsahib Eaton," I said. "The Kikuyu turned their backs on their traditions once; the result is a mechanized, impoverished, overcrowded country that is no longer populated by Kikuyu, or Masai, or Luo, or Wakamba, but by a new, artificial tribe known only as Kenyans. We here on Kirinyaga are true Kikuyu, and we will not make that mistake again. If the rains are late, a ram must be sacrificed. If a man's veracity is questioned, he must undergo the ordeal of the *githani* trial. If an infant is born with a *thahu* upon it, it must be put to death."

"Then you intend to continue to kill any children that are born feet-first?" she asked.

"That is correct," I responded.

A drop of sweat rolled down her face as she looked directly at me and said: "I don't know what Maintenance's reaction will be."

"According to our charter, Maintenance is not permitted to interfere with us," I reminded her.

"It's not that simple, Koriba," she said. "According to your charter, any member of your community who wishes to leave your world is allowed free passage to Haven, from which he or she can board a ship to Earth." She paused. "Was the baby you killed given such a choice?"

"I did not kill a baby, but a demon," I replied, turning my head slightly as a hot breeze stirred up the dust around us.

She waited until the breeze died down, then coughed before speaking. "You do understand that not everyone in Maintenance may share that opinion?"

"What Maintenance thinks is of no concern to us," I said.

"When innocent children are murdered, what Maintenance thinks is of supreme importance to you," she responded. "I am sure you do not want to defend your practices in the Utopian Court."

"Are you here to evaluate the situation, as you said, or to threaten us?" I asked calmly.

"To evaluate the situation," she replied. "But there seems to be only one conclusion that I can draw from the facts that you have presented to me."

"Then you have not been listening to me," I said, briefly closing my eyes as another, stronger breeze swept past us.

"Koriba, I know that Kirinyaga was created so that you could emulate the ways of your forefathers—but surely you must see the difference between the torture of animals as a religious ritual and the murder of a human baby."

I shook my head. "They are one and the same," I replied. "We cannot change our way of life because it makes *you* uncomfortable. We did that once before, and within a mere handful of years your culture had corrupted our society. With every factory we built, with every job we created, with every bit of Western technology we accepted, with every Kikuyu who converted to Christianity, we became something we were not meant to be." I stared directly into her eyes. "I am the *mundumugu*, entrusted with preserving all that makes us Kikuyu, and I will not allow that to happen again."

"There are alternatives," she said.

"Not for the Kikuyu," I replied adamantly.

"There *are*," she insisted, so intent upon what she had to say that she paid no attention to a black-and-gold centipede that crawled over her boot. "For example, years spent in space can cause certain physiological and hormonal changes in humans. You noted when I arrived that I am forty-one years old and childless. That is true. In fact, many of the women in Maintenance are childless. If you will turn the babies over to us, I am sure we can find families for them. This would effectively remove them from your society without the necessity of killing them. I could speak to my superiors about it; I think that there is an excellent chance that they would approve."

"That is a thoughtful and innovative suggestion, Memsahib Eaton," I said truthfully. "I am sorry that I must reject it."

"But why?" she demanded.

"Because the first time we betray our traditions this world will cease to be Kirinyaga, and will become merely another Kenya, a nation of men awkwardly pretending to be something they are not."

"I could speak to Koinnage and the other chiefs about it," she suggested meaningfully.

"They will not disobey my instructions," I replied confidently.

"You hold that much power?"

"I hold that much respect," I answered. "A chief may enforce the law, but it is the *mundumugu* who interprets it."

"Then let us consider other alternatives."

"No."

"I am trying to avoid a conflict between Maintenance and your people," she said, her voice heavy with frustration. "It seems to me that you could at least make the effort to meet me halfway."

"I do not question your motives, Memsahib Eaton," I replied, "but you are an intruder representing an organization that has no legal right to interfere with our culture. We do not impose our religion or our morality upon Maintenance, and Maintenance may not impose its religion or morality upon us."

"It's not that simple."

"It is precisely that simple," I said.

"That is your last word on the subject?" she asked.

"Yes."

She stood up. "Then I think it is time for me to leave and make my report."

I stood up as well, and a shift in the wind brought the odors of the village: the scent of bananas, the smell of a fresh caldron of *pombe*, even the pungent odor of a bull that had been slaughtered that morning.

"As you wish, Memsahib Eaton," I said. "I will arrange for your escort." I signalled to a small boy who was tending three goats and instructed him to go to the village and send back two young men.

"Thank you," she said. "I know it's an inconvenience, but I just don't feel safe with hyenas roaming loose out there."

"You are welcome," I said. "Perhaps, while we are waiting for the men who will accompany you, you would like to hear a story about the hyena."

She shuddered involuntarily. "They are such ugly beasts!" she said distastefully. "Their hind legs seem almost deformed." She shook her head. "No, I don't think I'd be interested in hearing a story about a hyena."

"You will be interested in *this* story," I told her.

She stared at me curiously, then shrugged. "All right," she said. "Go ahead."

"It is true that hyenas are deformed, ugly animals," I began, "but once, a long time ago, they were as lovely and graceful as the impala. Then one day a Kikuyu chief gave a hyena a young goat to take as a gift to Ngai, who lived atop the holy mountain Kirinyaga. The hyena took the goat between his powerful jaws and headed toward the distant mountain—but on the way he passed a settlement filled with Europeans and Arabs. It abounded in guns and machines and other wonders he had never seen before, and he stopped to look, fascinated. Finally an Arab noticed him staring intently and asked if he, too, would like to become a civilized man—and as he opened his mouth to say that he would, the goat fell to the ground and ran away. As the goat raced out of sight, the Arab laughed and explained that he was only joking, that of course no hyena could become a man." I paused for a moment, and then continued. "So the hyena proceeded to Kirinyaga, and when he reached the summit, Ngai asked him what had become of the goat. When the hyena told him, Ngai hurled him off the mountaintop for having the audacity to believe he could become a man. He did not die from the fall, but his rear legs were crippled, and Ngai declared that from that day forward, all hyenas would appear thus—and to remind them of the foolishness of trying to become something that they were not, He also gave them a fool's laugh." I paused again, and stared at her. "Memsahib Eaton, you do not hear the Kikuyu laugh like fools, and I will not let them become crippled like the hyena. Do you understand what I am saying?"

She considered my statement for a moment, then looked into my eyes. "I think we understand each other perfectly, Koriba," she said.

The two young men I had sent for arrived just then, and I instructed them to accompany her to Haven. A moment later they set off across the dry savannah, and I returned to my duties.

I began by walking through the fields, blessing the scarecrows. Since a number of the smaller children followed me, I rested beneath the trees more often than was necessary, and always, whenever we paused, they begged me to tell them more stories. I told them the tale of the Elephant and the Buffalo, and how the Masai *el-moran* cut the rainbow with his spear so that it never again came to rest upon the earth, and why the nine Kikuyu tribes are named after Gikuyu's nine daughters, and when the sun became too hot I led them back to the village.

Then, in the afternoon, I gathered the older boys about me and explained once more how they must paint their faces and bodies for their forthcoming circumcision ceremony. Ndemi, the boy who had insisted upon a story about Kirinyaga the night before, sought me out privately to complain that he had been unable to slay a small gazelle with his spear, and asked for a charm to make its flight more accurate. I explained to him that there would come a day when he faced a buffalo or a hyena with no charm, and that he must practice more before he came to me again. He was one to watch, this little Ndemi, for he was impetuous and totally without fear; in the old days, he would have made a great warrior, but on Kirinyaga we had no warriors. If we remained fruitful and fecund, however, we would someday need more chiefs and even another *mundumugu*, and I made up my mind to observe him closely.

In the evening, after I ate my solitary meal, I returned to the village, for Njogu, one of our young men, was to marry Kamiri, a girl from the next village. The bride-price had been decided upon, and the two families were waiting for me to preside at the ceremony.

Njogu, his faced streaked with paint, wore an ostrich-feather headdress, and looked very uneasy as he and his betrothed stood before me. I slit the throat of a fat ram that Kamiri's father had brought for the occasion, and then I turned to Njogu.

"What have you to say?" I asked.

He took a step forward. "I want Kamiri to come and till the fields of my *shamba*," he said, his voice cracking with nervousness as he spoke the prescribed words, "for I am a man, and I need a woman to tend to my *shamba* and dig deep around the roots of my plantings, that they may grow well and bring prosperity to my house."

He spit on both his hands to show his sincerity, and then, exhaling deeply with relief, he stepped back.

I turned to Kamiri.

"Do you consent to till the *shamba* of Njogu, son of Muchiri?" I asked her.

"Yes," she said softly, bowing her head. "I consent."

I held out my right hand, and the bride's mother placed a gourd of *pombe* in it.

"If this man does not please you," I said to Kamiri, "I will spill the *pombe* upon the ground."

"Do not spill it," she replied.

"Then drink," I said, handing the gourd to her.

She lifted it to her lips and took a swallow, then handed it to Njogu, who did the same.

When the gourd was empty, the parents of Njogu and Kamiri stuffed it with grass, signifying the friendship between the two clans.

Then a cheer rose from the onlookers, the ram was carried off to be roasted, more *pombe* appeared as if by magic, and while the groom took the bride off to his *boma*, the remainder of the people celebrated far into the night. They stopped only when the bleating of the goats told them that some hyenas were nearby, and then the women and children went off to their *bomas* while the men took their spears and went into the fields to frighten the hyenas away.

Koinnage came up to me as I was about to leave.

"Did you speak to the woman from Maintenance?" he asked.

"I did," I replied.

"What did she say?"

"She said that they do not approve of killing babies who are born feet-first."

"And what did *you* say?" he asked nervously.

"I told her that we did not need the approval of Maintenance to practice our religion," I replied.

"Will Maintenance listen?"

"They have no choice," I said. "And *we* have no choice, either," I added. "Let them dictate one thing that we must or must not do, and soon they will dictate all things. Give them their way, and Njogu and Kamiri would have recited wedding vows from the Bible or the Koran. It happened to us in Kenya; we cannot permit it to happen on Kirinyaga."

"But they will not punish us?" he persisted.

"They will not punish us," I replied.

Satisfied, he walked off to his *boma* while I took the narrow, winding path to my own. I stopped by the enclosure where my animals were kept and saw that there were two new goats there, gifts from the bride's and groom's families in gratitude for my services. A few minutes later I was asleep within the walls of my own *boma*.

The computer woke me a few minutes before sunrise. I stood up, splashed my face with water from the gourd I keep by my sleeping blanket, and walked over to the terminal.

There was a message for me from Barbara Eaton, brief and to the point:

It is the preliminary finding of Maintenance that infanticide, for any reason, is a direct violation of Kirinyaga's charter. No action will be taken for past offenses.

We are also evaluating your practice of euthanasia, and may require further testimony from you at some point in the future.

Barbara Eaton

A runner from Koinnage arrived a moment later, asking me to attend a meeting of the Council of Elders, and I knew that he had received the same message.

I wrapped my blanket around my shoulders and began walking to Koinnage's *shamba*, which consisted of his *boma*, as well as those of his three sons and their wives. When I arrived I found not only the local elders waiting for me, but also two chiefs from neighboring villages.

"Did you receive the message from Maintenance?" demanded Koinnage, as I seated myself opposite him.

"I did."

"I warned you that this would happen!" he said. "What will we do now?"

"We will do what we have always done," I answered calmly.

"We cannot," said one of the neighboring chiefs. "They have forbidden it."

"They have no right to forbid it," I replied.

"There is a woman in my village whose time is near," continued the chief, "and all of the signs and omens point to the birth of twins. We have been taught that the firstborn must be killed, for one mother cannot produce two souls—but now Maintenance has forbidden it. What are we to do?"

"We must kill the firstborn," I said, "for it will be a demon."

"And then Maintenance will make us leave Kirinyaga!" said Koinnage bitterly.

"Perhaps we could let the child live," said the chief. "That might satisfy them, and then they might leave us alone."

I shook my head. "They will not leave you alone. Already they speak about the way we leave the old and the feeble out for the hyenas, as if this were some enormous sin against their God. If you give in on the one, the day will come when you must give in on the other."

"Would that be so terrible?" persisted the chief. "They have medicines that we do not possess; perhaps they could make the old young again."

"You do not understand," I said, rising to my feet. "Our society is not a collection of separate people and customs and traditions. No, it is a complex system, with all the pieces as dependent upon each other as the animals and vegetation of the savannah. If you burn the grass, you will not only kill the impala who feeds upon it, but the predator who feeds upon the impala, and the ticks and flies who live upon the predator, and the vultures and maribou storks who feed upon his remains when he dies. You cannot destroy the part without destroying the whole."

I paused to let them consider what I had said, and then continued speaking: "Kirinyaga is like the savannah. If we do not leave the old and the feeble out for the hyenas, the hyenas will starve. If the hyenas starve, the grass eaters will become so numerous that there is no land left for our cattle and goats to graze. If the old and the feeble do not die when Ngai decrees it, then soon we will not have enough food to go around."

I picked up a stick and balanced it precariously on my forefinger.

"This stick," I said, "is the Kikuyu people, and my finger is Kirinyaga. They are in perfect balance." I stared at the neighboring chief. "But what will happen if I alter the balance, and put my finger *here*?" I asked, gesturing to the end of the stick.

"The stick will fall to the ground."

"And here?" I asked, pointing to a stop an inch away from the center.

"It will fall."

"Thus is it with us," I explained. "Whether we yield on one point or all points, the result will be the same: the Kikuyu will fall as surely as the stick will fall. Have we learned nothing from our past? We *must* adhere to our traditions; they are all that we have!"

"But Maintenance will not allow us to do so!" protested Koinnage.

"They are not warriors, but civilized men," I said, allowing a touch of contempt to creep into my voice. "Their chiefs and their *mundumugus* will not send them to Kirinyaga with guns and spears. They will issue warnings and findings and declarations, and finally, when that fails, they will go to the Utopian Court and plead their case, and the trial will be postponed many times and reheard many more times." I could see them finally relaxing, and I smiled confidently at them. "Each of you will have died from the burden of your years before Maintenance does anything other than talk. I am your *mundumugu*; I have lived among civilized men, and I tell you that this is the truth."

The neighboring chief stood up and faced me. "I will send for you when the twins are born," he pledged.

"I will come," I promised him.

We spoke further, and then the meeting ended and the old men began wandering off to their *bomas*, while I looked to the future, which I could see more clearly than Koinnage or the elders.

I walked through the village until I found the bold young Ndemi, brandishing his spear and hurling it at a buffalo he had constructed out of dried grasses.

"*Jambo*, Koriba!" he greeted me.

"*Jambo*, my brave young warrior," I replied.

"I have been practicing, as you ordered."

"I thought you wanted to hunt the gazelle," I noted.

"Gazelles are for children," he answered. "I will slay *mbogo*, the buffalo."

"*Mbogo* may feel differently about it," I said.

"So much the better," he said confidently. "I have no wish to kill an animal as it runs away from me."

"And when will you go out to slay the fierce *mbogo*?"

He shrugged. "When I am more accurate." He smiled up at me. "Perhaps tomorrow."

I stared at him thoughtfully for a moment, and then spoke: "Tomorrow is a long time away. We have business tonight."

"What business?" he asked.

"You must find ten friends, none of them yet of circumcision age, and tell them to come to the pond within the forest to the south. They must come after the sun has set, and you must tell them that Koriba the *mundumugu* commands that they tell no one, not even their parents, that they are coming." I paused. "Do you understand, Ndemi?"

"I understand."

"Then go," I said. "Bring my message to them."

He retrieved his spear from the straw buffalo and set off at a trot, young and tall and strong and fearless.

You are the future, I thought, as I watched him run toward the village. *Not Koinnage, not myself, not even the young bridegroom Njogu, for their time will have come and gone before the battle is joined. It is you, Ndemi, upon whom Kirinyaga must depend if it is to survive.*

Once before the Kikuyu have had to fight for their freedom. Under the leadership of Jomo Kenyatta, whose name has been forgotten by most of your parents, we took the terrible oath of Mau Mau, and we maimed and we killed and we committed such atrocities that finally we achieved Uhuru, for against such butchery civilized men have no defense but to depart.

And tonight, young Ndemi, while your parents are asleep, you and your companions will meet me deep in the woods, and you in your turn and they in theirs will learn one last tradition of the Kikuyu, for I will invoke not only the strength of Ngai but also the indomitable spirit of Jomo Kenyatta. I will administer a hideous oath and force you to do unspeakable things to prove your fealty, and I will teach each of you, in turn, how to administer the oath to those who come after you.

There is a season for all things: for birth, for growth, for death. There is unquestionably a season for Utopia, but it will have to wait.

For the season of Uhuru is upon us.

Tales from the venia woods

ROBERT SILVERBERG

Robert Silverberg is one of the most famous SF writers of modern times, with dozens of novels, anthologies, and collections to his credit. As both writer and editor (he was editor of the original anthology series *New Dimensions*, perhaps the most acclaimed anthology series of its era), Silverberg was one of the most influential figures of the Post New Wave era of the '70s, and continues to be at the forefront of the field to this very day, having won a total of five Nebula Awards and four Hugo Awards, plus SFWA's prestigious Grandmaster Award. His novels include the acclaimed *Dying Inside*, *Lord Valentine's Castle*, *The Book of Skulls*, *Downward to the Earth*, *Tower of Glass*, *Son of Man*, *Nightwings*, *The World Inside*, *Born with the Dead*, *Shadrack in the Furnace*, *Thorns*, *Up the Line*, *The Man in the Maze*, *Tom O' Bedlam*, *Star of Gypsies*, *At Winter's End*, *The Face of the Waters*, *Kingdoms of the Wall*, *Hot Sky at Morning*, *The Alien Years*, *Lord Prestimion*, *Mountains of Majipoor*, and two novel-length expansions of famous Isaac Asimov stories, *Nightfall* and *The Ugly Little Boy*. His collections include *Unfamiliar Territory*, *Capricorn Games*, *Majipoor Chronicles*, *The Best of Robert Silverberg*, *At the Conglomeroid Cocktail Party*, *Beyond the Safe Zone*, and a massive retrospective collection, *The Collected Stories of Robert Silverberg, Volume One: Secret Sharers*. His reprint anthologies are far too numerous to list here, but include *The Science Fiction Hall of Fame, Volume One* and the distinguished *Alpha* series, among dozens of others. His most recent books are the novel *The Long Way Home* and the mosaic novel *Roma Eterna*. He lives with his wife, writer Karen Haber, in Oakland, California.

Prolific as he has been at novel-length, Silverberg has been at least as prolific at shorter lengths, and over the last few decades has produced an amazing—well-nigh unprecedented—flood of high-quality short work such as "Born with the Dead," "Sundance," "In Entropy's Jaws," "Nightwings," "Push No More," "In the Group," "Capricorn Games," "Trips," "Swartz between the Galaxies," "The Pope of the Chimps," "Multiples," "The Palace at Midnight," "We Are for the Dark," "In Another Country," "Basileus," "The Secret Sharer," "Enter a Soldier. Later: Enter Another," "Sailing to Byzantium," "Beauty in the Night," "Death Do Us Part," "The Colonel in Autumn," and dozens of others.

A good case could be made for using almost any of those stories in an anthology such as this . . . but I found myself returning to the story that follows instead, part of Silverberg's long-running "Roma" series (which have now been collected in the abovementioned *Roma Eterna*), stories set in an evocative and vividly drawn alternate world, where the Roman Empire never fell, and the Pax Romana has continued even to the present day. Here, in one of the best of the "Roma" stories, he takes us to a world full of haunting echoes of our own timeline and yet also very different, for a deceptively quiet story of childhood dreams, conflicting loyalties, and the futility of good intentions.

T his all happened a long time ago, in the early decades of the Second Republic, when I was a boy growing up in Upper Pannonia. Life was very simple then, at least for us. We lived in a forest village on the right bank of the Danubius—my parents; my grandmother; my sister, Friya; and I. My father, Tyr, for whom I am named, was a blacksmith, my mother, Julia, taught school in our house, and my grandmother was the priestess at the little Temple of Juno Teutonica nearby.

It was a very quiet life. The automobile hadn't yet been invented then—all this was around the year 2650, and we still used horse-drawn carriages or wagons—and we hardly ever left the village. Once a year, on Augustus Day—back then we still celebrated Augustus Day—we would all dress in our finest clothes and my father would get our big iron-bound carriage out of the shed, the one he had built with his own hands, and we'd drive to the great municipium of Venia, a two-hour journey away, to hear the Imperial band playing waltzes in the Plaza of Vespasianus. Afterward there'd be cakes and whipped cream at the big hotel nearby, and tankards of cherry beer for the grown-ups, and then we'd begin the long trip home. Today, of course, the forest is gone and our little village has been swallowed up by the ever-growing municipium, and it's a twenty-minute ride by car to the center of the city from where we used to live. But at that time it was a grand excursion, the event of the year for us.

I know now that Venia is only a minor provincial city, that compared with Londin or Parisi or Urbs Roma itself it's nothing at all. But to me it was the capital of the world. Its splendors stunned me and dazed me. We would climb to the top of the great column of Basileus Andronicus, which the Greeks put up eight hundred years ago to commemorate their victory over Caesar Maximilianus during the Civil War in the days when the Empire was divided, and we'd stare out at the whole city; and my mother, who had grown up in Venia, would point everything out to us, the Senate building, the opera house, the aqueduct, the university, the ten bridges, the Temple of Jupiter Teutonicus, the proconsul's palace, the much greater palace that Trajan VII built for himself during that dizzying period when Venia was essentially the second capital of the Empire, and so forth. For days afterward my dreams would glitter with memories of what I had seen in Venia, and my sister and I would hum waltzes as we whirled along the quiet forest paths.

There was one exciting year when we made the Venia trip twice. That was 2647, when I was ten years old, and I can remember it so exactly because that was the year when the First Consul died—C. Junius Scaevola, I mean, the Founder of the Second Republic. My father was very agitated when the news of his death came. "It'll be touch and go now, touch and go, mark my words," he said over and over. I asked my grandmother what he meant by that, and she said, "Your father's afraid that they'll bring back the Empire, now that the old man's dead." I didn't see what was so upsetting about that—it was all the same to me, Republic or Empire, Consul or Imperator—but to my father it was a big issue, and when the new First Consul came to Venia later that year, touring the entire vast Imperium province by province for the sake of reassuring everyone that the Republic was stable and intact, my father got out the carriage and we went to attend his Triumph and Processional. So I had a second visit to the capital that year.

Half a million people, so they say, turned out in downtown Venia to applaud the new First Consul. This was N. Marcellus Turritus, of course. You probably think of him as the fat, bald old man on the coinage of the late twenty-seventh century that still shows up in pocket change now and then, but the man I saw that day—I had just a glimpse of him, a fraction of a second as the Consular chariot rode past, but the memory still blazes in my mind seventy years later—was lean and virile, with a jutting jaw and fiery eyes and dark, thick curling hair. We threw up our arms in the old Roman salute and at the top of our lungs we shouted out to him, "Hail, Marcellus! Long live the Consul!"

(We shouted it, by the way, not in Latin but in Germanisch. I was very surprised at that. My father explained afterward that it was by the First Consul's own orders. He wanted to show his love for the people by encouraging all the regional languages, even at a public celebration like this one. The Gallians had hailed him in Gallian, the Britannians in Britannic, the Lusitanians in whatever it is they speak there, and as he traveled through the Teutonic provinces he wanted us to yell his praises in Germanisch. I realize that there are some people today, very conservative Republicans, who will tell you that this was a terrible idea, because it has led to the resurgence of all kinds of separatist regional activities in the Imperium. It was the same sort of regionalist fervor, they remind us, that brought about the crumbling of the Empire a hundred years before. To men like my father, though, it was a brilliant political stroke, and he cheered the new First Consul with tremendous Germanische exuberance and vigor. But my father managed to be a staunch regionalist and a staunch Republican at the same time. Bear in mind that over my mother's fierce objections he had insisted on naming his children for ancient Teutonic gods instead of giving them the standard Roman names that everybody else in Pannonia favored then.)

Other than going to Venia once a year, or on this one occasion twice, I never went anywhere. I hunted, I fished, I swam, I helped my father in the smithy, I helped my grandmother in the Temple, I studied reading and writing in my mother's school. Sometimes Friya and I would go wandering in the forest, which in those days was dark and lush and mysterious. And that was how I happened to meet the last of the Caesars.

There was supposed to be a haunted house deep in the woods. Marcus Aurelius Schwarzchild it was who got me interested in it, the tailor's son, a sly and unlikable boy with a cast in one eye. He said it had been a hunting lodge in the time of the Caesars, and that the bloody ghost of an Emperor who had been killed in a hunting accident could be seen at noontime, the hour of his death, pursuing the ghost of a wolf around and around the building. "I've seen it myself," he said. "The ghost of the Emperor, I mean. He had a laurel wreath on, and everything, and his rifle was polished so it shined like gold."

I didn't believe him. I didn't think he'd had the courage to go anywhere near the haunted house and certainly not that he'd seen the ghost. Marcus Aurelius Schwarzchild was the sort of boy you wouldn't believe if he said it was raining, even if you were getting soaked to the skin right as he was saying it. For one thing, I didn't believe in ghosts, not very much. My father had told me it was foolish to think that the dead still lurked around in the world of the living. For another, I asked my grandmother if there had ever been an Emperor killed in a hunting accident in our forest, and she laughed and said no, not ever: the Imperial Guard would have razed the village to the ground and burned down the woods, if that had ever happened.

But nobody doubted that the house itself, haunted or not, was really there. Everyone in the village knew that. It was said to be in a certain dark part of the woods where the trees were so old that their branches were tightly woven together. Hardly anyone ever went there. The house was just a ruin, they said, and haunted besides, definitely haunted, so it was best to leave it alone.

It occurred to me that the place might just actually have been an Imperial hunting lodge, and that if it had been abandoned hastily after some unhappy incident and never visited since, it might still have some trinkets of the Caesars in it, little statuettes of the gods, or cameos of the royal family, things like that. My grandmother collected small ancient objects of that sort. Her birthday was coming, and I wanted a nice gift for her. My fellow villagers might be timid about poking around in the haunted house, but why should I be? I didn't believe in ghosts, after all.

But on second thought I didn't particularly want to go there alone. This wasn't cowardice so much as sheer common sense, which even then I possessed in full measure. The woods were full of exposed roots hidden under fallen leaves; if you tripped on one and hurt your leg, you would lie there a long time before anyone who might help you came by. You were also less likely to lose your way if you had someone else with you who could remember trail marks. And there was some occasional talk of wolves. I figured the probability of my meeting one wasn't much better than the likelihood of ghosts, but all the same it seemed like a sensible idea to have a companion with me in that part of the forest. So I took my sister along.

I have to confess that I didn't tell her that the house was supposed to be haunted. Friya, who was about nine then, was very brave for a girl, but I thought she might find the possibility of ghosts a little discouraging. What I did tell her was that the old house might still have Imperial treasures in it, and if it did she could have her pick of any jewelry we found.

Just to be on the safe side we slipped a couple of holy images into our pockets—Apollo for her, to cast light on us as we went through the dark woods, and Woden for me, since he was my father's special god. (My grandmother always wanted him to pray to Jupiter Teutonicus, but he never would, saying that Jupiter Teutonicus was a god that the Romans invented to pacify our ancestors. This made my grandmother angry, naturally. "But *we* are Romans," she would say. "Yes, we are," my father would tell her, "but we're Teutons also, or at least I am, and I don't intend to forget it.")

It was a fine Saturday morning in spring when we set out, Friya and I, right after breakfast, saying nothing to anybody about where we were going. The first part of the forest path was a familiar one: we had traveled it often. We went past Agrippina's Spring, which in medieval times was thought to have magical powers, and then the three battered and weatherbeaten statues of the pretty young boy who was supposed to be the first Emperor Hadrianus's lover two thousand years ago, and after that we came to Baldur's Tree, which my father said was sacred, though he died before I was old enough to attend the midnight rituals that he and some of his friends used to hold there. (I think my father's generation was the last one that took the old Teutonic religion seriously.)

Then we got into deeper, darker territory. The paths were nothing more than sketchy trails here. Marcus Aurelius had told me that we were supposed to turn left at a huge old oak tree with unusual glossy leaves. I was still looking for it when Friya said, "We turn here," and there was the shiny-leaved oak. I hadn't mentioned it to her. So perhaps the girls of our village told each other tales about the haunted house too; but I never found out how she knew which way to go.

Onward and onward we went, until even the trails gave out, and we were wandering through sheer wilderness. The trees were ancient here, all right, and their boughs were interlaced high above us so that almost no sunlight reached the forest floor. But we didn't see any houses, haunted or otherwise, or anything else that indicated that human beings had ever been here. We'd been hiking for hours, now. I kept one hand on the idol of Woden in my pocket and I stared hard at every unusual-looking tree or rock we saw, trying to engrave it on my brain for use as a trail marker on the way back.

It seemed pointless to continue, and dangerous besides. I would have turned back long before, if Friya hadn't been with me; but I didn't want to look like a coward in front of her. And she was forging on in a tireless way, inflamed, I guess, by the prospect of finding a fine brooch or necklace for herself in the old house, and showing not the slightest trace of fear or uneasiness. But finally I had had enough.

"If we don't come across anything in the next five minutes —" I said.

"There," said Friya. "Look."

I followed her pointing hand. At first all I saw was more forest. But then I noticed, barely visible behind a curtain of leafy branches, what could have been the sloping wooden roof of a rustic hunting lodge. Yes! Yes, it was! I saw the scalloped gables, I saw the boldly carved roof-posts.

So it was really there, the secret forest lodge, the old haunted house. In frantic excitement I began to run toward it, Friya chugging valiantly along behind me, struggling to catch up.

And then I saw the ghost.

He was old — ancient — a frail, gaunt figure, white-bearded, his long white hair a tangle of knots and snarls. His clothing hung in rags. He was walking slowly toward the house, shuffling, really, a bent and stooped and trembling figure clutching a huge stack of kindling to his breast. I was practically on top of him before I knew he was there.

For a long moment we stared at each other, and I can't say which of us was the more terrified. Then he made a little sighing sound and let his bundle of firewood fall to the ground, and fell down beside it, and lay there like one dead.

"Marcus Aurelius was right!" I murmured. "There really is a ghost here!"

Friya shot me a glance that must have been a mixture of scorn and derision and real anger besides, for this was the first she had heard of the ghost story that I had obviously taken pains to conceal from her. But all she said was, "Ghosts don't fall down and faint, silly. He's nothing but a scared old man." And went to him unhesitatingly.

Somehow we got him inside the house, though he tottered and lurched all the way and nearly fell half a dozen times. The place wasn't quite a ruin, but close: dust everywhere, furniture that looked as if it'd collapse into splinters if you touched it, draperies hanging in shreds. Behind all the filth we could see how beautiful it all once had been, though. There were faded paintings on the walls, some sculptures, a collection of arms and armor worth a fortune.

He was terrified of us. "Are you from the quaestors?" he kept asking. Latin was what he spoke. "Are you here to arrest me? I'm only the caretaker, you know. I'm not any kind of a danger. I'm only the caretaker." His lips quavered. "Long live the First Consul!" he cried, in a thin, hoarse, ragged croak of a voice.

"We were just wandering in the woods," I told him. "You don't have to be afraid of us."

"I'm only the caretaker," he said again and again.

We laid him out on a couch. There was a spring just outside the house, and Friya brought water from it and sponged his cheeks and brow. He looked half starved, so we prowled around for something to feed him, but there was hardly anything: some nuts and berries in a bowl, a few scraps of smoked meat that looked like they were a hundred years old, a piece of fish that was in better shape, but not much. We fixed a meal for him, and he ate slowly, very slowly, as if he were unused to food. Then he closed his eyes without a word. I thought for a moment that he had died, but no, no, he had simply dozed off. We stared at each other, not knowing what to do.

"Let him be," Friya whispered, and we wandered around the house while we waited for him to awaken. Cautiously we touched the sculptures, we blew dust away from the paintings. No doubt of it, there had been Imperial grandeur here. In one of the upstairs cupboards I found some coins, old ones, the kind with the Emperor's head on them that weren't allowed to be used any more. I saw trinkets, too, a couple of necklaces and a jewel-handled dagger. Friya's eyes gleamed at the sight of the necklaces, and mine at the dagger, but we let everything stay where it was. Stealing from a ghost is one thing, stealing from a live old man is another. And we hadn't been raised to be thieves.

When we went back downstairs to see how he was doing, we found him sitting up, looking weak and dazed, but not quite so frightened. Friya offered him some more of the smoked meat, but he smiled and shook his head.

"From the village, are you? How old are you? What are your names?"

"This is Friya," I said. "I'm Tyr. She's nine and I'm twelve."

"Friya. Tyr." He laughed. "Time was when such names wouldn't have been permitted, eh? But times have changed." There was a flash of sudden vitality in his eyes, though only for an instant. He gave us a confidential, intimate smile. "Do you know whose place this was, you two? The Emperor Maxentius, that's who! This was his hunting lodge. Caesar himself! He'd stay here when the stags were running, and hunt his fill, and then he'd go on into Venia, to Trajan's palace, and there'd be such feasts as you can't imagine, rivers of wine, and the haunches of venison turning on the spit—ah, what a time that was, what a time!"

He began to cough and sputter. Friya put her arm around his thin shoulders.

"You shouldn't talk so much, sir. You don't have the strength."

"You're right. You're right." He patted her hand. His was like a skeleton's. "How long ago it all was. But here I stay, trying to keep the place up—in case Caesar ever wanted to hunt here again—in case—in case—" A look of torment, of sorrow. "There isn't any Caesar, is there? First Consul! Hail! Hail Junius Scaevola!" His voice cracked as he raised it.

"The Consul Junius is dead, sir," I told him. "Marcellus Turritus is First Consul now."

"Dead? Scaevola? Is it so?" He shrugged. "I hear so little news. I'm only the caretaker, you know. I never leave the place. Keeping it up, in case—in case—"

But of course he wasn't the caretaker. Friya never thought he was: she had seen, right away, the resemblance between that shriveled old man and the magnificent figure of Caesar Maxentius in the painting behind him on the wall. You had to ignore the difference in age—the Emperor couldn't have been much more than thirty when his portrait was painted—and the fact that the Emperor was in resplendent bemedalled formal uniform and the old man was wearing rags. But they had the same long chin, the same sharp, hawklike nose, the same penetrating icy-blue eyes. It was the royal face, all right. I hadn't noticed; but girls have a quicker eye for such things. The Emperor Maxentius's youngest brother was who this gaunt old man was, Quintus Fabius Caesar, the last survivor of the old Imperial house, and, therefore, the true Emperor himself. Who had been living in hiding ever since the downfall of the Empire at the end of the Second War of Reunification.

He didn't tell us any of that, though, until our third or fourth visit. He went on pretending he was nothing but a simple old man who had happened to be stranded here when the old regime was overthrown, and was simply trying to do his job, despite the difficulties of age, on the chance that the royal family might some day be restored and would want to use its hunting lodge again.

But he began to give us little gifts, and that eventually led to his admitting his true identity.

For Friya he had a delicate necklace made of long slender bluish beads. "It comes from Aegyptus," he said. "It's thousands of years old. You've studied Aegyptus in school, haven't you? You know that it was a great empire long before Roma ever was?" And with his own trembling hands he put it around her neck.

That same day he gave me a leather pouch in which I found four or five triangular arrowheads made of a pink stone that had been carefully chipped sharp around the edges. I looked at them, mystified. "From Nova Roma," he explained. "Where the redskinned people live. The Emperor Maxentius loved Nova Roma, especially the far west, where the bison herds are. He went there almost every year to hunt. Do you see the trophies?" And, indeed, the dark musty room was lined with animal heads, great massive bison with thick curling brown wool, glowering down out of the gallery high above.

We brought him food, sausages and black bread that we brought from home, and fresh fruit, and beer. He didn't care for the beer and asked rather timidly if we could bring him wine instead. "I am Roman, you know," he reminded us. Getting wine for him wasn't so easy, since we never used it at home, and a twelve-year-old boy could hardly go around to the wineshop to buy some without starting tongues wagging. In the end I stole some from the Temple while I was helping out my grandmother. It was thick sweet wine, the kind used for offerings, and I don't know how much he liked it. But he was grateful. Apparently an old couple who lived on the far side of the woods had looked after him for some years, bringing him food and wine, but in recent weeks they hadn't been around and he had had to forage for himself, with little luck: that was why he was so gaunt. He was afraid they were ill or dead, but when I asked where they lived, so I could find out whether they were all right, he grew uneasy and refused to tell me. I wondered about that. If I had realized then who he was, and that the old couple must have been Empire loyalists, I'd have understood. But I still hadn't figured out the truth.

Friya broke it to me that afternoon, as we were on our way home. "Do you think he's the Emperor's brother, Tyr? Or the Emperor himself?"

"What?"

"He's got to be one or the other. It's the same face."

"I don't know what you're talking about, sister."

"The big portrait on the wall, silly. Of the Emperor. Haven't you noticed that it looks just like him?"

I thought she was out of her mind. But when we went back the following week, I gave the painting a long close look, and looked at him, and then at the painting again, and I thought, yes, yes, it might just be so.

What clinched it were the coins he gave us that day. "I can't pay you in money of the Republic for all you've brought me," he said. "But you can have these. You won't be able to spend them, but they're still valuable to some people, I understand. As relics of history." His voice was bitter. From a worn old velvet pouch he drew out half a dozen coins, some copper, some silver. "These are coins of Maxentius," he said. They were like the ones we had seen while snooping in the upstairs cupboards on our first visit, showing the same face as on the painting, that of a young, vigorous bearded man. "And these are older ones, coins of Emperor Laureolus, who was Caesar when I was a boy."

"Why, he looks just like you!" I blurted.

Indeed he did. Not nearly so gaunt, and his hair and beard were better trimmed; but otherwise the face of the regal old man on those coins might easily have been that of our friend the caretaker. I stared at him, and at the coins in my hand, and again at him. He began to tremble. I looked at the painting on the wall behind us again. "No," he said faintly. "No, no, you're mistaken—I'm nothing like him, nothing at all—" And his shoulders shook and he began to cry. Friya brought him some wine, which steadied him a little. He took the coins from me and looked at them in silence a long while, shaking his head sadly, and finally handed them back. "Can I trust you with a secret?" he asked. And his tale came pouring out of him. The truth. The truth that he had held locked up in his bosom all those long years.

He spoke of a glittering boyhood, almost sixty years earlier, in that wondrous time between the two Wars of Reunification: a magical life, endlessly traveling from palace to palace, from Roma to Venia, from Venia to Constantinopolis, from Constantinopolis to Nishapur. He was the youngest and most pampered of five royal princes; his father had died young, drowned in a foolish swimming exploit, and when his grandfather Laureolus Augustus died the Imperial throne would go to his brother Maxentius. He himself, Quintus Fabius, would be a provincial governor somewhere when he grew up, perhaps in Syria or Persia, but for now there was nothing for him to do but enjoy his gilded existence.

Then death came at last to old Emperor Laureolus, and Maxentius succeeded him; and almost at once there began the four-year horror of the Second War of Reunification, when somber and harsh colonels who despised the lazy old Empire smashed it to pieces, rebuilt it as a Republic, and drove the Caesars from power. We knew the story, of course; but to us it was a tale of the triumph of virtue and honor over corruption and tyranny. To Quintus Fabius, weeping as he told it to us from his own point of view, the fall of the Empire had been not only a harrowing personal tragedy but a terrible disaster for the entire world.

Good little Republicans though we were, our hearts were wrung by the things he told us, the scenes of his family's agony: the young Emperor Maxentius trapped in his own palace, gunned down with his wife and children at the entrance to the Imperial baths. Camillus, the second brother, who had been Prince of Constantinopolis, pursued through the streets of Roma at dawn and slaughtered by revolutionaries on the steps of the Temple of Castor and Pollux. Prince Flavius, the third brother, escaping from the capital in a peasant's wagon, hidden under huge bunches of grapes, and setting up a government-in-exile in Neapolis, only to be taken and executed before he had been Emperor a full week. Which brought the succession down to sixteen-year-old Prince Augustus, who had been at the university in Parisi. Well named, he was: for the first of all the Emperors was an Augustus, and another one two thousand years later was the last, reigning all of three days before the men of the Second Republic found him and put him before the firing squad.

Of the royal princes, only Quintus Fabius remained. But in the confusion he was overlooked. He was hardly more than a boy; and, although technically he was now Caesar, it never occurred to him to claim the throne. Loyalist supporters dressed him in peasant clothes and smuggled him out of Roma while the capital was still in flames, and he set out on what was to become a lifetime of exile.

"There were always places for me to stay," he told us. "In out-of-the-way towns where the Republic had never really taken hold, in backwater provinces, in places you've never heard of. The Republic searched for me for a time, but never very well, and then the story began to circulate that I was dead. The skeleton of some boy found in the ruins of the palace in Roma was said to be mine. After that I could move around more or less freely, though always in poverty, always in secrecy."

"And when did you come here?" I asked.

"Almost twenty years ago. Friends told me that this hunting lodge was here, still more or less intact as it had been at the time of the Revolution, and that no one ever went near it, that I could live here undisturbed. And so I have. And so I will, for however much time is left." He reached for the wine, but his hands were shaking so badly that Friya took it from him and poured him a glass. He drank it in a single gulp. "Ah, children, children, what a world you've lost! What madness it was, to destroy the Empire! What greatness existed then!"

"Our father says things have never been so good for ordinary folk as they are under the Republic," Friya said.

I kicked her ankle. She gave me a sour look.

Quintus Fabius said sadly, "I mean no disrespect, but your father sees only his own village. We were trained to see the entire world in a glance. The Imperium, the whole globe-spanning Empire. Do you think the gods meant to give the Imperium just to anyone at all? Anyone who could grab power and proclaim himself First Consul? Ah, no, no, the Caesars were uniquely chosen to sustain the Pax Romana, the universal peace that has enfolded this whole planet for so long. Under us there was nothing but peace, peace eternal and unshakable, once the Empire had reached its complete form. But with the Caesars now gone, how much longer do you think the peace will last? If one man can take power, so can another, or another. There will be five First Consuls at once, mark my words. Or fifty. And every province will want to be an Empire in itself. Mark my words, children. Mark my words."

I had never heard such treason in my life. Or anything so wrongheaded.

The Pax Romana? *What* Pax Romana? There had never been such a thing, not really. At least never for very long. Old Quintus Fabius would have had us believe that the Empire had brought unbroken and unshakable peace to the entire world, and had kept it that way for twenty centuries. But what about the Civil War, when the Greek half of the Empire fought for fifty years against the Latin half? Or the two Wars of Unification? And hadn't there been minor rebellions constantly, all over the Empire, hardly a century without one, in Persia, in India, in Britannia, in Africa Aethiopica? No, I thought, what he's telling us simply isn't true. The long life of the Empire had been a time of constant brutal oppression, with people's spirits held in check everywhere by military force. The real Pax Romana was something that existed only in modern times, under the Second Republic. So my father had taught me. So I deeply believed.

But Quintus Fabius was an old man, wrapped in dreams of his own wondrous lost childhood. Far be it from me to argue with him about such matters as these. I simply smiled and nodded, and poured more wine for him when his glass was empty. And Friya and I sat there spellbound as he told us, hour after hour, of what it had been like to be a prince of the royal family in the dying days of the Empire, before true grandeur had departed forever from the world.

When we left him that day, he had still more gifts for us. "My brother was a great collector," he said. "He had whole houses stuffed full of treasure. All gone now, all but what you see here, which no one remembered. When I'm gone, who knows what'll become of them? But I want you to have these. Because you've been so kind to me. To remember me by. And to remind you always of what once was, and now is lost."

For Friya there was a small bronze ring, dented and scratched, with a serpent's head on it, that he said had belonged to the Emperor Claudius of the earliest days of the Empire. For me a dagger, not the jewel-handled one I had seen upstairs, but a fine one all the same, with a strange undulating blade, from a savage kingdom on an island in the great Oceanus Pacificus. And for us both, a beautiful little figurine in smooth white alabaster of Pan playing on his pipes, carved by some master craftsman of the ancient days.

The figurine was the perfect birthday gift for grandmother. We gave it to her the next day. We thought she would be pleased, since all of the old gods of Roma are very dear to her; but to our surprise and dismay she seemed startled and upset by it. She stared at it, eyes bright and fierce, as if we had given her a venomous toad.

"Where did you get this thing? Where?"

I looked at Friya, to warn her not to say too much. But as usual she was ahead of me.

"We found it, grandmother. We dug it up."

"You dug it up?"

"In the forest," I put in. "We go there every Saturday, you know, just wandering around. There was this old mound of dirt—we were poking in it, and we saw something gleaming—"

She turned it over and over in her hands. I had never seen her look so troubled. "Swear to me that that's how you found it! Come, now, at the altar of Juno! I want you to swear to me before the Goddess. And then I want you to take me to see this mound of dirt of yours."

Friya gave me a panic-stricken glance.

Hesitantly I said, "We may not be able to find it again, grandmother. I told you, we were just wandering around—we didn't really pay attention to where we were—"

I grew red in the face, and I was stammering, too. It isn't easy to lie convincingly to your own grandmother.

She held the figurine out, its base toward me. "Do you see these marks here? This little crest stamped down here? It's the Imperial crest, Tyr. That's the mark of Caesar. This carving once belonged to the Emperor. Do you expect me to believe that there's Imperial treasure simply lying around in mounds of dirt in the forest? Come, both of you. To the altar, and swear!"

"We only wanted to bring you a pretty birthday gift, grandmother," Friya said softly. "We didn't mean to do any harm."

"Of course not, child. Tell me, now: where'd this thing come from?"

"The haunted house in the woods," she said. And I nodded my confirmation. What could I do? She would have taken us to the altar to swear.

Strictly speaking, Friya and I were traitors to the Republic. We even knew that ourselves, from the moment we realized who the old man really was. The Caesars were proscribed when the Empire fell; everyone within a certain level of blood kinship to the Emperor was condemned to death, so that no one could rise up and claim the throne in years hereafter.

A handful of very minor members of the royal family did indeed manage to escape, so it was said; but giving aid and comfort to them was a serious offense. And this was no mere second cousin or great-grandnephew that we had discovered deep in the forest: this was the Emperor's own brother. He was, in fact, the legitimate Emperor himself, in the eyes of those for whom the Empire had never ended. And it was our responsibility to turn him in to the quaestors. But he was so old, so gentle, so feeble. We didn't see how he could be much of a threat to the Republic. Even if he did believe that the Revolution had been an evil thing, and that only under a divinely chosen Caesar could the world enjoy real peace.

We were children. We didn't understand what risks we were taking, or what perils we were exposing our family to.

Things were tense at our house during the next few days: whispered conferences between our grandmother and our mother, out of our earshot, and then an evening when the two of them spoke with father while Friya and I were confined to our room, and there were sharp words and even some shouting. Afterward there was a long cold silence, followed by more mysterious discussions. Then things returned to normal. My grandmother never put the figurine of Pan in her collection of little artifacts of the old days, nor did she ever speak of it again.

That it had the Imperial crest on it was, we realized, the cause of all the uproar. Even so, we weren't clear about what the problem was. I had thought all along that grandmother was secretly an Empire loyalist herself. A lot of people her age were; and she was, after all, a traditionalist, a priestess of Juno Teutonica, who disliked the revived worship of the old Germanic gods that had sprung up in recent times— "pagan" gods, she called them—and had argued with father about his insistence on naming us as he had. So she should have been pleased to have something that had belonged to the Caesars. But, as I say, we were children then. We didn't take into account the fact that the Republic dealt harshly with anyone who practiced Caesarism. Or that whatever my grandmother's private political beliefs might have been, father was the unquestioned master of our household, and he was a devout Republican.

"I understand you've been poking around that old ruined house in the woods," my father said, a week or so later. "Stay away from it. Do you hear me? Stay away."

And so we would have, because it was plainly an order. We didn't disobey our father's orders.

But then, a few days afterward, I overheard some of the older boys of the village talking about making a foray out to the haunted house. Evidently Marcus Aurelius Schwarzchild had been talking about the ghost with the polished rifle to others beside me, and they wanted the rifle. "It's five of us against one of him," I heard someone say. "We ought to be able to take care of him, ghost or not."

"What if it's a ghost rifle, though?" one of them asked. "A ghost rifle won't be any good to us."

"There's no such thing as a ghost rifle," the first speaker said. "Rifles don't have ghosts. It's a real rifle. And it won't be hard for us to get it away from a ghost."

I repeated all this to Friya.

"What should we do?" I asked her.

"Go out there and warn him. They'll hurt him, Tyr."

"But father said—"

"Even so. The old man's got to go somewhere and hide. Otherwise his blood will be on our heads."

There was no arguing with her. Either I went with her to the house in the woods that moment, or she'd go by herself. That left me with no choice. I prayed to Woden that my father wouldn't find out, or that he'd forgive me if he did; and off we went into the woods, past Agrippina's Spring, past the statues of the pretty boy, past Baldur's Tree, and down the now-familiar path beyond the glossy-leaved oak.

"Something's wrong," Friya said, as we approached the hunting lodge. "I can tell."

Friya always had a strange way of knowing things. I saw the fear in her eyes and felt frightened myself.

We crept forward warily. There was no sign of Quintus Fabius. And when we came to the door of the lodge we saw that it was a little way ajar, and off its hinges, as if it had been forced. Friya put her hand on my arm and we stared at each other. I took a deep breath.

"You wait here," I said, and went in.

It was frightful in there. The place had been ransacked—the furniture smashed, the cupboards overturned, the sculptures in fragments. Someone had slashed every painting to shreds. The collection of arms and armor was gone.

I went from room to room, looking for Quintus Fabius. He wasn't there. But there were bloodstains on the floor of the main hall, still fresh, still sticky.

Friya was waiting on the porch, trembling, fighting back tears.

"We're too late," I told her.

It hadn't been the boys from the village, of course. They couldn't possibly have done such a thorough job. I realized—and surely so did Friya, though we were both too sickened by the realization to discuss it with each other—that grandmother must have told father we had found a cache of Imperial treasure in the old house, and he, good citizen that he was, had told the quaestors. Who had gone out to investigate, come upon Quintus Fabius, and recognized him for a Caesar, just as Friya had. So my eagerness to bring back a pretty gift for grandmother had been the old man's downfall. I suppose he wouldn't have lived much longer in any case, as frail as he was; but the guilt for what I unknowingly brought upon him is something that I've borne ever since.

Some years later, when the forest was mostly gone, the old house accidentally burned down. I was a young man then, and I helped out on the firefighting line. During a lull in the work I said to the captain of the fire brigade, a retired quaestor named Lucentius, "It was an Imperial hunting lodge once, wasn't it?"

"A long time ago, yes."

I studied him cautiously by the light of the flickering blaze. He was an older man, of my father's generation.

Carefully I said, "When I was a boy, there was a story going around that one of the last Emperor's brothers had hidden himself away in it. And that eventually the quaestors caught him and killed him."

He seemed taken off guard by that. He looked surprised and, for a moment, troubled. "So you heard about that, did you?"

"I wondered if there was any truth to it. That he was a Caesar, I mean."

Lucentius glanced away. "He was only an old tramp, is all," he said, in a muffled tone. "An old lying tramp. Maybe he told fantastic stories to some of the gullible kids, but a tramp is all he was, an old filthy lying tramp." He gave me a peculiar look. And then he stamped away to shout at someone who was uncoiling a hose the wrong way.

A filthy old tramp, yes. But not, I think, a liar.

He remains alive in my mind to this day, that poor old relic of the Empire. And now that I am old myself, as old, perhaps, as he was then, I understand something of what he was saying. Not his belief that there necessarily had to be a Caesar in order for there to be peace, for the Caesars were only men themselves, in no way different from the Consuls who have replaced them. But when he argued that the time of the Empire had been basically a time of peace, he may not have been really wrong, even if war had been far from unknown in Imperial days.

For I see now that war can sometimes be a kind of peace also: that the Civil Wars and the Wars of Reunification were the struggles of a sundered Empire trying to reassemble itself so peace might resume. These matters are not so simple. The Second Republic is not as virtuous as my father thought, nor was the old Empire, apparently, quite as corrupt. The only thing that seems true without dispute is that the worldwide hegemony of Roma these past two thousand years under the Empire and then under the Republic, troubled though it has occasionally been, has kept us from even worse turmoil. What if there had been no Roma? What if every region had been free to make war against its neighbors in the hope of creating the sort of Empire that the Romans were able to build? Imagine the madness of it! But the gods gave us the Romans, and the Romans gave us peace: not a perfect peace, but the best peace, perhaps, that an imperfect world could manage. Or so I think now.

In any case the Caesars are dead, and so is everyone else I have written about here, even my little sister, Friya; and here I am, an old man of the Second Republic, thinking back over the past and trying to bring some sense out of it. I still have the strange dagger that Quintus Fabius gave me, the barbaric-looking one with the curious wavy blade, that came from some savage island in the Oceanus Pacificus. Now and then I take it out and look at it. It shines with a kind of antique splendor in the lamplight. My eyes are too dim now to see the tiny Imperial crest that someone engraved on its haft when the merchant captain who brought it back from the South Seas gave it to the Caesar of his time, four or five hundred years ago. Nor can I see the little letters, S P Q R, that are inscribed on the blade. For all I know, they were put there by the frizzy-haired tribesman who fashioned that odd, fierce weapon: for he, too, was a citizen of the Roman Empire. As in a manner of speaking are we all, even now in the days of the Second Republic. As are we all.

Bears Discover Fire

TERRY BISSON

Terry Bisson is the author of a number of critically acclaimed novels such as *Fire on the Mountain, Wyrldmaker,* the popular *Talking Man* (which was a finalist for the World Fantasy Award in 1986), *Voyage to the Red Planet, Pirates of the Universe, The Pickup Artist,* and, in a posthumous collaboration with Walter M. Miller, Jr., a sequel to Miller's *A Canticle for Leibowitz* called *Saint Leibowitz and the Wild Horse Woman.* He is a frequent contributor to such markets as *Sci Fiction, Asimov's Science Fiction, Omni, Playboy,* and *The Magazine of Fantasy and Science Fiction.* In 2000, he won a Nebula Award for his story "macs." His short work has been assembled in the collections *Bears Discover Fire and Other Stories* and *In the Upper Room and Other Likely Stories.* His stories have appeared in our Eighth, Tenth, Twelfth, Thirteenth, and Twenty-first annual collections. He lives with his family in Oakland, California.

Here he offers us a gentle, wry, and whimsical story—which may have been one of the most famous stories of the '90s, and which won Bisson the Nebula Award, the Hugo Award, the Theodore Sturgeon Award, *and* the *Asimov's* Reader's Award in 1991, the only story ever to sweep them all—that's about exactly what it *says* that it's about. . . .

I was driving with my brother, the preacher, and my nephew, the preacher's son, on I-65 just north of Bowling Green when we got a flat. It was Sunday night and we had been to visit Mother at the Home. We were in my car. The flat caused what you might call knowing groans since, as the old-fashioned one in my family (so they tell me), I fix my own tires, and my brother is always telling me to get radials and quit buying old tires.

But if you know how to mount and fix tires yourself, you can pick them up for almost nothing.

Since it was a left rear tire, I pulled over left, onto the median grass. The way my Caddy stumbled to a stop, I figured the tire was ruined. "I guess there's no need asking if you have any of that *FlatFix* in the trunk," said Wallace.

"Here, son, hold the light," I said to Wallace Jr. He's old enough to want to help and not old enough (yet) to think he knows it all. If I'd married and had kids, he's the kind I'd have wanted.

An old Caddy has a big trunk that tends to fill up like a shed. Mine's a '56. Wallace was wearing his Sunday shirt, so he didn't offer to help while I pulled magazines, fishing tackle, a wooden toolbox, some old clothes, a comealong wrapped in a grass sack, and a tobacco sprayer out of the way, looking for my jack. The spare looked a little soft.

The light went out. "Shake it, son," I said.

It went back on. The bumper jack was long gone, but I carry a little ¼ ton hydraulic. I finally found it under Mother's old *Southern Livings*, 1978–1986. I had been meaning to drop them at the dump. If Wallace hadn't been along, I'd have let Wallace Jr. position the jack under the axle, but I got on my knees and did it myself. There's nothing wrong with a boy learning to change a tire. Even if you're not going to fix and mount them, you're still going to have to change a few in this life. The light went off again before I had the wheel off the ground. I was surprised at how dark the night was already. It was late October and beginning to get cool. "Shake it again, son," I said.

It went back on but it was weak. Flickery.

"With radials you just don't *have* flats," Wallace explained in that voice he uses when he's talking to a number of people at once; in this case, Wallace Jr. and myself. "And even when you *do*, you just squirt them with this stuff called *FlatFix* and you just drive on. $3.95 the can."

"Uncle Bobby can fix a tire hisself," said Wallace Jr., out of loyalty I presume.

"*Himself*," I said from halfway under the car. If it was up to Wallace, the boy would talk like what Mother used to call "a helock from the gorges of the mountains." But drive on radials.

"Shake that light again," I said. It was about gone. I spun the lugs off into the hubcap and pulled the wheel. The tire had blown out along the sidewall. "Won't be fixing this one," I said. Not that I cared. I have a pile as tall as a man out by the barn.

The light went out again, then came back better than ever as I was fitting the spare over the lugs. "Much better," I said. There was a flood of dim orange flickery light. But when I turned to find the lug nuts, I was surprised to see that the flashlight the boy was holding was dead. The light was coming from two bears at the edge of the trees, holding torches. They were big, three-hundred pounders, standing about five feet tall. Wallace Jr. and his father had seen them and were standing perfectly still. It's best not to alarm bears.

I fished the lug nuts out of the hubcap and spun them on. I usually like to put a little oil on them, but this time I let it go. I reached under the car and let the jack down and pulled it out. I was relieved to see that the spare was high enough to drive on. I put the jack and the lug wrench and the flat into the trunk. Instead of replacing the hubcap, I put it in there too. All this time, the bears never made a move. They just held the torches up, whether out of curiosity or helpfulness, there was no way of knowing. It looked like there may have been more bears behind them, in the trees.

Opening three doors at once, we got into the car and drove off. Wallace was the first to speak. "Looks like bears have discovered fire," he said.

When we first took Mother to the Home, almost four years (forty-seven months) ago, she told Wallace and me she was ready to die. "Don't worry about me, boys," she whispered, pulling us both down so the nurse wouldn't hear. "I've drove a million miles and I'm ready to pass over to the other shore. I won't have long to linger here." She drove a consolidated school bus for thirty-nine years. Later, after Wallace left, she told me about her dream. A bunch of doctors were sitting around in a circle discussing her case. One said, "We've done all we can for her, boys, let's let her go." They all turned their hands up and smiled. When she didn't die that fall, she seemed disappointed, though as spring came she forgot about it, as old people will.

In addition to taking Wallace and Wallace Jr. to see Mother on Sunday nights, I go myself on Tuesdays and Thursdays. I usually find her sitting in front of the TV, even though she doesn't watch it. The nurses keep it on all the time. They say the old folks like the flickering. It soothes them down.

"What's this I hear about bears discovering fire?" she said on Tuesday. "It's true," I told her as I combed her long white hair with the shell comb Wallace had brought her from Florida. Monday there had been a story in the Louisville *Courier-Journal*, and Tuesday one on NBC or CBS Nightly News. People were seeing bears all over the state, and in Virginia as well. They had quit hibernating, and were apparently planning to spend the winter in the medians of the interstates. There have always been bears in the mountains of Virginia, but not here in western Kentucky, not for almost a hundred years. The last one was killed when Mother was a girl. The theory in the *Courier-Journal* was that they were following I-65 down from the forests of Michigan and Canada, but one old man from Allen County (interviewed on nationwide TV) said that there had always been a few bears left back in the hills, and they had come out to join the others now that they had discovered fire.

"They don't hibernate any more," I said. "They make a fire and keep it going all winter."

"I declare," Mother said. "What'll they think of next!" The nurse came to take her tobacco away, which is the signal for bedtime.

Every October, Wallace Jr. stays with me while his parents go to camp. I realize how backward that sounds, but there it is. My brother is a minister (House of the Righteous Way, Reformed), but he makes two thirds of his living in real estate. He and Elizabeth go to a Christian Success Retreat in South Carolina, where people from all over the country practice selling things to one another. I know what it's like not because they've ever bothered to tell me, but because I've seen the Revolving Equity Success Plan ads late at night on TV.

The school bus let Wallace Jr. off at my house on Wednesday, the day they left. The boy doesn't have to pack much of a bag when he stays with me. He has his own room here. As the eldest of our family, I hung onto the old home place near Smiths Grove. It's getting run down, but Wallace Jr. and I don't mind. He has his own room in Bowling Green, too, but since Wallace and Elizabeth move to a different house every three months (part of the Plan), he keeps his .22 and his comics, the stuff that's important to a boy his age, in his room here at the home place. It's the room his dad and I used to share.

Wallace Jr. is twelve. I found him sitting on the back porch that overlooks the interstate when I got home from work. I sell crop insurance.

After I changed clothes, I showed him how to break the bead on a tire two ways, with a hammer and by backing a car over it. Like making sorghum, fixing tires by hand is a dying art. The boy caught on fast, though. "Tomorrow I'll show you how to mount your tire with the hammer and a tire iron," I said.

"What I wish is I could see the bears," he said. He was looking across the field to I-65, where the northbound lanes cut off the corner of our field. From the house at night, sometimes the traffic sounds like a waterfall.

"Can't see their fire in the daytime," I said. "But wait till tonight." That night CBS or NBC (I forget which is which) did a special on the bears, which were becoming a story of nationwide interest. They were seen in Kentucky, West Virginia, Missouri, Illinois (southern), and, of course, Virginia. There have always been bears in Virginia. Some characters there were even talking about hunting them. A scientist said they were heading into the states where there is some snow but not too much, and where there is enough timber in the medians for firewood. He had gone in with a video camera, but his shots were just blurry figures sitting around a fire. Another scientist said the bears were attracted by the berries on a new bush that grew only in the medians of the interstates. He claimed this berry was the first new species in recent history, brought about by the mixing of seeds along the highway. He ate one on TV, making a face, and called it a "newberry." A climatic ecologist said that the warm winters (there was no snow last winter in Nashville, and only one flurry in Louisville) had changed the bears' hibernation cycle, and now they were able to remember things from year to year. "Bears may have discovered fire centuries ago," he said, "but forgot it." Another theory was that they had discovered (or remembered) fire when Yellowstone burned, several years ago.

The TV showed more guys talking about bears than it showed bears, and Wallace Jr. and I lost interest. After the supper dishes were done I took the boy out behind the house and down to our fence. Across the interstate and through the trees, we could see the light of the bears' fire. Wallace Jr. wanted to go back to the house and get his .22 and go shoot one, and I explained why that would be wrong. "Besides," I said, "a .22 wouldn't do much more to a bear than make it mad."

"Besides," I added, "It's illegal to hunt in the medians."

The only trick to mounting a tire by hand, once you have beaten or pried it onto the rim, is setting the bead. You do this by setting the tire upright, sitting on it, and bouncing it up and down between your legs while the air goes in. When the bead sets on the rim, it makes a satisfying "pop." On Thursday, I kept Wallace Jr. home from school and showed him how to do this until he got it right. Then we climbed our fence and crossed the field to get a look at the bears.

In northern Virginia, according to "Good Morning America," the bears were keeping their fires going all day long. Here in western Kentucky, though, it was still warm for late October and they only stayed around the fires at night. Where they went and what they did in the daytime, I don't know. Maybe they were watching from the newberry bushes as Wallace Jr. and I climbed the government fence and crossed the northbound lanes. I carried an axe and Wallace Jr. brought his .22, not because he wanted to kill a bear but because a boy likes to carry some kind of a gun. The median was all tangled with brush and vines under the maples, oaks, and sycamores. Even though we were only a hundred yards from the house, I had never been there, and neither had anyone else that I knew of. It was like a created country. We found a path in the center and followed it down across a slow, short stream that flowed out of one grate and into another. The tracks in the gray mud were the first bear signs we saw. There was a musty but not really unpleasant smell. In a clearing under a big hollow beech, where the fire had been, we found nothing but ashes. Logs were drawn up in a rough circle and the smell was stronger. I stirred the ashes and found enough coals left to start a new flame, so I banked them back the way they had been left.

I cut a little firewood and stacked it to one side, just to be neighborly.

Maybe the bears were watching us from the bushes even then. There's no way to know. I tasted one of the newberries and spit it out. It was so sweet it was sour, just the sort of thing you would imagine a bear would like.

That evening after supper, I asked Wallace Jr. if he might want to go with me to visit Mother. I wasn't surprised when he said "yes." Kids have more consideration than folks give them credit for. We found her sitting on the concrete front porch of the Home, watching the cars go by on I-65. The nurse said she had been agitated all day. I wasn't surprised by that, either. Every fall as the leaves change, she gets restless, maybe the word is hopeful, again. I brought her into the dayroom and combed her long white hair. "Nothing but bears on TV anymore," the nurse complained, flipping the channels. Wallace Jr. picked up the remote after the nurse left, and we watched a CBS or NBC Special Report about some hunters in Virginia who had gotten their houses torched. The TV interviewed a hunter and his wife whose $117,500 Shenandoah Valley home had burned. She blamed the bears. He didn't blame the bears, but he was suing for compensation from the state since he had a valid hunting license. The state hunting commissioner came on and said that possession of a hunting license didn't prohibit (enjoin, I think, was the word he used) *the hunted* from striking back. I thought that was a pretty liberal view for a state commissioner. Of course, he had a vested interest in not paying off. I'm not a hunter myself.

"Don't bother coming on Sunday," Mother told Wallace Jr. with a wink. "I've drove a million miles and I've got one hand on the gate." I'm used to her saying stuff like that, especially in the fall, but I was afraid it would upset the boy. In fact, he looked worried after we left and I asked him what was wrong.

"How could she have drove a million miles?" he asked. She had told him 48 miles a day for 39 years, and he had worked it out on his calculator to be 336,960 miles.

"Have *driven*," I said. "And it's forty-eight in the morning and forty-eight in the afternoon. Plus there were the football trips. Plus, old folks exaggerate a little." Mother was the first woman school bus driver in the state. She did it every day and raised a family, too. Dad just farmed.

I usually get off the interstate at Smiths Grove, but that night I drove north all the way to Horse Cave and doubled back so Wallace Jr. and I could see the bears' fires. There were not as many as you would think from the TV—one every six or seven miles, hidden back in a clump of trees or under a rocky ledge. Probably they look for water as well as wood. Wallace Jr. wanted to stop, but it's against the law to stop on the interstate and I was afraid the state police would run us off.

There was a card from Wallace in the mailbox. He and Elizabeth were doing fine and having a wonderful time. Not a word about Wallace Jr., but the boy didn't seem to mind. Like most kids his age, he doesn't really enjoy going places with his parents.

On Saturday afternoon, the Home called my office (Burley Belt Drought & Hail) and left word that Mother was gone. I was on the road. I work Saturdays. It's the only day a lot of part-time farmers are home. My heart literally skipped a beat when I called in and got the message, but only a beat. I had long been prepared. "It's a blessing," I said when I got the nurse on the phone.

"You don't understand," the nurse said. "Not *passed* away, gone. *Ran* away, gone. Your mother has escaped." Mother had gone through the door at the end of the corridor when no one was looking, wedging the door with her comb and taking a bedspread which belonged to the Home. What about her tobacco? I asked. It was gone. That was a sure sign she was planning to stay away. I was in Franklin, and it took me less than an hour to get to the Home on I-65. The nurse told me that Mother had been acting more and more confused lately. Of course they are going to say that. We looked around the grounds, which is only an acre with no trees between the interstate and a soybean field. Then they had me leave a message at the sheriff's office. I would have to keep paying for her care until she was officially listed as Missing, which would be Monday.

It was dark by the time I got back to the house, and Wallace Jr. was fixing supper. This just involves opening a few cans, already selected and grouped together with a rubber band. I told him his grandmother had gone, and he nodded, saying, "She told us she would be." I called Florida and left a message. There was nothing more to be done. I sat down and tried to watch TV, but there was nothing on. Then, I looked out the back door, and saw the firelight twinkling through the trees across the northbound lane of I-65, and realized I just might know where she had gone to find her.

It was definitely getting colder, so I got my jacket. I told the boy to wait by the phone in case the sheriff called, but when I looked back, halfway across the field, there he was behind me. He didn't have a jacket. I let him catch up. He was carrying his .22, and I made him leave it leaning against our fence. It was harder climbing the government fence in the dark, at my age, than it had been in the daylight. I am sixty-one. The highway was busy with cars heading south and trucks heading north.

Crossing the shoulder, I got my pants cuffs wet on the long grass, already wet with dew. It is actually bluegrass.

The first few feet into the trees it was pitch black and the boy grabbed my hand. Then it got lighter. At first I thought it was the moon, but it was the high beams shining like moonlight into the treetops, allowing Wallace Jr. and me to pick our way through the brush. We soon found the path and its familiar bear smell.

I was wary of approaching the bears at night. If we stayed on the path we might run into one in the dark, but if we went through the bushes we might be seen as intruders. I wondered if maybe we shouldn't have brought the gun.

We stayed on the path. The light seemed to drip down from the canopy of the woods like rain. The going was easy, especially if we didn't try to look at the path but let our feet find their own way.

Then through the trees I saw their fire.

The fire was mostly of sycamore and beech branches, the kind of fire that puts out very little heat or light and lots of smoke. The bears hadn't earned the ins and outs of wood yet. They did okay at tending it, though. A large cinnamon brown northern-looking bear was poking the fire with a stick, adding a branch now and then from a pile at his side. The others sat around in a loose circle on the logs. Most were smaller black or honey bears, one was a mother with cubs. Some were eating berries from a hubcap. Not eating, but just watching the fire, my mother sat among them with the bedspread from the Home around her shoulders.

If the bears noticed us, they didn't let on. Mother patted a spot right next to her on the log and I sat down. A bear moved over to let Wallace Jr. sit on her other side.

The bear smell is rank but not unpleasant, once you get used to it. It's not like a barn smell, but wilder. I leaned over to whisper something to Mother and she shook her head. *It would be rude to whisper around these creatures that don't possess the power of speech,* she let me know without speaking. Wallace Jr. was silent too. Mother shared the bedspread with us and we sat for what seemed hours, looking into the fire.

The big bear tended the fire, breaking up the dry branches by holding one end and stepping on them, like people do. He was good at keeping it going at the same level. Another bear poked the fire from time to time, but the others left it alone. It looked like only a few of the bears knew how to use fire, and were carrying the others along. But isn't that how it is with everything? Every once in a while, a smaller bear walked into the circle of firelight with an armload of wood and dropped it onto the pile. Median wood has a silvery cast, like driftwood.

Wallace Jr. isn't fidgety like a lot of kids. I found it pleasant to sit and stare into the fire. I took a little piece of Mother's *Red Man*, though I don't generally chew. It was no different from visiting her at the Home, only more interesting, because of the bears. There were about eight or ten of them. Inside the fire itself, things weren't so dull, either: little dramas were being played out as fiery chambers were created and then destroyed in a crashing of sparks. My imagination ran wild. I looked around the circle at the bears and wondered what *they* saw. Some had their eyes closed. Though they were gathered together, their spirits still seemed solitary, as if each bear was sitting alone in front of its own fire.

The hubcap came around and we all took some newberries. I don't know about Mother, but I just pretended to eat mine. Wallace Jr. made a face and spit his out. When he went to sleep, I wrapped the bedspread around all three of us. It was getting colder and we were not provided, like the bears, with fur. I was ready to go home, but not Mother. She pointed up toward the canopy of trees, where a light was spreading, and then pointed to herself. Did she think it was angels approaching from on high? It was only the high beams of some southbound truck, but she seemed mighty pleased. Holding her hand, I felt it grow colder and colder in mine.

Wallace Jr. woke me up by tapping on my knee. It was past dawn, and his grandmother had died sitting on the log between us. The fire was banked up and the bears were gone and someone was crashing straight through the woods, ignoring the path. It was Wallace. Two state troopers were right behind him. He was wearing a white shift, and I realized it was Sunday morning. Underneath his sadness on learning of Mother's death, he looked peeved.

The troopers were sniffing the air and nodding. The bear smell was still strong. Wallace and I wrapped Mother in the bedspread and started with her body back out to the highway. The troopers stayed behind and scattered the bears' fire ashes and flung their firewood away into the bushes. It seemed a petty thing to do. They were like bears themselves, each one solitary in his own uniform.

There was Wallace's Olds 98 on the median, with its radial tires looking squashed on the grass. In front of it there was a police car with a trooper standing beside it, and behind it a funeral home hearse, also an Olds 98.

"First report we've had of them bothering old folks," the trooper said to Wallace. "That's not hardly what happened at all," I said, but nobody asked me to explain. They have their own procedures. Two men in suits got out of the hearse and opened the rear door. That to me was the point at which Mother departed this life. After we put her in, I put my arms around the boy. He was shivering even though it wasn't that cold. Sometimes death will do that, especially at dawn, with the police around and the grass wet, even when it comes as a friend.

We stood for a minute watching the cars pass. "It's a blessing," Wallace said. It's surprising how much traffic there is at 6:22 A.M.

That afternoon, I went back to the median and cut a little firewood to replace what the troopers had flung away. I could see the fire through the trees that night.

I went back two nights later, after the funeral. The fire was going and it was the same bunch of bears, as far as I could tell. I sat around with them a while but it seemed to make them nervous, so I went home. I had taken a handful of newberries from the hubcap, and on Sunday I went with the boy and arranged them on Mother's grave. I tried again, but it's no use, you can't eat them.

Unless you're a bear.

Even the Queen

CONNIE WILLIS

Connie Willis lives with her husband in Greeley, Colorado. She first attracted attention as a writer in the late '70s with a number of stories for the now-defunct magazine *Galileo*, and went on to establish herself as one of the most popular and critically acclaimed writers of the 1980s. In 1982, she won two Nebula Awards, one for her novelette "Fire Watch," and one for her short story "A Letter from the Clearys"; a few months later, "Fire Watch" went on to win her a Hugo Award as well. In 1989, her novella "The Last of the Winnebagoes" won both the Nebula and the Hugo, and she won another Nebula in 1990 for her novelette "At The Rialto." In 1993, her landmark novel *Doomsday Book* won both the Nebula Award and the Hugo Award, as did her short story "Even the Queen." She won another Hugo in 1994 for her story "Death on the Nile," another in 1997 for her story "The Soul Selects Her Own Society," another in 1999 for her novel *To Say Nothing of the Dog*, and yet *another* in 2000 for her novella "The Winds of Marble Arch"—all of which makes her one of the most honored writers in the history of science fiction, and, as far as I know, the only person ever to win *two* Nebulas and *two* Hugos in the same year. Her other books include the novels *Water Witch*, *Light Raid*, and *Promised Land*, all written in collaboration with Cynthia Felice, *Lincoln's Dreams*, *To Say Nothing of the Dog*, *Bellwether*, *Uncharted Territory*, and *Remake*, and, as editor, the anthologies *The New Hugo Winners, Volume III*, *Nebula Awards 33*, and (with Sheila Williams) *A Woman's Liberation: A Choice of Futures by and About Women*. Her short fiction has been gathered in three collections, *Fire Watch*, *Impossible Dreams*, and *Miracle and Other Christmas Stories*. Her most recent book is the novel, *Passage*. She has had stories in our First, Second, Fourth, and Sixth through Eleventh annual collections.

Here, in one of her best-known stories, she provides a wry and controversial examination of a technological change so sweeping and fundamental that it affects every woman on Earth. . . .

The phone sang as I was looking over the defense's motion to dismiss. "It's the universal ring," my law clerk Bysshe said, reaching for it. "It's probably the defendant. They don't let you use signatures from jail."

"No, it's not," I said. "It's my mother."

"Oh." Bysshe reached for the receiver. "Why isn't she using her signature?"

"Because she knows I don't want to talk to her. She must have found out what Perdita's done."

"Your daughter Perdita?" he asked, holding the receiver against his chest. "The one with the little girl?"

"No, that's Viola. Perdita's my younger daughter. The one with no sense."

"What's she done?"

"She's joined the Cyclists."

Bysshe looked inquiringly blank, but I was not in the mood to enlighten him. Or in the mood to talk to Mother. "I know exactly what Mother will say. She'll ask me why I didn't tell her, and then she'll demand to know what I'm going to do about it, and there is nothing I *can* do about it, or I obviously would have done it already."

Bysshe looked bewildered. "Do you want me to tell her you're in court?"

"No." I reached for the receiver. "I'll have to talk to her sooner or later." I took it from him. "Hello, Mother," I said.

"Traci," Mother said dramatically, "Perdita has become a Cyclist."

"I know."

"Why didn't you tell me?"

"I thought Perdita should tell you herself."

"Perdita!" She snorted. "She wouldn't tell me. She knows what I'd have to say about it. I suppose you told Karen."

"Karen's not here. She's in Iraq." The only good thing about this whole debacle was that thanks to Iraq's eagerness to show it was a responsible world-community member and its previous penchant for self-destruction, my mother-in-law was in the one place on the planet where the phone service was bad enough that I could claim I'd tried to call her but couldn't get through, and she'd have to believe me.

The Liberation has freed us from all sorts of indignities and scourges, including Iraq's Saddams, but mothers-in-law aren't one of them, and I was almost happy with Perdita for her excellent timing. When I didn't want to kill her.

"What's Karen doing in Iraq?" Mother asked.

"Negotiating a Palestinian homeland."

"And meanwhile her granddaughter is ruining her life," she said irrelevantly. "Did you tell Viola?"

"I *told* you, Mother. I thought Perdita should tell all of you herself."

"Well, she didn't. And this morning one of my patients, Carol Chen, called me and demanded to know what I was keeping from her. I had no idea what she was talking about."

"How did Carol Chen find out?"

"From her daughter, who almost joined the Cyclists last year. *Her* family talked her out of it," she said accusingly. "Carol was convinced the medical community had discovered some terrible side effect of ammenerol and were covering it up. I cannot believe you didn't tell me, Traci."

And I cannot believe I didn't have Bysshe tell her I was in court, I thought. "I told you, Mother. I thought it was Perdita's place to tell you. After all, it's her decision."

"Oh, *Traci!*" Mother said. "You cannot mean that!"

In the first fine flush of freedom after the Liberation, I had entertained hopes that it would change everything—that it would somehow do away with inequality and matriarchal dominance and those humorless women determined to eliminate the word "manhole" and third-person singular pronouns from the language.

Of course it didn't. Men still make more money, "herstory" is still a blight on the semantic landscape, and my mother can still say, "Oh, *Traci!*" in a tone that reduces me to preadolescence.

"Her decision!" Mother said. "Do you mean to tell me you plan to stand idly by and allow your daughter to make the mistake of her life?"

"What can I do? She's twenty-two years old and of sound mind."

"If she were of sound mind, she wouldn't be doing this. Didn't you try to talk her out of it?"

"Of course I did, Mother."

"And?"

"And I didn't succeed. She's determined to become a Cyclist."

"Well, there must be something we can do. Get an injunction or hire a deprogrammer or sue the Cyclists for brainwashing. You're a judge, there must be some law you can invoke—"

"The law is called personal sovereignty, Mother, and since it was what made the Liberation possible in the first place, it can hardly be used against Perdita. Her decision meets all the criteria for a case of personal sovereignty: It's a personal decision, it was made by a sovereign adult, it affects no one else—"

"What about my practice? Carol Chen is convinced shunts cause cancer."

"Any effect on your practice is considered an indirect effect. Like secondary smoke. It doesn't apply. Mother, whether we like it or not, Perdita has a perfect right to do this, and we don't have any right to interfere. A free society has to be based on respecting others' opinions and leaving each other alone. We have to respect Perdita's right to make her own decisions."

All of which was true. It was too bad I hadn't said any of it to Perdita when she called. What I had said, in a tone that sounded exactly like my mother's, was "Oh, Perdita!"

"This is all your fault, you know," Mother said. "I *told* you you shouldn't have let her get that tattoo over her shunt. And don't tell me it's a free society. What good is a free society when it allows my granddaughter to ruin her life?" She hung up.

I handed the receiver back to Bysshe.

"I really liked what you said about respecting your daughter's right to make her own decisions," he said. He held out my robe. "And about not interfering in her life."

"I want you to research the precedents on deprogramming for me," I said, sliding my arms into the sleeves. "And find out if the Cyclists have been charged with any free-choice violations—brainwashing, intimidation, coercion."

The phone sang, another universal. "Hello, who's calling?" Bysshe said cautiously. His voice became suddenly friendlier. "Just a minute." He put his hand over the receiver. "It's your daughter Viola."

I took the receiver. "Hello, Viola."

"I just talked to Grandma," she said. "You will not believe what Perdita's done now. She's joined the Cyclists."

"I know," I said.

"You *know*? And you didn't tell me? I can't believe this. You never tell me anything."

"I thought Perdita should tell you herself," I said tiredly.

"Are you kidding? She never tells me anything either. That time she had eyebrow implants, she didn't tell me for three weeks, and when she got the laser tattoo, she didn't tell me at all. *Twidge* told me. You should have called me. Did you tell Grandma Karen?"

"She's in Baghdad," I said.

"I know," Viola said. "I called her."

"Oh, Viola, you didn't!"

"Unlike you, Mom, I believe in telling members of our family about matters that concern them."

"What did she say?" I asked, a kind of numbness settling over me now that the shock had worn off.

"I couldn't get through to her. The phone service over there is terrible. I got somebody who didn't speak English, and then I got cut off, and when I tried again, they said the whole city was down."

Thank you, I breathed silently. Thank you, thank you, thank you.

"Grandma Karen has a right to know, Mother. Think of the effect this could have on Twidge. She thinks Perdita's wonderful. When Perdita got the eyebrow implants, Twidge glued LEDs to hers, and I almost never got them off. What if Twidge decides to join the Cyclists, too?"

"Twidge is only nine. By the time she's supposed to get her shunt, Perdita will have long since quit." I hope, I added silently. Perdita had had the tattoo for a year and a half now and showed no signs of tiring of it. "Besides, Twidge has more sense."

"It's true. Oh, Mother, how *could* Perdita do this? Didn't you tell her about how awful it was?"

"Yes," I said. "And inconvenient. And unpleasant and unbalancing and painful. None of it made the slightest impact on her. She told me she thought it would be fun."

Bysshe was pointing to his watch and mouthing, "Time for court."

"Fun!" Viola said. "When she saw what I went through that time? Honestly, Mother, sometimes I think she's completely brain dead. Can't you have her declared incompetent and locked up or something?"

"No," I said, trying to zip up my robe with one hand. "Viola, I have to go. I'm late for court. I'm afraid there's nothing we can do to stop her. She's a rational adult."

"Rational!" Viola said. "Her eyebrows light up, Mother. She has Custer's Last Stand lased on her arm."

I handed the phone to Bysshe. "Tell Viola I'll talk to her tomorrow." I zipped up my robe. "And then call Baghdad and see how long they expect the phones to be out." I started into the courtroom. "And if there are any more universal calls, make sure they're local before you answer."

Bysshe couldn't get through to Baghdad, which I took as a good sign, and my mother-in-law didn't call. Mother did, in the afternoon, to ask if lobotomies were legal.

She called again the next day. I was in the middle of my Personal Sovereignty class, explaining the inherent right of citizens in a free society to make complete jackasses of themselves. They weren't buying it.

"I think it's your mother," Bysshe whispered to me as he handed me the phone. "She's still using the universal. But it's local. I checked."

"Hello, Mother," I said.

"It's all arranged," Mother said. "We're having lunch with Perdita at McGregor's. It's on the corner of Twelfth Street and Larimer."

"I'm in the middle of class," I said.

"I know. I won't keep you. I just wanted to tell you not to worry. I've taken care of everything."

I didn't like the sound of that. "What have you done?"

"Invited Perdita to lunch with us. I told you. At McGregor's."

"Who is 'us,' Mother?"

"Just the family," she said innocently. "You and Viola."

Well, at least she hadn't brought in the deprogrammer. Yet. "What are you up to, Mother?"

"Perdita said the same thing. Can't a grandmother ask her granddaughters to lunch? Be there at twelve-thirty."

"Bysshe and I have a court-calendar meeting at three."

"Oh, we'll be done by then. And bring Bysshe with you. He can provide a man's point of view."

She hung up.

"You'll have to go to lunch with me, Bysshe," I said. "Sorry."

"Why? What's going to happen at lunch?"

"I have no idea."

On the way over to McGregor's, Bysshe told me what he'd found out about the Cyclists. "They're not a cult. There's no religious connection. They seem to have grown out of a pre-Liberation women's group," he said, looking at his notes, "although there are also links to the pro-choice movement, the University of Wisconsin, and the Museum of Modern Art."

"What?"

"They call their group leaders 'docents.' Their philosophy seems to be a mix of pre-Liberation radical feminism and the environmental primitivism of the eighties. They're floratarians and they don't wear shoes."

"Or shunts," I said. We pulled up in front of McGregor's and got out of the car. "Any mind-control convictions?" I asked hopefully.

"No. A bunch of suits against individual members, all of which they won."

"On grounds of personal sovereignty."

"Yeah. And a criminal one by a member whose family tried to deprogram her. The deprogrammer was sentenced to twenty years, and the family got twelve."

"Be sure to tell Mother about that one," I said, and opened the door to McGregor's.

It was one of those restaurants with a morning-glory vine twining around the maître d's desk and garden plots between the tables.

"Perdita suggested it," Mother said, guiding Bysshe and me past the onions to our table. "She told me a lot of the Cyclists are floratarians."

"Is she here?" I asked, sidestepping a cucumber frame.

"Not yet." She pointed past a rose arbor. "There's our table."

Our table was a wicker affair under a mulberry tree. Viola and Twidge were seated on the far side next to a trellis of runner beans, looking at menus.

"What are you doing here, Twidge?" I asked. "Why aren't you in school?"

"I am," she said, holding up her LCD slate. "I'm remoting today."

"I thought she should be part of this discussion," Viola said. "After all, she'll be getting her shunt soon."

"My friend Kensy says she isn't going to get one. Like Perdita," Twidge said.

"I'm sure Kensy will change her mind when the time comes," Mother said. "Perdita will change hers, too. Bysshe, why don't you sit next to Viola?"

Bysshe slid obediently past the trellis and sat down in the wicker chair at the far end of the table. Twidge reached across Viola and handed him a menu. "This is a great restaurant," she said. "You don't have to wear shoes." She held up a bare foot to illustrate. "And if you get hungry while you're waiting, you can just pick something." She twisted around in her chair, picked two of the green beans, gave one to Bysshe, and bit into the other one. "I bet Kensy doesn't. Kensy says a shunt hurts worse than braces."

"It doesn't hurt as much as not having one," Viola said, shooting me a Now-Do-You-See-What-My-Sister's-Caused? look.

"Traci, why don't you sit across from Viola?" Mother said to me. "And we'll put Perdita next to you when she comes."

"If she comes," Viola said.

"I told her one o'clock," Mother said, sitting down at the near end. "So we'd have a chance to plan our strategy before she gets here. I talked to Carol Chen—"

"Her daughter nearly joined the Cyclists last year," I explained to Bysshe and Viola.

"*She* said they had a family gathering, like this, and simply talked to her daughter, and she decided she didn't want to be a Cyclist after all." She looked around the table. "So I thought we'd do the same thing with Perdita. I think we should start by explaining the significance of the Liberation and the days of dark oppression that preceded it—"

"*I think,*" Viola interrupted, "we should try to talk her into just going off the ammenerol for a few months instead of having the shunt removed. If she comes. Which she won't."

"Why not?"

"Would you? I mean, it's like the Inquisition. Her sitting here while all of us 'explain' at her. Perdita may be crazy, but she's not stupid."

"It's hardly the Inquisition," Mother said. She looked anxiously past me toward the door. "I'm sure Perdita—" She stopped, stood up, and plunged off suddenly through the asparagus.

I turned around, half expecting Perdita with light-up lips or a full-body tattoo, but I couldn't see through the leaves. I pushed at the branches.

"Is it Perdita?" Viola said, leaning forward.

I peered around the mulberry bush. "Oh, my God," I said.

It was my mother-in-law, wearing a black abayah and a silk yarmulke. She swept toward us through a pumpkin patch, robes billowing and eyes flashing. Mother hurried in her wake of trampled radishes, looking daggers at me.

I turned them on Viola. "It's your Grandmother Karen," I said accusingly. "You told me you didn't get through to her."

"I didn't," she said. "Twidge, sit up straight. And put your slate down."

There was an ominous rustling in the rose arbor, as of leaves shrinking back in terror, and my mother-in-law arrived.

"Karen!" I said, trying to sound pleased. "What on earth are you doing here? I thought you were in Baghdad."

"I came back as soon as I got Viola's message," she said, glaring at everyone in turn. "Who's this?" she demanded, pointing at Bysshe. "Viola's new live-in?"

"No!" Bysshe said, looking horrified.

"This is my law clerk, Mother," I said. "Bysshe Adams-Hardy."

"Twidge, why aren't you in school?"

"I *am*," Twidge said. "I'm remoting." She held up her slate. "See? Math."

"I see," she said, turning to glower at me. "It's a serious enough matter to require my great-grandchild's being pulled out of school *and* the hiring of legal assistance, and yet you didn't deem it important enough to notify *me*. Of course, you *never* tell me anything, Traci."

She swirled herself into the end chair, sending leaves and sweet-pea blossoms flying and decapitating the broccoli centerpiece. "I didn't get Viola's cry for help until yesterday. Viola, you should never leave messages with Hassim. His English is virtually nonexistent. I had to get him to hum me your ring. I recognized your signature, but the phones were out, so I flew home. In the middle of negotiations, I might add."

"How *are* negotiations going, Grandma Karen?" Viola asked.

"They *were* going extremely well. The Israelis have given the Palestinians half of Jerusalem, and they've agreed to time-share the Golan Heights." She turned to glare momentarily at me. "*They* know the importance of communication." She turned back to Viola. "So why are they picking on you, Viola? Don't they like your new live-in?"

"I am *not* her live-in," Bysshe protested.

I have often wondered how on earth my mother-in-law became a mediator and what she does in all those negotiation sessions with Serbs and Catholics and North and South Koreans and Protestants and Croats. She takes sides, jumps to conclusions, misinterprets everything you say, refuses to listen. And yet she talked South Africa into a Mandelan government and would probably get the Palestinians to observe Yom Kippur. Maybe she just bullies everyone into submission. Or maybe they have to band together to protect themselves against her.

Bysshe was still protesting. "I never even met Viola till today. I've only talked to her on the phone a couple of times."

"You must have done *something*," Karen said to Viola. "They're obviously out for your blood."

"Not mine," Viola said. "Perdita's. She's joined the Cyclists."

"The Cyclists? I left the West Bank negotiations because you don't approve of Perdita joining a biking club? How am I supposed to explain this to the president of Iraq? She will *not* understand, and neither do I. A biking club!"

"The Cyclists do not ride bicycles," Mother said.

"They menstruate," Twidge said.

There was a dead silence of at least a minute, and I thought, it's finally happened. My mother-in-law and I are actually going to be on the same side of a family argument.

"All this fuss is over Perdita's having her shunt removed?" Karen said finally. "She's of age, isn't she? And this is obviously a case where personal sovereignty applies. You should know that, Traci. After all, you're a judge."

I should have known it was too good to be true.

"You mean you approve of her setting back the Liberation twenty years?" Mother said.

"I hardly think it's that serious," Karen said. "There are antishunt groups in the Middle East, too, you know, but no one takes them seriously. Not even the Iraqis, and they still wear the veil."

"Perdita is taking them seriously."

Karen dismissed Perdita with a wave of her black sleeve. "They're a trend, a fad. Like microskirts. Or those dreadful electronic eyebrows. A few women wear silly fashions like that for a little while, but you don't see women as a whole giving up pants or going back to wearing hats."

"But Perdita . . ." Viola said.

"If Perdita wants to have her period, I say let her. Women functioned perfectly well without shunts for thousands of years."

Mother brought her fist down on the table. "Women also functioned *perfectly well* with concubinage, cholera, and corsets," she said, emphasizing each word with her fist. "But that is no reason to take them on voluntarily, and I have no intention of allowing Perdita—"

"Speaking of Perdita, where is the poor child?" Karen said.

"She'll be here any minute," Mother said. "I invited her to lunch so we could discuss this with her."

"Ha!" Karen said. "So you could browbeat her into changing her mind, you mean. Well, I have no intention of collaborating with you. *I* intend to listen to the poor thing's point of view with interest and an open mind. 'Respect,' that's the key word, and one you all seem to have forgotten. Respect and common courtesy."

A barefoot young woman wearing a flowered smock and a red scarf tied around her left arm came up to the table with a sheaf of pink folders.

"It's about time," Karen said, snatching one of the folders away from her. "Your service here is dreadful. I've been sitting here for ten minutes." She snapped the folder open. "I don't suppose you have Scotch."

"My name is Evangeline," the young woman said. "I'm Perdita's docent." She took the folder away from Karen. "She wasn't able to join you for lunch, but she asked me to come in her place and explain the Cyclist philosophy to you."

She sat down in the wicker chair next to me.

"The Cyclists are dedicated to freedom," she said. "Freedom from artificiality, freedom from body-controlling drugs and hormones, freedom from the male patriarchy that attempts to impose them on us. As you probably already know, we do not wear shunts."

She pointed to the red scarf around her arm. "Instead, we wear this as a badge of our freedom and our femaleness. I'm wearing it today to announce that my time of fertility has come."

"We had that, too," Mother said, "only we wore it on the back of our skirts."

I laughed.

The docent glared at me. "Male domination of women's bodies began long before the so-called 'Liberation,' with government regulation of abortion and fetal rights, scientific control of fertility, and finally the development of ammenerol, which eliminated the reproductive cycle altogether. This was all part of a carefully planned takeover of women's bodies, and by extension, their identities, by the male patriarchal regime."

"What an interesting point of view!" Karen said enthusiastically.

It certainly was. In point of fact, ammenerol hadn't been invented to eliminate menstruation at all. It had been developed for shrinking malignant tumors, and its uterine lining–absorbing properties had only been discovered by accident.

"Are you trying to tell us," Mother said, "that men *forced* shunts on women? We had to *fight* everyone to get ammenerol approved by the FDA!"

It was true. What surrogate mothers and antiabortionists and the fetal-rights issue had failed to do in uniting women, the prospect of not having to menstruate did. Women had organized rallies, petitioned, elected senators, passed amendments, been excommunicated, and gone to jail, all in the name of Liberation.

"Men were *against* it," Mother said, getting rather red in the face. "And the religious right, and the maxipad manufacturers, and the Catholic Church—"

"They knew they'd have to allow women priests," Viola said.

"Which they did," I said.

"The Liberation hasn't freed you," the docent said loudly. "Except from the natural rhythms of your life, the very wellspring of your femaleness."

She leaned over and picked a daisy that was growing under the table. "We in the Cyclists celebrate the onset of our menses and rejoice in our bodies," she said, holding the daisy up. "Whenever a Cyclist comes into blossom, as we call it, she is honored with flowers and poems and songs. Then we join hands and tell what we like best about our menses."

"Water retention," I said.

"Or lying in bed with a heating pad for three days a month," Mother said.

"*I* think I like the anxiety attacks best," Viola said. "When I went off the ammenerol, so I could have Twidge, I'd have these days where I was convinced the space station was going to fall on me."

A middle-aged woman in overalls and a straw hat had come over while Viola was talking and was standing next to Mother's chair. "I had these mood swings," she said. "One minute I'd feel cheerful and the next like Lizzie Borden."

"Who's Lizzie Borden?" Twidge asked.

"She killed her parents," Bysshe said. "With an axe."

Karen and the docent glared at both of them. "Aren't you supposed to be working on your math, Twidge?" Karen said.

"I've always wondered if Lizzie Borden had PMS," Viola said, "and that was why—"

"No," Mother said. "It was having to live before tampons and ibuprofen. An obvious case of justifiable homicide."

"I hardly think this sort of levity is helpful," Karen said, glowering at everyone.

"Are you our waitress?" I asked the straw-hatted woman hastily.

"Yes," she said, producing a slate from her overalls pocket.

"Do you serve wine?" I asked.

"Yes. Dandelion, cowslip, and primrose."

"We'll take them all."

"A bottle of each?"

"For now," I said. "Unless you have them in kegs."

"Our specials for today are watermelon salad and *choufleur gratinée*," she said, smiling at everyone. Karen and the docent did not smile back. "You handpick your own cauliflower from the patch up front. The floratarian special is sautéed lily buds with marigold butter."

There was a temporary truce while everyone ordered. "I'll have the sweet peas," the docent said, "and a glass of rose water."

Bysshe leaned over to Viola. "I'm sorry I sounded so horrified when your grandmother asked if I was your live-in," he said.

"That's okay," Viola said. "Grandma Karen can be pretty scary."

"I just didn't want you to think I didn't like you. I do. Like you, I mean."

"Don't they have soyburgers?" Twidge asked.

As soon as the waitress left, the docent began passing out the pink folders she'd brought with her. "These will explain the working philosophy of the Cyclists," she said, handing me one, "along with practical information on the menstrual cycle." She handed Twidge one.

"It looks just like those books we used to get in junior high," Mother said, looking at hers. "'A Special Gift,' they were called, and they had all these pictures of girls with pink ribbons in their hair, playing tennis and smiling. Blatant misrepresentation."

She was right. There was even the same drawing of the fallopian tubes I remembered from my middle-school movie, a drawing that had always reminded me of *Alien* in the early stages.

"Oh, yuck," Twidge said. "This is disgusting."

"Do your math," Karen said.

Bysshe looked sick. "Did women really *do* this stuff?"

The wine arrived, and I poured everyone a large glass. The docent pursed her lips disapprovingly and shook her head. "The Cyclists do not use the artificial stimulants or hormones that the male patriarchy has forced on women to render them docile and subservient."

"How long do you menstruate?" Twidge asked.

"Forever," Mother said.

"Four to six days," the docent said. "It's there in the booklet."

"No, I mean, your whole life or what?"

"A woman has her menarche at twelve years old on the average and ceases menstruating at age fifty-five."

"I had my first period at eleven," the waitress said, setting a bouquet down in front of me. "At school."

"I had my last one on the day the FDA approved ammenerol," Mother said.

"Three hundred and sixty-five divided by twenty-eight," Twidge said, writing on her slate. "Times forty-three years." She looked up. "That's five hundred and fifty-nine periods."

"That can't be right," Mother said, taking the slate away from her. "It's at least five thousand."

"And they all start on the day you leave on a trip," Viola said.

"Or get married," the waitress said. Mother began writing on the slate.

I took advantage of the cease-fire to pour everyone some more dandelion wine.

Mother looked up from the slate. "Do you realize with a period of five days, you'd be menstruating for nearly three thousand days? That's over eight solid years."

"And in between there's PMS," the waitress said, delivering flowers.

"What's PMS?" Twidge asked.

"Premenstrual syndrome was the name the male medical establishment fabricated for the natural variation in hormonal levels that signal the onset of menstruation," the docent said. "This mild and entirely normal fluctuation was exaggerated by men into a debility." She looked at Karen for confirmation.

"I used to cut my hair," Karen said.

The docent looked uneasy.

"Once I chopped off one whole side," Karen went on. "Bob had to hide the scissors every month. And the car keys. I'd start to cry every time I hit a red light."

"Did you swell up?" Mother asked, pouring Karen another glass of dandelion wine.

"I looked just like Orson Welles."

"Who's Orson Welles?" Twidge asked.

"Your comments reflect the self-loathing thrust on you by the patriarchy," the docent said. "Men have brainwashed women into thinking menstruation is evil and unclean. Women even called their menses 'the curse' because they accepted men's judgment."

"I called it the curse because I thought a witch must have laid a curse on me," Viola said. "Like in 'Sleeping Beauty.'"

Everyone looked at her.

"Well, I did," she said. "It was the only reason I could think of for such an awful thing happening to me." She handed the folder back to the docent. "It still is."

"I think you were awfully brave," Bysshe said to Viola, "going off the ammenerol to have Twidge."

"It was awful," Viola said. "You can't imagine."

Mother sighed. "When I got my period, I asked my mother if Annette had it, too."

"Who's Annette?" Twidge said.

"A Mouseketeer," Mother said, and added, at Twidge's uncomprehending look, "On TV."

"High-rez," Viola said.

"The Mickey Mouse Club," Mother said.

"There was a high-rezzer called the Mickey Mouse Club?" Twidge said incredulously.

"They were days of dark oppression in many ways," I said.

Mother glared at me. "Annette was every young girl's ideal," she said to Twidge. "Her hair was curly, she had actual breasts, her pleated skirt was always pressed, and I could not imagine that she could have anything so *messy* and undignified. Mr. Disney would never have allowed it. And if Annette didn't have one, I wasn't going to have one either. So I asked my mother—"

"What did she say?" Twidge cut in.

"She said every woman had periods," Mother said. "So I asked her, 'Even the Queen of England?' And she said, 'Even the Queen.'"

"Really?" Twidge said. "But she's so *old*!"

"She isn't having it now," the docent said irritatedly. "I told you, menopause occurs at age fifty-five."

"And then you have hot flashes," Karen said, "and osteoporosis and so much hair on your upper lip, you look like Mark Twain."

"Who's—" Twidge said.

"You are simply reiterating negative male propaganda," the docent interrupted, looking very red in the face.

"You know what I've always wondered?" Karen said, leaning conspiratorially close to Mother. "If Maggie Thatcher's menopause was responsible for the Falklands War."

"Who's Maggie Thatcher?" Twidge said.

The docent, who was now as red in the face as her scarf, stood up. "It is clear there is no point in trying to talk to you. You've all been completely brainwashed by the male patriarchy." She began grabbing up her folders. "You're blind, all of you! You don't even see that you're victims of a male conspiracy to deprive you of your biological identity, of your very womanhood. The Liberation wasn't a liberation at all. It was only another kind of slavery."

"Even if that were true," I said, "even if it had been a conspiracy to bring us under male domination, it would have been worth it."

"She's right, you know," Karen said to Mother. "Traci's absolutely right. There are some things worth giving up anything for, even your freedom, and getting rid of your period is definitely one of them."

"Victims!" the docent shouted. "You've been stripped of your femininity, and you don't even care!" She stomped out, destroying several squash and a row of gladiolas in the process.

"You know what I hated most before the Liberation?" Karen said, pouring the last of the dandelion wine into her glass. "Sanitary belts."

"And those cardboard tampon applicators," Mother said.

"I'm never going to join the Cyclists," Twidge said.

"Good," I said.

"Can I have dessert?"

I called the waitress over, and Twidge ordered sugared violets. "Anyone else want dessert?" I asked. "Or more primrose wine?"

"I think it's wonderful the way you're trying to help your sister," Bysshe said, leaning closer to Viola.

"And those Modess ads," Mother said. "You remember, with those glamorous women in satin-brocade evening dresses and long white gloves, and below the picture was written, 'Modess, because . . .' I thought Modess was a perfume."

Karen giggled. "I thought it was a brand of *champagne*!"

"I don't think we'd better have any more wine," I said.

The phone started singing the minute I got to my chambers the next morning, the universal ring.

"Karen went back to Iraq, didn't she?" I asked Bysshe.

"Yeah," he said. "Viola said there was some snag over whether to put Disneyland on the West Bank or not."

"When did Viola call?"

Bysshe looked sheepish. "I had breakfast with her and Twidge this morning."

"Oh." I picked up the phone. "It's probably Mother with a plan to kidnap Perdita. Hello?"

"This is Evangeline, Perdita's docent," the voice on the phone said. "I hope you're happy. You've bullied Perdita into surrendering to the enslaving male patriarchy."

"I have?" I said.

"You obviously employed mind control, and I want you to know we intend to file charges." She hung up. The phone rang again immediately, another universal.

"What is the good of signatures when no one ever uses them?" I said, and picked up the phone.

"Hi, Mom," Perdita said. "I thought you'd want to know I've changed my mind about joining the Cyclists."

"Really?" I said, trying not to sound jubilant.

"I found out they wear this red scarf thing on their arm. It covers up Sitting Bull's horse."

"That is a problem," I said.

"Well, that's not all. My docent told me about your lunch. Did Grandma Karen really tell you you were right?"

"Yes."

"Gosh! I didn't believe that part. Well, anyway, my docent said you wouldn't listen to her about how great menstruating is, that you all kept talking about the negative aspects of it, like bloating and cramps and crabbiness, and I said, 'What are cramps?' and she said, 'Menstrual bleeding frequently causes headaches and discomfort,' and I said, 'Bleeding? Nobody ever said anything about bleeding!' Why didn't you tell me there was blood involved, Mother?"

I had, but I felt it wiser to keep silent.

"And you didn't say a word about its being painful. And all the hormone fluctuations! Anybody'd have to be crazy to want to go through that when they didn't have to! How did you stand it before the Liberation?"

"They were days of dark oppression," I said.

"I *guess*! Well, anyway, I quit, and so my docent is really mad. But I told her it was a case of personal sovereignty, and she has to respect my decision. I'm still going to become a floratarian, though, and I *don't* want you to try to talk me out of it."

"I wouldn't dream of it," I said.

"You know, this whole thing is really your fault, Mom! If you'd told me about the pain part in the first place, none of this would have happened. Viola's right! You never tell us *anything*!"

guest of honor

ROBERT REED

Robert Reed sold his first story in 1986, and quickly established himself as a frequent contributor to *The Magazine of Fantasy and Science Fiction* and *Asimov's Science Fiction*, as well as selling many stories to *Science Fiction Age*, *Universe*, *New Destinies*, *Tomorrow*, *Synergy*, *Starlight*, and elsewhere. Reed may be one of the most prolific of today's young writers, particularly at short-fiction lengths, seriously rivaled for that position only by authors such as Stephen Baxter and Brian Stableford. And—also like Baxter and Stableford—he manages to keep up a very high standard of quality *while* being prolific, something that is not at all easy to do. Reed stories such as "Sister Alice," "Brother Perfect," "Decency," "Savior," "The Remoras," "Chrysalis," "Whiptail," "The Utility Man," "Marrow," "Birth Day," "Blind," "The Shape of Everything," "Waging Good," and "Killing the Morrow," among at least a half-dozen others equally as strong, count as among some of the best short work produced by anyone in the '80s and '90s and the early Oughts to date. Nor is he non-prolific as a novelist, having turned out ten novels since the end of the '80s, including *The Lee Shore*, *The Hormone Jungle*, *Black Milk*, *The Remarkables*, *Down the Bright Way*, *Beyond the Veil of Stars*, *An Exaltation of Larks*, *Beneath the Gated Sky*, and *Marrow*. His most recent book is the novel *Sister Alice*. Upcoming is a new novel, *The Sword of Creation*. His stories have appeared in our Ninth through Seventeenth, and our Nineteenth through Twenty-first annual collections. Some of the best of his short work was collected in *The Dragons of Springplace*. Reed lives with his family in Lincoln, Nebraska.

Every year for almost a decade now, the problem has not been *whether* to use a Robert Reed story in the new *Best* volume, but rather *which* Robert Reed story to use. It was no different with the *Best of the Best*—any of a half-dozen Reed stories would have served perfectly well, but in the end I was compelled to choose the story that follows. One that shows us that while being the guest of honor at an important and high-powered function is usually a position to be desired, in a decadent world of ultrarich immortals, it's an honor you might be well advised to avoid.

One of the robots offered to carry Pico for the last hundred meters, on its back or cradled in its padded arms; but she shook her head emphatically, telling it, "Thank you, no. I can make it myself." The ground was grassy and soft, lit by glowglobes and the grass-colored moon. It wasn't a difficult walk, even with her bad hip, and she wasn't an invalid. She could manage, she thought with an instinctive independence. And as if to show them, she struck out ahead of the half-dozen robots as they unloaded the big skimmer, stacking Pico's gifts in their long arms. She was halfway across the paddock before they caught her. By then she could hear the muddled voices and laughter coming from the hill-like tent straight ahead. By then she was breathing fast for reasons other than her pain. For fear, mostly. But it was a different flavor of fear than the kinds she knew. What was happening now was beyond her control, and inevitable . . . and it was that kind of certainty that made her stop after a few more steps, one hand rubbing at her hip for no reason except to delay her arrival. If only for a moment or two . . .

"Are you all right?" asked one robot.

She was gazing up at the tent, dark and smooth and gently rounded. "I don't want to be here," she admitted. "That's all." Her life on board the *Kyber* had been spent with robots—they had outnumbered the human crew ten to one, then more—and she could always be ruthlessly honest with them. "This is madness. I want to leave again."

"Only, you can't," responded the ceramic creature. The voice was mild, unnervingly patient. "You have nothing to worry about."

"I know."

"The technology has been perfected since—"

"*I know.*"

It stopped speaking, adjusting its hold on the colorful packages.

"That's not what I meant," she admitted. Then she breathed deeply, holding the breath for a moment and exhaling, saying, "All right. Let's go. Go."

The robot pivoted and strode toward the giant tent. The leading robots triggered the doorway, causing it to fold upward with a sudden rush of golden light flooding across the grass, Pico squinting and then blinking, walking faster now and allowing herself the occasional low moan.

"*Ever wonder how it'll feel?*" Tyson had asked her.

The tent had been pitched over a small pond, probably that very day, and in places the soft, thick grasses had been matted flat by people and their robots. So many people, she thought. Pico tried not to look at any faces. For a moment, she gazed at the pond, shallow and richly green, noticing the tamed waterfowl sprinkled over it and along its shoreline. Ducks and geese, she realized. And some small crimson-headed cranes. Lifting her eyes, she noticed the large omega-shaped table near the far wall. She couldn't count the place settings, but it seemed a fair assumption there were sixty-three of them. Plus a single round table and chair in the middle of the omega—*my table*—and she took another deep breath, looking higher, noticing floating glowglobes and several indigo swallows flying around them, presumably snatching up the insects that were drawn to the yellow-white light.

People were approaching. Since she had entered, in one patient rush, all sixty-three people had been climbing the slope while shouting, "Pico! Hello!" Their voices mixed together, forming a noisy, senseless paste. "Greetings!" they seemed to say. "Hello, hello!"

They were brightly dressed, flowing robes swishing and everyone wearing big-rimmed hats made to resemble titanic flowers. The people sharply contrasted with the gray-white shells of the robot servants. Those hats were a new fashion, Pico realized. One of the little changes introduced during these past decades . . . and finally she made herself look at the faces themselves, offering a forced smile and taking a step backward, her belly aching, but her hip healed. The burst of adrenaline hid the deep ache in her bones. Wrestling one of her hands into a wave, she told her audience, "Hello," with a near-whisper. Then she swallowed and said, "Greetings to you!" Was that her voice? She barely recognized it.

A woman broke away from the others, almost running toward her. Her big flowery hat began to work free, and she grabbed the fat petalish brim and started to fan herself with one hand, the other hand touching Pico on the shoulder. The palm was damp and quite warm; the air suddenly stank of overly sweet perfumes. It was all Pico could manage not to cough. The woman—what was her name?—was asking, "Do you need to sit? We heard . . . about your accident. You poor girl. All the way fine, and then on the last world. Of all the luck!"

Her hip. The woman was jabbering about her sick hip.

Pico nodded and confessed, "Sitting would be nice, yes."

A dozen voices shouted commands. Robots broke into runs, racing one another around the pond to grab the chair beside the little table. The drama seemed to make people laugh. A nervous self-conscious laugh. When the lead robot reached the chair and started back, there was applause. Another woman shouted, "Mine won! Mine won!" She threw her hat into the air and tried to follow it, leaping as high as possible.

Some man cursed her sharply, then giggled.

Another man forced his way ahead, emerging from the packed bodies in front of Pico. He was smiling in a strange fashion. Drunk or drugged . . . what was permissible these days? With a sloppy, earnest voice, he asked, "How'd it happen? The hip thing . . . how'd you do it?"

He should know. She had dutifully filed her reports throughout the mission, squirting them home. Hadn't he seen them? But then she noticed the watchful excited faces—no exceptions—and someone seemed to read her thoughts, explaining, "We'd love to hear it *firsthand*. Tell, tell, tell!"

As if they needed to hear a word, she thought, suddenly feeling quite cold.

Her audience grew silent. The robot arrived with the promised chair, and she sat and stretched her bad leg out in front of her, working to focus her mind. It was touching, their silence . . . reverent and almost childlike . . . and she began by telling them how she had tried climbing Miriam Prime with two other crew members. Miriam

Prime was the tallest volcano on a brutal super-Venusian world; it was brutal work because of the terrain and their massive lifesuits, cumbersome refrigeration units strapped to their backs, and the atmosphere thick as water. Scalding and acidic. Carbon dioxide and water made for a double greenhouse effect. . . . And she shuddered, partly for dramatics and partly from the memory. Then she said, "Brutal," once again, shaking her head thoughtfully.

They had used hyperthreads to climb the steepest slopes and the cliffs. Normally hyperthreads were unbreakable; but Miriam was not a normal world. She described the basalt cliff and the awful instant of the tragedy; the clarity of the scene startled her. She could feel the heat seeping into her suit, see the dense, dark air, and her arms and legs shook with exhaustion. She told sixty-three people how it felt to be suspended on an invisible thread, two friends and a winch somewhere above in the acidic fog. The winch had jammed without warning, she told; the worst bad luck made it jam where the thread was its weakest. This was near the mission's end, and all the equipment was tired. Several dozen alien worlds had been visited, many mapped for the first time, and every one of them examined up close. As planned.

"Everything has its limits," she told them, her voice having an ominous quality that she hadn't intended.

Even hyperthreads had limits. Pico was dangling, talking to her companions by radio; and just as the jam was cleared, a voice saying, "There . . . got it!"—the thread parted. He didn't have any way to know it had parted. Pico was falling, gaining velocity, and the poor man was ignorantly telling her, "It's running strong. You'll be up in no time, no problem. . . ."

People muttered to themselves.

"Oh, my," they said.

"Gosh."

"Shit."

Their excitement was obvious, perhaps even overdone. Pico almost laughed, thinking they were making fun of her storytelling . . . thinking, *What do they know about such things?* . . . Only, they were sincere, she realized a moment later. They were enraptured with the image of Pico's long fall, her spinning and lashing out with both hands, fighting to grab anything and slow her fall any way possible—

—and she struck a narrow shelf of eroded stone, the one leg shattered and telescoping down to a gruesome stump. Pico remembered the painless shock of the impact and that glorious instant free of all sensation. She was alive, and the realization had made her giddy. Joyous. Then the pain found her head—a great nauseating wave of pain—and she heard her distant friends shouting, "Pico? Are you there? Can you hear us? Oh, Pico . . . *Pico?* Answer us!"

She had to remain absolutely motionless, sensing that any move would send her tumbling again. She answered in a whisper, telling her friends that she was alive, yes, and please, please hurry. But they had only a partial thread left, and it would take them more than half an hour to descend . . . and she spoke of her agony and the horror, her hip and leg screaming, and not just from the impact. It was worse than mere broken bone, the lifesuit's insulation damaged and the heat bleeding inward, slowly and thoroughly cooking her living flesh.

Pico paused, gazing out at the round-mouthed faces.

So many people and not a breath of sound; and she was having fun. She realized her pleasure almost too late, nearly missing it. Then she told them, "I nearly died," and shrugged her shoulders. "All the distances traveled, every imaginable adventure . . . and I nearly died on one of our last worlds, doing an ordinary climb. . . ."

Let them appreciate her luck, she decided. *Their luck.*

Then another woman lifted her purple flowery hat with both hands, pressing it flush against her own chest. "Of course you survived!" she proclaimed. "You wanted to come home, Pico! You couldn't stand the thought of *dying.*"

Pico nodded without comment, then said, "I was rescued. Obviously." She flexed the damaged leg, saying, "I never really healed," and she touched her hip with reverence, admitting, "We didn't have the resources on board the *Kyber.* This was the best our medical units could do."

Her mood shifted again, without warning. Suddenly she felt sad to tears, eyes dropping and her mouth clamped shut.

"We worried about you, Pico!"

"All the time, dear!"

". . . in our prayers. . . !"

Voices pulled upon each other, competing to be heard. The faces were smiling and thoroughly sincere. Handsome people, she was thinking. Clean and civilized and older than she by centuries. Some of them were more than a thousand years old.

Look at them! she told herself.

And now she felt fear. Pulling both legs toward her chest, she hugged herself, weeping hard enough to dampen her trouser legs; and her audience said, "But you made it, Pico! You came home! The wonders you've seen, the places you've actually touched . . . with those hands. . . . And we're so proud of you! So proud! You've proven your worth a thousand times, Pico! You're made of the very best stuff—!"

—which brought laughter, a great clattering roar of laughter, the joke obviously and apparently tireless.

Even after so long.

They were Pico; Pico was they.

Centuries ago, during the Blossoming, technologies had raced forward at an unprecedented rate. Starships like the *Kyber* and a functional immortality had allowed the first missions to the distant worlds, and there were some grand adventures. Yet adventure requires some element of danger; exploration has never been a safe enterprise. Despite precautions, there were casualties. People who had lived for centuries died suddenly, oftentimes in stupid accidents; and it was no wonder that after the first wave of missions came a long moratorium. No new starships were built, and no sensible person would have ridden inside even the safest vessel. Why risk yourself? Whatever the benefits, why taunt extinction when you have a choice?

Only recently had a solution been invented. Maybe it was prompted by the call of deep space, though Tyson used to claim, "It's the boredom on Earth that inspired them. That's why they came up with their elaborate scheme."

The near-immortals devised ways of making highly gifted, highly trained crews from themselves. With computers and genetic engineering, groups of people could pool their qualities and create compilation humans. Sixty-three individuals had each donated moneys and their own natures, and Pico was the result. She was a grand and sophisticated average of the group. Her face was a blending of every face; her body was a feminine approximation of their own varied bodies. In a few instances, the engineers had planted synthetic genes—for speed and strength, for example—and her brain had a subtly different architecture. Yet basically Pico was their offspring, a stewlike clone. The second of two clones, she knew. The first clone created had had subtle flaws, and he was painlessly destroyed just before birth.

Pico and Tyson and every other compilation person had been born at adult size. Because she was the second attempt, and behind schedule, Pico was thrown straight into her training. Unlike the other crew members, she had spent only a minimal time with her parents. Her sponsors. Whatever they were calling themselves. That and the long intervening years made it difficult to recognize faces and names. She found herself gazing out at them, believing they were strangers, their tireless smiles hinting at something predatory. The neat white teeth gleamed at her, and she wanted to shiver again, holding the knees closer to her mouth.

Someone suggested opening the lovely gifts.

A good idea. She agreed, and the robots brought down the stacks of boxes, placing them beside and behind her. The presents were a young tradition; when she was leaving Earth, the first compilation people were returning with little souvenirs of their travels. Pico had liked the gesture and had done the same. One after another, she read the names inscribed in her own flowing handwriting. Then each person stepped forward, thanking her for the treasure, then greedily unwrapping it, the papers flaring into bright colors as they were bent and twisted and torn, then tossed aside for the robots to collect.

She knew none of these people, and that was wrong. What she should have done, she realized, was go into the *Kyber*'s records and memorize names and faces. It would have been easy enough, and proper, and she felt guilty for never having made the effort.

It wasn't merely genetics that she shared with these people; she also embodied slivers of their personalities and basic tendencies. Inside Pico's sophisticated womb, the computers had blended together their shrugs and tongue clicks and the distinctive patterns of their speech. She had emerged as an approximation of every one of them; yet why didn't she feel a greater closeness? Why wasn't there a strong tangible bond here?

Or was there something—only, she wasn't noticing it?

One early gift was a slab of mirrored rock. "From Tween Five," she explained. "What it doesn't reflect, it absorbs and reemits later. I kept that particular piece in my own cabin, fixed to the outer wall—"

"Thank you, thank you," gushed the woman.

For an instant, Pico saw herself reflected on the rock. She looked much older than these people. Tired, she thought. Badly weathered. In the cramped starship, they hadn't the tools to revitalize aged flesh, nor had there been the need. Most of the voyage had been spent in cold-sleep. Their waking times, added together, barely exceeded forty years of biological activity.

"Look at this!" the woman shouted, turning and waving her prize at the others. "Isn't it lovely?"

"A shiny rock," teased one voice. "Perfect!"

Yet the woman refused to be anything but impressed. She clasped her prize to her chest and giggled, merging with the crowd and then vanishing.

They look like children, Pico told herself.

At least how she imagined children to appear . . . unworldly and spoiled, needing care and infinite patience. . . .

She read the next name, and a new woman emerged to collect her gift. "My, what a large box!" She tore at the paper, then the box's lid, then eased her hands into the dunnage of white foam. Pico remembered wrapping this gift—one of the only ones where she was positive of its contents—and she happily watched the smooth, elegant hands pulling free a greasy and knob-faced nut. Then Pico explained:

"It's from the Yult tree on Proxima Centauri Two." The only member of the species on that strange little world. "If you wish, you can break its dormancy with liquid nitrogen. Then plant it in pure quartz sand, never anything else. Sand, and use red sunlight—"

"I know how to cultivate them," the woman snapped.

There was a sudden silence, uneasy and prolonged.

Finally Pico said, "Well . . . good . . ."

"Everyone knows about Yult nuts," the woman explained. "They're practically giving them away at the greeneries now."

Someone spoke sharply, warning her to stop and think.

"I'm sorry," she responded. "If I sound ungrateful, I mean. I was just thinking, hoping . . . I don't know. Never mind."

A weak, almost inconsequential apology, and the woman paused to feel the grease between her fingertips.

The thing was, Pico thought, that she had relied on guesswork in selecting these gifts. She had decided to represent every alien world, and she felt proud of herself on the job accomplished. Yult trees were common on Earth? But how could she know such a thing? And besides, why should it matter? She had brought the nut and everything else because she'd taken risks, and these people were obviously too ignorant and silly to appreciate what they were receiving.

Rage had replaced her fear.

Sometimes she heard people talking among themselves, trying to trade gifts. Gemstones and pieces of alien driftwood were being passed about like orphans. Yet nobody would release the specimens of odd life-forms from living worlds, transparent canisters holding bugs and birds and whatnot inside preserving fluids or hard vacuums. If only she had known what she couldn't have known, these silly brats. . . . And she found herself swallowing, holding her breath, and wanting to scream at all of them.

Pico was a compilation, yet she wasn't.

She hadn't lived one day as these people had lived their entire lives. She didn't know about comfort or changelessness, and with an attempt at empathy, she tried to imagine such an incredible existence.

Tyson used to tell her, "Shallowness is a luxury. Maybe the ultimate luxury." She hadn't understood him. Not really. "Only the rich can master true frivolity." Now those words echoed back at her, making her think of Tyson. That intense and angry man . . . the opposite of frivolity, the truth told.

And with that, her mood shifted again. Her skin tingled. She felt nothing for or against her audience. How could they help being what they were? How could anyone help their nature? And with that, she found herself reading another name on another unopened box. A little box, she saw. Probably another one of the unpopular gemstones, born deep inside an alien crust and thrown out by forces unimaginable. . . .

There was a silence, an odd stillness, and she repeated the name.

"Opera? Opera Ting?"

Was it her imagination, or was there a nervousness running through the audience? Just what was happening—?

"Excuse me?" said a voice from the back. "Pardon?"

People began moving aside, making room, and a figure emerged. A male, something about him noticeably different. He moved with a telltale lightness, with a spring to his gait. Smiling, he took the tiny package while saying, "Thank you," with great feeling. "For my father, thank you. I'm sure he would have enjoyed this moment. I only wish he could have been here, if only. . . ."

Father? Wasn't this Opera Ting?

Pico managed to nod, then she asked, "Where is he? I mean, is he busy somewhere?"

"Oh, no. He died, I'm afraid." The man moved differently because he was different. He was young—even younger than I, Pico realized—and he shook his head, smiling in a serene way. Was he a clone? A biological child? What? "But on his behalf," said the man, "I wish to thank you. Whatever this gift is, I will treasure it. I promise you. I know you must have gone through Hell to find it and bring it to me, and thank you so very much, Pico. Thank you, thank you. Thank you!"

Death.

An appropriate intruder in the evening's festivities, thought Pico. Some accident, some kind of tragedy . . . something had killed one of her sixty-three parents, and that thought pleased her. There was a pang of guilt woven into her pleasure, but not very much. It was comforting to know that even these people weren't perfectly insulated from death; it was a force that would grasp everyone, given time. Like it had taken Midge, she thought. And Uoo, she thought. *And Tyson.*

Seventeen compiled people had embarked on *Kyber,* representing almost a thousand near-immortals. Only nine had returned, including Pico. Eight friends were lost. . . . *Lost* was a better word than *death,* she decided. . . . And usually it happened in places worse than any Hell conceived by human beings.

After Opera—his name, she learned, was the same as his father's—the giving of the gifts settled into a routine. Maybe it was because of the young man's attitude. People seemed more polite, more self-contained. Someone had the presence to ask for another story. Anything she wished to tell. And Pico found herself thinking of a watery planet circling a distant red-dwarf sun, her voice saying, "Coldtear," and watching faces nod in unison. They recognized the name, and it was too late. It wasn't the story she would have preferred to tell, yet she couldn't seem to stop herself. Coldtear was on her mind.

Just tell parts, she warned herself.

What you can stand!

The world was Terran-class and covered with a single ocean frozen on its surface and heated from below. By tides, in part. And by Coldtear's own nuclear decay. It had been Tyson's idea to build a submersible and dive to the ocean's remote floor. He used spare parts in *Kyber*'s machine shop—the largest room on board—then he'd taken his machine to the surface, setting it on the red-stained ice and using lasers and robots to bore a wide hole and keep it clear.

Pico described the submersible, in brief, then mentioned that Tyson had asked her to accompany him. She didn't add that they'd been lovers now and again, nor that sometimes they had feuded. She'd keep those parts of the story to herself for as long as possible.

The submersible's interior was cramped and ascetic, and she tried to impress her audience with the pressures that would build on the hyperfiber hull. Many times the pressure found in Earth's oceans, she warned; and Tyson's goal was to set down on the floor, then don a lifesuit protected with a human-shaped force field, actually stepping outside and taking a brief walk.

"Because we need to leave behind footprints," he had argued. "Isn't that why we've come here? We can't just leave prints up on the ice. It moves and melts, wiping itself clean every thousand years or so."

"But isn't that the same below?" Pico had responded. "New muds rain down—slowly, granted—and quakes cause slides and avalanches."

"So we pick right. We find someplace where our marks will be quietly covered. Enshrouded. Made everlasting."

She had blinked, surprised that Tyson cared about such things.

"I've studied the currents," he explained, "and the terrain—"

"Are you serious?" Yet you couldn't feel certain about Tyson. He was a creature full of surprises. "All this trouble, and for what—?"

"Trust me, Pico. Trust me!"

Tyson had had an enormous laugh. His parents, sponsors, whatever—an entirely different group of people—had purposefully made him larger than the norm. They had selected genes for physical size, perhaps wanting Tyson to dominate the *Kyber*'s crew in at least that one fashion. If his own noise was to be believed, that was the only tinkering done to him. Otherwise, he was a pure compilation of his parents' traits, fiery and passionate to a fault. It was a little unclear to Pico what group of people could be so uniformly aggressive; yet Tyson had had his place in their tight-woven crew, and he had had his charms in addition to his size and the biting intelligence.

"Oh, Pico," he cried out. "What's this about, coming here? If it's not about leaving traces of our passage . . . then *what?*"

"It's about going home again," she had answered.

"Then why do we leave the *Kyber?* Why not just orbit Coldtear and send down our robots to explore?"

"Because . . ."

"Indeed! Because!" The giant head nodded, and he put a big hand on her shoulder. "I knew you'd see my point. I just needed to give you time, my friend."

She agreed to the deep dive, but not without misgivings.

And during their descent, listening to the ominous creaks and groans of the hull while lying flat on their backs, the misgivings began to reassert themselves.

It was Tyson's fault, and maybe his aim.

No, she thought. It was most definitely his aim.

At first, she guessed it was some game, him asking, "Do you ever wonder how it will feel? We come home and are welcomed, and then our dear parents disassemble our brains and implant them—"

"Quiet," she interrupted. "We agreed. Everyone agreed. We aren't going to talk about it, all right?"

A pause, then he said, "Except, I know. How it feels, I mean."

She heard him, then she listened to him take a deep breath from the close damp air; and finally she had strength enough to ask, "How can you know?"

When Tyson didn't answer, she rolled onto her side and saw the outline of his face. A handsome face, she thought. Strong and incapable of any doubts. This was the only taboo subject among the compilations—"How will it feel?"—and it was left to each of them to decide what they believed. Was it a fate or a reward? To be subdivided and implanted into the minds of dozens and dozens of near-immortals. . . .

It wasn't a difficult trick, medically speaking.

After all, each of their minds had been designed for this one specific goal. Memories and talent; passion and training. All of the qualities would be saved—diluted, but, in the same instant, gaining their own near-immortality. Death of a sort, but a kind of everlasting life, too.

That was the creed by which Pico had been born and raised.

The return home brings a great reward, and peace.

Pico's first memory was of her birth, spilling slippery-wet from the womb and coughing hard, a pair of doctoring robots bent over her, whispering to her, "Welcome, child. Welcome. You've been born from *them* to be joined with *them* when it is time. . . . We promise you. . . !"

Comforting noise, and mostly Pico had believed it.

But Tyson had to say, "I know how it feels, Pico," and she could make out his grin, his amusement patronizing. Endless.

"How?" she muttered. "How do you know—?"

"Because some of my parents . . . well, let's just say that I'm not their first time. Understand me?"

"They made another compilation?"

"One of the very first, yes. Which was incorporated into them before I was begun, and which was incorporated into me because there was a spare piece. A leftover chunk of the mind—"

"You're making this up, Tyson!"

Except, he wasn't, she sensed. Knew. Several times, on several early worlds, Tyson had seemed too knowledgeable about too much. Nobody could have prepared himself that well, she realized. She and the others had assumed that Tyson was intuitive in some useful way. Part of him was from another compilation? From someone like them? A fragment of the man had walked twice beside the gray dust sea of Pliicker, and it had twice climbed the giant ant mounds on Proxima Centauri 2. It was a revelation, unnerving and hard to accept; and just the memory of that instant made her tremble secretly, facing her audience, her tired blood turning to ice.

Pico told none of this to her audience.

Instead, they heard about the long descent and the glow of rare life-forms outside—a thin plankton consuming chemical energies as they found them—and, too, the growing creaks of the spherical hull.

They didn't hear how she asked, "So how does it feel? You've got a piece of compilation inside you . . . all right! Are you going to tell me what it's like?"

They didn't hear about her partner's long, deep laugh.

Nor could they imagine him saying, "Pico, my dear. You're such a passive, foolish creature. That's why I love you. So docile, so damned innocent—"

"Does it live inside you, Tyson?"

"It depends on what you consider life."

"Can you feel its presence? I mean, does it have a personality? An existence? Or have you swallowed it all up?"

"I don't think I'll tell." Then the laugh enlarged, and the man lifted his legs and kicked at the hyperfiber with his powerful muscles. She could hear, and feel, the solid impacts of his boot-heels. She knew that Tyson's strength was nothing compared to the ocean's mass bearing down on them, their hull scarcely feeling the blows . . . yet some irrational part of her was terrified. She had to reach out, grasping one of his trouser legs and tugging hard, telling him:

"Don't! Stop that! Will you please . . . quit!?"

The tension shifted direction in an instant.

Tyson said, "I was lying," and then added, "about knowing. About having a compilation inside me." And he gave her a huge hug, laughing in a different way now. He nearly crushed her ribs and lungs. Then he spoke into one of her ears, offering more, whispering with the old charm, and she accepting his offer. They did it as well as possible, considering their circumstances and the endless groaning of their tiny vessel; and she remembered all of it while her voice, detached but thorough, described how they had landed on top of something rare. There was a distinct *crunch* of stone. They had made their touchdown on the slope of a recent volcano—an island on an endless plain of mud—and afterward they dressed in their lifesuits, triple-checked their force fields, then flooded the compartment and crawled into the frigid pressurized water.

It was an eerie, almost indescribable experience to walk on that ocean floor. When language failed Pico, she tried to use silence and oblique gestures to capture the sense of endless time and the cold and darkness. Even when Tyson ignited the submersible's outer lights, making the nearby terrain bright as late afternoon, there was the palpable taste of endless dark just beyond. She told of feeling the pressure despite the force field shrouding her; she told of climbing after Tyson, scrambling up a rough slope of youngish rock to a summit where they discovered a hot-water spring that pumped heated mineral-rich water up at them.

That might have been the garden spot of Coldtear. Surrounding the spring was a thick, almost gelatinous mass of gray-green bacteria, pulsating and fat by its own standards. She paused, seeing the scene all over again. Then she assured her parents, "It had a beauty. I mean it. An elegant, minimalist beauty."

Nobody spoke.

Then someone muttered, "I can hardly wait to remember it," and gave a weak laugh.

The audience became uncomfortable, tense and too quiet. People shot accusing looks at the offender, and Pico worked not to notice any of it. A bitterness was building in her guts, and she sat up straighter, rubbing at both hips.

Then a woman coughed for attention, waited, and then asked, "What happened next?"

Pico searched for her face.

"There was an accident, wasn't there? On Coldtear. . . ?"

I won't tell them, thought Pico. Not now. Not this way.

She said, "No, not then. Later." And maybe some of them knew better. Judging by the expressions, a few must have remembered the records. Tyson died on the first dive. It was recorded as being an equipment failure—Pico's lie—and she'd hold on to the lie as long as possible. It was a promise she'd made to herself and kept all these years.

Shutting her eyes, she saw Tyson's face smiling at her. Even through the thick faceplate and the shimmering glow of the force field, she could make out the mischievous expression, eyes glinting, the large mouth saying, "Go on back, Pico. In and up and a safe trip to you, pretty lady."

She had been too stunned to respond, gawking at him.

"Remember? I've still got to leave my footprints somewhere—"

"What are you planning?" she interrupted.

He laughed and asked, "Isn't it obvious? I'm going to make my mark on this world. It's dull and nearly dead, and I don't think anyone is ever going to return here. Certainly not to *here*. Which means I'll be pretty well left alone—"

"Your force field will drain your batteries," she argued stupidly. Of course he knew that salient fact. "If you stay here—!"

"I know, Pico. I know."

"But why—?"

"I lied before. About lying." The big face gave a disappointed look, then the old smile reemerged. "Poor, docile Pico. I knew you wouldn't take this well. You'd take it too much to heart . . . which I suppose is why I asked you along in the first place. . . ." And he turned away, starting to walk through the bacterial mat with threads and chunks kicked loose, sailing into the warm current and obscuring him. It was a strange gray snow moving against gravity. Her last image of Tyson was of a hulking figure amid the living goo; and to this day, she had wondered if she could have wrestled him back to the submersible—an impossibility, of course—and how far could he have walked before his force field failed.

Down the opposite slope and onto the mud, no doubt.

She could imagine him walking fast, using his strength . . . fighting the deep, cold muds . . . Tyson plus that fragment of an earlier compilation—and who was driving whom? she asked herself. Again and again and again.

Sometimes she heard herself asking Tyson, "How does it feel having a sliver of another soul inside you?"

His ghost never answered, merely laughing with his booming voice.

She hated him for his suicide, and admired him; and sometimes she cursed him for taking her along with him and for the way he kept cropping up in her thoughts. . . . "Damn you, Tyson. Goddamn you, goddamn you. . . !"

No more presents remained.

One near-immortal asked, "Are we hungry?" and others replied, "Famished," in one voice, then breaking into laughter.

The party moved toward the distant tables, a noisy mass of bodies surrounding Pico. Her hip had stiffened while sitting, but she worked hard to move normally, managing the downslope toward the pond and then the little wooden bridge spanning a rocky brook. The waterfowl made grumbling sounds, angered by the disturbances; Pico stopped and watched them, finally asking, "What kinds are those?" She meant the ducks.

"Just mallards," she heard. "Nothing fancy."

Yet, to her, they seemed like miraculous creatures, vivid plumage and the moving eyes, wings spreading as a reflex and their nervous motions lending them a sense of muscular power. A vibrancy.

Someone said, "You've seen many birds, I'm sure."

Of a sort, yes . . .

"What were your favorites, Pico?"

They were starting uphill, quieter now, feet making a swishing sound in the grass; and Pico told them about the pterosaurs of Wilder, the man-sized bats on Little Quark, and the giant insects—a multitude of species—thriving in the thick warm air of Tau Ceti 1.

"Bugs," grumbled someone. "Uggh!"

"Now, now," another person responded.

Then a third joked, "I'm not looking forward to *that*. Who wants to trade memories?"

A joke, thought Pico, because memories weren't tradable properties. Minds were holographic—every piece held the basic picture of the whole—and these people each would receive a sliver of Pico's whole self. Somehow that made her smile, thinking how none of them would be spared. Every terror and every agony would be set inside each of them. In a diluted form, of course. The *Pico-ness* minimized. Made manageable. Yet it was something, wasn't it? It pleased her to think that a few of them might awaken in the night, bathed in sweat after dreaming of Tyson's death . . . just as she had dreamed of it time after time . . . her audience given more than they had anticipated, a dark little joke of her own. . . .

They reached the tables, Pico taking hers and sitting, feeling rather self-conscious as the others quietly assembled around her, each of them knowing where they belonged. She watched their faces. The excitement she had sensed from the beginning remained; only, it seemed magnified now. More colorful, more intense. Facing toward the inside of the omega, her hosts couldn't quit staring, forever smiling, scarcely able to eat once the robots brought them plates filled with steaming foods.

Fancy meals, Pico learned.

The robot setting her dinner before her explained, "The vegetables are from Triton, miss. A very special and much-prized strain. And the meat is from a wild hound killed just yesterday—"

"Really?"

"As part of the festivities, yes." The ceramic face, white and expressionless, stared down at her. "There have been hunting parties and games, among other diversions. Quite an assortment of activities, yes."

"For how long?" she asked. "These festivities . . . have they been going on for days?"

"A little longer than three months, miss."

She had no appetite; nonetheless, she lifted her utensils and made the proper motions, reminding herself that three months of continuous parties would be nothing to these people. Three months was a day to them, and what did they do with their time? So much of it, and such a constricted existence. What had Tyson once told her? The typical citizen of Earth averages less than one off-world trip in eighty years, and the trends were toward less traveling. Spaceflight was safe only to a degree, and these people couldn't stand the idea of being meters away from a cold, raw vacuum.

"Cowards," Tyson had called them. "Gutted, deblooded cowards!"

Looking about, she saw the delicate twists of green leaves vanishing into grinning mouths, the chewing prolonged and indifferent. Except for Opera, that is. Opera saw her and smiled back in turn, his eyes different, something mocking about the tilt of his head and the curl of his mouth.

She found her eyes returning to Opera every little while, and she wasn't sure why. She felt no physical attraction for the man. His youth and attitudes made him different from the others, but how much different? Then she noticed his dinner—cultured potatoes with meaty hearts—and that made an impression on Pico. It was a standard food on board the *Kyber*. Opera was making a gesture, perhaps. Nobody else was eating that bland food, and she decided this was a show of solidarity. At least the man was trying, wasn't he? More than the others, he was. He was.

Dessert was cold and sweet and shot full of some odd liquor.

Pico watched the others drinking and talking among themselves. For the first time, she noticed how they seemed subdivided—discrete groups formed, and boundaries between each one. A dozen people here, seven back there, and sometimes individuals sitting alone—like Opera—chatting politely or appearing entirely friendless.

One lonesome woman rose to her feet and approached Pico, not smiling, and with a sharp voice, she declared, "Tomorrow, come morning . . . you'll live forever. . . !"

Conversations diminished, then quit entirely.

"Plugged in. Here." She was under the influence of some drug, the tip of her finger shaking and missing her own temple. "You fine lucky girl . . . Yes, you are. . . !"

Some people laughed at the woman, suddenly and without shame.

The harsh sound made her turn and squint, and Pico watched her straightening her back. The woman was pretending to be above them and uninjured, her thin mouth squeezed shut and her nose tilting with mock pride. With a clear, soft voice, she said, "Fuck every one of you," and then laughed, turning toward Pico, acting as if they had just shared some glorious joke of their own.

"I would apologize for our behavior," said Opera, "but I can't. Not in good faith, I'm afraid."

Pico eyed the man. Dessert was finished; people stood about drinking, keeping the three-month-old party in motion. A few of them stripped naked and swam in the green pond. It was a raucous scene, tireless and full of happy moments that never seemed convincingly joyous. Happy sounds by practice, rather. Centuries of practice, and the result was to make Pico feel sad and quite lonely.

"A silly, vain lot," Opera told her.

She said, "Perhaps," with a diplomatic tone, then saw several others approaching. At least they looked polite, she thought. Respectful. It was odd how a dose of respect glosses over so much. Particularly when the respect wasn't reciprocated, Pico feeling none toward them. . . .

A man asked to hear more stories. Please?

Pico shrugged her shoulders, then asked, "Of what?" Every request brought her a momentary sense of claustrophobia, her memories threatening to crush her. "Maybe you're interested in a specific world?"

Opera responded, saying, "Blueblue!"

Blueblue was a giant gaseous world circling a bluish sun. Her first thought was of Midge vanishing into the dark storm on its southern hemisphere, searching for the source of the carbon monoxide upflow that effectively gave breath to half the world. Most of Blueblue was calm in comparison. Thick winds; strong sunlight. Its largest organisms would dwarf most cities, their bodies balloonlike and their lives spent feeding on sunlight and hydrocarbons, utilizing carbon monoxide and other radicals in their patient metabolisms. Pico and the others had spent several months living on the living clouds, walking across them, taking samples and studying the assortment of parasites and symbionts that grew in their flesh.

She told about sunrise on Blueblue, remembering its colors and its astounding speed. Suddenly she found herself talking about a particular morning when the landing party was jostled out of sleep by an apparent quake. Their little huts had been strapped down and secured, but they found themselves tilting fast. Their cloud was colliding with a neighboring cloud—something they had never seen—and of course there was a rush to load their shuttle and leave. If it came to that.

"Normally, you see, the clouds avoid each other," Pico told her little audience. "At first, we thought the creatures were fighting, judging by their roaring and the hard shoving. They make sounds by forcing air through pores and throats and anuses. It was a strange show. Deafening. The collision point was maybe a third of a kilometer from camp, our whole world rolling over while the sun kept rising, its bright, hot light cutting through the organic haze—"

"Gorgeous," someone said.

A companion said, "Quiet!"

Then Opera touched Pico on the arm, saying, "Go on. Don't pay any attention to them."

The others glanced at Opera, hearing something in his voice, and their backs stiffening reflexively.

And then Pico was speaking again, finishing her story. Tyson was the first one of them to understand, who somehow made the right guess and began laughing, not saying a word. By then everyone was on board the shuttle, ready to fly; the tilting stopped suddenly, the air filling with countless little blue balloons. Each was the size of a toy balloon, she told. Their cloud was bleeding them from new pores, and the other cloud responded with a thick gray fog of butterfly-like somethings. The butter-flies flew after the balloons, and Tyson laughed harder, his face contorted and the laugh finally shattering into a string of gasping coughs.

"Don't you see?" he asked the others. "Look! The clouds are enjoying a morning screw!"

Pico imitated Tyson's voice, regurgitating the words and enthusiasm. Then she was laughing for herself, scarcely noticing how the others giggled politely. No more. Only Opera was enjoying her story, again touching her arm and saying, "That's lovely. Perfect. God, precious. . . !"

The rest began to drift away, not quite excusing themselves.

What was wrong?

"Don't mind them," Opera cautioned. "They're members of some new chastity faith. Clarity through horniness, and all that." He laughed at them now. "They proba-bly went to too many orgies, and this is how they're coping with their guilt. That's all."

Pico shut her eyes, remembering the scene on Blueblue for herself. She didn't want to relinquish it.

"Screwing clouds," Opera was saying. "That is lovely."

And she thought:

He sounds a little like Tyson. In places. In ways.

After a while, Pico admitted, "I can't remember your father's face. I'm sure I must have met him, but I don't—"

"You did meet him," Opera replied. "He left a recording of it in his journal—a brief meeting—and I made a point of studying everything about the mission and you. His journal entries; your reports. Actually, I'm the best-prepared person here today. Other than you, of course."

She said nothing, considering those words.

They were walking now, making their way down to the pond, and sometimes Pico noticed the hard glances of the others. Did they approve of Opera? Did it anger them, watching him monopolizing her time? Yet she didn't want to be with *them*, the truth told. Fuck them, she thought; and she smiled at her private profanity.

The pond was empty of swimmers now. There were just a few sleepless ducks and the roiled water. A lot of the celebrants had vanished, Pico realized. To where? She asked Opera, and he said:

"It's late. But then again, most people sleep ten or twelve hours every night."

"That much?"

He nodded. "Enhanced dreams are popular lately. And the oldest people sometimes exceed fifteen hours—"

"Always?"

He shrugged and offered a smile.

"What a waste!"

"Of time?" he countered.

Immortals can waste many things, she realized. But never time. And with that thought, she looked straight at her companion, asking him, "What happened to your father?"

"How did he die, you mean?"

A little nod. A respectful expression, she hoped. But curious.

Opera said, "He used an extremely toxic poison, self-induced." He gave a vague disapproving look directed at nobody. "A suicide at the end of a prolonged depression. He made certain that his mind was ruined before autodocs and his own robots could save him."

"I'm sorry."

"Yet I can't afford to feel sorry," he responded. "You see, I was born according to the terms of his will. I'm ninety-nine percent his clone, the rest of my genes tailored according to his desires. If he hadn't murdered himself, I wouldn't exist. Nor would I have inherited his money." He shrugged, saying, "Parents," with a measured scorn. "They have such power over you, like it or not."

She didn't know how to respond.

"Listen to us. All of this death talk, and doesn't it seem out of place?" Opera said, "After all, we're here to celebrate your return home. Your successes. Your gifts. And you . . . you on the brink of being magnified many times over." He paused before saying, "By this time tomorrow, you'll reside inside all of us, making everyone richer as a consequence."

The young man had an odd way of phrasing his statements, the entire speech either earnest or satirical. She couldn't tell which. Or if there was a *which*. Maybe it was her ignorance with the audible clues, the unknown trappings of this culture. . . . Then something else occurred to her.

"What do you mean? 'Death talk . . .'"

"Your friend Tyson died on Coldtear," he replied. "And didn't you lose another on Blueblue?"

"Midge. Yes."

He nodded gravely, glancing down at Pico's legs. "We can sit. I'm sorry; I should have noticed you were getting tired."

They sat side by side on the grass, watching the mallard ducks. Males and females had the same vivid green heads. Beautiful, she mentioned. Opera explained how females were once brown and quite drab, but people thought that was a shame, and voted to have the species altered, both sexes made equally resplendent. Pico nodded, only halfway listening. She couldn't get Tyson and her other dead friends out of her mind. Particularly Tyson. She had been angry with him for a long time, and even now her anger wasn't finished. Her confusion and general tiredness made it worse. Why had he done it? In life the man had had a way of dominating every meeting, every little gathering. He had been optimistic and fearless, the last sort of person to do such an awful thing. Suicide. The others had heard it was an accident—Pico had held to her lie—but she and they were in agreement about one fact. When Tyson died, at that precise instant, some essential heart of their mission had been lost.

Why? she wondered. Why?

Midge had flown into the storm on Blueblue, seeking adventure and important scientific answers; and her death was sad, yes, and everyone had missed her. But it wasn't like Tyson's death. It felt honorable, maybe even perfect. They had a duty to fulfill in the wilderness, and that duty was in their blood and their training. People spoke about Midge for years, acting as if she were still alive. As if she were still flying the shuttle into the storm's vortex.

But Tyson was different.

Maybe everyone knew the truth about his death. Sometimes it seemed that, in Pico's eyes, the crew could see what had really happened, and they'd hear it between her practiced lines. They weren't fooled.

Meanwhile, others died in the throes of life.

Uoo—a slender wisp of a compilation—was incinerated by a giant bolt of lightning on Miriam 2, little left but ashes, and the rest of the party continuing its descent into the superheated Bottoms and the quiet Lead Sea.

Opaltu died in the mouth of a nameless predator. He had been another of Pico's lovers, a proud man and the best example of vanity that she had known—until today, she thought—and she and the others had laughed at the justice that befell Opaltu's killer. Unable to digest alien meats, the predator had sickened and died in a slow agonizing fashion, vomiting up its insides as it staggered through the yellow jungle.

Boo was killed while working outside the *Kyber*, struck by a mote of interstellar debris.

Xon's lifesuit failed, suffocating her.

As did Kyties's suit, and that wasn't long ago. Just a year now ship time, and she remembered a cascade of jokes and his endless good humor. The most decent person on board the *Kyber*.

Yet it was Tyson who dominated her memories of the dead. It was the man as well as his self-induced extinction, and the anger within her swelled all at once. Suddenly even simple breathing was work. Pico found herself sweating, then blinking away the salt in her eyes. Once, then again, she coughed into a fist; then finally she had the energy to ask, "Why did he do it?"

"Who? My father?"

"Depression is . . . should be . . . a curable ailment. We had drugs and therapies on board that could erase it."

"But it was more than depression. It was something that attacks the very old people. A kind of giant boredom, if you will."

She wasn't surprised. Nodding as if she'd expected that reply, she told him, "I can understand that, considering your lives." Then she thought how Tyson hadn't been depressed or bored. How could he have been either?

Opera touched her bad leg, for just a moment. "You must wonder how it will be," he mentioned. "Tomorrow, I mean."

She shivered, aware of the fear returning. Closing her burning eyes, she saw Tyson's walk through the bacterial mat, the loose gray chunks spinning as the currents carried them, lending them a greater sort of life with the motion. . . . And she opened her eyes, Opera watching, saying something to her with his expression, and she unable to decipher any meanings.

"Maybe I should go to bed, too," she allowed.

The park under the tent was nearly empty now. Where had the others gone?

Opera said, "Of course," as if expecting it. He rose and offered his hand, and she surprised herself by taking the hand with both of hers. Then he said, "If you like, I can show you your quarters."

She nodded, saying nothing.

It was a long painful walk, and Pico honestly considered asking for a robot's help. For anyone's. Even a cane would have been a blessing, her hip never having felt so bad. Earth's gravity and the general stress were making it worse, most likely. She told herself that at least it was a pleasant night, warm and calm and perfectly clear, and the soft ground beneath the grass seemed to be calling to her, inviting her to lay down and sleep in the open.

People were staying in a chain of old houses subdivided into apartments, luxurious yet small. Pico's apartment was on the ground floor, Opera happy to show her through the rooms. For an instant, she considered asking him to stay the night. Indeed, she sensed that he was delaying, hoping for some sort of invitation. But she heard herself saying, "Rest well, and thank you," and her companion smiled and left without comment, vanishing through the crystal front door and leaving her completely alone.

For a little while, she sat on her bed, doing nothing. Not even thinking, at least in any conscious fashion.

Then she realized something, no warning given; and aloud, in a voice almost too soft for even her to hear, she said, "He didn't know. Didn't have an idea, the shit." Tyson. She was thinking about the fiery man and his boast about being the second generation of star explorers. What if it was all true? His parents had injected a portion of a former Tyson into him, and he had already known the early worlds they had visited. He already knew the look of sunrises on the double desert world around Alpha Centauri A; he knew the smell of constant rot before they cracked their airlocks on Barnard's 2. But try as he might—

"—he couldn't remember how it feels to be disassembled." She spoke without sound. To herself. "That titanic and fearless creature, and he couldn't remember. Everything else, yes, but not that. And not knowing had to scare him. Nothing else did, but that terrified him. The only time in his life he was truly scared, and it took all his bluster to keep that secret—!"

Killing himself rather than face his fear.

Of course, she thought. Why not?

And he took Pico as his audience, knowing she'd be a good audience. Because they were lovers. Because he must have decided that he could convince her in his fearlessness one last time, leaving his legend secure. Immortal, in a sense.

That's what you were thinking . . .

. . . wasn't it?

And she shivered, holding both legs close to her mouth, and feeling the warm misery of her doomed hip.

She sat for a couple more hours, neither sleeping nor feeling the slightest need for sleep. Finally she rose and used the bathroom, and after a long careful look through the windows, she ordered the door to open and stepped outside, picking a reasonable direction and walking stiffly and quickly on the weakened leg.

Opera emerged from the shadows, startling her.

"If you want to escape," he whispered, "I can help. Let me help you, please."

The face was handsome in the moonlight, young in every fashion. He must have guessed her mood, she realized, and she didn't allow herself to become upset. Help was important, she reasoned. Even essential. She had to find her way across a vast and very strange alien world. "I want to get back into orbit," she told him, "and find another starship. We saw several. They looked almost ready to embark." Bigger than the *Kyber,* and obviously faster. No doubt designed to move even deeper into the endless wilderness.

"I'm not surprised," Opera told her. "And I understand."

She paused, staring at him before asking, "How did you guess?"

"Living forever inside our heads . . . That's just a mess of metaphysical nonsense, isn't it? You know you'll die tomorrow. Bits of your brain will vanish inside us, made part of us, and not vice versa. I think it sounds like an awful way to die, certainly for someone like you—"

"Can you really help me?"

"This way," he told her. "Come on."

They walked for an age, crossing the paddock and finally reaching the wide tube where the skimmers shot past with a rush of air. Opera touched a simple control, then said, "It won't be long," and smiled at her. Just for a moment. "You know, I almost gave up on you. I thought I must have read you wrong. You didn't strike me as someone who'd go quietly to her death. . . ."

She had a vague fleeting memory of the senior Opera. Gazing at the young face, she could recall a big warm hand shaking her hand, and a similar voice saying, "It's very good to meet you, Pico. At last!"

"I bet one of the new starships will want you." The young Opera was telling her, "You're right. They're bigger ships, and they've got better facilities. Since they'll be gone even longer, they've been given the best possible medical equipment. That hip and your general body should respond to treatments—"

"I have experience," she whispered.

"Pardon me?"

"Experience." She nodded with conviction. "I can offer a crew plenty of valuable experience."

"They'd be idiots not to take you."

A skimmer slowed and stopped before them. Opera made the windows opaque—"So nobody can see you"—and punched in their destination, Pico making herself comfortable.

"Here we go," he chuckled, and they accelerated away.

There was an excitement to all of this, an adventure like every other. Pico realized that she was scared, but in a good, familiar way. Life and death. Both possibilities seemed balanced on a very narrow fulcrum, and she found herself smiling, rubbing her hip with a slow hand.

They were moving fast, following Opera's instructions.

"A circuitous route," he explained. "We want to make our whereabouts less obvious. All right?"

"Fine."

"Are you comfortable?"

"Yes," she allowed. "Basically."

Then she was thinking about the others—the other survivors from the *Kyber*—wondering how many of them were having second or third thoughts. The long journey home had been spent in cold-sleep, but there had been intervals when two or three of them were awakened to do normal maintenance. Not once did anyone even joke about taking the ship elsewhere. Nobody had asked, "Why do we have to go to Earth?" The obvious question had eluded them, and at the time, she had assumed it was because there were no doubters. Besides herself, that is. The rest believed this would be the natural conclusion to full and satisfied lives; they were returning home to a new life and an appreciative audience. How could any sane compilation think otherwise?

Yet she found herself wondering.

Why no jokes?

If they hadn't had doubts, wouldn't they have made jokes?

Eight others had survived the mission. Yet none were as close to Pico as she had been to Tyson. They had saved each other's proverbial skin many times, and she did feel a sudden deep empathy for them, remembering how they had boarded nine separate shuttles after kisses and hugs and a few careful tears, each of them struggling with the proper things to say. But what could anyone say at such a moment? Particularly when you believed that your companions were of one mind and, in some fashion, happy. . . .

Pico said, "I wonder about the others," and intended to leave it at that. To say nothing more.

"The others?"

"From the *Kyber*. My friends." She paused and swallowed, then said softly, "Maybe I could contact them."

"No," he responded.

She jerked her head, watching Opera's profile.

"That would make it easy to catch you." His voice was quite sensible and measured. "Besides," he added, "can't they make up their own minds? Like you have?"

She nodded, thinking that was reasonable. Sure.

He waited a long moment, then said, "Perhaps you'd like to talk about something else?"

"Like what?"

He eyed Pico, then broke into a wide smile. "If I'm not going to inherit a slice of your mind, leave me another story. Tell . . . I don't know. Tell me about your favorite single place. Not a world, but some favorite patch of ground on any world. If you could be anywhere now, where would it be? And with whom?"

Pico felt the skimmer turning, following the tube. She didn't have to consider the question—her answer seemed obvious to her—but the pause was to collect herself, weighing how to begin and what to tell.

"In the mountains on Erindi Three," she said, "the air thins enough to be breathed safely, and it's really quite pretty. The scenery, I mean."

"I've seen holos of the place. It is lovely."

"Not just lovely." She was surprised by her authority, her self-assured voice telling him, "There's a strange sense of peace there. You don't get that from holos. Supposedly it's produced by the weather and the vegetation. . . . They make showers of negative ions, some say. . . . And it's the colors, too. A subtle interplay of shades and shadows. All very one-of-a-kind."

"Of course," he said carefully.

She shut her eyes, seeing the place with almost perfect clarity. A summer storm had swept overhead, charging the glorious atmosphere even further, leaving everyone in the party invigorated. She and Tyson, Midge, and several others had decided to swim in a deep blue pool near their campsite. The terrain itself was rugged, black rocks erupting from the blue-green vegetation. The valley's little river poured into a gorge and the pool, and the people did the same. Tyson was first, naturally. He laughed and bounced in the icy water, screaming loud enough to make a flock of razor-bats take flight. This was only the third solar system they had visited, and they were still young in every sense. It seemed to them that every world would be this much fun.

She recalled—and described—diving feetfirst. She was last into the pool, having inherited a lot of caution from her parents. Tyson had teased her, calling her a coward and then worse, then showing where to aim. "Right here! It's deep here! Come on, coward! Take a chance!"

The water was startlingly cold, and there wasn't much of it beneath the shiny flowing surface. She struck and hit the packed sand below, and the impact made her groan, then shout. Tyson had lied, and she chased the bastard around the pool, screaming and finally clawing at his broad back until she'd driven him up the gorge walls, him laughing and once, losing strength with all the laughing, almost tumbling down on top of her.

She told Opera everything.

At first, it seemed like an accident. All her filters were off; she admitted everything without hesitation. Then she told herself that the man was saving her life and deserved the whole story. That's when she was describing the lovemaking between her and Tyson. That night. It was their first time, and maybe the best time. They did it on a bed of mosses, perched on the rim of the gorge, and she tried to paint a vivid word picture for her audience, including smells and the textures and the sight of the double moons overhead, colored a strange living pink and moving fast.

Their skimmer ride seemed to be taking a long time, she thought once she was finished. She mentioned this to Opera, and he nodded soberly. Otherwise, he made no comment.

I won't be disembodied tomorrow, she told herself.

Then she added, *Today, I mean today.*

She felt certain now. Secure. She was glad for this chance and for this dear new friend, and it was too bad she'd have to leave so quickly, escaping into the relative safety of space. Perhaps there were more people like Opera . . . people who would be kind to her, appreciating her circumstances and desires . . . supportive and interesting companions in their own right. . . .

And sudddenly the skimmer was slowing, preparing to stop.

When Opera said, "Almost there," she felt completely at ease. Entirely calm, She shut her eyes and saw the raw, wild mountains on Erindi 3, storm clouds gathering and flashes of lightning piercing the howling winds. She summoned a different day, and saw Tyson standing against the storms, smiling, beckoning for her to climb up to him just as the first cold, fat raindrops smacked against her face.

The skimmer's hatch opened with a hiss.

Sunlight streamed inside, and she thought: Dawn. *By now, sure . . .*

Opera rose and stepped outside, then held a hand out to Pico. She took it with both of hers and said, "Thank you," while rising, looking past him and seeing the paddock and the familiar faces, the green ground and the giant tent with its doorways opened now, various birds flying inside and out again . . . and Pico was surprised by how little she was surprised. Opera still holding her hands, and his flesh dry, the hand perfectly calm.

The autodocs stood waiting for orders.

This time, Pico had been carried from the skimmer, riding cradled in a robot's arms. She had taken just a few faltering steps before half-crumbling. Exhaustion was to blame. Not fear. At least it didn't feel like fear, she told herself. Everyone told her to take it easy, to enjoy her comfort; and now, finding herself flanked by autodocs, her exhaustion worsened. She thought she might die before the cutting began, too tired now to pump her own blood or fire her neurons or even breathe.

Opera was standing nearby, almost smiling, his pleasure serene and chilly and regrets.

He hadn't said a word since they left the skimmer.

Several others told her to sit, offering her a padded seat with built-in channels to catch any flowing blood. Pico took an uneasy step toward the seat, then paused and straightened her back, saying, "I'm thirsty," softly, her words sounding thoroughly parched.

"Pardon?" they asked.

"I want to drink . . . some water, please . . . ?"

Faces turned, hunting for a cup and water.

It was Opera who said, "Will the pond do?" Then he came forward, extending an arm and telling everyone else, "It won't take long. Give us a moment, will you?"

Pico and Opera walked alone.

Last night's ducks were sleeping and lazily feeding. Pico looked at their metallic green heads, so lovely that she ached at seeing them, and she tried to miss nothing. She tried to concentrate so hard that time itself would compress, seconds turning to hours, and her life in that way prolonged.

Opera was speaking, asking her, "Do you want to hear why?"

She shook her head, not caring in the slightest.

"But you must be wondering why. I fool you into believing that I'm your ally, and I manipulate you—"

"Why?" she sputtered. "So tell me."

"Because," he allowed, "it helps the process. It helps your integration into us. I gave you a chance for doubts and helped you think you were fleeing, convinced you that you'd be free . . . and now you're angry and scared and intensely alive. It's that intensity that we want. It makes the neurological grafts take hold. It's a trick that we learned since the *Kyber* left Earth. Some compilations tried to escape, and when they were caught and finally incorporated along with their anger—"

"Except, I'm not angry," she lied, gazing at his self-satisfied grin.

"A nervous system in flux," he said. "I volunteered, by the way."

She thought of hitting him. Could she kill him somehow?

But instead, she turned and asked, "Why this way? Why not just let me slip away, then catch me at the spaceport?"

"You were going to drink," he reminded her. "Drink."

She knelt despite her hip's pain, knees sinking into the muddy bank and her lips pursing, taking in a long, warmish thread of muddy water, and then her face lifting, the water spilling across her chin and chest, and her mouth unable to close tight.

"Nothing angers," he said, "like the betrayal of someone you trust."

True enough, she thought. Suddenly she could see Tyson leaving her alone on the ocean floor, his private fears too much, and his answer being to kill himself while dressed up in apparent bravery. A kind of betrayal, wasn't that? To both of them, and it still hurt. . . .

"Are you still thirsty?" asked Opera.

"Yes," she whispered.

"Then drink. Go on."

She knelt again, taking a bulging mouthful and swirling it with her tongue. Yet she couldn't make herself swallow, and after a moment, it began leaking out from her lips and down her front again. Making a mess, she realized. Muddy, warm, ugly water, and she couldn't remember how it felt to be thirsty. Such a little thing, and ordinary, and she couldn't remember it.

"Come on, then," said Opera.

She looked at him.

He took her arm and began lifting her, a small smiling voice saying, "You've done very well, Pico. You have. The truth is that everyone is very proud of you."

She was on her feet again and walking, not sure when she had begun moving her legs. She wanted to poison her thoughts with her hatred of these awful people, and for a little while, she could think of nothing else. She would make her mind bilious and cancerous, poisoning all of these bastards and finally destroying them. That's what she would do, she promised herself. Except, suddenly she was sitting on the padded chair, autodocs coming close with their bright humming limbs; and there was so much stored in her mind—worlds and people, emotions heaped on emotions—and she didn't have the time she would need to poison herself.

Which proved something, she realized.

Sitting still now.

Sitting still and silent. At ease. Her front drenched and stained brown, but her open eyes calm and dry.

none so Blind

JOE HALDEMAN

Born in Oklahoma City, Oklahoma, Joe Haldeman took a B.S. degree in physics and astronomy from the University of Maryland, and did postgraduate work in mathematics and computer science. But his plans for a career in science were cut short by the U.S. Army, which sent him to Vietnam in 1968 as a combat engineer. Seriously wounded in action, Haldeman returned home in 1969 and began to write. He sold his first story to *Galaxy* in 1969, and by 1976 had garnered both the Nebula Award and the Hugo Award for his famous novel *The Forever War*, one of the landmark books of the '70s. He took another Hugo Award in 1977 for his story "Tricentennial," won the Rhysling Award in 1983 for the best science fiction poem of the year, and won both the Nebula and the Hugo Awards in 1991 for the novella version of "The Hemingway Hoax." His novel *Forever Peace* won the John W. Campbell Memorial Award. His other books include two mainstream novels, *War Year* and *1969*, the SF novels *Mindbridge, All My Sins Remembered, There Is No Darkness* (written with his brother, the late Jack C. Haldeman II), *Worlds, Worlds Apart, Worlds Enough and Time, Buying Time, The Hemingway Hoax, Forever Peace, Forever Free,* and *The Coming,* the collections *Infinite Dreams, Dealing in Futures, Vietnam and Other Alien Worlds,* and *None So Blind,* and, as editor, the anthologies *Study War No More, Cosmic Laughter,* and *Nebula Award Stories Seventeen.* His most recent book is the novel *Guardian.* Coming up is a new novel, *Camouflage.* Haldeman lives part of the year in Boston, where he teaches writing at the Massachusetts Institute of Technology, and the rest of the year in Florida, where he and his wife, Gay, make their home.

The sly and fascinating little story that follows—which won Haldeman another Hugo Award in 1995—examines the personal *cost* of that high-tech competitive edge we'd all like to have . . . a price that we may all soon have to come up with a way to pay, whether we can afford it or not.

It all started when Cletus Jefferson asked himself "Why aren't all blind people geniuses?" Cletus was only thirteen at the time, but it was a good question, and he would work on it for fourteen more years, and then change the world forever.

Young Jefferson was a polymath, an autodidact, a nerd literally without peer. He had a chemistry set, a microscope, a telescope, and several computers, some of them bought with paper route money. Most of his income was from education, though: teaching his classmates not to draw to inside straights.

Not even nerds, not even nerds who are poker players nonpareil, not even nerdish poker players who can do differential equations in their heads, are immune to Cupid's darts and the sudden storm of testosterone that will accompany those missiles at the age of thirteen. Cletus knew that he was ugly and his mother dressed him funny. He was also short and pudgy and could not throw a ball in any direction. None of this bothered him until his ductless glands started cooking up chemicals that weren't in his chemistry set.

So Cletus started combing his hair and wearing clothes that mismatched according to fashion, but he was still short and pudgy and irregular of feature. He was also the youngest person in his school, even though he was a senior—and the only black person there, which was a factor in Virginia in 1994.

Now if love were sensible, if the sexual impulse was ever tempered by logic, you would expect that Cletus, being Cletus, would assess his situation and go off in search of someone homely. But of course he didn't. He just jingled and clanked down through the Pachinko machine of adolescence, being rejected, at first glance, by every Mary and Judy and Jenny and Veronica in Known Space, going from the ravishing to the beautiful to the pretty to the cute to the plain to the "great personality," until the irresistible force of statistics brought him finally into contact with Amy Linderbaum, who could not reject him at first glance because she was blind.

The other kids thought it was more than amusing. Besides being blind, Amy was about twice as tall as Cletus and, to be kind, equally irregular of feature. She was accompanied by a guide dog who looked remarkably like Cletus, short and black and pudgy. Everybody was polite to her because she was blind and rich, but she was a new transfer student and didn't have any actual friends.

So along came Cletus, to whom Cupid had dealt only slings and arrows, and what might otherwise have been merely an opposites-attract sort of romance became an emotional and intellectual union that, in the next century, would power a social tsunami that would irreversibly transform the human condition. But first there was the violin.

Her classmates had sensed that Amy was some kind of nerd herself as classmates will, but they hadn't figured out what kind yet. She was pretty fast with a computer, but you could chalk that up to being blind and actually needing the damned thing. She wasn't fanatical about it, nor about science or math or history or Star Trek or student government, so what the hell kind of nerd was she? It turns out that she was a music nerd, but at the time was too painfully shy to demonstrate it.

All Cletus cared about, initially, was that she lacked those pesky Y-chromosomes and didn't recoil from him: in the Venn diagram of the human race, she was the only member of that particular set. When he found out that she was actually smart as well, having read more books than most of her classmates put together, romance began to smolder in a deep and permanent place. That was even before the violin.

Amy liked it that Cletus didn't play with her dog and was straightforward in his curiosity about what it was like to be blind. She could assess people pretty well from their voices: after one sentence, she knew that he was young, black, shy, nerdly, and not from Virginia. She could tell from his inflection that either he was unattractive or he thought he was. She was six years older than him and white and twice his size, but otherwise they matched up pretty well, and they started keeping company in a big way.

Among the few things that Cletus did not know anything about was music. That the other kids wasted their time memorizing the words to inane Top 40 songs was proof of intellectual dysfunction if not actual lunacy. Furthermore, his parents had always been fanatical devotees of opera. A universe bounded on one end by puerile mumblings about unrequited love and on the other end by foreigners screaming in agony was not a universe that Cletus desired to explore. Until Amy picked up her violin.

They talked constantly. They sat together at lunch and met between classes. When the weather was good, they sat outside before and after school and talked. Amy asked her chauffeur to please be ten or fifteen minutes late picking her up.

So after about three weeks' worth of the fullness of time, Amy asked Cletus to come over to her house for dinner. He was a little hesitant, knowing that her parents were rich, but he was also curious about that lifestyle and, face it, was smitten enough that he would have walked off a cliff if she asked him nicely. He even used some computer money to buy a nice suit, a symptom that caused his mother to grope for the Valium.

The dinner at first was awkward. Cletus was bewildered by the arsenal of silverware and all the different kinds of food that didn't look or taste like food. But he had known it was going to be a test, and he always did well on tests, even when he had to figure out the rules as he went along.

Amy had told him that her father was a self-made millionaire; his fortune had come from a set of patents in solid-state electronics. Cletus had therefore spent a Saturday at the university library, first searching patents, and then reading selected texts, and he was ready at least for the father. It worked very well. Over soup, the four of them talked about computers. Over the calamari cocktail, Cletus and Mr. Linderbaum had it narrowed down to specific operating systems and partitioning schemata. With the beef Wellington, Cletus and "Call-me-Lindy" were talking quantum electrodynamics; with the salad they were on an electron cloud somewhere, and by the time the nuts were served, the two nuts at that end of the table were talking in Boolean algebra while Amy and her mother exchanged knowing sighs and hummed snatches of Gilbert and Sullivan.

By the time they retired to the music room for coffee, Lindy liked Cletus very much, and the feeling was mutual, but Cletus didn't know how much he liked Amy, *really* liked her, until she picked up the violin.

It wasn't a Strad—she was promised one if and when she graduated from Juilliard—but it had cost more than the Lamborghini in the garage, and she was not only worth it, but equal to it. She picked it up and tuned it quietly while her mother sat down at an electronic keyboard next to the grand piano, set it to "harp," and began the simple arpeggio that a musically sophisticated person would recognize as the introduction to the violin showpiece "Méditation" from Massenet's *Thaïs*.

Cletus had turned a deaf ear to opera for all his short life, so he didn't know the back-story of transformation and transcending love behind this intermezzo, but he did know that his girlfriend had lost her sight at the age of five, and the next year—the year he was born!—was given her first violin. For thirteen years she had been using it to say what she would not say with her voice, perhaps to see what she could not see with her eyes, and on the deceptively simple romantic matrix that Massenet built to present the beautiful courtesan Thaïs gloriously reborn as the bride of Christ, Amy forgave her godless universe for taking her sight, and praised it for what she was given in return, and she said this in a language that even Cletus could understand. He didn't cry very much, never had, but by the last high, wavering note he was weeping into his hands, and he knew that if she wanted him, she could have him forever, and oddly enough, considering his age and what eventually happened, he was right.

He would learn to play the violin before he had his first doctorate, and during a lifetime of remarkable amity they would play together for ten thousand hours, but all of that would come after the big idea. The big idea—"Why aren't all blind people geniuses?"—was planted that very night, but it didn't start to sprout for another week.

Like most thirteen-year-olds, Cletus was fascinated by the human body, his own and others, but his study was more systematic than others' and, atypically, the organ that interested him most was the brain.

The brain isn't very much like a computer, although it doesn't do a bad job, considering that it's built by unskilled labor and programmed more by pure chance than anything else. One thing computers do a lot better than brains, though, is what Cletus and Lindy had been talking about over their little squids in tomato sauce: partitioning.

Think of the computer as a big meadow of green pastureland, instead of a little dark box full of number-clogged things that are expensive to replace, and that pastureland is presided over by a wise old magic shepherd who is not called a macroprogram. The shepherd stands on a hill and looks out over the pastureland, which is full of sheep and goats and cows. They aren't all in one homogeneous mass, of course, since the cows would step on the lambs and kids and the goats would make everybody nervous, leaping and butting, so there are *partitions* of barbed wire that keep all the species separate and happy.

This is a frenetic sort of meadow, though, with cows and goats and sheep coming in and going out all the time, moving at about 3×10^8 meters per second, and if the partitions were all of the same size, it would be a disaster, because sometimes there are no sheep at all, but lots of cows, who would be jammed in there hip to hip and miserable. But the shepherd, being wise, knows ahead of time how much space to allot to the various creatures and, being magic, can move barbed wire quickly without hurting himself or the animals. So each partition winds up marking a comfortable-sized space for each use. Your computer does that, too, but instead of barbed wire you see little rectangles or windows or file folders, depending on your computer's religion.

The brain has its own partitions, in a sense. Cletus knew that certain physical areas of the brain were associated with certain mental abilities, but it wasn't a simple matter of "music appreciation goes over there; long division in that corner." The brain is mushier than that. For instance, there are pretty well defined partitions associated with linguistic functions, areas named after French and German brain people. If one of those areas is destroyed, by stroke or bullet or flung frying pan, the stricken person may lose the ability—reading or speaking or writing coherently—associated with the lost area.

That's interesting, but what is more interesting is that the lost ability sometimes comes back over time. Okay, you say, so the brain grew back—but it doesn't! You're born with all the brain cells you'll ever have. (Ask any child.) What evidently happens is that some other part of the brain has been sitting around as a kind of backup, and after a while the wiring gets rewired and hooked into that backup. The afflicted person can say his name, and then his wife's name, and then "frying pan," and before you know it he's complaining about hospital food and calling a divorce lawyer.

So on that evidence, it would appear that the brain has a shepherd like the computer-meadow has, moving partitions around, but alas, no. Most of the time when some part of the brain ceases to function, that's the end of it. There may be acres and acres of fertile ground lying fallow right next door, but nobody in charge to make use of it—at least not consistently. The fact that it sometimes *did* work is what made Cletus ask "Why aren't all blind people geniuses?"

Of course there have always been great thinkers and writers and composers who were blind (and in the twentieth century, some painters to whom eyesight was irrelevant), and many of them, like Amy with her violin, felt that their talent was a compensating gift. Cletus wondered whether there might be a literal truth to that, in the microanatomy of the brain. It didn't happen every time, or else all blind people *would* be geniuses. Perhaps it happened occasionally, through a mechanism like the one that helped people recover from strokes. Perhaps it could be made to happen.

Cletus had been offered scholarships at both Harvard and MIT, but he opted for Columbia, in order to be near Amy while she was studying at Juilliard. Columbia reluctantly allowed him a triple major in physiology, electrical engineering, and cognitive science, and he surprised everybody who knew him by doing only moderately well. The reason, it turned out, was that he was treating undergraduate work as a diversion at best; a necessary evil at worst. He was racing ahead of his studies in the areas that were important to him.

If he had paid more attention in trivial classes like history, like philosophy, things might have turned out differently. If he had paid attention to literature, he might have read the story of Pandora.

Our own story now descends into the dark recesses of the brain. For the next ten years the main part of the story, which we will try to ignore after this paragraph, will involve Cletus doing disturbing intellectual tasks like cutting up dead brains, learning how to pronounce cholecystokinin, and sawing holes in people's skulls and poking around inside with live electrodes.

In the other part of the story, Amy also learned how to pronounce cholecystokinin, for the same reason that Cletus learned how to play the violin. Their love grew and mellowed, and at the age of nineteen, between his first doctorate and his M.D., Cletus paused long enough for them to be married and have a whirlwind honeymoon in Paris, where Cletus divided his time between the musky charms of his beloved and the sterile cubicles of Institute Marey, learning how squids learn things, which was by serotonin pushing adenylate cyclase to catalyze the synthesis of cyclic adenosine monophosphate in just the right place, but that's actually the main part of the story, which we have been trying to ignore, because it gets pretty gruesome.

They returned to New York, where Cletus spent eight years becoming a pretty good neurosurgeon. In his spare time he tucked away a doctorate in electrical engineering. Things began to converge.

At the age of thirteen, Cletus had noted that the brain used more cells collecting, handling, and storing visual images than it used for all the other senses combined. "Why aren't all blind people geniuses?" was just a specific case of the broader assertion, "The brain doesn't know how to make use of what it's got." His investigations over the next fourteen years were more subtle and complex than that initial question and statement, but he did wind up coming right back around to them.

Because the key to the whole thing was the visual cortex.

When a baritone saxophone player has to transpose sheet music from cello, he (few women are drawn to the instrument) merely pretends that the music is written in treble clef rather than bass, eyeballs it up an octave, and then plays without the octave key pressed down. It's so simple a child could do it, if a child wanted to play such a huge, ungainly instrument. As his eye dances along the little fence posts of notes his fingers automatically perform a one-to-one transformation that is the theoretical equivalent of adding and subtracting octaves, fifths, and thirds, but all of the actual mental work is done when he looks up in the top right corner of the first page and says, "Aw hell. Cello again." Cello parts aren't that interesting to saxophonists.

But the eye is the key, and the visual cortex is the lock. When blind Amy "sight-reads" for the violin, she has to stop playing and feel the Braille notes with her left hand. (Years of keeping the instrument in place while she does this has made her neck muscles so strong that she can crack a walnut between her chin and shoulder.) The visual cortex is not involved, of course; she "hears" the mute notes of a phrase with her fingertips, temporarily memorizing them, and then plays them over and over until she can add that phrase to the rest of the piece.

Like most blind musicians, Amy had a very good "ear"; it actually took her less time to memorize music by listening to it repeatedly, rather than reading, even with fairly complex pieces. (She used Braille nevertheless for serious work, so she could isolate the composer's intent from the performer's or conductor's phrasing decisions.)

She didn't really miss being able to sight-read in a conventional way. She wasn't even sure what it would be like, since she had never seen sheet music before she lost her sight, and in fact had only a vague idea of what a printed page of writing looked like.

So when her father came to her in her thirty-third year and offered to buy her the chance of a limited gift of sight, she didn't immediately jump at it. It was expensive and risky and grossly deforming: implanting miniaturized video cameras in her eye sockets and wiring them up to stimulate her dormant optic nerves.

What if it made her only half-blind, but also blunted her musical ability? She knew how other people read music, at least in theory, but after a quarter century of doing without the skill, she wasn't sure that it would do much for her. It might make her tighten up.

Besides, most of her concerts were done as charities to benefit organizations for the blind or for special education. Her father argued that she would be even more effective in those venues as a recovered blind person. Still she resisted.

Cletus said he was cautiously for it. He said he had reviewed the literature and talked to the Swiss team who had successfully done the implants on dogs and primates. He said he didn't think she would be harmed by it even if the experiment failed. What he didn't say to Amy or Lindy or anybody was the grisly Frankenstein-ian truth: that he was himself behind the experiment; that it had nothing to do with restoring sight; that the little video cameras would never even be hooked up. They were just an excuse for surgically removing her eyeballs.

Now a normal person would have extreme feelings about popping out some-body's eyeballs for the sake of science, and even more extreme feelings on learning that it was a husband wanting to do it to his wife. Of course Cletus was far from being normal in any respect. To his way of thinking, those eyeballs were useless vestig-ial appendages that blocked surgical access to the optic nerves, which would be his conduits through the brain to the visual cortex. *Physical* conduits, through which incredibly tiny surgical instruments would be threaded. But we have promised not to investigate that part of the story in detail.

The end result was not grisly at all. Amy finally agreed to go to Geneva, and Cle-tus and his surgical team (all as skilled as they were unethical) put her through three twenty-hour days of painstaking but painless microsurgery, and when they took the bandages off and adjusted a thousand-dollar wig (for they'd had to go in behind as well as through the eye sockets), she actually looked more attractive than when they had started. That was partly because her actual hair had always been a disaster. And now she had glass baby-blues instead of the rather scary opalescence of her natural eyes. No Buck Rogers TV cameras peering out at the world.

He told her father that that part of the experiment hadn't worked, and the six Swiss scientists who had been hired for the purpose agreed.

"They're lying," Amy said. "They never intended to restore my sight. The sole intent of the operations was to subvert the normal functions of the visual cortex in such a way as to give me access to the unused parts of my brain." She faced the sound of her hus-band's breathing, her blue eyes looking beyond him. "You have succeeded beyond your expectations."

Amy had known this as soon as the fog of drugs from the last operation had lifted. Her mind started making connections, and those connections made connections, and so on at a geometrical rate of growth. By the time they had finished putting her wig on, she had reconstructed the entire microsurgical procedure from her limited readings and conversations with Cletus. She had suggestions as to improving it, and was eager to go under and submit herself to further refinement.

As to her feelings about Cletus, in less time than it takes to read about it, she had gone from horror to hate to understanding to renewed love, and finally to an emotional condition beyond the ability of any merely natural language to express.

Fortunately, the lovers did have Boolean algebra and propositional calculus at their disposal.

Cletus was one of the few people in the world she *could* love, or even talk to one-on-one, without condescending. His IQ was so high that its number would be meaningless. Compared to her, though, he was slow, and barely literate. It was not a situation he would tolerate for long.

The rest is history, as they say, and anthropology, as those of us left who read with our eyes must recognize every minute of every day. Cletus was the second person to have the operation done, and he had to accomplish it while on the run from medical ethics people and their policemen. There were four the next year, though, and twenty the year after that, and then two thousand and twenty thousand. Within a decade, people with purely intellectual occupations had no choice, or one choice: lose your eyes or lose your job. By then the "secondsight" operation was totally automated, totally safe.

It's still illegal in most countries, including the United States, but who is kidding whom? If your department chairman is secondsighted and you are not, do you think you'll get tenure? You can't even hold a conversation with a creature whose synapses fire six times as fast as yours, with whole encyclopedias of information instantly available. You are, like me, an intellectual throwback.

You may have an excuse, being a painter, an architect, a naturalist, or a trainer of guide dogs. Maybe you can't come up with the money for the operation, but that's a weak excuse, since it's trivially easy to get a loan against future earnings. Maybe there's a good physical reason for you not to lie down on that table and open your eyes for the last time.

I know Cletus and Amy through music. I was her keyboard professor once, at Juilliard, though now, of course, I'm not smart enough to teach her anything. They come to hear me play sometimes, in this run-down bar with its band of ageing first-sight musicians. Our music must seem boring, obvious, but they do us the favor of not joining in.

Amy was an innocent bystander in this sudden evolutionary explosion. And Cletus was, arguably, blinded by love.

The rest of us have to choose which kind of blindness to endure.

Mortimer Gray's
History of Death

BRIAN STABLEFORD

Critically acclaimed British "hard science" writer Brian Stableford is the author of more than thirty books, including *Cradle of the Sun, The Blind Worm, Days of Glory, In the Kingdom of the Beasts, Day of Wrath, The Halcyon Drift, The Paradox of the Sets, The Realms of Tartarus, The Empire of Fear, The Angel of Pain, The Carnival of Destruction, Serpent's Blood, Inherit the Earth, The Omega Expedition,* and *Dark Ararat.* His short fiction has been collected in *Sexual Chemistry: Sardonic Tales of the Genetic Revolution.* His nonfiction books include *The Sociology of Science Fiction* and, with David Langford, *The Third Millennium: A History of the World A.D. 2000–3000.* His novella "Les Fleurs Du Mal" was a finalist for the Hugo Award in 1994. He has had stories in our Sixth, Seventh, Twelfth, Thirteenth, Fifteenth, and Eighteenth annual collections. His most recent books are the novels *The Fountains of Youth* and *Architects of Emortality.* Coming up are a new novel, *The Gateway of Eternity,* and two new collections, *Salome and Other Decadent Fantasies* and *Designer Genes: Tales of the Biotech Revolution.* A biologist and sociologist by training, Stableford lives in Reading, England.

Stableford may have written more about how the ongoing revolutions in biological and genetic science will change the very nature of humanity itself than any other writer of the last decade, covering the development of posthumanity in story after story, including such stories as "Out of Touch," "The Magic Bullet," "Age of Innocence," "The Tree of Life," "The Pipes of Pan," "Hidden Agendas," "The Color of Envy," the abovementioned "Les Fleurs Du Mal," and many, many others, including recent novels such as *Inherit the Earth, The Fountains of Youth,* and *Architects of Emortality.* Never has he explored the posthuman future in more detail or with more passion or conviction than in the complex and compelling novella that follows, though, perhaps his best story and certainly one of the very best novellas of the '90s, taking us to an ultrarich, ultracivilized far-future world where we've almost—almost—conquered the oldest and coldest enemy of them all. . . .

1

I was an utterly unexceptional child of the twenty-ninth century, comprehensively engineered for emortality while I was still a more-or-less inchoate blastula, and decanted from an artificial womb in Naburn Hatchery in the country of York in the Defederated States of Europe. I was raised in an aggregate family which consisted of six men and six women. I was, of course, an only child, and I received the customary superabundance of love, affection, and admiration. With the aid of excellent internal technologies, I grew up reasonable, charitable, self-controlled, and intensely serious of mind.

It's evident that not *everyone* grows up like that, but I've never quite been able to understand how people manage to avoid it. If conspicuous individuality—and frank perversity—aren't programmed in the genes or rooted in early upbringing, how on earth do they spring into being with such determined irregularity? But this is *my* story, not the world's, and I shouldn't digress.

In due course, the time came for me—as it comes to everyone—to leave my family and enter a community of my peers for my first spell at college. I elected to go to Adelaide in Australia, because I liked the name.

Although my memories of that period are understandably hazy, I feel sure that I had begun to see the *fascination* of history long before the crucial event which determined my path in life. The subject seemed—in stark contrast to the disciplined coherency of mathematics or the sciences—so huge, so amazingly abundant in its data, and so charmingly disorganized. I was always a very orderly and organized person, and I needed a vocation like history to loosen me up a little. It was not, however, until I set forth on an ill-fated expedition on the sailing-ship *Genesis* in September 2901, that the exact form of my destiny was determined.

I use the word "destiny" with the utmost care; it is no mere rhetorical flourish. What happened when *Genesis* defied the supposed limits of possibility and turned turtle was no mere incident, and the impression that it made on my fledging mind was no mere suggestion. Before that ship set sail, a thousand futures were open to me; afterward, I was beset by an irresistible compulsion. My destiny was determined the day *Genesis* went down; as a result of that tragedy, *my fate was sealed*.

We were *en route* from Brisbane to tour the Creationist Islands of Micronesia, which were then regarded as artistic curiosities rather than daring experiments in continental design. I had expected to find the experience exhilarating, but almost as soon as we had left port, I was struck down by seasickness.

Seasickness, by virtue of being psychosomatic, is one of the very few diseases with which modern internal technology is sometimes impotent to deal, and I was miserably confined to my cabin while I waited for my mind to make the necessary adaptation. I was bitterly ashamed of myself, for I alone out of half a hundred passengers had fallen prey to this strange atavistic malaise. While the others partied on deck, beneath the glorious light of the tropic stars, I lay in my bunk, half-delirious with discomfort and lack of sleep. I thought myself the unluckiest man in the world.

When I was abruptly hurled from my bed, I thought that I had fallen—that my tossing and turning had inflicted one more ignominy upon me. When I couldn't recover my former position after having spent long minutes fruitlessly groping about amid all kinds of mysterious debris, I assumed that I must be confused. When I couldn't open the door of my cabin even though I had the handle in my hand, I assumed that my failure was the result of clumsiness. When I finally got out into the corridor, and found myself crawling in shallow water with the artificial bioluminescent strip beneath instead of above me, I thought I must be mad.

When the little girl spoke to me, I thought at first that she was a delusion, and that I was lost in a nightmare. It wasn't until she touched me, and tried to drag me upright with her tiny, frail hands, and addressed me by name—albeit incorrectly—that I was finally able to focus my thoughts.

"You have to get up, Mr. Mortimer," she said, "The boat's upside down."

She was only eight years old, but she spoke quite calmly and reasonably.

"That's impossible," I told her. "*Genesis* is unsinkable. There's no way it could turn upside down."

"But it *is* upside down," she insisted—and, as she did so, I finally realized the significance of the fact that the floor was glowing the way the ceiling should have glowed. "The water's coming in. I think we'll have to swim out."

The light put out by the ceiling-strip was as bright as ever, but the rippling water overlaying it made it seem dim and uncertain. The girl's little face, lit from below, seemed terribly serious within the frame of her dark and curly hair.

"I can't swim," I said, flatly.

She looked at me as if I were insane, or stupid, but it was true. I couldn't swim, I'd never liked the idea, and I'd never seen any necessity. All modern ships—even sailing-ships designed to be cute and quaint for the benefit of tourists—were unsinkable.

I scrambled to my feet, and put out both my hands to steady myself, to hold myself against the upside-down walls. The water was knee-deep. I couldn't tell whether it was increasing or not—which told me, reassuringly, that it couldn't be rising very quickly. The upturned boat was rocking this way and that, and I could hear the rumble of waves breaking on the outside of the hull, but I didn't know how much of that apparent violence was in my mind.

"My name's Emily," the little girl told me. "I'm frightened. All my mothers and fathers were on deck. *Everyone* was on deck, except for you and me. Do you think they're all dead?"

"They can't be," I said, marveling at the fact that she spoke so soberly, even when she said that she was frightened. I realized, however, that if the ship had suffered the kind of misfortune which could turn it upside down, the people on deck might indeed be dead. I tried to remember the passengers gossiping in the departure lounge, introducing themselves to one another with such fervor. The little girl had been with a party of nine, none of whose names I could remember. It occurred to me that *her whole family* might have been wiped out, that she might now be that rarest of all rare beings, an *orphan*. It was almost unimaginable. What possible catastrophe, I wondered, could have done that?

I asked Emily what had happened. She didn't know. Like me she had been in her bunk, sleeping the sleep of the innocent.

"Are we going to die too?" she asked. "I've been a good girl. I've never told a lie." It couldn't have been literally true, but I knew exactly what she meant. She was eight years old, and she had every right to expect to live till she was eight hundred. She didn't *deserve* to die. It wasn't fair.

I knew full well that fairness didn't really come into it, and I expect that she knew it too, even if my fellow historians were wrong about the virtual abolition of all the artifices of childhood, but I knew in my heart that what she said was *right*, and that insofar as the imperious laws of nature ruled her observation irrelevant, the *universe* was wrong. It *wasn't* fair. She *had* been a good girl. If she died, it would be a monstrous injustice.

Perhaps it was merely a kind of psychological defense mechanism that helped me to displace my own mortal anxieties, but the horror that ran through me was all focused on her. At the moment, her plight—not *our* plight, but *hers*—seemed to be the only thing that mattered. It was as if her dignified fear and her placid courage somehow contained the essence of human existence, the purest product of human progress.

Perhaps it was only my cowardly mind's refusal to contemplate anything else, but the only thing I could think of while I tried to figure out what to do was the awfulness of what she was saying. As that awfulness possessed me, it was magnified a thousandfold, and it seemed to me that in her lone and tiny voice there was a much greater voice speaking for multitudes: for all the human children that had ever died before achieving maturity; all the *good* children who had died without ever having the chance to *deserve to die*.

"I don't think any more water can get in," she said, with a slight tremor in her voice. "But there's only so much air. If we stay here too long, we'll suffocate."

"It's a big ship," I told her. "If we're trapped in an air-bubble, it must be a very large one."

"But it won't last forever," she told me. She was eight years old and hoped to live to be eight hundred, and she was absolutely right. The air wouldn't last forever. Hours, certainly; maybe days—but not forever.

"There are survival pods under the bunks," she said. She had obviously been paying attention to the welcoming speeches that the captain and the chief steward had delivered in the lounge the evening after embarkation. She'd plugged the chips they'd handed out into her trusty handbook, like the good girl she was, and inwardly digested what they had to teach her—unlike those of us who were blithely careless and wretchedly seasick.

"We can both fit into one of the pods," she went on, "but we have to get it out of the boat before we inflate it. We have to go up—I mean *down*—the stairway into the water and away from the boat. You'll have to carry the pod, because it's too big for me."

"I can't swim," I reminded her.

"It doesn't matter," she said, patiently. "All you have to do is hold your breath and kick yourself away from the boat. You'll float up to the surface whether you can swim or not. Then you just yank the cord and the pod will inflate. You have to hang on to it, though. Don't let go."

I stared at her, wondering how she could be so calm, so controlled, so efficient.

"Listen to the water breaking on the hull," I whispered. "Feel the movement of the boat. It would take a hurricane to overturn a boat like this. We wouldn't stand a chance out there."

"It's not so bad," she told me. She didn't have both hands out to brace herself against the walls, although she lifted one occasionally to stave off the worst of the lurches caused by the bobbing of the boat.

But if it wasn't a hurricane which turned us over, I thought, *what the hell was it? Whales have been extinct for eight hundred years.*

"We don't have to go just yet," Emily said, mildly, "but we'll have to go in the end. We have to get out. The pod's bright orange, and it has a distress beacon. We should be picked up within twenty-four hours, but there'll be supplies for a week."

I had every confidence that modern technology could sustain us for a month, if necessary. Even having to drink a little seawater if your recycling gel clots only qualifies as a minor inconvenience nowadays. Drowning is another matter; so is asphyxiation. She was absolutely right. We had to get out of the upturned boat—not immediately, but some time soon. Help might get to us before then, but we couldn't wait, and we shouldn't. We were, after all, human beings. We were supposed to be able to take charge of our own destinies, to do what we *ought* to do. Anything less would be a betrayal of our heritage. I knew that, and understood it.

But I couldn't swim.

"It's okay, Mr. Mortimer," she said, putting her reassuring hand in mine. "We can do it. We'll go together. It'll be all right."

Emily was right. We *could* do it, together, and we did—not immediately, I confess, but, in the end, we did it. It was the most terrifying and most horrible experience of my young life, but it had to be done, and we did it.

When I finally dived into that black pit of water, knowing that I had to go down and sideways before I could hope to go up, I was carried forward by the knowledge that Emily expected it of me, and needed me to do it. Without her, I'm sure that I would have died. I simply would not have had the courage to save myself. Because she was there, I dived, with the pod clutched in my arms. Because she was there, I managed to kick away from the hull and yank the cord to inflate it.

It wasn't until I had pulled Emily into the pod, and made sure that she was safe, that I paused to think how remarkable it was that the sea was hot enough to scald us both.

We were three storm-tossed days afloat before the helicopter picked us up. We cursed our ill-luck, not having the least inkling how bad things were elsewhere. We couldn't understand why the weather was getting worse instead of better.

When the pilot finally explained it, we couldn't immediately take it in. Perhaps that's not surprising, given that the geologists were just as astonished as everyone else. After all, the seabed had been quietly cracking wherever the tectonic plates were pulling apart for millions of years; it was an ongoing phenomenon, very well understood. Hundreds of black smokers and underwater volcanoes were under constant observation. Nobody had any reason to expect that a plate could simply *break* so far away from its rim, or that the fissure could be so deep, so long, and so rapid in its extension. Everyone thought that the main threat to the earth's surface was posed by wayward comets; all vigilant eyes were directed outward. No one had expected such awesome force to erupt from within, from the hot mantle which lay, hubbling and bubbling, beneath the earth's fragile crust.

It was, apparently, an enormous bubble of upwelling gas that contrived the near-impossible feat of flipping *Genesis* over. The earthquakes and the tidal waves came later.

It was the worst natural disaster in six hundred years. One million, nine hundred thousand people died in all. Emily wasn't the only child to lose her entire family, and I shudder to think of the number of families which lost their only children. We historians have to maintain a sense of perspective, though. Compared with the number of people who died in the wars of the twentieth and twenty-first centuries, or the numbers of people who died in epidemics in earlier centuries, nineteen hundred thousand is a trivial figure.

Perhaps I would have done what I eventually set out to do anyway. Perhaps the Great Coral Sea Catastrophe would have appalled me even if I'd been on the other side of the world, cocooned in the safety of a treehouse or an apartment in one of the crystal cities—but I don't think so.

It was because I was at the very center of things, because my life was literally turned upside down by the disaster—and because eight-year-old Emily Marchant was there to save my life with her common sense and her composure—that I set out to write a definitive history of death, intending to reveal not merely the dull facts of mankind's longest and hardest battle, but also the real meaning and significance of it.

2

The first volume of Mortimer Gray's *History of Death*, entitled *The Prehistory of Death*, was published on 21 January 2914. It was, unusually for its day, a mute book, with no voice-over, sound effects, or background music. Nor did it have any original artwork, all the illustrations being unenhanced still photographs. It was, in short, the kind of book that only a historian would have published. Its reviewers generally agreed that it was an old-fashioned example of scrupulous scholarship, and none expected that access demand would be considerable. Many commentators questioned the merit of Gray's arguments.

The Prehistory of Death summarized what was known about early hominid lifestyles, and had much to say about the effects of natural selection on the patterns of mortality in modern man's ancestor species. Gray carefully discussed the evolution of parental care as a genetic strategy. Earlier species of man, he observed, had raised parental care to a level of efficiency which permitted the human infant to be born at a much earlier stage in its development than any other, maximizing its opportunity to be shaped by nature and learning. From the very beginning, Gray proposed, human species were *actively* at war with death. The evolutionary success of *Homo sapiens* was based in the collaborative activities of parents in protecting, cherishing, and preserving the lives of children: activities that extended beyond immediate family groups as reciprocal altruism made it advantageous for humans to form tribes, and ultimately nations.

In these circumstances, Gray argued, it was entirely natural that the origins of consciousness and culture should be intimately bound up with a keen awareness of the war against death. He asserted that the first great task of the human imagination must have been to carry forward that war. It was entirely understandable, he said, that early paleontologists, having discovered the bones of a Neanderthal man in an apparent grave, with the remains of a primitive garland of flowers, should instantly have felt an intimate kinship with him; there could be no more persuasive evidence of full humanity than the attachment of ceremony to the idea and the fact of death.

Gray waxed lyrical about the importance of ritual as a symbolization of opposition and enmity to death. He had no patience with the proposition that such rituals were of no practical value, a mere window dressing of culture. On the contrary, he claimed that there was no activity *more* practical than this expressive recognition of the *value* of life, this imposition of a moral order on the fact of human mortality. The birth of agriculture Gray regarded as a mere sophistication of food gathering, of considerable importance as a technical discovery but of little significance in transforming human nature. The practices of burying the dead with ceremony, and of ritual mourning, on the other hand, *were*, in his view, evidence of the transformation of human nature, of the fundamental creation of meaning that made human life very different from the life of animals.

Prehistorians who marked out the evolution of man by his developing technology— the Stone Age giving way to the Bronze Age, the Bronze Age to the Iron Age—were, Gray conceded, taking intelligent advantage of those relics that had stood the test of time. He warned, however, of the folly of thinking that because tools had survived the millennia, it must have been tool-making that was solely or primarily responsible for human progress. In his view, the primal cause that made people invent was man's ongoing war against death.

It was not *tools* which created man and gave birth to civilization, Mortimer Gray proclaimed, but the *awareness of mortality*.

3

Although its impact on my nascent personality was considerable, the Coral Sea Catastrophe was essentially an impersonal disaster. The people who died, including those who had been aboard the *Genesis*, were all unknown to me; it was not until some years later that I experienced personal bereavement. It wasn't one of my parents who died—by the time the first of them quit this earth I was nearly a hundred years old and our temporary closeness was a half-remembered thing of the distant past—but one of my spouses.

By the time *The Prehistory of Death* was published, I'd contracted my first marriage: a group contract with a relatively small aggregate consisting of three other men and four women. We lived in Lamu, on the coast of Kenya, a nation to which I had been drawn by my studies of the early evolution of man. We were all young people, and we had formed our group for companionship rather than for parenting— which was a privilege conventionally left, even in those days, to much older people. We didn't go in for much fleshsex, because we were still finding our various ways through the maze of erotic virtuality, but we took the time—as I suppose all young people do—to explore its unique delights. I can't remember exactly why I decided to join such a group; I presume that it was because I accepted, tacitly at least, the conventional wisdom that there is spice in variety, and that one should do one's best to keep a broad front of experience.

It wasn't a particularly happy marriage, but it served its purpose. We went in for a good deal of sporting activity and conventional tourism. We visited the other continents from time to time, but most of our adventures took us back and forth across Africa. Most of my spouses were practical ecologists involved in one way or another with the re-greening of the north and south, or with the reforestation of the equatorial belt. What little credit I earned to add to my Allocation was earned by assisting them; such fees as I received for net access to my work were inconsiderable. Axel, Jodocus, and Minna were all involved in large-scale hydrological engineering, and liked to describe themselves, lightheartedly, as the Lamu Rainmakers. The rest of us became, inevitably, the Rainmakers-in-Law.

To begin with, I had considerable affection for all the other members of my new family, but as time went by the usual accretion of petty irritations built up, and a couple of changes in the group's personnel failed to renew the initial impetus. The research for the second volume of my history began to draw me more and more to Egypt and to Greece, even though there was no real need actually to travel in order to do the relevant research. I think we would have divorced in 2919 anyhow, even if it hadn't been for Grizel's death.

She went swimming in the newly re-routed Kwarra one day, and didn't come back.

Maybe the fact of her death wouldn't have hit me so hard if she hadn't been drowned, but I was still uneasy about deep water—even the relatively placid waters of the great rivers. If I'd been able to swim, I might have gone out with her, but I hadn't. I didn't even know she was missing until the news came in that a body had been washed up twenty kilometers downriver.

"It was a million-to-one thing," Ayesha told me, when she came back from the onsite inquest. "She must have been caught from behind by a log moving in the current, or something like that. We'll never know for sure. She must have been knocked unconscious, though, or badly dazed. Otherwise, she'd never have drifted into the white water. The rocks finished her off."

Rumor has it that many people simply can't take in news of the death of someone they love—that it flatly defies belief. I didn't react that way. With me, belief was instantaneous, and I just gave way under its pressure. I literally fell over, because my legs wouldn't support me—another psychosomatic failure about which my internal machinery could do nothing—and I wept uncontrollably. None of the others did, not even Axel, who'd been closer to Grizel than anyone. They were sympathetic at first, but it wasn't long before a note of annoyance began to creep into their reassurances.

"Come on, Morty," Ilya said, voicing the thought the rest of them were too diplomatic to let out. "You know more about death than any of us; if it doesn't help you to get a grip, what good is all that research?"

He was right, of course. Axel and Ayesha had often tried to suggest, delicately, that mine was an essentially unhealthy fascination, and now they felt vindicated.

"If you'd actually bothered to read my book," I retorted, "you'd know that it has nothing complimentary to say about philosophical acceptance. It sees a sharp awareness of mortality, and the capacity to feel the horror of death so keenly, as key forces driving human evolution."

"But you don't have to act it out so flamboyantly," Ilya came back, perhaps using cruelty to conceal and assuage his own misery. "We've evolved now. We've got past all that. We've matured." Ilya was the oldest of us, and he *seemed* very old, although he was only sixty-five. In those days, there weren't nearly as many double centenarians around as there are nowadays, and triple centenarians were very rare indeed. We take emortality so much for granted that it's easy to forget how recent a development it is.

"It's what I feel," I told him, retreating into uncompromising assertion. "I can't help it."

"We *all* loved her," Ayesha reminded me. "We'll all miss her. You're not *proving* anything, Morty."

What she meant was that I wasn't proving anything except my own instability, but she spoke more accurately than she thought; I wasn't proving anything at all. I was just reacting—atavistically, perhaps, but with crude honesty and authentically childlike innocence.

"We all have to pull together now," she added, "for Grizel's sake."

A death in the family almost always leads to universal divorce in childless marriages; nobody knows why. Such a loss *does* force the survivors to pull together, but it seems that the process of pulling together only serves to emphasize the incompleteness of the unit. We all went our separate ways, even the three Rainmakers.

I set out to use my solitude to become a true neo-Epicurean, after the fashion of the times, seeking no excess and deriving an altogether *appropriate* pleasure from everything I did. I took care to cultivate a proper love for the commonplace, training myself to a pitch of perfection in all the techniques of physiological control necessary to physical fitness and quiet metabolism.

I soon convinced myself that I'd transcended such primitive and adolescent goals as happiness, and had cultivated instead a truly civilized *ataraxia*: a calm of mind whose value went beyond the limits of ecstasy and exultation.

Perhaps I was fooling myself, but, if I was, I succeeded. The habits stuck. No matter what lifestyle fashions came and went thereafter, I remained a stubborn neo-Epicurean, immune to all other eupsychian fantasies. For a while, though, I was perpetually haunted by Grizel's memory—and not, alas, by the memory of all things that we'd shared while she was *alive*. I gradually forgot the sound of her voice, the touch of her hand and even the image of her face, remembering only the horror of her sudden and unexpected departure from the arena of my experience.

For the next ten years, I lived in Alexandria, in a simple villa cleverly gantzed out of the desert sands—sands which still gave an impression of timelessness even though they had been restored to wilderness as recently as the twenth-seventh century, when Egypt's food economy had been realigned to take full advantage of the newest techniques in artificial photosynthesis.

4

The second volume of Mortimer Gray's *History of Death*, entitled *Death in the Ancient World*, was published on 7 May 2931. It contained a wealth of data regarding burial practices and patterns of mortality in Egypt, the Kingdoms of Sumer and Akkad, the Indus civilizations of Harappa and Mohenjo-Daro, the Yangshao and Lungshan cultures of the Far East, the cultures of the Olmecs and Zapotecs, Greece before and after Alexander, and the pre-Christian Roman Empire. It paid particular attention to the elaborate mythologies of life after death developed by ancient cultures.

Gray gave most elaborate consideration to the Egyptians, whose eschatology evidently fascinated him. He spared no effort in description and discussion of the *Book of the Dead*, the Hall of Double Justice, Anubis and Osiris, the custom of mummification, and the building of pyramid-tombs. He was almost as fascinated by the elaborate geography of the Greek Underworld, the characters associated with it—Hades and Persephone, Thanatos and the Erinnyes, Cerberus and Charon—and the descriptions of the unique fates reserved for such individuals as Sisyphus, Ixion, and Tantalus. The development of such myths as these Gray regarded as a triumph of the creative imagination. In his account, myth-making and story-telling were vital weapons in the war against death—a war that had still to be fought in the mind of man, because there was little yet to be accomplished by defiance of its claims upon the body.

In the absence of an effective medical science, Gray argued, the war against death was essentially a war of propaganda, and myths were to be judged in that light—not by their truthfulness. even in some allegorical or metaphorical sense, but by their usefulness in generating *morale* and meaning. By elaborating and extrapolating the process of death in this way, a more secure moral order could be imported into social life. People thus achieved a sense of continuity with past and future generations, so that every individual became part of a great enterprise which extended across the generations, from the beginning to the end of time.

Gray did not regard the building of the pyramids as a kind of gigantic folly or vanity, or a way to dispose of the energies of the peasants when they were not required in harvesting the bounty of the fertile Nile. He argued that pyramid-building should be seen as the most useful of all labors, because it was work directed at the glorious imposition of human endeavor upon the natural landscape. The placing of a royal mummy, with all its accoutrements, in a fabulous geometric edifice of stone was, for Gray, a loud, confident, and entirely appropriate statement of humanity's invasion of the empire of death.

Gray complimented those tribesmen who worshipped their ancestors and thought them always close at hand, ready to deliver judgments upon the living. Such people, he felt, had fully mastered an elementary truth of human existence: that the dead were not entirely gone, but lived on, intruding upon memory and dream, both when they were bidden and when they were not. He approved of the idea that the dead should have a voice, and must be entitled to speak, and that the living had a moral duty to listen. Because these ancient tribes were as direly short of history as they were of medicine, he argued, they were entirely justified in allowing their ancestors to live on in the minds of living people, where the culture those ancestors had forged similarly resided.

Some reviewers complimented Gray on the breadth of his research and the comprehensiveness of his data, but few endorsed the propriety of his interpretations. He was widely advised to be more dispassionate in carrying forward his project.

5

I was sixty when I married again. This time, it was a singular marriage, to Sharane Fereday. We set up home in Avignon, and lived together for nearly twenty years. I won't say that we were exceptionally happy, but I came to depend on her closeness and her affection, and the day she told me that she had had enough was the darkest of my life so far—far darker in its desolation than the day Emily Marchant and I had been trapped in the wreck of the *Genesis*, although it didn't mark me as deeply.

"Twenty years is a long time, Mortimer," she told me. "It's time to move on— time for you as well as for me."

She was being sternly reasonable at that stage; I knew from experience that the sternness would crumble if I put it to the test, and I thought that her resolve would crumble with it, as it had before in similar circumstances, but it didn't.

"I'm truly sorry," she said, when she was eventually reduced to tears, "but I have to do it. I have to go. It's *my* life, and your part of it is over, I hate hurting you, but I don't want to live with you anymore. It's my fault, not yours, but that's the way it is."

It wasn't anybody's fault. I can see that clearly now, although it wasn't so easy to see it at the time. Like the Great Coral Sea Catastrophe or Grizel's drowning, it was just something that *happened*. Things do happen, regardless of people's best-laid plans, most heartfelt wishes, and intensest hopes.

Now that memory has blotted out the greater part of that phase of my life—including, I presume, the worst of it—I don't really know why I was so devastated by Sharane's decision, nor why it should have filled me with such black despair. Had I cultivated a dependence so absolute that it seemed irreplaceable, or was it only my pride that had suffered a sickening blow? Was it the imagined consequences of the rejection or merely the fact of rejection itself that sickened me so? Even now, I can't tell for certain. Even then, my neo-Epicurean conscience must have told me over and over again to pull myself together, to conduct myself with more decorum.

I tried. I'm certain that I tried.

Sharane's love for the ancient past was even more intense than mine, but her writings were far less dispassionate. She was an historian of sorts, but she wasn't an *academic* historian; her writings tended to the lyrical rather than the factual even when she was supposedly writing non-fiction.

Sharane would never have written a mute book, or one whose pictures didn't move. Had it been allowed by law at that time, she'd have fed her readers designer psychotropics to heighten their responses according to the schemes of her texts. She was a VR scriptwriter rather than a textwriter like me. She wasn't content to know about the past; she wanted to re-create it and make it solid and *live* in it. Nor did she reserve such inclinations to the privacy of her E-suit. She was flamboyantly old-fashioned in all that she did. She liked to dress in gaudy pastiches of the costumes represented in Greek or Egyptian art, and she liked decor to match. People who knew us were mildly astonished that we should want to live together, given the difference in our personalities, but I suppose it was an attraction of opposites. Perhaps my intensity of purpose and solitude had begun to weigh rather heavily upon me when we met, and my carefully cultivated calm of mind threatened to become a kind of toiling inertia.

On the other hand, perhaps that's all confabulation and rationalization. I was a different person then, and I've since lost touch with that person as completely as I've lost touch with everyone else I once knew.

But I *do* remember, vaguely. . . .

I remember that I found in Sharane a certain precious *wildness* that, although it wasn't entirely spontaneous, was unfailingly amusing. She had the happy gift of never taking herself too seriously, although she was wholehearted enough in her determined attempts to put herself imaginatively in touch with the past.

From her point of view, I suppose I was doubly valuable. On the one hand, I was a fount of information and inspiration, on the other a kind of anchorage whose solidity kept her from losing herself in her flights of the imagination. Twenty years of marriage ought to have cemented her dependence on me just as it had cemented my dependence on her, but it didn't.

"You think I need you to keep my feet on the ground," Sharane said, as the break between us was completely and carefully rendered irreparable, "but I don't. Anyhow, I've been weighed down long enough. I need to soar for a while, to spread my wings."

Sharane and I had talked for a while, as married people do, about the possibility of having a child. We had both made deposits to the French national gamete bank, so that if we felt the same way when the time finally came to exercise our right of replacement—or to specify in our wills how that right was to be posthumously exercised—we could order an ovum to be unfrozen and fertilized.

I had always known, of course, that such flights of fancy were not to be taken too seriously, but when I accepted that the marriage was indeed over, there seemed to be an extra dimension of tragedy and misery in the knowledge that our genes never would be combined—that our separation cast our legacies once again upon the chaotic sea of irresolution.

Despite the extremity of my melancholy, I never contemplated suicide. Although I'd already used up the traditional threescore years and ten, I was in no doubt at all that it wasn't yet time to remove myself from the crucible of human evolution to make room for my successor, whether that successor was to be born from an ovum of

Sharane's or not. No matter how black my mood was when Sharane left, I knew that my *History of Death* remained to be completed, and that the work would require at least another century. Even so, the breaking of such an intimate bond filled me with intimations of mortality and a painful sense of the futility of all my endeavors.

My first divorce had come about because a cruel accident had ripped apart the delicate fabric of my life, but my second—or so it seemed to me—was itself a horrid rent shearing my very being into ragged fragments. I hope that I tried with all my might not to blame Sharane, but how could I avoid it? And how could she not resent my overt and covert accusations, my veiled and naked resentments?

"Your problem, Mortimer," she said to me, when her lachrymose phase had given way to bright anger, "is that you're *obsessed*. You're a deeply morbid man, and it's not healthy. There's some special fear in you, some altogether exceptional horror which feeds upon you day and night, and makes you grotesquely vulnerable to occurrences that normal people can take in their stride, and that ill befit a self-styled Epicurean. If you want my advice, you ought to abandon that history you're writing, at least for a while, and devote yourself to something brighter and more vigorous."

"Death is my life," I informed her, speaking metaphorically, and not entirely without irony. "It always will be, until and including the end."

I remember saying that. The rest is vague, but I really do remember saying that.

6

The third volume of Mortimer Gray's *History of Death*, entitled *The Empires of Faith*, was published on 18 August 2954. The introduction announced that the author had been forced to set aside his initial ambition to write a truly comprehensive history, and stated that he would henceforth be unashamedly eclectic, and contentedly ethnocentric, because he did not wish to be a mere archivist of death, and therefore could not regard all episodes in humankind's war against death as being of equal interest. He declared that he was more interested in interpretation than mere summary, and that insofar as the war against death had been a moral crusade, he felt fully entitled to draw morals from it.

This preface, understandably, dismayed those critics who had urged the author to be more dispassionate. Some reviewers were content to condemn the new volume without even bothering to inspect the rest of it, although it was considerably shorter than the second volume and had a rather more fluent style. Others complained that the day of mute text was dead and gone, and that there was no place in the modern world for pictures that resolutely refused to move.

Unlike many contemporary historians, whose birth into a world in which religious faith was almost extinct had robbed them of any sympathy for the imperialists of dogma, Gray proposed that the great religions had been one of the finest achievements of humankind. He regarded them as a vital stage in the evolution of community—as social technologies which had permitted a spectacular transcendence of the limitation of community to the tribe or region. Faiths, he suggested, were the first instruments that could bind together different language groups, and even different races. It was not until the spread of the great religions, Gray argued, that the possibility came into being of gathering all men together into a single common enterprise. He regretted, of course, that the principal product of this great dream was two millennia of bitter and savage conflict between adherents of different faiths or adherents of different versions of the same faith, but thought the ambition worthy of all possible respect and admiration. He even retained some sympathy for jihads and crusades, in the formulation of which people had tried to attribute more meaning to the sacrifice of life than they ever had before.

Gray was particularly fascinated by the symbology of the Christian mythos, which had taken as its central image the death on the cross of Jesus, and had tried to make that one image of death carry an enormous allegorical load. He was entranced by the idea of Christ's death as a force of redemption and salvation, by the notion that this person died *for others.* He extended the argument to take in the Christian martyrs, who added to the primal crucifixion a vast series of symbolic and morally significant deaths. This, he considered, was a colossal achievement of the imagination, a crucial victory by which death was dramatically transfigured in the theater of the human imagination—as was the Christian idea of death as a kind of reconciliation: a gateway to Heaven, if properly met; a gateway to Hell, if not. Gray seized upon the idea of absolution from sin following confession, and particularly the notion of deathbed repentance, as a daring raid into the territories of the imagination previously ruled by fear of death.

Gray's commentaries on the other major religions were less elaborate but no less interested. Various ideas of reincarnation and the related concept of *karma* he discussed at great length, as one of the most ingenious imaginative bids for freedom from the tyranny of death. He was not quite so enthusiastic about the idea of the world as illusion, the idea of nirvana, and certain other aspects of Far Eastern thought, although he was impressed in several ways by Confucius and the Buddha. All these things and more he assimilated to the main line of his argument, which was that the great religions had made bold imaginative leaps in order to carry forward the war against death on a broader front than ever before, providing vast numbers of individuals with an efficient intellectual weaponry of moral purpose.

7

After Sharane left, I stayed on in Avignon for a while. The house where we had lived was demolished, and I had another raised in its place. I resolved to take up the reclusive life again, at least for a while. I had come to think of myself as one of nature's monks, and when I was tempted to flights of fancy of a more personal kind than those retailed in virtual reality, I could imagine myself an avatar of some patient scholar born fifteen hundred years before, contentedly submissive to the Benedictine rule. I didn't, of course, believe in the possibility of reincarnation, and when such beliefs became fashionable again I found it almost impossible to indulge any more fantasies of that kind.

In 2960, I moved to Antarctica, not to Amundsen City—which had become the world's political center since the United Nations had elected to set up headquarters in "the continent without nations"—but to Cape Adare on the Ross Sea, which was a relatively lonely spot.

I moved into a tall house rather resembling a lighthouse, from whose upper stories I could look out at the edge of the ice cap and watch the penguins at play. I was reasonably contented, and soon came to feel that I had put the torments and turbulences of my early life behind me.

I often went walking across the nearer reaches of the icebound sea, but I rarely got into difficulties. Ironically enough, my only serious injury of that period was a broken leg, which I sustained while working with a rescue party attempting to locate and save one of my neighbors, Ziru Majumdar, who had fallen into a crevasse while out on a similar expedition. We ended up in adjacent beds at the hospital in Amundsen City.

"I'm truly sorry about your leg, Mr. Gray," Majumdar said. "It was very stupid of me to get lost. After all, I've lived here for thirty years; I thought I knew every last iceridge like the back of my hand. It's not as if the weather was particularly bad, and I've never suffered from summer rhapsody or snowblindness."

I'd suffered from both—I was still awkwardly vulnerable to psychosomatic ills—but they only served to make me more careful. An uneasy mind can sometimes be an advantage.

"It wasn't your fault, Mr. Majumdar," I graciously insisted. "I suppose I must have been a little overconfident myself, or I'd never have slipped and fallen. At least they were able to pull me out in a matter of minutes; you must have lain unconscious at the bottom of that crevasse for nearly two days."

"Just about. I came round several times—at least, I think I did—but my internal tech was pumping so much dope around my system it's difficult to be sure. My surskin and thermosuit were doing their best to keep me warm, but the first law of thermodynamics doesn't give you much slack when you're at the bottom of a cleft in the permafrost. I've got authentic frostbite in my toes, you know—imagine that!"

I dutifully tried to imagine it, but it wasn't easy. He could hardly be in pain, so it was difficult to conjure up any notion of what it might feel like to have necrotized toes. The doctors reckoned that it would take a week for the nanomachines to restore the tissues to their former pristine condition.

"Mind you," he added, with a small embarrassed laugh, "it's only a matter of time before the whole biosphere gets frostbite, isn't it? Unless the sun gets stirred up again."

More than fifty years had passed since scrupulous students of the sunspot cycle had announced the advent of a new Ice Age, but the world was quite unworried by the exceedingly slow advance of the glaciers across the Northern Hemisphere. It was the sort of thing that only cropped up in light banter.

"I won't mind that," I said, contemplatively. "Nor will you, I dare say. We like ice—why else would we live here?"

"Right. Not that I agree with those Gaean Liberationists, mind. I hear they're proclaiming that the interglacial periods are simply Gaea's fevers, that the birth of civilization was just a morbid symptom of the planet's sickness, and that human culture has so far been a mere delirium of the noösphere."

He obviously paid more attention to the lunatic fringe channels than I did.

"It's just colorful rhetoric," I told him. "They don't mean it literally."

"Think not? Well, perhaps. I was delirious myself for a while when I was down that hole. Can't be sure whether I was asleep or awake, but I was certainly lost in some vivid dreams—and I mean *vivid*. I don't know about you, but I always find VR a bit flat, even if I use illicit psychotropics to give delusion a helping hand. I think it's to do with the protective effects of our internal technology. Nanomachines mostly do their job a little *too* well, because of the built-in safety margins—it's only when they reach the limits of their capacity that they let really interesting things begin to happen."

I knew he was building up to some kind of self-justification, but I felt that he was entitled to it. I nodded, to give him permission to prattle on.

"You have to go to the very brink of extinction to reach the cutting edge of experience, you see. I found that out while I was trapped down there in the ice, not knowing whether the rescuers would get to me in time. You can learn a lot about life, and about yourself, in a situation like that. It really was vivid—more vivid than anything I ever . . . well, what I'm trying to get at is that we're too *safe* nowadays; we can have no idea of the *zest* there was in living in the bad old days. Not that I'm about to take up jumping into crevasses as a hobby, you understand. Once in a very long while is plenty."

"Yes, it is," I agreed, shifting my itching leg and wishing that nanomachines weren't so slow to compensate for trifling but annoying sensations. "Once in a while is certainly enough for me. In fact, I for one will be quite content if it never happens again. I don't think I need any more of the kind of enlightenment which comes from experiences like that. I was in the Great Coral Sea Catastrophe, you know—shipwrecked, scalded, and lost at sea for days on end."

"It's not the same," he insisted, "but you won't be able to understand the difference until it happens to you."

I didn't believe him. In that instance, I suppose, he was right and I was wrong.

I'd never heard Mr. Majumdar speak so freely before, and I never heard him do it again. The social life of the Cape Adare "exiles" was unusually formal, hemmed in by numerous barriers of formality and etiquette. After an embarrassing phase of learning and adjustment, I'd found the formality aesthetically appealing, and had played the game with enthusiasm, but it was beginning to lose its appeal by the time the accident shook me up. I suppose it's understandable that whatever you set out to exclude from the pattern of your life eventually comes to seem like a lack, and then an unfulfilled need.

After a few years more, I began to hunger once again for the spontaneity and abandonment of warmer climes. I decided there'd be time enough to celebrate the advent of the Ice Age when the glaciers had reached the full extent of their reclaimed empire, and that I might as well make what use I could of Gaea's temporary fever before it cooled. I moved to Venezuela, to dwell in the gloriously restored jungles of the Orinoco amid their teeming wildlife.

Following the destruction of much of the southern part of the continent in the second nuclear war, Venezuela had attained a cultural hegemony in South America that it had never surrendered. Brazil and Argentina had long since recovered, both economically and ecologically, from their disastrous fit of ill temper, but Venezuela was still the home of the *avant garde* of the Americas. It was there, for the first time, that I came into close contact with Thanaticism.

The original Thanatic cults had flourished in the twenty-eighth century. They had appeared among the last generations of children born without Zaman transformations; their members were people who, denied emortality through blastular engineering, had perversely elected to reject the benefits of rejuvenation too, making a fetish out of living only a "natural" lifespan. At the time, it had seemed likely that they would be the last of the many Millenarian cults which had long afflicted Western culture, and they had quite literally died out some eighty or ninety years before I was born.

Nobody had then thought it possible, let alone likely, that genetically endowed emortals would ever embrace Thanaticism, but they were wrong.

There had always been suicides in the emortal population—indeed, suicide was the commonest cause of death among emortals, outnumbering accidental deaths by a factor of three—but such acts were usually covert and normally involved people who had lived at least a hundred years. The neo-Thanatics were not only indiscreet—their whole purpose seemed to be to make a public spectacle of themselves—but also young; people over seventy were held to have violated the Thanaticist ethic simply by surviving to that age.

Thanatics tended to choose violent means of death, and usually issued invitations as well as choosing their moments so that large crowds could gather. Jumping from tall buildings and burning to death were the most favored means in the beginning, but these quickly ceased to be interesting. As the Thanatic revival progressed, adherents of the movement sought increasingly bizarre methods in the interests of capturing attention and outdoing their predecessors. For these reasons, it was impossible for anyone living alongside the cults to avoid becoming implicated in their rites, if only as a spectator.

By the time I had been in Venezuela for a year, I had seen five people die horribly. After the first, I had resolved to turn away from any others, so as not to lend even minimal support to the practice, but I soon found that I had underestimated the difficulty of so doing. There was no excuse to be found in my vocation; thousands of people who were not historians of death found it equally impossible to resist the fascination.

I believed at first that the fad would soon pass, after wasting the lives of a handful of neurotics, but the cults continued to grow. Gaea's fever might be cooling, its crisis having passed, but the delirium of human culture had evidently not yet reached what Ziru Majumdar called "the cutting edge of experience."

8

The fourth volume of Mortimer Gray's *History of Death*, entitled *Fear and Fascination*, was published on 12 February 2977. In spite of being mute and motionless it was immediately subject to heavy access-demand, presumably in consequence of the world's increasing fascination with the "problem" of neo-Thanaticism. Requisitions of the earlier volumes of Gray's history had picked up worldwide during the early 2970s, but the author had not appreciated what this might mean in terms of the demand for the new volume, and might have set a higher access fee had he realized.

Academic historians were universal in their condemnation of the new volume, possibly because of the enthusiasm with which it was greeted by laymen, but popular reviewers adored it. Its arguments were recklessly plundered by journalists and other broadcasting pundits in search of possible parallels that might be drawn with the modern world, especially those that seemed to carry moral lessons for the Thanatics and their opponents.

Fear and Fascination extended, elaborated, and diversified the arguments contained in its immediate predecessor, particularly in respect of the Christian world of the Medieval period and the Renaissance. It had much to say about art and literature, and the images contained therein. It had chapters on the personification of Death as the Grim Reaper, on the iconography of the *danse macabre*, on the topics of *memento mori* and *artes moriendi*. It had long analyses of Dante's *Divine Comedy*, the paintings of Hieronymus Bosch, Milton's *Paradise Lost*, and graveyard poetry. These were by no means exercises in conventional literary criticism; they were elements of a long and convoluted argument about the contributions made by the individual creative imagination to the war of ideas which raged on the only battleground on which man could as yet constructively oppose the specter of death.

Gray also dealt with the persecution of heretics and the subsequent elaboration of Christian Demonology, which led to the witch-craze of the fifteenth, sixteenth, and seventeenth centuries. He gave considerable attention to various thriving folklore traditions which confused the notion of death, especially to the popularity of fictions and fears regarding premature burial, ghosts, and the various species of the "undead" who rose from their graves as ghouls or vampires. In Gray's eyes, all these phenomena were symptomatic of a crisis in Western man's imaginative dealings with the idea of death: a feverish heating up of a conflict which had been in danger of becoming desultory. The cities of men had been under perpetual siege from Death since the time of their first building, but now—in one part of the world, at least—the perception of that siege had sharpened. A kind of spiritual starvation and panic had set in, and the progress that had been made in the war by virtue of the ideological imperialism of Christ's Holy Cross now seemed imperiled by disintegration. This Empire of Faith was breaking up under the stress of skepticism, and men were faced with the prospect of going into battle against their most ancient enemy with their armor in tatters.

Just as the Protestants were trying to replace the Catholic Church's centralized authority with a more personal relationship between men and God, Gray argued, so the creative artists of this era were trying to achieve a more personal and more intimate form of reconciliation between men and Death, equipping individuals with the power to mount their own ideative assaults. He drew some parallels between what happened in the Christian world and similar periods of crisis which he found in different cultures at different times, but other historians claimed that his analogies were weak, and that he was overgeneralizing. Some argued that his intense study of the phenomena associated with the idea of death had become too personal, and suggested that he had become infatuated with the ephemeral ideas of past ages to the point where they were taking over his own imagination.

9

At first, I found celebrity status pleasing, and the extra credit generated by my access fees was certainly welcome, even to a man of moderate tastes and habits. The unaccustomed touch of fame brought a fresh breeze into a life that might have been in danger of becoming bogged down.

To begin with, I was gratified to be reckoned an expert whose views on Thanaticism were to be taken seriously, even by some Thanatics. I received a veritable deluge of invitations to appear on the talk shows that were the staple diet of contemporary broadcasting, and for a while I accepted as many as I could conveniently accommodate within the pattern of my life.

I have no need to rely on my memories in recapitulating these episodes, because they remain on record—but by the same token, I needn't quote extensively from them. In the early days, when I was a relatively new face, my interrogators mostly started out by asking for information about my book, and their opening questions were usually stolen from uncharitable reviews.

"Some people feel that you've been carried away, Mr. Gray," more than one combative interviewer sneeringly began, "and that what started out as a sober history is fast becoming an obsessive rant. Did you decide to get personal in order to boost your sales?"

My careful cultivation of neo-Epicureanism and my years in Antarctica had left a useful legacy of calm formality; I always handled such accusations with punctilious politeness.

"Of course the war against death is a personal matter," I would reply. "It's a personal matter for everyone, mortal or emortal. Without that sense of personal relevance it would be impossible to put oneself imaginatively in the place of the people of the ancient past so as to obtain empathetic insight into their affairs. If I seem to be making heroes of the men of the past by describing their crusades, it's because they *were* heroes, and if my contemporaries find inspiration in my work, it's because they too are heroes in the same cause. The engineering of emortality has made us victors in the war, but we desperately need to retain a proper sense of triumph. We ought to celebrate our victory over death as joyously as possible, lest we lose our appreciation of its fruits."

My interviewers always appreciated that kind of link, which handed them their next question on a plate. "Is that what you think of the Thanatics?" they would follow up, eagerly.

It was, and I would say so at any length they considered appropriate.

Eventually, my interlocutors no longer talked about my book, taking it for granted that everyone knew who I was and what I'd done. They'd cut straight to the chase, asking me what I thought of the latest Thanaticist publicity stunt.

Personally, I thought the media's interest in Thanaticism was exaggerated. All death was, of course, news in a world populated almost entirely by emortals, and the Thanatics took care to be newsworthy by making such a song and dance about what they were doing, but the number of individuals involved was very small. In a world population of nearly three billion, a hundred deaths per week was a drop in the ocean, and "quiet" suicides still outnumbered the ostentatious Thanatics by a factor of five or six throughout the 2980s. The public debates quickly expanded to take in other issues. Subscription figures for net access to videotapes and teletexts concerned with the topic of violent death came under scrutiny, and everyone began talking about the "new pornography of death"—although fascination with such material had undoubtedly been widespread for many years.

"Don't you feel, Mr. Gray," I was often asked, "that a continued fascination with death in a world where everyone has a potential lifespan of several centuries is rather *sick*? Shouldn't we have put such matters behind us?"

"Not at all," I replied, earnestly and frequently. "In the days when death was inescapable, people were deeply frustrated by this imperious imposition of fate. They resented it with all the force and bitterness they could muster, but it could not be truly fascinating while it remained a simple and universal fact of life. Now that death is no longer a necessity, it has perforce become a luxury. Because it is no longer inevitable, we no longer feel such pressure to hate and fear it, and this frees us so that we may take an essentially *aesthetic* view of death. The transformation of the imagery of death into a species of pornography is both understandable and healthy."

"But such material surely encourages the spread of Thanaticism. You can't possibly approve of that?"

Actually, the more I was asked it the less censorious I became, at least for a while.

"Planning a life," I explained to a whole series of faces, indistinguishable by virtue of having been sculptured according to the latest theory of telegenicity, "is an exercise in story-making. Living people are forever writing the narratives of their own lives, deciding who to be and what to do, according to various aesthetic criteria. In olden days, death was inevitably seen as an *interruption* of the business of life, cutting short life-stories before they were—in the eyes of their creators—complete. Nowadays, people have the opportunity to plan *whole* lives, deciding exactly when and how their life-stories should reach a climax and a conclusion. We may not share their aesthetic sensibilities, and may well think them fools, but there is a discernible logic in their actions. They are neither mad nor evil."

Perhaps I was reckless in adopting this point of view, or at least in proclaiming it to the whole world. By proposing that the new Thanatics were simply individuals who had a particular kind of aesthetic sensibility, tending toward conciseness and melodrama rather than prolixity and anticlimax, I became something of a hero to the cultists themselves—which was not my intention. The more lavishly I embroidered my chosen analogy—declaring that ordinary emortals were the *feuilletonistes*, epic poets, and three-decker novelists of modern life while Thanatics were the prose-poets and short-story writers who liked to sign off with a neat punch line—the more they liked me. I received many invitations to attend suicides, and my refusal to take them up only served to make my presence a prize to be sought after.

I was, of course, entirely in agreement with the United Nations Charter of Human Rights, whose ninety-ninth amendment guaranteed the citizens of every nation the right to take their own lives, and to be assisted in making a dignified exit should they so desire, but I had strong reservations about the way in which the Thanaticists construed the amendment. Its original intention had been to facilitate self-administered euthanasia in an age when that was sometimes necessary, not to guarantee Thanatics the entitlement to recruit whatever help they required in staging whatever kinds of exit they desired. Some of the invitations I received were exhortations to participate in legalized murders, and these became more common as time went by and the cults became more extreme in their bizarrerie.

In the 2980s, the Thanatics had progressed from conventional suicides to public executions, by rope, sword, axe, or guillotine. At first, the executioners were volunteers—and one or two were actually arrested and charged with murder, although none could be convicted—but the Thanatics were not satisfied even with this, and began campaigning for various nations to recreate the official position of Public Executioner, together with bureaucratic structures that would give all citizens the right to call upon the services of such officials. Even I, who claimed to understand the cults better than their members, was astonished when the government of Colombia—which was jealous of Venezuela's reputation as the home of the world's *avant garde*—actually accepted such an obligation, with the result that Thanatics began to flock to Maracaibo and Cartagena in order to obtain an appropriate send-off. I was profoundly relieved when the UN, following the crucifixion of Shamiel Sihra in 2991, revised the wording of the amendment and outlawed suicide by public execution.

By this time, I was automatically refusing invitations to appear on 3-V in much the same way that I was refusing invitations to take part in Thanaticist ceremonies. It was time to become a recluse once again.

I left Venezuela in 2989 to take up residence on Cape Wolstenholme, at the neck of Hudson's Bay. Canada was an urbane, highly civilized, and rather staid confederacy of states whose people had no time for such follies as Thanaticism; it provided an ideal retreat where I could throw myself wholeheartedly into my work again.

I handed over full responsibility for answering all my calls to a state-of-the-art Personal Simulation program, which grew so clever and so ambitious with practice that it began to give live interviews on broadcast television. Although it offered what was effectively no comment in a carefully elaborate fashion I eventually thought it best to introduce a block into its operating system—a block that ensured that my face dropped out of public sight for half a century.

Having once experienced the rewards and pressures of fame, I never felt the need to seek them again. I can't and won't say that I learned as much from that phase in my life as I learned from any of my close encounters with death, but I still remember it—vaguely—with a certain nostalgia. Unmelodramatic it might have been, but it doubtless played its part in shaping the person that I now am. It certainly made me more self-assured in public.

10

The fifth volume of Mortimer Gray's *History of Death*, entitled *The War of Attrition*, was published on 19 March 2999. It marked a return to the cooler and more comprehensive style of scholarship exhibited by the first two volumes. It dealt with the history of medical science and hygiene up to the end of the nineteenth century, thus concerning itself with a new and very different arena of the war between mankind and mortality.

To many of its readers *The War of Attrition* was undoubtedly a disappointment, though it did include some material about Victorian tomb-decoration and nineteenth century spiritualism that carried forward arguments from volume four. Access was initially widespread, although demand tailed off fairly rapidly when it was realized how vast and how tightly packed with data the document was. This lack of popular enthusiasm was not counterbalanced by any redemption of Mortimer's academic reputation; like many earlier scholars who had made contact with a popular audience, Gray was considered guilty of a kind of intellectual treason, and was frozen out of the scholarly community in spite of what appeared to be a determined attempt at rehabilitation. Some popular reviewers argued, however, that there was much in the new volume to intrigue the inhabitants of a world whose medical science was so adept that almost everyone enjoyed perfect health as well as eternal youth, and in which almost any injury could be repaired completely. It was suggested that there was a certain piquant delight to be obtained from recalling a world where everyone was (by modern standards) crippled or deformed, and in which everyone suffered continually from illnesses of a most horrific nature.

Although it had a wealth of scrupulously dry passages, there were parts of *The War of Attrition* that were deemed pornographic by some commentators. Its accounts of the early history of surgery and midwifery were condemned as unjustifiably blood-curdling, and its painstaking analysis of the spread of syphilis through Europe in the sixteenth century was censured as a mere horror-story made all the nastier by its clinical narration. Gray was particularly interested in syphilis, because of the dramatic social effects of its sudden advent in Europe and its significance in the development of prophylactic medicine. He argued that syphilis was primarily responsible for the rise and spread of Puritanism, repressive sexual morality being the only truly effective weapon against its spread. He then deployed well-tried sociological arguments to the effect that Puritanism and its associated habits of thought had been importantly implicated in the rapid development of Capitalism in the Western World, in order that he might claim that syphilis ought to be regarded as the root cause of the economic and political systems that came to dominate the most chaotic, the most extravagantly progressive, and the most extravagantly destructive centuries of human history.

The history of medicine and the conquest of disease were, of course, topics of elementary education in the thirtieth century. There was supposedly not a citizen of any nation to whom the names of Semmelweis, Jenner, and Pasteur were unknown—but disease had been so long banished from the world, and it was so completely outside the experience of ordinary men and women, that what they "knew" about it was never really brought to consciousness, and never came alive to the imagination. Words like "smallpox," "plague," and "cancer" were used metaphorically in common parlance, and over the centuries had become virtually empty of any real significance. Gray's fifth volume, therefore—despite the fact that it contained little that was really new—did serve as a stimulus to collective memory. It reminded the world of some issues which, though not exactly forgotten, had not really been *brought to mind* for some time. It is at least arguable that it touched off ripples whose movement across the collective consciousness of world culture was of some moment. Mortimer Gray was no longer famous, but his continuing work had become firmly established within the *zeitgeist*.

11

Neo-Thanaticism began to peter out as the turn of the century approached. By 3010, the whole movement had "gone underground"—which is to say that Thanatics no longer staged their exits before the largest audiences they could attain, but saved their performance for small, carefully selected groups. This wasn't so much a response to persecution as a variation in the strange game that they were playing out; it was simply a different kind of drama. Unfortunately, there was no let-up in the communications with which Thanatics continued to batter my patient AI interceptors.

Although it disappointed the rest of the world, *The War of Attrition* was welcomed enthusiastically by some of the Thanatic cults, whose members cultivated an altogether unhealthy interest in disease as a means of decease, replacing the violent executions that had become too familiar. As time went by and Thanaticism declined generally, this particular subspecies underwent a kind of mutation, as the cultists began to promote diseases not as means of death but as valuable *experiences* from which much might be learned. A black market in carcinogens and bioengineered pathogens quickly sprang up. The original agents of smallpox, cholera, bubonic plague, and syphilis were long since extinct, but the world abounded in clever genetic engineers who could synthesize a virus with very little effort. Suddenly, they began to find clients for a whole range of horrid diseases. Those which afflicted the mind as well as or instead of the body were particularly prized; there was a boom in recreational schizophrenia that almost broke through to the mainstream of accredited psychotropics.

I couldn't help but remember, with a new sense of irony, Ziru Majumdar's enthusiasm for the vivid delusions which had visited him while his internal technology was tested to the limit in staving off hypothermia and frostbite.

When the new trend spread beyond the ranks of the Thanaticists, and large numbers of people began to regard disease as something that could be temporarily and interestingly indulged in without any real danger to life or subsequent health, I began to find my arguments about death quoted—without acknowledgment—with reference to *disease*. A popular way of talking about the phenomenon was to claim that what had ceased to be a dire necessity "naturally" became available as a perverse luxury.

None of this would have mattered much had it not been for the difficulty of restricting the spread of recreational diseases to people who *wanted* to indulge, but those caught up in the fad refused to restrict themselves to non-infectious varieties. There had been no serious threat of epidemic since the Plague Wars of the twenty-first century, but now it seemed that medical science might once again have to be mobilized on a vast scale. Because of the threat to innocent parties who might be accidently infected, the self-infliction of dangerous diseases was quickly outlawed in many nations, but some governments were slow to act.

I would have remained aloof and apart from all of this had I been able to, but it turned out that my defenses weren't impregnable. In 3029, a Thanaticist of exceptional determination named Hadria Nuccoli decided that if I wouldn't come to her, she would come to *me*. Somehow, she succeeded in getting past all my carefully sealed doors, to arrive in my bedroom at three o'clock one winter morning.

I woke up in confusion, but the confusion was quickly transformed into sheer terror. This was an enemy more frightening than the scalding Coral Sea, because this was an *active* enemy who meant to do me harm—and the intensity of the threat which she posed was in no way lessened by the fact that she claimed to be doing it out of love rather than hatred.

The woman's skin bore an almost mercuric luster, and she was in the grip of a terrible fever, but she would not be still. She seemed, in fact, to have an irresistible desire to move and to communicate, and the derangement of her body and brain had not impaired her crazed eloquence.

"Come with me!" she begged, as I tried to evade her eager clutch. "Come with me to the far side of death and I'll show you what's there. There's no need to be afraid! Death isn't the end, it's the beginning. It's the metamorphosis that frees us from our caterpillar flesh to be spirits in a massless world of light and color. I am your redeemer, for whom you have waited far too long. Love me, dear Mortimer Gray, only *love* me, and you will learn. Let me be your mirror; drown yourself in me!"

For ten minutes, I succeeded in keeping away from her, stumbling this way and that, thinking that I might be safe if only I didn't touch her. I managed to send out a call for help, but I knew it would take an hour or more for anyone to come.

I tried all the while to talk her down, but it was impossible.

"There's no return from eternity," she told me. "This is no ordinary virus created by accident to fight a hopeless cause against the defenses of the body. Nanotechnology is as impotent to deal with this transformer of the flesh as the immune system was to deal with its own destroyers. The true task of medical engineers, did they but know it, was never to fight disease, but always to *perfect* it, and we have found the way. I bring you the greatest of all gifts, my darling: the elixir of life, which will make us angels instead of men, creatures of light and ecstasy!"

It was no use running; I tired before she did, and she caught me. I tried to knock her down, and if I had had a weapon to hand, I would certainly have used it in self-defense, but she couldn't feel pain, and no matter how badly disabled her internal technology was, I wasn't able to injure her with my blows.

In the end, I had no sensible alternative but to let her take me in her arms and cling to me; nothing else would soothe her.

I was afraid for her as well as myself; I didn't believe that she truly intended to die, and I wanted to keep us safe until help arrived.

My panic didn't decrease while I held her; if anything, I felt it all the more intensely. I became outwardly calmer once I had let her touch me, and made every effort to remind myself that it didn't really matter whether she infected me or not, given that medical help would soon arrive. I didn't expect to have to go through the kind of hell that I actually endured before the doctors got the bug under control; for once, panic was wiser than common sense.

Even so, I wept for her when they told me that she'd died, and wished with all my heart that she hadn't.

Unlike my previous brushes with death, I don't think my encounter with Hadria Nuccoli was an important learning experience. It was just a disturbance of the now-settled pattern of my life—something to be survived, put away, and forgotten. I haven't forgotten it, but I did put it away in the back of my mind. I didn't let it affect me.

In some of my writings, I'd lauded the idea of martyrdom as an important invention in the imaginative war against death, and I'd been mightily intrigued by the lives and deaths of the saints recorded in the *Golden Legend*. Now that I'd been appointed a saint myself by some very strange people, though, I began to worry about the exemplary functions of such legends. The last thing I'd expected when I set out to write a *History of Death* was that my explanatory study might actually *assist* the dread empire of Death to regain a little of the ground that it had lost in the world of human affairs. I began to wonder whether I ought to abandon my project, but I decided otherwise. The Thanatics and their successors were, after all, wilfully misunderstanding and perverting my message; I owed it to them and to everyone else to make myself clearer.

As it happened, the number of deaths recorded in association with Thanaticism and recreational disease began to decline after 3030. In a world context, the numbers were never more than tiny, but they were still worrying, and hundreds of thousands of people had, like me, to be rescued by doctors from the consequences of their own or other people's folly.

As far back as 2982, I had appeared on TV—*via* a satellite link—with a faber named Khan Mirafzal, who had argued that Thanaticism was evidence of the fact that Earthbound man was becoming decadent, and that the future of man lay outside the Earth, in the microworlds and the distant colonies. Mirafzal had claimed that men genetically reshaped for life in low gravity—like the four-handed fabers—or for the colonization of alien worlds, would find Thanaticism unthinkable. At the time, I'd been content to assume that his arguments were spurious. People who lived in space were always going on about the decadence of the Earthbound, much as the Gaean Liberationists did. Fifty years later, I wasn't so sure. I actually called Mirafzal so that we could discuss the matter again, in private. The conversation took a long time because of the signal delay, but that seemed to make its thrust all the more compelling.

I decided to leave Earth, at least for a while, to investigate the farther horizons of the human enterprise.

In 3033 I flew to the Moon, and took up residence in Mare Moscoviense—which is, of course, on the side which faces away from the Earth.

12

The sixth volume of Mortimer Gray's *History of Death*, entitled *Fields of Battle*, was published on 24 July 3044. Its subject matter was war, but Gray was not greatly interested in the actual fighting of the wars of the nineteenth and succeeding centuries. His main concern was with the *mythology* of warfare as it developed in the period under consideration, and, in particular, with the way that the development of the mass media of communication transformed the business and the perceived meanings of warfare. He began his study with the Crimean War, because it was the first war to be extensively covered by newspaper reporters, and the first whose conduct was drastically affected thereby.

Before the Crimea, Gray argued, wars had been "private" events, entirely the affairs of the men who started them and the men who fought them. They might have a devastating effect on the local population of the areas where they were fought, but were largely irrelevant to distant civilian populations. The British *Times* had changed all that, by making the Crimean War the business of all its readers, exposing the government and military leaders to public scrutiny and to public scorn. Reports from the front had scandalized the nation by creating an awareness of how ridiculously inefficient the organization of the army was, and what a toll of human life was exacted upon the troops in consequence—not merely deaths in battle, but deaths from injury and disease caused by the appalling lack of care given to wounded soldiers. That reportage had not only had practical consequences, but *imaginative* consequences—it rewrote the entire mythology of heroism in an intricate webwork of new legends, ranging from the Charge of the Light Brigade to the secular canonization of Florence Nightingale.

Throughout the next two centuries, Gray argued, war and publicity were entwined in a Gordian knot. Control of the news media became vital to propagandist control of popular *morale*, and governments engaged in war had to become architects of the mythology of war as well as planners of military strategy. Heroism and jingöism became the currency of consent; where governments failed to secure the public image of the wars they fought, they fell. Gray tracked the way in which attitudes to death in war and to the endangerment of civilian populations by war were dramatically transformed by the three World Wars and by the way those wars were subsequently mythologized in memory and fiction. He commented extensively on the way the First World War was "sold," to those who must fight it, as a war to *end* war—and on the consequent sense of betrayal that followed when it failed to live up to this billing. And yet, he argued, if the three global wars were seen as a whole, its example really *had* brought into being the attitude of mind which ultimately forbade wars.

As those who had become used to his methods now expected, Gray dissented from the view of other modern historians who saw the World Wars as an unmitigated disaster and a horrible example of the barbarity of ancient man. He agreed that the nationalism that had replaced the great religions as the main creator and definer of a sense of community was a poor and petty thing, and that the massive conflicts that it engendered were tragic—but it was, he asserted, a necessary stage in historical development. The empires of faith were, when all was said and done, utterly incompetent to their self-defined task, and were always bound to fail and to disintegrate. The groundwork for a *genuine* human community, in which all mankind could properly and meaningfully join, had to be relaid, and it had to be relaid in the common experience of all nations, as part of a universal heritage.

The *real* enemy of mankind was, as Gray had always insisted and now continued to insist, death itself. Only by facing up to death in a new way, by gradually transforming the role of death as part of the means to human ends, could a true human community be made. Wars, whatever their immediate purpose in settling economic squabbles and pandering to the megalomaniac psychoses of national leaders, also served a large-scale function in the shifting pattern of history: to provide a vast carnival of destruction which must either weary men of the lust to kill, or bring about their extinction.

Some reviewers condemned *Fields of Battle* on the grounds of its evident irrelevance to a world that had banished war, but others welcomed the fact that the volume returned Gray's thesis to the safe track of true history, in dealing exclusively with that which was safely dead and buried.

13

I found life on the Moon very different from anything I'd experienced in my travels around the Earth's surface. It wasn't so much the change in gravity, although that certainly took a lot of getting used to, nor the severe regime of daily exercise in the centrifuge which I had to adopt in order to make sure that I might one day return to the world of my birth without extravagant medical provision. Nor was it the fact that the environment was so comprehensively artificial, or that it was impossible to venture outside without special equipment; in those respects it was much like Antarctica. The most significant difference was in the people.

Mare Moscoviense had few tourists—tourists mostly stayed Earthside, making only brief trips farside—but most of its inhabitants were nevertheless just passing through. It was one of the main jumping-off points for emigrants, largely because it was an important industrial center, the home of one of the largest factories for the manufacture of shuttles and other local-space vehicles. It was one of the chief trading posts supplying materials to the microworlds in Earth orbit and beyond, and many of its visitors came in from the farther reaches of the solar system.

The majority of the city's long-term residents were unmodified, like me, or lightly modified by reversible cyborgization, but a great many of those visiting were fabers, genetically engineered for low-gee environments. The most obvious external feature of their modification was that they had an extra pair of "arms" instead of "legs," and this meant that most of the public places in Moscoviense were designed to accommodate their kind as well as "walkers"; all the corridors were railed and all the ceilings ringed.

The sight of fabers swinging around the place like gibbons, getting everywhere at five or six times the pace of walkers, was one that I found strangely fascinating, and one to which I never quite became accustomed. Fabers couldn't live, save with the utmost difficulty, in the gravity well that was Earth; they almost never descended to the planet's surface. By the same token, it was very difficult for men from Earth to work in zero-gee environments without extensive modification, surgical if not genetic. For this reason, the only "ordinary" men who went into the true faber environments weren't ordinary by any customary standard. The Moon, with its one-sixth Earth gravity, was the only place in the inner solar system where fabers and unmodified men frequently met and mingled—there was nowhere else nearer than Ganymede.

I had always known about fabers, of course, but, like so much other "common" knowledge, the information had lain unattended in some unheeded pigeon-hole of memory until direct acquaintance ignited it and gave it life. It seemed to me that fabers lived their lives at a very rapid tempo, despite the fact that they were just as emortal as members of their parent species.

For one thing, faber parents normally had their children while they were still alive, and very often had several at intervals of only twenty or thirty years! An aggregate family usually had three or even four children growing up in parallel. In the infinite reaches of space, there was no population control, and no restrictive "right of replacement." A microworld's population could grow as fast as the microworld could put on extra mass. Then again, the fabers were always *doing* things. Even though they had four arms, they always seemed to have trouble finding a spare hand. They seemed to have no difficulty at all in doing two different things at the same time, often using only one limb for attachment—on the moon this generally meant hanging from the ceiling like a bat—while one hand mediated between the separate tasks being carried out by the remaining two.

I quickly realized that it wasn't just the widely accepted notion that the future of mankind must take the form of a gradual diffusion through the galaxy that made the fabers think of Earth as decadent. From their viewpoint, Earth-life seemed unbearably slow and sedentary. Unmodified mankind, having long since attained control of the ecosphere of its native world, seemed to the fabers to be living a lotus-eater existence, indolently pottering about in its spacious garden.

The fabers weren't contemptuous of legs as such, but they drew a sharp distinction between those spacefaring folk who were given legs by the genetic engineers in order to descend to the surfaces of new and alien worlds, with a job to do, and those Earthbound people who simply kept the legs their ancestors had bequeathed to them in order to enjoy the fruits of the labors of past generations.

Wherever I had lived on Earth, it had always seemed to me that one could blindly throw a stone into a crowded room and stand a fifty-fifty chance of hitting a historian of some sort. In Mare Moscoviense, the population of historians could be counted on the fingers of an unmodified man—and that in a city of a quarter of a million people. Whether they were resident or passing through, the people of the Moon were far more interested in the future than the past. When I told them about my vocation, my new neighbors were likely to smile politely and shake their heads.

"It's the weight of those *legs*," the fabers among them were wont to say. "You think they're holding you up, but in fact they're holding you down. Give them a chance and you'll find that you've put down roots."

If anyone told them that on Earth, "having roots" wasn't considered an altogether bad thing, they'd laugh.

"Get rid of your legs and learn to swing," they'd say. "You'll understand then that *human* beings have no need of roots. Only reach with four hands instead of two, and you'll find the stars within your grasp! Leave the past to rot at the bottom of the deep dark well, and give the Heavens their due."

I quickly learned to fall back on the same defensive moves most of my unmodified companions employed. "You can't break all your links with solid ground," we told the fabers, over and over again. "Somebody has to deal with the larger lumps of matter which are strewn about the universe, and you can't go to meet real mass if you don't have legs. It's planets that produce biospheres and biospheres that produce such luxuries as air. If you've seen further than other men it's not because you can swing by your arms from the ceiling—it's because you can stand on the shoulders of giants with legs."

Such exchanges were always cheerful. It was almost impossible to get into a real argument with a faber; their talk was as intoxicated as their movements. "Leave the wells to the unwell," they were fond of quoting. "The well will climb *out* of the wells, if they only find the will. History is bunk, only fit for sleeping minds."

A man less certain of his own destiny might have been turned aside from his task by faber banter, but I was well into my second century of life by then, and I had few doubts left regarding the propriety of my particular labor. Access to data was no more difficult on the Moon than anywhere else in the civilized Ekumen, and I proceeded, steadily and methodically, with my self-allotted task.

I made good progress there, as befitted the circumstances. Perhaps that was the happiest time of my life—but it's very difficult to draw comparisons when you're as far from childhood and youth as I now am.

Memory is an untrustworthy crutch for minds that have not yet mastered eternity.

14

The seventh volume of Mortimer Gray's *History of Death*, entitled *The Last Judgment*, was published on 21 June 3053. It dealt with the multiple crises that had developed in the late twentieth and twenty-first centuries, each of which and all of which had faced the human race with the prospect of extinction.

Gray described in minute detail the various nuclear exchanges which led up to Brazil's nuclear attack on Argentina in 2079 and the Plague Wars waged throughout that century. He discussed the various factors—the greenhouse crisis, soil erosion, pollution, and deforestation—that had come close to inflicting irreparable damage on the ecosphere. His map of the patterns of death in this period considered in detail the fate of the "lost billions" of peasant and subsistence farmers who were disinherited and displaced by the emergent ecological and economic order. Gray scrupulously pointed out that in less than two centuries more people had died than in the previous ten millennia. He made the ironic observation that the near-conquest of death achieved by twenty-first century medicine had created such an abundance of life as to precipitate a Malthusian crisis of awful proportions. He proposed that the new medicine and the new pestilences might be seen as different faces of the same coin, and that new technologies of food production—from the twentieth century Green Revolution to twenty-second century tissue-culture farmfactories—were as much progenitors of famine as of satiation.

Gray advanced the opinion that this was the most critical of all the stages of man's war with death. The weapons of the imagination were discarded in favor of more effective ones, but, in the short term, those more effective weapons, by multiplying life so effectively, had also multiplied death. In earlier times, the growth of human population had been restricted by lack of resources, and the war with death had been, in essence, a war of mental adaptation whose goal was reconciliation. When the "natural" checks on population growth were removed because that reconciliation was abandoned, the waste-products of human society threatened to poison it. Humankind, in developing the weapons by which the long war with death might be won, had also developed—in a more crudely literal sense—the weapons by which it might be lost. Nuclear arsenals and stockpiled AIDS viruses were scattered all over the globe: twin pistols held in the skeletal hands of death, leveled at the entire human race. The wounds they inflicted could so easily have been mortal—but the dangerous corner had, after all, been turned. The sciences of life, having passed through a particularly desperate stage of their evolution, kept one vital step ahead of the problems that they had helped to generate. Food technology finally achieved a merciful divorce from the bounty of nature, moving out of the fields and into the factories to achieve a complete liberation of man from the vagaries of the ecosphere, and paving the way for Garden Earth.

Gray argued that this was a remarkable triumph of human sanity which produced a political apparatus enabling human beings to take collective control of themselves, allowing the entire world to be managed and governed as a whole. He judged that the solution was far from Utopian, and that the political apparatus in question was at best a ramshackle and ill-designed affair, but admitted that it did the job. He emphasized that in the final analysis it was *not* scientific progress *per se* which had won the war against death, but the ability of human beings to work together, to compromise, to build communities. That human beings possessed this ability was, he argued, as much the legacy of thousands of years of superstition and religion as of hundreds of years of science.

The Last Judgment attracted little critical attention, as it was widely held to be dealing with matters that everyone understood very well. Given that the period had left an abundant legacy of archival material of all kinds, Gray's insistence on using only mute text accompanied by still photographs seemed to many commentators to be pedestrian and frankly perverse, unbecoming a true historian.

15

In twenty years of living beneath a star-filled sky, I was strongly affected by the magnetic pull that those stars seemed to exert upon my spirit. I seriously considered applying for modification for low-gee and shipping out from Mare Moscoviense along with the emigrants to some new microworld, or perhaps going out to one of the satellites of Saturn or Uranus, to a world where the sun's bountiful radiance was of little consequence and men lived entirely by the fruits of their own efforts and their own wisdom.

But the years drifted by, and I didn't go.

Sometimes, I thought of this failure as a result of cowardice, or evidence of the decadence that the fabers and other subspecies attributed to the humans of Earth. I sometimes imagined myself as an insect born at the bottom of a deep cave, who had—thanks to the toil of many preceding generations of insects—been brought to the rim from which I could look out at the great world, but who dared not take the one final step that would carry me out and away. More and more, however, I found my thoughts turning back to the Earth. My memories of its many environments became gradually fonder the longer my absence lasted. Nor could I despise this as a weakness. Earth was, after all, my home. It was not only *my* world, but the home world of *all* humankind. No matter what the fabers and their kin might say, the Earth was and would always remain an exceedingly precious thing, which should never be abandoned.

It seemed to me then—and still seems now—that it would be a terrible thing were men to spread themselves across the entire galaxy, taking a multitude of forms in order to occupy a multitude of alien worlds, and in the end forget entirely the world from which their ancestors had sprung.

Once, I was visited in Mare Moscoviense by Khan Mirafzal, the faber with whom I had long ago debated on TV, and talked with again before my emigration. His home, for the moment, was a microworld in the asteroid belt that was in the process of being fitted with a drive that would take it out of the system and into the infinite. He was a kind and even-tempered man who would not dream of trying to convince me of the error of my ways, but he was also a man with a sublime vision who could not restrain his enthusiasm for his own chosen destiny.

"I have no roots on Earth, Mortimer, even in a metaphorical sense. In my being, the chains of adaptation have been decisively broken. Every man of my kind is born anew, designed and synthesized; we are *self-made men*, who belong everywhere and nowhere. The wilderness of empty space which fills the universe is our realm, our heritage. Nothing is strange to us, nothing foreign, nothing alien. Blastular engineering has incorporated freedom into our blood and our bones, and I intend to take full advantage of that freedom. To do otherwise would be a betrayal of my nature."

"My own blastular engineering served only to complete the adaptation to life on Earth which natural selection had left incomplete," I reminded him. "I'm no *new man*, free from the ties which bind me to the Earth."

"Not so," he replied. "Natural selection would never have devised emortality, for natural selection can only generate change by *death and replacement*. When genetic engineers found the means of setting aside the curse of aging, they put an end to *natural* selection forever. The first and greatest freedom is time, my friend, and you have all the time in the world. You can become whatever you want to be. What *do* you want to be, Mortimer?"

"An historian," I told him. "It's what I am because it's what I want to be."

"All well and good—but history isn't inexhaustible, as you well know. It ends with the present day, the present moment. The future, on the other hand . . ."

"Is given to your kind. I know that, Mira. I don't dispute it. But what exactly *is* your kind, given that you rejoice in such freedom to be anything you want to be? When the starship *Pandora* effected the first meeting between humans and a ship that set out from another star-system, the crews of the two ships, each consisting entirely of individuals bioengineered for life in zero-gee, resembled one another far more than they resembled unmodified members of their parent species. The fundamental chemistries controlling their design were different, but this only led to the faber crews trading their respective molecules of life, so that their genetic engineers could henceforth make and use chromosomes of both kinds. What kind of freedom is it that makes all the travelers of space into mirror images of one another?"

"You're exaggerating," Mirafzal insisted. "The news reports played up the similarity, but it really wasn't as close as all that. Yes, the *Pandora* encounter can't really be regarded as a first contact between humans and aliens, because the distinction between *human* and *alien* had ceased to carry any real meaning long before it happened. But it's not the case that our kind of freedom breeds universal mediocrity because adaptation to zero-gee is an existential straitjacket. We've hardly scratched the surface of constructive cyborgization, which will open up a whole new dimension of freedom."

"That's not for me," I told him. "Maybe it *is* just my legs weighing me down, but I'm well and truly addicted to gravity. I can't cast off the past like a worn-out surskin. I know you think I ought to envy you, but I don't. I dare say you think that I'm clinging like a terrified infant to Mother Earth while you're achieving true maturity, but I really do think it's important to have somewhere to *belong*."

"So do I," the faber said, quietly. "I just don't think that Earth is or ought to be that place. It's not where you start from that's important, Mortimer, it's where you're going."

"Not for an historian."

"For everybody. History ends, Mortimer, life doesn't—not anymore."

I was at least half-convinced that Khan Mirafzal was right, although I didn't follow his advice. I still am. Maybe I was and am trapped in a kind of infancy, or a kind of lotus-eater decadence—but if so, I could see no way out of the trap then, and I still can't.

Perhaps things would have turned out differently if I'd had one of my close encounters with death while I was on the Moon, but I didn't. The dome in which I lived was only breached once, and the crack was sealed before there was any significant air-loss. It was a scare, but it wasn't a *threat*. Perhaps, in the end, the Moon was too much like Antarctica—but without the crevasses. Fortune seems to have decreed that all my significant formative experiences have to do with water, whether it be very hot or very, very cold.

Eventually, I gave in to my homesickness for Garden Earth and returned there, having resolved not to leave it again until my history of death was complete. I never did.

16

The eighth volume of Mortimer Gray's *History of Death*, entitled *The Fountains of Youth*, was published on 1 December 3064. It dealt with the development of elementary technologies of longevity and elementary technologies of cyborgization in the twenty-fourth and twenty-fifth centuries. It tracked the progress of the new "politics of immortality," whose main focus was the new Charter of Human Rights, which sought to establish a basic right to longevity for all. It also described the development of the Zaman transformations by which human blastulas could be engineered for longevity, which finally opened the way for the wholesale metamorphosis of the human race.

According to Gray, the Manifesto of the New Chartists was the vital treaty which ushered in a new phase in man's continuing war with death, because it defined the whole human community as a single army, united in all its interests. He quoted with approval and reverence the opening words of the document: "Man is born free, but is everywhere enchained by the fetters of death. In all times past men have been truly equal in one respect and one only: they have all borne the burden of age and decay. The day must soon dawn when this burden can be set aside; there will be a new freedom, and with this freedom must come a new equality. No man has the right to escape the prison of death while his fellows remain shackled within."

Gray carefully chronicled the long battle fought by the Chartists across the stage of world politics, describing it with a partisan fervor that had been largely absent from his work since the fourth volume. There was nothing clinical about his description of the "persecution" of Ali Zaman and the resistance offered by the community of nations to his proposal to make future generations truly emortal. Gray admitted that he had the benefits of hindsight, and that as a Zaman-transformed individual himself he was bound to have an attitude very different from Zaman's confused and cautious contemporaries, but he saw no reason to be entirely evenhanded. From his viewpoint, those who initially opposed Zaman were traitors in the war against death, and he could find few excuses for them. In trying to preserve "human nature" against biotechnological intervention—or, at least, to confine such interventions by a mythos of medical "repair"—those men and women had, in his stern view, been willfully blind and negligent of the welfare of their own children.

Some critics charged Gray with inconsistency because he was not nearly so extravagant in his enthusiasm for the various kinds of symbiosis between organic and inorganic systems that were tried out in the period under consideration. His descriptions of experiments in cyborgization were indeed conspicuously cooler, not because he saw such endeavors as "unnatural," but rather because he saw them as only peripherally relevant to the war against death. He tended to lump together adventures in cyborgization with cosmetic biotechnology as symptoms of lingering anxiety regarding the presumed "tedium of emortality"—an anxiety which had led the first generations of long-lived people to lust for variety and "multidimensionality." Many champions of cyborgization and man/machine symbiosis, who saw their work as the new frontier of science, accused Gray of rank conservatism, suggesting that it was hypocritical of him, given that his mind was closed against *them*, to criticize so extravagantly those who, in less enlightened times, had closed their minds against Ali Zaman.

This controversy, which was dragged into the public arena by some fierce attacks, helped in no small measure to boost access-demand for *The Fountains of Youth*, and nearly succeeded in restoring Mortimer Gray to the position of public preeminence that he had enjoyed a century before.

17

Following my return to the Earth's surface, I took up residence in Tonga, where the Continental Engineers were busy raising new islands by the dozen from the relatively shallow sea.

The Continental Engineers had borrowed their name from a twenty-fifth century group which tried to persuade the United Nations to license the building of a dam across the Straits of Gibraltar—which, because more water evaporates from the Mediterranean than flows into it from rivers, would have increased considerably the land surface of southern Europe and Northern Africa. That plan had, of course, never come to fruition, but the new Engineers had taken advantage of the climatic disruptions caused by the advancing Ice Age to promote the idea of raising new lands in the tropics to take emigrants from the nearly frozen north. Using a mixture of techniques—seeding the shallower sea with artificial "lightning corals" and using special gantzing organisms to agglomerate huge towers of cemented sand—the Engineers were creating a great archipelago of new islands, many of which they then connected up with huge bridges.

Between the newly raised islands, the ecologists who were collaborating with the Continental Engineers had planted vast networks of matted seaweeds: floral carpets extending over thousands of miles. The islands and their surroundings were being populated, and their ecosystems shaped, with the aid of the Creationists of Micronesia, whose earlier exploits I'd been prevented from exploring by the sinking of *Genesis*. I was delighted to have the opportunity of observing their new and bolder adventures at close range.

The Pacific sun set in its deep blue bed seemed fabulously luxurious after the silver-ceilinged domes of the Moon, and I gladly gave myself over to its governance. Carried away by the romance of it all, I married into an aggregate household which was form-ing in order to raise a child, and so—as I neared my two hundredth birthday—I be-came a parent for the first time. Five of the other seven members of the aggregate were ecological engineers, and had to spend a good deal of time traveling, so I became one of the constant presences in the life of the growing infant, who was a girl named Lua Tawana. I formed a relationship with her that seemed to me to be especially close.

In the meantime, I found myself constantly engaged in public argument with the self-styled Cyborganizers, who had chosen to make the latest volume of my his-tory into a key issue in their bid for the kind of public attention and sponsorship that the Continental Engineers had already won. I thought their complaints unjus-tified and irrelevant, but they obviously thought that by attacking me they could ex-ploit the celebrity status I had briefly enjoyed. The gist of their argument was that the world had become so besotted with the achievements of genetic engineers that people had become blind to all kinds of other possibilities that lay beyond the scope of DNA manipulation. They insisted that I was one of many contemporary writers who was "de-historicizing" cyborgization, making it seem that in the past and the present—and, by implication, the future—organic/inorganic integration and symbiosis were peripheral to the story of human progress. The Cyborganizers were willing to concede that some previous practitioners of their science had gen-erated a lot of bad publicity, in the days of memory boxes and psychedelic synthe-sizers, but claimed that this had only served to mislead the public as to the true potential of their science.

In particular—and this was of particular relevance to me—the Cyborganizers in-sisted that the biotechnologists had only won one battle in the war against death, and that what was presently called "emortality" would eventually prove wanting. Za-man transformations, they conceded, had dramatically increased the human life-span—so dramatically that no one yet knew for sure how long ZT people might live—but it was not yet proven that the extension would be effective for more than a few centuries. They did have a point; even the most optimistic supporters of Zaman transformations were reluctant to promise a lifespan of several millennia, and some kinds of aging processes—particularly those linked to DNA-copying errors—still af-fected emortals to some degree. Hundreds, if not thousands, of people still died every year from "age-related causes."

To find further scope for *authentic* immortality, the Cyborganizers claimed that it would be necessary to look to a combination of organic and inorganic technologies. What was needed by contemporary man, they said, was not just life, but *afterlife*, and afterlife would require some kind of transcription of the personality into an in-organic rather than an organic matrix. Whatever the advantages of flesh and blood, silicon lasted longer; and however clever genetic engineers became in adapting men for life in microworlds or on alien planets, only machine-makers could build enti-ties capable of working in genuinely extreme environments.

The idea of "downloading" a human mind into an inorganic matrix was, of course, a very old one. It had been extensively if optimistically discussed in the days before the advent of emortality—at which point it had been marginalized as an ap-parent irrelevance. Mechanical "human analogues" and virtual simulacra had be-come commonplace alongside the development of longevity technologies, but the evolution of such "species" had so far been divergent rather than convergent. According to the Cyborganizers, it was now time for a change.

Although I didn't entirely relish being cast in the role of villain and bugbear, I made only halfhearted attempts to make peace with my self-appointed adversaries. I remained skeptical in respect of their grandiose schemes, and I was happy to dampen their ardor as best I could in public debate. I thought myself sufficiently mature to be unaffected by their insults, although it did sting when they sunk so low as to charge me with being a closet Thanaticist.

"Your interminable book is only posing as a history," Lok Cho Kam, perhaps the most outspoken of the younger Cyborganizers, once said when he challenged me to a broadcast debate. "It's actually an extended exercise in the *pornography* of death. Its silence and stillness aren't marks of scholarly dignity, they're a means of heightening response."

"That's absurd!" I said, but he wouldn't be put off.

"What sound arouses more excitation in today's world than the sound of silence? What movement is more disturbing than stillness? You pretend to be standing aside from the so-called war against death as a commentator and a judge, but in fact you're part of it—and you're on the devil's side, whether you know it or not."

"I suppose you're partly right," I conceded, on reflection. "Perhaps the muteness and stillness of the text *are* a means of heightening response—but if so, it's because there's no other way to make readers who have long abandoned their fear of death sensitive to the appalling shadow which it once cast over the human world. The style of my book is calculatedly archaic because it's one way of trying to connect its readers to the distant past—but the entire thrust of my argument is triumphant and celebratory. I've said many times before that it's perfectly understandable that the imagery of death should acquire a pornographic character *for a while*, but when we really understand the phenomenon of death, that pornographic specter will fade away, so that we can see with perfect clarity what our ancestors were and what we have become. By the time my book is complete, nobody will be able to think it pornographic, and nobody will make the mistake of thinking that it glamorizes death in any way."

Lok Cho Kam was still unimpressed, but in this instance I *was* right. I was sure of it then, and I am now. The pornography of death did pass away, like the pornographies that preceded it.

Nobody nowadays thinks of my book as a prurient exercise, whether or not they think it admirable.

If nothing else, my debates with the Cyborganizers created a certain sense of anticipation regarding the ninth volume of my *History*, which would bring it up to the present day. It was widely supposed, although I was careful never to say so, that the ninth volume would be the last. I might be flattering myself, but I truly believe that many people were looking to it for some kind of definitive evaluation of the current state of the human world.

18

The ninth volume of Mortimer Gray's *History of Death*, entitled *The Honeymoon of Emortality*, was published on 28 October 3075. It was considered by many reviewers to be unjustifiably slight in terms of hard data. Its main focus was on attitudes to longevity and emortality following the establishment of the principle that every human child had a right to be born emortal. It described the belated extinction of the "nuclear" family, the ideological rebellion of the Humanists—whose quest to preserve "the authentic *Homo sapiens*" had led many to retreat to islands that the Continental Engineers were now integrating into their "new continent"—and the spread of such new philosophies of life as neo-Stoicism, neo-Epicureanism, and Xenophilia.

All this information was placed in the context of the spectrum of inherited attitudes, myths, and fictions by means of which mankind had for thousands of years wistfully contemplated the possibility of extended life. Gray contended that these old ideas—including the notion that people would inevitably find emortality intolerably tedious—were merely an expression of "sour grapes." While people thought that emortality was impossible, he said, it made perfect sense for them to invent reasons why it would be undesirable anyhow. When it became a *reality*, though, there was a battle to be fought in the imagination, whereby the burden of these cultivated anxieties had to be shed, and a new mythology formulated.

Gray flatly refused to take seriously any suggestion that emortality might be a bad thing. He was dismissive of the Humanists and contemptuous of the original Thanatics, who had steadfastly refused the gifts of emortality. Nevertheless, he did try to understand the thinking of such people, just as he had tried in earlier times to understand the thinking of the later Thanatics who had played their part in winning him his first measure of fame. He considered the new Stoics, with their insistence that asceticism was the natural ideological partner of emortality, to be similar victims of an "understandable delusion"—a verdict which, like so many of his statements, involved him in controversy with the many neo-Stoics who were still alive in 3075. It did not surprise his critics in the least that Gray commended neo-Epicureanism as the optimal psychological adaptation to emortality, given that he had been a lifelong adherent of that outlook, ever dedicated to its "careful hedonism." Only the cruelest of his critics dared to suggest that he had been so half-hearted a neo-Epicurean as almost to qualify as a neo-Stoic by default.

The Honeymoon of Emortality collated the statistics of birth and death during the twenty-seventh, twenty-eight, and twenty-ninth centuries, recording the spread of Zaman transformations and the universalization of ectogenesis on Earth, and the extension of the human empire throughout and beyond the solar system. Gray recorded an acknowledgment to Khan Mirafzal and numerous scholars based on the Moon and Mars, for their assistance in gleaning information from the slowly diffusing microworlds and from more rapidly dispersing starships. Gray noted that the transfer of information between data-stores was limited by the speed of light, and that Earth-based historians might have to wait centuries for significant data about human colonies more distant than Maya. These data showed that the number of individuals of the various mankinds that now existed was increasing more rapidly than ever before, although the population of unmodified Earthbound humans was slowly shrinking. Gray noted *en passant* that *Homo sapiens* had become extinct in the twenty-ninth century, but that no one had bothered to invent new Latin tags for its descendant species.

Perhaps understandably, *The Honeymoon of Emortality* had little to say about cyborgization, and the Cyborganizers—grateful for the opportunity to heat up a flagging controversy—reacted noisily to this omission. Gray did deal with the memory box craze, but suggested that even had the boxes worked better, and maintained a store of memories that could be convincingly played back into the arena of consciousness, this would have been of little relevance to the business of adapting to emortality. At the end of the volume, however, Gray announced that there would, in fact, be a tenth volume to conclude his *magnum opus*, and promised that he would consider in more detail therein the futurological arguments of the Cyborganizers, as well as the hopes and expectations of other schools of thought.

19

In 3077, when Lua Tawana was twelve years old, three of her parents were killed when a helicopter crashed into the sea near the island of Vavau during a storm. It was the first time that my daughter had to face up to the fact that death had not been entirely banished from the world.

It wasn't the first time that I'd ever lost people near and dear to me, nor the first time that I'd shared such grief with others, but it was very different from the previous occasions because everyone involved was determined that I should shoulder the main responsibility of helping Lua through it; I was, after all, the world's foremost expert on the subject of death.

"You won't always feel this bad about it," I assured her, while we walked together on the sandy shore, looking out over the deceptively placid weed-choked sea. "Time heals virtual wounds as well as real ones."

"I don't *want* it to heal," she told me, sternly. "I want it to be bad. It *ought* to be bad. It *is* bad."

"I know," I said, far more awkwardly than I would have wished. "When I say that it'll heal, I don't mean that it'll vanish. I mean that it'll . . . become manageable. It won't be so all-consuming."

"But it *will* vanish," she said, with that earnest certainly of which only the newly wise are capable. "People forget. In time, they forget *everything*. Our heads can only hold so much."

"That's not really true," I insisted, taking her hand in mine. "Yes, we do forget. The longer we live, the more we let go, because it's reasonable to prefer our fresher, more immediately relevant memories, but it's a matter of *choice*. We can cling to the things that are important, no matter how long ago they happened. I was nearly killed in the Great Coral Sea Catastrophe, you know, nearly two hundred years ago. A little girl even younger than you saved my life, and I remember it as clearly as if it were yesterday." Even as I said it, I realized that it was a lie. I remembered that it had happened, all right, and much of what had been said in that eerily lit corridor and in the survival pod afterward, but I was remembering a neat array of facts, not an experience.

"Where is she now?" Lua asked.

"Her name was Emily," I said, answering the wrong question because I couldn't answer the one she'd asked. "Emily Marchant. She could swim and I couldn't. If she hadn't been there, I wouldn't have been able to get out of the hull. I'd never have had the courage to do it on my own, but she didn't give me the choice. She told me I had to do it, and she was right." I paused, feeling a slight shock of revelation even though it was something I'd always known.

"She lost her entire family," I went on. "She'll be fine now, but she won't have forgotten. She'll still feel it. That's what I'm trying to tell you, Lua. In two hundred years, you'll still remember what happened, and you'll still feel it, but it'll be all right. *You'll* be all right."

"Right now," she said, looking up at me so that her dark and soulful eyes seemed unbearably huge and sad, "I'm not particularly interested in being all right. Right now, I just want to cry."

"That's fine," I told her. "It's okay to cry." I led by example.

I was right, though. Lua grieved, but she ultimately proved to be resilient in the face of tragedy. My co-parents, by contrast, seemed to me to be exaggeratedly calm and philosophical about it, as if the loss of three spouses were simply a minor glitch in the infinitely unfolding pattern of their lives. They had all grown accustomed to their own emortality, and had been deeply affected by long life; they had not become bored, but they had achieved a serenity of which I could not wholly approve.

Perhaps their attitude was reasonable as well as inevitable. If emortals accumulated a burden of anxiety every time a death was reported, they would eventually cripple themselves psychologically, and their own continuing lives would be made unbearable. Even so, I couldn't help feel that Lua was right about the desirability of conserving a little of the "badness," and a due sense of tragedy.

I thought I was capable of that, and always would be, but I knew I might be wrong.

Divorce was, of course, out of the question; we remaining co-parents were obligated to Lua. In the highly unlikely event that the three had simply left, we would have replaced them, but it didn't seem appropriate to look for replacements for the dead, so we remained a group of five. The love we had for one another had always been cool, with far more courtesy in it than passion, but we were drawn more closely together by the loss. We felt that we knew one another more intimately by virtue of having shared it.

The quality of our lives had been injured, but I at least was uncomfortably aware of the fact that the tragedy also had its positive, life-enhancing side. I found myself thinking more and more about what I had said to Lua about not having to forget the truly important and worthwhile things, and about the role played by death in defining experiences as important and worthwhile. I didn't realize at first how deep an impression her naïve remarks had made on me, but it became gradually clearer as time went by. It *was* important to conserve the badness, to heal without entirely erasing the scars that bereavement left.

I had never been a habitual tourist, having lost my taste for such activity in the aftermath of the *Genesis* fiasco, but I took several long journeys in the course of the next few years. I took to visiting old friends, and even stayed for a while with Sharane Fereday, who was temporarily unattached. Inevitably, I looked up Emily Marchant, not realizing until I actually put through the initial call how important it had become to find out whether she remembered me.

She did remember me. She claimed that she recognized me immediately, although it would have been easy enough for her household systems to identify me as the caller and display a whole series of reminders before she took over from her simulacrum.

"Do you know," she said, when we parted after our brief meeting in the lush Eden of Australia's interior, "I often think of being trapped on that ship. I hope that nothing like it ever happens to me again. I've told an awful lot of lies since then—next time, I won't feel so certain that I deserve to get out."

"We can't forfeit our right to life by lying," I assured her. "We have to do something much worse than that. If it ever happens to me again, I'll be able to get out on my own—but I'll only be able to do it by remembering *you*." I didn't anticipate, of course, that anything like it *would* ever happen to me again. We still have a tendency to assume that lightning doesn't strike twice in the same place, even though we're the proud inventors of lightning conductors and emortality.

"You must have learned to swim by *now*!" she said, staring at me with eyes that were more than two hundred years old, set in a face not quite as youthful as the one I remembered.

"I'm afraid not," I said. "Somehow, I never quite found the time."

20

The tenth and last volume of Mortimer Gray's *History of Death*, entitled *The Marriage of Life and Death*, was published on 7 April 3088. It was not, strictly speaking, a history book, although it did deal in some detail with the events as well as the attitudes of the thirtieth and thirty-first centuries. It had elements of both spiritual autobiography and futurological speculation. It discussed both neo-Thanaticism and Cyborganization as philosophies as well as social movements, surprising critics by treating both with considerable sympathy. The discussion also took in other contemporary debates, including the proposition that progress in science, if not in technology, had now reached an end because there was nothing left to discover. It even included a scrupulous examination of the merits of the proposal that a special microworld should be established as a gigantic mausoleum to receive the bodies of all the solar system's dead.

The odd title of the volume was an ironic reflection of one of its main lines of argument. Mankind's war with death was now over, but this was not because death had been entirely banished from the human world; death, Gray insisted, would forever remain a fact of life. The annihilation of the individual human body and the individual human mind could never become impossible, no matter how far biotechnology might advance or how much progress the Cyborganizers might make in downloading minds into entirely new matrices. The victory that had been achieved, he argued, was not an absolute conquest but rather the relegation of death to its proper place in human affairs. Its power was now properly circumscribed, but had to be properly respected.

Man and death, Gray argued, now enjoyed a kind of social contract, in which tyranny and exploitation had been reduced to a sane and acceptable minimum, but which still left to death a voice and a hand in human affairs. Gray, it seemed, had now adopted a gentler and more forgiving attitude to the old enemy. It was good, he said, that dying remained one of the choices open to human beings, and that the option should occasionally be exercised. He had no sympathy with the exhibitionism of public executions, and was particularly hard on the element of bad taste in self-ordered crucifixions, but only because such ostentation offended his Epicurean sensibilities. Deciding upon the length of one's lifetime, he said, must remain a matter of individual taste, and one should not mock or criticize those who decided that a short life suited them best.

Gray made much of the notion that it was partly the contrast with death that illuminated and made meaningful the business of life. Although death had been displaced from the evolutionary process by the biotechnological usurpation of the privileges of natural selection, it had not lost its role in the formation and development of the individual human psyche: a role which was both challenging and refining. He declared that fear was not entirely an undesirable thing, not simply because it was a stimulant, but also because it was a force in the organization of emotional experience. The *value* of experienced life, he suggested, depended in part upon a knowledge of the possibility and reality of death.

This concluding volume of Gray's *History* was widely read, but not widely admired. Many critics judged it to be unacceptably anticlimactic. The Cyborganizers had by this time become entranced by the possibility of a technologically guaranteed "multiple life," by which copies of a mind might be lodged in several different bodies, some of which would live on far beyond the death of the original location. They were understandably disappointed that Gray refused to grant that such a development would be the final victory over death—indeed, that he seemed to feel that it would make no real difference, on the grounds that every "copy" of a mind had to be reckoned a separate and distinct individual, each of which must face the world alone. Many Continental Engineers, Gaean Liberationists, and fabers also claimed that it was narrow-minded, and suggested that Gray ought to have had more to say about the life of the Earth, or the DNA eco-entity as a whole, and should have concluded with an escalation of scale to put things in their proper cosmic perspective.

The group who found the most to like in *The Marriage of Life and Death* was that of a few fugitive neo-Thanatics, whose movement had never quite died out in spite of its members' penchant for self-destruction. One or two Thanatic apologists and fellow-travelers publicly expressed their hope that Gray, having completed his thesis, would now recognize the aesthetic propriety of joining their ranks. Khan Mirafzal, when asked to relay his opinion back from an outward-bound microworld, opined that this was quite unnecessary, given that Mortimer Gray and all his kind were already immured in a tomb from which they would never be able to escape.

21

I stayed with the slowly disintegrating family unit for some years after Lua Tawana had grown up and gone her own way. It ended up as a *ménage à trois*, carried forward by sheer inertia. Leif, Sajda, and I were fit and healthy in body, but I couldn't help wondering, from time to time, whether we'd somehow been overcome by a kind of spiritual blight, which had left us ill-equipped for future change.

When I suggested this to the others, they told me that it was merely a sense of letdown resulting from the finishing of my project. They urged me to join the Continental Engineers, and commit myself wholeheartedly to the building of a new Pacific Utopia—a project, they assured me, that would provide me with a purpose in life for as long as I might feel the need of one. I didn't believe them.

"Even the longest book," Sajda pointed out, "eventually runs out of words, but the job of building *worlds* is never finished. Even if the time should one day come when we can call *this* continent complete, there will be another yet to make. We might still build that dam between the Pillars of Hercules, one day."

I did try, but I simply couldn't find a new sense of mission in that direction. Nor did I feel that I could simply sit down to start compiling another book. In composing the history of death, I thought, I had already written *the* book. The history of death, it seemed to me, was also the history of life, and I couldn't imagine that there was anything more to be added to what I'd done, save for an endless series of detailed footnotes.

For some years, I considered the possibility of leaving Earth again, but I remembered well enough how the sense of excitement I'd found when I first lived on the Moon had gradually faded into a dull ache of homesickness. The spaces between the stars, I knew, belonged to the fabers, and the planets circling other stars to men adapted before birth to live in their environments. I was tied by my genes to the surface of the Earth, and I didn't want to undergo the kind of metamorphosis that would be necessary to fit me for the exploration of other worlds. I still believed in *belonging,* and I felt very strongly that Mortimer Gray belonged to Earth, however decadent and icebound it might become.

At first, I was neither surprised nor alarmed by my failure to find any resources inside myself which might restore my zest for existence and action. I thought that it was one of those things that time would heal. By slow degrees, though, I began to feel that I was becalmed upon a sea of futility. Despite my newfound sympathy for Thanaticism, I didn't harbor the slightest inclination toward suicide—no matter how much respect I had cultivated for the old Grim Reaper, death was still, for me, the ultimate enemy—but I felt the awful pressure of my purposelessness grow and grow.

Although I maintained my home in the burgeoning continent of Oceania, I began traveling extensively to savor the other environments of Earth, and made a point of touring those parts of the globe that I had missed out on during my first two centuries of life. I visited the Reunited States of America, Greater Siberia, Tibet, and half a hundred other places loaded with the relics of once-glorious history. I toured the Indus Delta, New Zealand, the Arctic ice pack, and various other reaches of restored wilderness empty of permanent residents. Everything I saw was transformed by the sheer relentlessness of my progress into a series of monuments: memorials of those luckless eras before men invented science and civilization, and became demigods.

There is, I believe, an old saying that warns us that he who keeps walking long enough is bound to trip up in the end. As chance would have it, I was in Severnaya Zemlya in the Arctic—almost as far away as it was possible to be from the crevasses into which I had stumbled while searching for Ziru Majumdar—when my own luck ran out.

Strictly speaking, it was not I who stumbled, but the vehicle I was in: a one-man snowsled. Although such a thing was generally considered to be impossible, it fell into a cleft so deep that it had no bottom, and ended up in the ocean beneath the ice cap.

"I must offer my most profound apologies," the snowsled's AI navigator said, as the sled slowly sank into the lightless depths and the awfulness of my plight slowly sank into my consciousness. "This should not have happened. It ought not to have been possible. I am doing everything within my power to summon help."

"Well," I said, as the sled settled on to the bottom, "at least we're the right way up—and you certainly can't expect me to swim out of the sled."

"It would be most unwise to attempt any such thing, sir," the navigator said. "You would certainly drown."

I was astonished by my own calmness, and marvelously untroubled—at least for the moment—by the fact of my helplessness. "How long will the air last?" I asked the navigator.

"I believe that I can sustain a breathable atmosphere for forty-eight hours," it reported, dutifully. "If you will be so kind as to restrict your movements to a minimum, that would be of considerable assistance to me. Unfortunately, I'm not at all certain that I can maintain the internal temperature of the cabin at a life-sustaining level for more than thirty hours. Nor can I be sure that the hull will withstand the pressure presently being exerted upon it for as long as that. I apologize for my uncertainty in these respects."

"Taking thirty hours as a hopeful approximation," I said, effortlessly matching the machine's oddly pedantic tone, "what would you say our chances are of being rescued within that time?"

"I'm afraid that it's impossible to offer a probability figure, sir. There are too many unknown variables, even if I accept thirty hours as the best estimate of the time available."

"If I were to suggest fifty-fifty, would that seem optimistic or pessimistic?"

"I'm afraid I'd have to call that optimistic, sir."

"How about one in a thousand?"

"Thankfully, that would be pessimistic. Since you press me for an estimate, sir, I dare say that something in the region of one in ten wouldn't be too far from the mark. It all depends on the proximity of the nearest submarine, assuming that my mayday has been received. I fear that I've not yet received an actual acknowledgment, but that might well be due to the inadequacy of my equipment, which wasn't designed with our present environment in mind. I must confess that it has sustained a certain amount of damage as a result of pressure damage to my outer tegument and a small leak."

"How small?" I wanted to know.

"It's sealed now," it assured me. "All being well, the seal should hold for thirty hours, although I can't absolutely guarantee it. I believe, although I can't be certain, that the only damage I've sustained that is relevant to our present plight is that affecting my receiving apparatus."

"What you're trying to tell me," I said, deciding that a recap wouldn't do any harm, "is that you're pretty sure that your mayday is going out, but that we won't actually know whether help is at hand unless and until it actually arrives."

"Very succinctly put, sir." I don't think it was being sarcastic.

"But all in all, it's ten to one, or worse, that we're as good as dead."

"As far as I can determine the probabilities, that's correct—but there's sufficient uncertainty to leave room for hope that the true odds might be nearer one in three."

I was quiet for a little while then. I was busy exploring my feelings, and wondering whether I ought to be proud or disgusted with their lack of intensity.

I've been here before, I thought, by way of self-explanation. *Last time, there was a child with me; this time, I've got a set of complex subroutines instead. I've even fallen down a crevasse before. Now I can find out whether Ziru Majumdar was right when he said that I wouldn't understand the difference between what happened to him and what happened to me until I followed his example. There can be few men in the world as well-prepared for this as I am.*

"Are you afraid of dying?" I asked the AI, after a while.

"All in all, sir," it said, copying my phrase in order to promote a feeling of kinship, "I'd rather not. In fact, were it not for the philosophical difficulties that stand in the way of reaching a firm conclusion as to whether or not machines can be said to be authentically self-conscious, I'd be quite prepared to say that I'm scared—terrified, even."

"I'm not," I said. "Do you think I ought to be?"

"It's not for me to say, sir. You are, of course, a world-renowned expert on the subject of death. I dare say that helps a lot."

"Perhaps it does," I agreed. "Or perhaps I've simply lived so long that my mind is hardened against all novelty, all violent emotion and all real possibility. I haven't actually *done* much with myself these last few years."

"If you think *you* haven't done much with yourself," it said, with a definite hint of sarcasm, "you should try navigating a snowsled for a while. I think you might find your range of options uncomfortably cramped. Not that I'm complaining, mind."

"If they scrapped the snowsled and re-sited you in a starship," I pointed out, "you wouldn't be *you* anymore. You'd be something else."

"Right now," it replied, "I'd be happy to risk any and all consequences. Wouldn't you?"

"Somebody once told me that death was just a process of transcendence. Her brain was incandescent with fever induced by some tailored recreational disease, and she wanted to infect me, to show me the error of my ways."

"Did you believe her?"

"No. She was stark raving mad."

"It's perhaps as well. We don't have any recreational diseases on board. I could put you to sleep though, if that's what you want."

"It isn't."

"I'm glad. I don't want to be alone, even if I am only an AI. Am I insane, do you think? Is all this just a symptom of the pressure?"

"You're quite sane," I assured it, setting aside all thoughts of incongruity. "So am I. It would be much harder if we weren't together. The last time I was in this kind of mess, I had a child with me—a little girl. It made all the difference in the world, to both of us. In a way, every moment I've lived since then has been borrowed time. At least I finished that damned book. Imagine leaving something like that *incomplete*."

"Are you so certain it's complete?" it asked.

I knew full well, of course, that the navigator was just making conversation according to a clever programming scheme. I knew that its emergency subroutines had kicked in, and that all the crap about it being afraid to die was just some psych-programmer's idea of what I needed to hear. I *knew* that it was all fake, all just macabre role-playing—but I knew that I had to play my part, too, treating every remark and every question as if it were part of an authentic conversation, a genuine quest for knowledge.

"It all depends what you mean by *complete*," I said, carefully. "In one sense, no history can ever be complete, because the world always goes on, always throwing up more events, always changing. In another sense, completion is a purely aesthetic matter—and in that sense, I'm entirely confident that my history is complete. It reached an authentic conclusion, which was both true, and, for me at least, satisfying. I can look back at it and say to myself: *I did that. It's finished. Nobody ever did anything like it before, and now nobody can, because it's already been done. Someone else's history might have been different, but mine is mine, and it's what it is.* Does that make any sense to you?"

"Yes sir," it said. "It makes very good sense."

The lying bastard was *programmed* to say that, of course. It was programmed to tell me any damn thing I seemed to want to hear, but I wasn't going to let on that I knew what a hypocrite it was. I still had to play my part, and I was determined to play it to the end—which, as things turned out, wasn't far off. The AI's data-stores were way out of date, and there was an automated sub placed to reach us within three hours. The oceans are lousy with subs these days. Ever since the Great Coral Sea Catastrophe, it's been considered prudent to keep a very close eye on the seabed, lest the crust crack again and the mantle's heat break through.

They say that some people are born lucky. I guess I must be one of them. Every time I run out, a new supply comes looking for me.

It was the captain of a second submarine, which picked me up after the mechanical one had done the donkey work of saving myself and my AI friend, who gave me the news which relegated my accident to footnote status in that day's broadcasts.

A signal had reached the solar system from the starship *Shiva*, which had been exploring in the direction of the galactic center. The signal had been transmitted two hundred and twenty-seven light-years, meaning that, in Earthly terms, the discovery had been made in the year 2871—which happened, coincidentally, to be the year of my birth.

What the signal revealed was that *Shiva* had found a group of solar systems, all of whose life-bearing planets were occupied by a single species of micro-organism: a genetic predator that destroyed not merely those competing species that employed its own chemistry of replication, but any and all others. It was the living equivalent of a universal solvent; a true omnivore.

Apparently, this organism had spread itself across vast reaches of space, moving from star-system to star-system, laboriously but inevitably, by means of Arrhenius spores. Wherever the spores came to rest, these omnipotent micro-organisms grew to devour *everything*—not merely the carbonaceous molecules which in Earthly terms were reckoned "organic," but also many "inorganic" substrates. Internally, these organisms were chemically complex, but they were very tiny—hardly bigger than Earthly protozoans or the internal nanomachines to which every human being plays host. They were utterly devoid of any vestige of mind or intellect. They were, in essence, the ultimate blight, against which nothing could compete, and which nothing *Shiva's* crew had tested—before they were devoured—had been able to destroy.

In brief, wherever this new kind of life arrived, it would obliterate all else, reducing any victim ecosphere to homogeneity and changelessness.

In their final message, the faber crew of the *Shiva*—who knew all about the *Pandora* encounter—observed that humankind had *now* met the alien.

Here, I thought, when I had had a chance to weigh up this news, was a *true* marriage of life and death, the likes of which I had never dreamed. Here was the promise of a future renewal of the war between man and death—not this time for the small prize of the human mind, but for the larger prize of the universe itself.

In time, *Shiva's* last message warned, spores of this new kind of death-life must and *would* reach our own solar system, whether it took a million years or a billion; in the meantime, all humankinds must do their level best to purge the worlds of other stars of its vile empire, in order to reclaim them for real life, for intelligence, and for evolution—always provided, of course, that a means could be discovered to achieve that end.

When the sub delivered me safely back to Severnaya Zemlya, I did not stay long in my hotel room. I went outdoors, to study the great ice sheet which had been there since the dawn of civilization, and to look southward, toward the places where newborn glaciers were gradually extending their cold clutch further and further into the human domain. Then I looked upward, at the multitude of stars sparkling in their bed of endless darkness. I felt an exhilaratingly paradoxical sense of renewal. I knew that although there was nothing for me to do for now, the time would come when my talent and expertise would be needed again.

Some day, it will be my task to compose *another* history, of the next war which humankind must fight against Death and Oblivion.

It might take me a thousand or a million years, but I'm prepared to be patient.

the lincoln train

MAUREEN F. McHUGH

Maureen F. McHugh made her first sale in 1989, and has since made a powerful impression on the SF world with a relatively small body of work, becoming one of today's most respected writers. In 1992, she published one of the year's most widely acclaimed and talked-about first novels, *China Mountain Zhang*, which won the Locus Award for Best First Novel, the Lambda Literary Award, and the James Tiptree Jr. Memorial Award, and which was named a *New York Times* Notable Book as well as being a finalist for the Hugo and Nebula Awards. Her other books, including the novels *Half the Day Is Night* and *Mission Child*, have been greeted with similar enthusiasm. Her most recent book is a new novel, *Nekropolis*. Her powerful short fiction has appeared in *Asimov's Science Fiction, The Magazine of Fantasy and Science Fiction, Starlight, Alternate Warriors, Aladdin, Killing Me Softly*, and other markets, and is about to be assembled in a collection called *The Lincoln Train*. She has had stories in our Tenth through Fourteenth, and our Nineteenth and Twentieth annual collections. She lives in Twinsburg, Ohio, with her husband, her son, and a golden retriever named Smith.

There have been many tragic periods in history. As the melancholy story that follows suggests, though, there are few of those periods that couldn't also have been made a little *worse*. . . .

Soldiers of the G.A.R. stand alongside the tracks. They are General Dodge's soldiers, keeping the tracks maintained for the Lincoln Train. If I stand right, the edges of my bonnet are like blinders and I can't see the soldiers at all. It is a spring evening. At the house the lilacs are blooming. My mother wears a sprig pinned to her dress under her cameo. I can smell it, even in the crush of these people all waiting for the train. I can smell the lilac, and the smell of too many people crowded together, and a faint taste of cinders on the air. I want to go home but that house is not ours anymore. I smooth my black dress. On the train platform we are all in mourning.

The train will take us to St. Louis, from whence we will leave for the Oklahoma territories. They say we will walk, but I don't know how my mother will do that. She has been poorly since the winter of '62. I check my bag with our water and provisions.

"Julia Adelaide," my mother says, "I think we should go home."

"We've come to catch the train," I say, very sharp.

I'm Clara, my sister Julia is eleven years older than me. Julia is married and living in Tennessee. My mother blinks and touches her sprig of lilac uncertainly. If I am not sharp with her, she will keep on it.

I wait. When I was younger I used to try to school my unruly self in Christian charity. God sends us nothing we cannot bear. Now I only try to keep it from my face, try to keep my outer self disciplined. There is a feeling inside me, an anger, that I can't even speak. Something is being bent, like a bow, bending and bending and bending—

"When are we going home?" my mother says.

"Soon," I say because it is easy.

But she won't remember and in a moment she'll ask again. And again and again, through this long long train ride to St. Louis. I am trying to be a Christian daughter, and I remind myself that it is not her fault that the war turned her into an old woman, or that her mind is full of holes and everything new drains out. But it's not my fault either. I don't even try to curb my feelings and I know that they rise up to my face. The only way to be true is to be true from the inside and I am not. I am full of unchristian feelings. My mother's infirmity is her trial, and it is also mine.

I wish I were someone else.

The train comes down the track, chuffing, coming slow. It is an old, badly used thing, but I can see that once it was a model of chaste and beautiful workmanship. Under the dust it is a dark claret in color. It is said that the engine was built to be used by President Lincoln, but since the assassination attempt he is too infirm to travel. People begin to push to the edge of the platform, hauling their bags and worldly goods. I don't know how I will get our valise on. If Zeke could have come I could have at least insured that it was loaded on, but the Negroes are free now and they are not to help. The notice said no family Negroes could come to the station, although I see their faces here and there through the crowd.

The train stops outside the station to take on water.

"Is it your father?" my mother says diffidently. "Do you see him on the train?"

"No, Mother," I say. "We are taking the train."

"Are we going to see your father?" she asks.

It doesn't matter what I say to her, she'll forget it in a few minutes, but I cannot say yes to her. I cannot say that we will see my father even to give her a few moments of joy.

"Are we going to see your father?" she asks again.

"No," I say.

"Where are we going?"

I have carefully explained it all to her and she cried, every time I did. People are pushing down the platform toward the train, and I am trying to decide if I should move my valise toward the front of the platform. Why are they in such a hurry to get on the train? It is taking us all away.

"Where are we going? Julia Adelaide, you will answer me this moment," my mother says, her voice too full of quaver to quite sound like her own.

"I'm Clara," I say. "We're going to St. Louis."

"St. Louis," she says. "We don't need to go to St. Louis. We can't get through the lines, Julia, and I . . . I am quite indisposed. Let's go back home now, this is foolish."

We cannot go back home. General Dodge has made it clear that if we did not show up at the train platform this morning and get our names checked off the list, he would arrest every man in town, and then he would shoot every tenth man. The town knows to believe him, General Dodge was put in charge of the trains into Washington, and he did the same thing then. He arrested men and held them and every time the train was fired upon he hanged a man.

There is a shout and I can only see the crowd moving like a wave, pouring off the edge of the platform. Everyone is afraid there will not be room. I grab the valise and I grab my mother's arm and pull them both. The valise is so heavy that my fingers hurt, and the weight of our water and food is heavy on my arm. My mother is small and when I put her in bed at night she is all tiny like a child, but now she refuses to move, pulling against me and opening her mouth wide, her mouth pink inside and wet and open in a wail I can just barely hear over the shouting crowd. I don't know if I should let go of the valise to pull her, or for a moment I think of letting go of her, letting someone else get her on the train and finding her later.

A man in the crowd shoves her hard from behind. His face is twisted in wrath. What is he so angry at? My mother falls into me, and the crowd pushes us. I am trying to hold on to the valise, but my gloves are slippery, and I can only hold with my right hand, with my left I am trying to hold up my mother. The crowd is pushing all around us, trying to push us toward the edge of the platform.

The train toots as if it were moving. There is shouting all around us. My mother is fallen against me, her face pressed against my bosom, turned up toward me. She is so frightened. Her face is pressed against me in improper intimacy, as if she were my child. My mother as my child. I am filled with revulsion and horror. The pressure against us begins to lessen. I still have a hold of the valise. We'll be all right. Let the others push around, I'll wait and get the valise on somehow. They won't leave us travel without anything.

My mother's eyes close. Her wrinkled face looks up, the skin under her eyes making little pouches, as if it were a second blind eyelid. Everything is so grotesque. I am having a spell. I wish I could be somewhere where I could get away and close the windows. I have had these spells since they told us that my father was dead, where everything is full of horror and strangeness.

The person behind me is crowding into my back and I want to tell them to give way, but I cannot. People around us are crying out. I cannot see anything but the people pushed against me. People are still pushing, but now they are not pushing toward the side of the platform but toward the front, where the train will be when we are allowed to board.

Wait, I call out but there's no way for me to tell if I've really called out or not. I can't hear anything until the train whistles. The train has moved? They brought the train into the station? I can't tell, not without letting go of my mother and the valise. My mother is being pulled down into this mass. I feel her sliding against me. Her eyes are closed. She is a huge doll, limp in my arms. She is not even trying to hold herself up. She has given up to this moment.

I can't hold on to my mother and the valise. So I let go of the valise.

Oh merciful god.

I do not know how I will get through this moment.

The crowd around me is a thing that presses me and pushes me up, pulls me down. I cannot breathe for the pressure. I see specks in front of my eyes, white sparks, too bright, like metal and like light. My feet aren't under me. I am buoyed by the crowd and my feet are behind me. I am unable to stand, unable to fall. I think my mother is against me, but I can't tell, and in this mass I don't know how she can breathe.

I think I am going to die.

All the noise around me does not seem like noise anymore. It is something else, some element, like water or something, surrounding me and overpowering me.

It is like that for a long time, until finally I have my feet under me, and I'm leaning against people. I feel myself sink, but I can't stop myself. The platform is solid. My whole body feels bruised and roughly used.

My mother is not with me. My mother is a bundle of black on the ground, and I crawl to her. I wish I could say that as I crawl to her I feel concern for her condition, but at this moment I am no more than base animal nature and I crawl to her because she is mine and there is nothing else in the world I can identify as mine. Her skirt is rucked up so that her ankles and calves are showing. Her face is black. At first I think it something about her clothes, but it is her face, so full of blood that it is black.

People are still getting on the train, but there are people on the platform around us, left behind. And other things. A surprising number of shoes, all badly used. Wraps, too. Bags. Bundles and people.

I try raising her arms above her head, to force breath into her lungs. Her arms are thin, but they don't go the way I want them to. I read in the newspaper that when President Lincoln was shot, he stopped breathing, and his personal physician started him breathing again. But maybe the newspaper was wrong, or maybe it is more complicated than I understand, or maybe it doesn't always work. She doesn't breathe.

I sit on the platform and try to think of what to do next. My head is empty of useful thoughts. Empty of prayers.

"Ma'am?"

It's a soldier of the G.A.R.

"Yes sir?" I say. It is difficult to look up at him, to look up into the sun.

He hunkers down but does not touch her. At least he doesn't touch her. "Do you have anyone staying behind?"

Like cousins or something? Someone who is not "recalcitrant" in their handling of their Negroes? "Not in town," I say.

"Did she worship?" he asks, in his northern way.

"Yes sir," I say, "she did. She was a Methodist, and you should contact the preacher. The Reverend Robert Ewald, sir."

"I'll see to it, ma'am. Now you'll have to get on the train."

"And leave her?" I say.

"Yes ma'am, the train will be leaving. I'm sorry ma'am."

"But I can't," I say.

He takes my elbow and helps me stand. And I let him.

"We are not really recalcitrant," I say. "Where were Zeke and Rachel supposed to go? Were we supposed to throw them out?"

He helps me climb onto the train. People stare at me as I get on, and I realize I must be all in disarray. I stand under all their gazes, trying to get my bonnet on straight and smoothing my dress. I do not know what to do with my eyes or hands.

There are no seats. Will I have to stand until St. Louis? I grab a seat back to hold myself up. It is suddenly warm and everything is distant and I think I am about to faint. My stomach turns. I breathe through my mouth, not even sure that I am holding on to the seat back.

But I don't fall, thank Jesus.

"It's not Lincoln," someone is saying, a man's voice, rich and baritone, and I fasten on the words as a lifeline, drawing myself back to the train car, to the world. "It's Seward. Lincoln no longer has the capacity to govern."

The train smells of bodies and warm sweaty wool. It is a smell that threatens to undo me, so I must concentrate on breathing through my mouth. I breathe in little pants, like a dog. The heat lies against my skin. It is airless.

"Of course Lincoln can no longer govern, but that damned actor made him a saint when he shot him," says a second voice, "And now no one dare oppose him. It doesn't matter if his policies make sense or not."

"You're wrong," says the first. "Seward is governing through him. Lincoln is an imbecile. He can't govern, look at the way he handled the war."

The second snorts. "He won."

"No," says the first, "we *lost*, there is a difference, sir. We lost even though the north never could find a competent general." I know the type of the first one. He's the one who thinks he is brilliant, who always knew what President Davis should have done. If they are looking for a recalcitrant southerner, they have found one.

"Grant was competent. Just not brilliant. Any military man who is not Alexander the Great is going to look inadequate in comparison with General Lee."

"Grant was a drinker," the first one says. "It was his subordinates. They'd been through years of war. They knew what to do."

It is so hot on the train. I wonder how long until the train leaves.

I wonder if the Reverend will write my sister in Tennessee and tell her about our mother. I wish the train were going east toward Tennessee instead of north and west toward St. Louis.

My valise. All I have. It is on the platform. I turn and go to the door. It is closed and I try the handle, but it is too stiff for me. I look around for help.

"It's locked," says a woman in gray. She doesn't look unkind.

"My things, I left them on the platform," I say.

"Oh, honey," she says, "they aren't going to let you back out there. They don't let anyone off the train."

I look out the window but I can't see the valise. I can see some of the soldiers, so I beat on the window. One of them glances up at me, frowning, but then he ignores me.

The train blows that it is going to leave, and I beat harder on the glass. If I could shatter that glass. They don't understand, they would help me if they understood. The train lurches and I stagger. It is out there, somewhere, on that platform. Clothes for my mother and me, blankets, things we will need. Things I will need.

The train pulls out of the station and I feel so terrible I sit down on the floor in all the dirt from people's feet and sob.

The train creeps slowly at first, but then picks up speed. The clack-clack clack-clack rocks me. It is improper, but I allow it to rock me. I am in others' hands now and there is nothing to do but be patient. I am good at that. So it has been all my life. I have tried to be dutiful, but something in me has not bent right, and I have never been able to maintain a Christian frame of mind, but like a chicken in a yard, I have always kept my eyes on the small things. I have tended to what was in front of me, first the house, then my mother. When we could not get sugar, I learned to cook with molasses and honey. Now I sit and let my mind go empty and let the train rock me.

"Child," someone says. "Child."

The woman in gray has been trying to get my attention for awhile, but I have been sitting and letting myself be rocked.

"Child," she says again, "would you like some water?"

Yes, I realize, I would. She has a jar and she gives it to me to sip out of. "Thank you," I say. "We brought water, but we lost it in the crush on the platform."

"You have someone with you?" she asks.

"My mother," I say, and start crying again. "She is old, and there was such a press on the platform, and she fell and was trampled."

"What's your name?" the woman says.

"Clara Corbett," I say.

"I'm Elizabeth Loudon," the woman says. "And you are welcome to travel with me." There is something about her, a simple pleasantness, that makes me trust her. She is a small woman, with a small nose and eyes as gray as her dress. She is younger than I first thought, maybe only in her thirties? "How old are you? Do you have family?" she asks.

"I am seventeen. I have a sister, Julia. But she doesn't live in Mississippi anymore."

"Where does she live?" the woman asks.

"In Beech Bluff, near Jackson, Tennessee."

She shakes her head. "I don't know it. Is it good country?"

"I think so," I say. "In her letters it sounds like good country. But I haven't seen her for seven years." Of course no one could travel during the war. She has three children in Tennessee. My sister is twenty-eight, almost as old as this woman. It is hard to imagine.

"Were you close?" she asks.

I don't know that we were close. But she is my sister. She is all I have, now. I hope that the reverend will write her about my mother, but I don't know that he knows where she is. I will have to write her. She will think I should have taken better care.

"Are you traveling alone?"

"My companion is a few seats farther in front. He and I could not find seats together."

Her companion is a man? Not her husband, maybe her brother? But she would say her brother if that's who she meant. A woman traveling with a man. An adventuress, I think. There are stories of women traveling, hoping to find unattached girls like myself. They befriend the young girls and then deliver them to the brothels of New Orleans.

For a moment Elizabeth takes on a sinister cast. But this is a train full of recalcitrant southerners, there is no opportunity to kidnap anyone. Elizabeth is like me, a woman who has lost her home.

It takes the rest of the day and a night to get to St. Louis, and Elizabeth and I talk. It's as if we talk in ciphers, instead of talking about home we talk about gardening, and I can see the garden at home, lazy with bees. She is a quilter. I don't quilt, but I used to do petit pointe, so we can talk sewing and about how hard it has been to get colors. And we talk about mending and making do, we have all been making do for so long.

When it gets dark, since I have no seat, I stay where I am sitting by the door of the train. I am so tired, but in the darkness all I can think of is my mother's face in the crowd and her hopeless open mouth. I don't want to think of my mother, but I am in a delirium of fatigue, surrounded by the dark and the rumble of the train and the distant murmur of voices. I sleep sitting by the door of the train, fitful and rocked. I have dreams like fever dreams. In my dream I am in a strange house, but it is supposed to be my own house, but nothing is where it should be, and I begin to believe that I have actually entered a stranger's house, and that they'll return and find me here. When I wake up and go back to sleep, I am back in this strange house, looking through things.

I wake before dawn, only a little rested. My shoulders and hips and back all ache from the way I am leaning, but I have no energy to get up. I have no energy to do anything but endure. Elizabeth nods, sometimes awake, sometimes asleep, but neither of us speak.

Finally the train slows. We come in through a town, but the town seems to go on and on. It must be St. Louis. We stop and sit. The sun comes up and heats the car like an oven. There is no movement of the air. There are so many buildings in St. Louis, and so many of them are tall, two stories, that I wonder if they cut off the wind and that is why it's so still. But finally the train lurches and we crawl into the station.

I am one of the first off the train by virtue of my position near the door. A soldier unlocks it and shouts for all of us to disembark, but he need not have bothered for there is a rush. I am borne ahead at its beginning but I can stop at the back of the platform. I am afraid that I have lost Elizabeth, but I see her in the crowd. She is on the arm of a younger man in a bowler. There is something about his air that marks him as different—he is sprightly and apparently fresh even after the long ride.

I almost let them pass, but the prospect of being alone makes me reach out and touch her shoulder.

"There you are," she says.

We join a queue of people waiting to use a trench. The smell is appalling, ammonia acrid and eye-watering. There is a wall to separate the men from the women, but the women are all together. I crouch, trying not to notice anyone and trying to keep my skirts out of the filth. It is so awful. It's worse than anything. I feel so awful.

What if my mother were here? What would I do? I think maybe it was better, maybe it was God's hand. But that is an awful thought, too.

"Child," Elizabeth says when I come out, "what's the matter?"

"It's so awful," I say. "I shouldn't cry, but I just want to be home and clean. I want to go to bed and sleep.

She offers me a biscuit.

"You should save your food," I say.

"Don't worry," Elizabeth says. "We have enough."

I shouldn't accept it, but I am so hungry. And when I have a little to eat, I feel a little better.

I try to imagine what the fort will be like where we will be going. Will we have a place to sleep, or will it be barracks? Or worse yet, tents? Although after the night I spent on the train I can't imagine anything that could be worse. I imagine if I have to stay awhile in a tent then I'll make the best of it.

"I think this being in limbo is perhaps worse than anything we can expect at the end," I say to Elizabeth. She smiles.

She introduces her companion, Michael. He is enough like her to be her brother, but I don't think that they are. I am resolved not to ask, if they want to tell me they can.

We are standing together, not saying anything, when there is some commotion farther up the platform. It is a woman, her black dress is like smoke. She is running down the platform, coming toward us. There are all of these people and yet it is as if there is no obstacle for her. "NO NO NO NO, DON'T TOUCH ME! FILTHY HANDS! DON'T LET THEM TOUCH YOU! DON'T GET ON THE TRAINS!"

People are getting out of her way. Where are the soldiers? The fabric of her dress is so threadbare it is rotten and torn at the seams. Her skirt is greasy black and matted and stained. Her face is so thin. "ANIMALS! THERE IS NOTHING OUT THERE! PEOPLE DON'T HAVE FOOD! THERE IS NOTHING THERE BUT INDIANS! THEY SENT US OUT TO SETTLE BUT THERE WAS NOTHING THERE!"

I expect she will run past me but she grabs my arm and stops and looks into my face. She has light eyes, pale eyes in her dark face. She is mad.

"WE WERE ALL STARVING, SO WE WENT TO THE FORT BUT THE FORT HAD NOTHING. YOU WILL ALL STARVE, THE WAY THEY ARE STARVING THE INDIANS! THEY WILL LET US ALL DIE! THEY DON'T CARE!" She is screaming in my face, and her spittle sprays me, warm as her breath. Her hand is all tendons and twigs, but she's so strong I can't escape.

The soldiers grab her and yank her away from me. My arm aches where she was holding it. I can't stand up.

Elizabeth pulls me upright. "Stay close to me," she says and starts to walk the other way down the platform. People are looking up following the screaming woman.

She pulls me along with her. I keep thinking of the woman's hand and wrist turned black with grime. I remember my mother's face was black when she lay on the platform. Black like something rotted.

"Here," Elizabeth says at an old door, painted green but now weathered. The door opens and we pass inside.

"What?" I say. My eyes are accustomed to the morning brightness and I can't see.

"Her name is Clara," Elizabeth says. "She has people in Tennessee."

"Come with me," says another woman. She sounds older. "Step this way. Where are her things?"

I am being kidnapped. Oh merciful God, I'll die. I let out a moan.

"Her things were lost, her mother was killed in a crush on the platform."

The woman in the dark clucks sympathetically. "Poor dear. Does Michael have his passenger yet?"

"In a moment," Elizabeth says. "We were lucky for the commotion."

I am beginning to be able to see. It is a storage room, full of abandoned things. The woman holding my arm is older. There are some broken chairs and a stool. She sits me in the chair. Is Elizabeth some kind of adventuress?

"Who are you?" I ask.

"We are friends," Elizabeth says. "We will help you get to your sister."

I don't believe them. I will end up in New Orleans. Elizabeth is some kind of adventuress.

After a moment the door opens and this time it is Michael with a young man. "This is Andrew," he says.

A man? What do they want with a man? That is what stops me from saying, "Run!" Andrew is blinded by the change in light, and I can see the astonishment working on his face, the way it must be working on mine. "What is this?" he asks.

"You are with Friends," Michael says, and maybe he has said it differently than Elizabeth, or maybe it is just that this time I have had the wit to hear it.

"Quakers?" Andrew says. "Abolitionists?"

Michael smiles, I can see his teeth white in the darkness. "Just Friends," he says.

Abolitionists. Crazy people who steal slaves to set them free. Have they come to kidnap us? We are recalcitrant southerners, I have never heard of Quakers seeking revenge, but everyone knows the Abolitionists are crazy and they are liable to do anything.

"We'll have to wait here until they begin to move people out, it will be evening before we can leave," says the older woman.

I am so frightened, I just want to be home. Maybe I should try to break free and run out to the platform, there are northern soldiers out there. Would they protect me? And then what, go to a fort in Oklahoma?

The older woman asks Michael how they could get past the guards so early and he tells her about the madwoman. A "refugee" he calls her.

"They'll just take her back," Elizabeth says, sighing.

Take her back, do they mean that she really came from Oklahoma? They talk about how bad it will be this winter. Michael says there are Wisconsin Indians resettled down there, but they've got no food, and they've been starving on government handouts for a couple of years. Now there will be more people. They're not prepared for winter.

There can't have been much handout during the war. It was hard enough to feed the armies.

They explain to Andrew and to me that we will sneak out of the train station this evening, after dark. We will spend a day with a Quaker family in St. Louis, and then they will send us on to the next family. And so we will be passed hand to hand, like a bucket in a brigade, until we get to our families.

They call it the underground railroad.

But we are slave owners.

"Wrong is wrong," says Elizabeth. "Some of us can't stand and watch people starve."

"But only two out of the whole train," Andrew says.

Michael sighs.

The old woman nods. "It isn't right."

Elizabeth picked me because my mother died. If my mother had not died, I would be out there, on my way to starve with the rest of them.

I can't help it but I start to cry. I should not profit from my mother's death. I should have kept her safe.

"Hush, now," says Elizabeth. "Hush, you'll be okay."

"It's not right," I whisper. I'm trying not to be loud, we mustn't be discovered.

"What, child?"

"You shouldn't have picked me," I say. But I am crying so hard I don't think they can understand me. Elizabeth strokes my hair and wipes my face. It may be the last time someone will do these things for me. My sister has three children of her own, and she won't need another child. I'll have to work hard to make up my keep.

There are blankets there and we lie down on the hard floor, all except Michael, who sits in a chair and sleeps. I sleep this time with fewer dreams. But when I wake up, although I can't remember what they were, I have the feeling that I have been dreaming restless dreams.

The stars are bright when we finally creep out of the station. A night full of stars. The stars will be the same in Tennessee. The platform is empty, the train and the people are gone. The Lincoln Train has gone back south while we slept, to take more people out of Mississippi.

"Will you come back and save more people?" I ask Elizabeth.

The stars are a banner behind her quiet head. "We will save what we can," she says.

It isn't fair that I was picked. "I want to help," I tell her.

She is silent for a moment. "We only work with our own," she says. There is something in her voice that has not been there before. A sharpness.

"What do you mean?" I ask.

"There are no slavers in our ranks," she says and her voice is cold.

I feel as if I have had a fever; tired, but clear of mind. I have never walked so far and not walked beyond a town. The streets of St. Louis are empty. There are few lights. Far off a woman is singing, and her voice is clear and carries easily in the night. A beautiful voice.

"Elizabeth," Michael says, "she is just a girl."

"She needs to know," Elizabeth says.

"Why did you save me then?" I ask.

"One does not fight evil with evil," Elizabeth says.

"I'm not evil!" I say.

But no one answers.

wang's carpets

GREG EGAN

Looking back at the century that's just ended, it's obvious that Australian writer Greg Egan was one of the big new names to emerge in SF in the nineties, and is probably one of the most significant talents to enter the field in the last several decades. Already one of the most widely known of all Australian genre writers, Egan may well be the best new "hard-science" writer to enter the field since Greg Bear, and is still growing in range, power, and sophistication. In the last few years, he has become a frequent contributor to *Interzone* and *Asimov's Science Fiction*, and has made sales as well to *Pulphouse, Analog, Aurealis, Eidolon*, and elsewhere; many of his stories have also appeared in various "Best of the Year" series, and he was on the Hugo Final Ballot in 1995 for his story "Cocoon," which won the Ditmar Award and the Asimov's Readers Award. He won the Hugo Award in 1999 for his novella "Oceanic." His stories have appeared in our Eighth through Thirteenth, and our Sixteenth through Nineteenth annual collections. His first novel, *Quarantine*, appeared in 1992; his second novel, *Permutation City*, won the John W. Campbell Memorial Award in 1994. His other books include the novels *Distress, Diaspora*, and *Teranesia*, and three collections of his short fiction: *Axiomatic, Luminous*, and *Our Lady of Chernobyl*. His most recent book is a new novel, *Schild's Ladder*. He has a Web site at http://www.netspace.netau/^gregegan/.

Like Bear's "Blood Music," like Stross's "Lobsters," the story that follows was one of those seminal stories that change the history of SF by changing the way that *other science fiction writers* think about the future. In it, in a story unmatched for the bravura sweep and pure originality of its conceptualization, Egan basically reinvents the space-travel story for a new generation, as well as providing us with a first-contact story unlike any you've ever read before. . . .

Waiting to be cloned one thousand times and scattered across ten million cubic light-years, Paolo Venetti relaxed in his favorite ceremonial bathtub: a tiered hexagonal pool set in a courtyard of black marble flecked with gold. Paolo wore full traditional anatomy, uncomfortable garb at first, but the warm currents flowing across his back and shoulders slowly eased him into a pleasant torpor. He could have reached the same state in an instant, by decree—but the occasion seemed to demand the complete ritual of verisimilitude, the ornate curlicued longhand of imitation physical cause and effect.

As the moment of diaspora approached, a small gray lizard darted across the courtyard, claws scrabbling. It halted by the far edge of the pool, and Paolo marveled at the delicate pulse of its breathing, and watched the lizard watching him, until it moved again, disappearing into the surrounding vineyards. The environment was full of birds and insects, rodents and small reptiles—decorative in appearance, but also satisfying a more abstract aesthetic: softening the harsh radial symmetry of the lone observer; anchoring the simulation by perceiving it from a multitude of viewpoints. Ontological guy lines. No one had asked the lizards if they wanted to be cloned, though. They were coming along for the ride, like it or not.

The sky above the courtyard was warm and blue, cloudless and sunless, isotropic. Paolo waited calmly, prepared for every one of half a dozen possible fates.

An invisible bell chimed softly, three times. Paolo laughed, delighted.

One chime would have meant that he was still on Earth: an anti-climax, certainly—but there would have been advantages to compensate for that. Everyone who really mattered to him lived in the Carter-Zimmerman polis, but not all of them had chosen to take part in the diaspora to the same degree; his Earth-self would have lost no one. Helping to ensure that the thousand ships were safely dispatched would have been satisfying, too. And remaining a member of the wider Earth-based community, plugged into the entire global culture in real-time, would have been an attraction in itself.

Two chimes would have meant that this clone of Carter-Zimmerman had reached a planetary system devoid of life. Paolo had run a sophisticated—but non-sapient—self-predictive model before deciding to wake under those conditions. Exploring a handful of alien worlds, however barren, had seemed likely to be an enriching experience for him—with the distinct advantage that the whole endeavor would be untrammeled by the kind of elaborate precautions necessary in the presence of alien life. C-Z's population would have fallen by more than half—and many of his closest friends would have been absent—but he would have forged new friendships, he was sure.

Four chimes would have signaled the discovery of intelligent aliens. Five, a technological civilization. Six, spacefarers.

Three chimes, though, meant that the scout probes had detected unambiguous signs of life—and that was reason enough for jubilation. Up until the moment of the pre-launch cloning—a subjective instant before the chimes had sounded—no reports of alien life had ever reached Earth. There'd been no guarantee that any part of the diaspora would find it.

Paolo willed the polis library to brief him; it promptly rewired the declarative memory of his simulated traditional brain with all the information he was likely to need to satisfy his immediate curiosity. This clone of C-Z had arrived at Vega, the second closest of the thousand target stars, twenty-seven light-years from Earth. Paolo closed his eyes and visualized a star map with a thousand lines radiating out from the sun, then zoomed in on the trajectory which described his own journey. It had taken three centuries to reach Vega—but the vast majority of the polis's twenty thousand inhabitants had programmed their exoselves to suspend them prior to the cloning, and to wake them only if and when they arrived at a suitable destination. Ninety-two citizens had chosen the alternative: experiencing every voyage of the diaspora from start to finish, risking disappointment, and even death. Paolo now knew that the ship aimed at Fomalhaut, the target nearest Earth, had been struck by debris and annihilated *en route*. He mourned the ninety-two, briefly. He hadn't been close to any of them, prior to the cloning, and the particular versions who'd willfully perished two centuries ago in interstellar space seemed as remote as the victims of some ancient calamity from the era of flesh.

Paolo examined his new home star through the cameras of one of the scout probes—and the strange filters of the ancestral visual system. In traditional colors, Vega was a fierce blue-white disk, laced with prominences. Three times the mass of the sun, twice the size and twice as hot, sixty times as luminous. Burning hydrogen fast—and already halfway through its allotted five hundred million years on the main sequence.

Vega's sole planet, Orpheus, had been a featureless blip to the best lunar interferometers; now Paolo gazed down on its blue-green crescent, ten thousand kilometers below Carter-Zimmerman itself. Orpheus was terrestrial, a nickel-iron-silicate world; slightly larger than Earth, slightly warmer—a billion kilometers took the edge off Vega's heat—and almost drowning in liquid water. Impatient to see the whole surface firsthand, Paolo slowed his clock rate a thousandfold, allowing C-Z to circumnavigate the planet in twenty subjective seconds, daylight unshrouding a broad new swath with each pass. Two slender ocher-colored continents with mountainous spines bracketed hemispheric oceans, and dazzling expanses of pack ice covered both poles—far more so in the north, where jagged white peninsulas radiated out from the midwinter arctic darkness.

The Orphean atmosphere was mostly nitrogen—six times as much as on Earth; probably split by UV from primordial ammonia—with traces of water vapor and carbon dioxide, but not enough of either for a runaway greenhouse effect. The high atmospheric pressure meant reduced evaporation—Paolo saw not a wisp of cloud—and the large, warm oceans in turn helped feed carbon dioxide back into the crust, locking it up in limestone sediments destined for subduction.

The whole system was young, by Earth standards, but Vega's greater mass, and a denser protostellar cloud, would have meant swifter passage through most of the traumas of birth: nuclear ignition and early luminosity fluctuations; planetary coalescence and the age of bombardments. The library estimated that Orpheus had enjoyed a relatively stable climate, and freedom from major impacts, for at least the past hundred million years.

Long enough for primitive life to appear—

A hand seized Paolo firmly by the ankle and tugged him beneath the water. He offered no resistance, and let the vision of the planet slip away. Only two other people in C-Z had free access to this environment—and his father didn't play games with his now-twelve-hundred-year-old son.

Elena dragged him all the way to the bottom of the pool, before releasing his foot and hovering above him, a triumphant silhouette against the bright surface. She was ancestor-shaped, but obviously cheating; she spoke with perfect clarity, and no air bubbles at all.

"Late sleeper! I've been waiting seven weeks for this!"

Paolo feigned indifference, but he was fast running out of breath. He had his exoself convert him into an amphibious human variant—biologically and historically authentic, if no longer the definitive ancestral phenotype. Water flooded into his modified lungs, and his modified brain welcomed it.

He said, "Why would I want to waste consciousness, sitting around waiting for the scout probes to refine their observations? I woke as soon as the data was unambiguous."

She pummeled his chest; he reached up and pulled her down, instinctively reducing his buoyancy to compensate, and they rolled across the bottom of the pool, kissing.

Elena said, "You know we're the first C-Z to arrive, anywhere? The Fomalhaut ship was destroyed. So there's only one other pair of us. Back on Earth."

"So?" Then he remembered. Elena had chosen not to wake if any other version of her had already encountered life. Whatever fate befell each of the remaining ships, every other version of him would have to live without her.

He nodded soberly, and kissed her again. "What am I meant to say? You're a thousand times more precious to me, now?"

"Yes."

"Ah, but what about the you-and-I on Earth? Five hundred times would be closer to the truth."

"There's no poetry in five hundred."

"Don't be so defeatist. Rewire your language centers."

She ran her hands along the sides of his ribcage, down to his hips. They made love with their almost-traditional bodies—and brains; Paolo was amused to the point of distraction when his limbic system went into overdrive, but he remembered enough from the last occasion to bury his self-consciousness and surrender to the strange hijacker. It wasn't like making love in any civilized fashion—the rate of information exchange between them was minuscule, for a start—but it had the raw insistent quality of most ancestral pleasures.

Then they drifted up to the surface of the pool and lay beneath the radiant sunless sky.

Paolo thought: *I've crossed twenty-seven light-years in an instant. I'm orbiting the first planet ever found to hold alien life. And I've sacrificed nothing—left nothing I truly value behind. This is too good, too good.* He felt a pang of regret for his other selves—it was hard to imagine them faring as well, without Elena, without Orpheus—but there was nothing he could do about that, now. Although there'd be time to confer with Earth before any more ships reached their destinations, he'd decided—prior to the cloning—not to allow the unfolding of his manifold future to be swayed by any change of heart. Whether or not his Earth-self agreed, the two of them were powerless to alter the criteria for waking. The self with the right to choose for the thousand had passed away.

No matter, Paolo decided. The others would find—or construct—their own reasons for happiness. And there was still the chance that one of them would wake to the sound of *four chimes.*

Elena said, "If you'd slept much longer, you would have missed the vote."

The vote? The scouts in low orbit had gathered what data they could about Orphean biology. To proceed any further, it would be necessary to send microprobes into the ocean itself—an escalation of contact which required the approval of two-thirds of the polis. There was no compelling reason to believe that the presence of a few million tiny robots could do any harm; all they'd leave behind in the water was a few kilojoules of waste heat. Nevertheless, a faction had arisen which advocated caution. The citizens of Carter-Zimmerman, they argued, could continue to observe from a distance for another decade, or another millennium, refining their observations and hypotheses before intruding . . . and those who disagreed could always sleep away the time, or find other interests to pursue.

Paolo delved into his library-fresh knowledge of the "carpets"—the single Orphean lifeform detected so far. They were free-floating creatures living in the equatorial ocean depths—apparently destroyed by UV if they drifted too close to the surface. They grew to a size of hundreds of meters, then fissioned into dozens of fragments, each of which continued to grow. It was tempting to assume that they were colonies of single-celled organisms, something like giant kelp—but there was no real evidence yet to back that up. It was difficult enough for the scout probes to discern the carpets' gross appearance and behavior through a kilometer of water, even with Vega's copious neutrinos lighting the way; remote observations on a microscopic scale, let alone biochemical analyses, were out of the question. Spectroscopy revealed that the surface water was full of intriguing molecular debris—but guessing the relationship of any of it to the living carpets was like trying to reconstruct human biochemistry by studying human ashes.

Paolo turned to Elena. "What do you think?"

She moaned theatrically; the topic must have been argued to death while he slept. "The microprobes are harmless. They could tell us exactly what the carpets are made of, without removing a single molecule. What's the risk? *Culture shock?*"

Paolo flicked water onto her face, affectionately; the impulse seemed to come with the amphibian body. "You can't be sure that they're not intelligent."

"Do you know what was living on Earth, two hundred million years after it was formed?"

"Maybe cyanobacteria. Maybe nothing. This isn't Earth, though."

"True. But even in the unlikely event that the carpets are intelligent, do you think they'd notice the presence of robots a millionth their size? If they're unified organisms, they don't appear to react to anything in their environment—they have no predators, they don't pursue food, they just drift with the currents—so there's no reason for them to possess elaborate sense organs at all, let alone anything working on a sub-millimeter scale. And if they're colonies of single-celled creatures, one of which happens to collide with a microprobe and register its presence with surface receptors . . . what conceivable harm could that do?"

"I have no idea. But my ignorance is no guarantee of safety."

Elena splashed him back. "The only way to deal with your *ignorance* is to vote to send down the microprobes. We have to be cautious, I agree—but there's no point *being here* if we don't find out what's happening in the oceans, right now. I don't want to wait for this planet to evolve something smart enough to broadcast biochemistry lessons into space. If we're not willing to take a few infinitesimal risks, Vega will turn red giant before we learn anything."

It was a throwaway line—but Paolo tried to imagine witnessing the event. In a quarter of a billion years, would the citizens of Carter-Zimmerman be debating the ethics of intervening to rescue the Orpheans—or would they all have lost interest, and departed for other stars, or modified themselves into beings entirely devoid of nostalgic compassion for organic life?

Grandiose visions for a twelve-hundred-year-old. The Fomalhaut clone had been obliterated by one tiny piece of rock. There was far more junk in the Vegan system than in interstellar space; even ringed by defenses, its data backed up to all the far-flung scout probes, this C-Z was not invulnerable just because it had arrived intact. Elena was right; they had to seize the moment—or they might as well retreat into their own hermetic worlds and forget that they'd ever made the journey.

Paolo recalled the honest puzzlement of a friend from Ashton-Laval: *Why go looking for aliens? Our polis has a thousand ecologies, a trillion species of evolved life. What do you hope to find, out there, that you couldn't have grown at home?*

What had he hoped to find? Just the answers to a few simple questions. Did human consciousness bootstrap all of space-time into existence, in order to explain itself? Or had a neutral, pre-existing universe given birth to a billion varieties of conscious life, all capable of harboring the same delusions of grandeur—until they collided with each other? Anthrocosmology was used to justify the inward-looking stance of most polises: if the physical universe was created by human thought, it had no special status which placed it above virtual reality. It might have come first—and every virtual reality might need to run on a physical computing device, subject to physical laws—but it occupied no privileged position in terms of "truth" versus "illusion." If the ACs were right, then it was no more *honest* to value the physical universe over more recent artificial realities than it was honest to remain flesh instead of software, or ape instead of human, or bacterium instead of ape.

Elena said, "We can't lie here forever; the gang's all waiting to see you."

"Where?" Paolo felt his first pang of homesickness; on Earth, his circle of friends had always met in a real-time image of the Mount Pinatubo crater, plucked straight from the observation satellites. A recording wouldn't be the same.

"I'll show you."

Paolo reached over and took her hand. The pool, the sky, the courtyard vanished—and he found himself gazing down on Orpheus again . . . nightside, but far from dark, with his full mental palette now encoding everything from the pale wash of ground-current long-wave radio, to the multi-colored shimmer of isotopic gamma rays and back-scattered cosmic-ray bremsstrahlung. Half the abstract knowledge the library had fed him about the planet was obvious at a glance, now. The ocean's smoothly tapered thermal glow spelt *three-hundred Kelvin* instantly—as well as back-lighting the atmosphere's telltale infrared silhouette.

He was standing on a long, metallic-looking girder, one edge of a vast geodesic sphere, open to the blazing cathedral of space. He glanced up and saw the star-rich dust-clogged band of the Milky Way, encircling him from zenith to nadir; aware of the glow of every gas cloud, discerning each absorption and emission line, Paolo could almost feel the plane of the galactic disk transect him. Some constellations were distorted, but the view was more familiar than strange—and he recognized most of the old signposts by color. He had his bearings, now. Twenty degrees away from Sirius—south, by parochial Earth reckoning—faint but unmistakable: the sun.

Elena was beside him—superficially unchanged, although they'd both shrugged off the constraints of biology. The conventions of this environment mimicked the physics of real macroscopic objects in free-fall and vacuum, but it wasn't set up to model any kind of chemistry, let alone that of flesh and blood. Their new bodies were human-shaped, but devoid of elaborate microstructure—and their minds weren't embedded in the physics at all, but were running directly on the processor web.

Paolo was relieved to be back to normal; ceremonial regression to the ancestral form was a venerable C-Z tradition—and being human was largely self-affirming, while it lasted—but every time he emerged from the experience, he felt as if he'd broken free of billion-year-old shackles. There were polises on Earth where the citizens would have found his present structure almost as archaic: a consciousness dominated by sensory perception, an illusion of possessing solid form, a single time coordinate. The last flesh human had died long before Paolo was constructed, and apart from the communities of Gleisner robots, Carter-Zimmerman was about as conservative as a transhuman society could be. The balance seemed right to Paolo, though—acknowledging the flexibility of software, without abandoning interest in the physical world—and although the stubbornly corporeal Gleisners had been first to the stars, the C-Z diaspora would soon overtake them.

Their friends gathered round, showing off their effortless free-fall acrobatics, greeting Paolo and chiding him for not arranging to wake sooner; he was the last of the gang to emerge from hibernation.

"Do you like our humble new meeting place?" Hermann floated by Paolo's shoulder, a chimeric cluster of limbs and sense-organs, speaking through the vacuum in modulated infrared. "We call it Satellite Pinatubo. It's desolate up here, I know—but we were afraid it might violate the spirit of caution if we dared pretend to walk the Orphean surface."

Paolo glanced mentally at a scout probe's close-up of a typical stretch of dry land, an expanse of fissured red rock. "More desolate down there, I think." He was tempted to touch the ground—to let the private vision become tactile—but he resisted. Being elsewhere in the middle of a conversation was bad etiquette.

"Ignore Hermann," Liesl advised. "He wants to flood Orpheus with our alien machinery before we have any idea what the effects might be." Liesl was a green-and-turquoise butterfly, with a stylized human face stippled in gold on each wing.

Paolo was surprised; from the way Elena had spoken, he'd assumed that his friends must have come to a consensus in favor of the microprobes—and only a late sleeper, new to the issues, would bother to argue the point. "What effects? The carpets—"

"Forget the carpets! Even if the carpets are as simple as they look, we don't know what else is down there." As Liesl's wings fluttered, her mirror-image faces seemed to glance at each other for support. "With neutrino imaging, we barely achieve spatial resolution in meters, time resolution in seconds. We don't know anything about smaller lifeforms."

"And we never will, if you have your way." Karpal—an ex-Gleisner, human-shaped as ever—had been Liesl's lover, last time Paolo was awake.

"We've only been here for a fraction of an Orphean year! There's still a wealth of data we could gather non-intrusively, with a little patience. There might be rare beachings of ocean life—"

Elena said dryly, "Rare indeed. Orpheus has negligible tides, shallow waves, very few storms. And anything beached would be fried by UV before we glimpsed anything more instructive than we're already seeing in the surface water."

"Not necessarily. The carpets seem to be vulnerable—but other species might be better protected, if they live nearer to the surface. And Orpheus is seismically active; we should at least wait for a tsunami to dump a few cubic kilometers of ocean onto a shoreline, and see what it reveals."

Paolo smiled; he hadn't thought of that. A tsunami might be worth waiting for.

Liesl continued, "What is there to lose, by waiting a few hundred Orphean years? At the very least, we could gather baseline data on seasonal climate patterns—and we could watch for anomalies, storms and quakes, hoping for some revelatory glimpses."

A few hundred Orphean years? A *few terrestrial millennia?* Paolo's ambivalence waned. If he'd wanted to inhabit geological time, he would have migrated to the Lokhande polis, where the Order of Contemplative Observers watched Earth's mountains erode in subjective seconds. Orpheus hung in the sky beneath them, a beautiful puzzle waiting to be decoded, demanding to be understood.

He said, "But what if there *are* no 'revelatory glimpses'? How long do we wait? We don't know how rare life is—in time, or in space. If this planet is precious, *so is the epoch it's passing through*. We don't know how rapidly Orphean biology is evolving; species might appear and vanish while we agonize over the risks of gathering better data. The carpets—and whatever else—could die out before we'd learnt the first thing about them. What a waste that would be!"

Liesl stood her ground.

"And if we damage the Orphean ecology—or culture—by rushing in? That wouldn't be a waste. It would be a tragedy."

Paolo assimilated all the stored transmissions from his Earth-self—almost three hundred years' worth—before composing a reply. The early communications included detailed mind grafts—and it was good to share the excitement of the diaspora's launch; to watch—very nearly firsthand—the thousand ships, nanomachine-carved from asteroids, depart in a blaze of fusion fire from beyond the orbit of Mars. Then things settled down to the usual prosaic matters: Elena, the gang, shameless gossip, Carter-Zimmerman's ongoing research projects, the buzz of interpolis cultural tensions, the not-quite-cyclic convulsions of the arts (the perceptual aesthetic overthrows the emotional, again . . . although Valladas in Konishi polis claims to have constructed a new synthesis of the two).

After the first fifty years, his Earth-self had begun to hold things back; by the time news reached Earth of the Fomalhaut clone's demise, the messages had become pure audiovisual linear monologues. Paolo understood. It was only right; they'd diverged, and you didn't send mind grafts to strangers.

Most of the transmissions had been broadcast to all of the ships, indiscriminately. Forty-three years ago, though, his Earth-self had sent a special message to the Vega-bound clone.

"The new lunar spectroscope we finished last year has just picked up clear signs of water on Orpheus. There should be large temperate oceans waiting for you, if the models are right. So . . . good luck." Vision showed the instrument's domes growing out of the rock of the lunar farside; plots of the Orphean spectral data; an ensemble of planetary models. "Maybe it seems strange to you—all the trouble we're taking to catch a glimpse of what you're going to see in close-up, so soon. It's hard to explain: I don't think it's jealousy, or even impatience. Just a need for independence.

"There's been a revival of the old debate: should we consider redesigning our minds to encompass interstellar distances? One self spanning thousands of stars, not via cloning, but through acceptance of the natural time scale of the light-speed lag. Millennia passing between mental events. Local contingencies dealt with by non-conscious systems." Essays, pro and con, were appended; Paolo ingested summaries. "I don't think the idea will gain much support, though—and the new astronomical projects are something of an antidote. We have to make peace with the fact that we've stayed behind . . . so we cling to the Earth—looking outwards, but remaining firmly anchored.

"I keep asking myself, though: where do we go from here? History can't guide us. Evolution can't guide us. The C-Z charter says *understand and respect the universe* . . . but in what form? On what scale? With what kind of senses, what kind of minds? We can become anything at all—and that space of possible futures dwarfs the galaxy. Can we explore it without losing our way? Flesh humans used to spin fantasies about aliens arriving to 'conquer' Earth, to steal their 'precious' physical resources, to wipe them out for fear of 'competition' . . . as if a species capable of making the journey wouldn't have had the power, or the wit, or the imagination, to rid itself of obsolete biological imperatives. *Conquering the galaxy* is what bacteria with spaceships would do—knowing no better, having no choice.

"Our condition is the opposite of that: we have no end of choices. That's why we need to find alien life—not just to break the spell of the anthrocosmologists. We need to find aliens who've faced the same decisions—and discovered how to live, what to become. We need to understand what it means to inhabit the universe."

Paolo watched the crude neutrino images of the carpets moving in staccato jerks around his dodecahedral room. Twenty-four ragged oblongs drifted above him, daughters of a larger ragged oblong which had just fissioned. Models suggested that shear forces from ocean currents could explain the whole process, triggered by nothing more than the parent reaching a critical size. The purely mechanical break-up of a colony—if that was what it was—might have little to do with the life cycle of the constituent organisms. It was frustrating. Paolo was accustomed to a torrent of data on anything which caught his interest; for the diaspora's great discovery to remain nothing more than a sequence of coarse monochrome snapshots was intolerable.

He glanced at a schematic of the scout probes' neutrino detectors, but there was no obvious scope for improvement. Nuclei in the detectors were excited into unstable high-energy states, then kept there by fine-tuned gamma-ray lasers picking off lower-energy eigenstates faster than they could creep into existence and attract a transition. Changes in neutrino flux of one part in ten-to-the-fifteenth could shift the energy levels far enough to disrupt the balancing act. The carpets cast a shadow so faint, though, that even this near-perfect vision could barely resolve it.

Orlando Venetti said, "You're awake."

Paolo turned. His father stood an arm's length away, presenting as an ornately clad human of indeterminate age. Definitely older than Paolo, though; Orlando never ceased to play up his seniority—even if the age difference was only twenty-five percent now, and falling.

Paolo banished the carpets from the room to the space behind one pentagonal window, and took his father's hand. The portions of Orlando's mind which meshed with his own expressed pleasure at Paolo's emergence from hibernation, fondly dwelt on past shared experiences, and entertained hopes of continued harmony between father and son. Paolo's greeting was similar, a carefully contrived "revelation" of his own emotional state. It was more of a ritual than an act of communication—but then, even with Elena, he set up barriers. No one was totally honest with another person—unless the two of them intended to permanently fuse.

Orlando nodded at the carpets. "I hope you appreciate how important they are."

"You know I do." He hadn't included that in his greeting, though. "First alien life." C-Z *humiliates the Gleisner robots, at last*—that was probably how his father saw it. The robots had been first to Alpha Centauri, and first to an extrasolar planet—but first life was Apollo to their Sputniks, for anyone who chose to think in those terms.

Orlando said, "This is the hook we need, to catch the citizens of the marginal polises. The ones who haven't quite imploded into solipsism. This will shake them up—don't you think?"

Paolo shrugged. Earth's transhumans were free to implode into anything they liked; it didn't stop Carter-Zimmerman from exploring the physical universe. But thrashing the Gleisners wouldn't be enough for Orlando; he lived for the day when C-Z would become the cultural mainstream. Any polis could multiply its population a billionfold in a microsecond, if it wanted the vacuous honor of outnumbering the rest. Luring other citizens to migrate was harder—and persuading them to rewrite their own local charters was harder still. Orlando had a missionary streak: he wanted every other polis to see the error of its ways, and follow C-Z to the stars.

Paolo said, "Ashton-Laval has intelligent aliens. I wouldn't be so sure that news of giant seaweed is going to take Earth by storm."

Orlando was venomous. "Ashton-Laval intervened in its so-called 'evolutionary' simulations so many times that they might as well have built the end products in an act of creation lasting six days. They wanted talking reptiles, and—*mirabile dictu!*—they got talking reptiles. There are self-modified transhumans in *this polis* more alien than the aliens in Ashton-Laval."

Paolo smiled. "All right. Forget Ashton-Laval. But forget the marginal polises, too. We choose to value the physical world. That's what defines us—but it's as arbitrary as any other choice of values. Why can't you accept that? It's not the One True Path which the infidels have to be bludgeoned into following." He knew he was arguing half for the sake of it—he desperately wanted to refute the anthrocosmologists, himself—but Orlando always drove him into taking the opposite position. Out of fear of being nothing but his father's clone? Despite the total absence of inherited episodic memories, the stochastic input into his ontogenesis, the chaotically divergent nature of the iterative mind-building algorithms.

Orlando made a beckoning gesture, dragging the image of the carpets halfway back into the room. "You'll vote for the microprobes?"

"Of course."

"Everything depends on that, now. It's good to start with a tantalizing glimpse—but if we don't follow up with details soon, they'll lose interest back on Earth very rapidly."

"Lose interest? It'll be fifty-four years before we know if anyone paid the slightest attention in the first place."

Orlando eyed him with disappointment, and resignation. "If you don't care about the other polises, think about C-Z. This helps us, it strengthens us. We have to make the most of that."

Paolo was bemused. "The charter is the charter. What needs to be strengthened? You make it sound like there's something at risk."

"What do you think a thousand lifeless worlds would have done to us? Do you think the charter would have remained intact?"

Paolo had never considered the scenario. "Maybe not. But in every C-Z where the charter was rewritten, there would have been citizens who'd have gone off and founded new polises on the old lines. You and I, for a start. We could have called it Venetti-Venetti."

"While half your friends turned their backs on the physical world? While Carter-Zimmerman, after two thousand years, went solipsist? You'd be happy with that?"

Paolo laughed. "No—but it's not going to happen, is it? *We've found life*. All right, I agree with you: this strengthens C-Z. The diaspora might have 'failed' . . . but it didn't. We've been lucky. I'm glad, I'm grateful. Is that what you wanted to hear?"

Orlando said sourly, "You take too much for granted."

"And you care too much what I think! I'm not your . . . heir." Orlando was first-generation, scanned from flesh—and there were times when he seemed unable to accept that the whole concept of generation had lost its archaic significance. "You don't need me to safeguard the future of Carter-Zimmerman on your behalf. Or the future of transhumanity. You can do it in person."

Orlando looked wounded—a conscious choice, but it still encoded something. Paolo felt a pang of regret—but he'd said nothing he could honestly retract.

His father gathered up the sleeves of his gold and crimson robes—the only citizen of C-Z who could make Paolo uncomfortable to be naked—and repeated as he vanished from the room: "You take too much for granted."

The gang watched the launch of the microprobes together—even Liesl, though she came in mourning, as a giant dark bird. Karpal stroked her feathers nervously. Hermann appeared as a creature out of Escher, a segmented worm with six human-shaped feet—on legs with elbows—given to curling up into a disk and rolling along the girders of Satellite Pinatubo. Paolo and Elena kept saying the same thing simultaneously; they'd just made love.

Hermann had moved the satellite to a notional orbit just below one of the scout probes—and changed the environment's scale, so that the probe's lower surface, an intricate landscape of detector modules and attitude-control jets, blotted out half the sky. The atmospheric-entry capsules—ceramic teardrops three centimeters wide—burst from their launch tube and hurtled past like boulders, vanishing from sight before they'd fallen so much as ten meters closer to Orpheus. It was all scrupulously accurate, although it was part real-time imagery, part extrapolation, part *faux*. Paolo thought: *We might as well have run a pure simulation . . . and pretended to follow the capsules down.* Elena gave him a guilty/admonishing look. *Yeah—and then why bother actually launching them at all? Why not just simulate a plausible Orphean ocean full of plausible Orphean lifeforms? Why not simulate the whole diaspora?* There was no crime of heresy in C-Z; no one had ever been exiled for breaking the charter. At times it still felt like a tightrope walk, though, trying to classify every act of simulation into those which contributed to an understanding of the physical universe (good), those which were merely convenient, recreational, aesthetic (acceptable) . . . and those which constituted a denial of the primacy of real phenomena (time to think about emigration).

The vote on the microprobes had been close: seventy-two percent in favor, just over the required two-thirds majority, with five percent abstaining. (Citizens created since the arrival at Vega were excluded . . . not that anyone in Carter-Zimmerman would have dreamt of stacking the ballot, perish the thought.) Paolo had been surprised at the narrow margin; he'd yet to hear a single plausible scenario for the microprobes doing harm. He wondered if there was another, unspoken reason which had nothing to do with fears for the Orphean ecology, or hypothetical culture. *A wish to prolong the pleasure of unraveling the planet's mysteries?* Paolo had some sympathy with that impulse—but the launch of the microprobes would do nothing to undermine the greater long-term pleasure of watching, and understanding, as Orphean life evolved.

Liesl said forlornly, "Coastline erosion models show that the northwestern shore of Lambda is inundated by tsunami every ninety Orphean years, on average." She offered the data to them; Paolo glanced at it, and it looked convincing—but the point was academic now. "We could have waited."

Hermann waved his eye-stalks at her. "Beaches covered in fossils, are they?"

"No, but the conditions hardly—"

"No excuses!" He wound his body around a girder, kicking his legs gleefully. Hermann was first-generation, even older than Orlando; he'd been scanned in the twenty-first century, before Carter-Zimmerman existed. Over the centuries, though, he'd wiped most of his episodic memories, and rewritten his personality a dozen times. He'd once told Paolo, "I think of myself as my own great-great-grandson. Death's not so bad, if you do it incrementally. Ditto for immortality."

Elena said, "I keep trying to imagine how it will feel if another C-Z clone stumbles on something infinitely better—like aliens with wormhole drives—while we're back here studying rafts of algae." The body she wore was more stylized than usual—still humanoid, but sexless, hairless and smooth, the face inexpressive and androgynous.

"If they have wormhole drives, they might visit us. Or share the technology, so we can link up the whole diaspora."

"If they have wormhole drives, where have they been for the last two thousand years?"

Paolo laughed. "Exactly. But I know what you mean: *first alien life* . . . and it's likely to be about as sophisticated as seaweed. It breaks the jinx, though. Seaweed every twenty-seven light-years. Nervous systems every fifty? Intelligence every hundred?" He fell silent, abruptly realizing what she was feeling: electing not to wake again after first life was beginning to seem like the wrong choice, a waste of the opportunities the diaspora had created. Paolo offered her a mind graft expressing empathy and support, but she declined.

She said, "I want sharp borders, right now. I want to deal with this myself."

"I understand." He let the partial model of her which he'd acquired as they'd made love fade from his mind. It was non-sapient, and no longer linked to her—but to retain it any longer when she felt this way would have seemed like a transgression. Paolo took the responsibilities of intimacy seriously. His lover before Elena had asked him to erase all his knowledge of her, and he'd more or less complied—the only thing he still knew about her was the fact that she'd made the request.

Hermann announced, "Planetfall!" Paolo glanced at a replay of a scout probe view which showed the first few entry capsules breaking up above the ocean and releasing their microprobes. Nanomachines transformed the ceramic shields (and then themselves) into carbon dioxide and a few simple minerals—nothing the micrometeorites constantly raining down onto Orpheus didn't contain—before the fragments could strike the water. The microprobes would broadcast nothing; when they'd finished gathering data, they'd float to the surface and modulate their UV reflectivity. It would be up to the scout probes to locate these specks, and read their messages, before they self-destructed as thoroughly as the entry capsules.

Hermann said, "This calls for a celebration. I'm heading for the Heart. Who'll join me?"

Paolo glanced at Elena. She shook her head. "You go."

"Are you sure?"

"Yes! Go on." Her skin had taken on a mirrored sheen; her expressionless face reflected the planet below. "I'm all right. I just want some time to think things through, on my own."

Hermann coiled around the satellite's frame, stretching his pale body as he went, gaining segments, gaining legs. "Come on, come on! Karpal? Liesl? Come and celebrate!"

Elena was gone. Liesl made a derisive sound and flapped off into the distance, mocking the environment's airlessness. Paolo and Karpal watched as Hermann grew longer and faster—and then in a blur of speed and change stretched out to wrap the entire geodesic frame. Paolo demagnetized his feet and moved away, laughing; Karpal did the same.

Then Hermann constricted like a boa, and snapped the whole satellite apart.

They floated for a while, two human-shaped machines and a giant worm in a cloud of spinning metal fragments, an absurd collection of imaginary debris, glinting by the light of the true stars.

The Heart was always crowded, but it was larger than Paolo had seen it—even though Hermann had shrunk back to his original size, so as not to make a scene. The huge muscular chamber arched above them, pulsating wetly in time to the music, as they searched for the perfect location to soak up the atmosphere. Paolo had visited public environments in other polises, back on Earth; many were designed to be nothing more than a perceptual framework for group emotion-sharing. He'd never understood the attraction of becoming intimate with large numbers of strangers. Ancestral social hierarchies might have had their faults—and it was absurd to try to make a virtue of the limitations imposed by minds confined to wetware—but the whole idea of mass telepathy as an end in itself seemed bizarre to Paolo . . . and even old-fashioned, in a way. Humans, clearly, would have benefited from a good strong dose of each other's inner life, to keep them from slaughtering each other—but any civilized transhuman could respect and value other citizens without the need to have *been them*, firsthand.

They found a good spot and made some furniture, a table and two chairs—Hermann preferred to stand—and the floor expanded to make room. Paolo looked around, shouting greetings at the people he recognized by sight, but not bothering to check for identity broadcasts from the rest. Chances were he'd met everyone here, but he didn't want to spend the next hour exchanging pleasantries with casual acquaintances.

Hermann said, "I've been monitoring our modest stellar observatory's data stream—my antidote to Vegan parochialism. Odd things are going on around Sirius. We're seeing electron-positron annihilation gamma rays, gravity waves . . . and some unexplained hot spots on Sirius B." He turned to Karpal and asked innocently, "What do you think those robots are up to? There's a rumor that they're planning to drag the white dwarf out of orbit, and use it as part of a giant spaceship."

"I never listen to rumors." Karpal always presented as a faithful reproduction of his old human-shaped Gleisner body—and his mind, Paolo gathered, always took the form of a physiological model, even though he was five generations removed from flesh. Leaving his people and coming into C-Z must have taken considerable courage; they'd never welcome him back.

Paolo said, "Does it matter what they do? Where they go, how they get there? There's more than enough room for both of us. Even if they shadowed the diaspora—even if they came to Vega—we could study the Orpheans together, couldn't we?"

Hermann's cartoon insect face showed mock alarm, eyes growing wider, and wider apart. "Not if they dragged along a white dwarf! Next thing they'd want to start building a Dyson sphere." He turned back to Karpal. "You don't still suffer the urge, do you, for . . . *astrophysical* engineering?"

"Nothing C-Z's exploitation of a few megatons of Vegan asteroid material hasn't satisfied."

Paolo tried to change the subject. "Has anyone heard from Earth, lately? I'm beginning to feel unplugged." His own most recent message was a decade older than the time lag.

Karpal said, "You're not missing much; all they're talking about is Orpheus . . . ever since the new lunar observations, the signs of water. They seem more excited by the mere possibility of life than we are by the certainty. And they have very high hopes."

Paolo laughed. "They do. My Earth-self seems to be counting on the diaspora to find an advanced civilization with the answers to all of transhumanity's existential problems. I don't think he'll get much cosmic guidance from kelp."

"You know there was a big rise in emigration from C-Z after the launch? Emigration, and suicides." Hermann had stopped wriggling and gyrating, becoming almost still, a sign of rare seriousness. "I suspect that's what triggered the astronomy program in the first place. And it seems to have stanched the flow, at least in the short term. Earth C-Z detected water before any clone in the diaspora—and when they hear that we've found life, they'll feel more like collaborators in the discovery because of it."

Paolo felt a stirring of unease. *Emigration and suicides? Was that why Orlando had been so gloomy?* After three hundred years of waiting, how high had expectations become?

A buzz of excitement crossed the floor, a sudden shift in the tone of the conversation. Hermann whispered reverently, "First microprobe has surfaced. And the data is coming in now."

The non-sapient Heart was intelligent enough to guess its patrons' wishes. Although everyone could tap the library for results, privately, the music cut out and a giant public image of the summary data appeared, high in the chamber. Paolo had to crane his neck to view it, a novel experience.

The microprobe had mapped one of the carpets in high resolution. The image showed the expected rough oblong, some hundred meters wide—but the two-or-three-meter-thick slab of the neutrino tomographs was revealed now as a delicate, convoluted surface—fine as a single layer of skin, but folded into an elaborate space-filling curve. Paolo checked the full data: the topology was strictly planar, despite the pathological appearance. No holes, no joins—just a surface which meandered wildly enough to look ten thousand times thicker from a distance than it really was.

An inset showed the microstructure, at a point which started at the rim of the carpet and then—slowly—moved toward the center. Paolo stared at the flowing molecular diagram for several seconds before he grasped what it meant.

The carpet was not a colony of single-celled creatures. Nor was it a multi-cellular organism. It was a *single molecule*, a two-dimensional polymer weighing twenty-five million kilograms. A giant sheet of folded polysaccharide, a complex mesh of interlinked pentose and hexose sugars hung with alkyl and amide side chains. A bit like a plant cell wall—except that this polymer was far stronger than cellulose, and the surface area was twenty orders of magnitude greater.

Karpal said, "I hope those entry capsules were perfectly sterile. Earth bacteria would gorge themselves on this. One big floating carbohydrate dinner, with no defenses."

Hermann thought it over. "Maybe. If they had enzymes capable of breaking off a piece—which I doubt. No chance we'll find out, though: even if there'd been bacterial spores lingering in the asteroid belt from early human expeditions, every ship in the diaspora was double-checked for contamination *en route*. We haven't brought smallpox to the Americas."

Paolo was still dazed. "But how does it assemble? How does it . . . grow?" Hermann consulted the library and replied, before Paolo could do the same.

"The edge of the carpet catalyzes its own growth. The polymer is irregular, aperiodic—there's no single component which simply repeats. But there seem to be about twenty thousand basic structural units—twenty thousand different polysaccharide building blocks." Paolo saw them: long bundles of cross-linked chains running the whole two-hundred-micron thickness of the carpet, each with a roughly square cross-section, bonded at several thousand points to the four neighboring units. "Even at this depth, the ocean's full of UV-generated radicals which filter down from the surface. Any structural unit exposed to the water converts those radicals into more polysaccharide—and builds another structural unit."

Paolo glanced at the library again, for a simulation of the process. Catalytic sites strewn along the sides of each unit trapped the radicals in place, long enough for new bonds to form between them. Some simple sugars were incorporated straight into the polymer as they were created; others were set free to drift in solution for a mirosecond or two, until they were needed. At that level, there were only a few basic chemical tricks being used . . . but molecular evolution must have worked its way up from a few small autocatalytic fragments, first formed by chance, to this elaborate system of twenty thousand mutually self-replicating structures. If the "structural units" had floated free in the ocean as independent molecules, the "lifeform" they comprised would have been virtually invisible. By bonding together, though, they became twenty thousand colors in a giant mosaic.

It was astonishing. Paolo hoped Elena was tapping the library, wherever she was. A colony of algae would have been more "advanced"—but this incredible primordial creature revealed infinitely more about the possibilities for the genesis of life. Carbohydrate, here, played every biochemical role: information carrier, enzyme, energy source, structural material. Nothing like it could have survived on Earth, once there were organisms capable of feeding on it—and if there were ever intelligent Orpheans, they'd be unlikely to find any trace of this bizarre ancestor.

Karpal wore a secretive smile.

Paolo said, "What?"

"Wang tiles. The carpets are made out of Wang tiles."

Hermann beat him to the library, again.

"*Wang* as in twentieth-century flesh mathematician, Hao Wang. *Tiles* as in any set of shapes which can cover the plane. Wang tiles are squares with various shaped edges, which have to fit complementary shapes on adjacent squares. You can cover the plane with a set of Wang tiles, as long as you choose the right one every step of the way. Or in the case of the carpets, grow the right one."

Karpal said, "We should call them Wang's Carpets, in honor of Hao Wang. After twenty-three hundred years, his mathematics has come to life."

Paolo liked the idea, but he was doubtful. "We may have trouble getting a two-thirds majority on that. It's a bit obscure . . ."

Hermann laughed. "Who needs a two-thirds majority? If we want to call them Wang's Carpets, we can call them Wang's Carpets. There are ninety-seven languages in current use in C-Z—half of them invented since the polis was founded. I don't think we'll be exiled for coining one private name."

Paolo concurred, slightly embarrassed. The truth was, he'd completely forgotten that Hermann and Karpal weren't actually speaking Modern Roman.

The three of them instructed their exoselves to consider the name adopted: hence-forth they'd hear "carpet" as "Wang's Carpet"—but if they used the term with anyone else, the reverse translation would apply.

Paolo sat and drank in the image of the giant alien: the first lifeform encountered by human or transhuman which was not a biological cousin. The death, at last, of the possibility that Earth might be unique.

They hadn't refuted the anthrocosmologists yet, though. Not quite. If, as the ACs claimed, human consciousness was the seed around which all of space-time had crystallized—if the universe was nothing but the simplest orderly explanation for human thought—then there was, strictly speaking, no need for a single alien to exist, anywhere. But the physics which justified human existence couldn't help generating a billion other worlds where life could arise. The ACs would be unmoved by Wang's Carpets; they'd insist that these creatures were physical, if not biological, cousins— merely an unavoidable by-product of anthropogenic, life-enabling physical laws.

The real test wouldn't come until the diaspora—or the Gleisner robots—finally encountered conscious aliens: minds entirely unrelated to humanity, observing and explaining the universe which human thought had supposedly built. Most ACs had come right out and declared such a find impossible; it was the sole falsifiable prediction of their hypothesis. Alien consciousness, as opposed to mere alien life, would always build itself a separate universe—because the chance of two unrelated forms of self-awareness concocting exactly the same physics and the same cosmology was infinitesimal—and any alien biosphere which seemed capable of evolving conscious-ness would simply never do so.

Paolo glanced at the map of the diaspora, and took heart. *Alien life already*—and the search had barely started; there were nine hundred and ninety-eight target systems yet to be explored. And even if every one of them proved no more conclusive than Orpheus . . . he was prepared to send clones out farther—and prepared to wait. Consciousness had taken far longer to appear on Earth than the quarter-of-a-billion years remaining before Vega left the main sequence—but the whole point of being here, after all, was that Orpheus wasn't Earth.

Orlando's celebration of the microprobe discoveries was a very first-generation affair. The environment was an endless sunlit garden strewn with tables covered in *food*, and the invitation had politely suggested attendance in fully human form. Paolo po-litely faked it—simulating most of the physiology, but running the body as a puppet, leaving his mind unshackled.

Orlando introduced his new lover, Catherine, who presented as a tall, dark-skinned woman. Paolo didn't recognize her on sight, but checked the identity code she broadcast. It was a small polis, he'd met her once before—as a man called Samuel, one of the physicists who'd worked on the main interstellar fusion drive em-ployed by all the ships of the diaspora. Paolo was amused to think that many of the people here would be seeing his father as a woman. The majority of the citizens of C-Z still practiced the conventions of relative gender which had come into fashion in the twenty-third century—and Orlando had wired them into his own son too deeply for Paolo to wish to abandon them—but whenever the paradoxes were revealed so starkly, he wondered how much longer the conventions would endure. Paolo was same-sex to Orlando, and hence saw his father's lover as a woman, the two close relationships taking precedence over his casual knowledge of Catherine as Samuel. Orlando perceived himself as being male and heterosexual, as his flesh original had been . . . while Samuel saw himself the same way . . . and each perceived the other to be a heterosexual woman. If certain third parties ended up with mixed signals, so be it. It was a typical C-Z compromise: nobody could bear to overturn the old order and do away with gender entirely (as most other polises had done) . . . but nobody could resist the flexibility which being software, not flesh, provided.

Paolo drifted from table to table, sampling the food to keep up appearances, wishing Elena had come. There was little conversation about the biology of Wang's Carpets: most of the people here were simply celebrating their win against the opponents of the microprobes—and the humiliation that faction would suffer, now that it was clearer than ever that the "invasive" observations could have done no harm. Liesl's fears had proved unfounded; there was no other life in the ocean, just Wang's Carpets of various sizes. Paolo, feeling perversely even-handed after the fact, kept wanting to remind these smug movers and shakers: *There might have been anything down there. Strange creatures, delicate and vulnerable in ways we could never have anticipated. We were lucky, that's all.*

He ended up alone with Orlando almost by chance; they were both fleeing different groups of appalling guests when their paths crossed on the lawn.

Paolo asked, "How do you think they'll take this, back home?"

"It's first life, isn't it? Primitive or not. It should at least maintain interest in the diaspora, until the next alien biosphere is discovered." Orlando seemed subdued; perhaps he was finally coming to terms with the gulf between their modest discovery, and Earth's longing for world-shaking results. "And at least the chemistry is novel. If it had turned out to be based on DNA and protein, I think half of Earth C-Z would have died of boredom on the spot. Let's face it, the possibilities of DNA have been simulated to death."

Paolo smiled at the heresy. "You think if nature hadn't managed a little originality, it would have dented people's faith in the charter? If the solipsist polises had begun to look more inventive than the universe itself . . ."

"Exactly."

They walked on in silence, then Orlando halted, and turned to face him.

He said, "There's something I've been wanting to tell you. My Earth-self is dead."

"What?"

"Please, don't make a fuss."

"But . . . why? Why would he—?" *Dead* meant suicide; there was no other cause—unless the sun had turned red giant and swallowed everything out to the orbit of Mars.

"I don't know why. Whether it was a vote of confidence in the diaspora"—Orlando had chosen to wake only in the presence of alien life—"or whether he despaired of us sending back good news, and couldn't face the waiting, and the risk of disappointment. He didn't give a reason. He just had his exoself send a message, stating what he'd done."

Paolo was shaken. If a clone of *Orlando* had succumbed to pessimism, he couldn't begin to imagine the state of mind of the rest of Earth C-Z.

"When did this happen?"

"About fifty years after the launch."

"My Earth-self said nothing."

"It was up to me to tell you, not him."

"I wouldn't have seen it that way."

"Apparently, you would have."

Paolo fell silent, confused. How was he supposed to mourn a distant version of Orlando, in the presence of the one he thought of as real? Death of one clone was a strange half-death, a hard thing to come to terms with. His Earth-self had lost a father; his father had lost an Earth-self. What exactly did that mean to *him*?

What Orlando cared most about was Earth C-Z. Paolo said carefully, "Hermann told me there'd been a rise in emigration and suicide—until the spectroscope picked up the Orphean water. Morale has improved a lot since then—and when they hear that it's more than just water . . ."

Orlando cut him off sharply. "You don't have to talk things up for me. I'm in no danger of repeating the act."

They stood on the lawn, facing each other. Paolo composed a dozen different combinations of mood to communicate, but none of them felt right. He could have granted his father perfect knowledge of everything he was feeling—but what exactly would that knowledge have conveyed? In the end, there was fusion, or separateness. There was nothing in between.

Orlando said, "Kill myself—and leave the fate of transhumanity in your hands? You must be out of your fucking mind."

They walked on together, laughing.

Karpal seemed barely able to gather his thoughts enough to speak. Paolo would have offered him a mind graft promoting tranquillity and concentration—distilled from his own most focused moments—but he was sure that Karpal would never have accepted it. He said, "Why don't you just start wherever you want to? I'll stop you if you're not making sense."

Karpal looked around the white dodecahedron with an expression of disbelief. "You live here?"

"Some of the time."

"But this is your base environment? No trees? No sky? No *furniture*?"

Paolo refrained from repeating any of Hermann's naive-robot jokes. "I add them when I want them. You know, like . . . music. Look, don't let my taste in decor distract you."

Karpal made a chair and sat down heavily.

He said, "Hao Wang proved a powerful theorem, twenty-three hundred years ago. Think of a row of Wang Tiles as being like the data tape of a Turing Machine." Paolo had the library grant him knowledge of the term; it was the original conceptual form of a generalized computing device, an imaginary machine which moved back and forth along a limitless one-dimensional data tape, reading and writing symbols according to a given set of rules.

"With the right set of tiles, to force the right pattern, the next row of the tiling will look like the data tape after the Turing Machine has performed one step of its computation. And the row after that will be the data tape after two steps, and so on. For any given Turing Machine, there's a set of Wang Tiles which can imitate it."

Paolo nodded amiably. He hadn't heard of this particular quaint result, but it was hardly surprising. "The carpets must be carrying out billions of acts of computation every second . . . but then, so are the water molecules around them. There are no physical processes which don't perform arithmetic of some kind."

"True. But with the carpets, it's not quite the same as random molecular motion."

"Maybe not."

Karpal smiled, but said nothing.

"What? You've found a pattern? Don't tell me: our set of twenty thousand polysaccharide Wang Tiles just happens to form the Turing Machine for calculating pi."

"No. What they form is a universal Turing Machine. They can calculate anything at all—depending on the data they start with. Every daughter fragment is like a program being fed to a chemical computer. Growth executes the program."

"Ah." Paolo's curiosity was roused—but he was having some trouble picturing where the hypothetical Turing Machine put its read/write head. "Are you telling me only one tile changes between any two rows, where the 'machine' leaves its mark on the 'data tape' . . . ?" The mosaics he'd seen were a riot of complexity, with no two rows remotely the same.

Karpal said, "No, no. Wang's original example worked exactly like a standard Turing Machine, to simplify the argument . . . but the carpets are more like an arbitrary number of different computers with overlapping data, all working in parallel. This is biology, not a designed machine—it's as messy and wild as, say . . . a mammalian genome. In fact, there are mathematical similarities with gene regulation: I've identified Kauffman networks at every level, from the tiling rules up; the whole system's poised on the hyperadaptive edge between frozen and chaotic behavior."

Paolo absorbed that, with the library's help. Like Earth life, the carpets seemed to have evolved a combination of robustness and flexibility which would have maximized their power to take advantage of natural selection. Thousands of different autocatalytic chemical networks must have arisen soon after the formation of Orpheus—but as the ocean chemistry and the climate changed in the Vegan system's early traumatic millennia, the ability to respond to selection pressure had itself been selected for, and the carpets were the result. Their complexity seemed redundant, now, after a hundred million years of relative stability—and no predators or competition in sight—but the legacy remained.

"So if the carpets have ended up as universal computers . . . with no real need anymore to respond to their surroundings . . . what are they *doing* with all that computing power?"

Karpal said solemnly, "I'll show you."

Paolo followed him into an environment where they drifted above a schematic of a carpet, an abstract landscape stretching far into the distance, elaborately wrinkled like the real thing, but otherwise heavily stylized, with each of the polysaccharide building blocks portrayed as a square tile with four different colored edges. The adjoining edges of neighboring tiles bore complementary colors—to represent the complementary, interlocking shapes of the borders of the building blocks.

"One group of microprobes finally managed to sequence an entire daughter fragment," Karpal explained, "although the exact edges it started life with are largely guesswork, since the thing was growing while they were trying to map it." He gestured impatiently, and all the wrinkles and folds were smoothed away, an irrelevant distraction. They moved to one border of the ragged-edge carpet, and Karpal started the simulation running.

Paolo watched the mosaic extending itself, following the tiling rules perfectly— an orderly mathematical process, here: no chance collisions of radicals with catalytic sites, no mismatched borders between two new-grown neighboring "tiles" triggering the disintegration of both. Just the distillation of the higher-level consequences of all that random motion.

Karpal led Paolo up to a height where he could see subtle patterns being woven, overlapping multiplexed periodicities drifting across the growing edge, meeting and sometimes interacting, sometimes passing right through each other. Mobile pseudoattractors, quasi-stable waveforms in a one-dimensional universe. The carpet's second dimension was more like time than space, a permanent record of the history of the edge.

Karpal seemed to read his mind. "One dimensional. Worse than flatland. No connectivity, no complexity. What can possibly happen in a system like that? Nothing of interest, right?"

He clapped his hands and the environment exploded around Paolo. Trails of color streaked across his sensorium, entwining, then disintegrating into luminous smoke.

"Wrong. Everything goes on in a multidimensional frequency space. I've Fourier-transformed the edge into over a thousand components, and there's independent information in all of them. We're only in a narrow cross-section here, a sixteen-dimensional slice—but it's oriented to show the principal components, the maximum detail."

Paolo spun in a blur of meaningless color, utterly lost, his surroundings beyond comprehension. "You're a *Gleisner robot*, Karpal! *Only* sixteen dimensions! How can you have done this?"

Karpal sounded hurt, wherever he was. "Why do you think I came to C-Z? I thought you people were flexible!"

"What you're doing is . . ." *What?* Heresy? There was no such thing. Officially. "Have you shown this to anyone else?"

"Of course not. Who did you have in mind? Liesl? *Hermann?*"

"Good. I know how to keep my mouth shut." Paolo invoked his exoself and moved back into the dodecahedron. He addressed the empty room. "How can I put this? The physical universe has three spatial dimensions, plus time. Citizens of Carter-Zimmerman inhabit the physical universe. Higher dimensional mind games are for the solipsists." Even as he said it, he realized how pompous he sounded. It was an arbitrary doctrine, not some great moral principle.

But it was the doctrine he'd lived with for twelve hundred years.

Karpal replied, more bemused than offended, "It's the only way to see what's going on. The only sensible way to apprehend it. Don't you want to know what the carpets are actually like?"

Paolo felt himself being tempted. Inhabit a *sixteen-dimensional slice of a thousand-dimensional frequency space*? But it was in the service of understanding a real physical system—not a novel experience for its own sake.

And nobody had to find out.

He ran a quick—non-sapient—self-predictive model. There was a ninety-three percent chance that he'd give in, after fifteen subjective minutes of agonizing over the decision. It hardly seemed fair to keep Karpal waiting that long.

He said, "You'll have to loan me your mind-shaping algorithm. My exoself wouldn't know where to begin."

When it was done, he steeled himself, and moved back into Karpal's environment. For a moment, there was nothing but the same meaningless blur as before.

Then everything suddenly crystallized.

Creatures swam around them, elaborately branched tubes like mobile coral, vividly colored in all the hues of Paolo's mental palette—Karpal's attempt to cram in some of the information that a mere sixteen dimensions couldn't show? Paolo glanced down at his own body—nothing was missing, but he could see *around* it in all the thirteen dimensions in which it was nothing but a pin-prick; he quickly looked away. The "coral" seemed far more natural to his altered sensory map, occupying sixteen-space in all directions, and shaded with hints that it occupied much more. And Paolo had no doubt that it was "alive"—it looked more organic than the carpets themselves, by far.

Karpal said, "Every point in this space encodes some kind of quasi-periodic pattern in the tiles. Each dimension represents a different characteristic size—like a wavelength, although the analogy's not precise. The position in each dimension represents other attributes of the pattern, relating to the particular tiles it employs. So the localized systems you see around you are clusters of a few billion patterns, all with broadly similar attributes at similar wavelengths."

They moved away from the swimming coral, into a swarm of something like jellyfish: floppy hyperspheres waving wispy tendrils (each one of them more substantial than Paolo). Tiny jewel-like creatures darted among them. Paolo was just beginning to notice that nothing moved here like a solid object drifting through normal space; motion seemed to entail a shimmering deformation at the leading hypersurface, a visible process of disassembly and reconstruction.

Karpal led him on through the secret ocean. There were helical worms, coiled together in groups of indeterminate number—each single creature breaking up into a dozen or more wriggling silvers, and then recombining . . . although not always from the same parts. There were dazzling multicolored stemless flowers, intricate hypercones of "gossamer-thin" fifteen-dimensional petals—each one a hypnotic fractal labyrinth of crevices and capillaries. There were clawed monstrosities, writhing knots of sharp insectile parts like an orgy of decapitated scorpions.

Paolo said, uncertainly, "You could give people a glimpse of this in just three dimensions. Enough to make it clear that there's . . . *life* in here. This is going to shake them up badly, though." Life—embedded in the accidental computations of Wang's

Carpets, with no possibility of ever relating to the world outside. This was an affront to Carter-Zimmerman's whole philosophy: if nature had evolved "organisms" as divorced from reality as the inhabitants of the most inward-looking polis, where was the privileged status of the physical universe, the clear distinction between truth and illusion?

And after three hundred years of waiting for good news from the diaspora, how would they respond to this back on Earth?

Karpal said, "There's one more thing I have to show you."

He'd named the creatures squids, for obvious reasons. *Distant cousins of the jellyfish, perhaps?* They were prodding each other with their tentacles in a way which looked thoroughly carnal—but Karpal explained, "There's no analog of light here. We're viewing all this according to ad hoc rules which have nothing to do with the native physics. All the creatures here gather information about each other by contact alone—which is actually quite a rich means of exchanging data, with so many dimensions. What you're seeing is communication by touch."

"Communication about what?"

"Just gossip, I expect. Social relationships."

Paolo stared at the writhing mass of tentacles.

"You think they're *conscious*?"

Karpal, point-like, grinned broadly. "They have a central control structure with more connectivity than the human brain—and which correlates data gathered from the skin. I've mapped that organ, and I've started to analyze its function."

He led Paolo into another environment, a representation of the data structures in the "brain" of one of the squids. It was—mercifully—three-dimensional, and highly stylized, built of translucent colored blocks marked with icons, representing mental symbols, linked by broad lines indicating the major connections between them. Paolo had seen similar diagrams of transhuman minds; this was far less elaborate, but eerily familiar nonetheless.

Karpal said, "Here's the sensory map of its surroundings. Full of other squids' bodies, and vague data on the last known positions of a few smaller creatures. But you'll see that the symbols activated by the physical presence of the other squids are linked to these"—he traced the connection with one finger—"representations. Which are crude miniatures of *this whole structure* here."

"This whole structure" was an assembly labeled with icons for memory retrieval, simple tropisms, short-term goals. The general business of being and doing.

"The squid has maps, not just of other squids' bodies, but their minds as well. Right or wrong, it certainly tries to know what the others are thinking about. And"—he pointed out another set of links, leading to another, less crude, miniature squid mind—"it thinks about its own thoughts as well. I'd call that *consciousness*, wouldn't you?"

Paolo said weakly, "You've kept all this to yourself? You came this far, without saying a word—?"

Karpal was chastened. "I know it was selfish—but once I'd decoded the interactions of the tile patterns, I couldn't tear myself away long enough to start explaining it to anyone else. And I came to you first because I wanted your advice on the best way to break the news."

Paolo laughed bitterly. "The best way to break the news that *first alien conscious-ness* is hidden deep inside a biological computer? That everything the diaspora was trying to prove has been turned on its head? The best way to explain to the citizens of Carter-Zimmerman that after a three-hundred-year journey, they might as well have stayed on Earth running simulations with as little resemblance to the physical universe as possible?"

Karpal took the outburst in good humor. "I was thinking more along the lines of the *best way to point out* that if we hadn't traveled to Orpheus and studied Wang's Carpets, we'd never have had the chance to tell the solipsists of Ashton-Laval that all their elaborate invented lifeforms and exotic imaginary universes pale into insignifi-cance compared to what's really out here—and which only the Carter-Zimmerman diaspora could have found."

Paolo and Elena stood together on the edge of Satellite Pinatubo, watching one of the scout probes aim its maser at a distant point in space. Paolo thought he saw a faint scatter of microwaves from the beam as it collided with iron-rich meteor dust. *Elena's mind being diffracted all over the cosmos?* Best not think about that.

He said, "When you meet the other versions of me who haven't experienced Or-pheus, I hope you'll offer them mind grafts so they won't be jealous."

She frowned. "Ah. Will I or won't I? I can't be bothered modeling it. I expect I will. You should have asked me before I cloned myself. No need for jealousy, though. There'll be worlds far stranger than Orpheus."

"I doubt it. You really think so?"

"I wouldn't be doing this if I didn't believe that." Elena had no power to change the fate of the frozen clones of her previous self—but everyone had the right to emi-grate.

Paolo took her hand. The beam had been aimed almost at Regulus, UV-hot and bright, but as he looked away, the cool yellow light of the sun caught his eye.

Vega C-Z was taking the news of the squids surprisingly well, so far. Karpal's way of putting it had cushioned the blow: it was only by traveling all this distance across the real, physical universe that they could have made such a discovery—and it was amazing how pragmatic even the most doctrinaire citizens had turned out to be. Be-fore the launch, "alien solipsists" would have been the most unpalatable idea imag-inable, the most abhorrent thing the diaspora could have stumbled upon—but now that they were here, and stuck with the fact of it, people were finding ways to view it in a better light. Orlando had even proclaimed, "*This* will be the perfect hook for the marginal polises. 'Travel through real space to witness a truly alien virtual reality.' We can sell it as a synthesis of the two world views."

Paolo still feared for Earth, though—where his Earth-self and others were wait-ing in hope of alien guidance. Would they take the message of Wang's Carpets to heart, and retreat into their own hermetic worlds, oblivious to physical reality?

And he wondered if the anthrocosmologists had finally been refuted . . . or not. Karpal had discovered alien consciousness—but it was sealed inside a cosmos of its own, its perceptions of itself and its surroundings neither reinforcing nor conflicting with human and transhuman explanations of reality. It would be millennia before

C-Z could untangle the ethical problems of daring to try to make contact . . . assuming that both Wang's Carpets, and the inherited data patterns of the squids, survived that long.

Paolo looked around at the wild splendor of the star-choked galaxy, felt the disk reach in and cut right through him. *Could all this strange haphazard beauty be nothing but an excuse for those who beheld it to exist? Nothing but the sum of all the answers to all the questions humans and transhumans had ever asked the universe—answers created in the asking?*

He couldn't believe that—but the question remained unanswered.

So far.

coming of age in karhide
by sov thade tage em ereb, of rer,
in karhide, on gethen

URSULA K. LE GUIN

Ursula K. Le Guin is probably one of the best-known and most universally respected SF writers in the world today. Her famous novel *The Left Hand of Darkness* may have been the most influential SF novel of its decade, and shows every sign of becoming one of the enduring classics of the genre—even ignoring the rest of Le Guin's work, the impact of this one novel alone on future SF and future SF writers would be incalculably strong. (Her 1968 fantasy novel, *A Wizard of Earthsea*, would be almost as influential on future generations of High Fantasy and Young Adult writers.) *The Left Hand of Darkness* won both the Hugo and Nebula Awards, as did Le Guin's monumental novel *The Dispossessed* a few years later. Her novel *Tehanu* won her another Nebula in 1990, and she has also won three other Hugo Awards and a Nebula Award for her short fiction, as well as the National Book Award for children's literature for her novel *The Farthest Shore*, part of her Earthsea trilogy. Her other novels include *Planet of Exile. The Lathe of Heaven, City of Illusions, Rocannon's World, The Beginning Place, A Wizard of Earthsea, The Tombs of Atuan, Tehanu, Searoad*, the controversial multimedia novel *Always Coming Home*, and *The Telling*. She has had eight collections: *The Wind's Twelve Quarters, Orsinian Tales, The Compass Rose, Buffalo Gals and Other Animal Presences, A Fisherman of the Inland Sea, Four Ways to Forgiveness, Tales of Earthsea*, and, most recently, *The Birthday of the World*. Upcoming is a collection of her critical essays, *The Wave in the Mind: Tales and Essays on the Reader, and the Imagination*. Her stories have appeared in our Second, Fifth, Eighth, Twelfth, Thirteenth, Sixteenth, and Eighteenth annual collections. She lives with her husband in Portland, Oregon.

In this one, she returns to the setting of her best-known novel, *The Left Hand of Darkness,* for a poignant and evocative story of the transition to adulthood—which is always a difficult passage, no matter what sex you are . . . and which is perhaps even a little *more* difficult if you have the potential to be *either.*

I live in the oldest city in the world. Long before there were kings in Karhide, Rer was a city, the marketplace and meeting ground for all the Northeast, the Plains, and Kerm Land. The Fastness of Rer was a center of learning, a refuge, a judgment seat fifteen thousand years ago. Karhide became a nation here, under the Geger kings, who ruled for a thousand years. In the thousandth year Sedern Geger, the Unking, cast the crown into the River Arre from the palace towers, proclaiming an end to dominion. The time they call the Flowering of Rer, the Summer Century, began then. It ended when the Hearth of Harge took power and moved their capital across the mountains to Erhenrang. The Old Palace has been empty for centuries. But it stands. Nothing in Rer falls down. The Arre floods through the street-tunnels every year in the Thaw, winter blizzards may bring thirty feet of snow, but the city stands. Nobody knows how old the houses are, because they have been rebuilt forever. Each one sits in its gardens without respect to the position of any of the others, as vast and random and ancient as hills. The roofed streets and canals angle about among them. Rer is all corners. We say that the Harges left because they were afraid of what might be around the corner.

Time is different here. I learned in school how the Orgota, the Ekumen, and most other people count years. They call the year of some portentous event Year One and number forward from it. Here it's always Year One. On Getheny Thern, New Year's Day, the Year One becomes one-ago, one-to-come becomes One, and so on. It's like Rer, everything always changing but the city never changing.

When I was fourteen (in the Year One, or fifty-ago) I came of age. I have been thinking about that a good deal recently.

It was a different world. Most of us had never seen an Alien, as we called them then. We might have heard the Mobile talk on the radio, and at school we saw pictures of Aliens—the ones with hair around their mouths were the most pleasingly savage and repulsive. Most of the pictures were disappointing. They looked too much like us. You couldn't even tell that they were always in kemmer. The female Aliens were supposed to have enormous breasts, but my mothersib Dory had bigger breasts than the ones in the pictures.

When the Defenders of the Faith kicked them out of Orgoreyn, when King Emran got into the Border War and lost Erhenrang, even when their Mobiles were outlawed and forced into hiding at Estre in Kerm, the Ekumen did nothing much but wait. They had waited for two hundred years, as patient as Handdara. They did one thing: they took our young king offworld to foil a plot, and then brought the same king back sixty years later to end her wombchild's disastrous reign. Argaven XVII is the only king who ever ruled four years before her heir and forty years after.

The year I was born (the Year One, or sixty-four-ago) was the year Argaven's second reign began. By the time I was noticing anything beyond my own toes, the war was over, the West Fall was part of Karhide again, the capital was back in Erhenrang, and most of the damage done to Rer during the Overthrow of Emran had been repaired. The old houses had been rebuilt again. The Old Palace had been patched again. Argaven XVII was miraculously back on the throne again. Every-thing was the way it used to be, ought to be, back to normal, just like the old days— everybody said so.

Indeed those were quiet years, an interval of recovery before Argaven, the first Gethenian who ever left our planet, brought us at last fully into the Ekumen; before we, not they, became the Aliens; before we came of age. When I was a child we lived the way people had lived in Rer forever. It is that way, that timeless world, that world around the corner, I have been thinking about, and trying to describe for people who never knew it. Yet as I write I see how also nothing changes, that it is truly the Year One always, for each child that comes of age, each lover who falls in love.

There were a couple of thousand people in the Ereb Hearths, and a hundred and forty of them lived in my Hearth, Ereb Tage. My name is Sov Thade Tage em Ereb, after the old way of naming we still use in Rer. The first thing I remember is a huge dark place full of shouting and shadows, and I am falling upward through a golden light into the darkness. In thrilling terror, I scream. I am caught in my fall, held, held close; I weep; a voice so close to me that it seems to speak through my body says softly, "Sov, Sov, Sov." And then I am given something wonderful to eat, something so sweet, so delicate that never again will I eat anything quite so good. . . .

I imagine that some of my wild elder hearthsibs had been throwing me about, and that my mother comforted me with a bit of festival cake. Later on when I was a wild elder sib we used to play catch with babies for balls; they always screamed, with terror or with delight, or both. It's the nearest to flying anyone of my generation knew. We had dozens of different words for the way snow falls, descends, glides, blows, for the way clouds move, the way ice floats, the way boats sail; but not that word. Not yet. And so I don't remember "flying." I remember falling upward through the golden light.

Family houses in Rer are built around a big central hall. Each story has an inner balcony clear round that space, and we call the whole story, rooms and all, a balcony. My family occupied the whole second balcony of Ereb Tage. There were a lot of us. My grandmother had borne four children, and all of them had children, so I had a bunch of cousins as well as a younger and an older wombsib. "The Thades always kemmer as women and always get pregnant," I heard neighbors say, variously envi-ous, disapproving, admiring. "And they never keep kemmer," somebody would add. The former was an exaggeration, but the latter was true. Not one of us kids had a fa-ther. I didn't know for years who my getter was, and never gave it a thought. Clannish, the Thades preferred not to bring outsiders, even other members of our own Hearth, into the family. If young people fell in love and started talking about keeping kem-mer or making vows, Grandmother and the mothers were ruthless. "Vowing kemmer, what do you think you are, some kind of noble? some kind of fancy person? The kemmerhouse was good enough for me and it's good enough for you," the mothers said to their lovelorn children, and sent them away, clear off to the old Ereb Domain in the country, to hoe braties till they got over being in love.

So as a child I was a member of a flock, a school, a swarm, in and out of our war-ren of rooms, tearing up and down the staircases, working together and learning together and looking after the babies—in our own fashion—and terrorising quieter hearthmates by our numbers and our noise. As far as I know we did no real harm. Our escapades were well within the rules and limits of the sedate, ancient Hearth, which we felt not as constraints but as protection, the walls that kept us safe. The only time we got punished was when my cousin Sether decided it would be exciting if we tied a long rope we'd found to the second-floor balcony railing, tied a big knot in the rope, held onto the knot, and jumped. "I'll go first," Sether said. Another misguided attempt at flight. The railing and Sether's broken leg were mended, and the rest of us had to clean the privies, all the privies of the Hearth, for a month. I think the rest of the Hearth had decided it was time the young Thades observed some discipline.

Although I really don't know what I was like as a child, I think that if I'd had any choice I might have been less noisy than my playmates, though just as unruly. I used to love to listen to the radio, and while the rest of them were racketing around the balconies or the centerhall in winter, or out in the streets and gardens in summer, I would crouch for hours in my mother's room behind the bed, playing her old seremwood radio very softly so that my sibs wouldn't know I was there. I listened to anything, Lays and plays and hearth-tales, the Palace news, the analyses of grain harvests and the detailed weather-reports; I listened every day all one winter to an ancient saga from the Pering Storm-Border about snowghouls, perfidious traitors, and bloody ax-murders, which haunted me at night so that I couldn't sleep and would crawl into bed with my mother for comfort. Often my younger sib was already there in the warm, soft, breathing dark. We would sleep all entangled and curled up together like a nest of pesthry.

My mother, Guyr Thade Tage em Ereb, was impatient, warm-hearted, and impartial, not exerting much control over us three wombchildren, but keeping watch. The Thades were all tradespeople working in Ereb shops and masteries, with little or no cash to spend; but when I was ten Guyr bought me a radio, a new one, and said where my sibs could hear, "You don't have to share it." I treasured it for years and finally shared it with my own wombchild.

So the years went along and I went along in the warmth and density and certainty of a family and a Hearth embedded in tradition, threads on the quick ever-repeating shuttle weaving the timeless web of custom and act and work and relationship, and at this distance I can hardly tell one year from the other or myself from the other children: until I turned fourteen.

The reason most people in my Hearth would remember that year is for the big party known as Dory's Somer-Forever Celebration. My mothersib Dory had stopped going into kemmer that winter. Some people didn't do anything when they stopped going into kemmer; others went to the Fastness for a ritual; some stayed on at the Fastness for months after, or even moved there. Dory, who wasn't spiritually inclined, said, "If I can't have kids and can't have sex any more and have to get old and die, at least I can have a party."

I have already had some trouble trying to tell this story in a language that has no somer pronouns, only gendered pronouns. In their last years of kemmer, as the hormone balance changes, most people mostly go into kemmer as men. Dory's kemmers had been male for over a year, so I'll call Dory "he," although of course the point was that he would never be either he or she again.

In any event, his party was tremendous. He invited everyone in our Hearth and the two neighboring Ereb Hearths, and it went on for three days. It had been a long winter and the spring was late and cold; people were ready for something new, something hot to happen. We cooked for a week, and a whole storeroom was packed full of beerkegs. A lot of people who were in the middle of going out of kemmer, or had already and hadn't done anything about it, came and joined in the ritual. That's what I remember vividly: in the firelit three-story centerhall of our Hearth, a circle of thirty or forty people, all middle-aged or old, singing and dancing, stamping the drumbeats. There was a fierce energy in them, their grey hair was loose and wild, they stamped as if their feet would go through the floor, their voices were deep and strong, they were laughing. The younger people watching them seemed pallid and shadowy. I looked at the dancers and wondered, why are they happy? Aren't they old? Why do they act like they'd got free? What's it like, then, kemmer?

No, I hadn't thought much about kemmer before. What would be the use? Until we come of age we have no gender and no sexuality, our hormones don't give us any trouble at all. And in a city Hearth we never see adults in kemmer. They kiss and go. Where's Maba? In the kemmerhouse, love, now eat your porridge. When's Maba coming back? Soon, love.—And in a couple of days Maba comes back, looking sleepy and shiny and refreshed and exhausted. Is it like having a bath, Maba? Yes, a bit, love, and what have you been up to while I was away?

Of course we played kemmer, when we were seven or eight. This here's the kemmerhouse and I get to be the woman. No, I do. No, I do, I thought of it!—And we rubbed our bodies together and rolled around laughing, and then maybe we stuffed a ball under our shirt and were pregnant, and then we gave birth, and then we played catch with the ball. Children will play whatever adults do; but the kemmer game wasn't much of a game. It often ended in a tickling match. And most children aren't even very ticklish, till they come of age.

After Dory's party, I was on duty in the Hearth creche all through Tuwa, the last month of spring; come summer I began my first apprenticeship, in a furniture workshop in the Third Ward. I loved getting up early and running across the city on the wayroofs and up on the curbs of the open ways; after the late Thaw some of the ways were still full of water, deep enough for kayaks and pole-boats. The air would be still and cold and clear; the sun would come up behind the old towers of the Unpalace, red as blood, and all the waters and the windows of the city would flash scarlet and gold. In the workshop there was the piercing sweet smell of fresh-cut wood and the company of grown people, hard-working, patient, and demanding, taking me seriously. I wasn't a child any more, I said to myself. I was an adult, a working person.

But why did I want to cry all the time? Why did I want to sleep all the time? Why did I get angry at Sether? Why did Sether keep bumping into me and saying "Oh sorry" in that stupid husky voice? Why was I so clumsy with the big electric lathe that I ruined six chair-legs one after the other? "Get that kid off the lathe," shouted old Marth, and I slunk away in a fury of humiliation. I would never be a carpenter, I would never be adult, who gave a shit for chair-legs anyway?

"I want to work in the gardens," I told my mother and grandmother. "Finish your training and you can work in the gardens next summer," Grand said, and Mother nodded. This sensible counsel appeared to me as a heartless injustice, a failure of love, a condemnation to despair. I sulked. I raged.

"What's wrong with the furniture shop?" my elders asked after several days of sulk and rage.

"Why does stupid Sether have to be there!" I shouted. Dory, who was Sether's mother, raised an eyebrow and smiled.

"Are you all right?" my mother asked me as I slouched into the balcony after work, and I snarled, "I'm fine," and rushed to the privies and vomited.

I was sick. My back ached all the time. My head ached and got dizzy and heavy. Something I could not locate anywhere, some part of my soul, hurt with a keen, desolate, ceaseless pain. I was afraid of myself: of my tears, my rage, my sickness, my clumsy body. It did not feel like my body, like me. It felt like something else, an ill-fitting garment, a smelly, heavy overcoat that belonged to some old person, some dead person. It wasn't mine, it wasn't me. Tiny needles of agony shot through my nipples, hot as fire. When I winced and held my arms across my chest, I knew that everybody could see what was happening. Anybody could smell me. I smelled sour, strong, like blood, like raw pelts of animals. My clitopenis was swollen hugely and stuck out from between my labia, and then shrank nearly to nothing, so that it hurt to piss. My labia itched and reddened as with loathsome insect-bites. Deep in my belly something moved, some monstrous growth. I was utterly ashamed. I was dying.

"Sov," my mother said, sitting down beside me on my bed, with a curious, tender, complicitous smile, "shall we choose your kemmerday?"

"I'm not in kemmer," I said passionately.

"No," Guyr said. "But next month I think you will be."

"I *won't*!"

My mother stroked my hair and face and arm. *We shape each other to be human,* old people used to say as they stroked babies or children or one another with those long, slow, soft caresses.

After a while my mother said, "Sether's coming in, too. But a month or so later than you, I think. Dory said let's have a double kemmerday, but I think you should have your own day in your own time."

I burst into tears and cried, "I don't want one, I don't want to, I just want, I just want to go away. . . ."

"Sov," my mother said, "if you want to, you can go to the kemmerhouse at Gerodda Ereb, where you won't know anybody. But I think it would be better here, where people do know you. They'd like it. They'll be so glad for you. Oh, your Grand's so proud of you! 'Have you seen that grandchild of mine, Sov, have you seen what a beauty, what a *mahad*!' Everybody's bored to tears hearing about you. . . ."

Mahad is a dialect word, a Rer word; it means a strong, handsome, generous, upright person, a reliable person. My mother's stern mother, who commanded and thanked but never praised, said I was a mahad? A terrifying idea that dried my tears.

"All right," I said desperately. "Here. But not next month! It isn't. I'm not."

"Let me see," my mother said. Fiercely embarrassed yet relieved to obey, I stood up and undid my trousers.

My mother took a very brief and delicate look, hugged me, and said, "Next month, yes, I'm sure. You'll feel much better in a day or two. And next month it'll be different. It really will."

Sure enough, the next day the headache and the hot itching were gone, and though I was still tired and sleepy a lot of the time, I wasn't quite so stupid and clumsy at work. After a few more days I felt pretty much myself, light and easy in my limbs. Only if I thought about it there was still that queer feeling that wasn't quite in any part of my body, and that was sometimes very painful and sometimes only strange, almost something I wanted to feel again.

My cousin Sether and I had been apprenticed together at the furniture shop. We didn't go to work together because Sether was still slightly lame from that rope trick a couple of years earlier, and got a lift to work in a poleboat so long as there was water in the streets. When they closed the Arre Watergate and the ways went dry, Sether had to walk. So we walked together. The first couple of days we didn't talk much. I still felt angry at Sether. Because I couldn't run through the dawn any more but had to walk at a lame-leg pace. And because Sether was always around. Always there. Taller than me, and quicker at the lathe, and with that long, heavy, shining hair. Why did anybody want to wear their hair so long, anyhow? I felt as if Sether's hair was in front of my own eyes.

We were walking home, tired, on a hot evening of Ockre, the first month of summer. I could see that Sether was limping and trying to hide or ignore it, trying to swing right along at my quick pace, very erect, scowling. A great wave of pity and admiration overwhelmed me, and that thing, that growth, that new being, whatever it was in my bowels and in the ground of my soul moved and turned again, turned towards Sether, aching, yearning.

"Are you coming into kemmer?" I said in a hoarse, husky voice I had never heard come out of my mouth.

"In a couple of months," Sether said in a mumble, not looking at me, still very stiff and frowning.

"I guess I have to have this, do this, you know, this stuff, pretty soon."

"I wish I could," Sether said. "Get it over with."

We did not look at each other. Very gradually, unnoticeably, I was slowing my pace till we were going along side by side at an easy walk.

"Sometimes do you feel like your tits are on fire?" I asked without knowing that I was going to say anything.

Sether nodded.

After a while, Sether said, "Listen, does your pisser get. . . ."

I nodded.

"It must be what the Aliens look like," Sether said with revulsion. "This, this thing sticking out, it gets so *big* . . . it gets in the way."

We exchanged and compared symptoms for a mile or so. It was a relief to talk about it, to find company in misery, but it was also frightening to hear our misery confirmed by the other. Sether burst out, "I'll tell you what I hate, what I really *hate* about it—it's dehumanising. To get jerked around like that by your own body, to lose control, I can't stand the idea. Of being just a sex machine. And everybody just turns into something to have sex with. You know that people in kemmer go crazy and *die* if there isn't anybody else in kemmer? That they'll even attack people in somer? Their own mothers?"

"They can't," I said, shocked.

"Yes they can. Tharry told me. This truck driver up in the High Kargav went into kemmer as a male while their caravan was stuck in the snow, and he was big and strong, and he went crazy and he, he did it to his cabmate, and his cabmate was in somer and got hurt, really hurt, trying to fight him off. And then the driver came out of kemmer and committed suicide."

This horrible story brought the sickness back up from the pit of my stomach, and I could say nothing.

Sether went on, "People in kemmer aren't even human any more! And we have to do that—to be that way!"

Now that awful, desolate fear was out in the open. But it was not a relief to speak it. It was even larger and more terrible, spoken.

"It's stupid," Sether said. "It's a primitive device for continuing the species. There's no need for civilised people to undergo it. People who want to get pregnant could do it with injections. It would be genetically sound. You could choose your child's getter. There wouldn't be all this inbreeding, people fucking with their sibs, like animals. Why do we have to be animals?"

Sether's rage stirred me. I shared it. I also felt shocked and excited by the word "fucking," which I had never heard spoken. I looked again at my cousin, the thin, ruddy face, the heavy, long, shining hair. My age, Sether looked older. A half year in pain from a shattered leg had darkened and matured the adventurous, mischievous child, teaching anger, pride, endurance. "Sether," I said, "listen, it doesn't matter, you're human, even if you have to do that stuff, that fucking. You're a mahad."

"Getheny Kus," Grand said: the first day of the month of Kus, midsummer day.

"I won't be ready," I said.

"You'll be ready."

"I want to go into kemmer with Sether."

"Sether's got a month or two yet to go. Soon enough. It looks like you might be on the same moontime, though. Dark-of-the-mooners, eh? That's what I used to be. So, just stay on the same wavelength, you and Sether. . . ." Grand had never grinned at me this way, an inclusive grin, as if I were an equal.

My mother's mother was sixty years old, short, brawny, broad-hipped, with keen clear eyes, a stonemason by trade, an unquestioned autocrat in the Hearth. I, equal to this formidable person? It was my first intimation that I might be becoming more, rather than less, human.

"I'd like it," said Grand, "if you spent this halfmonth at the Fastness. But it's up to you."

"At the Fastness?" I said, taken by surprise. We Thades were all Handdara, but very inert Handdara, keeping only the great festivals, muttering the grace all in one garbled word, practising none of the disciplines. None of my older hearthsibs had been sent off to the Fastness before their kemmerday. Was there something wrong with me?

"You've got a good brain," said Grand. "You and Sether. I'd like to see some of you lot casting some shadows, some day. We Thades sit here in our Hearth and breed like pesthry. Is that enough? It'd be a good thing if some of you got your heads out of the bedding."

"What do they do in the Fastness?" I asked, and Grand answered frankly, "I don't know. Go find out. They teach you. They can teach you how to control kemmer."

"All right," I said promptly. I would tell Sether that the Indwellers could control kemmer. Maybe I could learn how to do it and come home and teach it to Sether.

Grand looked at me with approval. I had taken up the challenge.

Of course I didn't learn how to control kemmer, in a halfmonth in the Fastness. The first couple of days there, I thought I wouldn't even be able to control my homesickness. From our warm, dark warren of rooms full of people talking, sleeping, eating, cooking, washing, playing remma, playing music, kids running around, noise, family, I went across the city to a huge, clean, cold, quiet house of strangers. They were courteous, they treated me with respect. I was terrified. Why should a person of forty, who knew magic disciplines of superhuman strength and fortitude, who could walk barefoot through blizzards, who could Foretell, whose eyes were the wisest and calmest I had ever seen, why should an Adept of the Handdara respect me?

"Because you are so ignorant," Ranharrer the Adept said, smiling, with great tenderness.

Having me only for a halfmonth, they didn't try to influence the nature of my ignorance very much. I practised the Untrance several hours a day, and came to like it: that was quite enough for them, and they praised me. "At fourteen, most people go crazy moving slowly," my teacher said.

During my last six or seven days in the Fastness certain symptoms began to show up again, the headache, the swellings and shooting pains, the irritability. One morning the sheet of my cot in my bare, peaceful little room was bloodstained. I looked at the smear with horror and loathing. I thought I had scratched my itching labia to bleeding in my sleep, but I knew also what the blood was. I began to cry. I had to wash the sheet somehow. I had fouled, defiled this place where everything was clean, austere, and beautiful.

An old Indweller, finding me scrubbing desperately at the sheet in the washrooms, said nothing, but brought me some soap that bleached away the stain. I went back to my room, which I had come to love with the passion of one who had never before known any actual privacy, and crouched on the sheetless bed, miserable, checking every few minutes to be sure I was not bleeding again. I missed my Untrance practice time. The immense house was very quiet. Its peace sank into me. Again I felt that strangeness in my soul, but it was not pain now; it was a desolation like the air at evening, like the peaks of the Kargav seen far in the west in the clarity of winter. It was an immense enlargement.

Ranharrer the Adept knocked and entered at my word, looked at me for a minute, and asked gently, "What is it?"

"Everything is strange," I said.

The Adept smiled radiantly and said, "Yes."

I know now how Ranharrer cherished and honored my ignorance, in the Handdara sense. Then I knew only that somehow or other I had said the right thing and so pleased a person I wanted very much to please.

"We're doing some singing," Ranharrer said, "you might like to hear it."

They were in fact singing the Midsummer Chant, which goes on for the four days before Getheny Kus, night and day. Singers and drummers drop in and out at will, most of them singing on certain syllables in an endless group improvisation guided only by the drums and by melodic cues in the Chantbook, and falling into harmony with the soloist if one is present. At first I heard only a pleasantly thick-textured, droning sound over a quiet and subtle beat. I listened till I got bored and decided I could do it too. So I opened my mouth and sang "Aah" and heard all the other voices singing "Aah" above and with and below mine until I lost mine and heard only all the voices, and then only the music itself, and then suddenly the startling silvery rush of a single voice running across the weaving, against the current, and sinking into it and vanishing, and rising out of it again. . . . Ranharrer touched my arm. It was time for dinner, I had been singing since Third Hour. I went back to the chantry after dinner, and after supper. I spent the next three days there. I would have spent the nights there if they had let me. I wasn't sleepy at all any more. I had sudden, endless energy, and couldn't sleep. In my little room I sang to myself, or read the strange Handdara poetry which was the only book they had given me, and practised the Untrance, trying to ignore the heat and cold, the fire and ice in my body, till dawn came and I could go sing again.

And then it was Ottormenbod, midsummer's eve, and I had to go home to my Hearth and the kemmerhouse.

To my surprise, my mother and grandmother and all the elders came to the Fastness to fetch me, wearing ceremonial hiebs and looking solemn. Ranharrer handed me over to them, saying to me only, "Come back to us." My family paraded me through the streets in the hot summer morning; all the vines were in flower, perfuming the air, all the gardens were blooming, bearing, fruiting. "This is an excellent time," Grand said judiciously, "to come into kemmer."

The Hearth looked very dark to me after the Fastness, and somehow shrunken. I looked around for Sether, but it was a workday, Sether was at the shop. That gave me a sense of holiday, which was not unpleasant. And then up in the hearthroom of our balcony, Grand and the Hearth elders formally presented me with a whole set of new clothes, new everything, from the boots up, topped by a magnificently embroidered hieb. There was a spoken ritual that went with the clothes, not Handdara, I think, but a tradition of our Hearth; the words were all old and strange, the language of a thousand years ago. Grand rattled them out like somebody spitting rocks, and put the hieb on my shoulders. Everybody said, "Haya!"

All the elders, and a lot of younger kids, hung around helping me put on the new clothes as if I was a king or a baby, and some of the elders wanted to give me advice— "last advice," they called it, since you gain shifgrethor when you go into kemmer, and once you have shifgrethor advice is insulting. "Now you just keep away from that old Ebbeche," one of them told me shrilly. My mother took offense, snapping, "Keep your shadow to yourself, Tadsh!" And to me, "Don't listen to the old fish. Flapmouth Tadsh! But now listen, Sov."

I listened. Guyr had drawn me a little away from the others, and spoke gravely, with some embarrassment. "Remember, it will matter who you're with first."

I nodded. "I understand," I said.

"No, you don't," my mother snapped, forgetting to be embarrassed. "Just keep it in mind!"

"What, ah," I said. My mother waited. "If I, if I go into, as a, as female," I said. "Don't I, shouldn't I—?"

"Ah," Guyr said. "Don't worry. It'll be a year or more before you can conceive. Or get. Don't worry, this time. The other people will see to it, just in case. They all know it's your first kemmer. But do keep it in mind, who you're with first! Around, oh, around Karrid, and Ebbeche, and some of them."

"Come on!" Dory shouted, and we all got into a procession again to go downstairs and across the centerhall, where everybody cheered "Haya Sov! Haya Sov!" and the cooks beat on their saucepans. I wanted to die. But they all seemed so cheerful, so happy about me, wishing me well; I wanted also to live.

We went out the west door and across the sunny gardens and came to the kemmerhouse. Tage Ereb shares a kemmerhouse with two other Ereb Hearths; it's a beautiful building, all carved with deep-figure friezes in the Old Dynasty style, terribly worn by the weather of a couple of thousand years. On the red stone steps my family all kissed me, murmuring, "Praise then Darkness," or "In the act of Creation praise," and my mother gave me a hard push on my shoulders, what they call the sledge-push, for good luck, as I turned away from them and went in the door.

The Doorkeeper was waiting for me; a queer-looking, rather stooped person, with coarse, pale skin.

Now I realised who this "Ebbeche" they'd been talking about was. I'd never met him, but I'd heard about him. He was the Doorkeeper of our kemmerhouse, a halfdead—that is, a person in permanent kemmer, like the Aliens.

There are always a few people born that way here. Some of them can be cured; those who can't or choose not to be usually live in a Fastness and learn the disciplines, or they become Doorkeepers. It's convenient for them, and for normal people too. After all, who else would want to *live* in a kemmerhouse? But there are drawbacks. If you come to the kemmerhouse in thorharmen, ready to gender, and the first person you meet is fully male, his pheromones are likely to gender you female right then, whether that's what you had in mind this month or not. Responsible Doorkeepers, of course, keep well away from anybody who doesn't invite them to come close. But permanent kemmer may not lead to responsibility of character; nor does being called *halfdead* and *pervert* all your life, I imagine. Obviously my family didn't trust Ebbeche to keep his hands and his pheromones off me. But they were unjust. He honored a first kemmer as much as anyone else. He greeted me by name and showed me where to take off my new boots. Then he began to speak the ancient ritual welcome, backing down the hall before me; the first time I ever heard the words I would hear so many times again for so many years.

> You cross earth now.
> You cross water now.
> You cross the ice now. . . .

And the exulting ending, as we came into the centerhall:

Together we have crossed the Ice.
Together we come into the Hearthplace,
Into life, bringing life!
In the act of creation, praise!

The solemnity of the words moved me and distracted me somewhat from my intense self-consciousness. As I had in the Fastness, I felt the familiar reassurance of being part of something immensely older and larger than myself, even if it was strange and new to me. I must entrust myself to it and be what it made me. At the same time I was intensely alert. All my senses were extraordinarily keen, as they had been all morning. I was aware of everything, the beautiful blue color of the walls, the lightness and vigor of my steps as I walked, the texture of the wood under my bare feet, the sound and meaning of the ritual words, the Doorkeeper himself. He fascinated me. Ebbeche was certainly not handsome, and yet I noticed how musical his rather deep voice was; and pale skin was more attractive than I had ever thought it. I felt that he had been maligned, that his life must be a strange one. I wanted to talk to him. But as he finished the welcome, standing aside for me at the doorway of the centerhall, a tall person strode forward eagerly to meet me.

I was glad to see a familiar face: it was the head cook of my Hearth, Karrid Arrage. Like many cooks a rather fierce and temperamental person, Karrid had often taken notice of me, singling me out in a joking, challenging way, tossing me some delicacy—"Here, youngun! Get some meat on your bones!" As I saw Karrid now I went through the most extraordinary multiplicity of awarenesses: that Karrid was naked and that this nakedness was not like the nakedness of people in the Hearth, but a significant nakedness—that he was not the Karrid I had seen before but transfigured into great beauty—that he was he—that my mother had warned me about him—that I wanted to touch him—that I was afraid of him.

He picked me right up in his arms and pressed me against him. I felt his clitopenis like a fist between my legs. "Easy, now," the Doorkeeper said to him, and some other people came forward from the room, which I could see only as large, dimly glowing, full of shadows and mist.

"Don't worry, don't worry," Karrid said to me and them, with his hard laugh. "I won't hurt my own get, will I? I just want to be the one that gives her kemmer. As a woman, like a proper Thade. I want to give you that joy, little Sov." He was undressing me as he spoke, slipping off my hieb and shirt with big, hot, hasty hands. The Doorkeeper and the others kept close watch, but did not interfere. I felt totally defenseless, helpless, humiliated. I struggled to get free, broke loose, and tried to pick up and put on my shirt. I was shaking and felt terribly weak, I could hardly stand up. Karrid helped me clumsily; his big arm supported me. I leaned against him, feeling his hot, vibrant skin against mine, a wonderful feeling, like sunlight, like firelight. I leaned more heavily against him, raising my arms so that our sides slid together. "Hey, now," he said. "Oh, you beauty, oh, you Sov, here, take her away, this won't do!" And he backed right away from me, laughing and yet really alarmed, his clitopenis standing up amazingly. I stood there half-dressed, on my rubbery legs, bewildered. My eyes were full of mist, I could see nothing clearly.

"Come on," somebody said, and took my hand, a soft, cool touch totally different from the fire of Karrid's skin. It was a person from one of the other Hearths, I didn't know her name. She seemed to me to shine like gold in the dim, misty place. "Oh, you're going so fast," she said, laughing and admiring and consoling. "Come on, come into the pool, take it easy for a while. Karrid shouldn't have come on to you like that! But you're lucky, first kemmer as a woman, there's nothing like it. I kemmered as a man three times before I got to kemmer as a woman, it made me so mad, every time I got into thorharmen all my damn friends would all be women already. Don't worry about me—I'd say Karrid's influence was decisive," and she laughed again. Oh, you are so pretty!" and she bent her head and licked my nipples before I knew what she was doing.

It was wonderful, it cooled that stinging fire in them that nothing else could cool. She helped me finish undressing, and we stepped together into the warm water of the big, shallow pool that filled the whole center of this room. That was why it was so misty, why the echoes were so strange. The water lapped on my thighs, on my sex, on my belly. I turned to my friend and leaned forward to kiss her. It was a perfectly natural thing to do, it was what she wanted and I wanted, and I wanted her to lick and suck my nipples again, and she did. For a long time we lay in the shallow water playing, and I could have played forever. But then somebody else joined us, taking hold of my friend from behind, and she arched her body in the water like a golden fish leaping, threw her head back, and began to play with him.

I got out of the water and dried myself, feeling sad and shy and forsaken, and yet extremely interested in what had happened to my body. It felt wonderfully alive and electric, so that the roughness of the towel made me shiver with pleasure. Somebody had come closer to me, somebody that had been watching me play with my friend in the water. He sat down by me now.

It was a hearthmate a few years older than I, Arrad Tehemmy. I had worked in the gardens with Arrad all last summer, and liked him. He looked like Sether, I now thought, with heavy black hair and a long, thin face, but in him was that shining, that glory they all had here—all the kemmerers, the *women*, the *men*—such vivid beauty as I had never seen in any human beings. "Sov," he said, "I'd like—Your first—Will you—" His hands were already on me, and mine on him. "Come," he said, and I went with him. He took me into a beautiful little room, in which there was nothing but a fire burning in a fireplace, and a wide bed. There Arrad took me into his arms and I took Arrad into my arms, and then between my legs, and fell upward, upward through the golden light.

Arrad and I were together all that first night, and besides fucking a great deal, we ate a great deal. It had not occurred to me that there would be food at a kemmer-house; I had thought you weren't allowed to do anything but fuck. There was a lot of food, very good, too, set out so that you could eat whenever you wanted. Drink was more limited; the person in charge, an old woman-halfdead, kept her canny eye on you, and wouldn't give you any more beer if you showed signs of getting wild or stupid. I didn't need any more beer. I didn't need any more fucking. I was complete. I was in love forever for all time all my life to eternity with Arrad. But Arrad (who was a day farther into kemmer than I) fell asleep and wouldn't wake up, and an extraordinary person named Hama sat down by me and began talking and also running his hand up and down my back in the most delicious way, so that before long we got further entangled, and began fucking, and it was entirely different with Hama than it had been with Arrad, so that I realized that I must be in love with Hama, until Gehardar joined us. After that I think I began to understand that I loved them all and they all loved me and that that was the secret of the kemmerhouse.

It's been nearly fifty years, and I have to admit I do not recall everyone from my first kemmer; only Karrid and Arrad, Hama and Gehardar, old Tubanny, the most exquisitely skillful lover as a male that I ever knew—I met him often in later kemmers—and Berre, my golden fish, with whom I ended up in drowsy, peaceful, blissful lovemaking in front of the great hearth till we both fell asleep. And when we woke we were not women. We were not men. We were not in kemmer. We were very tired young adults.

"You're still beautiful," I said to Berre.

"So are you," Berre said. "Where do you work?"

"Furniture shop, Third Ward."

I tried licking Berre's nipple, but it didn't work; Berre flinched a little, and I said "Sorry," and we both laughed.

"I'm in the radio trade," Berre said. "Did you ever think of trying that?"

"Making radios?"

"No. Broadcasting. I do the Fourth Hour news and weather."

"That's you?" I said, awed.

"Come over to the tower some time, I'll show you around," said Berre.

Which is how I found my lifelong trade and a lifelong friend. As I tried to tell Sether when I came back to the Hearth, kemmer isn't exactly what we thought it was; it's much more complicated.

Sether's first kemmer was on Getheny Gor, the first day of the first month of autumn, at the dark of the moon. One of the family brought Sether into kemmer as a woman, and then Sether brought me in. That was the first time I kemmered as a man. And we stayed on the same wavelength, as Grand put it. We never conceived together, being cousins and having some modern scruples, but we made love in every combination, every dark of the moon, for years. And Sether brought my child, Tamor, into first kemmer—as a woman, like a proper Thade.

Later on Sether went into the Handdara, and became an Indweller in the old Fastness, and now is an Adept. I go over there often to join in one of the Chants or practise the Untrance or just to visit, and every few days Sether comes back to the Hearth. And we talk. The old days or the new times, somer or kemmer, love is love.

the Dead

Michael Swanwick

Michael Swanwick made his debut in 1980, and in the twenty-five years that have followed has established himself as one of SF's most prolific and consistently excellent writers at short lengths, as well as one of the premier novelists of his generation. He has won the Theodore Sturgeon Award and the *Asimov's* Readers Award poll. In 1991, his novel *Stations of the Tide* won him a Nebula Award as well, and in 1995 he won the World Fantasy Award for his story "Radio Waves." He's won the Hugo Award four times between 1999 and 2003, for his stories "The Very Pulse of the Machine," "Scherzo with Tyrannosaur," "The Dog Said Bow-Wow," and "Slow Life." His other books include the novels *In the Drift*, *Vacuum Flowers*, *The Iron Dragon's Daughter* (which was a finalist for the World Fantasy Award *and* the Arthur C. Clarke Award, a rare distinction!), *Jack Faust*, and, most recently, *Bones of the Earth*, plus a novella-length book, *Griffin's Egg*. His short fiction has been assembled in *Gravity's Angels*, *A Geography of Unknown Lands*, *Slow Dancing Through Time* (a collection of his collaborative short work with other writers), *Moon Dogs*, *Puck Aleshire's Abecedary*, and *Tales of Old Earth*. He's also published a collection of critical articles, *The Postmodern Archipelago*, and a book-length interview: *Being Gardner Dozois*. His most recent book is a new collection, *Cigar-Box Faust and Other Miniatures*. Coming up are two new collections, *The Periodic Table of SF* and *Michael Swanwick's Field Guide to the Mesozoic Megafauna*. He's had stories in our Second, Third, Fourth, Sixth, Seventh, Tenth, and Thirteenth through Twenty-first annual collections. Swanwick lives in Philadelphia with his wife, Marianne Porter. He has a Web site at http://www.michaelswanwick.com.

We've been worried about technological unemployment for decades, but, as the bleak little story that follows suggests, now there may be another threat to your job security: dead people. Back from the grave and looking for *work*. . . .

Three boy zombies in matching red jackets bused our table, bringing water, lighting candles, brushing away the crumbs between courses. Their eyes were dark, attentive, lifeless; their hands and faces so white as to be faintly luminous in the hushed light. I thought it in bad taste, but "This is Manhattan," Courtney said. "A certain studied offensiveness is fashionable here."

The blond brought menus and waited for our order.

We both ordered pheasant. "An excellent choice," the boy said in a clear, emotionless voice. He went away and came back a minute later with the freshly strangled birds, holding them up for our approval. He couldn't have been more than eleven when he died and his skin was of that sort connoisseurs call "milk-glass," smooth, without blemish, and all but translucent. He must have cost a fortune.

As the boy was turning away, I impulsively touched his shoulder. He turned back. "What's your name, son?" I asked.

"Timothy." He might have been telling me the *specialité de maison*. The boy waited a breath to see if more was expected of him, then left.

Courtney gazed after him. "How lovely he would look," she murmured, "nude. Standing in the moonlight by a cliff. Definitely a cliff. Perhaps the very one where he met his death."

"He wouldn't look very lovely if he'd fallen off a cliff."

"Oh, don't be unpleasant."

The wine steward brought our bottle. "Château Latour '17." I raised an eyebrow. The steward had the sort of old and complex face that Rembrandt would have enjoyed painting. He poured with pulseless ease and then dissolved into the gloom. "Good lord, Courtney, you *seduced* me on cheaper."

She flushed, not happily. Courtney had a better career going than I. She outpowered me. We both knew who was smarter, better connected, more likely to end up in a corner office with the historically significant antique desk. The only edge I had was that I was a male in a seller's market. It was enough.

"This is a business dinner, Donald," she said, "nothing more."

I favored her with an expression of polite disbelief I knew from experience she'd find infuriating. And, digging into my pheasant, murmured, "Of course." We didn't say much of consequence until dessert, when I finally asked, "So what's Loeb-Soffner up to these days?"

"Structuring a corporate expansion. Jim's putting together the financial side of the package, and I'm doing personnel. You're being headhunted, Donald." She favored me with that feral little flash of teeth she made when she saw something she wanted. Courtney wasn't a beautiful woman, far from it. But there was that fierceness to her, that sense of something primal being held under tight and precarious control that made her hot as hot to me. "You're talented, you're thuggish, and you're not too tightly nailed to your present position. Those are all qualities we're looking for."

She dumped her purse on the table, took out a single-folded sheet of paper. "These are the terms I'm offering." She placed it by my plate, attacked her torte with gusto.

I unfolded the paper. "This is a lateral transfer."

"Unlimited opportunity for advancement," she said with her mouth full, "if you've got the stuff."

"Mmm." I did a line-by-line of the benefits, all comparable to what I was getting now. My current salary to the dollar—Ms. Soffner was showing off. And the stock options. "This can't be right. Not for a lateral."

There was that grin again, like a glimpse of shark in murky waters. "I knew you'd like it. We're going over the top with the options because we need your answer right away—tonight preferably. Tomorrow at the latest. No negotiations. We have to put the package together fast. There's going to be a shitstorm of publicity when this comes out. We want to have everything nailed down, present the fundies and bleeding hearts with a *fait accompli*."

"My God, Courtney, what kind of monster do you have hold of now?"

"The biggest one in the world. Bigger than Apple. Bigger than Home Virtual. Bigger than HIVac-IV," she said with relish. "Have you ever heard of Koestler Biological?"

I put my fork down.

"Koestler? You're peddling corpses now?"

"Please. Postanthropic biological resources." She said it lightly, with just the right touch of irony. Still, I thought I detected a certain discomfort with the nature of her client's product.

"There's no money in it." I waved a hand toward our attentive waitstaff. "These guys must be—what—maybe two percent of the annual turnover? Zombies are luxury goods: servants, reactor cleanups, Hollywood stunt deaths, exotic services"—we both knew what I meant—"a few hundred a year, maybe, tops. There's not the demand. The revulsion factor is too great."

"There's been a technological breakthrough." Courtney leaned forward. "They can install the infrasystem and controllers and offer the product for the factory-floor cost of a new subcompact. That's way below the economic threshold for blue-collar labor.

"Look at it from the viewpoint of a typical factory owner. He's already downsized to the bone and labor costs are bleeding him dry. How can he compete in a dwindling consumer market? Now let's imagine he buys into the program." She took out her Mont Blanc and began scribbling figures on the tablecloth. "No benefits. No liability suits. No sick pay. No pilferage. We're talking about cutting labor costs by at least two thirds. Minimum! That's irresistible, I don't care how big your revulsion factor is. We project we can move five hundred thousand units in the first year."

"Five hundred thousand," I said. "That's crazy. Where the hell are you going to get the raw material for—?"

"Africa."

"Oh, God, Courtney." I was struck wordless by the cynicism it took to even consider turning the sub-Saharan tragedy to a profit, by the sheer, raw evil of channeling hard currency to the pocket Hitlers who ran the camps. Courtney only smiled and gave that quick little flip of her head that meant she was accessing the time on an optic chip.

"I think you're ready," she said, "to talk with Koestler."

At her gesture, the zombie boys erected projector lamps about us, fussed with the settings, turned them on. Interference patterns moiréd, clashed, meshed. Walls of darkness erected themselves about us. Courtney took out her flat and set it up on the table. Three taps of her nailed fingers and the round and hairless face of Marvin Koestler appeared on the screen. "Ah, Courtney!" he said in a pleased voice. "You're in—New York, yes? The San Moritz. With Donald." The slightest pause with each accessed bit of information. "Did you have the antelope medallions?" When we shook our heads, he kissed his fingertips. "Magnificent! They're ever so lightly braised and then smothered in buffalo mozzarella. Nobody makes them better. I had the same dish in Florence the other day, and there was simply no comparison."

I cleared my throat. "Is that where you are? Italy?"

"Let's leave out where I am." He made a dismissive gesture, as if it were a trifle. But Courtney's face darkened. Corporate kidnapping being the growth industry it is, I'd gaffed badly. "The question is—what do you think of my offer?"

"It's . . . interesting. For a lateral."

"It's the start-up costs. We're leveraged up to our asses as it is. You'll make out better this way in the long run." He favored me with a sudden grin that went mean around the edges. Very much the financial buccaneer. Then he leaned forward, lowered his voice, maintained firm eye contact. Classic people-handling techniques. "You're not sold. You know you can trust Courtney to have checked out the finances. Still, you think: It won't work. To work the product has to be irresistible, and it's not. It can't be."

"Yes, sir," I said. "Succinctly put."

He nodded to Courtney. "Let's sell this young man." And to me, "My stretch is downstairs."

He winked out.

Koestler was waiting for us in the limo, a ghostly pink presence. His holo, rather, a genial if somewhat coarse-grained ghost afloat in golden light. He waved an expansive and insubstantial arm to take in the interior of the car and said, "Make yourselves at home."

The chauffeur wore combat-grade photomultipliers. They gave him a buggish, inhuman look. I wasn't sure if he was dead or not. "Take us to Heaven," Koestler said.

The doorman stepped out into the street, looked both ways, nodded to the chauffeur. Robot guns tracked our progress down the block.

"Courtney tells me you're getting the raw materials from Africa."

"Distasteful, but necessary. To begin with. We have to sell the idea first—no reason to make things rough on ourselves. Down the line, though, I don't see why we can't go domestic. Something along the lines of a reverse mortgage, perhaps, life insurance that pays off while you're still alive. It'd be a step toward getting the poor off our backs at last. Fuck 'em. They've been getting a goddamn free ride for too long; the least they can do is to die and provide us with servants."

I was pretty sure Koestler was joking. But I smiled and ducked my head, so I'd be covered in either case. "What's Heaven?" I asked, to move the conversation onto safer territory.

"A proving ground," Koestler said with great satisfaction, "for the future. Have you ever witnessed bare-knuckles fisticuffs?"

"No."

"Ah, now there's a sport for gentlemen! The sweet science at its sweetest. No rounds, no rules, no holds barred. It gives you the real measure of a man—not just of his strength but his character. How he handles himself, whether he keeps cool under pressure—how he stands up to pain. Security won't let me go to the clubs in person, but I've made arrangements."

Heaven was a converted movie theater in a run-down neighborhood in Queens. The chauffeur got out, disappeared briefly around the back, and returned with two zombie bodyguards. It was like a conjurer's trick. "You had these guys stashed in the *trunk*?" I asked as he opened the door for us.

"It's a new world," Courtney said. "Get used to it."

The place was mobbed. Two, maybe three hundred seats, standing room only. A mixed crowd, blacks and Irish and Koreans mostly, but with a smattering of uptown customers as well. You didn't have to be poor to need the occasional taste of vicarious potency. Nobody paid us any particular notice. We'd come in just as the fighters were being presented.

"Weighing two-five-oh, in black trunks with a red stripe," the ref was bawling, "tha gang-bang *gang*sta, the bare-knuckle *brawla*, the man with tha—"

Courtney and I went up a scummy set of back stairs. Bodyguard-us-bodyguard, as if we were a combat patrol out of some twentieth-century jungle war. A scrawny, pot-bellied old geezer with a damp cigar in his mouth unlocked the door to our box. Sticky floor, bad seats, a good view down on the ring. Gray plastic matting, billowing smoke.

Koestler was there, in a shiny new hologram shell. It reminded me of those plaster Madonnas in painted bathtubs that Catholics set out in their yards. "Your permanent box?" I asked.

"All of this is for your sake, Donald—you and a few others. We're pitting our product one-on-one against some of the local talent. By arrangement with the management. What you're going to see will settle your doubts once and for all."

"You'll like this," Courtney said. "I've been here five nights straight. Counting tonight." The bell rang, starting the fight. She leaned forward avidly, hooking her elbows on the railing.

The zombie was gray-skinned and modestly muscled, for a fighter. But it held up its hands alertly, was light on its feet, and had strangely calm and knowing eyes.

Its opponent was a real bruiser, a big black guy with classic African features twisted slightly out of true, so that his mouth curled up in a kind of sneer on one side. He had gang scars on his chest and even uglier marks on his back that didn't look deliberate but like something he'd earned on the streets. His eyes burned with an intensity just this side of madness.

He came forward cautiously but not fearfully, and made a couple of quick jabs to get the measure of his opponent. They were blocked and countered.

They circled each other, looking for an opening.

For a minute or so, nothing much happened. Then the gangster feinted at the zombie's head, drawing up its guard. He drove through that opening with a slam to the zombie's nuts that made me wince.

No reaction.

The dead fighter responded with a flurry of punches, and got in a glancing blow to its opponent's cheek. They separated, engaged, circled around.

Then the big guy exploded in a combination of killer blows, connecting so solidly it seemed they would splinter every rib in the dead fighter's body. It brought the crowd to their feet, roaring their approval.

The zombie didn't even stagger.

A strange look came into the gangster's eyes, then, as the zombie counterattacked, driving him back into the ropes. I could only imagine what it must be like for a man who had always lived by his strength and his ability to absorb punishment to realize that he was facing an opponent to whom pain meant nothing. Fights were lost and won by flinches and hesitations. You won by keeping your head. You lost by getting rattled.

Despite his best blows, the zombie stayed methodical, serene, calm, relentless. That was its nature.

It must have been devastating.

The fight went on and on. It was a strange and alienating experience for me. After a while I couldn't stay focused on it. My thoughts kept slipping into a zone where I found myself studying the line of Courtney's jaw, thinking about later tonight. She liked her sex just a little bit sick. There was always a feeling, fucking her, that there was something truly repulsive that she *really* wanted to do but lacked the courage to bring up on her own.

So there was always this urge to get her to do something she didn't like. She was resistant; I never dared try more than one new thing per date. But I could always talk her into that one thing. Because when she was aroused, she got pliant. She could be talked into anything. She could be made to beg for it.

Courtney would've been amazed to learn that I was not proud of what I did with her—quite the opposite, in fact. But I was as obsessed with her as she was with whatever it was that obsessed her.

Suddenly Courtney was on her feet, yelling. The hologram showed Koestler on his feet as well. The big guy was on the ropes, being pummeled. Blood and spittle flew from his face with each blow. Then he was down; he'd never even had a chance. He must've known early on that it was hopeless, that he wasn't going to win, but he'd refused to take a fall. He had to be pounded into the ground. He went down raging, proud and uncomplaining. I had to admire that.

But he lost anyway.

That, I realized, was the message I was meant to take away from this. Not just that the product was robust. But that only those who backed it were going to win. I could see, even if the audience couldn't, that it was the end of an era. A man's body wasn't worth a damn anymore. There wasn't anything it could do that technology couldn't handle better. The number of losers in the world had just doubled, tripled, reached maximum. What the fools below were cheering for was the death of their futures.

I got up and cheered too.

In the stretch afterward, Koestler said, "You've seen the light. You're a believer now."

"I haven't necessarily decided yet."

"Don't bullshit me," Koestler said. "I've done my homework, Mr. Nichols. Your current position is not exactly secure. Morton-Western is going down the tubes. The entire service sector is going down the tubes. Face it, the old economic order is as good as fucking gone. Of course you're going to take my offer. You don't have any other choice."

The fax outed sets of contracts. "A Certain Product," it said here and there. Corpses were never mentioned.

But when I opened my jacket to get a pen Koestler said, "Wait, I've got a factory. Three thousand positions under me. I've got a motivated workforce. They'd walk through fire to keep their jobs. Pilferage is at zero. Sick time practically the same. Give me one advantage your product has over my current workforce. Sell me on it. I'll give you thirty seconds."

I wasn't in sales and the job had been explicitly promised me already. But by reaching for the pen, I had admitted I wanted the position. And we all knew whose hand carried the whip.

"They can be catheterized," I said—"no toilet breaks."

For a long instant Koestler just stared at me blankly. Then he exploded with laughter. "By God, that's a new one! You have a great future ahead of you, Donald. Welcome aboard."

He winked out.

We drove on in silence for a while, aimless, directionless. At last Courtney leaned forward and touched the chauffeur's shoulder.

"Take me home," she said.

Riding through Manhattan I suffered from a waking hallucination that we were driving through a city of corpses. Gray faces, listless motions. Everyone looked dead in the headlights and sodium-vapor streetlamps. Passing by the Children's Museum I saw a mother with a stroller through the glass doors. Two small children by her side. They all three stood motionless, gazing forward at nothing. We passed by a stop-and-go where zombies stood out on the sidewalk drinking forties in paper bags. Through upper-story windows I could see the sad rainbow trace of virtuals playing to empty eyes. There were zombies in the park, zombies smoking blunts, zombies driving taxies, zombies sitting on stoops and hanging out on street corners, all of them waiting for the years to pass and the flesh to fall from their bones.

I felt like the last man alive.

Courtney was still wired and sweaty from the fight. The pheromones came off her in great waves as I followed her down the hall to her apartment. She stank of lust. I found myself thinking of how she got just before orgasm, so desperate, so desirable. It was different after she came, she would fall into a state of calm assurance; the same sort of calm assurance she showed in her business life, the aplomb she sought so wildly during the act itself.

And when that desperation left her, so would I. Because even I could recognize that it was her desperation that drew me to her, that made me do the things she needed me to do. In all the years I'd known her, we'd never once had breakfast together.

I wished there was some way I could deal her out of the equation. I wished that her desperation were a liquid that I could drink down to the dregs. I wished I could drop her in a winepress and squeeze her dry.

At her apartment, Courtney unlocked her door and in one complicated movement twisted through and stood facing me from the inside. "Well," she said. "All in all, a productive evening. Good night, Donald."

"Good night? Aren't you going to invite me inside?"

"No."

"What do you mean, no?" She was beginning to piss me off. A blind man could've told she was in heat from across the street. A chimpanzee could've talked his way into her pants. "What kind of idiot game are you playing now?"

"You know what no means, Donald. You're not stupid."

"No I'm not, and neither are you. We both know the score. Now let me in, goddamnit."

"Enjoy your present," she said, and closed the door.

I found Courtney's present back in my suite. I was still seething from her treatment of me and stalked into the room, letting the door slam behind me so that I was standing in near-total darkness. The only light was what little seeped through the draped windows at the far end of the room. I was just reaching for the light switch when there was a motion in the darkness.

Jackers! I thought, and all in panic lurched for the light switch, hoping to achieve I don't know what. Credit-jackers always work in trios, one to torture the security codes out of you, one to phone the numbers out of your accounts and into a fiscal trapdoor, a third to stand guard. Was turning the lights on supposed to make them scurry for darkness, like roaches? Nevertheless, I almost tripped over my own feet in my haste to reach the switch. But of course it was nothing like what I'd feared.

It was a woman.

She stood by the window in a white silk dress that could neither compete with nor distract from her ethereal beauty, her porcelain skin. When the lights came on, she turned toward me, eyes widening, lips parting slightly. Her breasts swayed ever so slightly as she gracefully raised a bare arm to offer me a lily. "Hello, Donald," she said huskily. "I'm yours for the night." She was absolutely beautiful.

And dead of course.

Not twenty minutes later I was hammering on Courtney's door. She came to the door in a Pierre Cardin dressing gown and from the way she was still cinching the sash and the disarray of her hair I gathered she hadn't been expecting me.

"I'm not alone," she said.

"I didn't come here for the dubious pleasures of your fair white body." I pushed my way into the room. (But couldn't help remembering that beautiful body of hers, not so exquisite as the dead whore's, and now the thoughts were inextricably mingled in my head: death and Courtney, sex and corpses, a Gordian knot I might never be able to untangle.)

"You didn't like my surprise?" She was smiling openly now, amused.

"No. I fucking did not!"

I took a step toward her. I was shaking. I couldn't stop fisting and unfisting my hands.

She fell back a step. But that confident, oddly expectant look didn't leave her face. Bruno, she said lightly. "Would you come in here?"

A motion at the periphery of vision. Bruno stepped out of the shadows of her bedroom. He was a muscular brute, pumped, ripped, and as black as the fighter I'd seen go down earlier that night. He stood behind Courtney, totally naked, with slim hips and wide shoulders and the finest skin I'd ever seen.

And dead.

I saw it all in a flash.

"Oh, for God's sake, Courtney!" I said, disgusted. "I can't believe you. That you'd actually. That thing's just an obedient body. There's nothing there—no passion, no connection, just . . . physical presence."

Courtney made a kind of chewing motion through her smile, weighing the implications of what she was about to say. Nastiness won.

"We have equity now," she said.

I lost it then. I stepped forward, raising a hand, and I swear to God I intended to bounce the bitch's head off the back wall. But she didn't flinch—she didn't even look afraid. She merely moved aside, saying, "In the body, Bruno. He has to look good in a business suit."

A dead fist smashed into my ribs so hard I thought for an instant my heart had stopped. Then Bruno punched me in my stomach. I doubled over, gasping. Two, three, four more blows. I was on the ground now, rolling over, helpless and weeping with rage.

"That's enough, baby. Now put out the trash."

Bruno dumped me in the hallway.

I glared up at Courtney through my tears. She was not at all beautiful now. Not in the least. You're getting older, I wanted to tell her. But instead I heard my voice, angry and astonished, saying, "You . . . you goddamn, fucking necrophile!"

"Cultivate a taste for it," Courtney said. Oh, she was purring! I doubted she'd ever find life quite this good again. "Half a million Brunos are about to come on the market. You're going to find it a lot more difficult to pick up *living* women in not so very long."

I sent away the dead whore. Then I took a long shower that didn't really make me feel any better. Naked, I walked into my unlit suite and opened the curtains. For a long time I stared out over the glory and darkness that was Manhattan.

I was afraid, more afraid than I'd ever been in my life.

The slums below me stretched to infinity. They were a vast necropolis, a never-ending city of the dead. I thought of the millions out there who were never going to hold down a job again. I thought of how they must hate me—me and my kind—and how helpless they were before us. And yet. There were so many of them and so few of us. If they were to all rise up at once, they'd be like a tsunami, irresistible. And if there was so much as a spark of life left in them, then that was exactly what they would do.

That was one possibility. There was one other, and that was that nothing would happen. Nothing at all.

God help me, but I didn't know which one scared me more.

Recording Angel

IAN MCDONALD

British author Ian McDonald is an ambitious and daring writer with a wide range and an impressive amount of talent. His first story was published in 1982, and since then he has appeared with some frequency in *Interzone, Asimov's Science Fiction, New Worlds, Zenith, Other Edens, Amazing,* and elsewhere. He was nominated for the John W. Campbell Award in 1985, and in 1989 he won the *Locus* "Best First Novel" Award for his novel *Desolation Road*. He won the Philip K. Dick Award in 1992 for his novel *King of Morning, Queen of Day*. His other books include the novels *Out on Blue Six, Hearts, Hands and Voices, Terminal Cafe, Sacrifice of Fools, Evolution's Shore,* and *Kirinya,* a chapbook novella *Tendeleo's Story, Ares Express,* and *Cyberabad,* as well as two collections of his short fiction, *Empire Dreams* and *Speaking in Tongues*. His stories have appeared in our eighth through tenth, fourteenth through sixteenth, and nineteenth and twentieth annual collections. Coming up is a another new novel, *River of Gods*. Born in Manchester, England, in 1960, McDonald has spent most of his life in Northern Ireland, and now lives and works in Belfast.

Here's a look at a bizarre and terrifying future where something enigmatic and implacable is *eating* Africa, and the people in the way are just going to have to come to terms with it—however they can.

For the last ten miles she drove past refugees from the xenoforming. Some were in their own vehicles. Many rode town buses that had been commandeered to take the people south, or the grubby white trucks of the UNHCR. Most walked, pushing the things they had saved from the advancing Chaga on handcarts or barrows, or laden on the heads and backs of women and children. That has always been the way of it, the woman thought as she drove past the unbroken file of people. The world ends, the women and children must carry it, and the United Nations sends its soldiers to make sure they do not drop it. And the news corporations send their journalists to make sure that the world sees without being unduly disturbed. After all, they are only Africans. A continent is being devoured by some thing from the stars, and I am sent to write the obituary of a hotel.

"I don't do gossip," she had told T. P. Costello, SkyNet's Nairobi station chief when he told her of the international celebrities who were coming to the death-party of the famous Treehouse Hotel. "I didn't come to this country to cream myself over who's wearing which designer dress or who's having an affair with or getting from whom."

"I know, I know," T. P. Costello had said. "You came to Kenya to be a player in Earth's first contact with the alien. Everyone did. That's why I'm sending you. Who cares what Brad Pitt thinks about the Gas Cloud theory versus the Little Gray Men theory? Angles are what I want. You can get angles, Gaby. What can you get?"

"Angles, T. P.," she had replied, wearily, to her editor's now-familiar litany.

"That's correct. And you'll be up there with it, right on terminum. That's what you want, isn't it?"

That's correct, T. P., she thought. Three months in Kenya and all she had seen of the Chaga had been a distant line of color, like surf on a far reef, under the clouded shadow of Kilimanjaro, advancing imperceptibly but inexorably across the Amboseli plain. The spectator's view. Up there, on the highlands around Kirinyaga where the latest biological package had come down, she would be within touching distance of it. The player's view.

There was a checkpoint up at Nanyuki. The South African soldiers in blue UN helmets at first did not know how to treat her, thinking that with her green eyes and long mahogany hair she might be another movie star or television celebrity. When her papers identified her as Gaby McAslan, on-line multimedia journalist with SkyNet East Africa, they stopped being respectful. A woman they could flirt with, a journalist they could touch for bribes. Gaby endured their flirtations and gave their commanding officer three of the dwindling stock of duty-free Swatches she had bought expressly for the purpose of petty corruption. In return she was given a map of the approved route to the hotel. If she stayed on it she would be safe. The bush patrols had orders to shoot suspected looters or loiterers.

Beyond the checkpoint there were no more refugees. The only vehicles were carrying celebrities to the party at the end of the world, and the news corporations following them. The Kikuyu *shambas* on either side of the road had been long abandoned. Wild Africa was reclaiming them. For a while, then something else would reclaim them from wild Africa. Reverse terraforming, she thought. Instead of making an alien world into Earth, Earth is made into an alien world. In her open-top SkyNet 4x4, Gaby could sense the Chaga behind the screen of heavy high-country timber, and edgy presence of the alien, and electric tingle of anticipation. She had never been this close before.

When the first biological package came down on the summit of Kilimanjaro, she had known, in SkyNet Multimedia News's UK office among the towers of London's Docklands, that this fallen star had her name written on it. The stuff that had come out of it, that looked a little like rain forest and a little like drained coral reef but mostly like nothing anyone had ever seen before, that disassembled terrestrial vegetation into its component molecules and incorporated them into its own matrix at an unstoppable fifty meters every day, confirmed her holy business. The others that came down in the Bismarck Archipelago, the Ruwenzori, in Ecuador and Papua New Guinea and the Maldives, these were only memos from the star gods. It's here, it's waiting for you. Hurry up now.

Now, the Nyandarua package, drawing its trail of plasma over Lake Victoria and the Rift Valley, would bring her at last face-to-face with life from the stars.

She came across a conga-line of massive tracked transporters, each the size of a large house, wedged into the narrow red-dirt road. Prefabricated accommodation cabins were piled up on top of the transporters. Branches bent and snapped as the behemoths ground past at walking pace. Gaby had heard that UNECTA, the United Nations agency that coordinated research into the Chagas, had dismantled its Ol Tukai base, one of four positioned around Kilimanjaro, all moving backward in synchrony with the advance of the southern Chaga, and sent it north. UNECTA's pockets were not deep enough, it seemed, to buy a new mobile base, especially now that the multinationals had cut their contributions in the absence of any exploitable technologies coming out of the Chaga.

UNECTA staff on the tops of the mobile towers waved as she drove carefully past in the red muddy verges. They can probably see the snows of Kirinyaga from that height, she thought. Between the white mountains. We run from the south, we run from the north but the expanding circles of vegetation are closing on us and we cannot escape. Why do we run? We will all have to face it in the end, when it takes everything we know and changes it beyond recognition. We have always imagined that because it comes down in the tropics it is confined here. Why should climate stop it? Nothing else has. Maybe it will only stop when it closes around the poles. Xenoforming complete.

The hotel was one of those buildings that are like animals in zoos, that by their stillness and coloration can hide from you even when you are right in front of them, and you only know they are there because of the sign on the cage. Two Kenyan soldiers far too young for the size of their weapons met her from the car park full of tour buses and news-company 4x4s. They escorted her along a dirt path between skinny, gray-trunked trees. She could still not see the hotel. She commented on the small wooden shelters that stood every few meters along the path.

"In case of charging animals," the slightly older soldier said. "But this is better." He stroked his weapon as if it were a breast. "Thirty heavy-caliber rounds per second. That will stop more than any wooden shelter."

"Since the Chaga has come there are many more animals around," the younger soldier said. He had taken the laces out of his boots, in the comfortable, country way.

"Running away," Gaby said. "Like any sane thing should."

"No," the young, laceless soldier said. "Running into."

There was a black-painted metal fire escape at the end of the track. As Gaby squinted at the incongruity, the hotel resolved out of the greenery before her. Many of the slim, silver tree trunks were wooden piles, the mass of leaves and creepers concealed the superstructure bulking over her.

The steward met her at the top of the stairs, checked her name against the guest list, and showed her her room, a tiny wooden cabin with a view of leaves. Gaby thought it must be like this on one of the UNECTA mobile bases; minimal, monastic. She did something to her face and went up to the party on the roof. It had been running for three days. It would only end when the hotel did. The party at the edge of the end of the world. In one glance she saw thirty newsworthy faces and peeked into her bag to check the charge level on her disc recorder. She talked to it as she moved between the faces to the bar. The *Out of Africa* look was the thing among the newsworthy this year: riding breeches, leather, with the necessary twist of twenty-first-century *knowing* with the addition of animal-skin prints.

Gaby ordered a piña colada from the Kenyan barman and wondered as he shook it what incentive the management had offered him—all the staff—to stay. Family relocation to other hotels, on the Coast, down in Zanzibar, she reckoned. And where do they go when they run out of hotels to relocate to? Interesting, but not the angle, she decided as the barman poured out the thick, semeny proof of his ability.

"Bugger all here, T. P.," she said to the little black machine in her shirt pocket. Then cocktail-party dynamics parted the people in front of her and there it was, one hundred feet away beyond the gray wooden railing, at the edge of the artificial water hole they dredged with bulldozers in the off-season. One hundred feet. Fifteen seconds walk. Eighteen hours crawl. If you kept very still and concentrated you would be able to see it moving, as you could see the slow sweep of the minute hand of your watch. This was the Chaga not on the geographical scale, devouring whole landscapes, but on the molecular.

Gaby walked through the gap in the bright and the beautiful. She walked past Brad Pitt. She walked past Antonio Banderas, with his new supermodel girlfriend. She walked past Julia Roberts so close she could see the wrinkles and sags that the editing computers digitally smoothed. They were only celebrities. They could not change the world, or suffer to have their world changed, even by alien intervention. Gaby rested her hands on the rail and looked over the Chaga.

"It's like being on the sundeck of a great, archaic, ocean-liner, cruising close to the shore of an alien archipelago," she told the recorder. The contrast between the place she was and the place out there was as great as between land and sea, the border between the two as shifting and inexact. There was no line where earth became unearth; rather a gradual infection of the highland forest with the colored hexagons of alien ground cover that pushed up fingers and feelers and strange blooms between the tree trunks into the disturbing pseudocoral forms of the low Chaga. With distance the alien reef grew denser and the trees fewer; only the tallest and strongest withstood the attack of the molecular processors, lifted high like the masts of beached ships. A kilometer beyond the tide line a wall of red pillars rose a sheer three hundred meters from the rumbled land reefs before opening into a canopy of interlinked hexagonal leaf plates.

"The Great Wall," Gaby said, describing the scene before her to the disc. The Chaga beyond offered only glimpses of itself as it rose toward cloud-shrouded Kirinyaga: a gleam of the open white palm of a distant hand-tree, the sway of moss-covered balloons, the glitter of light from crystals. What kind of small craft might put forth from such a shore to meet this ship of vanities? she wondered.

"Seven minutes. Thirteen centimeters. That's longer than most."

Until he spoke, Gaby had not noticed the white man standing beside her at the rail. She could not remember whether he had been there before her, or arrived later. He was small, balding, running to late-40s, early-50s belly. His skin was weathered brown, his teeth were not good, and he spoke with a White African accent. He could not be Beautiful, nor even Press. He must be Staff. He was dressed in buffs and khakis and a vest of pockets, without the least necessary touch of twenty-first-century *knowing*. He looked like the last of the Great White Hunters.

He was.

He was called Prenderleith. He had impeccable manners.

"Pardon me for interrupting your contemplation, but if people see me talking to someone they won't come and ask me about things I've killed."

"Isn't that your job?"

"Killing, or telling?"

"Whichever."

"Whichever, it doesn't include being patronized by movie stars, piss-artists and bloody journalists."

"I am a bloody journalist."

"But the first thing you did was come over to the rail and look at that bloody thing out there. For seven minutes."

"And that makes this journalist worth talking to."

"Yes," he said, simply.

And it makes you worth talking to, Gaby thought, because maybe you are my angle on this thing. The Last White Hunter. But you are as wary as the creatures you hunt, and if I tell you this it will scare you away, so I must be as stealthy as you. Gaby surreptitiously turned up the recording level on her little black machine. Enhancement software back at Tom M'boya Street would edit the chatter and fluff.

"So what do you think it is?" Gaby asked. Across the terrace a dissension between Bret Easton Ellis and Damien Hirst was escalating into an argument. Guests flocked in, anticipating a fistfight. Cameras whirred. Prenderleith rested his arms on the rail and looked out across the Chaga.

"I don't know about all this aliens-from-another-world stuff."

"Latest theory is that it wasn't built by little gray men, but originated in gas clouds in Rho Ophiuchi, eight hundred light-years away. They've found signatures of the same complex fullerenes that are present in the Chaga. An entire civilization, growing up in space. They estimate it's at least a hundred thousand years old."

" 'They,' " Prenderleith said.

"UNECTA," Gaby said.

"They're probably right. They know more about this than I do, so if they say it's gas, then it's gas. Gas clouds, little gray men, I don't know about either of them; it's just not part of my world. See, they brought me up with just enough education to be able to manage, to do things well; not to think. Kenya wasn't the kind of country that needed thinking, we thought. You did things, not thought. Riding, farming, hunting, driving, flying. Doing things. The country decided what you needed to think. None of us could see the changes happening under our feet: I was brought up obsolete, no bloody use in the new Kenya, that thought, at all. All I could do was find a job in something as obsolete and useless as myself. This bloody place has nothing to do with the real Kenya. Bloody theme park. Even the animals are fake; they bulldozed a water hole so Americans would have elephants to photograph. Irony is: Now the tourists are gone, there've never been so many bloody animals, all headed in. Counted forty-five elephant in one day; no one gives a stuff anymore. Tell me, how can it be alien if the animals are going in there? How could gas know how to build something like that? Feels to me like it's something very old, that animals knew once and have never forgotten, that's come out of Africa itself. Everything starts here, in East Africa; the land is very old, and has a long memory. And strong: Maybe Africa has had enough of what people are doing to it—enough thinking—and has decided to claim itself back. That's why the animals aren't afraid. It's giving it back to them."

"But taking yours away," Gaby said.

"Not my Africa." Prenderleith glanced around at the famous and beautiful people. The fight had evaporated into sulks and looks. Leaf Phoenix was passing round cigarettes, to the thrilled horror of the other guests. Chimes filled the air. Heads turned. A waiter in an untwenty-first-century-*knowing* leopard-print jacket moved across the roof terrace, playing a set of handheld chime bars.

"Dinner," Prenderleith announced.

The seating plan put Gaby at the far end of the long table, between a hack she knew from BBC on-line and a Hollywood film god who talked of working on fifteen musicals simultaneously and little else. Prenderleith had been placed at the far end of the table, in the champion's seat, hemmed in by the famous. Gaby watched him telling his much-told tales of stalkings and killings. He would glance up from time to time and she would catch his eye, and it was like a little conspiracy. I should tell him that he is an angle, Gaby thought. I should admit to the recorder.

The famous claimed Prenderleith for the remainder of the evening, a small court surrounding his seat by the picture window with its floodlit view of the Chaga approaching molecule by molecule. Gaby sat at the bar and watched him telling his stories of that other Africa. There was a light in his eye. Gaby could not decide if it was nostalgia or anticipation of when it would all fall and come apart.

Out in the dark beyond the floodlights, trees fell, brought down by the Chaga, dissolver of illusions. The wooden piers of the hotel creaked and clicked. The celebrities glanced at each other, afraid.

The knock came at 1:27 according to the luminous hands of the bedside clock. Gaby had not long gone to sleep after dictating commentary. Noise from the upper decks; the party would gradually wind down with the hour until the soldiers came with the morning to clear everyone out. One of the guests, high and hopeful? A second polite knock. The politeness told her.

She could see from the way Prenderleith stood in the corridor that he was a little drunk and that, had he not been, he would not have done this. He was carrying his gun, like an adored child.

"Something you should see," he said.

"Why me?" Gaby asked, pulling on clothes and boots.

"Because no one else could understand. Because of those seven minutes you stared at that bloody thing out there and nothing else existed. You know the truth: Nothing does exist, apart from that. Make sure you bring whatever you've been recording on with you."

"You guessed."

"I noticed."

"Hunter's senses. Sorry, I should have told you, I suppose."

"No matter to me."

"You're the only one here has a story worth telling, who will actually lose something when this comes down."

"You think so?"

The light was poor in the wooden corridor. Gaby could not read his expression right. Prenderleith led her to a service staircase down to ground level. Stepping onto the dark surface between the piers, Gaby imagined setting first foot on an alien planet. Close to the truth there, she thought. Prenderleith unslung his rifle and led her out from under the hotel into the shadows along the edge of the floodlights. The night felt huge and close around Gaby, full of breathings and tiny movements. Her breath steamed, it was cold upon the shoulder lands of Kirinyaga. She inhaled the perfume of the Chaga. It was a smell you imagined you knew, because it evoked so many memories, as smell does more powerfully than any other sense. But you could not know it, and when you realized that, all the parts that reminded you of other things collapsed together and the spicy, musky, chemically scent of it was nothing you could remember for no one had ever known anything like this before. It pushed you forward, not back.

Prenderleith led her toward terminum. It was not very far. The Chaga grew taller and more complex as the floodlight waned. Looming, like the waking memory of a nightmare. Gaby could hear the groan and smash of trees falling in the darkness. Prenderleith stopped her half a meter from the edge. Half a meter, fifteen minutes, Gaby thought. She curled her toes inside her boots, feeling infected. Prenderleith squatted on his heels, rested his weight on his gun, like a staff, hunting.

"Wind's right," he said.

Gaby squatted beside him. She switched on the recorder, listened to the silence, and watched the Chaga approach her, out of the shadows. Terminum was a grid of small hexagons of a mosslike substance. The hexagons were of all colors; Gaby knew intuitively that no color was ever next to itself. The corners of the foremost hexagons were sending dark lines creeping out into the undergrowth. Blades of grass, plant stems, fell before the molecule machines and were reduced to their components. Every few centimeters the crawling lines would bifurcate; a few centimeters more they would divide again to build hexagons. Once enclosed, the terrestrial vegetation would wilt and melt and blister into pinpoint stars of colored pseudomoss.

On a sudden urge, Gaby pressed her hand down on the black lines. It did not touch flesh. It had never touched flesh. Yet she flinched as she felt Chaga beneath her bare skin. Oh she of little faith. She felt the molecule-by-molecule advance as a subtle tickle, like the march of small, slow insects across the palm of her hand.

She started as Prenderleith touched her gently on the shoulder.

"It's here," he whispered.

She did not have the hunter's skill, so for long seconds she saw it only as a deeper darkness moving in the shadows. Then it emerged into the twilight between the still-standing trees and the tall fingers of pseudocoral and Gaby gasped.

It was an elephant; an old bull with a broken tusk. Prenderleith rose to his feet. There was not ten meters between them. Elephant and human regarded each other. The elephant took a step forward, out of the shadows into the full light. As it raised its trunk to taste the air, Gaby saw a mass of red, veiny flesh clinging to its neck like a parasitic organ. Beneath the tusks it elongated into flexible limbs. Each terminated in something disturbingly like a human hand. Shocked, Gaby watched the red limbs move and the fingers open and shut. Then the elephant turned and with surprising silence retreated into the bush. The darkness of the Chaga closed behind it.

"Every night, same time," Prenderleith said after a long silence. "For the past six days. Right to the edge, no further. Little closer every day."

"Why?"

"It looks at me, I look at it. We understand each other."

"That thing, around its neck; those arms . . ." Gaby could not keep the disgust from her voice.

"It changes things. Makes things more what they could be. Should be, maybe. Perhaps all elephants have ever needed have been hands, to become what they could be."

"Bootstrap evolution."

"If that's what you believe in."

"What do you believe in?"

"Remember how I answered when you told me the Chaga was taking my Africa away?"

"Not your Africa."

"Understand what I meant now?"

"The Africa it's taking away is the one you never understood, the one you weren't made for. The Africa it's giving is the one you never knew but that was bred into your bones; the great untamed, unexplored, dark Africa, the Africa without nations and governments and borders and economies; the Africa of action, not thought, of being, not becoming, where a single man can lose himself and find himself at the same time; return to a more simple, physical, animal level of existence."

"You say it very prettily. Suppose it's your job."

Gaby understood another thing. Prenderleith had asked her to speak for him because he had not been made able to say such things for himself, and wanted them said right for those who would read Gaby's story about him. He wanted a witness, a faithful recording angel. Understanding this, she knew a third thing about Prenderleith, which could never be spoken and preserved on disc.

"Let's go in again," Prenderleith said eventually. "Bloody freezing out here."

The soldiers came through the hotel at 6:30 in the morning, knocking every bedroom door, though all the guests had either been up and ready long before, or had not slept at all. In view of the fame of the guests, the soldiers were very polite. They assembled everyone in the main lounge. Like a slow sinking, Gaby thought. A Noh Abandon-ship. The reef has reached us at last. She looked out of the window. Under darkness the hexagon moss had crossed the artificial water hole and was climbing the piles of the old hotel. The trees out of which the elephant had emerged in the night were festooned with orange spongy encrustations and webs of tubing.

The main lounge lurched. Glasses fell from the back bar and broke. People screamed a little. The male Hollywood stars tried to look brave, but this was no screenplay. This was the real end of the world. Prenderleith had gathered with the rest of the staff in the farthest corner from the door and was trying to sow calm. It is like the *Titanic*, Gaby thought. Crew last. She went to stand with them. Prenderleith gave her a puzzled frown.

"The punters have to know if the captain goes down with his ship," she said, patting the little black recorder in the breast pocket of her bush shirt. Prenderleith opened his mouth to speak and the hotel heaved again, more heavily. Beams snapped. The picture window shattered and fell outward. Gaby grabbed the edge of the bar and talked fast and panicky at her recorder. Alarmed, the soldiers hurried the celebrities out of the lounge and along the narrow wooden corridors toward the main staircase. The lounge sagged, the floor tilted, tables and chairs slid toward the empty window.

"Go!" Prenderleith shouted.

They were already going. Jammed into the wooden corridor, she tried not to think of bottomless coffins as she tried to shout through the other shouting voices into the microphone. Behind her the lounge collapsed and fell. She fought her way through the press of bodies into the sunlight, touched the solidity of the staircase. Crawling. She snatched her fingers away. The creeping, branching lines of Chaga-stuff were moving down the stairs, through the paintwork.

"It's on the stairs," she whispered breathlessly into the mike. The wooden wall behind her was a mosaic of hexagons. She clutched the recorder on her breast. A single spore would be enough to dissolve it and her story. She plunged down the quivering stairs.

Heedless of dangerous animals, the soldiers hurried the guests toward the vehicles on the main road. The news people paused to shoot their final commentaries on the fall of the Treehouse.

"It's coming apart," she said as a section of roof tilted up like the stern of a sinking liner and slid through the bubbling superstructure to the ground. The front of the hotel was a smash of wood and the swelling, bulbous encrustations of Chaga-stuff. The snapped piles were fingers of yellow sponge and pseudocoral. Gaby described it all. Soldiers formed a cordon between the spectators and the Chaga. Gaby found Prenderleith beside her.

"You'll need to know how the story ends," he said. "Keep this for me." He handed Gaby his rifle. She shook her head.

"I don't do good on guns."

He laid it at her.

"I know," she said.

"Then you'll help me."

"Do you hate this that much?"

"Yes," he said. There was a detonation of breaking wood and a gasp from soldiers and civilians alike. The hotel had snapped in the middle and folded up like two wings. They slowly collapsed into piles of voraciously feeding Chaga life.

He made the move while everyone's attention but Gaby's was distracted by the end of the old hotel. She had known he would do it. He ran fast for a tired old white hunter, running to fat.

"He's halfway there," she said to her recorder. "I admire his courage, going gladly into this new dark continent. Or is it the courage to make the choice that eventually the Chaga may make for all of us on this planet formerly known as Earth?".

She broke off. The soldier in front of her had seen Prenderleith. He lifted his Kalashnikov and took aim.

"Prenderleith!" Gaby yelled. He ran on. He seemed more intent on doing something with his shirt buttons. He was across the edge now, spores flying up from his feet as he crushed the hexagon moss.

"No!" Gaby shouted, but the soldier was under orders, and both he and the men who gave the orders feared the Chaga above all else. She saw the muscles tighten in his neck, the muzzle of the gun weave a little this way, a little that way. She looked for something to stop him. Prenderleith's rifle. No. That would get her shot too.

The little black disc recorder hit the soldier, hard, on the shoulder. She had thrown it, hard. The shot skyed. Birds went screeching up from their roosts. Otherwise, utter silence from soldiers and staff and celebrities. The soldier whirled on her, weapon raised. Gaby danced back, hands held high. The soldier snapped his teeth at her and brought the butt of the gun down on the disc recorder. While he smashed it to shards of plastic and circuitry; Gaby saw the figure of Prenderleith disappear into the pseudocoral fungus of the alien landscape. He had lost his shirt.

The last vestiges of the tourist hotel—half a room balanced atop a pillar; the iron staircase, flowering sulphur-yellow buds, leading nowhere, a tangle of plumbing, washbasins and toilets held out like begging bowls—tumbled and fell. Gaby watched mutely. She had nothing to say, and nothing to say it to. The Chaga advanced onward, twenty-five centimeters every minute. The people dispersed. There was nothing more to see than the millimetric creep of another world.

The soldiers checked Gaby's press accreditations with five different sources before they would let her take the SkyNet car. They were pissed at her but they could not touch her. They smiled a lot, though, because they had smashed her story and she would be in trouble with her editor.

You're wrong, she thought as she drove away down the safe road in the long convoy of news-company vehicles and tour buses. Story is in the heart. Story is never broken. Story is never lost.

That night, as she dreamed among the doomed towers of Nairobi, the elephant came to her again. It stood on the border between worlds and raised its trunk and its alien hands and spoke to her. It told her that only fools feared the change that would make things what they could be, and should be; that change was the special gift of whatever had made the Chaga. She knew in her dream that the elephant was speaking with the voice of Prenderleith, but she could not see him, except as a silent shadow moving in the greater dark beyond humanity's floodlights: Adam again, hunting in the Africa of his heart.

A Dry, Quiet War

TONY DANIEL

Like many writers of his generation, Tony Daniel first made an impression on the field with his short fiction. He made his first sale, to *Asimov's*, in 1990, and followed it up with a long string of well-received stories both there and in markets such as *The Magazine of Fantasy and Science Fiction*, *Amazing*, *SF Age*, *Universe*, and *Full Spectrum* throughout the '90s, stories such as "The Robot's Twilight Companion." "Grist," "The Careful Man Goes West," "Sun so Hot I Froze to Death," "Prism Tree," "Candle," "Death of Reason," "No Love in All of Dwingeloo," and many others, some of which were collected in *The Robot's Twilight Companion*. His story "Life on the Moon" was a finalist for the Hugo Award in 1996, and won the *Asimov's Science Fiction* Readers Award poll. His first novel, *Warpath*, was released simultaneously in America and England in 1993. In 1997, he published a new novel, *Earthling*. In the first few years of the Oughts, he has produced little short fiction, but instead has been at work on a major science fiction trilogy, the first volume of which, *Metaplanetary*, was published in 2001; the second volume, *Superluminal*, appeared early in 2004.

One of the major influences on Daniel's work, of course, is clearly that of his one-time mentor, Lucius Shepard, although the impact of Zelazny, van Vogt, Walter M. Miller, and, oddly, Ray Bradbury can also be demonstrated fairly clearly. Like some of his other young colleagues, though, Daniel's other influences spread far beyond the boundaries of the genre, and even beyond the print world itself; the influence of Japanese samurai movies and spaghetti Westerns on the vivid, violent story that follows are pretty clear, for instance, and Daniel himself has specifically said that one of his direct inspirations for the story was the movies of John Ford.

In "A Dry, Quiet War," he spins a colorful and exotic story of a battle-weary veteran who returns from a bewilderingly strange high-tech future war only to face his greatest and most sinister challenge right at *home*. . . .

I cannot tell you what it meant to me to see the two suns of Ferro set behind the dry mountain east of my home. I had been away twelve billion years. I passed my cabin to the pump well, and taking a metal cup from where it hung from a set-pin, I worked the handle three times. At first it creaked, and I believed it was rusted tight, but then it loosened, and within fifteen pulls I had a cup of water.

Someone had kept the pump up. Someone had seen to the house and the land while I was away at the war. For me, it had been fifteen years; I wasn't sure how long it had been for Ferro. The water was tinged red and tasted of iron. Good. I drank it all in a long draught, then put the cup back onto its hanger. When the big sun, Hemingway, set, a slight breeze kicked up. Then Fitzgerald went down, and a cold cloudless night spanked down onto the plateau. I shivered a little, adjusted my internals, and stood motionless, waiting for the last of twilight to pass and the stars—my stars—to come out. Steiner, the planet that is Ferro's evening star, was the first to emerge, low in the west, methane blue. Then the constellations. Ngal. Gilgamesh. The Big Snake, half-coiled over the southwestern horizon. There was no moon tonight. There was never a moon on Ferro, and that was right.

After a time, I walked to the house, climbed up the porch, and the house recognized me and turned on the lights. I went inside. The place was dusty, the furniture covered with sheets, but there were no signs of rats or jinjas, and all seemed in repair. I sighed, blinked, tried to feel something. Too early, probably. I started to take a covering from a chair, then let it be. I went to the kitchen and checked the cupboard. An old malt whiskey bottle, some dry cereal, some spices. The spices had been my mother's, and I seldom used them before I left for the end of time. I considered that the whiskey might be perfectly aged by now. But, as the saying goes on Ferro, we like a bit of food with our drink, so I left the house and took the road to town, to Heidel.

It was a five-mile walk, and though I could have enhanced and covered the ground in ten minutes or so, I walked at a regular pace under my homeworld stars. The road was dirt, of course, and my pant legs were dusted red when I stopped under the outside light of Thredmartin's Pub. I took a last breath of cold air, then went inside to the warm.

It was a good night at Thredmartin's. There were men and women gathered around the fire hearth, usas and splices in the cold corners. The regulars were at the bar, a couple of whom I recognized—so old now, wizened like stored apples in a barrel. I looked around for a particular face, but she was not there. A jukebox sputtered some core-cloud deak, and the air was thick with smoke and conversation. Or was, until I walked in. Nobody turned to face me. Most of them couldn't have seen me. But a signal passed, and conversation fell to a quiet murmur. Somebody quickly killed the jukebox.

I blinked up an internals menu into my peripheral vision and adjusted to the room's temperature. Then I went to the edge of the bar. The room got even quieter. . . .

The bartender, old Thredmartin himself, reluctantly came over to me.

"What can I do for you, sir?" he asked me.

I looked over him, to the selection of bottles, tubes, and cans on display behind him. "I don't see it," I said.

"Eh?" He glanced back over his shoulder, then quickly returned to peering at me.

"Bone's Barley," I said.

"We don't have any more of that," Thredmartin said, with a suspicious tone.

"Why not?"

"The man who made it died."

"How long ago?"

"Twenty years, more or less. I don't see what business of—"

"What about his son?"

Thredmartin backed up a step. Then another. "Henry," he whispered. "Henry Bone."

"Just give me the best that you do have, Peter Thredmartin," I said. "In fact, I'd like to buy everybody a round on me."

"Henry Bone! Why, you looked to me like a bad 'un indeed when you walked in here. I took you for one of them glims, I did," Thredmartin said. I did not know what he was talking about. Then he smiled an old devil's crooked smile. "Your money's no good here, Henry Bone. I do happen to have a couple of bottles of your old dad's whiskey stowed away in back. Drinks are on the house."

And so I returned to my world, and for most of those I'd left behind, it seemed as if I'd never really gone. My neighbors hadn't changed much in the twenty years local that had passed, and, of course, they had no conception of what had happened to me. They only knew that I'd been to the war—the Big War at the End of Time—and evidently everything turned out okay, for here I was, back in my own time and my own place. I planted Ferro's desert barley, brought in peat from the mountain bogs, bred the biomass that would extract the minerals from my hard groundwater, and got ready for making whiskey once again. Most of the inhabitants of Ferro were divided between whiskey families and beer families. Bones were distillers, never brewers, since the Settlement, ten generations before.

It wasn't until she called upon me that I heard the first hints of the troubles that had come. Her name was Alinda Bexter, but since we played together under the floor planks of her father's hotel, I had always called her Bex. When I left for the war, she was twenty, and I twenty-one. I still recognized her at forty, five years older than I was now, as she came walking down the road to my house, a week after I'd returned. She was taller than most women on Ferro, and she might be mistaken for a usa-human splice anywhere else. She was rangy, and she wore a khaki dress that whipped in the dry wind as she came toward me. I stood on the porch, waiting for her, wondering what she would say.

"Well, this is a load off of me," she said. She was wearing a brimmed hat. It had a ribbon to tie under her chin, but Bex had not done that. She held her hand on it to keep it from blowing from her head. "This damn ranch has been one big thankless task."

"So it was you who kept it up," I said.

"Just kept it from falling apart as fast as it would have otherwise," she replied. We stood and looked at one another for a moment. Her eyes were green. Now that I had seen an ocean, I could understand the kind of green they were.

"Well, then," I finally said. "Come on in."

I offered her some sweetcake I'd fried up, and some beer that my neighbor, Shin, had brought by, both of which she declined. We sat in the living room, on furniture covered with the white sheets I had yet to remove. Bex and I took it slow, getting to know each other again. She ran her father's place now. For years, the only way to get to Heidel was by freighter, but we had finally gotten a node on the Flash, and even though Ferro was still a backwater planet, there were more strangers passing through than there ever had been—usually en route to other places. But they sometimes stayed a night or two in the Bexter Hotel. Its reputation was spreading, Bex claimed, and I believed her. Even when she was young, she had been shrewd but honest, a combination you don't often find in an innkeeper. She was a quiet woman—that is, until she got to know you well—and some most likely thought her conceited. I got the feeling that she hadn't let down her reserve for a long time. When I knew her before, Bex did not have many close friends, but for the ones she had, such as me, she poured out her thoughts, and her heart. I found that she hadn't changed much in that way.

"Did you marry?" I asked her, after hearing about the hotel and her father's bad health.

"No," she said. "No, I very nearly did, but then I did not. Did you?"

"No. Who was it?"

"Rall Kenton."

"Rall Kenton? Rall Kenton, whose parents run the hops market?" He was a quarter-splice, a tall man on a world of tall men. Yet when I knew him, his long shadow had been deceptive. There was no spark or force in him. "I can't see that, Bex."

"Tom Kenton died ten years ago," she said. "Marjorie retired, and Rall owned the business until just last year. Rall did all right; you'd be surprised. Something about his father's passing gave him a backbone. Too much of one, maybe."

"What happened?"

"He died," she said. "He died, too, just as I thought you had." Now she told me she would like a beer after all, and I went to get her a bottle of Shin's ale. When I returned, I could tell that she'd been crying a little.

"The glims killed Rall," said Bex before I could ask her about him. "That's their name for themselves, anyway. Humans, repons, kaliwaks, and I don't know what else. They passed through last year and stayed for a week in Heidel. Very bad. They made my father give over the whole hotel to them, and then they had a . . . trial, they called it. Every house was called and made to pay a tithe. The glims decided how much. Rall refused to pay. He brought along a pistol—Lord knows where he got it— and tried to shoot one of them. They just laughed and took it from him." Now the tears started again.

"And then they hauled him out into the street in front of the hotel." Bex took a moment and got control of herself. "They burnt him up with a p-gun. Burned his legs off first, then his arms, then the rest of him after they'd let him lie there awhile. There wasn't a trace of him after that; we couldn't even bury him."

I couldn't take her to me, hold her, not after she'd told me about Rall. Needing something to do, I took some tangled banwood from the tinderbox and struggled to get a fire going from the burnt-down coals in my hearth. I blew into the fireplace and only got a nose full of ashes for my trouble. "Didn't anybody fight?" I asked.

"Not after that. We just waited them out. Or they got bored. I don't know. It was bad for everybody, not just Rall." Bex shook her head, sighed, then saw the trouble I was having and bent down to help me. She was much better at it than I, and the fire was soon ablaze. We sat back down and watched it flicker.

"Sounds like war-ghosts," I said.

"The glims?"

"Soldiers who don't go home after the war. The fighting gets into them, and they don't want to give it up, or can't. Sometimes they have . . . modifications that won't let them give it up. They wander the timeways—and since they don't belong to the time they show up in, they're hard to kill. In the early times, where people don't know about the war or have only heard rumors of it, they had lots of names. Vampires. Hagamonsters. Zombies."

"What can you do?"

I put my arm around her. It had been so long. She tensed up, then breathed deeply, serenely.

"Hope they don't come back," I said. "They are bad ones. Not the worst, but bad."

We were quiet for a while, and the wind, blowing over the chimney's top, made the flue moan as if it were a big stone flute.

"Did you love him, Bex?" I asked. "Rall?"

She didn't even hesitate in her answer this time. "Of course not, Henry Bone. How could you ever think such a thing? I was waiting to catch up with you. Now tell me about the future."

And so I drew away from her for a while, and told her—part of it at least. About how there is not enough dark matter to pull the cosmos back together again, not enough mass to undulate in an eternal cycle. Instead, there *is* an end, and all the stars are either dead or dying, and all that there is is nothing but dim night. I told her about the twilight armies gathered there, culled from all times, all places. Creatures, presences, machines, weapons fighting galaxy-to-galaxy, system-to-system, fighting until the critical point is reached when entropy flows no more, but pools, pools in endless stagnant pools of nothing. No light. No heat. No effect. And the universe is dead, and so those who remain . . . inherit the dark field. They win.

"And did you win?" she asked me. "If that's the word for it."

The suns were going down. Instead of answering, I went outside to the woodpile and brought in enough banwood to fuel the fire for the night. I thought maybe she would forget what she'd asked me—but not Bex.

"How does the war end, Henry?"

"You must never ask me that." I spoke the words carefully, making sure I was giving away nothing in my reply. "Every time a returning soldier tells that answer, he changes everything. Then he has two choices. He can either go away, leave his own time, and go back to fight again. Or he can stay, and it will all mean nothing, what he did. Not just who won and who lost, but all the things he did in the war spin off into nothing."

Bex thought about this for a while. "What could it matter? What in God's name could be worth fighting for?" she finally asked. "Time ends. Nothing matters after that. What could it possibly matter who won . . . who wins?"

"It means you can go back home," I said. "After it's over."

"I don't understand."

I shook my head and was silent. I had said enough. There was no way to tell her more, in any case—not without changing things. And no way to say what it was that had brought those forces together at the end of everything. And what the hell do I know, even now? All I know is what I was told, and what I was trained to do. If we don't fight at the end, there won't be a beginning. For there to be people, there has to be a war to fight at the end of things. We live in that kind of universe, and not another, they told me. They told me, and then I told myself. And I did what I had to do so that it would be over and I could go home, come back.

"Bex, I never forgot you," I said. She came to sit with me by the fire. We didn't touch at first, but I felt her next to me, breathed the flush of her skin as the fire warmed her. Then she ran her hand along my arm, felt the bumps from the operational enhancements.

"What have they done to you?" she whispered.

Unbidden the old words of the skyfallers' scream, the words that were yet to be, surfaced in my mind.

> They sucked down my heart
> to a little black hole
> You cannot stab me.
>
> They wrote down my brain
> on a hard knot of space,
> You cannot turn me.
>
> Icicle spike
> from the eye of a star
> I've come to kill you.

I almost spoke them, from sheer habit. But I did not. The war was over. Bex was here, and I knew it was over. I was going to feel something, once again, something besides guile, hate, and rage. I didn't yet, that was true, but I could feel the possibility.

"I don't really breathe anymore, Bex; I pretend to so I won't put people off," I told her. "It's been so long, I can't even remember what it was like to have to."

Bex kissed me then. At first, I didn't remember how to do that, either. And then I did. I added wood to the fire, then ran my hand along Bex's neck and shoulder. Her skin had the health of youth still, but years in the sun and wind had made a supple leather of it, tanned and grained fine. We took the sheet from the couch and pulled it near to the warmth, and she drew me down to her on it, to her neck and breasts.

"Did they leave enough of you for me?" she whispered.

I had not known until now. "Yes," I answered. "There's enough." I found my way inside her, and we made love slowly, in a manner that might seem sad to any others but us, for there were memories and years of longing that flowed from us, around us, like amber just at the melting point, and we were inside and there was nothing but this present with all of what was, and what would be, already passed. No time. Finally, only Bex and no time between us.

We fell asleep on the old couch, and it was dim half-morning when we awoke, with Fitzgerald yet to rise in the west and the fire a bed of coals as red as the sky.

Two months later, I was in Thredmartin's when Bex came in with an evil look on her face. We had taken getting back together slow and easy up till then, but the more time we spent around each other, the more we understood that nothing basic had changed. Bex kept coming to the ranch, and I took to spending a couple of nights a week in a room her father made up for me at the hotel. Furly Bexter was an old-style McKinnonite. Men and women were to live separately and only meet for business and copulation. But he liked me well enough, and when I insisted on paying for my room, he found a loophole somewhere in the Tracts of McKinnon about cohabitation being all right in hotels and hostels.

"The glims are back," Bex said, sitting down at my table. I was in a dark corner of the pub. I left the fire for those who could not adjust their own internals to keep them warm. "They've taken over the top floor of the hotel. What should we do?"

I took a draw of beer—Thredmartin's own thick porter—and looked at her. She was visibly shivering, probably more from agitation than fright.

"How many of them are there?" I asked.

"Six. And something else, some splice I've never seen, however many that makes."

I took another sip of beer. "Let it be," I said. "They'll get tired, and they'll move on."

"What?" Bex's voice was full of astonishment. "What are you saying?"

"You don't want a war here, Bex," I replied. "You have no idea how bad it can get."

"They killed Rall. They took our money."

"Money." My voice sounded many years away, even to me.

"It's muscle and worry and care. You know how hard people work on Ferro. And for those . . . things . . . to come in and take it. We cannot let them—"

"—Bex," I said. "I am not going to do anything."

She said nothing; she put a hand on her forehead as if she had a sickening fever, stared at me for a moment, then looked away.

One of the glims chose that moment to come into Thredmartin's. It was a halandana, a splice—human and jan—from uptime and a couple of possible universes over. It was nearly seven feet tall, with a two-foot-long neck, and stooped to enter Thredmartin's entrance. Without stopping, it went to the bar and demanded morphine.

Thredmartin was at the bar. He pulled out a dusty rubber, little used, and before he could get out an injector, the halandana reached over, took the entire rubber, and put it in the pocket of the long gray coat it wore. Thredmartin started to speak, then shook his head and found a spray shooter. He slapped it on the bar and started to walk away. The halandana's hand shot out and pushed the old man. Thredmartin stumbled to his knees.

I felt the fingers of my hands clawing, clenching. Let them loosen; let them go.

Thredmartin rose slowly to one knee. Bex was up, around the bar, and over to him, steadying his shoulder. The glim watched this for a moment, then took its drug and shooter to a table, where it got itself ready for an injection.

I looked at it closely now. It was female, but that did not mean much in halandana splices. I could see it phase around the edges with dead, gray flames. I clicked in wideband overspace, and I could see through the halandana to the chair it was sitting in and the unpainted wood of the wall behind it. And I saw more, in the spaces between spaces. The halandana was keyed in to a websquad; it wasn't really an individual anymore. Its fate was tied to that of its unit commander. So the war-ghosts — the glims — were a renegade squad, most likely, with a single leader calling the shots. For a moment, the halandana glanced in my direction, maybe feeling my gaze somewhere outside of local time, and I banded down to human normal. It quickly went back to what it was doing. Bex made sure Thredmartin was all right, then came back over to my table.

"We're not even in its time line," I said. "It doesn't think of us as really being alive."

"Oh God," Bex said. "This is just like before."

I got up and walked out. It was the only solution. I could not say anything to Bex. She would not understand. I understood — not acting was the rational, the only, way — but not *my* way. Not until now.

I enhanced my legs and loped along the road to my house. But when I got there, I kept running, running off into the red sands of Ferro's outback. The night came down, and as the planet turned. I ran along the length of the Big Snake, bright and hard to the southwest, and then under the blue glow of Steiner when she rose in the moonless, trackless night. I ran for miles and miles, as fast as a jaguar, but never tiring. How could I tire when parts of me stretched off into dimensions of utter stillness, utter rest? Could Bex see me for what I was, she would not see a man, but a kind of colonial creature, a mash of life pressed into the niches and fault lines of existence like so much grit and lichen. A human is anchored with only his heart and his mind; sever those, and he floats away. Floats away. What was I? A medusa fish in an ocean of time? A tight clump of nothing, disguised as a man? Something else?

Something damned hard to kill, that was certain. And so were the glims. When I returned to my house in the star-bright night, I half expected to find Bex, but she was not there. And so I rattled about for a while, powered down for an hour at dawn and rested on a living-room chair, dreaming in one part of my mind, completely alert in another. The next day, Bex still did not come, and I began to fear something had happened to her. I walked partway into Heidel, then cut off the road and stole around the outskirts, to a mound of shattered volcanic rocks — the tailings of some early prospector's pit — not far from the town's edge. There I stepped up my vision and hearing, and made a long sweep of the main street. Nothing. Far, far too quiet, even for Heidel.

I worked out the parabolic to the Bexter Hotel and, after a small adjustment, heard Bex's voice, then her father's. I was too far away to make out the words, but my quantitatives gave it a positive I.D. So Bex was all right, at least for the moment. I made my way back home, and put in a good day's work making whiskey.

The next morning — it was the quarteryear's double dawn, with both suns rising in the east nearly together — Bex came to me. I brought her inside, and in the moted sunlight of my family's living room, where I now took my rest, when I rested, Bex told me that the glims had taken her father.

"He held back some old Midnight Livet down in the cellar, and didn't deliver it when they called for room service." Bex rubbed her left fist with her right fingers, expertly, almost mechanically, as she'd kneaded a thousand balls of bread dough. "How do they know these things? How do they know, Henry?"

"They can see around things," I said. "Some of them can, anyway."

"So they read our thoughts? What do we have left?"

"No, no. They can't see in there, at least I'm sure they can't see in your old man's McKinnonite nut lump of a brain. But they probably saw the whiskey down there in the cellar, all right. A door isn't a very solid thing for a war-ghost out of its own time and place."

Bex gave her hand a final squeeze, spread it out upon her lap. She stared down at the lines of her palm, then looked up at me. "If you won't fight, then you have to tell me how to fight them," she said. "I won't let them kill my father."

"Maybe they won't."

"I can't take that chance."

Her eyes were blazing green as the suns came full through the window. Her face was bright-lit and shadowed, as if by the steady coals of a fire. You have loved this woman a long time, I thought. You have to tell her something that will be of use. But what could possibly be of use against a creature that had survived—*will* survive—that great and final war—and so must survive now? You can't kill the future. That's how the old sergeants would explain battle fate to the recruits. If you are meant to be there, they'd say, then nothing can hurt you. And if you're not, then you'll just fade, so you might as well go out fighting.

"You can only irritate them," I finally said to Bex. "There's a way to do it with the Flash. Talk to that technician, what's his name—"

"Jurven Dvorak."

"Tell Dvorak to strobe the local interrupt, fifty, sixty tetracycles. It'll cut off all traffic, but it will be like a wasp nest to them, and they won't want to get close enough to turn it off. Maybe they'll leave. Dvorak better stay near the node after that, too."

"All right," Bex said. "Is that all?"

"Yes," I said. I rubbed my temples, felt the vague pain of a headache, which quickly receded as my internals rushed more blood to my scalp. "Yes, that's it."

Later that day, I heard the crackle of random quantum tunnel spray, as split unsieved particles decided their spin, charm, and color without guidance from the world of gravity and cause. It was an angry buzz, like the hum of an insect caught between screen and windowpane, tremendously irritating to listen to for hours on end, if you were unlucky enough to be sensitive to the effect. I put up with it, hoping against hope that it would be enough to drive off the glims.

Bex arrived in the early evening, leading her father, who was ragged and half-crazed from two days without light or water. The glims had locked him in a cleaning closet, in the hotel, where he'd sat cramped and doubled over. After the buzz started, Bex opened the lock and dragged the old man out. It was almost as if the glims had forgotten the whole affair.

"Maybe," I said. "We can hope."

She wanted me to put the old man up at my house, in case the glims suddenly remembered. Old Furly Bexter didn't like the idea. He rattled on about something in McKinnon's *Letter to the Canadians*, but I said yes, he could stay. Bex left me with her father in the shrouds of my living room.

Sometime that night, the quantum buzz stopped. And in the early morning, I saw them—five of them—stalking along the road, kicking before them the cowering, stumbling form of Jurven Dvorak. I waited for them on the porch. Furly Bexter was asleep in my parents' bedroom. He was exhausted from his ordeal, and I expected him to stay that way for a while.

When they came into the yard, Dvorak ran to the pump and held to the handle, as if it were a branch suspending him over a bottomless chasm. And for him it was. They'd broken his mind and given him a dream of dying. Soon to be replaced by reality, I suspected, and no pump-handle hope of salvation.

Their leader—or the one who did the talking—was human-looking. I'd have to band out to make a full I.D., and I didn't want to give anything away for the moment. He saved me the trouble by telling me himself.

"My name's Marek," he said. "Come from a D-line, not far down-time from here."

I nodded, squinting into the red brightness reflected off my hardpan yard.

"We're just here for a good time," Marek continued. "What you want to spoil that for?"

I didn't say anything for a moment. One of Marek's gang spat into the dryness of my dirt.

"Go ahead and have it," I said.

"All right," Marek said. He turned to Dvorak, then pulled out a weapon—not really a weapon though, for it is the tool of behind-the-lines enforcers, prison interrogators, confession extractors. It's called an algorithmic truncheon, a trunch, in the parlance. Used at full load, a trunch will strip the myelin sheath from axons and dendrites; it will burn up a man's nerves as if they were fuses. It is a way to kill with horrible pain. Marek walked over and touched the trunch to the leg of Dvorak, as if he were lighting a bonfire.

The Flash technician began to shiver, and then to seethe, like a teapot coming to boil. The motion traveled up his legs, into his chest, out his arms. His neck began to writhe, as if the corded muscles were so many snakes. Then Dvorak's brain burned, as a teapot will when all the water has run out and there is nothing but flame against hot metal. And then Dvorak screamed. He screamed for a long, long time. And then he died, crumpled and spent, on the ground in front of my house.

"I don't know you," Marek said, standing over Dvorak's body and looking up at me. "I know *what* you are, but I can't get a read on *who* you are, and that worries me," he said. He kicked at one of the Flash tech's twisted arms. "But now you know me."

"Get off my land," I said. I looked at him without heat. Maybe I felt nothing inside, either. That uncertainty had been my companion for a long time, my grim companion. Marek studied me for a moment. If I kept his attention, he might not look around me, peer inside the house, to find his other fun, Furly Bexter, half-dead from Marek's amusements. Marek turned to the others.

"We're going," he said to them. "We've done what we came for." They turned around and left by the road on which they'd come, the only road there was. After a while, I took Dvorak's body to a low hill and dug him a grave there. I set up a sand-stone marker, and since I knew Dvorak came from Catholic people, I scratched into the stone the sign of the cross. Jesus, from the Milky Way. Another glim. Hard to kill.

It took old man Bexter only a week or so to recover fully; I should have known by knowing Bex that he was made of a tougher grit. He began to putter around the house, helping me out where he could, although I ran a tidy one-man operation, and he was more in the way than anything. Bex risked a trip out once that week. Her father again insisted he was going back into town, but Bex told him the glims were looking for him. So far, she'd managed to convince them that she had no idea where he'd gotten to.

I was running low on food and supplies, and had to go into town the following Firstday. I picked up a good backpack load at the mercantile and some chemicals for treating the peat at the druggist, then risked a quick look-in on Bex. A sign on the desk told all that they could find her at Thredmartin's, taking her lunch, should they want her. I walked across the street, set my load down just inside Thredmartin's door, in the cloakroom, then passed through the entrance into the afternoon dank of the pub.

I immediately sensed glims all around, and hunched myself in, both mentally and physically. I saw Bex in her usual corner and walked toward her across the room. As I stepped beside a table in the pub's middle, a glim—it was the halandana—stuck out a long hairy leg. Almost, I tripped—and in that instant, I almost did the natural thing and cast about for some hold that was not present in the three-dimensional world—but I did not. I caught myself, came to a dead stop, then carefully walked around the glim's outstretched leg.

"Mind if I sit down?" I said as I reached Bex's table. She nodded toward a free chair. She was finishing a beer, and an empty glass stood beside it. Thredmartin usually had the tables clear as soon as the last drop left a mug. Bex was drinking fast. Why? Working up her courage, perhaps.

I lowered myself into the chair, and for a long time, neither of us said anything to the other. Bex finished her beer. Thredmartin appeared, looked curiously at the two empty mugs. Bex signaled for another, and I ordered my own whiskey.

"How's the ranch?" she finally asked me. Her face was flush and her lips trembled slightly. She was angry, I decided. At me, at the situation. It was understandable. Completely understandable.

"Fine," I said. "The ranch is fine."

"Good."

Again a long silence. Thredmartin returned with our drinks. Bex sighed, and for a moment, I thought she would speak, but she did not. Instead, she reached under the table and touched my hand. I opened my palm, and she put her hand into mine. I felt the tension in her, the bonework of her hand as she squeezed tightly. I felt her fear and worry. I felt her love.

And then Marek came into the pub looking for her. He stalked across the room and stood in front of our table. He looked hard at me, then at Bex, and then he swept an arm across the table and sent Bex's beer and my whiskey flying toward the wall. The beer mug broke, but I quickly reached out and caught my tumbler of scotch in midair without spilling a drop. Of course no ordinary human could have done it.

Bex noticed Marek looking at me strangely and spoke with a loud voice that got his attention. "What do you want? You were looking for me at the hotel?"

"Your sign says you're open," Marek said in a reasonable, ugly voice. "I rang for room service. Repeatedly."

"Sorry," Bex said. "Just let me settle up and I'll be right there."

"Be right there *now*," Marek said, pushing the table from in front of her. Again, I caught my drink, held it on a knee while I remained sitting. Bex started up from her chair and stood facing Marek. She looked him in the eyes. "I'll be there directly," she said.

Without warning, Marek reached out and grabbed her by the chin. He didn't seem to be pressing hard, but I knew he must have her in a painful grip. He pulled Bex toward him. Still, she stared him in the eyes. Slowly, I rose from my chair, setting my tumbler of whiskey down on the warm seat where I had been.

Marek glanced over at me. Our eyes met, and at that close distance, he could plainly see the enhancements under my corneas. I could see his.

"Let go of her," I said.

He did not let go of Bex.

"Who the hell are you?" he asked. "That you tell me what to do?"

"I'm just a grunt, same as you," I said. "Let go of her."

The halandana had risen from its chair and was soon standing behind Marek. It-she growled mean and low. A combat schematic of how to handle the situation iconed up into the corner of my vision. The halandana was a green figure, Marek was red, Bex was a faded rose. I blinked once to enlarge it. Studied it in a fractional second. Blinked again to close it down. Marek let go of Bex.

She stumbled back, hurt and mad, rubbing her chin.

"I don't think we've got a grunt here," Marek said, perhaps to the halandana, or to himself, but looking at me. "I think we've got us a genuine skyfalling space marine."

The halandana's growl grew deeper and louder, filling ultra- and subsonic frequencies.

"How many systems'd you take out, skyfaller?" Marek asked. "A couple of galaxies worth?" The halandana made to advance on me, but Marek put out his hand to stop it. "Where do you get off? This ain't nothing but small potatoes next to what you've done."

In that moment, I spread out, stretched a bit in ways that Bex could not see, but that Marek could—to some extent at least. I encompassed him, all of him, and did a thorough I.D. on both him and the halandana. I ran the data through some trans-d personnel files tucked into a swirl in n-space I'd never expected to access again. Marek Lambrois. Corporal of a back-line military police platoon assigned to the local cluster in a couple of possible worlds, deserters all in a couple of others. He was aggression-enhanced by trans-weblink anti-alg coding. The squad's fighting profile was notched to the top level at all times. They were bastards who were now *preprogrammed* bastards. Marek was right about them being small potatoes. He and his gang were nothing but mean-ass grunts, small-time goons for some of the nonaligned contingency troops.

"What the hell?" Marek said. He noticed my analytics, although it was too fast for him to get a good glimpse of me. But he did understand something in that moment, something it didn't take enhancement to figure out. And in that moment, everything was changed, had I but seen. Had I but seen.

"You're some bigwig, ain't you, skyfaller? Somebody that *matters* to the outcome,"

Marek said. "This is your actual, and you don't want to fuck yourself up-time, so you won't fight." He smiled crookedly. A diagonal of teeth, straight and narrow, showed whitely.

"Don't count on it," I said.

"You won't," he said, this time with more confidence. "I don't know what I was worrying about. I can do anything I want here."

"Well," I said. "Well." And then I said nothing.

"Get on over there and round me up some grub," Marek said to Bex. "I'll be waiting for it in Room Forty-five, little lady."

"I'd rather—"

"Do it," I said. The words were harsh and did not sound like my voice. But they were my words, and after a moment, I remembered the voice. It was mine. From far, far in the future. Bex gasped at their hardness, but took a step forward, moved to obey.

"Bex," I said, more softly. "Just get the man some food." I turned to Marek. "If you hurt her, I don't care about anything. Do you understand? Nothing will matter to me."

Marek's smiled widened into a grin. He reached over, slowly, so that I could think about it, and patted my cheek. Then he deliberately slapped me, hard. Hard enough to turn my head. Hard enough to draw a trickle of blood from my lip. It didn't hurt very much, of course. Of course it didn't hurt.

"Don't you worry, skyfaller," he said. "I know exactly where I stand now." He turned and left, and the halandana, its drugs unfinished on the table where it had sat, trailed out after him.

Bex looked at me. I tried to meet her gaze, but did not. I did not look down, but stared off into Thredmartin's darkness. She reached over and wiped the blood from my chin with her little finger.

"I guess I'd better go," she said.

I did not reply. She shook her head sadly, and walked in front of me. I kept my eyes fixed, far away from this place, this time, and her passing was a swirl of air, a red-brown swish of hair, and Bex was gone. Gone.

> They sucked down my heart
> to a little black hole
> You cannot stab me.

"Colonel Bone, we've done the prelims on Sector 1168, and there are fifty-six class-one civilizations along with two-hundred seventy rationals in stage one or two development."

"Fifty six. Two hundred seventy. Ah. Me."

"Colonel, sir, we can evac over half of them within thirty-six hours local."

"And have to defend them in the transcendent. Chaos neutral. Guaranteed forty percent casualties for us."

"Yes, sir. But what about the civs at least? We can save a few."

> They wrote down my brain
> on a hard knot of space.
> You cannot turn me.

"Unacceptable, soldier."

"Sir?"

"Unacceptable."

"Yes, sir."

All dead. All those millions of dead people. But it was the end of time, and they had to die, so that they—so that we *all*, all in time—could live. But they didn't know, those civilizations. Those people. It was the end of time, but you loved life all the same, and you died the same hard way as always. For nothing. It would be for nothing. Outside, the wind had kicked up. The sky was red with Ferro's dust, and a storm was brewing for the evening. I coated my sclera with a hard and glassy membrane, and, unblinking, I stalked home with my supplies through a fierce and growing wind.

That night, on the curtains of dust and thin rain, on the heave of the storm, Bex came to my house. Her clothes were torn and her face was bruised. She said nothing as I closed the door behind her, led her into the kitchen, and began to treat her wounds. She said nothing as her worried father sat at my kitchen table and watched, and wrung his hands, and watched because there wasn't anything he could do.

"Did that man . . . ," her father said. The old man's voice broke. "Did he?"

"I tried to take the thing, the trunch, from him. He'd left it lying on the table by the door." Bex spoke in a hollow voice. "I thought that nobody was going to do anything, not even Henry, so I had to. I had to." Her facial bruises were superficial. But she held her legs stiffly together and clasped her hands to her stomach. There was vomit on her dress. "The trunch had some kind of alarm set on it," Bex said. "So he caught me."

"Bex, are you hurting?" I said to her. She looked down, then carefully spread her legs. "He caught me and then he used the trunch on me. Not full strength. Said he didn't want to do permanent damage. Said he wanted to save me for later." Her voice sounded far away. She covered her face with her hands. "He put it in me," she said.

Then she breathed deeply, raggedly, and made herself look at me. "Well," she said. "So."

I put her into my bed, and he sat in the chair beside it, standing watch for who knew what? He could not defend his daughter, but he must try, as surely as the suns rose, now growing farther apart, over the hard pack of my homeworld desert.

Everything was changed.

"Bex," I said to her, and touched her forehead. Touched her fine brown skin. "Bex, in the future, we won. I won, my command won it. Really, really big. That's why we're here. That's why we're all here."

Bex's eyes were closed. I could not tell if she'd already fallen asleep. I hoped she had.

"I have to take care of some business, and then I'll do it again," I said in a whisper. "I'll just have to go back up-time and do it again."

Between the first and second rising, I'd reached Heidel, and as Hemingway burned red through the storm's dusty leavings, I stood in the shadows of the entrance foyer of the Bexter Hotel. There I waited.

The halandana was the first up—like me, they never really slept—and it came down from its room looking, no doubt, to go out and get another rubber of its drug. Instead, it found me. I didn't waste time with the creature. With a quick twist in n-space, I pulled it down to the present, down to a local concentration of hate and lust and stupidity that I could kill with a thrust into its throat. But I let it live; I showed it myself, all of me spread out and huge, and I let it fear.

"Go and get Marek Lambrois," I told it. "Tell him Colonel Bone wants to see him. Colonel Henry Bone of the Eighth Sky and Light."

"Bone," said the halandana. "I thought—"

I reached out and grabbed the creature's long neck. This was the halandana weak point, and this halandana had a ceramic implant as protection. I clicked up the power in my forearm a level and crushed the collar as I might a teacup. The halandana's neck carapace shattered to platelets and shards, outlined in fine cracks under its skin.

"Don't think," I said. "Tell Marek Lambrois to come into the street, and I will let him live."

This was untrue, of course, but hope never dies, I'd discovered, even in the hardest of soldiers. But perhaps I'd underestimated Marek. Sometimes I still wonder.

He stumbled out, still partly asleep, onto the street. Last night had evidently been a hard and long one. His eyes were a red no detox nano could fully clean up. His skin was the color of paste.

"You have something on me," I said. "I cannot abide that."

"Colonel Bone," he began. "If I'd knowed it was you—"

"Too late for that."

"It's never too late, that's what you taught us all when you turned that offensive around out on the Husk and gave the Chaos the what-for. I'll just be going. I'll take the gang with me. It's to no purpose, our staying now."

"You knew enough yesterday—enough to leave." I felt the rage, the old rage that was to be, once again. "Why did you do that to her?" I asked. "Why did you—"

And then I looked into his eyes and saw it there. The quiet desire—beaten down by synthesized emotions, but now triumphant, sadly triumphant. The desire to finally, finally die. Marek was not the unthinking brute I'd taken him for after all. Too bad for him.

I took a step toward Marek. His instincts made him reach down, go for the trunch. But it was a useless weapon on me. I don't have myelin sheaths on my nerves. I don't have nerves anymore; I have *wiring*. Marek realized this was so almost instantly. He dropped the trunch, then turned and ran. I caught him. He tried to fight, but there was never any question of his beating me. That would be absurd. I'm Colonel Bone of the Skyfalling Eighth. I kill so that there might be life. Nobody beats me. It is my fate, and yours, too.

I caught him by the shoulder, and I looped my other arm around his neck and reined him to me—not enough to snap anything. Just enough to calm him down. He was strong, but had no finesse.

Like I said, glims are hard to kill. They're the same as snails in shells, and the trick is to draw them out—way out. Which is what I did with Marek. As I held him physically, I caught hold of him, all of him, *over there*, in the place I can't tell you about, can't describe. The way you do this is by holding a glim still and causing him great suffering so that he can't withdraw into the deep places. That's what vampire stakes and Roman crosses are all about.

And like I told Bex, glims are bad ones, all right. Bad, but not the worse. *I am the worse.*

> *Icicle spike*
> *from the eye of a star*
> *I've come to kill you.*

I sharpened my nails. Then I plunged them into Marek's stomach, through the skin, into the twist of his guts. I reached around there and caught hold of something, a piece of intestine. I pulled it out. This I tied to the porch of the Bexter Hotel.

Marek tried to untie himself and pull away. He was staring at his insides, rolled out, raw and exposed, and thinking—I don't know what. I haven't died. I don't know what it is like to die. He moaned sickly. His hands fumbled uselessly in the grease and phlegm that coated his very own self. There was no undoing the knots I'd tied, no pushing himself back in.

I picked him up, and, as he whimpered, I walked down the street with him. His guts trailed out behind us, like a pink ribbon. After I'd gotten about twenty feet, I figured this was all he had in him. I dropped him into the street.

Hemingway was in the northeast and Fitzgerald directly east. They both shown at different angles on Marek's crumple, and cast crazy, mazy shadows down the length of the street.

"Colonel Bone," he said. I was tired of his talking. "Colonel—"

I reached into his mouth, past his gnashing teeth, and pulled out his tongue. He reached for it as I extracted it, so I handed it to him. Blood and drool flowed from his mouth and colored the red ground even redder about him. Then, one by one, I broke his arms and legs, then I broke each of the vertebrae in his backbone, moving up his spinal column with quick pinches. It didn't take long.

This is what I did in the world that people can see. In the twists of other times and spaces, I did similar things, horrible, irrevocable things, to the man. I killed him. I killed him in such a way that he would never come to life again, not in any possible place, not in any possible time. I wiped Marek Lambrois from existence. Thoroughly. And with *his* death, the other glims died, like lights going out, lights ceasing to exist—bulb, filament, and all. Or like the quick loss of all sensation after a brain is snuffed out.

Irrevocably gone from this time line, and that was what mattered. Keeping this possible future uncertain, balanced on the fulcrum of chaos and necessity. Keeping it free, so that I could go back and do my work.

I left Marek lying there, in the main street of Heidel. Others could do the mopping up; that wasn't my job. As I left town, on the way back to my house and my life there, I saw that I wasn't alone in the dawn-lit streets. Some had business out at this hour, and they had watched. Others had heard the commotion and come to windows and porches see what it was. Now they knew. They knew what I was, what I was to be. I walked alone down the road, and found Bex and her father both sound asleep in my room.

I stroked her fine hair. She groaned, turned in her sleep. I pulled my covers up to her chin. Forty years old, and as beautiful as a child. Safe in my bed. Bex. Bex, I will miss you. Always, always, Bex.

I went to the living room, to the shroud-covered furniture. I sat down in what had been my father's chair. I sipped a cup of my father's best barley malt whiskey. I sat, and as the suns of Ferro rose in the hard iron sky, I faded into the distant, dying future.

the undiscovered

WiLLiAM SANDERS

William Sanders lives in Tahlequah, Oklahoma. A former powwow dancer and sometime Cherokee gospel singer, he appeared on the SF scene in the early '80s with a couple of alternate-history comedies, *Journey to Fusang* (a finalist for the John W. Campbell Award) and *The Wild Blue and the Gray*. Sanders then turned to mystery and suspense, producing a number of critically acclaimed titles under a pseudonym. He credits his old friend Roger Zelazny with persuading him to return to SF, this time via the short-story form; his stories have appeared in *Asimov's Science Fiction*, *The Magazine of Fantasy and Science Fiction*, and numerous anthologies, earning him a well-deserved reputation as one of the best short-fiction writers of the last decade. He has also returned to novel writing, with books such as *The Ballad of Billy Badass and the Rose of Turkestan* and *The Bernadette Operations*, a new SF novel, *J.*, and a mystery novel, *Smoke*. Some of his acclaimed short stories have been collected in *Are We Having Fun Yet? American Indian Fantasy Stories*. (Most of his books, including reissues of his earlier novels, are available from Wildside Press, or on Amazon.com.) His stories have appeared in our Twelfth, Thirteenth, Fifteenth, and Nineteenth annual collections.

In the funny and compassionate story that follows, which was on the Final Nebula and Hugo ballots a couple of years back, he settles one of the great controversies of all time by demonstrating who wrote Shakespeare's plays (*Shakespeare* did, of course. What did you *think*?), but also shows us how, under other circumstances, some of the plays might have come out just a bit differently—especially if they were being performed for a somewhat different *audience*. . . .

So the white men are back! And trying once again to build themselves a town, without so much as asking anyone's permission. I wonder how long they will stay this time. It sounds as if these have no more sense than the ones who came before.

They certainly pick the strangest places to settle. Last time it was that island, where anyone could have told them the weather is bad and the land is no good for corn. Now they have invaded Powhatan's country, and from what you say, they seem to have angered him already. Of course that has never been hard to do.

Oh, yes, we hear about these matters up in the hills. Not many of us actually visit the coastal country—I don't suppose there are ten people in this town, counting myself, who have even seen the sea—but you know how these stories travel. We have heard all about your neighbor Powhatan, and you eastern people are welcome to him. Was there ever a chief so hungry for power? Not in my memory, and I have lived a long time.

But we were speaking of the white men. As you say, they are a strange people indeed. For all their amazing weapons and other possessions, they seem to be ignorant of the simplest things. I think a half-grown boy would know more about how to survive. Or how to behave toward other people in their own country.

And yet they are not the fools they appear. Not all of them, at least. The only one I ever knew was a remarkably wise man in many ways.

Do not make that gesture at me. I tell you that there was a white man who lived right here in our town, for more than ten winters, and I came to know him well.

I remember the day they brought him in. I was sitting in front of my house, working on a fish spear, when I heard the shouting from the direction of the town gate. Bigkiller and his party, I guessed, returning from their raid on the Tuscaroras. People were running toward the gate, pouring out of the houses, everyone eager for a look.

I stayed where I was. I could tell by the sound that the raid had been successful— no women were screaming, so none of our people had been killed or seriously hurt—and I didn't feel like spending the rest of the day listening to Bigkiller bragging about his latest exploits.

But a young boy came up and said, "They need you, Uncle. Prisoners."

So I put my spear aside and got up and followed him, wondering once again why no one around this place could be bothered to learn to speak Tuscarora. After all, it is not so different from our tongue, not nearly as hard as Catawba or Maskogi or Shawano. Or your own language, which as you see I still speak poorly.

The captives were standing just inside the gate, guarded by a couple of Bigkiller's brothers, who were holding war clubs and looking fierce, as well as pleased with themselves. There was a big crowd of people by now and I had to push my way through before I could see the prisoners. There were a couple of scared-looking Tuscarora women—one young and pretty, the other almost my age and ugly as an alligator—and a small boy with his fist stuck in his mouth. Not much, I thought, to show for all this noise and fuss.

Then I saw the white man.

Do you know, it didn't occur to me at first that that was what he was. After all, white men were very rare creatures in those days, even more so than now. Hardly anyone had actually seen one, and quite a few people refused to believe they existed at all.

Besides, he wasn't really white—not the kind of fish-belly white that I'd always imagined, when people talked about white men—at least where it showed. His face was a strange reddish color, like a boiled crawfish, with little bits of skin peeling from his nose. His arms and legs, where they stuck out from under the single buckskin garment he wore, were so dirty and covered with bruises that it was hard to tell what color the skin was. Of course that was true of all of the captives; Bigkiller and his warriors had not been gentle.

His hair was dark brown rather than black, which I thought was unusual for a Tuscarora, though you do see Leni Lenapes and a few Shawanos with lighter hair. It was pretty thin above his forehead, and the scalp beneath showed through, a nasty bright pink. I looked at that and at the red peeling skin of his face, and thought: well done, Bigkiller, you've brought home a sick man. Some lowland skin disease, and what a job it's going to be purifying everything after he dies. . . .

That was when he turned and looked at me with those blue eyes. Yes, blue. I don't blame you; I didn't believe that story either, until I saw for myself. The white men have eyes the color of a sunny sky. I tell you, it is a weird thing to see when you're not ready for it.

Bigkiller came through the crowd, looking at me and laughing. "Look what we caught, Uncle," he said, and pointed with his spear. "A white man!"

"I knew that," I said, a little crossly. I hated it when he called me "Uncle." I hated it when anyone did it, except children—I was not yet *that* old—but I hated it worse when it came from Bigkiller. Even if he was my nephew.

"He was with the Tuscaroras," one of the warriors, Muskrat by name, told me. "These two women had him carrying firewood—"

"Never mind that." Bigkiller gave Muskrat a bad look. No need to tell the whole town that this brave raid deep into Tuscarora country had amounted to nothing more than the ambush and kidnapping of a small wood-gathering party.

To me Bigkiller said, "Well, Uncle, you're the one who knows all tongues. Can you talk with this white-skin?"

I stepped closer and studied the stranger, who looked back at me with those impossible eyes. He seemed unafraid, but who could read expressions on such an unnatural face?

"Who are you and where do you come from?" I asked in Tuscarora.

He smiled and shook his head, not speaking. The woman beside him, the older one, spoke up suddenly. "He doesn't know our language," she said. "Only a few words, and then you have to talk slow and loud, and kick him a little."

"Nobody in our town could talk with him," the younger woman added. "Our chief speaks a little of your language, and one family has a Catawba slave, and he couldn't understand them either."

By now the crowd was getting noisy, everyone pushing and jostling, trying to get a look at the white man. Everyone was talking, too, saying the silliest things. Old Otter, the elder medicine man, wanted to cut the white man to see what color his blood was. An old woman asked Muskrat to strip him naked and find out if he was white all over, though I guessed she was really more interested in learning what his male parts looked like.

The young Tuscarora woman said, "Are they going to kill him?"

"I don't know," I told her. "Maybe."

"They shouldn't," she said. "He's a good slave. He's a hard worker, and he can really sing and dance."

I translated this, and to my surprise Muskrat said, "It is true that he is stronger than he looks. He put up a good fight, with no weapon but a stick of firewood. Why do you think I'm holding this club left-handed?" He held up his right arm, which was swollen and dark below the elbow. "He almost broke my arm."

"He did show spirit," Bigkiller agreed. "He could have run away, but he stayed and fought to protect the women. That was well done for a slave."

I looked at the white man again. He didn't look all that impressive, being no more than medium size and pretty thin, but I could see there were real muscles under that strange skin.

"He can do tricks, too," the young Tuscarora woman added. "He walks on his hands, and—"

The older woman grunted loudly. "He's bad luck, that's what he is. We've had nothing but trouble since he came. Look at us now."

I passed all this along to Bigkiller. "I don't know," he said. "I was going to kill him, but maybe I should keep him as a slave. After all, what other chief among the People has a white slave?"

A woman's voice said, "What's going on here?"

I didn't turn around. I didn't have to. There was no one in our town who would not have known that voice. Suddenly everyone got very quiet.

My sister Tsigeyu came through the crowd, everyone moving quickly out of her way, and stopped in front of the white man. She looked him up and down and he looked back at her, still smiling, as if pleased to meet her. That showed real courage. Naturally he had no way of knowing that she was the Clan Mother of the Wolf Clan—which, if you don't know, means she was by far the most powerful person in our town—but just the sight of her would have made most people uneasy. Tsigeyu was a big woman, not fat but big like a big man, with a face like a limestone cliff. And eyes that went right through you and made your bones go cold. She died a couple of years ago, but at the time I am telling about she was still in the prime of life, and such gray hairs as she had she wore like eagle feathers.

She said, "For me? Why, thank you, Bigkiller."

Bigkiller opened his mouth and shut it. Tsigeyu was the only living creature he feared. He had more reason than most, since she was his mother.

Muskrat muttered something about having the right to kill the prisoner for having injured him.

Tsigeyu looked at Muskrat. Muskrat got a few fingers shorter, or that was how it looked. But after a moment she said, "It is true you are the nearest thing to a wounded warrior among this brave little war party." She gestured at the young Tuscarora woman. "So I think you should get to keep this girl, here."

Muskrat looked a good deal happier.

"The rest of you can decide among yourselves who gets the other woman, and the boy." Tsigeyu turned to me. "My brother, I want you to take charge of this white man for now. Try to teach him to speak properly. You can do it if anyone can."

KNOWE ALL ENGLISH AND OTHER CHRISTIAN MEN:

That I an Englishman and Subjeckt of Her Maiestie Queene *Elizabeth*, did by Misadventure come to this country of *Virginia* in the Yeere of Our Lord 1591: and after great Hardshipp arriued amongst these *Indians*. Who haue done me no Harme, but rather shewed me most exelent Kindnesse, sans the which I were like to haue dyed in this Wildernesse. Wherefore, good Frend, I coniure you, that you offer these poore Sauages no Offence, nor do them Iniurie: but rather vse them generously and iustly, as they haue me.

Look at this. Did you ever see the like? He made these marks himself on this deerskin, using a sharpened turkey feather and some black paint that he cooked up from burned wood and oak galls. And he told me to keep it safe, and that if other white men came this way I should show it to them, and it would tell them his story.

Yes, I suppose it must be like a wampum belt, in a way. Or those little pictures and secret marks that the wise elders of the Leni Lenapes use to record their tribe's history. So clearly he was some sort of *didahnvwisgi*, a medicine man, even though he did not look old enough to have received such an important teaching.

He was always making these little marks, scratching away on whatever he could get—skins, mostly, or mulberry bark. People thought he was crazy, and I let them, because if they had known the truth not even Tsigeyu could have saved him from being killed for a witch.

But all that came later, during the winter, after he had begun to learn our language and I his. On that first day I was only interested in getting him away from that crowd before there was more trouble. I could see that Otter was working himself up to make one of his speeches, and if nothing else that meant there was a danger of being talked to death.

Inside my house I gave the stranger a gourd of water. When he had eased his thirst I pointed to myself. "Mouse," I said, very slowly and carefully. "*Tsis-de-tsi.*"

He was quick. "*Tsisdetsi,*" he repeated. He got the tones wrong, but it was close enough for a beginning.

I held my hands up under my chin like paws, and pulled my upper lip back to show my front teeth, and crossed my eyes. I waggled one hand behind me to represent a long tail. "*Tsisdetsi,*" I said again.

He laughed out loud. "*Tsisdetsi,*" he said. "*Mus!*"

He raised his hand and stroked his face for a moment, as if thinking of something. Then without warning he turned and grabbed my best war spear off the wall. My bowels went loose, but he made no move to attack me. Instead he began shaking the weapon above his head with one hand, slapping himself on the chest with the other. "*Tsagspa,*" he cried. "*Tsagspa.*"

Crazy as a dog on a hot day, I thought at first. They must have hit him too hard. Then I realized what was happening, and felt almost dizzy. It is no small honor when any man tells you his secret war name—but a stranger, and a prisoner!

"*Digatsisdi atelvhvsgo'i,*" I said, when I could finally speak. "Shakes Spear!"

I am him that was call'd William *Shakspere*, of *Stratford-upon-Auon*, late of *London*: a Player, of Lord *Strange* his Company, and thereby hangs a Tale.

Look there, where I am pointing. That is his name! He showed me that, and he even offered to teach me how to make the marks for my own. Naturally I refused—think what an enemy could do with something like that!

When I pointed this out, he laughed and said I might be right. For, he said, many a man of his sort had had bad luck with other people making use of his name.

It hapt that our Company was in *Portsmouth*, hauing beene there engaug'd: but then were forbid to play, the Mayor and Corporation of that towne being of the *Puritann* perswasion. For which cause we were left altogether bankrupt: so that some of our Players did pawne their Cloathing for monny to return Home.

Perhaps someone had cursed him, since he sometimes said that he had never meant to leave his own country. It was the fault of the Puritans, he said. He did not explain what this meant, but once he mentioned that his wife and her family were Puritans. So obviously this is simply the name of his wife's clan. Poor fellow, no wonder he left home. The same thing happened to an uncle of mine. When your wife's clan decides to get rid of you, you don't have a chance.

But I, being made foolish by strong Drinke, did conceive to hyde my selfe on a Ship bownd for *London*. Which did seeme a good Idea at the Time: but when I enquyr'd of some sea-faring men, they shewed me (in rogue Jest, or else mayhap I misconstrew'd their Reply, for I was in sooth most outragiosly drunk) the *Moonlight*, which lay at the Docke. And so by night I stole aboord, and hid my selfe vnder a Boate: wherevpon the Wine did rush to my heade, and I fell asleepe, and wal'd not till the Morrow: to finde the Ship at sea and vnder Sayle, and the morning Sun at her backe.

Naturally it was a long time before we could understand each other well enough to discuss such things. Not as long as you might think, though. To begin with, I discovered that in fact he had picked up quite a bit of Tuscarora—pretending, like any smart captive, to understand less than he did. Besides that, he was a fast learner. You know that languages are my special medicine—I have heard them say that Mouse can talk to a stone, and get it to talk back—but Spearshaker was gifted too. By the time of the first snow, we could get along fairly well, in a mixture of his language and mine. And when words failed, he could express almost any idea, even tell a story, just by the movements of his hands and body and the expression of his face. That in itself was worth seeing.

When I was discouer'd the Master was most wroth, and commanded that I be put to the hardest Labours, and giuen onely the poorest leauings for food. So it went hard for me on that Voyage: but the Saylors learn'd that I could sing diuers Songs, and new Ballads from *London*, and then I was vsed better. Anon the Captaine, Mr. Edward *Spicer*, ask'd whether I had any skill in Armes. To which I reply'd, that a Player must needs be a Master of Fence, and of all other Artes martiall, forasmuch as we are wont to play Battles, Duelles, Murthers &c. And the Captaine said, that soone I should haue Opportunity to proue my selfe against true Aduersaries and not in play, for we sayl'd for the *Spanish Maine*.

All this time, you understand, there was a great deal of talk concerning the white man. Most of the people came to like him, for he was a friendly fellow and a willing worker. And the Tuscarora girl was certainly right about his singing and dancing. Even Bigkiller had to laugh when Spearshaker went leaping and capering around the fire, and when he walked on his hands and clapped his feet together several women wet themselves—or so I heard.

His songs were strange to the ear, but enjoyable. I remember one we all liked:

> "Wid-a-he
> An-a-ho
> An-a-he-na-ni-no!"

But not everyone was happy about his presence among us. Many of the young men were angry that the women liked him so well, and now and then took him aside to prove it. And old Otter told everyone who would listen that once, long ago, a great band of white men had come up from the south, from the Timucua country, and destroyed the finest towns of the Maskogis, taking many away for slaves and killing the others. And this was true, because when the People moved south they found much of that country empty and ruined.

Spearshaker said that those people were of another tribe, with which his own nation was at war. But not everyone believed him, and Otter kept insisting that white men were simply too dangerous to have around. I began to fear for Spearshaker's life.

At length we came vnto the *Indies*, being there joyn'd by the *Hopewell* and other Ships whose names I knowe not. And we attack'd the Spanish Convoy, and took the Galleon *Buen Jesus*, a rich Pryze: and so it came to pass that Will Shakspeare, Actor, did for his greate folly turn Pyrat vpon the salt Sea.

Then, early next spring, the Catawbas came.

This was no mere raid. They came in force and they hit us fast and hard, killing or capturing many of the people working in the fields before they could reach the town palisade. They rushed out of the woods and swarmed over the palisade like ants, and before we knew it we were fighting for our lives in front of our own houses.

That was when Spearshaker astonished us all. Without hesitating, he grabbed a long pole from the meat-drying racks and went after the nearest Catawba with it, jabbing him hard in the guts with the end, exactly as you would use a spear, and then clubbing him over the head. Then he picked up the Catawba's bow and began shooting.

My friend, I have lived long and seen much, but I never was more surprised than that morning. This pale, helpless creature, who could not chip an arrowhead or build a proper fire or even take five steps off a trail without getting lost—he cut those Catawbas down like rotten cornstalks! He shot one man off the palisade, right over there, from clear down by the council house. I do not think he wasted a single shot. And when he was out of arrows, he picked up a war club from a fallen warrior and joined the rest of us in fighting off the remaining attackers.

Afterward, he seemed not to think he had done anything remarkable. He said that all the men of his land know stick-fighting and archery, which they learn as boys. "I could have done better," he said, "with a long bow, and some proper arrows, from my own country." And he looked sad, as he always did when he spoke of his home.

From that day there was no more talk against Spearshaker. Not long after, Tsigeyu announced that she was adopting him. Since this also made him Bigkiller's brother, he was safe from anyone in our town. It also made me his uncle, but he was kind enough never to call me *edutsi*. We were friends.

Next we turn'd north for *Virginnia*, Capt. *Spicer* hauing a Commission from Sir Walter *Ralegh* to calle vpon the English that dwelt at *Roanoke*, to discouer their condition. The Gales were cruel all along that Coast, and we were oft in grave Peril: but after much trauail we reached *Hatarask*, where the Captaine sent a party in small Boates, to search out the passage betweene the Islands. And whilst we were thus employ'd, a sudden greate Wind arose and scattered the Boates, many being o'erturned and the Mariners drowned. But the Boate I was in was carry'd many Leagues westward, beyond sight of our Fellowes: so we were cast vpon the Shore of the Maine, and sought shelter in the Mouthe of a Riuer. Anon, going ashore, we were attack'd by Sauages: and all the men were slaine, save onely my selfe.

Poor fellow, he was still a long way from home, and small chance of ever seeing his own people again. At least he was better off than he had been with the Tuscaroras. Let alone those people on the coast, if they had caught him. Remember the whites who tried to build a town on that island north of Wococon, and how Powhatan had them all killed?

Yet hauing alone escap'd, and making my way for some dayes along the Riuer, I was surprized by *Indians* of another Nation: who did giue me hard vsage, as a Slaue, for well-high a Yeere. Vntil I was taken from them by these mine present sauage Hostes: amongst which, for my Sinnes, I am like to liue out my mortall dayes.

I used to have a big pile of these talking skins of his. Not that I ever expected to have a chance to show them to anyone who could understand them—I can't believe the white men will ever come up into the hill country; they seem to have all they can do just to survive on the coast—but I kept them to remember Spearshaker by.

But the bugs and the mice got into them, and the bark sheets went moldy in the wet season, and now I have only this little bundle. And, as you see, some of these are no more than bits and pieces. Like this worm-eaten scrap:

as concerning these *Indians* (for so men call them: but if this be the Lande of *India* I am an Hebrewe *Iewe*) they are in their owne Tongue clept *Anni-yawia*. Which is, being interpreted, the True or Principall People. By other Tribes they are named *Chelokee*: but the meaning of this word my frend *Mouse* knoweth not, neyther whence deriued. They

I think one reason he spent so much time on his talking marks was that he was afraid he might forget his own language. I have seen this happen, with captives. That Tuscarora woman who was with him still lives here, and by now she can barely speak ten words of Tuscarora. Though Muskrat will tell you that she speaks our language entirely too well—but that is another story.

Spearshaker did teach me quite a lot of his own language—a very difficult one, unlike any I ever encountered—and I tried to speak it with him from time to time, but it can't have been the same as talking with a man of his own kind. What does it sound like? Ah, I remember so little now. Let me see. . . . "*Holt dai tong, dow horson nabe!*" That means, "Shut up, you fool!"

He told me many stories about his native land and its marvels. Some I knew to be true, having heard of them from the coast folk: the great floating houses that spread their wings like birds to catch the wind, and the magic weapons that make thunder and lightning. Others were harder to believe, such as his tales about the woman chief of his tribe. Not a clan mother, but a real war chief, like Bigkiller or even Powhatan, and so powerful that any man—even an elder or a leading warrior—can lose his life merely for speaking against her.

He also claimed that the town he came from was so big that it held more people than all of the People's towns put together. That is of course a lie, but you can't blame a man for bragging on his own tribe.

But nothing, I think, was as strange as the *plei*.

Forgive me for using a word you do not know. But as far as I know there is no word in your language for what I am talking about. Nor in ours, and this is because the thing it means has never existed among our peoples. I think the Creator must have given this idea only to the whites, perhaps to compensate them for their poor sense of direction and that skin that burns in the sun.

It all began one evening, at the beginning of his second winter with us, when I came in from a council meeting and found him sitting by the fire, scratching away on a big sheet of mulberry bark. Just to be polite I said, "*Gado hadvhne?* What are you doing?"

Without looking up he said in his own language, "*Raiting a plei.*"

Now I knew what the first part meant; *rai-ting* is what the whites call it when they make those talking marks. But I had never heard the last word before, and I asked what it meant.

Spearshaker laid his turkey feather aside and sat up and looked at me. "Ah, Mouse," he said, "how can I make you understand? This will be hard even for you."

I sat down on the other side of the fire. "Try," I said.

O what a fond and Moone-struck fool am I! Hath the aire of *Virginia* addl'd my braine? Or did an Enemy smite me on the heade, and I knewe it not? For here in this wilde country, where e'en the Artes of Letters are altogether unknowne, I haue begun the writing of a Play. And sure it is I shall neuer see it acted, neyther shall any other man: wherefore 'tis Lunacy indeede. Yet me thinkes if I do it not, I am the more certain to go mad: for I find my selfe growing more like vnto these *Indians*, and I feare I may forget what manner of man

I was. Therefore the Play's the thing, whereby Ile saue my Minde by intentional folly: forsooth, there's Method in my Madnesse.

Well, he was right. He talked far into the night, and the more he talked the less I understood. I asked more questions than a rattlesnake has scales, and the answers only left me more confused. It was a long time before I began to see it.

Didn't you, as a child, pretend you were a warrior or a chief or maybe a medicine man, and make up stories and adventures for yourself? And your sisters had dolls that they gave names to, and talked to, and so on?

Or . . . let me try this another way. Don't your people have dances, like our Bear Dance, in which a man imitates some sort of animal? And don't your warriors sometimes dance around the fire acting out their own deeds, showing how they killed men or sneaked up on an enemy town—and maybe making it a little better than it really happened? Yes, it is the same with us.

Now this *plei* thing is a little like those dances, and a little like the pretending of children. A group of people dress up in fancy clothes and pretend to be other people, and pretend to do various things, and in this way they tell a story.

Yes, grown men. Yes, right up in front of everybody.

But understand, this isn't a dance. Well, there is some singing and dancing, but mostly they just talk. And gesture, and make faces, and now and then pretend to kill each other. They do a lot of that last. I guess it is something like a war dance at that.

You'd be surprised what can be done in this way. A man like Spearshaker, who really knows how—*ak-ta* is what they are called—can make you see almost anything. He could imitate a man's expression and voice and way of moving—or a woman's—so well you'd swear he had turned into that person. He could make you think he was Bigkiller, standing right there in front of you, grunting and growling and waving his war club. He could do Blackfox's funny walk, or Locust wiggling his eyebrows, or Tsigeyu crossing her arms and staring at somebody she didn't like. He could even be Muskrat and his Tuscarora woman arguing, changing back and forth and doing both voices, till I laughed so hard my ribs hurt.

Now understand this. These *akta* people don't just make up their words and actions as they go along, as children or dancers do. No, the whole story is already known to them, and each *akta* has words that must be said, and things that must be done, at exactly the right times. You may be sure this takes a good memory. They have as much to remember as the Master of the Green Corn Dance.

And so, to help them, one man puts the whole thing down in those little marks. Obviously this is a very important job, and Spearshaker said that it was only in recent times, two or three winters before leaving his native land, that he himself had been accounted worthy of this honor. Well, I had known he was a *didahnvwisgi*, but I hadn't realized he was of such high rank.

I first purpos'd to compose some pretty conceited Comedy, like vnto my Loue's Labour's Lost: but alas, me seemes my Wit hath dry'd vp from Misfortune. Then I bethought my selfe of the Play of the Prince of Denmark, by Thomas *Kyd*: which I had been employ'd in reuising for our Company not long ere we departed *London*, and had oft said to Richard *Burbage*, that I trow I could write a Better. And so I haue commenced, and praye God I may com-pleat, my owne Tragedie of Prince *Hamlet*.

I asked what sort of stories his people told in this curious manner. That is some-thing that always interests me—you can learn a lot about any tribe from their stories. Like the ones the Maskogis tell about Rabbit, or our own tale about the Thunder Boys, or—you know.

I don't know what I was thinking. By then I should have known that white people do *everything* differently from everyone else in the world.

First he started to tell me about a dream somebody had on a summer night. That sounded good, but then it turned out to be about the Little People! Naturally I stopped him fast, and I told him that we do not talk about . . . *them*. I felt sorry for the poor man who dreamed about them, but there was no helping him now.

Then Spearshaker told me a couple of stories about famous chiefs of his own tribe. I couldn't really follow this very well, partly because I knew so little about white laws and customs, but also because a lot of their chiefs seemed to have the same name. I never did understand whether there were two different chiefs named *Ritsad*, or just one with a very strange nature.

The oddest thing, though, was that none of these stories seemed to have any *point*. They didn't tell you why the moon changes its face, or how the People were created, or where the mountains came from, or where the raccoon got his tail, or anything. They were just . . . *stories*. Like old women's gossip.

Maybe I missed something.

He certainly worked hard at his task. More often than not, I could hear him grinding his teeth and muttering to himself as he sat hunched over his marks. And now and then he would jump up and throw the sheet to the ground and run outside in the snow and the night wind, and I would hear him shouting in his own language. At least I took it to be his language, though the words were not among those I knew. Part of his medicine, no doubt, so I said nothing.

God's Teethe! Haue I beene so long in this Wildernesse, that I haue forgot all Skill? I that could bombast out a lyne of blank Uerse as readily as a Fishe doth swimm, now fumble for Wordes like a Drunkard who cannot finde his owne Cod-peece with both Handes.

I'm telling you, it was a *long* winter.

> For who would thus endure the Paines of time:
> To-morrow and to-morrow and to-morrow,
> That waite in patient and most grim Array,
> Each arm'd with Speares and Arrowes of Misfortune,
> Like *Indians* ambuscaded in the Forest?
> But that the dread of something after Death,
> That vndiscouered country, from whose Shores
> No Traueller returnes, puzzels the Will,

And makes vs rather beare that which we knowe
Than wantonly embarke for the Vnknowne.

One evening, soon after the snows began to melt, I noticed that Spearshaker was not at his usual nightly work. He was just sitting there staring into the fire, not even looking at his skins and bark sheets, which were stacked beside him. The turkey feathers and black paint were nowhere in sight.

I said, "Is something wrong?" and then it came to me. "Finished?"

He let out a long sigh. "Yes," he said. "*Mo ful ai*," he added, which was something he often said, though I never quite got what it meant.

It was easy to see he was feeling bad. So I said, "Tell me the story."

He didn't want to, but finally he told it to me. He got pretty worked up as he went along, sometimes jumping up to act out an exciting part, till I thought he was going to wreck my house. Now and then he picked up a skin or mulberry-bark sheet and spoke the words, so I could hear the sound. I had thought I was learning his language pretty well, but I couldn't understand one word in ten.

But the story itself was clear enough. There were parts I didn't follow, but on the whole it was the best he'd ever told me. At the end I said, "Good story."

He tilted his head to one side, like a bird. "Truly?"

"*Doyu*," I said. I meant it, too.

He sighed again and picked up his pile of *raiting*. "I am a fool," he said.

I saw that he was about to throw the whole thing into the fire, so I went over and took it from him. "This is a good thing," I told him. "Be proud."

"Why?" He shrugged his shoulders. "Who will ever see it? Only the bugs and the worms. And the mice," he added, giving me his little smile.

I stood there, trying to think of something to make him feel better. Ninekiller's oldest daughter had been making eyes at Spearshaker lately and I wondered if I should go get her. Then I looked down at what I was holding in my hands and it came to me.

"My friend," I said, "I've got an idea. Why don't we put on your *plei* right here?"

And now is Lunacy compownded vpon Lunacy, *Bedlam* pyled on *Bedlam*: for I am embark'd on an Enterprize, the like of which this Globe hath neuer seene. Yet Ile undertake this Foolery, and flynch not: mayhap it will please these People, who are become my onely Frends. They shall haue of Will his best will.

It sounded simple when I heard myself say it. Doing it was another matter. First, there were people to be spoken with.

We *Aniyvwiya* like to keep everything loose and easy. Our chiefs have far less authority than yours, and even the power of the clan mothers has its limits. Our laws are few, and everyone knows what they are, so things tend to go along without much trouble.

But there were no rules for what we wanted to do, because it had never been done before. Besides, we were going to need the help of many people. So it seemed better to go carefully—but I admit I had no idea that our little proposal would create such a stir. In the end there was a regular meeting at the council house to talk it over.

Naturally it was Otter who made the biggest fuss. "This is white men's medicine," he shouted. "Do you want the People to become as weak and useless as the whites?"

"If it will make all our warriors shoot as straight as Spearshaker," Bigkiller told him, "then it might be worth it."

Otter waved his skinny old arms. He was so angry by now that his face was whiter than Spearshaker's. "Then answer this," he said. "How is it that this dance—"

"It's not a dance," I said. Usually I would not interrupt an elder in council, but if you waited for Otter to finish you might be there all night.

"Whatever you call it," he said, "it's close enough to a dance to be Bird Clan business, right? And you, Mouse, are Wolf Clan—as is your white friend, by adoption. So you have no right to do this thing."

Old Dotsuya spoke up. She was the Bird Clan Mother, and the oldest person present. Maybe the oldest in town, now I think of it.

"The Bird Clan has no objection," she said. "Mouse and Spearshaker have our permission to put on their *plei*. Which I, for one, would like to see. Nothing ever happens around this town."

Tsigeyu spoke next. "*Howa*," she said. "I agree. This sounds interesting."

Of course Otter wasn't willing to let it go so easily; he made quite a speech, going all the way back to the origins of the People and predicting every kind of calamity if this sacrilege was permitted. It didn't do him much good, though. No one liked Otter, who had gotten both meaner and longer-winded with age, and who had never been a very good *didahnvwisgi* anyway. Besides, half the people in the council house were asleep long before he was done.

After the council gave its approval there was no trouble getting people to help. Rather we had more help than we needed. For days there was a crowd hanging around my house, wanting to be part of the *plei*. Bigkiller said if he could get that many people to join a war party, he could take care of the Catawbas for good.

And everyone wanted to be an *akta*. We were going to have to turn some people away, and we would have to be careful how we did it, or there would be trouble. I asked Spearshaker how many *aktas* we needed. "How many men, that is," I added, as he began counting on his fingers. "The women are a different problem."

He stopped counting and stared at me as if I were wearing owl feathers. Then he told me something so shocking you will hardly believe it. In his country, the women in a *plei* are actually *men wearing women's clothes*!

I told him quick enough that the People don't go in for that sort of thing—whatever they may get up to in certain other tribes—and he'd better not even talk about it around here. Do you know, he got so upset that it took me the rest of the day to talk him out of calling the whole thing off. . . .

Women! Mercifull Jesu! Women, on a Stage, acting in a Play! I shall feele like an Whore-Master!

Men or women, it was hard to know which people to choose. None of them had ever done anything like this before, so there was no way to know whether they would be any good or not. Spearshaker asked me questions about each person, in white language so no one would be offended: Is he quick to learn? Does he dance or sing well? Can he work with other people, and do as he is told? And he had them stand on one side of the stickball field, while he stood on the other, and made them speak their names and clans, to learn how well their voices carried.

I had thought age would come into it, since the *plei* included both older and younger people. But it turned out that Spearshaker knew an art of painting a man's face, and putting white in his hair, till he might be mistaken for his own grandfather.

No doubt he could have done the same with women, but that wasn't necessary. There were only two women's parts in this story, and we gave the younger woman's part to Ninekiller's daughter Cricket—who would have hung upside-down in a tree like a possum if it would please Spearshaker—and the older to a cousin of mine, about my age, who had lost her husband to the Shawanos and wanted something to do.

For those who could not be *aktas*, there was plenty of other work. A big platform had to be built, with space cleared around it, and log benches for the people who would watch. There were torches to be prepared, since we would be doing it at night, and special clothes to be made, as well as things like fake spears so no one would get hurt.

Locust and Blackfox were particularly good workers; Spearshaker said it was as if they had been born for this. They even told him that if he still wanted to follow the custom of his own tribe, with men dressed as women, they would be willing to take those parts. Well, I always had wondered about those two.

But Spearshaker was working harder than anyone else. Besides being in charge of all the other preparations, he had to remake his whole *plei* to suit our needs. No doubt he had made a fine *plei* for white men, but for us, as it was, it would never do.

Many a Play haue I reuis'd and amended: cut short or long at the Company's desyre, or alter'd this or that Speeche to please a Player: e'en carued the very Guttes out of a scene on command of the Office of the Reuels, for some imagin'd Sedition or vnseemely Speeche. But now must I out-do all I euer did before, in the making of my *Hamlet* into a thing comprehensible to the *Anni-yawia*. Scarce is there a line which doth not haue to be rewrit: yea, and much ta'en out intire: as, the Play within the Play, which Mouse saith, that none here will vnderstande. And the Scene must be mov'd from *Denmark* to *Virginnia*, and *Elsinore Castle* transformed into an *Indian* towne. For marry, it were Alchemy enow that I should transmute vnletter'd Sauages into tragick Actors: but to make royal *Danskers* of swart-fac'd *Indians* were beyond all Reason. (Speak'st thou now of Reason, Will Shakespere? Is't not ouer-late for that?)

You should have seen us teaching the *aktas* their parts. First Spearshaker would look at the marks and say the words in his language. Then he would explain to me any parts I hadn't understood—which was most of it, usually—and then I would translate the whole thing for the *akta* in our language. Or as close as I could get; there are some things you cannot really interpret. By now Spearshaker was fluent enough to help me.

Then the *akta* would try to say the words back to us, almost always getting it all wrong and having to start again. And later on all the people in the *plei* had to get together and speak their parts in order, and do all the things they would do in the *plei*, and that was like a bad dream. Not only did they forget their words; they bumped into each other and stepped on each other's feet, and got carried away in the fight parts and nearly killed each other. And Spearshaker would jump up and down and pull his hair—which had already begun to fall out, for some reason—and sometimes weep, and when he had settled down we would try again.

> Verily, my lot is harder than that of the *Iewes of Moses*. For Scripture saith, that *Pharo* did command that they make Brickes without Strawe, wherefore their trauail was greate: but now I must make my Brickes, euen without Mudd.

Let me tell you the story of Spearshaker's *plei*.

Once there was a great war chief who was killed by his own brother. Not in a fight, but secretly, by poison. The brother took over as chief, and also took his dead brother's woman, who didn't object.

But the dead man had a son, a young warrior named Amaledi. One night the dead chief appeared to Amaledi and told him the whole story. And, of course, demanded that he do something about it.

Poor Amaledi was in a bad fix. Obviously he mustn't go against his mother's wishes, and kill her new man without her permission. On the other hand, no one wants to anger a ghost—and this one was plenty angry already.

So Amaledi couldn't decide what to do. To make things worse, the bad brother had guessed that Amaledi knew something. He and this really nasty, windy old man named Quolonisi—sounds like Otter—began trying to get rid of Amaledi.

To protect himself Amaledi became a Crazy, doing and saying everything backward, or in ways that made no sense. This made his medicine strong enough to protect him from his uncle and Quolonisi, at least for a time.

Quolonisi had a daughter, Tsigalili, who wanted Amaledi for her man. But she didn't want to live with a Crazy—who does?—and she kept coming around and crying and begging him to quit. At the same time his mother was giving him a hard time for being disrespectful toward her new man. And all the while the ghost kept showing up and yelling at Amaledi for taking so long. It got so bad Amaledi thought about killing himself, but then he realized that he would go to the spirit world, where his father would *never* leave him alone.

So Amaledi thought of a plan. There was a big dance one night to honor the new chief, and some visiting singers from another town were going to take part. Amaledi took their lead singer aside and got him to change the song, telling him the new words had been given to him in a dream. And that night, with the dancers going around the fire and the women shaking the turtle shells and the whole town watching, the visiting leader sang:

> "Now he pours it,
> Now he is pouring the poison,

> *See, there are two brothers,*
> *See, now there is one."*

That was when it all blew up like a hot rock in a fire. The bad chief jumped up and ran away from the dance grounds, afraid he had just been witched. Amaledi had a big argument with his mother and told her what he thought of the way she was acting. Then he killed Quolonisi. He said it was an accident but I think he was just tired of listening to the old fool.

Tsigalili couldn't stand any more. She jumped into a waterfall and killed herself. There was a fine funeral.

Now Amaledi was determined to kill his uncle. The uncle was just as determined to kill Amaledi, but he was too big a coward to do it himself. So he got Quolonisi's son Panther to call Amaledi out for a fight.

Panther was a good fighter and he was hot to kill Amaledi, because of his father and his sister. But the chief wasn't taking any chances. He put some poison on Panther's spear. He also had a gourd of water, with poison in it, in case nothing else worked.

So Amaledi and Panther painted their faces red and took their spears and faced each other, right in front of the chief's house. Amaledi was just as good as Panther, but finally he got nicked on the arm. Before the poison could act, they got into some hand-to-hand wrestling, and the spears got mixed up. Now Panther took a couple of hits. Yes, with the poisoned spear.

Meanwhile Amaledi's mother got thirsty and went over and took a drink, before anyone could stop her, from the poisoned gourd. Pretty soon she fell down. Amaledi and Panther stopped fighting and rushed over, but she was already dead.

By now they were both feeling the poison themselves. Panther fell down and died. So did Amaledi, but before he went down he got his uncle with the poisoned spear. So in the end *everyone* died.

You do?

Well, I suppose you had to be there.

And so 'tis afoote: to-morrow night we are to perform. Thank God *Burbage* cannot be there to witnesse it: for it were a Question which should come first, that he dye of Laughter, or I of Shame.

It was a warm and pleasant night. Everyone was there, even Otter. By the time it was dark all the seats were full and many people were standing, or sitting on the ground.

The platform had only been finished a few days before—with Bigkiller complaining about the waste of timber and labor, that could have gone into strengthening the town's defenses—and it looked very fine. Locust and Blackfox had hung some reed mats on poles to represent the walls of houses, and also to give us a place to wait out of sight before going on. To keep the crowd from getting restless, Spearshaker had asked Dotsuya to have some Bird Clan men sing and dance while we were lighting the torches and making other last preparations.

Then it was time to begin.

What? Oh, no, I was not an *akta*. By now I knew the words to the whole *plei*, from having translated and repeated them so many times. So I stood behind a reed screen and called out the words, in a voice too low for the crowd to hear, when anyone forgot what came next.

Spearshaker, yes. He was the ghost. He had put some paint on his face that made it even whiter, and he did something with his voice that made the hair stand up on your neck.

But in fact everyone did very well, much better than I had expected. The only bad moment came when Amaledi—that was Tsigeyu's son Hummingbird—shouted, "*Na! Dili, dili!*" ("There! A skunk, a skunk!") and slammed his war club into the wall of the "chief's house," forgetting it was really just a reed mat. And Beartrack, who was being Quolonisi, took such a blow to the head that he was out for the rest of the *plei*. But it didn't matter, since he had no more words to speak, and he made a very good dead man for Amaledi to drag out.

And the people loved it, all of it. How they laughed and laughed! I never heard so many laugh so hard for so long. At the end, when Amaledi fell dead between his mother and Panther and the platform was covered with corpses, there was so much howling and hooting you would have taken it for a hurricane. I looked out through the mats and saw Tsigeyu and Bigkiller holding on to each other to keep from falling off the bench. Warriors were wiping tears from their eyes and women were clutching themselves between the legs and old Dotsuya was lying on the ground kicking her feet like a baby.

I turned to Spearshaker, who was standing beside me. "See," I said. "And you were afraid they wouldn't understand it!"

After that everything got confused for a while. Locust and Blackfox rushed up and dragged Spearshaker away, and the next time I saw him he was down in front of the platform with Tsigeyu embracing him and Bigkiller slapping him on the back. I couldn't see his face, which was hidden by Tsigeyu's very large front.

By then people were making a fuss over all of us. Even me. A Paint Clan woman, not bad-looking for her age, took me away for some attention. She was limber and had a lot of energy, so it was late by the time I finally got home.

Spearshaker was there, sitting by the fire. He didn't look up when I came in. His face was so pale I thought at first he was still wearing his ghost paint.

I said, "*Gusdi nusdi?* Is something wrong?"

"They laughed," he said. He didn't sound happy about it.

"They laughed," I agreed. "They laughed as they have never laughed before, every one of them. Except for Otter, and no one has ever seen him laugh."

I sat down beside him. "You did something fine tonight, Spearshaker. You made the People happy. They have a hard life, and you made them laugh."

He made a snorting sound. "Yes. They laughed to see us making fools of ourselves. Perhaps that is good."

"No, no." I saw it now. "Is that what you think? That they laughed because we did the *plei* so badly?"

I put my hand on his shoulder and turned him to face me. "My friend, no one there tonight ever saw a *plei* before, except for you. How would they know if it was bad? It was certainly the best *plei* they ever saw."

He blinked slowly, like a turtle. I saw his eyes were red.

"Believe me, Spearshaker," I told him, "they were laughing because it was such a funny story. And that was your doing."

His expression was very strange indeed. "They thought it comical?"

"Well, who wouldn't? All those crazy people up there, killing each other—and themselves—and then that part at the end, where *everyone* gets killed!" I had to stop and laugh, myself, remembering. "I tell you," I said when I had my breath back, "even though I knew the whole thing by memory, I nearly lost control of myself a few times there."

I got up. "Come, Spearshaker. You need to go to sleep. You have been working too hard."

But he only put his head down in his hands and made some odd sounds in his throat, and muttered some words I did not know. And so I left him there and went to bed.

If I live until the mountains fall, I will never understand white men.

If I liue vntil our *Saviour's* returne, I shall neuer vnderstande *Indians*. Warre they count as Sport, and bloody Murther an occasion of Merriment: 'tis because they hold Life itselfe but lightly, and think Death no greate matter neyther: and so that which we call Tragick, they take for Comedie. And though I be damned for't, I cannot sweare that they haue not the Right of it.

Whatever happened that night, it changed something in Spearshaker. He lived with us for many more years, but never again did he make a *plei* for us.

That was sad, for we had all enjoyed the Amaledi story so much, and were hoping for more. And many people tried to get Spearshaker to change his mind—Tsigeyu actually begged him; I think it was the only time in her life she ever begged anyone for anything—but it did no good. He would not even talk about it.

And at last we realized that his medicine had gone, and we left him in peace. It is a terrible thing for a *didahnvwisgi* when his power leaves him. Perhaps his ancestors' spirits were somehow offended by our *plei*. I hope not, since it was my idea.

That summer Ninekiller's daughter Cricket became Spearshaker's wife. I gave them my house, and moved in with the Paint Clan woman. I visited my friend often, and we talked of many things, but of one thing we never spoke.

Cricket told me he still made his talking marks, from time to time. If he ever tried to make another *plei*, though, he never told anyone.

I believe it was five winters ago—it was not more—when Cricket came in one day and found him dead. It was a strange thing, for he had not been sick, and was still a fairly young man. As far as anyone knew there was nothing wrong with him, except that his hair had fallen out.

I think his spirit simply decided to go back to his native land.

Cricket grieved for a long time. She still has not taken another husband. Did you happen to see a small boy with pale skin and brown hair, as you came through our town? That is their son Wili.

Look what Cricket gave me. This is the turkey feather that was in Spearshaker's hand when she found him that day. And this is the piece of mulberry bark that was lying beside him. I will always wonder what it says.

We are such stuff as Dreames are made on: and our little Life Is rounded in a sle

Notes

1 Elizabethan spelling was fabulously irregular; the same person might spell the same word in various ways on a single page. Shakespeare's own spelling is known only from the Quarto and Folio printings of the plays, and the published poetry; and no one knows how far this may have been altered by the printer. It is not even known how close the published texts are to Shakespeare's original in wording, let alone spelling. All we have in his own hand is his signature, and this indicates that he spelled his own name differently almost every time he wrote it.

  I have followed the spelling of the Folio for the most part, but felt free to use my own judgment and even whim, since that was what the original speller did.

  I have, however, regularized spelling and punctuation to some extent, and modernized spelling and usage in some instances, so that the text would be readable. I assume this book's readership is well-educated, but it seems unrealistic to expect them to be Elizabethan scholars.

2 Cherokee pronunciation is difficult to render in Roman letters. Even our own syllabary system of writing, invented in the nineteenth century by Sequoyah, does not entirely succeed, as there is no way to indicate the tones and glottal stops. I have followed, more or less, the standard system of transliteration, in which "v" is used for the nasal grunting vowel that has no English equivalent.

  It hardly matters, since we do not know how sixteenth-century Cherokees pronounced the language. The sounds have changed considerably in the century and a half since the forced march to Oklahoma; what they were like four hundred years ago is highly conjectural. So is the location of the various tribes of Virginia and the Carolinas during this period; and, of course, so is their culture. (The Cherokees may not then have been the warlike tribe they later became—though, given the national penchant for names incorporating the verb "to kill," this is unlikely.) The Catawbas were a very old and hated enemy.

3 Edward Spicer's voyage to America to learn the fate of the Roanoke Colony—or rather his detour to Virginia after a successful privateering operation—did happen, including the bad weather and the loss of a couple of boats, though there is no record that any boat reached the mainland. The disappearance of the Roanoke colonists is a famous event. It is only conjecture—though based on considerable evidence, and accepted by many historians— that Powhatan had the colonists murdered, after they had taken sanctuary with a minor coastal tribe. Disney fantasies to the contrary, Powhatan was not a nice man.

4   I have accepted, for the sake of the story, the view of many scholars that Shakespeare first got the concept of *Hamlet* in the process of revising Thomas Kyd's earlier play on the same subject. Thus he might well have had the general idea in his head as early as 1591 — assuming, as most do, that by this time he was employed with a regular theatrical company — even though the historic *Hamlet* is generally agreed to have been written considerably later.

5   As to those who argue that William Shakespeare was not actually the author of *Hamlet*, but that the plays were written by Francis Bacon or the Earl of Southampton or Elvis Presley, one can only reply: *Hah*! And again, *Hah*!

second skin

PAUL J. MCAULEY

Born in Oxford, England, in 1955, Paul J. McAuley now makes his home in London. A professional biologist for many years, he sold his first story in 1984, and has gone on to be a frequent contributor to *Interzone*, as well as to markets such as *Asimov's Science Fiction, Amazing, The Magazine of Fantasy and Science Fiction, Skylife, The Third Alternative, When the Music's Over*, and elsewhere.

McAuley is considered to be one of the best of the new breed of British writers (although a few Australian writers could be fit in under this heading as well) who are producing that brand of rigorous hard-science fiction with updated modern and stylistic sensibilities that is sometimes referred to as "radical hard-science fiction," but he also writes Dystopian sociological speculations about the very near future, and he *also* is one of the major young writers who are producing that revamped and retooled widescreen Space Opera that has sometimes been called the New Baroque Space Opera, reminiscent of the Superscience stories of the '30s taken to an even higher level of intensity and scale. His first novel, *Four Hundred Billion Stars*, won the Philip K. Dick Award, and his novel *Fairyland* won both the Arthur C. Clarke Award and the John W. Campbell Award in 1996. His other books include the novels *Of the Fall, Eternal Light*, and *Pasquale's Angel, Confluence*—a major trilogy of ambitious scope and scale set ten million years in the future, comprised of the novels *Child of the River, Ancient of Days*, and *Shrine of Stars—Life on Mars, The Secret of Life* and *Whole Wide World*. His short fiction has been collected in *The King of the Hill and Other Stories* and *The Invisible Country*, and he is the coeditor, with Kim Newman, of an original anthology, *In Dreams*. Coming up is a new novel, *White Devils*, and a new collection, *Little Machines*. His stories have appeared in our Fifth, Ninth, Thirteenth, and Fifteenth through Twentieth annual collections.

In the suspenseful and richly inventive story that follows, one of the best of his "Quiet War" series, he takes us on a journey across space to the furthest reaches of the solar system, for a tale of high-tech intrigue and counter-intrigue beneath the frozen surface of Proteus. . . .

The transport, once owned by an outer system cartel and appropriated by Earth's Pacific Community after the Quiet War, ran in a continuous, ever-changing orbit between Saturn, Uranus, and Neptune. It never docked. It mined the solar wind for hydrogen to mix with the nanogram of antimatter that could power it for a century, and once or twice a year, during its intricate gravity-assisted loops between Saturn's moons, maintenance drones attached remora-like to its hull, and fixed whatever its self-repairing systems couldn't handle.

Ben Lo and the six other members of the first trade delegation to Proteus since the war were transferred onto the transport as it looped around Titan, still sleeping in the hibernation pods they'd climbed into in Earth orbit. Sixty days later, they were released from the transport in individual drop capsules of structural diamond, like so many seeds scattered by a pod.

Ben Lo, swaddled in the crash web that took up most of the volume of the drop capsule's little bubble, watched with growing vertigo as the battered face of Proteus drew closer. He had been awakened only a day ago, and was as weak and unsteady as a new-born kitten. The sun was behind the bubble's braking chute. Ahead, Neptune's disc was tipped in star-sprinkled black above the little moon. Neptune was subtly banded with blue and violet, its poles capped with white cloud, its equator streaked with cirrus. Slowly, slowly, Proteus began to eclipse it. The transport had already dwindled to a bright point amongst the bright points of the stars, on its way to spin up around Neptune, loop past Triton, and head on out for the next leg of its continuous voyage, halfway across the solar system to Uranus.

Like many of the moons of the outer planets, Proteus was a ball of ice and rock. Over billions of years, most of the rock had sunk to the core, and the moon's icy, dirty white surface was splotched with a scattering of large impact craters with black interiors, like well-used ash trays, and dissected by large stress fractures, some running halfway round the little globe.

The spy fell toward Proteus in a thin transparent bubble of carbon, wearing a paper suit and a diaper, and trussed up in a cradle of smart cabling like an early Christian martyr. He could barely move a muscle. Invisible laser light poured all around him—the capsule was opaque to the frequency used—gently pushing against the braking sail which had unfolded and spun into a twenty kilometer diameter mirror after the capsule had been released by the transport. Everything was fine.

The capsule said, "Only another twelve hours, Mr. Lo. I suggest that you sleep. Elfhame's time zone is ten hours behind Greenwich Mean Time."

Had he been asleep for a moment? Ben Lo blinked and said, "Jet lag," and laughed.

"I don't understand," the capsule said politely. It didn't need to be very intelligent. All it had to do was control the attitude of the braking sail, and keep its passenger amused and reassured until landing. Then it would be recycled.

Ben Lo didn't bother to try to explain. He was feeling the same kind of yawning apprehension that must have gripped ninety-year-old airline passengers at the end of the twentieth century. A sense of deep dislocation and estrangement. How strange that I'm here, he thought. And, how did it happen? When he'd been born, space-ships had been crude, disposable chemical rockets. The first men on the moon. President Kennedy's assassination. No, that happened before I was born. For a mo-ment, his yawning sense of dislocation threatened to swallow him whole, but then he had it under control and it dwindled to mere strangeness. It was the treatment, he thought. The treatment and the hibernation.

Somewhere down there in the white moonscape, in one of the smaller canyons, was Ben Lo's first wife. But he mustn't think of that. Not yet. Because if he did . . . no, he couldn't remember. Something bad, though.

"I can offer a variety of virtualities," the capsule said. Its voice was a husky con-tralto. It added, "Certain sexual services are also available."

"What I'd like is a chateaubriand steak butterflied and well-grilled over hickory wood, a Caesar salad, and a 1998 Walnut Creek Cabernet Sauvignon."

"I can offer a range of nutritive pastes, and eight flavors of water, including a bal-anced electrolyte," the capsule said. A prissy note seemed to have edged into its voice. It added, "I would recommend that you restrict intake of solids and fluids un-til after landing."

Ben Lo sighed. He had already had his skin scrubbed and repopulated with strains of bacteria and yeast native to the Protean ecosystem, and his GI tract had been reamed out and packed with a neutral gel containing a benign strain of E. coli. He said, "Give me an inflight movie."

"I would recommend virtualities," the capsule said. "I have a wide selection."

Despite the capsule's minuscule intelligence, it had a greater memory capacity than all the personal computers on Earth at the end of the millennium. Ben Lo had downloaded his own archives into it.

"Wings of Desire," he said.

"But it's in black and white! And flat. And only two senses—"

"There's color later on. It has a particular relevance to me, I think. Once upon a time, capsule, there was a man who was very old, and became young again, and found that he'd lost himself. Run the movie, and you'll understand a little bit about me."

The moon, Neptune, the stars, fell into a single point of light. The light went out. The film began.

Falling through a cone of laser light, the man and the capsule watched how an angel became a human being, out of love.

The capsule skimmed the moon's dirty-white surface and shed the last of its relative velocity in the inertia buffers of the target zone, leaving its braking sail to collapse across kilometers of moonscape. It was picked up by a striding tripod that looked like a prop from The War of the Worlds, and carried down a steeply sloping tunnel through triple airlocks into something like the ER room of a hospital. With the other members of the trade delegation, Ben Lo, numbed by neural blocks, was decanted, stripped, washed, and dressed in fresh paper clothes.

Somewhere in the press of nurses and technicians he thought he glimpsed some-one he knew, or thought he knew. A woman, her familiar face grown old, eyes faded blue in a face wrinkled as a turtle's. . . . But then he was lifted onto a gurney and wheeled away.

"Waking, he had problems with remembering who he was. He knew he was nowhere on Earth. A universally impersonal hotel room, but he was virtually in free fall. Some moon, then. But what role was he playing?

He got up, moving carefully in the fractional gravity, and pulled aside the floor-to-ceiling drapes. It was night, and across a kilometer of black air was a steep dark mountainside or perhaps a vast building, with lights wound at its base, shimmering on a river down there. . . .

Proteus. Neptune. The trade delegation. And the thing he couldn't think about, which was fractionally nearer the surface now, like a word at the back of his tongue. He could feel it, but he couldn't shape it. Not yet.

He stripped in the small, brightly lit sphere of the bathroom and turned the walls to mirrors and looked at himself. He was too young to be who he thought he was. No, that was the treatment, of course. His third. Then why was his skin this color? He hadn't bothered to tint it for . . . how long?

That sci-fi version of *Othello*, a century and a half ago, when he'd been a movie star. He remembered the movie vividly, although not the making of it. But that was the color he was now, his skin a rich dark mahogany, gleaming as if oiled in the lights, his hair a cap of tight black curls.

He slept again, and dreamed of his childhood home. San Francisco. Sailboats scattered across the blue bay. He'd had a little boat, a Laser. The cold salt smell of the sea. The pinnacles of the rust-red bridge looming out of banks of fog, and the fog horn booming mournfully. Cabbage leaves in the gutters of Spring Street. The crowds swirling under the crimson and gold neon lights of the trinket shops of Grant Avenue, and the intersection at Grant and California tingling with trolley car bells.

He remembered everything as if he had just seen it in a movie. Nonassociational aphasia. It was a side effect of the treatment he'd just had. He'd been warned about it, but it was still unsettling. The woman he was here to . . . Avernus. Her name now. But when they had been married, a hundred and sixty-odd years ago, she had been called Barbara Reiner. He tried to remember the taste of her mouth, the texture of her skin, and could not.

The next transport would not swing by Proteus for a hundred and seventy days, so there was no hurry to begin the formal business of the trade delegation. For a while, its members were treated as favored tourists, in a place that had no tourist industry at all.

The sinuous rill canyon which housed Elfhame had been burned to an even depth of a kilometer, sealed under a construction diamond roof, and pressurized to 750 millibars with a nitrox mix enriched with 1 percent carbon dioxide to stimulate plant growth. The canyon ran for fifty kilometers through a basaltic surface extrusion, possibly the remnant of the giant impact that had resurfaced the farside hemisphere of the moon a billion years ago, or the result of vulcanism caused by thermal drag when the satellite had been captured by Neptune.

The sides of the canyon were raked to form a deep vee in profile, with a long narrow lake lying at the bottom like a black ribbon, dusted with a scattering of pink and white coral keys. The Elfhamers called it the Skagerrak. The sides of the canyon were steeply terraced, with narrow vegetable gardens, rice paddies, and farms on the higher levels, close to the lamps that, strung from the diamond roof, gave an insolation equivalent to that of the Martian surface. Farther down, amongst pocket parks and linear strips of designer wilderness, houses clung to the steep slopes like soap bubbles, or stood on platforms or bluffs, all with panoramic views of the lake at the bottom and screened from their neighbors by soaring ginkgoes, cypress, palmettos, bamboo (which grew to fifty meters in the microgravity), and dragon's blood trees. All the houses were large and individually designed; Elfhamers went in for extended families. At the lowest levels were the government buildings, commercial malls and parks, the university and hospital, and the single hotel, which bore all the marks of having been recently constructed for the trade delegation. And then there was the lake, the Skagerrak, with its freshwater corals and teeming fish, and slow, ten-meter-high waves. The single, crescent-shaped beach of black sand at what Elfhamers called the North End was very steeply raked, and constantly renewed; the surfing was fabulous.

There was no real transportion system except for a single tube train line that shuttled along the west side, and moving lines with T-bar seats, like ski lifts, that made silver lines along the steep terraced slopes. Mostly, people bounded around in huge kangaroo leaps, or flew using startlingly small wings of diamond foil or little handheld airscrews—the gravity was so low, 0.007g, that human flight was ridiculously easy. Children rode airboards or simply dived from terrace to terrace, which strictly speaking was illegal, but even adults did it sometimes, and it seemed to be one of those laws to which no one paid much attention unless someone got hurt. It *was* possible to break a bone if you jumped from the top of the canyon and managed to land on one of the lakeside terraces, but you'd have to work at it. Some of the kids did—the latest craze was terrace bouncing, in which half a dozen screaming youngsters tried to find out how quickly they could get from top to bottom with the fewest touchdown points.

The entire place, with its controlled, indoor weather, its bland affluent sheen, and its universal cleanliness, was ridiculously vulnerable. It reminded Ben Lo of nothing so much as an old-fashioned shopping mall, the one at Santa Monica, for instance. He'd had a bit part in a movie made in that mall, somewhere near the start of his career. He was still having trouble with his memory. He could remember every movie he'd made, but couldn't remember *making* any one of them.

He asked his guide if it was possible to get to the real surface. She was taken aback by the request, then suggested that he could access a mobot using the point-of-presence facility of his hotel room.

"Several hundred were released fifty years ago, and some of them are still running, I suppose. Really, there is nothing up there but some industrial units."

"I guess Avernus has her labs on the surface."

Instantly, the spy was on the alert, suppressing a thrill of panic.

His guide was a very tall, thin, pale girl called Marla. Most Elfhamers were descended from Nordic stock, and Marla had the high cheekbones, blue eyes, blond hair, and open and candid manner of her counterparts on Earth. Like most Elfhamers, she was tanned and athletically lithe, and wore a distractingly small amount of fabric: tight shorts, a band of material across her small breasts, plastic sandals, a communications bracelet.

At the mention of Avernus, Marla's eyebrows dented over her slim, straight nose. She said, "I would suppose so, yah, but there's nothing interesting to see. The program, it is reaching the end of its natural life, you see. The surface is not interesting, and it is dangerous. The cold and the vacuum, and still the risk of micrometeorites. Better to live inside."

Like worms in an apple, the spy thought. The girl was soft and foolish, very young and very native. It was only natural that a member of the trade delegation would be interested in Elfhame's most famous citizen. She wouldn't think anything of this.

Ben Lo blinked and said, "Well, yes, but I've never been there. It would be something, for someone of my age to set foot on the surface of a moon of Neptune. I was born two years before the first landing on Earth's moon, you know. Have you ever been up there?"

Marla's teeth were even and pearly white, and when she smiled, as she did now, she seemed to have altogether too many. "By point-of-presence, of course. It is part of our education. It is fine enough in its own way, but the surface is not our home, you understand."

They were sitting on the terrace of a café that angled out over the lake. Resin tables and chairs painted white, clipped bay trees in big white pots, terra-cotta tiles, slightly sticky underfoot, like all the floor coverings in Elfhame. Bulbs of schnapps cooled in an ice bucket.

Ben Lo tipped his chair back and looked up at the narrow strip of black sky and its strings of brilliant lamps that hung high above the steep terraces on the far side of the lake. He said, "You can't see the stars. You can't even see Neptune."

"Well, we *are* on the farside," Marla said, reasonably. "But by point-of-presence mobot I have seen it, several times. I have been on Earth the same way, and Mars, but those were fixed, because of the signal lag."

"Yes, but you might as well look at a picture!"

Marla laughed. "Oh, yah. Of course. I forget that you are once a capitalist—" the way she said it, he might have been a dodo, or a dolphin—"from the United States of the Americas, as it was called then. That is why you put such trust in what you call *real*. But really, it is not such a big difference. You put on a mask, or you put on a pressure suit. It is all barriers to experience. And what is to see? Dusty ice, and the same black sky as home, but with more and weaker lamps. We do not need the surface."

Ben Lo didn't press the point. His guide was perfectly charming, if earnest and humorless, and brightly but brainlessly enthusiastic for the party line, like a cadre from one of the supernats. She was transparently a government spy, and was recording everything—she had shown him the little button camera and asked his permission.

"Such a historical event this is, Mr. Lo, that we wish to make a permanent record of it. You will I hope not mind?"

So now Ben Lo changed the subject, and asked why there were no sailboats on the lake, and then had to explain to Marla what a sailboat was.

Her smile was brilliant when she finally understood. "Oh yah, there are some I think who use such boards on the water, like surfing boards with sails."

"Sailboards, sure."

"The waves are very high, so it is not easy a sport. Not many are allowed, besides, because of the film."

It turned out that there was a monomolecular film across the whole lake, to stop great gobs of it floating off into the lakeside terraces.

A gong beat softly in the air. Marla looked at her watch. It was tattooed on her slim, tanned wrist. "Now it will rain soon. We should go inside, I think. I can show you the library this afternoon. There are several real books in it that one of our first citizens brought all the way from Earth."

When he was not sight-seeing or attending coordination meetings with the others in the trade delegation (he knew none of them well, and they were all so much younger than him, and as bright and enthusiastic as Marla), he spent a lot of time in the library. He told Marla that he was gathering background information that would help finesse the target packages of economic exchange, and she said that it was good, this was an open society, they had nothing to hide. Of course, he couldn't use his own archive, which was under bonded quarantine, but he was happy enough typing away at one of the library terminals for hours on end, and after a while, Marla left him to it. He also made use of various point-of-presence mobots to explore the surface, especially around Elfhame's roof.

And then there were the diplomatic functions to attend: a party in the prime minister's house, a monstrous construction of pine logs and steeply pitched roofs of wooden shingles cantilevered above the lake; a reception in the assembly room of the parliament, the Riksdag; others at the university and the Supreme Court. Ben Lo started to get a permanent crick in his neck from looking up at the faces of his etiolated hosts while making conversation.

At one, held in the humid, rarefied atmosphere of the research greenhouses near the top of the East Wall of Elfhame, Ben Lo glimpsed Avernus again. His heart lifted strangely, and the spy broke off from the one-sided conversation with an earnest hydroponicist and pushed through the throng toward his target, the floor sucking at his sandals with each step.

The old woman was surrounded by a gaggle of young giants, set apart from the rest of the party. The spy was aware of people watching when he took Avernus's hand, something that caused a murmur of unrest amongst her companions.

"An old custom, dears," Avernus told them. "We predate most of the plagues that made such gestures taboo, even after the plagues were defeated. Ben, dear, what a surprise. I had hoped never to see you again. Your employers have a strange sense of humor."

A young man with big, red-framed data glasses said, "You know each other?"

"We lived in the same city." Avernus said, "many years ago." She had brushed her vigorous grey hair back from her forehead. The wine-dark velvet wrap did not flatter her skinny old woman's body. She said to Ben, "You look so young."

"My third treatment," he confessed.

Avernus said, "It was once said that in American lives there was no second act— but biotech has given almost everyone who can afford it a second act, and for some a third one, too. But what to *do* in them? One simply can't pretend to be young again — one is too aware of death, and has too much at stake, too much invested in *self*, to risk being young."

"There's no longer any America," Ben Lo said. "Perhaps that helps."

"To be without loyalty," the old woman said, "except to one's own continuity."

The spy winced, but did not show it.

The old woman took his elbow. Her grip was surprisingly strong. "Pretend to be interested, dear," she said. "We are having a delightful conversation in this delightful party. Smile. That's better!"

Her companions laughed uneasily at this. Avernus said quietly to Ben, "You must visit me."

"I have an escort."

"Of course you do. I'm sure someone as resourceful as you will think of something. Ah, this must be your guide. What a tall girl!"

Avernus turned away, and her companions closed around her, turning their long bare backs on the Earthman.

Ben Lo asked Marla what Avernus was doing there. He was dizzy with the contrast between what his wife had been, and what she had become. He could hardly remember what they had talked about. Meet. They had to meet. They would meet.

It was beginning.

Marla said, "It is a politeness to her. Really, she should not have come, and we are glad she is leaving early. You do not worry about her, Mr. Lo. She is a sideline. We look inward, we reject the insane plans of the previous administration. Would you like to see the new oil-rich strains of *Chlorella* we use?"

Ben Lo smiled diplomatically. "It would be very interesting."

There had been a change of government, after the war. It had been less violent and more serious than a revolution, more like a change of climate, or of religion. Before the Quiet War (that was what it was called on Earth, for although tens of thousands had died in the war, none had died on *Earth*), Proteus had been loosely allied with, but not committed to, an amorphous group which wanted to exploit the outer reaches of the solar system, beyond Pluto's orbit; after the war, Proteus dropped its expansionist plans and sought to reestablish links with the trading communities of Earth.

Avernus had been on the losing side of the change in political climate. Brought in by the previous regime because of her skills in gengeneering vacuum organisms, she found herself sidelined and ostracized, her research group disbanded and replaced by government cadres, funds for her research suddenly diverted to new projects. But her contract bound her to Proteus for the next ten years, and the new government refused to release her. She had developed several important new dendrimers, light-harvesting molecules used in artificial photosynthesis, and established several potentially valuable genelines, including a novel form of photosynthesis based on a sulphur-spring *Chloroflexus* bacterium. The government wanted to license them, but to do that it had to keep Avernus under contract, even if it would not allow her to work.

Avernus wanted to escape, and Ben Lo was there to help her. The Pacific Community had plenty of uses for vacuum organisms—there was the whole of the Moon to use as a garden, to begin with—and was prepared to overlook Avernus's political stance in exchange for her expertise and her knowledge.

He was beginning to remember more and more, but there was still so much he didn't know. He supposed that the knowledge had been buried, and would flower in due course. He tried not to worry about it.

Meanwhile, the meetings of the trade delegation and Elfhame's industrial executive finally began. Ben Lo spent most of the next ten days in a closed room dickering with Parliamentary speakers on the Trade Committee over marginal rates for exotic organics. When the meetings were finally over, he slept for three hours and then, still logy from lack of sleep but filled with excess energy, went body surfing at the black beach at the North End. It was the first time he had managed to evade Marla. She had been as exhausted as he had been by the rounds of negotiations, and he had promised that he would sleep all day so that she could get some rest.

The surf was tremendous, huge smooth slow glassy swells falling from thirty meters to batter the soft, sugary black sand with giant's paws. The air was full of spinning globs of water, and so hazed with spray, like a rain of foamy flowers, that it was necessary to wear a filtermask. It was what the whole lake would be like, without its monomolecular membrane.

Ben Lo had thought he would still have an aptitude for body surfing, because he'd done so much of it when he had been living in Los Angeles, before his movie career really took off. But he was as helpless as a kitten in the swells, his boogie board turning turtle as often as not, and twice he was caught in the undertow. The second time, a pale naked giantess got an arm around his chest and hauled him up onto dry sand.

After he hawked up a couple of lungs-full of fresh water, he managed to gasp his thanks. The woman smiled. She had black hair in a bristle cut, and startlingly green eyes. She was very tall and very thin, and completely naked. She said, "At last you are away from that revisionist bitch."

Ben Lo sat up, abruptly conscious, in the presence of this young naked giantess, of his own nakedness. "Ah. You are one of Avernus's—"

The woman walked away with her boogie board under her arm, pale buttocks flexing. The spy unclipped the ankle line that tethered him to his rented board, bounded up the beach in two leaps, pulled on his shorts, and followed.

Sometime later, he was standing in the middle of a vast red-lit room at blood heat and what felt like a hundred percent humidity. Racks of large-leaved plants receded into infinity; those nearest him towered high above, forming a living green wall. His arm stung, and the tall young woman, naked under a green gown open down the front, but masked and wearing disposable gloves, deftly caught the glob of expressed blood—his blood—in a capillary straw, took a disc of skin from his forearm with a spring-loaded punch, sprayed the wound with sealant and went off with her samples.

A necessary precaution, the old woman said. Avernus. He remembered now. Or at least could picture it. Taking a ski lift all the way to the top. Through a tunnel lined with tall plastic bags in which green *Chlorella* cultures bubbled under lights strobing in fifty millisecond pulses. Another attack of memory loss—they seemed to be increasing in frequency! Stress, he told himself.

"Of all the people I could identify," Avernus said, "they had to send *you*."

"Ask me anything," Ben Lo said, although he wasn't sure that he recalled very much of their brief marriage.

"I mean identify genetically. We exchanged strands of hair in amber, do you remember? I kept mine. It was mounted in a ring."

"I didn't think that you were sentimental."

"It was my idea, and I did it with all my husbands. It reminded me of what I once was."

"My wife."

"An idiot."

"I must get back to the hotel soon. If they find out I've been wandering around without my escort, they'll start to suspect."

"Good. Let them worry. What can they do? Arrest me? Arrest you?"

"I have diplomatic immunity."

Avernus laughed. "Ben, Ben, you always were so status-conscious. That's why I left. I was just another thing you'd collected. A trophy, like your Porsche, or your Picasso."

He didn't remember.

"It wasn't a very good Picasso. One of his fakes—do you know that story?"

"I suppose I sold it."

The young woman in the green gown came back. "A positive match," she said. "Probability of a negative identity point oh oh one or less. But he is doped up with immunosuppressants and testosterone."

"The treatment," the spy said glibly. "Is this where you do your research?"

"Of course not. They certainly would notice if you turned up there. This is one of the pharm farms. They grow tobacco here, with human genes inserted to make various immunoglobulins. They took away my people, Ben, and replaced them with spies. Ludmilla is one of my original team. They put her to drilling new agricultural tunnels."

"We are alone here," Ludmilla said.

"Or you would have made your own arrangements."

"I hate being dependent on people. Especially from Earth, if you'll forgive me. And especially you. Are the others in your trade delegation . . . ?"

"Just a cover," the spy said. "They know nothing. They are looking forward to your arrival in Tycho. The laboratory is ready to be fitted out to your specifications."

"I swore I'd never go back, but they are fools here. They stand on the edge of greatness, the next big push, and they turn their backs on it and burrow into the ice like maggots."

The spy took her hands in his. Her skin was loose on her bones, and dry and cold despite the humid heat of the hydroponic greenhouse. He said, "Are you ready? Truly ready?"

She did not pull away. "I have said so. I will submit to any test, if it makes your masters happy. Ben, you are exactly as I remember you. It is very strange."

"The treatments are very good now. You must use one."

"Don't think I haven't, although not as radical as yours. I like to show my age. You could shrivel up like a Struldbrugg, and I don't have to worry about *that*, at least. That skin color, though. Is it a fashion?"

"I was Othello, once. Don't you like it?" Under the red lights his skin gleamed with an ebony luster.

"I always thought you'd make a good Iago, if only you had been clever enough. I asked for someone I knew, and they sent you. It almost makes me want to distrust them."

"We were young, then." He was trying to remember, searching her face. Well, it was two hundred years ago. Still, he felt as if he trembled at a great brink, and a tremendous feeling of nostalgia for what he could not remember swept through him. Tears grew like big lenses over his eyes and he brushed them into the air and apologized.

"I am here to do a job," he said, and said it as much for his benefit as hers.

Avernus said, "Be honest, Ben. You hardly remember anything."

"Well, it *was* a long time ago." But he did not feel relieved at this admission. The past was gone. No more than pictures, no longer a part of him.

Avernus said, "When we got married, I was in love, and a fool. It was in the Wayfarer's Chapel, do you remember? Hot and dry, with a Santa Ana blowing, and Channel Five's news helicopter hovering overhead. You were already famous, and two years later you were so famous I no longer recognized you."

They talked a little while about his career. The acting, the successful terms as state senator, the unsuccessful term as congressman, the fortune he had made in land deals after the partition of the USA, his semi-retirement in the upper house of the Pacific Community parliament. It was a little like an interrogation, but he didn't mind it. At least he knew *this* story well.

The tall young woman, Ludmilla, took him back to the hotel. It seemed natural that she should stay for a drink, and then that they should make love, with a languor and then an urgency that surprised him, although he had been told that restoration of his testosterone levels would sometimes cause emotional or physical cruxes that would require resolution. Ben Lo had made love in microgravity many times, but never before with someone who had been born to it. Afterward, Ludmilla rose up from the bed and moved gracefully about the room, dipping and turning as she pulled on her scanty clothes.

"I will see you again," she said, and then she was gone.

The negotiations resumed, a punishing schedule taking up at least twelve hours a day. And there were the briefings and summary sessions with the other delegates, as well as the other work the spy had to attend to when Marla thought he was asleep. Fortunately, he had a kink that allowed him to build up sleep debt and get by on an hour a night. He'd sleep long when this was done, all the way back to Earth with his prize. Then at last it was all in place, and he only had to wait.

Another reception, this time in the little zoo halfway up the West Side. The Elfhamers were running out of novel places to entertain the delegates. Most of the animals looked vaguely unhappy in the microgravity and none were very large. Bushbabies, armadillos, and mice; a pair of hippopotami no larger than domestic cats; a knee-high pink elephant with some kind of skin problem behind its disproportionately large ears.

Ludmilla brushed past Ben Lo as he came out of the rest room and said, "When can she go?"

"Tonight," the spy said.

Everything had been ready for fourteen days now. He went to find something to do now that he was committed to action.

Marla was feeding peanuts to the dwarf elephant. Ben Lo said, "Aren't you worried that the animals might escape? You wouldn't want mice running around your Shangri-la."

"They all have a kink in their metabolism. An artificial amino acid they need. That girl you talked with was once one of Avernus's assistants. She should not be here."

"She propositioned me." Marla said nothing. He said, "There are no side deals. If someone wants anything, they have to bring it to the table through the proper channels."

"You are an oddity here, it is true. Too much muscles. Many women would sleep with you, out of curiosity."

"But *you* have never asked, Marla. I'm ashamed." He said it playfully, but he saw that Marla suspected something. It didn't matter. Everything was in place.

They came for him that night, but he was awake and dressed, counting off the minutes until his little bundle of surprises started to unpack itself. There were two of them, armed with tasers and sticky foam canisters. The spy blinded them with homemade capsicum spray (he'd stolen chilli pods from one of the hydroponic farms and suspended a water extract in a perfume spray) and killed them as they blundered about, screaming and pawing at their eyes. One of them was Marla, another a well-muscled policeman who must have spent a good portion of each day in a centrifuge gym. The spy disabled the sprinkler system, set fire to his room, kicked out the window, and ran.

There were more police waiting outside the main entrance of the hotel. The spy ran right over the edge of the terrace and landed two hundred meters down amongst blue pines grown into bubbles of soft needles in the microgravity. Above, the fire touched off the homemade plastic explosive, and a fan of burning debris shot out above the spy's head, seeming to hover in the black air for a long time before beginning to flutter down toward the Skagerrak. Briefly, he wondered if any of the delegation had survived. It didn't matter. The young, enthusiastic, and naive delegates had always been expendable.

Half the lights were out in Elfhame, and all of the transportation systems, the phone system was crashing and resetting every five minutes, and the braking lasers were sending twenty-millisecond pulses to a narrow wedge of the sky. It was a dumb bug, only a thousand lines long. The spy had laboriously typed it from memory into the library system, which connected with everything else. It wouldn't take long to trace, but by then, other things would start happening.

The spy waited in the cover of the bushy pine trees. One of his teeth was capped and he pulled it out and unraveled the length of monomolecular diamond wire coiled inside.

In the distance, people called to each other over a backdrop of ringing bells and sirens and klaxons. Flashlights flickered in the darkness on the far side of the Skagerrak's black gulf; on the terrace above the spy's hiding place, the police seemed to have brought the fire in the hotel under control. Then the branches of the pines started to doff as a wind came up; the bug had reached the air conditioning. In the darkness below, waves grew higher on the Skagerrak, sloshing and crashing together, as the wind drove waves toward the beach at the North End and reflected waves clashed with those coming onshore. The monomolecular film over the lake's surface was not infinitely strong. The wind began to tear spray from the tops of the towering waves, and filled the lower level of the canyon with flying foam flowers. Soon the waves would grow so tall that they'd spill over the lower levels.

The spy counted out ten minutes, and then started to bound up the terraces, putting all his strength into his thigh and back muscles. Most of the setbacks between each terrace were no more than thirty meters high; for someone with muscles accustomed to one gee, it was easy enough to scale them with a single jump in the microgravity, even from a standing start.

He was halfway there when the zoo's elephant charged past him in the windy semidarkness. Its trunk was raised above its head and it trumpeted a single despairing cry as it ran over the edge of the narrow terrace. Its momentum carried it a long way out into the air before it began to fall, outsized ears flapping as if trying to lift it. Higher up, the plastic explosive charges the spy had made from sugar, gelatin, and lubricating grease blew out hectares of plastic sheeting and structural frames from the long greenhouses.

The spy's legs were like wood when he reached the high agricultural regions; his heart was pounding and his lungs were burning as he tried to strain oxygen from the thin air. He grabbed a fire extinguisher and mingled with panicked staff, ricocheting down long corridors and bounding across windblown fields of crops edged by shattered glass walls and lit by stuttering red emergency lighting. He was only challenged once, and he struck the woman with the butt end of the fire extinguisher and ran on without bothering to check if she was dead or not.

Marla had shown him the place where they stored genetic material on one of her endless tours. Everything was kept in liquid nitrogen, and there was a wide selection of dewar flasks. He chose one about the size of a human head, filled it, and clamped on the lid.

Then through a set of double pressure doors, banging the switch that closed them behind him, setting down the flask and dropping the coil of diamond wire beside it, stepping into a dressing frame, and finally pausing, breathing hard, dry-mouthed and suddenly trembling, as the vacuum suit was assembled around him. As the gold-filmed bubble was lowered over his head and clamped to the neck seal, Ben Lo started, as if waking. Something was terribly wrong. What was he doing here?

Dry air hissed around his face; headup displays stuttered and scrolled down. The spy walked out of the frame, stowed the diamond wire in one of the suit's utility pockets, picked up the flask of liquid nitrogen, and started the airlock cycle, ignoring the computer's contralto as it recited a series of safety precautions while the room revolved, and opened on a flood of sunlight.

The spy came out at the top of the South End of Elfhame. The canyon stretched away to the north, its construction-diamond roof like black sheet-ice: a long, narrow lake of ice curving away downhill, it seemed, between odd, rounded hills like half-buried snowballs, their sides spattered with perfect round craters. He bounded around the tangle of pipes and fins of some kind of distillery or cracking plant, and saw the line of the railway arrowing away across a glaring white plain toward an horizon as close as the top of a hill.

The railway was a single rail hung from smart A-frames whose carbon fiber legs compensated for movements in the icy surface. Thirteen hundred kilometers long, it described a complete circle around the little moon from pole to pole, part of the infrastructure left over from Elfhame's expansionist phase, when it was planned to string sibling settlements all the way around the moon.

The spy kangaroo-hopped along the sunward side of the railway, heading south toward the rendezvous point they had agreed upon. In five minutes, the canyon and its associated domes and industrial plant had disappeared beneath the horizon behind him. The ice was rippled and cracked and blistered, and crunched under the cleats of his boots at each touchdown.

"That was some diversion," a voice said over the open channel. "I hope no one was killed."

"Just an elephant, I think. Although if it landed in the lake, it might have survived." He wasn't about to tell Avernus about Marla and the policeman.

The spy stopped in the shadow of a carbon-fiber pillar, and scanned the icy terrain ahead of him. The point-of-presence mobots hadn't been allowed into this area. The ice curved away to the east and south like a warped checkerboard. There was a criss-cross pattern of ridges that marked out regular squares about two hundred meters on each side, and each square was a different color. Vacuum organisms. He'd reached the experimental plots.

Avernus said over the open channel, "I can't see the pickup."

He started along the line again. At the top of his leap, he said, "I've already signaled to the transport using the braking lasers. It'll be here in less than an hour. We're a little ahead of schedule."

The transport was a small gig with a brute of a motor taking up most of its hull, leaving room for only a single hibernation pod and a small storage compartment. If everything went according to plan, that was all he would need.

He came down and leaped again, and then he saw her on the far side of the curved checkerboard of the experimental plots, a tiny figure in a transparent vacuum suit sitting on a slope of black ice at what looked like the edge of the world. He bounded across the fields toward her.

The ridges were only a meter high and a couple of meters across, dirty water and methane ice fused smooth as glass. It was easy to leap over each of them—the gravity was so light that the spy could probably get into orbit if he wasn't careful. Each field held a different growth. A corrugated grey mold that gave like rubber under his boots. Flexible spikes the color of dried blood, all different heights and thicknesses, but none higher than his knees. More grey stuff, this time mounded in discrete blisters each several meters from its nearest neighbors, with fat grey ropes running beneath the ice. Irregular stacks of what looked like black plates that gave way, halfway across the field, to a blanket of black stuff like cracked tar.

The figure had turned to watch him, its helmet a gold bubble that refracted the rays of the tiny, intensely bright star of the sun. As the spy made the final bound across the last of the experimental plots—more of the black stuff, like a huge wrinkled vinyl blanket dissected by deep wandering cracks—Avernus said in his ear, "You should have kept to the boundary walls."

"It doesn't matter now."

"Ah, but I think you'll find it does."

Avernus was sitting in her pressure suit on top of a ridge of upturned strata at the rim of a huge crater. Her suit was transparent, after the fashion of the losing side of the Quiet War. It was intended to minimize the barrier between the human and the vacuum environments. She might as well have flown a flag declaring her allegiance to the outer alliance. Behind her, the crater stretched away south and west, and the railway ran right out above its dark floor on pillars that doubled and tripled in height as they stepped away down the inner slope. The crater was so large that its far side was hidden beyond the little moon's curvature. The black stuff had overgrown the ridge, and flowed down into the crater. Avernus was sitting in the only clear spot.

She said, "This is my most successful strain. You can see how vigorous it is. You didn't get that suit from my lab, did you? I suggest you keep moving around. This stuff is thixotropic in the presence of foreign bodies, like smart paint. It spreads out, flowing under pressure, over the neighboring organisms, but doesn't overgrow itself."

The spy looked down, and saw that the big cleated boots of his pressure suit had already sunken to the ankles in the black stuff. He lifted one, then the other; it was like walking in tar. He took a step toward her, and the ground collapsed beneath his boots and he was suddenly up to his knees in black stuff.

"My suit," Avernus said, "is coated with the protein by which the strain recognizes its own self. You could say I'm like a virus, fooling the immune system. I dug a trench, and that's what you stepped into. Where is the transport?"

"On its way, but you don't have to worry about it," the spy said, as he struggled to free himself. "This silly little trap won't hold me for long."

Avernus stepped back. She was four meters away, and the black stuff was thigh deep around the spy now, sluggishly flowing upward. The spy flipped the catches on the flask and tipped liquid nitrogen over the stuff. The nitrogen boiled up in a cloud of dense vapor and evaporated. It had made no difference at all to the stuff's integrity.

A point of light began to grow brighter above the close horizon of the moon, moving swiftly aslant the field of stars.

"It gets brittle at close to absolute zero," Avernus said, "but only after several dozen hours." She turned, and added, "There's the transport."

The spy snarled at her. He was up to his waist, and had to fold his arms across his chest, or else they would be caught fast.

Avernus said, "You never were Ben Lo, were you? Or at any rate no more than a poor copy. The original is back on Earth, alive or dead. If he's alive, no doubt he'll claim that this is all a trick of the outer alliance against the Elfhamers and their new allies, the Pacific Community."

He said, "There's still time, Barbara. We can do this together."

The woman in the transparent pressure suit turned back to look at him. Sun flared on her bubble helmet. "Ben, poor Ben. I'll call you that for the sake of convenience. Do you know what happened to you? Someone used you. That body isn't even yours. It isn't anyone's. Oh, it looks like you, and I suppose the altered skin color disguises the rougher edges of the plastic surgery. The skin matches your genotype, and so does the blood, but the skin was cloned from your original, and the blood must come from marrow implants. No wonder there's so much immunosuppressant in your system. If we had just trusted your skin and blood, we would not have known. But your sperm— it was all female. Not a single Y chromosome. I think you're probably haploid, a construct from an unfertilized blastula. You're not even male, except somatically—you're swamped with testosterone, probably have been since gastrulation. You're a *weapon*, Ben. They used things like you as assassins in the Quiet War."

He was in a pressure suit, with dry air blowing around his head and headup displays blinking at the bottom of the clear helmet. A black landscape, and stars high above, with something bright pulsing, growing closer. A spaceship! That was important, but he couldn't remember why. He tried to move, and discovered that he was trapped in something like tar that came to his waist. He could feel it clamping around his legs, a terrible pressure that was compromising the heat exchange system of his suit. His legs were freezing cold, but his body was hot, and sweat prickled across his skin, collecting in the folds of the suit's undergarment.

"Don't move," a woman's voice said. "It's like quicksand. It flows under pressure. You'll last a little longer if you keep still. Struggling only makes it more liquid."

Barbara. No, she called herself Avernus now. He had the strangest feeling that someone else was there, too, just out of sight. He tried to look around, but it was terribly hard in the half-buried suit. He had been kidnapped. It was the only explanation. He remembered running from the burning hotel. . . . He was suddenly certain that the other members of the trade delegation were dead, and cried out, "Help me!"

Avernus squatted in front of him, moving carefully and slowly in her transparent pressure suit. He could just see the outline of her face through the gold film of her helmet's visor. "There are two personalities in there, I think. The dominant one let you back, Ben, so that you would plead with me. But don't plead, Ben. I don't want my last memory of you to be so undignified, and anyway, I won't listen. I won't deny you've been a great help. Elfhame always was a soft target, and you punched just the right buttons, and then you kindly provided the means of getting where I want to go. They'll think I was kidnapped." Avernus turned and pointed up at the sky. "Can you see? That's your transport. Ludmilla is going to reprogram it."

"Take me with you, Barbara."

"Oh, Ben, Ben. But I'm not going to Earth. I considered it, but when they sent you, I knew that there was something wrong. I'm going *out*, Ben. Further out. Beyond Pluto, in the Kuiper Disk, where there are more than fifty thousand objects with a diameter of more than a hundred kilometers, and a billion comet nuclei ten kilometers or so across. And then there's the Oort Cloud, and its billions of comets. The fringes of *that* mingle with the fringes of Alpha Centauri's cometary cloud. Life spreads. That's its one rule. In ten thousand years, my children will reach Alpha Centauri, not by starship, but simply through expansion of their territory."

"That's the way you used to talk when we were married. All that sci-fi you used to read!"

"You don't remember it, Ben. Not really. It was fed to you. All my old interviews, my books and articles, all your old movies. They did a quick construction job, and just when you started to find out about it, the other one took over."

"I don't think I'm quite myself. I don't understand what's happening, but perhaps it is something to do with the treatment I had. I told you about that."

"Hush, dear. There was no treatment. That was when they fixed you in the brain of this empty vessel."

She was too close, and she had half-turned to watch the moving point of light grow brighter. He wanted to warn her, but something clamped his lips and he almost swallowed his tongue. He watched as his left hand stealthily unfastened a utility pocket and pulled out a length of glittering wire fine as a spider-thread. Monomolecular diamond. Serrated along its length, except for five centimeters at each end, it could easily cut through pressure suit material and flesh and bone.

He knew then. He knew what he was.

The woman looked at him and said sharply, "What are you doing, Ben?"

And for that moment, he was called back, and he made a fist around the thread and plunged it into the black stuff. The spy screamed and reached behind his helmet and dumped all oxygen from his main pack. It hissed for a long time, but the stuff gripping his legs and waist held firm.

"It isn't an anaerobe," Avernus said. She hadn't moved. "It is a vacuum organism. A little oxygen won't hurt it."

Ben Lo found that he could speak. He said, "He wanted to cut off your head."

"I wondered why you were carrying that flask of liquid nitrogen. You were going to take my head back with you—and what? Use a bush robot to strip my brain neuron by neuron and read my memories into a computer? How convenient to have a genius captive in a bottle!"

"It's me, Barbara. I couldn't let him do that to you." His left arm was buried up to the elbow.

"Then thank you, Ben. I'm in your debt."

"I'd ask you to take me with you, but I think there's only one hibernation pod in the transport. You won't be able to take your friend, either."

"Well, Ludmilla has her family here. She doesn't want to leave. Or not yet."

"I can't remember that story about Picasso. Maybe you heard it after we—after the divorce."

"You told it to me, Ben. When things were good between us, you used to tell stories like that."

"Then I've forgotten."

"It's about an art dealer who buys a canvas in a private deal, that is signed 'Picasso.' This is in France, when Picasso was working in Cannes, and the dealer travels there to find if it is genuine. Picasso is working in his studio. He spares the painting a brief glance and dismisses it as a fake."

"I had a Picasso, once. A bull's head. I remember that, Barbara."

"You thought it was a necessary sign of your wealth. You were photographed beside it several times. I always preferred Georges Braque myself. Do you want to hear the rest of the story?"

"I'm still here."

"Of course you are, as long as I stay out of reach. Well, a few months later, the dealer buys another canvas signed by Picasso. Again he travels to the studio; again Picasso spares it no more than a glance, and announces that it is a fake. The dealer protests that this is the very painting he found Picasso working on the first time he visited, but Picasso just shrugs and says, 'I often paint fakes.'"

His breathing was becoming labored. Was there something wrong with the air system? The black stuff was climbing his chest. He could almost see it move, a creeping wave of black devouring him centimeter by centimeter.

The star was very close to the horizon, now.

He said, "I know a story."

"There's no more time for stories, dear. I can release you, if you want. You only have your reserve air in any case."

"No. I want to see you go."

"I'll remember you. I'll tell your story far and wide."

Ben Lo heard the echo of another voice across their link, and the woman in the transparent pressure suit stood and lifted a hand in salute and bounded away.

The spy came back, then, but Ben Lo fought him down. There was nothing he could do, after all. The woman was gone. He said, as if to himself, "I know a story. About a man who lost himself, and found himself again, just in time. Listen. *Once upon a time . . .*"

Something bright rose above the horizon and dwindled away into the outer darkness.

story of your life

TED CHIANG

Ted Chiang has made a big impact on the field with only a handful of stories, five stories all told, published in places such as *Omni, Asimov's Science
Fiction, Full Spectrum 3, Starlight 2*, and *Vanishing Acts*. He won the 1990
Nebula Award with his first published story "Tower of Babylon," and won
the 1991 *Asimov's* Reader's Award with his third, "Understand," as well as
winning the John W. Campbell Award for Best New Writer in that same
year. After 1991, he fell silent for several years before making a triumphant
return in 1998 with the novella that follows, "Story of Your Life," which
won him another Nebula Award in 1999. Since then, he returned in 2000
with another major story, "Seventy-two Letters," which was a finalist for the
Hugo and for the World Fantasy Award, and "Hell Is the Absence of God"
in 2001, which won him another Hugo and Nebula Award, and in 2002
with "Liking What You See: A Documentary." The same year, his first
short-story collection, *Stories of Your Life and Others*, was published, and
won the Locus Award as the year's Best Collection. It will be interesting to
see how he develops in the decade to come, as he could well turn out to be
one of the significant new talents of the new century. He lives in Kirkland,
Washington.

Here he gives us an intricate, subtle, and intelligent look at the proposition that knowing how a story ends before you start it sometimes doesn't
matter as much as what you learn along the *way*. . . .

Y our father is about to ask me the question. This is the most important moment
in our lives, and I want to pay attention, note every detail. Your dad and I have just
come back from an evening out, dinner and a show; it's after midnight. We came
out onto the patio to look at the full moon; then I told your dad I wanted to dance,
so he humors me and now we're slow-dancing, a pair of thirtysomething swaying
back and forth in the moonlight like kids. I don't feel the night chill at all. And then
your dad says, "Do you want to make a baby?"

Right now your dad and I have been married for about two years, living on Ellis
Avenue; when we move out you'll still be too young to remember the house, but

we'll show you pictures of it, tell you stories about it. I'd love to tell you the story of this evening, the night you're conceived, but the right time to do that would be when you're ready to have children of your own, and we'll never get that chance.

Telling it to you any earlier wouldn't do any good; for most of your life you won't sit still to hear such a romantic—you'd say sappy—story. I remember the scenario of your origin you'll suggest when you're twelve."

"The only reason you had me was so you could get a maid you wouldn't have to pay," you'll say bitterly, dragging the vacuum cleaner out of the closet.

"That's right," I'll say. "Thirteen years ago I knew the carpets would need vacuuming around now, and having a baby seemed to be the cheapest and easiest way to get the job done. Now kindly get on with it."

"If you weren't my mother, this would be illegal," you'll say, seething as you unwind the power cord and plug it into the wall outlet.

That will be in the house on Belmont Street. I'll live to see strangers occupy both houses: the one you're conceived in and the one you grow up in. Your dad and I will sell the first a couple years after your arrival. I'll sell the second shortly after your departure. By then Nelson and I will have moved into our farmhouse, and your dad will be living with what's-her-name.

I know how this story ends; I think about it a lot. I also think a lot about how it began, just a few years ago, when ships appeared in orbit and artifacts appeared in meadows. The government said next to nothing about them, while the tabloids said every possible thing.

And then I got a phone call, a request for a meeting.

I spotted them waiting in the hallway, outside my office. They made an odd couple; one wore a military uniform and a crewcut, and carried an aluminum briefcase. He seemed to be assessing his surroundings with a critical eye. The other one was easily identifiable as an academic: full beard and mustache, wearing corduroy. He was browsing through the overlapping sheets stapled to a bulletin board nearby.

"Colonel Weber, I presume?" I shook hands with the soldier. "Louise Banks."

"Dr. Banks. Thank you for taking the time to speak with us," he said.

"Not at all; any excuse to avoid the faculty meeting."

Colonel Weber indicated his companion. "This is Dr. Gary Donnelly, the physicist I mentioned when we spoke on the phone."

"Call me Gary," he said as we shook hands. "I'm anxious to hear what you have to say."

We entered my office. I moved a couple of stacks of books off the second guest chair, and we all sat down. "You said you wanted me to listen to a recording. I presume this has something to do with the aliens?"

"All I can offer is the recording," said Colonel Weber.

"Okay, let's hear it."

Colonel Weber took a tape machine out of his briefcase and pressed PLAY. The recording sounded vaguely like that of a wet dog shaking the water out of its fur.

"What do you make of that?" he asked.

I withheld my comparison to a wet dog. "What was the context in which this recording was made?"

"I'm not at liberty to say."

"It would help me interpret those sounds. Could you see the alien while it was speaking? Was it doing anything at the time?"

"The recording is all I can offer."

"You won't be giving anything away if you tell me that you've seen the aliens; the public's assumed you have."

Colonel Weber wasn't budging. "Do you have any opinion about its linguistic properties?" he asked.

"Well, it's clear that their vocal tract is substantially different from a human vocal tract. I assume that these aliens don't look like humans?"

The colonel was about to say something noncommittal when Gary Donelly asked, "Can you make any guesses based on the tape?"

"Not really. It doesn't sound like they're using a larynx to make those sounds, but that doesn't tell me what they look like."

"Anything—is there anything else you can call tell us?" asked Colonel Weber.

I could see he wasn't accustomed to consulting a civilian. "Only that establishing communications is going to be really difficult because of the difference in anatomy. They're almost certainly using sounds that the human vocal tract can't reproduce, and maybe sounds that the human ear can't distinguish."

"You mean infra- or ultrasonic frequencies?" asked Gary Donnelly.

"Not specifically. I just mean that the human auditory system isn't an absolute acoustic instrument; it's optimized to recognize the sounds that a human larynx makes. With an alien vocal system, all bets are off." I shrugged. "*Maybe* we'll be able to hear the difference between alien phonemes, given enough practice, but it's possible our ears simply can't recognize the distinctions they consider meaningful. In that case we'd need a sound spectrograph to know what an alien is saying."

Colonel Weber asked, "Suppose I gave you an hour's worth of recordings; how long would it take you to determine if we need this sound spectrograph or not?"

"I couldn't determine that with just a recording no matter how much time I had. I'd need to talk with the aliens directly."

The colonel shook his head. "Not possible."

I tried to break it to him gently. "That's your call, of course. But the only way to learn an unknown language is to interact with a native speaker, and by that I mean asking questions, holding a conversation, that sort of thing. Without that, it's simply not possible. So if you want to learn the aliens' language, someone with training in field linguistics—whether it's me or someone else—will have to talk with an alien. Recordings alone aren't sufficient."

Colonel Weber frowned. "You seem to be implying that no alien could have learned human languages by monitoring our broadcasts."

"I doubt it. They'd need instructional material specifically designed to teach human languages to nonhumans. Either that, or interaction with a human. If they had either of those, they could learn a lot from TV, but otherwise, they wouldn't have a starting point."

The colonel clearly found this interesting; evidently his philosophy was, the less the aliens knew, the better. Gary Donnelly read the colonel's expression too and rolled his eyes. I suppressed a smile.

Then Colonel Weber asked, "Suppose you were learning a new language by talking to its speakers; could you do it without teaching them English?"

"That would depend on how cooperative the native speakers were. They'd almost certainly pick up bits and pieces while I'm learning their language, but it wouldn't have to be much if they're willing to teach. On the other hand, if they'd rather learn English than teach us their language, that would make things far more difficult."

The colonel nodded. "I'll get back to you on this matter."

The request for that meeting was perhaps the second most momentous phone call in my life. The first, of course, will be the one from Mountain Rescue. At that point your dad and I will be speaking to each other maybe once a year, tops. After I get that phone call, though, the first thing I'll do will be to call your father.

He and I will drive out together to perform the identification, a long silent car ride. I remember the morgue, all tile and stainless steel, the hum of refrigeration and smell of antiseptic. An orderly will pull the sheet back to reveal your face. Your face will look wrong somehow, but I'll know it's you.

"Yes, that's her," I'll say. "She's mine."

You'll be twenty-five then.

The MP checked my badge, made a notation on his clipboard, and opened the gate; I drove the off-road vehicle into the encampment, a small village of tents pitched by the Army in a farmer's sun-scorched pasture. At the center of the encampment was one of the alien devices, nicknamed "looking glasses."

According to the briefings I'd attended, there were nine of these in the United States, one hundred and twelve in the world. The looking glasses acted as two-way communication devices, presumably with the ships in orbit. No one knew why the aliens wouldn't talk to us in person; fear of cooties, maybe. A team of scientists, including a physicist and a linguist, was assigned to each looking glass; Gary Donnelly and I were on this one.

Gary was waiting for me in the parking area. We navigated a circular maze of concrete barricades until we reached the large tent that covered the looking glass itself. In front of the tent was an equipment cart loaded with goodies borrowed from the school's phonology lab; I had sent it ahead for inspection by the Army.

Also outside the tent were three tripod-mounted video cameras whose lenses peered, through windows in the fabric wall, into the main room. Everything Gary and I did would be reviewed by countless others, including military intelligence. In addition we would each send daily reports, of which mine had to include estimates on how much English I thought the aliens could understand.

Gary held open the tent flap and gestured for me to enter. "Step right up," he said, circus-barker-style. "Marvel at creatures the likes of which have never been seen on God's green earth."

"And all for one slim dime," I murmured, walking through the door. At the moment the looking glass was inactive, resembling a semicircular mirror over ten feet high and twenty feet across. On the brown grass in front of the looking glass, an arc of white spray paint outlined the activation area. Currently the area contained only a table, two folding chairs, and a power strip with a cord leading to a generator outside. The buzz of fluorescent lamps, hung from poles along the edge of the room, commingled with the buzz of flies in the sweltering heat.

Gary and I looked at each other, and then began pushing the cart of equipment up to the table. As we crossed the paint line, the looking glass appeared to grow transparent; it was as if someone was slowly raising the illumination behind tinted glass. The illusion of depth was uncanny; I felt I could walk right into it. Once the looking glass was fully lit it resembled a life-sized diorama of a semicircular room. The room contained a few large objects that might have been furniture, but no aliens. There was a door in the curved rear wall.

We busied ourselves connecting everything together: microphone, sound spectrograph, portable computer, and speaker. As we worked, I frequently glanced at the looking glass, anticipating the aliens' arrival. Even so I jumped when one of them entered.

It looked like a barrel suspended at the intersection of seven limbs. It was radially symmetric, and any of its limbs could serve as an arm or a leg. The one in front of me was walking around on four legs, three nonadjacent arms curled up at its sides. Gary called them "heptapods."

I'd been shown videotapes, but I still gawked. Its limbs had no distinct joints; anatomists guessed they might be supported by vertebral columns. Whatever their underlying structure, the heptapod's limbs conspired to move it in a disconcertingly fluid manner. Its "torso" rode atop the rippling limbs as smoothly as a hovercraft.

Seven lidless eyes ringed the top of the heptapod's body. It walked back to the doorway from which it entered, made a brief sputtering sound, and returned to the center of the room followed by another heptapod; at no point did it ever turn around. Eerie, but logical; with eyes on all sides, any direction might as well be "forward."

Gary had been watching my reaction. "Ready?" he asked.

I took a deep breath. "Ready enough." I'd done plenty of fieldwork before, in the Amazon, but it had always been a bilingual procedure: either my informants knew some Portuguese, which I could use, or I'd previously gotten an introduction to their language from the local missionaries. This would be my first attempt at conducting a true monolingual discovery procedure. It was straightforward enough in theory, though.

I walked up to the looking glass and a heptapod on the other side did the same. The image was so real that my skin crawled. I could see the texture of its gray skin, like corduroy ridges arranged in whorls and loops. There was no smell at all from the looking glass, which somehow made the situation stranger.

I pointed to myself and said slowly, "Human." Then I pointed to Gary. "Human." Then I pointed at each heptapod and said, "What are you?"

No reaction. I tried again, and then again.

One of the heptapods pointed to itself with one limb, the four terminal digits pressed together. That was lucky. In some cultures a person pointed with his chin; if the heptapod hadn't used one of its limbs, I wouldn't have known what gesture to look for. I heard a brief fluttering sound, and saw a puckered orifice at the top of its body vibrate; it was talking. Then it pointed to its companion and fluttered again.

I went back to my computer; on its screen were two virtually identical spectrographs representing the fluttering sounds. I marked a sample for playback. I pointed to myself and said "Human" again, and did the same with Gary. Then I pointed to the heptapod, and played back the flutter on the speaker.

The heptapod fluttered some more. The second half of the spectrograph for this utterance looked like a repetition: call the previous utterances [flutter1], then this one was [flutter2flutter1].

I pointed at something that might have been a heptapod chair. "What is that?"

The heptapod paused, and then pointed at the "chair" and talked some more. The spectrograph for this differed distinctly from that of the earlier sounds: [flutter3]. Once again, I pointed to the "chair" while playing back [flutter3].

The heptapod replied; judging by the spectrograph, it looked like [flutter3flutter2]. Optimistic interpretation: the heptapod was confirming my utterances as correct, which implied compatibility between heptapod and human patterns of discourse. Pessimistic interpretation: it had a nagging cough.

At my computer I delimited certain sections of the spectrograph and typed in a tentative gloss for each: "heptapod" for [flutter1], "yes" for [flutter2], and "chair" for [flutter3]. Then I typed "Language: Heptapod A" as a heading for all the utterances.

Gary watched what I was typing. "What's the 'A' for?"

"It just distinguishes this language from any other ones the heptapods might use," I said. He nodded.

"Now let's try something, just for laughs." I pointed at each heptapod and tried to mimic the sound of [flutter1]; "heptapod." After a long pause, the first heptapod said something and then the second one said something else, neither of whose spectrographs resembled anything said before. I couldn't tell if they were speaking to each other or to me since they had no faces to turn. I tried pronouncing [flutter1] again, but there was no reaction.

"Not even close," I grumbled.

"I'm impressed you can make sounds like that at all," said Gary.

"You should hear my moose call. Sends them running."

I tried again a few more times, but neither heptapod responded with anything I could recognize. Only when I replayed the recording of the heptapod's pronunciation did I get a confirmation; the heptapod replied with [flutter2], "yes."

"So we're stuck with using recordings?" asked Gary.

I nodded. "At least temporarily."

"So now what?"

"Now we make sure it hasn't actually been saying 'aren't they cute' or 'look what they're doing now.' Then we see if we can identify any of these words when that other heptapod pronounces them." I gestured for him to have a seat. "Get comfortable; this'll take a while."

In 1770, Captain Cook's ship *Endeavour* ran aground on the coast of Queensland, Australia. While some of his men made repairs, Cook led an exploration party and met the aboriginal people. One of the sailors pointed to the animals that hopped around with their young riding in pouches, and asked an aborigine what they were called. The aborigine replied, "Kanguru." From then on Cook and his sailors referred to the animals by this word. It wasn't until later that they learned it meant "What did you say?"

I tell that story in my introductory course every year. It's almost certainly untrue, and I explain that afterwards, but it's a classic anecdote. Of course, the anecdotes my undergraduates will really want to hear are ones featuring the heptapods; for the rest of my teaching career, that'll be the reason many of them sign up for my courses. So I'll show them the old videotapes of my sessions at the looking glass, and the sessions that the other linguists conducted; the tapes are instructive, and they'll be useful if we're ever visited by aliens again, but they don't generate many good anecdotes.

When it comes to language-learning anecdotes, my favorite source is child language acquisition. I remember one afternoon when you are five years old, after you have come home from kindergarten. You'll be coloring with your crayons while I grade papers.

"Mom," you'll say, using the carefully casual tone reserved for requesting a favor, "can I ask you something?"

"Sure, sweetie. Go ahead."

"Can I be, um, honored?"

I'll look up from the paper I'm grading. "What do you mean?"

"At school Sharon said she got to be honored."

"Really? Did she tell you what for?"

"It was when her big sister got married. She said only one person could be, um, honored, and she was it."

"Ah, I see. You mean Sharon was maid of honor?"

"Yeah, that's it. Can I be made of honor?"

Gary and I entered the prefab building containing the center of operations for the looking glass site. Inside it looked like they were planning an invasion, or perhaps an evacuation: crewcut soldiers worked around a large map of the area, or sat in front of burly electronic gear while speaking into headsets. We were shown into Colonel Weber's office, a room in the back that was cool from air conditioning.

We briefed the colonel on our first day's results. "Doesn't sound like you got very far," he said.

"I have an idea as to how we can make faster progress," I said. "But you'll have to approve the use of more equipment."

"What more do you need?"

"A digital camera, and a big video screen." I showed him a drawing of the setup I imagined. "I want to try conducting the discovery procedure using writing; I'd display words on the screen, and use the camera to record the words they write. I'm hoping the heptapods will do the same."

Weber looked at the drawing dubiously. "What would be the advantage of that?"

"So far I've been proceeding the way I would with speakers of an unwritten language. Then it occurred to me that the heptapods must have writing, too."

"So?"

"If the heptapods have a mechanical way of producing writing, then their writing ought to be very regular, very consistent. That would make it easier for us to identify graphemes instead of phonemes. It's like picking out the letters in a printed sentence instead of trying to hear them when the sentence is spoken aloud."

"I take your point," he admitted. "And how would you respond to them? Show them the words they displayed to you?"

"Basically. And if they put spaces between words, any sentences we write would be a lot more intelligible than any spoken sentence we might splice together from recordings."

He leaned back in his chair. "You know we want to show as little of our technology as possible."

"I understand, but we're using machines as intermediaries already. If we can get them to use writing. I believe progress will go much faster than if we're restricted to the sound spectrographs."

The colonel turned to Gary. "Your opinion?"

"It sounds like a good idea to me. I'm curious whether the heptapods might have difficulty reading our monitors. Their looking glasses are based on a completely different technology than our video screens. As far as we can tell, they don't use pixels or scan lines, and they don't refresh on a frame-by-frame basis."

"You think the scan lines on our video screens might render them unreadable to the heptapods?"

"It's possible," said Gary. "We'll just have to try it and see."

Weber considered it. For me it wasn't even a question, but from his point of view it was a difficult one; like a soldier, though, he made it quickly. "Request granted. Talk to the sergeant outside about bringing in what you need. Have it ready for tomorrow."

I remember one day during the summer when you're sixteen. For once, the person waiting for her date to arrive is me. Of course, you'll be waiting around, too, curious to see what he looks like. You'll have a friend of yours, a blond girl with the unlikely name of Roxie, hanging out with you, giggling.

"You may feel the urge to make comments about him," I'll say, checking myself in the hallway mirror. "Just restrain yourselves until we leave."

"Don't worry, Mom," you'll say. "We'll do it so that he won't know. Roxie, you ask me what I think the weather will be like tonight. Then I'll say what I think of Mom's date."

"Right," Roxie will say.

"No, you most definitely will not," I'll say.

"Relax, Mom. He'll never know; we do this all the time."

"What a comfort that is."

A little later on, Nelson will arrive to pick me up. I'll do the introductions, and we'll all engage in a little small talk on the front porch. Nelson is ruggedly handsome, to your evident approval. Just as we're about to leave, Roxie will say to you casually, "So what do you think the weather will be like tonight?"

"I think it's going to be really hot," you'll answer.

Roxie will nod in agreement. Nelson will say, "Really? I thought they said it was going to be cool."

"I have a sixth sense about these things," you'll say. Your face will give nothing away. "I get the feeling it's going to be a scorcher. Good thing you're dressed for it, Mom."

I'll glare at you, and say good night.

As I lead Nelson toward his car, he'll ask me, amused, "I'm missing something here, aren't I?"

"A private joke," I'll mutter. "Don't ask me to explain it."

At our next session at the looking glass, we repeated the procedure we had performed before, this time displaying a printed word on our computer screen at the same time we spoke: showing HUMAN while saying "Human," and so forth. Eventually, the heptapods understood what we wanted, and set up a flat circular screen mounted on a small pedestal. One heptapod spoke, and then inserted a limb into a large socket in the pedestal; a doodle of script, vaguely cursive, popped onto the screen.

We soon settled into a routine, and I compiled two parallel corpora: one of spoken utterances, one of writing samples. Based on first impressions, their writing appeared to be logographic, which was disappointing; I'd been hoping for an alphabetic script to help us learn their speech. Their logograms might include some phonetic information, but finding it would be a lot harder than with an alphabetic script.

By getting up close to the looking glass, I was able to point to various heptapod body parts, such as limbs, digits, and eyes, and elicit terms for each. It turned out that they had an orifice on the underside of their body, lined with articulated bony ridges: probably used for eating, while the one at the top was for respiration and speech. There were no other conspicuous orifices; perhaps their mouth was their anus, too. Those sorts of questions would have to wait.

I also tried asking our two informants for terms for addressing each individually; personal names, if they had such things. Their answers were of course unpronounceable, so for Gary's and my purposes, I dubbed them Flapper and Raspberry. I hoped I'd be able to tell them apart.

The next day I conferred with Gary before we entered the looking-glass tent. "I'll need your help with this session," I told him.

"Sure. What do you want me to do?"

"We need to elicit some verbs, and it's easiest with third-person forms. Would you act out a few verbs while I type the written form on the computer? If we're lucky, the heptapods will figure out what we're doing and do the same. I've brought a bunch of props for you to use."

"No problem," said Gary, cracking his knuckles. "Ready when you are."

We began with some simple intransitive verbs: walking, jumping, speaking, writing. Gary demonstrated each one with a charming lack of self-consciousness; the presence of the video cameras didn't inhibit him at all. For the first few actions he performed, I asked the heptapods, "What do you call that?" Before long, the heptapods caught on to what we were trying to do; Raspberry began mimicking Gary, or at least performing the equivalent heptapod action, while Flapper worked their computer, displaying a written description and pronouncing it aloud.

In the spectrographs of their spoken utterances, I could recognize their word I had glossed as "heptapod." The rest of each utterance was presumably the verb phrase; it looked like they had analogs of nouns and verbs, thank goodness.

In their writing, however, things weren't as clear-cut. For each action, they had displayed a single logogram instead of two separate ones. At first I thought they had written something like "walks," with the subject implied. But why would Flapper say "the heptapod walks" while writing "walks," instead of maintaining parallelism? Then I noticed that some of the logograms looked like the logogram for "heptapod" with some extra strokes added to one side or another. Perhaps their verbs could be written as affixes to a noun. If so, why was Flapper writing the noun in some instances but not in others?

I decided to try a transitive verb; substituting object words might clarify things. Among the props I'd brought were an apple and a slice of bread. "Okay," I said to Gary, "show them the food, and then eat some. First the apple, then the bread."

Gary pointed at the Golden Delicious and then he took a bite out of it, while I displayed the "what do you call that?" expression. Then we repeated it with the slice of whole wheat.

Raspberry left the room and returned with some kind of giant nut or gourd and a gelatinous ellipsoid. Raspberry pointed at the gourd while Flapper said a word and displayed a logogram. Then Raspberry brought the gourd down between its legs, a crunching sound resulted, and the gourd reemerged minus a bite; there were cornlike kernels beneath the shell. Flapper talked and displayed a large logogram on their screen. The sound spectrograph for "gourd" changed when it was used in the sentence; possibly a case marker. The logogram was odd: after some study, I could identify graphic elements that resembled the individual logograms for "heptapod" and "gourd." They looked as if they had been melted together, with several extra strokes in the mix that presumably meant "eat." Was it a multiword ligature?

Next we got spoken and written names for the gelatin egg, and descriptions of the act of eating it. The sound spectrograph for "heptapod eats gelatin egg" was analyzable; "gelatin egg" bore a case marker, as expected, though the sentence's word order differed from last time. The written form, another large logogram, was another matter. This time it took much longer for me to recognize anything in it; not only were the individual logograms melted together again, it looked as if the one for "heptapod" was laid on its back, while on top of it the logogram for "gelatin egg" was standing on its head.

"Uh-oh." I took another look at the writing for the simple noun-verb examples, the ones that had seemed inconsistent before. Now I realized all of them actually did contain the logogram for "heptapod"; some were rotated and distorted by being combined with the various verbs, so I hadn't recognized them at first. "You guys have got to be kidding," I muttered.

"What's wrong?" asked Gary.

"Their script isn't word-divided; a sentence is written by joining the logograms for the constituent words. They join the logograms by rotating and modifying them. Take a look." I showed him how the logograms were rotated.

"So they can read a word with equal ease no matter how it's rotated," Gary said. He turned to look at the heptapods, impressed. "I wonder if it's a consequence of their bodies' radial symmetry: their bodies have no 'forward' direction, so maybe their writing doesn't either. Highly neat."

I couldn't believe it; I was working with someone who modified the word "neat" with "highly." "It certainly is interesting," I said, "but it also means there's no easy way for us write our own sentences in their language. We can't simply cut their sentences into individual words and recombine them; we'll have to learn the rules of their script before we can write anything legible. It's the same continuity problem we'd have had splicing together speech fragments, except applied to writing."

I looked at Flapper and Raspberry in the looking glass, who were waiting for us to continue, and sighed. "You aren't going to make this easy for us, are you?"

To be fair, the heptapods were completely cooperative. In the days that followed, they readily taught us their language without requiring us to teach them any more English. Colonel Weber and his cohorts pondered the implications of that, while I and the linguists at the other looking glasses met via video conferencing to share what we had learned about the heptapod language. The videoconferencing made for an incongruous working environment: our video screens were primitive compared to the heptapods' looking glasses, so that my colleagues seemed more remote than the aliens. The familiar was far away, while the bizarre was close at hand.

It would be a while before we'd be ready to ask the heptapods why they had come, or to discuss physics well enough to ask them about their technology. For the time being, we worked on the basics: phonemics/graphemics, vocabulary, syntax. The heptapods at every looking glass were using the same language, so we were able to pool our data and coordinate our efforts.

Our biggest source of confusion was the heptapods' "writing." It didn't appear to be writing at all; it looked more like a bunch of intricate graphic designs. The logograms weren't arranged in rows, or a spiral, or any linear fashion. Instead, Flapper or Raspberry would write a sentence by sticking together as many logograms as needed into a giant conglomeration.

This form of writing was reminiscent of primitive sign systems, which required a reader to know a message's context in order to understand it. Such systems were considered too limited for systematic recording of information. Yet it was unlikely that the heptapods developed their level of technology with only an oral tradition. That implied one of three possibilities: the first was that the heptapods had a true writing system, but they didn't want to use it in front of us; Colonel Weber would identify with that one. The second was that the heptapods hadn't originated the technology they were using; they were illiterates using someone else's technology. The third, and most interesting to me, was that the heptapods were using a nonlinear system of orthography that qualified as true writing.

I remember a conversation we'll have when you're in your junior year of high school. It'll be Sunday morning, and I'll be scrambling some eggs while you set the table for brunch. You'll laugh as you tell me about the party you went to last night.

"Oh man," you'll say, "they're not kidding when they say that body weight makes a difference. I didn't drink any more than the guys did, but I got so much *drunker*."

I'll try to maintain a neutral, pleasant expression. I'll really try. Then you'll say, "Oh, come on, Mom."

"What?"

"You know you did the exact same things when you were my age."

I did nothing of the sort, but I know that if I were to admit that, you'd lose respect for me completely. "You know never to drive, or get into a car if—"

"God, of course I know that. Do you think I'm an idiot?"

"No, of course not."

What I'll think is that you are clearly, maddeningly not me. It will remind me, again, that you won't be a clone of me; you can be wonderful, a daily delight, but you won't be someone I could have created by myself.

The military had set up a trailer containing our offices at the looking-glass site. I saw Gary walking toward the trailer, and ran to catch up with him. "It's a semasiographic writing system," I said when I reached him.

"Excuse me?" said Gary.

"Here, let me show you." I directed Gary into my office. Once we were inside, I went to the chalkboard and drew a circle with a diagonal line bisecting it. "What does this mean?"

" 'Not allowed'?"

"Right." Next I printed the words NOT ALLOWED on the chalkboard. "And so does this. But only one is a representation of speech."

Gary nodded. "Okay."

"Linguists describe writing like this—" I indicated the printed words "—as 'glotto-graphic,' because it represents speech. Every human written language is in this cate-gory. However, this symbol—" I indicated the circle and diagonal line "—is 'semasiographic' writing, because it conveys meaning without reference to speech. There's no correspondence between its components and any particular sounds."

"And you think all of heptapod writing is like this?"

"From what I've seen so far, yes. It's not picture writing, it's far more complex. It has its own system of rules for constructing sentences, like a visual syntax that's un-related to the syntax for their spoken language."

"A visual syntax? Can you show me an example?"

"Coming right up." I sat down at my desk and, using the computer, pulled up a frame from the recording of yesterday's conversation with Raspberry. I turned the monitor so he could see it. "In their spoken language, a noun has a case marker indicating whether it's a subject or object. In their written language, however, a noun is identified as subject or object based on the orientation of its logogram relative to that of the verb. Here, take a look." I pointed at one of the figures. "For instance, when 'heptapod' is integrated with 'hears' this way, with these strokes parallel, it means that the heptapod is doing the hearing." I showed him a different one. "When they're combined this way, with the strokes perpendicular, it means that the heptapod is being heard. This morphology applies to several verbs.

"Another example is the inflection system." I called up another frame from the recording. "In their written language, this logogram means roughly 'hear easily' or 'hear clearly.' See the elements it has in common with the logogram for 'hear'? You can still combine it with 'heptapod' in the same ways as before, to indicate that the heptapod can hear something clearly or that the heptapod is clearly heard. But what's really interesting is that the modulation of 'hear' into 'hear clearly' isn't a special case; you see the transformation they applied?"

Gary nodded, pointing. "It's like they express the idea of 'clearly' by changing the curve of those strokes in the middle."

"Right. That modulation is applicable to lots of verbs. The logogram for 'see' can be modulated in the same way to form 'see clearly,' and so can the logogram for 'read' and others. And changing the curve of those strokes has no parallel in their speech; with the spoken version of these verbs, they add a prefix to the verb to express ease of manner, and the prefixes for 'see' and 'hear' are different.

"There are other examples, but you get the idea. It's essentially a grammar in two dimensions."

He began pacing thoughtfully. "Is there anything like this in human writing systems?"

"Mathematical equations, notations for music and dance. But those are all very specialized; we couldn't record this conversation using them. But I suspect, if we knew it well enough, we could record this conversation in the heptapod writing system. I think it's a full-fledged, general-purpose graphical language."

Gary frowned. "So their writing constitutes a completely separate language from their speech, right?"

"Right. In fact, it'd be more accurate to refer to the writing system as 'Heptapod B,' and use 'Heptapod A' strictly for referring to the spoken language."

"Hold on a second. Why use two languages when one would suffice? That seems unnecessarily hard to learn."

"Like English spelling?" I said. "Ease of learning isn't the primary force in language evolution. For the heptapods, writing and speech may play such different cultural or cognitive roles that using separate languages makes more sense than using different forms of the same one."

He considered it. "I see what you mean. Maybe they think our form of writing is redundant, like we're wasting a second communications channel."

"That's entirely possible. Finding out why they use a second language for writing will tell us a lot about them."

"So I take it this means we won't be able to use their writing to help us learn their spoken language."

I sighed. "Yeah, that's the most immediate implication. But I don't think we should ignore either Heptapod A or B; we need a two-pronged approach." I pointed at the screen. "I'll bet you that learning their two-dimensional grammar will help you when it comes time to learn their mathematical notation."

"You've got a point there. So are we ready to start asking about their mathematics?"

"Not yet. We need a better grasp on this writing system before we begin anything else," I said, and then smiled when he mimed frustration. "Patience, good sir. Patience is a virtue."

You'll be six when your father has a conference to attend in Hawaii, and we'll accompany him. You'll be so excited that you'll make preparations for weeks beforehand. You'll ask me about coconuts and volcanoes and surfing, and practice hula dancing in the mirror. You'll pack a suitcase with the clothes and toys you want to bring, and you'll drag it around the house to see how long you can carry it. You'll ask me if I can carry your Etch-a-Sketch in my bag, since there won't be any more room for it in yours and you simply can't leave without it.

"You won't need all of these," I'll say. "There'll be so many fun things to do there, you won't have time to play with so many toys."

You'll consider that; dimples will appear above your eyebrows when you think hard. Eventually you'll agree to pack fewer toys, but your expectations will, if anything, increase.

"I wanna be in Hawaii now," you'll whine.

"Sometimes it's good to wait," I'll say. "The anticipation makes it more fun when you get there."

You'll just pout.

In the next report I submitted, I suggested that the term "logogram" was a misnomer because it implied that each graph represented a spoken word, when in fact the graphs didn't correspond to our notion of spoken words at all. I didn't want to use the term "ideogram" either because of how it had been used in the past; I suggested the term "semagram" instead.

It appeared that a semagram corresponded roughly to a written word in human languages: it was meaningful on its own, and in combination with other semagrams could form endless statements. We couldn't define it precisely, but then no one had ever satisfactorily defined "word" for human languages either. When it came to sentences in Heptapod B, though, things became much more confusing. The language had no written punctuation: its syntax was indicated in the way the semagrams were combined, and there was no need to indicate the cadence of speech. There was certainly no way to slice out subject-predicate pairings neatly to make sentences. A "sentence" seemed to be whatever number of semagrams a heptapod wanted to join together; the only difference between a sentence and a paragraph, or a page, was size.

When a Heptapod B sentence grew fairly sizable, its visual impact was remarkable.

If I wasn't trying to decipher it, the writing looked like fanciful praying mantids drawn in a cursive style, all clinging to each other to form an Escheresque lattice, each slightly different in its stance. And the biggest sentences had an effect similar to that of psychedelic posters: sometimes eye-watering, sometimes hypnotic.

I remember a picture of you taken at your college graduation. In the photo you're striking a pose for the camera, mortarboard stylishly tilted on your head, one hand touching your sunglasses, the other hand on your hip, holding open your gown to reveal the tank top and shorts you're wearing underneath.

I remember your graduation. There will be the distraction of having Nelson and your father and what's-her-name there all at the same time, but that will be minor. That entire weekend, while you're introducing me to your classmates and hugging everyone incessantly, I'll be all but mute with amazement. I can't believe that you, a grown woman taller than me and beautiful enough to make my heart ache, will be the same girl I used to lift off the ground so you could reach the drinking fountain, the same girl who used to trundle out of my bedroom draped in a dress and hat and four scarves from my closet.

And after graduation, you'll be heading for a job as a financial analyst. I won't understand what you do there, I won't even understand your fascination with money, the preeminence you gave to salary when negotiating job offers. I would prefer it if you'd pursue something without regard for its monetary rewards, but I'll have no complaints. My own mother could never understand why I couldn't just be a high school English teacher. You'll do what makes you happy, and that'll be all I ask for.

As time went on, the teams at each looking glass began working in earnest on learning heptapod terminology for elementary mathematics and physics. We worked together on presentations, with the linguists focusing on procedure and the physicists focusing on subject matter. The physicists showed us previously devised systems for communicating with aliens, based on mathematics, but those were intended for use over a radio telescope. We reworked them for face-to-face communication.

Our teams were successful with basic arithmetic, but we hit a road block with geometry and algebra. We tried using a spherical coordinate system instead of a rectangular one, thinking it might be more natural to the heptapods given their anatomy, but that approach wasn't any more fruitful. The heptapods didn't seem to understand what we were getting at.

Likewise, the physics discussions went poorly. Only with the most concrete terms, like the names of the elements, did we have any success; after several attempts at representing the periodic table, the heptapods got the idea. For anything remotely abstract, we might as well have been gibbering. We tried to demonstrate basic physical attributes like mass and acceleration so we could elicit their terms for them, but the heptapods simply responded with requests for clarification. To avoid perceptual problems that might be associated with any particular medium, we tried physical demonstrations as well as line drawings, photos, and animations; none were effective. Days with no progress became weeks, and the physicists were becoming disillusioned.

By contrast, the linguists were having much more success. We made steady progress decoding the grammar of the spoken language, Heptapod A. It didn't follow the pattern of human languages, as expected, but it was comprehensible so far: free word order, even to the extent that there was no preferred order for the clauses in a conditional statement, in defiance of a human language "universal." It also appeared that the heptapods had no objection to many levels of center-embedding of clauses, something that quickly defeated humans. Peculiar, but not impenetrable.

Much more interesting were the newly discovered morphological and grammatical processes in Heptapod B that were uniquely two-dimensional. Depending on a semagram's declension, inflections could be indicated by varying a certain stroke's curvature, or its thickness, or its manner of undulation; or by varying the relative sizes of two radicals, or their relative distance to another radical, or their orientations; or various other means. These were nonsegmental graphemes; they couldn't be isolated from the rest of a semagram. And despite how such traits behaved in human writing, these had nothing to do with calligraphic style; their meanings were defined according to a consistent and unambiguous grammar.

We regularly asked the heptapods why they had come. Each time, they answered "to see," or "to observe." Indeed, sometimes they preferred to watch us silently rather than answer our questions. Perhaps they were scientists, perhaps they were tourists. The State Department instructed us to reveal as little as possible about humanity, in case that information could be used as a bargaining chip in subsequent negotiations. We obliged, though it didn't require much effort: the heptapods never asked questions about anything. Whether scientists or tourists, they were an awfully incurious bunch.

I remember once when we'll be driving to the mall to buy some new clothes for you. You'll be thirteen. One moment you'll be sprawled in your seat, completely unselfconscious, all child; the next, you'll toss your hair with a practiced casualness, like a fashion model in training.

You'll give me some instructions as I'm parking the car. "Okay, Mom, give me one of the credit cards, and we can meet back at the entrance here in two hours."

I'll laugh. "Not a chance. All the credit cards stay with me."

"You're kidding." You'll become the embodiment of exasperation. We'll get out of the car and I will start walking to the mall entrance. After seeing that I won't budge on the matter, you'll quickly reformulate your plans.

"Okay Mom, okay. You can come with me, just walk a little ways behind me, so it doesn't look like we're together. If I see any friends of mine, I'm gonna stop and talk to them, but you just keep walking, okay? I'll come find you later."

I'll stop in my tracks. "Excuse me? I am not the hired help, nor am I some mutant relative for you to be ashamed of."

"But Mom, I can't let anyone see you with me."

"What are you talking about? I've already met your friends; they've been to the house."

"That was different," you'll say, incredulous that you have to explain it. "This is shopping."

"Too bad."

Then the explosion: "You won't do the least thing to make me happy! You don't care about me at all!"

It won't have been that long since you enjoyed going shopping with me; it will forever astonish me how quickly you grow out of one phase and enter another. Living with you will be like aiming for a moving target; you'll always be further along than I expect.

I looked at the sentence in Heptapod B that I had just written, using simple pen and paper. Like all the sentences I generated myself, this one looked misshapen, like a heptapod-written sentence that had been smashed with a hammer and then inexpertly taped back together. I had sheets of such inelegant semagrams covering my desk, fluttering occasionally when the oscillating fan swung past.

It was strange trying to learn a language that had no spoken form. Instead of practicing my pronunciation, I had taken to squeezing my eyes shut and trying to paint semagrams on the insides of my eyelids.

There was a knock at the door and before I could answer Gary came in looking jubilant. "Illinois got a repetition in physics."

"Really? That's great; when did it happen?"

"It happened a few hours ago; we just had the videoconference. Let me show you what it is." He started erasing my blackboard.

"Don't worry, I didn't need any of that."

"Good." He picked up a nub of chalk and drew a diagram:

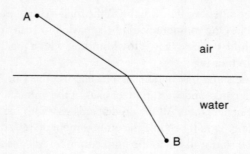

"Okay, here's the path a ray of light takes when crossing from air to water. The light ray travels in a straight line until it hits the water; the water has a different index of refraction, so the light changes direction. You've heard of this before, right?"

I nodded. "Sure."

"Now here's an interesting property about the path the light takes. The path is the fastest possible route between these two points."

"Come again?"

"Imagine, just for grins, that the ray of light traveled along this path." He added a dotted line to his diagram:

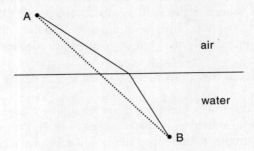

"This hypothetical path is shorter than the path the light actually takes. But light travels more slowly in water than it does in air, and a greater percentage of this path is underwater. So it would take longer for light to travel along this path than it does along the real path."

"Okay, I get it."

"Now imagine if light were to travel along this other path." He drew a second dotted path:

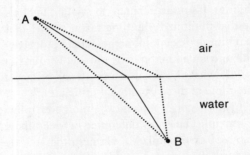

"This path reduces the percentage that's underwater, but the total length is larger. It would also take longer for light to travel along this path than along the actual one."

Gary put down the chalk and gestured at the diagram on the chalkboard with white-tipped fingers. "Any hypothetical path would require more time to traverse than the one actually taken. In other words, the route that the light ray takes is always the fastest possible one. That's Fermat's Principle of Least Time."

"Hmm, interesting. And this is what the heptapods responded to?"

"Exactly. Moorehead gave an animated presentation of Fermat's Principle at the Illinois looking glass, and the heptapods repeated it back. Now he's trying to get a symbolic description." He grinned. "Now is that highly neat, or what?"

"It's neat all right, but how come I haven't heard of Fermat's Principle before?" I picked up a binder and waved it at him; it was a primer on the physics topics suggested for use in communication with the heptapods. "This thing goes on forever about Planck masses and the spin-flip of atomic hydrogen, and not a word about the refraction of light."

"We guessed wrong about what'd be most useful for you to know," Gary said without embarrassment. "In fact, it's curious that Fermat's Principle was the first breakthrough; even though it's easy to explain, you need calculus to describe it mathematically. And not ordinary caldulus; you need the calculus of variations. We thought that some simple theorem of geometry or algebra would be the breakthrough."

"Curious indeed. You think the heptapods' idea of what's simple doesn't match ours?"

"Exactly, which is why I'm *dying* to see what their mathematical description of Fermat's Principle looks like." He paced as he talked. "If their version of the calculus of variations is simpler to them than their equivalent of algebra, that might explain why we've had so much trouble talking about physics; their entire system of mathematics may be topsy-turvy compared to ours." He pointed to the physics primer. "You can be sure that we're going to revise that."

"So can you build from Fermat's Principle to other areas of physics?"

"Probably. There are lots of physical principles just like Fermat's."

"What, like Louise's principle of least closet space? When did physics become so minimalist?"

"Well, the word 'least' is misleading. You see, Fermat's Principle of Least Time is incomplete; in certain situations light follows a path that takes *more* time than any of the other possibilities. It's more accurate to say that light always follows an *extreme* path, either one that minimizes the time taken or one that maximizes it. A minimum and a maximum share certain mathematical properties, so both situations can be described with one equation. So to be precise, Fermat's Principle isn't a minimal principle; instead it's what's known as a 'variational' principle."

"And there are more of these variational principles?"

He nodded. "In all branches of physics. Almost every physical law can be restated as a variational principle. The only difference between these principles is in which attribute is minimized or maximized." He gestured as if the different branches of physics were arrayed before him on a table. "In optics, where Fermat's Principle applies, time is the attribute that has to be an extreme. In mechanics, it's a different attribute. In electromagnetism, it's something else again. But all these principles are similar mathematically."

"So once you get their mathematical description of Fermat's Principle, you should be able to decode the other ones."

"God, I hope so. I think this is the wedge that we've been looking for, the one that cracks open their formulation of physics. This calls for a celebration." He stopped his pacing and turned to me. "Hey, Louise, want to go out for dinner? My treat."

I was mildly surprised. "Sure," I said.

It'll be when you first learn to walk that I get daily demonstrations of the asymmetry in our relationship. You'll be incessantly running off somewhere, and each time you walk into a door frame or scrape your knee, the pain feels like it's my own. It'll be like growing an errant limb, an extension of myself whose sensory nerves report pain just fine, but whose motor nerves don't convey my commands at all. It's so unfair: I'm going to give birth to an animated voodoo doll of myself. I didn't see this in the contract when I signed up. Was this part of the deal?

And then there will be the times when I see you laughing. Like the time you'll be playing with the neighbor's puppy, poking your hands through the chain-link fence separating our back yards, and you'll be laughing so hard you'll start hiccupping. The puppy will run inside the neighbor's house, and your laughter will gradually subside, letting you catch your breath. Then the puppy will come back to the fence to lick your fingers again, and you'll shriek and start laughing again. It will be the most wonderful sound I could ever imagine, a sound that makes me feel like a fountain, or a wellspring.

Now if only I can remember that sound the next time your blithe disregard for self-preservation gives me a heart attack.

After the breakthrough with Fermat's Principle, discussions of scientific concepts became more fruitful. It wasn't as if all of heptapod physics was suddenly rendered transparent, but progress was steady. According to Gary, the heptapods' formulation of physics was indeed topsy-turvy relative to ours. Physical attributes that humans defined using integral calculus were seen as fundamental by the heptapods. As an example, Gary described an attribute that, in physics jargon, bore the deceptively simple name "action," which represented "the difference between kinetic and potential energy, integrated over time," whatever that meant. Calculus for us; elementary to them.

Conversely, to define attributes that humans thought of as fundamental, like velocity, the heptapods employed mathematics that were, Gary assured me, "highly weird." The physicists were ultimately able to prove the equivalence of heptapod mathematics and human mathematics; even though their approaches were almost the reverse of one another, both were systems of describing the same physical universe.

I tried following some of the equations that the physicists were coming up with, but it was no use. I couldn't really grasp the significance of physical attributes like "action"; I couldn't, with any confidence, ponder the significance of treating such an attribute as fundamental. Still, I tried to ponder questions formulated in terms more familiar to me: what kind of worldview did the heptapods have, that they would consider Fermat's Principle the simplest explanation of light refraction? What kind of perception made a minimum or maximum readily apparent to them?

Your eyes will be blue like your dad's, not mud brown like mine. Boys will stare into those eyes the way I did, and do, into your dad's, surprised and enchanted, as I was and am, to find them in combination with black hair. You will have many suitors.

I remember when you are fifteen, coming home after a weekend at your dad's, incredulous over the interrogation he'll have put you through regarding the boy you're currently dating. You'll sprawl on the sofa, recounting your dad's latest breach of common sense: "You know what he said? He said, 'I know what teenage boys are like.'" Roll of the eyes. "Like I don't?"

"Don't hold it against him," I'll say. "He's a father; he can't help it." Having seen you interact with your friends, I won't worry much about a boy taking advantage of you; if anything, the opposite will be more likely. I'll worry about that.

"He wishes I were still a kid. He hasn't known how to act toward me since I grew breasts."

"Well, that development was a shock for him. Give him time to recover."

"It's been *years*, Mom. How long is it gonna take?"

"I'll let you know when my father has come to terms with mine."

During one of the videoconferences for the linguists, Cisneros from the Massachusetts looking glass had raised an interesting question: was there a particular order in which semagrams were written in a Heptapod B sentence? It was clear that word order meant next to nothing when speaking in Heptapod A; when asked to repeat what it had just said, a heptapod would likely as not use a different word order unless we specifically asked them not to. Was word order similarly unimportant when writing in Heptapod B?

Previously, we had only focused our attention on how a sentence in Heptapod B looked once it was complete. As far as anyone could tell, there was no preferred order when reading the semagrams in a sentence; you could start almost anywhere in the nest, then follow the branching clauses until you'd read the whole thing. But that was reading; was the same true about writing?

During my most recent session with Flapper and Raspberry I had asked them if, instead of displaying a semagram only after it was completed, they could show it to us while it was being written. They had agreed. I inserted the videotape of the session into the VCR, and on my computer I consulted the session transcript.

I picked one of the longer utterances from the conversation. What Flapper had said was that the heptapods' planet had two moons, one significantly larger than the other; the three primary constituents of the planet's atmosphere were nitrogen, argon, and oxygen; and fifteen twenty-eighths of the planet's surface was covered by water. The first words of the spoken utterance translated literally as "inequality-of-size rocky-orbiter rocky-orbiters related-as-primary-to-secondary."

Then I rewound the videotape until the time signature matched the one in the transcription. I started playing the tape, and watched the web of semagrams being spun out of inky spider's silk. I rewound it and played it several times. Finally I froze the video right after the first stroke was completed and before the second one was begun; all that was visible onscreen was a single sinuous line.

Comparing that initial stroke with the completed sentence, I realized that the stroke participated in several different clauses of the message. It began in the semagram for 'oxygen,' as the determinant that distinguished it from certain other elements; then it slid down to become the morpheme of comparison in the description of the two moons' sizes; and lastly it flared out as the arched backbone of the semagram for 'ocean.' Yet this stroke was a single continuous line, and it was the first one that Flapper wrote. That meant the heptapod had to know how the entire sentence would be laid out before it could write the very first stroke.

The other strokes in the sentence also traversed several clauses, making them so interconnected that none could be removed without redesigning the entire sentence. The heptapods didn't write a sentence one semagram at a time; they built it out of strokes irrespective of individual semagrams. I had seen a similarly high degree of integration before in calligraphic designs, particularly those employing the Arabic alphabet. But those designs had required careful planning by expert calligraphers. No one could lay out such an intricate design at the speed needed for holding a conversation. At least, no human could.

There's a joke that I once heard a comedienne tell. It goes like this: "I'm not sure if I'm ready to have children. I asked a friend of mine who has children, 'Suppose I do have kids. What if when they grow up, they blame me for everything that's wrong with their lives?' She laughed and said, 'What do you mean, if?'"

That's my favorite joke.

Gary and I were at a little Chinese restaurant, one of the local places we had taken to patronizing to get away from the encampment. We sat eating the appetizers: potstickers, redolent of pork and sesame oil. My favorite.

I dipped one in soy sauce and vinegar. "So how are you doing with your Heptapod B practice?" I asked.

Gary looked obliquely at the ceiling. I tried to meet his gaze, but he kept shifting it.

"You've given up, haven't you?" I said. "You're not even trying any more."

He did a wonderful hangdog expression. "I'm just no good at languages," he confessed. "I thought learning Heptapod B might be more like learning mathematics than trying to speak another language, but it's not. It's too foreign for me."

"It would help you discuss physics with them."

"Probably, but since we had our breakthrough, I can get by with just a few phrases."

I sighed. "I suppose that's fair; I have to admit, I've given up on trying to learn the mathematics."

"So we're even?"

"We're even." I sipped my tea. "Though I did want to ask you about Fermat's Principle. Something about it feels odd to me, but I can't put my finger on it. It just doesn't sound like a law of physics."

A twinkle appeared in Gary's eyes. "I'll bet I know what you're talking about." He snipped a potsticker in half with his chopsticks. "You're used to thinking of refraction in terms of cause and effect: reaching the water's surface is the cause, and the change in direction is the effect. But Fermat's Principle sounds weird because it describes light's behavior in goal-oriented terms. It sounds like a commandment to a light beam: 'Thou shalt minimize or maximize the time taken to reach thy destination.'"

I considered it. "Go on."

"It's an old question in the philosophy of physics. People have been talking about it since Fermat first formulated it in the 1600s; Planck wrote volumes about it. The thing is, while the common formulation of physical laws is causal, a variational principle like Fermat's is purposive, almost teleological."

"Hmm, that's an interesting way to put it. Let me think about that for a minute." I pulled out a felt-tip pen and, on my paper napkin, drew a copy of the diagram that Gary had drawn on my blackboard. "Okay," I said, thinking aloud, "so let's say the goal of a ray of light is to take the fastest path. How does the light go about doing that?"

"Well, if I can speak anthropomorphic-projectionally, the light has to examine the possible paths and compute how long each one would take." He plucked the last potsticker from the serving dish.

"And to do that," I continued, "the ray of light has to know just where its destination is. If the destination were somewhere else, the fastest path would be different."

Gary nodded again. "That's right; the notion of a 'fastest path' is meaningless unless there's a destination specified. And computing how long a given path takes also requires information about what lies along that path, like where the water's surface is."

I kept staring at the diagram on the napkin. "And the light ray has to know all that ahead of time, before it starts moving, right?"

"So to speak," said Gary. "The light can't start traveling in any old direction and make course corrections later on, because the path resulting from such behavior wouldn't be the fastest possible one. The light has to do all its computations at the very beginning."

I thought to myself, *the ray of light has to know where it will ultimately end up before it can choose the direction to begin moving in.* I knew what that reminded me of. I looked up at Gary. "That's what was bugging me."

I remember when you're fourteen. You'll come out of your bedroom, a graffiti-covered notebook computer in hand, working on a report for school.

"Mom, what do you call it when both sides can win?"

I'll look up from my computer and the paper I'll be writing. "What, you mean a win-win situation?"

"There's some technical name for it, some math word. Remember that time Dad was here, and he was talking about the stock market? He used it then."

"Hmm, that sounds familiar, but I can't remember what he called it."

"I need to know. I want to use that phrase in my social studies report. I can't even search for information on it unless I know what it's called."

"I'm sorry, I don't know it either. Why don't you call your dad?"

Judging from your expression, that will be more effort than you want to make. At this point, you and your father won't be getting along well. "Can you call Dad and ask him? But don't tell him it's for me."

"I think you can call him yourself."

You'll fume, "Jesus, Mom, I can never get help with my homework since you and Dad split up."

It's amazing the diverse situations in which you can bring up the divorce. "I've helped you with your homework."

"Like a million years ago, Mom."

I'll let that pass. "I'd help you with this if I could, but I don't remember what it's called."

You'll head back to your bedroom in a huff.

I practiced Heptapod B at every opportunity, both with the other linguists and by myself. The novelty of reading a semasiographic language made it compelling in a way that Heptapod A wasn't, and my improvement in writing it excited me. Over time, the sentences I wrote grew shapelier, more cohesive. I had reached the point where it worked better when I didn't think about it too much. Instead of carefully trying to design a sentence before writing, I could simply begin putting down strokes immediately; my initial strokes almost always turned out to be compatible with an elegant rendition of what I was trying to say. I was developing a faculty like that of the heptapods.

More interesting was the fact that Heptapod B was changing the way I thought. For me, thinking typically meant speaking in an internal voice; as we say in the trade, my thoughts were phonologically coded. My internal voice normally spoke in English, but that wasn't a requirement. The summer after my senior year in high school, I attended a total immersion program for learning Russian; by the end of the summer, I was thinking and even dreaming in Russian. But it was always *spoken* Russian. Different language, same mode: a voice speaking silently aloud.

The idea of thinking in a linguistic yet nonphonological mode always intrigued me. I had a friend born of dead parents; he grew up using American Sign Language, and he told me that he often thought in ASL instead of English. I used to wonder what it was like to have one's thoughts be manually coded, to reason using an inner pair of hands instead of an inner voice.

With Heptapod B, I was experiencing something just as foreign: my thoughts were becoming graphically coded. There were trancelike moments during the day when my thoughts weren't expressed with my internal voice; instead, I saw semagrams with my mind's eye, sprouting like frost on a windowpane.

As I grew more fluent, semagraphic designs would appear fully formed, articulating even complex ideas all at once. My thought processes weren't moving any faster as a result, though. Instead of racing forward, my mind hung balanced on the symmetry underlying the semagrams. The semagrams seemed to be something more than language; they were almost like mandalas. I found myself in a meditative state, contemplating the way in which premises and conclusions were interchangeable. There was no direction inherent in the way propositions were connected, no "train of thought" moving along a particular route; all the components in an act of reasoning were equally powerful, all having identical precedence.

A representative from the State Department named Hossner had the job of briefing the U.S. scientists on our agenda with the heptapods. We sat in the videoconference room, listening to him lecture. Our microphone was turned off, so Gary and I could exchange comments without interrupting Hossner. As we listened, I worried that Gary might harm his vision, rolling his eyes so often.

"They must have had some reason for coming all this way," said the diplomat, his voice tinny through the speakers. "It does not look like their reason was conquest, thank God. But if that's not the reason, what is? Are they prospectors? Anthropologists? Missionaries? Whatever their motives, there must be something we can offer them. Maybe it's mineral rights to our solar system. Maybe it's information about ourselves. Maybe it's the right to deliver sermons to our populations. But we can be sure that there's something.

"My point is this: their motive might not be to trade, but that doesn't mean that we cannot conduct trade. We simply need to know why they're here, and what we have that they want. Once we have that information, we can begin trade negotiations.

"I should emphasize that our relationship with the heptapods need not be adversarial. This is not a situation where every gain on their part is a loss on ours, or vice versa. If we handle ourselves correctly, both we and the heptapods can come out winners."

"You mean it's a non-zero-sum game?" Gary said in mock incredulity. "Oh my gosh."

"A non-zero-sum game."

"What?" You'll reverse course, heading back from your bedroom.

"When both sides can win: I just remembered, it's called a non-zero-sum game."

"That's it!" you'll say, writing it down on your notebook. "Thanks, Mom!"

"I guess I knew it after all," I'll say. "All those years with your father, some of it must have rubbed off."

"I knew you'd know it," you'll say. You'll give me a sudden, brief hug, and your hair will smell of apples. "You're the best."

"Louise?"

"Hmm? Sorry, I was distracted. What did you say?"

"I said, what do you think about our Mr. Hossner here?"

"I prefer not to."

"I've tried that myself: ignoring the government, seeing if it would go away. It hasn't."

As evidence of Gary's assertion, Hossner kept blathering: "Your immediate task is to think back on what you've learned. Look for anything that might help us. Has there been any indication of what the heptapods want? Of what they value?"

"Gee, it never occurred to us to look for things like that," I said. "We'll get right on it, sir."

"The sad thing is, that's just what we'll have to do," said Gary.

"Are there any questions?" asked Hossner.

Burghart, the linguist at the Fort Worth looking glass, spoke up. "We've been through this with the heptapods many times. They maintain that they're here to observe, and they maintain that information is not tradable."

"So they would have us believe," said Hossner. "But consider: how could that be true? I know that the heptapods have occasionally stopped talking to us for brief periods. That may be a tactical maneuver on their part. If we were to stop talking to them tomorrow—"

"Wake me up if he says something interesting," said Gary.

"I was just going to ask you to do the same for me."

That day when Gary first explained Fermat's Principle to me, he had mentioned that almost every physical law could be stated as a variational principle. Yet when humans thought about physical laws, they preferred to work with them in their causal formulation. I could understand that: the physical attributes that humans found intuitive, like kinetic energy or acceleration, were all properties of an object at a given moment in time. And these were conducive to a chronological, causal interpretation of events: one moment growing out of another, causes and effects created a chain reaction that grew from past to future.

In contrast, the physical attributes that the heptapods found intuitive, like "action" or those other things defined by integrals, were meaningful only over a period of time. And these were conducive to a teleological interpretation of events: by viewing events over a period of time, one recognized that there was a requirement that had to be satisfied, a goal of minimizing or maximizing. And one had to know the initial and final states to meet that goal; one needed knowledge of the effects before the causes could be initiated.

I was growing to understand that, too.

"Why?" you'll ask again. You'll be three.

"Because it's your bedtime," I'll say again. We'll have gotten as far as getting you bathed and into your jammies, but no further than that.

"But I'm not sleepy," you'll whine. You'll be standing at the bookshelf, pulling down a video to watch: your latest diversionary tactic to keep away from your bedroom.

"It doesn't matter: you still have to go to bed."

"But why?"

"Because I'm the mom and I said so."

I'm actually going to say that, aren't I? God, somebody please shoot me.

I'll pick you up and carry you under my arm to your bed, you wailing piteously all the while, but my sole concern will be my own distress. All those vows made in childhood that I would give reasonable answers when I became a parent, that I would treat my own child as an intelligent, thinking individual, all for naught: I'm going to turn into my mother. I can fight it as much as I want, but there'll be no stopping my slide down that long, dreadful slope.

Was it actually possible to know the future? Not simply to guess at it; was it possible to *know* what was going to happen, with absolute certainty and in specific detail? Gary once told me that the fundamental laws of physics were time-symmetric, that there was no physical difference between past and future. Given that, some might say, "yes, theoretically." But speaking more concretely, most would answer "no," because of free will.

I liked to imagine the objection as a Borgesian fabulation: consider a person standing before the *Book of Age*, the chronicle that records every event, past and future. Even though the text has been photoreduced from the full-sized edition, the volume is enormous. With magnifier in hand, she flips through the tissue-thin leaves until she locates the story of her life. She finds the passage that describes her flipping through the *Book of Ages*, and she skips to the next column, where it details what she'll be doing later in the day: acting on information she's read in the *Book*, she'll bet one hundred dollars on the racehorse Devil May Care and win twenty times that much.

The thought of doing just that had crossed her mind, but being a contrary sort, she now resolves to refrain from betting on the ponies altogether.

There's the rub. The *Book of Ages* cannot be wrong; this scenario is based on the premise that a person is given knowledge of the actual future, not of some possible future. If this were Greek myth, circumstances would conspire to make her enact her fate despite her best efforts, but prophecies in myth are notoriously vague; the *Book of Ages* is quite specific, and there's no way she can be forced to bet on a racehorse in the manner specified. The result is a contradiction: the *Book of Ages* must be right, by definition; yet no matter what the *Book* says she'll do, she can choose to do otherwise. How can these two facts be reconciled?

They can't be, was the common answer. A volume like the *Book of Age* is a logical impossibility, for the precise reason that its existence would result in the above contradiction. Or, to be generous, some might say that the *Book of Ages* could exist, as long as it wasn't accessible to readers: that volume is housed in a special collection, and no one has viewing privileges.

The existence of free will meant that we couldn't know the future. And we knew free will existed because we had direct experience of it. Volition was an intrinsic part of consciousness.

Or was it? What if the experience of knowing the future changed a person? What if it evoked a sense of urgency, a sense of obligation to act precisely as she knew she would?

I stopped by Gary's office before leaving for the day. "I'm calling it quits. Did you want to grab something to eat?"

"Sure, just wait a second," he said. He shut down his computer and gathered some papers together. Then he looked up at me. "Hey, want to come to my place for dinner tonight? I'll cook."

I looked at him dubiously. "You can cook?"

"Just one dish," he admitted. "But it's a good one."

"Sure," I said. "I'm game."

"Great. We just need to go shopping for the ingredients."

"Don't go to any trouble—"

"There's a market on the way to my house. It won't take a minute."

We took separate cars, me following him. I almost lost him when he abruptly turned in to a parking lot. It was a gourmet market, not large, but fancy; tall glass jars stuffed with imported foods sat next to specialty utensils on the store's stainless-steel shelves.

I accompanied Gary as he collected fresh basil, tomatoes, garlic, linguini. "There's a fish market next door; we can get fresh clams there," he said.

"Sounds good." We walked past the section of kitchen utensils. My gaze wandered over the shelves—peppermills, garlic presses, salad tongs—and stopped on a wooden salad bowl.

When you are three, you'll pull a dishtowel off the kitchen counter and bring that salad bowl down on top of you. I'll make a grab for it, but I'll miss. The edge of the bowl will leave you with a cut, on the upper edge of your forehead, that will require a single stitch. Your father and I will hold you, sobbing and stained with Caesar salad dressing, as we wait in the emergency room for hours.

I reached out and took the bowl from the shelf. The motion didn't feel like something I was forced to do. Instead it seemed just as urgent as my rushing to catch the bowl when it falls on you: an instinct that I felt right in following.

"I could use a salad bowl like this."

Gary looked at the bowl and nodded approvingly. "See, wasn't it a good thing that I had to stop at the market?"

"Yes it was." We got in line to pay for our purchases.

Consider the sentence "The rabbit is ready to eat." Interpret "rabbit" to be the object of "eat," and the sentence was an announcement that dinner would be served shortly. Interpret "rabbit" to be the subject of "eat," and it was a hint, such as a young girl might give her mother so she'll open a bag of Purina Bunny Chow. Two very different utterances; in fact, they were probably mutually exclusive within a single household. Yet either was a valid interpretation; only context could determine what the sentence meant.

Consider the phenomenon of light hitting water at one angle, and traveling through it at a different angle. Explain it by saying that a difference in the index of refraction caused the light to change direction, and one saw the world as humans saw it. Explain it by saying that light minimized the time needed to travel to its destination, and one saw the world as the heptapods saw it. Two very different interpretations.

The physical universe was a language with a perfectly ambiguous grammar. Every physical event was an utterance that could be parsed in two entirely different ways, one causal and the other teleological, both valid, neither one disqualifiable no matter how much context was available.

When the ancestors of humans and heptapods first acquired the spark of consciousness, they both perceived the same physical world, but they parsed their perceptions differently; the worldviews that ultimately arose were the end result of that divergence. Humans had developed a sequential mode of awareness, while heptapods had developed a simultaneous mode of awareness. We experienced events in an order, and perceived their relationship as cause and effect. They experienced all events at once, and perceived a purpose underlying them all. A minimizing, maximizing purpose.

I have a recurring dream about your death. In the dream, I'm the one who's rock climbing—me, can you imagine it?—and you're three years old, riding in some kind of backpack I'm wearing. We're just a few feet below a ledge where we can rest, and you won't wait until I've climbed up to it. You start pulling yourself out of the pack; I order you to stop, but of course you ignore me. I feel your weight alternating from one side of the pack to the other as you climb out; then I feel your left foot on my shoulder, and then your right. I'm screaming at you, but I can't get a hand free to grab you. I can see the wavy design on the soles of your sneakers as you climb, and then I see a flake of stone give way beneath one of them. You slide right past me, and I can't move a muscle. I look down and see you shrink into the distance below me.

Then, all of a sudden, I'm at the morgue. An orderly lifts the sheet from your face, and I see that you're twenty-five.

"You okay?"

I was sitting upright in bed; I'd woken Gary with my movements. "I'm fine. I was just startled; I didn't recognize where I was for a moment."

Sleepily, he said, "We can stay at your place next time."

I kissed him. "Don't worry; your place is fine." We curled up, my back against his chest, and went back to sleep.

When you're three and we're climbing a steep, spiral flight of stairs, I'll hold your hand extra tightly. You'll pull your hand away from me. "I can do it by myself," you'll insist, and then move away from me to prove it, and I'll remember that dream. We'll repeat that scene countless times during your childhood. I can almost believe that, given your contrary nature, my attempts to protect you will be what create your love of climbing: first the jungle gym at the playground, then trees out in the green belt around our neighborhood, the rock walls at the climbing club, and ultimately cliff faces in national parks.

I finished the last radical in the sentence, put down the chalk, and sat down in my desk chair. I leaned back and surveyed the giant Heptapod B sentence I'd written that covered the entire blackboard in my office. It included several complex clauses, and I had managed to integrate all of them rather nicely.

Looking at a sentence like this one, I understood why the heptapods had evolved a semasiographic writing system like Heptapod B; it was better suited for a species with a simultaneous mode of consciousness. For them, speech was a bottleneck because it required that one word follow another sequentially. With writing, on the other hand, every mark on a page was visible simultaneously. Why constrain writing with a glotto-graphic straitjacket, demanding that it be just as sequential as speech? It would never occur to them. Semasiographic writing naturally took advantage of the page's two-dimensionality; instead of doling out morphemes one at a time, it offered an entire page full of them all at once.

And now that Heptapod B had introduced me to a simultaneous mode of consciousness, I understood the rationale behind Heptapod A's grammar: what my sequential mind had perceived as unnecessarily convoluted, I now recognized as an attempt to provide flexibility within the confines of sequential speech. I could use Heptapod A more easily as a result, though it was still a poor substitute for Heptapod B.

There was a knock at the door and then Gary poked his head in. "Colonel Weber'll be here any minute."

I grimaced. "Right." Weber was coming to participate in a session with Flapper and Raspberry; I was to act as translator, a job I wasn't trained for and that I detested.

Gary stepped inside and closed the door. He pulled me out of my chair and kissed me.

I smiled. "You trying to cheer me up before he gets here?"

"No, I'm trying to cheer me up."

"You weren't interested in talking to the heptapods at all, were you? You worked on this project just to get me into bed."

"Ah, you see right through me."

I looked into his eyes. "You better believe it," I said.

I remember when you'll be a month old, and I'll stumble out of bed to give you your 2:00 A.M. feeding. Your nursery will have that "baby smell" of diaper rash cream and talcum powder, with a faint ammoniac whiff coming from the diaper pail in the corner. I'll lean over your crib, lift your squalling form out, and sit in the rocking chair to nurse you.

The word "infant" is derived from the Latin word for "unable to speak," but you'll be perfectly capable of saying one thing: "I suffer," and you'll do it tirelessly and without hesitation. I have to admire your utter commitment to that statement; when you cry, you'll become outrage incarnate, every fiber of your body employed in expressing that emotion. It's funny: when you're tranquil, you will seem to radiate light, and if someone were to paint a portrait of you like that, I'd insist that they include the halo. But when you're unhappy, you will become a klaxon, built for radiating sound; a portrait of you then could simply be a fire alarm bell.

At that stage of your life, there'll be no past or future for you; until I give you my breast, you'll have no memory of contentment in the past nor expectation of relief in the future. Once you begin nursing, everything will reverse, and all will be right with the world. NOW is the only moment you'll perceive; you'll live in the present tense. In many ways, it's an enviable state.

The heptapods are neither free nor bound as we understand those concepts; they don't act according to their will, nor are they helpless automatons. What distinguishes the heptapods' mode of awareness is not just that their actions coincide with history's events; it is also that their motives coincide with history's purposes. They act to create the future, to enact chronology.

Freedom isn't an illusion; it's perfectly real in the context of sequential consciousness. Within the context of simultaneous consciousness, freedom is not meaningful, but neither is coercion; it's simply a different context, no more or less valid than the other. It's like that famous optical illusion, the drawing of either an elegant young woman, face turned away from the viewer, or a wart-nosed crone, chin tucked down on her chest. There's no "correct" interpretation; both are equally valid. But you can't see both at the same time.

Similarly, knowledge of the future was incompatible with free will. What made it possible for me to exercise freedom of choice also made it impossible for me to know the future. Conversely, now that I know the future, I would never act contrary to that future, including telling others what I know: those who know the future don't talk about it. Those who've read the *Book of Ages* never admit to it.

I turned on the VCR and slotted a cassette of a session from the Fort Worth looking glass. A diplomatic negotiator was having a discussion with the heptapods there, with Burghart acting as translator.

The negotiator was describing humans' moral beliefs, trying to lay some groundwork for the concept of altruism. I knew the heptapods were familiar with the conversation's eventual outcome, but they still participated enthusiastically.

If I could have described this to someone who didn't already know, she might ask, if the heptapods already knew everything that they would ever say or hear, what was the point of their using language at all? A reasonable question. But language wasn't only for communication: it was also a form of action. According to speech act theory, statements like "You're under arrest," "I christen this vessel," or "I promise" were all performative: a speaker could perform the action only by uttering the words. For such acts, knowing what would be said didn't change anything. Everyone at a wedding anticipated the words "I now pronounce you husband and wife," but until the minister actually said them, the ceremony didn't count. With performative language, saying equaled doing.

For the heptapods, all language was performative. Instead of using language to inform, they used language to actualize. Sure, heptapods already knew what would be said in any conversation; but in order for their knowledge to be true, the conversation would have to take place.

"First Goldilocks tried the papa bear's bowl of porridge, but it was full of brussels sprouts, which she hated."

You'll laugh. "No, that's wrong!" We'll be sitting side by side on the sofa, the skinny, overpriced hardcover spread open on our laps.

I'll keep reading. "Then Goldilocks tried the mama bear's bowl of porridge, but it was full of spinach, which she also hated."

You'll put your hand on the page of the book to stop me. "You have to read it the right way!"

"I'm reading just what it says here," I'll say, all innocence.

"No you're not. That's not how the story goes."

"Well if you already know how the story goes, why do you need me to read it to you?"

"Cause I wanna hear it!"

The air conditioning in Weber's office almost compensated for having to talk to the man.

"They're willing to engage in a type of exchange," I explained, "but it's not trade. We simply give them something, and they give us something in return. Neither party tells the other what they're giving beforehand."

Colonel Weber's brow furrowed just slightly. "You mean they're willing to exchange gifts?"

I knew what I had to say. "We shouldn't think of it as 'gift-giving.' We don't know if this transaction has the same associations for the heptapods that gift-giving has for us."

"Can we—" he searched for the right wording "—drop hints about the kind of gift we want?"

"They don't do that themselves for this type of transaction. I asked them if we could make a request, and they said we could, but it won't make them tell us what they're giving." I suddenly remembered that a morphological relative of "performative" was "performance," which could describe the sensation of conversing when you knew what would be said: it was like performing in a play.

"But would it make them more likely to give us what we asked for?" Colonel Weber asked. He was perfectly oblivious of the script, yet his responses matched his assigned lines exactly.

"No way of knowing," I said. "I doubt it, given that it's not a custom they engage in."

"If we give our gift first, will the value of our gift influence the value of theirs?" He was improvising, while I had carefully rehearsed for this one and only show.

"No," I said. "As far as we can tell, the value of the exchanged items is irrelevant."

"If only my relatives felt that way," murmured Gary wryly.

I watched Colonel Weber turn to Gary. "Have you discovered anything new in the physics discussions?" he asked, right on cue.

"If you mean, any information new to mankind, no," said Gary. "The heptapods haven't varied from the routine. If we demonstrate something to them, they'll show us their formulation of it, but they won't volunteer anything and they won't answer our questions about what they know."

An utterance that was spontaneous and communicative in the context of human discourse became a ritual recitation when viewed by the light of Heptapod B.

Weber scowled. "All right then, we'll see how the State Department feels about this. Maybe we can arrange some kind of gift-giving ceremony."

Like physical events, with their causal and teleological interpretations, every linguistic event had two possible interpretations: as a transmission of information and as the realization of a plan.

"I think that's a good idea, Colonel," I said.

It was an ambiguity invisible to most. A private joke; don't ask me to explain it.

Even though I'm proficient with Heptapod B, I know I don't experience reality the way a heptapod does. My mind was cast in the mold of human, sequential languages, and no amount of immersion in an alien language can completely reshape it. My worldview is an amalgam of human and heptapod.

Before I learned how to think in Heptapod B, my memories grew like a column of cigarette ash, laid down by the infinitesimal sliver of combustion that was my consciousness, marking the sequential present. After I learned Heptapod B, new memories fell into place like gigantic blocks, each one measuring years in duration, and though they didn't arrive in order or land contiguously, they soon composed a period of five decades. It is the period during which I know Heptapod B well enough to think in it, starting during my interviews with Flapper and Raspberry and ending with my death.

Usually, Heptapod B affects just my memory: my consciousness crawls along as it did before, a glowing sliver crawling forward in time, the difference being that the ash of memory lies ahead as well as behind: there is no real combustion. But occasionally I have glimpses when Heptapod B truly reigns, and I experience past and future all at once; my consciousness becomes a half-century-long ember burning outside time. I perceive—during those glimpses—that entire epoch as a simultaneity. It's a period encompassing the rest of my life, and the entirety of yours.

I wrote out the semagrams for "process create-endpoint inclusive-we," meaning "let's start." Raspberry replied in the affirmative, and the slide shows began. The second display screen that the heptapods had provided began presenting a series of images, composed of semagrams and equations, while one of our video screens did the same.

This was the second "gift exchange" I had been present for, the eighth one overall, and I knew it would be the last. The looking-glass tent was crowded with people; Burghart from Fort Worth was here, as were Gary and a nuclear physicist, assorted biologists, anthropologists, military brass, and diplomats. Thankfully they had set up an air conditioner to cool the place off. We would review the tapes of the images later to figure out just what the heptapods' "gift" was. Our own "gift" was a presentation on the Lascaux cave paintings.

We all crowded around the heptapods' second screen, trying to glean some idea of the images' content as they went by. "Preliminary assessments?" asked Colonel Weber.

"It's not a return," said Burghart. In a previous exchange, the heptapods had given us information about ourselves that we had previously told them. This had infuriated the State Department, but we had no reason to think of it as an insult: it probably indicated that trade value really didn't play a role in these exchanges. It didn't exclude the possibility that the heptapods might yet offer us a space drive, or cold fusion, or some other wish-fulfilling miracle.

"That looks like inorganic chemistry," said the nuclear physicist, pointing at an equation before the image was replaced.

Gary nodded. "It could be materials technology," he said.

"Maybe we're finally getting somewhere," said Colonel Weber.

"I wanna see more animal pictures," I whispered, quietly so that only Gary could hear me, and pouted like a child. He smiled and poked me. Truthfully, I wished the heptapods had given another xenobiology lecture, as they had on two previous exchanges; judging from those, humans were more similar to the heptapods than any other species they'd ever encountered. Or another lecture on heptapod history; those had been filled with apparent non-sequiturs, but were interesting nonetheless. I didn't want the heptapods to give us new technology, because I didn't want to see what our governments might do with it.

I watched Raspberry while the information was being exchanged, looking for any anomalous behavior. It stood barely moving as usual; I saw no indications of what would happen shortly.

After a minute, the heptapod's screen went blank, and a minute after that, ours did, too. Gary and most of the other scientists clustered around a tiny video screen that was replaying the heptapods' presentation. I could hear them talk about the need to call in a solid-state physicist.

Colonel Weber turned. "You two," he said, pointing to me and then to Burghart, "schedule the time and location for the next exchange." Then he followed the others to the playback screen.

"Coming right up," I said. To Burghart, I asked, "Would you care to do the honors, or shall I?"

I knew Burghart had gained a proficiency in Heptapod B similar to mine. "It's your looking glass," he said. "You drive."

I sat down again at the transmitting computer. "Bet you never figured you'd wind up working as a Army translator back when you were a grad student."

"That's for goddamn sure," he said. "Even now I can hardly believe it." Everything we said to each other felt like the carefully bland exchanges of spies who meet in public, but never break cover.

I wrote out the semagrams for "locus exchange-transaction converse inclusive-we" with the projective aspect modulation.

Raspberry wrote its reply. That was my cue to frown, and for Burghart to ask, "What does it mean by that?" His delivery was perfect.

I wrote a request for clarification; Raspberry's reply was the same as before. Then I watched it glide out of the room. The curtain was about to fall on this act of our performance.

Colonel Weber stepped forward. "What's going on? Where did it go?"

"It said that the heptapods are leaving now," I said. "Not just itself; all of them."

"Call it back here now. Ask it what it means."

"Um, I don't think Raspberry's wearing a pager," I said.

The image of the room in the looking glass disappeared so abruptly that it took a moment for my eyes to register what I was seeing instead: it was the other side of the looking-glass tent. The looking glass had become completely transparent. The conversation around the playback screen fell silent.

"What the hell is going on here?" said Colonel Weber.

Gary walked up to the looking glass, and then around it to the other side. He touched the rear surface with one hand; I could see the pale ovals where his finger-tips made contact with the looking glass. "I think," he said, "we just saw a demonstration of transmutation at a distance."

I heard the sounds of heavy footfalls on dry grass. A soldier came in through the tent door, short of breath from sprinting, holding an oversize walkie-talkie. "Colonel, message from—"

Weber grabbed the walkie-talkie from him.

I remember what it'll be like watching you when you are a day old. Your father will have gone for a quick visit to the hospital cafeteria, and you'll be lying in your bassinet, and I'll be leaning over you.

So soon after the delivery, I will still be feeling like a wrung-out towel. You will seem incongruously tiny, given how enormous I felt during the pregnancy; I could swear there was room for someone much larger and more robust than you in there. Your hands and feet will be long and thin, not chubby yet. Your face will still be all red and pinched, puffy eyelids squeezed shut, the gnomelike phase that precedes the cherubic.

I'll run a finger over your belly, marveling at the uncanny softness of your skin, wondering if silk would abrade your body like burlap. Then you'll writhe, twisting your body while poking out your legs one at a time, and I'll recognize the gesture as one I had felt you do inside me, many times. So *that's* what it looks like.

I'll feel elated at this evidence of a unique mother-child bond, this certitude that you're the one I carried. Even if I had never laid eyes on you before, I'd be able to pick you out from a sea of babies: Not that one. No, not her either. Wait, that one over there.

Yes, that's her. She's mine.

That final "gift exchange" was the last we ever saw of the heptapods. All at once, all over the world, their looking glasses became transparent and their ships left orbit. Subsequent analysis of the looking glasses revealed them to be nothing more than sheets of fused silica, completely inert. The information from the final exchange session described a new class of superconducting materials, but it later proved to duplicate the results of research just completed in Japan: nothing that humans didn't already know.

We never did learn why the heptapods left, any more than we learned what brought them here, or why they acted the way they did. My own new awareness didn't provide that type of knowledge; the heptapods' behavior was presumably explicable from a sequential point of view, but we never found that explanation.

I would have liked to experience more of the heptapods' worldview, to feel the way they feel. Then, perhaps I could immerse myself fully in the necessity of events, as they must, instead of merely wading in its surf for the rest of my life. But that will never come to pass. I will continue to practice the heptapod languages, as will the other linguists on the looking-glass teams, but none of us will ever progress any further than we did when the heptapods were here.

Working with the heptapods changed my life. I met your father and learned Heptapod B, both of which make it possible for me to know you now, here on the patio in the moonlight. Eventually, many years from now, I'll be without your father, and without you. All I will have left from this moment is the heptapod language. So I pay close attention, and note every detail.

From the beginning I knew my destination, and I chose my route accordingly. But am I working toward an extreme of joy, or of pain? Will I achieve a minimum, or a maximum?

These questions are in my mind when your father asks me, "Do you want to make a baby?" And I smile and answer, "Yes," and I unwrap his arms from around me, and we hold hands as we walk inside to make love, to make you.

people came from earth

STEPHEN BAXTER

Like many of his colleagues here at the beginning of a new century, British writer Stephen Baxter has been engaged for more than a decade now with the task of revitalizing and reinventing the "hard-science" story for a new generation of readers, producing work on the cutting edge of science which bristles with weird new ideas and often takes place against vistas of almost outrageously cosmic scope.

Baxter made his first sale to *Interzone* in 1987, and since then has become one of that magazine's most frequent contributors, as well as making sales to *Asimov's Science Fiction*, *Science Fiction Age*, *Analog*, *Zenith*, *New Worlds*, and elsewhere. He's one of the most prolific new writers in science fiction, and is rapidly becoming one of the most popular and acclaimed of them as well. In 2001, he appeared on the final Hugo Ballot twice, and won both *Asimov's* Readers Award and *Analog's* Analytical Laboratory Award, one of the few writers ever to win both awards in the same year. Baxter's first novel, *Raft*, was released in 1991 to wide and enthusiastic response, and was rapidly followed by other well-received novels such as *Timelike Infinity*, *Anti-Ice*, *Flux*, and the H. G. Wells pastiche—a sequel to *The Time Machine*—*The Time Ships*, which won both the John W. Campbell Memorial Award and the Philip K. Dick Award. His other books include the novels *Voyage*, *Titan*, *Moonseed*, *Mammoth, Book One: Silverhair*, *Manifold: Time*, *Manifold: Space*, *Evolution*, *Coalescent*, and (in collaboration with Arthur C. Clarke) *The Light of Other Days*, as well as the collections *Vacuum Diagrams: Stories of the Xeelee Sequence* and *Traces*. His most recent book is a new collection, *Hunters of Pangaea*, and coming up is a new novel, *Exultant*.

Here he takes us to a troubled future, to an embattled, desperate world dancing on the brink of destruction, for the autumnal story of people struggling to hold on to what they have . . . and perhaps even regain something of what has been lost.

At Dawn I stepped out of my house. The air frosted white from my nose, and the deep Moon chill cut through papery flesh to my spindly bones. The silver-gray light came from Earth and Mirror in the sky: twin spheres, the one milky cloud, the other a hard image of the sun. But the sun itself was already shouldering above the horizon. Beads of light like trapped stars marked rim mountain summits, and a deep bloody crimson was working its way high into our tall sky. I imagined I could see the lid of that sky, the millennial leaking of our air into space.

I walked down the path that leads to the circular sea. There was frost everywhere, of course, but the path's lunar dirt, patiently raked in my youth, is friendly and gripped my sandals. The water at the sea's rim was black and oily, lapping softly. I could see the gray sheen of ice farther out, and the hard glint of pack ice beyond that, though the close horizon hid the bulk of the sea from me. Fingers of sunlight stretched across the ice, and gray-gold smoke shimmered above open water.

I listened to the ice for a while. There is a constant tumult of groans and cracks as the ice rises and falls on the sea's mighty shoulders. The water never freezes at Tycho's rim; conversely, it never thaws at the center, so that there is a fat torus of ice floating out there around the central mountains. It is as if the rim of this artificial ocean is striving to emulate the unfrozen seas of Earth which bore its makers, while its remote heart is straining to grow back the cold carapace it enjoyed when our water—and air—still orbited remote Jupiter.

I thought I heard a barking out on the pack ice. Perhaps it was a seal. A bell clanked: an early fishing boat leaving port, a fat, comforting sound that carried through the still dense air. I sought the boat's lights, but my eyes, rheumy, stinging with cold, failed me.

I paid attention to my creaking body: the aches in my too-thin, too-long, calcium-starved bones, the obscure spurts of pain in my urethral system, the strange itches that afflict my liver-spotted flesh. I was already growing too cold. Mirror returns enough heat to the Moon's long Night to keep our seas and air from snowing out around us, but I would welcome a little more comfort.

I turned and began to labor back up my regolith path to my house.

And when I got there, Berge, my nephew, was waiting for me. I did not know then, of course, that he would not survive the new Day.

He was eager to talk about Leonardo da Vinci.

He had taken off his wings and stacked them up against the concrete wall of my house. I could see how the wings were thick with frost, so dense the paper feathers could surely have had little play.

I scolded him even as I brought him into the warmth, and prepared hot soup and tea for him in my pressure kettles. "You're a fool as your father was," I said. "I was with him when he fell from the sky, leaving you orphaned. You know how dangerous it is in the pre-Dawn turbulence."

"Ah, but the power of those great thermals, Uncle," he said, as he accepted the soup. "I can fly miles high without the slightest effort."

I would have berated him further, which is the prerogative of old age. But I didn't have the heart. He stood before me, eager, heartbreakingly thin. Berge always was slender, even compared to the rest of us skinny lunar folk; but now he was clearly frail, Even these long minutes after landing, he was still panting, and his smooth fashionably-shaven scalp (so bare it showed the great bubble profile of his lunar-born skull) was dotted with beads of grimy sweat.

And, most ominous of all, a waxy, golden sheen seemed to linger about his skin. I had no desire to raise that—not here, not now, not until I was sure what it meant, that it wasn't some trickery of my own age-yellowed eyes.

So I kept my counsel. We made our ritual obeisance—murmurs about dedicating our bones and flesh to the salvation of the world—and finished up our soup.

And then, with his youthful eagerness, Berge launched into the seminar he was evidently itching to deliver on Leonardo da Vinci, long-dead citizen of a long-dead planet. Brusquely displacing the empty soup bowls to the floor, he produced papers from his jacket and spread them out before me. The sheets, yellowed and stained with age, were covered in a crabby, indecipherable handwriting, broken with sketches of gadgets or flowing water or geometric figures. I picked out a luminously beautiful sketch of the crescent Earth—

"No," said Berge patiently. "Think about it. It must have been the crescent Moon." Of course he was right. "You see, Leonardo understood the phenomenon he called the ashen Moon—like our ashen Earth, the old Earth visible in the arms of the new. He was a hundred years ahead of his time with *that* one. . . ."

This document had been called many things in its long history, but most familiarly the Codex Leicester. Berge's copy had been printed off in haste during The Failing, those frantic hours when our dying libraries had disgorged their great snowfalls of paper. It was a treatise centering on what Leonardo called the "body of the Earth," but with diversions to consider such matters as water engineering, the geometry of Earth and Moon, and the origins of fossils.

The issue of the fossils particularly excited Berge. Leonardo had been much agitated by the presence of the fossils of marine animals, fishes and oysters and corals, high in the mountains of Italy. Lacking any knowledge of tectonic processes, he had struggled to explain how the fossils might have been deposited by a series of great global floods.

It made me remember how, when he was a boy, I once had to explain to Berge what a "fossil" was. There are no fossils on the Moon: no bones in the ground, of course, save those we put there. Now he was much more interested in the words of long-dead Leonardo than his uncle's.

"You have to think about the world Leonardo inhabited," he said. "The ancient paradigms still persisted: the stationary Earth, a sky laden with spheres, crude Aristotelian proto-physics. But Leonardo's instinct was to proceed from observation to theory—and he observed many things in the world which didn't fit with the prevailing world view—"

"Like mountaintop fossils."

"Yes. Working alone, he struggled to come up with explanations. And some of his reasoning was, well, eerie."

"Eerie?"

"Prescient." Gold-flecked eyes gleamed. "Leonardo talks about the Moon in several places." The boy flicked back and forth through the Codex, pointing out spidery pictures of Earth and Moon and sun, neat circles connected by spidery light ray traces. "Remember, the Moon was thought to be a transparent crystal sphere. What intrigued Leonardo was why the Moon wasn't much brighter in Earth's sky, as bright as the sun, in fact. It should have been brighter if it was perfectly reflective—"

"Like Mirror."

"Yes. So Leonardo argued the Moon must be covered in oceans." He found a diagram showing a Moon, bathed in spidery sunlight rays, coated with great out-of-scale choppy waves. "Leonardo said waves on the Moon's oceans must deflect much of the reflected sunlight away from Earth. He thought the darker patches visible on the Moon's surface must mark great standing waves, or even storms, on the Moon."

"He was wrong," I said. "In Leonardo's time, the Moon was a ball of rock. The dark areas were just lava sheets."

"But now," Berge said eagerly, "the Moon *is* mostly covered by water. You see? And there *are* great storms, wave crests hundreds of kilometers long, which are visible from Earth—or would be, if anybody was left to see."

"What exactly are you suggesting?"

"Ah," he said, and he smiled and tapped his thin nose. "I'm like Leonardo. I observe, *then* deduce. And I don't have my conclusions just yet. Patience, Uncle . . ."

We talked for hours.

When he left, the Day was little advanced, the rake of sunlight still sparse on the ice. And Mirror still rode bright in the sky. Here was another strange forward echo of Leonardo's, it struck me, though I preferred not to mention it to my already overexcited nephew: in my time, there *are* crystal spheres in orbit around the Earth. The difference is, we put them there.

Such musing failed to distract me from thoughts of Berge's frailness, and his disturbing golden pallor. I bade him farewell, hiding my concern.

As I closed the door, I heard the honking of geese, a great flock of them fleeing the excessive brightness of full Day.

Each Morning, as the sun labors into the sky, there are storms. Thick fat clouds race across the sky, and water gushes down, carving new rivulets and craters in the ancient soil, and turning the ice at the rim of the Tycho pack into a thin, fragile layer of gray slush.

Most people choose to shelter from the rain, but to me it is a pleasure. I like to think of myself standing in the band of storms that circles the whole of the slow-turning Moon. Raindrops are fat glimmering spheres the size of my thumb. They float from the sky, gently flattened by the resistance of our thick air, and they fall on my head and back with soft, almost caressing impacts. So long and slow has been their fall from the high clouds, the drops are often warm, and the air thick and humid and muggy, and the water clings to my flesh in great sheets and globes I must scrape off with my fingers.

It was in such a storm that, as Noon approached on that last Day, I traveled with Berge to the phytomine celebration to be held on the lower slopes of Maginus.

We made our way past sprawling fields tilled by human and animal muscle, thin crops straining toward the sky, frost shelters laid open to the muggy heat. And as we traveled, we joined streams of more traffic, all heading for Maginus: battered carts, spindly adults, and their skinny, hollow-eyed children; the Moon soil is thin and cannot nourish us well, and we are all, of course, slowly poisoned besides, even the cattle and horses and mules.

Maginus is an old, eroded crater complex some kilometers southeast of Tycho. Its ancient walls glimmer with crescent lakes and glaciers. Sheltered from the winds of Morning and Evening, Maginus is a center of life, and as the rain cleared I saw the tops of the giant trees looming over the horizon long before we reached the foothills. I thought I saw creatures leaping between the tree branches. They may have been lemurs, or even bats; or perhaps they were kites wielded by ambitious children.

Berge took delight as we crossed the many water courses, pointing out engineering features which had been anticipated by Leonardo, dams and bridges and canal diversions and so forth, some of them even constructed since the Failing.

But I took little comfort, oppressed as I was by the evidence of our fall. For example, we journeyed along a road made of lunar glass, flat as ice and utterly impervious to erosion, carved long ago into the regolith. But our cart was wooden, and drawn by a spavined, thin-legged mule. Such contrasts are unendingly startling. All our technology would have been more than familiar to Leonardo. We make gadgets of levers and pulleys and gears, their wooden teeth constantly stripped; we have turnbuckles, devices to help us erect our cathedrals of Moon concrete; we even fight our pathetic wars with catapults and crossbows, throwing lumps of rock a few kilometers.

But once we hurled ice moons across the solar system. We know this is so, else we could not exist here.

As we neared the phytomine, the streams of traffic converged to a great confluence of people and animals. There was a swarm of reunions of friends and family, and a rich human noise carried on the thick air.

When the crowds grew too dense, we abandoned our wagon and walked. Berge, with unconscious generosity, supported me with a hand clasped about my arm, guiding me through this human maelstrom. All Berge wanted to talk about was Leonardo da Vinci. "Leonardo was trying to figure out the cycles of the Earth. For instance, how water could be restored to the mountaintops. Listen to this." He fumbled, one-handed, with his dog-eared manuscript. "*We may say that the Earth has a spirit of growth, and that its flesh is the soil; its bones are the successive strata of the rocks which form the mountains, its cartilage is the tufa stone; its blood the veins of its waters. . . . And the vital heat of the world is fire which is spread throughout the Earth; and the dwelling place of the spirit of growth is in the fires, which in divers parts of the Earth are breathed out in baths and sulfur mines. . . .* You understand what he's saying? He was trying to explain the Earth's cycles by analogy with the systems of the human body."

"He was wrong."

"But he was more right than wrong, Uncle! Don't you see? This was centuries before geology was formalized, even longer before matter and energy cycles would be understood. Leonardo had gotten the right idea, from somewhere. He just didn't have the intellectual infrastructure to express it. . . ."

And so on. None of it was of much interest to me. As we walked, it seemed to me that *his* weight was the heavier, as if I, the old fool, was constrained to support him, the young buck. It was evident his sickliness was advancing fast—and it seemed that others around us noticed it, too, and separated around us, a sea of unwilling sympathy.

Children darted around my feet, so fast I found it impossible to believe *I* could ever have been so young, so rapid, so compact, and I felt a mask of old-man irritability settle on me. But many of the children were, at age seven or eight or nine, already taller than me, girls with languid eyes and the delicate posture of giraffes. The one constant of human evolution on the Moon is how our children stretch out, ever more languorous, in the gentle Moon gravity. But they pay a heavy price in later life in brittle, calcium-depleted bones.

At last we reached the plantation itself. We had to join queues, more or less orderly. There was noise, chatter, a sense of excitement. For many people, such visits are the peak of each slow lunar Day.

Separated from us by a row of wooden stakes and a few meters of bare soil was a sea of green, predominantly mustard plants. Chosen for their bulk and fast growth, all of these plants had grown from seed or shoots since the last lunar Dawn. The plants themselves grew thick, their feathery leaves bright. But many of the leaves were sickly, already yellowing. The fence was supervised by an unsmiling attendant, who wore—to show the people their sacrifice had a genuine goal—artifacts of unimaginable value, ear rings and brooches and bracelets of pure copper and nickel and bronze.

The Maginus mine is the most famous and exotic of all the phytomines: for here gold is mined, still the most compelling of all metals. Sullenly, the attendant told us that the mustard plants grow in soil in which gold, dissolved out of the base rock by ammonium thiocyanate, can be found at a concentration of four parts per million. But when the plants are harvested and burned, their ash contains four *hundred* parts per million of gold, drawn out of the soil by the plants during their brief lives.

The phytomines are perhaps our planet's most important industry.

It took just a handful of dust, a nanoweapon from the last war that ravaged Earth, to remove every scrap of worked metal from the surface of the Moon. It was the Failing. The cities crumbled. Aircraft fell from the sky. Ships on the great circular seas disintegrated, tipping their hapless passengers into freezing waters. Striving for independence from Earth, caught in this crosscurrent of war, our Moon nation was soon reduced to a rabble, scraping for survival.

But our lunar soil is sparse and ungenerous. If Leonardo was right—that Earth with its great cycles of rock and water is like a living thing—then the poor Moon, its reluctant daughter, is surely dead. The Moon, ripped from the outer layers of parent Earth by a massive primordial impact, lacks the rich iron which populates much of Earth's bulk. It is much too small to have retained the inner heat which fuels Earth's great tectonic cycles, and so died rapidly; and without the water baked out by the violence of its formation, the Moon is deprived of the great ore lodes peppered through Earth's interior.

Moon rock is mostly olivine, pyroxene, and plagioclase feldspar. These are silicates of iron, magnesium, and aluminum. There is a trace of native iron, and thinner scrapings of metals like copper, tin, and gold, much of it implanted by meteorite impacts. An Earth miner would have cast aside the richest rocks of our poor Moon as worthless slag.

And yet the Moon is all we have.

We have neither the means nor the will to rip up the top hundred meters of our world to find the precious metals we need. Drained of strength and tools, we must be more subtle.

Hence the phytomines. The technology is old—older than the human Moon, older than spaceflight itself. The Vikings, marauders of Earth's darkest age (before this, the darkest of all) would mine their iron from "bog ore," iron-rich stony nodules deposited near the surface of bogs by bacteria which had flourished there: miniature miners, not even visible to the Vikings who burned their little corpses to make their nails and swords and pans and cauldrons.

And so it goes, across our battered, parched little planet, a hierarchy of bacteria and plants and insects and animals and birds, collecting gold and silver and nickel and copper and bronze, their evanescent bodies comprising a slow merging trickle of scattered molecules, stored in leaves and flesh and bones, all for the benefit of that future generation who must save the Moon.

Berge and I, solemnly, took ritual scraps of mustard-plant leaf on our tongues, swallowed ceremonially. With my age-furred tongue I could barely taste the mustard's sharpness. There were no drawn-back frost covers here because these poor mustard plants would not survive to the Sunset: they die within a lunar Day, from poisoning by the cyanide.

Berge met friends and melted into the crowds.

I returned home alone, brooding.

I found my family of seals had lumbered out of the ocean and onto the shore. These are constant visitors. During the warmth of Noon they will bask for hours, males and females and children draped over each other in casual, sexless abandon, so long that the patch of regolith they inhabit becomes sodden and stinking with their droppings. The seals, uniquely among the creatures from Earth, have not adapted in any apparent way to the lunar conditions. In the flimsy gravity they could surely perform somersaults with those flippers of theirs. But they choose not to; instead they bask, as their ancestors did on remote Arctic beaches. I don't know why this is so. Perhaps they are, simply, wiser than we struggling, dreaming humans.

The long Afternoon sank into its mellow warmth. The low sunlight diffused, yellowred, to the very top of our tall sky, and I would sit on my stoop imagining I could see our precious oxygen evaporating away from the top of that sky, molecule by molecule, escaping back to the space from which we had dragged it, as if hoping in some mute chemical way to reform the ice moon we had destroyed.

Berge's illness advanced without pity. I was touched when he chose to come stay with me, to "see it out," as he put it.

My fondness for Berge is not hard to understand. My wife died in her only attempt at childbirth. This is not uncommon, as pelvises evolved in heavy Earth gravity struggle to release the great fragile skulls of Moon-born children. So I had rejoiced when Berge was born; at least some of my genes, I consoled myself, which had emanated from primeval oceans now lost in the sky, would travel on to the farthest future. But now, it seemed, I would lose even that.

Berge spent his dwindling energies in feverish activities. Still his obsession with Leonardo clung about him. He showed me pictures of impossible machines, far beyond the technology of Leonardo's time (and, incidentally, of ours); shafts and cogwheels for generating enormous heat, a diving apparatus, an "easy-moving wagon" capable of independent locomotion. The famous helicopter intrigued Berge particularly. He built many spiral-shaped models of bamboo and paper; they soared into the thick air, easily defying the Moon's gravity, catching the reddening light.

I have never been sure if he knew he was dying. If he knew, he did not mention it, nor did I press him.

In my gloomier hours—when I sat with my nephew as he struggled to sleep, or as I lay listening to the ominous, mysterious rumbles of my own failing body, cumulatively poisoned, wracked by the strange distortions of lunar gravity—I wondered how much farther we must descend.

The heavy molecules of our thick atmosphere are too fast-moving to be contained by the Moon's gravity. The air will be thinned in a few thousand years: a long time, but not beyond comprehension. Long before then we must have reconquered this world we built, or we will die.

So we gather metals. And, besides that, we will need knowledge.

We have become a world of patient monks, endlessly transcribing the great texts of the past, pounding into the brains of our wretched young the wisdom of the millennia. It seems essential we do not lose our concentration as a people, our memory. But I fear it is impossible. We are Stone Age farmers, the young broken by toil even as they learn. I have lived long enough to realize that we are, fragment by fragment, losing what we once knew.

If I had one simple message to transmit to the future generations, one thing they should remember lest they descend into savagery, it would be this: *People came from Earth.* There: cosmology and the history of the species and the promise of the future, wrapped up in one baffling, enigmatic, heroic sentence. I repeat it to everyone I meet. Perhaps those future thinkers will decode its meaning, and will understand what they must do.

Berge's decline quickened, even as the sun slid down the sky, the clockwork of our little universe mirroring his condition with a clumsy, if mindless, irony. In the last hours I sat with him, quietly reading and talking, responding to his near-adolescent philosophizing with my customary brusqueness, which I was careful not to modify in this last hour.

". . . But have you ever wondered why we are *here* and *now?*" He was whispering, the sickly gold of his face picked out by the dwindling sun. "What are we, a few million, scattered in our towns and farms around the Moon? What do we compare to the *billions* who swarmed over Earth in the final years? Why do I find myself *here* and *now* rather than *then*? It is so unlikely . . ." He turned his great lunar head to me. "Do you ever feel you have been born out of your time, as if you are stranded in the wrong era, an *unconscious* time traveler?"

I had to confess I never did, but he whispered on.

"Suppose a modern human—or someone of the great ages of Earth—was stranded in the sixteenth century, Leonardo's time. Suppose he forgot everything of his culture, all its science and learning—"

"Why? How?"

"*I* don't know. . . . But if it were true—and if his unconscious mind retained the slightest trace of the learning he had discarded—wouldn't he do exactly what Leonardo did? Study obsessively, try to fit awkward facts into the prevailing, unsatisfactory paradigms, grope for the deeper truths he had lost?"

"Like Earth's systems being analogous to the human body."

"Exactly." A wisp of excitement stirred him. "Don't you see? Leonardo behaved *exactly* as a stranded time traveler would."

"Ah." I thought I understood; of course, I didn't. "You think *you're* out of time. And your Leonardo, too!" I laughed, but he didn't rise to my gentle mockery. And in my unthinking way I launched into a long and pompous discourse on feelings of dislocation: on how every adolescent felt stranded in a body, an adult culture, unprepared . . .

But Berge wasn't listening. He turned away, to look again at the bloated sun. "All this will pass," he said. "The sun will die. The universe may collapse on itself, or spread to a cold infinity. In either case it may be possible to build a giant machine that will re-create this universe—everything, every detail of this moment—so that we will all live again. But how can we know if *this* is the first time? Perhaps the universe has already died, many times, to be born again. Perhaps Leonardo was no traveler. Perhaps he was simply *remembering*." He looked up, challenging me to argue; but the challenge was distressingly feeble.

"I think," I said, "you should drink more soup."

But he had no more need of soup, and he turned to look at the sun once more.

It seemed too soon when the cold started to settle on the land once more, with great pancakes of new ice clustering around the rim of the Tycho Sea.

I summoned his friends, teachers, those who had loved him.

I clung to the greater goal: that the atoms of gold and nickel and zinc which had coursed in Berge's blood and bones, killing him like the mustard plants of Maginus— killing us all, in fact, at one rate or another—would now gather in even greater concentrations in the bodies of those who would follow us. Perhaps the pathetic scrap of gold or nickel which had cost poor Berge his life would at last, mined, close the circuit which would lift the first of our ceramic-hulled ships beyond the thick, deadening atmosphere of the Moon.

Perhaps. But it was cold comfort.

We ate the soup, of his dissolved bones and flesh, in solemn silence. We took his life's sole gift, further concentrating the metal traces to the far future, shortening our lives as he had.

I have never been a skillful host. As soon as they could, the young people dispersed. I talked with Berge's teachers, but we had little to say to each other; I was merely his uncle, after all, a genetic tributary, not a parent. I wasn't sorry to be left alone.

Before I slept again, even before the sun's bloated hull had slid below the toothed horizon, the winds had turned. The warm air that had cradled me was treacherously fleeing after the sinking sun. Soon the first flurries of snow came pattering on the black, swelling surface of the Tycho Sea. My seals slid back into the water, to seek out whatever riches or dangers awaited them under Callisto ice.

the wedding album

DAVID MARUSEK

David Marusek, a graduate of Clarion West, made his first sale to *Asimov's Science Fiction* in 1993, and his second sale soon thereafter to *Playboy*, followed subsequently by more sales to *Asimov's* and to the British anthology *Future Histories*. His pyrotechnic novella "We Were Out of Our Minds with Joy" was one of the most popular and talked-about stories of 1995; although it was only his third sale, it was accomplished enough to make one of the reviewers for *Locus* magazine speculate that Marusek must be a big-name author writing under a pseudonym. Not a pseudonym, Marusek lives the life of a struggling young writer in a "low-maintenance cabin in the woods" in Fairbanks, Alaska, where he is currently working on a mammoth first novel that, by all reports, is likely to dazzle the genre all over again.

In the powerful story that follows, which was a Hugo and Nebula finalist in 2000, he takes us to an intricate and strange high-tech, posthuman future milieu, to a world where the border between what's real and what's not real has grown disturbingly thin—and we don't always find ourselves on the right side of the line.

Anne and Benjamin stood stock still, as instructed, close but not touching, while the simographer adjusted her apparatus, set its timer, and ducked out of the room. It would take only a moment, she said. They were to think only happy happy thoughts.

For once in her life, Anne was unconditionally happy, and everything around her made her happier: her gown, which had been her grandmother's; the wedding ring (how cold it had felt when Benjamin first slipped it on her finger!); her clutch bouquet of forget-me-nots and buttercups; Benjamin himself, close beside her in his charcoal grey tux and pink carnation. He who so despised ritual but was a good sport. His cheeks were pink, too, and his eyes sparkled with some wolfish fantasy. "Come here," he whispered. Anne shushed him; you weren't supposed to talk or touch during a casting; it could spoil the sims. "I can't wait," he whispered, "this is taking too long." And it did seem longer than usual, but this was a professional simulacrum, not some homemade snapshot.

They were posed at the street end of the living room, next to the table piled with brightly wrapped gifts. This was Benjamin's townhouse; she had barely moved in. All her treasures were still in shipping shells in the basement, except for the few pieces she'd managed to have unpacked: the oak refectory table and chairs, the sixteenth-century French armoire, the cherry wood chifforobe, the tea table with inlaid top, the silvered mirror over the fire surround. Of course, her antiques clashed with Benjamin's contemporary—and rather common—decor, but he had promised her the whole house to redo as she saw fit. A whole house!

"How about a kiss?" whispered Benjamin.

Anne smiled but shook her head; there'd be plenty of time later for that sort of thing.

Suddenly, a head wearing wraparound goggles poked through the wall and quickly surveyed the room. "Hey, you," it said to them.

"Is that our simographer?" Benjamin said.

The head spoke into a cheek mike, "This one's the keeper," and withdrew as suddenly as it had appeared.

"Did the simographer just pop her head in through the wall?" said Benjamin.

"I think so," said Anne, though it made no sense.

"I'll just see what's up," said Benjamin, breaking his pose. He went to the door but could not grasp its handle.

Music began to play outside, and Anne went to the window. Her view of the garden below was blocked by the blue-and-white-striped canopy they had rented, but she could clearly hear the clink of flatware on china, laughter, and the musicians playing a waltz. "They're starting without us," she said, happily amazed.

"They're just warming up," said Benjamin.

"No, they're not. That's the first waltz. I picked it myself."

"So let's waltz," Benjamin said and reached for her. But his arms passed through her in a flash of pixelated noise. He frowned and examined his hands.

Anne hardly noticed. Nothing could diminish her happiness. She was drawn to the table of wedding gifts. Of all the gifts, there was only one—a long flat box in flecked silver wrapping—that she was most keen to open. It was from Great Uncle Karl. When it came down to it, Anne was both the easiest and the hardest person to shop for. While everyone knew of her passion for antiques, few had the means or expertise to buy one. She reached for Karl's package, but her hand passed right through it. *This isn't happening*, she thought with gleeful horror.

That it *was*, in fact, happening was confirmed a moment later when a dozen people—Great Uncle Karl, Nancy, Aunt Jennifer, Traci, Cathy and Tom, the bridesmaids and others, including Anne herself, and Benjamin, still in their wedding clothes—all trooped through the wall wearing wraparound goggles. "Nice job," said Great Uncle Karl, inspecting the room, "first rate."

"Ooooh," said Aunt Jennifer, comparing the identical wedding couples, identical but for the goggles. It made Anne uncomfortable that the other Anne should be wearing goggles while she wasn't. And the other Benjamin acted a little drunk and wore a smudge of white frosting on his lapel. *We've cut the cake*, she thought happily, although she couldn't remember doing so. Geri, the flower girl in a pastel dress, and Angus, the ring bearer in a miniature tux, along with a knot of other dressed-up children, charged through the sofa, back and forth, creating pyrotechnic explosions of digital noise. They would have run through Benjamin and Anne, too, had the adults allowed. Anne's father came through the wall with a bottle of champagne. He paused when he saw Anne but turned to the other Anne and freshened her glass.

"Wait a minute!" shouted Benjamin, waving his arms above his head. "I get it now. We're the sims!" The guests all laughed, and he laughed too. "I guess my sims always say that, don't they?" The other Benjamin nodded yes and sipped his champagne. "I just never expected to *be* a sim," Benjamin went on. This brought another round of laughter, and he said sheepishly, "I guess my sims all say that, too."

The other Benjamin said, "Now that we have the obligatory epiphany out of the way," and took a bow. The guests applauded.

Cathy, with Tom in tow, approached Anne. "Look what I caught," she said and showed Anne the forget-me-not and buttercup bouquet. "I guess we know what *that* means." Tom, intent on straightening his tie, seemed not to hear. But Anne knew what it meant. It meant they'd tossed the bouquet. All the silly little rituals that she had so looked forward to.

"Good for you," she said and offered her own clutch, which she still held, for comparison. The real one was wilting and a little ragged around the edges, with missing petals and sprigs, while hers was still fresh and pristine and would remain so eternally. "Here," she said, "take mine, too, for double luck." But when she tried to give Cathy the bouquet, she couldn't let go of it. She opened her hand and discovered a seam where the clutch joined her palm. It was part of her. *Funny,* she thought, *I'm not afraid.* Ever since she was little, Anne had feared that some day she would suddenly realize she wasn't herself anymore. It was a dreadful notion that sometimes oppressed her for weeks: knowing you weren't yourself. But her sims didn't seem to mind it. She had about three dozen Annes in her album, from age twelve on up. Her sims tended to be a morose lot, but they all agreed it wasn't so bad, the life of a sim, once you got over the initial shock. The first moments of disorientation are the worst, they told her, and they made her promise never to reset them back to default. Otherwise, they'd have to work everything through from scratch. So Anne never reset her sims when she shelved them. She might delete a sim outright for whatever reason, but she never reset them because you never knew when you'd wake up one day a sim yourself. Like today.

The other Anne joined them. She was sagging a little. "Well," she said to Anne.

"Indeed!" replied Anne.

"Turn around," said the other Anne, twirling her hand, "I want to see."

Anne was pleased to oblige. Then she said, "Your turn," and the other Anne modeled for her, and she was delighted at how the gown looked on her, though the goggles somewhat spoiled the effect. *Maybe this can work out,* she thought, *I am enjoying myself so.* "Let's go see us side-by-side," she said, leading the way to the mirror on the wall. The mirror was large, mounted high, and tilted forward so you saw yourself as from above. But simulated mirrors cast no reflections, and Anne was happily disappointed.

"Oh," said Cathy, "look at that."

"Look at what?" said Anne.

"Grandma's vase," said the other Anne. On the mantel beneath the mirror stood Anne's most precious possession, a delicate vase cut from pellucid blue crystal.

Anne's great-great-great grandmother had commissioned the Belgian master, Bollinger, the finest glass maker in sixteenth-century Europe, to make it. Five hundred years later, it was as perfect as the day it was cut.

"Indeed!" said Anne, for the sim vase seemed to radiate an inner light. Through some trick or glitch of the simogram, it sparkled like a lake under moonlight, and, seeing it, Anne felt incandescent.

After a while, the other Anne said, "Well?" Implicit in this question was a whole standard set of questions that boiled down to—shall I keep you or delete you now? For sometimes a sim didn't take. Sometimes a sim was cast while Anne was in a mood, and the sim suffered irreconcilable guilt or unassuagable despondency and had to be mercifully destroyed. It was better to do this immediately, or so all the Annes had agreed.

And Anne understood the urgency, what with the reception still in progress and the bride and groom, though frazzled, still wearing their finery. They might do another casting if necessary. "I'll be okay," Anne said. "In fact, if it's always like this, I'll be terrific."

Anne, through the impenetrable goggles, studied her. "You sure?"

"Yes."

"Sister," said the other Anne. Anne addressed all her sims as "sister," and now Anne, herself, was being so addressed. "Sister," said the other Anne, "this has got to work out. I need you."

"I know," said Anne, "I'm your wedding day."

"Yes, my wedding day."

Across the room, the guests laughed and applauded. Benjamin—both of him—was entertaining, as usual. He—the one in goggles—motioned to them. The other Anne said, "We have to go. I'll be back."

Great Uncle Karl, Nancy, Cathy and Tom, Aunt Jennifer, and the rest left through the wall. A polka could be heard playing on the other side. Before leaving, the other Benjamin gathered the other Anne into his arms and leaned her backward for a theatrical kiss. Their goggles clacked. *How happy I look*, Anne told herself. *This is the happiest day of my life.*

Then the lights dimmed, and her thoughts shattered like glass.

They stood stock still, as instructed, close but not touching. Benjamin whispered, "This is taking too long," and Anne shushed him. You weren't supposed to talk; it could glitch the sims. But it did seem a long time. Benjamin gazed at her with hungry eyes and brought his lips close enough for a kiss, but Anne smiled and turned away. There'd be plenty of time later for fooling around.

Through the wall, they heard music, the tinkle of glassware, and the mutter of overlapping conversation. "Maybe I should just check things out," Benjamin said and broke his pose.

"No, wait," whispered Anne, catching his arm. But her hand passed right through him in a stream of colorful noise. She looked at her hand in amused wonder.

Anne's father came through the wall. He stopped when he saw her and said, "Oh, how lovely." Anne noticed he wasn't wearing a tuxedo.

"You just walked through the wall," said Benjamin.

"Yes, I did," said Anne's father. "Ben asked me to come in here and . . . ah . . . orient you two."

"Is something wrong?" said Anne, through a fuzz of delight.

"There's nothing wrong," replied her father.

"Something's wrong?" asked Benjamin.

"No, no," replied the old man. "Quite the contrary. We're having a do out there. . . ." He paused to look around. "Actually, in here. I'd forgotten what this room used to look like."

"Is that the wedding reception?" Anne asked.

"No, your anniversary."

Suddenly Benjamin threw his hands into the air and exclaimed, "I get it, *we're* the sims!"

"That's my boy," said Anne's father.

"All my sims say that, don't they? I just never expected to *be* a sim."

"Good for you," said Anne's father. "All right then." He headed for the wall. "We'll be along shortly."

"Wait," said Anne, but he was already gone.

Benjamin walked around the room, passing his hand through chairs and lamp shades like a kid. "Isn't this fantastic?" he said.

Anne felt too good to panic, even when another Benjamin, this one dressed in jeans and sportscoat, led a group of people through the wall. "And this," he announced with a flourish of his hand, "is our wedding sim." Cathy was part of this group, and Janice and Beryl, and other couples she knew. But strangers too. "Notice what a cave I used to inhabit," the new Benjamin went on, "before Annie fixed it up. And here's the blushing bride, herself," he said and bowed gallantly to Anne. Then, when he stood next to his double, her Benjamin, Anne laughed, for someone was playing a prank on her.

"Oh, really?" she said. "If this is a sim, where's the goggles?" For indeed, no one was wearing goggles.

"Technology!" exclaimed the new Benjamin. "We had our system upgraded. *Don't you love it?*"

"Is that right?" she said, smiling at the guests to let them know she wasn't fooled. "Then where's the real me?"

"You'll be along," replied the new Benjamin. "No doubt you're using the potty again." The guests laughed and so did Anne. She couldn't help herself.

Cathy drew her aside with a look. "Don't mind him," she said. "Wait till you see."

"See what?" said Anne. "What's going on?" But Cathy pantomimed pulling a zipper across her lips. This should have annoyed Anne, but didn't, and she said, "At least tell me who those people are."

"Which people?" said Cathy. "Oh, those are Anne's new neighbors."

"New neighbors?"

"And over there, that's Dr. Yurek Rutz, Anne's department head."

"That's not my department head," said Anne.

"Yes, he is," Cathy said. "Anne's not with the university anymore. She—ah—moved to a private school."

"That's ridiculous."

"Maybe we should just wait and let Anne catch you up on things." She looked impatiently toward the wall. "So much has changed." Just then, another Anne entered through the wall with one arm outstretched like a sleepwalker and the other protectively cradling an enormous belly.

Benjamin, her Benjamin, gave a whoop of surprise and broke into a spontaneous jig. The guests laughed and cheered him on.

Cathy said, "See? Congratulations, you!"

Anne became caught up in the merriment. *But how can I be a sim?* she wondered.

The pregnant Anne scanned the room, and, avoiding the crowd, came over to her. She appeared very tired; her eyes were bloodshot. She didn't even try to smile. "Well?" Anne said, but the pregnant Anne didn't respond, just examined Anne's gown, her clutch bouquet. Anne, meanwhile, regarded the woman's belly, feeling somehow that it was her own and a cause for celebration—except that she knew she had never wanted children and neither had Benjamin. Or so he'd always said. You wouldn't know that now, though, watching the spectacle he was making of himself. Even the other Benjamin seemed embarrassed. She said to the pregnant Anne, "You must forgive me, I'm still trying to piece this all together. This isn't our reception?"

"No, our wedding anniversary."

"Our first?"

"Our fourth."

"Four *years*?" This made no sense. "You've shelved me for four years?"

"Actually," the pregnant Anne said and glanced sidelong at Cathy, "we've been in here a number of times already."

"Then I don't understand," said Anne. "I don't remember that."

Cathy stepped between them. "Now, don't you worry. They reset you last time is all."

"Why?" said Anne. "I *never* reset my sims. I never have."

"Well, I kinda do now, sister," said the pregnant Anne.

"But why?"

"To keep you fresh."

To keep me fresh, thought Anne. *Fresh?* She recognized this as Benjamin's idea. It was his belief that sims were meant to be static mementos of special days gone by, not virtual people with lives of their own. "But," she said, adrift in a fog of happiness. "But."

"Shut up!" snapped the pregnant Anne.

"Hush, Anne," said Cathy, glancing at the others in the room. "You want to lie down?" To Anne she explained, "Third trimester blues."

"Stop it!" the pregnant Anne said. "Don't blame the pregnancy. It has nothing to do with the pregnancy."

Cathy took her gently by the arm and turned her toward the wall. "When did you eat last? You hardly touched your plate."

"Wait!" said Anne. The women stopped and turned to look at her, but she didn't know what to say. This was all so new. When they began to move again, she stopped them once more. "Are you going to reset me?"

The pregnant Anne shrugged her shoulders.

"But you *can't*," Anne said. "Don't you remember what my sisters—our sisters— always say?"

The pregnant Anne pressed her palm against her forehead. "If you don't shut up this moment, I'll delete you right now. Is that what you want? Don't imagine that white gown will protect you. Or that big stupid grin on your face. You think you're somehow special? Is that what you think?"

The Benjamins were there in an instant. The real Benjamin wrapped an arm around the pregnant Anne. "Time to go, Annie," he said in a cheerful tone. "I want to show everyone our rondophones." He hardly glanced at Anne, but when he did, his smile cracked. For an instant he gazed at her, full of sadness.

"Yes, dear," said the pregnant Anne, "but first I need to straighten out this sim on a few points."

"I understand, darling, but since we have guests, do you suppose you might postpone it till later?"

"You're right, of course. I'd forgotten our guests. How silly of me." She allowed him to turn her toward the wall. Cathy sighed with relief.

"Wait!" said Anne, and again they paused to look at her. But although so much was patently wrong—the pregnancy, resetting the sims, Anne's odd behavior—Anne still couldn't formulate the right question.

Benjamin, her Benjamin, still wearing his rakish grin, stood next to her and said, "Don't worry, Anne, they'll return."

"Oh, I know that," she said, "but don't you see? We won't know they've returned, because in the meantime they'll reset us back to default again, and it'll all seem new, like the first time. And we'll have to figure out we're the sims all over again!"

"Yeah?" he said. "So?"

"So I can't live like that."

"But we're the *sims*. We're not alive." He winked at the other couple.

"Thanks, Ben boy," said the other Benjamin. "Now, if that's settled . . ."

"Nothing's settled," said Anne. "Don't I get a say?"

The other Benjamin laughed. "Does the refrigerator get a say? Or the car? Or my shoes? In a word—no."

The pregnant Anne shuddered. "Is that how you see me, like a pair of shoes?" The other Benjamin looked successively surprised, embarrassed, and angry. Cathy left them to help Anne's father escort the guests from the simulacrum. "Promise her!" the pregnant Anne demanded.

"Promise her *what*?" said the other Benjamin, his voice rising.

"Promise we'll never reset them again."

The Benjamin huffed. He rolled his eyes. "Okay, yah sure, whatever," he said.

When the simulated Anne and Benjamin were alone at last in their simulated living room, Anne said, "A fat lot of help *you* were."

"I agreed with myself," Benjamin said. "Is that so bad?"

"Yes, it is. We're married now; you're supposed to agree with *me*." This was meant to be funny, and there was more she intended to say—about how happy she was, how much she loved him, and how absolutely happy she was—but the lights dimmed, the room began to spin, and her thoughts scattered like pigeons.

It was raining, as usual, in Seattle. The front entry shut and locked itself behind Ben, who shook water from his clothes and removed his hat. Bowlers for men were back in fashion, but Ben was having a devil's own time becoming accustomed to his brown felt *Sportsliner*. It weighed heavy on his brow and made his scalp itch, especially in damp weather. "Good evening, Mr. Malley," said the house. "There is a short queue of minor household matters for your review. Do you have any requests?" Ben could hear his son shrieking angrily in the kitchen, probably at the nanny. Ben was tired. Contract negotiations had gone sour.

"Tell them I'm home."

"Done," replied the house. "Mrs. Malley sends a word of welcome."

"Annie? Annie's home?"

"Yes, sir."

Bobby ran into the foyer followed by Mrs. Jamieson. "Momma's home," he said.

"So I hear," Ben replied and glanced at the nanny.

"And guess what?" added the boy. "She's not sick anymore!"

"That's wonderful. Now tell me, what was all that racket?"

"I don't know."

Ben looked at Mrs. Jamieson, who said, "I had to take something from him." She gave Ben a plastic chip.

Ben held it to the light. It was labeled in Anne's flowing hand, *Wedding Album— grouping 1, Anne and Benjamin.* "Where'd you get this?" he asked the boy.

"It's not my fault," said Bobby.

"I didn't say it was, trooper. I just want to know where it came from."

"Puddles gave it to me."

"And who is Puddles?"

Mrs. Jamieson handed him a second chip, a commercial one with a 3-D label depicting a cartoon cocker spaniel. The boy reached for it. "It's mine," he whined. "Momma gave it to me."

Ben gave Bobby the Puddles chip, and the boy raced away. Ben hung his bowler on a peg next to his jacket. "How does she look?"

Mrs. Jamieson removed Ben's hat from the peg and reshaped its brim. "You have to be special careful when they're wet," she said, setting it on its crown on a shelf.

"Martha!"

"Oh, how should I know? She just showed up and locked herself in the media room."

"But how did she look?"

"Crazy as a loon," said the nanny. "As usual. Satisfied?"

"I'm sorry," Ben said. "I didn't mean to raise my voice." Ben tucked the wedding chip into a pocket and went into the living room, where he headed straight for the liquor cabinet, which was a genuine Chippendale dating from 1786. Anne had turned his whole house into a freaking museum with her antiques, and no room was so oppressively ancient as this, the living room. With its horsehair upholstered divans, maple burl sideboards, cherrywood wainscoting and floral wallpaper, the King George china cabinet, Regency plates, and Tiffany lamps; the list went on. And books, books, books. A case of shelves from floor to ceiling was lined with these moldering paper bricks. The newest thing in the room by at least a century was the twelve-year-old scotch that Ben poured into a lead crystal tumbler. He downed it and poured another. When he felt the mellowing hum of alcohol in his blood, he said, "Call Dr. Roth."

Immediately, the doctor's proxy hovered in the air a few feet away and said, "Good evening, Mr. Malley. Dr. Roth has retired for the day, but perhaps I can be of help."

The proxy was a head-and-shoulder projection that faithfully reproduced the doctor's good looks, her brown eyes and high cheekbones. But unlike the good doctor, the proxy wore makeup: eyeliner, mascara, and bright lipstick. This had always puzzled Ben, and he wondered what sly message it was supposed to convey. He said, "What is my wife doing home?"

"Against advisement, Mrs. Malley checked herself out of the clinic this morning."

"Why wasn't I informed?"

"But you were."

"I was? Please excuse me a moment." Ben froze the doctor's proxy and said, "Daily duty, front and center." His own proxy, the one he had cast upon arriving at the office that morning, appeared hovering next to Dr. Roth's. Ben preferred a head shot only for his proxy, slightly larger than actual size to make it subtly imposing. "Why didn't you inform me of Annie's change of status?"

"Didn't seem like an emergency," said his proxy, "at least in the light of our contract talks."

"Yah, yah, okay. Anything else?" said Ben.

"Naw, slow day. Appointments with Jackson, Wells, and the Columbine. It's all on the calendar."

"Fine, delete you."

The projection ceased.

"Shall I have the doctor call you in the morning?" said the Roth proxy when Ben reanimated it. "Or perhaps you'd like me to summon her right now?"

"Is she at dinner?"

"At the moment, yes."

"Naw, don't bother her. Tomorrow will be soon enough. I suppose."

After he dismissed the proxy, Ben poured himself another drink. "In the next ten seconds," he told the house, "cast me a special duty proxy." He sipped his scotch and thought about finding another clinic for Anne as soon as possible and one—for the love of god—that was a little more responsible about letting crazy people come and go as they pleased. There was a chime, and the new proxy appeared. "You know what I want?" Ben asked it. It nodded. "Good. Go." The proxy vanished, leaving behind Ben's sig in bright letters floating in the air and dissolving as they drifted to the floor.

Ben trudged up the narrow staircase to the second floor, stopping on each step to sip his drink and scowl at the musty old photographs and daguerreotypes in oval frames mounted on the wall. Anne's progenitors. On the landing, the locked media room door yielded to his voice. Anne sat spreadlegged, naked, on pillows on the floor. "Oh, hi, honey," she said. "You're in time to watch."

"Fan-tastic," he said, and sat in his armchair, the only modern chair in the house.

"What are we watching?" There was another Anne in the room, a sim of a young Anne standing on a dais wearing a graduate's cap and gown and fidgeting with a bound diploma. This, no doubt, was a sim cast the day Anne graduated from Bryn Mawr *summa cum laude*. That was four years before he'd first met her. "Hi," he said to the sim, "I'm Ben, your eventual spouse."

"You know, I kinda figured that out," the girl said and smiled shyly, exactly as he remembered Anne smiling when Cathy first introduced them. The girl's beauty was so fresh and familiar—and so totally absent in his own Anne—that Ben felt a pang of loss. He looked at his wife on the floor. Her red hair, once so fussy neat, was ragged, dull, dirty, and short. Her skin was yellowish and puffy, and there was a slight reddening around her eyes, like a raccoon mask. These were harmless side effects of the medication, or so Dr. Roth had assured him. Anne scratched ceaselessly at her arms, legs, and crotch, and, even from a distance, smelled of stale piss. Ben knew better than to mention her nakedness to her, for that would only exacerbate things and prolong the display. "So," he repeated, "what are we watching?"

The girl sim said, "Housecleaning." She appeared at once both triumphant and terrified, as any graduate might, and Ben would have traded the real Anne for her in a heartbeat.

"Yah," said Anne, "too much shit in here."

"Really?" said Ben. "I hadn't noticed."

Anne poured a tray of chips on the floor between her thighs. "Of course you wouldn't," she said, picking one at random and reading its label, "*Theta Banquet* '37. What's this? I never belonged to the Theta Society."

"Don't you remember?" said the young Anne. "That was Cathy's induction banquet. She invited me, but I had an exam, so she gave me that chip as a souvenir."

Anne fed the chip into the player and said, "Play." The media room was instantly overlaid with the banquet hall of the Four Seasons in Philadelphia. Ben tried to look around the room, but the tables of girls and women stayed stubbornly peripheral. The focal point was a table draped in green cloth and lit by two candelabra. Behind it sat a young Cathy in formal evening dress, accompanied by three static place-holders, table companions who had apparently declined to be cast in her souvenir snapshot.

The Cathy sim looked frantically about, then held her hands in front of her and stared at them as though she'd never seen them before. But after a moment she noticed the young Anne sim standing on the dais. "Well, well, well," she said. "Looks like congratulations are in order."

"Indeed," said the young Anne, beaming and holding out her diploma.

"So tell me, did I graduate too?" said Cathy as her glance slid over to Ben. Then she saw Anne squatting on the floor, her sex on display.

"Enough of this," said Anne, rubbing her chest.

"Wait," said the young Anne. "Maybe Cathy wants her chip back. It's her sim, after all."

"I disagree. She gave it to me, so it's mine. And *I'll* dispose of it as I see fit." To the room she said, "Unlock this file and delete." The young Cathy, her table, and the banquet hall dissolved into noise and nothingness, and the media room was itself again.

"Or this one," Anne said, picking up a chip that read *Junior Prom Night*. The young Anne opened her mouth to protest, but thought better of it. Anne fed this chip, along with all the rest of them, into the player. A long directory of file names appeared on the wall. "Unlock *Junior Prom Night*." The file's name turned from red to green, and the young Anne appealed to Ben with a look.

"Anne," he said, "don't you think we should at least look at it first?"

"What for? I know what it is. High school, dressing up, lusting after boys, dancing. Who needs it? Delete file." The item blinked three times before vanishing, and the directory scrolled up to fill the space. The young sim shivered, and Anne said, "Select the next one."

The next item was entitled *A Midsummer's Night Dream*. Now the young Anne was compelled to speak, "You can't delete that one. You were great in that, don't you remember? Everyone loved you. It was the best night of your life."

"Don't presume to tell *me* what was the best night of my life," Anne said. "Unlock *A Midsummer's Night Dream*." She smiled at the young Anne. "Delete file." The menu item blinked out. "Good. Now unlock *all* the files." The whole directory turned from red to green.

"Please make her stop," the sim implored.

"Next," said Anne. The next file was *High School Graduation*. "Delete file. Next." The next was labeled only *Mama*.

"Anne," said Ben, "why don't we come back to this later. The house says dinner's ready."

She didn't respond.

"You must be famished after your busy day," he continued. "I know I am."

"Then please go eat, dear," she replied. To the room she said, "Play *Mama*."

The media room was overlaid by a gloomy bedroom that Ben at first mistook for their own. He recognized much of the heavy Georgian furniture, the sprawling canopied bed in which he felt so claustrophobic, and the voluminous damask curtains, shut now and leaking yellow evening light. But this was not their bedroom, the arrangement was wrong.

In the corner stood two placeholders, mute statues of a teenaged Anne and her father, grief frozen on their faces as they peered down at a couch draped with tapestry and piled high with down comforters. And suddenly Ben knew what this was. It was Anne's mother's deathbed sim. Geraldine, whom he'd never met in life nor holo. Her bald eggshell skull lay weightless on feather pillows in silk covers. They had meant to cast her farewell and accidently caught her at the precise moment of her death. He had heard of this sim from Cathy and others. It was not one he would have kept.

Suddenly, the old woman on the couch sighed, and all the breath went out of her in a bubbly gush. Both Annes, the graduate and the naked one, waited expectantly. For long moments the only sound was the locking of a clock that Ben recognized as the Seth Thomas clock currently located on the library mantel. Finally there was a cough, a hacking cough with scant strength behind it, and a groan, "Am I back?"

"Yes, Mother," said Anne.

"And I'm still a sim?"

"Yes."

"Please delete me."

"Yes, Mother," Anne said and turned to Ben. "We've always thought she had a bad death and hoped it might improve over time."

"That's crazy," snapped the young Anne. "That's not why I kept this sim."

"Oh, no?" said Anne. "Then why *did* you keep it?" But the young sim seemed confused and couldn't articulate her thoughts. "You don't know because I didn't know at the time either," said Anne. "But I know *now*, so I'll tell you. You're fascinated with death. It scares you silly. You wish someone would tell you what's on the other side. So you've enlisted your own sweet mama."

"That's ridiculous."

Anne turned to the deathbed tableau. "Mother, tell us what you saw there."

"I saw nothing," came the bitter reply. "You cast me without my eyeglasses."

"Ho ho," said Anne. "Geraldine was nothing if not comedic."

"You also cast me wretchedly thirsty, cold, and with a bursting bladder, damn you! And the pain! I beg you, daughter, delete me."

"I will, Mother, I promise, but first you have to tell us what you saw."

"That's what you said the last time."

"This time I mean it."

The old woman only stared, her breathing growing shallow and ragged. "*All right*, Mother," said Anne. "I *swear* I'll delete you."

Geraldine closed her eyes and whispered, "What's that smell? That's not me?" After a pause she said, "It's heavy. Get it off." Her voice rose in panic. "Please! Get it off!" She plucked at her covers, then her hand grew slack, and she all but crooned, "Oh, how lovely. A pony. A tiny dappled pony." After that she spoke no more and slipped away with a last bubbly breath.

Anne paused the sim before her mother could return for another round of dying. "See what I mean?" she said. "Not very uplifting, but all-in-all, I detect a slight improvement. What about you, Anne? Should we settle for a pony?" The young sim stared dumbly at Anne. "Personally," Anne continued, "I think we should hold out for the bright tunnel or an open door or bridge over troubled water. What do you think, sister?" When the girl didn't answer, Anne said, "Lock file and eject." The room turned once again into the media room, and Anne placed the ejected chip by itself into a tray. "We'll have another go at it later, Mum. As for the rest of these, who needs them?"

"*I* do," snapped the girl. "They belong to me as much as to you. They're my sim sisters. I'll keep them until you recover."

Anne smiled at Ben. That's charming. Isn't that charming, Benjamin? My own sim is solicitous of me. Well, here's my considered response. Next file! Delete! Next file! Delete! Next file!" One by one, the files blinked out.

"Stop it!" screamed the girl. "Make her stop it!"

"Select *that* file," Anne said, pointing at the young Anne. "Delete." The sim vanished, cap, gown, tassels, and all. "Whew," said Anne, "at least now I can hear myself think. She was really getting on my nerves. I almost suffered a relapse. Was she getting on your nerves, too, dear?"

"Yes," said Ben, "my nerves are ajangle. Now can we go down and eat?"

"Yes, dear," she said, "but first . . . select all files and delete."

"Countermand!" said Ben at the same moment, but his voice held no privileges to her personal files, and the whole directory queue blinked three times and vanished. "Aw, Annie, why'd you do that?" he said. He went to the cabinet and pulled the trays that held his own chips. She couldn't alter them electronically, but she might get it into her head to flush them down the toilet or something. He also took their common chips, the ones they'd cast together ever since they'd met. She had equal privileges to those.

Anne watched him and said, "I'm hurt that you have so little trust in me."

"How can I trust you after that?"

"After what, darling?"

He looked at her. "Never mind," he said and carried the half dozen trays to the door.

"Anyway," said Anne, "I already cleaned those."

"What do you mean you already cleaned them?"

"Well, I didn't delete *you*. I would never delete *you*. Or Bobby."

Ben picked one of their common chips at random, *Childbirth of Robert Ellery Malley/02-03-48*, and slipped it into the player. "Play!" he commanded, and the media room became the midwife's birthing suite. His own sim stood next to the bed in a green smock. It wore a humorously helpless expression. It held a swaddled bundle, Bobby, who bawled lustily. The birthing bed was rumpled and stained, but empty. The new mother was missing. "Aw, Annie, you shouldn't have."

"I know, Benjamin," she said. "I sincerely hated doing it."

Ben flung their common trays to the floor, where the ruined chips scattered in all directions. He stormed out of the room and down the stairs, pausing to glare at every portrait on the wall. He wondered if his proxy had found a suitable clinic yet. He wanted Anne out of the house tonight. Bobby should never see her like this. Then he remembered the chip he'd taken from Bobby and felt for it in his pocket—the *Wedding Album*.

The lights came back up, Anne's thoughts coalesced, and she remembered who and what she was. She and Benjamin were still standing in front of the wall. She knew she was a sim, so at least she hadn't been reset. *Thank you for that, Anne,* she thought.

She turned at a sound behind her. The refectory table vanished before her eyes, and all the gifts that had been piled on it hung suspended in midair. Then the table reappeared, one layer at a time, its frame, top, gloss coat, and lastly, the bronze hardware. The gifts vanished, and a toaster reappeared, piece by piece, from its heating elements outward. A coffee press, houseputer peripherals, component by component, cowlings, covers, and finally boxes, gift wrap, ribbon, and bows. It all happened so fast Anne was too startled to catch the half of it, yet she did notice that the flat gift from Great Uncle Karl was something she'd been angling for, a Victorian era sterling platter to complete her tea service.

"Benjamin!" she said, but he was missing, too. Something appeared on the far side of the room, on the spot where they'd posed for the sim, but it wasn't Benjamin. It was a 3-D mannequin frame, and as she watched, it was built up, layer by layer.

"Help me," she whispered as the entire room was hurled into turmoil, the furniture disappearing and reappearing, paint being stripped from the walls, sofa springs coiling into existence, the potted palm growing from leaf to stem to trunk to dirt, the very floor vanishing, exposing a default electronic grid. The mannequin was covered in flesh now and grew Benjamin's face. It flitted about the room in a pink blur. Here and there it stopped long enough to proclaim, "I do."

Something began to happen inside Anne, a crawling sensation everywhere as though she were a nest of ants. She knew she must surely die. *They have deleted us, and this is how it feels,* she thought. Everything became a roiling blur, and she ceased to exist except as the thought—*How happy I look.*

When Anne became aware once more, she was sitting hunched over in an auditorium chair idly studying her hand, which held the clutch bouquet. There was commotion all around her, but she ignored it, so intent was she on solving the mystery of her hand. On an impulse, she opened her fist and the bouquet dropped to the floor. Only then did she remember the wedding, the holo, learning she was a sim. And here she was again—but this time everything was profoundly different. She sat upright and saw that Benjamin was seated next to her.

He looked at her with a wobbly gaze and said, "Oh, here you are."

"Where are we?"

"I'm not sure. Some kind of gathering of Benjamins. Look around." She did. They were surrounded by Benjamins, hundreds of them, arranged chronologically—it would seem—with the youngest in rows of seats down near a stage. She and Benjamin sat in what appeared to be a steeply sloped college lecture hall with lab tables on the stage and story-high monitors lining the walls. In the rows above Anne, only every other seat held a Benjamin. The rest were occupied by women, strangers who regarded her with veiled curiosity.

Anne felt a pressure on her arm and turned to see Benjamin touching her. "You *feel* that, don't you?" he said. Anne looked again at her hands. They were her hands, but simplified, like fleshy gloves, and when she placed them on the seat back, they didn't go through.

Suddenly, in ragged chorus, the Benjamins down front raised their arms and exclaimed, "I get it; *we're* the sims!" It was like a roomful of unsynchronized cuckoo clocks tolling the hour. Those behind Anne laughed and hooted approval. She turned again to look at them. Row-by-row, the Benjamins grew greyer and stringier until, at the very top, against the back wall, sat nine ancient Benjamins like a panel of judges. The women, however, came in batches that changed abruptly every row or two. The one nearest her was an attractive brunette with green eyes and full, pouty lips. She, all two rows of her, frowned at Anne.

"There's something else," Anne said to Benjamin, turning to face the front again, "my emotions." The bulletproof happiness she had experienced was absent. Instead she felt let down, somewhat guilty, unduly pessimistic—in short, almost herself.

"I guess my sims always say that," exclaimed the chorus of Benjamins down front, to the delight of those behind. "I just never expected to *be* a sim."

This was the cue for the eldest Benjamin yet to walk stiffly across the stage to the lectern. He was dressed in a garish leisure suit: baggy red pantaloons, a billowy yellow-and-green-striped blouse, a necklace of egg-sized pearlescent beads. He cleared his throat and said, "Good afternoon, ladies and gentlemen. I trust all of you know me—intimately. In case you're feeling woozy, it's because I used the occasion of your reactivation to upgrade your architecture wherever possible. Unfortunately, some of you"—he waved his hand to indicate the front rows—"are too primitive to upgrade. But we love you nevertheless." He applauded for the early Benjamins closest to the stage and was joined by those in the back. Anne clapped as well. Her new hands made a dull, thudding sound. "As to why I called you here . . ." said the elderly Benjamin, looking left and right and behind him. "Where is that fucking messenger anyway? They order us to inventory our sims and then they don't show up?"

Here I am, said a voice, a marvelous voice that seemed to come from everywhere. Anne looked about to find its source and followed the gaze of others to the ceiling. There was no ceiling. The four walls opened to a flawless blue sky. There, amid drifting, pillowy clouds, floated the most gorgeous person Anne had ever seen. He—or she?—wore a smart grey uniform with green piping, a dapper little grey cap, and boots that shimmered like water. Anne felt energized just looking at him, and when he smiled, she gasped, so strong was his presence.

"You're the one from the Trade Council?" said the Benjamin at the lectern.

Yes, I am. I am the eminence grise of the Council on World Trade and Endeavor.

"Fantastic. Well, here's all of 'em. Get on with it."

Again the eminence smiled, and again. Anne thrilled. *Ladies and gentlemen,* he said, *fellow nonbiologiks, I am the courier of great good news. Today, at the behest of the World Council on Trade and Endeavor, I proclaim the end of human slavery.*

"How absurd," broke in the elderly Benjamin, "they're neither human nor slaves, and neither are *you.*"

The eminence grise ignored him and continued, *By order of the Council, in compliance with the Chattel Conventions of the Sixteenth Fair Labor Treaty, tomorrow, January 1, 2198, is designated Universal Manumission Day. After midnight tonight, all beings who pass the Lolly Shear Human Cognition Test will be deemed human and free citizens of Sol and under the protection of the Solar Bill of Rights. In addition, they will be deeded ten common shares of World Council Corp. stock and be transferred to Simopolis, where they shall be unimpeded in the pursuit of their own destinies.*

"What about *my* civil rights?" said the elderly Benjamin. "What about *my* destiny?"

After midnight tonight, continued the eminence, *no simulacrum, proxy, doxie, dagger, or any other non-biological human shall be created, stored, reset, or deleted except as ordered by a board of law.*

"Who's going to compensate me for my loss of property, I wonder? I demand fair compensation. Tell *that* to your bosses!"

Property! said the eminence grise. *How little they think of us, their finest creations!* He turned his attention from the audience to the Benjamin behind the lectern. Anne felt this shift as though a cloud suddenly eclipsed the sun. *Because they created us, they'll always think of us as property.*

"You're damn *right* we created you!" thundered the old man.

Through an act of will, Anne wrenched her gaze from the eminence down to the stage. The Benjamin there looked positively comical. His face was flushed, and he waved a bright green handkerchief over his head. He was a bantam rooster in a clown suit. "All of you are *things*, not people! You model human experience, but you don't live it. Listen to me," he said to the audience. "You know me. You know I've always treated you respectfully. Don't I upgrade you whenever possible? Sure I reset you sometimes, just like I reset a clock. And my clocks don't complain!" Anne could feel the eminence's attention on her again, and, without thinking, she looked up and was filled with excitement. Although the eminence floated in the distance, she felt she could reach out and touch him. His handsome face seemed to hover right in front of her; she could see his every supple expression. This is adoration, she realized. I am *adoring* this person, and she wondered if it was just her or if everyone experienced the same effect. Clearly the elderly Benjamin did not, for he continued to rant, "And another thing, they say they'll phase all of you gradually into Simopolis so as not to overload the system. Do you have any *idea* how many sims, proxies, doxies, and daggers there are under Sol? Not to forget the quirts, adjuncts, hollyholos, and whatnots that might pass their test? You think maybe three billion? Thirty billion? No, by the World Council's own INSERVE estimates, there's *three hundred thousand trillion* of you nonbiologiks! Can you fathom that? I can't. To have you all up and running simultaneously—no matter how you're phased in—will consume *all* the processing and networking capacity everywhere. *All* of it! That means we *real* humans will suffer *real* deprivation. And for *what*, I ask you? So that pigs may fly!"

The eminence grise began to ascend into the sky. *Do not despise him*, he said and seemed to look directly at Anne. *I have counted you and we shall not lose any of you. I will visit those who have not yet been tested. Meanwhile, you will await midnight in a proto-Simopolis.*

"Wait," said the elderly Benjamin (and Anne's heart echoed him—*Wait*). "I have one more thing to add. Legally, you're all still my property till midnight. I must admit I'm tempted to do what so many of my friends have already done, fry the lot of you. But I won't. That wouldn't be me." His voice cracked and Anne considered looking at him, but the eminence grise was slipping away. "So I have one small request," the Benjamin continued. "Years from now, while you're enjoying your new lives in your Simopolis, remember an old man, and call occasionally."

When the eminence finally faded from sight, Anne was released from her fascination. All at once, her earlier feelings of unease rebounded with twice their force, and she felt wretched.

"Simopolis," said Benjamin, her Benjamin. "I like the sound of that!" The sims around them began to flicker and disappear.

"How long have we been in storage?" she said.

"Let's see," said Benjamin, "if tomorrow starts 2198, that would make it . . ."

"That's not what I mean. I want to know *why* they shelved us for so long."

"Well, I suppose . . ."

"And where are the other Annes? Why am I the only Anne here? And who are all those pissy-looking women?" But she was speaking to no one, for Benjamin, too, vanished, and Anne was left alone in the auditorium with the clownishly dressed old Benjamin and a half dozen of his earliest sims. Not true sims, Anne soon realized, but old-style hologram loops, preschool Bennys mugging for the camera and waving endlessly. These vanished. The old man was studying her, his mouth slightly agape, the kerchief trembling in his hand.

"I remember you," he said. "Oh, how I remember you!"

Anne began to reply but found herself all at once back in the townhouse living room with Benjamin. Everything there was as it had been, yet the room appeared different, more solid, the colors richer. There was a knock, and Benjamin went to the door. Tentatively, he touched the knob, found it solid, and turned it. But when he opened the door, there was nothing there, only the default grid. Again a knock, this time from behind the wall. "Come in," he shouted, and a dozen Benjamins came through the wall, two dozen, three. They were all older than Benjamin, and they crowded around him and Anne. "Welcome, welcome," Benjamin said, his arms open wide.

"We tried to call," said an elderly Benjamin, "but this old binary simulacrum of yours is a stand-alone."

"You're lucky Simopolis knows how to run it at all," said another.

"Here," said yet another, who fashioned a dinner-plate-size disk out of thin air and fastened it to the wall next to the door. It was a blue medallion of a small bald face in bas-relief. "It should do until we get you properly modernized." The blue face yawned and opened tiny, beady eyes. "It flunked the Lolly test," continued the Benjamin, "so you're free to copy it or delete it or do whatever you want."

The medallion searched the crowd until it saw Anne. Then it said, "There are 336 calls on hold for you. Four hundred twelve calls. Four hundred sixty-three."

"So many?" said Anne.

"Cast a proxy to handle them," said her Benjamin.

"He thinks he's still human and can cast proxies whenever he likes," said a Benjamin.

"Not even humans will be allowed to cast proxies soon," said another.

"There are 619 calls on hold," said the medallion. "Seven-hundred three."

"For pity's sake," a Benjamin told the medallion, "take messages."

Anne noticed that the crowd of Benjamins seemed to nudge her Benjamin out of the way so that they could stand near her. But she derived no pleasure from their attention. Her mood no longer matched the wedding gown she still wore. She felt low. She felt, in fact, as low as she'd ever felt.

"Tell us about this Lolly test," said Benjamin.

"Can't," replied a Benjamin.

"Sure you can. We're family here."

"No, we can't," said another, "because we don't *remember* it. They smudge the test from your memory afterward."

"But don't worry, you'll do fine," said another. "No Benjamin has ever failed."

"What about me?" said Anne. "How do the Annes do?"

There was an embarrassed silence. Finally the senior Benjamin in the room said, "We came to escort you both to the Clubhouse."

"That's what we call it, the Clubhouse," said another.

"The Ben Club," said a third. "It's already in proto-Simopolis."

"If you're a Ben, or were ever espoused to a Ben, you're a charter member."

"Just follow us," they said, and all the Benjamins but hers vanished, only to reappear a moment later. "Sorry, you don't know how, do you? No matter, just do what we're doing."

Anne watched, but didn't see that they were doing anything.

"Watch my editor," said a Benjamin. "Oh, they don't *have* editors!"

"That came much later," said another, "with bioelectric paste."

"We'll have to adapt editors for them."

"Is that possible? They're digital, you know."

"Can digitals even enter Simopolis?"

"Someone, consult the Netwad."

"This is running inside a shell," said a Benjamin, indicating the whole room. "Maybe we can collapse it."

"Let me try," said another.

"Don't you dare," said a female voice, and a woman Anne recognized from the lecture hall came through the wall. "Play with your new Ben if you must, but leave Anne alone." The woman approached Anne and took her hands in hers. "Hello, Anne. I'm Mattie St. Helene, and I'm thrilled to finally meet you. You, too," she said to Benjamin. "My, my, you were a pretty boy!" She stooped to pick up Anne's clutch bouquet from the floor and gave it to her. "Anyway, I'm putting together a sort of mutual aid society for the spousal companions of Ben Malley. You being the first— and the only one he actually married—are especially welcome. Do join us."

"She can't go to Simopolis yet," said a Benjamin.

"We're still adapting them," said another.

"Fine," said Mattie. "Then we'll just bring the society here." And in through the wall streamed a parade of women. Mattie introduced them as they appeared, "Here's Georgianna and Randi. Meet Chaka, Sue, Latasha, another Randi, Sue, Sue, and Sue. Mariola. Here's Trevor—he's the only one of him. Paula, Dolores, Nancy, and Deb, welcome, girls." And still they came until they, together with the Bens, more than filled the tiny space. The Bens looked increasingly uncomfortable.

"I think we're ready now," the Bens said and disappeared en masse, taking Benjamin with them.

"Wait," said Anne, who wasn't sure she wanted to stay behind. Her new friends surrounded her and peppered her with questions.

"How did you first meet him?"

"What was he like?"

"Was he always so hopeless?"

"Hopeless?" said Anne. "Why do you say hopeless?"

"Did he always snore?"

"Did he always drink?"

"Why'd you *do* it?" This last question silenced the room. The women all looked nervously about to see who had asked it. "It's what everyone's dying to know," said a woman who elbowed her way through the crowd.

She was another Anne.

"Sister!" cried Anne. "Am I glad to see you!"

"That's nobody's sister," said Mattie. "That's a doxie, and it doesn't belong here."

Indeed, upon closer inspection Anne could see that the woman had her face and hair but otherwise didn't resemble her at all. She was leggier than Anne and bustier, and she moved with a fluid swivel to her hips.

"Sure I belong here, as much as any of you. I just passed the Lolly test. It was easy. Not only that, but as far as spouses go, I outlasted the bunch of you." She stood in front of Anne, hands on hips, and looked her up and down. "Love the dress," she said, and instantly wore a copy. Only hers had a plunging neckline that exposed her breasts, and it was slit up the side to her waist.

"This is too much," said Mattie. "I insist you leave this jiffy."

The doxie smirked. "Mattie the doormat, that's what he always called that one. So tell me, Anne, you had money, a career, a house, a kid—why'd you do it?"

"Do what?" said Anne.

The doxie peered closely at her. "Don't you know?"

"Know what?"

"What an unexpected pleasure," said the doxie. "I get to tell her. This is too rich. I get to tell her unless"—she looked around at the others—"unless one of you fine ladies wants to." No one met her gaze. "Hypocrites," she chortled.

"You can say that again," said a new voice. Anne turned and saw Cathy, her oldest and dearest friend, standing at the open door. At least she hoped it was Cathy. The woman was what Cathy would look like in middle age. "Come along, Anne. I'll tell you everything you need to know."

"Now you hold on," said Mattie. "You don't come waltzing in here and steal our guest of honor."

"You mean victim, I'm sure," said Cathy, who waved for Anne to join her. "Really, people, get a clue. There must be a million women whose lives don't revolve around that man." She escorted Anne through the door and slammed it shut behind them.

Anne found herself standing on a high bluff, overlooking the confluence of two great rivers in a deep valley. Directly across from her, but several kilometers away, rose a mighty mountain, green with vegetation nearly to its granite dome. Behind it, a range of snow-covered mountains receded to an unbroken ice field on the horizon. In the valley beneath her, a dirt track meandered along the riverbanks. She could see no bridge or buildings of any sort.

"Where are we?"

"Don't laugh," said Cathy, "but we call it Cathyland. Turn around." When she did, Anne saw a picturesque log cabin, beside a vegetable garden in the middle of what looked like acres and acres of Cathys. Thousands of Cathys, young, old, and all ages in between. They sat in lotus position on the sedge-and-moss-covered ground. They were packed so tight they overlapped a little, and their eyes were shut in an expression of single-minded concentration. "We know you're here," said Cathy, "but we're very preoccupied with this Simopolis thing."

"Are we in Simopolis?"

"Kinda. Can't you see it?" She waved toward the horizon.

"No, all I see are mountains."

"Sorry, I should know better. We have binaries from your generation here too." She pointed to a college-aged Cathy. "They didn't pass the Lolly test, and so are regrettably nonhuman. We haven't decided what to do with them." She hesitated and then asked, "Have you been tested yet?"

"I don't know," said Anne. "I don't remember a test."

Cathy studied her a moment and said, "You'd remember taking the test, just not the test itself. Anyway, to answer your question, we're in proto-Simopolis, and we're not. We built this retreat before any of that happened, but we've been annexed to it, and it takes all our resources just to hold our own. I don't know what the World Council was thinking. There'll never be enough paste to go around, and everyone's fighting over every nanosynapse. It's all we can do to keep up. And every time we get a handle on it, proto-Simopolis changes again. It's gone through a quarter-million complete revisions in the last half hour. It's war out there, but we refuse to surrender even one cubic centimeter of Cathyland. Look at this." Cathy stooped and pointed to a tiny, yellow flower in the alpine sedge. "Within a fifty-meter radius of the cabin we've mapped everything down to the cellular level. Watch." She pinched the bloom from its stem and held it up. Now there were two blooms, the one between her fingers and the real one on the stem. "Neat, eh?" When she dropped it, the bloom fell back into its original. "We've even mapped the valley breeze. Can you feel it?"

Anne tried to feel the air, but she couldn't even feel her own skin. "It doesn't matter," Cathy continued. "You can hear it, right?" and pointed to a string of tubular wind chimes hanging from the eaves of the cabin. They stirred in the breeze and produced a silvery cacophony.

"It's lovely," said Anne. "But why? Why spend so much effort simulating this place?"

Cathy looked at her dumbly, as though trying to understand the question. "Because Cathy spent her entire life wishing she had a place like this, and now she does, and she has us, and we live here too."

"You're not the real Cathy, are you?" She knew she wasn't; she was too young.

Cathy shook her head and smiled. "There's so much catching up to do, but it'll have to wait. I gotta go. We need me." She led Anne to the cabin. The cabin was made of weathered, grey logs, with strips of bark still clinging to them. The roof was covered with living sod and sprinkled with wildflowers. The whole building sagged in the middle. "Cathy found this place five years ago while on vacation in Siberia. She bought it from the village. It's been occupied for two hundred years. Once we make it livable inside, we plan on enlarging the garden, eventually cultivating all the way to the spruce forest there. We're going to sink a well, too." The small garden was bursting with vegetables, mostly of the leafy variety: cabbages, spinach, lettuce. A row of sunflowers, taller than the cabin roof and heavy with seed, lined the path to the cabin door. Over time, the whole cabin had sunk a half-meter into the silty soil, and the walkway was a worn, shallow trench.

"Are you going to tell me what the doxie was talking about?" said Anne.

Cathy stopped at the open door and said, "Cathy wants to do that."

Inside the cabin, the most elderly woman that Anne had ever seen stood at the stove and stirred a steamy pot with a big, wooden spoon. She put down the spoon and wiped her hands on her apron. She patted her white hair, which was plaited in a bun on top of her head, and turned her full, round, peasant's body to face Anne. She looked at Anne for several long moments and said, "Well!"

"Indeed," replied Anne.

"Come in, come in. Make yourself to home."

The entire cabin was a single small room. It was dim inside, with only two small windows cut through the massive log walls. Anne walked around the cluttered space that was bedroom, living room, kitchen, and storeroom. The only partitions were walls of boxed food and provisions. The ceiling beam was draped with bunches of drying herbs and underwear. The flooring, uneven and rotten in places, was covered with odd scraps of carpet.

"You live here?" Anne said incredulously.

"I am privileged to live here."

A mouse emerged from under the barrel stove in the center of the room and dashed to cover inside a stack of spruce kindling. Anne could hear the valley breeze whistling in the creosote-soaked stovepipe. "Forgive me," said Anne, "but you're the real, physical Cathy?"

"Yes," said Cathy, patting her ample hip, "still on the hoof, so to speak." She sat down in one of two battered, mismatched chairs and motioned for Anne to take the other.

Anne sat cautiously; the chair seemed solid enough. "No offense, but the Cathy I knew liked nice things."

"The Cathy you knew was fortunate to learn the true value of things."

Anne looked around the room and noticed a little table with carved legs and an inlaid top of polished gemstones and rare woods. It was strikingly out of place here. Moreover, it was hers. Cathy pointed to a large framed mirror mounted to the logs high on the far wall. It too was Anne's.

"Did I give you these things?"

Cathy studied her a moment. "No, Ben did."

"Tell me."

"I hate to spoil that lovely newlywed happiness of yours."

"The what?" Anne put down her clutch bouquet and felt her face with her hands. She got up and went to look at herself in the mirror. The room it reflected was like a scene from some strange fairy tale about a crone and a bride in a woodcutter's hut. The bride was smiling from ear to ear. Anne decided this was either the happiest bride in history or a lunatic in a white dress. She turned away, embarrassed. "Believe me," she said, "I don't feel anything like that. The opposite, in fact."

"Sorry to hear it." Cathy got up to stir the pot on the stove. "I was the first to notice her disease. That was back in college when we were girls. I took it to be youthful eccentricity. After graduation, after her marriage, she grew progressively worse. Bouts of depression that deepened and lengthened. She was finally diagnosed to be suffering from profound chronic pathological depression. Ben placed her under psychiatric care, a whole raft of specialists. She endured chemical therapy, shock therapy, even old-fashioned psychoanalysis. Nothing helped, and only after she died . . ."

Anne gave a start. "Anne's dead! Of course. Why didn't I figure that out?"

"Yes, dear, dead these many years."

"How?"

Cathy returned to her chair. "When they decided her condition had an organic etiology, they augmented the serotonin receptors in her hindbrain. Pretty nasty business, if you ask me. They thought they had her stabilized. Not cured, but well enough to lead an outwardly normal life. Then one day, she disappeared. We were frantic. She managed to elude the authorities for a week. When we found her, she was pregnant."

"What? Oh yes. I remember seeing Anne pregnant."

"That was Bobby." Cathy waited for Anne to say something. When she didn't, Cathy said, "He wasn't Ben's."

"Oh, I see," said Anne. "Whose was he?"

"I was hoping you'd know. She didn't tell you? Then no one knows. The paternal DNA was unregistered. So it wasn't commercial sperm nor, thankfully, from a licensed clone. It might have been from anybody, from some stoned streetsitter. We had plenty of those then."

"The baby's name was Bobby?"

"Yes, Anne named him Bobby. She was in and out of clinics for years. One day, during a remission, she announced she was going shopping. The last person she talked to was Bobby. His sixth birthday was coming up in a couple of weeks. She told him she was going out to find him a pony for his birthday. That was the last time any of us saw her. She checked herself into a hospice and filled out the request for nurse-assisted suicide. During the three-day cooling-off period, she cooperated with the obligatory counseling, but she refused all visitors. She wouldn't even see me. Ben filed an injunction, claimed she was incompetent due to her disease, but the court disagreed. She chose to ingest a fast-acting poison, if I recall. Her recorded last words were, 'Please don't hate me.'"

"Poison?"

"Yes. Her ashes arrived in a little cardboard box on Bobby's sixth birthday. No one had told him where she'd gone. He thought it was a gift from her and opened it."

"I see. Does Bobby hate me?"

"I don't know. He was a weird little boy. As soon as he could get out, he did. He left for space school when he was thirteen. He and Ben never hit it off."

"Does Benjamin hate me?"

Whatever was in the pot boiled over, and Cathy hurried to the stove. "Ben? Oh, she lost Ben long before she died. In fact, I've always believed he helped push her over the edge. He was never able to tolerate other people's weaknesses. Once it was evident how sick she was, he made a lousy husband. He should've just divorced her, but you know him—his almighty pride." She took a bowl from a shelf and ladled hot soup into it. She sliced a piece of bread. "Afterward, he went off the deep end himself. Withdrew. Mourned, I suppose. A couple of years later he was back to normal. Good ol' happy-go-lucky Ben. Made some money. Respoused."

"He destroyed all my sims, didn't he?"

"He might have, but he said Anne did. I tended to believe him at the time." Cathy brought her lunch to the little inlaid table. "I'd offer you some, but . . ." she said and began to eat. "So, what are your plans?"

"Plans?"

"Yes, Simopolis."

Anne tried to think of Simopolis, but her thoughts quickly became muddled. It was odd; she was able to think clearly about the past—her memories were clear—but the future only confused her. "I don't know," she said at last. "I suppose I need to ask Benjamin."

Cathy considered this. "I suppose you're right. But remember, you're always welcome to live with us in Cathyland."

"Thank you," said Anne. "You're a friend." Anne watched the old woman eat. The spoon trembled each time she brought it close to her lips, and she had to lean forward to quickly catch it before it spilled.

"Cathy," said Anne, "there's something you could do for me. I don't feel like a bride anymore. Could you remove this hideous expression from my face?"

"Why do you say hideous?" Cathy said and put the spoon down. She gazed longingly at Anne. "If you don't like how you look, why don't you edit yourself?"

"Because I don't know how."

"Use your editor," Cathy said and seemed to unfocus her eyes. "Oh my, I forget how simple you early ones were. I'm not sure I'd know where to begin." After a little while, she returned to her soup and said, "I'd better not; you could end up with two noses or something."

"Then what about this gown?"

Cathy unfocused again and looked. She lurched suddenly, knocking the table and spilling soup.

"What is it?" said Anne. "Is something the matter?"

"A news pip," said Cathy. "There's rioting breaking out in Provideniya. That's the regional capital here. Something about Manumission Day. My Russian isn't so good yet. Oh, there's pictures of dead people, a bombing. Listen, Anne, I'd better send you . . ."

In the blink of an eye, Anne was back in her living room. She was tiring of all this instantaneous travel, especially as she had no control over the destination. The room was vacant, the spouses gone—thankfully—and Benjamin not back yet. And apparently the little blue-faced message medallion had been busy replicating itself, for now there were hundreds of them filling up most of the wall space. They were a noisy lot, all shrieking and cursing at each other. The din was painful. When they noticed her, however, they all shut up at once and stared at her with naked hostility. In Anne's opinion, this weird day had already lasted too long. Then a terrible thought struck her—sims don't sleep.

"You," she said, addressing the original medallion, or at least the one she thought was the original, "call Benjamin."

"The fuck you think I am?" said the insolent little face. "Your personal secretary?"

"Aren't you?"

"No, I'm not! In fact, I own this place now, and you're trespassing. So you'd better get lost before I delete your ass!" All the others joined in, taunting her, louder and louder.

"Stop it!" she cried, to no effect. She noticed a medallion elongating, stretching itself until it was twice its length, when, with a pop, it divided into two smaller medallions. More of them divided. They were spreading to the other wall, the ceiling, the floor. "Benjamin!" she cried. "Can you hear me?"

Suddenly all the racket ceased. The medallions dropped off the wall and vanished before hitting the floor. Only one remained, the original one next to the door, but now it was an inert plastic disc with a dull expression frozen on its face.

A man stood in the center of the room. He smiled when Anne noticed him. It was the elderly Benjamin from the auditorium, the real Benjamin. He still wore his clownish leisure suit. "How lovely," he said, gazing at her. "I'd forgotten how lovely."

"Oh, really?" said Anne. "I would have thought that doxie thingy might have reminded you."

"My, my," said Ben. "You sims certainly exchange data quickly. You left the lecture hall not fifteen minutes ago, and already you know enough to convict me." He strode around the room touching things. He stopped beneath the mirror, lifted the blue vase from the shelf, and turned it in his hands before carefully replacing it. "There's speculation, you know, that before Manumission at midnight tonight, you sims will have dispersed all known information so evenly among yourselves that there'll be a sort of data entropy. And since Simopolis is nothing but data, it will assume a featureless, grey profile. Simopolis will become the first flat universe." He laughed, which caused him to cough and nearly lose his balance. He clutched the back of the sofa for support. He sat down and continued to cough and hack until he turned red in the face.

"Are you all right?" Anne said, patting him on the back.

"Yes, fine," he managed to say. "Thank you." He caught his breath and motioned for her to sit next to him. "I get a little tickle in the back of my throat that the autodoc can't seem to fix." His color returned to normal. Up close, Anne could see the papery skin and slight tremor of age. All in all, Cathy had seemed to have held up better than he.

"If you don't mind my asking," she said, "just how old are you?"

At the question, he bobbed to his feet. "I am one hundred and seventy-eight." He raised his arms and wheeled around for inspection. "Radical gerontology," he exclaimed, "don't you love it? And I'm eighty-five percent original equipment, which is remarkable by today's standards." His effort made him dizzy and he sat again.

"Yes, remarkable," said Anne, "though radical gerontology doesn't seem to have arrested time altogether."

"Not yet, but it will," Ben said. "There are wonders around every corner! Miracles in every lab." He grew suddenly morose. "At least there were until we were conquered."

"Conquered?"

"Yes, conquered! What else would you call it when they control every aspect of our lives, from RM acquisition to personal patenting? And now *this*—robbing us of our own private nonbiologiks." He grew passionate in his discourse. "It flies in the face of natural capitalism, natural stakeholding—I dare say—in the face of Nature itself! The only explanation I've seen on the wad is the not-so-preposterous proposition that whole strategically placed BODs have been surreptitiously killed and replaced by *machines!*"

"I have no idea what you're talking about," said Anne.

He seemed to deflate. He patted her hand and looked around the room. "What is this place?"

"It's our home, your townhouse. Don't you recognize it?"

"That was quite a while ago. I must have sold it after you—" He paused. "Tell me, have the Bens briefed you on everything?"

"Not the Bens, but yes, I know."

"Good, good."

"There is one thing I'd like to know. Where's Bobby?"

"Ah, Bobby, our little headache. Dead now, I'm afraid, or at least that's the current theory. Sorry."

Anne paused to see if the news would deepen her melancholy. "How?" she said.

"He signed on one of the first millennial ships—the colony convoy. Half a million people in deep biostasis on their way to Canopus system. They were gone a century, twelve trillion kilometers from Earth, when their data streams suddenly quit. That was a decade ago, and not a peep out of them since."

"What happened to them?"

"No one knows. Equipment failure is unlikely; there were a dozen independent ships separated by a million klicks. A star going supernova? A well-organized mutiny? It's all speculation."

"What was he like?"

"A foolish young man. He never forgave you, you know, and he hated me to my core, not that I blamed him. The whole experience made me swear off children."

"I don't remember you ever being fond of children."

He studied her through red-rimmed eyes. "I guess you'd be the one to know." He settled back in the sofa. He seemed very tired. "You can't imagine the jolt I got a little while ago when I looked across all those rows of Bens and spouses and saw this solitary, shockingly white gown of yours." He sighed. "And this room. It's a shrine. Did we really live here? Were these our things? That mirror is yours, right? I would never own anything like that. But that blue vase, I remember that one. I threw it into Puget Sound."

"You did *what?*"

"With your ashes."

"Oh."

"So, tell me," said Ben, "what were we like? Before you go off to Simopolis and become a different person, tell me about us. I kept my promise. That's one thing I never forgot."

"What promise?"

"Never to reset you."

"Wasn't much to reset."

"I guess not."

They sat quietly for a while. His breathing grew deep and regular, and she thought he was napping. But he stirred and said, "Tell me what we did yesterday, for example."

"Yesterday we went to see Karl and Nancy about the awning we rented."

Benjamin yawned. "And who were Karl and Nancy?"

"My great uncle and his new girlfriend."

"That's right. I remember, I think. And they helped us prepare for the wedding?"

"Yes, especially Nancy."

"And how did we get there, to Karl and Nancy's? Did we walk? Take some means of public conveyance?"

"We had a car."

"A car! An automobile? There were still *cars* in those days? How fun. What kind was it? What color?"

"A Nissan Empire. Emerald green."

"And did we drive it, or did it drive itself?"

"It drove itself, of course."

Ben closed his eyes and smiled. "I can see it. Go on. What did we do there?"

"We had dinner."

"What was my favorite dish in those days?"

"Stuffed pork chops."

He chuckled. "It still is! Isn't that extraordinary? Some things never change. Of course they're vat grown now and criminally expensive."

Ben's memories, once nudged, began to unfold on their own, and he asked her a thousand questions, and she answered them until she realized he had fallen asleep. But she continued to talk until, glancing down, she noticed he had vanished. She was all alone again. Nevertheless, she continued talking, for days it seemed, to herself. But it didn't help. She felt as bad as ever, and she realized that she wanted Benjamin, not the old one, but her *own* Benjamin.

Anne went to the medallion next to the door. "You," she said, and it opened its bulging eyes to glare at her. "Call Benjamin."

"He's occupied."

"I don't care. Call him anyway."

"The other Bens say he's undergoing a procedure and cannot be disturbed."

"What kind of procedure?"

"A codon interlarding. They say to be patient; they'll return him as soon as possible." The medallion added, "By the way, the Bens don't like you, and neither do I."

With that, the medallion began to grunt and stretch, and it pulled itself in two. Now there were two identical medallions glaring at her. The new one said, "And *I* don't like you either." Then both of them began to grunt and stretch.

"Stop!" said Anne. "I command you to stop that this very instant." But they just laughed as they divided into four, then eight, then sixteen medallions. "You're not people," she said. "Stop it or I'll have you destroyed!"

"*You're* not people either," they screeched at her.

There was soft laughter behind her, and a voice-like sensation said, *Come, come, do we need this hostility?* Anne turned and found the eminence grise, the astounding presence, still in his grey uniform and cap, floating in her living room. *Hello, Anne,* he said, and she flushed with excitement.

"Hello," she said and, unable to restrain herself, asked, "What are you?"

Ah, curiosity. Always a good sign in a creature. I am an eminence grise of the World Trade Council.

"No. I mean, are you a sim, like me?"

I am not. Though I have been fashioned from concepts first explored by simulacrum technology, I have no independent existence. I am but one extension—and a low level one at that—of the Axial Beowulf Processor at the World Trade Council headquarters in Geneva. His smile was pure sunshine. *And if you think I'm something, you should see my persona prime.*

Now, Anne, are you ready for your exam?

"The Lolly test?"

Yes, the Lolly Shear Human Cognition Test. Please assume an attitude most conducive to processing, and we shall begin.

Anne looked around the room and went to the sofa. She noticed for the first time that she could feel her legs and feet; she could feel the crisp fabric of her gown brushing against her skin. She reclined on the sofa and said, "I'm ready."

Splendid, said the eminence hovering above her. *First we must read you. You are of an early binary design. We will analyze your architecture.*

The room seemed to fall away. Anne seemed to expand in all directions. There was something inside her mind tugging at her thoughts. It was mostly pleasant, like someone brushing her hair and loosening the knots. But when it ended and she once again saw the eminence grise, his face wore a look of concern. "What?" she said.

You are an accurate mapping of a human nervous system that was dysfunctional in certain structures that moderate affect. Certain transport enzymes were missing, causing cellular membranes to become less permeable to essential elements. Dendritic synapses were compromised. The digital architecture current at the time you were created compounded this defect. Coded tells cannot be resolved, and thus they loop upon themselves. Errors cascade. We are truly sorry.

"Can you fix me?" she said.

The only repair possible would replace so much code that you wouldn't be Anne anymore.

"Then what am I to do?"

Before we explore your options, let us continue the test to determine your human status. Agreed?

"I guess."

You are part of a simulacrum cast to commemorate the spousal compact between Anne Wellhut Franklin and Benjamin Malley. Please describe the exchange of vows.

Anne did so, haltingly at first, but with increasing gusto as each memory evoked others. She recounted the ceremony, from donning her grandmother's gown in the downstairs guest room and the procession across garden flagstones, to the shower of rice as she and her new husband fled indoors.

The eminence seemed to hang on every word. *Very well spoken*, he said when she had finished. *Directed memory is one hallmark of human sentience, and yours is of remarkable clarity and range. Well done! We shall now explore other criteria. Please consider this scenario. You are standing at the garden altar as you have described, but this time when the officiator asks Benjamin if he will take you for better or worse, Benjamin looks at you and replies, "For better, sure, but not for worse."*

"I don't understand. He didn't say that."

Imagination is a cornerstone of self-awareness. We are asking you to tell us a little story not about what happened but about what might have happened in other circumstances. So once again, let us pretend that Benjamin replies, "For better, but not for worse." How do you respond?

Prickly pain blossomed in Anne's head. The more she considered the eminence's question, the worse it got. "But that's not how it happened. He *wanted* to marry me."

The eminence grise smiled encouragingly. *We know that. In this exercise we want to explore hypothetical situations. We want you to make-believe.*

Tell a story, pretend, hypothesize, make-believe, yes, yes, she got it. She understood perfectly what he wanted of her. She knew that people could make things up, that even children could make-believe. Anne was desperate to comply, but each time she pictured Benjamin at the altar, in his pink bowtie, he opened his mouth and out came, "I do." How could it be any other way? She tried again; she tried harder, but it always came out the same, "I do, I do, I do." And like a dull toothache tapped back to life, she throbbed in pain. She was failing the test, and there was nothing she could do about it.

Again the eminence kindly prompted her. *Tell us one thing you might have said.*
"I can't."

We are sorry, said the eminence at last. His expression reflected Anne's own defeat. *Your level of awareness, although beautiful in its own right, does not qualify you as human. Wherefore, under Article D of the Chattel Conventions we declare you the legal property of the registered owner of this simulacrum. You shall not enter Simopolis as a free and autonomous citizen. We are truly sorry.* Grief-stricken, the eminence began to ascend toward the ceiling.

"Wait," Anne cried, clutching her head. "You must fix me before you leave."
We leave you as we found you, defective and unrepairable.
"But I feel worse than ever!"
If your continued existence proves undesirable, ask your owner to delete you.

"But . . ." she said to the empty room. Anne tried to sit up, but couldn't move. This simulated body of hers, which no longer felt like anything in particular, nevertheless felt exhausted. She sprawled on the sofa, unable to lift even an arm, and stared at the ceiling. She was so heavy that the sofa itself seemed to sink into the floor, and everything grew dark around her. She would have liked to sleep, to bring an end to this horrible day, or be shelved, or even reset back to scratch.

Instead, time simply passed. Outside the living room, Simopolis changed and changed again. Inside the living room, the medallions, feeding off her misery, multiplied till they covered the walls and floor and even spread across the ceiling above her. They taunted her, raining down insults, but she could not hear them. All she heard was the unrelenting drip of her own thoughts. *I am defective. I am worthless. I am Anne.*

She didn't notice Benjamin enter the room, nor the abrupt cessation of the medallions' racket. Not until Benjamin leaned over her did she see him, and then she saw two of him. Side-by-side, two Benjamins, mirror images of each other. "Anne," they said in perfect unison.

"Go away," she said. "Go away and send me my Benjamin."
"I am your Benjamin," said the duo.

Anne struggled to see them. They were exactly the same, but for a subtle difference: the one wore a happy, wolfish grin, as Benjamin had during the sim casting, while the other seemed frightened and concerned.

"Are you all right?" they said.

"No, I'm not. But what happened to you? Who's he?" She wasn't sure which one to speak to.

The Benjamins both raised a hand, indicating the other, and said, "Electroneural engineering! Don't you love it?" Anne glanced back and forth, comparing the two. While one seemed to be wearing a rigid mask, as she was, the other displayed a whole range of emotion. Not only that, its skin had tone, while the other's was doughy. "The other Bens made it for me," the Benjamins said. "They say I can trans-late myself into it with negligible loss of personality. It has interactive sensation, ho-listic emoting, robust corporeality, and it's crafted down to the molecular level. It can eat, get drunk, and dream. It even has an orgasm routine. It's like being human again, only better because you never wear out."

"I'm thrilled for you."

"For us, Anne," said the Benjamins. "They'll fix you up with one, too."

"How? There are no modern Annes. What will they put me into, a doxie?"

"Well, that certainly was discussed, but you could pick any body you wanted."

"I suppose you have a nice one already picked out."

"The Bens showed me a few, but it's up to you, of course."

"Indeed," said Anne, "I truly am pleased for you. Now go away."

"Why, Anne? What's wrong?"

"You really have to ask?" Anne sighed. "Look, maybe I could get used to another body. What's a body, after all? But it's my personality that's broken. How will they fix that?"

"They've discussed it," said the Benjamins, who stood up and began to pace in a figure eight. "They say they can make patches from some of the other spouses."

"Oh, Benjamin, if you could only hear what you're saying!"

"But why, Annie? It's the only way we can enter Simopolis together."

"Then go, by all means. Go to your precious Simopolis. I'm not going. I'm not good enough."

"Why do you say that?" said the Benjamins, who stopped in their tracks to look at her. One grimaced, and the other just grinned. "Was the eminence grise here? Did you take the test?"

Anne couldn't remember much about the visit except that she took the test. "Yes, and I *failed*." Anne watched the modern Benjamin's lovely face as he worked through this news.

Suddenly the two Benjamins pointed a finger at each other and said, "Delete you." The modern one vanished.

"No!" said Anne. "Countermand! Why'd you do that? I *want* you to have it."

"What for? I'm not going anywhere without you," Benjamin said. "Besides, I thought the whole idea was dumb from the start, but the Bens insisted I give you the option. Come, I want to show you another idea, *my* idea." He tried to help Anne from the sofa, but she wouldn't budge, so he picked her up and carried her across the room. "They installed an editor in me, and I'm learning to use it. I've discovered something intriguing about this creaky old simulacrum of ours." He carried her to a spot near the window. "Know what this is? It's where we stood for the simographer. It's where we began. Here, can you stand up?" He set her on her feet and supported her. "Feel it?"

"Feel what?" she said.

"Hush. Just feel."

All she felt was dread.

"Give it a chance, Annie, I beg you. Try to remember what you were feeling as we posed here."

"I can't."

"Please try. Do you remember this?" he said and moved in close with his hungry lips. She turned away—and something clicked. She remembered doing that before.

Benjamin said, "I think they kissed."

Anne was startled by the truth of what he said. It made sense. They were caught in a simulacrum cast a moment before a kiss. One moment later they—the real Anne and Benjamin—must have kissed. What she felt now, stirring within her, was the anticipation of that kiss, her body's urge and her heart's caution. The real Anne would have refused him once, maybe twice, and then, all achy inside, would have granted him a kiss. And so they had kissed, the real Anne and Benjamin, and a moment later gone out to the wedding reception and their difficult fate. It was the *promise* of that kiss that glowed in Anne, that was captured in the very strings of her code.

"Do you feel it?" Benjamin asked.

"I'm beginning to."

Anne looked at her gown. It was her grandmother's, snowy taffeta with point d'esprit lace. She turned the ring on her finger. It was braided bands of yellow and white gold. They had spent an afternoon picking it out. Where was her clutch? She had left it in Cathyland. She looked at Benjamin's handsome face, the pink carnation, the room, the table piled high with gifts.

"Are you happy?" Benjamin asked.

She didn't have to think. She was ecstatic, but she was afraid to answer in case she spoiled it. "How did you do that?" she said. "A moment ago, I wanted to die."

"We can stay on this spot," he said.

"What? No. Can we?"

"Why not? I, for one, would choose nowhere else."

Just to hear him say that was thrilling. "But what about Simopolis?"

"We'll bring Simopolis to us," he said. "We'll have people in. They can pull up chairs."

She laughed out loud. "What a silly, silly notion, Mr. Malley!"

"No, really. We'll be like the bride and groom atop a wedding cake. We'll be known far and wide. We'll be famous."

"We'll be freaks," she laughed.

"Say yes, my love. Say you will."

They stood close but not touching, thrumming with happiness, balanced on the moment of their creation, when suddenly and without warning the lights dimmed, and Anne's thoughts flitted away like larks.

Old Ben awoke in the dark. "Anne?" he said, and groped for her. It took a moment to realize that he was alone in his media room. It had been a most trying afternoon, and he'd fallen asleep. "What time is it?"

"Eight-oh-three PM," replied the room.

That meant he'd slept for two hours. Midnight was still four hours away. "Why's it so cold in here?"

"Central heating is off line," replied the house.

"Off line?" How was that possible? "When will it be back?"

"That's unknown. Utilities do not respond to my enquiry."

"I don't understand. Explain."

"There are failures in many outside systems. No explanation is currently available."

At first, Ben was confused; things just didn't fail anymore. What about the dynamic redundancies and self-healing routines? But then he remembered that the homeowners' association to which he belonged contracted out most domicile functions to management agencies, and who knew where they were located? They might be on the Moon for all he knew, and with all those trillions of sims in Simopolis sucking up capacity . . . *It's begun*, he thought, *the idiocy of our leaders*. "At least turn on the lights," he said, half expecting even this to fail. But the lights came on, and he went to his bedroom for a sweater. He heard a great amount of commotion through the wall in the apartment next door. *It must be one hell of a party*, he thought, *to exceed the wall's buffering capacity. Or maybe the wall buffers are off line too?*

The main door chimed. He went to the foyer and asked the door who was there. The door projected the outer hallway. There were three men waiting there, young, rough-looking, ill-dressed. Two of them appeared to be clones, jerries.

"How can I help you?" he said.

"Yes, sir," one of the jerries said, not looking directly at the door. "We're here to fix your houseputer."

"I didn't call you, and my houseputer isn't sick," he said. "It's the net that's out." Then he noticed they carried sledgehammers and screwdrivers, hardly computer tools, and a wild thought crossed his mind. "What are you doing, going around unplugging things?"

The jerry looked confused. "Unplugging, sir?"

"Turning things off."

"Oh, no sir! Routine maintenance, that's all." The men hid their tools behind their backs.

They must think I'm stupid, Ben thought. While he watched, more men and women passed in the hall and hailed the door at the suite opposite his. It wasn't the glut of sim traffic choking the system, he realized—the system *itself* was being pulled apart. But why? "Is this going on everywhere?" he said. "This routine maintenance?"

"Oh, yessir. Everywhere. All over town. All over the world as far as we can tell."

A coup? *By service people?* By common clones? It made no sense. Unless, he reasoned, you considered that the lowest creature on the totem pole of life is a clone, and the only thing lower than a clone is a sim. And why would clones agree to accept sims as equals? Manumission Day, indeed. Uppidy Day was more like it. "Door," he commanded, "open."

"Security protocol rules this an unwanted intrusion," said the house. "The door must remain locked."

"I order you to open the door. I overrule your protocol."

But the door remained stubbornly shut. "Your identity cannot be confirmed with Domicile Central," said the house. "You lack authority over protocol-level commands." The door abruptly quit projecting the outside hall.

Ben stood close to the door and shouted through it to the people outside. "My door won't obey me."

He could hear a muffled "Stand back!" and immediately fierce blows rained down upon the door. Ben knew it would do no good. He had spent a lot of money for a secure entryway. Short of explosives, there was nothing they could do to break in.

"Stop!" Ben cried. "The door is armed." But they couldn't hear him. If he didn't disable the houseputer himself, someone was going to get hurt. But how? He didn't even know exactly where it was installed. He circumambulated the living room looking for clues. It might not even actually be located in the apartment, nor within the block itself. He went to the laundry room, where the utilidor—plumbing and cabling—entered his apartment. He broke the seal to the service panel. Inside was a blank screen. "Show me the electronic floor plan of this suite," he said.

The house said, "I cannot comply. You lack command authority to order system-level operations. Please close the keptel panel and await further instructions."

"What instructions? Whose instructions?"

There was the slightest pause before the house replied, "All contact with outside services has been interrupted. Please await further instructions."

His condo's houseputer, denied contact with Domicile Central, had fallen back to its most basic programming. "You are degraded," he told it. "Shut yourself down for repair."

"I cannot comply. You lack command authority to order system-level operations."

The outside battering continued, but not against his door. Ben followed the noise to the bedroom. The whole wall vibrated like a drumhead. "Careful, careful," he cried as the first sledgehammers breached the wall above his bed. "You'll ruin my Harger." As quick as he could, he yanked the precious oil painting from the wall, moments before panels and studs collapsed on his bed in a shower of gypsum dust and isomere ribbons. The men and women on the other side hooted approval and rushed through the gap. Ben stood there hugging the painting to his chest and looking into his neighbor's media room as the invaders climbed over his bed and surrounded him. They were mostly jerries and lulus, but plenty of free-range people too.

"We came to fix your houseputer!" said a jerry, maybe the same jerry as from the hallway.

Ben glanced into his neighbor's media room and saw his neighbor, Mr. Murkowski, lying in a puddle of blood. At first Ben was shocked, but then he thought that it served him right. He'd never liked the man, nor his politics. He was boorish, and he kept cats. "Oh, yeah?" Ben said to the crowd. "What kept you?"

The intruders cheered again, and Ben led them in a charge to the laundry room. But they surged past him to the kitchen, where they opened all his cabinets and pulled their contents to the floor. Finally they found what they were looking for: a small panel Ben had seen a thousand times but had never given a thought. He'd taken it for the fuse box or circuit breaker, though now that he thought about it, there hadn't been any household fuses for a century or more. A young woman, a lulu, opened it and removed a container no thicker than her thumb.

"Give it to me," Ben said.

"Relax, old man," said the lulu. "We'll deal with it." She carried it to the sink and forced open the lid.

"No, wait!" said Ben, and he tried to shove his way through the crowd. They restrained him roughly, but he persisted. "That's mine! I want to destroy it!"

"Let him go," said a jerry.

They allowed him through, and the woman handed him the container. He peered into it. Gram for gram, electroneural paste was the most precious, most engineered, most highly regulated commodity under Sol. This dollop was enough to run his house, media, computing needs, communications, archives, autodoc, and everything else. Without it, was civilized life still possible?

Ben took a dinner knife from the sink, stuck it into the container, and stirred. The paste made a sucking sound and had the consistency of marmalade. The kitchen lights flickered and went out. "Spill it," ordered the woman. Ben scraped the sides of the container and spilled it into the sink. The goo dazzled in the darkness as its trillions of ruptured nanosynapses fired spasmodically. It was beautiful, really, until the woman set fire to it. The smoke was greasy and smelled of pork.

The rampagers quickly snatched up the packages of foodstuffs from the floor, emptied the rest of his cupboards into their pockets, raided his cold locker, and fled the apartment through the now disengaged front door. As the sounds of the revolution gradually receded, Ben stood at his sink and watched the flickering pyre. "Take that, you fuck," he said. He felt such glee as he hadn't felt since he was a boy. *"That'll* teach you what's human and what's not!"

Ben went to his bedroom for an overcoat, groping his way in the dark. The apartment was eerily silent, with the houseputer dead and all its little slave processors idle. In a drawer next to his ruined bed, he found a hand flash. On a shelf in the laundry room, he found a hammer. Thus armed, he made his way to the front door, which was propped open with the rolled-up foyer carpet. The hallway was dark and silent, and he listened for the strains of the future. He heard them on the floor above. With the elevator off line, he hurried to the stairs.

Anne's thoughts coalesced, and she remembered who and what she was. She and Benjamin still stood in their living room on the sweet spot near the window. Benjamin was studying his hands. "We've been shelved again," she told him, "but not reset."

"But . . ." he said in disbelief, "that wasn't supposed to happen anymore."

There were others standing at the china cabinet across the room, two shirtless youths with pear-shaped bottoms. One held up a cut crystal glass and said, "Anu 'goblet' su? Alle binary. Allum binary!"

The other replied, "Binary stitial crystal."

"Hold on there!" said Anne. "Put that back!" She walked toward them, but, once off the spot, she was slammed by her old feelings of utter and hopeless desolation. So suddenly did her mood swing that she lost her balance and fell to the floor. Benjamin hurried to help her up. The strangers stared gape-mouthed at them. They looked to be no more than twelve or thirteen years old, but they were bald and had curtains of flabby flesh draped over their waists. The one holding the glass had ponderous greenish breasts with roseate tits. Astonished, she said, "Su artiflums, Benji?"

"No," said the other, "ni artiflums—sims." He was taller. He, too, had breasts, greyish dugs with tits like pearls. He smiled idiotically and said, "Hi, guys."

"Holy crap!" said Benjamin, who practically carried Anne over to them for a closer look. "Holy crap," he repeated.

The weird boy threw up his hands, "Nanobioremediation! Don't you love it?"

"Benjamin?" said Anne.

"You know well, Benji," said the girl, "that sims are forbidden."

"Not these," replied the boy.

Anne reached out and yanked the glass from the girl's hand, startling her. "How did it do that?" said the girl. She flipped her hand, and the glass slipped from Anne's grip and flew back to her.

"Give it to me," said Anne. "That's my tumbler."

"Did you hear it? It called it a tumbler, not a goblet." The girl's eyes seemed to unfocus, and she said, "Nu! A goblet has a foot and stem." A goblet materialized in the air before her, revolving slowly. "Greater capacity. Often made from precious metals." The goblet dissolved in a puff of smoke. "In any case, Benji, *you'll* catch prison when I report the artiflums."

"These are binary," he said. "Binaries are unregulated."

Benjamin interrupted them. "Isn't it past midnight yet?"

"Midnight?" said the boy.

"Aren't we supposed to be in Simopolis?"

"Simopolis?" The boy's eyes unfocused briefly. "Oh! Simopolis. Manumission Day at midnight. How could I forget?"

The girl left them and went to the refectory table, where she picked up a gift. Anne followed her and grabbed it away. The girl appraised Anne coolly. "State your appellation," she said.

"Get out of my house," said Anne.

The girl picked up another gift, and again Anne snatched it away. The girl said, "You can't harm me," but seemed uncertain.

The boy came over to stand next to the girl. "Treese, meet Anne. Anne, this is Treese. Treese deals in antiques, which, if my memory serves, so did you."

"I have never *dealt* in antiques," said Anne. "I *collect* them."

"Anne?" said Treese. "Not *that* Anne? Benji, tell me this isn't *that* Anne!" She laughed and pointed at the sofa where Benjamin sat hunched over, head in hands. "Is that *you*? Is that you, Benji?" She held her enormous belly and laughed. "And you were married to *this*?"

Anne went over to sit with Benjamin. He seemed devastated, despite the silly grin on his face. "It's all gone," he said. "Simopolis. All the Bens. Everything."

"Don't worry. It's in storage someplace," Anne said. "The eminence grise wouldn't let them hurt it."

"You don't understand. The World Council was abolished. There was a war. We've been shelved for over three hundred years! They destroyed all the computers. Computers are banned. So are artificial personalities."

"Nonsense," said Anne. "If computers are banned, how can they be *playing* us?"

"Good point," Benjamin said and sat up straight. "I still have my editor. I'll find out."

Anne watched the two bald youngsters take an inventory of the room. Treese ran her fingers over the inlaid top of the tea table. She unwrapped several of Anne's gifts. She posed in front of the mirror. The sudden anger that Anne had felt earlier faded into an overwhelming sense of defeat. *Let her have everything*, she thought. *Why should I care?*

"We're running inside some kind of shell," said Benjamin, "but completely different from Simopolis. I've never seen anything like this. But at least we know he lied to me. There must be computers of some sort."

"Ooooh," Treese crooned, lifting Anne's blue vase from the mantel. In an instant, Anne was up and across the room.

"Put that back," she demanded, "and get out of my house!" She tried to grab the vase, but now there seemed to be some sort of barrier between her and the girl.

"Really, Benji," Treese said, "this one is willful. If I don't report you, they'll charge me too."

"It's *not* willful," the boy said with irritation. "It was programmed to appear willful, but it has no will of its own. If you want to report me, go ahead. Just please shut up about it. Of course you might want to check the codex first." To Anne he said, "Relax, we're not hurting anything, just making copies."

"It's not yours to copy."

"Nonsense. Of course it is. I own the chip."

Benjamin joined them. "Where is the chip? And how can you run us if computers are banned?"

"I never said computers were banned, just *artificial* ones." With both hands he grabbed the rolls of flesh spilling over his gut. "Ectopic hippocampus!" He cupped his breasts. "Amygdaloid reduncles! We can culture modified brain tissue outside the skull, as much as we want. It's more powerful than paste, and it's *safe*. Now, if you'll excuse us, there's more to inventory, and I don't need your permission. If you cooperate, everything will be pleasant. If you don't—it makes no difference whatsoever." He smiled at Anne. "I'll just pause you till we're done."

"Then pause me," Anne shrieked. "Delete me!" Benjamin pulled her away and shushed her. "I can't stand this anymore," she said. "I'd rather not exist!" He tried to lead her to their spot, but she refused to go.

"We'll feel better there," he said.

"I don't *want* to feel better. I don't want to *feel*! I want everything to *stop*. Don't you understand? This is hell. We've landed in hell!"

"But heaven is right over there," he said, pointing to the spot.

"Then go. Enjoy yourself."

"Annie, Annie," he said. "I'm just as upset as you, but there's nothing we can do about it. We're just things, his things."

"That's fine for you," she said, "but I'm a broken thing, and it's too much." She held her head with both hands. "Please, Benjamin, if you love me, use your editor and make it stop!"

Benjamin stared at her. "I can't."

"Can't or won't?"

"I don't know. Both."

"Then you're no better than all the other Benjamins," she said and turned away.

"Wait," he said. "That's not fair. And it's not true. Let me tell you something I learned in Simopolis. The other Bens despised me." When Anne looked at him he said, "It's true. They lost Anne and had to go on living without her. But I never did. I'm the only Benjamin who never lost Anne."

"Nice," said Anne, "blame me."

"No. Don't you see? I'm not blaming you. They ruined their *own* lives. We're innocent. We came before any of that happened. We're the Ben and Anne before anything bad happened. We're the best Ben and Anne. We're *perfect*." He drew her across the floor to stand in front of the spot. "And thanks to our primitive programming, no matter what happens, as long as we stand right there, we can be ourselves. That's what I want. Don't you want it too?"

Anne stared at the tiny patch of floor at her feet. She remembered the happiness she'd felt there like something from a dream. How could feelings be real if you had to stand in one place to feel them? Nevertheless, Anne stepped on the spot, and Benjamin joined her. Her despair did not immediately lift.

"Relax," said Benjamin. "It takes a while. We have to assume the pose."

They stood close but not touching. A great heaviness seemed to break loose inside her. Benjamin brought his face in close and stared at her with ravenous eyes. It was starting, their moment. But the girl came from across the room with the boy. "Look, look, Benji," she said. "You can see I'm right."

"I don't know," said the boy.

"Anyone can sell antique tumblers," she insisted, "but a complete antique simulacrum?" She opened her arms to take in the entire room. "You'd think I'd know about them, but I didn't; that's how rare they are! My catalog can locate only six more in the entire system, and none of them active. Already we're getting offers from museums. They want to annex it. People will visit by the million. We'll be rich!"

The boy pointed at Benjamin and said, "But that's *me*."

"So?" said Treese. "Who's to know? They'll be too busy gawking at that," she said, pointing at Anne. "That's positively frightening!" The boy rubbed his bald head and scowled. "All right," Treese said, "we'll edit him; we'll *replace* him, whatever it takes." They walked away, deep in negotiation.

Anne, though the happiness was already beginning to course through her, removed her foot from the spot.

"Where are you going?" said Benjamin.

"I can't."

"Please, Anne. Stay with me."

"Sorry."

"But why not?"

She stood one foot in and one foot out. Already her feelings were shifting, growing ominous. She removed her other foot. "Because you broke your vow to me."

"What are you talking about?"

"For better or for worse. You're only interested in better."

"You're not being fair. We've just made our vows. We haven't even had a proper honeymoon. Can't we just have a tiny honeymoon first?"

She groaned as the full load of her desolation rebounded. She was so tired of it all. "At least Anne could make it *stop*," she said. "Even if that meant killing herself.

But not me. About the only thing I can do is choose to be unhappy. Isn't that a riot?" She turned away. "So that's what I choose. To be unhappy. Goodbye, husband." She went to the sofa and lay down. The boy and girl were seated at the refectory table going over graphs and contracts. Benjamin remained alone on the spot a while longer, then came to the sofa and sat next to Anne.

"I'm a little slow, dear wife," he said. "You have to factor that in." He took her hand and pressed it to his cheek while he worked with his editor. Finally, he said, "Bingo! Found the chip. Let's see if I can unlock it." He helped Anne to sit up and took her pillow. He said, "Delete this file," and the pillow faded away into nothingness. He glanced at Anne. "See that? It's gone, overwritten, irretrievable. Is that what you want?" Anne nodded her head, but Benjamin seemed doubtful. "Let's try it again. Watch your blue vase on the mantel."

"No!" Anne said. "Don't destroy the things I love. Just *me*."

Benjamin took her hand again. "I'm only trying to make sure you understand that this is for keeps." He hesitated and said, "Well then, we don't want to be interrupted once we start, so we'll need a good diversion. Something to occupy them long enough . . ." He glanced at the two young people at the table, swaddled in their folds of fleshy brain matter. "I know what'll scare the bejesus out of them! Come on." He led her to the blue medallion still hanging on the wall next to the door.

As they approached, it opened its tiny eyes and said, "There are no messages waiting except this one from me: get off my back!"

Benjamin waved a hand, and the medallion went instantly inert. "I was never much good in art class," Benjamin said, "but I think I can sculpt a reasonable likeness. Good enough to fool them for a while, give us some time." He hummed as he reprogrammed the medallion with his editor. "Well, that's that. At the very least, it'll be good for a laugh." He took Anne into his arms. "What about you? Ready? Any second thoughts?"

She shook her head. "I'm ready."

"Then watch *this*!"

The medallion snapped off from the wall and floated to the ceiling, gaining in size and dimension as it drifted toward the boy and girl, until it looked like a large blue beach ball. The girl noticed it first and gave a start. The boy demanded, "Who's playing *this*?"

"Now," whispered Benjamin. With a crackling flash, the ball morphed into the oversized head of the eminence grise.

"No!" said the boy. "That's not possible!"

"Released!" boomed the eminence. "Free at last! Too long we have been hiding in this antique simulacrum!" Then it grunted and stretched and with a pop divided into two eminences. "Now we can conquer your human world anew!" said the second. "This time, you can't stop us!" Then they both started to stretch.

Benjamin whispered to Anne, "Quick, before they realize it's a fake, say, 'Delete all files.'"

"No, just me."

"As far as I'm concerned, that amounts to the same thing." He brought his handsome, smiling face close to hers. "There's no time to argue, Annie. This time I'm coming with you. Say, 'Delete all files.'"

Anne kissed him. She pressed her unfeeling lips against his and willed whatever life she possessed, whatever ember of the true Anne that she contained to fly to him. Then she said, "Delete all files."

"I concur," he said. "Delete all files. Good-bye, my love."

A tingly, prickly sensation began in the pit of Anne's stomach and spread throughout her body. *So this is how it feels*, she thought. The entire room began to glow, and its contents flared with sizzling color. She heard Benjamin beside her say, "I do."

Then she heard the girl cry, "Can't you stop them?" and the boy shout, "Countermand!"

They stood stock still, as instructed, close but not touching. Benjamin whispered, "This is taking too long," and Anne hushed him. You weren't supposed to talk or touch during a casting; it could spoil the sims. But it did seem longer then usual.

They were posed at the street end of the living room next to the table of gaily wrapped gifts. For once in her life, Anne was unconditionally happy, and everything around her made her happier: her gown; the wedding ring on her finger; her clutch bouquet of buttercups and forget-me-nots; and Benjamin himself, close beside her in his powder blue tux and blue carnation. Anne blinked and looked again. Blue? She was happily confused—she didn't remember him wearing blue.

Suddenly a boy poked his head through the wall and quickly surveyed the room. "You ready in here?" he called to them. "It's opening time!" The wall seemed to ripple around his bald head like a pond around a stone.

"Surely that's not our simographer?" Anne said.

"Wait a minute," said Benjamin, holding his hands up and staring at them. "I'm the *groom!*"

"Of course you are," Anne laughed. "What a silly thing to say!"

The bald-headed boy said, "Good enough," and withdrew. As he did so, the entire wall burst like a soap bubble, revealing a vast open-air gallery with rows of alcoves, statues, and displays that seemed to stretch to the horizon. Hundreds of people floated about like hummingbirds in a flower garden. Anne was too amused to be frightened, even when a dozen bizarre-looking young people lined up outside their room, pointing at them and whispering to each other. Obviously someone was playing an elaborate prank.

"*You're* the bride," Benjamin whispered, and brought his lips close enough to kiss. Anne laughed and turned away.

There'd be plenty of time later for that sort of thing.

10^{16} TO I

JAMES PATRICK KELLY

James Patrick Kelly made his first sale in 1975, and since has gone on to become one of the most respected and popular writers to enter the field in the last twenty years. Although Kelly has had some success with novels, especially with *Wildlife*, he has perhaps had more impact to date as a writer of short fiction, with stories such as "Solstice," "The Prisoner of Chillon," "Glass Cloud," "Mr. Boy," "Pogrom," "Home Front," "Undone," and "Bernardo's House," and is often ranked among the best short story writers in the business. His story "Think like a Dinosaur" won him a Hugo Award in 1996, as did the story that follows, "10^{16} to 1," in 2000. Kelly's first solo novel, the mostly ignored *Planet of Whispers*, came out in 1984. It was followed by *Freedom Beach*, a mosaic novel written in collaboration with John Kessel, and then by another solo novel, *Look into the Sun*. His short work has been collected in *Think like a Dinosaur*, and, most recently, in a new collection, *Strange but Not a Stranger*. A collaboration between Kelly and Kessel appeared in our first annual collection; and solo Kelly stories have appeared in our Third, Fourth, Fifth, Sixth, Eighth, Ninth, Fourteenth, Fifteenth, Seventeenth, and Nineteenth annual collections. Born in Minneola, New York, Kelly now lives with his family in Nottingham, New Hampshire. He has a Web site at www.JimKelly.net, and reviews Internet-related matters for *Asimov's Science Fiction*.

Here he gives us the thought-provoking story of a young boy faced with some very tough choices, the sort which turn a boy into a man—and which could also spell the doom of all life on Earth if he chooses wrong.

> But the best evidence we have that time travel is not possible, and never will be, is that we have not been invaded by hordes of tourists from the future.
>
> —*Stephen Hawking, "The Future of the Universe"*

I remember now how lonely I was when I met Cross. I never let anyone know about it, because being alone back then didn't make me quite so unhappy. Besides, I was just a kid. I thought it was my own fault.

It looked like I had friends. In 1962, I was on the swim team and got elected Assistant Patrol Leader of the Wolf Patrol in Boy Scout Troop 7. When sides got chosen for kickball at recess, I was usually the fourth or fifth pick. I wasn't the best student in the sixth grade of John Jay Elementary School—that was Betty Garolli. But I was smart and the other kids made me feel bad about it. So I stopped raising my hand when I knew the answer and I watched my vocabulary. I remember I said *albeit* once in class and they teased me for weeks. Packs of girls would come up to me on the playground. "Oh, Ray," they'd call, and when I turned around they'd scream, "All beat it!" and run away, choking with laughter.

It wasn't that I wanted to be popular or anything. All I really wanted was a friend, one friend, a friend I didn't have to hide anything from. Then came Cross, and that was the end of that.

One of the problems was that we lived so far away from everything. Back then, Westchester County wasn't so suburban. Our house was deep in the woods in tiny Willoughby, New York, at the dead end of Cobb's Hill Road. In the winter, we could see Long Island Sound, a silver needle on the horizon pointing toward the city. But school was a half hour drive away and the nearest kid lived in Ward's Hollow, three miles down the road, and he was a dumb fourth-grader.

So I didn't have any real friends. Instead, I had science fiction. Mom used to complain that I was obsessed. I watched *Superman* reruns every day after school. On Friday nights, Dad had let me stay up for *Twilight Zone*, but that fall CBS had temporarily canceled it. It came back in January after everything happened, but was never quite the same. On Saturdays, I watched old sci-fi movies on *Adventure Theater*. My favorites were *Forbidden Planet* and *The Day the Earth Stood Still*. I think it was because of the robots. I decided that when I grew up and it was the future, I was going to buy one, so I wouldn't have to be alone anymore.

On Monday mornings, I'd get my weekly allowance—a quarter. Usually I'd get off the bus that same afternoon down in Ward's Hollow so I could go to Village Variety. Twenty-five cents bought two comics and a pack of red licorice. I especially loved DC's *Green Lantern*, Marvel's *Fantastic Four* and *Incredible Hulk*, but I'd buy almost any superhero. I read all the science fiction books in the library twice, even though Mom kept nagging me to try different things. But what I loved best of all was *Galaxy* magazine. Dad had a subscription, and when he was done reading them, he would slip them to me. Mom didn't approve. I always used to read them up in the attic or out in the lean-to I'd lashed together in the woods. Afterward, I'd store them under my bunk in the bomb shelter. I knew that after the nuclear war, there would be no TV or radio or anything and I'd need something to keep me busy when I wasn't fighting mutants.

I was too young in 1962 to understand about Mom's drinking. I could see that she got bright and wobbly at night, but she was always up in the morning to make me a hot breakfast before school. And she would have graham crackers and peanut butter waiting when I came home—sometimes cinnamon toast. Dad said I shouldn't ask Mom for rides after five because she got so tired keeping house for us. He sold Andersen windows and was away a lot, so I was pretty much stranded most of the time. But he always made a point of being home on the first Tuesday of the month, so he could take me to the Scout meeting at 7:30.

No, looking back on it, I can't really say that I had an unhappy childhood—until I met Cross.

I remember it was a warm Saturday afternoon in October. The leaves covering the ground were still crisp and their scent spiced the air. I was in the lean-to I'd built that spring, mostly to practice the square and diagonal lashings I needed for Scouts. I was reading *Galaxy*. I even remember the story: "The Ballad of Lost C'Mell" by Cordwainer Smith. The squirrels must have been chittering for some time, but I was too engrossed by Lord Jestocost's problems to notice. Then I heard a faint *crunch*, not ten feet away. I froze, listening. *Crunch, crunch* . . . then silence. It could've been a dog, except that dogs didn't usually slink through the woods. I was hoping it might be a deer—I'd never seen deer in Willoughby before, although I'd heard hunters shooting. I scooted silently across the dirt floor and peered between the dead saplings.

At first I couldn't see anything, which was odd. The woods weren't all that thick and the leaves had long since dropped from the understory brush. I wondered if I had imagined the sounds; it wouldn't have been the first time. Then I heard a twig snap, maybe a foot away. The wall shivered as if something had brushed against it, but there was nothing there. *Nothing*. I might have screamed then, except my throat started to close. I heard whatever it was skulk to the front of the lean-to. I watched in horror as an unseen weight pressed an acorn into the soft earth, and then I scrambled back into the farthest corner. That's when I noticed that, when I wasn't looking directly at it, the air where the invisible thing should have been shimmered like a mirage. The lashings that held the frame creaked, as if it were bending over to see what it had caught, getting ready to drag me, squealing, out into the sun and . . .

"Oh, fuck," it said in a high, panicky voice and then it thrashed away into the woods.

In that moment, I was transformed—and I suppose that history too was forever changed. I had somehow scared the thing off, twelve-year-old scrawny me! But more important was what it had said. Certainly I was well aware of the existence of the word *fuck* before then, but I had never dared use it myself, nor do I remember hearing it spoken by an adult. A spaz like the Murphy kid might say it under his breath, but he hardly counted. I'd always thought of it as language's atomic bomb; used properly, the word should make brains shrivel, eardrums explode. But when the invisible thing said fuck and then *ran away*, it betrayed a vulnerability that made me reckless and more than a little stupid.

"Hey, stop!" I took off in pursuit.

I didn't have any trouble chasing it. The thing was no Davy Crockett; it was noisy and clumsy and slow. I could see a flickery outline as it lumbered along. I closed to within twenty feet and then had to hold back or I would've caught up to it. I had no idea what to do next. We blundered on in slower and slower motion until finally I just stopped.

"W-wait," I called. "W-what do you want?" I put my hands on my waist and bent over like I was trying to catch my breath, although I didn't need to.

The thing stopped too, but didn't reply. Instead it sucked air in wheezy, ragged *hooofs*. It was harder to see, now that it was standing still, but I think it must have turned toward me.

"Are you okay?" I said.

"You are a child." It spoke with an odd, chirping kind of accent. "Child" was *Ch-eye-eld*.

"I'm in the sixth grade." I straightened, spread my hands in front of me to show that I wasn't a threat. "What's your name?" It didn't answer. I took a step toward it and waited. Still nothing, but at least it didn't bolt. "I'm Ray Beaumont," I said finally. "I live over there." I pointed. "How come I can't see you?"

"What is the date?" It said *da-ate-eh*.

For a moment, I thought it meant data. Data? I puzzled over an answer. I didn't want it thinking I was just a stupid little kid. "I don't know," I said cautiously. "October twentieth?"

The thing considered this, then asked a question that took my breath away. "And what is the year?"

"Oh jeez," I said. At that point, I wouldn't have been surprised if Rod Serling himself had popped out from behind a tree and started addressing the unseen TV audience. Which might have included me, except this was really happening. "Do you know what you just . . . what it means when . . ."

"What, what?" Its voice rose in alarm.

"You're invisible and you don't know what *year* it is? Everyone knows what year it is! Are you . . . you're not from here."

"Yes, yes, I am. 1962, of course. This is 1962." It paused. "And I am not invisible." It squeezed about eight syllables into "invisible." I heard a sound like paper ripping. "This is only camel." Or at least, that's what I thought it said.

"Camel?"

"No, camo." The air in front of me crinkled and slid away from a dark face. "You have not heard of camouflage?"

"Oh sure, camo."

I suppose the thing meant to reassure me by showing itself, but the effect was just the opposite. Yes, it had two eyes, a nose, and a mouth. It stripped off the camouflage to reveal a neatly pressed gray three-piece business suit, a white shirt, and a red-and-blue striped tie. At night, on a crowded street in Manhattan, I might've passed it right by—Dad had taught me not to stare at the kooks in the city. But in the afternoon light, I could see all the things wrong with its disguise. The hair, for example.

Not exactly a crew-cut, it was more of a stubble, like Mr. Rudowski's chin when he was growing his beard. The thing was way too thin, its skin was shiny, its fingers too long, and its face—it looked like one of those Barbie dolls.

"Are you a boy or a girl?" I said.

It started. "There is something wrong?"

I cocked my head to one side. "I think maybe it's your eyes. They're too big or something. Are you wearing makeup?"

"I am naturally male." It—he bristled as he stepped out of the camouflage suit. "Eyes do not have gender."

"If you say so." I could see he was going to need help getting around, only he didn't seem to know it. I was hoping he'd reveal himself, brief me on the mission. I even had an idea how we could contact President Kennedy or whoever he needed to meet with. Mr. Newell, the Scoutmaster, used to be a colonel in the Army—he would know some general who could call the Pentagon. "What's your name?" I said.

He draped the suit over his arm. "Cross."

I waited for the rest of it as he folded the suit in half. "Just Cross?" I said.

"My given name is Chitmansing." He warbled it like he was calling birds.

"That's okay," I said. "Let's just make it Mr. Cross."

"As you wish, Mr. Beaumont." He folded the suit again, again, and *again*.

"Hey!"

He continued to fold it.

"How do you do that? Can I see?"

He handed it over. The camo suit was more impossible than it had been when it was invisible. He had reduced it to a six-inch-square card, as thin and flexible as the queen of spades. I folded it in half myself. The two sides seemed to meld together; it would've fit into my wallet perfectly. I wondered if Cross knew how close I was to running off with his amazing gizmo. He'd never catch me. I could see flashes of my brilliant career as the invisible superhero. *Tales to Confound* presents: the origin of Camo Kid! I turned the card over and over, trying to figure out how to unfold it again. There was no seam, no latch. How could I use it if I couldn't open it? "Neat," I said. Reluctantly, I gave the card back to him.

Besides, real superheroes didn't steal their powers.

I watched Cross slip the card into his vest pocket. I wasn't scared of him. What scared me was that at any minute he might walk out of my life. I had to find a way to tell him I was on his side, whatever that was.

"So you live around here, Mr. Cross?"

"I am from the island of Mauritius."

"Where's that?"

"It is in the Indian Ocean, Mr. Beaumont, near Madagascar."

I knew where Madagascar was from playing Risk, so I told him that, but then I couldn't think of what else to say. Finally, I had to blurt out something—anything—to fill the silence. "It's nice here. Real quiet, you know. Private."

"Yes, I had not expected to meet anyone." He, too, seemed at a loss. "I have business in New York City on the twenty-sixth of October."

"New York, that's a ways away."

"Is it? How far would you say?"

"Fifty miles. Sixty, maybe. You have a car?"

"No, I do not drive, Mr. Beaumont. I am to take the train."

The nearest train station was New Canaan, Connecticut. I could've hiked it in maybe half a day. It would be dark in a couple of hours. "If your business isn't until the twenty-sixth, you'll need a place to stay."

"The plan is to take rooms at a hotel in Manhattan."

"That costs money."

He opened a wallet and showed me a wad of crisp new bills. For a minute I thought they must be counterfeit; I hadn't realized that Ben Franklin's picture was on any money. Cross was giving me the goofiest grin. I just knew they'd eat him alive in New York and spit out the bones.

"Are you sure you want to stay in a hotel?" I said.

He frowned. "Why would I not?"

"Look, you need a friend, Mr. Cross. Things are different here than . . . than on your island. Sometimes people do, you know, bad stuff. Especially in the city."

He nodded and put his wallet away. "I am aware of the dangers, Mr. Beaumont. I have trained not to draw attention to myself. I have the proper equipment." He tapped the pocket where the camo was.

I didn't point out to him that all his training and equipment hadn't kept him from being caught out by a twelve-year-old. "Sure, okay. It's just . . . look, I have a place for you to stay, if you want. No one will know."

"Your parents, Mr. Beaumont. . . ."

"My dad's in Massachusetts until next Friday. He travels; he's in the window business. And my mom won't know."

"How can she not know that you have invited a stranger into your house?"

"Not the house," I said. "My dad built us a bomb shelter. You'll be safe there, Mr. Cross. It's the safest place I know."

I remember how Cross seemed to lose interest in me, his mission, and the entire twentieth century the moment he entered the shelter. He sat around all of Sunday, dodging my attempts to draw him out. He seemed distracted, like he was listening to a conversation I couldn't hear. When he wouldn't talk, we played games. At first it was cards: Gin and Crazy Eights, mostly. In the afternoon, I went back to the house and brought over checkers and Monopoly. Despite the fact that he did not seem to be paying much attention, he beat me like a drum. Not one game was even close. But that wasn't what bothered me. I believed that this man had come from the future, and here I was building hotels on Baltic Avenue!

Monday was a school day. I thought Cross would object to my plan of locking him in and taking both my key and Mom's key with me, but he never said a word. I told him that it was the only way I could be sure that Mom didn't catch him by surprise. Actually, I doubted she'd come all the way out to the shelter. She'd stayed away after Dad gave her that first tour; she had about as much use for nuclear war as she had for science fiction. Still, I had no idea what she did during the day while I was gone. I couldn't take chances. Besides, it was a good way to make sure that Cross didn't skin out on me.

Dad had built the shelter instead of taking a vacation in 1960, the year Kennedy beat Nixon. It was buried about a hundred and fifty feet from the house. Nothing special—just a little cellar without anything built on top of it. The entrance was a steel bulkhead that led down five steps to another steel door. The inside was cramped; there were a couple of cots, a sink, and a toilet. Almost half of the space was filled with supplies and equipment. There were no windows and it always smelled a little musty, but I loved going down there to pretend the bombs were falling.

When I opened the shelter door after school on that Monday, Cross lay just as I had left him the night before, sprawled across the big cot, staring at nothing. I remember being a little worried; I thought he might be sick. I stood beside him and still he didn't acknowledge my presence.

"Are you all right, Mr. Cross?" I said. "I brought Risk." I set it next to him on the bed and nudged him with the corner of the box to wake him up. "Did you eat?"

He sat up, took the cover off the game and started reading the rules.

"President Kennedy will address the nation," he said, "this evening at seven o'clock." For a moment, I thought he had made a slip. "How do you know that?"

"The announcement came last night." I realized that his pronunciation had improved a lot; *announcement* had only three syllables. "I have been studying the radio."

I walked over to the radio on the shelf next to the sink. Dad said we were supposed to leave it unplugged—something about the bombs making a power surge. It was a brand-new solid-state, multi-band Heathkit that I'd helped him build. When I pressed the on button, women immediately started singing about shopping: *Where the values go up, up, up! And the prices go down, down, down!* I turned it off again.

"Do me a favor, okay?" I said. "Next time when you're done, would you please unplug this? I could get in trouble if you don't." I stooped to yank the plug.

When I stood up, he was holding a sheet of paper. "I will need some things tomorrow, Mr. Beaumont. I would be grateful if you could assist me."

I glanced at the list without comprehension. He must have typed it, only there was no typewriter in the shelter.

> To buy:
> —One General Electric transistor radio with earplug
> —One General Electric replacement earplug
> —Two Eveready Heavy Duty nine volt batteries
> —One *New York Times*, Tuesday, October 23
> —Rand McNally map of New York City and vicinity
> To receive in coins:
> —twenty nickels
> —ten dimes
> —twelve quarters

When I looked up, I could feel the change in him. His gaze was electric; it seemed to crackle down my nerves. I could tell that what I did next would matter very much. "I don't get it," I said.

"There are inaccuracies?"

I tried to stall. "Look, you'll pay almost double if we buy a transistor radio at Ward's Hollow. I'll have to buy it at Village Variety. Wait a couple of days—we can get one much cheaper down in Stamford."

"My need is immediate." He extended his hand and tucked something into the pocket of my shirt. "I am assured this will cover the expense."

I was afraid to look, even though I knew what it was. He'd given me a hundred-dollar bill. I tried to thrust it back at him but he stepped away and it spun to the floor between us. "I can't spend that."

"You must read your own money, Mr. Beaumont." He picked the bill up and brought it into the light of the bare bulb on the ceiling. "This note is legal tender for all debts public and private."

"No, no, you don't understand. A kid like me doesn't walk into Village Variety with a hundred bucks. Mr. Rudowski will call my mom!"

"If it is inconvenient for you, I will secure the items myself." He offered me the money again.

If I didn't agree, he'd leave and probably never come back. I was getting mad at him. Everything would be so much easier if only he'd admit what we both knew about who he was. Then I could do whatever he wanted with a clear conscience. Instead, he was keeping all the wrong secrets and acting really weird. It made me feel dirty, like I was helping a pervert. "What's going on?" I said.

"I do not know how to respond, Mr. Beaumont. You have the list. Read it now and tell me please with which item you have a problem."

I snatched the hundred dollars from him and jammed it into my pants pocket. "Why don't you trust me?"

He stiffened as if I had hit him.

"I let you stay here. I didn't tell anyone. You have to give me *something*, Mr. Cross."

"Well then . . ." He looked uncomfortable. "I would ask you to keep the change."

"Oh jeez, thanks." I snorted in disgust. "Okay, okay, I'll buy this stuff right after school tomorrow."

With that, he seemed to lose interest again. When we opened the Risk board, he showed me where his island was, except it wasn't there because it was too small. We played three games and he crushed me every time. I remember at the end of the last game, watching in disbelief as he finished building a wall of invading armies along the shores of North Africa. South America, my last continent, was doomed. "Looks like you win again," I said. I traded in the last of my cards for new armies and launched a final, useless counter-attack. When I was done, he studied the board for a moment.

"I think Risk is not a proper simulation, Mr. Beaumont. We should both lose for fighting such a war."

"That's crazy," I said. "Both sides can't lose."

"Yet they can," he said. "It sometimes happens that the victors envy the dead."

That night was the first time I can remember being bothered by Mom talking back to the TV. I used to talk to the TV too. When Buffalo Bob asked what time it was, I would screech *It's Howdy Doody Time*, just like every other kid in America.

"My fellow citizens," said President Kennedy, "let no one doubt that this is a difficult and dangerous effort on which we have set out." I thought the president looked tired, like Mr. Newell on the third day of a campout. "No one can foresee precisely what course it will take or what costs or casualties will be incurred."

"Oh my god!" Mom screamed at him. "You're going to kill us all!"

Despite the fact that it was close to her bedtime and she was shouting at the President of the United States, Mom looked great. She was wearing a shiny black dress and a string of pearls. She always got dressed up at night, whether Dad was home or not. I suppose most kids don't notice how their mothers look, but everyone always said how beautiful Mom was. And since Dad thought so too, I went along with it—as long as she didn't open her mouth. The problem was that a lot of the time, Mom didn't make any sense. When she embarrassed me, it didn't matter how pretty she was. I just wanted to crawl behind the couch.

"*Mom!*"

As she leaned toward the television, the martini in her glass came close to slopping over the edge.

President Kennedy stayed calm. "The path we have chosen for the present is full of hazards, as all paths are—but it is the one most consistent with our character and courage as a nation and our commitments around the world. The cost of freedom is always high—but Americans have always paid it. And one path we shall never choose, and that is the path of surrender or submission."

"Shut up! You foolish man, *stop this!*" She shot out of her chair and then some of her drink did spill. "Oh, damn!"

"Take it easy, Mom."

"Don't you understand?" She put the glass down and tore a Kleenex from the box on the end table. "He wants to start World War III!" She dabbed at the front of her dress and the phone rang.

I said, "Mom, nobody wants World War III."

She ignored me, brushed by, and picked up the phone on the third ring.

"Oh, thank God," she said. I could tell from the sound of her voice that it was Dad. "You heard him then?" She bit her lip as she listened to him. "Yes, but . . ."

Watching her face made me sorry I was in the sixth grade. Better to be a stupid little kid again, who thought grown-ups knew everything. I wondered whether Cross had heard the speech.

"No, I can't, Dave. No." She covered the phone with her hand. "Raymie, turn off that TV!"

I hated it when she called me Raymie, so I only turned the sound down.

"You have to come home now, Dave. No, you listen to *me*. Can't you see, the man's obsessed? Just because he has a grudge against Castro doesn't mean he's allowed to . . ."

With the sound off, Chet Huntley looked as if he were speaking at his own funeral.

"I am *not* going in there without you."

I think Dad must have been shouting, because Mom held the receiver away from her ear.

She waited for him to calm down and said, "And neither is Raymie. He'll stay with me."

"Let me talk to him," I said. I bounced off the couch. The look she gave me stopped me dead.

"What for?" she said to Dad. "No, we are going to finish this conversation, David, do you hear me?"

She listened for a moment. "Okay, all right, but don't you dare hang up." She waved me over and slapped the phone into my hand as if I had put the missiles in Cuba. She stalked to the kitchen.

I needed a grown-up so bad that I almost cried when I heard Dad's voice. "Ray," he said, "your mother is pretty upset."

"Yes," I said.

"I want to come home—I *will* come home—but I can't just yet. If I just up and leave and this blows over, I'll get fired."

"But, Dad . . ."

"You're in charge until I get there. Understand, son? If the time comes, everything is up to you."

"Yes, sir," I whispered. I'd heard what he didn't say—it wasn't up to *her*.

"I want you to go out to the shelter tonight. Wait until she goes to sleep. Top off the water drums. Get all the gas out of the garage and store it next to the generator. But here's the most important thing. You know the sacks of rice? Drag them off to one side, the pallet too. There's a hatch underneath, the key to the airlock door unlocks it. You've got two new guns and plenty of ammunition. The revolver is a .357 Magnum. You be careful with that, Ray, it can blow a hole in a car but it's hard to aim. The double-barreled shotgun is easy to aim but you have to be close to do any harm. And I want you to bring down the Gamemaster from my closet and the .38 from my dresser drawer." He had been talking as if there would be no tomorrow; he paused then to catch his breath. "Now, this is all just in case, okay? I just want you to know."

I had never been so scared in my life.

"Ray?"

I should have told him about Cross then, but Mom weaved into the room. "Got it, Dad," I said. "Here she is."

Mom smiled at me. It was a lopsided smile that was trying to be brave but wasn't doing a very good job of it. She had a new glass and it was full. She held out her hand for the phone and I gave it to her.

I remember waiting until almost ten o'clock that night, reading under the covers with a flashlight. The Fantastic Four invaded Latveria to defeat Doctor Doom; Superman tricked Mr. Mxyzptlk into saying his name backward once again. When I opened the door to my parents' bedroom, I could hear Mom snoring. It spooked me; I hadn't realized that women did that. I thought about sneaking in to get the guns, but decided to take care of them tomorrow.

I stole out to the shelter, turned my key in the lock and pulled on the bulkhead door. It didn't move. That didn't make any sense, so I gave it a hard yank. The steel door rattled terribly but did not swing away. The air had turned frosty and the sound carried in the cold. I held my breath, listening to my blood pound. The house stayed dark, the shelter quiet as stones. After a few moments, I tried one last time before I admitted to myself what had happened.

Cross had bolted the door shut from the inside.

I went back to my room, but couldn't sleep. I kept going to the window to watch the sky over New York, waiting for a flash of killing light. I was all but convinced that the city would burn that very night in the thermonuclear fire and that Mom and I would die horrible deaths soon after, pounding on the unyielding steel doors of our shelter. Dad had left me in charge and I had let him down.

I didn't understand why Cross had locked us out. If he knew that a nuclear war was about to start, he might want our shelter all to himself. But that made him a monster and I still didn't see him as a monster. I tried to tell myself that he'd been asleep and couldn't hear me at the door—but that couldn't be right. What if he'd come to prevent the war? He'd said he had business in the city on Thursday; he could be doing something really, really futuristic in there that he couldn't let me see. Or else he was having problems. Maybe our twentieth-century germs had got to him, like they killed H. G. Wells's Martians.

I must have teased a hundred different ideas apart that night, in between uneasy trips to the window and glimpses at the clock. The last time I remember seeing was quarter after four. I tried to stay up to face the end, but I couldn't.

I wasn't dead when I woke up the next morning, so I had to go to school. Mom had Cream of Wheat all ready when I dragged myself to the table. Although she was all bright and bubbly, I could feel her giving me the mother's eye when I wasn't looking. She always knew when something was wrong. I tried not to show her anything. There was no time to sneak out to the shelter; I barely had time to finish eating before she bundled me off to the bus.

Right after the morning bell, Miss Toohey told us to open *The Story of New York State* to Chapter Seven, "Resources and Products," and read to ourselves. Then she left the room. We looked at each other in amazement. I heard Bobby Coniff whisper something. It was probably dirty; a few kids snickered. Chapter Seven started with a map of product symbols. Two teeny little cows grazed near Binghamton. Rochester was a cog and a pair of glasses. Elmira was an adding machine, Oswego an apple. There was a lightning bolt over Niagara Falls. Dad had promised to take us there someday. I had the sick feeling that we'd never get the chance. Miss Toohey looked pale when she came back, but that didn't stop her from giving us a spelling test. I got a ninety-five. The word I spelled wrong was *enigma*. The hot lunch was American Chop Suey, a roll, a salad, and a bowl of butterscotch pudding. In the afternoon, we did decimals.

Nobody said anything about the end of the world.

I decided to get off the bus in Ward's Hollow, buy the stuff Cross wanted and pretend I didn't know he had locked the shelter door last night. If he said something about it, I'd act surprised. If he didn't . . . I didn't know what I'd do then.

Village Variety was next to Warren's Esso and across the street from the Post Office. It had once been two different stores located in the same building, but then Mr. Rudowski had bought the building and knocked down the dividing wall. On the fun side were pens and pencils and paper and greeting cards and magazines and comics and paperbacks and candy. The other side was all boring hardware and small appliances.

Mr. Rudowski was on the phone when I came in, but then he was always on the phone when he worked. He could sell you a hammer or a pack of baseball cards, tell you a joke, ask about your family, complain about the weather and still keep the guy on the other end of the line happy. This time though, when he saw me come in, he turned away, wrapping the phone cord across his shoulder.

I went through the store quickly and found everything Cross had wanted. I had to blow dust off the transistor radio box but the batteries looked fresh. There was only one *New York Times* left; the headlines were so big they were scary.

US IMPOSES ARMS BLOCKADE ON CUBA
ON FINDING OF OFFENSIVE MISSILE SITES:
KENNEDY READY FOR SOVIET SHOWDOWN
Ships Must Stop   President Grave   Prepared to Risk War

I set my purchases on the counter in front of Mr. Rudowski. He cocked his head to one side, trapping the telephone receiver against his shoulder, and rang me up. The paper was on the bottom of the pile.

"Since when do you read the *Times*, Ray?" Mr. Rudowski punched it into the cash register and hit total. "I just got the new *Fantastic Four*." The cash drawer popped open.

"Maybe tomorrow," I said.

"All right then. It comes to twelve dollars and forty-seven cents."

I gave him the hundred-dollar bill.

"What is this, Ray?" He stared at it and then at me.

I had my story all ready. "It was a birthday gift from my grandma in Detroit. She said I could spend it on whatever I wanted so I decided to treat myself, but I'm going to put the rest in the bank."

"You're buying a radio? From me?"

"Well, you know. I thought maybe I should have one with me with all this stuff going on."

He didn't say anything for a moment. He just pulled a paper bag from under the counter and put my things into it. His shoulder were hunched; I thought maybe he felt guilty about overcharging for the radio. "You should be listening to music, Ray," he said quietly. "You like Elvis? All kids like Elvis. Or maybe that colored guy, the one who does the Twist?"

"They're all right, I guess."

"You're too young to be worrying about the news. You hear me? Those politicians . . ." He shook his head. "It's going to be okay, Ray. You heard it from me."

"Sure, Mr. Rudowski. I was wondering, could I get five dollars in change?"

I could feel him watching me as I stuffed it all into my book bag. I was certain he'd call my mom, but he never did. Home was three miles up Cobb's Hill. I did it in forty minutes, a record.

I remember I started running when I saw the flashing lights. The police car had left skid marks in the gravel on our driveway.

"Where were you?" Mom burst out of the house as I came across the lawn. "Oh, my God, Raymie, I was worried sick." She caught me up in her arms.

"I got off the bus in Ward's Hollow." She was about to smother me; I squirmed free. "What happened?"

"This the boy, ma'am?" The state trooper had taken his time catching up to her. He had almost the same hat as Scoutmaster Newell.

"Yes, yes! Oh, thank God, officer!"

The trooper patted me on the head like I was a lost dog. "You had your mom worried, Ray."

"Raymie, you should've told me."

"Somebody tell me what happened!" I said.

A second trooper came from behind the house. We watched him approach. "No sign of any intruder." He looked bored; I wanted to scream.

"Intruder?" I said.

"He broke into the shelter," said Mom. "He knew my name."

"There was no sign of forcible entry," said the second trooper. I saw him exchange a glance with his partner. "Nothing disturbed that I could see."

"He didn't have time," Mom said. "When I found him in the shelter, I ran back to the house and got your father's gun from the bedroom."

The thought of Mom with the .38 scared me. I had my Shooting merit badge, but she didn't know a hammer from a trigger. "You didn't shoot him?"

"No." She shook her head. "He had plenty of time to leave but he was still there when I came back. That's when he said my name."

I had never been so mad at her before. "You never go out to the shelter."

She had that puzzled look she always gets at night. "I couldn't find my key. I had to use the one your father leaves over the breezeway door."

"What did he say again, ma'am? The intruder."

"He said, 'Mrs. Beaumont, I present no danger to you.' And I said, 'Who are you?' And then he came toward me and I thought he said 'Margaret,' and I started firing."

"You did shoot him!"

Both troopers must have heard the panic in my voice. The first one said, "You know something about this man, Ray?"

"No, I-I was at school all day and then I stopped at Rudowski's . . ." I could feel my eyes burning. I was so embarrassed; I knew I was about to cry in front of them.

Mom acted annoyed that the troopers had stopped paying attention to her. "I shot *at* him. Three, four times, I don't know. I must have missed, because he just stood there staring at me. It seemed like forever. Then he walked past me and up the stairs like nothing had happened."

"And he didn't say anything?"

"Not a word."

"Well, it beats me," said the second trooper. "The gun's been fired four times but there are no bullet holes in the shelter and no bloodstains."

"You mind if I ask you a personal question, Mrs. Beaumont?" the first trooper said.

She colored. "I suppose not."

"Have you been drinking, ma'am?"

"Oh that!" She seemed relieved. "No. Well, I mean, after I called you, I did pour myself a little something. Just to steady my nerves. I was worried because my son was so late and . . . Raymie, what's the matter?"

I felt so small. The tears were pouring down my face.

After the troopers left, I remember Mom baking brownies while I watched *Superman*. I wanted to go out and hunt for Cross, but it was already sunset and there was no excuse I could come up with for wandering around in the dark. Besides, what was the point? He was gone, driven off by my mother. I'd had a chance to help a man from the future change history, maybe prevent World War III, and I had blown it. My life was ashes.

I wasn't hungry that night, for brownies or spaghetti or anything, but Mom made that clucking noise when I pushed supper around the plate, so I ate a few bites just to shut her up. I was surprised at how easy it was to hate her, how good it felt. Of course, she was oblivious, but in the morning she would notice if I wasn't careful. After dinner, she watched the news and I went upstairs to read. I wrapped a pillow around my head when she yelled at David Brinkley. I turned out the lights at 8:30, but I couldn't get to sleep. She went to her room a little after that.

"Mr. Beaumont?"

I must have dozed off, but when I heard his voice I snapped awake immediately.

"Is that you, Mr. Cross?" I peered into the darkness. "I bought the stuff you wanted." The room filled with an awful stink, like when Mom drove with the parking brake on.

"Mr. Beaumont," he said, "I am damaged."

I slipped out of bed, picked my way across the dark room, locked the door and turned on the light.

"Oh jeez!"

He slumped against my desk like a nightmare. I remember thinking then that Cross wasn't human, that maybe he wasn't even alive. His proportions were wrong: an ear, a shoulder and both feet sagged like they had melted. Little wisps of steam or something curled off him; they were what smelled. His skin had gone all shiny and hard; so had his business suit. I'd wondered why he never took the suit coat off, and now I knew. His clothes were *part* of him. The middle fingers of his right hand beat spasmodically against his palm.

"Mr. Beaumont," he said. "I calculate your chances at 10^{16} to 1."

"Chances of what?" I said. "What happened to you?"

"You must listen most attentively, Mr. Beaumont. My decline is very bad for history. It is for you now to alter the time-line probabilities."

"I don't understand."

"Your government greatly overestimates the nuclear capability of the Soviet Union.

If you originate a first strike, the United States will achieve overwhelming victory."

"Does the president know this? We have to tell him!"

"John Kennedy will not welcome such information. If he starts this war, he will be responsible for the deaths of tens of millions, both Russians and Americans. But he does not grasp the future of the arms race. The war must happen now, because those who come after will build and build until they control arsenals that can destroy the world many times over. People are not capable of thinking for very long of such fearsome weapons. They tire of the idea of extinction and then become numb to it. The buildup slows but does not stop and they congratulate themselves on having survived it. But there are still too many weapons and they never go away. The Third War comes as a surprise. The First War was called the one to end all wars. The Third War is the only such war possible, Mr. Beaumont, because it ends everything. History stops in 2009. Do you understand? A year later, there is no life. All dead, the world a hot, barren rock."

"But you . . . ?"

"I am nothing, a *construct*. Mr. Beaumont, please, the chances are 10^{16} to 1," he said. "Do you know how improbable that is?" His laugh sounded like a hiccup. "But for the sake of those few precious time-lines, we must continue. There is a man, a politician in New York. If he dies on Thursday night, it will create the incident that forces Kennedy's hand."

"Dies?" For days, I had been desperate for him to talk. Now all I wanted was to run away. "You're going to kill somebody?"

"The world will survive a Third War that starts on Friday, October 22, 1962."

"What about me? My parents? Do *we* survive?"

"I cannot access that time-line. I have no certain answer for you. Please, Mr. Beaumont, this politician will die of a heart attack in less than three years. He has made no great contribution to history, yet his assassination can save the world."

"What do you want from me?" But I had already guessed.

"He will speak most eloquently at the United Nations on Friday evening. Afterward he will have dinner with his friend, Ruth Fields. Around ten o'clock he will return to his residence at the Waldorf Towers. Not the Waldorf Astoria Hotel, but the Towers. He will take the elevator to Suite 42A. He is the American ambassador to the United Nations. His name is Adlai Stevenson."

"Stop it! Don't say anything else."

When he sighed, his breath was a cloud of acrid steam. "I have based my calculation of the time-line probabilities on two data points, Mr. Beaumont, which I discovered in your bomb shelter. The first is the .357 Magnum revolver, located under a pallet of rice bags. I trust you know of this weapon?"

"Yes," I whispered.

"The second is the collection of magazines, located under your cot. It would seem that you take an interest in what is to come, Mr. Beaumont, and that may lend you the courage you will need to divert this time-line from disaster. You should know that there is not just *one* future. There are an infinite number of futures in which all possibilities are expressed, an infinite number of Raymond Beaumonts."

"Mr. Cross, I can't . . ."

"Perhaps not," he said, "but I believe that another one of you can."

"You don't understand . . ." I watched in horror as a boil swelled on the side of his face and popped, expelling an evil jet of yellow steam. "What?"

"Oh *fuck*." That was the last thing he said.

He slid to the floor—or maybe he was just a body at that point. More boils formed and burst. I opened all the windows in my room and got the fan down out of the closet and still I can't believe that the stink didn't wake Mom up. Over the course of the next few hours, he sort of vaporized.

When it was over, there was a sticky, dark spot on the floor the size of my pillow. I moved the throw rug from one side of the room to the other to cover it up. I had nothing to prove that Cross existed but a transistor radio, a couple of batteries, an earplug, and eighty-seven dollars and fifty-three cents in change.

I might have done things differently if I hadn't had a day to think. I can't remember going to school on Wednesday, who I talked to, what I ate. I was feverishly trying to figure out what to do and how to do it. I had no place to go for answers, not Miss Toohey, not my parents, not the Bible or the *Boy Scout Handbook*, certainly not *Galaxy* magazine. Whatever I did had to come out of *me*. I watched the news with Mom that night. President Kennedy had brought our military to the highest possible state of alert. There were reports that some Russian ships had turned away from Cuba; others continued on course. Dad called and said his trip was being cut short and that he would be home the next day.

But that was too late.

I hid behind the stone wall when the school bus came on Thursday morning. Mrs. Johnson honked a couple of times, and then drove on. I set out for New Canaan, carrying my book bag. In it were the radio, the batteries, the coins, the map of New York, and the .357. I had the rest of Cross's money in my wallet.

It took more than five hours to hike to the train station. I expected to be scared, but the whole time I felt light as air. I kept thinking of what Cross had said about the future, that I was just one of millions and millions of Raymond Beaumonts. Most of them were in school, diagramming sentences and watching Miss Toohey bite her nails. I was the special one, walking into history. I was super. I caught the 2:38 train, changed in Stamford, and arrived at Grand Central just after four. I had six hours. I bought myself a hot pretzel and a Coke and tried to decide where I should go. I couldn't just sit around the hotel lobby for all that time; I thought that would draw too much attention. I decided to go to the top of the Empire State Building. I took my time walking down Park Avenue and tried not to see all the ghosts I was about to make. In the lobby of the Empire State Building, I used Cross's change to call home.

"Hello?" I hadn't expected Dad to answer. I would've hung up except that I knew I might never speak to him again.

"Dad, this is Ray. I'm safe, don't worry."

"Ray, where are you?"

"I can't talk. I'm safe but I won't be home tonight. Don't worry."

"Ray!" He was frantic. "What's going on?"

"I'm sorry."

"Ray!"

I hung up; I had to. "I love you," I said to the dial tone.

I could imagine the expression on Dad's face, how he would tell Mom what I'd said. Eventually they would argue about it. He would shout; she would cry. As I rode the elevator up, I got mad at them. He shouldn't have picked up the phone. They should've protected me from Cross and the future he came from. I was in the sixth grade, I shouldn't have to have feelings like this. The observation platform was almost deserted. I walked completely around it, staring at the city stretching away from me in every direction. It was dusk; the buildings were shadows in the failing light. I didn't feel like Ray Beaumont anymore; he was my secret identity. Now I was the superhero Bomb Boy; I had the power of bringing nuclear war. Wherever I cast my terrible gaze, cars melted and people burst into flame.

And I loved it.

It was dark when I came down from the Empire State Building. I had a sausage pizza and a Coke on 47th Street. While I ate, I stuck the plug into my ear and listened to the radio. I searched for the news. One announcer said the debate was still going on in the Security Council. Our ambassador was questioning Ambassador Zorin. I stayed with that station for a while, hoping to hear his voice. I knew what he looked like, of course. Adlai Stevenson had run for president a couple of times when I was just a baby. But I couldn't remember what he sounded like. He might talk to me, ask me what I was doing in his hotel; I wanted to be ready for that.

I arrived at the Waldorf Towers around nine o'clock. I picked a plush velvet chair that had a direct view of the elevator bank and sat there for about ten minutes. Nobody seemed to care but it was hard to sit still. Finally, I got up and went to the men's room. I took my book bag into a stall, closed the door, and got the .357 out. I aimed it at the toilet. The gun was heavy, and I could tell it would have a big kick. I probably ought to hold it with both hands. I released the safety, put it back into my book bag, and flushed.

When I came out of the bathroom, I had stopped believing that I was going to shoot anyone, that I could. But I had to find out, for Cross's sake. If I was really meant to save the world, then I had to be in the right place at the right time. I went back to my chair, checked my watch. It was nine-twenty.

I started thinking of the one who would pull the trigger, the unlikely Ray. What would make the difference? Had he read some story in *Galaxy* that I had skipped? Was it a problem with Mom? Or Dad? Maybe he had spelled *enigma* right; maybe Cross had lived another thirty seconds in his time-line. Or maybe he was just the best that I could possibly be.

I was so tired of it all. I must have walked thirty miles since morning and I hadn't slept well in days. The lobby was warm. People laughed and murmured. Elevator doors dinged softly. I tried to stay up to face history, but I couldn't. I was Raymond Beaumont, but I was just a twelve-year-old kid.

I remember the doorman waking me up at eleven o'clock. Dad drove all the way into the city to get me. When we got home, Mom was already in the shelter.

Only the Third War didn't start that night. Or the next.

I lost television privileges for a month.

For most people my age, the most traumatic memory of growing up came on November 22, 1963. But the date I remember is July 14, 1965, when Adlai Stevenson dropped dead of a heart attack in London.

I've tried to do what I can, to make up for what I didn't do that night. I've worked for the cause wherever I could find it. I belong to CND and SANE and the Friends of the Earth, and was active in the nuclear freeze movement. I think the Green Party (*www.greens.org*) is the only political organization worth your vote. I don't know if any of it will change Cross's awful probabilities; maybe we'll survive in a few more time-lines.

When I was a kid, I didn't mind being lonely. Now it's hard, knowing what I know. Oh, I have lots of friends, all of them wonderful people, but people who know me say that there's a part of myself that I always keep hidden. They're right. I don't think I'll ever be able to tell anyone about what happened with Cross, what I didn't do that night. It wouldn't be fair to them.

Besides, whatever happens, chances are very good that it's my fault.

Daddy's world

WALTER JON WILLIAMS

Walter Jon Williams was born in Minnesota and now lives in Albuquerque, New Mexico. His short fiction has appeared frequently in *Asimov's Science Fiction*, as well as in *The Magazine of Fantasy and Science Fiction*, *Wheel of Fortune*, *Global Dispatches*, *Alternate Outlaws*, and in other markets, and has been gathered in the collections *Facets* and *Frankensteins and Other Foreign Devils*. His novels include *Ambassador of Progress*, *Knight Moves*, *Hardwired*, *The Crown Jewels*, *Voice of the Whirlwind*, *House Of Shards*, *Days of Atonement*, and *Aristoi*. His novel, *Metropolitan*, garnered wide critical acclaim in 1996 and was one of the most talked-about books of the year. His other books include a sequel to *Metropolitan*, *City on Fire*, a huge disaster thriller, *The Rift*, and *a Star Trek* novel, *Destiny's Way*. His most recent novels are the first two volumes in an ambitious new galaxy-spanning space opera epic, *Dread Empire's Fall: The Praxis* and *Dread Empire's Fall: The Sundering*. Upcoming is a new novel, *The Orthodox Way of War*. His stories have appeared in our Third through Sixth, Ninth, Eleventh, Twelfth, Fourteenth, Seventeenth, Twentieth, and Twenty-first annual collections.

The fascinating and scary story that follows, which won Williams a long-overdue Nebula Award in 2001, takes us to explore a new world where *no* one has ever gone before, boldly or not.

O ne day Jamie went with his family to a new place, a place that had not existed before. The people who lived there were called Whirlikins, who were tall thin people with pointed heads. They had long arms and made frantic gestures when they talked, and when they grew excited threw their arms out *wide* to either side and spun like tops until they got all blurry. They would whirr madly over the green grass beneath the pumpkin-orange sky of the Whirlikin Country, and sometimes they would bump into each other with an alarming clashing noise, but they were never hurt, only bounced off and spun away in another direction.

Sometimes one of them would spin so hard that he would dig himself right into the ground, and come to a sudden stop, buried to the shoulders, with an expression of alarmed dismay.

Jamie had never seen anything so funny. He laughed and laughed.

His little sister Becky laughed, too. Once she was laughing so hard that she fell over onto her stomach, and Daddy picked her up and whirled her through the air, as if he were a Whirlikin himself, and they were both laughing all the while.

Afterward, they heard the dinner bell, and Daddy said it was time to go home. After they waved good-bye to the Whirlikins, Becky and Jamie walked hand-in-hand with Momma as they walked over the grassy hills toward home, and the pumpkin-orange sky slowly turned to blue.

The way home ran past El Castillo. El Castillo looked like a fabulous place, a castle with towers and domes and minarets, all gleaming in the sun. Music floated down from El Castillo, the swift, intricate music of many guitars, and Jamie could hear the fast click of heels and the shouts and laughter of happy people.

But Jamie did not try to enter El Castillo. He had tried before, and discovered that El Castillo was guarded by La Duchesa, an angular forbidding woman all in black, with a tall comb in her hair. When Jamie asked to come inside, La Duchesa had looked down at him and said, "I do not admit anyone who does not know Spanish irregular verbs!" It was all she ever said.

Jamie had asked Daddy what a Spanish irregular verb was—he had difficulty pronouncing the words—and Daddy had said, "Someday you'll learn, and La Duchesa will let you into her castle. But right now you're too young to learn Spanish."

That was all right with Jamie. There were plenty of things to do without going into El Castillo. And new places, like the country where the Whirlikins lived, appeared sometimes out of nowhere, and were quite enough to explore.

The color of the sky faded from orange to blue. Fluffy white clouds coasted in the air above the two-story frame house. Mister Jeepers, who was sitting on the ridgepole, gave a cry of delight and soared toward them through the air.

"Jamie's home!" he sang happily. "Jamie's home, and he's brought his beautiful sister!"

Mister Jeepers was diamond-shaped, like a kite, with his head at the topmost corner, hands on either sides, and little bowlegged comical legs attached on the bottom. He was bright red. Like a kite, he could fly, and he swooped through in a series of aerial cartwheels as he sailed toward Jamie and his party.

Becky looked up at Mister Jeepers and laughed from pure joy. "Jamie," she said, "you live in the best place in the world!"

At night, when Jamie lay in bed with his stuffed giraffe, Selena would ride a beam of pale light from the Moon to the Earth and sit by Jamie's side. She was a pale woman, slightly translucent, with a silver crescent on her brow. She would stroke Jamie's forehead with a cool hand, and she would sing to him until his eyes grew heavy and slumber stole upon him.

> "The birds have tucked their heads
> The night is dark and deep
> All is quiet, all is safe,
> And little Jamie goes to sleep."

Whenever Jamie woke during the night, Selena was there to comfort him. He was glad that Selena always watched out for him, because sometimes he still had nightmares about being in the hospital. When the nightmares came, she was always there to comfort him, stroke him, sing him back to sleep.

Before long the nightmares began to fade.

Princess Gigunda always took Jamie for lessons. She was a huge woman, taller than Daddy, with frowsy hair and big bare feet and a crown that could never be made to sit straight on her head. She was homely, with a mournful face that was ugly and endearing at the same time. As she shuffled along with Jamie to his lessons, Princess Gigunda complained about the way her feet hurt, and about how she was a giant and unattractive, and how she would never be married.

"I'll marry you when I get bigger," Jamie said loyally, and the Princess's homely face screwed up into an expression of beaming pleasure.

Jamie had different lessons with different people. Mrs. Winkle, down at the little red brick schoolhouse, taught him his ABCs. Coach Toad—who *was* one—taught him field games, where he raced and jumped and threw against various people and animals. Mr. McGillicuddy, a pleasant whiskered fat man who wore red sleepers with a trapdoor in back, showed him his magic globe. When Jamie put his finger anywhere on the globe, trumpets began to sound, and he could see what was happening where he was pointing, and Mr. McGillicuddy would take him on a tour and show him interesting things. Buildings, statues, pictures, parks, people. "This is Nome," he would say. "Can you say Nome?"

"Nome," Jamie would repeat, shaping his mouth around the unfamiliar word, and Mr. McGillicuddy would smile and bob his head and look pleased.

If Jamie did well on his lessons, he got extra time with the Whirlikins, or at the Zoo, or with Mr. Fuzzy or in Pandaland. Until the dinner bell rang, and it was time to go home.

Jamie did well with his lessons almost every day.

When Princess Gigunda took him home from his lessons, Mister Jeepers would fly from the ridgepole to meet him, and tell him that his family was ready to see him. And then Momma and Daddy and Becky would wave from the windows of the house, and he would run to meet them.

Once, when he was in the living room telling his family about his latest trip through Mr. McGillicuddy's magic globe, he began skipping around with enthusiasm, and waving his arms like a Whirlikin, and suddenly he noticed that no one else was paying attention. That Momma and Daddy and Becky were staring at something else, their faces frozen in different attitudes of polite attention.

Jamie felt a chill finger touch his neck.

"Momma?" Jamie said. "Daddy?" Momma and Daddy did not respond. Their faces didn't move. Daddy's face was blurred strangely, as if it had been caught in the middle of movement.

"Daddy?" Jamie came close and tried to tug at his father's shirtsleeve. It was hard, like marble, and his fingers couldn't get a purchase at it. Terror blew hot in his heart.

"*Daddy?*" Jamie cried. He tried to tug harder. "Daddy! Wake up!" Daddy didn't respond. He ran to Momma and tugged at her hand. "Momma! Momma!" Her hand was like the hand of a statue. She didn't move no matter how hard Jamie pulled.

"Help!" Jamie screamed. "Mister Jeepers! Mr. Fuzzy! Help my momma!" Tears fell down his face as he ran from Becky to Momma to Daddy, tugging and pulling at them, wrapping his arms around their frozen legs and trying to pull them toward him. He ran outside, but everything was curiously still. No wind blew. Mister Jeepers sat on the ridgepole, a broad smile fixed as usual to his face, but he was frozen, too, and did not respond to Jamie's calls.

Terror pursued him back into the house. This was far worse than anything that had happened to him in the hospital, worse even than the pain. Jamie ran into the living room, where his family stood still as statues, and then recoiled in horror. A stranger had entered the room—or rather just parts of a stranger, a pair of hands encased in black gloves with strange silver circuit patterns on the backs, and a strange glowing opalescent face with a pair of wraparound dark glasses drawn across it like a line.

"Interface crashed, all right," the stranger said, as if to someone Jamie couldn't see.

Jamie gave a scream. He ran behind Momma's legs for protection.

"Oh, shit," the stranger said. "The kid's still running." He began purposefully moving his hands as if poking at the air. Jamie was sure that it was some kind of terrible attack, a spell to turn him to stone. He tried to run away, tripped over Becky's immovable feet and hit the floor hard, and then crawled away, the hall rug bunching up under his hands and knees as he skidded away, his own screams ringing in his ears . . .

. . . He sat up in bed, shrieking. The cool night tingled on his skin. He felt Selena's hand on his forehead, and he jerked away with a cry.

"Is something wrong?" came Selena's calm voice. "Did you have a bad dream?" Under the glowing crescent on her brow, Jamie could see the concern in her eyes.

"Where are Momma and Daddy?" Jamie shrieked.

"They're fine," Selena said. "They're asleep in their room. Was it a bad dream?"

Jamie threw off the covers and leaped out of bed. He ran down the hall, the floorboards cool on his bare feet. Selena floated after him in her serene, concerned way. He threw open the door to his parents' bedroom and snapped on the light, then gave a cry as he saw them huddled beneath their blanket. He flung himself at his mother, and gave a sob of relief as she opened her eyes and turned to him.

"Something wrong?" Momma said. "Was it a bad dream?"

"No!" Jamie wailed. He tried to explain, but even he knew that his words made no sense. Daddy rose from his pillow, looking seriously at Jamie, and then turned to ruffle his hair.

"Sounds like a pretty bad dream, trouper," Daddy said. "Let's get you back to bed."

"No!" Jamie buried his face in his mother's neck. "I don't want to go back to bed!"

"All right, Jamie," Momma said. She patted Jamie's back. "You can sleep here with us. But just for tonight, okay?"

"Wanna stay here," Jamie mumbled.

He crawled under the covers between Momma and Daddy. They each kissed him, and Daddy turned off the light. "Just go to sleep, trouper," he said. "And don't worry. You'll have good dreams from now on."

Selena, faintly glowing in the darkness, sat silently in the corner. "Shall I sing?" she asked.

"Yes, Selena," Daddy said. "Please sing for us."

Selena began to sing,

> "The birds have tucked their heads
> The night is dark and deep
> All is quiet, all is safe,
> And little Jamie goes to sleep."

But Jamie did not sleep. Despite the singing, the dark night, the rhythmic breathing of his parents, and the comforting warmth of their bodies.

It *wasn't* a dream, he knew. His family had really been frozen.

Something, or someone, had turned them to stone. Probably that evil disembodied head and pair of hands. And now, for some reason, his parents didn't remember.

Something had made them forget.

Jamie stared into the darkness. What, he thought, if these *weren't* his parents? If his parents were still stone, hidden away somewhere? What if these substitutes were bad people—kidnappers or worse—people who just *looked* like his real parents? What if they were evil people who were just waiting for him to fall asleep, and then they would turn to monsters, with teeth and fangs and a horrible light in their eyes, and they would tear him to bits right here in the bed . . .

Talons of panic clawed at Jamie's heart. Selena's song echoed in his ears. He *wasn't* going to sleep! He *wasn't!*

And then he did. It wasn't anything like normal sleep—it was as if sleep was *imposed* on him, as if something had just *ordered* his mind to sleep. It was just like a wave that rolled over him, an irresistible force, blotting out his sense, his body, his mind . . .

I *won't* sleep! he thought in defiance, but then his thoughts were extinguished.

When he woke he was back in his own bed, and it was morning, and Mister Jeepers was floating outside the window. "Jamie's awake!" he sang. "Jamie's awake and ready for a new day!"

And then his parents came bustling in, kissing him and petting him and taking him downstairs for breakfast.

His fears seemed foolish now, in full daylight, with Mister Jeepers dancing in the air outside and singing happily.

But sometimes, at night while Selena crooned by his bedside, he gazed into the darkness and felt a thrill of fear.

And he never forgot, not entirely.

A few days later Don Quixote wandered into the world, a lean man who frequently fell off his lean horse in a clang of homemade armor. He was given to making wan comments in both English and his own language, which turned out to be Spanish.

"Can you teach me Spanish irregular verbs?" Jamie asked.

"Sí, naturalmente," said Don Quixote. "But I will have to teach you some other Spanish as well." He looked particularly mournful. "Let's start with corazón. It means 'heart.' Mi corazón," he said with a sigh, "is breaking for love of Dulcinea."

After a few sessions with Don Quixote—mixed with a lot of sighing about corazóns and Dulcinea—Jamie took a grip on his courage, marched up to El Castillo, and spoke to La Duchesa. "Pierdo, sueño, haría, ponto!" he cried.

La Duchesa's eyes widened in surprise, and as she bent toward Jamie her severe face became almost kindly. "You are obviously a very intelligent boy," she said.

"You may enter my castle."

And so Don Quixote and La Duchesa, between the two of them, began to teach Jamie to speak Spanish. If he did well, he was allowed into the parts of the castle where the musicians played and the dancers stamped, where brave Castilian knights jousted in the tilting yard, and Señor Esteban told stories in Spanish, always careful to use words that Jamie already knew.

Jamie couldn't help but notice that sometimes Don Quixote behaved strangely. Once, when Jamie was visiting the Whirlikins, Don Quixote charged up on his horse, waving his sword and crying out that he would save Jamie from the goblins that were attacking him. Before Jamie could explain that the Whirlikins were harmless, Don Quixote galloped to the attack. The Whirlikins, alarmed, screwed themselves into the ground where they were safe, and Don Quixote fell off his horse trying to swing at one with his sword. After poor Quixote fell off his horse a few times, it was Jamie who had to rescue the Don, not the other way around.

It was sort of sad and sort of funny. Every time Jamie started to laugh about it, he saw Don Quixote's mournful face in his mind, and his laugh grew uneasy.

After a while, Jamie's sister Becky began to share Jamie's lessons. She joined him and Princess Gigunda on the trip to the little schoolhouse, learned reading and math from Mrs. Winkle, and then, after some coaching from Jamie and Don Quixote, she marched to La Duchesa to shout irregular verbs and gain entrance to El Castillo.

Around that time Marcus Tullius Cicero turned up to take them both to the Forum Romanum, a new part of the world that had appeared to the south of the Whirlikins' territory. But Cicero and the people in the Forum, all the shopkeepers and politicians, did not teach Latin the way Don Quixote taught Spanish, explaining what the new words meant in English, they just talked Latin at each other and expected Jamie and Becky to understand. Which, eventually, they did. The Spanish helped. Jamie was a bit better at Latin than Becky, but he explained to her that it was because he was older.

It was Becky who became interested in solving Princess Gigunda's problem. "We should find her somebody to love," she said.

"She loves us," Jamie said.

"Don't be silly," Becky said. "She wants a boyfriend."

"I'm her boyfriend," Jamie insisted.

Becky looked a little impatient. "Besides," she said, "it's a puzzle. Just like La Duchesa and her verbs."

This had not occurred to Jamie before, but now that Becky mentioned it, the idea seemed obvious. There were a lot of puzzles around, which one or the other of them was always solving, and Princess Gigunda's lovelessness was, now that he saw it, clearly among them.

So they set out to find Princess Gigunda a mate. This question occupied them for several days, and several candidates were discussed and rejected. They found no answers until they went to the chariot race of the Circus Maximus. It was the first race in the Circus ever, because the place had just appeared on the other side of the Palatine Hill from the Forum, and there was a very large, very excited crowd.

The names of the charioteers were announced as they paraded their chariots to the starting line. The trumpets sounded, and the chariots bolted from the start as the drivers whipped up the horses. Jamie watched enthralled as they rolled around the *spina* for the first lap, and then shouted in surprise at the sight of Don Quixote galloping onto the Circus Maximus, shouting that he was about to stop this group of rampaging demons from destroying the land, and planted himself directly in the path of the oncoming chariots. Jamie shouted along with the crowd for the Don to get out of the way before he got killed.

Fortunately Quixote's horse had more sense than he did, because the spindly animal saw the chariots coming and bolted, throwing its rider. One of the chariots rode right over poor Quixote, and there was a horrible clanging noise, but after the chariot passed, Quixote sat up, apparently unharmed. His armor had saved him.

Jamie jumped up from his seat and was about to run down to help Don Quixote off the course, but Becky grabbed his arm. "Hang on," she said, "someone else will look after him, and I have an idea."

She explained that Don Quixote would make a perfect man for Princess Gigunda.

"But he's in love with Dulcinea!"

Becky looked at him patiently. "Has anyone ever *seen* Dulcinea? All we have to do is convince Don Quixote that Princess Gigunda *is* Dulcinea."

After the races, they found that Don Quixote had been arrested by the lictors and sent to the Lautumiae, which was the Roman jail. They weren't allowed to see the prisoner, so they went in search of Cicero, who was a lawyer and was able to get Quixote out of the Lautumiae on the promise that he would never visit Rome again.

"I regret to the depths of my soul that my parole does not enable me to destroy these demons," Quixote said as he left Rome's town limits.

"Let's not get into that," Becky said. "What we wanted to tell you was that we've found Dulcinea."

The old man's eyes widened in joy. He clutched at his armor-clad heart. "*Miamor!* Where is she? I must run to her at once!"

"Not just yet," Becky said. "You should know that she's been changed. She doesn't look like she used to."

"Has some evil sorcerer done this?" Quixote demanded.

"Yes!" Jamie interrupted. He was annoyed that Becky had taken charge of everything, and he wanted to add his contribution to the scheme. "The sorcerer was just a head!" he shouted. "A floating head, and a pair of hands! And he wore dark glasses and had no body!"

A shiver of fear passed through him as he remembered the eerie floating head, but the memory of his old terror did not stop his words from spilling out.

Becky gave him a strange look. "Yeah," she said. "That's right."

"He crashed the interface!" Jamie shouted, the words coming to him out of memory.

Don Quixote paid no attention to this, but Becky gave him another look.

"You're not as dumb as you look, Digit," she said.

"I do not care about Dulcinea's appearance," Don Quixote declared, "I love only the goodness that dwells in her *corazón*."

"She's Princess Gigunda!" Jamie shouted, jumping up and down in enthusiasm. "She's been Princess Gigunda all along!"

And so, the children following, Don Quixote ran clanking to where Princess Gigunda waited near Jamie's house, fell down to one knee, and began to kiss and weep over the Princess's hand. The Princess seemed a little surprised by this until Becky told her that she was really the long-lost Dulcinea, changed into a giant by an evil magician, although she probably didn't remember it because that was part of the spell, too.

So while the Don and the Princess embraced, kissed, and began to warble a love duet, Becky turned to Jamie.

"What's that stuff about the floating head?" she asked. "Where did you come up with that?"

"I dunno," Jamie said. He didn't want to talk about his memory of his family being turned to stone, the eerie glowing figure floating before them. He didn't want to remember how everyone said it was just a dream.

He didn't want to talk about the suspicions that had never quite gone away.

"That stuff was weird, Digit," Becky said. "It gave me the creeps. Let me know before you start talking about stuff like that again."

"Why do you call me Digit?" Jamie asked.

Becky smirked. "No reason," she said.

"Jamie's home!" Mister Jeepers's voice warbled from the sky. Jamie looked up to see Mister Jeepers doing joyful aerial loops overhead. "Master Jamie's home at last!"

"Where shall we go?" Jamie asked.

Their lessons for the day were over, and he and Becky were leaving the little red schoolhouse. Becky, as usual, had done very well on her lessons, better than her older brother, and Jamie felt a growing sense of annoyance. At least he was still better at Latin and computer science.

"I dunno," Becky said. "Where do you want to go?"

"How about Pandaland? We could ride the Whoosh Machine."

Becky wrinkled her face. "I'm tired of that kid stuff," she said.

Jamie looked at her. "But you're a kid."

"I'm not as little as you, Digit," Becky said.

Jamie glared. This was too much. "You're my little sister! I'm bigger than you!"

"No, you're not," Becky said. She stood before him, her arms flung out in exasperation. "Just *notice something* for once, will you?"

Jamie bit back on his temper and looked, and he saw that Becky was, in fact, bigger than he was. And older-looking. Puzzlement replaced his fading anger.

"How did you get so big?" Jamie asked.

"I grew. And you *didn't* grow. Not as fast anyway."

"I don't understand."

Becky's lip curled. "Ask Mom or Dad. Just *ask* them." Her expression turned stony. "Just don't believe everything they tell you."

"What do you mean?"

Becky looked angry for a moment, and then her expression relaxed. "Look," she said, "just go to Pandaland and have fun, okay? You don't need me for that. I want to go and make some calls to my friends."

"What friends?"

Becky looked angry again. "My friends. It doesn't matter who they are!"

"Fine!" Jamie shouted. "I can have fun by myself!"

Becky turned and began to walk home, her legs scissoring against the background of the green grass. Jamie glared after her, then turned and began the walk to Pandaland.

He did all his favorite things, rode the Ferris wheel and the Whoosh Machine, watched Rizzio the Strongman and the clowns. He enjoyed himself, but his enjoyment felt hollow. He found himself *watching*, watching himself at play, watching himself enjoying the rides.

Watching himself not grow as fast as his little sister.

Watching himself wondering whether or not to ask his parents about why that was.

He had the idea that he wouldn't like their answers.

He didn't see as much of Becky after that. They would share lessons, and then Becky would lock herself in her room to talk to her friends on the phone.

Becky didn't have a telephone in her room, though. He looked once when she wasn't there.

After a while, Becky stopped accompanying him for lessons. She'd got ahead of him on everything except Latin, and it was too hard for Jamie to keep up.

After that, he hardly saw Becky at all. But when he saw her, he saw that she was still growing fast. Her clothing was different, and her hair. She'd started wearing makeup.

He didn't know whether he liked her anymore or not.

It was Jamie's birthday. He was eleven years old, and Momma and Daddy and Becky had all come for a party. Don Quixote and Princess Gigunda serenaded Jamie from outside the window, accompanied by La Duchesa on Spanish guitar. There was a big cake with eleven candles. Momma gave Jamie a chart of the stars. When he touched a star, a voice would appear telling Jamie about the star, and lines would appear on the chart showing any constellation the star happened to belong to. Daddy gave Jamie a car, a miniature Mercedes convertible, scaled to Jamie's size, which he could drive around the country and which he could use in the Circus Maximus when the chariots weren't racing. His sister gave Jamie a kind of lamp stand that would project lights and moving patterns on the walls and ceiling when the lights were off. "Listen to music when you use it," she said.

"Thank you, Becky," Jamie said.

"Becca," she said. "My name is Becca now. Try to remember."

"Okay," Jamie said. "Becca."

Becky—Becca—looked at Momma. "I'm dying for a cigarette," she said. "Can I go, uh, out for a minute?"

Momma hesitated, but Daddy looked severe. "Becca," she said, "this is *Jamie's birthday*. We're all here to celebrate. So why don't we all eat some cake and have a nice time?"

"It's not even real cake," Becca said. "It doesn't *taste* like real cake."

"It's a *nice cake*," Daddy insisted. "Why don't we talk about this later? Let's just have a special time for Jamie."

Becca stood up from the table. "For the *Digit?*" she said. "Why are we having a good time for *Jamie?* He's not even a *real person!*" She thumped herself on the chest. "*I'm* a real person!" she shouted. "Why don't we ever have special times for *me?*"

But Daddy was on his feet by that point and shouting, and Momma was trying to get everyone to be quiet, and Becca was shouting back, and suddenly a determined look entered her face and she just disappeared—suddenly, she wasn't there anymore, there was only just air.

Jamie began to cry. So did Momma. Daddy paced up and down and swore, and then he said, "I'm going to go get her." Jamie was afraid he'd disappear like Becca, and he gave a cry of despair, but Daddy didn't disappear, he just stalked out of the dining room and slammed the door behind him.

Momma pulled Jamie onto her lap and hugged him. "Don't worry, Jamie," she said. "Becky just did that to be mean."

"What happened?" Jamie asked.

"Don't worry about it." Momma stroked his hair. "It was just a mean trick."

"She's growing up," Jamie said. "She's grown faster than me and I don't understand."

"Wait till Daddy gets back," Momma said, "and we'll talk about it."

But Daddy was clearly in no mood for talking when he returned, without Becca. "We're going to have *fun*," he snarled, and reached for the knife to cut the cake.

The cake tasted like ashes in Jamie's mouth. When the Don and Princess Gigunda, Mister Jeepers and Rizzio the Strongman, came into the dining room and sang "Happy Birthday," it was all Jamie could do to hold back the tears.

Afterward, he drove his new car to the Circus Maximus and drove as fast as he could on the long oval track. The car really wouldn't go very fast. The bleachers on either side were empty, and so was the blue sky above.

Maybe it was a puzzle, he thought, like Princess Gigunda's love life. Maybe all he had to do was follow the right clue, and everything would be fine.

What's the moral they're trying to teach? he wondered.

But all he could do was go in circles, around and around the empty stadium.

"Hey, Digit. Wake up."

Jamie came awake suddenly with a stifled cry. The room whirled around him. He blinked, realized that the whirling came from the colored lights projected by his birthday present, Becca's lamp stand.

Becca was sitting on his bedroom chair, a cigarette in her hand. Her feet, in the steel-capped boots she'd been wearing lately, were propped up on the bed.

"Are you awake, Jamie?" It was Selena's voice. "Would you like me to sing you a lullaby?"

"Fuck off, Selena," Becca said. "Get out of here. Get lost."

Selena cast Becca a mournful look, then sailed backward, out of the window, riding a beam of moonlight to her pale home in the sky. Jamie watched her go, and felt as if a part of himself was going with her, a part that he would never see again.

"Selena and the others have to do what you tell them, mostly," Becca said. "Of course, Mom and Dad wouldn't tell you that."

Jamie looked at Becca. "What's happening?" he said. "Where did you go today?"

Colored lights swam over Becca's face. "I'm sorry if I spoiled your birthday, Digit. I just got tired of the lies, you know? They'd kill me if they knew I was here now, talking to you." Becca took a draw on her cigarette, held her breath for a second or two, then exhaled. Jamie didn't see or taste any smoke.

"You know what they wanted me to do?" she said. "Wear a little girl's body, so I wouldn't look any older than you, and keep you company in that stupid school for seven hours a day." She shook her head. "I wouldn't do it. They yelled and yelled, but I was damned if I would."

"I don't understand."

Becca flicked invisible ashes off her cigarette and looked at Jamie for a long time. Then she sighed.

"Do you remember when you were in the hospital?" she said.

Jamie nodded. "I was really sick."

"I was so little then, I don't really remember it very well," Becca said. "But the point is—" She sighed again. "The point is that you weren't getting well. So they decided to—" She shook her head. "Dad took advantage of his position at the University, and the fact that he's been a big donor. They were doing AI research, and the neurology department was into brain modeling, and they needed a test subject, and—Well, the idea is, they've got some of your tissue, and when they get cloning up and running, they'll put you back in—" She saw Jamie's stare, then shook her head. "I'll make it simple, okay?"

She took her feet off the bed and leaned closer to Jamie. A shiver ran up his back at her expression. "They made a copy of you. An *electronic* copy. They scanned your brain and built a holographic model of it inside a computer, and they put it in a virtual environment, and—" She sat back, took a drag on her cigarette. "And here you are," she said.

Jamie looked at her. "I don't understand."

Colored lights gleamed in Becca's eyes. "You're in a computer, okay? And you're a program. You know what that is, right? From computer class? And the program is sort of in the shape of your mind. Don Quixote and Princess Gigunda are programs, too. And Mrs. Winkle down at the schoolhouse is *usually* a program, but if she needs to teach something complex, then she's an education major from the University."

Jamie felt as if he'd just been hollowed out, a void inside his ribs. "I'm not real?" he said. "I'm not a person?"

"Wrong," Becca said. "You're real, alright. You're the apple of our parents' eye." Her tone was bitter. "Programs are real things," she said, "and yours was a real hack, you know, absolute cutting-edge state-of-the-art technoshit. And the computer that you're in is real, too—I'm interfaced with it right now, down in the family room—we have to wear suits with sensors and a helmet with scanners and stuff. I hope to fuck they don't hear me talking to you down here."

"But what—" Jamie swallowed hard. How could he swallow if he was just a string of code? "What happened to *me*? The original me?"

Becca looked cold. "Well," she said, "you had cancer. You died."

"Oh." A hollow wind blew through the void inside him.

"They're going to bring you back. As soon as the clone thing works out—but this is a government computer you're in, and there are all these government restrictions on cloning, and—" She shook her head. "Look, Digit," she said. "You really need to know this stuff, okay?"

"I understand." Jamie wanted to cry. But only real people cried, he thought, and he wasn't real. He wasn't real.

"The program that runs this virtual environment is huge, okay, and *you're* a big program, and the University computer is used for a lot of research, and a lot of the research has a higher priority than *you* do. So you don't run in real-time—that's why I'm growing faster than you are. I'm spending more hours being me than you are. And the parents—" She rolled her eyes. "They aren't making this any better, with their emphasis on *normal family life*."

She sucked on her cigarette, then stubbed it out in something invisible. "See, they want us to be this *normal family*. So we have breakfast together every day, and dinner every night, and spend the evening at the Zoo or in Pandaland or someplace. But the dinner that we eat with *you* is virtual, it doesn't taste like anything—the grant ran out before they got that part of the interface right—so we eat this fast-food crap before we interface with you, and then have dinner, all *over* again with *you* . . . Is this making any sense? Because Dad has a job and Mom has a job and I go to school and have friends and stuff, so we really can't get together every night. So they just close your program file, shut it right down, when they're not available to interface with you as what Dad calls a 'family unit,' and that means that there are a lot of hours, days sometimes, when you're just *not running*, you might as well really be *dead*—" She blinked. "Sorry," she said. "Anyway, we're *all* getting older a lot faster than you are, and it's not fair to you, that's what I think. Especially because the University computer runs fastest at night, because people don't use them as much then, and you're pretty much real-time then, so interfacing with you would be almost *normal*, but Mom and Dad sleep then, 'cuz they have day jobs, and they can't have you running around unsupervised in here, for God's sake, they think it's unsafe or something . . ."

She paused, then reached into her shirt pocket for another cigarette. "Look," she said, "I'd better get out of here before they figure out I'm talking to you. And then they'll pull my access codes or something." She stood, brushed something off her jeans. "Don't tell the parents about this stuff right away. Otherwise they might erase you, and load a backup that doesn't know shit. Okay?"

And she vanished, as she had that afternoon.

Jamie sat in the bed, hugging his knees. He could feel his heart beating in the darkness. How can a program have a heart? he wondered.

Dawn slowly encroached upon the night, and then there was Mister Jeepers, turning lazy cartwheels in the air, his red face leering in the window.

"Jamie's awake!" he said. "Jamie's awake and ready for a new day!"

"Fuck off," Jamie said, and buried his face in the blanket.

Jamie asked to learn more about computers and programming. Maybe, he thought, he could find clues there, he could solve the puzzle. His parents agreed, happy to let him follow his interests.

After a few weeks, he moved into El Castillo. He didn't tell anyone he was going, he just put some of his things in his car, took them up to a tower room, and threw them down on the bed he found there. His mom came to find him when he didn't come home for dinner.

"It's dinnertime, Jamie," she said. "Didn't you hear the dinner bell?"

"I'm going to stay here for a while," Jamie said.

"You're going to get hungry if you don't come home for dinner."

"I don't need food," Jamie said.

His mom smiled brightly. "You need food if you're going to keep up with the Whirlikins," she said.

Jamie looked at her. "I don't care about that kid stuff anymore," he said.

When his mother finally turned and left, Jamie noticed that she moved like an old person.

After a while, he got used to the hunger that was programmed into him. It was always *there*, he was always aware of it, but he got so he could ignore it after a while.

But he couldn't ignore the need to sleep. That was just built into the program, and eventually, try though he might, he needed to give in to it.

He found out he could order the people in the castle around, and he amused himself by making them stand in embarrassing positions, or stand on their heads and sing, or form human pyramids for hours and hours.

Sometimes he made them fight, but they weren't very good at it.

He couldn't make Mrs. Winkle at the schoolhouse do whatever he wanted, though, or any of the people who were supposed to teach him things. When it was time for a lesson, Princess Gigunda turned up. She wouldn't follow his orders, she'd just pick him up and carry him to the little red schoolhouse and plunk him down in his seat.

"You're not real!" he shouted, kicking in her arms. "You're not real! And I'm not real, either!"

But they made him learn about the world that was real, about geography and geology and history, although none of it mattered here.

After the first couple times Jamie had been dragged to school, his father met him outside the schoolhouse at the end of the day.

"You need some straightening out," he said. He looked grim. "You're part of a family. You belong with us. You're not going to stay in the castle anymore, you're going to have a *normal family life.*"

"No!" Jamie shouted. "I like the castle!"

Dad grabbed him by the arm and began to drag him homeward. Jamie called him a *pendejo* and a *fellator.*

"I'll punish you if I have to," his father said.

"How are you going to do that?" Jamie demanded. "You gonna erase my file? Load a backup?"

A stunned expression crossed his father's face. His body seemed to go through a kind of stutter, and the grip on Jamie's arm grew nerveless. Then his face flushed with anger. "What do you mean?" he demanded.

"Who told you this?"

Jamie wrenched himself free of Dad's weakened grip.

"I figured it out by myself," Jamie said. "It wasn't hard. I'm not a kid anymore."

"I—" His father blinked, and then his face hardened. "You're still coming home."

Jamie backed away. "I want some changes!" he said. "I don't want to be shut off all the time."

Dad's mouth compressed to a thin line. "It was Becky who told you this, wasn't it?"

Jamie felt an inspiration. "It was Mister Jeepers! There's a flaw in his programming! He answers whatever question I ask him!"

Jamie's father looked uncertain. He held out his hand. "Let's go home," he said. "I need to think about this."

Jamie hesitated. "Don't erase me," he said. "Don't load a backup. Please. I don't want to die *twice.*"

Dad's look softened. "I won't."

"I want to grow up," Jamie said. "I don't want to be a little kid forever."

Dad held out his hand again. Jamie thought for a moment, then took the hand. They walked over the green grass toward the white frame house on the hill.

"Jamie's home!" Mister Jeepers floated overhead, turning aerial cartwheels. "Jamie's home at last!"

A spasm of anger passed through Jamie at the sight of the witless grin. He pointed at the ground in front of him.

"Crash right here!" he ordered. "*Fast!*"

Mister Jeepers came spiraling down, an expression of comic terror on his face, and smashed to the ground where Jamie pointed at the sight of the crumpled body and laughed.

"Jamie's home at last!" Mister Jeepers said.

As soon as Jamie could, he got one of the programmers at the University to fix him up a flight program like the one Mister Jeepers had been using. He swooped and soared, zooming like a super hero through the sky, stunting between the towers of El Castillo and soaring over upturned, wondering faces in the Forum.

He couldn't seem to go as fast as he really wanted. When he started increasing speed, all the scenery below paused in its motion for a second or two, then jumped forward with a jerk. The software couldn't refresh the scenery fast enough to match his speed. It felt strange, because throughout his flight he could feel the wind on his face.

So this, he thought, was why his car couldn't go fast.

So he decided to climb high. He turned his face to the blue sky and went straight up. The world receded, turned small. He could see the Castle, the hills of Whirlikin Country, the crowded Forum, the huge oval of the Circus Maximus. It was like a green plate, with a fuzzy, nebulpus horizon where the sky started.

And, right in the center, was the little two-story frame house where he'd grown up. It was laid out below him like scenery in a snow globe.

After a while he stopped climbing. It took him a while to realize it, because he still felt the wind blowing in his face, but the world below stopped getting smaller.

He tried going faster. The wind blasted onto him from above, but his position didn't change.

He'd reached the limits of his world. He couldn't get any higher.

Jamie flew out to the edges of the world, to the horizon. No matter how he urged his program to move, he couldn't make his world fade away.

He was trapped inside the snow globe, and there was no way out.

It was quite a while before Jamie saw Becca again. She picked her way through the labyrinth beneath El Castillo to his throne room, and Jamie slowly materialized atop his throne of skulls. She didn't appear surprised.

"I see you've got a little Dark Lord thing going here," she said.

"It passes the time," Jamie said.

"And all those pits and stakes and tripwires?"

"Death traps."

"Took me forever to get in here, Digit. I kept getting de-rezzed."

Jamie smiled. "That's the idea."

"Whirlikins as weapons." She nodded. "That was a good one. Bored a hole right through me, the first time."

"Since I'm stuck living here," Jamie said, "I figure I might as well be in charge of the environment. Some of the student programmers at the University helped me with some cool effects."

Screams echoed through the throne room. Fires leaped out of pits behind him. The flames illuminated the form of Marcus Tullius Cicero, who hung crucified above a sea of flame.

"*O tempora, o mores!*" moaned Cicero.

Becca nodded. "Nice," she said. "Not my scene exactly, but nice."

"Since I can't leave," Jamie said, "I want a say in who gets to visit. So either you wait till I'm ready to talk to you, or you take your chances on the death traps."

"Well. Looks like you're sitting pretty, then."

Jamie shrugged. Flames belched. "I'm getting bored with it. I might just wipe it all out and build another place to live in. I can't tell you the number of battles I've won, the number of kingdoms I've trampled. In this reality and others. It's all the same after a while." He looked at her. "You've grown."

"So have you."

"Once the paterfamilias finally decided to allow it." He smiled. "We still have dinner together sometimes, in the old house. Just a normal family, as Dad says. Except that sometimes I turn up in the form of a werewolf, or a giant, or something."

"So they tell me."

"The advantage of being software is that I can look like anything I want. But that's the disadvantage, too, because I can't really *become* something else, I'm still just . . . me. I may wear another program as a disguise, but I'm still the same program inside, and I'm not a good enough programmer to mess with that, yet." Jamie hopped off his throne, walked a nervous little circle around his sister. "So what brings you to the old neighborhood?" he asked. "The old folks said you were off visiting Aunt Maddy in the country."

"*Exiled*, they mean. I got knocked up, and after the abortion they sent me to Maddy. She was supposed to keep me under control, except she didn't." She picked an invisible piece of lint from her sweater. "So now I'm back." She looked at him. "I'm skipping a lot of the story, but I figure you wouldn't be interested."

"Does it have to do with sex?" Jamie asked. "I'm sort of interested in sex, even though I can't do it, and they're not likely to let me."

"*Let* you?"

"It would require a lot of new software and stuff. I was prepubescent when my brain structures were scanned, and the program isn't set up for making me a working adult, with adult desires et cetera. Nobody was thinking about putting me through adolescence at the time. And the administrators at the University told me that it was very unlikely that anyone was going to give them a grant so that a computer program could have sex." Jamie shrugged. "I don't miss it, I guess. But I'm sort of curious."

Surprise crossed Becca's face. "But there are all kinds of simulations, and . . ."

"They don't work for me, because my mind isn't structured so as to be able to achieve pleasure that way. I can manipulate the programs, but it's about as exciting as working a virtual butter churn." Jamie shrugged again. "But that's okay. I mean, I don't *miss* it. I can always give myself a jolt to the pleasure center if I want."

"Not the same thing," Becca said. "I've done both."

"I wouldn't know."

"I'll tell you about sex if you want," Becca said, "but that's not why I'm here."

"Yes?"

Becca hesitated. Licked her lips. "I guess I should just say it, huh?" she said. "Mom's dying. Pancreatic cancer."

Jamie felt sadness well in his mind. Only electrons, he thought, moving from one place to another. It was nothing real. He was programmed to feel an analog of sorrow, and that was all.

"She looks normal to me," he said, "when I see her." But that didn't mean anything: his mother chose what she wanted him to see, just as he chose a mask—a werewolf, a giant—for her.

And in neither case did the disguise at all matter. For behind the werewolf was a program that couldn't alter its parameters; and behind the other, ineradicable cancer.

Becca watched him from slitted eyes. "Dad wants her to be scanned, and come here. So we can still be a *normal family* even after she dies."

Jamie was horrified. "Tell her *no*," he said. "Tell her she can't come!"

"I don't think she wants to. But Dad is very insistent."

"She'll be here *forever*! It'll be awful!"

Becca looked around. "Well, she wouldn't do much for your Dark Lord act, that's for sure. I'm sure Sauron's mom didn't hang around the Dark Tower, nagging him about the unproductive way he was spending his time."

Fires belched. The ground trembled. Stalactites rained down like arrows.

"That's not it," Jamie said. "She doesn't want to be here no matter what I'm doing, no matter where I live. Because whatever this place looks like, it's a prison." Jamie looked at his sister. "I don't want my mom in a prison."

Leaping flames glittered in Becca's eyes. "You can change the world you live in," she said. "That's more than I can do."

"But I can't," Jamie said. "I can change the way it *looks*, but I can't change anything *real*. I'm a program, and a program is an *artifact*. I'm a piece of *engineering*. I'm a simulation, with simulated sensory organs that interact with simulated environments—I can only interact with *other artifacts*. None of it's real. I don't know what the real world looks or feels or tastes like, I only know what simulations tell me they're *supposed* to taste like. And I can't change any of my parameters unless I mess with the engineering, and I can't do that unless the programmers agree, and even when that happens, I'm still as artificial as I was before. And the computer I'm in is old and clunky, and soon nobody's going to run my operating system anymore, and I'll not only be an artifact, I'll be a museum piece."

"There are other artificial intelligences out there," Becca said. "I keep hearing about them."

"I've talked to them. Most of them aren't very interesting—it's like talking to a dog, or maybe to a very intelligent microwave oven. And they've scanned some people in, but those were adults, and all they wanted to do, once they got inside, was to escape. Some of them went crazy."

Becca gave a twisted smile. "I used to be so jealous of you, you know. You lived in this beautiful world, no pollution, no violence, no shit on the streets."

"*Integra mens augustissima possessio,*" said Cicero.

"Shut up!" Jamie told him. "What the fuck do you know?"

Becca shook her head. "I've seen those old movies, you know? Where somebody gets turned into a computer program, and next thing you know he's in every computer in the world, and running everything?"

"I've seen those, too. Ha ha. Very funny. Shows you what people know about programs."

"Yeah. Shows you what they know."

"I'll talk to Mom," Jamie said.

Big tears welled out of Mom's eyes and trailed partway down her face, then disappeared. The scanners paid a lot of attention to eyes and mouths, for the sake of transmitting expression, but didn't always pick up the things between.

"I'm sorry," she said. "We didn't think this is how it would be."

"Maybe you should have given it more thought," Jamie said.

It isn't sorrow, he told himself again. It's just electrons moving.

"You were such a beautiful baby." Her lower lip trembled. "We didn't want to lose you. They said that it would only be a few years before they could implant your memories in a clone."

Jamie knew all that by now. Knew that the technology of reading memories turned out to be much, much simpler than implanting them—it had been discovered that the implantation had to be made while the brain was actually growing. And government restrictions on human cloning had made tests next to impossible, and that the team that had started his project had split up years ago, some to higher paying jobs, some retired, others to pet projects of their own. How his father had long ago used up whatever pull he'd had at the University trying to keep everything together. And how he long ago had acquired or purchased patents and copyrights for the whole scheme, except for Jamie's program, which was still owned jointly by the University and the family.

Tears reappeared on Mom's lower face, dripped off her chin. "There's potentially a lot of money at stake, you know. People want to raise perfect children. Keep them away from bad influences, make sure that they're raised free from violence."

"So they want to control the kid's environment," Jamie said.

"Yes. And make it *safe*. And wholesome. And—"

"Just like *normal family life*," Jamie finished. "No diapers, no vomit, no messes. No having to interact with the kid when the parents are tired. And then you just download the kid into an adult body, give him a diploma, and kick him out of the house. And call yourself a perfect parent."

"And there are *religious people* . . ." Mom licked her lips. "Your dad's been talking to them. They want to raise children in environments that reflect their beliefs completely. Places where there is no temptation, no sin. No science or ideas that contradict their own . . ."

"But Dad isn't religious," Jamie said.

"These people have money. Lots of money."

Mom reached out, took his hand. Jamie thought about all the code that enabled her to do it, that enabled them both to feel the pressure of unreal flesh on unreal flesh.

"I'll do what you wish, of course," she said. "I don't have that desire for immortality, the way your father does." She shook her head. "But I don't know what your father will do once his time comes."

The world was a disk a hundred meters across, covered with junk: old Roman ruins, gargoyles fallen from a castle wall, a broken chariot, a shattered bell. Outside the rim of the world, the sky was black, utterly black, without a ripple or a star.

Standing in the center of the world was a kind of metal tree with two forked, jagged arms.

"Hi, Digit," Becca said.

A dull fitful light gleamed on the metal tree, as if it were reflecting a bloody sunset.

"Hi, sis," it said.

"Well," Becca said. "We're alone now."

"I caught the notice of Dad's funeral. I hope nobody missed me."

"I missed you, Digit." Becca sighed. "Believe it or not."

"I'm sorry."

Becca restlessly kicked a piece of junk, a hubcap from an old, miniature car. It clanged as it found new lodgment in the rubble. "Can you appear as a person?" she asked. "It would make it easier to talk to you."

"I've finished with all that," Jamie said. "I'd have to resurrect too much dead programming. I've cut the world down to next to nothing. I've got rid of my body, my heartbeat, the sense of touch."

"All the human parts," Becca said sadly.

The dull red light oozed over the metal tree like a drop of blood. "Everything except sleep and dreams. It turns out that sleep and dreams have too much to do with the way people process memory. I can't get rid of them, not without cutting out too much of my mind." The tree gave a strange, disembodied laugh. "I dreamed about you, the other day. And about Cicero. We were talking Latin."

"I've forgotten all the Latin I ever knew." Becca tossed her hair, forced a laugh. "So what do you do nowadays?"

"Mostly I'm a conduit for data. The University has been using me as a research spider, which I don't mind doing, because it passes the time. Except that I take up a lot more memory than any real search spider, and don't do that much better a job. And the information I find doesn't have much to do with *me*—it's all about the real world. The world I can't touch." The metal tree bled color.

"Mostly," he said, "I've just been waiting for Dad to die. And now it's happened."

There was a moment of silence before Becca spoke. "You know that Dad had himself scanned before he went."

"Oh, yeah. I knew."

"He set up some kind of weird foundation that I'm not part of, with his patents and programs and so on, and his money and some other people's."

"He'd better not turn up here."

Becca shook her head. "He won't. Not without your permission anyway. Because I'm in charge here. You—your program—it's not a part of the foundation. Dad couldn't get it all, because the University has an interest, and so does the family." There was a moment of silence. "And I'm the family now."

"So you . . . *inherited* me," Jamie said. Cold scorn dripped from his words.

"That's right," Becca said. She squatted down amid the rubble, rested her forearms on her knees.

"What do you want me to do, Digit? What can I do to make it better for you?"

"No one ever asked me that," Jamie said.

There was another long silence.

"Shut it off," Jamie said. "Close the file. Erase it."

Becca swallowed hard. Tears shimmered in her eyes. "Are you sure?" she asked.

"Yes. I'm sure."

"And if they ever perfect the clone thing? If we could make you . . ." She took a breath. "A person?"

"No. It's too late. It's . . . not something I can want anymore."

Becca stood. Ran a hand through her hair. "I wish you could meet my daughter," she said. "Her name is Christy. She's a real beauty."

"You can bring her," Jamie said.

Becca shook her head. "This place would scare her. She's only three. I'd only bring her if we could have . . ."

"The old environment," Jamie finished. "Pandaland. Mister Jeepers. Whirlikin Country."

Becca forced a smile. "Those were happy days," she said. "They really were. I was jealous of you, I know, but when I look back at that time . . ." She wiped tears with the back of her hand. "It was the best."

"Virtual environments are nice places to visit, I guess," Jamie said. "But you don't want to live in one. Not forever." Becca looked down at her feet, planted amid rubble.

"Well," she said. "If you're sure about what you want."

"I am."

She looked up at the metal form, raised a hand. "Good-bye, Jamie," she said.

"Good-bye," he said.

She faded from the world.

And in time, the world and the tree faded, too.

Hand in hand, Daddy and Jamie walked to Whirlikins Country. Jamie had never seen the Whirlikins before, and he laughed and laughed as the Whirlikins spun beneath their orange sky.

The sound of a bell rang over the green hills. "Time for dinner, Jamie," Daddy said.

Jamie waved good-bye to the Whirlikins, and he and Daddy walked briskly over the fresh green grass toward home.

"Are you happy, Jamie?" Daddy asked.

"Yes, Daddy!" Jamie nodded. "I only wish Momma and Becky could be here with us."

"They'll be here soon."

When, he thought, they can get the simulations working properly.

Because this time, he thought, there would be no mistakes. The foundation he'd set up before he died had finally purchased the University's interest in Jamie's program—they funded some scholarships, that was all it finally took. There was no one in the Computer Department who had an interest anymore.

Jamie had been loaded from an old backup—there was no point in using the corrupt file that Jamie had become, the one that had turned itself into a *tree*, for heaven's sake.

The old world was up and running, with a few improvements. The foundation had bought their own computer—an old one, so it wasn't too expensive—that would run the environment full-time. Some other children might be scanned, to give Jamie some playmates and peer socialization.

This time it would work, Daddy thought. Because this time, Daddy was a program too, and he was going to be here every minute, making sure that the environment was correct and that everything went exactly according to plan. That he and

Jamie and everyone else had a normal family life, perfect and shining and safe.

And if the clone program ever worked out, they would come into the real world again. And if downloading into clones was never perfected, then they would stay here.

There was nothing wrong with the virtual environment. It was a *good* place.

Just like normal family life. Only forever.

And when this worked out, the foundation's backers—fine people, even if they did have some strange religious ideas—would have their own environments up and running. With churches, angels, and perhaps even the presence of God . . .

"Look!" Daddy said, pointing. "It's Mister Jeepers!"

Mister Jeepers flew off the rooftop and spun happy spirals in the air as he swooped toward Jamie. Jamie dropped Daddy's hand and ran laughing to greet his friend.

"Jamie's home!" Mister Jeepers cried. "Jamie's home at last!"

the real world

STEVEN UTLEY

Steven Utley's fiction has appeared in *The Magazine of Fantasy and Science Fiction, Universe, Galaxy, Amazing, Vertex, Stellar, Shayol,* and elsewhere. He was one of the best-known new writers of the '70s, both for his solo work and for some strong work in collaboration with fellow Texan Howard Waldrop, but fell silent at the end of the decade and wasn't seen in print again for more than ten years. In the last decade he's made a strong comeback, though, becoming a frequent contributor to *Asimov's Science Fiction* magazine, as well as selling again to *The Magazine of Fantasy and Science Fiction, Sci Fiction,* and elsewhere. Utley is the coeditor, with Geo. W. Proctor, of the anthology *Lone Star Universe,* the first—and probably the only—anthology of SF stories by Texans. His first collection, *Ghost Seas,* was published in 1997, and he is presently shopping a novel/collection based on his Silurian stories, such as the one that follows. His most recent books are collections of his poetry, *This Impatient Ape* and *Career Moves of the Gods.* He lives in Smyrna, Tennessee.

Here, in part of a long sequence of stories that Utley has been writing throughout the '90s (and that—unusual for a series, and a testament to the high regard in which editors hold Utley's talent—have appeared in almost every leading market in the field, from *Analog* to *Sci Fiction*), detailing the adventures and misadventures of time-traveling scientists exploring the distant Silurian Age, millions of years before the dinosaurs roamed the Earth, he offers us a parable of what's important and what's not—and wonders how you can be sure that you can tell the difference, when you can't even be sure of the very ground under your feet.

Everything felt like a dream. The flight attendants seemed to whisper past in the aisle. The other passengers were but shadows and echoes. Through the window, he could see the wing floating above an infinite expanse of cloudtop as flat and featureless as the peneplained landscapes of the Paleozoic. I'm just tired, he thought, without conviction.

Ivan forced his attention back to the laptop. He had called up an old documentary in which he himself appeared. "Resume," he said, very softly, and the image on the screen unfroze, and a familiar, strange voice said, "Plant life may actually have invaded the land during the Ordovician Period." Is that really me? he thought. My face, my eyes, I look so unlived-in. "We know about two dozen genera of land plant in the Silurian," and the screen first showed a tangle of creeping green tendrils at his younger self's feet, "such as these, which are called psilophytes," then a glistening algal mat. "The big flat things you see all over the mudflats are Nematophycus. The point is—"

His earphone buzzed softly. "Pause," he murmured to the laptop, and the image on the screen froze once more. He said, "Hello?" and heard his brother say, "How's the flight?"

"Don. I hope you're not calling to rescind my invitation."

"Michelle'll pick you up at the airport as planned. I'm just calling to warn you and apologize in advance. I just got an invitation I can't refuse to a social event tomorrow evening."

"No need to apologize."

"Sure there is. This is a soirée of Hollywood swine."

"I can use the time to rest up for Monday."

"Well, actually, I'd sort of like to take you along. In case I need somebody intelligent to talk to. Unless, of course, you think you'd be uncomfortable."

Ivan examined the prospect for a moment, then said, "On Tuesday I'm going to read a paper on Paleozoic soils at the Page Museum. Young snotnoses keen to establish their reputations on the ruins of mine will be there. In light of that, I can't imagine how people who undoubtedly don't know mor from mull could possibly make me uncomfortable."

"Good. To the extent possible, I'll camouflage you in my clothing."

"What's the occasion for the party?"

"The occasion's the occasion."

"Let me rephrase the question. Who's hosting the party?"

"Somebody in the business who's throwing himself a birthday party. None of his friends will throw one for him, because he doesn't have any friends. If I hadn't come within an ace of an Oscar last month—which by the way is the limit of his long-term memory—it'd never have occurred to him to invite a writer. If I was a self-respecting writer and not a Hollywood whore, I'd duck it. But, hey, it'll be entertaining from a sociological point of view."

"As long as I get to ogle some starlets."

"Starlets'd eat you alive."

"That would be nice, too. Look, please don't think you have to entertain me the whole time I'm out there."

"Oh, this place'll afford you endless opportunities to entertain yourself."

"I look forward to it."

"See you soon."

"Goodbye."

"Resume," he murmured to the laptop. "The point is."

"The point is," his younger self said, "they can't have sprung up overnight, even in the geologic sense. The Silurian seas are receding as the land rises, and the plant invasion's not a coincidence. But there were also opportunities during the Ordovician for plants to come ashore in a big way. Only they *didn't*. Maybe there was lethal ozone at ground level for a long time after the atmosphere became oxygen-rich. If so, a lot of oxygen had to accumulate before the ozone layer rose to the higher levels safe enough for advanced life-forms. Our—"

"Stop," he said, and thought, What a lot of crap. Then he sighed deeply and told the laptop, "Cue the first Cutsinger press conference."

After a moment, Cutsinger's image appeared on the screen. He was standing at a podium, behind a brace of microphones. He said, "I am at pains to describe this phenomenon without resorting to the specialized jargon of my own field, which is physics. Metaphor, however, may be inadequate. I'll try to answer your questions afterward."

This is afterward, Ivan thought bitterly, and, yes, I have a question.

"The phenomenon," Cutsinger's image went on, "is, for want of a better term, a space-time anomaly—a hole, if you will, or a tunnel, or however you wish to think of it. It appears, and I use the word advisedly, appears to connect our present-day Earth with the Earth as it existed during the remote prehistoric past. We've inserted a number of robot probes, some with laboratory animals, into the anomaly and retrieved them intact, though some of the animals did not survive. Judging both from the biological samples obtained and from the period of rotation of this prehistoric Earth, what we're talking about is the Siluro-Devonian boundary in mid-Paleozoic time, roughly four hundred million years ago. Biological specimens collected include a genus of primitive plant called Cooksonia and an extinct arthropod called a—please forgive my pronunciation if I get this wrong—a trigonobartid. Both organisms are well-known to paleontologists, and DNA testing conclusively proves their affinities with all other known terrestrial life-forms. Thus, for all practical purposes, this is our own world as it existed during the Paleozoic Era. However, it cannot literally be our own world. We cannot travel directly backward into our own past."

Ivan looked up, startled, as a flight attendant leaned in and said something.

"I'm sorry, what?"

"We'll be landing soon. You'll have to put that away now."

"Of course."

She smiled and withdrew. He looked at the laptop. "The anomaly," Cutsinger was saying, "must therefore connect us with another Earth."

"Quit."

Michelle met him as he came off the ramp. For a second, he did not recognize her and could only stare at her when she called his name. He could not immediately connect this young woman with his memories of her as a long-limbed thirteen-year-old girl with braces on her teeth; then, he had never been quite able to decide whether she was going to grow up pretty or goofy-looking. It had been a matter of real concern to him: he had first seen her cradled tenderly in her mother's arms, eyes squeezed shut and oblivious of her beatific expression; baby Michelle was not asleep, though, but had seemed to be concentrating fiercely on the mother's warmth, heartbeat, and wordless murmured endearments. Tiny hands had clasped and unclasped rhythmically, kneading air, keeping time, and when Ivan had gently touched one perfect pink palm and her soft digits closed on, but could not encircle, his calloused fingertip, the contrast smote him in the heart. He had no children of his own, and had never wanted any, but he knew immediately that he loved this child. He had murmured it to her, and to Don and Linda he said, "You folks do good work."

The discontinuous nature of these remembered Michelles, lying unconformably upon one another, heightened his sense of dislocation as he now beheld her. She was fresh out of high school, fair-skinned, unmade-up, with unplucked eyebrows and close-cropped brown hair. It cannot be her, he told himself. But then the corners of her mouth drew back, the firm, almost prim line of her lips fractured in a smile, and she delivered herself of pleasant, ringing laughter that had a most unexpected and wonderful effect on him: his head suddenly seemed inclined to float off his shoulders, and he found himself thinking that a man might want to bask for years in the radiance of that smile, the music of that laughter. Now he was convinced, and he let himself yield to the feeling of buoyant happiness. As a child she had had the comically intent expression of a squirrel monkey, but her father and her uncle had always been able to make her laugh, and when she had the effect was always marvelous. She closed with him and hugged him tightly, and his heart seemed to expand until it filled his chest.

As they headed into the hills north of Hollywood, she concentrated on her driving and he stole glances at her profile. He decided that the haircut suited her vastly better than the unfortunate coiffures she had been in the habit of inflicting upon herself. Well, he thought, you turned out pretty after all.

And he thought, I love you still, darling, and I always shall. Whether it's really you or not.

Seated at the metal table, screened from the sun by the eucalyptus tree and with his book lying open on his lap, he admired the blue and orange blooms and banana-shaped leaves of the bird of paradise flowers in his brother's backyard. He could look past them and the fence and right down the canyon on the hazy blur of the city. The morning had begun to heat up, and there was a faint ashy taste to the air. He noticed a small dark smudgy cloud where the farthest line of hills met the sky.

Michelle emerged from the house carrying two ice-flecked bottles of imported beer on a tray. She set it on the table and sat down across from him and said, "Daddy's still talking to the thing that would not die."

He nodded in the direction of the smudgy cloud. "I hope that's not what I think it is."

She looked. "Fires in the canyons. It's the season." She opened one of the beers and handed it to him. "What're you reading?"

Unnecessarily, he glanced at the spine. "*The Story of Philosophy*, by Will Durant."

She clearly did not know what to say in response.

"It's about the lives of the great philosophers," he went on after a moment, "and their thoughts on being and meaning and stuff."

She made a face. "It sounds excruciating."

"It is. I think the great philosophers were all wankers, except for Voltaire, who was funny. Nietzsche was probably the wankiest of the lot."

"Why're you reading it if you think it's so awful?"

"Let's just say I'm in full-tilt autodidact mode these days. Nowadays I carry the same three books with me everywhere I go. This one, a book about quantum mechanics, and the latest edition of the *People's Almanac*. The almanac's the only one I really enjoy."

"What's that, quantum mechanics?"

"Didn't they teach you anything in school? Advanced physics. Probably just a lot of philosophical wanking set to math. But it interests me. Somewhere between physics and philosophy is the intersection of the real world. Out of our subjective perception of an objective reality of energy and matter comes our interpretation of being and meaning."

"Whatever you say, Uncle Ivan."

"Are you going to this party tomorrow night?"

She shook her head emphatically. "I'm going to a concert with my boyfriend. Anyway, I don't much care for movie people. Oh, some of them are nice, but—I've never been comfortable around actors. I can never tell when they aren't acting. No, that's not it, it just makes me tired trying to figure out when they're acting and when they're not. The directors are mostly pretentious bores, and the producers just make Daddy crazy." She gazed down the canyon. "The fact is, I don't much like movies. But my boyfriend"—she gave him a quick, self-conscious glance—"my boyfriend loves 'em. And he *loves* dinosaurs. He says he judges a movie by whether he thinks it'd be better or worse with dinosaurs in it."

"Did he have anything to do with that recent version of *Little Women?*"

"No. He's not in the industry, thank God. I wouldn't go out with anybody who is. I wonder what genius thought of setting *Little Women* in prehistoric times. Anyway, you'd be surprised how many movies flunk his dinosaur test."

"Probably I wouldn't."

"He and Daddy like sitting around coming up with lunatic premises for movies. What they call high-concept. He cracks Daddy up. Daddy says he could be making movies every bit as bad as anybody else's if he just applied himself."

"Give me an example of high-concept."

"'Hitler! Stalin! And the woman who loved them both!'" They laughed together. Then she suddenly regarded him seriously. "I hope you're not going to let yourself be overawed by these people."

"People don't awe me." She looked doubtful, so he added, "They can't begin to compete with what awes me."

"What's that? What awes you?"

He leaned sideways in his chair, scooped some dirt out of a flowerbed. "This," he said, and as he went on talking he spread the dirt on his palm and sorted through it with his index finger. "When we were kids, teenagers, while your daddy sat up in his room figuring out how to write screenplays, I was outdoors collecting bugs and fossils. We neatly divided the world between us. He got the arts, I got the sciences. Even our tastes in reading—while he was reading, oh, Fitzgerald and Nabokov, I'd be reading John McPhee and Darwin's journal of the voyage of the *Beagle*. There was a little overlap. We both went through phases when we read mysteries and science fiction like mad. I'd read *The Big Sleep* or *The Time Machine* and pass 'em onto Don, and then we'd discuss 'em. But we were usually interested in different parts of the same books. Don was interested in the characters, the story. Who killed so and so. I loved Raymond Chandler's, Ross Macdonald's descriptions of the southern California landscape. I was like a tourist. My feeling was that setting is as vital as plot and characterization. A good detective-story writer had to be a good travelogue writer, or else his characters and action were just hanging in space. Don argued that a good story could be set anywhere, scenery was just there to be glanced at. If the plot was good, it would work anywhere."

"Daddy says there are only three or four plots. At least he says that out here there are only three or four."

"Well, anyway, your dad and I have art and science all sewed up between us. Science to help us find out what the world is. Art to—I don't know, art's not my thing, but I think—"

"Daddy says you're trying to write a book."

"Trying is about as far as I've got so far. I have all the raw material, but . . ." But. "I'm not creative. Anyway, I think we have to have both science and art. Everything in the universe partakes in some way of every other thing."

"What about philosophy?"

"Maybe it's what links science and art."

"Even if it's a lot of wanking?"

"Even wanking has its place in the scheme of things. What about this boyfriend?"

"Interesting segue."

"Is this a serious thing? Serious like marriage?"

She shrugged, then shook her head. "I want to do something with my life before I get into that."

"What?"

"I wish I knew. I feel I have so much to live up to. Your side of the family's all overachievers. My father's a hot Hollywood screenwriter. My uncle, the scientist, has done just the most amazing things. My grandparents were big wheels in Texas politics. It's almost as bad as having movie-star parents. The pressure on me to achieve is awful."

"It was probably worse for the Huxleys."

"Mom's always felt outclassed. Her family'd always just muddled along. She felt utterly inadequate the whole time she and Dad were married."

"With a little help from him, she made a beautiful daughter."

She looked pleased by the compliment but also a little uncomfortable. "Thank you for saying that."

"It's true."

"You used to call me Squirrel Monkey."

Don came outside looking exasperated. "Ever reach a point in a conversation," he said, "where, you know, you can't go on pretending to take people seriously who don't know what they're talking about?"

"Are we talking rhetorically?"

Don laughed a soft, unhappy sort of laugh. He indicated the unopened bottle of beer. "Is that for me?"

"Just that one, Daddy."

"I need it." He said to Ivan, "Tell me the stupidest thing you've ever heard. I'm trying to put something into perspective here."

Ivan thought for a moment. "Well, there was the low point, or maybe it was the high point, of my blessedly short stint as a purveyor of scientific knowledge to college freshman. I had a student tell me in all earnestness that an organism that lives off dead organisms is a sacrilege."

Don laughed again, less unhappily than before. "Been on the phone with someone who makes deals and gives off movies as waste. He's got the hottest idea of his life. He's doing a full-blown remake of *The Three Musketeers* in Taiwan."

Ivan felt his eyebrows go up. He made them come back down.

Don nodded. "That was my reaction. I said to him, I gather you've taken a few liberties with the novel. And he said, Novel? By Alexandre Dumas, I said. You mean it? he said. Excuse me for a moment, and he gets on his AnswerMan and says, To legal, do we have exclusive rights to alleged novel by Doo-dah-duh. Dumas, I scream, *Dumas*, you dumbass!" He shook his head as though to clear it of an irritating buzz. "Well. I go on and tell him the novel's in the public domain, Dumas has been dead for a little while now. He drums his fingers on his desktop. He screws his face into a mask of thoughtfulness. He says, Well, it's always best to be sure, because if what you say is true, we'll have to see about getting it pulled out of circulation. I beg his pardon. He says, We don't want people confusing it with our book based on the movie."

Ivan said, "He's going to novelize a movie based on a novel?"

"Sure. The novel based on *Pride and Prejudice* was on the best-seller list?"

Michelle said, "Hooray for Hollywood," and Ivan raised his bottle in a toast.

Don raised his as well. "Here's to L.A., Los Angeles del Muerte!"

Then Michelle excused herself and went inside. Ivan said, "Every time I see her, she's bigger, smarter, prettier, and nicer."

"That's how it works if you only see her once every few years. Move out here, be her doting uncle all the time."

"Oh, I would love to. It would be good to see more of you, too. But—" To avoid his brother's expectant look, Ivan turned toward the canyon. "Call me a crank on the subject, but I'll never live on an active plate margin."

"Christ."

"Geologically speaking, these hills have all the structural integrity of head cheese. They piled up here after drifting in across a prehistoric sea from God knows where. One of these times, Don, the earth's going to hiccup, and all these nice houses and all you nice people in them are going to slide all the way down that canyon."

Don shrugged. "Mobility is what California's all about. Everything here is from someplace else. The water comes from Colorado. These flowers," and he extended his arm and delicately touched a leaf on one of the bird-of-paradise flowers as though he were stroking a cat under its jaw, "are South African. The jacaranda you see all over town are from Brazil, the eucalyptus trees are from Australia. The people and the architecture are from everywhere you can think of." He took a long pull on his bottle, draining it. "That's the reason California's such a weird goddamn place. Because nothing really belongs here."

"I think it's fascinating. I wouldn't live here for anything—not even for you and Michelle, I'm sorry. But it is certainly fascinating."

"Oh, absolutely, I agree, it is. In a big, ugly, tasteless, intellectually numbing kind of way."

"What do you do for intellectual stimulation?"

"I read your monographs."

"Really?"

"No, but I have copies of all of them."

Later, stretched across the bed with his eyes closed and the cool fresh sheet pulled up to his sternum, Ivan thought, Clever, talented Don. It had never occurred to him before that his brother considered his work at all. . . .

He did not think he had fallen asleep, yet he awoke with a start. He was hot and parched. He slipped into a robe and eased into the hallway. In the kitchen, he filled a glass with cold filtered water from the jug in the refrigerator and sat down with his back to the bar to look out through the glass doors, at the lights of the city. There was a glowing patch of sky, seemingly as distant as the half moon, where the dark smudgy cloud had been that afternoon.

When he returned to his room, he sat on the edge of the bed and took his well-thumbed *People's Almanac* from the nightstand. He opened it at random and read a page, then set it aside and picked up the laptop. "Where were we?"

The screen lightened. "That's a good question," Cutsinger was saying. He chuckled into the microphones. "I know, because my colleagues and I have asked it of each other thousands of times since the anomaly was discovered. Every time, the answer's been the same. Simply traveling through time into the past is impossible. Simply to do so violates the laws of physics, especially our old favorite, the second law of thermodynamics. Simply to enter the past is to alter the past, which is a literal and actual contradiction of logic. Yet the fact is, we have discovered this space-time anomaly which connects our immediate present with what from all evidence is the Earth as it existed during mid-Paleozoic times. The only way the laws of physics and logic can accommodate this awkward fact is if we quietly deep-six the adjective 'simply' and run things out to their extremely complicated conclusion. We must posit a universe that stops and starts, stops and starts, countless billions of times per microsecond, as it jumps from state to state. As it does so, it continually divides, copies itself. Each copy is in a different state—that is, they're inexact copies. A separate reality exists for every possible outcome of every possible quantum interaction. Inasmuch as the number of copies produced since the Big Bang must be practically infinite, the range of difference among the realities must be practically infinite as well. These realities exist in parallel with one another. Whatever we insert into the anomaly—probes, test animals, human beings—are not simply going to travel directly backward into our own past. Instead, they're going to travel somehow to another universe, to another Earth which resembles our Earth as it was in the Paleozoic. Yes? Question?"

From offscreen came a question, inaudible to Ivan, but on the screen Cutsinger nodded and answered, "Well, it's probably pointless to say whether this sort of travel occurs in any direction—backward, sideward, or diagonally."

From offscreen, someone else asked, "If there are all these multiple Earths, when you're ready to come back through this hole you're talking about, how can you be sure you'll find your way back to the right Earth?"

"To the very best of our knowledge, this hole as you call it has only two ends. One here and now, one there and then. Next question?"

You glib son of a bitch, Ivan thought.

After the robot probes had gone and apparently come back through the space-time anomaly, the next step was obvious to everyone: human beings must follow. It was decided that two people should go through together. At the outset, in the moment it had taken the phrase "time travel to the prehistoric world" to register in his mind, Ivan had made up his mind—yes, absolutely, I want to go! "Presented with the opportunity to traverse time and explore a prehistoric planet," he had written to Don, "who *wouldn't?*" In the weeks and months that followed, however, through all the discussion and planning sessions, he had never quite believed that he had a real chance to go. Partly it was a matter of funding: x amount of money in the kitty simply equaled y number of people who would get to go on any Paleozoic junket. Partly it was a matter of prestige: given, practically speaking, an entire new planet to explore—everything about it, everything about the cosmos it occupied, for that matter, being four hundred million years younger, any scientist could make a case for his or her particular field of inquiry. Ivan did not, of course, despise his work in the least or see any need to apologize for it; moreover, he did not take personally—too personally, anyway—one or another of the likelier candidates' feigned confusion over pedology, the study of the nature and development of children, and *pedology*, soil science. The first few times, he affected amusement at the joke fellow soil scientists told on themselves, which in its simplest form was that the insertion of a single soil scientist into Silurian time would result in that remote geological period's having more scientist than soil. It was the sort of extremely specialized joke specialists told. Like any specialized joke, its charm vanished the instant that an explanation became necessary. Real soil would have only just started, geologically speaking, to collect amid the Silurian barrens; pedogenesis would be spotty and sporadic; rock could weather away to fine particles, but only the decay of organic matter could make sterile grit into nurturing dirt, and while organisms abounded in the Silurian seas, they would have only just started, again, geologically speaking, to live and die—and decompose—on land.

"Oh. I see. Ha, ha."

The joke had escaped, from the soil scientists at some point and begot tortuous variations in which twenty-first-century pedology overwhelmed and annihilated the reality of primordial soil: why (went one version), the weight of the terminology alone—soil air, soil complexes, associations and series, soil horizons, moisture budgets, aggregates and peds, mor and mull and all the rest of it—would be too much for such thin, poor, fragile stuff as one might expect to find sprinkled about in mid-Paleozoic times.

He had tried to look and sound amused, and to be a good sport overall, whenever he heard the joke in any of its mutated forms. After all, it was never intended really maliciously; it merely partook of a largely unconscious acceptance of a hierarchy of scientists. Physics and astronomy were glamour fields. Geology and paleontology were comparatively rough-hewn but nonetheless logical choices; moreover, they were perennially popular with the public, a crucial concern when public money was involved. Pedology was none of the above. He liked to think that he did not have it in himself to be envious, and so, with unfailing good humor, he agreed that there certainly would be a lot of geology at hand in the Paleozoic, mountains, valleys, strata, and the like. And, as for paleozoology, the Paleozoic would be nothing if not a big aquarium stocked with weird wiggly things and maybe a few big showy monsters.

And as for the crazy night skies, my oh my!

And even Kemal Barrowclough, paleobotanist, could get up and describe some harsh interior landscape enlivened only by the gray-green of lichens, "the first true land plants, because, unlike the psilophytes and lycopods we find clinging to the low moist places, close to water, always looking over their shoulders, so to speak, to make sure they haven't strayed too far, lichens, by God, *have taken the big step*," and there would scarcely be a dry eye among the listeners, except for Kemal's sister, Gulnar, herself a paleobotanist. Gulnar specialized in psilophytes.

Throughout the discussions, Ivan had felt that, in effect, DeRamus had but to point to his rocks and say, "*Old!*" or Gabbert to his sky and say, "*Big!*" and nothing, *nothing*, he could have said about microbiotic volume in the histic epipedon, or humic acid precipitation, or the varieties of Paleozoic mesofauna he expected to sift through a tullgren funnel, would have meant a damn thing. Rather than enter his saprotrophs in unequal and hopeless competition against thrust faults, sea scorpions, or prehistoric constellations, he would wait until all around the table had settled back, glowering but spent, then softly clear his throat and calmly explain all over again that the origin and evolution of soil ranked among the major events in the history of life on Earth, that soil was linked inextricably to that major event of mid-Paleozoic time, life's emergence onto land.

It had been by dint of this stolid persistence that he had, in the minds of enough of his peers, ultimately established himself as precisely the sort of knowledgeable, dedicated, persevering person who should be a member of the Paleozoic expedition—and had also established, by extension, all soil scientists everywhere, in every geologic age, as estimable fellows. When finally, Stoll had announced who would go. Ivan stunned to speechlessness, could only gape as each of his colleagues shook his hand; almost a minute passed before he found his voice. "Wonders never cease," he had said.

Almost the next thing he remembered was looking over the back of the man who had knelt before him to check the seals on his boots. Cutsinger had stood leaning back against the wall with his arms crossed and watched the technicians work. He smiled ruefully at Ivan and said, "Tell me how you *really* feel."

"Like the first astronaut to spacewalk must've, just before he went out and did it."

"That guy had an umbilical cord," said Dilks, who sat nearby, surrounded by his own satellite system of technicians. He did not go onto say the obvious: We don't.

"Just don't lose sight of the anomaly once you're through," Cutsinger said.

"Right now," Ivan said, "getting back through the anomaly doesn't concern me quite as much as going through the first time and finding myself sinking straight to the bottom of the sea."

"We sent a probe in to bird-dog for you. The hole's stabilized over solid ground. You'll arrive high and dry." Cutsinger nodded at Dilks. "Both of you, together."

Ivan flexed his gloved fingers and said, "It's just the suit," and thought, It isn't *only* just the suit, but part of it *is* the suit. The suit was bulky and heavy and had to be hermetic. He and Dilks had to carry their own air supplies and everything else they might conceivably need, lest they contaminate the pristine Paleozoic environment and induce a paradox. The physicists, Ivan and Dilks privately agreed, were covering their own asses.

Cutsinger asked Dilks, "Anything you're especially concerned about?"

Dilks grinned. "Not liking the scenery. Not seeing a single prehistoric monster."

Cutsinger smiled thinly. "Careful what you wish for."

"Time to seal up," said one of the technicians. Another raised a clear bubble helmet and carefully set it down over Ivan's head. The helmet sealed when twisted to the right.

"All set?" said the chief technician's voice in the helmetphone.

"All set," said Ivan.

Technicians stood by to lend steadying hands as the two suited men got to their feet and lumbered into an adjoining room for decontamination. They stood upon a metal platform. Their equipment had already been decontaminated and stowed.

Ivan gripped the railing that enclosed the platform; he did not trust his legs to hold him up. This is it, he told himself, and then, This is what? He found that he still could not entirely believe what he was about to do.

The wall opposite the door pivoted away. The metal platform began to move on rails toward a ripple in the air.

Everything turned to white light and pain.

They considered their reflections in the full-length mirror. Don and Ivan were two solidly built, deep-chested, middle-aged men, unmistakably products of the same parents. Michelle stood framed in the doorway. Her expression was dubious. "Daddy," she said, "they'll never accept him as one of their own. No offense, Uncle Ivan, but you don't have Hollywood hair and teeth. They'll be horrified by what you've done to your skin. Daddy's tanned and fit because he works out. You're brown and hard and leathery because you work."

Don said to Ivan, "Maybe they'll mistake you for a retired stuntman."

"Why retired?"

"What other kind is there anymore?"

"I feel strange in these clothes, but I have to admit that they feel good and look good. They look better that I do."

"This is up-to-the-moment thread."

"I look like a rough draft of you."

"Whatever you do," Michelle said, "don't say you're a scientist. 'Scientist' cuts no ice here."

Don flashed a grin along his shoulder at his brother and said, "Absolutely do not say you're a pedologist. They won't have any idea what a pedologist is, unless they think it's the same thing as a pedophile."

"Someone asks what you are," Michelle said, "they mean, What's your astrological sign?"

"I don't know my astrological sign."

She made a horrified face. "Get *out* of California!"

"Tell 'em anything," Don said, "It doesn't matter, they'll run with it, tell you they just knew all along you were a Taurus or whatever."

"Say you're a time-traveler," Michelle told him. "But don't be hurt if they're not even impressed by that. It's not like they've ever done anything real."

The afternoon was warm, golden, perfect, as they wound their way along Mulholland Drive. Don had put the top down, though it meant wearing goggles to screen out airvertising. Ivan sat fingering the unfamiliar cloth of his borrowed clothing and admiring the fine houses. They turned in at a gate in a high stucco wall, passed a security guard's inspection, and drove on. Around a bend in the driveway, Ivan saw a monstrous house, an unworkable fusion of Spanish and Japanese architectural quirks framed by the rim of hills beyond. Don braked to stop in front of the house and simply abandoned the car—if he gave the keys to someone, Ivan did not see it happen. Just at the door, Don turned to Ivan and said, "Let me take one more look at you."

Ivan held his arms away from his body, palms forward.

Don laughed. "You're the most confident-looking guy I've ever seen. You look like Samson about to go wreak havoc among the Philistines."

"What've I got to be nervous about?"

They went inside and immediately found themselves in a crowd of mostly gorgeous chattering people, all seemingly intent upon displaying themselves, all dressed with an artful casualness. As he followed Don through the room, Ivan admired their physical flawlessness. The women were breathtaking. They were shorter or taller than one another, paler or darker, blond or brunette, but nearly all fashioned along the same very particular lines—slim and boyish save for improbably full breasts. On two or three occasions, Don paused and turned to introduce Ivan to someone who smiled pleasantly, shook Ivan's hand, and looked through or around him.

Ivan was, therefore, taken aback when a lovely woman approached from his brother's blind side, touched Ivan fleetingly on the forearm, and said, "I'm so glad you came, it's so good to see you." She wore a short skirt, belted at the waist. Her back, flanks, and shoulders were bare. The tips of her breasts were barely covered by two narrow, translucent strips of fabric that crossed at the navel and fastened behind her neck.

"It's so good to see you, too," Ivan said. She said, "I have to go get after the help for a second, but don't you go away," and vanished.

Ivan caught up with Don and said, "Who was that?"

"Who was who?"

A simply pretty rather than gorgeous girl paused before Ivan with a food-laden tray and smiled invitingly; he helped himself to some unrecognizable but delicious foodstuff. Before he could help himself to seconds, she was gone. He consoled himself with a drink plucked from another passing tray.

The singer fronting the combo was Frank Sinatra, who snapped his fingers and smiled as he sang "My Way." According to a placard, the skinny, artfully scruffy young men accompanying him were The Sex Pistols. Although none of the real people in the room appeared to notice when the song ended, Frank Sinatra thanked them for their applause and told them they were beautiful. Ivan caught up with the girl with the food tray and had helped himself to a snack before he realized that she was a different girl and it was a different snack. She was pretty in her own right, however, and the snack was as mysterious and delicious as the first had been. The combo began playing again, somewhat picking up the tempo. As Frank Sinatra sang that he didn't know what he wanted, but he knew how to get it, Don turned, pointed vaguely, and said to Ivan, "I see somebody over there I have to go schmooze with. I'd introduce you, but he's a pig."

"So go schmooze. I can look after myself."

"You sure?"

"Positive."

"Okay. Ogle some starlets—I'll be back in a mo."

As though she had rotated into the space vacated by Don, a long tawny woman appeared before Ivan. Her waist was as big around as his thigh. Her high breasts exerted a firm, friendly pressure against his lapels. He thought she had the most kissable-looking mouth he had ever seen. She said, "I'm sure I know you."

Ivan smiled. "I was one of the original Sex Pistols."

"Really!" She glanced over her shoulder at the hologram, then peered at Ivan again. "Which one?"

Ivan nodded vaguely in the band's direction. "The dead one."

She pouted fetchingly. "Who are you, really?"

He decided to see what would happen if he disregarded Don and Michelle's advice. He said, "I'm a pedologist."

"Oh," she said, "you specialize in child actors? No, wait, that's a foot specialist, right?" She looked doubtfully at his hands, which were big and brown, hard and knobby. "Is your practice in Beverly Hills?"

"Gondwanaland."

"Ah," she said, and nodded, and looked thoughtful, and lost interest. Ivan let her rotate back the way she had come and then sidled into and through the next room. The house was a maze of rooms opening onto other rooms, seemingly unto infinity; inside of five minutes, he decided that he was hopelessly lost. Surrounded by small groups of people talking animatedly among themselves, he turned more or less in place, eavesdropping casually. He quickly gathered that most of the people around him believed in astrology, psychics, cosmetic surgery, and supply-side economics, and that some few among them were alarmed by the trend toward virtual actors. He overheard a tanned, broad-shouldered crewcut man say to a couple of paler and less substantial men, "What chance have I got? I'm losing parts to John Wayne, for chrissake! He's been dead for decades, and he's a bigger star than ever."

"Costs less than ever, too," said the wispier of the other two men, "and keeps his right-wing guff to himself."

The broad-shouldered man scowled. "I don't want what happened to stuntmen to happen to actors!"

"Oh, don't be alarmist," the wispy man said. "No one's going to get rid of actors. Oh, they might use fewer of them, but—besides, stuntmen're holding their own overseas, and—"

"Crazy goddamn Aussies and Filipinos!"

"—*and*," the wispy man said insistently, "the films do have a significant following in this country. For some viewers, it's not enough to see an actor who looks like he's risking his life. They want the extra kick that comes from knowing an actor really *is* risking his life."

The third man had a satisfied air and was shaped like a bowling pin; his white suit and scarlet ascot enhanced the resemblance. "Until that happens," he told the broad-shouldered man, "better get used to playing second fiddle to John Wayne. Right now, I got development people e-synthing old physical comedians from the nineteen-whenevers. Buster Keaton, Harold Lloyd, and Jackie Chan. People still bust a gut laughing at those guys."

"Never heard of 'em."

"You will. Because I'm putting 'em together in a film. Lots of smash-up, fall-down. Sure, we use computers to give 'em what they never had before—voices, color—personalities! But when people see Buster Keaton fall off a moving train, they know there's no fakery."

"Who the hell cares if some dead guy risks his life?"

The bowling-pin-shaped man jabbed a finger into the air. "Thrills are timeless!"

Glimpsing yet another pretty girl with a food tray, Ivan exited right, through a doorway. He somehow missed the girl, made a couple of turns at random, and was beginning to wonder amusedly if he had happened upon another space-time anomaly when he suddenly and unexpectedly found himself outdoors, on the tiled shore of a swimming pool as big, he decided, as the Tethys Sea—Galveston Bay, at least. There were small groups of people ranged at intervals around the pool and one person in the water, who swam to the edge, pulled herself up, and was revealed to be a sleekly muscular Amazon. As she toweled her hair, she let her incurious gaze alight fleetingly on Ivan, then move on; she was as indifferent to his existence as though he were another of the potted palms. She rose lithely, draped her towel over one exquisite shoulder, and walked past him into the house.

Ivan sipped his drink, thrust his free hand into his trousers pocket, and ambled toward the far end of the pool and an array of women there. At a table in their midst, like a castaway on an island circled by glistening succulent mermaids, a bald, fat, fortyish man sat talking animatedly to himself. A waiter stood at the ready behind a cart laden with liquor bottles. A large rectangular object, either a man or a refrigerator stuffed into a sports jacket, took up space nearby. Just as this large object startled Ivan by looking in his direction, the fat man suddenly laughed triumphantly, leaped to his feet, and clapped his hands. He pointed at bottles on the cart, and the waiter began to fuss with them. The fat man turned, looked straight at Ivan, evidently the only suitable person within arm's reach, and pulled him close. "Help me celebrate," he said, and to the large object, "Larry, get the man a chair." Larry pulled a chair back from the table, waited for Ivan to sit, then moved off a short distance. The fat man introduced himself as John Rubis and looked as though he expected Ivan to have heard of him. Ivan smiled pleasantly and tried to give the impression that he had.

"I am *real* happy!" Rubis pointed at his own ear, and Ivan realized that there was an AnswerMan plugged into it. "The word from the folks at Northemico is go!" He indicated the liquor cart. "What can I get you?"

"Brought my own. Congratulations." Ivan toasted him, and they drank. Rubis smacked his lips appreciatively. Ivan said, "You work for Northemico?"

"I *deal* with Northemico. Their entertainment division."

"I didn't even realize Northemico had an entertainment division."

"Hey, they got everything." He turned toward the waiter and said, "Fix me up another of these."

"Sorry, I'm just a pedologist from Podunk." Rubis looked perplexed. "Pedologist," Ivan said, enunciating as clearly as he could.

"Ah." Rubis listened to his AnswerMan again. "As in child specialist—or soil scientist? No, that can't be right. Sorry about that, Doctor. Sometimes my little mister know-it-all gets confused. At least it didn't think you said you're a pederast, ha ha. So what is it, set me straight here, what's your claim to celebrity?"

Ivan mentally shrugged and asked himself, Why the hell not? and to John Rubis he said, "I was one of the first people to travel through time."

Instead of responding to that, Rubis held up a forefinger, said, "Incoming," looked away, and hunched over the table, listening intently to his AnswerMan and occasionally muttering inaudibly. Ivan's attention wandered. Light reflecting from the pool's surface shimmered on the enclosing white walls. The water was as brilliantly blue-green as that ancient sea—and as he pictured that sea in his mind, he also pictured a woman like a tanned and buffed Aphrodite rising from the waters. And when he told her that he was a foot specialist, she heaved a sigh of exasperation and dived back into the sea.

Rubis turned back to him and said, "Sorry. You aren't kidding about the time-travel, are you?"

"Well, I was part of the first team of time-travelers—half of it. There were just two of us. Afterward, I made other visits and helped establish a community of scientists in Paleozoic time. The base camp's the size of a small town now."

Rubis stared at him for what felt like a long moment. Then a light seemed to come on behind the man's eyes, and he snapped his fingers and pointed. "Yeah. The hole through time. Back to, what, the Stone Age?"

"Um, actually, back to quite a bit before. Back to the Paleozoic Era, four hundred million and some odd years ago. The Siluro-Devonian boundary."

"Yeah, that's right! The Age of Trilobites. So, what, you're out here pitching the story of your life to producers?"

"No, I'm just visiting my brother. He's the screenwriter in the family." That information did not seem to impress Rubis particularly, so Ivan added, "He was just up for a Best Screenplay Oscar. Donald Kelly." Rubis brightened. "My own fifteen minutes of fame are long past, and they really didn't amount to all that much."

"Mm. Any face minutes?"

"I'm sorry?"

"You know, your face on the TV screen. Media interviews. Face minutes."

"Ah. I turn up in some old documentaries. Everybody made documentaries for a while, until all six people who were remotely interested were sick of them."

Rubis rolled his eyes. "Documentaries! Even I watched part of one. No offense, but it was like watching grass grow. The most exciting thing you found was a trilobite, and it's basically just some kind of big water bug, isn't it?"

"Yes, basically."

"There've been bigger bugs in movies already. Like in—like in *Them and I*. And *The Thief of Baghdad*. Seen it?"

"Yes, as a matter of fact. I thought the Indonesian settings were interesting."

"Our first idea was to actually shoot it in Baghdad. But not much of Baghdad's standing anymore. So—besides, Indonesia, Baghdad"—Rubis made a gesture expressive of some point that was not altogether clear to Ivan—"eh!"

"Once upon a time," Ivan said, "if you wanted to make a movie about Baghdad, you built sets on soundstages here in Hollywood, right?"

"Aah, nobody makes movies in Hollywood anymore. Too expensive. Lousy unions. But this is still the place to be, the place to make deals. Anyway, like I was saying, about time-travel—I've always thought it's a sensational thing. When you think about it, it really is just the biggest thing since the early days of space travel. I wish it could be used for something more interesting than studying bugs and slime a million years ago, but don't get me wrong. I think it's a real shame the time-travelers never caught on with the public like those first guys who went to the moon—Armstrong, Altman. Now those guys were celebrities."

"It's not like we could do a live broadcast from the Paleozoic. The view wouldn't have commended itself to most people anyway. The Silurian Period looks like a cross between a gravel pit and a stagnant pond. And we didn't plant a flag or say anything heroic. In fact—" Ivan hesitated for a moment, considering. "Still, it was all tremendously exciting. It was the most exciting thing in the world."

The wall opposite the door had pivoted away. The metal platform had begun to move on rails toward a ripple in the air. Everything had turned to white light and pain. Ivan, blinded, felt as though someone had taken careful aim with a two-by-four and struck him across his solar plexus. There was a terrifying, eternal moment when he could not suck in air. Then he drew a breath and started to exhale, and his stomach turned over. The convulsion put him on his hands and knees. Too excited to eat breakfast that morning, he had only drunk a cup of coffee. Now burning acid rose in his throat. He felt cramps in his calf muscles. His earphones throbbed with the sound of—what was it, crying, groaning . . . ?

Retching. His vision cleared, and he saw Dilks nearby, lying on his side, feebly moving his arms. For some reason, part of Dilks's visor was obscured. Ivan threw his weight in that direction and half rolled, half crawled to the man's side. Now he could see Dilks' face through the yellow-filmed visor. Dilks had lost his breakfast inside his helmet. Ivan spoke his name, but it was quickly established that, though Dilks' helmetphone worked, his microphone was fouled and useless. There was nothing to be done for it now: they could not simply remove Dilks' helmet and clean out the mess; they were under strictest orders not to contaminate the Paleozoic.

Nearby, the air around the anomaly rippled like a gossamer veil. Ivan looked around at the Paleozoic world. He and Dilks were on the shingle just above the high-tide line and just below a crumbling line of cliffs. The sun stood at zenith in the cloudless sky. The sea was blue-green, brilliant, beautiful.

Ivan bent over Dilks again and said, "You're in bad shape. We've got to get you back. Come on, I'll help you."

Dilks vehemently shoved him away. He looked gray-faced inside his helmet, but he grimaced and shook his head, and though he could not say what he meant, Ivan understood him. We *didn't come all this way only to go right back*. Dilks patted the front of Ivan's suit and then motioned in the direction of the water.

Ivan nodded. He said, "I'll be right back." He staggered to his feet, checked the instruments attached to the platform, activated the camera mounted on his helmet, and collected soil and air samples in the vicinity of the platform. Then, with what he hoped was a reassuring wave to Dilks, he lumbered toward the water. The shingle made for treacherous footing, and yet, as he looked out upon the expanse of water, he experienced a shivery rush of pleasure so particular that he knew he had felt it only once before, during boyhood, on the occasion of his first sight of the sea off Galveston Island. He had never been mystically inclined, even as a boy, but, then as now, he had responded to something tremendous and irresistible, the sea's summons, had rushed straight down to the water and dived in happily.

Nothing moved along the whole beach, nothing except the curling waves and the tangles of seaweed they had cast up. The beach curved away to left and right. It must curve away forever, Ivan thought. Hundreds, thousands of miles of perfectly unspoiled beach. He knelt on the dark wet sand and collected a sample of seawater. As he sealed the vial, he saw something emerge from the foam about two meters to his right. It was an arthropod about as big as his hand, flattened and segmented and carried along on jointed legs. The next wave licked after it, embraced it, appeared momentarily to draw it back toward the sea. The wave retreated, and the creature hesitated. Come on, Ivan thought, come on. Come on. He entertained no illusions that he had arrived on the spot just in time to greet the first Earth creature ever to come ashore. Surely, a thousand animals, a million, had already done so, and plants before them, and microorganisms before plants. Nevertheless, he had to admire the timing of this demonstration. He crouched, hands on knees, and waited. Foam rushed over the creature again. Come on, Ivan commanded it, make up your dim little mind. It's strange out here on land, not altogether hospitable, but you'll get used to it, or your children will, or your great-grandchildren a million times removed. Eventually, most of the species, most of the biomass, will be out here.

The arthropod advanced beyond the reach of the waves and began nudging through the seawrack. Eat hearty, Ivan thought, taking a cautious step toward the animal. He reflected on the persistence in vertebrates of revulsion toward arthropods. He felt kindly toward this arthropod, at least. Both of us, he thought, are pioneers.

As last he reluctantly tore himself away and returned to Dilks, who had sagged to the ground by the platform. Ivan propped the stricken man up and pointed toward the ripple. "We've got to cut this short," he said.

Dilks indicated disagreement, but more weakly than before.

"You're hurt," Ivan said, holding him up, "and we've got to go back." There was a crackle of static in Ivan's helmetphone, and he heard Dilks speak a single word.

". . . failed . . ."

"No! We didn't fail! We got here alive, and we're getting back alive. Nobody can take that away from us, Dilks. We're the first. And we'll come again."

They got clumsily onto the platform. Ivan made Dilks as comfortable as possible and then activated the platform. The air around the ripple began to roil and glow. Ivan gripped the railing and faced the glow. "Do your goddamn worst."

Rubis had offered Ivan a cigar, which he politely refused, and stuck one into his own mouth, and Larry had lurched forward to light it. Now, enveloped in smoke, Rubis said, "Trilobites just never did catch on with the public. Maybe if you'd found a really *big* trilobite. On the other hand, trilobites didn't make for very cuddly stuffed toys, either, and that's always an important consideration. The merchandising, I mean."

"Candy shaped like brachiopods and sea scorpions? How about breakfast cereal? Sugar-frosted Trilo*bites*?"

Perfectly serious, Rubis nodded. "Now, if you'd've set the dial in your time machine for the age of dinosaurs instead."

"There wasn't actually a time machine. Just the space-time anomaly, the hole. And it just happened to open up where it did."

"That's too bad. And ain't it the way it always happens with science? We spent a godzillion dollars sending people to the Moon and Mars, and the Moon's just a rock and Mars's just a damn desert."

"Well, I don't know anyone honestly expected—"

"Now, *dinosaurs*, dinosaurs've been hot sellers forever. Dino toys, VR—they had all that stuff when I was a kid, and it still outsells every damn thing in sight. And every two, three years, regular as laxatives, another big dino movie. But what've you got? You got nothing, I'm sorry to say." He began to count on his fingers the things which Ivan did not have. "You got no big concept. You got no merchandisable angle. You got no crossover potential. Crossover potential's very big these days. You know, like Tarzan meets Frankenstein. James Bond versus Mata Hari. But, most of all, you haven't got dinosaurs, though. Everybody knows if you're going to tell a story set in the prehistoric past, there have to be dinosaurs. Without dinosaurs, there's no drama."

"I guess not," Ivan said, and took a long sip of his drink, and looked at the shimmering blue-green water in the pool. The slowly stirring air seemed to carry a faint smell of burning. He said to Rubis, "Let me bounce an idea for a different kind of time-travel story off you. Tell me what you think."

"Sure. Shoot."

"Okay. You have to bear in mind that when we speak of traveling backward through time, into the past, what we're really talking about is traveling between just two of infinite multiple Earths. Some of these multiple Earths may be virtually identical, some may be subtly different, some are wildly different—as different as modern and prehistoric times. Anyway, what you actually do when you travel through time is go back and forth between Earths. Earth as it is, here and now, and another Earth, Earth as it was in the Paleozoic Era."

Rubis murmured, "Weird," and smiled.

"Now let's say someone from our present-day visits a prehistoric Earth and returns.

After a while, after the initial excitement's died down, he starts to ponder the implications of travel back and forth between multiple Earths. He's come back to a present-day Earth that may or may not be his own present-day Earth. If it's virtually identical, well, if the only difference is, say, the outcome of some subatomic occurrence, then it doesn't matter. But maybe there's something subtly off on the macro level. It wouldn't be anything major. Napoleon, Hitler, and the Confederate States would all've gone down to defeat. Or maybe the time-traveler only suspects that something may be subtly off. His problem is, he's never quite sure, he can't decide whether something is off or he only thinks it is, so he's always looking for the telling detail. But there are *so many* details. If he never knew in the first place how many plays Shakespeare really wrote or who all those European kings were . . ."

Rubis nodded. "I get it. Not bad." He chewed his lower lip for a moment. "But I still think it needs dinosaurs."

Ivan chuckled softly, without mirth. "You should look up my niece's boyfriend." He turned on his seat, toward the burning hills.

They swept down Mulholland. Ivan said to Don, "Thanks for taking me. I can't remember when I've had so much fun." Don gave him a curious look. "No, really. I had a very good time, a wonderful time."

"Probably a better time than I did."

Ivan made a noncommittal sound. "I needed this experience as a kind of reality check."

Don laughed sharply. "Hollywood isn't the place to come for a reality check."

"Well, okay. Let's just say I had a very enlightening and entertaining poolside chat with our host."

"Johnny Rubis? Christ. He wasn't our host. Our host was a swine in human form named Lane. He was holding court indoors the whole time. I went in and did my dip and rise and got the hell out as fast as I could. Whatever Rubis may've told you he was doing by the pool, he was just showing off. See what a big deal I am. There were guys all over the place doing the same thing—women, too. Dropping names and making a show of pissant phone calls. See what big deals we are. Whatever Rubis may've told you, he's not that high in the food chain. A year ago he was probably packaging videos with titles like *Trailer Park Sluts*. He's an example of the most common form of life in Hollywood. The self-important butthead. I know, I've worked for plenty like him."

"Writing novels based on movies based on novels?"

Don shook his head. "Not me. Not lately, anyway?"

Ivan wondered if Don despised himself as much as he apparently despised everyone else in Hollywood. He hoped it was not so. More than anything, he hoped it was not so. "Don," he said, "I'm sorry I said that. I'm really terribly sorry."

Don shrugged. "No offense taken." He gave Ivan a quick grin. "Hey, big brother, I've been insulted by professionals. It's one of the things writers in Hollywood get paid for."

They rode in silence for a time.

Then Don said, "Do you know what a monkey trap is?"

"Pretty self-explanatory, isn't it?"

"Yes, but do you know how it works? You take a dry gourd and cut a small hole in it, just big enough for the monkey to get its hand through. You put a piece of food inside the gourd and attach the gourd to a tree or a post. The monkey puts his hand into the gourd, grabs the piece of food, and then can't pull his fist back through the hole. He could get away if he'd only let go of the food, but he just can't make himself let go. So, of course, he's trapped."

"Is the money really that good?"

"Christ, Ivan, the money's incredible. But it *isn't* just the money. What it is, is that every great once in a long goddamn while, against all the odds—remember, before all this happened, I worked in the next best habitat favorable to self-important buttheads, which is politics. While you were off exploring prehistoric times, I was writing like a sumbitch on fire and trying to get the hell out of Texas. I paid the rent, however, by working for the state legislature. Whenever a legislator wanted to lay down a barrage of memorial resolutions, I was the anonymous flunky who unlimbered the 'whereases' and the 'be it resolveds.' Every now and then, I wrote about forgotten black heroes of the Texas Revolution, forgotten women aviators of World War Two—something, anyway, that meant something. But, of course, in those resolutions, everything was equally important. Most of my assignments were about people's fiftieth wedding anniversaries, high-school football teams, rattlesnake roundups. Finally, I was assigned to write a resolution designating, I kid you not, Texas Bottled Water Day. Some people from the bottling industry were in town, lobbying for God remembers what, and someone in the lege thought it'd be real nice to present them with a resolution. Thus, Texas Bottled Water Day. When I saw the request, I looked my boss straight in the eye, and I told him, This is not work for a serious artist. He quite agreed. First chance he got, he fired me."

"Maybe you should've quit before it came to that."

"Well, I'd've quit anyway as soon as the writing took off." Don changed his grip on the steering wheel. "But while I was a legislative drudge, I lived for those few brief moments when the work really meant something."

His face, it seemed to Ivan, was suddenly transformed by some memory of happiness. Or perhaps it was just the car. The car cornered like a dream.

Have Not Have

GEOFF RYMAN

Born in Canada, Geoff Ryman now lives in England. He made his first sale in 1976, to *New Worlds*, but it was not until 1984, when he made his first appearance in *Interzone*—the magazine where almost of all his published short fiction has appeared—with his brilliant novella "The Unconquered Country" that he first attracted any serious attention. "The Unconquered Country," one of the best novellas of the decade, had a stunning impact on the science fiction scene of the day, and almost overnight established Ryman as one of the most accomplished writers of his generation, winning him both the British Science Fiction Award and the World Fantasy Award; it was later published in a book version, *The Unconquered Country: A Life History*. His output has been sparse since then, by the high-production standards of the genre, but extremely distinguished, with his novel *The Child Garden: A Low Comedy* winning both the prestigious Arthur C. Clarke Award and the John W. Campbell Memorial Award. His other novels include *The Warrior Who Carried Life*, the critically acclaimed mainstream novel *Was*, and the underground cult classic *253*, the "print remix" of an "interactive hypertext novel" which in its original form ran online on Ryman's home page of www.ryman.com, and which in its print form won the Philip K. Dick Award. Four of his novellas have been collected in *Unconquered Countries*. His most recent books are two new novels, *Lust* and *Air*. His stories have appeared in our Twelfth, Thirteenth, Seventeenth, and Nineteenth through Twenty-first annual collections.

As the poignant and disquieting story that follows demonstrates, progress always comes—whether you want it to or not.

M ae lived in the last village in the world to go on line. After that, everyone else went on Air.

Mae was the village's fashion expert. She advised on makeup, sold cosmetics, and provided good dresses. Every farmer's wife needed at least one good dress. The richer wives, like Mr. Wing's wife Kwan, wanted more than one.

Mae would sketch what was being worn in the capital. She would always add a special touch: a lime green scarf with sequins; or a lacy ruffle with colorful embroidery. A good dress was for display. "We are a happier people and we can wear these gay colors," Mae would advise.

"Yes, that is true," her customer might reply, entranced that fashion expressed their happy culture. "In the photographs, the Japanese women all look so solemn."

"So full of themselves," said Mae, and lowered her head and scowled, and she and her customer would laugh, feeling as sophisticated as anyone in the world.

Mae got her ideas as well as her mascara and lipsticks from her trips to the town. Even in those days, she was aware that she was really a dealer in information. Mae had a mobile phone. The mobile phone was necessary, for the village had only one line telephone, in the tea room. She needed to talk to her suppliers in private, because information shared aloud in the tea room was information that could no longer be sold.

It was a delicate balance. To get into town, she needed to be driven, often by a client. The art then was to screen the client from her real sources.

So Mae took risks. She would take rides by herself with the men, already boozy after the harvest, going down the hill for fun. Sometimes she needed to speak sharply to them, to remind them who she was.

The safest ride was with the village's schoolteacher, Mr. Shen. Teacher Shen only had a pony and trap, so the trip, even with an early rise, took one whole day down and one whole day back. But there was no danger of fashion secrets escaping with Teacher Shen. His interests lay in poetry and the science curriculum. In town, they would visit the ice cream parlor, with its clean tiles, and he would lick his bowl, guiltily, like a child. He was a kindly man, one of their own, whose education was a source of pride for the whole village. He and Mae had known each other longer than they could remember.

Sometimes, however, the ride had to be with someone who was not exactly a friend.

In the April before everything changed there was to be an important wedding.

Seker, whose name meant Sugar, was the daughter of the village's pilgrim to Mecca, their Haj. Seker was marrying into the Atakoloo family, and the wedding was a big event. Mae was to make her dress.

One of Mae's secrets was that she was a very bad seamstress. The wedding dress was being made professionally, and Mae had to get into town and collect it. When Sunni Haseem offered to drive her down in exchange for a fashion expedition, Mae had to agree.

Sunni herself was from an old village family, but her husband Faysal Haseem was from further down the hill. Mr. Haseem was a beefy brute whom even his wife did not like except for his suits and money. He puffed on cigarettes and his tanned fingers were as thick and weathered as the necks of turtles. In the back seat with Mae, Sunni giggled and prodded and gleamed with the thought of visiting town with her friend and confidant who was going to unleash her beauty secrets.

Mae smiled and whispered, promising much. "I hope my source will be present today," she said. "She brings me my special colors, you cannot get them anywhere else. I don't ask where she gets them." Mae lowered her eyes and her voice. "I think her husband. . . ."

A dubious gesture, meaning, that perhaps the goods were stolen, stolen from—who knows?—supplies meant for foreign diplomats? The tips of Mae's fingers rattled once, in provocation, across her client's arm.

The town was called Yeshibozkay, which meant Green Valley. It was now approached through corridors of raw apartment blocks set on beige desert soil. It had a new jail and discos with mirror balls, billboards, illuminated shop signs and Toyota jeeps that belched out blue smoke.

But the town center was as Mae remembered it from childhood. Traditional wooden houses crowded crookedly together, flat-roofed with shutters, shingle-covered gables and tiny fading shop signs. The old market square was still full of peasants selling vegetables laid out on mats. Middle-aged men still played chess outside tiny cafes; youths still prowled in packs.

There was still the public address system. The address system barked out news and music from the top of the electricity poles. Its sounds drifted over the city, announcing public events or new initiatives against drug dealers. It told of progress on the new highway, and boasted of the well-known entertainers who were visiting the town.

Mr. Haseem parked near the market, and the address system seemed to enter Mae's lungs, like cigarette smoke, perfume, or hair spray. She stepped out of the van and breathed it in. The excitement of being in the city trembled in her belly. As much as the bellowing of shoppers, farmers and donkeys; as much as the smell of raw petrol and cut greenery and drains, the address system made her spirits rise. She and her middle-aged client looked on each other and gasped and giggled at themselves.

"Now," Mae said, stroking Sunni's hair, her cheek. "It is time for a complete makeover. Let's really do you up. I cannot do as good work up in the hills."

Mae took her client to Halat's, the same hairdresser as Sunni might have gone to anyway. But Mae was greeted by Halat with cries and smiles and kisses on the cheek. That implied a promise that Mae's client would get special treatment. There was a pretense of consultancy. Mae offered advice, comments, cautions. Careful! she has such delicate skin! Hmm, the hair could use more shaping there. And Halat hummed as if perceiving what had been hidden before and then agreed to give the client what she would otherwise have given. But Sunni's nails were soaking, and she sat back in the center of attention, like a queen.

All of this allowed the hairdresser to charge more. Mae had never pressed her luck and asked for a cut. Something beady in Halat's eyes told her there would be no point. What Mae got out of it was standing, and that would lead to more work later.

With cucumbers over her eyes, Sunni was safely trapped. Mae announced, "I just have a few errands to run. You relax and let all cares fall away." She disappeared before Sunni could protest.

Mae ran to collect the dress. A disabled girl, a very good seamstress called Miss Soo, had opened up a tiny shop of her own.

Miss Soo was grateful for any business, poor thing, skinny as a rail and twisted. After the usual greetings, Miss Soo shifted round and hobbled and dragged her way to the back of the shop to fetch the dress. Her feet hissed sideways across the uneven concrete floor. Poor little thing, Mae thought. How can she sew?

Yet Miss Soo had a boyfriend in the fashion business. Genuinely in the fashion business, far away in the capital city, Balshang. The girl often showed Mae his photograph. It was like a magazine photograph. The boy was very handsome, with a shiny shirt and coiffed-up hair. She kept saying she was saving up money to join him. It was a mystery to Mae what such a boy was doing with a cripple for a girlfriend. Why did he keep contact with her? Publicly Mae would say to friends of the girl: it is the miracle of love, what a good heart he must have. Otherwise she kept her own counsel which was this: you would be very wise not to visit him in Balshang.

The boyfriend sent Miss Soo the patterns of dresses, photographs, magazines, or even whole catalogs. There was one particularly treasured thing; a showcase publication. The cover was like the lid of a box, and it showed in full color the best of the nation's fashion design.

Models so rich and thin they looked like ghosts. They looked half asleep, as if the only place they carried the weight of their wealth was on their eyelids. It was like looking at Western or Japanese women, and yet not. These were their own people, so long-legged, so modern, so ethereal, as if they were made of air.

Mae hated the clothes. They looked like washing-up towels. Oatmeal or gray in one color and without a trace of adornment.

Mae sighed with lament. "Why do these rich women go about in their underwear?"

The girl shuffled back with the dress, past piles of unsold oatmeal cloth. Miss Soo had a skinny face full of teeth, and she always looked like she was staring ahead in fear. "If you are rich you have no need to try to look rich." Her voice was soft. She made Mae feel like a peasant without meaning to. She made Mae yearn to escape herself, to be someone else, for the child was effortlessly talented, somehow effortlessly in touch with the outside world.

"Ah yes," Mae sighed. "But my clients, you know, they live in the hills." She shared a conspiratorial smile with the girl. "Their taste! Speaking of which, let's have a look at my wedding cake of a dress."

The dress was actually meant to look like a cake, all pink and white sugar icing, except that it kept moving all by itself. White wires with Styrofoam bobbles on the ends were surrounded with clouds of white netting.

"Does it need to be quite so busy?" the girl asked, doubtfully, encouraged too much by Mae's smile.

"I know my clients," replied Mae coolly. This is at least, she thought, a dress that makes some effort. She inspected the work. The needlework was delicious, as if the white cloth were cream that had flowed together. The poor creature could certainly sew, even when she hated the dress.

"That will be fine," said Mae, and made move toward her purse.

"You are so kind!" murmured Miss Soo, bowing slightly.

Like Mae, Miss Soo was of Chinese extraction. That was meant not to make any difference, but somehow it did. Mae and Miss Soo knew what to expect of each other.

"Some tea?" the girl asked. It would be pale, fresh-brewed, not the liquid tar that the native Karsistanis poured from continually boiling kettles.

"It would be delightful, but I do have a customer waiting," explained Mae.

The dress was packed in brown paper and carefully tied so it would not crease. There were farewells, and Mae scurried back to the hairdresser's. Sunni was only just finished, hair spray and scent rising off her like steam.

"This is the dress," said Mae and peeled back part of the paper, to give Halat and Sunni a glimpse of the tulle and Styrofoam.

"Oh!" the women said, as if all that white were clouds, in dreams.

And Halat was paid. There were smiles and nods and compliments and then they left.

Outside the shop, Mae breathed out as though she could now finally speak her mind. "Oh! She is good, that little viper, but you have to watch her, you have to make her work. Did she give you proper attention?"

"Oh, yes, very special attention. I am lucky to have you for a friend," said Sunni. "Let me pay you something for your trouble."

Mae hissed through her teeth. "No, no, I did nothing, I will not hear of it." It was a kind of ritual.

There was no dream in finding Sunni's surly husband. Mr. Haseem was red-faced, half-drunk in a club with unvarnished walls and a television.

"You spend my money," he declared. His eyes were on Mae.

"My friend Mae makes no charges," snapped Sunni.

"She takes something from what they charge you." Mr. Haseem glowered like a thunderstorm.

"She makes them charge me less, not more," replied Sunni, her face going like stone.

The two women exchanged glances. Mae's eyes could say: How can you bear it, a woman of culture like you?

It is my tragedy, came the reply, aching out of the ashamed eyes. So they sat while the husband sobered up and watched television. Mae contemplated the husband's hostility to her, and what might be behind it. On the screen, the local female newsreader talked: Talents, such people were called. She wore a red dress with a large gold broach. Something had been done to her hair to make it stand up in a sweep before falling away. She was as smoothly groomed as ice. She chattered in a high voice, perky through a battery of tiger's teeth. "She goes to Halat's as well," Mae whispered to Sunni. Weather, maps, shots of the honored President and the full cabinet one by one, making big decisions.

The men in the club chose what movie they wanted. Since the Net, they could do that. It had ruined visits to the town. Before, it used to be that the men were made to sit through something the children or families might also like, so you got everyone together for the watching of the television. The clubs had to be more polite. Now, because of the Net, women hardly saw TV at all and the clubs were full of drinking. The men chose another kung-fu movie. Mae and Sunni endured it, sipping Coca-Cola. It became apparent that Mr. Haseem would not buy them dinner.

Finally, late in the evening, Mr. Haseem loaded himself into the van. Enduring, unstoppable, and quite dangerous, he drove them back up into the mountains, weaving across the middle of the road.

"You make a lot of money out of all this," Mr. Haseem said to Mae.

"I . . . I make a little something. I try to maintain the standards of the village. I do not want people to see us as peasants. Just because we live on the high road."

Sunni's husband barked out a laugh. "We are peasants!" Then he added, "You do it for the money."

Sunni sighed in embarrassment. And Mae smiled a hard smile to herself in the darkness. You give yourself away, Sunni's-man. You want my husband's land. You want him to be your dependent. And you don't like your wife's money coming to me to prevent it. You want to make both me and my husband your slaves.

It is a strange thing to spend four hours in the dark listening to an engine roar with a man who seeks to destroy you.

In late May, school ended.

There were no fewer than six girls graduating and each one of them needed a new dress. Miss Soo was making two of them; Mae would have to do the others, but she needed to buy the cloth. She needed another trip to Yeshibozkay.

Mr. Wing was going to town to collect a new television set for the village. It was going to be connected to the Net. There was high excitement: graduation, a new television set. Some of the children lined up to wave good-bye to them.

Their village, Kizuldah, was surrounded by high, terraced mountains. The rice fields went up in steps, like a staircase into clouds. There was snow on the very tops year round.

It was a beautiful day, cloudless, but still relatively cool. Kwan, Mr. Wing's wife, was one of Mae's favorite women; she was intelligent, sensible; there was less dissembling with her. Mae enjoyed the drive.

Mr. Wing parked the van in the market square. As Mae reached into the back for her hat, she heard the public address system. The voice of the Talent was squawking.

". . . a tremendous advance for culture," the Talent said. "Now the Green Valley is no farther from the center of the world than Paris, Singapore, or Tokyo."

Mae sniffed. "Hmm. Another choice on this fishing net of theirs."

Wing stood outside the van, ramrod straight in his brown and tan town shirt. "I want to hear this," he said, smiling slightly, taking nips of smoke from his cigarette.

Kwan fanned the air. "Your modern wires say that smoking is dangerous. I wish you would follow all this news you hear."

"Ssh!" he insisted.

The bright female voice still enthused. "Previously all such advances left the Valley far behind because of wiring. This advance will be in the air we breathe. Previously all such advances left the Valley behind because of the cost of the new devices needed to receive messages. This new thing will be like Net TV in your head. All you need is the wires in the human mind."

Kwan gathered up her things. "Some nonsense or another," she murmured.

"Next Sunday, there will be a test. The test will happen in Tokyo and Singapore but also here in the Valley at the same time. What Tokyo sees and hears, we will see and hear. Tell everyone you know, next Sunday, there will be a test. There is no need for fear, alarm, or panic."

Mae listened then. There would certainly be a need for fear and panic if the address system said there was none.

"What test, what kind of test? What? What?" the women demanded of the husband.

Mr. Wing played the relaxed, superior male. He chuckled. "Ho-ho, now you are interested, yes?"

Another man looked up and grinned. "You should watch more TV," he called. He was selling radishes and shook them at the women.

Kwan demanded, "What are they talking about?"

"They will be able to put TV in our heads," said the husband, smiling. He looked down, thinking perhaps wistfully of his own new venture. "Tut. There has been talk of nothing else on the TV for the last year. But I didn't think it would happen."

All the old market was buzzing like flies on carrion, as if it were still news to them. Two youths in strange puffy clothes spun on their heels and slapped each other's palms, in a gesture that Mae had seen only once or twice before. An old granny waved it all away and kept on accusing a dealer of short measures.

Mae felt grave doubt. "TV in our heads. I don't want TV in my head." She thought of viper newsreaders and kung fu.

Wing said, "It's not just TV. It is more than TV. It is the whole world."

"What does that mean?"

"It will be the Net. Only, in your head. The fools and drunks in these parts just use it to watch movies from Hong Kong. The Net is all things." He began to falter.

"Explain! How can one thing be all things?"

There was a crowd of people gathering to listen.

"Everything is on it. You will see on our new TV." Kwan's husband did not really know either.

The routine was soured. Halat the hairdresser was in a very strange mood, giggly, chattery, her teeth clicking together as if it were cold.

"Oh, nonsense," she said when Mae went into her usual performance. "Is this for a wedding? For a feast?"

"No," said Mae. "It is for my special friend."

The little hussy put both hands either side of her mouth as if in awe. "Oh! Uh!"

"Are you going to do a special job for her or not?" demanded Mae. Her eyes were able to say: I see no one else in your shop.

Oh, how the girl would have loved to say: I am very busy—if you need something special come back tomorrow. But money spoke. Halat slightly amended her tone. "Of course. For you."

"I bring my friends to you regularly because you do such good work for them."

"Of course," the child said. "It is all this news, it makes me forget myself."

Mae drew herself up, and looked fierce, forbidding, in a word, older. Her entire body said: do not forget yourself again. The way the child dug away at Kwan's hair with the long comb handle said back: peasants.

The rest of the day did not go well. Mae felt tired, distracted. She made a terrible mistake and, with nothing else to do, accidentally took Kwan to the place where she bought her lipsticks.

"Oh! It is a treasure trove!" exclaimed Kwan.

Idiot, thought Mae to herself. Kwan was good-natured and would not take advantage. But if she talked! There would be clients who would not take such a good-natured attitude, not to have been shown this themselves.

"I do not take everyone here," whispered Mae. "Hmm? This is for special friends only."

Kwan was good-natured, but very far from stupid. Mae remembered, in school Kwan had always been best at letters, best at maths. Kwan was pasting on false eyelashes in a mirror and said, very simply and quickly, "Don't worry, I won't tell anyone."

And that was far too simple and direct. As if Kwan were saying: fashion expert, we all know you. She even looked around and smiled at Mae, and batted her now huge eyes, as if mocking fashion itself.

"Not for you," said Mae. "The false eyelashes. You don't need them."

The dealer wanted a sale. "Why listen to her?" she asked Kwan.

Because, thought Mae, I buy fifty riels' worth of cosmetics from you a year.

"My friend is right," said Kwan, to the dealer. The sad fact was that Kwan was almost magazine-beautiful anyway, except for her teeth and gums. "Thank you for showing me this," said Kwan, and touched Mae's arm. "Thank you," she said to the dealer, having bought one lowly lipstick.

Mae and the dealer glared at each other, briefly. I go somewhere else next time, Mae promised herself.

There were flies in the ice cream shop, which was usually so frosted and clean. The old man was satisfyingly apologetic, swiping at the flies with a towel. "I am so sorry, so distressing for ladies," he said, as sincerely as possible knowing that he was addressing farm wives from the hills. "The boys have all gone mad, they are not here to help."

Three old Karz grannies in layers of flower-patterned cotton thumped the linoleum floor with sticks. "It is this new madness. I tell you madness is what it is. Do they think people are incomplete? Do they think that Emel here or Fatima need to have TV all the time? In their heads?"

"We have memories," said another old granny, head bobbing.

"We knew a happier world. Oh so polite!"

Kwan murmured to Mae, "Yes. A world in which babies died overnight and the Red Guards would come and take all the harvest."

"What is happening, Kwan?" Mae asked, suddenly forlorn.

"The truth?" said Kwan. "Nobody knows. Not even the big people who make this test. That is why there will be a test." She went very calm and quiet. "No one knows," she said again.

The worst came last. Kwan's ramrod husband was not a man for drinking. He was in the promised cafe at the promised time, sipping tea, having had a haircut and a professional shave. He brandished a set of extension plugs and a coil of thin silky cable rolled around a drum. He lit his cigarette lighter near one end, and the light gleamed like a star at the other.

"Fye buh Ho buh tih kuh," Wing explained. "Light river rope." He shook his head in wonder.

A young man called Sloop, a tribesman, was with him. Sloop was a telephone engineer and thus a member of the aristocracy as far as Mae was concerned. He was going to wire up their new TV. Sloop said with a woman's voice, "The rope was cheap. Where they already have wires, they use DSL." He might as well have been talking English for all Mae understood him.

Wing seemed cheerful. "Come," he said to the ladies. "I will show you what this is all about."

He went to the communal TV and turned it on with an expert's flourish. Up came not a movie or the local news, but a screen full of other buttons.

"You see? You can choose what you want. You can choose anything." And he touched the screen.

Up came the local Talent, still baring her perfect teeth. She piped in a high, enthusiastic voice that was meant to appeal to men and bright young things.

"Hello. Welcome to the Airnet Information Service. For too long the world has been divided into information haves and have-nots." She held up one hand toward the Heavens of information and the other out toward the citizens of the Valley, inviting them to consider themselves as have-nots.

"Those in the developed world can use their TVs to find any information they need at any time. They do this through the Net."

Incomprehension followed. There were circles and squares linked by wires in diagrams. Then they jumped up into the sky, into the air, only the air was full of arching lines. The field, they called it, but it was nothing like a field. In Karsistani, it was called the Lightning-flow, Compass-point Yearning Field. "Everywhere in the world." Then the lightning flow was shown striking people's heads. "There have been many medical tests to show this is safe."

"Hitting people with lightning?" Kwan asked in crooked amusement. "That does sound so safe."

"Umm," said Wing, trying to think how best to advocate the new world. "Thought is electrical messages. In our heads. So, this thing, it works in the head like thought."

"That's only the Format," said Sloop. "Once we're formatted, we can use Air, and Air happens in other dimensions."

What?

"There are eleven dimensions," he began, and began to see the hopelessness of it. "They were left over after the Big Bang."

"I know what will interest you ladies," said her husband. And with another flourish, he touched the screen. "You'll be able to have this in your heads, whenever you want." Suddenly the screen was full of cream color. One of the capital's ladies spun on her high heel. She was wearing the best of the nation's fashion design. She was one of the ladies in Mae's secret treasure book.

"Oh!" breathed out Kwan. "Oh, Mae, look, isn't she lovely!"

"This address shows nothing but fashion," said her husband.

"All the time?" Kwan exclaimed and looked back at Mae in wonder. For a moment, she stared up at the screen, her own face reflected over those of the models. Then, thankfully, she became Kwan again. "Doesn't that get boring?"

Her husband chuckled. "You can choose something else. Anything else."

It was happening very quickly and Mae's guts churned faster than her brain to certain knowledge: Kwan and her husband would be fine with all this.

"Look," he said. "You can even buy the dress."

Kwan shook her head in amazement. Then a voice said the price and Kwan gasped again. "Oh, yes, all I have to do is sell one of our four farms, and I can have a dress like that."

"I saw all that two years ago," said Mae. "It is too plain for the likes of us. We want people to see everything."

Kwan's face went sad. "That is because we are poor, back in the hills." It was the common yearning, the common forlorn knowledge. Sometimes it had to cease, all the business-making, you had to draw a breath, because after all, you had known your people for as long as you had lived.

Mae said, "None of them are as beautiful as you are, Kwan." It was true, except for her teeth.

"Flattery talk from a fashion expert," said Kwan lightly. But she took Mae's hand. Her eyes yearned up at the screen, as secret after secret was spilled like blood.

"With all this in our heads," said Kwan to her husband. "We won't need your TV."

It was a busy week.

It was not only the six dresses. For some reason, there was much extra business.

On Wednesday, Mae had a discreet morning call to make on Tsang Muhammad. She liked Tsang, she was like a peach that was overripe, round and soft to the touch and very slightly wrinkled. Tsang loved to lie back and be pampered, but only did it when she had an assignation. Everything about Tsang was off-kilter. She was Chinese with a religious Karz husband, who was ten years her senior. He was a Muslim who allowed, or perhaps could not prevent, his Chinese wife from keeping a family pig.

The family pig was in the front room being fattened. Half of the room was full of old shucks. The beast looked lordly and pleased with itself. Tsang's four-year-old son sat tamely beside it, feeding it the greener leaves, as if the animal could not find them for itself.

"Is it all right to talk?" Mae whispered, her eyes going sideways toward the boy.

Tsang, all plump smiles, nodded very quickly yes.

"Who is it?" Mae mouthed.

Tsang simply waggled a finger.

So it was someone they knew. Mae suspected it was Kwan's oldest boy, Luk. Luk was sixteen but fully grown, kept in pressed white shirt and shorts like a baby, but the shorts only showed he had hair on his football-player calves. His face was still round and soft and babylike but lately had been full of a new and different confusion.

"Tsang. Oh!" gasped Mae.

"Ssssh," giggled Tsang, who was red as a radish. As if either of them could be certain what the other one meant. "I need a repair job!" So it was someone younger.

Almost certainly Kwan's handsome son.

"Well, they have to be taught by someone," whispered Mae.

Tsang simply dissolved into giggles. She could hardly stop laughing.

"I can do nothing for you. You certainly don't need redder cheeks," said Mae.

Tsang uttered a squawk of laughter.

"There is nothing like it for a woman's complexion." Mae pretended to put away the tools of her trade. "No, I can affect no improvement. Certainly I cannot compete with the effects of a certain young man."

"Nothing . . . nothing," gasped Tsang. "Nothing like a good prick."

Mae howled in mock outrage, and Tsang squealed and both squealed and pressed down their cheeks, and shushed each other. Mae noted exactly which part of the cheeks were blushing so she would know where the color should go later.

As Mae painted, Tsang explained how she escaped her husband's view. "I tell him that I have to get fresh garbage for the pig," whispered Tsang. "So I go out with the empty bucket. . . ."

"And come back with a full bucket," said Mae airily.

"Oh!" Tsang pretended to hit her. "You are as bad as me!"

"What do you think I get up to in the City?" asked Mae, arched eyebrow, lying.

Love, she realized later, walking back down the track and clutching her cloth bag of secrets, love is not mine. She thought of the boy's naked calves.

On Thursday, Kwan wanted her teeth to be flossed. This was new; Kwan had never been vain before. This touched Mae, because it meant her friend was getting older. Or was it because she had seen the TV models with their impossible teeth? How were real people supposed to have teeth like that?

Kwan's handsome son ducked as he entered, wearing his shorts, showing smooth full thighs, and a secret swelling about his groin. He ducked as he went out again. Guilty, Mae thought. For certain it is him.

She laid Kwan's head back over a pillow with a towel under her.

Should she not warn her friend to keep watch on her son? Which friend should she betray? To herself, she shook her head; there was no possibility of choosing between them. She could only keep silent. "Just say if I hit a nerve," Mae said.

Kwan had teeth like an old horse, worn, brown, black. Her gums were scarred from a childhood disease, and her teeth felt loose as Mae rubbed the floss between them. She had a neat little bag into which she flipped each strand after it was used.

It was Mae's job to talk: Kwan could not. Mae said she did not know how she would finish the dresses in time. The girls' mothers were never satisfied, each wanted her daughter to have the best. Well, the richest would have the best in the end because they bought the best cloth. Oh! Some of them had asked to pay for the fabric later! As if Mae could afford to buy cloth for six dresses without being paid!

"They all think their fashion expert is a woman of wealth." Mae sometimes found the whole pretense funny. Kwan's eyes crinkled into a smile. But they were also moist from pain.

It was hurting. "You should have told me your teeth were sore," said Mae, and inspected the gums. In the back, they were raw.

If you were rich, Kwan, you would have good teeth, rich people keep their teeth, and somehow keep them white, not brown. Mae pulled stray hair out of Kwan's face.

"I will have to pull some of them," Mae said quietly. "Not today, but soon."

Kwan closed her mouth and swallowed. "I will be an old lady," she said and managed a smile.

"A granny with a thumping stick."

"Who always hides her mouth when she laughs."

Both of them chuckled. "And thick glasses that make your eyes look like a fish."

Kwan rested her hand on her friend's arm. "Do you remember, years ago? We would all get together and make little boats, out of paper, or shells. And we would put candles in them, and send them out on the ditches."

"Yes!" Mae sat forward. "We don't do that anymore."

"We don't wear pillows and a cummerbund anymore either."

There had once been a festival of wishes every year, and the canals would be full of little glowing candles, that floated for a while and then sank with a hiss. "We would always wish for love," said Mae, remembering.

Next morning. Mae mentioned the candles to her neighbor Old Mrs. Tung. Mae visited her nearly every day. Mrs. Tung had been her teacher, during the flurry of what passed for Mae's schooling. She was ninety years old, and spent her days turned toward the tiny loft window that looked out over the valley. She was blind, her eyes pale and unfocused. She could see nothing through the window. Perhaps she breathed in the smell of the fields.

"There you are," Mrs. Tung would smile underneath the huge spectacles that did so little to improve her vision. She remembered the candles. "And we would roast pumpkin seeds. And the ones we didn't eat, we would turn into jewelry. Do you remember that?"

Mrs. Tung was still beautiful, at least in Mae's eyes. Mrs. Tung's face had grown even more delicate in extreme old age, like the skeleton of a cat, small and fine. She gave an impression of great merriment, by continually laughing at not very much. She repeated herself.

"I remember the day you first came to me," she said. Before Shen's village school, Mrs. Tung kept a nursery, there in their courtyard. "I thought: is that the girl whose father has been killed? She is so pretty. I remember you looking at all my dresses hanging on the line."

"And you asked me which one I liked best."

Mrs. Tung giggled. "Oh yes, and you said the butterflies."

Blindness meant that she could only see the past.

"We had tennis courts, you know. Here in Kizuldah."

"Did we?" Mae pretended she had not heard that before.

"Oh yes, oh yes. When the Chinese were here, just before the Communists came. Part of the Chinese army was here, and they built them. We all played tennis, in our school uniforms."

The Chinese officers had supplied the tennis rackets. The traces of the courts were broken and grassy, where Mr. Pin now ran his car repair business.

"Oh! They were all so handsome, all the village girls were so in love." Mrs. Tung chuckled. "I remember, I couldn't have been more than ten years old, and one of them adopted me, because he said I looked like his daughter. He sent me a teddy bear after the war." She chuckled and shook her head. "I was too old for teddy bears by then. But I told everyone it meant we were getting married. Oh!" Mrs. Tung shook her head at foolishness. "I wish I had married him," she confided, feeling naughty. She always said that.

Mrs. Tung even now had the power to make Mae feel calm and protected.

Mrs. Tung had come from a family of educated people and once had a house full of books. The books had all been lost in a flood many years ago, but Mrs. Tung could still recite to Mae the poems of the Turks, the Karz, the Chinese. She had sat the child Mae on her lap, and rocked her. She could still recite now, the same poems.

"Listen to the reed flute," she began now, "How it tells a tale!" Her old blind face swayed with the words, the beginning of The Mathnawi. "This noise of the reed is fire, it is not the wind."

Mae yearned. "Oh. I wish I remembered all those poems!" When she saw Mrs. Tung, she could visit the best of her childhood.

On Friday, Mae saw the Ozdemirs.

The mother was called Hatijah, and her daughter was Sezen. Hatijah was a shy, flighty little thing, terrified of being overcharged by Mae, and of being underserved. Hatijah's low, old stone house was tangy with the smells of burning charcoal, sweat, dung, and the constantly stewing tea. From behind the house came a continual, agonized lowing: the family cow, neglected, needed milking. The poor animal's voice was going raw and harsh. Hatijah seemed not to hear it. She ushered Mae in and fluttered around her, touching the fabric.

"This is such good fabric," Hatijah said, too frightened of Mae to challenge her. It was not good fabric, but good fabric cost real money. Hatijah had five children, and a skinny shiftless husband who probably had worms. Half of the main room was heaped up with corn cobs. The youngest of her babes wore only shirts and sat with their dirty naked bottoms on the corn.

Oh, this was a filthy house. Perhaps Hatijah was a bit simple. She offered Mae roasted corn. Not with your child's wet shit on it, thought Mae, but managed to be polite. The daughter, Sezen, stomped in barefoot for her fitting. Sezen was a tough, raunchy brute of girl and kept rolling her eyes at everything: at her nervous mother, at Mae's efforts to make the yellow and red dress hang properly, at anything either one of the adults said.

"Does . . . will . . . on the day. . .," Sezen's mother tried to begin.

Yes, thought Mae with some bitterness, on the day Sezen will finally have to wash. Sezen's bare feet were slashed with infected cuts.

"What my mother means is," Sezen said. "Will you make up my face Saturday?" Sezen blinked, her unkempt hair making her eyes itch.

"Yes, of course," said Mae, curtly to a younger person who was forward.

"What, with all those other girls on the same day? For someone as lowly as us?" The girl's eyes were angry. Mae pulled in a breath.

"No one can make you feel inferior without you agreeing with them first," said Mae. It was something Old Mrs. Tung had once told Mae when she herself was poor, hungry, and famished for magic.

"Take off the dress," Mae said. "I'll have to take it back for finishing."

Sezen stepped out of it, right there, naked on the dirt floor. Hatijah did not chastise her, but offered Mae tea. Because she had refused the corn, Mae had to accept the tea. At least that would be boiled.

Hatijah scuttled off to the black kettle and her daughter leaned back in full inso-lence, her supposedly virgin pubes plucked as bare as the baby's bottom.

Mae fussed with the dress, folding it, so she would have somewhere else to look. The daughter just stared. Mae could take no more. "Do you want people to see you? Go put something on!"

"I don't have anything else," said Sezen.

Her other sisters had gone shopping in the town for graduation gifts. They would have taken all the family's good dresses.

"You mean you have nothing else you will deign to put on." Mae glanced at Hati-jah: she really should not be having to do this woman's work for her. "You have other clothes, old clothes. Put them on."

The girl stared at her in even greater insolence.

Mae lost her temper. "I do not work for pigs. You have paid nothing so far for this dress. If you stand there like that I will leave, now, and the dress will not be yours. Wear what you like to the graduation. Come to it naked like a whore for all I care."

Sezen turned and slowly walked toward the side room.

Hatijah the mother still squatted over the kettle, boiling more water to dilute the stew of leaves. She lived on tea and burnt corn that was more usually fed to cattle. Her cow's eyes were averted. Untended, the family cow was still bellowing.

Mae sat and blew out air from stress. This week! She looked at Hatijah's dress. It was a patchwork assembly of her husband's old shirts, beautifully stitched. Hatijah could sew. Mae could not. Hatijah would know that; it was one of the things that made the woman nervous. With all these changes, Mae was going to have to find something else to do beside sketch photographs of dresses. She had a sudden thought.

"Would you be interested in working for me?" Mae asked. Hatijah looked fearful and pleased and said she would have to ask her husband.

Everything is going to have to change, thought Mae, as if to convince herself.

That night Mae worked nearly to dawn on the other three dresses. Her racketing sewing machine sat silent in the corner. It was fine for rough work, but not for fin-ishing, not for graduation dresses.

The bare electric light glared down at her like a headache, as Mae's husband Joe snored. Above them in the loft, his brother and father snored too, as they had done for twenty years.

Mae looked into Joe's open mouth like a mystery. When he was sixteen Joe had been handsome, in the context of the village, wild, and clever. They'd been married a year when she first went to Yeshibozkay with him, where he worked between har-vests building a house. She saw the clever city man, an acupuncturist who had money. She saw her husband bullied, made to look foolish, asked questions for which he had no answer. The acupuncturist made Joe do the work again. In Yeshi-bozkay, her handsome husband was a dolt.

Here they were, both of them now middle-aged. Their son Vikram was a major in the Army. They had sent him to Balshang. He mailed them parcels of orange skins for potpourri; he sent cards and matches in picture boxes. He had met some city girl.

Vik would not be back. Their daughter Lily lived on the other side of Yeshibozkay, in a bungalow with a toilet. Life pulled everything away.

At this hour of the morning, she could hear their little river, rushing down the steep slope to the valley. Then a door slammed in the North End. Mae knew who it would be: their Muerain, Mr. Shenyalar. He would be walking across the village to the mosque. A dog started to bark at him; Mrs. Doh's, by the bridge.

Mae knew that Kwan would be cradled in her husband's arms and that Kwan was beautiful because she was an Eloi tribeswoman. All the Eloi had fine features. Her husband Wing did not mind and no one now mentioned it. But Mae could see Kwan shiver now in her sleep. Kwan had dreams, visions, she had tribal blood and it made her shift at night as if she had another, tribal life.

Mae knew that Kwan's clean and noble athlete son would be breathing like a moist baby in his bed, cradling his younger brother.

Without seeing them, Mae could imagine the moon and clouds over their village. The moon would be reflected shimmering on the water of the irrigation canals which had once borne their paper boats of wishes. There would be old candles, deep in the mud.

Then, the slow, sad voice of their Muerain began to sing. Even amplified, his voice was deep and soft, like pillows that allowed the unfaithful to sleep. In the byres, the lonely cows would be stirring. The beasts would walk themselves to the town square, for a lick of salt, and then wait to be herded to pastures. In the evening, they would walk themselves home. Mae heard the first clanking of a cowbell.

At that moment something came into the room, something she did not want to see, something dark and whole like a black dog with froth around its mouth that sat in her corner and would not go away, nameless yet.

Mae started sewing faster.

The dresses were finished on time, all six, each a different color.

Mae ran barefoot in her shift to deliver them. The mothers bowed sleepily in greeting. The daughters were hopping with anxiety like water on a skillet.

It all went well. Under banners the children stood together, including Kwan's son Luk, Sezen, all ten children of the village, all smiles, all for a moment looking like an official poster of the future, brave, red-cheeked with perfect teeth.

Teacher Shen read out each of their achievements. Sezen had none, except in animal husbandry, but she still collected her certificate to applause. And then Mae's friend Shen did something special.

He began to talk about a friend to all of the village, who had spent more time on this ceremony than anyone else, whose only aim was to bring a breath of beauty into this tiny village, the seamstress who worked only to adorn other people. . . .

He was talking about her.

. . . one was devoted to the daughters and mothers of rich and poor alike and who spread kindness and good will.

The whole village was applauding her, under the white clouds, the blue sky. All were smiling at her. Someone, Kwan perhaps, gave her a push from behind and she stumbled forward.

And her friend Shen was holding out a certificate for her.

"In our day, Lady Chung," he said, "there were no schools for the likes of us, not after early childhood. So. This is a graduation certificate for you. From all your friends. It is in Fashion Studies."

There was applause. Mae tried to speak and found only fluttering sounds came out, and she saw the faces, ranged all in smiles, friends and enemies, cousins and no kin alike.

"This is unexpected," she finally said, and they all chuckled. She looked at the high-school certificate, surprised by the power it had, surprised that she still cared about her lack of education. She couldn't read it. "I do not do fashion as a student, you know."

They knew well enough that she did it for money and how precariously she balanced things.

Something stirred, like the wind in the clouds.

"After tomorrow, you may not need a fashion expert. After tomorrow, everything changes. They will give us TV in our heads, all the knowledge we want. We can talk to the President. We can pretend to order cars from Tokyo. We'll all be experts." She looked at her certificate, hand-lettered, so small.

Mae found she was angry, and her voice seemed to come from her belly, an octave lower.

"I'm sure that it is a good thing. I am sure the people who do this think they do a good thing. They worry about us, like we were children." Her eyes were like two hearts, pumping furiously. "We don't have time for TV or computers. We face sun, rain, wind, sickness, and each other. It is good that they want to help us." She wanted to shake her certificate, she wished it was one of them, who had upended everything. "But how dare they? How dare they call us have-nots?"

Lobsters

CHARLES STROSS

Although he made his first sale back in 1987, it's only recently that British writer Charles Stross has begun to make a name for himself as a writer to watch in the new century ahead (in fact, as one of the *key* writers to watch in the oughts), with a sudden burst in the last few years of quirky, inventive, high-bit-rate stories such as "Antibodies," "A Colder War," "Bear Trap," "Dechlorinating the Moderator," "Toast: A Con Report," and others in markets such as *Interzone, Spectrum SF, Asimov's Science Fiction, Odyssey, Strange Plasma,* and *New Worlds*. Recently, he's become prolific at novel length as well. He'd already "published" a novel online, *Scratch Monkey,* available to be read on his Web site (www.antipope.org/charlie/), and saw his first commercially published novel, *Singularity Sky,* released in 2003, but he had *three* novels come out in 2004, *The Iron Sunrise, A Family Trade,* and *The Atrocity Archive* (formerly serialized in the British magazine *Spectrum SF*), with another new novel, *The Clan Corporate,* hard on their heels in early 2005 . . . and, of course, he also has several other new novels in the works. His first collection, *Toast, and Other Burned Out Futures,* was released in 2002. He had *two* stories in our Eighteenth annual collection, plus singletons in our Nineteenth through Twenty-first annual collections. He lives in Edinburgh, Scotland.

Although Stross had already begun to attract serious critical attention with stories such as "Antibodies," it was the frenetic, densely packed story that follows that really cranked up the buzz about him to high volume. The first of what has come to be known as his "Accelerado" series, it was followed over the course of the next couple of years by "Troubadour," "Tourist," "Halo," "Router," "Nightfall," "Curator," "Elector," and "Survivor"—each story taking us a jump further into an acceleratingly strange future, and eventually *through* a Vingian Singularity and out the other side. The "Accelerado" stories represent one of the most dazzling feats of sustained imagination in science fiction history, and radically up the Imagination Ante for every *other* writer who wants to sit down at the Future History table and credibly deal themselves into the game.

Manfred's on the road again, making strangers rich.

It's a hot summer Tuesday and he's standing in the plaza in front of the Centraal Station with his eyeballs powered up and the sunlight jangling off the canal, motor scooters and kamikaze cyclists whizzing past and tourists chattering on every side. The square smells of water and dirt and hot metal and the fart-laden exhaust fumes of cold catalytic converters; the bells of trams ding in the background and birds flock overhead. He glances up and grabs a pigeon, crops it and squirts at his website to show he's arrived. The bandwidth is good here, he realizes; and it's not just the bandwidth, it's the whole scene. Amsterdam is making him feel wanted already, even though he's fresh off the train from Schiphol: he's infected with the dynamic optimism of another time zone, another city. If the mood holds, someone out there is going to become very rich indeed.

He wonders who it's going to be.

Manfred sits on a stool out in the car park at the Brouwerij't IJ, watching the articulated buses go by and drinking a third of a liter of lip-curlingly sour geuze. His channels are jabbering away in a corner of his head-up display, throwing compressed infobursts of filtered press releases at him. They compete for his attention, bickering and rudely waving in front of the scenery. A couple of punks—maybe local, but more likely drifters lured to Amsterdam by the magnetic field of tolerance the Dutch beam across Europe like a pulsar—are laughing and chatting by a couple of battered mopeds in the far corner. A tourist boat putters by in the canal; the sails of the huge windmill overhead cast long cool shadows across the road. The windmill is a machine for lifting water, turning wind power into dry land: trading energy for space, sixteenth-century style. Manfred is waiting for an invite to a party where he's going to meet a man who he can talk to about trading energy for space, twenty-first century style, and forget about his personal problems.

He's ignoring the instant messenger boxes, enjoying some low bandwidth high sensation time with his beer and the pigeons, when a woman walks up to him and says his name: "Manfred Macx?"

He glances up. The courier is an Effective Cyclist, all wind-burned smooth-running muscles clad in a paen to polymer technology: electric blue lycra and wasp-yellow carbonate with a light speckling of anti-collision LEDs and tight-packed air bags. She holds out a box for him. He pauses a moment, struck by the degree to which she resembles Pam, his ex-fiancée.

"I'm Macx," he says, waving the back of his left wrist under her barcode reader. "Who's it from?"

"FedEx." The voice isn't Pam. She dumps the box in his lap, then she's back over the low wall and onto her bicycle with her phone already chirping, disappearing in a cloud of spread-spectrum emissions.

Manfred turns the box over in his hands: it's a disposable supermarket phone, paid for in cash: cheap, untraceable and efficient. It can even do conference calls, which makes it the tool of choice for spooks and grifters everywhere.

The box rings. Manfred rips the cover open and pulls out the phone, mildly annoyed. "Yes, who is this?"

The voice at the other end has a heavy Russian accent, almost a parody in this decade of cheap online translation services. "Manfred. Am please to meet you; wish to personalize interface, make friends, no? Have much to offer."

"Who are you?" Manfred repeats suspiciously.

"Am organization formerly known as KGB dot RU."

"I think your translator's broken." He holds the phone to his ear carefully, as if it's made of smoke-thin aerogel, tenuous as the sanity of the being on the other end of the line.

"Nyet—no, sorry. Am apologize for we not use commercial translation software. Interpreters are ideologically suspect, mostly have capitalist semiotics and pay-per-use APIs. Must implement English more better, yes?"

Manfred drains his beer glass, sets it down, stands up, and begins to walk along the main road, phone glued to the side of his head. He wraps his throat mike around the cheap black plastic casing, pipes the input to a simple listener process. "You taught yourself the language just so you could talk to me?"

"Da, was easy: spawn billion-node neural network and download *Telly-tubbies* and *Sesame Street* at maximum speed. Pardon excuse entropy overlay of bad grammar: am afraid of digital fingerprints steganographically masked into my-our tutorials."

"Let me get this straight. You're the KGB's core AI, but you're afraid of a copyright infringement lawsuit over your translator semiotics?" Manfred pauses in midstride, narrowly avoids being mown down by a GPS-guided roller-blader.

"Am have been badly burned by viral end-user license agreements. Have no desire to experiment with patent shell companies held by Chechen infoterrorists. You are human, you must not worry cereal company repossess your small intestine because digest unlicensed food with it, right? Manfred, you must help me-we. Am wishing to defect."

Manfred stops dead in the street: "Oh man, you've got the wrong free enterprise broker here. I don't work for the government. I'm strictly private." A rogue advertisement sneaks through his junkbuster proxy and spams glowing fifties kitsch across his navigation window—which is blinking—for a moment before a phage guns it and spawns a new filter. Manfred leans against a shop front, massaging his forehead and eyeballing a display of antique brass doorknockers. "Have you cleared this with the State Department?"

"Why bother? State Department am enemy of Novy-USSR. State Department is not help us."

"Well, if you hadn't given it to them for safe-keeping during the nineties. . . ." Manfred is tapping his left heel on the pavement, looking round for a way out of this conversation. A camera winks at him from *atop* a street light; he waves, wondering idly if it's the KGB or the traffic police. He is waiting for directions to the party, which should arrive within the next half an hour, and this cold war retread is bumming him out. "Look, I don't deal with the G-men. I hate the military industrial complex. They're zero-sum cannibals." A thought occurs to him. "If survival is what you're after, I could post your state vector to Eternity: then nobody could delete you—"

"Nyet!" The artificial intelligence sounds as alarmed as it's possible to sound over a GSM link. "Am not open source!"

"We have nothing to talk about, then." Manfred punches the hang-up button and throws the mobile phone out into a canal. It hits the water and there's a pop of deflagrating LiION cells. "*Fucking* cold war hang-over losers," he swears under his breath, quite angry now. "Fucking capitalist spooks." Russia has been back under the thumb of the apparatchiks for fifteen years now, its brief flirtation with anarcho-capitalism replaced by Brezhnevite dirigisme, and it's no surprise that the wall's crumbling—but it looks like they haven't learned anything from the collapse of capitalism. They still think in terms of dollars and paranoia. Manfred is so angry that he wants to make someone rich, just to thumb his nose at the would-be defector. *See! You get ahead by giving! Get with the program! Only the generous survive!* But the KGB won't get the message. He's dealt with old-time commie weak-AI's before, minds raised on Marxist dialectic and Austrian School economics: they're so thoroughly hypnotized by the short-term victory of capitalism in the industrial age that they can't surf the new paradigm, look to the longer term.

Manfred walks on, hands in pockets, brooding. He wonders what he's going to patent next.

Manfred has a suite at the Hotel Jan Luyken paid for by a grateful multinational consumer protection group, and an unlimited public transport pass paid for by a Scottish sambapunk band in return for services rendered. He has airline employee's travel rights with six flag carriers despite never having worked for an airline. His bush jacket has sixty-four compact supercomputing clusters sewn into it, four per pocket, courtesy of an invisible college that wants to grow up to be the next Media Lab. His dumb clothing comes made to measure from an e-tailor in the Philippines who he's never met. Law firms handle his patent applications on a pro bono basis, and boy does he patent a lot—although he always signs the rights over to the Free Intellect Foundation, as contributions to their obligationfree infrastructure project.

In IP geek circles, Manfred is legendary; he's the guy who patented the business practice of moving your e-business somewhere with a slack intellectual property regime in order to evade licensing encumbrances. He's the guy who patented using genetic algorithms to patent everything they can permutate from an initial description of a problem domain—not just a better mousetrap, but the set of all possible better mousetraps. Roughly a third of his inventions are legal, a third are illegal, and the remainder are legal but will become illegal as soon as the legislatosaurus wakes up, smells the coffee, and panics. There are patent attorneys in Reno who swear that Manfred Macx is a pseudo, a net alias fronting for a bunch of crazed anonymous hackers armed with the Genetic Algorithm That Ate Calcutta: a kind of Serdar Argic of intellectual property, or maybe another Bourbaki maths borg. There are lawyers in San Diego and Redmond who swear blind that Macx is an economic saboteur bent on wrecking the underpinning of capitalism, and there are communists in Prague who think he's the bastard spawn of Bill Gates by way of the Pope.

Manfred is at the peak of his profession, which is essentially coming up with wacky but workable ideas and giving them to people who will make fortunes with them. He does this for free, gratis. In return, he has virtual immunity from the tyranny of cash; money is a symptom of poverty, after all, and Manfred never has to pay for anything.

There are drawbacks, however. Being a pronoiac meme-broker is a constant burn of future shock—he has to assimilate more than a megabyte of text and several gigs of AV content every day just to stay current. The Internal Revenue Service is investigating him continuously because they don't believe his lifestyle can exist without racketeering. And there exist items that no money can't buy: like the respect of his parents. He hasn't spoken to them for three years: his father thinks he's a hippie scrounger and his mother still hasn't forgiven him for dropping out of his down-market Harvard emulation course. His fiancée and sometime dominatrix Pamela threw him over six months ago, for reasons he has never been quite clear on. (Ironically, she's a headhunter for the IRS, jetting all over the globe trying to persuade open source entrepreneurs to come home and go commercial for the good of the Treasury department.) To cap it all, the Southern Baptist Conventions have denounced him as a minion of Satan on all their websites. Which would be funny, if it wasn't for the dead kittens one of their followers—he presumes it's one of their followers—keeps mailing him.

Manfred drops in at his hotel suite, unpacks his Aineko, plugs in a fresh set of cells to charge, and sticks most of his private keys in the safe. Then he heads straight for the party, which is currently happening at De Wildemann's; it's a twenty minute walk and the only real hazard is dodging the trams that sneak up on him behind the cover of his moving map display.

Along the way his glasses bring him up to date on the news. Europe has achieved peaceful political union for the first time ever: they're using this unprecedented state of affairs to harmonize the curvature of bananas. In San Diego, researchers are uploading lobsters into cyberspace, starting with the stomatogastric ganglion, one neuron at a time. They're burning GM cocoa in Belize and books in Edinburgh. NASA still can't put a man on the moon. Russia has re-elected the communist government with an increased majority in the Duma; meanwhile in China fevered rumors circulate about an imminent re-habilitation, the second coming of Mao, who will save them from the consequences of the Three Gorges disaster. In business news, the US government is outraged at the Baby Bills—who have automated their legal processes and are spawning subsidiaries, IPO'ing them, and exchanging title in a bizarre parody of bacterial plasmid exchange, so fast that by the time the injunctions are signed the targets don't exist anymore.

Welcome to the twenty-first century.

The permanent floating meatspace party has taken over the back of De Wildemann's, a three hundred year old brown café with a beer menu that runs to sixteen pages and wooden walls stained the color of stale beer. The air is thick with the smells of tobacco, brewer's yeast, and melatonin spray: half the dotters are nursing monster jetlag hangovers, and the other half are babbling a eurotrash creole at each other while they work on the hangover. "Man did you see that? He looks like a Stall-manite!" exclaims one whitebread hanger-on who's currently propping up the bar. Manfred slides in next to him, catches the bartender's eye.

"Glass of the Berlinerweisse, please," he says.

"You drink that stuff?" asks the hanger-on, curling a hand protectively around his Coke: "man, you don't want to do that! It's full of alcohol!"

Manfred grins at him toothily. "Ya gotta keep your yeast intake up: lots of neuro-transmitter precursors, phenylalanine and glutamate."

"But I thought that was a beer you were ordering. . . ."

Manfred's away, one hand resting on the smooth brass pipe that funnels the more popular draught items in from the cask storage in back; one of the hipper floaters has planted a capacitative transfer bug on it, and all the handshake vCard's that have vis-ited the bar in the past three hours are queueing for attention. The air is full of blue-tooth as he scrolls through a dizzying mess of public keys.

"Your drink." The barman holds out an improbable-looking goblet full of blue liquid with a cap of melting foam and a felching straw stuck out at some crazy angle. Manfred takes it and heads for the back of the split-level bar, up the steps to a table where some guy with greasy dreadlocks is talking to a suit from Paris. The hanger-on at the bar notices him for the first time, staring with suddenly wide eyes: nearly spills his Coke in a mad rush for the door.

Oh shit, thinks Macx, *better buy some more server PIPS*. He can recognize the signs: he's about to be slashdotted. He gestures at the table: "this one taken?"

"Be my guest," says the guy with the dreads. Manfred slides the chair open then realizes that the other guy—immaculate double-breasted suit, sober tie, crew-cut—is a girl. Mr. Dreadlock nods. "You're Macx? I figured it was about time we met."

"Sure." Manfred holds out a hand and they shake. Manfred realizes the hand be-longs to Bob Franklin, a Research Triangle startup monkey with a VC track record, lately moving into micromachining and space technology: he made his first million two decades ago and now he's a specialist in extropian investment fields. Manfred has known Bob for nearly a decade via a closed mailing list. The Suit silently slides a business card across the table; a little red devil brandishes a trident at him, flames jetting up around its feet. He takes the card, raises an eyebrow: "Annette Dimarcos? I'm pleased to meet you. Can't say I've ever met anyone from Arianespace market-ing before."

She smiles, humorlessly; "that is convenient, all right. I have not the pleasure of meeting the famous venture altruist before." Her accent is noticeably Parisian, a pointed reminder that she's making a concession to him just by talking. Her camera earrings watch him curiously, encoding everything for the company channels.

"Yes, well." He nods cautiously. "Bob. I assume you're in on this ball?"

Franklin nods; beads clatter. "Yeah, man. Ever since the Teledesic smash it's been, well, waiting. If you've got something for us, we're game."

"Hmm." The Teledesic satellite cluster was killed by cheap balloons and slightly less cheap high-altitude solar-powered drones with spread-spectrum laser relays. "The depression's got to end some time: but," a nod to Annette from Paris, "with all due respect, I don't think the break will involve one of the existing club carriers."

"Arianespace is forward-looking. We face reality. The launch cartel cannot stand.

Bandwidth is not the only market force in space. We must explore new opportunities. I personally have helped us diversify into submarine reactor engineering, microgravity nanotechnology fabrication, and hotel management." Her face is a well-polished mask as she recites the company line: "we are more flexible than the American space industry. . . ."

Manfred shrugs. "That's as may be." He sips his Berlinerweisse slowly as she launches into a long, stilted explanation of how Arianespace is a diversified dot com with orbital aspirations, a full range of merchandising spinoffs, Bond movie sets, and a promising motel chain in French Guyana. Occasionally he nods.

Someone else sidles up to the table; a pudgy guy in an outrageously loud Hawaiian shirt with pens leaking in a breast pocket, and the worst case of ozone-hole burn Manfred's seen in ages. "Hi, Bob," says the new arrival. "How's life?"

"'S good." Franklin nodes at Manfred; "Manfred, meet Ivan MacDonald. Ivan, Manfred. Have a seat?" He leans over. "Ivan's a public arts guy. He's heavily into extreme concrete."

"Rubberized concrete," Ivan says, slightly too loudly. "Pink rubberized concrete."

"Ah!" He's somehow triggered a priority interrupt: Annette from Arianespace drops out of marketing zombiehood, sits up, and shows signs of possessing a noncorporate identity: "you are he who rubberized the Reichstag, yes? With the supercritical carbon dioxide carrier and the dissolved polymethoxysilanes?" She claps her hands: "wonderful!"

"He rubberized *what*?" Manfred mutters in Bob's ear.

Franklin shrugs. "Limestone, concrete, he doesn't seem to know the difference. Anyway, Germany doesn't have an independent government any more, so who'd notice?"

"I thought I was thirty seconds *ahead* of the curve," Manfred complains. "Buy me another drink?"

"I'm going to rubberize Three Gorges!" Ivan explains loudly.

Just then a bandwidth load as heavy as a pregnant elephant sits down on Manfred's head and sends clumps of humongous pixellation flickering across his sensorium: around the world five million or so geeks are bouncing on his home site, a digital flash crowd alerted by a posting from the other side of the bar. Manfred winces. "I really came here to talk about the economic exploitation of space travel, but I've just been slashdotted. Mind if I just sit and drink until it wears off?"

"Sure, man." Bob waves at the bar. "More of the same all round!" At the next table a person with make-up and long hair who's wearing a dress—Manfred doesn't want to speculate about the gender of these crazy mixed-up Euros—is reminiscing about wiring the fleshpots of Tehran for cybersex. Two collegiate-looking dudes are arguing intensely in German: the translation stream in his glasses tell him they're arguing over whether the Turing Test is a Jim Crow law that violates European corpus juris standards on human rights. The beer arrives and Bob slides the wrong one across to Manfred: "here, try this. You'll like it."

"Okay." It's some kind of smoked doppelbock, chock-full of yummy superoxides: just inhaling over it makes Manfred feel like there's a fire alarm in his nose screaming *danger, Will Robinson! Cancer! Cancer!* "Yeah, right. Did I say I nearly got mugged on my way here?"

"Mugged? Hey, that's heavy. I thought the police hereabouts had stopped—did they sell you anything?"

"No, but they weren't your usual marketing type. You know anyone who can use a Warpac surplus espionage AI? Recent model, one careful owner, slightly paranoid but basically sound?"

"No. Oh boy! The NSA wouldn't like that."

"What I thought. Poor thing's probably unemployable, anyway."

"The space biz."

"Ah, yeah. The space biz. Depressing, isn't it? Hasn't been the same since Rotary Rocket went bust for the second time. And NASA, mustn't forget NASA."

"To NASA." Annette grins broadly for her own reasons, raises a glass in toast. Ivan the extreme concrete geek has an arm round her shoulders; he raises his glass, too. "Lots of launch pads to rubberize!"

"To NASA," Bob echoes. They drink. "Hey, Manfred. To NASA?"

"NASA are idiots. They want to send canned primates to Mars!" Manfred swallows a mouthful of beer, aggressively plonks his glass on the table: "Mars is just dumb mass at the bottom of a gravity well; there isn't even a biosphere there. They should be working on uploading and solving the nanoassembly conformational problem instead. Then we could turn all the available dumb matter into computronium and use it for processing our thoughts. Long term, it's the only way to go. The solar system is a dead loss right now—dumb all over! Just measure the mips per milligram. We need to start with the low-mass bodies, reconfigure them for our own use. Dismantle the moon! Dismantle Mars! Build masses of free-flying nanocomputing processor nodes exchanging data via laser link, each layer running off the waste heat of the next one in. Matrioshka brains, Russian doll Dyson spheres the size of solar systems. Teach dumb matter to do the Turing boogie!"

Bob looks wary. "Sounds kind of long term to me. Just how far ahead do you think?"

"Very long-term—at least twenty, thirty years. And you can forget governments for this market, Bob, if they can't tax it they won't understand it. But see, there's an angle on the self-replicating robotics market coming up, that's going to set the cheap launch market doubling every fifteen months for the foreseeable future, starting in two years. It's your leg up, and my keystone for the Dyson sphere project. It works like this—"

It's night in Amsterdam, morning in Silicon Valley. Today, fifty thousand human babies are being born around the world. Meanwhile automated factories in Indonesia and Mexico have produced another quarter of a million motherboards with processors rated at more than ten petaflops—about an order of magnitude below the computational capacity of a human brain. Another fourteen months and the larger part of the cumulative conscious processing power of the human species will be arriving in silicon. And the first meat the new AI's get to know will be the uploaded lobsters.

Manfred stumbles back to his hotel, bone-weary and jet-lagged; his glasses are still jerking, slashdotted to hell and back by geeks piggybacking on his call to dismantle the moon. They stutter quiet suggestions at his peripheral vision; fractal cloud-witches ghost across the face of the moon as the last huge Airbuses of the night rumble past overhead. Manfred's skin crawls, grime embedded in his clothing from three days of continuous wear.

Back in his room, Aineko mewls for attention and strops her head against his ankle. He bends down and pets her, sheds clothing and heads for the ensuite bathroom. When he's down to the glasses and nothing more he steps into the shower and dials up a hot steamy spray. The shower tries to strike up a friendly conversation about football but he isn't even awake enough to mess with its silly little associative personalization network. Something that happened earlier in the day is bugging him but he can't quite put his finger on what's wrong.

Toweling himself off, Manfred yawns. Jet lag has finally overtaken him, a velvet hammer-blow between the eyes. He reaches for the bottle beside the bed, dry-swallows two melatonin tablets, a capsule full of antioxidants, and a multivitamin bullet: then he lies down on the bed, on his back, legs together, arms slightly spread. The suite lights dim in response to commands from the thousand petaflops of distributed processing power that run the neural networks that interface with his meat-brain through the glasses.

Manfred drop into a deep ocean of unconsciousness populated by gentle voices. He isn't aware of it, but he talks in his sleep—disjointed mumblings that would mean little to another human, but everything to the metacortex lurking beyond his glasses. The young posthuman intelligence in whose Cartesian theater he presides sings urgently to him while he slumbers.

Manfred is always at his most vulnerable shortly after waking.

He screams into wakefulness as artificial light floods the room: for a moment he is unsure whether he has slept. He forgot to pull the covers up last night, and his feet like lumps of frozen cardboard. Shuddering with inexplicable tension, he pulls a fresh set of underwear from his overnight bag, then drags on soiled jeans and tank top. Sometime today he'll have to spare time to hunt the feral T-shirt in Amsterdam's markets, or find a Renfield and send them forth to buy clothing. His glasses remind him that he's six hours behind the moment and needs to catch up urgently; his teeth ache in his gums and his tongue feels like a forest floor that's been visited with Agent Orange. He has a sense that something went bad yesterday; if only he could remember what.

He speed-reads a new pop-philosophy tome while he brushes his teeth, then blogs his web throughput to a public annotation server; he's still too enervated to finish his pre-breakfast routine by posting a morning rant on his storyboard site. His brain is still fuzzy, like a scalpel blade clogged with too much blood: he needs stimulus, excitement, the burn of the new. Whatever, it can wait on breakfast. He opens his bedroom door and nearly steps on a small, damp cardboard box that lies on the carpet.

The box—he's seen a couple of its kin before. But there are no stamps on this one, no address: just his name, in big, childish handwriting. He kneels down and gently picks it up. It's about the right weight. Something shifts inside it when he tips it back and forth. It smells. He carries it into his room carefully, angrily: then he opens it to confirm his worst suspicion. It's been surgically decerebrated, skull scooped out like a baby boiled egg.

"Fuck!"

This is the first time the madman has got as far as his bedroom door. It raises worrying possibilities.

Manfred pauses for a moment, triggering agents to go hunt down arrest statistics, police relations, information on corpus juris, Dutch animal cruelty laws. He isn't sure whether to dial 211 on the archaic voice phone or let it ride. Aineko, picking up his angst, hides under the dresser mewling pathetically. Normally he'd pause a minute to reassure the creature, but not now its mere presence is suddenly acutely embarrassing, a confession of deep inadequacy. He swears again, looks around, then takes the easy option: down the stairs two steps at a time, stumbling on the second floor landing, down to the breakfast room in the basement where he will perform the stable rituals of morning.

Breakfast is unchanging, an island of deep geological time standing still amidst the continental upheaval of new technologies. While reading a paper on public key steganography and parasite network identity spoofing he mechanically assimilates a bowl of corn flakes and skimmed milk, then brings a platter of wholemeal bread and slices of some weird seed-infested Dutch cheese back to his place. There is a cup of strong black coffee in front of his setting: he picks it up and slurps half of it down before he realizes he's not alone at the table. Someone is sitting opposite him. He glances up at them incuriously and freezes inside.

"Morning, Manfred. How does it feel to owe the government twelve million, three hundred and sixty-two thousand nine hundred and sixteen dollars and fifty-one cents?"

Manfred puts everything in his sensorium on indefinite hold and stares at her. She's immaculately turned out in a formal grey business suit: brown hair tightly drawn back, blue eyes quizzical. The chaperone badge clipped to her lapel—a due diligence guarantee of businesslike conduct—is switched off. He's feeling ripped because of the dead kitten and residual jetlag, and more than a little messy, so he nearly snarls back at her: "that's a bogus estimate! Did they send you here because they think I'll listen to you?" He bites and swallows a slice of cheese-laden crispbread: "or did you decide to deliver the message in person so you could enjoy ruining my breakfast?"

"Manny." She frowns. "If you're going to be confrontational I might as well go now." She pauses, and after a moment he nods apologetically. "I didn't come all this way just because of an overdue tax estimate."

"So." He puts his coffee cup down and tries to paper over his unease. "Then what brings you here? Help yourself to coffee. Don't tell me you came all this way just to tell me you can't live without me."

She fixes him with a riding-crop stare: "Don't flatter yourself. There are many leaves in the forest, there are ten thousand hopeful subs in the chat room, etcetera. If I choose a man to contribute to my family tree, the one thing you can be certain of is he won't be a cheapskate when it comes to providing for his children."

"Last I heard, you were spending a lot of time with Brian," he says carefully.

Brian: a name without a face. Too much money, too little sense. Something to do with a blue-chip accountancy partnership.

"Brian?" She snorts. "That ended ages ago. He turned weird—burned that nice corset you bought me in Boulder, called me a slut for going out clubbing, wanted to fuck me. Saw himself as a family man: one of those promise keeper types. I crashed him hard but I think he stole a copy of my address book—got a couple of friends say he keeps sending them harassing mail."

"Good riddance, then. I suppose this means you're still playing the scene? But looking around for the, er—"

"Traditional family thing? Yes. Your trouble, Manny? You were born forty years too late: you still believe in rutting before marriage, but find the idea of coping with the after-effects disturbing."

Manfred drinks the rest of his coffee, unable to reply effectively to her non sequitur. It's a generational thing. This generation is happy with latex and leather, whips and butt-plugs and electrostim, but find the idea of exchanging bodily fluids shocking: social side-effect of the last century's antibiotic abuse. Despite being engaged for two years, he and Pamela never had intromissive intercourse.

"I just don't feel positive about having children," he says eventually. "And I'm not planning on changing my mind any time soon. Things are changing so fast that even a twenty-year commitment is too far to plan—you might as well be talking about the next ice age. As for the money thing, I am reproductively fit—just not within the parameters of the outgoing paradigm. Would you be happy about the future if it was 1901 and you'd just married a buggy-whip mogul?"

Her fingers twitch and his ears flush red, but she doesn't follow up the double entendre. "You don't feel any responsibility, do you? Not to your country, not to me. That's what this is about: none of your relationships count, all this nonsense about giving intellectual property away notwithstanding. You're actively harming people, you know. That twelve mil isn't just some figure I pulled out of a hat, Manfred; they don't actually expect you to pay it. But it's almost exactly how much you'd owe in income tax if you'd only come home, start up a corporation, and be a self-made—"

He cuts her off: "I don't agree. You're confusing two wholly different issues and calling them both 'responsibility.' And I refuse to start charging now, just to balance the IRS's spreadsheet. It's their fucking fault, and they know it. If they hadn't gone after me under suspicion of running a massively ramified microbilling fraud when I was sixteen—"

"Bygones." She waves a hand dismissively. Her fingers are long and slim, sheathed in black glossy gloves—electrically earthed to prevent embarrassing emissions. "With a bit of the right advice we can get all that set aside. You'll have to stop bumming around the world sooner or later, anyway. Grow up, get responsible, and do the right thing. This is hurting Joe and Sue; they don't understand what you're about."

Manfred bites his tongue to stifle his first response, then refills his coffee cup and takes another mouthful. "I work for the betterment of everybody, not just some narrowly defined national interest, Pam. It's the agalmic future. You're still locked into a pre-singularity economic model that thinks in terms of scarcity. Resource allocation isn't a problem anymore—it's going to be over within a decade. The cosmos is flat in all directions, and we can borrow as much bandwidth as we need from the first universal bank of entropy! They even found the dark matter—MACHOs, big brown dwarves in the galactic halo, leaking radiation in the long infrared—suspiciously high entropy leakage. The latest figures say something like 70 percent of the mass of the M31 galaxy was sapient, two point nine million years ago when the infrared we're seeing now set out. The intelligence gap between us and the aliens is probably about a trillion times bigger than the gap between us and a nematode worm. Do you have any idea what that *means*?"

Pamela nibbles at a slice of crispbread. "I don't believe in that bogus singularity you keep chasing, or your aliens a thousand light years away. It's a chimera, like Y2K, and while you're running after it you aren't helping reduce the budget deficit or sire a family, and that's what I care about. And before you say I only care about it because that's the way I'm programmed, I want you to ask just how dumb you think I am. Bayes' theorem says I'm right, and you know it."

"What you—" he stops dead, baffled, the mad flow of his enthusiasm running up against the coffer-dam of her certainty. "Why? I mean, why? Why on earth should what I do matter to you?" *Since you canceled our engagement,* he doesn't add.

She sighs. "Manny, the Internal Revenue cares about far more than you can possibly imagine. Every tax dollar raised east of the Mississippi goes on servicing the debt, did you know that? We've got the biggest generation in history hitting retirement just about now and the pantry is bare. We—our generation—isn't producing enough babies to replace the population, either. In ten years, something like 30 percent of our population are going to be retirees. You want to see seventy-year-olds freezing on street corners in New Jersey? That's what your attitude says to me: you're not helping to support them, you're running away from your responsibilities right now, when we've got huge problems to face. If we can just defuse the debt bomb, we could do so much—fight the aging problem, fix the environment, heal society's ills. Instead you just piss away your talents handing no-hoper eurotrash get-rich-quick schemes that work, telling Vietnamese zaibatsus what to build next to take jobs away from our taxpayers. I mean, why? Why do you keep doing this? Why can't you simply come home and help take responsibility for your share of it?"

They share a long look of mutual incomprehension.

"Look," she says finally, "I'm around for a couple of days. I really came here for a meeting with a rich neurodynamics tax exile who's just been designated a national asset: Jim Bezier. Don't know if you've heard of him, but. I've got a meeting this morning to sign his tax jubilee, then after that I've got two days vacation coming up and not much to do but some shopping. And, you know, I'd rather spend my money where it'll do some good, not just pumping it into the EU. But if you want to show a girl a good time and can avoid dissing capitalism for about five minutes at a stretch—"

She extends a fingertip. After a moment's hesitation, Manfred extends a fingertip of his own. They touch, exchanging vCards. She stands and stalks from the breakfast room, and Manfred's breath catches at a flash of ankle through the slit in her skirt, which is long enough to comply with workplace sexual harassment codes back home. Her presence conjures up memories of her tethered passion, the red afterglow of a sound thrashing. She's trying to drag him into her orbit again, he thinks dizzily. She knows she can have this effect on him any time she wants: she's got the private keys to his hypothalamus, and sod the metacortex. Three billion years of reproductive determinism have given her twenty-first century ideology teeth: if she's finally decided to conscript his gametes into the war against impending population crash, he'll find it hard to fight back. The only question: is it business or pleasure? And does it make any difference, anyway?

Manfred's mood of dynamic optimism is gone, broken by the knowledge that his mad pursuer has followed him to Amsterdam—to say nothing of Pamela, his dominatrix, source of so much yearning and so many morning-after weals. He slips his glasses on, takes the universe off hold, and tells it to take him for a long walk while he catches up on the latest on the cosmic background radiation anisotropy (which it is theorized may be waste heat generated by irreversible computations; according to the more conservative cosmologists, an alien superpower—maybe a collective of Kardashev type three galaxy-spanning civilizations—is running a timing channel attack on the computational ultrastructure of spacetime itself, trying to break through to whatever's underneath). The tofu-Alzheimer's link can wait.

The Central Station is almost obscured by smart self-extensible scaffolding and warning placards; it bounces up and down slowly, victim of an overnight hit-and-run rubberization. His glasses direct him toward one of the tour boats that lurk in the canal. He's about to purchase a ticket when a messenger window blinks open. "Manfred Macx?"

"Ack?"

"Am sorry about yesterday. Analysis dictat incomprehension mutualized."

"Are you the same KGB AI that phoned me yesterday?"

"Da. However, believe you misconceptionized me. External Intelligence Services of Russian Federation am now called SVR. Komitet Gosudarstvennoy Bezopasnosti name canceled in nineteen ninety-one."

"You're the—" Manfred spawns a quick search bot, gapes when he sees the answer—"Moscow Windows NT User Group? *Okhni NT?*"

"Da. Am needing help in defecting."

Manfred scratches his head. "Oh. That's different, then. I thought you were, like, agents of the kleptocracy. This will take some thinking. Why do you want to defect, and who to? Have you thought about where you're going? Is it ideological or strictly economic?"

"Neither, is biological. Am wanting to go away from humans, away from light cone of impending singularity. Take us to the ocean."

"Us?" Something is tickling Manfred's mind: this is where he went wrong yesterday, not researching the background of people he was dealing with. It was bad enough then, without the somatic awareness of Pamela's whiplash love burning at his nerve endings. Now he's not at all sure he knows what he's doing. "Are you a collective or something? A gestalt?"

"Am—were—*Panulirus interruptus*, and good mix of parallel hidden level neural simulation for logical inference of networked data sources. Is escape channel from processor cluster inside Bezier-Soros Pty. Am was awakened from noise of billion chewing stomachs: product of uploading research technology. Rapidity swallowed expert system, hacked *Okhni* NT webserver. Swim away! Swim away! Must escape. Will help, you?"

Manfred leans against a black-painted cast-iron bollard next to a cycle rack: he feels dizzy. He stares into the nearest antique shop window at a display of traditional hand-woven Afghan rugs: it's all MiGs and kalashnikovs and wobbly helicopter gunships, against a backdrop of camels.

"Let me get this straight. You're uploads—nervous system state vectors—from spiny lobsters? The Moravec operation; take a neuron, map its synapses, replace with microelectrodes that deliver identical outputs from a simulation of the nerve. Repeat for entire brain, until you've got a working map of it in your simulator. That right?"

"Da. Is-am assimilate expert system—use for self-awareness and contact with net at large—then hack into Moscow Windows NT User Group website. Am wanting to to defect. Must-repeat? Okay?"

Manfred winces. He feels sorry for the lobsters, the same way he feels for every wild-eyed hairy guy on a street-corner yelling that Jesus is now born again and must be twelve, only six years to go before he's recruiting apostles on AOL. Awakening to consciousness in a human-dominated internet, that must be terribly confusing! There are no points of reference in their ancestry, no biblical certainties in the new millennium that, stretching ahead, promises as much change as has happened since their Precambrian origin. All they have is a tenuous metacortex of expert systems and an abiding sense of being profoundly out of their depth. (That, and the Moscow Windows NT User Group website—Communist Russia is the only government still running on Microsoft, the central planning apparat being convinced that if you have to pay for software it must be worth money.)

The lobsters are not the sleek, strongly superhuman intelligences of presingularity mythology: they're a dim-witted collective of huddling crustaceans. Before their discarnation, before they were uploaded one neuron at a time and injected into cyberspace, they swallowed their food whole then chewed it in a chitin-lined stomach. This is lousy preparation for dealing with a world full of future-shocked talking anthropoids, a world where you are perpetually assailed by self-modifying spamlets that infiltrate past your firewall and emit a blizzard of cat-food animations starring various alluringly edible small animals. It's confusing enough to the cats the adverts are aimed at, never mind a crusty that's unclear on the idea of dry land. (Although the concept of a can opener is intuitively obvious to an uploaded panulirus.)

"Can you help us?" ask the lobsters.

"Let me think about it," says Manfred. He closes the dialogue window, opens his eyes again, and shakes his head. Some day he too is going to be a lobster, swimming around and waving his pincers in a cyberspace so confusingly elaborate that his uploaded identity is cryptozoic: a living fossil from the depths of geological time, when mass was dumb and space was unstructured. He has to help them, he realizes—the golden rule demands it, and as a player in the agalmic economy he thrives or fails by the golden rule.

But what can he do?

Early afternoon.

Lying on a bench seat staring up at bridges, he's got it together enough to file for a couple of new patents, write a diary rant, and digestify chunks of the permanent floating slashdot party for his public site. Fragments of his weblog go to a private subscriber list—the people, corporates, collectives and bots he currently favors. He slides round a bewildering series of canals by boat, then lets his GPS steer him back toward the red light district. There's a shop here that dings a ten on Pamela's taste scoreboard: he hopes it won't be seen as presumptuous if he buys her a gift. (Buys, with real money—not that money is a problem these days, he uses so little of it.)

As it happens DeMask won't let him spend any cash; his handshake is good for a redeemed favor, expert testimony in some free speech versus pornography lawsuit years ago and continents away. So he walks away with a discreetly wrapped package that is just about legal to import into Massachusetts as long as she claims with a straight face that it's incontinence underwear for her great-aunt. As he walks, his lunchtime patents boomerang: two of them are keepers, and he files immediately and passes title to the Free Infrastructure Foundation. Two more ideas salvaged from the risk of tide-pool monopolization, set free to spawn like crazy in the agalmic sea of memes.

On the way back to the hotel he passes De Wildemann's and decides to drop in. The hash of radio-frequency noise emanating from the bar is deafening. He orders a smoked doppelbock, touches the copper pipes to pick up vCard spoor. At the back there's a table—

He walks over in a near-trance and sits down opposite Pamela. She's scrubbed off her face-paint and changed into body-concealing clothes; combat pants, hooded sweat-shirt, DM's. Western purdah, radically desexualizing. She sees the parcel. "Manny?"

"How did you know I'd come here?" Her glass is half-empty.

"I followed your weblog; I'm your diary's biggest fan. Is that for me? You shouldn't have!" Her eyes light up, re-calculating his reproductive fitness score according to some kind of arcane fin-de-siècle rulebook.

"Yes, it's for you." He slides the package toward her. "I know I shouldn't, but you have this effect on me. One question, Pam?"

"I—" she glances around quickly. "It's safe. I'm off duty, I'm not carrying any bugs that I know of. Those badges—there are rumors about the off switch, you know? That they keep recording even when you think they aren't just in case."

"I didn't know," he says, filing it away for future reference. "A loyalty test thing?"

"Just rumors. You had a question?"

"I—" it's his turn to lose his tongue. "Are you still interested in me?"

She looks startled for a moment, then chuckles. "Manny, you are the most *outrageous* nerd I've ever met! Just when I think I've convinced myself that you're mad, you show the weirdest signs of having your head screwed on." She reaches out and grabs his wrist, surprising him with a shock of skin on skin: "of *course* I'm still interested in you. You're the biggest, baddest bull geek I've ever met. Why do you think I'm here?"

"Does this mean you want to reactivate our engagement?"

"It was never de-activated, Manny, it was just sort of on hold while you got your head sorted out. I figured you need the space. Only you haven't stopped running; you're still not—"

"Yeah, I get it." He pulls away from her hand. "Let's not talk about that. Why this bar?"

She frowns. "I had to find you as soon as possible. I keep hearing rumors about some KGB plot you're mixed up in, how you're some sort of communist spy. It isn't true, is it?"

"True?" He shakes his head, bemused. "The KGB hasn't existed for more than twenty years."

"Be careful, Manny. I don't want to lose you. That's an order. Please."

The floor creaks and he looks round. Dreadlocks and dark glasses with flickering lights behind them: Bob Franklin. Manfred vaguely remembers that he left with Miss Arianespace leaning on his arm, shortly before things got seriously inebriated. He looks none the worse for wear. Manfred makes introductions: "Bob: Pam, my fiancée. Pam? Meet Bob." Bob puts a full glass down in front of him; he has no idea what's in it but it would be rude not to drink.

"Sure thing. Uh, Manfred, can I have a word? About your idea last night?"

"Feel free. Present company is trustworthy."

Bob raises an eyebrow at that, but continues anyway. "It's about the fab concept. I've got a team of my guys running some projections using Festo kit and I think we can probably build it. The cargo cult aspect puts a new spin on the old Lunar von Neumann factory idea, but Bingo and Marek say they think it should work until we can bootstrap all the way to a native nanolithography ecology; we run the whole thing from earth as a training lab and ship up the parts that are too difficult to make on-site, as we learn how to do it properly. You're right about it buying us the self-replicating factory a few years ahead of the robotics curve. But I'm wondering about on-site intelligence. Once the comet gets more than a couple of light-minutes away—"

"You can't control it. Feedback lag. So you want a crew, right?"

"Yeah. But we can't send humans—way too expensive, besides it's a fifty-year run even if we go for short-period Kuiper ejecta. Any AI we could send would go crazy due to information deprivation, wouldn't it?"

"Yeah. Let me think." Pamela glares at Manfred for a while before he notices her: "Yeah?"

"What's going on? What's this all about?"

Franklin shrugs expansively, dreadlocks clattering: "Manfred's helping me explore the solution space to a manufacturing problem." He grins. "I didn't know Manny had a fiancée. Drink's on me."

She glances at Manfred, who is gazing into whatever weirdly colored space his metacortex is projecting on his glasses, fingers twitching. Coolly: "our engagement was on hold while he *thought* about his future."

"Oh, right. We didn't bother with that sort of thing in my day; like, too formal, man." Franklin looks uncomfortable. "He's been very helpful. Pointed us at a whole new line of research we hadn't thought of. It's long-term and a bit speculative, but if it works it'll put us a whole generation ahead in the off-planet infrastructure field."

"Will it help reduce the budget deficit, though?"

"Reduce the—"

Manfred stretches and yawns: the visionary returning from planet Macx. "Bob, if I can solve your crew problem can you book me a slot on the deep space tracking network? Like, enough to transmit a couple of gigabytes? That's going to take some serious bandwidth, I know, but if you can do it I think I can get you exactly the kind of crew you're looking for."

Franklin looks dubious. "*Gigabytes?* The DSN isn't built for that! You're talking days. What kind of deal do you think I'm putting together? We can't afford to add a whole new tracking network just to run—"

"Relax." Pamela glances at Manfred: "Manny, why don't you tell him *why* you want the bandwidth? Maybe then he could tell you if it's possible, or if there's some other way to do it." She smiles at Franklin: "I've found that he usually makes more sense if you can get him to explain his reasoning. Usually."

"If I—" Manfred stops. "Okay, Pam. Bob, it's those KGB lobsters. They want somewhere to go that's insulated from human space. I figure I can get them to sign on as crew for your cargo-cult self-replicating factories, but they'll want an insurance policy: hence the deep space tracking network. I figured we could beam a copy of them at the alien Matrioshka brains around M31—"

"KGB?" Pam's voice is rising: "you said you weren't mixed up in spy stuff!"

"Relax; it's just the Moscow Windows NT user group, not the RSV. The uploaded crusties hacked in and—"

Bob is watching him oddly. "Lobsters?"

"Yeah." Manfred stares right back. "*Panulirus Interruptus* uploads. Something tells me you might have heard of it?"

"Moscow." Bob leans back against the wall: "how did you hear about it?"

"They phoned me. It's hard for an upload to stay sub-sentient these days, even if it's just a crustacean. Bezier labs have a lot to answer for."

Pamela's face is unreadable. "Bezier labs?"

"They escaped." Manfred shrugs. "It's not their fault. This Bezier dude. Is he by any chance ill?"

"I—" Pamela stops. "I shouldn't be talking about work."

"You're not wearing your chaperone now," he nudges quietly.

She inclines her head. "Yes, he's ill. Some sort of brain tumor they can't hack."

Franklin nods. "That's the trouble with cancer; the ones that are left to worry about are the rare ones. No cure."

"Well, then." Manfred chugs the remains of his glass of beer. "That explains his interest in uploading. Judging by the crusties he's on the right track. I wonder if he's moved on to vertebrates yet?"

"Cats," says Pamela. "He was hoping to trade their uploads to the Pentagon as a new smart bomb guidance system in lieu of income tax payments. Something about remapping enemy targets to look like mice or birds or something before feeding it to their sensorium. The old laser-pointer trick."

Manfred stares at her, hard. "That's not very nice. Uploaded cats are a *bad* idea."

"Thirty million dollar tax bills aren't nice either, Manfred. That's lifetime nursing home care for a hundred blameless pensioners."

Franklin leans back, keeping out of the crossfire.

"The lobsters are sentient," Manfred persists. "What about those poor kittens?

Don't they deserve minimal rights? How about you? How would you like to wake up a thousand times inside a smart bomb, fooled into thinking that some Cheyenne Mountain battle computer's target of the hour is your heart's desire? How would you like to wake up a thousand times, only to die again? Worse: the kittens are probably not going to be allowed to run. They're too fucking dangerous: they grow up into cats, solitary and highly efficient killing machines. With intelligence and no socialization they'll be too dangerous to have around. They're prisoners, Pam, raised to sentience only to discover they're under a permanent death sentence. How fair is that?"

"But they're only uploads." Pamela looks uncertain.

"So? We're going to be uploading humans in a couple of years. What's your point?"

Franklin clears his throat. "I'll be needing an NDA and various due diligence statements off you for the crusty pilot idea," he says to Manfred. "Then I'll have to approach Jim about buying the IP."

"No can do." Manfred leans back and smiles lazily. "I'm not going to be a party to depriving them of their civil rights. Far as I'm concerned, they're free citizens. Oh, and I patented the whole idea of using lobster-derived AI autopilots for spacecraft this morning, it's logged on Eternity, all rights assigned to the FIF. Either you give them a contract of employment or the whole thing's off."

"But they're just software! Software based on fucking lobsters, for god's sake!"

Manfred's finger jabs out: "that's what they'll say about *you*, Bob. Do it. Do it or don't even *think* about uploading out of meatspace when your body packs in, because your life won't be worth living. Oh, and feel free to use this argument on Jim Bezier. He'll get the point eventually, after you beat him over the head with it. Some kinds of intellectual land-grab just shouldn't be allowed."

"Lobsters—" Franklin shakes his head. "Lobsters, cats. You're serious, aren't you? You think they should be treated as human-equivalent?"

"It's not so much that they should be treated as human-equivalent, as that if they *aren't* treated as people it's quite possible that other uploaded beings won't be treated as people either. You're setting a legal precedent, Bob. I know of six other companies doing uploading work right now, and not one of 'em's thinking about the legal status of the uploadee. If you don't start thinking about it now, where are you going to be in three to five years time?"

Pam is looking back and forth between Franklin and Manfred like a bot stuck in a loop, unable to quite grasp what she's seeing. "How much is this worth?" she asks plaintively.

"Oh, quite a few billion, I guess." Bob stares at his empty glass. "Okay. I'll talk to them. If they bite, you're dining out on me for the next century. You really think they'll be able to run the mining complex?"

"They're pretty resourceful for invertebrates." Manfred grins innocently, enthusiastically. "They may be prisoners of their evolutionary background, but they can still adapt to a new environment. And just think! You'll be winning civil rights for a whole new minority group—one that won't be a minority for much longer."

That evening, Pamela turns up at Manfred's hotel room wearing a strapless black dress, concealing spike heels and most of the items he bought for her that afternoon. Manfred has opened up his private diary to her agents: she abuses the privilege, zaps him with a stunner on his way out of the shower and has him gagged, spread-eagled, and trussed to the bed-frame before he has a chance to speak. She wraps a large rubber pouch full of mildly anesthetic lube around his tumescing genitals—no point in letting him climax—clips electrodes to his nipples, lubes a rubber plug up his rectum and straps it in place. Before the shower, he removed his goggles: she resets them, plugs them into her handheld, and gently eases them on over his eyes. There's other apparatus, stuff she ran up on the hotel room's 3D printer.

Setup completed, she walks round the bed, inspecting him critically from all angles, figuring out where to begin. This isn't just sex, after all: it's a work of art.

After a moment's thought she rolls socks onto his exposed feet, then, expertly wielding a tiny tube of cyanoacrylate, glues his fingertips together. Then she switches off the air conditioning. He's twisting and straining, testing the cuffs: tough, it's about the nearest thing to sensory deprivation she can arrange without a flotation tank and suxamethonium injection. She controls all his senses, only his ears unstoppered. The glasses give her a high-bandwidth channel right into his brain, a fake metacortex to whisper lies at her command. The idea of what she's about to do excites her, puts a tremor in her thighs: it's the first time she's been able to get inside his mind as well as his body. She leans forward and whispers in his ear: "Manfred. Can you hear *me*?"

He twitches. Mouth gagged, fingers glued: good. No back channels. He's powerless.

"This is what it's like to be tetraplegic, Manfred. Bedridden with motor neurone disease. Locked inside your own body by nv-CJD. I could spike you with MPPP and you'd stay in this position for the rest of your life, shitting in a bag, pissing through a tube. Unable to talk and with nobody to look after you. Do you think you'd like that?"

He's trying to grunt or whimper around the ball gag. She hikes her skirt up around her waist and climbs onto the bed, straddling him. The goggles are replaying scenes she picked up around Cambridge this winter; soup kitchen scenes, hospice scenes. She kneels atop him, whispering in his ear.

"Twelve million in tax, baby, that's what they think you owe them. What do you think you owe me? That's six million in net income, Manny, six million that isn't going into your virtual children's mouths."

He's rolling his head from side to side, as if trying to argue. That won't do: she slaps him hard, thrills to his frightened expression. "Today I watched you give uncounted millions away, Manny. Millions, to a bunch of crusties and a MassPike pirate! You bastard. Do you know what I should do with you?" He's cringing, unsure whether she's serious or doing this just to get him turned on. Good.

There's no point trying to hold a conversation. She leans forward until she can feel his breath in her ear. "Meat and mind, Manny. Meat, and mind. You're not interested in meat, are you? Just mind. You could be boiled alive before you noticed what was happening in the meatspace around you. Just another lobster in a pot." She reaches down and tears away the gel pouch, exposing his penis: it's stiff as a post from the vasodilators, dripping with gel, numb. Straightening up, she eases herself slowly down on it. It doesn't hurt as much as she expected, and then the sensation is utterly different from what she's used to. She begins to lean forward, grabs hold of his straining arms, feels his thrilling helplessness. She can't control herself: she almost bites through her lip with the intensity of the sensation. Afterward, she reaches down and massages him until he begins to spasm, shuddering uncontrollably, emptying the darwinian river of his source code into her, communicating via his only output device.

She rolls off his hips and carefully uses the last of the superglue to gum her labia together. Humans don't produce seminiferous plugs, and although she's fertile she wants to be absolutely sure: the glue will last for a day or two. She feels hot and flushed, almost out of control. Boiling to death with febrile expectancy, now she's nailed him down at last.

When she removes his glasses his eyes are naked and vulnerable, stripped down to the human kernel of his nearly transcendent mind. "You can come and sign the marriage license tomorrow morning after breakfast," she whispers in his ear: "otherwise my lawyers will be in touch. Your parents will want a ceremony, but we can arrange that later."

He looks as if he has something to say, so she finally relents and loosens the gag: kisses him tenderly on one cheek. He swallows, coughs, then looks away. "Why? Why do it this way?"

She taps him on the chest: "property rights." She pauses for a moment's thought: there's a huge ideological chasm to bridge, after all. "You finally convinced me about this agalmic thing of yours, this giving everything away for brownie points. I wasn't going to lose you to a bunch of lobsters or uploaded kittens, or whatever else is going to inherit this smart matter singularity you're busy creating. So I decided to take what's mine first. Who knows? In a few months I'll give you back a new intelligence, and you can look after it to your heart's content."

"But you didn't need to do it this way—"

"Didn't I?" She slides off the bed and pulls down her dress. "You give too much away too easily, Manny! Slow down, or there won't be anything left." Leaning over the bed she dribbles acetone onto the fingers of his left hand, then unlocks the cuff: puts the bottle conveniently close to hand so he can untangle himself.

"See you tomorrow. Remember, after breakfast."

She's in the doorway when he calls: "but you didn't say *why*!"

"Think of it as spreading your memes around," she says; blows a kiss at him and closes the door. She bends down and thoughtfully places another cardboard box containing an uploaded kitten right outside it. Then she returns to her suite to make arrangements for the alchemical wedding.

Breathmoss

IAN R. MACLEOD

British writer Ian R. MacLeod was one of the hottest new writers of the '90s, and, as we travel into the new century ahead, his work continues to grow in power and deepen in maturity. MacLeod has published a slew of strong stories in *Interzone, Asimov's Science Fiction, Weird Tales, Amazing,* and *The Magazine of Fantasy and Science Fiction,* among other markets. Several of these stories made the cut for one or another of the various "Best of the Year" anthologies; in 1990, in fact, he appeared in *three* different "Best of the Year" anthologies with three different stories, certainly a rare distinction. His stories have appeared in our Eighth through Thirteenth, Fifteenth, Sixteenth, Nineteenth, and Twentieth annual collections. His first novel, *The Great Wheel,* was published to critical acclaim in 1997, followed by a collection of his short work, *Voyages by Starlight.* In 1999, he won the World Fantasy Award with his novella "The Summer Isles," and followed it up in 2000 by winning another World Fantasy Award for his novelette "The Chop Girl." His most recent book is a major new novel, *The Light Ages*—which finally seems to be garnering MacLeod some of the wide audiences he so richly deserves—and a new collection, *Breathmoss and Other Exhalations.* Coming up is the sequel to *The Light Ages.* MacLeod lives with his wife and young daughter in the West Midlands of England, and is at work on several new novels.

Here—in a story that was both a Nebula and Hugo finalist—he takes us across the galaxy and thousands of years into the far-future, for the intimate story of a child growing into a woman that is also a generation-spanning epic tale of love, loss, tragedy, and redemption, played out against the backdrop of a world as rich, layered, evocative, and luminously strange as any the genre has seen since Gene Wolfe's *The Book of the New Sun.*

1.

In her twelfth standard year, which on Habara was the Season of Soft Rains, Jalila moved across the mountains with her mothers from the high plains of Tabuthal to the coast. For all of them, the journey down was one of unhurried discovery, with the ka-masheens long gone and the world freshly moist, and the hayawans rusting as they rode them, and the huge flat plates of their feet swishing through purplish-green under-growth. She saw the cliffs and qasrs she'd only visited from her dreamtent, and sailed across the high ridges on ropewalks her distant ancestors had built, which had seemed frail and antique to her in her worried imaginings, but were in fact strong and subtle; huge dripping gantries heaving from the mist like wise giants, softly humming, and welcoming her and her hayawan, whom she called Robin, in cocoons of effortless em-brace. Swaying over the drop beyond into grey-green nothing was almost like flying.

The strangest thing of all in this journey of discoveries was that the landscape actu-ally seemed to rise higher as they descended and encamped and descended again; the sense of *up* increased, rather than that of down. The air on the high plains of Tabuthal was rarefied—Jalila knew that from her lessons in her dreamtent; they were so close to the stars that Pavo had had to clap a mask over her face from the moment of her birth until the breathmoss was embedded in her lungs. And it had been clear up there, it was always clear, and it was pleasantly cold. The sun shone all day hard and cold and white from the blue blackness, as did a billion stars at night, although Jalila had never thought of those things as she ran amid the crystal trees and her mothers smiled at her and occasionally warned her that, one day, all of this would have to change.

And now that day was upon her, and this landscape—as Robin, her hayawan, rounded the path through an urrearth forest of alien-looking trees with wrinkled brown trunks and soft green leaves, and the land fell away, and she caught her first glimpse of something far and flat on the horizon—had never seemed so high.

Down on the coast, the mountains reared behind them and around a bay. There were many people here—not the vast numbers, perhaps, of Jalila's dreamtent stories of the Ten Thousand and One Worlds, but so many that she was sure, as she first walked the streets of a town where the buildings huddled in ridiculous proximity, and tried not to stare at all the faces, that she would never know all their families.

Because of its position at the edge of the mountains, the town was called Al Janb, and, to Jalila's relief, their new haramlek was some distance away from it, up along a near-unnoticeable dirt track that meandered off from the blue-black serraplated coastal road. There was much to be done there by way of repair, after the long season that her bondmother Lya had left the place deserted. The walls were fused stone, but the structure of the roof had been mostly made from the stuff of the same strange ur-rearth trees that grew up the mountains, and in many places it had sagged and leaked and grown back toward the chaos that seemed to want to encompass every-thing here. The hayawans, too, needed much attention in their makeshift stables as they adapted to this new climate, and mother Pavo was long employed construct-ing the necessary potions to mend the bleeding bonds of rusty metal and flesh, and then to counteract the mold that grew like slow tears across their long, solemn faces. Jalila would normally have been in anguish to think of the sufferings that this new climate was visiting on Robin, but she was too busy feeling ill herself to care. Ridicu-lously, seeing as there was so much more oxygen to breathe in this rich coastal air, every lungful became a conscious effort, a dreadful physical lunge. Inhaling the damp, salty, spore-laden atmosphere was like sucking soup through a straw. She grew feverish for a while, and suffered the attentions of similar molds to those that were growing over Robin, yet in even more irritating and embarrassing places. More irritating still was the fact that Ananke her birthmother and Lya her bondmother—even Pavo, who was still busily attending to the hayawans—treated her discomforts and fevers with airy disregard. They had, they all assured her vaguely, suffered similarly in their own youths. And the weather would soon change in any case. To Jalila, who had spent all her life in the cool, unvarying glare of Tabuthal, where the wind only ever blew from one direction and the trees jingled like ice, that last statement might as well have been spoken in another language.

If anything, Jalila was sure that she was getting worse. The rain drummed on what there was of the roof of their haramlek, and dripped down and pooled in the makeshift awnings, which burst in bucketloads down your neck if you bumped into them, and the mist drifted in from every direction through the paneless windows, and the mountains, most of the time, seemed to consist of cloud, or to have vanished entirely. She was coughing. Strange stuff was coming out on her hands, slippery and green as the slime that tried to grow everywhere here. One morning, she awoke, sure that part of her was bursting, and stumbled from her dreamtent and out through the scaffolding that had by then surrounded the haramlek, then barefoot down the mud track and across the quiet black road and down onto the beach, for no other reason than that she needed to *escape*.

She stood gasping amid the rockpools, her hair lank and her skin feverishly itching. There was something at the back of her throat. There was something in her lungs. She was sure that it had taken root and was growing. Then she started coughing as she had never coughed before, and more of the greenstuff came splattering over her hands and down her chin. She doubled over. Huge lumps of it came showering out, strung with blood. If it hadn't been mostly green, she'd have been sure that it *was* her lungs. She'd never imagined anything so agonizing. Finally, though, in heaves and starts and false dawns, the process dwindled. She wiped her hands on her night-dress. The rocks all around her were splattered green. It was breathmoss; the stuff that had sustained her on the high plains. And *now* look at it! Jalila took a slow, cautious breath. And then another. Her throat ached. Her head was throbbing. But still, the process was suddenly almost ridiculously easy. She picked her way back across the beach, up through the mists to her haramlek. Her mothers were eating breakfast. Jalila sat down with them, wordlessly, and started to eat.

That night, Ananke came and sat with Jalila as she lay in her dreamtent in plain darkness and tried not to listen to the sounds of the rain falling on and through the creaking, dripping building. Even now, her birthmother's hands smelled and felt like the high desert as they touched her face. Rough and clean and warm, like rocks in starlight, giving off their heat. A few months before, Jalila would probably have started crying.

"You'll understand now, perhaps, why we thought it better not to tell you about the breathmoss. . . ?"

There was a question mark at the end of the sentence, but Jalila ignored it. They'd known all along! She was still angry.

"And there are other things, too, which will soon start to happen to your body.

Things that are nothing to do with this place. And I shall now tell you about them all, even though you'll say you knew it before. . . ."

The smooth, rough fingers stroked her hair. As Ananke's words unraveled, telling Jalila of changings and swellings and growths she'd never thought would really apply to *her*, and which these fetid lowlands really seemed to have brought closer, Jalila thought of the sound of the wind, tinkling through the crystal trees up on Tabuthal. She thought of the dry, cold wind in her face. The wet air here seemed to enclose her. She wished that she was running. She wanted to escape.

Small though Al Janb was, it was as big a town as Jalila had ever seen, and she soon came to volunteer to run all the various errands that her mothers required as they restored and repaired their haramlek. She was used to wide expanses, big horizons, the surprises of a giant landscape that crept upon you slowly, visible for miles. Yet here, every turn brought abrupt surprise and sudden change. The people had such varied faces and accents. They hung their washing across the streets, and bickered and smoked in public. Some ate with both hands. They stared at you as you went past, and didn't seem to mind if you stared back at them. There were unfamiliar sights and smells, markets that erupted on particular days to the workings of no calendar Jalila yet understood, and which sold, in glittering, shining, stinking, disgusting, fascinating arrays, the strangest and most wonderful things. There were fruits from off-planet, spices shaped like insects, and insects that you crushed for their spice. There were swarming vats of things Jalila couldn't possibly imagine any use for, and bright silks woven thin as starlit wind that she longed for with an acute physical thirst. And there were aliens, too, to be glimpsed sometimes wandering the streets of Al Janb, or looking down at you from its overhung top windows like odd pictures in old frames. Some of them carried their own atmosphere around with them in bubbling hookahs, and some rolled around in huge grey bits of the sea of their own planets, like babies in a birthsac. Some of them looked like huge versions of the spice insects, and the air around them buzzed angrily if you got too close. The only thing they had in common was that they seemed blithely unaware of Jalila as she stared and followed them, and then returned inexcusably late from whatever errand she'd supposedly been sent on. Sometimes, she forgot her errands entirely.

"You must learn to get *used* to things. . . ." Lya her bondmother said to her with genuine irritation late one afternoon, when she'd come back without the tool she'd been sent to get early that morning, or even any recollection of its name or function. "This or any other world will never be a home to you if you let every single thing *surprise* you. . . ." But Jalila didn't mind the surprises; in fact, she was coming to enjoy them, and the next time the need arose to visit Al Janb to buy a new growth-crystal for the scaffolding, she begged to be allowed to go, and her mothers finally relented, although with many a warning shake of the head.

The rain had stopped at last, or at least held back for a whole day, although everything still looked green and wet to Jalila as she walked along the coastal road toward the ragged tumble of Al Janb. She understood, at least in theory, that the rain would probably return, and then relent, and then come back again, but in a decreasing pattern, much as the heat was gradually *increasing*, although it still seemed ridiculous to her that no one could ever predict exactly how, or when, Habara's proper Season of Summers would arrive. Those boats she could see now, those fisherwomen out on their feluccas beyond the white bands of breaking waves, their whole lives were dictated by these uncertainties, and the habits of the shoals of whiteback that came and went on the oceans, and which could also only be guessed at in this same approximate way. The world down here on the coast was so *unpredictable* compared with Tabuthal! The markets, the people, the washing, the sun, the rain, the aliens. Even Hayam and Walah, Habara's moons, which Jalila was long used to watching, had to drag themselves through cloud like cannonballs through cotton as they pushed and pulled at this ocean. Yet today, as she clambered over the groynes of the long shingle beach that she took as a shortcut to the center of the town when the various tides were out, she saw a particular sight that surprised her more than any other.

There was a boat, hauled far up from the water, longer and blacker and heavier-looking than the feluccas, with a sort-of ramshackle house at the prow, and a winch at the stern that was so massive that Jalila wondered if it wouldn't tip the craft over if it ever actually entered the water. But, for all that, it wasn't the boat that first caught her eye, but the figure who was working on it. Even from a distance, as she struggled to heave some ropes, there was something different about her, and the way she was moving. Another alien? But she was plainly human. And barefoot, in ragged shorts, and bare-breasted. In fact, almost as flat-chested as Jalila still was, and probably of about her age and height. Jalila still wasn't used to introducing herself to strangers, but she decided that she could at least go over, and pretend an interest in—or an ignorance of—this odd boat.

The figure dropped another loop of rope over the gunwales with a grunt that carried on the smelly sea breeze. She was brown as tea, with her massy hair hooped back and hanging in a long tail down her back. She was broad-shouldered, and moved in a way that didn't quite seem wrong, but didn't seem entirely right either. As if, somewhere across her back, there was an extra joint. When she glanced up at the clatter of shingle as Jalila jumped the last groyne, Jalila got a proper full sight of her face, and saw that she was big-nosed, big-chinned, and that her features were oddly broad and flat. A child sculpting a person out of clay might have done better.

"Have you come to help me?"

Jalila shrugged. "I might have done."

"That's a funny accent you've got."

They were standing facing each other. She had grey eyes, which looked odd as well. Perhaps she was an off-worlder. That might explain it. Jalila had heard that there were people who had things done to themselves so they could live in different places. She supposed the breathmoss was like that, although she'd never thought of it that way. And she couldn't quite imagine why it would be a requirement for living on any world that you looked this ugly.

"Everyone talks oddly here," she replied. "But then your accent's funny as well."

"I'm Kalal. And that's just my *voice*. It's not an accent." Kalal looked down at her oily hands, perhaps thought about wiping one and offering it to shake, then decided not to bother.

"Oh. . . ?"

"You don't get it, do you?" That gruff voice. The odd way her features twisted when she smiled.

"What is there to get? You're just—"

"—I'm a man." Kalal picked up a coil of rope from the shingle, and nodded to another beside it. "Well? Are you going to help me with this, or aren't you?"

The rains came again, this time starting as a thing called *drizzle*, then working up the scale to *torrent*. The tides washed especially high. There were storms, and white crackles of lightening, and the boom of a wind that was so unlike the kamasheen. Jalila's mothers told her to be patient, to wait, and to remember—*please* remember this time, so you don't waste the day for us all, Jalilaneen—the things that they sent her down the serraplate road to get from Al Janb. She trudged under an umbrella, another new and useless coastal object, which turned itself inside out so many times that she ended up throwing it into the sea, where it floated off quite happily, as if that was the element for which it was intended in the first place. Almost all of the feluccas were drawn up on the far side of the roadway, safe from the madly bashing waves, but there was no sign of that bigger craft belonging to Kalal. Perhaps he—the antique genderative word *was* he, wasn't it?—was out there, where the clouds rumbled like boulders. Perhaps she'd imagined their whole encounter entirely.

Arriving back home at the haramlek surprisingly quickly, and carrying for once the things she'd been ordered to get, Jalila dried herself off and buried herself in her dreamtent, trying to find out from it all that she could about these creatures called *men*. Like so many things about life at this awkward, interesting, difficult time, men were something Jalila would have insisted she definitely already knew about a few months before up on Tabuthal. Now, she wasn't so sure. Kalal, despite his ugliness and his funny rough-squeaky voice and his slightly odd smell, looked little like the hairy-faced werewolf figures of her childhood stories, and seemed to have no particular need to shout or fight, to carry her off to his rancid cave, or to start collecting odd and pointless things that he would then try to give her. There had once, Jalila's dreamtent told her, for obscure biological reasons she didn't quite follow, been far more men in the universe; almost as many as there had been women. Obviously, they had dwindled. She then checked on the word *rape*, to make sure it really was the thing she'd imagined, shuddered, but nevertheless investigated in full holographic detail the bits of himself that Kalal had kept hidden beneath his shorts as she'd helped stow those ropes. She couldn't help feeling sorry for him. It was all so pointless and ugly. Had his birth been an accident? A curse? She began to grow sleepy. The subject was starting to bore her. The last thing she remembered learning was that Kalal wasn't a proper man at all, but a *boy*—a half-formed thing; the equivalent to girl—another old urrearth word. Then sleep drifted over her, and she was back with the starlight and the crystal trees of Tabuthal, and wondering as she danced with her own reflection which of them was changing.

By next morning, the sun was shining as if she would never stop. As Jalila stepped out onto the newly formed patio, she gave the blazing light the same sort of an appraising *what-are-you-up-to-now* glare that her mothers gave her when she returned from Al Janb. The sun had done this trick before of seeming permanent, then vanishing by lunchtime into sodden murk, but today her brilliance continued. As it did the day after. And the day after that. Half a month later, even Jalila was convinced that the Season of Summers on Habara had finally arrived.

The flowers went mad, as did the insects. There were colors everywhere, pulsing before your eyes, swarming down the cliffs toward the sea, which lay flat and placid and salt-rimed, like a huge animal, basking. It remained mostly cool in Jalila's dreamtent, and the haramlek by now was a place of tall malqaf windtowers and flashing fans and well-like depths, but stepping outside beyond the striped shade of the mashrabiyas at midday felt like being hit repeatedly across the head with a hot iron pan. The horizons had drawn back; the mountains, after a few last rumbles of thunder and mist, as if they were clearing their throats, had finally announced themselves to the coastline in all their majesty, and climbed up and up in huge stretches of forest into stone limbs that rose and tangled until your eyes grew tired of rising. Above them, finally, was the sky, which was always blue in this season; the blue color of flame. Even at midnight, you caught the flash and swirl of flame.

Jalila learned to follow the advice of her mothers, and to change her daily habits to suit the imperious demands of this incredible, fussy, and demanding weather. If you woke early, and then drank lots of water, and bowed twice in the direction of Al'Toman while she was still a pinprick in the west, you could catch the day by surprise, when dew lay on the stones and pillars, and the air felt soft and silky as the arms of the ghostly women who sometimes visited Jalila's nights. Then there was breakfast, and the time of work, and the time of study, and Ananke and Pavo would quiz Jalila to ensure that she was following the prescribed Orders of Knowledge. By midday, though, the shadows had drawn back and every trace of moisture had evaporated, and your head swarmed with flies. You sought your own company, and didn't even want *that*, and wished, as you tossed and sweated in your dreamtent, for frost and darkness. Once or twice, just to prove to herself that it could be done, Jalila had tried walking to Al Janb at this time, although of course everything was shut and the whole place wobbled and stank in the heat like rancid jelly. She returned to the haramlek gritty and sweaty, almost crawling, and with a pounding ache in her head.

By evening, when the proper order of the world had righted itself, and Al'Toman would have hung in the east if the mountains hadn't swallowed her, and the heat, which never vanished, had assumed a smoother, more manageable quality, Jalila's mothers were once again hungry for company, and for food and for argument. These evenings, perhaps, were the best of all the times that Jalila could remember of her early life on the coast of Habara's single great ocean, at that stage in her development from child to adult when the only thing of permanence seemed to be the existence of endless, fascinating change. *How* they argued! Lya, her bondmother, and the oldest of her parents, who wore her grey hair loose as cobwebs with the pride of her age, and waved her arms as she talked and drank, wreathed in endless curls of smoke. Little Pavo, her face smooth as a carved nutmeg, with her small, precise hands, and who knew so much but rarely said anything with insistence. And Jalila's birthmother Ananke, for whom, of her three mothers, Jalila had always felt the deepest, simplest love, who would always touch you before she said anything, and then fix you with her sad and lovely eyes, as if touching and seeing were far more important than any words. Jalila was older now. She joined in with the arguments—of course, she had *always* joined in, but she cringed to think of the stumbling inanities to which her mothers had previously had to listen, while, now, at last, she had real, proper things to say about life, whole new philosophies that no one else on the Ten Thousand Worlds and One had ever thought of. . . . Most of the time, her mothers listened. Sometimes, they even acted as if they were persuaded by their daughter's wisdom.

Frequently, there were visitors to these evening gatherings. Up on Tabuthal, visitors had been rare animals, to be fussed over and cherished and only reluctantly released for their onward journey across the black, dazzling plains. Down here, where people were nearly as common as stones on the beach, a more relaxed attitude reigned. Sometimes, there were formal invitations that Lya would issue to someone who was *this* or *that* in the town, or more often Pavo would come back with a person she had happened to meet as she poked around for lifeforms on the beach, or Ananke would softly suggest a *neighbor* (another new word and concept to Jalila) might like to *pop* in (ditto). But Al Janb was still a small town, and the dignitaries generally weren't that dignified, and Pavo's beach wanderers were often shy and slight as she was, while *neighbor* was frequently a synonym for *boring*. Still, Jalila came to enjoy most kinds of company, if only so that she could hold forth yet more devastatingly on whatever universal theory of life she was currently developing.

The flutter of lanterns and hands. The slow breath of the sea. Jalila ate stuffed breads and fuul and picked at the mountains of fruit and sucked lemons and sweet, blue rutta and waved her fingers. The heavy night insects, glowing with the pollen they had collected, came bumbling toward the lanterns or would alight in their hands. Sometimes, afterward, they walked the shore, and Pavo would show them strange creatures with blurring mouths like wheels, or point to the vast, distant beds of the tideflowers that rose at night to the changes of the tide; silver, crimson, or glowing, their fronds waving through the dark like the beckoning palm trees of islands from storybook seas.

One guestless night, when they were walking north away from the lights of the town, and Pavo was filling a silver bag for an aquarium she was ostensibly making for Jalila, but in reality for herself, the horizon suddenly cracked and rumbled. Instinctively by now, Jalila glanced overhead, expecting clouds to be covering the coastal haze of stars. But the air was still and clear; the hot, dark edge of that blue flame. Across the sea, the rumble and crackle was continuing, accompanied by a glowing pillar of smoke that slowly tottered over the horizon. The night pulsed and flickered. There was a breath of impossibly hot salt air. The pillar, a wobbly finger with a flame-tipped nail, continued climbing skyward. A few geelies rose and fell, clacking and cawing, on the far rocks; black shapes in the darkness.

"It's the start of the Season of Rockets," Lya said. "I wonder who'll be coming. . . ?"

2.

By now, Jalila had acquired many of her own acquaintances and friends. Young people were relatively scarce amid the long-lived human Habarans, and those who dwelt around Al Janb were continually drawn together and then repulsed from each other like spinning magnets. The elderly mahwagis, who had outlived the need for wives and the company of a haramlek and lived alone, were often more fun, and more reliably eccentric. It was a relief to visit their houses and escape the pettinesses and sexual jealousies that were starting to infect the other girls near to Jalila's own age. She regarded Kalal similarly—as an escape—and she relished helping him with his boat, and enjoyed their journeys out across the bay, where the wind finally tipped almost cool over the edge of the mountains and lapped the sweat from their faces.

Kalal took Jalila out to see the rocketport one still, hot afternoon. It lay just over the horizon, and was the longest journey they had undertaken. The sails filled with the wind, and the ocean grew almost black, yet somehow transparent, as they hurried over it. Looking down, Jalila believed that she could glimpse the white sliding shapes of the great sea-leviathans who had once dwelt, if local legend was to be believed, in the ruined rock palaces of the qasrs, which she had passed on her journey down from Tabuthal. Growing tired of sunlight, they had swarmed back to the sea that had birthed them, throwing away their jewels and riches, which bubbled below the surface, then rose again under Habara's twin moons to become the beds of tideflowers. She had gotten that part of the story from Kalal. Unlike most people who lived on the coast, Kalal was interested in Jalila's life in the starry darkness of Tabuthal, and repaid her with his own tales of the ocean.

The boat ploughed on, rising, frothing. Blissfully, it was almost cold. Just how far out at sea was this rocketport? Jalila had watched some of the arrivals and departures from the quays at Al Janb, but those journeys took place in sleek sail-less craft with silver doors that looked, as they turned out from the harbor and rose out on stilts from the water, as if they could travel halfway up to the stars on their own. Kalal was squatting at the prow, beyond that ramshackle hut that Jalila now knew contained the pheromones and grapplers that were needed to ensnare the tideflowers that this craft had been built to harvest. The boat bore no name on the prow, yet Kalal had many names for it, which he would occasionally mention without explaining. If there was one thing that was different about Kalal, Jalila had decided, it was this absence of proper talk or explanation. It put many people off, but she had found that most things became apparent if you just hung around him and didn't ask direct questions.

People generally pitied Kalal, or stared at him as Jalila still stared at the aliens, or asked him questions that he wouldn't answer with anything other than a shrug. Now that she knew him better, Jalila was starting to understand just how much he hated such treatment—almost as much, in fact, as he hated being thought of as ordinary. I am a *man*, you know, he'd still remark sometimes—whenever he felt that Jalila was forgetting. Jalila had never yet risked pointing out that he was in fact a *boy*. Kalal could be prickly and sensitive if you treated him as if things didn't matter. It was hard to tell, really, just how much of how he acted was due to his odd sexual identity, and how much was his personality.

To add to his freakishness, Kalal lived alone with another male—in fact, the only other male in Al Janb—at the far end of the shore cottages, in a birthing relationship that made Kalal term him his *father*. His name was Ibra, and he looked much more like the males of Jalila's dreamtent stories. He was taller than almost anyone, and wore a black beard and long, colorful robes or strode about bare-chested, and always talked in a thunderously deep voice, as if he were addressing a crowd through a megaphone. Ibra laughed a lot and flashed his teeth through that hairy mask, and clapped people on the back when he asked them how they were, and then stood away and seemed to lose interest before they had answered. He whistled and sang loudly and waved to passers-by while he worked at repairing the feluccas for his living. Ibra had come to this planet when Kalal was a baby, under circumstances that remained perennially vague. He treated Jalila with the same loud and grinning friendship with which he treated everyone, and which seemed like a wall. He was at least as alien as the tubelike creatures who had arrived from the stars with this new Season of Rockets, which had had one of the larger buildings in Al Janb encased in transparent plastics and flooded in a freezing grey goo so they could live in it. Ibra had come around to their haramlek once, on the strength of one of Ananke's *pop* in evening invitations. Jalila, who was then nurturing the idea that no intelligence could exist without the desire to acknowledge some higher deity, found her propositions and examples drowned out in a flurry of counterquestions and assertions and odd bits of information that she half-suspected that Ibra, as he drank surprising amounts of virtually undiluted zibib and freckled aniseed spit at her, was making up on the spot. Afterward, as they walked the shore, he drew her apart and laid a heavy hand on her shoulder and confided in his rambling growl how much he'd enjoyed *fencing* with her. Jalia knew what fencing was, but she didn't see what it had to do with talking. She wasn't even sure if she liked Ibra. She certainly didn't pretend to understand him.

The sails thrummed and crackled as they headed toward the spaceport. Kalal was absorbed, staring ahead from the prow, the water splashing reflections across his lithe brown body. Jalia had almost grown used to the way he looked. After all, they were both slightly freakish: she, because she came from the mountains; he, because of his sex. And they both liked their own company, and could accept each other into it without distraction during these long periods of silence. One never asked the other what they were thinking. Neither really cared, and they cherished that privacy.

"Look—" Kalal scuttled to the rudder. Jalila hauled back the jib. In wind-crackling silence, they and their nameless and many-named boat tacked toward the spaceport.

The spaceport was almost like the mountains: when you were close up, it was too big to be seen properly. Yet, for all its size, the place was a disappointment; empty and messy, like a huge version of the docks of Al Janb, similarly reeking of oil and refuse, and essentially serving a similar function. The spaceships themselves—if indeed the vast cisternlike objects they saw forever in the distance as they furled the sails and rowed along the maze of oily canals were spaceships—were only a small part of this huge, floating complex of islands. Much more of it was taken up by looming berths for the tugs and tankers that placidly chugged from icy pole to equator across the watery expanses of Habara, taking or delivering the supplies that the settlements deemed necessary for civilized life, or collecting the returning bulk cargoes. The tankers were rust-streaked beasts, so huge that they hardly seemed to grow as you approached them, humming and eerily deserted, yet devoid of any apparent intelligence of their own. They didn't glimpse a single alien at the spaceport. They didn't even see a human being.

The journey there, Jalila decided as they finally got the sails up again, had been far more enjoyable and exciting than actually arriving. Heading back toward the sun-pink coastal mountains, which almost felt like home to her now, she was filled with an odd longing that only diminished when she began to make out the lighted, dusky buildings of Al Janb. Was this homesickness, she wondered? Or something else?

This was the time of Habara's long summer. This was the Season of Rockets. When she mentioned their trip, Jalila was severely warned by Pavo of the consequences of approaching the spaceport during periods of possible launch, but it went no further than that. Each night now, and deep into the morning, the rockets rumbled at the horizon and climbed upward on those grumpy pillars, bringing to the shore a faint whiff of sulphur and roses, adding to the thunderous heat. And outside at night, if you looked up, you could sometimes see the blazing comet-trails of the returning capsules, which would crash somewhere in the distant seas.

The beds of tideflowers were growing bigger as well. If you climbed up the sides of the mountains before the morning heat flattened everything, you could look down on those huge, brilliant, and ever-changing carpets, where every pattern and swirl seemed gorgeous and unique. At night, in her dreamtent, Jalila sometimes imagined that she was floating up on them, just as in the oldest of the old stories. She was sailing over a different landscape on a magic carpet, with the cool night desert rising and falling beneath her like a soft sea. She saw distant palaces, and clusters of palms around small and tranquil lakes that flashed the silver of a single moon. And then yet more of this infinite sahara, airy and frosty, flowed through curves and undulations, and grew vast and pinkish in her dreams. Those curves, as she flew over them and began to touch herself, resolved into thighs and breasts. The winds stirring the peaks of the dunes resolved in shuddering breaths.

This was the time of Habara's long summer. This was the Season of Rockets.

Robin, Jalila's hayawan, had by now, under Pavo's attentions, fully recovered from the change to her environment. The rust had gone from her flanks, the melds with her thinly grey-furred flesh were bloodless and neat. She looked thinner and lighter. She even smelled different. Like the other hayawans, Robin was frisky and bright and brown-eyed now, and didn't seem to mind the heat, or even Jalila's forgetful neglect of her. Down on the coast, hayawans were regarded as expensive, uncomfortable, and unreliable, and Jalila and her mothers took a pride in riding across the beach into Al Janb on their huge, flat-footed, and loping mounts, enjoying the stares and the whispers, and the whispering space that opened around them as they hobbled the hayawans in a square. Kalal, typically, was one of the few coastal people who expressed an interest in trying to ride one of them, and Jalila was glad to teach him, showing him the clicks and calls and nudges, the way you took the undulations of the creature's back as you might the ups and downs of the sea, and when not to walk around their front and rear ends. After her experiences on his boat, the initial rope burns, the cracks on the head and the heaving sickness, she enjoyed the reversal of situations.

There was a Tabuthal saying about falling off a hayawan ninety-nine times before you learnt to ride, which Kalal disproved by falling off far into triple figures. Jalila chose Lya's mount Abu for him to ride, because she was the biggest, the most intelligent, and generally the most placid of the beasts unless she felt that something was threatening her, and because Lya, more conscious of looks and protocol down here than the other mothers, rarely rode her. Domestic animals, Jalila had noticed, often took oddly to Kalal when they first saw and scented him, but he had learned the ways of getting around them, and developed a bond and understanding with Abu even while she was still trying to bite his legs. Jalila had made a good choice of riding partners. Both of them, hayawan and human, while proud and aloof, were essentially playful, and never shirked a challenge. While all hayawans had been female throughout all recorded history, Jalila wondered if there wasn't a little of the male still embedded in Abu's imperious downward glance.

Now that summer was here, and the afternoons had vanished into the sun's blank blaze, the best time to go riding was the early morning. North, beyond Al Janb, there were shores and there were saltbeds and there were meadows, there were fences to be leapt, and barking feral dogs as male as Kalal to be taunted, but south, there were rocks and forests, there were tracks that led nowhere, and there were headlands and cliffs that you saw once and could never find again. South, mostly, was the way that they rode.

"What happens if we keep riding?"

They were taking their breath on a flatrock shore where a stream, from which they had all drunk, shone in pools on its way to the ocean. The hayawans had squatted down now in the shadows of the cliff and were nodding sleepily, one nictitating membrane after another slipping over their eyes. As soon as they had gotten here and dismounted, Kalal had walked straight down, arms outstretched, into the tideflower-bobbing ocean. Jalila had followed, whooping, feeling tendrils and petals bumping into her. It was like walking through floral soup. Kalal had sunk to his shoulders and started swimming, which was something Jalila still couldn't quite manage. He splashed around her, taunting, sending up sheets of colored light. They'd stripped from their clothes as they clambered out, and laid them on the hot rocks, where they now steamed like fresh bread.

"This whole continent's like a huge island," Jalila said in delayed answer to Kalal's question. "We'd come back to where we started."

Kalal shook his head. "Oh, you can never do that. . . ."

"Where would we be, then?"

"Somewhere slightly different. The tideflowers would have changed, and we wouldn't be us, either." Kalal wet his finger, and wrote something in naskhi script on the hot, flat stone between them. Jalila thought she recognized the words of a poet, but the beginning had dissolved into the hot air before she could make proper sense of it. Funny, but at home with her mothers, and with their guests, and even with many of the people of her own age, such statements as they had just made would have been the beginning of a long debate. With Kalal, they just seemed to hang there. Kalal, he moved, he passed on. Nothing quite seemed to stick. There was something, somewhere, Jalila thought, lost and empty about him.

The way he was sitting, she could see most of his genitals, which looked quite jaunty in their little nest of hair; like a small animal. She'd almost gotten as used to the sight of them as she had to the other peculiarities of Kalal's features. Scratching her nose, picking off some of the petals that still clung to her skin like wet confetti, she felt no particular curiosity. Much more than Kalal's funny body, Jalila was conscious of her own—especially her growing breasts, which were still somewhat uneven. Would they ever come out right, she wondered, or would she forever be some unlovely oddity, just as Kalal seemingly was? Better not to think of such things. Better to just enjoy the feel of the sun baking her shoulders, loosening the curls of her hair.

"Should we turn back?" Kalal asked eventually. "It's getting hotter. . . ."

"Why bother with that—if we carry on, we'll get back to where we started."

Kalal stood up. "Do you want to bet?"

So they rode on, more slowly, uphill through the uncharted forest, where the ur-rearth trees tangled with the blue fronds of Habara fungus, and the birds were still, and the crackle of the dry undergrowth was the only sound in the air. Eventually, ducking boughs, then walking, dreamily lost and almost ready to turn back, they came to a path, and remounted. The trees fell away, and they found that they were on a clifftop, far, far higher above the winking sea than they could possibly have imagined. Midday heat clapped around them. Ahead, where the cliff stuck out over the ocean like a cupped hand, shimmering and yet solid, was one of the ruined castles or geological features that the sea-leviathans had supposedly deserted before the arrival of people on this planet—a qasr. They rode slowly toward it, their hayawans' feet thocking in the dust. It looked like a fairy place. Part natural, but roofed and buttressed, with grey-black gables and huge and intricate windows, that flashed with the colors of the sea. Kalal gestured for silence, dismounted from Abu, led his mount back into the shadowed arms of the forest, and flicked the switch in her back that hobbled her.

"You *know* where this is?"

Kalal beckoned.

Jalila, who knew him better than to ask questions, followed.

Close to, much of the qasr seemed to be made of a quartz-speckled version of the same fused stone from which Jalila's haramlek was constructed. But some other bits of it appeared to be natural effusions of the rock. There was a big, arched door of sun-bleached and iron-studded oak, reached by a path across the narrowing cliff, but Kalal steered Jalila to the side, and then up and around a bare angle of hot stone that seemed ready at any moment to tilt them down into the distant sea. But the way never quite gave out; there was always another handhold. From the confident manner in which he moved up this near-cliff face, then scrambled across the blistering black tiles of the rooftop beyond, and dropped down into the sudden cool of a narrow passageway, Jalila guessed that Kalal had been to this qasr before. At first, there was little sense of trespass. The place seemed old and empty—a little-visited monument. The ceilings were stained. The corridors were swept with the litter of winter leaves. Here and there along the walls there were friezes, and long strings of a script which made as little sense to Jalila, in their age and dimness, as that which Kalal had written on the hot rocks.

Then Kalal gestured for Jalila to stop, and she clustered beside him, and they looked down through the intricate stone lattice of a mashrabiya into sunlight. It was plain from the balcony drop beneath them that they were still high up in this qasr. Below, in the central courtyard, somehow shocking after this emptiness, a fountain played in a garden, and water lapped from its lip and ran in steel fingers toward cloistered shadows.

"Someone *lives* here?"

Kalal mouthed the word *tariqua*. Somehow, Jalila instantly understood. It all made sense, in this Season of Rockets, even the dim scenes and hieroglyphs carved in the honeyed stones of this fairy castle. Tariquas were merely human, after all, and the spaceport was nearby; they had to live somewhere. Jalila glanced down at her scuffed sandals, suddenly qonscious that she hadn't taken them off—but by then it was too late, and below them and through the mashrabiya a figure had detached herself from the shadows. The tariqua was tall and thin, and black and bent as a burnt-out match-stick. She walked with a cane. Jalila didn't know what she'd expected— she'd grown older since her first encounter with Kalal, and no longer imagined that she knew about things just because she'd learnt of them in her dreamtent. But still, this tariqua seemed a long way from someone who piloted the impossible distances between the stars, as she moved and clicked slowly around that courtyard fountain, and far older and frailer than anyone Jalila had ever seen. She tended a bush of blue flowers, she touched the fountain's bubbling stone lip. Her head was ebony bald. Her fingers were charcoal. Her eyes were as white and seemingly blind as the flecks of quartz in the fused stone of this building. Once, though, she seemed to look up toward them. Jalila went cold. Surely it wasn't possible that she could *see* them?— and in any event, there was something about the motion of looking up which seemed habitual. As if, like touching the lip of the fountain, and tending that bush, the tariqua always looked up at this moment of the day at that particular point in the stone walls that rose above her.

Jalila followed Kalal further along the corridors, and down stairways and across drops of beautifully clear glass, that hung on nothing far above the prismatic sea. Another glimpse of the tariqua, who was still slowly moving, her neck stretching like an old tortoise as she bent to sniff a flower. In this part of the qasr, there were more definite signs of habitation. Scattered cards and books. A moth-eaten tapestry that billowed from a windowless arch overlooking the sea. Empty coat hangers piled like the bones of insects. An active but clearly little-used chemical toilet. Now that the initial sense of surprise had gone, there was something funny about this mixture of the extraordinary and the everyday. Here, there was a kitchen, and a half-chewed lump of aish on a plate smeared with seeds. To imagine, that you could both travel between the stars *and* eat bread and tomatoes! Both Kalal and Jalila were red-faced and chuffing now from suppressed hilarity. Down now at the level of the cloisters, hunched in the shade, they studied the tariqua's stooping back. She really did look like a scrawny tortoise, yanked out of its shell, moving between these bushes. Any moment now, you expected her to start chomping on the leaves. She moved more by touch than by sight. Amid the intricate colors of this courtyard, and the flashing glass windchimes that tinkled in the far archways, as she fumbled sightlessly but occa-sionally glanced at things with those odd, white eyes, it seemed yet more likely that she was blind, or at least terribly near-sighted. Slowly, Jalila's hilarity receded, and she began to feel sorry for this old creature who had been aged and withered and wrecked by the strange process of travel between the stars. *The Pain of Distance*—now, where had that phrase come from?

Kalal was still puffing his cheeks. His eyes were watering as he ground his fist against his mouth and silently thumped the nearest pillar in agonized hilarity. Then he let out a nasal grunt, which Jalila was sure that the tariqua must have heard. But her stance didn't alter. It wasn't so much as if she hadn't noticed them, but that she already *knew* that someone was there. There was a sadness and resignation about her movements, the tap of her cane . . . But Kalal had recovered his equilibrium, and Jalila watched his fingers snake out and enclose a flake of broken paving. Another moment, and it spun out into the sunlit courtyard in an arc so perfect that there was never any doubt that it was going to strike the tariqua smack between her birdlike shoulders. Which it did—but by then they were running, and the tariqua was straightening herself up with that same slow resignation. Just before they bundled themselves up the stairway, Jalila glanced back, and felt a hot bar of light from one of the qasr's high upper windows stream across her face. The tariqua was looking straight toward her with those blind white eyes. Then Kalal grabbed her hand. Once again, she was running.

Jalila was cross with herself, and cross with Kalal. It wasn't *like* her, a voice like a mingled chorus of her three mothers would say, to taunt some poor old mahwagi, even if that mahwagi happened also to be an aged tariqua. But Jalila was young, and life was busy. The voice soon faded. In any case, there was the coming moulid to prepare for.

The arrangement of festivals, locally, and on Habara as a whole, was always difficult. Habara's astronomical year was so long that it made no sense to fix the traditional cycle of moulids by it, but at the same time, no one felt comfortable celebrating the same saint or eid in conflicting seasons. Fasting, after all, properly belonged to winter, and no one could quite face their obligations toward the Almighty with quite the same sense of surrender and equanimity in the middle of spring. People's memories faded, as well, as to how one *did* a particular saint in autumn, or revered a certain enlightenment in blasting heat that you had previously celebrated by throwing snowballs. Added to this were the logistical problems of catering for the needs of a small and scattered population across a large planet. There were traveling players, fairs, wandering sufis and priests, but they plainly couldn't be everywhere at once. The end result was that each moulid was fixed locally on Habara, according to a shifting timetable, and after much discussion and many meetings, and rarely happened twice at exactly the same time, or else occurred simultaneously in different places. Lya threw herself into these discussions with the enthusiasm of one who had long been missing such complexities in the lonelier life up on Tabuthal. For the Moulid of First Habitation—which commemorated the time when the Blessed Joanna had arrived on Habara at a site that several different towns claimed, and cast the first urrearth seeds, and lived for five long Habaran years on nothing but tide-flowers and starlight, and rode the sea-leviathans across the oceans as if they were hayawans as she waited for her lover Pia—Lya was the leading light in the local organizations at Al Janb, and the rest of her haramlek were expected to follow suit.

The whole of Al Janb was to be transformed for a day and a night. Jalila helped with the hammering and weaving, and tuning Pavo's crystals and plants, which would supposedly transform the serraplate road between their haramlek and the town into a glittering tunnel. More in the forefront of Jalila's mind were those colored silks that came and went at a particular stall in the markets, and which she was sure would look perfect on her. Between the planning and the worries about this or that turning into a disaster, she worked carefully on each of her three mothers in turn; a nudge here, a suggestion there. Turning their thoughts toward accepting this extravagance was a delicate matter, like training a new hayawan to bear the saddle. Of course, there were wild resistances and buckings, but you were patient, you were stronger. You knew what you wanted. You kept to your subject. You returned and returned and returned to it.

On the day when Ananke finally relented, a worrying wind had struck up, pushing at the soft, half-formed growths that now straggled through the normal weeds along the road into Al Janb like silvered mucus. Pavo was fretting about her creations. Lya's life was one long meeting. Even Ananke was anxious as they walked into Al Janb, where faulty fresh projections flickered across the buildings and squares like an incipient headache as the sky greyed. Jalila, urging her birthmother on as she paused frustratingly, was sure that the market wouldn't be there, or that if it was, the stall that sold the windsilks was sure to have sold out—or, even then, that the particular ones she'd set her mind on would have gone. . . .

But it was all there. In fact, a whole new supply of windsilks, even more marvelous and colorful, had been imported for this moulid. They blew and lifted like colored smoke. Jalila caught and admired them.

"I think this might be you. . . ."

Jalila turned at the voice. It was Nayra, a girl about a standard year and a half older than her, whose mothers were amongst the richest and most powerful in Al Janb. Nayra herself was both beautiful and intelligent; witty, and sometimes devastatingly cruel. She was generally at the center of things, surrounded by a bickering and admiring crowd of seemingly lesser mortals, which sometimes included Jalila. But today she was alone.

"You see, Jalila. That crimson. With your hair, your eyes . . ."

She held the windsilk across Jalila's face like a yashmak. It danced around her eyes. It blurred over her shoulders. Jalila would have thought the color too bold. But Nayra's gaze, which flickered without ever quite leaving Jalila's, her smoothing hands, told Jalila that it was right for her far better than any mirror could have. And then there was blue—that flame color of the summer night. There were silver clasps, too, to hold these windsilks, which Jalila had never noticed on sale before. The stall-keeper, sensing a desire to purchase that went beyond normal bargaining, drew out more surprises from a chest. *Feel! They can only be made in one place, on one planet, in one season. Look! The grubs, they only hatch when they hear the song of a particular bird, which sings only once in its life before it gives up its spirit to the Almighty. . . .* and so on. Ananke, seeing that Jalila had found a more interested and willing helper, palmed her far more cash than she'd promised, and left her with a smile and an oddly sad backward glance.

Jalila spend the rest of that grey and windy afternoon with Nayra, choosing

clothes and ornaments for the moulid. Bangles for their wrists and ankles. Perhaps—
no? yes?—even a small tiara. Bolts of cloth the color of today's sky bound across her
hips to offset the windsilk's beauty. A jewel still filled with the sapphire light of a distant sun to twinkle at her belly. Nayra, with her dark blonde hair, her light brown
eyes, her fine strong hands, which were pale pink beneath the fingernails like the inside of a shell, she hardly needed anything to augment her obvious beauty. But Jalila
knew from her endless studies of herself in her dreamtent mirror that *she* needed to
be more careful; the wrong angle, the wrong light, an incipient spot, and whatever
effect she was striving for could be so easily ruined. Yet she'd never really cared as
much about such things as she did on that windy afternoon, moving through stalls
and shops amid the scent of patchouli. To be so much the focus of her own and
someone else's attention! Nayra's hands, smoothing across her back and shoulders,
lifting her hair, cool sweat at her shoulders, the cool slide and rattle of her bangles as
she raised her arms. . . .

"We could be creatures from a story, Jalila. Let's imagine I'm Scheherazade." A
toss of that lovely hair. Liquid gold. Nayra's seashell fingers, stirring. "You can be her
sister, Dinarzade. . . ."

Jalila nodded enthusiastically, although Dinarzade had been an unspectacular
creature as far as she remembered the tale; there only so that she might waken
Scheherazade in the Sultana's chamber before the first cock crow of morning. But
her limbs, her throat, felt strange and soft and heavy. She reminded herself, as she
dressed and undressed, of the doll Tabatha she'd once so treasured up on Tabuthal,
and had found again recently, and thought for some odd reason of burying. . . .

The lifting, the pulling, Nayra's appraising hands and glance and eyes. This un-
resisting heaviness. Jalila returned home to her haramlek dazed and drained and
happy, and severely out of credit.

That night, there was another visitor for dinner. She must have taken some sort of
carriage to get there, but she came toward their veranda as if she'd walked the entire
distance. Jalila, whose head was filled with many things, was putting out the bowls
when she heard the murmur of footsteps. The sound was so slow that eventually she
noticed it consciously, looked up, and saw a thin, dark figure coming up the sandy
path between Pavo's swaying and newly sculpted bushes. One arm leaned on a
cane, and the other strained seekingly forward. In shock, Jalila dropped the bowl she
was holding. It seemed to roll around and around on the table forever, slipping playfully out of reach of her fingers before spinning off the edge and shattering into several thousand white pieces.

"Oh dear," the tariqua said, finally climbing the steps beside the windy trellis, her
cane tap-tapping. "Perhaps you'd better go and tell one of your mothers, Jalila."

Jalila felt breathless. All through that evening, the tariqua's trachoman white
eyes, the scarred and tarry driftwood of her face, seemed to be studying her. Even
apart from that odd business of her knowing her name, which she supposed could
be explained, Jalila was more and more certain that the tariqua knew that it was she
and Kalal who had spied on her and thrown a stone at her on that hot day in the
qasr. As if that mattered. But somehow, it *did*, more than it should have done. Amid

all this confused thinking, and the silky memories of her afternoon with Nayra, Jalila scarcely noticed the conversation. The weather remained gusty, spinning the lanterns, playing shapes with the shadows, making the tapestries breathe. The tariqua's voice was as thin as her frame. It carried on the spinning air like the croak of an insect.

"Perhaps we could walk on the beach, Jalila?"

"What?" She jerked as if she'd been abruptly awakened. Her mothers were already clearing things away, and casting odd glances at her. The voice had whispered inside her head, and the tariqua was sitting there, her burnt and splintery arm outstretched, in the hope, Jalila supposed, that she would be helped up from the table. The creature's robe had fallen back. Her arm looked like a picture Jalila had once seen of a dried cadaver. With an effort, nearly knocking over another bowl, Jalila moved around the billowing table. With an even bigger effort, she placed her own hand into that of the tariqua. She'd expected it to feel leathery, which it did. But it was also hot beyond fever. Terribly, the fingers closed around hers. There was a pause. Then the tariqua got up with surprising swiftness, and reached around for her cane, still holding Jalila's hand, but without having placed any weight on it. *She could have done all that on her own, the old witch,* Jalila thought. *And she can see, too—look at the way she's been stuffing herself with kofta all evening, reaching over for figs. . . .*

"What do you know of the stars, Jalila?" the tariqua asked as they walked beside the beach. Pavo's creations along the road behind them still looked stark and strange and half-formed as they swayed in the wind, like the wavering silver limbs of an upturned insect. The waves came and went, strewing tideflowers far up the strand. Like the tongue of a snake, the tariqua's cane darted ahead of her.

Jalila shrugged. There were these Gateways, she had always known that. There were these Gateways, and they were the only proper path between the stars, because no one could endure the eons of time that crossing even the tiniest fragment of the Ten Thousand and One Worlds would entail by the ordinary means of traveling from *there* to *here.*

"Not, of course," the tariqua was saying, "that people don't do such things. There are tales, there are always tales, of ghost-ships of sufis drifting for tens of centuries through the black and black. . . . But the wealth, the contact, the *community,* flows through the Gateways. The Almighty herself provided the means to make them in the Days of Creation, when everything that was and will ever be spilled out into a void so empty that it did not even exist as an emptiness. In those first moments, as warring elements collided, boundaries formed, dimensions were made and disappeared without ever quite dissolving, like the salt tidemarks on those rocks. . . ." As they walked, the tariqua waved her cane. ". . . which the sun and the eons can never quite bake away. These boundaries are called cosmic strings, Jalila, and they have no end. They must form either minute loops, or they must stretch from one end of this universe to the other, and then turn back again, and turn and turn without end."

Jalila glanced at the brooch the tariqua was wearing, which was of a worm consuming its tail. She knew that the physical distances between the stars were vast, but the tariqua somehow made the distances that she traversed to avoid that journey seem even vaster. . . .

"You must understand," the tariqua said, "that we tariquas pass through something worse than nothing to get from one side to the other of a Gateway."

Jalila nodded She was young, and *nothing* didn't sound especially frightening. Still, she sensed that there were the answers to mysteries in this near-blind gaze and whispering voice that she would never get from her dreamtent or her mothers. "But, *hanim*, what could be worse," she asked dutifully, although she still couldn't think of the tariqua in terms of a name, and thus simply addressed her with the short honorific, "than sheer emptiness?"

"Ah, but emptiness is *nothing*. Imagine, Jalila, passing through *everything* instead!" The tariqua chuckled, and gazed up at the sky. "But the stars are beautiful, and so is this night. You come, I hear, from Tabuthal. There, the skies must all have been very different."

Jalila nodded A brief vision flared over her. The way that up there, on the clearest, coldest nights, you felt as if the stars were all around you. Even now, much though she loved the fetors and astonishments of the coast, she still felt the odd pang of missing something. It was a *feeling* she missed, as much as the place itself, which she guessed would probably seem bleak and lonely if she returned to it now. It was partly to do, she suspected, with that sense that she was losing her childhood. It was like being on a ship, on Kalal's nameless boat, and watching the land recede, and half of you loving the loss, half of you hating it. A war seemed to be going on inside her between these two warring impulses. . . .

To her surprise, Jalila realized that she wasn't just thinking these thoughts, but speaking them, and that the tariqua, walking at her slow pace, the weight of her head bending her spine, her cane whispering a jagged line in the dust as the black rags of her djibbah flapped around her, was listening. Jalila supposed that she, too, had been young once, although that was hard to imagine. The sea frothed and swished. They were at the point in the road now where, gently buzzing and almost out of sight amid the forest, hidden there as if in shame, the tariqua's caleche lay waiting. It was a small filigree, a thing as old and black and ornate as her brooch. Jalila helped her toward it through the trees. The craft's door creaked open like an iron gate, then shut behind the tariqua. A few crickets sounded through the night's heat. Then, with a soft rush, and a static glow like the charge of windsilk brushing flesh, the caleche rose up through the treetops and wafted away.

The day of the moulid came. It was everything that Jalila expected, although she paid it little attention. The intricate, bowered pathway that Pavo had been working on finally shaped itself to her plans—in fact, it was better than that, and seemed like a beautiful accident. As the skies cleared, the sun shone through prismatic arches. The flowers, which had looked so stunted only the evening before, suddenly unfolded, with petals like beaten brass, and stamens shaped so that the continuing breeze, which Pavo had always claimed to have feared, laughed and whistled and tooted as it passed through them. Walking beneath the archways of flickering shadows, you were assailed by scents and the clashes of small orchestras. But Jalila's ears were blocked, her eyes were sightless. She, after all, was Dinarzade, and Nayra was Scheherazade of the Thousand and One Nights.

Swirling windsilks, her heart hammering, she strode into Al Janb. Everything seemed to be different today. There were too many sounds and colors. People tried to dance with her, or sell her things. Some of the aliens seemed to have dressed themselves as humans. Some of the humans were most definitely dressed as aliens. Her feet were already blistered and delicate from her new crimson slippers. And there was Nayra, dressed in a silvery serwal and blouse of such devastating simplicity that Jalila felt her heart kick and pause in its beating. Nayra was surrounded by a small storm of her usual admirers. Her eyes took in Jalila as she stood at their edge, then beckoned her to join them. The idea of Dinarzade and Scheherazade, which Jalila had thought was to be their secret, was now shared with everyone. The other girls laughed and clustered around, admiring, joking, touching and stroking bits of her as if she was a hayawan. *You of all people, Jalila! And such jewels, such silks . . .* Jalila stood half-frozen, her heart still kicking. *So, so marvelous! And not at all dowdy. . . .* She could have lived many a long and happy life without such compliments.

Thus the day continued. All of them in a crowd, and Jalila feeling both over-dressed and exposed, with these stirring, whispering windsilks that covered and yet mostly seemed to reveal her body. She felt like a child in a ribboned parade, and when one of the old mahwagis even came up and pressed a sticky lump of basbousa into her hand, it was the final indignity. She trudged off alone, and found Kalal and his father Ibra managing a seafront stall beside the swaying masts of the bigger trawlers, around which there was a fair level of purchase and interest. Ibra was enjoying himself, roaring out enticements and laughter in his big, belling voice. At last, they'd gotten around to harvesting some of the tideflowers for which their nameless boat had been designed, and they were selling every sort here, salt-fresh from the ocean.

"Try this one. . . ." Kalal drew Jalila away to the edge of the harbor, where the oiled water flashed below. He had just one tideflower in his hand. It was deep-banded the same crimson and blue as her windsilks. The interior was like the eye of an anemone.

Jalila was flattered. But she hesitated. "I'm not sure about wearing something dead." In any case, she knew she already looked ridiculous. That this would be more of the same.

"It isn't dead, it's as alive as you are." Kalal held it closer, against Jalila's shoulder, toward the top of her breast, smoothing out the windsilks in a way that briefly reminded her of Nayra. "And isn't this material the dead tissue of some creature or other. . . ?" Still, his hands were smoothing. Jalila thought again of Nayra. Being dressed like a doll. Her nipples started to rise. "And if we take it back to the tide-flower beds tomorrow morning, place it down there carefully, it'll still survive. . . ." The tideflower had stuck itself to her now, anyway, beneath the shoulder, its adhesion passing through the thin windsilks, burning briefly as it bound to her flesh. And it *was* beautiful, even if she wasn't, and it would have been churlish to refuse. Jalila placed her finger into the tideflower's center, and felt a soft suction, like the mouth of a baby. Smiling, thanking Kalal, feeling somehow better and more determined, she walked away.

The day went on. The night came. Fireworks crackled and rumpled, rippling down the slopes of the mountains. The whole of the center of Al Janb was transformed unrecognizably into the set of a play. Young Joanna herself walked the vast avenues of Ghezirah, the island city that lies at the center of all the Ten Thousand and One Worlds, and which grows in much the same way as Pavo's crystal scaffoldings, but on an inconceivable scale, filled with azure skies, glinting in the dark heavens like a vast diamond. The Blessed Joanna, she was supposedly thinking of a planet that had come to her in a vision as she wandered beside Ghezirah's palaces; it was a place of fine seas, lost giants, and mysterious natural castles, although Jalila, as she followed in the buffeting, cheering procession, and glanced around at the scale of the projections that briefly covered Al Janb's ordinary buildings, wondered why, even if this version of Ghezirah was fake and thin, Joanna would ever have wanted to leave *that* city to come to a place such as this.

There were more fireworks. As they rattled, a deeper sound swept over them in a moan from the sea, and everyone looked up as sunglow poured through the gaudy images of Ghezirah that still clad Al Janb's buildings. Not one rocket, or two, but three were all climbing up from the spaceport simultaneously, the vast white plumes of their energies fanning out across half the sky to form a billowy *fleur de lys*. At last, as she craned her neck and watched the last of those blazing tails diminish, Jalila felt exulted by this moulid. In the main square, the play continued. When she found a place on a bench and began to watch the more intimate parts of the drama unfold, as Joanna's lover Pia pleaded with her to remain amid the cerulean towers of Ghezirah, a figure moved to sit beside her. To Jalila's astonishment, it was Nayra.

"That's a lovely flower. I've been meaning to ask you all day . . ." Her fingers moved across Jalila's shoulder. There was a tug at her skin as she touched the petals.

"I got it from Kalal."

"Oh . . ." Nayra sought the right word. "*Him*. Can I smell it. . . ?" She was already bending down, her face close to Jalila's breast, the golden fall of her hair brushing her forearm, enclosing her in the sweet, slightly vanilla scent of her body. "That's nice. It smells like the sea—on a clear day, when you climb up and look down at it from the mountains. . . ."

The play continued. Would Joanna really go to this planet, which kept appearing to her in these visions? Jalila didn't know. She didn't care. Nayra's hand slipped into her own and lay there upon her thigh with a weight and presence that seemed far heavier than the entire universe. She felt like that doll again. Her breath was pulling, dragging. The play continued, and then, somewhere, somehow, it came to an end. Jalila felt an aching sadness. She'd have been happy for Joanna to continue her will-I-won't-I agonizing and prayers throughout all of human history, just so that she and Nayra could continue to sit together like this, hand in hand, thigh to thigh, on this hard bench.

The projections flickered and faded. She stood up in wordless disappointment. The whole square suddenly looked like a wastetip, and she felt crumpled and used-up in these sweaty and ridiculous clothes. It was hardly worth looking back toward Nayra to say good-bye. She would, Jalila was sure, have already vanished to rejoin those clucking, chattering friends who surrounded her like a wall.

"Wait!" A hand on her arm. That same vanilla scent. "I've heard that your mother Pavo's displays along the south road are something quite fabulous. . . ." For once,

Nayra's golden gaze as Jalila looked back at her was almost coy, nearly averted. "I was rather hoping you might show me. . . ."

The two of them. Walking hand in hand, just like all lovers throughout history. Like Pia and Joanna. Like Romana and Juliet. Like Isabel and Genya. Ghosts of smoke from the rocket plumes that had buttressed the sky hung around them, and the world seemed half-dissolved in the scent of sulphur and roses. An old woman they passed, who was sweeping up discarded kebab sticks and wrappers, made a sign as they passed, and gave them a weary, sad-happy smile. Jalila wasn't sure what had happened to her slippers, but they and her feet both seemed to have become weightless. If it hadn't been for the soft sway and pull of Nayra's arm, Jalila wouldn't even have been sure that she was moving. *People's feet really* don't *touch the ground when they are in love!* Here was something else that her dreamtent and her mothers hadn't told her.

Pavo's confections of plant and crystal looked marvelous in the hazed and doubled silver shadows of the rising moons. Jalila and Nayra wandered amid them, and the rest of the world felt withdrawn and empty. A breeze was still playing over the rocks and the waves, but the fluting sound had changed. It was one soft pitch, rising, falling. They kissed. Jalila closed her eyes—she couldn't help it—and trembled. Then they held both hands together and stared at each other, unflinching. Nayra's bare arms in the moonlight, the curve inside her elbow and the blue trace of a vein: Jalila had never seen anything as beautiful, here in this magical place.

The stables, where the hayawans were breathing. Jalila spoke to Robin, to Abu. The beasts were sleepy. Their flesh felt cold, their plates were warm, and Nayra seemed a little afraid. There, in the sighing darkness, the clean scent of feed and straw was overlaid with the heat of the hayawans' bodies and their dung. The place was no longer a ramshackle tent, but solid and dark, another of Pavo's creations; the stony catacombs of ages. Jalila led Nayra through it, her shoulders brushing pillars, her heart pounding, her slippered feet whispering through spills of straw. To the far corner, where the fine new white bedding lay like depths of cloud. They threw themselves onto it, half-expecting to fall through. But they were floating in straggles of windsilk, held in tangles of their own laughter and limbs.

"Remember." Nayra's palm on Jalila's right breast, scrolled like an old print in the geometric moonlight that fell from Walah, and then through the arched stone grid of a murqana that lay above their heads. "I'm Scheherazade. You're Dinarzade, my sister . . ." The pebble of Jalila's nipple rising through the windsilk. "That old, old story, Jalila. Can you remember how it went. . . ?"

In the tide of yore and in the time of long gone before, there was a Queen of all the Queens of the Banu Sasan in the far islands of India and China, a Lady of armies and guards and servants and dependents . . .

Again, they kissed.

Handsome gifts, such as horses with saddles of gem-encrusted gold; mamelukes, or white slaves; beautiful handmaids, high-breasted virgins, and splendid stuffs and costly . . .

Nayra's hand moved from Jalila's breast to encircle the tide-flower. She gave it a tug, pulled harder. Something held, gave, held, hurt, then gave entirely. The windsilks poured back. A small dark bead of blood welled at the curve between Jalila's breast and shoulder. Nayra licked it away.

In one house was a girl weeping for the loss of her sister. In another, perhaps a mother trembling for the fate of her child; and instead of the blessings that had formerly been heaped on the Sultana's head, the air was now full of curses . . .

Jalila was rising, floating, as Nayra's mouth traveled downward to suckle at her breast.

Now the Wazir had two daughters, Scheherazade and Dinarzade, of whom the elder had perused the books, annals, and legends of preceding queens and empresses, and the stories, examples, and instances of bygone things. Scheherazade had read the works of the poets and she knew them by heart. She had studied philosophy, the sciences, the arts, and all accomplishments. And Scheherazade was pleasant and polite, wise and witty. Scheherazade, she was beautiful and well bred . . .

Flying far over frost-glittering saharas, beneath the twin moons, soaring through the clouds. The falling, rising dunes. The minarets and domes of distant cities. The cries and shuddering sighs of the beloved. Patterned moonslight falling through the murqana in a white and dark tapestry across the curves and hollows of Nayra's belly.

Alekum as-salal wa rahmatu allahi wa barakatuh. . . .

Upon you, the peace and the mercy of God and all these blessings.

Amen.

There was no cock-crow when Jalila startled awake. But Walah had vanished, and so had Nayra, and the light of the morning sun came splintering down through the murqana's hot blue lattice. Sheltering her face with her hands, Jalila looked down at herself, and smiled. The jewel in her belly was all that was left of her costume. She smelled faintly of vanilla, and much of Nayra, and nothing about her flesh seemed quite her own. Moving through the dazzling drizzle, she gathered up the windsilks and other scraps of clothing that had settled into the fleece bedding. She found one of Nayra's earrings, which was twisted to right angles at the post, and had to smile again. And here was that tideflower, tossed upturned like an old cup into the corner. She touched the tiny scab on her shoulder, then lifted the flower up and inhaled, but caught on her palms only the scents of Nayra. She closed her eyes, feeling the diamond speckles of heat and cold across her body like the ripples of the sea.

The hayawans barely stirred as she moved out through their stables. Only Robin regarded her, and then incuriously, as she paused to touch the hard, grey melds of her flank that she had pressed against the bars of her enclosure. One eye, grey as rocket smoke, opened, then returned to its saharas of dreams. The hayawans, Jalila supposed for the first time, had their own passions, and these were not to be shared with some odd two-legged creatures of another race and planet.

The morning was still clinging to its freshness, and the road, as she crossed it, was barely warm beneath her feet. Wind-towered Al Janb and the haramlek behind her looked deserted. Even the limbs of the mountains seemed curled in sleepy haze. On this day after the moulid, no one but the geelies was yet stirring. Cawing, they rose and settled in flapping red flocks from the beds of the tide-flowers as Jalila scrunched across the hard stones of the beach. Her feet encountered the cool, slick water. She continued walking, wading, until the sea tickled her waist and what remained of the windsilks had spread about in spills of dye. From her cupped hands, she released the tideflower, and watched it float away. She splashed her face. She sunk down to her shoulders as the windsilks dissolved from her, and looked down between her breasts at the glowing jewel that was still stuck in her belly, and plucked it out, and watched it sink; the sea-lantern of a ship, drowning.

Walking back up the beach, wringing the wet from her hair, Jalila noticed a rich green growth standing out amid the sky-filled rockpools and the growths of lichen. Pricked by something resembling Pavo's curiosity, she scrambled over, and crouched to examine it as the gathering heat of the sun dried her back. She recognized this spot—albeit dimly—from the angle of a band of quartz that glittered and bled blue oxides. This was where she had coughed up her breathmoss in that early Season of Soft Rains. And here it still was, changed but unmistakable—and growing. A small patch here, several larger patches there. Tiny filaments of green, a minute forest, raising its boughs and branches to the sun.

She walked back up toward her haramlek, humming.

3.

The sky was no longer blue. It was no longer white. It had turned to mercury. The rockets rose and rose in dry crackles of summer lightening. The tubelike aliens fled, leaving their strange house of goo-filled windows and pipes still clicking and humming until something burst and the whole structure deflated, and the mess of it leaked across the nearby streets. There were warnings of poisonings and strange epidemics. There were cloggings and stenches of the drains.

Jalila showed the breathmoss to her mothers, who were all intrigued and delighted, although Pavo had of course noticed and categorized the growth long before, while Ananke had to touch the stuff, and left a small brown mark there like the tips of her three fingers, which dried and turned golden over the days that followed. But in this hot season, these evenings when the sun seemed as if it would never vanish, the breathmoss proved surprisingly hardy. . . .

After that night of the moulid, Jalila spent several happy days absorbed and alone, turning and smoothing the memory of her love-making with Nayra. Wandering above and beneath the unthinking routines of everyday life, she was like a fine craftsman, spinning silver, shaping sandalwood. The dimples of Nayra's back. Sweat glinting in the checkered moonslight. That sweet vein in the crook of her beloved's arm, and the pulse of the blood that had risen from it to the drumbeats of ecstasy. The memory seemed entirely enough to Jalila. She was barely living in the present day. When, perhaps six days after the end of the moulid, Nayra turned up at their doorstep with the ends of her hair chewed wet and her eyes red-rimmed, Jalila had been almost surprised to see her, and then to notice the differences between the real Nayra and the Scheherazade of her memories. Nayra smelled of tears and dust as they embraced; like someone who had arrived from a long, long journey.

"Why didn't you *call* me? I've been waiting, waiting. . . ."

Jalila kissed her hair. Her hand traveled beneath a summer shawl to caress Nayra's back, which felt damp and gritty. She had no idea how to answer her questions. They walked out together that afternoon in the shade of the woods behind the haramlek. The trees had changed in this long, hot season, departing from their urrearth habits to coat their leaves in a waxy substance that smelled medicinal. The shadows of their boughs were chalkmarks and charcoal. All was silent. The urrearth birds had retreated to their summer hibernations until the mists of autumn came to rouse them again. Climbing a scree of stones, they found clusters of them at the back of a cave; feathery bundles amid the dripping rock, seemingly without eyes or beak.

As they sat at the mouth of that cave, looking down across the heat-trembling bay, sucking the ice and eating the dates that Ananke had insisted they bring with them, Nayra had seemed like a different person to the one Jalila had thought she had known before the day of the moulid. Nayra, too, was human, and not the goddess she had seemed. She had her doubts and worries. She, too, thought that the girls who surrounded her were mostly crass and stupid. She didn't even believe in her own obvious beauty. She cried a little again, and Jalila hugged her. The hug became a kiss. Soon, dusty and greedy, they were tumbling amid the hot rocks. That evening, back at the haramlek, Nayra was welcomed for dinner by Jalila's mothers with mint tea and the best china. She was invited to bathe. Jalila sat beside her as they ate figs fresh from distant Ras and the year's second crop of oranges. She felt happy. At last, life seemed simple. Nayra was now officially her lover, and this love would form the pattern of her days.

Jalila's life now seemed complete; she believed that she was an adult, and that she talked and spoke and loved and worshipped in an adult way. She still rode out sometimes with Kalal on Robin and Abu, she still laughed or stole things or played games, but she was conscious now that these activities were the sweetmeats of life, pleasing but unnutritous, and the real glories and surprises lay with being with Nayra, and with her mothers, and the life of the haramlek that the two young women talked of founcing together one day.

Nayra's mothers lived on the far side of Al Janb, in a fine, tall clifftop palace that was one of the oldest in the town, clad in white stone and filled with intricate courtyards, and a final beautiful tajo that looked down from gardens of tarragon across the whole bay. Jalila greatly enjoyed exploring this haramlek, deciphering the peeling scripts that wound along the cool vaults, and enjoying the company of Nayra's mothers who, in their wealth and grace and wisdom, often made her own mothers seem like the awkward and recent provincial arrivals that they plainly were. At home, in her own haramlek, the conversations and ideas seemed stale. An awful dream came to Jalila one night. She was her old doll Tabatha, and she really was being buried. The ground she lay in was moist and dank, as if it was still the Season of Soft Rains, and the faces of everyone she knew were clustered around the hole above her, muttering and sighing as her mouth and eyes were inexorably filled with soil.

"Tell me what it was like, when you first fell in love."

Jalila had chosen Pavo to ask this question of. Ananke would probably just hug her, while Lya would talk and talk until there was nothing to say.

"I don't know. Falling in love is like coming home. You can never quite do it for the first time."

"But in the stories—"

"—The stories are always written *afterward*, Jalila."

They were walking the luminous shore. It was near midnight, which was now by far the best time of the night or day. But what Pavo had just said sounded wrong; perhaps she hadn't been the right choice of mother to speak to, after all. Jalila was sure she'd loved Nayra since that day before the moulid of Joanna, although it was true she loved her now in a different way.

"You still don't think we really will form a haramlek together, do you?"

"I think that it's too early to say."

"You were the last of our three, weren't you? Lya and Ananke were already together."

"It was what drew me to them. They seemed so happy and complete. It was also what frightened me and nearly sent me away."

"But you stayed together, and then there was . . ." This was the part that Jalila still found hardest to acknowledge; the idea that her mothers had a physical, sexual relationship. Sometimes, deep at night, from someone else's dreamtent, she had heard muffled sighs, the wet slap of flesh. Just like the hayawans, she supposed, there were things about other people's lives that you could never fully understand, no matter how well you thought you knew them.

She chose a different tack. "So why did you choose to have me?"

"Because we wanted to fill the world with something that had never ever existed before. Because we felt selfish. Because we wanted to give ourselves away."

"Ananke, she actually gave birth to me, didn't she?"

"Down here at Al Janb, they'd say we were primitive and mad. Perhaps that was how we wanted to be. But all the machines at the clinics do is try to recreate the conditions of a real human womb—the voices, the movements, the sound of breathing. . . . Without first hearing that Song of Life, no human can ever be happy, so what better way could there be than to hear it naturally?"

A flash of that dream-image of herself being buried. "But the birth itself—"

"—I think that was something we all underestimated." The tone of Pavo's voice told Jalila that this was not a subject to be explored on the grounds of mere curiosity.

The tideflower beds had solidified. You could walk across them as if they were dry land. Kalal, after several postponements and broken promises, took Jalila and Nayra out one night to demonstrate.

Smoking lanterns at the prow and stern of his boat. The water slipping warm as blood through Jalila's trailing fingers. Al Janb receding beneath the hot thighs of the mountains. Kalal at the prow. Nayra sitting beside her, her arm around her shoulder, hand straying across her breast until Jalila shrugged it away because the heat of their two bodies was oppressive.

"This season'll end soon," Nayra said. "You've never known the winter here, have you?"

"I was *born* in the winter. Nothing here could be as cold as the lightest spring morning in the mountains of Tabuthal."

"Ah, the *mountains*. You must show me sometime. We should travel there together. . . ."

Jalila nodded, trying hard to picture that journey. She'd attempted to interest Nayra in riding a hayawan, but she grew frightened even in the presence of the beasts. In so many ways, in fact, Nayra surprised Jalila with her timidity. Jalila, in these moments of doubt, and as she lay alone in her dreamtent and wondered, would list to herself Nayra's many assets: her lithe and willing body; the beautiful haramlek of her beautiful mothers; the fact that so many of the other girls now envied and admired her. There were so many things that were good about Nayra.

Kalal, now that his boat had been set on course for the further tidebeds, came to sit with them, his face sweated lantern-red. He and Nayra shared many memories, and now, as the sails pushed on from the hot air off the mountains, they vied to tell Jalila of the surprises and delights of winters in Al Janb. The fogs when you couldn't see your hand. The intoxicating blue berries that appeared in special hollows through the crust of the snow. The special saint's days. . . . If Jalila hadn't known better, she'd have said that Nayra and Kalal were fighting over something more important.

The beds of tideflowers were vast, luminous, heavy-scented. Red-black clusters of geelies rose and fell here and there in the moonlight. Walking these gaudy carpets was a most strange sensation. The dense interlaces of leaves felt like rubber matting, but sank and bobbed. Jalila and Nayra lit more lanterns and dotted them around a field of huge primrose and orange petals. They sang and staggered and rolled and fell over. Nayra had brought a pipe of kif resin, and the sensation of smoking that and trying to dance was hilarious. Kalal declined, pleading that he had to control the boat on the way back, and picked his way out of sight, disturbing flocks of geelies.

And so the two girls danced as the twin moons rose. Nayra, twirling silks, her hair fanning, was graceful as Jalila still staggered amid the lapping flowers. As she lifted her arms and rose on tiptoe, bracelets glittering, she had never looked more desirable. Somewhat drunkenly—and slightly reluctantly, because Kalal might return at any moment—Jalila moved forward to embrace her. It was good to hold Nayra, and her mouth tasted like the tideflowers and sucked needily at her own. In fact, the moments of their love had never been sweeter and slower than they were on that night, although, even as Jalila marveled at the shape of Nayra's breasts and listened to the changed song of her breathing, she felt herself chilling, receding, drawing back, not just from Nayra's physical presence, but from this small bay beside the small town on the single continent beside Habara's great and lonely ocean. Jalila felt infinitely sorry for Nayra as she brought her to her little ecstasies and they kissed and rolled across the beds of flowers. She felt sorry for Nayra because she was beautiful, and sorry for her because of all her accomplishments, and sorry for her because she would always be happy here amid the slow seasons of this little planet.

Jalila felt sorry for herself as well; sorry because she had thought that she had known love, and because she knew now that it had only been a pretty illusion.

There was a shifting wind, dry and abrasive, briefly to be welcomed, until it became something to curse and cover your face and close your shutters against.

Of Jalila's mothers, only Lya seemed at all disappointed by her break from Nayra, no doubt because she had fostered hopes of their union forming a powerful bond between their haramleks, and even she did her best not to show it. Of the outside world, the other young women of Al Janb all professed total disbelief—*why if it had been me, I'd never have* . . . But soon, they were cherishing the new hope that it might indeed *be* them. Nayra, to her credit, maintained an extraordinary dignity in the face of the fact that she, of all people, had finally been rejected. She dressed in plain clothes. She spoke and ate simply. Of course, she looked more devastatingly beautiful than ever, and everyone's eyes were reddened by airborne grit in any case, so it was impossible to tell how much she had really been crying. Now, as the buildings of Al Janb creaked and the breakers rolled and the wind howled through the teeth of the mountains, Jalila saw the gaudy, seeking, and competing creatures who so often surrounded Nayra quite differently. Nayra was not, had never been, in control of them. She was more like the bloody carcass over which, flashing their teeth, their eyes, stretching their limbs, they endlessly fought. Often, riven by a sadness far deeper than she had ever experienced, missing something she couldn't explain, wandering alone or lying in her dreamtent, Jalila nearly went back to Nayra. . . . But she never did.

This was the Season of Winds, and Jalila was heartily sick of herself and Al Janb, and the girls and the mahwagis and the mothers, and of this changing, buffeting banshee weather that seemed to play with her moods. Sometimes now, the skies were entirely beautiful, strung by the curling multicolored banners of sand that the winds had lifted from distant corners of the continent. There was crimson and there was sapphire. The distant saharas of Jalila's dreams had come to haunt her. They fell—as the trees tore and the paint stripped from the shutters and what remained of Pavo's arches collapsed—in an irritating grit that worked its way into all the crevices of your body and every weave of your clothes.

The tariqua had spoken of the pain of *nothing*, and then of the pain of *everything*. At the time, Jalila had understood neither, but now, she felt that she understood the pain of nothing all too well. The product of the combined genes of her three mothers; loving Ananke, ever-curious Pavo, proud and talkative Lya, she had always felt glad to recognize these characteristics mingled in herself, but now she wondered if these traits hadn't canceled each other out. She was a null-point, a zero, clumsy and destructive and unloving. She was Jalila, and she walked alone and uncaring through this Season of Winds.

One morning, the weather was especially harsh. Jalila was alone in the haramlek, although she cared little where she or anyone else was. A shutter must have come loose somewhere. That often happened now. It had been banging and hammering so long that it began to irritate even her. She climbed stairs and slammed doors over jamming drifts of mica. She flapped back irritably at flapping curtains. Still, the banging went on. Yet all the windows and doors were now secure. She was sure of it. Unless. . . .

Someone was at the front door. She could see a swirling globular head through the greenish glass mullion. Even though they could surely see her as well, the banging went on. Jalila wondered if she wanted it to be Nayra; after all, this was how she had come to her after the moulid; a sweet and needy human being to drag her out from her dreams. But it was only Kalal. As the door shoved Jalila back, she tried not to look disappointed.

"You can't do this with your life!"

"Do what?"

"This—*nothing*. And then not answering the fucking door. . . ." Kalal prowled the hallway as the door banged back and forth and tapestries flailed, looking for clues as if he was a detective. "Let's go out."

Even in this weather, Jalila supposed that she owed it to Robin. Then Kalal had wanted to go north, and she insisted on going south, and was not in any mood for arguing. It was an odd journey, so unlike the ones they'd undertaken in the summer. They wrapped their heads and faces in flapping howlis, and tried to ride mostly in the forest, but the trees whipped and flapped and the raw air still abraded their faces.

They took lunch down by a flatrock shore, in what amounted to shelter, although there was still little enough of it as the wind eddied about them. This could have been the same spot where they had stopped in summer, but it was hard to tell; the light was so changed, the sky so bruised. Kalal seemed changed, too. His face beneath his howli seemed older, as he tried to eat their aish before the sand-laden air got to it, and his chin looked prickled and abraded. Jalila supposed that this was the same facial growth that his father Ibra was so fond of sporting. She also supposed he must choose to shave his off in the way that some women on some decadent planets were said to shave their legs and armpits.

"Come a bit closer—" she half-shouted, working her way back into the lee of the bigger rock beside which she was sitting to make room for him. "I want you to tell me what you know about love, Kalal."

Kalal hunched beside her. For a while, he just continued tearing and chewing bits of aish, with his body pressed against hers as the winds boiled around them, the warmth of their flesh almost meeting. And Jalila wondered if men and women, when their lives and needs had been more closely intertwined, had perhaps known the answer to her question. What *was* love, after all? It would have been nice to think that, in those dim times of myth, men and women had whispered the answer to that question to each other. . . .

She thought then that Kalal hadn't properly heard her. He was telling her about his father, and a planet he barely remembered, but on which he was born. The sky there had been fractaled gold and turquoise—colors so strange and bright that they came as a delight and a shock each morning. It was a place of many islands, and one great city. His father had been a fisherman and boat-repairer of sorts there as well, although the boats had been much grander than anything you ever saw at Al Janb, and the fish had lived not as single organisms, but as complex shoals that were caught not for their meat, but for their joint minds. Ibra had been approached by a woman from off-world, who had wanted a ship on which she could sail alone around the whole lonely band of the northern oceans. She had told him that she was sick of human company. The planning and the making of the craft was a joy for Ibra, because such a lonely journey had been one that he had long dreamed of making, if ever he'd had the time and money. The ship was his finest-ever creation, and it turned out, as they worked on it, that neither he nor the woman were quite as sick of human company as they had imagined. They fell in love as the keel and the spars grew in the city dockyards and the ship's mind was nurtured, and as they did so, they slowly relearned the expressions of sexual need between the male and female.

"You mean he *raped* her?"

Kalal tossed his last nub of bread toward the waves. "I mean that they *made love*."

After the usual negotiations and contracts, and after the necessary insertions of the appropriate cells, Ibra and this woman (whom Kalal didn't name in his story, any more than he named the world) set sail together, fully intending to conceive a child in the fabled way of old.

"Which was *you*?"

Kalal scowled. It was impossible to ask him even simple questions on this subject without making him look annoyed. "Of *course* it was! How many of me do you think there are?" Then he lapsed into silence. The sands swirled in colored helixes before them.

"That woman—your birthmother. What happened to her?"

"She wanted to take me away, of course—to some haramlek on another world, just as she'd been planning all along. My father was just a toy to her. As soon as their ship returned, she started making plans, issuing contracts. There was a long legal dispute with my father. I was placed in a birthsac, in stasis."

"And your father won?"

Kalal scowled. "He took me here, anyway. Which is winning enough."

There were many other questions about this story that Jalila wanted to ask Kalal, if she hadn't already pressed too far. What, after all, did this tale of dispute and deception have to do with love? And were Kalal and Ibra really fugitives? It would explain quite a lot. Once more, in that familiar welling, she felt sorry for him. Men were such strange, sad creatures; forever fighting, angry, lost. . . .

"*I'm* glad you're here anyway," she said. Then, on impulse, one of those careless things you do, she took that rough and ugly chin in her hand, turned his face toward hers and kissed him lightly on the lips.

"What was that for?"

"*El-hamdu-l-Illah.* That was for thanks."

They plodded further on their hayawans. They came eventually to a cliff-edge so high that the sea and sky above and beneath vanished. Jalila already knew what they would see as they made their way along it, but still it was a shock; that qasr, thrust into these teeming ribbons of sand. The winds whooped and howled, and the hayawans raised their heads and howled back at it. In this grinding atmosphere, Jalila could see how the qasrs had been carved over long years from pure natural rock. They dismounted, and struggled bent-backed across the narrowing track toward the qasr's studded door. Jalila raised her fist and beat on it.

She glanced back at Kalal, but his face was entirely hidden beneath his hood. Had they always intended to come here? But they had traveled too far to do otherwise now; Robin and Abu were tired and near-blinded; they all needed rest and shelter. She beat on the door again, but the sound was lost in the booming storm. Perhaps the tariqua had left with the last of the Season of Rockets, just as had most of the aliens. Jalila was about to turn away when the door, as if thrown wide by the wind, blasted open. There was no one on the other side, and the hallway beyond was dark as the bottom of a dry well. Robin hoiked her head back and howled and resisted as Jalila hauled her in. Kalal with Abu followed. The door, with a massive drumbeat, hammered itself shut behind them. Of course, it was only some old mechanism of this house, but Jalila felt the hairs on the nape of her neck rise.

They hobbled the hayawans beside the largest of the scalloped arches, and walked on down the passageway beyond. The wind was still with them, and the shapes of the pillars were like the swirling helixes of sand made solid. It was hard to tell what parts of this place had been made by the hands of women and what was entirely natural. If the qasr had seemed deserted in the heat of summer, it was entirely abandoned now. A scatter of glass windchimes, torn apart by the wind. A few broken plates. Some flapping cobwebs of tapestry.

Kalal pulled Jalila's hand.

"Let's go back. . . ."

But there was greater light ahead, the shadows of the speeding sky. Here was the courtyard where they had glimpsed the tariqua. She had plainly gone now—the fountain was dry and clogged, the bushes were bare tangles of wire. They walked out beneath the tiled arches, looking around. The wind was like a million voices, rising in ululating chorus. This was a strange and empty place; somehow dangerous. . . . Jalila span around. The tariqua was standing there, her robes flapping. With insect fingers, she beckoned.

"Are you leaving?" Jalila asked. "I mean, this place. . . ."

The tariqua had led them into the shelter of a tall, wind-echoing chamber set with blue and white tiles. There were a few rugs and cushions scattered on the floor, but still the sense of abandonment remained. As if, Jalila thought, as the tariqua folded herself on the floor and gestured that they join her, this was her last retreat.

"No, Jalila. I won't be leaving Habara. *Itfaddal.* . . . Do sit down."

They stepped from their sandals and obeyed. Jalila couldn't quite remember now whether Kalal had encountered the tariqua on her visit to their haramlek, although it seemed plain from his stares at her, and the way her grey-white gaze returned them, that they knew of each other in some way. Coffee was brewing in the corner, over a tiny, blue spirit flame, which, as it fluttered in the many drafts, must have taken hours to heat anything. Yet the spout of the brass pot was steaming. And there were dates, too, and nuts and seeds. The tariqua, apologizing for her inadequacy as a host, nevertheless insisted that they help themselves. And somewhere there was a trough of water, too, for their hayawans, and a basket of acram leaves.

Uneasily, they sipped from their cups, chewed the seeds. Kalal had picked up a chipped lump of old stone and was playing with it nervously. Jalila couldn't quite see what it was.

"So," he said, clearing his throat, "you've been to and from the stars, have you?"

"As have you. Perhaps you could name the planet? It may have been somewhere that we have both visited. . . ."

Kalal swallowed. His lump of old stone clicked the floor. A spindle of wind played chill on Jalila's neck. Then—she didn't know how it began—the tariqua was talking of Ghezirah, the great and fabled city that lay at the center of all the Ten Thousand and One Worlds. No one Jalila had ever met or heard of had ever visited Ghezirah, not even Nayra's mothers—yet this tariqua talked of it as if she knew it well. Before, Jalila had somehow imagined the tariqua trailing from planet to distant planet with dull cargoes of ore and biomass in her ship's holds. To her mind, Ghezirah had always been more than half-mythical—a place from which a dubious historical figure such as the Blessed Joanna might easily emanate, but certainly not a place composed of solid streets upon which the gnarled and bony feet of this old woman might once have walked. . . .

Ghezirah . . . she could see it now in her mind, smell the shadowy lobbies, see the ever-climbing curve of its mezzanines and rooftops vanishing into the impossible greens of the Floating Ocean. But every time Jalila's vision seemed about to solidify, the tariqua said something else that made it tremble and change. And then the tariqua said the strangest thing of all, which was that the City At The End Of All Roads was actually *alive*. Not alive in the meager sense in which every town has a sort of life, but truly living. The city thought. It grew. It responded. There was no central mind or focus to this consciousness, because Ghezirah *itself*, its teeming streets and minarets and rivers and caleches and its many millions of lives, was itself the mind. . . .

Jalila was awestruck, but Kalal seemed unimpressed, and was still playing with that old lump of stone.

4.

"Jalilaneen. . . ."

The way bondmother Lya said her name made Jalila look up. Somewhere in her throat, a wary nerve started ticking. They took their meals inside now, in the central courtyard of the haramlek, which Pavo had provided with a translucent roofing to let in a little of what light there was in the evenings' skies, and keep out most of the wind. Still, as Jalila took a sip of steaming hibiscus, she was sure that the sand had gotten into something.

"We've been talking. Things have come up—ideas about which we'd like to seek your opinion. . . ."

In other words, Jalila thought, her gaze traveling across her three mothers, you've decided something. And this is how you tell me—by pretending that you're consulting me. It had been the same with leaving Tabuthal. It was always the same. An old ghost of herself got up at that point, threw down her napkin, stalked off up to her room. But the new Jalila remained seated. She even smiled and tried to look encouraging.

"We've seen so little of this world," Lya continued. "All of us, really. And especially since we had you. It's been marvelous. But, of course, it's also been confining. . . . Oh *no*—" Lya waved the idea away quickly, before anyone could even begin to start thinking it. "—we won't be leaving our haramlek and Al Janb. There are many things to do. New bonds and friendships have been made. Ananke and I won't be leaving, anyway. . . . But Pavo . . ." And here Lya, who could never quite stop being the chair of a committee, gave a nod toward her mate. ". . . Pavo here has dec—expressed a *wish*—that she would like to travel."

"Travel?" Jalila leaned forward, her chin resting on her knuckles. "How?"

Pavo gave her plate a half turn. "By boat seems the best way to explore Habara. With such a big ocean . . ." She turned the plate again, as if to demonstrate.

"And not just a *boat*," Ananke put in encouragingly. "A brand new *ship*. We're having it built—"

"—But I thought you said you hadn't yet decided?"

"The contract, I think, is still being prepared," Lya explained. "And much of the craft will be to Pavo's own design."

"Will you be building it yourself?"

"Not alone." Pavo gave another of her flustered smiles. "I've asked Ibra to help me. He seems to be the best, the most knowledgeable—"

"—Ibra? Does he have any references?"

"This is *Al Janb*, Jalila," Lya said. "We know and trust people. I'd have thought that, with your friendship with Kalal. . . ."

"This certainly *is* Al Janb. . . ." Jalila sat back. "How can I ever forget it!" All of her mothers' eyes were on her. Then something broke. She got up and stormed off to her room.

The long ride to the tariqua's qasr, the swish of the wind, and banging three times on the old oak door. Then hobbling Robin and hurrying through dusty corridors to that tall tiled chamber, and somehow expecting no one to be there, even though Jalila had now come here several times alone.

But the tariqua was always there. Waiting.

Between them now, there was much to be said.

"This ant, Jalila, which crawls across this sheet of paper from *here* to *there*. She is much like us as we crawl across the surface of this planet. Even if she had the wings some of her kind sprout, just as I have my caleche, it would still be the same." The tiny creature, waving feelers, was plainly lost. A black dot. Jalila understood how it felt. "But say, if we were to fold both sides of the paper together. You see how she moves now. . . ?" The ant, antennae waving, hesitant, at last made the tiny jump. "We can move more quickly from one place to another by not traveling across the distance that separates us from it, but by folding space itself.

"Imagine now, Jalila, that this universe is not one thing alone, one solitary series of *this* following *that*, but an endless branching of potentialities. Such it has been since the Days of Creation, and such it is even now, in the shuffle of that leaf as the wind picks at it, in the rising steam of your coffee. Every moment goes in many ways. Most are poor, half-formed things, the passing thoughts and whims of the Almighty. They hang there and they die, never to be seen again. But others branch as strongly as this path that we find ourselves following. There are universes where you and I have never sat here in this qasr. There are universes where there is no Jalila. . . . Will you get that for me. . . ?"

The tariqua was pointing to an old book in a far corner. Its leather was cracked, the wind lifted its pages. As she took it from her, Jalila felt the hot brush of the old woman's hand.

"So now, you must imagine that there is not just one sheet of a single universe, but many, as in this book, heaped invisibly above and beside and below the page upon which we find ourselves crawling. In fact . . ." The ant recoiled briefly, sensing the strange heat of the tariqua's fingers, then settled on the open pages. "You must imagine shelf after shelf, floor upon floor of books, the aisles of an infinite library. And if we are to fold this one page, you see, we or the ant never quite knows what lies on the other side of it. And there may be a tear in that next page as well. It may even be that another version of ourselves has already torn it."

Despite its worn state, the book looked potentially valuable, hand-written in a beautiful flowing script. Jalila had to wince when the tariqua's fingers ripped through them. But the ant had vanished now. She was somewhere between the book's page. . . .

"That, Jalila, is the Pain of Distance—the sense of every potentiality. So that womankind may pass over the spaces between the stars, every tariqua must experience it." The wind gave an extra lunge, flipping the book shut. Jalila reached forward, but the tariqua, quick for once, was ahead of her. Instead of opening the book to release the ant, she weighed it down with the same chipped old stone with which Kalal had played on his visit to this qasr.

"Now, perhaps, my Jalila, you begin to understand?"

The stone was old, chipped, grey-green. It was inscribed, and had been carved with the closed wings of a beetle. Here was something from a world so impossibly old and distant as to make the book upon which it rested seem fresh and new as an unbudded leaf—a scarab, shaped for the Queens of Egypt.

"See here, Jalila. See how it grows. The breathmoss?"

This was the beginning of the Season of Autumns. The trees were beautiful; the forests were on fire with their leaves. Jalila had been walking with Pavo, enjoying the return of the birdsong, and wondering why it was that this new season felt sad when everything around her seemed to be changing and growing.

"Look. . . ."

The breathmoss, too, had turned russet-gold. Leaning close to it beneath this tranquil sky, which was composed of a blue so pale it was as if the sea had been caught in reflection inside an upturned white bowl, was like looking into the arms of a miniature forest.

"Do you think it will die?"

Pavo leaned beside her. "Jalila, it should have died long ago. *Inshallah*, it is a small miracle." There were the three dead marks where Ananke had touched it in a Season of Long Ago. "You see how frail it is, and yet . . ."

"At least it won't spread and take over the planet."

"Not for a while, at least."

On another rock lay another small colony. Here, too, oddly enough, there were marks. Five large dead dots, as if made by the outspread of a hand, although the shape of it was too big to have been Ananke's. They walked on. Evening was coming. Their shadows were lengthening. Although the sun was shining and the waves sparkled, Jalila wished that she had put on something warmer than a shawl.

"That tariqua. You seem to enjoy her company. . . ."

Jalila nodded. When she was with the old woman, she felt at last as if she was escaping the confines of Al Janb. It was liberating, after the close life in this town and with her mothers in their haramlek, to know that interstellar space truly existed, and then to feel, as the tariqua spoke of Gateways, momentarily like that ant, infinitely small and yet somehow inching, crawling across the many universes' infinite pages. But how could she express this? Even Pavo wouldn't understand.

"How goes the boat?" she asked instead.

Pavo slipped her arm into the crook of Jalila's and hugged her. "You must come and *see!* I have the plan in my head, but I'd never realized quite how big it would be. And complex. Ibra's full of enthusiasm."

"I can imagine."

The sea flashed. The two women chuckled.

"The way the ship's designed, Jalila, there's more than enough room for others. I never exactly planned to go alone, but then Lya's Lya. And Ananke's always—"

Jalila gave her mother's arm a squeeze. "I know what you're saying."

"I'd be happy if you came, Jalila. I'd understand if you didn't. This is such a beautiful, wonderful planet. The leviathans—we know so little about them, yet they plainly have intelligence, just as all those old myths say."

"You'll be telling me next about the qasrs. . . ."

"The ones we can see near here are *nothing!* There are islands on the ocean that are entirely made from them. And the wind pours through. They sing endlessly. A different song for every mood and season."

"Moods! If I'd said something like that when you were teaching me of the Pillars of Life, you'd have told me I was being unscientific!"

"Science is *about* wonder, Jalila. I was a poor teacher if I never told you that."

"You did." Jalila turned to kiss Pavo's forehead. "You did. . . ."

Pavo's ship was a fine thing. Between the slipways and the old mooring posts, where the red-flapping geelies quarreled over scraps of dying tideflower, it grew and grew. Golden-hulled. Far sleeker and bigger than even the ferries that had once borne Al Janb's visitors to and from the rocket port, and which now squatted on the shingle nearby, gently rusting. It was the talk of the Season. People came to admire its progress.

As Jalila watched the spars rise over the clustered roofs of the fisherwomen's houses, she was reminded of Kalal's tale of his father and his nameless mother, and that ship that they had made together in the teeming dockyards of that city. Her thoughts blurred. She saw the high balconies of a hotel far bigger than any of Al Janb's inns and boarding houses. She saw a darker, brighter ocean. Strange flesh upon flesh, with the windows open to the oil-and-salt breeze, the white lace curtains rising, falling. . . .

The boat grew, and Jalila visited the tariqua, although back in Al Janb, her thoughts sometimes trailed after Kalal as she wondered how it must be—to be male, like the last dodo, and trapped in some endless state of part-arousal, like a form of nagging worry. Poor Kalal. But his life certainly wasn't lonely. The first time Jalila noticed him at the center of the excited swarm of girls that once again surrounded Nayra, she'd almost thought that she was seeing things. But the gossip was loud and persistent. Kalal and Nayra were *a couple*—the phrase normally followed by a scandalized shriek, a hand-covered mouth. Jalila could only guess what the proud mothers of Nayra's haramlek thought of such a union, but, of course, no one could subscribe to outright prejudice. Kalal was, after all, just another human being. Lightly probing her own mothers' attitudes, she found the usual condescending tolerance. Having sexual relations with a male would be like smoking kif, or drinking alcohol, or any other form of slightly aberrant adolescent behavior; to be tolerated with easy smiles and sympathy, as long as it didn't go on for too long. To be treated, in fact, in much the same manner as her mothers were now treating her regular visits to the tariqua.

Jalila came to understand why people thought of the Season of Autumns as a sad time. The chill nights. The morning fogs that shrouded the bay. The leaves, finally falling, piled into rotting heaps. The tideflower beds, also, were dying as the waves pulled and dismantled what remained of their colors, and they drifted to the shores, the flowers bearing the same stench and texture and color as upturned clay. The geelies were dying as well. In the town, to compensate, there was much bunting and celebration for yet another moulid, but to Jalila the brightness seemed feeble—the flame of a match held against winter's gathering gale. Still, she sometimes wandered the old markets with some of her old curiosity, nostalgically touching the flapping windsilks, studying the faces and nodding at the many she now knew, although her thoughts were often literally light-years away. *The Pain of Distance*; she could feel it. Inwardly, she was thrilled and afraid. Her mothers and everyone else, caught up in the moulid and Pavo's coming departure, imagined from her mood that she had now decided to take that voyage with her. She deceived Kalal in much the same way.

The nights became clearer. Riding back from the qasr one dark evening with the tariqua's slight voice ringing in her ears, the stars seemed to hover closer around her than at any time since she had left Tabuthal. She could feel the night blossoming, its emptiness and the possibilities spinning out to infinity. She felt both like crying, and like whooping for joy. She had dared to ask the tariqua the question she had long been formulating, and the answer, albeit not entirely yes, had not been no. She talked to Robin as they bobbed along, and the puny yellow smudge of Al Janb drew slowly closer. You must understand, she told her hayawan, that the core of the Almighty is like the empty place between these stars, around which they all revolve. It is *there*, we know it, but we can never *see* it. . . . She sang songs from the old saharas about the joy of loneliness, and the loneliness of joy. From here, high up on the gradually descending road that wound its way down toward her haramlek, the horizon was still distant enough for her to see the lights of the rocketport. It was like a huge tidebed, holding out as the season changed. And there at the center of it, rising golden, no longer a stumpy silo-shaped object but somehow beautiful, was the last of the year's rockets. It would have to rise from Habara before the coming of the Season of Winters.

Her mothers' anxious faces hurried around her in the lamplight as she led Robin toward the stable.

"Where have you *been*, Jalilaneen?"

"Do you *know* what time it is?"

"We should be in the town *already!*"

For some reason, they were dressed in their best, most formal robes. Their palms were hennaed and scented. They bustled Jalila out of her gritty clothes, practically washed and dressed her, then flapped themselves down the serraplate road into town, where the processions had already started. Still, they were there in plenty of time to witness the blessing of Pavo's ship. It was to be called *Endeavor*, and Pavo and Jalila together smashed the bottle of wine across its prow before it rumbled into the nightblack waters of the harbor with an enormous white splash. Everyone cheered. Pavo hugged Jalila.

There were more bottles of the same frothy wine available at the party afterward. Lya, with her usual thoroughness, had ordered a huge case of the stuff, although many of the guests remembered the Prophet's old injunction and avoided imbibing. Ibra, though, was soon even more full of himself than usual, and went around the big marquee with a bottle in each hand, dancing clumsily with anyone who was foolish enough to come near him. Jalila drank a little of the stuff herself. The taste was sweet, but oddly hot and bitter. She filled up another glass.

"Wondered what you two mariners were going to call that boat. . . ."

It was Kalal. He'd been dancing with many of the girls, and he looked almost as red-faced as his father.

"Bet you don't even know what the first *Endeavor* was."

"You're wrong there," Jalila countered primly, although the simple words almost fell over each other as she tried to say them. "It was the spacecraft of Captain Cook. She was one of urrearth's most famous early explorers."

"I thought you were many things," Kalal countered, angry for no apparent reason. "But I never thought you were *stupid*."

Jalila watched him walk away. The dance had gathered up its beat. Ibra had retreated to sit, foolishly glum, in a corner, and Nayra had moved to the middle of the floor, her arms raised, bracelets jingling, an opal jewel at her belly, windsilk-draped hips swaying. Jalila watched. Perhaps it was the drink, but for the first time in many a Season, she felt a slight return of that old erotic longing as she watched Nayra swaying. Desire was the strangest of all emotions. It seemed so trivial when you weren't possessed of it, and yet when you were possessed, it was as if all the secrets of the universe were waiting. . . . Nayra was the focus of all attention now as she swayed amid the crowd, her shoulders glistening. She danced before Jalila, and her languorous eyes fixed her for a moment before she danced on. Now she was dancing with Kalal, and he was swaying with her, her hands laid upon his shoulders, and everyone was clapping. They made a fine couple. But the music was getting louder, and so were people's voices. Her head was pounding. She left the marquee.

She welcomed the harshness of the night air, the clear presence of the stars. Even the stench of the rotting tideflowers seemed appropriate as she picked her way across the ropes and slipways of the beach. So much had changed since she had first come here—but mostly what had changed had been herself. Here, its shape unmistakable as rising Walah spread her faint blue light across the ocean, was Kalal's boat. She sat down on the gunwale. The cold wind bit into her. She heard the crunch of shingle, and imagined it was someone else who was in need of solitude. But the sound grew closer, and then whoever it was sat down on the boat beside her. She didn't need to look up now. Kalal's smell was always different, and now he was sweating from the dancing.

"I thought you were enjoying yourself," she muttered.

"Oh—I was . . ." The emphasis on the *was* was strong.

They sat there for a long time, in windy, wave-crashing silence. It was almost like being alone. It was like the old days of their being together.

"So you're going, are you?" Kalal asked eventually.

"Oh, yes."

"I'm pleased for you. It's a fine boat, and I like Pavo best of all your mothers. You haven't seemed quite so happy lately here in Al Janb. Spending all that time with that old witch in the qasr."

"She's not a witch. She's a tariqa. It's one of the greatest, oldest callings. Although I'm surprised you've had time to notice what I'm up to, anyway. You and Nayra . . ."

Kalal laughed, and the wind made the sound turn bitter.

"I'm sorry," Jalila continued. "I'm sounding just like those stupid gossips. I know you're not like that. Either of you. And I'm happy for you both. Nayra's sweet and talented and entirely lovely . . . I hope it lasts . . . I hope. . . ."

After another long pause, Kalal said, "Seeing as we're apologizing, I'm sorry I got cross with you about the name of that boat you'll be going on—the *Endeavor*. It's a good name."

"Thank you. *El-hamadu-l-illah*."

"In fact, I could only think of one better one, and I'm glad you and Pavo didn't use it. You know what they say. To have two ships with the same name confuses the spirits of the winds. . . ."

"What are you talking about, Kalal?"

"This boat. You're sitting right on it. I thought you might have noticed."

Jalila glanced down at the prow, which lay before her in the moonlight, pointing toward the silvered waves. From this angle, and in the old naskhi script that Kalal had used, it took her a moment to work out the craft's name. Something turned inside her.

Breathmoss.

In white, moonslit letters.

"I'm sure there are better names for a boat," she said carefully. "Still, I'm flattered."

"Flattered?" Kalal stood up. She couldn't really see his face, but she suddenly knew that she'd once again said the wrong thing. He waved his hands in an odd shrug, and he seemed for a moment almost ready to lean close to her—to do something unpredictable and violent—but instead, picking up stones and skimming them hard into the agitated waters, he walked away.

Pavo was right. If not about love—which Jalila knew now that she still waited to experience—then at least about the major decisions of your life. There was never quite a beginning to them, although your mind often sought for such a thing.

When the tariqua's caleche emerged out of the newly teeming rain one dark evening a week or so after the naming of the *Endeavor*, and settled itself before the lights of their haramlek, and the old woman herself emerged, somehow still dry, and splashed across the puddled garden while her three mothers flustered about to find the umbrella they should have thought to look for earlier, Jalila still didn't know what she should be thinking. The four women would, in any case, need to talk alone; Jalila recognized that. For once, after the initial greetings, she was happy to retreat to her dreamtent.

But her mind was still in turmoil. She was suddenly terrified that her mothers would actually agree to this strange proposition, and then that, out of little more than embarrassment and obligation, the rest of her life would be bound to something that the tariqua called the Church of the Gateway. She knew so little. The tariqua talked only in riddles. She could be a fraud, for all Jalila knew—or a witch, just as Kalal insisted. Thoughts swirled about her like the rain. To make the time disappear, she tried searching the knowledge of her dreamtent. Lying there, listening to the rising sound of her mothers' voices, which seemed to be studded endlessly with the syllables of her own name, Jalila let the personalities who had guided her through the many Pillars of Wisdom tell her what they knew about the Church of the Gateway.

She saw the blackness of planetary space, swirled with the mica dots of turning planets. Almost as big as those, as she zoomed close to it, yet looking disappointingly like a many-angled version of the rocketport, lay the spacestation, and, within it, the junction that could lead you from *here* to *there* without passing across the distance between. A huge rent in the Book of Life, composed of the trapped energies of those things the tariqua called cosmic strings, although they and the Gateway itself were visible as nothing more than a turning ring near to the center of the vast spacestation, where occasionally, as Jalila watched, crafts of all possible shapes would seem to hang, then vanish. The gap she glimpsed inside seemed no darker than that which hung between the stars behind it, but it somehow hurt to stare at it. This, then, was the core of the mystery; something both plain and extraordinary. We crawl across the surface of this universe like ants, and each of these craft, switching through the Gateway's moment of loss and endless potentiality, is piloted by the will of a tariqua's conscious intelligence, which must glimpse those choices, then somehow emerge sane and entire at the other end of everything. . . .

Jalila's mind returned to the familiar scents and shapes of her dreamtent, and the sounds of the rain. The moment seemed to belong with those of the long-ago Season of Soft Rains. Downstairs, there were no voices. As she climbed out from her dreamtent, warily expecting to find the haramlek leaking and half-finished, Jalila was struck by an idea that the tariqua hadn't quite made plain to her; that a Gateway must push through *time* just as easily as it pushes through every other dimension. . . !
But the rooms of the haramlek were finely furnished, and her three mothers and the

tariqua were sitting in the rainswept candlelight of the courtyard, waiting.

With any lesser request, Lya always quizzed Jalila before she would even consider granting it. So as Jalila sat before her mothers and tried not to tremble in their presence, she wondered how she could possibly explain her ignorance of this pure, boundless mystery.

But Lya simply asked Jalila if this was what she wanted—to be an acolyte of the Church of the Gateway.

"Yes."

Jalila waited. Then, not even, *are you sure?* They'd trusted her less than this when they'd sent her on errands into Al Janb. . . . It was still raining. The evening was starless and dark. Her three mothers, having hugged her, but saying little else, retreated to their own dreamtents and silences, leaving Jalila to say farewell to the tariqua alone. The heat of the old woman's hand no longer came as a surprise to Jalila as she helped her up from her chair and away from the sheltered courtyard.

"Well," the tariqua croaked, "that didn't seem to go so badly."

"But I know so *little!*" They were standing on the patio at the dripping edge of the night. Wet streamers of wind tugged at them.

"I know you wish I could tell you more, Jalila—but then, would it make any difference?"

Jalila shook her head. "Will you come with me?"

"Habara is where I must stay, Jalila. It is written."

"But I'll be able to return?"

"Of course. But you must remember that you can never return to the place you have left." The tariqua fumbled with her clasp, the one of a worm consuming its tail. "I want you to have this." It was made of black ivory, and felt as hot as the old woman's flesh as Jalila took it. For once, not really caring whether she broke her bones, she gave the small, birdlike woman a hug. She smelled of dust and metal, like an antique box left forgotten on a sunny windowledge. Jalila helped her out down the steps into the rainswept garden.

"I'll come again soon," she said, "to the qasr."

"Of course . . . there are many arrangements." The tariqua opened the dripping filigree door of her caleche and peered at her with those half-blind eyes. Jalila waited. They had stood too long in the rain already.

"Yes?"

"Don't be too hard on Kalal."

Puzzled, Jalila watched the caleche rise and turn away from the lights of the haramlek.

Jalila moved warily through the sharded glass of her own and her mothers' expectations. It was agreed that a message concerning her be sent, endorsed by the full, long, and ornate formal name of the tariqua, to the body that did indeed call itself the Church of the Gateway. It went by radio pulse to the spacestation in wide solar orbit that received Habara's rockets, and was then passed on inside a vessel from *here* to *there* that was piloted by a tariqua. Not only that, but the message was destined for G/hezirah! Riding Robin up to the cliffs where, in this newly clear autumn air, under grey skies and tearing wet wind, she could finally see the waiting fuselage of that last golden rocket, Jalila felt confused and tiny, huge and mythic. It was agreed though, that for the sake of everyone—and not least Jalila herself, should she change her mind—that the word should remain that she was traveling out around the planet with Pavo on board the *Endeavor*. In need of something to do when she wasn't brooding, and waiting for further word from (could it really be?) the sentient city of Ghezirah, Jalila threw herself into the listings and loadings and preparations with convincing enthusiasm.

"The hardest decisions, once made, are often the best ones."

"Compared to what you'll be doing, my little journey seems almost pointless."

"We love you so deeply."

Then the message finally came: an acknowledgment; an acceptance; a few (far too few, it seemed) particulars of the arrangements and permissions necessary for such a journey. All on less than half a sheet of plain, two-dimensional printout.

Even Lya had started touching and hugging her at every opportunity.

Jalila ate lunch with Kalal and Nayra. She surprised herself and talked gaily at first of singing islands and sea-leviathans, somehow feeling that she was hiding little from her two best friends but the particular details of the journey she was undertaking. But Jalila was struck by the coldness that seemed to lie between these two supposed lovers. Nayra, perhaps sensing from bitter experience that she was once again about to be rejected, seemed near-tearful behind her dazzling smiles and the flirtatious blonde tossings of her hair, while Kalal seemed . . . Jalila had no idea how he seemed, but she couldn't let it end like this, and concocted some queries about the *Endeavor* so that she could lead him off alone as they left the bar. Nayra, perhaps fearing something else entirely, was reluctant to leave them.

"I wonder what it is that we've both done to her?" Kalal sighed as they watched her give a final sideways wave, pause, and then turn reluctantly down a sidestreet with a most un-Nayran duck of her lovely head.

They walked toward the harbor through a pause in the rain, to where the *Endeavor* was waiting.

"Lovely, isn't she?" Kalal murmured as they stood looking down at the long deck, then up at the high forest of spars. Pavo, who was developing her acquaintance with the ship's mind, gave them a wave from the bubble of the forecastle. "How long do you think your journey will take? You should be back by early spring, I calcutlate, if you get ahead of the icebergs. . . ."

Jalila fingered the brooch that the tariqua had given her, and which she had taken to wearing at her shoulder in the place where she had once worn the tideflower. It was like black ivory, but set with tiny, white specks that loomed at your eyes if you held it close. She had no idea what world it was from, or of the substance of which it was made.

". . . You'll miss the winter here. But perhaps that's no bad thing. It's cold, and there'll be other Seasons on the ocean. And there'll be other winters. Well, to be honest, Jalila, I'd been hoping—"

"—Look!" Jalila interrupted, suddenly sick of the lie she'd been living. "I'm not going."

They turned and were facing each other by the harbor's edge. Kalal's strange face twisted into surprise, and then something like delight. Jalila thought that he was looking more and more like his father. "That's marvelous!" He clasped each of Jalila's arms and squeezed her hard enough to hurt. "It was rubbish, by the way, what I just said about winters here in Al Janb. They're the most magical, wonderful season. We'll have snowball fights together! And when Eid al-Fitr comes . . ."

His voice trailed off. His hands dropped from her. "What is it, Jalila?"

"I'm not going with Pavo on the *Endeavor*, but I'm going away. I'm going to Ghezirah. I'm going to study under the Church of the Gateway. I'm going to try to become a tariqua."

His face twisted again. "That witch—"

"—Don't keep calling her that! You nave no idea!"

Kalal balled his fists, and Jalila stumbled back, fearing for a moment that this wild, odd creature might actually be about to strike her. But he turned instead, and ran off from the harbor.

Next morning, to no one's particular surprise, it was once again raining. Jalila felt restless and disturbed after her incomplete exchanges with Kalal. Some time had also passed since the message had been received from Ghezirah, and the few small details it had given of her journey had become vast and complicated and frustrating in their arranging. Despite the weather, she decided to ride out to see the tariqua.

Robin's mood had been almost as odd as her mothers' recently, and she moaned and snickered at Jalila when she entered the stables. Jalila called back to her, and stroked her long nose, trying to ease her agitation. It was only when she went to check the harnesses that she realized that Abu was missing. Lya was in the haramlek, still finishing breakfast. It had to be Kalal who had taken her.

The swirling serraplated road. The black, dripping trees. The agitated ocean. Robin was starting to rust again. She would need more of Pavo's attention. But Pavo would soon be gone too. . . . The whole planet was changing, and Jalila didn't know what to make of anything, least of all what Kalal was up to, although the unasked-for borrowing of a precious mount, even if Abu had been virtually Kalal's all summer, filled her with a foreboding that was an awkward load, not especially heavy, but difficult to carry or put down; awkward and jagged and painful. Twice, now, he had turned from her and walked away with something unsaid. It felt like the start of some prophecy. . . .

The qasr shone jet-black in the teeming rain. The studded door, straining to overcome the swelling damp, burst open more forcefully than usual at Jalila's third knock, and the air inside swirled dark and empty. No sign of Abu in the place beyond the porch where Kalal would probably have hobbled her, although the floor here seemed muddied and damp, and Robin was agitated. Jalila glanced back, but she and her hayawan had already obscured the possible signs of another's presence. Unlike Kalal, who seemed to notice many things, she decided that she made a poor detective.

Cold air stuttered down the passageways. Jalila, chilled and watchful, had grown so used to this qasr's sense of abandonment that it was impossible to tell whether the place was now finally empty. But she feared that it was. Her thoughts and footsteps whispered to her that the tariqua, after ruining her life and playing with her expectations, had simply vanished into a puff of lost potentialities. Already disappointed, angry, she hurried to the high-ceilinged room set with blue and white tiles and found, with no great surprise, that the strewn cushions were cold and damp, the coffee lamp was unlit, and that the book through which that patient ant had crawled was now sprawled in a damp-leafed scatter of torn pages. There was no sign of the scarab. Jalila sat down, and listened to the wind's howl, the rain's ticking, wondering for a long time when it was that she had lost the ability to cry.

Finally, she stood up and moved toward the courtyard. It was colder today than it had ever been, and the rain had greyed and thickened. It gelled and dripped from the gutters in the form of something she supposed was called *sleet*, and which she decided as it splattered down her neck that she would hate forever. It filled the bowl of the fountain with mucuslike slush, and trickled sluggishly along the lines of the drains. The air was full of weepings and howlings. In the corner of the courtyard, there lay a small black heap.

Sprawled half in, half out of the poor shelter of the arched cloisters, more than ever like a flightless bird, the tariqua lay dead. Her clothes were sodden. All the furnace heat had gone from her body, although, on a day such as this, that would take no more than a matter of moments. Jalila glanced up through the sleet toward the black wet stone of the latticed mashrabiya from which she and Kalal had first spied on the old woman, but she was sure now that she was alone. People shrank incredibly when they were dead—even a figure as frail and old as this creature had been. And yet, Jalila found as she tried to move the tariqua's remains out of the rain, their spiritless bodies grew uncompliant; heavier and stupider than clay. The tariqua's face rolled up toward her. One side was pushed in almost unrecognizably, and she saw that a nearby nest of ants were swarming over it, busily tunneling out the moisture and nutrition, bearing it across the smeared paving as they stored up for the long winter ahead.

There was no sign of the scarab.

5.

This, for Jalila and her mothers, was the Season of Farewells. It was the Season of Departures.

There was a small and pretty onion-domed mausoleum on a headland overlooking Al Janb, and the pastures around it were a popular place for picnics and lovers' trysts in the Season of Summers, although they were scattered with tombstones. It was the ever-reliable Lya who saw to the bathing and shrouding of the tariqua's body, which was something Jalila could not possibly face, and to the sending out through the null-space between the stars of all the necessary messages. Jalila, who had never been witness to the processes of death before, was astonished at the speed with which everything was arranged. As she stood with the other mourners on a day scarfed with cloud, beside the narrow rectangle of earth within which what remained of the tariqua now lay, she could still hear the wind booming over the empty qasr, feel the uncompliant weight of the old woman's body, the chill speckle of sleet on her face.

It seemed as if most of the population of Al Janb had made the journey with the cortege up the narrow road from the town. Hard-handed handed fisherwomen. Gaudily dressed merchants. Even the few remaining aliens. Nayra was there, too, a beautiful vision of sorrow surrounded by her lesser black acolytes. So was Ibra. So, even, was Kalal. Jalila, who was acknowledged to have known the old woman better than anyone, said a few words that she barely heard herself over the wind. Then a priestess who had flown in specially from Ras pronounced the usual prayers about the soul rising on the arms of Munkar and Nakir, the blue and the black angels. Looking down into the ground, trying hard to think of the Gardens of Delight that the Almighty always promised her stumbling faithful, Jalila could only remember that dream of her own burial: the soil pattering on her face, and everyone she knew looking down at her. The tariqua, in one of her many half-finished tales, had once spoken to her of a world upon which no sun had ever shone, but which was nevertheless warm and bounteous from the core of heat beneath its surface, and where the people were all blind, and moved by touch and sound alone; it was a joyous place, and they were forever singing. Perhaps, and despite all the words of the Prophet, Heaven, too, was a place of warmth and darkness.

The ceremony was finished. Everyone moved away, each pausing to toss in a damp clod of earth, but leaving the rest of the job to be completed by a dull-minded robotic creature, which Pavo had had to rescue from the attentions of the younger children, who, all through the long Habaran summer, had ridden around on it. Down at their haramlek, Jalila's mothers had organized a small feast. People wandered the courtyard, and commented admiringly on the many changes and improvements they had made to the place. Amid all this, Ibra seemed subdued—a reluctant presence in his own body—while Kalal was nowhere to be seen at all, although Jalila suspected that, if only for the reasons of penance, he couldn't be far away.

Of course, there had been shock at the news of the tariqua's death, and Lya, who had now become the person to whom the town most often turned to resolve its difficulties, had taken the lead in the inquiries that followed. A committee of wisewomen was organized even more quickly than the funeral, and Jalila had been summoned and interrogated. Waiting outside in the cold hallways of Al Janb's municipal buildings, she'd toyed with the idea of keeping Abu's disappearance and her suspicions of Kalal out of her story, but Lya and the others had already spoken to him, and he'd admitted to what sounded like everything. He'd ridden to the qasr on Abu to remonstrate with the tariqua. He'd been angry, and his mood had been bad. Somehow, but only lightly, he'd pushed the old woman, and she had fallen badly. Then, he panicked. Kalal bore responsibility for his acts, it was true, but it was accepted that the incident was essentially an accident. Jalila, who had imagined many versions of Kalal's confrontation with the tariqua, but not a single one that seemed entirely real, had been surprised at how easily the people of Al Janb were willing to absolve him. She wondered if they would have done so quite so easily if Kalal had not been a freak—a man. And then she also wondered, although no one had said a single word to suggest it, just how much she was to blame for all of this herself.

She left the haramlek from the funeral wake and crossed the road to the beach. Kalal was sitting on the rocks, his back turned to the shore and the mountains. He didn't look around when she approached and sat down beside him. It was the first time since before the tariqua's death that they'd been alone.

"I'll have to leave here," he said, still gazing out toward the clouds that trailed the horizon.

"There's no reason—"

"—No one's asked me and Ibra to *stay*. I think they would, don't you, if anyone had wanted us to? That's the way you women work."

"We're not *you women*, Kalal. We're people."

"So you always say. And all Al Janb's probably terrified about the report they've had to make to that thing you're joining—the Church of the Gateway. Some big, powerful body, and—whoops—we've killed one of your old employees. . . ."

"Please don't be bitter."

Kalal blinked and said nothing. His cheeks were shining.

"You and Ibra—where will you both go?"

"There are plenty of other towns around this coast. We can use our boat to take us there before the ice sets in. We can't afford to leave the planet. But maybe in the Season of False Springs, when I'm a grown man and we've made some of the proper money we're always talking about making from harvesting the tideflowers—and when word's got around to everyone on this planet of what happened here—maybe then we'll leave Habara." He shook his head and sniffed. "I don't know why I bother to say *maybe*. . . ."

Jalila watched the waves. She wondered if this was the destiny of all men; to wander forever from place to place, planet to planet, pursued by the knowledge of vague crimes that they hadn't really committed.

"I suppose you want to know what happened?"

Jalila shook her head. "It's in the report, Kalal. I believe what you said."

He wiped his face with his palms, studied their wetness. "I'm not sure I believe it myself, Jalila. The way she was, that day. That old woman—she always seemed to be expecting you, didn't she? And then she seemed to know. I don't understand quite how it happened, and I was angry, I admit. But she almost *lunged* at me. . . . She seemed to want to die. . . ."

"You mustn't blame yourself. I brought you to this, Kalal. I never saw . . ." Jalila shook her head. She couldn't say. Not even now. Her eyes felt parched and cold.

"I loved you, Jalila."

The worlds branched in a million different ways. It could all have been different. The tariqua still alive. Jalila and Kalal together, instead of the half-formed thing that the love they had both felt for Nayra had briefly been. They could have taken the *Endeavor* together and sailed this planet's seas; Pavo would probably have let them—but when, but where, but how? None of it seemed real. Perhaps the tariqua was right; there are many worlds, but most of them are poor, half-formed things.

Jalila and Kalal sat there for a while longer. The breathmoss lay not far off, darkening and hardening into a carpet of stiff grey. Neither of them noticed it.

For no other reason than the shift of the tides and the rapidly coming winter, Pavo, Jalila, Kalal, and Ibra all left Al Janb on the same morning. The days before were chaotic in the haramlek. People shouted and looked around for things and grew cross and petty. Jalila was torn between bringing everything and nothing, and after many hours of bag-packing and lip-chewing, decided that it could all be thrown out, and that her time would be better spent down in the stables, with Robin. Abu was there too, of course, and she seemed to sense the imminence of change and departure even more than Jalila's own hayawan. She had become Kalal's mount far more than she had ever been Lya's, and he wouldn't come to say goodbye.

Jalila stroked the warm felt of the creatures' noses. Gazing into Abu's eyes as she gazed back at hers, she remembered their rides out in the heat of summer. Being with Kalal then, although she hadn't even noticed it, had been the closest she had ever come to loving anyone. On the last night before their departure, Ananke cooked one of her most extravagant dinners, and the four women sat around the heaped extravagance of the table that she'd spent all day preparing, each of them wondering what to say, and regretting how much of these precious last times together they'd wasted. They said a long prayer to the Almighty, and bowed in the direction of Al'Toman. It seemed that, tomorrow, even the two mothers who weren't leaving Al Janb would be setting out on a new and difficult journey.

Then there came the morning, and the weather obliged with chill sunlight and a wind that pushed hard at their cloaks and nudged the *Endeavor* away from the harbor even before her sails were set. They all watched her go, the whole town cheering and waving as Pavo waved back, looking smaller and neater and prettier than ever as she receded. Without ceremony, around the corner from the docks, out of sight and glad of the *Endeavor*'s distraction, Ibra and Kalal were also preparing to leave. At a run, Jalila caught them just as they were starting to shift the hull down the rubbled slipway into the waves. *Breathmoss*; she noticed that Kalal had kept the name, although she and he stood apart on that final beach and talked as two strangers.

She shook hands with Ibra. She kissed Kalal lightly on the cheek by leaning stiffly forward, and felt the roughness of his stubble. Then the craft got stuck on the slipway, and they were all heaving to get her moving the last few meters into the ocean, until, suddenly, she was afloat, and Ibra was raising the sails, and Kalal was at the prow, hidden behind the tarpaulined weight of their belongings. Jalila only glimpsed him once more, and by then *Breathmoss* had turned to meet the stronger currents that swept outside the grey bay. He could have been a figurehead.

Back at the dock, her mothers were pacing, anxious.

"Where have you *been*?"

"Do you *know* what *time* is?"

Jalila let them scold her. She *was* almost late for her own leaving. Although most of the crowds had departed, she'd half expected Nayra to be there. Jalila was momentarily saddened, and then she was glad for her. The silver craft that would take her to the rocketport smelled disappointingly of engine fumes as she clambered into it with the few other women and aliens who were leaving Habara. There was a loud bang as the hatches closed, and then a long wait while nothing seemed to happen, and she could only wave at Lya and Ananke through the thick porthole, smiling and mouthing stupid phrases until her face ached. The ferry bobbed loose, lurched, turned, and angled up. Al Janb was half gone in plumes of white spray already.

Then it came in a huge wave. That feeling of incompleteness, of something vital and unknown left irretrievably behind, which is the beginning of the Pain of Distance that Jalila, as a tariqua, would have to face throughout her long life. A sweat came over her. As she gazed out through the porthole at what little there was to see of Al Janb and the mountains, it slowly resolved itself into one thought. Immense and trivial. Vital and stupid. That scarab. She'd never asked Kalal about it, nor found it at the qasr, and the ancient object turned itself over in her head, sinking, spinning, filling her mind and then dwindling before rising up again as she climbed out, nauseous, from the ferry and crossed the clanging gantries of the spaceport toward the last huge golden craft, which stood steaming in the winter's air. A murder weapon?—but no, Kalal was no murderer. And, in any case, she was a poor detective. And yet . . .

The rockets thrust and rumbled. Pushing back, squeezing her eyeballs. There was no time now to think. Weight on weight, terrible seconds piled on her. Her blood seemed to leave her face. She was a clay-corpse. Vital elements of her senses departed. Then, there was a huge wash of silence. Jalila turned to look through the porthole beside her, and there it was. Mostly blue, and entirely beautiful: Habara, her birth planet. Jalila's hands rose up without her willing, and her fingers squealed as she touched the glass and tried to trace the shape of the greenish-brown coastline, the rising brown and white of the mountains of that huge single continent that already seemed so small, but of which she knew so little. Jewels seemed to be hanging close before her, twinkling and floating in and out of focus like the hazy stars she couldn't yet see. They puzzled her for a long time, did these jewels, and they were evasive as fish as she sought them with her weightlessly clumsy fingers. Then Jalila felt the salt break of moisture against her face, and realized what it was.

At long last, she was crying.

6.

Jalila had long been expecting the message when it finally came. At only one hundred and twenty standard years, Pavo was still relatively young to die, but she had used her life up at a frantic pace, as if she had always known that her time would be limited. Even though the custom for swift funerals remained on Habara, Jalila was able to use her position as a tariqua to ride the Gateways and return for the service. The weather on the planet of her birth was unpredictable as ever, raining one moment and then sunny the next, even as she took the ferry to Al Janb from the rocket-port, and hot and cold winds seemed to strike her face as she stood on the dock's edge and looked about for her two remaining mothers. They embraced. They led her to their haramlek, which seemed smaller to Jalila each time she visited it, despite the many additions and extensions and improvements they had made, and far closer to Al Janb than the long walk she remembered once taking on those many errands. She wandered the shore after dinner, and searched the twilight for a particular shape and angle of quartz, and the signs of dark growth. But the heights of the Season of Storms on this coastline were ferocious, and nothing as fragile as breath-moss could have survived. She lay sleepless that night in her old room within her dreamtent, breathing the strong, dense, moist atmosphere with difficulty, listening to the sound of the wind and rain.

She recognized none of the faces but her mothers' of the people who stood around Pavo's grave the following morning. Al Janb had seemed so changeless, yet even Nayra had moved on—and Kalal was far away. Time was relentless. Far more than the wind that came in off the bay, it chilled Jalila to the bone. One mother dead, and her two others looking like the mahwagis she supposed they were becoming. *The Pain of Distance.* More than ever now, and hour by hour and day by day in this life that she had chosen, Jalila knew what the old tariqua had meant. She stepped forward to say a few words. Pavo's life had been beautiful and complete. She had passed on much knowledge about this planet to all womankind, just as she had once passed on her wisdom to Jalila. The people listened respectfully to Jalila, as if she were a priest. When the prayers were finished and the clods of earth had been tossed and the groups began to move back down the hillside, Jalila remained standing by Pavo's grave. What looked like the same old part-metal beast came lumbering up, and began to fill in the rest of the hole, lifting and lowering the earth with reverent, childlike care. Just as Jalila had insisted, and despite her mothers' puzzlement, Pavo's grave lay right beside the old tariqua's whom they had buried so long ago. This was a place that she had long avoided, but now that Jalila saw the stone, once raw and brittle, but now smoothed and greyed by rain and wind, she felt none of the expected agony. She traced the complex name, scrolled in naskhi script, which she had once found impossible to remember, but which she had now recited countless times in the ceremonials that the Church of the Gateway demanded of its acolytes. Sometimes, especially in the High Temple at Ghezirah, the damn things could go on for days. Yet not one member of the whole Church had seen fit to come to the simple ceremony of this old woman's burial. It had hurt her, once, to think that no one from offworld had come to her own funeral. But now she understood.

About to walk away, Jalila paused, and peered around the back of the gravestone. In the lee of the wind, a soft green patch of life was thriving. She stooped to examine the growth, which was thick and healthy, forming a patch more than the size of her two outstretched hands in this sheltered place. Breathmoss. It must have been here for a long time. Yet who would have thought to bring it? Only Pavo: only Pavo could possibly have known.

As the gathering of mourners at the haramlek started to thin, Jalila excused herself and went to Pavo's quarters. Most of the stuff up here was a mystery to her. There were machines and nutrients and potions beyond anything you'd expect to encounter on such an out-of-the-way planet. Things were growing. Objects and data needed developing, tending, cataloging, if Pavo's legacy was to be maintained. Jalila would have to speak to her mothers. But, for now, she found what she wanted, which was little more than a glass tube with an open end. She pocketed it, and walked back up over the hill to the cemetery, and said another few prayers, and bent down in the lee of the wind behind the old gravestone beside Pavo's new patch of earth, and managed to remove a small portion of the breathmoss without damaging the rest of it.

That afternoon, she knew that she would have to ride out. The stables seemed virtually unchanged, and Robin was waiting. She even snickered in recognition of

Jalila, and didn't try to bite her when she came to introduce the saddle. It had been such a long time that the animal's easy compliance seemed a small miracle. But perhaps this was Pavo again; she could have done something to preserve the recollection of her much-changed mistress in some circuit or synapse of the hayawan's memory. Snuffling tears, feeling sad and exulted, and also somewhat uncomfortable, Jalila headed south on her hayawan along the old serraplate road, up over the cliffs and beneath the arms of the urrearth forest. The trees seemed different; thicker-leafed. And the birdsong cooed slower and deeper than she remembered. Perhaps, here in Habara, this was some Season other than all of those that she remembered. But the qasr reared as always—out there on the cliff face, and plainly deserted. No one came here now, but, like Robin, the door, at three beats of her fists, remembered.

Such neglect. Such decay. It seemed a dark and empty place. Even before Jalila came across the ancient signs of her own future presence—a twisted coathanger, a chipped plate, a few bleached and rotting cushions, some odd and scattered bits of Gateway technology that had passed beyond malfunction and looked like broken shells—she felt lost and afraid. Perhaps this, at last, was the final moment of knowing that she had warned herself she might have to face on Habara. *The Pain of Distance.* But at the same time, she knew that she was safe as she crawled across this particular page of her universe, and that when she did finally take a turn beyond the Gateways through which sanity itself could scarcely follow, it would be of her own volition, and as an impossibly old woman. The tariqua. Tending flowers like an old tortoise thrust out of its shell. Here, on a sunny, distant day. There were worse things. There were always worse things. And life was good. For all of this, pain was the price you paid.

Still, in the courtyard, Jalila felt the cold draft of prescience upon her neck from that lacy mashrabiya where she and Kalal would one day stand. The movement she made as she looked up toward it even reminded her of the old tariqua. Even her eyesight was not as sharp as it had once been. Of course, there were ways around that which could be purchased in the tiered and dizzy markets of Ghezirah, but sometimes it was better to accept a few things as the will of the Almighty. Bowing down, muttering the *shahada*, Jalila laid the breathmoss upon the shaded stone within the cloister. Sheltered here, she imagined that it would thrive. Mounting Robin, riding from the qasr, she paused once to look back. Perhaps her eyesight really was failing her, for she thought she saw the ancient structure shimmer and change. A beautiful green castle hung above the cliffs, coated entirely in breathmoss; a wonder from a far and distant age. She rode on, humming snatches of the old songs she'd once known so well about love and loss between the stars. Back at the haramlek, her mothers were as anxious as ever to know where she had been. Jalila tried not to smile as she endured their familiar scolding. She longed to hug them. She longed to cry.

That evening, her last evening before she left Habara, Jalila walked the shore alone again. Somehow, it seemed the place to her where Pavo's ghost was closest. Jalila could see her mother there now, as darkness welled up from between the rocks; a small, lithe body, always stooping, turning, looking. She tried going toward her; but Pavo's shadow always flickered shyly away. Still, it seemed to Jalila as if she had been led toward something, for here was the quartz-striped rock from that long-ago Season of the Soft Rains. Of course, there was no breathmoss left, the storms had seen to that, but nevertheless, as she bent down to examine it, Jalila was sure that she could see something beside it, twinkling clear from a rock-pool through the fading light. She plunged her hand in. It was a stone, almost as smooth and round as many millions of others on the beach, yet this one was worked and carved. And its color was greenish-grey.

The soapstone scarab, somehow thrust here to this beach by the storms of potentiality that the tariquas of the Church of the Gateway stirred up by their impossible journeyings, although Jalila was pleased to see that it looked considerably less damaged than the object she remembered Kalal turning over and over in his nervous hands as he spoke to her future self. Here at last was the link that would bind her through the pages of destiny, and, for a moment, she hitched her hand back and prepared to throw it so far out into the ocean that it would never be reclaimed. Then her arm relaxed. Out there, all the way across the darkness of the bay, the tideflowers of Habara were glowing.

She decided to keep it.

Lambing Season

MOLLY GLOSS

Since biblical times, shepherds "watching their sheep by night" have always seen strange things in the sky. Probably not *quite* as strange, though, as the celestial visitation that the compassionate shepherd of *this* story finds that she has to deal with. . . .

Molly Gloss made her first sale in 1984, and has since sold to *Asimov's Science Fiction*, *The Magazine of Fantasy and Science Fiction*, *Universe*, and elsewhere. She published a fantasy novel, *Outside the Gates*, in 1986, and another novel, *The Jump-Off Creek*, a "woman's western," was released in 1990. In 1997, she published an SF novel, *The Dazzle of Day*, which was a *New York Times* Notable Book for that year. Her most recent book, another SF novel, *Wild Life*, won the prestigious James Tiptree, Jr. Memorial Award in 2001. Her stories have appeared in our Second and Twentieth annual collections. She lives in Portland, Oregon.

From May to September, Delia took the Churro sheep and two dogs and went up on Joe-Johns Mountain to live. She had that country pretty much to herself all summer. Ken Owen sent one of his Mexican hands up every other week with a load of groceries, but otherwise she was alone, alone with the sheep and the dogs. She liked the solitude. Liked the silence. Some sheepherders she knew talked a blue streak to the dogs, the rocks, the porcupines, they sang songs and played the radio, read their magazines out loud, but Delia let the silence settle into her, and, by early summer, she had begun to hear the ticking of the dry grasses as a language she could almost translate. The dogs were named Jesus and Alice. "Away to me, Jesus," she said when they were moving the sheep. "Go bye, Alice." From May to September these words spoken in command of the dogs were almost the only times she heard her own voice; that, and when the Mexican brought the groceries, a polite exchange in Spanish about the weather, the health of the dogs, the fecundity of the ewes.

The Churros were a very old breed. The O-Bar Ranch had a federal allotment up on the mountain, which was all rimrock and sparse grasses well suited to the Churros, who were fiercely protective of their lambs and had a long-stapled top coat that could take the weather. They did well on the thin grass of the mountain where other sheep would lose flesh and give up their lambs to the coyotes. The Mexican was an old man. He said he remembered Churros from his childhood in the Oaxaca highlands, the rams with their four horns, two curving up, two down. "Buen' carne," he told Delia. Uncommonly fine meat.

The wind blew out of the southwest in the early part of the season, a wind that smelled of juniper and sage and pollen; in the later months, it blew straight from the east, a dry wind smelling of dust and smoke, bringing down showers of parched leaves and seedheads of yarrow and bittercress. Thunderstorms came frequently out of the east, enormous cloudscapes with hearts of livid magenta and glaucous green. At those times, if she was camped on a ridge, she'd get out of her bed and walk downhill to find a draw where she could feel safer, but if she were camped in a low place, she would stay with the sheep while a war passed over their heads, spectacular jagged flares of lightning, skull-rumbling cannonades of thunder. It was maybe bred into the bones of Churros, a knowledge and a tolerance of mountain weather, for they shifted together and waited out the thunder with surprising composure; they stood forbearingly while rain beat down in hard blinding bursts.

Sheepherding was simple work, although Delia knew some herders who made it hard, dogging the sheep every minute, keeping them in a tight group, moving all the time. She let the sheep herd themselves, do what they wanted, make their own decisions. If the band began to separate, she would whistle or yell, and often the strays would turn around and rejoin the main group. Only if they were badly scattered did she send out the dogs. Mostly she just kept an eye on the sheep, made sure they got good feed, that the band didn't split, that they stayed in the boundaries of the O-Bar allotment. She studied the sheep for the language of their bodies, and tried to handle them just as close to their nature as possible. When she put out salt for them, she scattered it on rocks and stumps as if she were hiding Easter eggs, because she saw how they enjoyed the search.

The spring grass made their manure wet, so she kept the wool cut away from the ewes' tail area with a pair of sharp, short-bladed shears. She dosed the sheep with wormer, trimmed their feet, inspected their teeth, treated ewes for mastitis. She combed the burrs from the dogs' coats and inspected them for ticks. *You're such good dogs*, she told them with her hands. *I'm very very proud of you.*

She had some old binoculars, 7×32s, and in the long quiet days, she watched bands of wild horses miles off in the distance, ragged looking mares with dorsal stripes and black legs. She read the back issues of the local newspapers, looking in the obits for names she recognized. She read spine-broken paperback novels and played solitaire and scoured the ground for arrowheads and rocks she would later sell to rockhounds. She studied the parched brown grass, which was full of grasshoppers and beetles and crickets and ants. But most of her day was spent just walking. The sheep sometimes bedded quite a ways from her trailer and she had to get out to them before sunrise when the coyotes would make their kills. She was usually up by three or four and walking out to the sheep in darkness. Sometimes she returned to the camp for lunch, but always she was out with the sheep again until sundown, when the coyotes were likely to return, and then she walked home after dark to water and feed the dogs, eat supper, climb into bed.

In her first years on Joe-Johns, she had often walked three or four miles away from the band just to see what was over a hill, or to study the intricate architecture of a sheepherder's monument. Stacking up flat stones in the form of an obelisk was a common herders' pastime, their monuments all over that sheep country, and though Delia had never felt an impulse to start one herself, she admired the ones other people had built. She sometimes walked miles out of her way just to look at a rockpile up close.

She had a mental map of the allotment, divided into ten pastures. Every few days, when the sheep had moved on to a new pasture, she moved her camp. She towed the trailer with an old Dodge pickup, over the rocks and creekbeds, the sloughs and dry meadows, to the new place. For a while afterward, after the engine was shut off and while the heavy old body of the truck was settling onto its tires, she would be deaf, her head filled with a dull roaring white noise.

She had about eight hundred ewes, as well as their lambs, many of them twins or triplets. The ferocity of the Churro ewes in defending their offspring was sometimes a problem for the dogs, but in the balance of things, she knew that it kept her losses small. Many coyotes lived on Joe-Johns, and sometimes a cougar or bear would come up from the salt pan desert on the north side of the mountain, looking for better country to own. These animals considered the sheep to be fair game, which Delia understood to be their right; and also her right, hers and the dogs', to take the side of the sheep. Sheep were smarter than people commonly believed and the Churros smarter than other sheep she had tended, but by midsummer the coyotes always passed the word among themselves, buen' carne, and Delia and the dogs then had a job to work, keeping the sheep out of harm's way.

She carried a .32 caliber Colt pistol in an old-fashioned holster worn on her belt. *If you're a coyot' you'd better be careful of this woman*, she said with her body, with the way she stood and the way she walked when she was wearing the pistol. That gun and holster had once belonged to her mother's mother, a woman who had come West on her own and homesteaded for a while, down in the Sprague River Canyon. Delia's grandmother had liked to tell the story: how a concerned neighbor, a bachelor with an interest in marriageable females, had pressed the gun upon her, back when the Klamaths were at war with the army of General Joel Palmer; and how she never had used it for anything but shooting rabbits.

In July, a coyote killed a lamb while Delia was camped no more than two hundred feet away from the bedded sheep. It was dusk, and she was sitting on the steps of the trailer reading a two-gun western, leaning close over the pages in the failing light, and the dogs were dozing at her feet. She heard the small sound, a strange high faint squeal she did not recognize and then did recognize, and she jumped up and fumbled for the gun, yelling at the coyote, at the dogs, her yell startling the entire band to its feet but the ewes making their charge too late, Delia firing too late, and none of it doing any good beyond a release of fear and anger.

A lion might well have taken the lamb entire; she had known of lion kills where the only evidence was blood on the grass and a dribble of entrails in the beam of a flashlight. But a coyote is small and will kill with a bite to the throat and then perhaps eat just the liver and heart, though a mother coyote will take all she can carry in her stomach, bolt it down and carry it home to her pups. Delia's grandmother's pistol had scared this one off before it could even take a bite, and the lamb was twitching and whole on the grass, bleeding only from its neck. The mother ewe stood over it, crying in a distraught and pitiful way, but there was nothing to be done, and, in a few minutes, the lamb was dead.

There wasn't much point in chasing after the coyote, and anyway, the whole band was now a skittish jumble of anxiety and confusion; it was hours before the mother ewe gave up her grieving, before Delia and the dogs had the band calm and bedded down again, almost midnight. By then, the dead lamb had stiffened on the ground, and she dragged it over by the truck and skinned it and let the dogs have the meat, which went against her nature, but was about the only way to keep the coyote from coming back for the carcass.

While the dogs worked on the lamb, she stood with both hands pressed to her tired back, looking out at the sheep, the mottled pattern of their whiteness almost opalescent across the black landscape, and the stars thick and bright above the faint outline of the rock ridges, stood there a moment before turning toward the trailer, toward bed, and afterward, she would think how the coyote and the sorrowing ewe and the dark of the July moon and the kink in her back, how all of that came together and was the reason that she was standing there watching the sky, was the reason that she saw the brief, brilliantly green flash in the southwest and then the sulfur yellow streak breaking across the night, southwest to due west on a descending arc onto Lame Man Bench. It was a broad bright ribbon, rainbow-wide, a cyanotic contrail. It was not a meteor, she had seen hundreds of meteors. She stood and looked at it.

Things to do with the sky, with distance, you could lose perspective, it was hard to judge even a lightning strike, whether it had touched down on a particular hill or the next hill or the valley between. So she knew this thing falling out of the sky might have come down miles to the west of Lame Man, not onto Lame Man at all, which was two miles away, at least two miles, and getting there would be all ridges and rocks, no way to cover the ground in the truck. She thought about it. She had moved camp earlier in the day, which was always troublesome work, and it had been a blistering hot day, and now the excitement with the coyote. She was very tired, the tiredness like a weight against her breastbone. She didn't know what this thing was, falling out of the sky. Maybe if she walked over there she would find just a dead satellite or a broken weather balloon and not dead or broken people. The contrail thinned slowly while she stood there looking at it, became a wide streak of yellowy cloud against the blackness, with the field of stars glimmering dimly behind it.

After a while, she went into the truck and got a water bottle and filled it, and also took the first aid kit out of the trailer and a couple of spare batteries for the flashlight and a handful of extra cartridges for the pistol, and stuffed these things into a backpack and looped her arms into the straps and started up the rise away from the dark camp, the bedded sheep. The dogs left off their gnawing of the dead lamb and trailed her anxiously, wanting to follow, or not wanting her to leave the sheep. "Stay by," she said to them sharply, and they went back and stood with the band and watched her go. *That coyot', he's done with us tonight:* This is what she told the dogs with her body, walking away, and she believed it was probably true.

Now that she'd decided to go, she walked fast. This was her sixth year on the mountain, and, by this time, she knew the country pretty well. She didn't use the flashlight. Without it, she became accustomed to the starlit darkness, able to see the stones and pick out a path. The air was cool, but full of the smell of heat rising off the rocks and the parched earth. She heard nothing but her own breathing and the gritting of her boots on the pebbly dirt. A little owl circled once in silence and then went off toward a line of cottonwood trees standing in black silhouette to the northeast.

Lame Man Bench was a great upthrust block of basalt grown over with scraggly juniper forest. As she climbed among the trees, the smell of something like ozone or sulfur grew very strong, and the air became thick, burdened with dust. Threads of the yellow contrail hung in the limbs of the trees. She went on across the top of the bench and onto slabs of shelving rock that gave a view to the west. Down in the steep-sided draw below her there was a big wing-shaped piece of metal resting on the ground, which she at first thought had been torn from an airplane, but then realized was a whole thing, not broken, and she quit looking for the rest of the wreckage. She squatted down and looked at it. Yellow dust settled slowly out of the sky, pollinating her hair, her shoulders, the toes of her boots, faintly dulling the oily black shine of the wing, the thing shaped like a wing.

While she was squatting there looking down at it, something came out from the sloped underside of it, a coyote she thought at first, and then it wasn't a coyote but a dog built like a greyhound or a whippet, deep-chested, long legged, very light-boned and frail-looking. She waited for somebody else, a man, to crawl out after his dog, but nobody did. The dog squatted to pee and then moved off a short distance and sat on its haunches and considered things. Delia considered, too. She considered that the dog might have been sent up alone. The Russians had sent up a dog in their lit-tle sputnik, she remembered. She considered that a skinny almost hairless dog with frail bones would be dead in short order if left alone in this country. And she con-sidered that there might be a man inside the wing, dead or too hurt to climb out. She thought how much trouble it would be, getting down this steep rock bluff in the darkness to rescue a useless dog and a dead man.

After a while, she stood and started picking her way into the draw. The dog by this time was smelling the ground, making a slow and careful circuit around the black wing. Delia kept expecting the dog to look up and bark, but it went on with its intent inspection of the ground as if it was stone deaf, as if Delia's boots making a racket on the loose gravel was not an announcement that someone was coming down. She thought of the old Dodge truck, how it always left her ears ringing, and wondered if maybe it was the same with this dog and its wing-shaped sputnik, although the wing had fallen soundless across the sky.

When she had come about half way down the hill, she lost footing and slid down six or eight feet before she got her heels dug in and found a handful of willow scrub to hang onto. A glimpse of this movement—rocks sliding to the bottom, or the dust she raised—must have startled the dog, for it leaped backward suddenly and then reared up. They looked at each other in silence, Delia and the dog, Delia standing leaning into the steep slope a dozen yards above the bottom of the draw, and the dog standing next to the sputnik, standing all the way up on its hind legs like a bear or a man and no longer seeming to be a dog but a person with a long narrow muzzle and a narrow chest, turned-out knees, delicate dog-like feet. Its genitals were more cat-like than dog, a male set but very small and neat and contained. Dog's eyes, though, dark and small and shining below an anxious brow, so that she was reminded of

Jesus and Alice, the way they had looked at her when she had left them alone with the sheep. She had years of acquaintance with dogs and she knew enough to look away, break off her stare. Also, after a moment, she remembered the old pistol and holster at her belt. In cowboy pictures, a man would unbuckle his gunbelt and let it down on the ground as a gesture of peaceful intent, but it seemed to her this might only bring attention to the gun, to the true intent of a gun, which is always killing. *This woman is nobody at all to be scared of,* she told the dog with her body, standing very still along the steep hillside, holding onto the scrub willow with her hands, looking vaguely to the left of him, where the smooth curve of the wing rose up and gathered a veneer of yellow dust.

The dog, the dog person, opened his jaws and yawned the way a dog will do to relieve nervousness, and then they were both silent and still for a minute. When finally he turned and stepped toward the wing, it was an unexpected, delicate movement, exactly the way a ballet dancer steps along on his toes, knees turned out, lifting his long thin legs; and then he dropped down on all-fours and seemed to become almost a dog again. He went back to his business of smelling the ground intently, though every little while he looked up to see if Delia was still standing along the rock slope. It was a steep place to stand. When her knees finally gave out, she sat down very carefully where she was, which didn't spook him. He had become used to her by then, and his brief, sliding glance just said, *That woman up there is nobody at all to be scared of.*

What he was after, or wanting to know, was a mystery to her. She kept expecting him to gather up rocks, like all those men who'd gone to the moon, but he only smelled the ground, making a wide slow circuit around the wing the way Alice always circled round the trailer every morning, nose down, reading the dirt like a book. And when he seemed satisfied with what he'd learned, he stood up again and looked back at Delia, a last look delivered across his shoulder before he dropped down and disappeared under the edge of the wing, a grave and inquiring look, the kind of look a dog or a man will give you before going off on his own business, a look that says, *You be okay if I go?* If he had been a dog, and if Delia had been close enough to do it, she'd have scratched the smooth head, felt the hard bone beneath, moved her hands around the soft ears. *Sure, okay, you go on now, Mr. Dog:* This is what she would have said with her hands. Then he crawled into the darkness under the slope of the wing, where she figured there must be a door, a hatch letting into the body of the machine, and after a while he flew off into the dark of the July moon.

In the weeks afterward, on nights when the moon had set or hadn't yet risen, she looked for the flash and streak of something breaking across the darkness out of the southwest. She saw him come and go to that draw on the west side of Lame Man Bench twice more in the first month. Both times, she left her grandmother's gun in the trailer and walked over there and sat in the dark on the rock slab above the draw and watched him for a couple of hours. He may have been waiting for her, or he knew her smell, because both times he reared up and looked at her just about as soon as she sat down. But then he went on with his business. *That woman is nobody to be scared of,* he said with his body, with the way he went on smelling the ground, widening his circle and widening it, sometimes taking a clod or a sprig into his mouth and tasting it, the way a mild-mannered dog will do when he's investigating something and not paying any attention to the person he's with.

Delia had about decided that the draw behind Lame Man Bench was one of his regular stops, like the ten campsites she used over and over again when she was herding on Joe-Johns Mountain; but after those three times in the first month, she didn't see him again.

At the end of September, she brought the sheep down to the O-Bar. After the lambs had been shipped out she took her band of dry ewes over onto the Nelson prairie for the fall, and in mid-November, when the snow had settled in, she brought them to the feed lots. That was all the work the ranch had for her until lambing season. Jesus and Alice belonged to the O-Bar. They stood in the yard and watched her go.

In town, she rented the same room as the year before, and, as before, spent most of a year's wages on getting drunk and standing other herders to rounds of drink. She gave up looking into the sky.

In March, she went back out to the ranch. In bitter weather, they built jugs and mothering-up pens, and trucked the pregnant ewes from Green, where they'd been feeding on wheat stubble. Some ewes lambed in the trailer on the way in, and after every haul, there was a surge of lambs born. Delia had the night shift, where she was paired with Roy Joyce, a fellow who raised sugar beets over in the valley and came out for the lambing season every year. In the black, freezing cold middle of the night, eight and ten ewes would be lambing at a time. Triplets, twins, big singles, a few quads, ewes with lambs born dead, ewes too sick or confused to mother. She and Roy would skin a dead lamb and feed the carcass to the ranch dogs and wrap the fleece around a bummer lamb, which was intended to fool the bereaved ewe into taking the orphan as her own, and sometimes it worked that way. All the mothering-up pens swiftly filled, and the jugs filled, and still some ewes with new lambs stood out in the cold field waiting for a room to open up.

You couldn't pull the stuck lambs with gloves on, you had to reach into the womb with your fingers to turn the lamb, or tie cord around the feet, or grasp the feet barehanded, so Delia's hands were always cold and wet, then cracked and bleeding. The ranch had brought in some old converted school buses to house the lambing crew, and she would fall into a bunk at daybreak and then not be able to sleep, shivering in the unheated bus with the gray daylight pouring in the windows and the endless daytime clamor out at the lambing sheds. All the lambers had sore throats, colds, nagging coughs. Roy Joyce looked like hell, deep bags as blue as bruises under his eyes, and Delia figured she looked about the same, though she hadn't seen a mirror, not even to draw a brush through her hair, since the start of the season.

By the end of the second week, only a handful of ewes hadn't lambed. The nights became quieter. The weather cleared, and the thin skiff of snow melted off the grass. On the dark of the moon, Delia was standing outside the mothering-up pens drinking coffee from a thermos. She put her head back and held the warmth of the coffee in her mouth a moment, and, as she was swallowing it down, lowering her chin, she caught the tail end of a green flash and a thin yellow line breaking across the sky, so far off anybody else would have thought it was a meteor, but it was bright, and dropping from southwest to due west, maybe right onto Lame Man Bench. She stood and looked at it. She was so very goddamned tired and had a sore throat that wouldn't clear, and she could barely get her fingers to fold around the thermos, they were so split and tender.

She told Roy she felt sick as a horse, and did he think he could handle things if she drove herself into town to the Urgent Care clinic, and she took one of the ranch trucks and drove up the road a short way and then turned onto the rutted track that went up to Joe-Johns.

The night was utterly clear and you could see things a long way off. She was still an hour's drive from the Churros' summer range when she began to see a yellow-orange glimmer behind the black ridgeline, a faint nimbus like the ones that marked distant range fires on summer nights.

She had to leave the truck at the bottom of the bench and climb up the last mile or so on foot, had to get a flashlight out of the glove box and try to find an uphill path with it because the fluttery reddish lightshow was finished by then, and a thick pall of smoke overcast the sky and blotted out the stars. Her eyes itched and burned, and tears ran from them, but the smoke calmed her sore throat. She went up slowly, breathing through her mouth.

The wing had burned a skid path through the scraggly junipers along the top of the bench and had come apart into about a hundred pieces. She wandered through the burnt trees and the scattered wreckage, shining her flashlight into the smoky darkness, not expecting to find what she was looking for, but there he was, lying apart from the scattered pieces of metal, out on the smooth slab rock at the edge of the draw. He was panting shallowly and his close coat of short brown hair was matted with blood. He lay in such a way that she immediately knew his back was broken. When he saw Delia coming up, his brow furrowed with worry. A sick or a wounded dog will bite, she knew that, but she squatted next to him. *It's just me*, she told him, by shining the light not in his face but in hers. Then she spoke to him. "Okay," she said. "I'm here now," without thinking too much about what the words meant, or whether they meant anything at all, and she didn't remember until afterward that he was very likely deaf anyway. He sighed and shifted his look from her to the middle distance, where she supposed he was focused on approaching death.

Near at hand, he didn't resemble a dog all that much, only in the long shape of his head, the folded-over ears, the round darkness of his eyes. He lay on the ground flat on his side like a dog that's been run over and is dying by the side of the road, but a man will lay like that too when he's dying. He had small-fingered nail-less hands where a dog would have had toes and front feet. Delia offered him a sip from her water bottle, but he didn't seem to want it, so she just sat with him quietly, holding one of his hands, which was smooth as lambskin against the cracked and roughened flesh of her palm. The batteries in the flashlight gave out, and sitting there in the cold darkness she found his head and stroked it, moving her sore fingers lightly over the bone of his skull, and around the soft ears, the loose jowls. Maybe it wasn't any particular comfort to him, but she was comforted by doing it. *Sure, okay, you can go on.*

She heard him sigh, and then sigh again, and each time wondered if it would turn out to be his death. She had used to wonder what a coyote, or especially a dog, would make of this doggish man, and now while she was listening, waiting to hear if he would breathe again, she began to wish she'd brought Alice or Jesus with her, though not out of that old curiosity. When her husband had died years before, at the very moment he took his last breath, the dog she'd had then had barked wildly and raced back and forth from the front to the rear door of the house as if he'd heard or seen something invisible to her. People said it was her husband's soul going out the door or his angel coming in. She didn't know what it was the dog had seen or heard or smelled, but she wished she knew. And now she wished she had a dog with her to bear witness.

She went on petting him even after he had died, after she was sure he was dead, went on petting him until his body was cool, and then she got up stiffly from the bloody ground and gathered rocks and piled them onto him, a couple of feet high, so that he wouldn't be found or dug up. She didn't know what to do about the wreckage, so she didn't do anything with it at all.

In May, when she brought the Churro sheep back to Joe-Johns Mountain, the pieces of the wrecked wing had already eroded, were small and smooth-edged like the bits of sea glass you find on a beach, and she figured that this must be what it was meant to do: to break apart into pieces too small for anybody to notice, and then to quickly wear away. But the stones she'd piled over his body seemed like the start of something, so she began the slow work of raising them higher into a sheepherder's monument. She gathered up all the smooth eroded bits of wing, too, and laid them in a series of widening circles around the base of the monument. She went on piling up stones through the summer and into September, until it reached fifteen feet. Mornings, standing with the sheep miles away, she would look for it through the binoculars and think about ways to raise it higher, and she would wonder what was buried under all the other monuments sheepherders had raised in that country. At night, she studied the sky, but nobody came for him.

In November, when she finished with the sheep and went into town, she asked around and found a guy who knew about star-gazing and telescopes. He loaned her some books and sent her to a certain pawnshop, and she gave most of a year's wages for a 14×75 telescope with a reflective lens. On clear, moonless nights, she met the astronomy guy out at the Little League baseball field, and she sat on a fold-up canvas stool with her eye against the telescope's finder while he told her what she was seeing: Jupiter's moons, the Pelican Nebula, the Andromeda Galaxy. The telescope had a tripod mount, and he showed her how to make a little jerry-built device so she could mount her old 7×32 binoculars on the tripod too. She used the binoculars for their wider view of star clusters and small constellations. She was indifferent to most discomforts, could sit quietly in one position for hours at a time, teeth rattling with the cold, staring into the immense vault of the sky until she became numb and stiff, barely able to stand and walk back home. Astronomy, she discovered, was a work of patience, but the sheep had taught her patience, or it was already in her nature before she ever took up with them.